Sun House

Sun House

David James Duncan

Little, Brown and Company
New York Boston London

Little, Brown and Company
Hachette Book Group
1290 Avenue of the Americas, New York, NY 10104
littlebrown.com

First Edition: August 2023

Little, Brown and Company is a division of Hachette Book Group, Inc. The Little, Brown name and logo are trademarks of Hachette Book Group, Inc.

The publisher is not responsible for websites (or their content) that are not owned by the publisher.

The Hachette Speakers Bureau provides a wide range of authors for speaking events. To find out more, go to hachettespeakersbureau.com or call (866) 376-6591.

Excerpted lines from "Statesboro Blues" and "Cottonwoods" © Chris Dombrowski from *Ragged Anthem* (Detroit: Wayne State University Press 2019), all rights reserved. Excerpted lines from "Brother Tree" © Chris Dombrowski; this poem is unpublished. Excerpted lines from "Fado" © Jane Hirshfield from *The Beauty* (New York: Knopf 2015), used by permission of Jane Hirshfield, all rights reserved. Excerpted lines from "The Kingdom of God" © Teddy Macker from *This World* (White Cloud Press, 2015), used by permission of Teddy Macker, all rights reserved. Gary Snyder, excerpts from "Breasts," "Changing Diapers," and "True Night" from *Axe Handles*. Copyright © 1983 by Gary Snyder. Reprinted with the permission of The Permissions Company, LLC on behalf of Counterpoint Press, counterpointpress.com. Excerpted lines from "Work Ethic" © Jessie van Eerden from *The Long Weeping* (Orison Books, 2017), used by permission of Jessie van Eerden, all rights reserved.

ISBN 9780316129374
LCCN 2022943306

Printing 1, 2023

LSC-C

Printed in the United States of America

Contents

Book One:

Moaning Is Connected with Hope

First Telling:

Magic Words

Magic words are the most difficult to get hold of, but they are also the strongest...Magic words or magic prayers are fragments of old songs or apparently meaningless sentences heard in the days when animals could talk, and remembered ever since by being passed from one generation to the next. In the very earliest time...when all spoke the same language, words were potent and the mind had mysterious powers. A word might suddenly come alive, and what people needed to happen *would* happen. Nobody could explain it. That's just the way it was.

—Nalungiaq (nineteenth-century Iglulik elder)

(Portland, Oregon, 1958 to 1968)

I. Dead Mother's Son

Assume you write for an audience consisting solely of terminal patients. That is, after all, the case. What would you begin writing if you knew you would die soon? What could you say to a dying person that would not enrage by its triviality?

—Annie Dillard, *The Writing Life*

EXTREMELY IMPLAUSIBLE ACCIDENTS do not feel innocent. When, for instance, an inch-long steel bolt shook loose and fell from an AeroMexico DC-8 cruising at 38,000 feet, drifted seven miles to Earth, and embedded itself in the skull of an eight-year-old girl hoeing weeds with her widower father in a Mexican cornfield, killing her almost instantly, the term "freak accident" did not begin to appease. The minds of everyone who loved the girl groped for explanations. *A thunderhead shook things loose... An airline skimped on maintenance inspections... A skilled maintenance man, distracted by a coworker's tale of a secret affair, failed to torque down the bolt despite the thousands he had faithfully inspected...* But no rational explanation, not even a "correct" one, purges the preposterousness from the event. *An inch-long bolt. Seven miles. The perfect timing. The tiny target.* Chance veered so far out of its way to kill this child that some sort of *premeditated attack* seemed to have been committed.

The question then became: *By whom?* Who was the unseen attacker? Destiny? Fate? God? One wants to know. And one doesn't want to know. Because say it *is* God. Suppose that not a sparrow or human-made meteor falls without His knowledge. Suppose the winds are His breath, and His exhalations oh-so-carefully steered the steel throughout its drifting, twisting, high-speed fall. Now say you're the girl's father. Suppose you call out to your daughter when she drops in the dirt, wondering what crazy game she's playing, smiling at her histrionics as she briefly writhes, then lies perfectly still. Suppose that, as the game grows protracted, you grow irritated, stroll over to her—and find the small, blood-filled cavity amid the raven hair you braided that morning. Suppose you look skyward as you shatter and glimpse, miles above, not even the departing jet but only a fast-vanishing contrail.

Now start trying to love that all-knowing, oh-so-careful God.

Suppose you're the Jesuit novice from El Norte, summoned in the old padre's absence to console the mourners at her grave. Suppose that, after heartsick consideration, you fall back on your Jesuit training, draw a troubled breath, but try to sound confident as, in your stiff foreign Spanish, you tell the girl's father and handful of ragged friends, "Yours is a terrible loss. I'm more sorry than I can say. But God loves those He takes as well as those He leaves behind. His purposes are beyond us. We must trust, even so, that all things are meant to bring us to holiness."

Suppose the father grows wild-eyed, leaps forward, and smashes your face repeatedly till you fall to the ground. Say he then sobs, "*You must trust that my fists have brought you to holiness!*"

How can you answer? Some human beings are singled out to suffer agonies of the heart. We don't know why. All we know is that any even slightly confident explanation or consolation we offer in Spanish, English, or any mortal tongue sounds glib in the face of every such event, and so merely insults the hearts in agony.

THE PORTLAND ACTOR and playwright James Lee Van Zandt once suffered a highly implausible blow: Jamey was born on January 30th, 1958, at Providence Hospital in Portland, Oregon. On January 30th, 1963—five years later to the day—his mother, Debbie Van Zandt, died of leukemia in the very same hospital.

When any conceivable Divine Being or Random Fate deletes your mother in the very place she gave birth to you, and on your birthday, the extreme odds against it suggest that a premeditated attack has been committed. The five-year-old Jamey struggled for months to grasp that his mother was never coming back. He struggled for years to accept that she'd been ripped away like a sweetly offered, viciously retracted birthday gift. His acceptance of these two facts, after all that struggle, led him to conclude that Fate, God, or whatever Power rules earthly life is so farcically cold and cruel that only a fool would place faith in "It" or "Him." He then began losing faith in other things the ruling Power was said to bestow upon humans—things as basic as the reality of his own feelings and experience; reality of his face in the mirror; reality of his very world and life.

This early wound began weathering Jamey's identity the way winter storms and summer thunderheads weather granite peaks. Psychologically, his wound sensitized him to farcical situations, disingenuous behavior, and cruel illusions of all kinds. Philosophically, the wound bequeathed him a seething hatred of any and every formulaic, theological, New Age, or piety-ridden consolation. Socially, the wound turned him into a sometimes hilarious, sometimes self-destructive iconoclast so unemployable that he had no choice but to employ himself, becoming a playwright, actor, and theatrical director. The wound also bequeathed his comedy a ruthlessness that at times delighted and at other times appalled his audiences.

But before any of these influences were clearly recognized by Jamey, his early wound and fierce rebellion against it nearly killed him several times over.

A BOY OF five, after suffering a heart-wound, doesn't rant and rail at the heavens. A boy of five plays the hand he's dealt, and if it kills him, oh well, and if it doesn't, what do ya know? The strongest suit in Jamey Van Zandt's hand was his nature. The weakest was his luck. An example of both:

When Jamey was born, his head was seventeen inches in circumference. The opening in his mother's pelvis was not. Debbie needed an emergency C-section to deliver him and days of rest afterward. Baby and mother were separated. In the hospital nursery, Jamey contracted staph boils, which were treated with sulfa drugs to which Jamey proved allergic. He ended up in Intensive Care. Prolonged separation delayed lactation. By the time mother and child were reunited it was impossible for Debbie to breastfeed her son. This was Jamey's luck. He grew into a big, happy, resentment-free lug of a baby anyway. This was his nature. Jamey's was not the sort of heart that cried out, *Where are the breasts that I deserve?* His was the sort that said, *Bottle? Cool. Formula?* Yum! From birth Jamey was blessed, despite his wretched luck, with a nature easily pleased by the world within his reach. If the kid in the backyard next door had a twenty-dollar action figure with kung-fu grip, fully articulated joints, and power-action waist, and Jamey had an old wet dishrag, Jamey set to work exploring the properties of his wet rag, inventing a personality for it, interacting and teasing and yucking it up with it till the neighbor kid would be pleading to trade his action figure for Jamey's rag.

Another of Jamey's strong suits: indefatigability. An invaluable asset for a lad destined for a life in the arts. An example: Jamey loved to crawl as an infant and became unusually proficient at it—so proficient that, long after other kids his age were walking, he took no particular interest in uprightness. Jamey was fifteen months old and his parents, Debbie and Jon, feared he was developmentally disabled in some way before he began to experiment with walking. But his experiments met with an odd setback: vertical toddling struck little Jamey as hilarious. Trying to convey a toy across a room by placing one tiny foot in front of the other when, on his hands and knees, he could nearly carry his mother on his back, made him laugh so hard he'd lose his balance, teeter into walls and furniture, bang his knees, hips, head, fall on his ass, laugh hysterically, stand back up, leg it into more crashes, and laugh even harder. When neighbors and relatives witnessed his hilarity-sabotaged toddling, word spread and small crowds would convene, soon laughing so hard that the future thespian experienced an early love of his ability to amuse an audience.

One morning during his Walk, Crash, and Laugh phase Jamey sat down on the floor, fell silent, and after a few minutes began to cry—a nearly unheard-of act for this ebullient little person. When Debbie tried to figure out why, the toddler could articulate nothing, but the crying grew so inconsolable that she took him to an emergency room. The problem was a hernia. Jamey underwent surgery that night. The operation left a seven-inch scar reaching from his groin's ground zero to his right hip bone. The surgeon warned Jamey's parents that it would be days before he tried to walk and that it would hurt like hell when he did. But this was where his *indefatigability* kicked in: on Jamey's first night home from the hospital, Jon woke to an eerie sound in the bedside crib, wakened Debbie, and in the glow of the night-light they beheld their son gripping the crib rail in his chubby fist as he staggered back and forth like King Lear in his late madness, cheeks streaked with tears, belly shaking with laughter. Even in pain, two-leggèd locomotion continued to strike Jamey as a scream.

THE BIRTHDAY DEATH of a mother does not unmake such a nature. Once in a while, though, his native ebullience would vanish, leaving him so inert that he appeared physically or mentally damaged. Not surprisingly, the worst of these cripplings came, as regularly and cynically as Santa Claus, on the birthdays that were also his mother's deathday.

On his first post-mom birthday his dad, Jon, and older sister, Judith, attempted to blow the family grief to smithereens by throwing Jamey an extra-big party. They decked the halls with synthetic jollies, hired a professional clown, amassed solid and liquid arsenals of multicolored forms of sugar, and invited an army of gift-bearing kids. The revelers buried Jamey, as planned, in hypoglycemic cheer. When the birthday boy began dashing about as gleefully and idiotically as his guests, Jon and Judith's plan seemed to be working. During the post-cake opening of presents, however, an officious-looking neighbor girl handed Jamey a gift and—with the cool neutrality of the mathematically precocious—announced, "You're six today, Jamey. And your mom is minus one."

Negative numbers. What a fascinating concept for the birthday boy. The instant Jamey began to consider Debbie's negative first deathday the gift in his hand vanished, the sounds in the room grew muted, the unopened mound of presents morphed into an emaciated body on a mechanical bed, and his mother's hollow eyes and chemo-swollen face turned to stare into and through him. Lost, Jamey stared back. He saw the blue eyes shine with love for a moment; then the head grew naked, the face turned yellow and puffy, and he saw himself faltering in his efforts to love this frighteningly changed face in return. Her hollow eyes saw him falter. In desperation he said to the face, *I love you, Momma,* but felt only fear of her state, causing the pained eyes to hurt even more.

Minus one.

Jamey stood frozen so long the math whiz finally tapped his shoulder, a wag called out, "Anybody home?" a circle of sugar-smeared faces burst into laughter, Debbie's swollen face vanished—and Jamey grew soul-sick. Mumbling to Jon that he didn't feel good, he deserted his guests, tottered to his room, put himself to bed, and remained there till every trace of the celebration was out of the house.

Jon and Judith's would-be exorcisms of Jamey's haunted birthday escalated like warfare: over the next three years they tried a swimming pool party, a roller rink party, and a Barnum & Bailey Circus party. But the neighbor girl's formula stuck:

I'm seven this year—and Mom is minus two . . .

I'm nine—and Mom's minus four . . .

The parties, for Jamey, were sulfa drugs. Allergic reactions made him more and more erratic. The day he turned eight, for instance, when it came time to make a wish and blow out the candles, he leaned carefully over the flames and stayed there, unflinching, until his hair began to singe and stink. When his father pulled him back and asked what he was trying to do, Jamey blurted, "Get my wish!" and ran from the room sobbing. When he turned nine and his big boisterous party was leaving the Barnum & Bailey Circus at Memorial Coliseum, Jamey eyed his entourage with allergic distaste, melted into the exit crowd, and vanished so completely that Jon, after a long and frantic search, called the police. Jamey was picked up after midnight by a squad car on a street three miles away. When his distraught dad again asked what he was trying to do, Jamey felt an answer, but couldn't yet speak it: what he truly wanted from his birthdays was a chance to grasp, by and for himself, the maddening gift he'd already been given: *a dead mother.*

A few weeks before Jamey's tenth birthday, Judith, in front of Jamey, began to query Jon, not Jamey, about the upcoming celebration. Jamey blew up. "Those parties are for *you*, not me! I hate them!" Judith then exploded in return, shrieking that their mother had given Jamey parties so she was doing the same. "Go ahead, Jude!" Jamey roared. "Play *Mommy* on my birthday. But I won't be there to watch!"

Jude fled the table in tears. Jamey stomped to his room. Jon gave his son time to cool, then went in and asked what he most wanted to do on his birthday. With great earnestness, Jamey said, "Treat it like a regular old day. No party, no nothing. I want to spend the day *alone* with . . . with whatever's left . . . you know . . . of *Mom.*"

Jon Van Zandt was a Stoic. His face showed nothing as he slowly nodded. But his voice quavered as he murmured, "Permission granted."

ON HIS FIRST party-free January 30th Jamey slept late, woke slowly, then remembered his new birthday freedom. Sighing with satisfaction, he stared up at the ceiling and commenced, as planned, to conjure every last thing he could remember about his mother. He managed to recall, at least faintly, a pleasing voice. He recalled a benign warmth bending down to praise him. He vaguely glimpsed a blue-eyed, pretty face. But before he could study that face, memorize it, convey his love to it, it broke up and melted into mist.

Distressed, Jamey summoned his indefatigability, jumped out of bed, dressed as fast as he could, and called to the mother mist, "*Come on!*" The mist made no reply—was no longer even a mist, really—but Jamey made a show of coaxing it downstairs even so.

He found Jon in the process of making his favorite breakfast: strawberry crepes topped with whipped cream. He found that Judith had placed, on his plate, a three-by-five card upon which she'd typed: "Happy Regular Old Day. —Jude." He noticed her staring at him so blankly she resembled a three-by-five card herself, and grinned. "No kidding, Jude," he said. "This is the best present you ever gave me! So thanks."

Judith stuck out her tongue, then bent to her crepes with seeming distaste. Jamey plowed into his with relish.

Jon joined them at the table. "So what will you do today, Mister Regular?"

Jamey peered out the window. "It's not raining and not too cold. I'd like to just go out on my bike, if that's okay, wander around all day, then come home for a regular ol' dinner here at the regular ol' ranch."

Poker-faced as ever, Jon said, "Two quick confessions. One, I broke the Regular Ol' Day Rule and got you a present. Two, I broke it again and gave Jude permission to bake a cake. If we ban all guests except Gramma Nan and if we don't sing 'Happy Birthday,' could you stand to blow out ten candles and eat a piece of the cake?"

Jamey tried to look put-upon, then grinned. "That's regular enough!"

"By four the daylight's going," Jon said. "I want you home at three. And no disappearing this year. Disappearing is not regular, Mister Regular."

"Deal," Jamey said with another grin.

HE SET OFF into Southeast Portland through a morning as bland as his plan for the day. The sky was a white so dull it looked like a ceiling, making the outdoors feel like the indoors of a giant unheated building. Jamey's bike, an old English three-speed, made a pleasing *clicketa-clicketa-clicketa* when he stopped pedaling, so he began to seek residential streets with downhill slants. Riding to the crest of each, he would put on a burst of speed, then glide, enjoying the *clicketa-clicketa* for as long as possible.

He'd been at this for half an hour and had set a record glide of three blocks, when he realized he hadn't thought of his mother once. Blushing with shame, he pulled up to the curb and looked at the empty air. "You're minus five today," he said softly. "Is there anything you'd like for...for your negative fifth deathday?"

He listened to the air's lack of answer long enough to grow sad. But sadness activated his indefatigability. "Come on!" he said. "There's gotta be *something*."

The nothing remained nothing. But Gramma Nan, Debbie's mother, often remarked that Debbie had been stubborn. Jamey refused to grow downhearted.

Looking around the neighborhood, getting his bearings, he realized he was only a block from the Woodstock public library. This struck him as more than nothing: Debbie used to take him and Jude there. Jon too had taken them a few times after Debbie died, but with Jon the visits had felt hollow—a Good Husband dutifully maintaining his Departed Wife's rite. Debbie had taken them to the library for an incomparably more enjoyable reason, and Jamey, briefly, could picture her declaring it: "I *love* books!" Then she'd prove it: every time they went to Woodstock public, Debbie checked out the maximum number from both the grown-up and kids' sections. She read Jamey and Jude to sleep every night. She also abandoned Jon at the TV most nights, preferring the novels she devoured in bed. Recalling all this with growing hope of contact, Jamey rode fast to the library, locked his bike in the rack, and stepped through the double glass doors.

Once inside, he stopped in the entrance area and stood quiet, hoping to sense Debbie somehow. He felt a faint pull from the children's book section but decided it was a memory, not a presence, so he stayed rooted where he was. *You're the booklover,* he thought. *Show me where you want me.* He then spread his feet a little, folded his arms over his chest, adopted a pleasant expression, and waited.

The library was nearly empty. A couple of codgers, winos to judge by a faint pall in the room, slumped in armchairs, perusing newspapers strung on wooden poles. The checkout counter was untended. Hearing a creak to his left, Jamey turned to see a gray-haired librarian halfway up an aluminum stepladder that let out rodent-like squeaks when she shifted her weight. On the wall before her was an enormous cork bulletin board topped by the words AROUND THE WORLD THIS DAY! The woman was push-pinning wire-service news clippings to the board.

Want to read those? Jamey whispered in his head.

Feeling no response, he waited a full minute—and felt more nothing. The librarian kept push-pinning. Invisible ladder-rodents kept squeaking. AROUND THE WORLD THIS DAY! the bulletin board kept proclaiming. Another minute passed. Jamey's hope for a prompt gave out. Still, he waited. He no longer believed anything was going to happen but felt that his patience, at least, and the pleasant expression he tried to keep on his face were gifts he could give to Debbie.

More minutes passed. The nothing responded with more nothing. The librarian turned twice and smiled at Jamey. Both times he dropped his eyes, knowing she was going to speak to him if he didn't move soon. He had a feeling her first words would be: *Waiting for someone?* If those were her words, he looked forward to replying, *Yes. My dead mom.*

I'll read anything you like, Jamey told the nothing.

Dead air.

Does this mean you want me to read what I wanna read? he asked.

Nothing moved or urged or whispered.

Taking care not to sigh with exasperation, keeping his expression pleasant, Jamey stepped up to the big bulletin board. The news clippings, he saw at once, all pertained to events of the past twenty-four hours. They were divided by continent. EUROPE had the most stories, but the librarian had cheated a little: she'd filed all news of the Soviet Union under EUROPE, but Jamey knew that most of the USSR was in Asia. AUSTRALIA had just four clippings. ANTARCTICA had nothing but a yellowed old photo of a blizzard-blown penguin with a chick standing on its feet. Jamey was surprised to see that the United States was not included under NORTH AMERICA. He guessed this was because the dozens of US papers, over where the codgers sat, contained too many stories to include.

He closed his eyes before the continents.

You choose, he thought. Then waited. And, as a special gift, waited some more. He faintly remembered the tone his mother had used, and glow he'd felt, when she'd tell him he was "*such* a good boy." But again, this was memory, not presence.

Sensing nothing, he opened his eyes, maintained his kind expression, and stepped up to ASIA. There were clippings from Hong Kong, Singapore, Taipei, Saigon, Peking, New Delhi, all telling of events that had taken place on this same January 30th. But Jamey's fifth grade teacher, Mr. Yaw, had explained how what he called "the make-believe known as the international date line" enabled certain news stories to travel impossibly fast. Inspecting the ASIA stories more closely, Jamey saw that several had partaken of "date line make-believe" by out-racing the clock. Something newsworthy would occur, a reporter would write it up, and if the story was wired from west to east, it could cross the date line and appear in print *before* the clocks said it had occurred. One such story, reported by the *New York Times,* was fresh in from India. On the library clock Jamey saw it was 10:50 a.m., yet in a *Times* photo taken at 11:00 a.m.—ten minutes into the future—a flood of humanity was washing through the streets of Calcutta.

The flood itself seized Jamey's imagination. "More than a million people," the caption said. A crowd twice the size of the entire population of Portland. Hard to believe. Yet the aerial photo showed a sea of dark heads and white clothes veering and sheering through the city streets in patterns that brought to mind vast flocks of migrating birds. Skimming the article to find out what had summoned the human flood, Jamey found they'd gathered in honor of a man shot to death, twenty years before, on this same 30th of January. A man named *Gandhi.* Not having heard of him, Jamey whispered it to rhyme with "candy." Another small photo showed the fallen hero to be a bald-headed, spindly-leggèd, grandfatherly little fellow in wire-rimmed glasses, smiling charmingly though he stood on the cold streets of London dressed in what looked like a dirty sheet, sandals, and no socks. The *Times* reporter praised this humble figure with a lavishness Jamey found distressing: "The father of a revolt based on strategic mass harmlessness." "Impossible odds against him from his first day in India to his last." "A once-invincible Empire brought to its knees by one man's weaponless rebellion." *How was it weaponless,* Jamey wanted to ask, *when Gandhi had been shot dead?* The vast crowd, worshipful praise, and murder of the sweetly grinning old man began to create a panic inside him. Was it random coincidence that Gandhi died on Debbie's deathday? Or was another premeditated *vicious coincidence* in the works? Feeling a desperate need to show "God" or "Fate" that he was keeping an eye on His or Its shenanigans, Jamey marched across the room to the checkout counter, borrowed a pencil, fished his library card out of his toy wallet, flipped it on its back, lay it on the counter, and in the humorless manner of a traffic cop filling out a reckless driving ticket, wrote:

> *Jan 30, 1948, Gandhi shot dead*
> *Jan 30, 1958, Jamey VZ born*
> *Jan 30, 1963, Debbie VZ dies of leukemia*
> *Jan 30, 1968, Dead Debbie Dead Gandhi and*
> *Live Jamey meet in Woodstock Library*

He glared at the empty air of the room, daring the Author of these vicious synchronicities to show His smirking face.

"Are you interested in Mahatma Gandhi?" an audible voice asked

Jamey froze. The gray-haired librarian. She'd come down off the ladder and followed him to the counter. The way she had said the name surprised him, softening the *a*'s to rhyme with "awe"—and that's what Jamey felt as she pronounced it. *Mahatma Gandhi.* What a string of syllables to own for a name!

But *was* Jamey interested in this man who, twenty long years after his assassination, was still adored not by a few forlorn mourners like Jamey, Jude, and Jon but by *millions*? Could he afford to learn more of this hero when, despite an ocean of adoration, he'd been murdered on Jamey and Debbie's already ridiculous birth and death day?

"Please follow me," the librarian said.

Jamey nearly snapped, *No!* But this was his mother's special library and day. She would have insisted on politeness. Directed at last by a palpable mothering force, he tagged along to the Young Adult section, where the librarian located and handed him a volume titled *The Man Who Won a War by Not Fighting.* But when the cover photo turned out to show him the same grandfatherly, sheet-and-sandals, happily grinning Gandhi he'd seen in the *Times,* everything that was happening felt deathly wrong. Hyperventilating as he spoke, Jamey reeled off the dates, "1948! 1958! 1963! 1968!!"

"What was that?" the librarian asked.

Jamey shook the book at her and blurted, "Does this tell about the *killing* of Gandhi?"

The woman stepped backward as if Jamey had physically shoved her. "I-I'm sure his death is mentioned."

"No! I mean, does it *describe* it? Like *how many bullets? Where they hit?* And what Muh…Maw…what he did after each bullet? And how long it took him to die?"

The librarian's jaw dropped. She took two more steps backward.

Seeing he'd horrified her, Jamey dropped the book, picked it back up, shoved it in her hands, turned to flee, but was so cramped up and burdened that he could only stagger toward the door. His plan for the day had succeeded! The instant the librarian had pronounced Gandhi's name correctly, Jamey felt magic in the sound. The word "Mahatma," especially, struck him as strong. So strong it had lured a million people into the streets this very day. So strong that even the likes of leukemia and bullets might have trouble dragging such a word to its grave. So strong that Jamey burned to know precisely how much violence was needed to tear the word from the man who'd answered to it.

But this was only half of what struck him: the instant he sensed the strength in the word "Mahatma" he compared it to another word: "Debbie." And his mother's yellowed face and wasted body grew so present, and her name struck him as so weak, that she collapsed onto him with a physical weight that caused him to sicken and stagger and sink. By the time he reached his bike he was too stricken to even stand, let alone mount or ride.

Deadly coincidence does not feel innocent. On January 30th, 1968, a million souls surged through the streets of Calcutta, pouring adoration into the legacy of a man who'd answered to the word "Mahatma" as, half a planet away yet in the same surging moment via date-line magic, an equally adoring boy hunched alone by an old English bicycle, crushed by the weight of his yearning to save his mother, even now, by giving her a more powerful name.

(Seattle, Washington, 1985)

II. Risa's Immaculate Conception

She saw the lightning in the east and she longed for the east,
but if it had flashed in the west she would have longed for
the west... The east wind whispered a hadith handed down,
successively, from distracted thoughts, from passion, from
anguish, from tribulation, from rapture, from reason, from
yearning, from ardor, from tears, from my eyelids, from fire,
from my heart:
  "He whom you love is between your ribs.
  Your breathing tosses him from side to side."
            —Ibn al-Arabi, *The Tarjumán Al-achwáq: XIV*

A UNIVERSITY OF Washington coed named Marisa Stella McKeig began
an affair on the very first day of college. Her lover, for several years, was
the ancient Indian language known as Sanskrit. Risa (rhymes with Lisa)
was drawn to the old tongue by an even older lure: smitten by the look of
a dark-eyed boy she saw registering for Intro to Sanskrit, she slipped in
line behind him. The attraction came to nothing: Risa fell for the tongue
instead.

On the first day of class the professor, Dr. Chagan Kuldunchari—a
seventyish, hawk-faced, outwardly calm, inwardly intense Indian—strode
into the room carrying nothing but an old-fashioned, yard-long wooden
pointer. The instant Risa saw the pointer she imagined it to be a relic of
the defunct British Raj and guessed—correctly as it turned out—that the
dignified man before her had been unjustly beaten with it.

Dr. Kuldunchari did not introduce himself. He didn't make any sort of
statement about the aims or methods of his course. He just walked over to
a movie screen that stood in front of a blackboard, moved it aside, and the
students saw words, written in pale blue chalk, covering the board. Standing to the left of the words, Kuldunchari set his body as if against a strong
wind. He then began chanting—to a roomful of ad-whacked, hormonally
skewed young Americans—in the incomprehensible, rhythmic, prehistoric
tongue of ancient rishis as he tapped with his pointer on the corresponding
English. The translation read:

The Lord of Love said, Let Me be born, Let Me be many!
And in the depths of His concentration He entered everything.
He the formless assumed myriad forms.
He the All-Knowing became ignorance.
He the Infinite became finite.
He the Real became the illusory.
He the Unseen became the universe.
The Lord of Love, unmanifest, became manifest,
drawing Himself out of Himself.
Therefore is He called "the Self-Existent."
Were He not here, who would breathe?

As the words entered her mind in English and her ears in Sanskrit, Risa felt what she could only describe as *the main Mystery* enter the room. For an unbounded moment, a Vastness breathed inside and outside her body, pervading campus and city, touching everyone and everything, near and far. She didn't understand any of this. She'd had no previous inkling that such experiences were possible. She just fell, sudden as a drunk into a swimming pool, into a glorious sense of connection and floated in it, blissful and effaced for a while.

When, in the silence that followed, Dr. Kuldunchari relaxed his stance, slid his wooden pointer like a sword into his belt, smiled the slightest of smiles, and asked, "Any questions?" Risa's heart did a little cartwheel and she had a new favorite professor as well as a new favorite tongue. Eighteen years old, guardedly fond of Beat poets, and a very occasional smoker with a weakness for menthol, she dubbed the tongue *Skrit* and the prof *Dr. Kool.*

As HER SKRIT studies commenced, India's oceanic scriptures, poetry, and mythology began whispering sweet nothings to Risa's entire sense of self. When she began learning, in other classes, how the world's last surviving oral cultures, Sanskrit included, were being obliterated by Maoist Mandarin, "Free Market" English, and a few other commerce-coronated tongues, she began rooting for her underdog language with the fervor of a sports fan. Enthusiasm intensified concentration. She grew aware of how inexact her American Teen English had been, and of what a muzzle it had placed over her thoughts. *Like, was it helpful,* she asked herself, *for my high school friends and me to like, use the word "like," like, four or five times per sentence?* The logic and structure of Skrit grammar soon brought such a powerful ordering force to her mind that her English, her thinking, and her daily life soon fell into unprecedentedly good working order. Then came a day and definition that changed her life.

On his same blackboard, in the same pale blue chalk, Dr. Kool wrote the word *sad.* No sooner did Risa ask herself *Why'd he do that?* than he changed the situation entirely by adding a dot under the *s,* converting the

English word *sad* into a Sanskrit syllable he pronounced "shod," and with the same blue chalk defined *ṣad* like so.

to sit down inwardly, and breathe, and attain the True

Dutifully writing down, "sad, *ṣad, ṣad*ness," dots and italics included, Risa had whispered the words, pronouncing them, "Sad, shod, shodness" as Dr. Kool advised, when something more happened: as the English word "sad" became the Sanskrit word *ṣad*, English and Skrit mated, the two words fused in a nonce word, *ṣad*ness, and she experienced an intuition she sensed might be profoundly true.

Feeling guilty to have gone mentally walkabout, she renewed her focus on the lecture and would have thought no more about the incident. But over the next few weeks, every time the sight of life's cruelty or humanity's inhumanity made her sad—a mother slapping her child in a supermarket, a homeless man babbling hundreds of words to no one on a rain-soaked sidewalk, a group of teen boys stoning a flightless gull on a Puget Sound beach— a transformative dot appeared beneath the cause of sadness, transforming it to *ṣad*ness, and *ṣad*ness caused her breath to come with a calm fullness, her mind and body to fill with a serenity she hadn't previously known how to summon, and interior doors to open in what had once seemed solid walls.

Risa was an exacting student. She knew the immaculate conception and birth of the word "*ṣad*ness" constituted the kind of magical Student-Think that drives language professors to liquor cabinets and Vedic rishis to remote mountain caves. The night after the word was born, she opened her English and Skrit dictionaries, discovered India's *ṣad* and England's *sad* to be as alien to each other as red roses and yellow catfish, and set out as dutifully as one of King Herod's soldiers to kill her bastard word. But before carrying out the execution she learned from a Skrit text that *ṣad* doesn't exist by itself: its meaning is created when preceded or followed by other letters. When, for instance, the *ṣad* in *Upaniṣad* becomes *ni-ṣad*, dot added, it *does* mean *to sit down*. Once she knew even this, her mind's attempts to sunder the sad/*ṣad*/sadness connection failed, and she recognized the cause: the serene inner state she called *ṣad*ness had not been born of an A-student's *mental* process; it was born of an *elemental* process. Cream is a far cry from coffee, but dump a little in a hot black cup and the coffee turns tan and stays tan whether you want its blackness back or not.

*Ṣad*ness proved the cream in every subsequent cup of Risa's sorrows. She developed a nightly habit of retrieving the thoughts that arose in response to spirit-soaked old Skrit words Dr. Kool had unpacked in class. If, say, *vyāna* or *dharma-kāya* set off reverberations over her nightly cup of green tea, she began, in the manner of her junior high anti-hero, Jack Kerouac, to write whatever the word's magic moved her to write in what Kerouac called *secret scribbled dumbsaint notebooks for yr own joy*. Her first such dumbsaint entry:

In Dr. Kool's class last week, in about two seconds flat, some old Vedic magic sprang to life & nuked my Constitutionally guaranteed right to feel like an Amerika-betrayed piece of crap. It was the words sad, ṣad, & ṣadness that did it – & I know! Ṣadness isn't even a word! So should I be worried? Are joss sticks, saffron robes, & Hare Krishna chants on street corners next? Or do most folks never try, when smacked by a wave of sadness, to sit down, breathe deep & slow, & sink into the black heart of it? And if they don't, how would they ever find what I've been finding in there?

I'm not asking for bad stuff to happen. (Hope you heard that, Grampa Shiva!) But when I sit quiet with my saddest feelings, letting them be what they are till they & I become silent & immovable, that little Skrit dot now & then appears beneath my sadness like the world's dinkiest Flying Carpet, wafting me into a place so dark, calm & spacious I not only don't dread it, I fall willingly inside it, growing dark, calm & spacious myself. To be honest in a way that pretty much terrifies Skeptical Me, this sad, sad, sadness mantra has carried me so deep into darkness that I have twice felt an expansion, looked inwardly skyward, & glimpsed some kind of actual inner stars. So what a rush it was, researching my Desert Fathers paper last week, to stumble upon this famous old saint, Isaac of Syria, who comes right out & says:

Make peace with yourself & heaven & earth
make peace with you. Take pains to enter
your innermost chamber & you will see the
chamber of heaven, for they are one & the same,
& in entering one you behold them both.

Wow! Or as Dr. Kool says, "Om shanti shanti shanti! That is full, this is full, peace! peace! peace!" By which I think he means: Wow!

Of course no inner chamber or starry sky solves an outward earthly problem, or even addresses its causes. But what if the way through the unending sadnesses—long wars, short lives, Congressional drivel, Seattle traffic—was never a matter of solving anything? What if it was always a matter of how small even the greatest sadness feels when you sit down without hope or fear, breathe in the darkness no matter how deep, & keep on breathing till blackness opens unto heaven's starry chamber & you realize, My God! I've got infinite insides!

(Portland, 1971)

III. Jamey's Gravitationally Collapsed Mother Object

I believed in God,
but I also believed that God was malign.
                                        —Nick Cave

ONCE IN A while, during the immeasurably long life of a galaxy, a random star is destroyed by a slow-motion explosion, burning for a while at thousands of times its former brightness, becoming the anomaly known as a supernova. Once in an even rarer while, a very large supernova— three times the mass of our sun seems the minimum requisite size— stops throwing its brilliance outward, turns on itself with inconceivable force, and collapses *inward,* causing this brightest of interstellar objects to vanish. Though the conflagrating star has disappeared, its inward collapse continues, creating a nuclear-powered gravitational implosion so fierce that not even that 186,000-mile-per-second speedster light can escape it. John Archibald Wheeler, the physicist who first discovered one of these unseen implosions, dubbed it a "gravitationally completely collapsed object." While giving a lecture one day, though, Wheeler had repeated his awkward term a few times when a woman in the audience called out, "Why not call the thing a *black hole?*" The nickname stuck.

Black holes, like God, are imperceptible. But the same light-devouring power that makes them invisible renders them detectable. Though astronomers have never seen a black hole, they chart their locations with precision when they detect the light, gases, and fire from neighboring stars or nebulas being sucked toward an invisible but specific point in space.

AFTER DEBBIE VAN Zandt died on her son's fifth birthday, her body was cremated. Her remains were then driven by Jon and his children to a headland Debbie had loved on the Oregon Coast, where they were to be thrown, handful by handful, off a cliff into the Pacific. The family's notion had been to watch the ashes fall to the waves so that, for the rest of their lives, they'd see something of blue-eyed Debbie every time they beheld the blue sea. But the Pacific that day was a gray-green riot, a twenty-knot wind was blowing straight onshore, and when Jon began flinging Debbie's remains toward the sea, little Jude and Jamey were soon hacking incinerated bits of Mom into the thrashing sedge grass and fingering her out of their eyes. Their misery sent the normally stoic Jon into a rage: with a roar he hurled the half-emptied urn as far as he could off the cliff. But how feeble, human fury, in the face of an ocean's power. The urn smashed on cobble far short of the breakers, startling a lone, napping harbor seal. When the seal then galloped like a quadruply amputated horse for the waves and disappeared, Jamey, from that moment on, identified his graceful blue-eyed mother not with the vast Pacific but with the land-hampered galumphing of a terrified seal.

Despite this mythic glitch, Debbie Van Zandt ceased on that day to exist by any method of measurement dealing with the perceptible. But one day each year—January 30th—the same disappearance that rendered Debbie invisible made her astronomically detectable, so to speak, when the light and energy of her son was violently drawn toward an invisible but specific point. To be as precise as possible: every year on Jamey and Debbie's joint birthday-deathday, a "gravitationally collapsed interior object" became his mom.

BASED ON THE evidence accrued, black holes don't make good mothers. But this isn't to say that they don't mother at all: on the day Jamey turned six, when the neighbor girl said that Debbie was now "minus one," a gravitationally collapsed interior object began to mother him so fiercely that the energy was sucked from his body in seconds, forcing him to abandon his guests and drag himself to bed. On the day he turned ten and compared the names Mahatma and Debbie, an interior force mothered him so vehemently that her unseen body added its mass to his own, making it impossible to mount and ride his bike. On ensuing birthday-deathdays, Jamey's link to his collapsed mother object grew increasingly problematic. Having loved and been loved by a physically appealing flesh-and-blood woman, Jamey longed to go on loving and being loved physically no matter how invisible she had become. Not only was he willing to be haunted by his vanished mother, he craved such a haunting. He wanted to feel noticed, feel watched over, sense maternal mists and ghostly emanations. He yearned for things as straightforward as an intuited voice saying: *My, you look handsome today!* Or: *You seem a bit down.* Or: *Good grades! Good game! Good joke!* But gravitationally collapsed interior objects implode so ferociously that not even light, let alone voices, can escape them. If Jamey's black hole mom was ever to emit a love palpable to her son, love's escape velocity would have to prove even faster and more powerful than light's.

There was also, in Jamey's mind, an increasingly troublesome "God factor" interfering with his efforts. When Debbie had died in his Providence Hospital birthplace on the day he turned five, a *vicious invasion* seemed to have been inflicted and his psyche received a stab from the Unseen. Whether the stabber was the loving God of his mother, the Random Fate of his father, or the ill-tempered heavenly Republican of his maternal grandmother made no difference to Jamey's psyche: the fifth-birthday blade had been driven in deep.

To add to his pain and confusion, Jamey deployed his indefatigable good cheer with panache, seeming never to have been wounded at all but on this one cursèd day of the year. His charming denial of his wound, however, created a profound interior blindness. And as generals, kings, presidents, popes, CEOs, and others have demonstrated throughout history, when the deeply wounded go inwardly blind, then pretend, with panache, that they can still see, they become monumentally destructive.

JAMEY'S THIRTEENTH JANUARY 30th dawned unseasonably bright and sunny despite the cold. Jon served up the usual strawberry birthday crepes. Judith grimly presented Jamey with her now traditional three-by-five "Have a Not Too Happy Regular Old Day" card. Jamey then set out, with the blitheness of a flamboyant blind man, in pursuit of the remnants of his gravitationally collapsed interior mother object.

Late morning found him riding a new Schwinn ten-speed—his birthday gift from Jon—down a small hill in Southeast Portland. No plan, no need to rush, no place he had to be. He was just gliding down the incline, enjoying the bike's speedometer and effortless twenty-mile-an-hour speed. But as he neared the intersection at the bottom of the hill, Jamey saw that the cross street was busy, that his own street had a stop sign, and that a four-story office building and parked truck blocked his view of cross traffic. Time to brake. His effortless glide was over, and something in him suddenly resented this. It was his and Debbie's thirteenth birthday and negative eighth deathday, damn it. *January 30th owes us!* he thought. *Mom and me have a God-caused or Fate-caused right to glide straight* through *this damned intersection. No slowing. No looking. No hesitation. Pure gift.*

So that's what they proceeded to do. Taking belligerent aim at the quiet street beyond the intersection—seeing that street as a kind of Hereafter he and Debbie deserved to reach and share—Jamey locked his arms, legs, brain, body, shut his eyes as if in prayer, shot past the office building and truck, shot past the stop sign, felt a presence on his right, *felt hugeness, heat, doom on his right,* opened his eyes, saw a Franz Bakery truck astoundingly close, coming *very* fast, the bulging-eyed driver swelling toward him, yards away, standing on his brakes, tires screaming, the braking not nearly enough. Expecting impact, expecting death, Jamey froze in terror, which kept his arms locked, kept the Gift Glide going. He watched the driver reef with all his might on the wheel, causing the truck to spin and miss him by an inch, then looked back over his shoulder as the now-out-of-control truck smashed into a parked pink Mustang on the cross street, flipped it onto its side, rammed it across the sidewalk, the truck flicking the shrieking, shattering car before it the way winds flick a dried leaf, candy wrapper, ashes of Mom, smashing it through a picket fence, over small trees and border shrubs, into the wall of a brick apartment house with a thud Jamey felt in his geologic roots, yet *still* the physics of truck mass kept crushing the car, trying to ram it *through* the bricks, out of this world, on into nothingness. Meanwhile the Cause of It All—young James Lee Van Zandt—shot unscathed as God up the side street, his deathday Gift Glide to negative-eight-year-old Debbie as intact as the intersection behind them was blighted.

Pedaling fast now, but repeatedly looking back, Jamey saw people pouring from houses, cars slamming on brakes, heard a chorus of horns, shouts, burning rubber, yelping dogs. Then—a sight that would follow him for life—the bakery truck driver, limping to the curb, holding his bleeding head and face in one hand, pointing at Jamey with the other, shouting, "*Come back here! You! Come back here!*"

Jamey tore on, turned a corner, zigzagged for six blocks, raced straight for several more; crossed a park, a ditch, a railroad track; reached a dirt driveway leading to an abandoned house; pulled into the overgrown yard behind the house.

Letting the birthday bike fall in winter-dead grass, he sank to his knees, covered his face with his hands, began reliving the scene, and fell into a chasm of feelings he'd never dreamed possible. Gargantuan defiance of he-knew-not-what ripped through him in shock waves. He began to babble and laugh convulsively: *Poor little bakery truck driver! Pointing at me! Bleeding at me! Bleeding and pointing. You! Come back here! And the culprit just rides on!*

"*Fuck you!*" Jamey roared into the palms of his hands, sobbing a little, choking a little, then laughing some more, for the world, his life, his grief, loss, birthday, felt wildly different. Better. Almost perfect. Why? *Because this time I didn't wait,* he told himself. No more innocent Jamey, tethered like a goat to the stone altar of his birthday, waiting for the God-Fate-Nothing Thing to come stab him and suck out his happiness. This time *he'd* sought the power. And found it. And worked it like a god. Hadn't he? *Hadn't he?*

Seeing the driver's bloodied face, tumbling pink car, crushed bricks of the apartment building—knowing real damage had been done and the driver's self-sacrifice was all that had saved him—Jamey felt waves of remorse. But with all his strength he defied them. He could have killed someone—sure! Could have died—of course! But what was real, now, was this surging power that filled him.

"*Screw you, little driver, and screw me!*" he roared into his palms, the smashed sound of his voice blasting hot back into his face. "*Screw the nice little job you'll prob'ly lose, an' your nice wrecked bakery crap, an' the cute little Mustang we obliterated!*" Jamey screamed, his palms dripping tears and snot as the power tore and thrilled him. Because...*because the Franz truck was leukemia,* wasn't it? And the parked car, pretty pink car, was Debbie, wasn't she? But who was the birthday maniac who had shot, blind and uncaring, into the cross traffic? Who was the senseless terror on the inexcusably speeding bike? The answer to this was what sent the surges blasting through him—because the world's most inarguable polarity had for once been reversed. The role of Random Havoc-Maker, Ruling Leukemia-and-Wreck-Bestower, All-Powerful Worldfucker, had been usurped, for a few shattering seconds, by Jamey himself.

"*See?*" he laughed and sobbed into his hands. "You're not the only One who can crush and maim and ruin!" Defiance fueled his implosion; the black energy billowed in on itself, and Jamey rode it blindly, letting the gyre spin him deeper down than most survivors ever go. He saw the bloodied driver, felt terrible guilt, kept gliding; saw his mother's lovely face melt into yellow hospital ruin, kept gliding; felt enraged love devouring his guilt, felt his stabbed heart devouring his humanity, felt the dark power plunging in and in till it was no longer Jamey, it was Collapsed Blackness itself that turned to any Being who dared visit such ruin on a young mother's face and shouted, "*You! Come back here! Because see? Even I can destroy for no reason! It's so easy! Sooooo easy! So screw You! You're Nobody! Do You hear me? Nobody!*"

Ah, Jamey, the half-good son, keeping the Fifth Commandment by smashing the First. Honoring the gravitationally collapsed implosion that was once his blue-eyed mom. Showing any conceivable Holiness how much he adored her still. "*Anybody can wreck, smash, and ruin!*" he sobbed into his palms. "*God! Shitheads! Nobodies on bikes and nobodies in heavens! So happy birthday to me and Mom, and screw You! Do You hear me? Do You hear? Come back here!*"

(Seattle, 1985)

IV. Veda U

Not by the out-breath nor by the in-breath does any mortal live. By a mystery immortal do we live, on which these two breaths depend. Come! I will show you this secret formulation!

—anonymous Vedic rishi

FOR HER FIRST eighteen years, Risa was an unusually bright but otherwise typical American child of TV, rock and roll, A.P. English and math classes; child of FM radio love songs inseparable from clogged Portland malls and sprawls and hi-speed girl chatter; child of parents whose dysfunctional marriage led to a divorce that simply chopped the dysfunction in two, bequeathing Risa two untenable homes instead of one; child increasingly aware, therefore, of the deep bewilderment of her parents' generation and the binge consumption, binge investment, binge drinking, eating, sex, religiosity, to which bewilderment led; child who, from the age of thirteen or so, was virtually self-raised amid a circle of smart, irony-addicted peers desperate to at least make black comedy out of their nation-state's willingness to sacrifice life, including children's lives, in the name of global markets, global shopping, tumorous growth, global golf.

But at eighteen a little Sanskrit sent some primordial magic into Risa's life. The myths and texts of ancient India soon struck her not as tales of an "exotic East" but as legible maps and gazetteers leading toward a preposterously wonderful yet conceivably reachable home. Her concept of the Divine leapt from Kerouac's adolescent "God, the Guy who ain't a guy" to the *Rig Veda's* "Unseen Unborn Guileless Perfection." Her descents into sorrow became occasions not for despondency but for a sad/ṣad/ṣadness-fueled dive into "a space so calm, dark & spacious I not only don't fear it, I fall willingly in, growing calm, dark & spacious myself." Her nights, after long days of diligent study, grew haunted by Skrit repetition loops that played like music on the edge of sleep: *Know the embodied soul. Though it hides in the hundredth part of the point of a hair divided a hundred times, it is infinite. Not female, not male, not neuter. What body it takes, with that it is united. It is the great in the sun, the food in the moon, the radiance in lightning, the sound in thunder, Indra in the wind, the fullness in space, the truth in waters, the resemblance in a mirror; it is the companion in a shadow, life in an echo, death in a sound, Yama in a dream, Prajāpati in the body, speech in the right eye, truth in the left.* Though most of her fellow students seemed satisfied, amid the U Dub's smorgasbord of intellectual goods, to have their brains filled like hard-drives by a sequence of professorial downloads, with Skrit as her ally Risa began to conduct herself more like a cagey barterer at a Rajasthan bazaar. Declaring an Art major and Asian Religions minor, she made Skrit scripture and mythology not her "academic focus," but her living guide to her inner self and native land, and as a result became almost constantly happy. Migrating into the old wisdom texts as instinctively and completely as a salmon migrates up its home river, she grew less and less interested in keeping up with "modern America," and ever more aware of the living continent and creatures upon which modern America remorselessly gorged. She studied Skrit each night as if her life depended on it, and by day the testimony of her senses pollinated the passions that bloomed by night. The marine light and vapor pouring in off Puget Sound moistened and localized the wisdom words. Mount Rainier and the peaks of the Olympic peninsula became a Himalayan realm of unmet gods. The meticulousness with which Dr. Kool and his rishis unpacked an ancient forest world inspired a meticulousness in Risa's love for her own world. She began keeping field journals of careful drawings and notes, capturing "swinging doors" she hoped to convert to canvases. She bought beat-up North American field guides to birds, plants, trees, mammals, bugs, and beat them up further. Her dad bequeathed her an old pair of binoculars that turned vague vistas into perceptible places, high-flying specks into migratory birds, and the moon into an intimate new neighbor.

She discovered certain Skrit words and teaching stories that telescope mysteriously inward, revealing ever more potent secrets the closer one looks. Remembering this as she poked around in a pawn shop one morning, Risa was drawn to an enormous old magnifying glass. The thing looked as goofy in her grip as Dr. Kool's wooden pointer in his belt. She bought it for that very reason, lugged it everywhere in her backpack, and the world poured forth subtleties in response. She trained her lens on the life-rife soil under compost piles, on the sand under rocks on the Puget Sound tideline, on the back sides of rotting tree bark, gravel beds of streams. Every such nook and cranny turned out to be crawling with weird little unmet citizens. She met a bright crimson spider, the size of an average freckle, that could sprint almost as fast as humans walk, though its legs were nearly invisible. She found inert brown obtect pupae she'd mistaken for rat turds without her glass, out of which the preposterous beauties known as butterflies much later emerged. She found lumps on cherry tree leaves which, broken open, revealed teeming feedlots of pale blue aphids being bred, fattened, and milked by ants who were basically dairying, using the trees as farms.

* * *

SHE MET A bumblebee she befriended for five entire days. The friendship began one fall morning as she was walking to her Roman history class as Seattle was getting pounded by a massive Pacific storm. Though most every pedestrian she passed was scowling, Risa couldn't stop smiling. The storm-driven raindrops were showing off like birds, flying sideways and even upward in places, and the rush hour traffic had lost its internal combustion roar due to shoals of water the myriad tires kept displacing. When she closed her eyes to listen, each passing vehicle became the foam fingers of a wave shallowing out on a Pacific beach.

As she was about to enter the history building she noticed a single autumn narcissus amid a bed of hundreds of motionless blossoms nodding vigorously, as if encouraging her pleasure in the storm. Imagining an invisible Vedic creature stashed in a subtle flower inside the ordinary flower, Risa returned the nods—causing her powers of reason to pull her over and issue a Woowoo Ticket. The fine was to get down on all fours, muddy her knees and the heels of her hands, and peer up into the blossom in search of the nods' rational cause—and there *was* a being present: a bumblebee had crawled into the narcissus to escape the torrential rain.

Risa reached for her magnifying glass and trained it on the blossom's occupant. The bee's hairy rump, bulging in the flower's gold corona, looked like a chunk of garish shag carpet stuffed in the bell of a tiny trumpet, but six surrounding white petals prevented the rain from reaching that bell, insulating the bee in a double wall of dryness. "*Ingenious!*" Risa murmured. With which she went to class.

An ordinary student wouldn't have given this encounter another thought. But at Green Tea Hour that evening, as the storm continued to pound Risa's dorm, an unseen thread flew from her interior, through the night, to the bee tucked in the narcissus. "*Poor guy!*" she whispered, grabbing her *Field Guide to Insects* to gauge her friend's chances. The dense hair that covered the bumbler, she learned, was called *pile,* and its obvious purpose was to insulate, but a more surprising function was to help the bee gather food. As a bumblebee flies, its pile gathers an electrostatic charge from the air. Because flowers are grounded, the instant the bee lands on a blossom, pollen leaps onto its pile, electromagnetically propelled by the grounding. As Risa marveled at this, rain smacked her windows with the violence of a carwash. Before reason could stop her, she closed her eyes and spent a long time sending well-being down invisible threads to her bee.

Two mornings later—after a Roman history lecture during which Risa's prof struck her as clinically obsessed with Emperor Caligula's spectacular gruesomeness—she checked the narcissus and found the bee still jammed inside the gold trumpet. "You okay?" she asked, lightly touching its pile. The bumbler remained motionless. Holding the narcissus stem to steady it, Risa blew warm breath into the little gold chamber. The bee responded with a whirring so faint she couldn't hear it, only felt it in her fingertips. "Please help us!" Risa prayed to she couldn't say what.

The storm lasted four days. On day five, a Friday, dawn sent Homeric rose fingertips up into a blue sky. Thanking *Surya* the Sun, Risa set off early on her morning run and arrived at the narcissus shortly after the first solar rays struck. The ground had begun to steam. The bee was still in the blossom, but motionless. Taking hold of the narcissus, Risa breathed into the trumpet. When a weak whir again met her fingertips, a Skrit verse came to Risa. Into the corona she whispered,

> *There is a path, extremely fine and extending far.*
> *It has touched you, you have discovered it!*
> *That beneath which the year revolves,*
> *the breathing behind breathing, the sight behind sight,*
> *the hearing behind hearing, the thinking behind thinking,*
> *the first, the ancient. With the heart alone, behold it!*

The bumbler didn't move. The hands of Risa's watch did. It was time to jog home, clean up, eat breakfast, and prep for more Roman Empire, post-Christ, pre-fall. But her bumblebee, she'd learned, was a *Bombus terrestris*. The Latin term and its small owner struck her as more interestingly Roman than anything likely to occur in class. She kept watch instead.

And a quarter hour later—on a far better Friday for her bee than Good Friday was for Jesus—it finally backed out of its sepulcher into a shaft of sunlight. Its wings turned out to be blades of thinnest ice. Its back legs wore jodhpurs of orange pollen. Its pile shone black and brilliant gold in the morning shine. "*Five days!*" Risa marveled. "You broke Christ's record!"

Bzzzt, her small friend faintly replied.

Balancing on the lip of a white petal, the bee cleaned its head and body with its forelegs, tested its wings with a few more *bzzzt*s, and with no further ado flew up the shaft of sunlight till it disappeared through the trees—no extra credit, no grade, no tenure.

But Risa stayed on in the same beam, gathering some kind of static charge, till she found herself whispering to an Unseen Guileless Unknown, "*I can't name You or see You. But You have touched me. With the heart alone I just felt it! Keep touching me. I'm coming to You...*"

MUCH AS SHE prized moments like this, Risa continued to throw herself not just into Sanskrit but into all her classes. She remained as capable as most of her professors and peers at asserting, denying, analyzing, explicating—attacking and deriding too, if necessary. She also continued to enjoy the hurly-burly of campus life—including a couple of hurly-burly boyfriends. Even so, the wall separating her inner and outer lives grew increasingly permeable, and her mental makeup began to change:

There'd been a time when Risa, amid groups of intellectually amped peers, enjoyed flaunting her mental adroitness and caustic wit as much as any raucous young scholar. But when Skrit Lit cautioned her with statements like "Restrain the mind as the charioteer restrains his vicious horses," Risa took the admonitions to heart. The difference between a stimulated mind and a frenetic one became obvious. Her behavior changed accordingly. She still enjoyed it when she and her classmates got amped up during a free-form discussion of, say, corporate oligarchy, or Milan Kundera's take on women, or Camille Paglia's on men, or Richard White's on the American West. When the word slinging and idea spraying grew wild, Risa had a fine old time tossing her own rhetoric around—until the moment her brain began to feel frenetic. She would then hear the ancient echo ("as the charioteer restrains his vicious horses... "), feel a loyalty to deep forest and nameless rishis, rein in her mind-horses, detach from the hubbub, slow and deepen her breath, and sink toward a peace that "hides in the hundredth part of the point of a hair divided a hundred times, and is infinite."

She dubbed these shifts of consciousness "strategic withdrawals." And her friends sometimes saw her make them. When this happened, they'd tease Risa, calling her "spaced," "sleep-deprived," "oversexed," "undersexed," anything to coax her back into the fray. But once she withdrew she was impervious to goading. At a time in life when most of her peers were only interested in making their mind-horses gallop, she was determined to learn how and when to rein her horses in.

The effort bore immediate fruit. Her ability to retreat to a calm center, for starters, enabled her to stay focused amid the irritations of campus life *right in the presence of the irritants*. This contemplative triumph would have earned her an A+ had Isaac of Syria been one of her profs. Her ability to occupy a place of observant inaction amid frenetic action helped her conserve energy she had formerly squandered. Her intellectual endurance increased dramatically as a result.

Strategic withdrawals also enabled her, in a genuine if temporary way, to drop out of college whenever she felt a need to do so. This in turn removed the pressure so many students feel to literally drop out, giving her even more focus and energy when she turned back to the college experience. The same brief but total internal retreats enabled Risa to grow less and less caustic, more and more patient, more capable of being kind, and more willing to risk revealing a childlike curiosity even in classes and in social groups. If her curiosity was then scoffed by the galloping mind-horses of a would-be cynic or sophisticate, another quick withdrawal enabled her to target the hurt caused by the scoffing, remove it like a silly hat the cynic had stuck on her head, and remain free of emotional stews.

Another fruit of her strategic withdrawals: Risa could, when needed, confront other people so gently, justly, and helpfully that, rather than humiliate them into a combative stance, she frequently earned their gratitude. An example of the sort of diplomacy she learned to bring to bear:

During her sophomore year Risa requested a note of recommendation from Dr. Kool to apply for a 400-level class called Intellectual History of the England-India Interface. All Dr. Kool ever told his students about the give-and-take between these nations was "India gave and gave and Britain took and took—until Gandhiji." Risa figured the exchange must've been more intricate than that. A quick thumbing through a biography revealed Gandhi wearing Western suits when he lived in South Africa, looking the proper British barrister. And it was the Westerner Henry David Thoreau whose "Civil Disobedience" cross-pollinated with Gandhi's beloved Bhagavad Gita and sent him back to India, and the astonishing life that ensued. Because of her equal loves for verities Eastern and landscapes Western, Risa loved instances in which the West had inspired rather than exploited the East and wanted to learn more about them.

The Interface class, it turned out, was taught by a Dr. Hans Dybok, a prof whose former students characterized him as "hard," "dry," and "unbearably encyclopedic." Though this sounded far from promising, Risa went to the University Book Store to peruse Dybok's proposed reading list. And she did find it "unbearably encyclopedic." But she also found an impressive list of the kind of positive cross-cultural East-West exchanges that fascinated her.

So it happened that, during Dr. Dybok's next office hours, she knocked on his door, heard him say, "Come in," and encountered an exceedingly tidy, slight-of-build, bespectacled man looking dead serious behind a meticulously trimmed beard. Taking a chair at his bidding, she smiled and studied him until he, growing uncomfortable, asked, "How may I help you?" She then greeted the poor fellow with this:

"My name is Risa McKeig. I'm an Art major and Asian Religions minor. England's relationship with India is a big deal to me. So I'm really interested in your Interface class. But when I checked out the reading list, I saw that you assigned six thick books of mostly theoretical, scholarly prose." She paused to shoot the prodigiously scowling Dybok an encouraging smile. He did not smile back.

"I'm here for a strange reason, Doctor. The speech I'm now making, when it's over, will have consisted of about three hundred words. I rehearsed it and counted. Weird of me, I know. But feel the effort needed to grasp all these words? Tiring, isn't it? Yet, believe it or not, you've asked your Interface students to grasp roughly *three thousand times* more words than I will have spoken when I'm done. Imagine me running up to your office three thousand more times in the next ten weeks to deliver speeches as long as this one. I'd lose my voice! You'd lose your *mind*!"

Risa and Hans Dybok began to laugh, she gleefully, he very nervously.

"I have no idea what's going on in your life, Professor. But I figure happy students could only brighten your life, no matter what. So I looked at some of your published articles. And wow! You're amazing. The one on 'East-West zingers'? Loved it! Bertrand Russell on Rabindranath Tagore. 'Unmitigated rubbish about rivers becoming one with the Ocean'! And that essay on Prince Albert? That guy was a saint. And who but you knew? You know so much we'll want to probe you with questions and mull all the cool stuff dancing in your head. But the glut of prose, I'm afraid, will prevent that. So. My hope, in visiting today, is that these three hundred or so words might convince you to cut back on the million or so words you assigned. If it does, see you in class! Thanks for considering this!"

With that, Risa jumped to her feet, shot the professor a gat-tooth grin that delightfully deconstructed her iconic beauty, spun on her heels, and vanished.

"Thank you, Miss, uh? Miss?" the "unbearably encyclopedic" Dr. Dybok sputtered to the energy, fragrances, and statistics still reverberating in his office. In response to three hundred words and a grin he couldn't stop seeing, he cut half a million words on cross-culturally influential art and architecture from his reading list, replacing them with films and slideshows he realized could accomplish the same purpose in one-tenth the time. Inspired now, he added a sort of anti-talent show of Raj-era Brits and Indians objectifying, slandering, lampooning, and deconstructing one another in editorials, verse, and drama, but balanced that with an equal-sized display of mutual Indian-English respect and détentes. For comic relief, he also showed, in class, the Beatles' inane treatment of so-called Indians in the aptly named stoner flick *Help!* Though he was too late to change his catalogue description, he advertised the course revamp on a poster he hung on the History Department bulletin board, on his office door, and at the University Book Store. And at his first class the following week, Dr. Dybok's stony face broke into a surprisingly boyish grin when he spied Risa beaming at him, as promised, from the second row.

THIS ABILITY TO charm, disarm, and sometimes reorient others improved the mood in some of Risa's classes immensely. As a result, a growing number of astute peers began to approach Risa and ask what classes she'd be taking the next term. By her junior year a small tribe of familiars was galloping through the U Dub curriculum alongside her, generating their own nourishing little subculture in class, and, after class, gently pressuring profs—via close attention, intrepid playfulness, truthfulness, and good-heartedness— to solicit student thought more, play and joke more, and expound less. Risa never connected this tribe to her own amiability, diplomacy, strategic withdrawals, radiant energy, crazy grin, or anything of the sort. She believed she'd just lucked into an unusually cool circle of friends. But though many people spend energy in search of some sort of calm and stable center, a very few people simply *are* such centers. Without realizing it, Risa had become one of these rare ones, and as a result was encircled by friends in almost every milieu she frequented.

Another Green Tea Hour reflection from the college-within-a-college she called "Veda U":

The flavor, rhythm, feel, taste & smell of Sanskrit doesn't sit in my head a little while, then evaporate like dew on a summer day the way most of what I study does. For two plus quarters now, the shapes, sounds, myths, dreams of Skrit Lit keep diving down into my heart, glands, gut, sex, hands, feet & maybe into some kind of fire underground. These full-bodied, high & low, inner & outer sensations are what "learning" now means to me. So to be asked, the way too many profs ask, to treat my brain as a Be-All & End-All leaves me feeling heartless, glandless, gutless, sexless, hand-less, footless & groundless. Paramatma gives each Atman its life sure as Ocean gives the cloud its raindrops & Fire, Earth, Water, Air give students the fluidity, solidity, spirit & sparks that carry us to class to learn. Giving thanks to Paramatma & the Elements therefore makes even academic sense. I have no wish to be "brainy." I wish to attend not just classes but the entire day, night, world & universe & not just with a brain but with my head, hair, aura, heart, glands, gut, organs, hands, feet & fire. That's why I keep stepping outside each dawn & dusk to sing little Skrit songs to Mt. Rainier, the Olympics & their gods.

"Inexcusable!" my A-student brain huffed at me this morn-ing. "Singing to mountains is a complete waste of time!"

"Think again, little brain," my heart told it. "When I'm done with this university & this body, the mountains & gods will still be here & might fondly remember some silly girl-soul's songs to them—whereas you won't be anywhere remembering anything at all."

"You need me!" my brain shouted. "Sanskrit's making you loony! Without me you'll flunk every class but Dr. K's & lose your scholarship money & end up sleeping on the couch at your mom's!"

"Loony," my heart told my brain, "is an English modifier stolen from a northern waterbird because the non-English tremolo songs of that bird stand human hair on end & the Atman that hides in the hundredth part of the point of every one of those loon-triggered hairs is infinite. Whereas you're not. Explain even to yourself, dear brain of mine, how par-taking of a behavior you just likened to the cry of a bird that stands my hidden infinities on end is a waste of time?"

My heart waited a long time for a reply.

None came.

I love how quiet it gets when my brain can't answer my heart.

V. Theology Face-First

> He has broken my bones...He has shut out my
> prayer. He has closed up my exits and ways with
> square stones...He is become to me like a bear lying
> in wait, as a lion in hiding. He has...broken me in pieces.
> —Book of Jeremiah

I, THE HOLY Goat, narrator in chief of these chronicles, have become so fond of the adult Jamey Van Zandt that I'd love to defend him from the shame of his potentially lethal teen responses to his mother's death on his birthdays. But at this early stage in his life I can only call a spade a spade: Debbie's death turned Jamey into a Grief Imbecile. For many birthday-deathdays to come he was given to such grandiose defiance that he felt he was waging war, sometimes successfully, upon God, whom Jamey conceived as a heavenly Couch Potato peering down upon Earth and His mortal children as if at a dull TV show. When God inevitably grew bored with humanity's clumsy attempts to find happiness, He'd then spice up the program by randomly assailing them with natural disasters, plagues, famines, wars, senseless loss of life, ceaseless injustice, obscene synchronicities, and so on.

On the day Jamey closed his eyes and rode blind into a busy street, wreaking havoc, he felt he had successfully stolen the remote control unit right out of the Divine Couch Potato's hand, switched a bunch of lives onto an unprecedented new channel, and forced the Old Despot to watch someone else's stupid script and idiot violence for a change. "Stealing the Remote" became his code phrase for spontaneous insurgencies of this kind—and as his fourteenth birthday approached, Jamey was fully determined to obtain God's Remote once again. True, the death-defying side of his plan made him queasy. He'd had nightmares of the bloody-headed bakery truck driver (*"You! Come back here!"*) whose self-sacrifice had saved his life. But nightmares didn't diminish his loathing for the heavenly Boob-Tube Addict created by his hormone-jangled blood and brain. "Why should I feel guilt over *one* hurt driver," he'd tell himself, "when God, if there is one, smashes entire cities and countries whenever the whim strikes Him? How come if a human hurts and kills somebody, it's a broken commandment that damns us to hell, but when God maims and kills, it's some big Power we're supposed to fall on our faces and worship?"

At thirteen Jamey had considered this kind of defiance daringly original—thus condemning himself to learn that fomentations like his were no more original than mating in the missionary position. On the day he shot blind into an intersection, scores of hermeneutical texts, had he studied them, would have forced him to concede that all he'd done was enact a street theatre version of the old "God's will versus free will" question, an existential dilemma so redundantly posed that it has created a veritable wallow in humanity's intellectual history. In the suspicious warmth and smell of that wallow, entire armies of the mud wrestlers known as "theologians" have been tossing one another about for centuries—and there are reasons why Nathaniel Hawthorne called theology "stupendous impertinence"; and Jim Harrison said, "Theologians and accountants, the same difference really"; and Emily Dickinson wrote, "They talk of Hallowed things...and embarrass my Dog." On the day Jamey turned fourteen and Debbie negative nine, he encountered these reasons face-first.

ON JANUARY 30TH, 1972, after the strawberry crepe breakfast from Jon and the "Have a Not Too Happy Regular Old Day" card from Jude, Jamey set out to anti-worship his mother's Unmaker via a rebel act that would rearrange Portland's plebeian script, God style. Exactly how he would ape God's havoc-wreaking Jamey didn't yet know. He *couldn't* know, he figured, or the Almighty would read his mind and usurp his will, turning it into God's own will. To avoid this, Jamey reasoned, his rebel act must be *perfectly spontaneous.*

Gliding out into the city on the same theologically inclined ten-speed he'd ridden the year before, again seeking the dark energies of Black Hole Mom, Jamey warmed to his task by trying to reverse habitual behaviors. Since he normally went out of his way to take quiet streets, he spontaneously decided on busy ones and headed for Powell Boulevard—a four-lane truck route leading to one of the Willamette River bridges that join the bustling East and West sides of Portland. But Powell turned out to be fuming with traffic spewing so much noise and pollution it was hard to even remember his name, let alone conjure a deathday gift for his gravitationally collapsed mother. Gulping carbon dioxide and monoxide, sulfur dioxide, benzene, formaldehyde, polycyclic hydrocarbon, and soot with every breath, Jamey exhorted himself by gasping the chant, *"Be spontaneous! Be spontaneous!"* only to recognize to his theological bewilderment that spontaneity becomes absolutely unattainable the instant an anti-theological rebel nonspontaneously makes it his stated goal.

"Our nature," wrote the famed French accountant John Calvin, "is not merely bereft of good, but is so productive of every kind of evil that it cannot be inactive." Unaware of the company he was keeping, Jamey took it into his head to start playing Chicken, right there on Powell Boulevard, with oncoming cars. Considering possible repercussions not at all, lest he diminish his spontaneity, Jamey steered his bike immediately toward a red Dodge Charger, forcing the driver to veer and nearly strike a truck in the lane beside it. Horns blared, curses were roared, every kind of evil grew potentially active, Jamey's pulse rate tripled, he sucked more exhaust, and his mind *and* his gut writhed with a queasiness born of shame.

"Whatever is in man, from intellect to will, from the soul to the flesh," averred J. Calvin, CPA, "is all defiled and crammed with concupiscence... [so that] the whole man is in himself nothing but concupiscence." Lusting ungovernably to prove his mother had not been a mere pawn sacrificed to the boob-tubular viewing whims of the Divine, Jamey chose as his second target a big black pickup. But when he swerved at this vehicle, the driver didn't notice or respond at all, causing his side mirror to miss Jamey's face by two inches, nip the shoulder of his winter jacket—and the ferocity of this light brush ripped a nine-inch gash in the nylon and nearly sent Jamey to the pavement. Two inches closer and his shoulder would have splintered.

Wobbling to the curb, our young accountant spent the next few minutes fighting an urge to vomit, and when the nauseousness passed, his theological condition worsened, for he now recognized that any close shave with death, when one's *aim* is close shaves with death, is entirely *non*spontaneous. Surprising God, he hated to admit, was bloody hard and dangerous work. Worse, even if his shoulder *had* shattered, even if he had been pulp on pavement, his Chicken playing as a *surprise attack* on the Divine was no surprise at all.

Exhausted by adrenaline rushes, exhaust fumes, and theological futility, Jamey wheeled in to a Plaid Pantry convenience store feeling desperate need for a Coke. But when he stepped inside and an enormous goateed cashier called out, "Mornin'," Jamey was seized by a cruel but, he hoped, spontaneous urge to rewrite the plebeian Plaid Pantry script.

"Good morning," he answered back, strolling up to the counter. He then looked the cashier in the face, snatched a pack of cigarettes off the stand right under the man's goatee, grabbed matches, chirped, "*Thanks,*" and sprinted for the door.

With a roar the cashier set out after him—and he was fast for a human haymow. Because Jamey had to grab and mount his bike, the big fellow nearly caught him. "Get *cancer,* ya punk!" he bellowed as Jamey streaked away. "Smoke till ya die, ya snot-nosed punk!"

Hoping the cashier would call the cops, creating unplanned complications for the Powers That Be, Jamey rode a diversionary zigzag through a maze of streets, just as he'd done after the Franz truck wrecked the pink Mustang. Pulling into a vacant lot, he dropped his bike in the grass, knelt beside it, covered his face with his hands, and started yelling at God as he'd done the year before. "*Fuck You, Ya Punk!*" he roared into his palms. "*Go to Your own hell and leave Mom and me and everybody on Earth alone, Ya snot-nosed invisible Punk!*" But his performance felt ludicrous. No surges of power, no righteous fire, no unstoppably fierce love flying into interior blackness. Jamey had stolen a pack of cigarettes from a friendly-looking overweight fellow, run away, and that was it. He was thirsty to the verge of pain now but, thanks to theology, had a pack of smokes in his pocket instead of a cold Coke in hand.

His attempts to Steal the Remote were failing so miserably that he began to second-guess his triumph of the previous year. Had his blind glide through the intersection *really* enabled him to seize hold of a greater-than-human Power? Had Jamey, Son of Debbie, stood defiant in the presence of the Great Leukemia Giver, exposing "God's love" as a monstrous hoax? Or had an idiot delinquent caused a senseless wreck, injured the driver who'd heroically saved his life, then fled like a coward to stand in dead grass, blubbering profanities and mucus into his own hands like a literally snot-nosed punk?

"I have no fucking idea!" Jamey muttered.

He was really doing some theology now.

IT GOT WORSE. Reasoning (incorrectly) that self-criticism leads nowhere, then reasoning (even more incorrectly) that there can be no act so spontaneous as an act one has already determined to be totally nonspontaneous, Jamey mounted his ten-speed, rode straight back to Powell Boulevard, and started playing Chicken *again*, this time with a vengeance. "Here's a present from a *snot-nosed punk!*" he yelled at God as he forced a man in a green sedan to veer so hard he nearly struck a power pole. "*Fuck God, fuck me, and fuck you too!*" he snarled as he forced a woman in a white VW van to wallop a curb and stop with two wheels on the sidewalk—then felt sick when, checking his mirror, he saw her turn to console a child in the back seat. He kept on, forcing more drivers into terrified responses, and saw ever more clearly that the spontaneity he sought was never his: it was all theirs, the drivers'. What's more, their spontaneity was invariably compassionate! Stranger after stranger, white-knuckled and gaping, veered reflexively to save the life of a lethal idiot threatening theirs. They began to move him like music, these drivers, began to shame him like saints. Their impulse to preserve life made him so sick with self-disgust he couldn't see straight.

He turned south off Powell, rode into a residential neighborhood, and spotted a stately old maple tree overhanging the street. Its naked limbs somehow beckoned. He pulled up to the tree, placed a hand on the ancient gray bark, and felt an immediate emanation of calm. Peering up into the barren branches, he glimpsed himself as a little boy walking with his mother, holding hands under trees like this one. *Is everything I'm doing wrong?* he asked, but she vanished as fast as she'd appeared. Only the maple remained, exuding silent integrity.

I'm dying of thirst, Jamey thought, or maybe whispered to the tree.

I'm drinking sweet water out of the earth, plucking sunlight out of the sky, and playing with a cold breeze, the tree silently replied to Jamey.

I'm screwing with people's heads and risking their lives playing Chicken, he confessed.

The tree heard, but didn't judge. This brought solace. His quick, shallow breathing began to deepen. The awful buzzing in his head and body eased. Gazing at the maple's sidewalk-shattering roots, he felt supported by the life force rising from below. Gazing at its massive limbs overhead, he felt sheltered from the heavens against which he was at war. "Is it a miracle I'm alive?" he asked the old tree.

The maple didn't speak, but neither did it turn away.

"All those people risking their lives for me, before they can even think," he whispered, "are as perfectly good as a tree in a breeze. I don't know shit, Tree. I don't know anything! Can you help me? If I stop thinking, can I become as good as you?"

The cold breeze picked up, sending a chill through him. Jamey turned up his collar, then leaned his face against the maple's bark. Rough ridges imprinted his cheek, making it feel a little like bark when he lightly touched it. He pretended he was the maple's child, a sapling. Though her roots were tearing up pavement with ease, she was also gently supporting him, bathing him in fresh oxygen, gestating latent leaves, kneading the sky. *Mothering,* Jamey thought, and he kept leaning, and he felt the first real solace he could ever remember feeling on his birthday-deathday. But his hands had grown cold, so he stuck them in his coat pockets—and discovered matches in one pocket, cigarettes in the other.

Smoke till ya die, ya snot-nosed punk!

He fished them out. *Larks.* He hadn't noticed he'd stolen a brand that named spontaneous frivolous actions. He turned skyward. "Are You fucking with me again?"

No answer. God was like Debbie that way.

Jamey had never smoked in his life. His father said the latest science proved it was deadly. Debbie was nine years dead. *What better birthday-deathday gift,* Jamey more or less prayed, *than to smoke my way closer to you?*

He struck a match, lit a Lark, drew his first-ever mouthful of smoke, went "*Blech!*" as he spat it out—and recognized his first truly spontaneous syllable of the day.

He looked up into the big maple. *Such integrity.* Looked at the smoldering cigarette. *Such stupidity.* Looked for traces of Debbie in the world. *Such invisibility.* He felt utterly defeated, but at peace with his defeat somehow. He had just decided to spit out the cigarette, enjoy the stately tree's presence a little longer, then ride carefully, nonvictoriously home when, no idea how it happened—a nicotine trigger, maybe?—Jamey's thoughts flew into hyperdrive:

To spit out the cigarette and ride home is sensible. But to be sensible is predictable, to be predictable is normal, and to be normal is to be obedient to the insane Sky Bozo and stand, head bowed, like all the other goats, sheep, and people waiting to see which of us will be Bozo's next meaningless sacrifice!

He lost contact with the beneficent old maple. He gripped the Lark in his teeth and his handlebars in his fists. "God damn *God!*" he shouted. "I love *Mom!* Fuck *You!*"

He set out to play Chicken a third time.

THE CLIMAX OF Jamey's theological bicycling career took place on Milwaukie Avenue, a two-lane thoroughfare that winds briefly along the bluff over the Willamette River. "*A scenic place to die!*" Jamey jibbered when the river came in sight.

Tightening his bite on the cigarette, he set out alongside the guardrail, picked up speed, passed a few cars without reacting, then spotted an on-coming gray utility van. Making eye contact with the burly, brown-bearded driver, Jamey swerved violently toward him. The man's eyes bulged as he hauled on his steering wheel. Jamey felt a wind as the vehicle's rear end whipped past, just missing him. He then turned to watch the van spin so hard it lifted onto two wheels, nearly rolling before it bounced back onto four. The van crossed the oncoming lane doing a 180-degree half spin, accidentally parking in a driveway with such precision it seemed a stunt driver was at the wheel. The white back-up lights flashed on. The engine roared. The rear tires screamed the driver's rage.

Jamey gulped, "*Uh-oh,*" and set out to escape, as he'd done last year, via a diversionary maze of side streets. But as he picked up speed he glanced back at his pursuer, brushed his cigarette against his upturned coat collar, and the bright coal fell inside his shirt and began burning his stomach. Slapping wildly at it, he heard a horn, looked up—and saw a maroon sedan about to kill him. The trajectories and speeds left but one split-second choice: Jamey turned his bike, head-on and *hard,* into the riverside guardrail.

During the slow-motion seconds that followed, an inordinate number of things happened. First, the white steel guardrail crushed Jamey's front wheel as if it were made of cardboard. Next, he and the ten-speed flew high over the rail and entered thin air above an incline that in the plains states would have qualified as a cliff. *What a terribly long way to the ground,* Jamey sadly noted as he let go of the handlebars, freeing his hands to try to deal with his reunion with Earth. As if seeking solace in Jamey's company, the Schwinn remained between his legs even after he'd freed it.

He landed, hands and chin first, on Himalayan-briar-and-gravel-covered reject asphalt, snapping both wrists even as he bit his tongue so hard he nearly severed it. He bounced twice, though human bodies filled with blood and bone are anything but bouncy. As the gravel-covered asphalt peeled his chin and the heels of both hands to bone, he shot toward a wall of solid briar trunks. Striking this wall face-first, he fractured his clavicle and nose, then slammed to such an abrupt halt that the sprocket of the faithful ten-speed drove itself into his right calf, leaving a half dozen chunks of meat poking out of a neat row of grease-blackened sprocket holes.

When he could move again—which was not soon—Jamey rolled onto his back, looked heavenward, and tried to groan, "*Fuck You anyway!*" But what flopped off the end of his gushing tongue was a faint "*Flhhuhh-nehwuh.*" Angered by his failure to voice defiance, he spat a mouthful of blood at the sky. After an exceedingly negligible journey, most of the blood plopped back onto his own face.

That pretty much spelled the end of Jamey's career as a renegade theologian. To his post-theological disbelief, however, Jamey sensed a presence, opened his eyes, and beheld a heavily bearded visage glowering down into his face. "You are *so* damned lucky you trashed *yourself,*" the being growled. "Otherwise I'd do *way* more than this!"

With which the utility van driver kicked Jamey with what doctors later guessed was a steel-toed work boot, given how easily it cracked two of his ribs. The pain of simple breathing then caused Jamey to black out.

WHEN HE CAME to, Jamey tried to free himself from the briars by rolling onto his stomach and inching forward. He had failed to progress even a foot before he was so pierced and hemmed in by briar trunks that he couldn't move at all. He tried calling for help, but the pain of a mere moan caused him to black out again.

The second time he woke, Jamey elected to just lie there and assess. The good thing about this was that the January cold began to numb some of the pain in his mouth, face, hands, wrists, collarbone, ribs, knees, calf. The bad thing was the assessment itself. The maroon sedan's driver had clearly failed to stop or Jamey would have been discovered by now. The utility van driver who'd kicked him had surely left him for dead. Jamey had left no sign of his existence up on the street except, possibly, a tiny black bike-tire scuff on a rusty white guardrail. He now lay thirty or so feet down an abrupt incline, unable to move, his body concealed by both brambles and the steep slope. *I'm going to die on Mom's negative ninth deathday,* he concluded. *And I deserve it.*

Then he pictured Jon and Jude throwing his ashes off the same Pacific cliff that had rejected Debbie's, missing the ocean and sending another seal galumphing into the waves. Realizing his dad and sister loved him and did not deserve another death in their family, his eyes filled with tears. How swiftly the tears grew frigid. He remembered, from a Jack London story maybe, that a person begins to feel warm as they begin to die of cold. He closed his eyes, looking forward to that warmth.

As he waited, he passed into a dream in which various creatures came snuffling through the briars that entrapped him. The possums, raccoons, and rats he expected, and silently thanked for not yet feeding upon him. A small vigilant bird of a kind his father called "little brown jobs" he also expected. But the three men in navy-blue jackets with crimson breast patches he did not expect. They were loud. They were gruff. Having already been savaged by a work boot, Jamey was terrified by the violence with which they stomped down the brambles as they came closer and closer to his head. When he began to pant with fear, his ribs electrocuted him. The men were rogue cops responding to phone calls from outraged motorists, he decided, come to off the snot-nosed punk who'd been terrorizing the city.

A stretcher appeared on the stomped briars beside him. Stunned to realize the men were paramedics, Jamey tried to say *Thank you!* but his wrecked tongue bleated, "*Llehlloo!*"

One of the men said, "Easy," as the other two touched him here and there, discussing injuries while the first man produced a syringe. "This will hurt a little," he said. "Then it won't hurt a *lot*. Sound like a bargain?"

Jamey faintly nodded, in went the needle, and the bargain came wonderfully true.

Six hands eased him onto the stretcher. More hands strapped down his ankles, thighs, chest, and forehead, then tied a rope to the uphill end of the stretcher. One man scrambled, with what sounded like great difficulty and lots of cursing, up to the street and vanished. An unseen tow truck then began winching Jamey up the near-vertical slope while the remaining two men did their best to keep the stretcher balanced as they free-climbed the nearly vertical embankment, using the winched stretcher to keep themselves upright.

The painkiller was stout. By the time Jamey reached the street his brain was a fuzz ball. He noticed two small mysteries he wished to solve even so. One: the front wheel of his defunct theological ten-speed, now crushed into the shape of a sloppy infinity sign, had been tied to the guardrail by a length of dirty yellow rope. Two: as the paramedics prepped the ambulance, Jamey heard a distant but familiar engine roar. He tried to lift his strapped head, couldn't, but by rolling his eyes managed to see, a hundred yards up Milwaukie Avenue, a gray utility van pulling away from the curb. Piecing it together, Jamey smiled, hurting his tongue and face terribly: the same bearded stranger who'd broken his ribs had somehow removed his bicycle wheel, found a length of plastic rope, tied wheel to guardrail to mark the spot where Jamey had flown off into oblivion, then driven to a phone booth and called for help—anonymously, no doubt, given his treatment of Jamey's ribs. He'd then returned and waited, making sure the twerp who'd nearly killed him was discovered and saved.

As the van's engine sound faded into the distance, Jamey's heart tried to leave his chest: he wanted to chase the driver down, embrace him, plead his forgiveness, thank and thank him, then run around Portland seeking and embracing every person he and his bike had terrorized. All day he'd placed people in danger as if their lives meant nothing. All day those same people had unthinkingly risked their lives to save his.

Act after act of spontaneous self-sacrifice does not feel random. When probabilities are defied to save us again and again, we feel blessed whether we believe in a Blesser or not. Feeling more like a tree in a breeze than he had since his mother lived and thrived, Jamey surfed waves of gratitude into unconsciousness.

AND WHEN HE woke in a hospital that was, thankfully, not Providence, the gratitude remained. Studying the faces of nurses, visitors, doctors, his dad and sister, other patients, he thought, *There's something good in people. Something way better than the way the people look and talk and feel. It's buried deeper than thought. But it was in every single person who swerved to save me, so it's in every one of these people too.*

AFTER SIX WEEKS of liquids sipped via straws through a wired jaw, Jamey returned home in dual wrist casts, possessed of a multitude of chin, heel-of-hand, and tongue stitches, with six permanent sprocket scars in his calf, a slightly asymmetrical but rather handsome forced-aquiline nose, and, due to tongue injuries, a slight speech impediment that would cause people to imagine a charming if not-quite-identifiable foreign accent for the rest of his life.

In the months and years that followed, Jamey also found he'd contracted a powerful new allergy: strong theological assertions of every kind—his own especially—had become as noxious to him as sulfa drugs. The symptoms? The instant he heard a knowing statement about God he felt as though he was about to fly off a cliff, smash his face, grind his flesh, snap bones, chomp his tongue, and send muscle meat gushing out of sprocket holes. This in turn sent him into a nauseated silence, in which he would wander off to seek such theology-free companions as stately old trees.

There are less helpful allergies. Sometimes the best a good boy can do is be bad, then be sorry. It's hard to lose your mom on the very day you turn five.

(Seattle, 1988)

VI. Mormons vs. Mojo

I believe God was in Christ, not will be, perhaps, maybe
if we're good boys and girls; it's over, it's done, we are
one people, race is a violation, nations are a violation.
                                        —Will Davis Campbell

RISA'S LAST CLASS of the day was her three o'clock: Southern US History.
A one-on-one teacher-student conference on the Desert Fathers had her
verging on tardy. Tardiness, in the eyes of her Southern History prof,
Dr. Lafayette Mboya, was a near capital crime. Mboya was a towering
and weighty African American whose fame was national, whose scholarship was impeccable, whose lectures were always packed, and whose
personality was impervious to Risa's or any other student's charm. More
orator than professor, dignified in bearing, lofty in rhetoric, overpowering
in delivery, Mboya had no interest, as he lectured, in give-and-take with
his students. But he was so insistent on receiving his class's full attention
as he spoke that he was infamous for occasionally spinning on his heel
in mid-sentence, sending a laser glare out into the lecture hall, and, for
seconds so intense they felt like hours, *frying* any student whose focus had
flagged. *So how unfortunate,* Risa thought as she rushed, late, toward his
lecture, *that I really, truly have to pee.*
    She reached the history building, dashed up three flights, ducked into the
restroom, locked herself in a stall, did her business, and was about to leave—
when she was thrown under a psychic bus: on the steel door before her,
someone had etched an image of a woman giving a standing but headless
man fellatio. Risa's brain reeled in revulsion, but also in reluctant wonder at
the engraver's skill. The stall's beige-orange paint was the color of Caucasian
flesh in firelight. The engraver had exploited this. Her incisions bit through
paint and primer into steel, creating bright silver lines, points, pixels, as
with minimal yet graphic strokes the artist had depicted the woman's breasts
crushed against the man's thighs as she knelt before him like a supplicant.
The headless male gripping the woman's hair, especially, made the graffiti's
take on eros so brutal that to simply flee it, Risa felt, would poison her somehow. She felt she must answer it instead, searched her memory for a shard of
Sanskrit that might defuse the image, half remembered a passage, and closed

her eyes to try to summon it: "*She who knows the bliss of,* uh, one of those God words," she whispered, "*Parabrahma,* let's say...*bliss that turns away words, bliss the mind never touches, is,* um, *afraid of nothing? Unassailed by the thought, 'Why do I do what is evil?' she knows good* and *evil as Ātman, and cherishes both as Ātman.*

"Hmm. Pretty close. *Amen* then, I guess." With which she opened her eyes—and the engraving had become an impotent act of lavatory vandalism, its power over her gone.

SHE ARRIVED IN Southern History six minutes late. Lafayette Mboya's lectures began *precisely* on time. He relished a riveted audience—and loathed being interrupted even by silent movement among his students. The two entrances to the lecture hall were down in front. The one hundred twenty desk chairs were bolted to the floor in a tiered semicircle uphill from the doors. To slip in without being seen was impossible. Risa knew this. What did it say about her that she'd felt compelled to combat and quiet a work of lavatory graffiti even so?

Steeling herself, she stepped into the hall. The instant she did so, Mboya spun, *drilling* her with his radioactive glower. Risa smiled, hunched her shoulders, and mouthed the word "Sorry." When Mboya went on glaring, it struck her as bullying. She felt an impulse to stop in her tracks, put her hands on her hips, and glare right back. Thinking better of it, she slipped behind a free desk.

Dr. Mboya did not speak when he lectured: he *intoned,* deploying a James Earl Jones basso profundo that had long since earned him the nickname Darth. (*Star Wars* was huge for Risa's generation.) After settling in and opening her notebook, she noticed that Darth wasn't pacing as usual. He stood by a portable stereo beside which lay a small stack of LPs. How odd. "But do not think, because you're hearing music," Mboya was warning, "that you can daydream. As you listen to these songs, I'll be tracing the journey from slavery to emancipation. A journey *far* from complete to this day. And you will take notes on lecture *and* music *and* the handouts I've distributed, or you will fail Friday's exam. Your choice, as *emancipated students.*" A corner of his mouth lifted. "I must warn," he added, "that the tension between music and lecture will prove painful. That very pain is a function of this class—an infinitesimal but instructive dose of the agonies that inspired these songs."

A pretty woman with beaded cornrows, two chairs to Risa's right, expended a forced exhalation in protest. Darth spun on her, skewered her with his gaze, and in seconds left her peering obsequiously down into her lap. "Today's focus is gospel music," Mboya said, "some of it born on the ships, some on plantations, two songs composed by Blacks, one by a penitent white. At our next class we'll delve into the far older African folk music, with its thankfully *pre*-Christian roots. Questions?"

No one moved or spoke. Just the way Darth liked it. "Let us commence."

Expecting an easy class despite the grim warnings, Risa half sighed with relief. Before she could exhale, Mboya spun up an a cappella baritone with a vibrato so slow and powerful it warped the air like a police siren. The song was "Amazing Grace." But before the sweet sound could save any wretches like Risa, Darth began intoning a litany of depravities suffered by Africans in the holds of slave ships that cut into the hope-filled hymn like a stylus into steel, creating a duet from hell:

'Tis Grace that brought me safe thus far, and Grace will lead me home... "as he watched his wife, ten feet away, in ankle, wrist, and neck chains, convulsing with fever for two days, moaning for another, then spasming, till she breathed no more..." *The Lord has promised good to me, his word my hope secures*... "For two more days and nights her body remained chained to the women on each side of her..." *was lost, but now am found*... "till her face began to collapse into itself, her ruinous flesh to reek..." *was blind, but now I see*... "so they unchained him long enough to drag her remains on deck, where he held her despite their threats and her condition, for a while enduring the beating that rained down until—after a club delivered a rib-cracking blow—he was made to toss her, like the bilge she had become, over the ship's side."

Risa called up the Vedic formula she'd invoked in the lavatory. *Bliss that turns away words, bliss the mind never touches*. But the incantation couldn't guard her from the pity she felt for the students around her. Tears filled the eyes of the pretty woman in cornrows. Others seemed to be falling into crushing guilt or nausea. Still others looked defiant, as if falsely accused of crimes they had not committed. Knowing how mercilessly Mboya graded, all were taking notes regardless. Risa too held pen over paper, but when a choir launched into "Swing Low, Sweet Chariot," Mboya scorched the hopeful harmonies with descriptions of Africans "yanked from shit- and vomit-strewn holds, forced up a gangplank, washed like lumber before its sale, displayed on a Carolina sales platform for the financial advancement of fine Christian gentlefolk..." and Risa fell into a déjà vu so strong that listening was impossible. She bent forward, placing a hand over her brow to hide her face from Mboya. Closing her eyes, she slowed her breath, whispered the sad, ṣad, ṣadness mantra, and tried to sink into the deep dark that transforms woe. But the déjà vu blocked her. *Musical warfare. The awful schism between happy choir and unbearable history.* Where and when had she lived all this before?

And it hit her: *Mormons versus Mojo.* Cold choral triumph versus weary old bluesmen. And Risa was seven again, and helpless against the schism that led her mother and father to toss each other, like bilge, out of each other's lives forever...

BOTH RISA'S PARENTS were music lovers. Both brought records home, played them often, and just as often invited her to listen. Moira's great love was choral music—gospel, classical, medieval, Russian, African. The higher the sopranos, lower the basses, and more overt the emotions the better. Risa's father, Dave, had very different tastes. During two college summers as a civil rights volunteer in the Jim Crow South he'd fallen for Delta blues, the more unadorned the better. The records he began collecting in '63 and '64 now ran from Robert Johnson to Taj Mahal via Blind Lemon, Muddy, Lightnin', Snooky, Mississippi John, Reverend Gary, and all the rest of that inspired riffraff.

Risa, at seven, loved Moira's choirs and Dave's Delta blues equally. But Moira, one seemingly ordinary morning when Dave was at work, suddenly disapproved of this lack of preference. Evening was the usual time for music. It struck Risa as odd when Moira invited her into the living room, sat her on the couch before the Magnavox cabinet stereo, and with an incomprehensible air of anger said, "You'll never hear music as beautiful as this when your *father's* home." She then put on the Mormon Tabernacle Choir and turned it up loud. A tremendous organ revved up. "*Eleven thousand six hundred twenty pipes!*" Moira shouted over the sound. "*Three hundred sixty voices! Eight-part harmonies!*" The song was "America the Beautiful." And Risa was transported.

But Moira's father, Grand-Da Finnegas, happened to be visiting. Hearing the explosion of sound, he appeared in the archway between living room and kitchen, his kind face creased in consternation. Over the music he called out, "Triumphalist balderdash. I'm off on a walk. Risa lass? Care to join me?"

Though flattered by the attention her musical tastes were receiving, it was no contest: Grand-Da, on a walk, was a bird imitator, Irish fairy-tale teller, dog-biscuit tosser, and milkshake lover. Turning to her mother, Risa sang out, "*Please? Can I?*"

Moira recoiled as if from a blow, gave Finnegas a furious look, turned the same look on Risa, and snapped, "*Like father, like daughter! Go!*"

When Risa froze in confusion, Finnegas gently took her hand and led her out the front door. As the door closed Moira cranked the choir so high the windows rattled.

That was the first musical skirmish. Unsettling, but not that memorable had escalating conflict not followed:

A few days later Dave got home from work a little early, found Risa out back on the swing, blazed his eyes at her, called, "*Lightnin' Time!*" and took off for the living room. Risa lit out after him. By the time she reached the Magnavox the LP was already spinning, the old guitar plunking. When Lightnin' Hopkins's world-weary voice sounded, Dave swept Risa up in his arms and began dancing her round the room. Recognizing a favorite, Risa chimed in. "*Whoa you know I'm my papa's baby, I'm my mama's baby child,*" she and Lightnin' sang.

Moira appeared in the same archway Finnegas had, looking as consternated over Lightnin' as Grand-Da had over the Mormon choir. *What is the problem with* music *all of a sudden?* Risa wondered. Feeling sure she could fix this, she beamed at Moira and sang her piping, off-key best: "*Yeah, you know I'm my papa's baby, I'm my mama's baby child!*"

Dave spun round and discovered Moira watching them. He extended a hand. "Join us," he said with a smile.

In an acidic tone Risa had never before heard, Moira snapped, "Join *that*? How? Same morbid and faithless stories forever. Same three chords, *boom-chuck, boom-chuck*. Dance to *that*? I don't see how you can even stand to listen."

Dave stopped dancing and stood graceless and flat-footed, his handsome face so fallen that Risa began molding it with her hands, trying to restore its cheer.

"Is it the *morality* that lures you, Dave?" Moira asked. "What *are* the bluesman's Seven Virtues? Let's see. *Betting on horses. Smoking. Drinking. Whoring.* There's four. *Sleeping with other men's wives.* Five. *Leaving town once the kids or job get a bit tiresome.* Six. Risa, honey, why don't you pick a seventh? Two-faced lying? Murdering somebody for their pocket watch then jumping, *poor weary you*, on a *long lonesome train?*"

The song ended. Dave gazed blankly at Moira. She glared bitterly back. Desperate to restore what she could see being lost, Risa again tried to mold her father's face.

"*Stop!*" he snapped, sliding her roughly to the floor.

"*You know I been wonderin',*" Lightnin' sang into the rift, "*what makes a well run dry . . .*"

Dave looked once more at Moira, then stepped round Risa and strode straight out the front door.

"*Whoa you know, I've been wonderin', wonderin', oh boy, what makes a well run dry . . .*"

Standing in the path of the abandoned song, Risa felt minuscule and alone.

"*You know that's when the earth done settle down on the water, ain't no more wa—*"

brrrEEEEET! Moira ripped the stylus from the record with a violence that made Risa jump. In the vacuum that followed they heard the car start. Dave hadn't packed a thing.

Feeling panic, Risa asked, "Where's he *going*?"

"Somewhere *his* music will justify!" Moira huffed, and stormed from the room.

Dave didn't return for a week. That was the second skirmish.

BUT THE RICH baritone she was hearing, Risa slowly realized, was no recording. She lowered her hand, looked, and sure enough, Lafayette Mboya's eyes were closed, his head was thrown back, his Darth intonation was gone, and his singing was a marvel:

I am a poor pilgrim of sorrow,
Tossed roun' the wide world, alone.
I heard of a city called heaven,
I'm trying to make it my home . . .

Risa had relaxed, ready to bask in the coming verses, when Mboya stopped cold, his eyes opened, and she saw at once: Darth was back.

"*That,*" he said bitterly, "is *Sabbath joy.* The only joy you'll be hearing today. The only joy you'll *ever* find in this music. Sabbath joy defined? A disembodied dream of real joy. A song of happiness, *deferred.* Song of love, *outlawed.* Song of any and every fulfillment exiled to realms we may enter only at death. When your best friend, your child, your bride is disbursed as merchandise, your comely ones raped for their beauty, gifted ones sold for their talent, spirited ones lynched for their courage, the threadbare solace of *Sabbath joy* is what remains. And on the day you embrace this solace, you've become a living dead man or woman, buried under your joyless *darkie* smile. Too harsh, some of you think? Study the Lawrence Levine and W. E. B. Du Bois handouts I gave you before you *dare* make that call from the safety of your white lives. In the meantime, here's Frederick Douglass, who knew no such safety: 'I have often been utterly astonished, since I came to the north, to find persons who could speak of the singing, among slaves, as evidence of their contentment and happiness. It is impossible to conceive of a greater mistake. Slaves sing most when they are most unhappy. The songs of the slave represent the sorrows of his heart; and he is relieved by them, only as an aching heart is relieved by its tears.' With that misery in mind, I offer you, *darkie* accent and all, another song of *Sabbath joy.*"

Mboya took a stance. His upper lip curled. His eyes blazed, till he shut them. And his voice, once again, was shockingly fine.

My Lord, what a mornin' when de stars begin to fall.
You'll see de world on fire when de stars begin to fall.
You'll see de moon ableedin' when you hear de saints a-singin'
O Lord, what a mornin' when de stars begin to fall...

Lowering her face, using her hand again for a burka, Risa closed her eyes, turned seven, and let herself be hijacked once more by warring music...

FOURTH OF JULY. Two dozen relatives from five states squeezed into Moira and Dave's little Portland backyard. O'Reilly clan, most of them, well into the keg, starting to circle the food, chatting and half listening as Dave and Moira's brother, Miles, played quiet blues turnarounds on their guitars. Then, from out of the house, a stupendous stereo blare! *Mormon Tabernacle Choir.* "*America the Beautiful.*" Moira's anthem, it seemed, since she had turned against her husband's favorite music.

Dave set his guitar aside. With every eye upon him, he walked over and slid the patio door closed, reducing the choir to a sonic moth batting red, white, and blue against the glass. Looking easy in his skin, nothing amiss, he then strolled to the keg for a fresh beer, returned to his chair, and began to chat with his wife's family as though he was perfectly pleased with the music on the other side of the plate glass. But Moira came off as crazed.

The entire O'Reilly clan looked uneasy, and Uncle Charlie McKeig shot Dave a look that pretty well shouted, *What the fuck!* At that very moment, Risa took sides: to her child mind it boiled down to a child's question: *Who started this?* Whatever he thought privately, Dave accepted Moira's choral music without so much as a frown. She did not do the same with his blues. The issue, as Risa saw it, was tolerance versus intolerance. She would need fifteen more years to realize she'd had no idea what the real issues had been.

HAVING JUDGED AND condemned her mother without a trial, Risa turned into a seven-year-old Delta blues activist. When Dave began replacing some of his scratched LPs with new ones, he gave Risa the rejects. She played them in her bedroom endlessly. If Moira made her turn them off, Risa would sing them, gratingly off-key. If Moira nixed that, she'd hum them. If Moira vetoed even that, Risa would affect a *g*-droppin' accent and plague her mother with mock-innocent blues-derived questions:

"When can I quit takin' piano an' start takin' guitar?"
"What's 'hoodoo,' Mama?"
"What is it we're s'posed to shake when they say 'Shake it'?"
"What's Lightnin' mean by she got too many drivers but only one steerin' wheel?"

There were nights, lots of them, when Dave didn't come home.

Then came the nights—lots of these too—when Moira disappeared into the small hours, wobbling home smoke-bleared and scary-smelling.

What did Dave's disappearances mean to his daughter? *Mom doesn't like Dad's music so he has to go out. Poor Daddy!* What did Moira's disappearances mean? *Oh boy! Dad will be taking care of me tonight!* Risa knew she'd stacked the deck against her mother but liked her stacked deck just fine, because when Dave vanished, Moira drank vodka and argued with the TV set while Risa hid in her room, but when Moira vanished, Dave turned into a melancholy charmer Risa never glimpsed when her mother was home.

The first thing he'd do was grab a pair of twelve-ounce glasses and pour them what he called "a couple o' tall cold ones." Root beer for Risa and "Miller Low Life" for himself. He'd then open his LP cupboard and start sliding out records till he had ten or twelve lined up. "Let's study us some *styles*," he'd say. And he'd play two or three tunes he called "cool," and a few he called "hot." Then, with increasingly fey funny commentary, he'd contrast some "upbeat" to some "downbeat" to some "beaten down" to some "plain ol' beat-up" while Risa laughed, loving every crazed explication and bizarre expression on Dave's face.

"How 'bout some story themes?" he'd say, shuffling LPs like big black playing cards. "Here's a couple tunes that pretty much agree, "My Baby's the Very Devil—an' I Pray She Keeps Me Here in Hell with Her Forever." And down would go the needle on the reliable chords and wildly unreliable lyrics that made Dave's eyes shine. "Now here's a couple tellin' how 'He Never Said Nuthin', He Never Once Complained, He Just One Night Up 'n' Gone.'"

Dave would speculate, as the themes were being sung, on who sang which storyline first, who'd influenced who, what tales and styles migrated from where to where. Then he might cock an eyebrow, adopt a whacked British accent, conjure "the musicologist, Sir David McKeig," and "prove" how Isaac Newton stole his law of gravity from Lightnin' Hopkins and Shakespeare stole the plot of *Macbeth* from Muddy Waters.

By the time a second root beer found its way into Risa's hand and a third "Miller Low Life" into Dave's, his faint Western drawl headed south in a hurry and he'd turn earnest under the influence, spinning Blues Hero yarns that made Risa hope her mother stayed out all night. And some nights she got that wish. With no sense at all of what it portended.

One night, over his third Low Life, Dave expounded on blues guitar itself. He began by discoursing—with snatches of grooves played in historical order—about which players influenced which. Then he got feisty and talked about who *didn't* influence who, even though so-and-so said they did, and played grooves to prove that. Next he stopped playing records altogether, pulled out his old cowboy guitar, and demonstrated a few nuances. "Here's how they bend the A-string to diminish the third. Hear the chord straight? Now listen to it bent. See how a bending string gets it to soundin' all *lonely* an' *sorry?*"

Oh, did she.

"But now look. In this tune B. B. King won't even play the fifth. He'll lift up on his *fourth,* like *this,* to throw a drunken wobble up into the fifth. Hear it? I can't do it right or I'd bust my string. But here's B. B. on his guitar, Lucille. Listen now. He's gonna set his strings to wobblin' till Lucille's arguing with herself like some poor ol' homeless lady."

On one of their last blues appreciation nights, Dave grew pensive at one point and said how wrong "some people" were to call this music "a three-chord *boom-chuck, boom-chuck*" show. Never naming names. Always the gentleman—even as his marriage and Risa's childhood happiness were quietly going up in flames. "There's so much nuance to how even *one chord* can be played," he said. "Look at John Lee Hooker, for God's sake. People deaf to that are missing out. The blues, I'm tellin' you, Risa, have helped *millions* through the hard things in life. An' not by soarin' up in some hot-air balloon of eight-part *righteousness.* The blues come find you in a low-down place and help you admit, damn right, sweet girl, we *are* down. We're so far down we might never make it back up. But by *bein'* down, if you'll set on down here with me, honey, we just might find us a way *through.*"

ONE NIGHT AFTER a few Miller Low Lifes had sent Dave's Western drawl clear down into the Gulf States, he told Risa about a blues joint he'd visited as a young Freedom Rider:

"Chickasaw County, Mississippi, 1963. Town called Stonecrop. Tiny place called The Fret. A Yalie, Edwin Something Something the Third, okay guy even so, came with me. And there was a hell of a guitar man going when we stepped inside. But it turned out Eddie and me were the only white people in the joint and *whooo*! Did we feel it! Our faces shone in there like hundred-watt light bulbs. It would've only made sense if somebody had walked over an' yelled, 'Shut that face off 'fore I shut it off for you!' "

Dave chuckled at his college-boy terror. "What happened instead was the guitar man took a break, and this old Black gent strolls over, kind faced and slow, extends his hand, shakes with each of us, and says, 'Earl Warren. Same as the chief justice. I'll bet you won't forget that.' Earl said he'd seen we were feelin' a little pale, so he'd decided to adopt us for a while. I was so relieved I jumped up an' pulled out a chair as if he was my date."

Dave jumped up and worked the big living-room armchair the way he'd done in '63, till Risa could see old Earl, same name as the chief justice, smiling at the overenthusiasm, sitting slowly down.

"We talked Delta blues awhile, since Earl saw we loved it. Then bottle-neck guitar came up. It was Son House played the first glass-slide solo I ever heard, Earl told us, and I could smell a great story coming. But Eddie Somethin' Somethin', being a Yalie, thought he had to know everything. So he piped up and said he heard Robert Johnson invented the use of slides 'Sure you heard that,' Earl tells Eddie. 'Everybody saints the early dead. But, the way the world is, I saint *survivors*. Like ol' Son.' "

When Dave nodded like he was Eddie, grateful to be set straight by Earl's words, Risa stared at the empty armchair, seeing Earl and The Fret as clear as dying saints see angels.

" 'Here's how it goes with survivors,' Earl says. Young Son was a preacher, first sermon at fifteen. Then he fell hard for a woman. Not some girl his age. A real-deal woman an' ever'thing goes with it. *Heh! Bye-bye preachin'*. Desperate for something to woo his woman with, Son gets himself a Stella steel guitar—good choice. Finds himself a teacher, Rube Lacy— good choice. Rube gets Son started, maybe even showed him a glass slide. But music gets made by a body, not a head, an' Son's young body wasn't ready for the magic o' no slide. 'The way a *survivor's* body learns,' Earl tells me and Eddie, 'is by *survivin'*.' "

Seven years old, mother out on the town, father shiny eyed, no idea what she was surviving, Risa's body learned and learned.

"How House's learnin' starts, he's playin' a juke joint, 1928, when some fella goes nuts, pulls a gun, starts shootin' the place up. Put a slug through Son's calf. 'I saw the in-scar an' the out-scar,' Earl says, pulling up his trouser leg, showing us where." (Dave did the same, Risa listening so hard she saw not a white leg but a black one, the in-scar and the out-scar.) "Son reaches in his guitar case, grabs his revolver, drops that shooter dead. Self-defense. Saved lives. But in *Mississippi. 1928*. Son has to do time. God-damn kangaroo bullshit." When Dave shook his head at the bullshit, Risa shook her head too, straining so hard to understand that she saw Australian kangaroos, defecating for some reason.

"Earl didn't remember which prison, or how long. But Son was free again, playing a Houston, Mississippi, roadhouse, 1934, when Earl heard him. House had warmed up, Earl tells Eddie and me, and was into his set, soundin' real solid, when a brawl broke out. Not a fistfight. Not *five* fistfights. 'Some crazy energy flew into the place an' havoc hit like I never seen,' Earl said. 'Too far to crawl out the door, but *Blessèd be the peace-makers*. I got me under a table. That crazy Son, though, kept right on playin'.'"

Dave began rocking back and forth like he was Son now, serenely play-ing. "Brawl keeps building, Earl keeps hiding, whole place a wrack an' ruin. Then, right in front o' Son, this big powerful fella starts gettin' creamed by a cat-quick boxer. Big Man could break Boxer in half if he could catch him. He can't. Boxer's pepperin' Big Man's face to pulp. Son sets watchin' this, keeps right on playin'."

As Dave kept rocking, Risa flew into a dark musical heaven that seated her at the foot of a throne. Upon that throne: nothing but Son, playin' and playin'.

"*Big Man goes off!*" Dave hollered and she jumped. "Busts a wine bottle to make a blade. But he's too damn mad, smashes too hard, ends up with an itty-bitty neck in his hand. Boxer grins, grabs his own wine bottle, taps it easy on a chairback, gets a *looooong* blade. Steps toward Big Man grinnin' ugly." Dave leaned in and grinned at Risa so ugly she gasped.

"'WAIT!' House shouts so big both men freeze. 'Gimme that,' he says, noddin' at Big Man's bitty bottleneck. It's all the poor guy's got, but he knows it's useless. Hands it over to Son. Son looks down his nose all schol-arly." Dave looked down his nose at an imaginary bottleneck all scholarly. "Boxer's curious now, half watchin' Big Man, but more than half watchin' House slide that neck onto fingers till he finds the one it fits. The fourth. It's still bottles-flyin', chairs-bustin', blood-spurtin' mayhem in there. Son don't care. He's *survivin'*."

Risa doesn't care either. She's *revering*.

"When Son starts playing again, a sound no one ever heard is born. Busted-glass-bottleneck-on-American-steel notes pourin' out all *slippery,* grabbin' men by the mind 'fore they know what hit 'em. Son builds it real slow but never backs off, till he gets his guitar crashin' six ways to Sunday. Then, real sudden, the crashin' stops and Son leaves just one lonesome string, the *survivor,* lettin' out this *loooooong* glassy moan. *Bam!* All over that room the fighting goes still. Son starts groan-growlin' over an' under his moaner string, eerie, dissonant, hittin' fifths, fourths, the same moan-note an octave down, the fighters turnin' from their enemies, leaving themselves all vulnerable, every wild damn one of 'em wonderin' *What. Is. That. Sound?* Till it's *church* in there, Earl tells us. *Pure church.* But Son don't know it. Son is eyes-closed head-back *bringin' it,* pullin' from a place so broke but overflowin' the brawlers take a fresh look at one another— and crooked little smiles start breakin' out. Pretty soon they're shakin' each other's bloody-knuckled hands, chucklin' quiet at the feeling Son's created, rippin' shirttails into bandages for the other guy, nursin' split lips, sweepin' broke glass with their shoe toe, proppin' broken tables with broken chairs, icin' the other fella's swole-up eye with the fist that swole it, Son still bringin' it while men mumble, 'Jeez, you okay? Why'd I wanna go an' do that? Can I help you with this here?' Brawlers turned to nurses, riot become a healin', bar become a church, because the glass-crashed steel of a blues father name o' Son grabbed hold of 'em then fell quiet, leavin' just one lonesome string, the *survivor,* moanin'.'"

Dave leaned back and eyed Risa with the saddest love she'd ever seen. "'First glass slide solo *I* ever heard anyway,' Earl says. *Son House. Houston, Mississippi. 1934.* So half his life later, *Chickasaw County, Mississippi, 1963,* Earl tells Eddie an' me. So, *Multnomah County, Oregon, 1975,* I'm tellin' *you,* sweet girl. Don't you ever forget."

Oh, Risa wouldn't. And Dave, so sad and handsome, fetched the pillow and blanket from her room, tucked her in on the living-room couch, took the armchair by the stereo. Earl's chair. Nursing the dregs of his Low Life, he then played one glass-on-steel cut after another, after another, till a seven-year-old Portland girl, 1975, fell asleep in Houston, Mississippi, 1934.

THE SHORT-TERM outcome of these motherless nights? Abject adoration. Risa worshipped her father, worshipped his blues, and openly pleaded with Moira to at least *try* to be kind to the man and his music—

to which Moira would cry, "You have no idea how hard I *already* tried!"—

until a few weeks shy of Christmas, two months after Risa turned eight, Dave *Never Said Nuthin', He Never Once Complained, He Just One Night Up 'n' Gone*—

taking with him the only music that made any sense of things—

leaving his long-memoried daughter not with the father and music she adored but with the mother and blaring choirs she believed had forced him to go.

(Portland, 1970s)

VII. Not Getting Schooled

Politics is high school with guns and more money.
—Frank Zappa

ACT AFTER ACT of spontaneous self-sacrifice does not feel random. On the day all those Portland strangers risked their lives and swerved their cars to save Jamey, he began, despite his refusal to believe in any kind of "Blesser," to feel blessed by an innate kindness within humans, and so began to find his life's trajectory. Though the signals remained faint and the detours plentiful, a sense of meaning and purpose had slipped into his heart. With the exception of his birthday-deathday flirtations with self-destruction, Jamey's young manhood then became about as enjoyable as late-twentieth-century American young manhoods got. At home he was adored, if harassed, by his jealous but doting big sister, Judith, and well provided for by, if largely incomprehensible to, his wooden but rock steady dad, Jon.

As he entered his teens Jamey's body grew long, strong, expressive, and energetic if not exactly athletic. Meanwhile his mind grew extra lively, his tongue witty to a fault, and his nature remained indefatigably upbeat. His voice at fourteen plunged from choirboy alto to some climate-change-threatened species of frog, then settled down into a pleasingly resonant baritone. In high school he proved so friendly and self-deprecatingly funny that he was liked by just about everybody from jocks, artistes, social climbers, and stoners to future CEOs, drag queens, and Marines.

Next adventure? His friendliness, voice, wit, height, exotic tongue-scar accent, and distinguished-looking bike-wreck-broken nose began to wow the opposite sex. Jamey's pull on girls was inadvertent at first. For a year or more he avoided flirts *especially* if he found them attractive, because his mother had been attractive and look what happened to her. But his capacity for evasive maneuvers was no match for his pursuers. By the time he set out for college he'd been caught and sampled by a variety of lassies, lionesses, and wahines, and the Circus McGurkus known as eros had become a potent new befuddlement in his life.

On the academic front, teachers in those days deployed two terms to describe the likes of Jamey: "talented and gifted" and "underachiever." The tension between compliment and insult was intended to spur the laggard to achievement, but Jamey threw his teachers an unhittable curve: he didn't consider underachievement negative at all. In a world as lethally misdirected as the one in which he found himself, *overachievement* struck him as the far greater danger. His distrust of institutions, born of his mother's demise in a fine-looking institution, proved lifelong. His problem with school systems, medical systems, militaries, governments, corporations, religions, political parties, was not that they didn't work but that they did. All such powers, according to Jamey, were *tremendously* skilled at changing the people who submitted to them, making them more predictable, medicalized, militarized, restricted, controllable, cloned, and afraid. Deploying the sort of rhetoric that young male renegades seem to acquire simultaneous to acne, Jamey espoused his distrust of this tendency in a sophomore-year Current Events paper titled "The Baitball Syndrome."

> Those who excel in the public school system do so because they're willing to be *schooled*. So are anchovies, herring, and sardines. What I can't work out is why people consider this to be a good thing. Rewarding kids for regurgitating a "school of thought" the way Maoists, Army recruiters, and Baptists do squeezes the thinking of the "schooled" into what fishermen call a "baitball." When a crisis then arises that requires creative response, *schooled* minds squeeze themselves into tightly closed ranks the same way sardines and anchovies do. Once in a baitball, the thoughts, words, and actions of "the schooled" respond to nothing but the surging movements of their own look-alike think-alike baitball, till it's *The Pope!* or *The Party!* or *Darwin!* or *Deutschland über Alles!* leaving the great god Neptune no choice but to send sharks, orcas, and other predators ripping into the baitball to gorge.

The poor grades such papers received came as a relief to Jamey: an A might suggest he'd been *schooled*. Of course his grades put prestigious colleges out of reach, but this suited him too. Yale, Stanford, the Air Force Academy, and such were, in his affected yet truly felt teen parlance, "just *Über High Schools,* same as the Pentagon, Wall Street, and Congress."

In his sixteenth year, moved by his post-bike-wreck insight that ordinary people, thanks to a compassion hidden deeper than thought, are much better than they know, Jamey began to counteract his schooling by simply wandering the streets of Portland and interacting with the populace in a wide-open state of mind. The result was magic: no sooner would he hit the streets than the chip fell off his shoulder, his curiosity and amiability kicked in, and he became an enthused student of ordinary human beings. Jamey was a natural at initiating deep contact via chitchat: by increments his curiosity would grow so genuine and his pleasure in people so pronounced that many fell open like books, becoming as fascinating as many humans in fact are. Jamey located the cafes where the nurse's aides and mechanics and window washers and off-duty cabbies and truckers and cops hung out, developed a taste for the same crappy coffee that refueled them, and truly relished hearing the ups, downs, and sideways of their lives. He found even bores fascinating for their unerring ability to be boring. He learned how a few lines of well-chosen poetry could cause a person speaking in slogans and received language to tap hidden depths. He learned to be, as Walt Whitman put it, "complacent, compassionating, idle, unitary...looking with side-curved head, curious what will come next." And Portland answered his curiosity with a stream of such unlikely, charming, scurrilous, frightening, fascinating people that street meanderings became the core curriculum of his education.

Jamey's life trajectory began to kick in when he realized he not only relished engaging with all kinds of people but also had a phenomenal memory for what they said and an uncanny ability to emulate the way they said it. He met a Delhi-born Sikh cabbie who harangued him for an hour on America's epidemic divorce rate, saying it was the result of our insane national preference for self-selected romance despite the far higher success rate of arranged marriages. For years afterward Jamey could replicate the Sikh's accent, arguments, indignation, and marriage statistics to perfection. He met a shy Salvadoran welder, Plinio by name, who had slipped across the border without passport or green card, taken a hopelessly low-paying job at Rick's Custom Mobile Homes on NE 33rd, and grown to miss his wife, Candelaria, so sorely that he memorized love poems, rehearsing them at work in the privacy of his welder's helmet, prepping for the day he'd be able to declaim them to his love. At Jamey's urging Plinio recited a few such poems, and sheer delight enabled Jamey to absorb Plinio's voice, manner, and delivery to perfection.

At his favorite low-end coffee shop, Jamey met a Jersey-accented plumber with a cement-mixer voice who asked what he thought of NFL football. When Jamey nervously admitted that he wasn't a fan, the plumber banged his back, growled, "Good lad!" and launched into a portrait of his linebacker brother, "a god at our Jersey high school, All-American in college, funniest, most charmin' guy ya ever met. *Thumper*, we called him." Turning surprisingly professorial, the plumber lectured Jamey on how changes in gridiron surfaces, greater player size and speed, and improved pain meds dovetailed, giving footballers the most battered brains of any athletes in sports history. "T'ree years on NFL special teams, hunnerds o' punts an' kick-offs an' five concussions later, my brudduh retires at twenny-four. Has enough league money left to buy a Caddy. Gets vanity plates. 'THUMPER,' they say. Turned out Thumpa can't work duh brakes. Rear-ends four drivers in a month. Loses his license for life. Now he lives wid no woman cuz who'd have him wid his neck pain, head pain, no concentration, no job, an' personality brown as a goddamn football. I tell ya, *James* was it? America's fav'ert sport puts *me* in duh mood for lawn bowlin'."

Jamey drank in such Portlanders the way the young Charles Dickens drank in 1840s Londoners, then replicated them with a wholeheartedness that went far beyond caricature. He could summon a hustler's or junkie's quirks and jerks as they slid from truth-telling to scam. He forgot no one's poignantly nervous gesture as they reached the emotionally raw part of their tale, or slid away from revealing rawness into a lie. The more peculiar the diction, stranger the obsession or realm of expertise, more intricate the person's tale, the more perfectly Jamey's ear, pliant body, and huge range of expressions and voices replicated them.

A NOT ATYPICAL adventure from his seventeenth year: legging his way through Southeast Portland one spring day in May, *complacent, compassionating, idle,* Jamey espied a seamstress's shop on Hawthorne Street with a bright-colored, new-looking, hand-painted sign that read: DAMSELS IN THIS DRESS. Typical of his modus operandi at the time, Jamey charged inside to inform whoever thought of the name that he or she was a genius.

The woman he found within—perched on a stool at a counter that doubled as her sewing table, hand-stitching spaghetti straps onto an altered prom dress—was the most spherical person Jamey had ever seen, yet also one of the most delicate. She struck Jamey as the thoroughly charming progeny of a Victorian-era porcelain doll and a beach ball—and when he began extolling the shop's name, the entire orb of her lit up!

"I was Lynette's Alterations for years," she said. "That's me, Lynette. But three months ago my bookkeeper, Gary, reads a dress label, spots the word 'damsel,' looks at me, an' says, 'Damsels in This Dress.' I says, 'Huh?' 'The new name of your shop,' Gary says. I says, 'Great idea,' an' laugh, but I don't have money to pay for no sign. Gary comes to work four days later toting the sign you just saw. Made it himself. Doubled my business in nuthin' flat. Which is one reason we're partners." Lynette had turned, as she was speaking, to two heavily loaded clothes racks directly behind her. When she mentioned her partnership with Gary, she began batting her lashes at the racks in a way that struck Jamey as downright erotic. *How strange to thank the clothes themselves for her improved business,* he thought.

Lynette then leaned toward Jamey and whispered, "He's altruistic, but *so sweet!*" Jamey had no idea what she was talking about. "An' the other reason we're partners," Lynette added, still making eyes at the clothes racks, "is we're engaged!"

It gave Jamey a start when a pair of pale hands, hovering perhaps two feet off the floor, emanated out from between the two clothes racks, followed by the white cuffs of a dress shirt, threadbare sleeves of a light brown polyester suit, matching brown shoes, shockingly pink socks, and, finally, the consternated face of a hunched little homunculus, rolling himself out of the clothing in a minuscule wooden office chair. The socks, Jamey intuited, were surely the doing of bright-pink Lynette, and "altruistic" must have been her attempt at "autistic."

"Gary!" Jamey said brightly. "Your sign is genius!"

Hearing himself named by a stranger, the little guy ducked as if a rock had been thrown at him, dropped his gaze to his lap, and began moving his hands as if he were washing them. Lynette beamed beneficently. Apparently this behavior was Gary's norm.

"So you're a bookkeeper too," Jamey said more quietly. "Multitalented guy."

Ducking still lower, Gary said, "I like to keep track."

Seeing that he held no pen or paper, and that there couldn't have been a desk squeezed in between the clothes, Jamey asked, "Are your bookkeeping supplies squeezed into the clothes racks with you?"

Gary's hands stopped dry-washing. He squinched up his face in concentration. He began to recite—in a monotone, but at the speed of a skilled auctioneer—what Jamey gradually realized was an inventory of every alteration Lynette had made since January 1st, five months ago. Gary never faltered, though his recitation took close to four minutes to reach May. When he finished, with poetic inevitability, with the prom dress Lynette now held in her fat, pretty hands, Jamey exclaimed, "*Gair!* You've got a mind like a steel trap!"

Gary looked like a scared squirrel in a suit as he went back to dry-washing his hands.

"I know a guy you'd dig big time, Gary," Jamey said. "Name's Plinio, from San Salvador. Makes dirt wages as a welder up on 33rd. Adores the wife he left behind. *Candelaria.* To 'keep her in my heart,' as Plinio puts it, he memorizes love poems, and practices them inside his welder's helmet where nobody else can hear. Maybe you could do that for Lynette back there in the clothes, Gair! The other day Plinio sprang some Lorca on me. 'Romance de la luna, luna.' I only remember part of it, but check it out."

Jamey's body took on the look of an overworked, cop-haunted, lovelorn migrant sending sheer adoration four thousand miles south as in accent he whispered:

> *The moon comes to the forge*
> *in her creamy pink petticoat.*
> *The child stares, stares,*
> *the child is staring at her.*
> *In the breeze, stirred,*
> *the moon stirs her arms,*
> *shows, pure, voluptuous,*
> *her breasts of shining metal.*

As Gary listened he rolled his chair a little forward so he could lean round the clothes and peer, expressionless but open-mouthed, at moonlike Lynette. Noticing, she glanced down at her voluptuous mounds and turned pink as Gary's socks. And Jamey left Damsels in This Dress in a euphoria, feeling strangely certain that his life's work would be bound to the miseducated, hardworking, half-broken, extraordinary creatures known as "ordinary people." He had no inkling what that work might be. He only knew that Lorca-quoting welders, sweet spherical seamstresses, and lovestruck homunculi with perfect recall were as far from human baitballs as you could get. What better reason did he need to draw such people out, archiving their skewed talents, quirks, and poetry in his lively mind, long body, and wounded tongue.

(Seattle, 1988)

VIII. Radiance vs. Reef

Maybe the sacred, today, is someone misspelling "scared,"
then loving the skewed meaning caused by their misspelling.
Maybe that reasonless loving is a sacred act.
                                                    —Thomas Soames

RISA HAD BEEN a gangly adolescent. But when her smile blazed forth, even
during her gawky years, she caused dogtails to wag, birds to sing, and boys
to attempt unperformable circus tricks. Young womanhood intensified the
effect, and after she fell for Sanskrit an increased connectivity between her
inner and outer worlds worked still greater magic: when she would fall into
Vedic reveries, or work to carry a sadness into the vast dark of ṣadness,
the little blue veins in her temples took on a bioluminescent quality and
her entire face glowed like campfire embers modulating in heavy night air,
resulting in a dignity reminiscent of a medieval madonna painting—*until*
the smile intensified to a grin. Then her lips parted, an utterly surprising
eighth-of-an-inch gap between her incisors exposed an unruly mirthfulness,
and the sanctity blew sky-high. From early childhood Dave made her
promise never to let an orthodontist touch what that cliché-shattering gap
did for her beauty.

At age twenty Risa's face was inspiring passersby to walk with some
frequency into phone poles, closed glass doors, parked cars, and one another. But other reactions set in at the same time. Now and then strangers
would take one look at her and their faces would harden as if her very
existence was a personal affront. Others would take her in, then assail
her with forced wit, bad poetry, dumb-shit hustle moves. Still others, some
of them so charming they were indistinguishable from potential friends,
would succeed in getting to know her before showing themselves to be
sexual conquistadors tracking her in hopes of bagging her the way hunters hope to bag trophy elk. Insulting encroachments, brushes with sleaze,
and a few modest harms befell her. Then Risa got lucky, or grace got
gracious and sent a friend who helped her come to terms with her strange
problem.

An ex–Jesuit novice a decade older than Risa, TJ McGraff, was attending Seattle Culinary Institute in preparation for opening a restaurant in

Portland, Oregon. For R&R he enrolled in an evening oil painting class at U Dub. Risa's own painting had flowered, winning her a work-study position co-teaching the class.

The first time she spoke with TJ, he introduced himself as "a failed Jesuit, a food fanatic, and an obsessed but awful painter, as we can see." The painting he nodded toward—a vaguely geometrical mass of orange, brown, and yellow chunks cluttering a canvas in a random strew—looked to Risa like the aftermath of a furniture-repair project attempted by a psychopath with no tools but a chainsaw and wood glue. "I see some potential there," she lied.

She began to like TJ the instant he snorted, "*Piffle!* Don't insult my astounding lack of talent with bogus encouragement. Come on, assistant instructor. Take another look and tell me what you *really* see."

Risa gave the painting another look. The thing remained such awful company that to speak of it honestly would violate her resolve to *Restrain the mind as the charioteer restrains his vicious horses.* But she had an idea. She'd been taking extracurricular Bharata natyam classes—one of the classical dance forms of southern India. Rather than comment on TJ's painting, she decided to concoct a faux Bharata natyam performance that would allow her to respond with no words at all.

Striking a sudden, full-bodied, wide-stanced, giant-eyed pose that caused TJ's jaw to drop, Risa arranged both hands in the "Live Long and Prosper" mudra of Mr. Spock of early *Star Trek.* Cocking her head with a look of "Bright Curiosity," she danced up to the painting. Contemplating the canvas, her brightness then dimmed, the Spock mudras spasmed into limpness, her mouth went slack and forehead and face seized up. Holding these gestures, she turned to TJ and maintained the pose for a good five seconds so he could see how totally his painting had fucked her up. TJ went hysterical with delight. The other students, hearing the ruckus, stopped working and watched.

As if to save herself, Risa danced ten steps away from TJ's painting, turned back, folded her hands over her breast, and gazed at the painting *yearningly.* This second study caused her to look as if she were being doused in radioactive waste. Mouth collapsed, forehead shriveled, hands quivering in some sort of "Bloodied Tuna Thrashing on the Deck of the Boat" mudra—and when she turned to TJ and again held the pose to reveal how he'd ruined her, he howled. The other students were laughing now too.

Dancing to her backpack, Risa reached inside, pulled out her trusty giant magnifying glass, pirouetted back to the painting, and used the glass to give TJ and the students a giant-eyeballed look that silently proclaimed: "A New Hope Dawns!" But when she held the glass close to the canvas, as if to study TJ's brushwork, she began puffing her cheeks and convulsing in the manner of an Afghan hound about to chunder on the carpet.

As TJ wiped his eyes, helpless with glee, the class broke out in applause.

Risa gave a smile to all, and a parting namaste to the godforsaken painting.

* * *

TJ APPEARED TO have money. He lived, during his chef school stint, in a pricey Queen Anne district bungalow with a heated garage he'd converted into a studio. On the day they'd met, he'd invited Risa to come see his studio and, if she liked, work in it free of charge. For fear of amorous intent, she resisted for a time, but the more she saw of TJ in class, the more he struck her as asexual. One rainy night, sinking into the ubiquitous annual Seattle Fall Melancholy, Risa drove over to Queen Anne, located TJ's place, saw lights on in the garage, and knocked on the door.

TJ answered, wearing a spattered green artist's apron, a tiny silk pouch on a cord hanging round his neck—and nothing else. Guessing that he was working with a live model, that she was completely wrong about his asexuality, and that activity was in the offing, Risa apologized for dropping in unannounced and turned to go. "No, no!" TJ cried. "I'm so glad you're here. Come in, come in!"

"You're...working alone?" she asked doubtfully.

"Of course I'm..." He glanced down at himself. "*Dear God.* Sorry about...*the obvious*!" Since his apron didn't close in back, TJ began backing toward the rear door of the studio, telling Risa, "William Blake contends the muses commune readily with the naked. My painting was so awful tonight I was trolling the heavens for help, using my body as a, uh...what do salmon fishermen call those lures? *Hoochies?*"

Risa had started laughing soon as TJ had gone into reverse. By the time he called himself a hoochie she was in pain.

"Art's hell! Don't you love it?" he declared. "When I get back we'll commiserate and drink way too much tea!" With which he turned and ran, leaving Risa gaping at his surprisingly furry, compact little butt.

She'd hardly finished grinning when he reappeared, wrapped in a dark blue silk dressing gown as distracting as the no-outfit outfit. Though elegant in its tailoring and sheen, the gown was covered with pale-faced geisha girls, every one of whom was wearing a smaller version of the same gown, each gown-within-a-gown covered with smaller geishas. Risa's head began to swim from the M. C. Escher effect. "What kind of tea?" TJ asked brightly.

"Lapsang if you've got it. I hardly ever smoke, but when I'm bumming I do. So smoky tea helps. A suicide substitute should taste believable."

Nodding Risa toward a rocker, TJ and the geishas went into high gear, putting a kettle on a hot plate, fetching a plastic honey bear from a cupboard, climbing onto a chair to fetch, from a high shelf, two diminutive Yixing teapots and a matching pair of teabowls no bigger than shot glasses. He placed a bamboo end table by Risa's rocker and a big wicker chair close by. But after he smiled at her, the geisha ensemble froze, his brow furrowed, and he began staring much more closely. "Okay, Risa," he said. "What's this talk of bumming and suicide substitutes? Who blew out the hurricane lamp I always see burning inside you?"

"I'm *fine,* TJ," she sighed.

"So long as you don't play poker," he replied. "You're the worst liar in Seattle."

"I came to *admire* your studio, not dump in it," she said.

The kettle whistled. TJ filled the little Yixing pots and delivered Risa's to the side table. With an athleticism that dazzled her for its strangeness he then balanced his tiny teabowl upside down atop his tiny pot, climbed up and stood on his wicker chair's seat, stayed perfectly balanced as he dropped to the seat by collapsing then folding his legs Buddha style with no help from his hands, smoothed his lapful of geishas, removed teabowl from pot, filled the tiny bowl with a dead-accurate high pour to cool the tea, squeezed in a drop of honey, stirred the tea with a tiny reed whisk, took a demure sip, and turned to face her.

"As my Jesuit novice master, Father Tom Schmidt, used to tell us," he began, "*Schmidt happens.* You've been schmadt upon, Risa. It's plain as day. So there's nothing for it but to find a friend, tell what happened, let him help scrape off the schmidt, and go figure. I'm your friend. If *I'd* been schmadt upon I'd want *you* to listen. So let me listen. Then we'll go figure."

She nodded indecisively, said nothing for several seconds, then drew a deep breath and nearly shouted, "It's my damned *face*!"

TJ blinked in surprise. "Your damned face," he said blankly.

"*This* thing!" she said, stabbing a finger at it.

"But it's...so...outstanding," he said, looking puzzled.

"Whatever it is," Risa said, "I have no choice but to live behind it. And something about it keeps causing certain...*strangelings*...to, well, *get in my face.* I never see them coming. I try to ignore them. But I need to get *way* better at ignoring and seeing them coming. And that's the whole story. So please, let's change the damned subject!"

TJ shook his head. "You think Father Schmidt would let you walk after a confession like *that*? He'd get down to it, Risa. He'd say, 'Describe a few of these *strangelings*.'"

She heaved a trauma-tinged sigh. "Well, there's the type who hate me point-blank—which is their right, I guess, but it always kind of shocks me. And there's the type who, despite lack of eye contact, lack of encouragement, lack of everything I can think to lack, attach to me like barnacles to a piling, then start venting all this hyper-personal...*stuff.* Then there's the Lotharios. Which is biological. You can't blame a guy, or now and then gal, for trying. But I draw the line at the man who, not an hour ago, on a sidewalk loaded with people, called across the street to me that he had ten inches and wouldn't I like to verify that by hand. The thing is, TJ, talking about this crap just smears around its sleazy residue. Life is good. Great, even. Mostly. Not one person in a thousand pulls this stuff."

"But there are two million people in Seattle, Risa. If these creeps are one in a thousand, that leaves you two thousand potential *strangelings* to have to deal with. This sounds like a pattern. Patterns need fixing. You can smoke in here, by the way."

"God, thanks!" Risa dug her battered Kools out of her backpack, fired one up, and filled her lungs. "I'd love to end these encounters, TJ. But I'm starting to fear I'm unconsciously doing something to cause them. Some days you'd think my face was a billboard that read: 'COME ON OVER AND TELL ME HOW FUCKED UP, UNFAIR, DULL, OR SEXUALLY WEIRD YOUR LIFE IS, FREE OF CHARGE, NO TIME LIMIT, NO THOUGHT TOO TEDIOUS OR KINKY. AND IF YOU'D RATHER JUST SCREW ME WITHOUT INTRODUCING YOURSELF, WHY, HOW FUN! THANKS FOR SHARING!' But see the problem? What a bitch I am to talk this way!"

"That was *not* bitchy," TJ said. "You're holding on to your humor despite your revulsion. And revulsion, under the circumstances you describe, is what à Kempis's *Imitation of Christ* would call 'a necessary sorrow of the soul.'"

Risa started giggling.

"What's funny?" TJ asked.

"A guy in a geisha robe quoting Thomas à Kempis," she said.

Ignoring the giggles, TJ leaned in toward her and stared at her with unapologetic directness. "That marvelous tooth gap in your grin," he said as if muttering over one of his own paintings, "really struck me when we met. It makes you look as if you know things it would delight others to know. Which you in fact do. But the come-ons, I suspect, have more to do with your iconographic features. In images of the saints, some faces draw us in with their serenity, some with their suffering, some with their eerily present eyes. With your face I'd say it's the smile. Sad or happy, good news or bad, a remarkably glowing smile is your default expression. Add the aura of dark, messy hair, the beauty, and those little blue veins at your temples and *wow*. You really light up the space around you."

"Just so you know," Risa said, "every time I hear words like 'aura' or 'glow' aimed my way I fight an urge to run away screaming."

"But just so *you* know," a dead serious TJ replied, "Seattle's Rembrandt-like reduction of light renders even a hint of radiance stunning. This isn't random harassment, Risa. Your face, to be nothing but an art historian about it, is *iconic*. And priests and religious artists for millennia have encouraged people not only to trust such a glow, but to light candles before it, pray to it, worship it. That history puts a face like yours in a *very* loaded position."

Risa groaned, and took a suicidal drag that finished off her cigarette.

"I sympathize," he said. "But I also think I've grasped the problem. Shall we cut to the advisory chase?"

"Please!"

"Jesus said, famously, that the poor are always with us. But he was apparently too loving to add that so are the haters, wheedlers, leeches, Lotharios, and self-proclaimed ten-inchers. Lost or fogbound souls are drawn to faces like yours as surely as lost and fogbound ships are drawn to guidance by lighthouses. If it's any consolation, I recently suffered a comparable fate. During my failed priest stint down in Chiapas, white clerical collars and black Jesuit shirts made a name-brand lighthouse out of me."

Risa was a parochial school veteran. She sensed TJ's priestly authority as he spoke. But boy did the gang of geishas modify the authority's frequency!

"What fogbound souls forget," he said, "is that every lighthouse on Earth stands on a stone cape or reef or sea stack signaling *the very opposite* of a safe harbor. This is where you have the power to change things."

"*How,* TJ? I don't see how."

"From the moment we met," TJ began, "I sensed your open, undefended heart. But I also sensed—when I asked you about my godawful painting, for instance—a strong determination to harm no one via word or thought or deed. My advice is, *lessen that determination.* Giving occasional offense is not the same as doing harm. An offense that shatters an illusion is a kindness in disguise. When you see a wheedler, whiner, or creeper sailing your way, be a lighthouse. Use the same beacon that draws people *to warn people away.* Don't let the fogbound even *think* about anchoring close to you. Allowing that is unfair to you *and them.*"

Risa nodded her head slowly, but faintly. Distractedly. And a quiet came over her. She sat very still for several seconds. She then bent at the waist, crossed her arms over her knees, lay her head down on her forearms and grew even more still. "I'm fine," she murmured toward the floor. "Back in a bit. This just happens."

A half minute passed. Her breath came slowly. TJ couldn't see her lowered face. Only the jumble of her hair. But he sensed she'd gone somewhere deep inside and far away.

When she returned to herself and sat up, Risa, being Risa, smiled and, alas, glowed. But her face was pale, her pupils enlarged, and she looked more than a little lost. "Your advice," she said weakly, "felt perfect. And then... something happened. Lately I sometimes... *get sent,* you could say, on these little... 'journeys' is a word. Gone in a flash, back in a flash. But the flash holds all this content that really whacks me. The content is... not like the thunder after a lightning flash. It's more like the cloudburst and downpour."

TJ received this with a deeply serious nod.

"Based on the downpour just now, TJ, can I ask you a strange question?"

Another serious nod.

"I have no siblings, and my parents divorced ages ago," she began. "But I've still felt I would. Have siblings, I mean. I felt I'd just need to find them. And in the place I just flew to, there was... a strong sense of having found the first."

TJ gazed at her evenly, showing no surprise.

"My question might sound like a New Age version of the pickup lines I've been bitching about. But it's not that at all. What I'm wondering, TJ, is whether you're willing to *be* the sibling I just sensed we somehow are."

For the first time since she'd met him, TJ looked ill at ease. "I too feel a closeness," he said quietly. "But before I commit to such an intimacy, there's a *but*."

"Tell me," she said.

"I've spoken of this to no one but my brother, Jervis, because when I've tried, people think I'm ineptly telling them I'm gay. I'm not. Or not *experientially*. It's more mysterious than that, harder to talk about. But I'll say this. Years ago, when reading an obscure text by Saint Augustine, I came upon the sentence 'I made myself a Mother of whom to be born.' And that phrase! It caused a cloudburst like the event you've described. And not just because I'm an orphan. What thrilled me was the possibility of a Mother one *can actually make of oneself*. A Mother so real she might be capable of bearing offspring. Say, a son. Maybe even *the* Son. Anyway, this...*insane maternal grandiosity*, let's call it"—TJ let out a tight little laugh—"spoke to something so alive in me that, if you and I were to have the depth of connection you seek, I'd need, in a way, to be both a brother *and* a mother to you."

Risa nodded. And again inadvertently glowed. "I've *felt* that!" she said. "I've sensed something like this in you, TJ. And given the mother I've got, *wow*, could I use an extra!"

TJ set aside his teapot and bowl, unraveled his legs, and stood, leaving thirty or so concentric geishas facing Risa from three feet away.

She set aside her teabowl, rose from the rocker, faced them back, and very slowly, very gently, they enclosed each other in each other's arms. "TJ," Risa whispered. "Mother-brother," she breathed. "It's so good to have found you."

(Columbia River Gorge, 1981)

IX. Jamey's Six-Cent Shopping Spree

The relationship between fathers and sons *should* be barbaric.
—Anatole Broyard, *Kafka Was the Rage*

JAMEY'S LOVE OF the innate kindness hidden in ordinary people did not come to include his father, Jon, until Jamey was twenty-three years old. The breakthrough began the last time the two of them went pheasant hunting. Jamey had skipped a year of college in order to work various itinerant jobs as he bummed his way happily around the US for a year. He then set out on a second working and bumming year in Europe. He was now a senior at the University of Oregon, still living in a dorm because his puny financial aid package helped with the cost. A more satisfyingly bohemian off-campus arrangement would have forced him to pay out of pocket; the only pockets in his life that weren't empty were Jon's, and Jon had not been happy about his two years on the road. "Stick with the dorm," his benefactor had advised.

Jamey was a good shot but didn't think much of pheasant hunting. Blasting birds out of Eastern Oregon skies made him feel a bit like the God who'd taken out his mother on his birthday for no sane reason. He'd agreed to the annual hunting trips so far because they were the only father-and-son undertaking that he and Jon shared. But this year he had an added reason for going: Jamey's course of study at U of O had secretly changed dramatically, and his determination to divulge this secret had him vibrating with nervous energy from the moment he met Jon at his home in Southeast Portland. When Jon asked Jamey to take the wheel of his three-quarter-ton Dodge truck and camper, negotiating that cumbersome beast through morning rush-hour traffic and up the Columbia River Gorge left Jamey so enervated that the disarming speech he'd rehearsed had vaporized. It was finally just racked nerves that made him blurt, "I've got a happy confession for you and it's huge! Are you ready?"

"Of course not if it's huge, but knock yourself out," Jon said, keeping his eyes on the approaching I-84 asphalt. As an engineer with the Oregon Department of Transportation, Jon stared at asphalt for a living. The giant camper was his home away from home.

"A year ago," Jamey said with nervous good cheer, "I dropped my pre-med major. Sorry not to fess up till now, but when setting sail on unknown seas an adventurer wants his sea legs under him and trade goods in the hold before he reports to his financial backers."

Jon continued to gaze at the approaching asphalt.

"I gave pre-med four semesters, but as you know, I was only drawn to doctoring because I'm a people person, and there *weren't* any people. It was all science classes. Hard labor from the neck up while the body we're supposedly learning how to heal molders away. When I'm with people, life has a vibrant flow to it. Pre-med, for me anyway, has no flow. So when I got back from Europe I jumped ship to a major *loaded* with people and vibrant flow."

Seeing no readable expression on his father's face, Jamey shrugged and dropped his bomb: "I switched to drama, Dad! *Pretty dramatic,* eh? And it turns out I've got a gift. *Several* gifts, actually! I love everything about theatre—casting, acting, directing, set and costume design, stage managing, writing plays. A play in production swallows me whole. All these folks with different skills—or almost no skills at all—come together with a short amount of time to unite and do something really difficult. But when we join forces, the skilled players cover for the low- to no-skill people, and it's amazing how often the realpolitik paradigm that belittles low-skill people gets stood on its head. Often as not, Dad, seeming theatrical losers end up delivering bolts to the heart that leave the realpolitik cynics gaping. I *love* that!"

Jon kept scowling at the approaching asphalt so diligently that Jamey silently cast him in a no-skill avant-garde role as Staring Person—and Jon was great at it! Nobody could stare at asphalt more authoritatively than Jon Van Zandt!

"I see you're thrilled," Jamey said. "But don't act so excited, because I haven't even told you the best news! You know the big indoor and outdoor Shakespeare company in Ashland? They're doing *Romeo and Juliet* this spring season—and *guess who just got cast as Mercutio*! I couldn't believe it! One of the best companies on Earth! I'll have to play hooky spring quarter to play the part, but this is huge. Nine actors tried out for Mercutio by invitation only, including this Royal Shakespeare Company pooh-bah Theo Bollingsworth, who flew all the way in from London thinking he had a lock. 'Fraid I sent him back to Crumpetland with a burr in his breechclout the size of Larch Mountain!"

Jamey's laugh was exultant. Jon continued to study pavement. And Jamey understood his father's funk: Jon had been in med school when he and Debbie had fallen in love. An unplanned pregnancy soon followed. When she refused to abort, Jon accepted her decision, but med school was brutal and there would be three more years of it even *after* the baby. When Jon learned that engineering created a quarter of the debt of med school and led to paychecks two years sooner, he reluctantly made the switch. But to this day he behaved like a doctor in exile. He kept medical journals by his

TV chair, in both bathrooms, and in the camper behind them, studied them assiduously, and on the rare occasions he initiated talk at the dinner table it was often to inform Jude and Jamey of what he called "breakthroughs in modern medicine." Always the same respectful *modern medicine*. Never "those greedy quacks" or "the American Medicators Association," or (Jamey's tag of choice) "the Detroit Automakers of Healing." It didn't help that, a short time after Debbie died, *modern medicine* developed a 75 percent effective treatment for the myelogenous leukemia that had killed her. Jamey's pre-med major had left Jon daydreaming that he could conceivably have saved three out of four dying Debbies in the future. Jamey had just told him he'd kissed those Debbies off for a chance to mince around a stage in tights.

Though his face remained unreadable, Jon sounded perfectly cordial when he said, "Congratulations, son. That all sounds grand. Do follow your heart and all that."

Jamey smiled with relief.

"Of course," his father added, still sounding cordial, "since our tuition arrangement was aimed at med school, I'm sure you're expecting no further assistance from me."

The fist hidden in Jon's last sentence caught Jamey flush on the jaw, as intended, and he reeled for a moment. But then his indefatigability kicked in. "*Assistance?*" he blurted. "As in *financial help*? For a *thespian*? What kind of fool do you think I take you for? Would-be *doctors* should be assisted, by all means. But would-be actors and playwrights? Poppycock! Actors and playwrights should be donated to *modern medicine* for drug and surgical experiments. Come to think of it—great idea, Dad!—volunteering for drug experiments can be my new source of tuition money! It worked for Ken Kesey!"

On that note, they drove through desert terrain in a silence so toxic that Jamey began to vibrate again. The unstable swaying of the camper and nine dollars in his checking account didn't help. And barreling down an endless strip of asphalt in silence was Jon's native terrain. As they neared the tiny Columbia Gorge town of Arlington, Jamey decided to remove his dad's home-court advantage by abruptly exiting the freeway. Jon's reaction was satisfying: "This isn't our *route*. We don't need *gas*. The backup tank is *full*. What are you *doing*?"

Jamey had no idea what he was doing till he spotted a roadside farm stand: ARLINGTON PRODUCE & PIES. He then pulled the big Dodge in so sharply that something fell with a crash in the camper behind them. Hopefully a stack of medical journals. "I always stop at the sight of fresh fruit," he lied.

"I packed more than enough fruit for both of us," Jon said.

"But my portion, I'm sure," Jamey said as he shut off the engine, "was pre-med fruit. We can't have that! I'll dart in and buy some drama major fruit of my own."

Jamey hopped down from the cab, sauntered in under the awning, pulled his wallet from his left butt pocket—and realized something tragic: the wallet was empty. *Shitfuck*. He'd emptied it on purpose, as always when he traveled with Jon, so he could produce it in front of cash registers, feign amazement at its lack of cash, and *sponge off of dear old Dad*.

Patting all four jeans pockets, Jamey came up empty. Though he considered it an idle gesture, he tried his little front right change pocket—and felt two wee disks. Dreading the sight of copper, he fished them out: *two dimes*! An entire fifth-of-a-dollar of discretionary funds! And on the international currency market this fine fruit and pheasant season, the US dollar was *strong*.

Jamey was normally a fast shopper. Drawn to a crate full of late Japanese plums, he leaned low to imbibe their fragrance, and had nearly made a selection when he noticed, out the corner of his eye, Jon glaring at him—a far more interesting expression than Staring Person's stare. This suggested possibilities. Feigning indecision, Jamey set off wandering down the long counter at a snail's pace, scrutinizing individual fruits one after another after another. Relishing the sight of Jon's face souring, he donned a look of perplexity as he examined unaffordable peaches and pears, sniffed hallock after hallock of exorbitant blue-, black-, and gooseberries, lusted after five types of apple, jammed his nose into the navels of cantaloupes, toyed with the apricots with the familiarity of a man minding his testicles in the shower, then set every piece of fruit back where he'd found it, looking mystified. And how *mesmerizing* the attributes of fruit become as one's ex-benefactor, imprisoned in an increasingly stuffy cab, realizes he's lost his right to urge his ex-benefactee to hurry the fuck up! As Jamey continued his devotions, the beige of Jon's face turned an irritated pink, moved inexorably on to crimson, then grew so eggplantish that Jamey began to feel genuine concern for Jon's life—inspiring the profoundly Shakespearean thought: *I'll inherit!* Meeting Jon's bulbous glare with more fake perplexity, Jamey turned on his heel and perused every bin in the farm stand yet again. *O Joy!* When he at last doddled back to the very crate where his marathon had commenced, he indolently, ostentatiously selected a single, perfect Japanese plum, set it upon the antique-looking farm scale, learned the price from the equally antique farmer, turned to Jon, held the plum up in triumph, and in the first Euro-twit accent he'd ever attempted, called out, "Puh*paw*! Look how *lovely*! And only *thix thenth*!"

Hmmm. The accent needed work. But what a pleasure to hear Jon gargle something fumious as Jamey handed the farmer a dime, placed the four pennies change in his now even bulkier change pocket, dropped the twit accent, and cross-examined the old agrarian about the year's growing season, the planetary prospects for weather in general, the suspicious fact that the collapse of the family farm coincided with the existence of liberals, the precarious state of our right to carry Uzis on the street due to said accursed liberals, and so on.

When Jamey glanced again at the cab, Jon looked to have aged several decades. Jamey started toward him, intending mercy. But he hadn't taken two steps when a muddy Ford flatbed roared up, died with a wrong-octane rattle, and in the dusty silence that followed Jamey heard what sounded like a half dozen opera sopranos vying to see how many ways they could sing the syllable "*Yike!*"

Seduced by a fresh excuse to dawdle, Jamey stepped round to the flatbed—and beheld six border collie pups in a coffin-sized crate, writhing round a tricolored bitch. The bitch was a beauty, her gaze intelligent, her coat the mottled black, white, and blue-gray of a sunlit forest floor after a dusting of December snow. A leathery woman in jeans and a battered straw Stetson hopped from the cab, turned green eyes as keen as the bitch's on Jamey, and announced, "All but the black-and-tan're fer sale."

Jamey hadn't remotely been considering a dog. But as a free enterprise fan with 14 percent of a strong American dollar still in his pocket, the rough-and-tumble of the marketplace felt suddenly irresistible. "How much?" he asked.

The rancher shook her head ruefully. "Thirty bucks. They just had their ten-week shots. Thirty'll just cover it. Them vets're gettin' greedy as people doctors."

Checking to be sure that Jon caught this shot at "modern medicine," and seeing that he had, Jamey set out to complicate the situation by pretending to want the pup that wasn't for sale. "Which is the black-and-tan?"

The woman pointed past the writhing swarm to a serene little face parked, chin on forepaws, in the crate's only tranquil corner. "That's my Romeo. With his daddy, the Big Duke, on guard at home and Momma Sheba there, queen of all she surveys, I s'pose the last thing I need's another canine. But look at them eyes."

Raising his face on cue, Romeo leveled *them eyes* on Jamey—and something kicked so hard inside him he felt pregnant! The pup was giving him the kind of serene smile Jamey had seen nowhere but on the faces of tribal elders in *National Geographic*. The littermates roiling around him looked like battery-operated toys in comparison. "Ten weeks old, you say?"

The rancher nodded.

"Your Romeo, at one-fifth of a year in age," Jamey said, "already smiles like the kind of person I've only dreamt of becoming at the end of a long, well-lived life."

Taking this odd statement in, the rancher assessed him more closely and liked what she saw. She strolled over, leaned her forearms on the flatbed next to Jamey, gazed at Romeo, and murmured, "Li'l heartbreaker, idn't he?"

Jamey shook his head just once, the way that means yes.

"Question is," the rancher said, "whose heart? Yours or mine?"

Jamey was taken aback. Was he in the running for a dog that wasn't even for sale?

The woman set a boot atop the truck's rear wheel, hoisted herself up, slipped a hand under Romeo's belly, lifted him out of the crate, then set him on the flatbed in front of Jamey. The perfect diplomat, Romeo smiled at his leathery owner, then up at the tall stranger, then turned back to smile at his mom. Sheba did not smile back. In fact she hopped out of the crate, slipped up to Jamey in the border collie's half-crouched, chaos-control gait, and began staring straight into his eyes. "*Don't meet her gaze,*" the rancher warned.

Looking off across the street, Jamey spotted a meadowlark perched on a fence post. "Our state bird," he remarked to no one.

Romeo's mom cooled her jets. Jamey's dad didn't. "Let's *go!*" Jon hollered. "You've got no business even *thinking* dog. No place to keep it, no money to care for it. And like I said, there will be *no help* from me."

"My financial advisor, Jon Van Zandt," Jamey said to the rancher.

She touched her Stetson brim to Jon, who scowled back. Romeo, meanwhile, leaned down to sniff the hand Jamey had rested on the flatbed and apparently liked what he smelled, because he sat his fuzzy haunches down on the back of it. At the same instant the meadowlark on the fence post burst into song. Chills flew up and down Jamey's entire body. In an endearingly diminutive voice the pup caused him to conjure on the spot, Jamey said, "I never met *anybody,* two leggèd or four, more charming than you." Romeo responded with a bottom wag that felt as perfect to the back of Jamey's hand as the pup's smile felt to his heart. When the meadowlark burst into song again, Jamey's feelings charged out ahead of the situation: he wanted this disarming little creature in his life.

And the rancher saw it. "That calm but intense way Romeo looks out his eyes? I see the same in you. 'Fey serenity' my husband calls it. You'd be a matched pair—if I were to pair you."

Jamey had held back till that moment. But Third World elder smiles, fuzzy haunches on hands, "fey serenity," meadowlarks? It ganged up on him. "Can I tell you three quick things about me?" he asked.

Knowing his "three things" might tip her scale, the rancher was clearly debating whether to risk hearing them at all. The nod she finally gave Jamey was *very* cautious.

"First thing," he said. "I switched majors this year, pre-med to drama, without my advisor's permission—as you can see." The rancher glanced over at Jon, whose head was shaking grimly. "He's not normally rude," Jamey said in a stage whisper he made audible to his father. "The trouble he's having is, he's cut me off at the purse strings due to my change of major, so now he can make rude faces at me all day and get no results."

The rancher smiled wryly. Jon made more faces.

"The second thing is this," Jamey said. "Next April, down in Ashland— please come if you can—I'm in Shakespeare's *Romeo and Juliet.* I'll be playing a guy called Mercutio."

The rancher rocked as if a gust of wind had hit her. "Romeo's best friend," she said. Seeing Jamey's surprise that she knew this, she extended her hand. "Name's Juliet. Juliet Tall. Which is why the pup's Romeo. Figured I'd pair

up the two tragedy tore apart. But now look." She sighed at the contentment with which Romeo remained parked on the back of Jamey's hand. "It
could be there's no settin' right what the Bard set wrong."

An engine roared. The tricolored bitch sprang to her feet. Jon had slid
across the cab, fired up the Dodge, and was now gunning it. "I'm *leaving*!"
he bellowed. Though he flinched at each roar, Romeo stayed seated on the
back of Jamey's hand.

"I'm going nowhere," Jamey said to Juliet, "till I tell you the third thing.
And my name is Jamey, by the way."

Again no reaction from the rancher. Just keen attention. But Jon, seeing
his bluster had failed, knew Jamey's indefatigable nature too well to fight
it. He shut off the engine.

Jamey looked down at the pup, then turned to Juliet. "The third thing is
this. One of us is gonna lose out, is one way of looking at it. But why see it
that way? Mercutio and Romeo together? Juliet and Romeo together? This
pup's gonna set right some of what the Bard set wrong, no matter how the
next minute or two go."

Juliet considered this, nodded agreement, but then something changed:
crossing her arms, she eyed Jamey with sudden suspicion. "What's wrong?"
he asked.

"I *wish* I was a perfect judge of character," she said. "You *might* be as
good-hearted as you sound. But if you're *not*, you're one of the slickest
fast-talkers I ever met. So let's back offa Thing Three a minute an' see some
proof of Thing Two." Arms still crossed, one boot tip tapping in the dirt,
she eyed Jamey expectantly.

It took the fledgling tragedian a moment to guess what she was after.
He then nodded, freed his hand from beneath Romeo, straightened his
back, loosened his shoulders and neck, filled his rib cage with an enormous
breath, began releasing the breath slowly. With no warning he then clutched
his gut, let out an awful *Hnnh!* sound, and doubled over.

Sheba crouched in fear. Jon's jaw dropped. Juliet saw the sword pierce
Mercutio.

"*'Tis not so deep as a well, nor so wide as a church door. But 'tis enough,
'twill serve!*" Jamey gasped in a voice so desperately damaged that Jon
found himself looking for the wound. "*Ask for me . . . tomorrow*"—Jamey's
cough made Jon fear a gout of blood—"*and you shall find me a grave man.
Zounds! Why came you between us, Romeo?*"

Jumping out of character, Jamey grabbed Romeo's forepaws, stood him
on his hind legs, and in the heartbreaking puppy voice lamented, "*I thought
all for the best!*"

Juliet's eyes shone. Jon gaped at his son, stunned. Sheba crouched and
began to growl.

Ignoring them, Jamey released the pup, coughed up a spume of unseen
yet mortal gore, and wheezed, "*A plague! On both your houses. They've
made worms' meat of me!*"

Collapsing the top half of his body onto the flatbed, Jamey expired briefly, then rose from the dead, stood Romeo on his hind legs again, turned him toward Juliet Tall, and made him cry out in heartbroken puppy-speak: "*This gentle man, my very friend, hath got this mortal hurt in my behalf. O sweet Juliet! Thy beauty hath made me effeminate!*"

That ended the scene, but not the drama: all in an instant Jon breathed, "Good *God*!" Juliet broke out in applause, Jamey spun Romeo toward each of them to take a bow, and Sheba shot forward and hit Jamey hard, on both cheekbones, with wide-open jaws and fangs. Not a bite. Just a blow. But it left blood-colored fang indentations, ended the curtain call, and got everyone's adrenaline flowing.

Maybe it was this adrenaline, Jamey felt, that gave Juliet the strength to do what she did next. "He's yours," she said without a word of apology for Sheba's blow to his face—which made sense to Jamey since, with those two words, Juliet had become by far the worst hurt.

"You're unbelievable!" he gushed as he fished out his wallet. Then he laughed and put it back. "I'm broke! But let's barter. I've got a Remington twelve-gauge worth a couple hundred. A warm red hunting jacket worth forty bucks or so."

"Mercutio," Juliet said fiercely, "I want *way* more from you than that."

Frozen by her seriousness, Jamey waited for her words.

"I've owned border collies all my life," she began. "Sheba's the best bitch I ever had. An' Romeo's the best pup she's ever given me. What you need to know is, he's gonna *worship* you. It's his heart. From now till you or he are done he's gonna watch every twitch of your hands an' legs an' body, movement of your lips, dart of your eyes, till he knows your next move the instant you do. He's gonna *adore* you, is what he's gonna do. *Unless you put him on a chain. Or in a pen. Or stuff him in a dorm room and leave him alone all day.* Do that to this animal and his great heart'll be ruined. What I want from you, Jamey, is to know there is *no* chance o' that. *Ever.*"

"I hear you," Jamey said, "and I promise. Zero chance. Ever."

"So you *say*," Juliet told him. "But I've raised 'em so long I'm a bit of a border collie myself. I wanna read your eyes and hands and body language while you swear to me to give Romeo his lifelong place at your side."

Moved by her demand, Jamey laid his hand on his heart. "I swear to you, Juliet Tall. I will honor Romeo's heart by making him my constant companion. He *will* live at my side. I don't know how yet, but he *will*. I swear it on Shakespeare's pen, Sheba's teeth, Romeo's wise elder smile, and your courage in entrusting him to me."

Juliet scrutinized him for a moment, nodded just once, turned to the truck, grabbed Sheba by the collar, and to Jamey snapped, "Be *quick*!"

Jamey took Romeo in his right hand, stood the perfect Japanese plum on the truck bed with his left, and said, "Ashland. April. Come see a vow being kept, Juliet."

She managed a strained smile as Sheba lunged and twisted against her grip. *"Go!"*

Jon started the Dodge, this time careful not to gun it. Jon, in fact, seemed a changed man. He had seen his son act and found him brilliant. He'd heard him make an impossible vow. And Jon believed Jamey would keep the vow, and was pondering ways to help him do it.

Jamey climbed up into the cab and set Romeo in the DMZ between himself and his father. The pup's diplomatic hot streak continued: he trundled up to Jon, placed his front paws on his thigh, looked up in his eyes, and turned on the wise elder smile.

"Romeo," Jon said gruffly. "It's a relief to know at least *one* of you two has good sense."

Jamey grinned straight ahead at the windshield.

"What d'ya think, Roams?" his father growled, shoving the Dodge into reverse. "They got any Milk-Bones or puppy chow in this one-horse, one-plum town?"

X. The Unbearable Lightness of Dave

You've got three minutes
to say what you want to say. Beyond that
no one hears a thing. So...
just say: There's a moon,
a boy walking, somebody crying. The rest of us
trying to mainline darkness
from the Little Dipper's spoon...
—Chris Dombrowski, "Statesboro Blues"

THROUGHOUT THE ELEVEN years between her parents' divorce and her falling in love with Sanskrit, Risa had attended four different Portland schools, two parochial, two public, nonstop. Over the same span of time she had paid her father an average of two visits a year in Seattle, twenty-two total, while Dave paid Risa just six one-day visits in Portland. Out of an increasingly scorched affection for him Risa had tried hard not to count. But single digits are dismayingly easy to remember.

He was better at phone calls. He telephoned to chat once a month or so and was an engaging talker. But even the most cordial calls didn't make up for the fact that he once let two years pass during which he never set eyes on his only child at all. When Risa was eight, ten, even twelve, she told herself that this abandonment wasn't abandonment, because that's what Dave told her. But when she turned thirteen and realized she'd ached ever since he left her with Moira, she decided to make him ache in return: she began referring to him, to his face, as "Dave." Never "Dad," "Father," "Daddy." The first time she reduced him to his name, her voice trembled as she spoke. But when Dave accepted his demotion without complaint, comment, or perhaps even notice, the hurt Risa had intended boomeranged back upon her, creating an even deeper sense of abandonment.

The main cause of Dave's ongoing fatherly abdications were what he called "serial romantic conflagrations." Since it won't be possible to understand Risa's romantic hesitancies otherwise, here's a brief summary of her father's misadventures.

* * *

DAVE MCKEIG WAS born on a family ranch in Montana. But to really tap into the emotional essence of his boyhood we need to imagine a moonless spring night, starshot and church quiet, the boy wide-awake in the wee hours, his love and awareness spilling out the open window, running uncontainable down the "sloeblack, slow, black, crowblack" Elkmoon River (Dylan Thomas a boyhood favorite of Dave's). The early May sky is ashimmer with starwinks through leaf buds, the cold air pungent with the fragrance of the century-old cottonwoods encircling the house. Weak-wooded trees, cottonwoods, potentially lethal in windstorms, but the McKeig family's allotment of thirty are all four feet in diameter and all magic to the boy for the grosbeaks, chickadees, and calliope hummingbirds asleep in their boles and bark caves by night, and the great horned owls hidden in their high branches by day. The owls (how the boy loves this!) so perfectly match the trees' rough gray bark and shadowing that visitors refuse to believe they're up there till Dave runs to his room, returns with a cigar box, and flips it open to show them the hundred or so owl-ejected vole and mouse skulls he's collected mowing the grass below. Magic too, his cottonwoods, for the way they share a single underground root network, so that one giant faery-ring organism encloses Dave and his family. "Dioecious" is the word Grandma Stella used to describe how male cottonwoods produce bullet blossoms that stain everything beneath them a sticky blood red, and females produce seed-bearing "cotton" capable of riding the breeze to start new faery rings hundreds of miles away. What a flight for the boy to ride this notion out into spring starlight, wander the world as far as his imagination can carry him, then wake to find himself as rooted as his family, sharing their ring of trees with hummingbirds safe in their silent night branches, and invisible owls raining vole skulls down by day.

Dave was a very good student despite his susceptibility to enchantment. He excelled at science and math and scored off the charts on standardized tests. Because prestigious East Coast colleges are often accused of being the bastions of elitism they in fact are, most make room for a few Western whiz kids. Dave's whizzery won him a full ride to Princeton.

A few months after he left the ranch and so emptied the family nest, his cattle-ranching parents, to his astonishment, wrote two separate letters to inform him that they had divorced and were moving to separate cities in the desert Southwest. Dave was beyond shocked. They'd been so hardworking and taciturn he hadn't even known they were struggling. To finance the split, they'd sold the ranch that Dave and his brother, Charlie, had assumed was their legacy. A worshipper of cottonwood faery rings was suddenly the rootless owner of nothing. The loss of the place she'd homesteaded sixty years before sent Grandma Stella into a tailspin, and a case of winter pneumonia became double pneumonia, then a headstone in the St. Luke's Parish graveyard before Dave could make it back to say goodbye.

The next time he set eyes on his Elkmoon Valley home, the following summer, the cottonwoods had become a polka-dot pattern of four-foot circles sawn level to the ground. As he knelt stunned on a circle, trying to find a last vole skull to take back to Princeton, a man stepped out of the house and told him he was trespassing. "Why'd you cut the cottonwoods?" Dave asked. "Damn things are dangerous," replied the new guardian of Dave's "sloeblack, slow, black, crowblack" boyhood nights and dreams.

Neither brother forgave his parents, but both greeted their loss with the laconic veneer popular among aspiring cowboys. A fraction of an inch beneath Charlie's veneer, impotent rage would simmer for the rest of his life. Dave, being more self-aware, made two attempts to heal his hurt. The first: hoping to resurrect some kind of idealism, he freedom-rode for civil rights in Mississippi for two successive early '60s summers. And he did feel briefly recharged. But over the long haul—especially after a brief blossoming of American idealism died with the assassinations of Martin Luther King and Bobby Kennedy—the legacy of those summers became Dave's full-bodied surrender to the music and moods celebrated by Delta blues.

His second attempt to heal: when his cattle-ranching career vaporized, Dave set out to explore alternative careers. He graduated magna cum laude from Princeton, spent two years as a Rhodes scholar studying diplomacy and economics at Oxford, got accepted into the Kennedy School at Harvard, and seemed briefly destined for a career as a diplomat, financier, politician, or some such shaker and mover. But, the summer before his graduate program started, Dave landed a decent-paying job at a Portland, Oregon, branch of the Pioneer Trail Bank chain. And there, at a college pal's wedding, he met the sexy, hard-partying Irish American Moira O'Reilly.

A loyal product of parochial schools, Moira was thrilled by the long-haired liberal priests of the era who held that while birth control is a mortal sin, the "rhythm method" was not a sin if confession absolved the rhythmic sinners. Once Moira and Dave got their rhythm thang goin', Moira grew more devout than ever. "I checked the calendar, checked my temp! *Go!*" she moaned all summer, instigating the zillionth shotgun wedding in Church history and, seven months later, the birth of Risa. (But let's not single out Catholics: Methodist Debbie and atheist Jon Van Zandt's daughter, Judith, was born of the same "method.")

When family life converted Dave's summer job at a dull suburban bank into his career, two traits he'd felt sure he possessed fell out of his possession. The first: ambition. The second: fidelity. Delta blues became the soundtrack for this exciting shift in perspective. *Damn right, Portland ladies, I'm down,* his night life began to croon. *I'm so far down I might never get back up. But by bein' down, if you'll get on down here with me, baby, we just might find us a way through.* Moira, meanwhile, fully believed the priests who said divorce is a mortal sin whether confessed or not, and so refused, out of genuine mortal terror, to accept Dave's demand for a divorce in spite of several years of infidelities.

When a split was granted, Dave headed north to a job as chief loan officer at the First State Bank of Puget Sound, the largest in Seattle at the time, and a promotion that could have taken him places, as the saying goes. But having lost his ambition, there was no place Dave much wanted to go except back through time to the Elkmoon Valley of his boyhood. His two-week Montana summer vacations became an annual fix, his laconic drawl and Western style became daily habits, and at certain cost to his career Dave took to wearing custom-tailored gray or indigo pin-striped suits, with the coats cut long to match his long brown hair. Black or brown Lucchese cowboy boots, immaculate white broadcloth shirts, mother-of-pearl cuff links, bolo ties with embossed silver tips and cattle-skull clasps, and natural good looks added to the ensembles, and a predictable result ensued.

Comely women walked into Dave's big downtown bank almost daily. After all, *there was money in there*! Not every day, but once or twice a month, a certain type of "looker" (Dave's term) would high-heel it across the marble floor, halt like an enemy officer in front of Chief Loan Officer McKeig's massive mahogany desk, seat herself in the lasciviously soft rawhide armchair, and level her gaze on the man in charge of the funds she hoped to extract. Having revved herself up to debate loan or mortgage rates with some soft-gutted steel-minded financial geek, the woman would feel confused, then disarmed, by the elegant gent eyeing her across a Great Plain of mahogany. Often it was not prime rates but Dave's garb that broke the ice. "Is that cattle skull on your bolo genuine ivory?" the woman might ask. "Oh, be sure," Dave would say of the Chinese plastic imitation, the lie making his eyes dance. As a discussion of loan contract details commenced he'd then hum snatches of such tried-and-true Western cowpies as "The Streets of Laredo," "El Paso," and "Tennessee Stud."

Was it fortunate that these performances worked? Not so much. As Jimmy Driftwood didn't quite sing it, "He had the nerve and he had the blood, but there never was a Dave like the Tennessee Stud," and on some level the women who succumbed to his cowboy banker act knew it. His phone chats with Risa throughout these years revealed a spate of conquests rote as a pulp Western plot. If a coffee date led to a dinner date and the dinner evoked what Dave called "chemistry," the "looker" would make every cell of her corporeal form and absolutely none of her net worth available. Dave's phraseology regarding the new "lady friend" would then morph, over the course of a few weeks, from an enthused "Astoundingly attractive!" or "This time it's different!" to a confused "A little high maintenance," or "Complicated, it turns out," then on to Risa's favorite deal breaker: "To quote Flannery O'Connor's misfit, 'She would of been a good woman if it had been somebody there to shoot her every minute of her life.'"

For a decade and a half following his divorce from Moira, Western Dave lured a veritable remuda of loan clients out onto a nonexistent home on the range. To his "credit"—in the overextended banking sense of that term—he married and divorced only two of them after Moira but struck up live-in relationships with another five. Each of these romances ended with Dave financially strafed and semi-catatonic due to the impossible incompatibilities that emerged once the brief dispensation of eros was spent. Each romance thus reminded his astute daughter of nothing so much as a man diving, with a gracefully high spring off the board, into a bone-dry swimming pool.

During each slow recovery Dave would call Risa more often and take her to dinner once or twice—the best father-daughter times they ever managed to have. By her late teens Risa also realized she had some influence. By glowering when Dave, under his breath, crooned faux cowpoke tunes, she could coax him back to Lightnin' Hopkins, Blind Willie Johnson, John Lee Hooker. And by refusing to pity his phone laments she could move him from melancholy to comic discourses upon, say, his determination to find a sizable woman by the name of May or Lula, with flour on her muumuu from the fruit pies she'd been baking all morning. But sooner or later another stiletto-heeled shape-shifter would staccato across the bank's marble floor, Dave would cowboy up, and Risa's heart would sink when her phone rang, and with an enthused "This time it's different!" Dave again vacated her life.

So her feelings remained loaded. Risa and her father were alike in sense of humor, long-leggedness, taste in music, facial expressions, and laugh—and she considered him a terrible role model. She found him one of the most charming people she'd ever met, watched him abuse and sully that charm to woo one ill-suited woman after another, asked herself what would stop her from exerting her own charm to win equally ill-suited men, and found no answer to her question.

Risa knew all along that Dave was not a phony. It was Great-Grandma Stella's word, "dioecious," that best described him. He remained so in love with the lost cottonwoods of his boyhood world that he took on the characteristics of a cottonwood's two genders. One side of him produced wistful, wind-riding talk that set a listener's imagination drifting for pleasant miles, like seed-laden cottonwood fluff. The other side exuded a sexuality reminiscent of the sticky red buds cottonwoods shed in high spring, adhering to and staining everything they touch in much the way Dave's come-ons eventually tainted every woman who responded, and the same taintedness in him.

Since there was no way to be charmed by one side of Dave without getting stained by the other, Risa was left praying that dioeciousness skipped generations.

THREE YEARS INTO her sojourn at U Dub, Dave invited Risa to dinner at the Seattle-Tacoma Airport two hours before he had to fly to Denver for a loan officers' convention.

Two hours. At SeaTac. Everything about the invitation hurt Risa's feelings. She then heard her Daddy-starved voice say, "I'll be there! Thanks so much for calling!"

They met at a newly opened fish house in the terminal with an atmosphere about as intimate as a Manhattan subway station. But the food and cabernet were surprisingly okay. And there were, for once, no droll tales of Dave's latest conflagration. Instead, despite the fact that his time was limited, Dave said he wanted to know "*everything*!" about Risa's studies, her living situation, her life, her art.

Feeling rushed from the start, Risa said she'd made friends with a pleasingly odd ex-Jesuit, TJ by name, and was sharing his private studio.

Dave's eyebrows shot up. "Love interest?" he asked.

"Spiritual littermate," Risa replied. "But if I take the time to explain how TJ and I discovered that, you'll miss your flight."

Dave nodded. "So what's going on with your art?"

"This will sound strange," Risa said, "but again, time's short, so I'll just say it. Sanskrit language and Vedic thought—more than any famed artist or school of painting—have become my mentors. But my love for them creates a yearning I want to explore for myself. I don't trust Academia with the mysterious yearnings of my heart. Whereas if I'm careful to dodge the expounders and self-appointed authorities, I do trust art."

"Your idealism is remarkable," Dave said. "I'm glad you're protecting it. But can those high ideals manifest in your art?"

"After I graduate, if I get scholarship help, I plan to pursue an art school MFA to explore that very question. What I very much like about art is that it doesn't compromise my spiritual ideals to practice it. My painting profs are good on technique, knowledge of materials, tricks of the trade, but are pretty good about leaving what I choose to paint up to me."

"So what are you choosing to paint these days?" Dave asked.

These days...Dave's questions were feeling so rote Risa considered punting. But their time was so short, and the bottle of cab so disarming, that she went for it. "I'm trying to capture landscapes with a...how to put this?...*swinging door quality*. A feeling that, even if I'm struck by something outward and study it as hard as I can, I have to turn inward to find the truest perception of the outward before I can turn it into art. My senior thesis paintings and writing will be about this somehow."

"Beautiful!" Dave exclaimed. "I'm picturing Monet. *Giverny*. The impossible pond more than the water lilies. Am I in the ballpark?"

Dave looked so pleased with his own concept that Risa felt irked, and shrugged. "John of the Cross said that words can be like a sun, doing for the heart what sunlight can do for a field. I want to make paintings that convey that heartward movement, and in a way I can't describe, certain Sanskrit words and phrases lead me into that sunlit field."

Dave looked briefly puzzled, then grinned and flitted to a new topic. "Love life?"

Risa turned self-protective. She confessed that a young man named Grady had come into her life, and that they were living together "on a trial basis." But when Dave cracked, "My entire love life has taken place on a trial basis," Risa's face turned stony.

Dave winced. "Sorry. And thank you for not laughing. I mean it, Risa. If you'd laughed at that dumb joke I'd *be* a dumb joke. Thanks for taking love and life seriously. I should try much harder to do the same. Tell me more about Grady."

She shared a few soundbytes suitable for dad ears, calling Grady, "Outdoorsy." "Funny." "Forthright." "Energetic."

" 'Trial basis' sounds like you're hesitant even so," Dave said.

He was right, but Risa didn't share her hesitations: not amid the hubbub of SeaTac with a *serial conflagration* addict about to take flight. Had she gone deeper she would have described Grady as a handsome, high-hearted, often hilarious, and almost mythologically horny young swain who charmed her most of the time but worshipped her body so obsessively he made her feel like a sham goddess at best, and a sex appliance at worst.

Seeing her uneasiness, Dave asked if she'd like a chilled Viognier for dessert. The goddess/appliance nodded eagerly. Dave waved down a waiter and put in the order.

"Once in a while," he remarked, "I'll meet a couple who seem 'made for each other,' as the saying goes. But every time I've learned such a couple's history, it turns out they found each other by sorting through a string of partners for whom they hadn't been 'made' at all. I wish I had greater wisdom for you, Risa. But I'm convinced that the part of us that falls in love might be the part of us we understand least."

Risa liked this observation. The Viognier arrived. Taking a sip, she prayed that Dave wouldn't make her regret a little genuine openness and said, "My main romantic problem is, my heart doesn't yearn much for a Mr. Right. It yearns for what the Vedas call the Unborn Unseen Guileless Perfection. The rub is, I feel romantic attractions, same as anybody, but the men I've been attracted to so far don't take spiritual yearning seriously. Yearning lies at the heart of every great culture, and can fill a body with energy, set off fireworks in minds and hearts, direct every moment of a life. But of the men I've known only Dr. Kool and TJ McGraff feel the same. And when a boy I'm drawn to pigeonholes my spiritual thirst as a weird little hobby of mine and no one else's, *wow*. Things cool down fast."

As she was speaking Dave was taking meditative sips of his wine and gazing at her intently. When she fell silent, he murmured, "*Remarkable!*"

Risa was so lost in thought she could only say, "Huh?"

"Your face. The way you speak, way you shine. Everything about you. Whatever's going on in your life, Risa, I've never seen you look more vibrant and alive. You don't seem madly in love, no offense to Grady. I sense something more rare here, perhaps *wed* to that yearning you speak of. Some enduring form of peace has found you."

Risa felt chills. Dave understood her a little! Just that shard of understanding left her ready to tell of a hundred beautiful things that had happened since her passion for what Dr. Kool called *hari-lila-amṛtam,* "the nectar of the play of the Lord," sprang to life.

Dave's eyes then dropped from her face to his watch. "*Damn.* Time for my flight."

Just that fast, Risa was eight years old. Same cold rock in her stomach. Same aching lump in her throat. *Daddy. Don't leave.*

"Please don't come to the gate," he said. "Too hard on us both. But what a delight it's been to see you, my girl."

Delight...My girl... Her throat closed. She couldn't have spoken if she'd tried.

"I brought you a little present. Just a book. But it's the best novel I've read in years. Kind of a take on my life, really"—he donned his dumb joke grin—"with Soviet tanks playing the part of former lady friends."

Don't say this. Don't be this. Don't leave me like this.

"But truly, Risa, I loved this novel like few I've ever read. And I love you like no one else on Earth. So it's yours."

When Dave bent to rummage for the book in his carry-on, Risa noticed for the first time that the rich head of hair she'd always taken for granted was vacating his crown. The sight of his pale, surprisingly pink scalp stunned her. She then flashed on TJ's phrase, *The offense that shatters an illusion is a kindness in disguise.* So she spoke her feeling:

"It doesn't feel right to me that a father and daughter can live in the same city but see each other so seldom that the father seems to his daughter to *suddenly* be going bald."

Dave looked up at her in shock. She kept shattering his illusion even so:

"Natural changes are gradual. So they should *feel* gradual. Is what I think. When gradual changes gain a power to startle us, it means too much time has passed since we saw each other. And that's not right. Not to your only child it isn't. And a quick dinner at an airport not only doesn't fix this. It makes it worse."

Dave wrestled with her words for a long time before he finally, reluctantly nodded. "The women in my life...keep me from the best woman in my life. The one I'm looking at. That's the bitter truth. And our lack of contact is my fault. But there's another truth here, Risa. A truth well expressed by a few lines in this novel. May I read them to you?"

Her shrug could not have been less encouraging. That didn't stop Dave.

The book's title, when he raised it, was *The Unbearable Lightness of Being.* The cover was a painting of a man's hat, a derby, floating impossibly up into the air as it escaped a woman's grasping hands. *Time for my flight. Kind of a take on my life.* No shit. Thanks, Daddy.

She expected him to paw through the book in search of the passage, but Dave always had a way of surprising. Opening to the novel's last page, he began reading at once: "'Tereza leaned her head on Tomas's shoulder. Just as she had when they flew together in the airplane through the storm clouds. She was experiencing the same odd happiness and odd sadness as then. The sadness meant: *we are at the last station.* The happiness meant: *we are together.* The sadness was form, the happiness content. Happiness filled the space of the sadness.'"

When Dave handed her the book, tears stood in his eyes—a sight so unexpected it made tears rise in Risa's. Dave noticed and, strangely, nodded. "Toward you more than anyone, my girl, my life hasn't been what I'd hoped. You deserve my steady love and attention. You get ragged scraps of it instead." He had to stop a moment to contain himself. "Yet every time I think of you—please, never forget this—you *do* fill the space of my sadness with happiness."

An embrace followed. An awkward father-to-daughter kiss. And Dave walked close beside her out of the restaurant. But at the entrance to his concourse he stopped, gave her a quick peck on the cheek, murmured a vacant-eyed goodbye, then strode away, his bald spot receding under the fluorescent lights, so that not two minutes after reading to her, he vanished.

Standing alone, holding Dave's book, Risa whispered, "We are at the last station."

Then: "We are *not* together."

And her feeling was the very opposite of what the novel had described: sadness poured into the diminishing space of her happiness, inundating her with hurts so long in the making that no imaginable act of her father's could assuage them.

Yet she attempted no strategic withdrawal. Uttered no sad, ṣad, ṣadness mantra. Sought no interior vastness, no escape. Not from this.

Standing motionless in the maw of the SeaTac D Concourse long after her father vanished, she used hurt itself to power a search for whatever kind of true fatherness, sans Dave, might hang unseen in the weary air.

(mostly Portland, 1982 into the 1990s)

XI. The Stumptown Shakespeare Ensemble

Love, and a bit with a dog! That's what they want!
    —the theater manager in *Shakespeare in Love*

ON THE DAY that Jamey, for the price of a parking lot Shakespeare performance, purchased a spectacular young border collie, his father's instant affection for Romeo caused him to begin to see his son the way Romeo saw him: as a marvel. Jamey's iconoclastic nature, spontaneity, ceaseless wit, and rule bending all worried Jon terribly when he believed he was headed into the medical profession. Career chaos! But the same nature aimed at theatre was ideal—and hunting pheasants with Jamey and Romeo was non-stop theatre. The pup's fearlessness in the face of shotgun blasts, tiny growls as he dragged around rooster pheasants the size of himself, and wise elder smiles for Jamey were already melting Jon's heart when the pup succumbed to exhaustion, spraddled legs down on Jamey's forearm, and slept sound as a bear in winter. Then came the last straw for Jon: the glowing look that Jamey gave the sleeping Romeo was exactly the look that Jon's long-gone wife, Debbie, used to give the infant Jamey as she held him.

Undone by that look, Jon experienced a depth of affection for what he began to call "the six-leggèd Jamey-Romeo Unit" that kept him awake every night of their hunt, pondering the problems they'd face upon their return to civilization. And Jon's sleeplessness bore fruit. On their last night in camp, sipping whiskeys by the fire, the father who rarely strung together more than a few words launched a veritable soliloquy:

"Jamey," he began. "You're an actor, not a doctor, and I was way off base for not supporting that. When you get to Ashland, rent a house on a quiet street with a safe, fenced yard. I've got you and Roams covered."

The nickname Roams, coupled with the sudden generosity, left Jamey speechless.

"As for the No Pets Allowed places that would break your promise to that good ranch woman to keep Roams with you, we three have special talents to meet that challenge. Look at Romeo, a total charmer. Look at you, Jamey, an actor-chameleon who can turn into whoever he needs to be at the drop of a hat. As for your old engineer dad, I've got a shop full of tools and an idea you're going to love. I'm going to build you two a conveyance that, with your acting skills, will accomplish outright magic! Any idea where I'm heading?"

"You've got me flying blind, Dad."

"I don't think I've ever told you that, when I was a boy, Jules Verne's *Twenty Thousand Leagues Under the Sea* was my bible. I loved the way Captain Nemo roamed the oceans in the Nautilus, free of the claims of any government, his travels detected by no one, his only allegiance to the wonders of the deep. Given your acting skills, Jamey, I believe you and Roams can duplicate that freedom on dry land."

As a crazy picture took shape in Jamey's mind, Jon confirmed it: "What Romeo needs to stay at your side is a Land Nautilus. And I'm going to build her for you."

ROMEO'S LAND-GOING SUBMARINE turned out to be a fiberglass instrument case that looked like it carried a stand-up bass. Jon didn't emulate the shape of a bass; he chose a simple right triangle to make the interior roomier and more versatile. He installed partitions that Jamey could configure in several ways, "depending on whether the Nautilus is under sail, or anchored," and installed comfortable foam-rubber padding, so one wall of the triangle became a comfortable dog bed if Jamey laid the Nautilus on its side. He eschewed the velvet lining of most instrument cases, preferring baize made of pure merino wool for its greater durability. He added a small internal oxygen tank, a side chamber for dry-ice blocks to serve as summertime AC, and gauges that let Jamey monitor the oxygen supply and temperature from outside the sub at a glance. He made the instrument case's stout lid lockable, added an axle and two electric golf cart tires for smoothness of ride, and a retractable handle allowed Jamey to tow the case with ease. At this point the sub still looked like a bass case, which was crucial for subterfuge. But Jon's love for the original Nautilus inspired a risky addition: two portholes with lockable covers allowed Romeo to study the passing world and its denizens as Captain Nemo had studied the environs and denizens of the seas.

Upon completion the Land Nautilus weighed 110 pounds, dog snacks, chew toys, Frisbees, leashes, and dog included, with plenty of room for Roams to grow. The instant the pup learned the sub led to adventures with Jamey, he took to jumping inside it, pulling the lid shut on himself, and smiling out a porthole in hope of an outing—which ploy often worked.

Enter Jamey's acting talent. His standard approach to a No Pets restaurant, lecture hall, hotel, or what have you involved inviting Romeo into the sub, giving him a hush command, locking the lid and porthole covers, and proceeding forthrightly into the danger zone. With his distinguished-looking bike-wrecked nose and great ear for accents Jamey then summoned the bearing of a classical bass player so effete, or a jazz bass player so hyper-cool, that the Nautilus didn't raise an eyebrow. Jamey's impersonations were so daunting that he enjoyed Romeo's occasional failures to maintain silence for the challenges they presented. Once, when they were checking into a Seattle hotel, for example, a desk clerk heard a muffled *wuff!* inside the case, scowled at Jamey, but before she could even speak he told her, "I must apologize *wuff!* for this damned nervous tic. I've got a *wuff!* concert in two hours, and nerves set it off. Worse, I've *wuff!* lost the key to my bass case! Would you be so kind as to *wuff!* recommend a locksmith I can call from my room?"

Embarrassed by her suspicion, the clerk gave Jamey the numbers of three locksmiths, and into the hotel his stowaway rolled.

MY SUMMARY OF Jamey's early acting career (*me* being the Holy Goat) will be brief, because fifteen years would pass before his life intersected with one of this chronicle's major figures in ways central to our overarching story. Suffice it to say that Jamey's repute with Ashland's Oregon Shakespeare Company (OSC) got a jump start when, a week before opening night, the man cast as Shakespeare's Romeo ripped a knee in a soccer match. He had no understudy. Though Jamey had only prepped his Mercutio role, he replaced Romeo on ridiculously short notice, unleashed his prodigious memory and great talent, and his Romeo was such a triumph that the OSC offered him a three-year contract and a string of major roles. When Jamey then called Jon with his news, he was stunned to hear his father say, "Time to drop out, Jamey. This is a huge step in the direction you've chosen. Don't worry. My support will continue."

Feeling he'd walked into an extended miracle, Jamey went to work playing Hamlet, Richard II, Shylock, Prince Hal in *Henry IV,* the same prince-become-king in *Henry V,* Mark Antony paired to a dazzling Cleopatra in *Antony and Cleopatra,* and a King Lear that astonished when a man in his twenties played a king so convincingly old and addled. Audiences loved him in role after role. But when reviewers and interviewers began to call him such ridiculous things as "Oregon's answer" to Peter O'Toole, Richard Burton, Patrick Stewart, Ian McKellen, or any other iconic British actor they happened to have heard of—as if Oregon could produce any such thing—the overpraise created a shift that left Jamey feeling stultified. He was already contemplating a sabbatical far from all things Shakespearean when disaster turned his plan into a necessity.

One night Jamey's phone rang near midnight, he picked up with a sinking feeling, and his sister, Judith, in tears, informed him that Jon had had a heart attack, undergone quadruple bypass surgery, and his recovery was less than certain.

Two days later Jamey and Roams moved into an apartment a short drive from Jamey's childhood home, where efforts to cheer Jon back to health occupied them for weeks, and were partially successful. Though Jon's energy was so reduced that he was forced into early retirement as a highway engineer, he was soon back in his shop refurbishing the Land Nautilus with his usual skill.

The performer in Jamey, meanwhile, had become broody. He began taking long city walks with Romeo again, rubbing shoulders in cafes and parks with the ordinary people who still oriented him like nothing else, and a direction began to present itself. Jamey had lost all desire to keep playing Shakespearean heroes with some renowned troupe. Instead he began pondering how a troupe of his own devising would allow him to stay in Portland to be near Jon, and solve some dramatic problems too. While the comedic and tragedic powers and over-the-top diction of Shakespeare still called to Jamey, in a world of shrinking spans of attention he couldn't justify being so loyal to the original plays that they induced exhaustion in his audience. On stage in Ashland playing roles like Lear and Hamlet, Jamey had often seen the Bard's verbosity cause good-hearted crowds to look bludgeoned.

And another possibility had begun to obsess Jamey: as Romeo evinced ever greater intelligence and a love for engaging his intelligence, Jamey ran his idea by Jon. "Dad. I'm thinking of creating roles for Roams that would let us perform together, and maybe reach a working-class audience like those Shakespeare started out with, but has nearly lost today."

Jon lit up. "What an idea, Jamey! What can I do to help?"

"Romeo excels at grasping certain commands. You've seen how he can bark as if laughing, whine as if heartbroken, make moon eyes at us when he wants a walk. I want to start teaching him more complex sounds and behaviors that I call for with signals so subtle that Romeo appears to initiate each sound and behavior himself. It would help a ton if you critiqued us once a week or so to make sure the commands are as invisible as they need to be."

"Sounds like a dream job for a forced retiree with too much time on his hands," Jon said, and the training began in earnest.

Soon Romeo was mastering sounds and actions surprisingly akin to humans: soft growls that sounded like intelligent questions rather than menace; groans of human-sounding disappointment; standing on his hind legs holding a paw to his ear mumbling, *"Rarrerr rawerr rawrrow,"* as if yammering on a pay phone. He mastered a fervidly overdone stage death for comedic purposes, a heartbreaking death for tragedic purposes, and three poses Jamey dubbed Inscrutable Buddha Dog, Disgusted by the Soliloquy Dog, and In Awe of the Soliloquy Dog. He learned to freeze in any position; to creep into a room with the guile of a burglar; to cover his eyes with his paws to avoid seeing a kiss, an act of violence, an unconscionable lie. He learned, in case of curtain calls, to stand on two legs next to Jamey, offer a paw, and do a tandem bow.

Sensing the dramatic power Roams was already capable of, Jamey began to pore over Shakespeare, seeking to devise roles that brought out Romeo's very best sounds and gestures. He warded off the Bludgeon Effect by condensing favorite plays by 15 to 30 percent. Well aware that purists would see this as heretical, he began to put together a lean, mean, eight-actor troupe, knowing that if he cast a single gifted actor in four or five different roles they would deflect the testy purists with their versatility. Auditioning more than thirty actors with classic Shakespearean chops but great improvisational skills as well, he hired three women and four men to the troupe he anchored, dubbed them the Stumptown Shakespeare Ensemble, and struck an inaugural six-play deal with the Ankeny Theatre in Southwest Portland. No one had ever seen the like of what resulted. The crowds were soon sellouts, and Romeo and Jamey *needed* their synchronized curtain call bow.

A few of the Stumptown troupe's more successful Bard alterations: the Stumptown troupe performed a *Macbeth* in which Romeo, wearing a small crown identical to the murdered King Duncan's, tracked Lady Macbeth everywhere wearing an ax-murderer smile that becomes the chief cause of her ultimate madness. They did a *Hamlet* in which Romeo played an empathetic companion to Jamey's Hamlet, doubling the power of his words with his In Awe of the Soliloquy expression, hiding his eyes from the machinations of Gertrude and Claudius, and when nearly the entire cast including Hamlet dies in a chaos of poisoned cups and blades, leaving only Hamlet's friend Horatio to explain the truth to a new king, Romeo sits at Horatio's side, the very picture of inconsolable grief, sustaining the cathartic sorrow of the audience. They did a *Richard III* that cast Roams as an obsequious toady dog whose ready nods and pants of agreement lured Jamey's Richard into all his most self-destructive decisions, infusing the play with black comedy that audiences welcomed with open arms. They tightened up *Lear,* casting Jamey as the mad king and Romeo as a clear-seeing companion achingly unable to convey Cordelia's loyalty or Goneril's treachery as Lear misapprehends both daughters, making Roams the very conscience of the play. As both the audience and Goneril grasped this and she ordered Romeo killed, he died so movingly that many wept, and others marveled at the Bard's canine characters and researched them, only to find that, until Jamey and Romeo, no such characters had existed. Reviewers raved in positive terms, the inevitable purists raved in negative terms, audiences chose to judge for themselves, and the buzz became tremendous.

Within three years the Stumptown Shakespeare Ensemble was touring university and independent theatres throughout the Pacific Northwest, Jon Van Zandt was one proud father, and Jamey and Roams were a six-leggèd, two-wheeled toast of Portland town.

XII. Risa's Vestigial Tongue

I am not the maiden who awaits her betrothed but the
unwelcome third who is with two betrothed lovers and
ought to go away so that they can really be together. If only
I knew how to disappear there would be a perfect union of
love between God and the earth I tread, the sea I hear.
                                —Simone Weil, *Gravity and Grace*

SHORTLY BEFORE HER fourth year of Skrit study was to commence, Risa
picked up a book she'd been avoiding. Dr. Kool had recommended the
Upaniṣads to her a year before, not as an assignment to be read against a
deadline but as an absolutely foundational text for anyone serious about
Vedic spirituality. Feeling she might be ready to tackle it, Risa obeyed an
impulse to ask the scripture itself if now was an auspicious time to read
it: closing her eyes, she opened the Upaniṣads and pointed blindly to a
page, hoping to touch down on a gem of wisdom. She was greeted instead
by this:

> *The highest mysteries must never be revealed*
> *to one whose passions have not been subdued,*
> *nor to one who is not a master's pupil,*
> *nor to one who is not a Brahmin's son.*

Implausible coincidence does not feel innocent. Stabbed by the words, Risa
desperately invoked her magic formula, whispering, "Sad. Ṣad. Ṣadness."
The very title of the scripture then stabbed her again: *Upaniṣad-ṣad-
ṣad*ness.

Her injury caught fire and flared into anger. How could this foundational
Vedic text be reserved for no one but Brahmin caste sons? Sanskrit tradition,
unlike Catholicism, didn't even give her hypocrite popes and chauvinist
cardinals with whom to argue, because the Upaniṣads weren't composed
by men: they were made up of "Self-Existent Knowledge Rays" that were
simply "heard" (*śruti*) by perfectly attentive rishis as the Rays hovered like
music in the primordial forest air—and Risa had trusted this legend so
deeply that it had greatly enhanced her own powers of listening. *How, in*

the name of Love, she asked, *could perfectly attentive forest rishis hear the very path to Perfection defined as a men's club?*

The silence that greeted her question felt like a door slammed in her face.

Storming over to the university library, Risa marched up to the stacks and found four scathing books of Hindu cultural criticism—two sociological and feminist, two by recent female survivors of Hindu religious, social, and sexual abuse. She tore through the books in an all-night fury, burning with shame to realize how little she'd known of centuries of sexist scriptural exegetics, ridiculously subservient roles for Hindu women, nightmare lives for widows, child brides, girl orphans. The books made her sick, as she had more or less hoped.

But they failed to kill her love. Her feelings for Sanskrit ran so deep that, like a woman returning to a lover who beat her, she returned home, slept off her research marathon, and dove back into the Upaniṣads, skipping classes for two days to read them through. To her dismay, with the exception of the Sons Only Verse, the scripture caused surge after intuitive surge to lift her like warm ocean swells:

Here in this body there is a dwelling place. Within the dwelling place is a small space. What is there in that space that we should seek to perceive? As vast as the space surrounding us is this small space within. Within this space are contained earth and sky, fire and wind, sun and moon, lightning and stars. The whole world, all beings, and all desires are contained in this small space. Those who come to possess this space obtain complete freedom of movement in all worlds and inhabit the heavens at all times.

Not only did her passion for Sanskrit survive the offending scripture, it intensified because of it. The Sons Only Verse declared her intensity worthless. She was left perfectly conflicted. Unable to deny the oceanic swells, just as unable to convert "Sons Only" into love, she sought psychic balance by breaking a few Vedic hearts in return.

SHE BEGAN BY scheduling an appointment with Dr. Chagan Kuldunchari. For a year and more she'd been like a favorite grandchild to him, free to drop by his office on any pretext: a sample of her ever-improving rice and dal for him to critique; a Kalidasa or Valmiki verse committed to memory and too beautiful to hold in; a batch of fudge brownies, a great Dr. Kool weakness.

At the sound of a knock the doctor always stood, so that when the door swung open his visitor was greeted by his joined palms. Some students blushed at this. Risa, from the start, simply returned the joined palms. This day was no different. But after taking the chair across his desk, she heard herself say, "Doctor. I've got some rough news. I've got to drop Sanskrit. Starting now."

Kuldunchari grew intensely still. Risa filled the awkward silence by nattering on about how she'd dropped the Asian religions half of her double major, had long since met her language requirement, was headed to art school, tons of paintings and a senior thesis to get done, blah-blah-blah. When she finally ran down, Dr. K's response was far from ambivalent:

"You will not do this," he said.

Hearing the dismay hiding inside his use of command form, Risa half wished he was right. But the Sons Only Verse, for her, was a world war declared against women by a traitor among the rishis of old, and the Upaniṣads had not come to womankind's rescue. Dr. Kool, in regard to this war, was like Switzerland.

He had strong views even so. Leveling his gaze upon her, he said, "You will not leave the refuge of Valmiki, Sankaracharya, Lord Krishna, Sita Ram. You will not rebuke the inward path and turn outward to the illusory. I have seen your heart and it is boiling with love. I have seen your mind and it is locked on truth. Tell me what has happened."

Risa felt so close to breaking that she hid behind vagaries. "Life got complicated. My feelings did too. I've loved working with you, but it's time I moved on. Time I focused." The strain of not confiding in her most trusted teacher then caused her eyes to well.

Seeing this, Dr. K ventured a brilliant guess: "Has the masculine bias of one of the old formulations wounded you?"

Though Risa said nothing, one of the welling tears spilled down her cheek.

Kuldunchari nodded. "I should have armed you against this. The Brahmin caste claim to own all scripture is infamous. *The Laws of Manu* are especially noxious in their hands."

Risa didn't just nod, she recited a riff from those very Laws: "'A woman should do nothing independently, even in her own house. In childhood subject to her father, in youth to her husband, and when her husband is dead, to her sons, she should never enjoy independence...Even if he has no good points at all, the virtuous wife should ever worship her husband as a god.'"

Dr. Kool nodded. "Another difficulty is English. In languages with grammatical gender, both masculine and feminine terms are applied to the divine, easing the seeming sexism."

"Bṛhadāraṇyaka Upaniṣad, and I quote," Risa said. "'The highest mysteries must never be revealed to one who is not a Brahmin's son.' Is there anything *seeming* about this sexism, Doctor? According to the most potent scripture I've read, my yearning for truth is banned!"

"That is not true and I'll help you see it," the old man said. "To begin, heed how the scripture works with the words 'child' and 'son.' Bṛhadāraṇyaka Upaniṣad: *the Father is Intellect, the Mother Word, the Child Life.* Don't chop Father, Mother, and Child in three, Risa. *Intellect, Word,* and *Life* are yours for the taking. When the Brahmins' superiority complex offends you, roll up your sleeves and fight back."

Risa said nothing.

"Fight as Kabir fights! Listen! 'You say you're a Brahmin, born of a mother who is a Brahmin. / Bring me this mother and show me the special Brahmin hole through which she squeezed you!'"

Risa couldn't help smiling. "Good one. The Upaniṣads themselves fight back. They say that Ātman can't be attained by study, by intelligence, or by the endless reading of holy books. Ātman is, quote, 'the Mystery to whom Brahmins and Kshatriyas are mere food and death itself a condiment.' The Sons Only Verse stands guard nonetheless, making sure silly girls like me don't even *think* about pursuing the divine Mystery."

Kuldunchari was shaking his head. "This is anger speaking," he said.

Risa stood up, trembling a little, but smiling even so. Circling Dr. K's desk, she took a stand right in front of his chair. "This is *heartbreak* speaking, Doctor. You're the best teacher I've ever had. I'll never forget you. I'll always be grateful to you. But the best way to help me now, if you still want to help, would be to stand up for just a moment."

Knowing what was coming, Dr. Kuldunchari refused to take his feet.

Risa's smile took on its lost radiance. "Your *Jiva* has become *Jada*. 'Immovable heaviness.' Another good one, Doctor! When *Jiva* becomes *Jada*, they say, Paramatma comes out to play. That's *my* strategy too. My *Jiva* is *Jada* to this Sons Only crap. But I'll *never* stop loving everything that you and Sanskrit have taught me!"

"Do not do this," Kuldunchari repeated.

"All I've done, Doctor, is step in a trap set for women ages ago. I must free myself. I refuse to spend my life married to a Truth that swears never to love me back. But I also refuse to leave this room till you bless the grandfather-granddaughter friendship we've both cherished."

Dr. Kool's expression remained immovably fierce, Risa's immovably tender. Silent seconds ticked by. When finally he stood, the good doctor appeared suddenly old and frail. But when Risa put her arms around him, his own arms went, by increments, from weakly holding her, to nearly crushing her, to quietly gasping as he crushed.

The instant he released her she spun on her heels. Not quite sobbing but not daring to look back, she strode out of his office and away.

QUITTING DR. KOOL was the worst. Her next few moves were enjoyable in a way.

First, to protect herself against any further "sacred sexism," she gathered up every last one of her Skrit-related class notebooks, texts, lexicons, mythology, and scriptures, boxed them up, taped the boxes tightly shut, drove them to her father's house, stored them in the rafters of his two-car garage, and swore never to open them again.

Next move: in hopes of venting and so purging the worst of her anger, Risa opened her latest secret scribbled dumbsaint notebook and penned a torrid if unmailable letter to the Sons Only Verse author:

Dear Pseudo Rishi,

I won't lie. The grenade you somehow slipped into the Upanishads broke my heart. But some of us lapsed Catholic girls know how to deal with this kind of shit. When Aristotle, Aquinas & the Church fathers teach that a woman is a mal-formed man known as a manqué, or when some big-shot early Xian like Tertullian teaches that the wombs of women are "filth" & the children in our wombs "loathsome curdled lumps feeding on muck," we turn as tough as this cruel foolishness forces us to be. When it comes to defining our minds, hearts & bodies, YOU, Sons Only Fool, are a manqué rishi; Aristotle, Tertullian & Aquinas are manqué theologians, & I thank the Unseen Guileless Perfection for the womb She gave me to distinguish me from the penis-fetishizing likes of you! My Skrit-fired heart burns for Truth in the body the Unseen bequeathed it, & if you think I'll let that fire die to passively await an incarnation as some niggle-scriptured Brahmin's pampered baby boy you've got another hundred thinks coming. There is a path, extremely fine & extending far! It has touched me, I have discovered it! That beneath which the year revolves, the breathing behind breathing, sight behind sight, hearing behind hearing, thinking behind thinking, the first, the ancient. With the heart alone I have beheld it, & that heart is beating inside a knowledge-body (sambodhakaya) & truth-body (dharmakaya) like yours, but a begotten-body (nirmanakaya) that, thanks to a Cathoholic Irish American, a philandering Montana Scot & my beloved Unseen Mother/Father, is double-breasted, girl-hipped & gratefully vaginaed & the time for you vaginaphobes to start freaking is NOW. This girl aims to show the Highest Myster-ies a love so true it will break even your mother-hating heart, causing the spurned word WOMAN to fall inside you, saving you, at long last, from YOU!

Risa's third move was her strangest: she launched perhaps the most poorly armed anti-sexist counterinsurgency of all time, consisting of a one-woman Sanskrit Oral Tradition of her own devising. In her downtime, off-time, waiting-in-grocery-lines or jammed-in-traffic time she began to recite, in an audible murmur, every Skrit word, verse, prayer fragment, or myth scrap she could recall. Since it was a written verse that had betrayed her, she refused to write down the scores of passages and couple thousand words she initially knew by heart. The only source for her recitations, she decided, would be her *female* memory. Her recitations, as a result, grew more unreliable by the day. But, over time, there turned out to be something soothing about the music her recitations made. Living in a computer-obsessed, car-clogged, espresso-wired Seattle that considered the previous decade a Nostalgia Product and previous civilizations off the radar entirely, the sound of ancient words like *prakṛiti, dharmakāya,* and *sahaj samādhi* stirred a place deep within that her Americanness might have anesthetized if not for her recitation habit. Her chief pleasure in reciting was auditory. The sound of her dwindling collection of Skrit scraps reminded her of the way the low *thud-thud-thud*ding of an old Norton, Indian, or Harley moves many an otherwise unadventurous middle-aged man to rise up in gypsy daring, suck in his gut, don leather, tie on a racy headscarf, and take off on multistate pilgrimages to nowhere, sans seat belts, antilock brakes, and helmet.

Years rolled by and life served up the usual roller coaster. She kept up her meditative efforts to convert sadnesses into interior night sky. She kept scribbling crazy-dumbsaint interpretations of her passing art passions, gratefully failed romances, epiphanies, metaphysical enthusiasms. She received the news, sent out of the blue by a U Dub classmate, that Dr. Chagan Kuldunchari had retired and returned to India to recite the Vedas with those who still can, only to take ill within a year and die, in a Pune hospital, of the jarringly non-Vedic term "dengue fever." She experienced daily angst, daily gridlock, daily blizzards of media-born info-pellets that buried everyone she knew beneath deep drifts of spiritual polystyrene. And—in the manner of a stubborn child dragging an ever more bedraggled old baby blanket off to kindergarten—she kept chanting scraps of Sanskrit during every lull in her day.

Why exactly? No reasonable reason. Her scraps had something mythic, sonic, and unreasoning to do with a time when animals could talk and the mind had mysterious powers. Something to do with fifty centuries of Indian women banned by the men to whom they'd given birth, sex, sons, breast milk, lives, from the wisdom that sustained those same fathers and sons. Something to do, too, with a recurring Earth-intuition she couldn't shake. In yet another dumbsaint notebook entry, she wrote:

> A language is not some orderly repository of words stockpiled by an academy or priesthood in a temperature-controlled warehouse. A language is a living, breathing creature made of millions of sounds wandering loose over the land, possessing, haunting & taunting its human hosts be they women, men, children, or any combination thereof. And of <u>course</u>, in a world like this one, the path to Truth is cluttered with tollbooths occupied by <u>Laws of Manu</u> cronies, corporate pretas, Brahmin banking twerps & Vatican mind police. Of <u>course</u> this Kali Age exudes a darkness so dense

that, by definition, reason can't see a glimmer of light. But some Irish poet I once read, Patrick Kavanagh maybe, had "a feeling / that through a hole in reason's ceiling / we can fly to knowledge / without ever going to college" & Skrit songs of unreason keep shooting me through that hole. I don't know why Skrit scraps are crucial. I only know that if I sit down in the smog of this mean, sweet incarnation, breathe slow as every lover of Big True since Prajapati, & chant, "A thousand heads hath Purusha, a thousand feet, a thousand eyes," hidden eyes sometimes actually open. I only know that, during a gyno exam last month, when Doc Jolene did a pap smear move that hurt like hell, without a thought I cried out, "_Avatara Tumha Dharaya Karana, Uddhraya jana jada jiva!_" Which is Hindi not Skrit & I don't even remember what it means! But no sooner was it out of my mouth than something wildly more mysterious than my legs opened & I felt the pangs of what I want to call the Mother Matrix straining to give birth to the desperately needed infant world destined to replace this shattered one. Out of some enormous dark joy I then began to sob, causing Jolene to gasp, "What is it, Risa?! What's wrong!" But how could I explain to my gyno that a Skrit scrap had just shot through reason's ceiling to soothe the Great Mother as She strains to deliver the infant world we'll soon be forced to leap aboard?

(Portland, winter 1991)

XIII. Tits vs. Gandhi

That guy you used to be, he's still in the car. He'll always be in the car. Just don't let him drive. He might be shouting out directions. But whatever you do, don't let him get behind the wheel.

—Eddie Vedder

My Mahatmaship is worthless.

—Mahatma Gandhi

As Jamey Van Zandt became a largish fish in the small pond of Portland's theatre scene, a gigantic fly continued to frolic in his champagne glass: every January on his and his mother's shared birthday-deathday he went as mad as King Lear. I've described the partial recovery inspired by the post-bike-crash realization that his near-victims kept selflessly saving his life. I wish I could say that this insight healed him permanently. But in his twenties, when drugs, alcohol, and women with gravitationally collapsed interior objects of their own entered the birthday-deathday equation, Jamey's January 30ths became a kind of Mardi Gras/New Year's Eve/Halloween/April Fools'/Day of the Dead rolled into one.

Among his darker misadventures was an LSD-fueled grocery-shopping excursion. Entering a busy Portland Safeway, Jamey perceived via acid logic that the existing global financial system is entirely bogus—which to LSD's credit did foretell the financial meltdown of 2008–2009 years in advance. To LSD's discredit, it also gave Jamey what he felt was an unerring ability to identify the Richly Deserving Poor among his fellow shoppers. Since all cash was now counterfeit, it made perfect sense to start dumping armloads of unpaid-for groceries into the carts of these souls. And because Jamey was egalitarian by nature, he also identified two police officers called to the scene as the Deserving Underpaid, and attempted to hand them each an armload of steaks. How odd it seemed, until the acid wore off hours later, that their response to his visionary generosity was throwing him facedown on the floor, cuffing him, hauling him to jail, and sending a terrified Romeo to Animal Control to await rescue by Jamey's long-suffering dad, Jon. Another misadventure involved a grain-alcohol-fueled encounter with a prostitute, leading to an unsuccessful proposal of marriage to said prostitute, but the successful contraction of a sexually transmitted disease.

More sad examples aren't needed. I, the Holy Goat, have already stated that Jamey was, for many years, entrapped in a split personality with a tragically strong preference for the friendlier of his two selves. Jamey's Princeling persona spent 364 days a year driving all thought of his mother down into darkness and comporting himself as if she'd never existed. On the 365th day an enraged Darkling then flew up out of blackness and "made it up to Debbie" by surrendering to almost any self-punishing act that presented itself. Sure, handing "free" Safeway T-bones to cops bodes ill for your legal record, but it sure frees up an alter ego boiling with repressed fury after 364 days locked up in a Princeling's mother-denying subconscious. Sure, prostitutes are almost never as good-hearted as Hollywood encourages us to believe, but when the sallow come-on smile of a streetwalker perfectly matches the yellow of your dying mother's leukemic face, the unhealed five-year-old within experiences a new brand of attraction altogether.

Because the sexually transmitted disease was a treatable case of gonorrhea and a Safeway manager chose not to press charges, Jamey remained physically and legally unscathed. But after every such fiasco the Princeling never wondered what had come over him. The sole strategy he used to stave off his next birthday-deathday disaster was to throw the Darkling back in prison, maintain the interior wall between his two selves, and weather fines, doctors' appointments, lawyers' fees, and physical recoveries with no attempt to grasp that grieving might be both a dire need and a kind of art form.

But one weird brand of energy remained capable of piercing the interior wall between his two selves. Its cause? The unrelated words "Mahatma" and "Debbie." Magic words are the most difficult to get hold of, but they're also the most powerful. And is any mother's name less than magic to those who evolve from gamete to fetus to infant inside the body bearing her name? Every time the weak word "Debbie" or strong word "Mahatma" entered Jamey's ears, the interior wall vanished, the Princeling and Darkling clearly saw and detested each other, and neither persona grasped that the death of his opposite would entail the death of himself. No kinder term than Grief Imbecile describes a man who refuses to try to resolve such an · intolerable psychic split.

ON JANUARY 30TH, 1991, the instant Jamey's eyes opened and his breathing grew wakeful, Romeo leapt from the Nautilus to the bed and stuck his cold nose in Jamey's face.

"I've been thinking," Jamey announced.

The dog smiled, doting on his funky morning breath and watching him eagerly.

"I'm thirty-three today, Roams, and my mom's negative twenty-eight.

So her corpse, had it remained, say, in this room with us, would be a pile of desiccated bones, splintered yellow teeth, cobwebs, and dust. Pondering that fact, I've decided upon this, my thirty-third born-date, to bid Mumsy farewell, sweep up the bones, cobwebs, and sad mess of her early death, toss it all out, and be done with this Fate-baiting birthday-deathday heaviness for the rest of my life. Sound like a plan?"

Despite the stupidity of Jamey's summary and the impossibility of his plan, his one true worshipper smiled and amiably nosed him. Is it any wonder humans have made an industry out of self-involved, book-length, nearly autoerotic odes to their dogs? Only our own sex organs are as cheerfully willing to share in our self-deluding impulses!

Taking Romeo's smile and tail wagging to be the "Yes" they weren't, Jamey began his Debbie Eradication Project by picking up the Kodachrome portrait on his nightstand, looking at his mother's blue eyes, happy smile, and comely face for the ten-thousandth time, and thought, *Mom, I figure the Buddhists have it right. Reincarnation's prob'ly the deal. So you, at this point, could be some winsome nineteen-year-old lass of Glasgow or deep-chested young potato farmer of Peru. But that lass or farmer can't hear a word I'm saying, doesn't care what I'm saying, and hasn't the faintest memory of Dad or Jude or me. Which is as it must be, whether we like it or not. So. Sorry as I am that you had to leave life so early, and pretty as you are in this old photo, yours is no longer a face I should be straining to recall. Trying to conjure you every birthday-deathday has messed with my life and other lives in inexcusable ways. You wouldn't want that. And Roams and I don't want it. Right, Roams?* Jamey turned the photo toward Romeo, who smiled and thumped his tail.

See how everyone visible agrees it's time we go our separate ways? You were my mom, I was your little boy, we loved each other. But time and space have stretched that love so thin it's time the link was allowed to snap. So to any part of you who might still be listening, hear me: go away. I don't say this to be mean. Only to make our farewell final so we can continue our separate journeys. Mother. Mom. Debbie. As of this moment, we're done. Fare well.

With that, Jamey carried the photo brusquely down the hall to his kitchen and bent to the lowest drawer to the left of the sink. "The junk drawer," he called it. Opening it and moving Romeo's investigative nose aside, he shoved around broken sunglasses, wood screws, a stale cigar in a cracked plastic tube, rubber bands, not-quite-empty Ronsonol lighter fluid and WD-40 cans, outmoded floppy disks, and reached the drawer's wood bottom. Placing Kodachrome Debbie on the bare wood, he unceremoniously scrambled the junk over it until the photo was buried. He then stood, shoved the drawer closed with his foot, but, as he was doing so, caught a last glimpse of one blue Mother eye peeking up at him through the junk.

A jolt of sick panic shot through his body. With effort, he repressed it. "That's that, Roams," he said, causing Romeo to smile on cue, and they turned to a birthday unhampered by such nuisances as gravitationally collapsed interior mom objects—

while on the opposite side of the interior wall the Darkling *seethed,* awaiting his moment.

THE PRINCELING'S PLANS for his 33rd-Birthday-and-First-Ever-No-Deathday Celebration had been laid for some time: a Northwest Portland movie house, Cinema 21, was hosting a traveling New York–based film festival called "Meetings with the Makers." The fest featured eight "art films" that arrived in town, one per week. Traveling with each film was a key actor, director, or cinematographer who, after the screening, would field questions from the audience. The 1981 Louis Malle cult hit *My Dinner with André* was part of the fest. Jamey hadn't seen the film in years and André Gregory was one of his theatrical heroes. But for purposes of his birthday celebration, the film's curious little co-star, Wallace Shawn, was Jamey's ace in the hole. Shawn was the "Maker" who'd be meeting the audience and answering questions. Shawn also happened to stand five foot two and was round faced and bald, while Jamey was six foot two, slender faced, and sported a thick brown ponytail, yet he could reproduce Shawn's voice, accent, lisp, and vexed rationalism to hilarious perfection.

He had major plans for this impersonation. His date for the evening was a stunning young woman by the name of Holly Brrhfygythsfyfth,[1] with whom he'd flirted off and on ever since college. Ms. Brrhfygythsfyfth had responded to his flirtations with cool indifference till his recent rise to Northwest theatre stardom, but after breaking up with a fiancé, she'd leaked news of renewed interest through a mutual friend. Jamey phoned her the same day, and Holly sounded nothing but thrilled to accept his invitation to "Meetings with the Makers." To unwind afterward, he'd reserved his favorite table at Café Cru, the late-night restaurant and jazz club, where his game plan was to await the perfect moment to launch an over-the-top seduction made sidesplitting by his Wallace Shawn lisp.

Moved by a suspicion that he might get lucky, Jamey spent the morning cleaning and romanticizing his apartment. He left his latest play, *Photographing Your Inner Child,* artfully strewn across one end of his dinner table. He built a winter "non-flower arrangement" of twigs and cattails for the same table and used a canning jar for a vase as if to say, "How casual!" He left a dashing red and gold robe he'd worn as King Lear visible in a not-quite-closed hall closet, not because he'd played Lear any time recently but because he had visions of a naked Ms. Brrhfygythsfyfth enwrapped and enraptured in the sumptuous robe.

In the belief that it was never too soon for a renowned actor—aka *professional multiple-personality-disordered exhibitionist*—to demonstrate

---

1   In light of how the evening turned out, Jamey advises the Holy Goat against the use of Ms. Brrhfygythsfyfth's actual name lest it lead to litigation.

that he is humble and kitchen literate, Jamey baked a batch of his irresistible homemade oatmeal raisin cookies, told Romeo, "We're prepped!" and off they went on a marathon walk. Jamey then showered, dressed for the film fest in his casual finest, and drove Romeo over to Jon's for the night, Jon being the one person with whom Romeo would cheerfully stay on the rare occasions when Jamey couldn't include a loaded Land Nautilus in his plans.

HOLLY BRRHFYGYTHSFYFTH DAZZLED Jamey the instant she opened her door. In his handsome ponytail, dark blue overcoat, and brown leather boots, the six-foot-two Jamey dazzled her in return. On the way to his pickup their strides fell effortlessly in sync. Holly then chose the center seat belt, sitting hip to hip with him cowgirl style on the drive. Once they'd parked and started for the theatre she then took his arm before he even offered it.

At the Cinema 21 entrance Jamey reached in his overcoat and gave three cookies to his friend and sometimes set carpenter Jimbo, the theatre's doorman. Saying nothing, Jimbo flashed the Stumptown Underground hand sign that meant they were clear to enter for free.

The theatre was crowded. *My Dinner with André* was already under way. Holly and Jamey didn't care. They found two open seats three rows from the very front, settled in, and Holly opened her purse, revealing four cute little bottles of airplane Côtes du Rhône, compliments of her Air France flight attendant housemate.

As they began sipping, nibbling, and zeroing in on the film, their smiles grew stuck. Soon they were breathing in sync, marveling at André Gregory's flights of Bohemian-mystic fancy, their senses of touch so sexualized that mere fingertips brushing fully clothed thighs began to drive them a little crazy. Up on the big screen, meanwhile, Jamey's ace in the hole, Wallace Shawn, also seemed to be going crazy. André, in response to Shawn's skein of workaday questions, had dived deep into an only marginally sane monologue, telling how he'd coaxed forty Jewish women—half older, who wanted out of theatre, half young, who wanted in—into performing a play in a forest in Poland. This play, "written" by André himself, had consisted of no script at all. The players just stood around till one of them suffered an impulse to do or say something. André's ecstatic description of the wonderments that resulted twisted Wallace Shawn's face into a nonstop cramp of skepticism. Hoping to bring the conversation down to Earth, Shawn finally interrupted André to say, "I-I'm just trying to survive. I mean, I'm just trying to earn a living, just trying to pay my rent and my bills. I mean, I live my life, I enjoy staying home with Debbie, I'm reading Charlton Heston's autobiography, and that's that."

While most of the audience was charmed by this droll attempt to establish mundanity, one viewer's reaction was unique: the instant the words *I enjoy staying home with Debbie* entered the theatre, a wall inside Jamey shattered and the Darkling rose up in a fury. *Debbie. Leukemia. Deathday. Birthday.*

"I mean, you know, I mean," Shawn lisped, "occasionally maybe Debbie and I will step outside, we'll go to a party or something. *Uh.* And if I can occasionally get my talent together and write a little play, why then that's just wonderful. But I don't know how anyone could enjoy anything more than I enjoy, *uh*, reading Charlton Heston's autobiography."

See her? the Darkling hissed as a blue eye suddenly peered up at the Princeling from under a pile of junk. *How dare you bury her in crap, then plot seduction by strewing your puling play across a table, leaving your Lear robe lying about, and rehearsing impersonations of this pampered nitwit!*

"Last Christmas," Shawn continued, his coyness and lisp magnified fortyfold by the screen and sound system, "Debbie and I were given an electric blanket, and I can tell you, it is *just such a marvelous advance* over our old way of life."

Jamey's right hand had become a fist. His left was squeezing Holly's arm painfully. She removed it and drew away. "What is *wrong?*" she whispered.

The Darkling usurped Jamey completely. Extending his yard-long arm and gripping his cookie with such fury that he rained raisins and oatmeal onto the heads of the couple in front of him, he pointed at Shawn's face and, in a whisper so resonant it seemed amplified by the theatre's own sound system, hissed, "What is *wrong?* What is WRONG? Listen to that Manhattan *hobbit fuck* burying his partner alive! *Debbie's job, Debbie's blanket, Debbie's this, Debbie's that.* The name *Debbie,* like the names *Buffy, Muffy,* and *Candy,* reduces a woman to the level of a house pet, a sex toy, an idiot's between-meal snack! Names like *Debbie* pasteurize a woman's brain like cow's milk, erase her wit, sap her immune system, and leave her so reduced and vulnerable that she can be whisked off to the first fatuous heaven to lower a fuckin' rope, there to frolic about—*forever,* we are to *biblically suppose*—with a bunch of grass-eating lions, lion-hugging lambs, and nutless Christs who might as well *all* go by the *ridiculous* fucking name of *Debbie!*"

With that, Jamey shoved the ruins of his cookie in his mouth, knocked his little wine bottle off his armrest in the process, and as it bounced around loudly, spilling its contents, barked, *"Balls!"*

Not a few members of the audience then burst into happy applause. They'd mistaken his outburst for experimental theatre intended to enhance the film—and among those who'd applauded, Jamey later learned, was Wallace Shawn himself. But others told Jamey to shut up. Then the theatre manager came bustling down the aisle, searching the crowd by flashlight till the beam found and lit up the Darkling's fury. When Jamey tried to straighten up and look civil, his boot kicked the little wine bottle, the flashlight beam dropped down on it, rose to illuminate an identical bottle in Holly Brrhfygythsfyfth's hand, then rose higher, spotlighting her lovely, horrified face. *"I want both of you to leave immediately!"* the manager said, inspiring another burst of applause. And he personally expelled them out onto the night sidewalk.

Need it be said that *My Dinner with André* was Jamey's last date with Ms. Brrhfygythsfyfth, or that her last four sentences to him were all declarative, said in a fury, and the fourth was punctuated by the taxi cab door she slammed in his face? The sentences: (1) "Don't *apologize,* don't *talk,* don't *call,* don't *write,* don't *telegraph*!"; (2) "If you contact me *ever,* for any reason, I'll say whatever it takes to get you arrested!"; (3) "My father is a judge!"; (4) "*GET*"—door slam in face—"*THERAPY!*"

"I've been conthidering that, acthually," Jamey said in his perfect Wallace Shawn lisp.

KICKED OUT OF his own little romantic comedy, Jamey stood on Northwest 21st, feeling the Darkling still seething inside him, eager to inflict greater disaster. "*Somehow,*" the Princeling begged Jamey, "*you've got to outlast this evil fucker!*"

Snow had begun falling. Jamey checked his watch: 8:20. Three hours and forty minutes till midnight. He looked north, down 21st Avenue. Cold. Dark. Lonely. He looked south. Saw a sign two blocks down: HOUCK'S VIDEO. He zombie-walked toward it.

When he reached the store, Jamey noticed, among the posters in the front window, a sun-faded image of the actor Ben Kingsley with his head shaved, nearly naked, wearing a pair of round wire-rimmed glasses. Realizing he was looking at the star of the Richard Attenborough movie *Gandhi,* Jamey froze, and to the falling snow murmured, "January 30th, 1991. Here stand thirty-three-year-old Jamey and negative-twenty-eight-year-old Debbie, staring at a poster of Ben Kingsley playing the negative-forty-three-year-old Gandhi."

Are you interested in Mahatma Gandhi? asked an invisible librarian.

"Am I?" Jamey asked the falling snow.

He pushed open the Houck's Video door and walked straight to the checkout counter. The clerk was visually genderless, henna haired, very thin, very pale. "Do you have the Attenborough *Gandhi* flick?" Jamey asked. "I see an old poster for it in the window."

Pecking at the computer, the clerk nodded, then pointed down an L-shaped aisle. "Should be in the elbow of the L. Two cassettes. Parts one and two might not be in the same place. We alphabetize, but our customers don't."

The clerk's voice did not reveal a gender, and Jamey was impressed by that neutrality. Even envied it after his disastrous date with Ms. Brrhfygythsfyfth. "I appreciate your help," he told the clerk, and meant it.

He found *Gandhi, Part One* immediately in the elbow of the L, and studied the photo of Kingsley on the box. The actor in Jamey was impressed. Very *Gandhian,* he thought. *Half Indian, Kingsley, isn't he?*

Lodged in his very chest, the Darkling hissed, *Who gives a shit?*

Trying to hold out, Jamey whispered the word "Mahatma," felt the familiar surge of power, found the hole in the wall within him, peered through it, and the Darkling and Princeling squared off. *Isn't there a Gandhi biography called* Freedom at Midnight? *the Princeling thought.*

Who gives a flying fuck? growled the Darkling.

Desperate, Jamey checked his watch: 8:27. The length of the movie, it said on the box, was three hours and eleven minutes. If he could find *Part Two* and get a semblance of himself safely home, the film would carry him to the end of his Mardi Gras/New Year's Eve/Halloween/April Fools'/Day of the Dead. He searched hard for several minutes before he spotted it, stashed by some random idiot among the musicals.

As he slid the box off the shelf he glimpsed what looked like female flesh on the adjacent box. Looking closer, he saw a title on the box: *The Mating Game.*

Holly Brrhfygythsfyfth gone bye-bye…Female flesh…Mating Game… Get therapy!

Jamey reached for the box and slid it out. His jaw dropped. The flesh that had caught his eye, so tantalizing when obscured on a dark shelf, belonged to the actress-dancer-entertainer *Debbie* Reynolds. *Run!* urged the Princeling.

But the Darkling's blood was already at full boil. This archetype of ingenues, this sexless sex symbol of the postwar subdivision, this *TickTock-TitTwatDebbieReynoldsPerson* was the very woman who'd inspired his mother to hamstring her name! Her expression on *The Mating Game* box— total self-confidence despite total vacuity; certainty that she was "cute in a perky sort of way"—was an eraser obliterating Jamey's weak memories of his mother's unique appearance and qualities. The Darkling seethed.

Outlast this fucker! the Princeling pleaded.

It occurred to Jamey to appease the Darkling with a quick act of vandalism. Peeking round the corner at the henna-haired clerk, who was facing the other way, Jamey slid *The Mating Game* out of its box, set the box back on the shelf, slid the cassette down the front of his pants, buttoned his overcoat to cover his rectangular crotch, and strode confidently up to the clerk. "Found 'em both," he said, setting *Gandhi One* and *Two* on the counter. "Gotta take a leak, though. Where's your john?"

The clerk nodded toward the far end of the store.

In the bathroom Jamey didn't need to pee. He needed to flush the toilet twice to cover the sound of his heel stomping *The Mating Game* to splinters before burying Debbie Reynolds's perky ass in the trash under a thousand used paper towels.

Washing his hands in triumph, he turned to go rent *Gandhi.* But on the inside door of the john was another poster, and the flesh on this one did not belong to some perky *Debbie.* Wearing red spiked heels, a red thong, and nothing else, a perfect-bodied, spectacularly naked woman crouched on taut haunches, leaning far forward over the supine, suit-and-tied chest of what looked like a fallen televangelist or businessman. Not that there's a difference. The woman had the man's tie wrapped in her right hand and her left plunged in his trousers. Her fabulous breasts squeezed outward between sinewy arms, their erect nipples not quite touching the tip of the man's nose. His expression was an insensate *Please-fuck-me-to-death* gape. Hers was a focused rage as willing to oblige and sure of inflicting fatal damage as an explosive-wrapped suicide bomber stepping onto a packed bus.

Endless Frenzy! proclaimed the title.

Gandhi! peeped the videos at the front counter.

8:40, said Jamey's watch. *Freedom at midnight.*

He backed away from the poster, turned to the bathroom's dirty mirror, and to his weary reflection whispered, "What'll it be, pal? British Ben Gandhi-Kingsley saving Injah from the Brits, shot dead as a dildo on Mommy's unbirthday? Or stupendous pretend tits and an idiotic birthday-deathday outing for the pocket rocket?"

Staph boils...Sulfa drugs...No breast milk...Leukemia...

Black hole Mommy emitted no light.

Jamey chose the tits.

BUT *ENDLESS FRENZY?* Come on! Jamey's late-night festivities were far from endless, and as for "frenzy," how swiftly the televised groans of a silicon-breasted porn queen morph from exciting to repugnant as she stuffs various parts of idiotic "businessmen" into various parts of her anatomy. Her rubberized tits and disingenuous gyrations did allow Jamey to forget his Holly Brrhfygythsfyfth humiliation long enough to spill a little seed. He then looked at the clock, saw it was 12:18, felt a wave of self-disgust, passed into the supposed safety of sleep—and the real frenzy began...

He fell into the most hideous dream of his life. The *Endless Frenzy* star was lying naked on a dining-room table. Six neatly dressed businessmen were seated on all sides of her, holding six ordinary teaspoons. Jamey was lying in a hospital bed in the corner of the same dining room, watching. When an unseen director said, "Roll 'em," the woman began to writhe and produce sexual noises. The businessmen grew excited, picked up their spoons, and dipped them into the woman's body. Her flesh parted like pudding, which the men eagerly ate. Grievous wounds appeared, leading to louder moans and wilder gyrations, each sound and movement a horrific conflation of lust and agony. This got the businessmen *really* excited. The teaspoons scooped faster and faster, targeting the parts of the woman they wanted most. Her breasts, sex, and inner thighs were gone in seconds, leaving behind horrific gore-filled hollows. Her mouth and nose became craters over which her blue eyes gaped at the men in an awful blend of come-on and horror. She couldn't die even so. A cheesy synth soundtrack forced her to keep groaning and writhing in time to the beat as the businessmen kept spooning her out till they found themselves carving a clean-stripped but still-writhing carcass. This gave them sufficient pause to turn to one another—and see blood and other less palatable substances running from their mouths onto their once-tidy suits, shirts, and ties. They then began to heave in unison like six very small, very sick dogs as Jamey, in his bed in the corner, looked down and saw a cascade of porn star goo running from his mouth down his naked torso, running to both sides of his still-erect penis. His attempt to scream was choked by the goo to a gurgle. Attracted by the sound, the blue-eyed carcass sat up and swiveled his way, extending the stripped bones of meatless arms to him in hope of further activity. With a second gurgling scream, Jamey woke to dirty gray daylight leaking in beneath his apartment window blind.

He had never been so grateful for dirty gray light in his life.

Shaking his head to clear it, he wondered why the adoring Romeo wasn't in his face, then remembered he'd left him at Jon's in the interests of everything that didn't happen with Ms. Brrhfygythsfyfth. He saw himself swearing on Shakespeare's pen, Sheba's teeth, and Romeo's smile that Roams would live at his side all his life. "I'm a drizzling piece of shit," he announced to the empty room.

Slapping himself hard on each side of the face, he jumped out of bed, ejected the porn from the VCR, threw it on the floor, slid on his boots, and gave *Endless Frenzy* the same treatment he'd given *The Mating Game*, barking in time to his stomps, "*Don't! Exploit! Drizzling! Pieces! Of shit!*" When the tape erupted from the splintered plastic, Jamey pronounced the film dead and stuffed it in the wastebasket. But the instant he turned his back on it, he imagined the blue-eyed carcass rising impossibly out of the wreckage, extending her bloody bones in attempted seduction. Hair on end, chanting, "*Fuckshit! Shitfuck!*" he threw on his Lear robe, ran the splintered video out to the garbage bins, dumped it, and ran back to his apartment, terrified to look behind him.

Inside, he stripped the bed for fear of psychic contamination, threw the sheets and pillowcases in his laundry bag, threw off his Lear robe, jumped in the shower, and turned on the cold, shouting, "*Penance! Brrrr! Cold! Arrrrr! NEVER! Fuckfuck! Shitshit! AGAIN!*"

AFTER HE'D DRIED off, dressed, made tea, and convinced himself his psychic airspace was safe, another act of penance occurred to him:

"Gandhi?" Jamey said to the empty room. "*Mohandas*, is it? Listen, man. I've made an annual event, for decades, out of disgracing your death-day, and I want to make it up to you. I don't know how yet. But I can at least find out why a million people loved you enough to march through the streets of Calcutta twenty years after you died. So don't give up on me, okay? I *mean* it, okay? Have we got a deal here, Mohandas? *I hope so.* Okay?"

But as soon as he drove over to Jon's, picked up Romeo and the Land Nautilus, and the six-leggèd Jamey-Roams Unit resumed their happily conjoined life, the Princeling shoved the Darkling so deep down inside himself that 364 days would pass before Jamey gave Mohandas Karamchand Gandhi another thought.

XIV. Wounded Eagle

I, unworthy sinner, was greeted overpoweringly by
the Holy Spirit in my twelfth year when I was alone.
                    —the Beguine, Mechthild of Magdeburg,
                        The Flowing Light of the Godhead

IN RISA, so far in our story, we've got a woman with standard-issue dysfunctional parents who wears a near-constant smile even so. On the psycho-spiritual front she has come to resemble a wrong-gendered 400 BC forest rishi surviving post-America America in a private India of her own creation thanks to a library of mystical classics, a few self-devised spiritual practices, and a daily litany of ever more unreliable "Skrit scraps." In an era when most women carried a few books on their hips, Risa barreled around in a backpack swollen not just with school texts and field guides but with a magnifying glass and binoculars through which she frequently stopped to scrutinize birds, mountains, anthills, runnels of rainwater, constellations, mosses, and Christic bumblebees that caused her to remind my cynical side of Disney's creepy paragon of "pure womanhood" Snow White. Though the same pack had been purged of its Skrit lexicons, dictionaries, and scriptures due to her war on the Sons Only Verse, it still contained a small library of metaphysics, mystical texts, poetry, and, for psycho-spiritual emergencies, a crushed-to-crap pack of Kools.

The time has come to ask whether all this accessorizing was enabling Risa to contact any genuine Presence, Truth, or Thou to hold in her heart or enclose in her arms and say, "Ah! *Here* You are!" And it dismays the skeptic in me to have to answer, *Yes. Apparently, yes.* The fact is, I came to know Risa rather well at U Dub and several times glimpsed her slipping into the throes of private reveries or raptures that, to be honest, gave me an uneasy sense of my own spiritual insensitivity. This in turn caused me to exude wry scorn toward her reveries and raptures. Taking note of this, Risa began to protect both my feelings and her own inner life by sharing nothing more with me than her intelligence, good nature, and wit. Fine with me at the time. But because she closed herself off from me I knew nothing, till I recorded several interviews with her, in 2012, of certain U Dub–era experiences she privately called "shooting star moments." A tale of one such moment:

* * *

RISA'S FAVORITE FORM of exercise was running, but her approach to this seemingly straightforward activity was typically crooked. Deploying oversized Huskies sweatshirts, sweatpants, and sunglasses to hide her face and contours and U Dub stocking caps or sweatbands to control her uncontrollable hair, she covered long distances over unplanned routes at a modest lope. Seattle was in a state of flux, and Risa liked to inspect the morphing city at four or five miles an hour to keep her pulse rate up without interfering with clear-eyed reconnoitering. She also carried a ten-dollar bill—the "Free Market Ten-Spot," she called it—in the key pocket of her sweats so that, if impulse overtook her, she could pop into an antique shop or book or health food store and make an impulse purchase. She'd acquired her magnifying glass and several fine old field guides in this way.

One bright fall morning a year or so after she'd quit her beloved Dr. Kool, Risa's run took her deep into the sprawled warehouse and shipping district bordering Puget Sound. The streets were bustling with industrial-strength activity and the men who perform it, but the warmth of the day required shorts, leaving her legs bare. By the time three separate huddles of hard hats had catcalled and whistled, Risa realized she'd long since left the orbit of the U District, where runners glean little more attention than passing cars. "Know...the embodied...soul..." she panted in antidote to the catcalls. "Though it hides...in the hundredth part...of the point of a hair...divided...a hundred times...it is infinite...Not female...Not male...Not neuter...What body...it takes...with that...it is united."

The streets smelled increasingly of diesel exhaust, salt water, and creosote from the docks and pilings in the Sound. The businesses occupied concrete, brick, or aluminum rectangles and sold stuff like truck parts, metal fabricators, fiberglass, neon signage, and sandblasting services. Because of the industrial nature of everything for the past mile or more, Risa was surprised when she jogged past a large corrugated metal quonset hut claiming to be a bookstore. She doubled back and, while running in place, inspected further.

The misplaced book biz was sandwiched between identical metal quonsets, one selling welding supplies, the other asphalt roofing. The book quonset had no visible name, but the word "BOOKS" was stenciled on a steel fire door and a knee-high rack of used paperbacks stood on the sidewalk near the door, looking grievously lost. The paperbacks, Risa saw at a glance, were in such bad shape that the BUCK A BOOK price on the cardboard sign struck her as greedy. The fire door contained a mail slot through which dollars were apparently to be slipped via the honor system. The door's small window was too filthy to see inside, but on its glass, in chartreuse and black greasepaint, stenciled block lettering proclaimed: "WE SPECIALIZE IN TRAVEL AND METAPHYSIQUES!!"

This hideous-hued claim struck Risa as so out of place that the fire door suddenly seemed a possible portal into another world. A ludicrous or dangerous world, most likely. But when she tested the door it was unlocked. Feeling like Goldilocks despite her dark hair, Risa opened the door and stepped inside.

The quonset's interior was cavernous, lit by a few faintly flickering fluorescent lights. No dollars on the concrete by the fire door. The twenty-foot ceiling was complicated by laminated wood struts and heat ducts. The floor was concrete smoothed to a shine. The air was cool but somehow unpleasant. Not toxic smelling. More...*soup-like*. And somehow *not safe.*

Rows of shelves filled the room, but not *bookshelves* exactly: they were eight-foot-tall metal racks, heavily loaded with literally tens of thousands of books. The portal-into-another-world feeling grew strong as Risa noticed every book, as far as she could see, was a used paperback in middling to wretched condition. Nor were they shelved in horizontal rows as in every bookstore on Earth: they were stacked vertically on pallets, in solid rectangular masses, so that all the books that lay behind the outermost row were impossible to even identify. Even the metal racks were unlabeled. This charnel house of literature must be a sort of clearinghouse that dealt in ravaged reading material by the pallet load. Who, Risa wondered, would *want* vast quantities of printed dreck? Corporate feedlots that added molasses and fed shredded literature to cattle? Fundamentalist cults of book-burning enthusiasts? Hippie architects hoping to expand the straw-bale housing fad to mashed paperback housing?

It began to bother Risa that she hadn't seen or heard an employee. The room was tomb-silent but for the buzz of the fluorescent lights and muffled engine noises leaking in from outside. The sole sign of commercial activity was a forklift, parked in a corner by a workbench covered with cardboard box-making material. Nothing about the room remotely suggested a "store." The owner apparently just hoped to pocket a few beer bucks by selling junk paperbacks to passersby—in which case Risa could be seen as trespassing and the Dobermans might even now be getting unmuzzled and unleashed in the back.

"How about *p* words?" she whispered to quell her fear. "Let's see. *Pani*. The hand. *Pada*. The foot. *Prana*. The breath of life. And *prada* is...something too, but all I can remember is the Italian fashion line. Then there's *Prabhu*, the Lord. And *Parameshwar*, the Lord of Lords. And uh, *prama*, which is, uh...which is eluding me, so maybe it's something ironic, like, uh...irrefutable knowledge! That's it! And *paramanu* is, uh, your Sanskrit atom. And *Paramatma* is the One so Replete there's no two. And *Purusha* is, um, the Supreme Self smashed into a billion pieces, each the size of a thumb, hidden in our bodies to give us life from the flame that gives no smoke. Whereas *pralaya* is, uh...Creole sounding, isn't it? Like 'jambalaya.' Which reminds me, I'm hungry! But what's *pralaya*? Something not too tasty, I'm thinking. Something down-right scary even…like, uh…total cosmic dissolution! That's it! Good doggie, brain! Let's feed you Cajun tonight. Perform *pralaya* on some jambalaya."

Glancing at a rack of books as she strolled past, she noticed a number of authors who looked like Saint Nick near the fatal end of a meth addiction and realized this must be the "METAPHYSIQUES" rack. The emaciated Santas were yogis and gurus whose abstemious faces made the room's aroma even more troubling, since they too looked repelled—

and she'd suddenly had enough. Yearning for open air, noise, exhaust fumes, fabricating and sandblasting services, she turned toward the now-distant fire door—to find her path blocked by an approaching figure so massive and multilayered that his movements brought to mind the world's largest sea slug. "Oh, hi!" Risa chirped, absurdly.

The man-mass didn't seem to hear. He just kept blalloping toward her, his four-chinned scowl doing nothing to brighten his approach. A scary line from the Rig Veda lurched into her mind: *Jyog eva dīrgham tama āsayiṣṭāh.* ("A great while hast Thou lain in the boundless darkness.") The words had been addressed, if she remembered right, to some sort of Titan or Balrog shortly before the hero who'd awakened it was beheaded in a single bite. Risa hated rudeness. Hated it so much she half wished she wasn't so fast on her feet. But as the hulking figure came within striking distance and his body turned out to be the source of the warehouse's soupy smell, the most polite move she could manage was to spin on her heel, sprint away down the row of meth Santas, circle up the next aisle over, and shout through the racks of heaped books, "Amazing place you've got! Thanks for the peek! Gotta run or I'm late for class!"

Charging out the steel door into blinding daylight, she took a hard right—and crashed full-bore into the knee-high BUCK A BOOK rack, sending herself and half a hundred junk paperbacks skidding down the sidewalk.

Her fall was slightly broken by some of the books she'd sent skittering. She sat up on the concrete, dazed and clammy, with both knees and one hand deeply skinned and bleeding. Her skid had ripped covers and pages from several books. She looked up and down the street. A few warehouses away a truck was pulling out, but no one seemed to have witnessed her folly. She turned to the fire door. It remained closed for the moment.

Anyone I know, in such circumstances, would have stood up and fled for fear that Sea Slug Man would pour onto the street through the portal, spew blinding exudates upon them, drag them back through the portal, and enslave them in a fetid alien galaxy. Not Risa. Though she did feel fear, it didn't occur to her to obey it. Instead, in untimely allegiance to *the great in the sun, food in the moon, Yama in a dream, Prajāpati in the body,* she picked herself up and set to work, limping badly as she fetched every book, reassembled every lost page and torn cover as best she could, and reshelved every volume she'd spilled.

When she gimped down the sidewalk and picked up the book she'd kicked farthest, she found herself holding a terribly abused copy of *The Collected Works of St. John of the Cross*. She remembered her late Grand-Da Finnegas expressing great respect for a work by this saint called "The Dark Night of the Soul." When she saw the battered paperback contained "The Dark Night," she began to experience what Finnegas would have called "a queer hum coming off it." Riffling through its pages, she discovered that a very hands-on reader had engaged in dharma combat with the author and worked hard to create the impression that John of the Cross had lost. *The Collected Works* were marred from beginning to end with cigarette burns, mad underlinings, a number of blacked-out phrases, and even madder marginalia ("You whacked!" "You call this syntax?" "Saint Cross of the John!"). But when Risa considered her bone-bruised shin, bloody knees, badly skinned hand, elusive father, Cathoholic mother, the book's wretched condition created a symmetry between it and her. Electing to slide money under the fire door and keep *The Collected Works*, she reached in her shorts pocket for the Free Market Ten-Spot.

Gone. She recalled a towering fruit dish and double cappuccino impulse-purchased a week or so before. Since she was too honest to steal even a ruined classic, she decided to close her eyes, open John of the Cross at random, point blindly to a line, memorize it, and at least take those few words home. Because of the Sons Only Verse devastation that followed her blind point at the Upaniṣads, however, she sought protection:

"*Lord of Love, unmanifest,*" she whispered. "*Become manifest. Draw Yourself out of Yourself. Touch me. Were You not here, who would breathe?*"

She shut her eyes, placed her fingertip on a page, opened her eyes, and found her finger resting on this:

I consider the fragile hairs
fluttering loose at the nape
of your neck, I gaze at them
hovering by your neck, and
they captivate Me. And
your shining eye wounds Me.

For a moment she felt not just seen but seen from inches away, as by a lover. "Wake up, Risa!" she muttered. "Do you truly think Love's Lord, unmanifest, in response to your little prayer, just popped in to say you wow Him to the point of wounding Him?"

Hoping for a less pretentious disclosure, she reopened the book but peeked through her lashes to be sure her finger lit on a blocky chunk of commentary, not a slim love verse. No relief: this time her fingertip rested upon this:

> With God, to gaze is to love. He sees that this soul's love is strong, without cowardice or fear, and that she is alone, without other loves. He sees her love fluttering fervently as the hairs flutter at her nape and these beauties capture Him...

Though her hair remained bound by a sweatband, the words made her reach to her nape—and sure enough, a swirl of frail hairs fluttered loose, just as John's impossible Gazer claimed. Tears rose. She felt not just seen but *loved* by Love's very Lord. But the same feeling made her whisper, "Will you please stop telling yourself Love Almighty is taking the trouble, here by Jabba the Hutt's Bookhaus, to say you and your pratfall and bloody knees and nape hairs have captivated Him? Just turn the page and point again, fool!"

She closed her eyes, turned the page, and pointed—only to read,

> A bird of lowly flight may indeed capture the royal Eagle of the heights if the Eagle descends with the desire of being captured. You have wounded My heart, beloved. You have wounded My heart with one shining eye and the fragile hairs of your neck...

Implausible coincidence does not feel innocent. The word "beloved," especially, caressed like the Unseen's own hand. She fought back a sob. "Don't You know how *corny* it is," she croaked, "in *this* stupid country especially, to call Yourself an *Eagle*?"

The air of the industrial district became a stillness. The sun froze. Nothing moved. Then a puff of air stirred the hair at her nape; she experienced it as the most intimate of exhalations, the Most Far became the Most Near, and it was all over: Love didn't just manifest, it stormed down upon her, causing a sob to rise so forcefully she moaned in the effort to contain it. She gazed through a blur of tears at the haunted book. The first words she could make out:

> Moaning is connected with hope.

With a second moan she dropped the book, picked it up, kissed it, placed it back on the rack, and took off running. Not jogging. *Running.* Because even as she dodged trucks, forklifts, sidewalk-blocking dumpsters, even as she watched for cars and heard the hard hats again whistling, she felt flood-lit by a gaze so adoring her mind went mad with joy. Running faster, her wild hair freeing itself, skin burning, heart hammering, she felt so physically pursued that her back, shoulders, head feared the grip of talons, causing her to jay-run, slowing for nothing, forcing cars to brake with wild two-armed waves. Overdosing on joy, tearing on in hope of cover, she found none. The inflaming hair flew and the Most Near assailed. Every step of the way home It assailed and insinuated and adored, up the stairs to her room, out of her clothes, to the thankfully dark shower where, alone and not alone, she staggered in and, with a racked sob, turned on the cold.

Frigid spray struck her full in the face and body. She stood in a vortex of water, Presence, and awe, answering with a flood of reciprocal love and tears.

Second Telling:

The One-Book-of-Poems-Long Marriage

For a short while,
they had been in love forever.
—Wisława Szymborska

Lore, Trey, and Snyder

PEOPLE NATIVE TO the American East, upon reading the meticulous, idio-syncratic, sometimes anti-lyrical lines of the poet Gary Snyder, can be baffled by his immense popularity out West. Westerners aren't similarly baffled. You cut your eyeteeth on a poet, grow up in the climes whose beauties and ravages he so painstakingly invokes, work the jobs he knows body and bone, hike the same high mountain ridgelines, drive a million or so miles over the same one-lane mountain byways, desert straightaways, river-hugging every-which-ways, you fall in love, fall out of love, live, revel, suffer in that world, and a bond forms. Earth-based poetry is not Esperanto. Wisdom sits in places, breeding aches, allegiances, and vernaculars too site-specific to be grasped by one and all. A single small example of a site-specific Western Snyder Experience:

The air was tropically humid by Rocky Mountain standards: July thunderhead season. The skies, though "not cloudy all day," were orange, not blue, thanks to regional forest fires. The sun was a neon salmon egg on the evening horizon. And Lorilee Shay and Trey Jantz had just summited a Southern Colorado mountain named Two Medicine Peak, drenching their clothes with sweat. Because they were twenty years old and unsure just how sweet they were on each other, they assured each other they were just drying those clothes, like at a laundromat, when they stripped and sat side by side, butt naked, on the baking summit. To pass the time Lore then produced a book of poetry, asked Trey if he'd like to hear a few, and he responded with a "*No thanks!*" so vehement it hurt her.

Protective of her love for poetry, she said, "You should come to a poetry reading with me sometime. I might surprise you."

Trey said, "Aw jeez, Lore. I get lost in two seconds listening to that heady mumbo jumbo."

Lorilee was a folklore major and music minor at Sangre de Cristo College in the town at the foot of the peak. She was also an aspiring songwriter, skilled mountain dulcimer player, and stand-your-hair-on-end singer with a particular love for mountain songs. Would Trey consider *her* lyrics *heady mumbo jumbo*? She feared so, started reading poems to herself. But when, atop that towering geophysical zafu, she came upon the Gary Snyder line

"The mountains are your mind," the words caused her mind to vanish as three separate waves of bliss washed through her. Turning to the blithe, physically beautiful free-climber and ski bum sharing a tentative nakedness, she yearned to share her bliss. And in his physical way, Trey adored mountains as much as she. Could the brash love that free-climbs granite faces and surfs powdered mountain shoulders learn to appreciate a quieter love that fashions music, rhyme, and insight out of the same ingredients? She decided to try to find out.

Catching Trey's ice-blue eyes with her black-rimmed gray ones, she said, "Trey. Listen to five words of poetry. Just five. I'm pretty sure you'll like 'em." Focusing, then, not on his face, which had a tendency to look anywhere-but-home at times, but on his impossibly smooth, summer-bronzed skin, Lorilee recited, "'The mountains are your mind.'"

Despite the heat, Trey's skin exploded. Every inch of chest, forearms, shoulders bristled with ranges of tiny answering peaks. Even his nipples stood on end.

His depth is in his body, Lorilee thought as a fresh wave of bliss washed through her.

Trey's eyes bore into hers, then dropped to her nipples, which were standing in answer to his own. They made love on the spot, sinking into Two Medicine as it purred like an eros-stunned mind beneath them.

Out East, read Snyder and maybe go figure.

Out West, events like this still sell a few books of poetry.

Trey's Poetry

LORILEE WAS IN bed, reading Snyder's *Riprap and Cold Mountain Poems.*

Trey, thigh to thigh with her, was reading a mountaineering journal.

Glancing from her poems to his journal, a pleasing thought occurred to Lorilee. She spoke it. "You know, you're a poet yourself, Trey. Your body's your pen. The mountains are your paper. Free-climbing vertical walls, you leave behind the lines your body traveled. And yeah, those lines are invisible once you come down off the wall. But I'll bet they've entered you. I'll bet those lines stay inside your mind and body the way a good mountain song or poem stays in my instruments and me. So who cares if others can't see what you wrote up there? It's *in* you."

Trey turned to Lorilee with that full-bodied attention unique to him, his bare chest as much a part of his visage as his face. Lorilee smiled. How strange, the way his skin and nipples could tell you more about what he was feeling than those bright blue eyes.

She ran with her idea: "This body-writing you do is so cool, Trey, that I wonder if there's a way to keep it from vanishing. I'm thinking you could *collect* your poems. I'm thinking, like, every time you tackle a big wall, you could take the best possible photo of it, make a big enlargement, then, right on your photo, you could draw the line you first imagined you'd take up the rock face. Maybe use a daydreamy color like pink or sky blue for that. Then, after the climb, you could use gold or silver or some color of, you know, valor, to show how the rock face argued with you during ascent and descent. Wouldn't a Before Photo of the imagined climbing line, then an After Photo of the route you actually climbed, portray a lot of what you did up there, so the rest of us could get a real feel for the impossible poems you write on those big vertical faces?"

Turning to see how Trey was taking this, Lore was stunned to find, what? Tears of joy in his eyes? She patted him the way one might an overexcited bird dog. *"Easy, boy."*

"But you're so *beautiful* to me!" Trey burst out. "You totally get me, Lore! God, I love how you get me!"

"Calm down now."

"But seriously! Non-climbers *never* get climbers. That you get me, without ever having climbed? That's *love,* Lore. And being loved like that? It effing *blows me away!*"

"Shucks," Lorilee said, a little blown away herself by the way Trey's cute little stand-up nipples kept staring her in the face.

"And something else about this poetry idea. The summit's everything to a summit-bagger. But it's no big deal to a free-climber. To free-climbers, summit-baggers are like...what d'ya call those people who *gobble, gobble* food? Eating disorders! They've got Summit Disorder. *Me Go 17,000 Feet Up. Prove Me Got Big Dick.* But to a free-climber it's like you say, it's the *whole poem* you're after! The ascent *and* the down-climb. People thinking *summit, summit, summit* blind themselves to the down. That's why so many fuck up and fall and die."

Picturing Trey plummeting off the rock and breaking, Lore said, "Don't you *dare* fuck up, fall, and die!"

"The reason I won't," he said, "is I really *do* climb for the poetry. Like, on a hard climb, when I get to a crux—we call them 'cruxes,' Lore, the parts that take us beyond what we know. Reaching a crux, I ascend that gnarly sucker, down-climb to a resting point, ascend again, up, down, up, working out the moves I'll need when I'm descending with much less energy. If you don't work the cruxes hard—if you're a summit hog going, *Oink, oink! Get me up there!*—you sooner or later reach the crux that makes you gamble your life on a crazy lunge to a distant hold, or do an up move you can't duplicate on the down. Which"—Trey gaped at Lorilee in a sudden rapture—"which isn't just *dangerous.* It's *sucky poetry.* You showed me that, Lore! And sucky poetry, on the vertical plane, can *kill* the effin' poet!"

His joy made Lorilee want to probe him more deeply. "Tell me why you're drawn to one rock face and not another, Trey. Tell me, start to finish, what you feel as your body and mind choose exactly where to write your invisible poem on stone."

With no idea how appealing he looked, Trey lifted his eyes as if studying a wall. "First thing. You don't jump outta the truck and head for the first damn dome or prow you see. Each climber's got his own kind of eye, which knows his body's strengths and weaknesses. So, eye and body together, you feel for the face that reaches down and grabs you on that valley floor. Why one and not another? You said it. *The line.* Those big masses are just a jumble, too much information, till mind and body *find that line.* Then it's a jumble no more, and all this beauty and drama calls down to you, energizing the living crap out of you! And when you start up the rock, actually *body-writing* like a Magic Marker on the photos I'm sure as heck gonna take and start drawing on, here's what non-climbers never get. Sure, it's dangerous. Sure, you're challenged to the max. But I swear, Lore, it's no scarier for me to climb a huge wall than it is for you to step onto a stage and sing. I mean, *jeez!* A stage and a crowd scare me *way* worse than any wall. But for you, the crowd's a high. For me on the wall, same deal. No dread. Just an effin' *high*."

Loving where the conversation had gone, Lore said, "I suspect this might be impossible to describe, but can you tell me what you actually *feel*? What the 'effin' *high*' is like?"

"Great question, Lore! A *crux question.* Let me work it up and down here a minute...

"Okay. Here's something. Those high faces we climb were ocean floors once. We often see fossil seashells up there. And what hits you, as you're inching past seashells buried in a super-high face, is...is that a mountain's made of everything we are. On a high face, more than any other place, I've felt how my body came up out of the ocean like the shells right there in my grip. And my climbing is...is the same kind of magic that made us want to crawl up out of the ocean! Your body grips that mountain ocean-bottom, skin to stone, stone to skin, every instant, till there's a point the badass climber Jeff Lowe calls 'the ecstasy point,' where you feel how you and that peak have danced together since *way, way* back. Then all this mystery about, I dunno, early life-forms, and those moving tectronic plate thingies, and the molten lava that shoves and stacks the plates comes pouring through you till you feel molten yourself. Then how you move, and what you *are,* hold after hold, is this seventy-two-inch ocean-and-lava creature flowing up a cooled piece of ocean floor, and huge feelings weld the mountain and ocean and you together, and the world's exact and perfect, and you're meeting that exactness so perfect you realize *you're* exact and perfect too!"

Trey was gaping into space, overcome with wonder at his own words. "That's *it,* Lore. That's the effing nail whacked on the head right there! And I never said it a tenth this good, or felt it so clear. And the reason I *could* is, the one listening is the one who totally gets me!"

Trey's eyes had filled with such joy, and the depths in his body were irradiating Lorilee so intensely, that she was speaking every thought in her head when she said, "*Gosh!*"

"And something else, Lore!" Trey said. "When you song-write, isn't it the same deal? Don't you, same as me, sit down and face a jumble, except for you it's human life and trouble, the things men and women do to each other? And when the song starts to work—I *watch* you, Lore, I see this!—isn't it because you *find that line,* same as me? I mean, *your* lines are people problems. Broken hearts. Dying towns. Dying loves. But your voice and words move up and down those cruxes of hurt just like a climber till you should see me some nights, driving home from my kind of climb, singing *your* sad lines about dying towns and hearts. And why? *To get happy!* I love cruxes so much, and your crux lines are sad in such a perfect heart-cracking way, that I'm driving along wishing *my* town would die and *my* heart crack so I'd be right there inside the song's crux with you!"

Trey was gazing with such abject adoration now that Lore's eyes began to fill. "And one more thing," he said. "Just one more thing. Feeling how totally you get me, I need for you to understand, and to grasp, and to feel how...*IT'S MY TURN TO GET YOU!*" With which he dove and Lorilee laughed and they rolled around a little, then began to up-and-down-climb each other till an art inaccessible to one body rose up in two. And it was singer on climber, climber on singer, cruxes mastered, songs on skin, exact and perfect to the point of ecstasy.

God's Rice

NOT MUCH LATER they married. On a 9,000-foot Colorado ridge, of course. And on Cinco de Mayo—"a holiday invented by beer companies!" the besotted best man happily reminded the wedding party.

Not all the guests were pleased by this. The solemnities had been greeted by a shockingly heavy flurry that soon buried them in seven inches of wet spring snow. "God's rice!" Trey laughed as it slammed down by the pound. "Basmati!" Lorilee added, licking a little off his cheekbone. Meanwhile the collective six divorced parents and step-spouses peered around at what Trey's second stepdad, the magniloquent Kenneth, kept calling "the high-altitude death trap into which our abominable snow children lured us."

"We'll be fine," Lorilee kept promising as the temperature dropped forty degrees, the nonalcoholic wedding punch froze, the children got smashed on the vodka-laden stuff, and Lorilee's hilariously named two-hundred-pound mom, Wren, began walking a besotted kid to a car to sleep it off, but instead stepped in a snow-covered marmot hole and sprained an ankle. Trey's stepbrother, Rhett, in a gallant attempt to rescue the downed Wren with the rented limo, then backed it into a boulder-filled ditch, inspiring Kenneth to produce a small silver flask, drain it, and commence to bellow, *"Welcome to the Donner Party!"*

But as bride and groom recited their homespun vows, the blizzard formed matching white crowns on their heads and mantles on their shoulders. "*You are my heart, and the mountains are our mind,*" Trey told Lorilee, his baby blues blazing joyously into her clear gray eyes. They then leaned so slowly forward and kissed so gently that the white crowns and mantles remained, making a small snowcapped peak, exact and perfect, of them both.

Love at 24 Percent Interest

SINCE LORILEE'S BRIDESMAIDS agreed that Lorilee and Trey's blue-lipped snowcapped kiss was the single most romantic thing they'd ever seen, they were taken aback when Trey sold a photo of the kiss to *Outside* magazine. But he and Lorilee needed *Outside*'s three hundred bucks to fund their dirt-cheap surfing honeymoon down in San Blas, Mexico.

Money turned out to be a problem for the newlyweds. Both came from highly leveraged families of the sinking middle class. Worse, Trey and Lorilee's financial union consisted of Lorilee's $56,000-Master's-Degree-in-Folklore Debt plus Trey's $62,000-Six-Years-of-Climbing-Partying-Shredding-the-Slopes-Changing-Majors-Shredding-Climbing-Partying-Never-Graduating Debt. To thicken the fiscal soup, postgraduate Lore remained as committed to singing and songwriting as nongraduate Trey remained committed to free-climbing, and Trey's passion more or less forced them to stay on in career-poor but mountain-rich Pipestone, Colorado, credit cards maxed, college debt immovable, interest rates crazed.

What they lived for, of course, were the body lines Trey kept inscribing on vertical granite and rhyming lines Lorilee kept fashioning out of hard lives, hollow wood, steel strings, and stunning voice. Every time Trey returned from a cliff face he'd tell Lore, "Never fear, darlin'. Looking down from the places I've been this day, every debt on Earth is microscopic!" Similarly, every time Lorilee played to an attentive crowd, at the moment she triggered truth with rhyme and the audience felt a quickening, she felt she lived not in debt but in grace.

THEN CAME A winter that trapped them in an Underworld. An inversion rolled in on Thanksgiving, throwing Pipestone under a blanket of what Lorilee dubbed "fmog," exiling every ray of light as the air filled with the carbon monoxide the Postal Service forthrightly acknowledged with the state's abbreviation: CO. Colors vanished. The slush grew so vile Trey dubbed it "fmush." The naked trees, splayed against the sky, looked like x-rays of nervous breakdowns. To inhale felt viral. The complexions of the Caucasian populace turned as gray as the fmog. When Trey joked that the

Defense Department was seeding the clouds with quaaludes, Lorilee couldn't even smile. The way she felt, it seemed plausible.

It did not help that they had moved, the previous fall, into a half-converted single-car garage apartment. The tiny place was in a high-end subdivision on the town-facing south slope of Two Medicine Peak. They'd chosen it for three reasons. One, Trey was handy with tools and could work out their rent by making improvements. Two, the garage was so cheap it allowed Trey and Lore to keep climbing and singing. Three, through the skylight over the bed in the tiny sleeping loft, they had an unobstructed view of the very summit upon which five words of Gary Snyder's had united their lives. The first time they'd climbed into the loft bed and peered up at the Peak, Trey said, "No worries, Lore. The steady sight of that Ol' Girl's gonna rebuild the fire we started up there." The Underworld Inversion then erased Two Medicine and all the rest of the Overworld from view, enabling Lorilee and Trey to see that their new home was exactly the size of two adjacent jail cells.

By January no one in Pipestone could remember what starry nights or sunny days looked like. Six days a week Lorilee and Trey slogged through fmog and fmush from garage, to work, back to garage, there to encounter a pale wraith vaguely reminiscent of a person they'd once sworn to love as long as mountains shall stand. Meanwhile, Lorilee read in the paper, hundreds of mountains out East had been targeted for annihilation for their coal.

Trey's six-day workweeks took place at the Pipestone Golf 'n' Ski Shoppe [sic], where he sold clubs, skis, boots, clothes, and outdoor goofus gear to a seemingly separate species of humanoids whose economic rise had given the males cloned politics and carry-on abdomens, the females surgically enhanced wallets for faces and voluptuous Silly Putty for breasts, and both genders titanium credit cards, which the little machine never beeped and refused the way it did Trey's. The Golf 'n' Ski clientele left him desperate for high summer granite or wild winter slopes. But his college debt still had him ball-and-chained to fifty-plus-hour weeks of hard labor amongst fmog, fmush, and titanium credit owners.

Lorilee, meanwhile, was secretarying for a Mormon real estate broker whose morose wife, five kids, ceaseless sexual innuendo, and frequently misplaced paws were fast making a radical feminist of her. Grubstake Realty, he called his firm. "In Honor of Pipestone's Proud Mining History," ran the motto, though that proud history consisted of a single large-scale hydraulic mining operation that made two tycoons rich, poisoned thousands of townsfolk, bequeathed them a Superfund site, then bilked broke taxpayers like Trey and Lorilee in perpetuity. Though no one phoned Grubstake in search of a home in the Underworld, hundreds yearned to flee, so the listing side of the business had Lorilee working overtime.

The overtime was welcome: she hoped to use the extra money to fund a May trip to a pair of North Carolina folk fests. Her need for the company of real musicians and sensitive crowds was dire. Her voice was ethereal, beautifully so, but required excellent acoustics for its magic to be heard. Her "rise" as a performer, meanwhile, had stalled out in the kinds of clubs and bars where any tune but a raucous pop cover gets smothered by the blore of bikers, skiers, and beer hounds. Her lyrics of late had come to reflect a blend of carbon-monoxide poisoning, thinly veiled real-estate-broker death threats, and beer-hound loathing. She needed fresh air and light to locate fresher, lighter lyrics. The Underworld offered none. She'd taken up zazen in the mornings, which brought enough clarity to make her feel guilty when she fell back into samsara at work. She still read poetry in the evenings in the hope that someone else's insight might revive her own. But no poet she could find explained to her how to service her giant debt while furthering a philanderer's career in Gaia sales.

Every evening in the double-jail-cell garage, Lorilee's misery reminded Trey of his own, and vice versa. Which was bad enough. Then, one fmushy March night they sat down to calculate what a winter of fifty- to seventy-hour workweeks had done to their battle against debt, discovered that the compound interest camouflaged by the microprint on their credit card applications had wiped out all headway—and something snapped. They began to keep score against each other. They began to hide their better selves from each other. They began to bore and to scorn each other. A couple of nasty cruxes in the marital down-climb:

Desperate for money, Lorilee took a singing gig at The Motherlode, the kind of honky-tonk she dreaded most. After a dismal day at the Golf 'n' Ski, Trey stopped by to listen to his partner-in-debt perform a set of her increasingly melancholy tunes. Two songs in, while singing her heart out, Lorilee saw Trey roll his baby blues at his drinking buddies, bend over to pantomime some sort of hunchbacked inbred-looking Appalachian dulcimer player, and start ad-libbing lampoon lyrics in time to the sincere words Lorilee was singing. When the buddies laughed big, her voice broke, she lost the lyrics, then fell out of the song completely. By staring, devastated, into the darkness inside the heart-shaped sound holes of her dulcimer, she was able to overcome her sick feeling and finish the song and set. But Trey and his pals never stopped bloring as she struggled her way through.

She was still feeling this hurt sharply, a week later, when Trey began to tear out and rebuild the rotting shower stall in their garage apartment. When she got home from Grubstake Realty one night, she found a note on the kitchen table. It said,

Oops. Wasn't thinking. We'll get a new one. Having a brewski with the guys. Home later.

—T.

Beside the note sat her Cuisinart food processor, in which Trey had tried to mix tile grout, destroying the work bowl and burning up the motor. Trying to calculate how many kinds of stupid you'd have to be to mix grout in a Cuisinart, Lorilee arrived not at a number but at fmog and fmush. The Underworld had swallowed the man she'd married. And this time Lore didn't hide her hurt.

When Trey took off on his next Sunday climbing adventure, she drove to the Safeway, bought a dozen discounted, wilting red roses, brought them home, put them in the oven, and turned it on 170 degrees to wilt them worse. She then stepped out behind the apartment, located a dirt-and-slush-covered cinder block, carried it inside, and set it, uncleaned and dripping, on the pinewood table Trey's uncle had given them for a wedding present. Next she fetched Trey's antique twelve-gauge over-and-under from the closet, his wedding gift from his grandpa. Violently jamming the immaculate walnut stock down into the cinder block to prop the gun upright, she poured tile grout down both Damascus steel barrels, began adding water, and used the bore snake to stir in more grout till it formed plugs that stopped the barrels from leaking. Filling both barrels to the top with water, she placed six rubber-necked roses in each, then stepped back to admire their blood red corpses drooping down the blue-black steel.

When Trey got home that night, he found no Lorilee and this note:

Needed a vase for the roses. Decided to try your shotgun, which needed propping and I didn't feel like thinking so I used a cinder block. "Oops." Then it leaked and I still didn't feel like thinking so I used grout to fix that. "Oops." And of course I'm lying. I _was_ thinking, Trey. This fucked-up floral arrangement, wrecked gun, scratched-up table, and dead Cuisinart are what are called _analogues_ of our marriage. I've gone to Bess's while you decide whether you're interested in staying married. If you are, I recommend you look up the word "analogue," think hard, and change your ways fast.

—Lore

Self-Arrest

TREY DID LOOK up "analogue," and for a while the marriage did better. But on yet another fmoggy Underworld morning in early April, trouble struck.

Trey was facing another dismal day's work at the Golf 'n' Ski. Lorilee had to work that day too, but she'd gotten up early to rehearse for the upcoming Carolina folk fests. Trey had wakened to the sound of a ballad she'd written a week or so before—a song he at first liked. But Lorilee's tolerance for repetition, at the woodshed stage, was heroic. As he lay in bed, her voice and dulcimer worked the same short phrase over ten, twelve, fourteen times in a home consisting of three hundred square feet of floor space. The sound of Trey urinating joined Lorilee in a perverse harmony. He then shuffled into the "kitchen" to find they had enough coffee for perhaps a quarter of a cup, opened the refrigerator to discover they were out of cream, honey, and every other food but limp celery, half an onion, a plastic bag of rotted salad greens, and a quarter jar of salsa topped like an analogue mountain by a cloud of blue-gray mold. When Lorilee lit again into the trouble verse, the mood inside the refrigerator flew into Trey, possessing him. Giving it voice, he said, "Would somebody please tell Malvina to wait till I'm fuckin' *outta here* before she soldiers on with *the high lonesome warbling?*"

Lorilee froze, then turned pale.

Seeing this, Trey turned crimson. Despite his self-deprecation about lack of word skill, he'd tossed an acid so corrosive he was amazed by the sound of it sizzling Lorilee's mind, heart, and skin. Her dulcimer hit the floor as she stood. In all their time together he'd never seen her drop even a bar of soap in the shower, let alone her beloved instrument. She didn't pick it up. Didn't look back to see if it had broken. It took her seconds to throw on clothes and flee the house. She hadn't brushed her hair or teeth, applied makeup, or said a word. But the instant the front door slammed, Trey heard her first desperately wounded sob. And he continued to hear her till she climbed in the car, started the engine, and drove away.

After picking up the dulcimer, unbroken, thank God, and casing it, Trey began pacing as he tried to justify himself to himself, but his thoughts seemed caged by the fact that, after five short paces, the garage walls forced him to do an about-face: *Her inability to learn an effing tune without singing it into the effing—* Stop. About-face. *She actually* likes *Malvina Reynolds, so there wasn't anything hurtful about that choice of—* Stop. About-face. *Am I supposed to like it when my day starts out in a musical Alzheimer's ward? Did I marry a broken record?*

When Trey stopped this time, he turned to stone: hanging at eye level before him was a framed photo of a tiny figure: Trey himself, shot with a telephoto, free-soloing the Grand Teton crux known as Black Ice Couloir. Two thousand feet of nothing below his boots, and back and forth he'd gone a second and third time for the sheer joy of it. As he stared at the photo he recalled how, hours before his alarm went off this morning, he'd half heard Lorilee, sitting on the toilet seat in their tiny bathroom, door shut, rehearsing in a polite whisper. The sound of soft voice and dulcimer had wafted him back into the sweetest sleep of the night. He then remembered this new song to be a storytelling ballad with complicated verses and an intricate melody that demanded her all—with which he realized what her obsessive rehearsing had been: *a crux.* She was working the hard passages to make them safe for her voice to traverse in public the same way Trey worked up and down cruxes to keep his body safe.

Malvina. High lonesome warbling. Lorilee's sobs as she'd fled.

"How has the man capable of such free-solos come to this?" he asked the empty room. And Trey's depth was in his body: seeing his face reflected in the glass, he pulled the picture off the wall, grabbed the frame in both hands, roared, "*You SUCK!*" and smashed the photo into his forehead. The glass shattered. Blood ran into his eyes and down his cheeks. Catching the blood by letting it shower onto the photo, Trey screamed, "*Go ahead! At least bleeding isn't SUCKING!*" As climber and peak began to vanish in a wash of crimson he swirled it around till the photo was gone. "*That was Lorilee, you fucking Suck!*" he shouted at his blood. "That beautiful woman is the one who *gets you! Who are you? What happened to you?*"

Then he too burst into sobs.

IN MID-APRIL, FRESH air and wildflowers returned to Pipestone and the summit of Two Medicine returned to the garage skylight, but another full week passed before Lorilee wrote to say she was coming home from her friend Bess Hern's.

Trey wasn't there when she arrived, but the house was remarkably clean. In the room's center, the pine table had been resurfaced and a dozen perfect red roses stood in a new crystal vase, alongside three objects: a new Cuisinart; Trey's ice axe; and this note:

Dearest Lore:

It's not uncommon, when a climber's alone on a slope covered with snow hard-crusted to ice, that his feet fly from under him and he's jetting down-mountain so fast he hardly knows what hit him. What I kept forgetting when the same thing happened to my heart this winter is the move that saves your sorry ass. It's called self-arrest. What you do is grip the ice axe in both hands, flip onto your belly if you're on your back, roar ARRRRRRR! and hold on with all your might as you smash the axe into the crust. I don't know why the ARRRRRRR! helps but it does. I also know it was me who left my feet and sent us into this awful slide, so it had to be me who self-arrested. And I have. PLEASE let me prove it. You will see, you will feel, you will know my slide is over. The hard crust has melted. The glacier lilies are coming out. And I love you more than anyone or anything. Even climbing. Let me show you. Please. ARRRRRRRRRRRRRRRR!

—Trey

Disappearing Origami

ON MAY 4TH, the day before Lorilee and Trey's fifth wedding anniversary, Trey took a secret day off work, donned a beret to cover the scar in his hairline, and set out for Base Camp Books up in Boulder. His destination was a poetry reading. The first of his life. The poet? Gary Snyder, author of Trey's favorite five words—and Lorilee's favorite man on Earth, Trey figured, now that her former favorite had learned how to fucking suck.

But he was determined to unsuck by launching a full-on eight-thousand-meter-peak effort for Lorilee. He would begin by driving two hundred miles north in sunlight, then two hundred south by moonlight—risky in a shit car with retreads, sure, but he'd made far longer drives on worse tires just to make overnight climbs, and once flew twenty-four thousand miles round trip, on credit, to Nepal, just to climb Pumori. He half wished Boulder was farther so his effort for Lorilee would amaze her all the more.

Trey found Base Camp Books a half hour before the reading. Because he'd arrived early, he was stunned to see a hundred or more people backed out the door onto the sidewalk, with a hundred more jammed inside the bookstore. He parked, hurried into line, but learned the store was full to capacity and some kind of fire marshal bullshit was in effect. Fuck. No poetry reading for Trey. And to make contact with Snyder and execute his plan would no doubt take hours. *But that's good!* Trey told himself. *Mashabrum, Chogolisa, K-6, Rakaposhi. They'll make you wait too, mofo. Eight-thousand-meter-peak effort! For Lore.*

The line of autograph seekers made Trey feel as though he was standing inside the pages of a *National Geographic*. The climbers and skiers he hung with, rough looking as some of them could be, were as clean-cut as Mormon boys compared to this crew. Snyder's fans, men and women alike, looked like ten or twelve kinds of Neolithic villagers in their rustic garb and weathered skin. Not far in front of Trey was a Maori-looking guy so paved with geometric tattoos that he looked like a contour map of himself, and his partner was a gal with the forked horn of a little blacktail buck woven into her dreads. Past them was a clutch of fellas who looked like four versions of Jesus if He'd been raised by pot growers instead of Mary and Joseph. It struck Trey that they, like he, had come from God-knows-where to hear their hero, only to be exiled by the same fire marshal bullshit. Yet there they all were, amiably chatting about the ten or so Snyder volumes in the window display with patience and cheer. *Who is this fucking guy?* Trey began to wonder.

In the display was a book called *No Nature*. No clues there. Also *Riprap and Cold Mountain Poems* and *Smokey the Bear Sutra*. Lore had both of those. Then he saw a blue one called *Axe Handles*. Thrilling concept. What might the sequel be? *Tire Irons?* But *Axe Handles* was Trey's target: he'd heard Lorilee, on the phone to Bess, say she'd begged the Pipestone Public Library to buy it. That she was dying to read a book named for a tool handle made no sense to Trey, but tonight wasn't about his notion of sense. Tonight was about fetching home something Lorilee loved, showing his own love by giving it to her without judgment.

Time passed. The reading started. No one on the sidewalk could see the poet or hear a word. Forty minutes later, judging by the muffled applause, the reading ended. But nobody left the store! The Neolithics were willing to wait till the next Ice Age to shake the hand of their chieftain! More time passed. Trey's legs and back ached. The night had turned cold. He was underdressed and beginning to shiver. Each time one of the hairy Ainus left the building Trey could only take two tiny steps forward. Noticing his irritation, he reminded himself: *irritated climbers make stupid moves.* The irritation itself, he realized, was a crux. To get through it, he imagined each two tiny steps toward the door were vertical instead of horizontal, imbuing them with his favorite value: *vertical gain.*

Another half hour and he was inside the store and warm. That helped. In another quarter hour the poet grew visible betwixt his tribespeople—a small, sturdy, leathery man with deeply crow's-footed eyes, steel-gray hair and beard, and a gold ring in one ear, seated at a table by a saleswoman who supplied whichever books the Neolithics requested.

Ten or so minutes later Trey found he could eavesdrop and things grew interesting. The first three folks in line identified themselves as members of a wilderness council and asked the poet if he'd serve on their board. Snyder begged off with such extreme fake horror it made them laugh. He then purchased three of his *own* books, signed them all, and donated them to be auctioned at the council's next fundraiser. He left the trio full of joy.

Two neo-hippie chicks approached. Though they weren't a third the age of the poet, they expressed such overt interest in what he was up to later that night that Snyder laughed as he gave them his appreciative regrets.

A young man with one eyebrow much higher than the other approached. Trey thought the brow might be scarred, perhaps from a burn. Then the guy introduced himself as "a very serious Buddhist," launched a question that turned out to be a lecture, and Trey realized the brow was being held·up by an act of willpower. Eyebrowman's lecture concerned how the influence of Yadda Yadda Roshi was so obvious in Snyder's work that it went without saying. Hearing this, Snyder signed the fellow's *Axe Handles* and waved the next person forward without saying a word. As Eyebrowman turned away, his face fell and brow plummeted in disappointment till it was level with the other brow and he looked like a normal human being. Trey couldn't wait to tell Lore, *Snyder's shunning healed the guy's eyebrow problem in two seconds! It was like something Jesus might have done!*

An old man in a blue flannel shirt, black jeans, and red suspenders stepped up and hung the cane he was using by its crook on the signing table.

He then slid a *No Nature* at the poet and stood smiling, saying nothing at all. "Would you like it signed?" Snyder asked.

As if he hadn't heard the question, the man said, "It's for a fella claims you, more than anyone, kept him going when he worked for the Forest Service. Which is to say, for the Pharaoh." (Snyder smiled at this.) "Time for a quick story?" the old man asked.

"Fire away," said the poet.

"Fella was a tree planter. Oregon Coast Range mostly. One point two million trees in twenty years. Half as many as lots of the planters he worked with. That cost him plenty in docked pay, but trees planted well enough to *grow* kinda seemed like the point, so he let it cost." (Again Snyder smiled.) "The part of his story I like best. Fella quit the Pharaoh a few years back, and on his own time and dime planted another quarter million, and that last gob of trees were all Port Orford cedar, western hemlock, and Sitka spruce." (Snyder let out a surprised *Hah!*) "For two decades, fella says, he'd set nothin' but Doug-fir in soil created by a seven-species climax forest. Made him sick to do it, but you know the story. Kids to raise, bills to pay, Weyerhaeuser and them dictating *monocrop*. His cedar, hemlock, and spruce he hand-planted low an' slow along creeks an' rivers the Pharaoh had clear-cut to the water, then lied that he didn't. That last quarter million left that planter proud to the day he died. And it was your words and songs, more than anything, he said, that moved him to plant 'em. 'So thank him,' he told me. And here I stand. *Thank you.*"

Snyder looked long and close at the man. "Time for two quick questions?" he asked.

"Fire away," the old man said.

"Might that worthy planter's death be slightly exaggerated? Might he in fact be standing in front of me?"

The tree-planter dipped his head, shy as a child. "If he is," he muttered, "he's so tired they got a special word for it. *Re*-tired."

Snyder nodded slowly, turned to the saleswoman, and asked for one of each of his books, nine titles in all. "Put those on my tab, please," he said. He then signed all nine, put them in a Base Camp Books bag, shoved them across the table, and said, "Try to pay for these and I'll send the royalties to the Pharaoh." The old man was already shaking a little at the gift when Snyder stood, circled the table, put his arms around the man, and firmly embraced him. "Thanks for the story. Thanks for the last quarter million. Thank you for your life."

The old planter nodded, took up his books and cane, and limped away, his face shining.

Snyder returned to his chair—and it was suddenly Trey reaching across the table to shake the small, tough hand. The poet looked up, briefly exploring his eyes, and Trey, like the old man, found himself flooded by shyness and...some kind of sadness. It was the encounters he'd witnessed that saddened him. This man was Lorilee's hero for rock-solid reasons, Trey now felt, and he'd never once asked Lore what those reasons might be, or opened a Snyder book to seek the reasons himself. This was gross neglect. This was what had caused the downhill slide. It was time to perform the self-arrest:

Trey asked Snyder for a copy of *Axe Handles*, as planned. Then he asked for *No Nature*, because it was the thickest, the most recent, hopefully the best. He might run out of gas before he reached Pipestone due to the unplanned purchase. If so, *good!* He'd show Lore how much he loved her by telling her how far he'd walked. *Eight-thousand-meter-peak effort.*

"Want them inscribed?" the poet asked.

Trey blushed. He didn't know what "inscribed" meant. "No thanks," he said, then leaned down, preparing to describe how he wanted them signed. But Snyder had already slid the two books across to him. Trey blushed deeper. Taking in his discomfort, the poet gave him a friendly nod and granted him space by turning to the couple behind him.

Bewildered by what had happened, Trey started to wander off, then recalled his eight-thousand-meter vow, spun on his heels, returned to the table, and leaned so abruptly back down that the couple startled and the poet leaned away with a frown.

"Sorry!" Trey said. "But...does 'inscribed' mean you sign the book to somebody?"

When Snyder nodded, Trey handed *Axe Handles* back to him. "Man, thanks! You're, like my wife's total hero. So if you could sign it to her, please? Plus, there's this five-word magic formula, *your formula,* we both love so much, me and her both, that it'd be *amazing* if you could add our magic words."

Looking harassed by all the directives, Snyder asked, "What formula is that?"

In a clear, at-last-confident voice, Trey said, "'The mountains are your mind.'"

A confusing thing then happened: hearing the words, Snyder looked up into Trey's eyes, sending him the most wide-open, uncanny, soul-to-soul smile Trey had ever received from anyone but Lorilee. But the very next instant (*In reaction to what?* Trey thought. *My face?*) the smile folded inscrutably in on itself and vanished, never to return. It was as if an origami called "Beaming Poet Face" had been created by invisible hands, then uncreated so completely it ended with the paper's disappearance. More confused than ever, Trey looked down at the book. Above Snyder's original signature it now said:

The mountains are your mind.
! !
—*Gary Snyder*

It did not say "for Lorilee." But the poet was talking with the couple Trey had already alarmed, and the vanished origami somehow made it impossible to interrupt again.

Trey carried the books to his car, set them carefully down on the seat, started the sorry-sounding engine, heaved a sigh rife with leaking exhaust fumes, and down-climbed the two hundred moonlit miles home.

Making Love, Making Home, Making Culture

THE NEXT NIGHT, Cinco de Mayo, an exhausted Lorilee dragged herself home from Grubstake Realty at 8:30, opened the front door of the grim garage apartment—and was greeted by candlelight and a barrage of fabulous smells.

"Happy anniversary!" Trey called. He was darting amongst pots, pans, cutting boards, and stove burners in tight jeans and one of the sleeveless little white T-shirts Lore called "Guido shirts," beaming like a feral but inarguably sexy mountain elf.

Lore's first reaction was mild horror. She'd just spent ten hours dodging a libidinous jerkwad who, though painstakingly trained never to touch her, left her feeling sexually slimed. She'd felt queasy all day. Ovulating maybe. But Trey was a very good cook. Lorilee smelled, without even trying, roasting game hens, garlic, fresh basil, basmati rice, cardamom, and her favorite squash soup made with coconut milk. But meals like this also created post-meal expectations. When Trey charmingly invited her to take a long hot shower in the stall he had so notoriously retiled, she felt like a pre-Columbian virgin being prepared for sacrifice, though she managed, with effort, not to show it.

In the shower she began to revive a little—till she heard the door open. "Privacy!" she barked, fearing Trey was coming for her already. But when she peeked, there was no one.

She stayed in the shower till the water heater emptied, stepped out into the steam, and discovered the cause of the door opening and closing: a package, gift wrapped in handmade coarse brown paper, sporting a little card that said: "OPEN NOW!" Command form. How loaded could a message be? But she couldn't figure out how not to obey.

Inside: a green and red kaftan. Handmade in Turkey. Stunning geometric embroidery at the throat and sleeves. Just her size. Lorilee sighed. A dozen red roses, a refinished pine table, and a Cuisinart on his credit card in the past month alone. And an anniversary snowboard for Trey, purchased on her card, stashed in the trunk of her car. Years of penury ahead. And now: this stunning kaftan.

But when she slipped into it, toweled the steam from the mirror, and considered herself, Lorilee saw beauty. Nothing less. She hadn't seen this in herself in months.

Next, a private debate: Is dressed in nothing but a kaftan dressed enough?

Only half of her heart answered yes. But this was the half she'd always gambled on. And how adorable Trey looked, when she stepped out of the bathroom, in his Guido shirt and sinews and muscle-sculpted jeans, dimple-cheeked, radar-eyed, struck speechless by the sight of her in the kaftan. "Thanks," she said, with a tiny cock of the hip.

Trey took Lorilee's elbow, seated her at a rose-petal-strewn and candlelit table, kissed the top of her head the way one kisses a child's, whispered, "Right back!" then darted out of the house. She looked round the room. The tiny space was spotless. Even the walls looked fresh-washed. Every pot and pan they owned had been deployed for the impending meal. The fragrances were intoxicating. How had he found time for all this?

She could feel herself melting a little when Trey stepped back inside, hands behind his back, looking so fluttery and shy he seemed effeminate—a rarity in her iron-bodied man. During what she'd come to think of as their Lost Glory Days, when Trey would try to surprise her with some small gift his flutteriness sometimes grew so intense that, even if the gift failed to appeal, he pleased her with his twitterpatedness. Seeing him aflutter once more, their Lost Glory Days didn't seem so lost. She melted a little more.

"Well?" Lore said as he beamed and quivered. "Whatcha got back there, fella?"

With his right arm Trey swung round a French Côtes du Rhône, which he presented with an awkward bow. Reading the ten-year-old date on the label, Lorilee had to stifle another monetary sigh. Then round Trey's left side came the second gift—a little brown paper quadrangle. A book of some kind? How unlike him. Yet look at him beaming.

He presented the gift with a trembling that hadn't accompanied the presentation of the wine, stepped behind her chair, rested his hands on her chairback, and waited. But Lore felt reluctant to move. *This moment. Just as it is.* The meal he'd made. The incredible cleaning he'd done. And now a Brown Paper Something given with so much expectancy and hope that her chair was trembling a little in his hands. What, more than this, could she want?

Then she began to wonder what sort of book would so appeal to Trey. Yikes. A compendium of mountain-climber aphorisms? One of those chicken-soup-for-dummies anthologies? A hand-bound journal in which Trey tried, with dreadful earnestness, to pen something about the Cruxes, Climbing Lines, Glare Ice, and Ice Axes of Love? How reluctantly she opened the brown paper. Then, there in her lap: *Axe Handles.*

She felt Trey fibrillating. Heard him whisper, "Look inside."

When Lore beheld the way Snyder's neat hand had inscribed their five magic words, she drew a sharp breath. Each of the two exclamation points gave her a chill. When a tear from overhead then landed on the shoulder of her kaftan, splashing her collarbone, she spun in her chair—and saw that every visible inch of Trey had broken out in goose bumps. Entirely melted now, she wrapped her free arm round his back, buried her face in his abdomen and felt how the strength, always evident in his hard belly, had given way to something so trembly and fragile she wanted to shelter it like a little bird. She then realized what this something was: Trey's terribly fragile hope for their marriage.

The fragility, even more than the hope, touched her core. A huge wave of love and first swoon of lust swashed through her. Pressing her lips into his belly, Lorilee said, "Would you like to know what your name is tonight?"

She felt, in Trey's abs, a faint shimmy from his eager nodding. Her free hand slid round to his buttocks. Pulling his belly tight to her lips, she said, "*Perrrrrrrrrrrrrrrrrfect!*" rolling the *r* on and on, feeling his muscles writhe with pleasure at the sensation. Fluttering her lashes into his abs, keeping her grip on his butt, she said, "Under the *cirrrrrrrrrrrrrcumstances,* I see no *alterrrrrrrrrrrrrrrrrrnative* but to change the name of the dude, formerly known as Trey, to *Perrrrrrrrrrrrrrrrrrrrrrrrrrrrrfect!*"

He pulled himself free. "Before I go back to being *Imperrrrrrfect,* let's drink to that!"

He opened the wine, then filled two pricey-looking new long-stemmed wineglasses. Lorilee let that go. They locked eyes: *clink*! When she tasted the wine, her coo was involuntary. She then tilted her head back, inviting Trey to kiss her wine-wet lips. Bending gallantly, he did so—but only briefly. When she felt how disappointed her body felt, she realized the smutty residue of the day's Grubstake sales had vanished.

"Hungry?" Trey asked, his baby blues blazing down at her, his body so statuesque, smile so boyish, face so blithely unaware of the off-center erection in the front of his jeans, that Lorilee suddenly couldn't get enough of him. She pulled him to her, replanted her lips on his belly, and repeated, "*Perrrrrrrrrrrrrrrrrrrrrrfect!*"

Somehow missing this gargantuan come-on, Trey pulled away, stepped over to the tiny counter, and proceeded to hand-build two honey-toasted-pecan, pear, and gorgonzola salads as lovely as the kaftan, the signed book, the fibrillating bronze-skinned man.

When he turned back to her, salads in hand, Lorilee was pleased to see that, despite his chef duties, the off-center erection remained intact. He presented her salad, fetched their plastic fake-wood grinder, and offered her freshly ground pepper.

Lorilee's hand shot out, hooking a belt loop of his jeans. "First listen," she said, opening *Axe Handles* to the first page. She then launched into the twenty-five-century-old *Shih Ching* folk song Snyder had placed on page one. Holding the book behind Trey so she could see it, she spoke not to his face but straight into the muscle and skin of his belly:

> *How do you shape an axe handle?*
> *Without an axe, it can't be done.*
> *How do you take a wife?*
> *Without a go-between, you can't get one.*

Shape a handle, shape a handle,
the pattern is not far off.
And here's a girl I know,
the wine and food in rows...

That's as far as the reading got. Pulling *Perrrrfect* closer, Lorilee set aside
the book, opened three buttons of his jeans, and reached deftly in, whispering, "*shape a handle, shape a handle.*" The fifth-yearly-weds then decided,
spur of the moment, to redecorate the apartment. Trey began by peeling his
jeans down his godlike legs with his feet and kicking them up onto a rafter
to serve as the forthcoming festivity's banner. In nothing but his Guido
shirt, his prong a stylish match for the pepper grinder he'd forgotten to set
aside, Trey looked so good to Lorilee that her kaftan lit out after the jeans,
becoming their second banner. Then she too flew, with total trust even as
the pepper grinder fell to the floor, up into the mighty arms that caught and
held her with such ease that, right there in the air, she offered all she owned.
Trey sampled her nakedness as he spun her in his arms, both of them
laughing, then not laughing as the vapor pressure within the beings known
as Lorilee and Trey surpassed atmospheric pressure, physics morphed into
metaphysics, the fresh-vacuumed fake Oriental rug transmogrified into the
loveliest bed imaginable, and Lore was all over Trey was all over Lore,
lips on lips, chest on breasts, lips on breasts, tongue on tongue, tongues on
thighs, dive down canyons, the wet warm winding, kiss the veins that pulse,
siphon skin where it peaks, breath entering, bliss rising, bodies fusing,
bloodstreams in rows, here's a girl I know oh *ohhhhhhh,* squash soup con-
gealing, feast charring in oven, salads wilting on table, legs sliding across
and around, lips and tongues everywhere, arms-mouths-hands-entwining-
ribs-breasts-thighs, so many cruxes to up-and-down-climb, portals to open,
fluids and metaphors to mix, credit cards to max, forms of physical and
financial gravity to defy, exactitudes and perfections to thank, convexities
and concavities to bliss-nuke, toe knuckles to crack, ecstasies to moan,
table shaking, candles quaking, *perrrrrrrfect handle entering perrrrrrrrfect*
holder, shape! shape! shape! Trey swooning on vertical mind-planes, Lore
singing *more lost, more lost,* Snyder's reputation fuckin' *soaring,* Trey and
Lorilee on the floor of the half-converted garage in Pipestone, CO, making
poetry fuck you debt, making song fuck you fmog and fmush, making love,
making home, making culture,
  without a condom.
  Ah, Blue Ridge Mountains.
  Ah, Carolina folk fests.
  Ah, truths triggered with rhyme. So long, so long, so long.

Old Mountain's Advice to Young Father

NINE MONTHS LATER, in a world again gone frigid, Lorilee's legs again opened, this time under the fluorescent lights of Pipestone Community Hospital, and Japheth Joshu Jantz slid alliteratively into this world to the tune of all two thousand of the baby-shower bucks that had constituted his parents' sole hope of a safer used car.

The newborn proved healthy. Nor were the patterns that *shape, shape, shaped* him far off. He had his father's perfect skin, strong resolve, and handle. He had his mother's small, fine-tuned body, calm nature, and exceptionally bright whites, though Japhy's irises were bright blue with a dark rim of indigo rather than the black rimming Lorilee's gray.

To AVOID THE cost of an all-night stay, Trey slipped out to the hospital parking lot around midnight, warmed the rusted-out twelve-year-old Celica that was the safer of their two bombs, opened the windows enough to clear the worst of the exhaust fumes that now leaked constantly up through the floorboards, then gathered the weakened Lorilee—holding the baby, helped by a nurse—out of the wheelchair and into the car.

He drove madonna and child home to the half-converted garage. He helped them inside, where they'd prepped a "nursery" half the size of a cut-rate hot tub. Trey then returned to the car for the rest of the baby gear, but as his arms filled with the stuff, he envisioned the bodily joy it always gave him, when prepping for an expedition, when his arms filled for the first time with everything he'd be carrying, to test its weight. The baby gear, in comparison, looked so deadly to his passion that, like a man who sees an inescapable avalanche coming, he sank to his knees. The baby crap fell to the driveway. With a sound close to a sob Trey threw himself forward like a Muslim at prayer. Eyes closed, forehead to the ice, he began groping for some shield or shelter or battle cry that might alter his sense of doom. When his hand lit instead upon a bloated bale of baby diapers, revulsion filled him. "*Noooo!*" he groaned. "This is *not* my path, *not* my fate, not my life!"

Realizing Lore might hear him, he gathered the baby things and got back on his feet. But when he turned toward the tiny house with his family inside, he felt he was facing the avalanche itself. Unable to take a step, he lifted his gaze to the one visible manifestation of the gods he worshipped. "*Two Medicine!*" he gasped. "*Please! Help me!*"

Looming over the tiny garage apartment, a silent, star-blotting blackness, the mountain gave Trey not the faintest signal, hope, or clue.

Three J's First Mountain

UNDER THE INFLUENCE of Gary Snyder, Lorilee had begun to think of herself as a Buddhist even before she met Trey. That was how she'd come to name their son after the Zen patriarch Joshu and the Snyder-inspired "Japhy Ryder" in Jack Kerouac's *The Dharma Bums*. Trey read enough of *The Dharma Bums*, during Lorilee's pregnancy, to approve her choice of name. But when faced with an actual bald-headed baby whose clear, gray-eyed gaze bore a disconcerting resemblance to the shaved-headed Zen teachers Lorilee had begun to study, Japheth Joshu Jantz struck Trey as far too highfalutin a name for a boy to tote around lowfalutin Pipestone. So he began to call the baby "Three J."

"*Please,*" Lorilee said. "You make him sound like a cattle ranch!"

"Okay," Trey said amiably. "Let's make it plain *Three.*"

"Making you *Trey,* father of *Three?*" Lorilee asked.

"Sure!" he said with a grin. "Shape, shape, shape! The pattern is not far off!"

His reference to the poem that had more or less impregnated her made Lore smile. The thought of a son named Three did not. "We agreed to call him Japhy, so that's what I'm going to call him," she said.

Trey said, "To each his own," stuck with "Three J" and "Three," and the baby began to experience himself as an entirely different being with each parent. Lack of confidence followed. Japhy proved clingy, afraid of strangers, afraid of being left alone in his crib, and utterly addicted to Lorilee's quiet voice, gentle care, and milky breasts.

Not liking the long-term implications of this, Trey obeyed an impulse one cold winter's morn: stepping over to the futon couch where madonna and child had long lain attached, he plucked his sated son up off Lorilee's chest. When the mouth-to-tit suction broke, there was an audible pop and rubbery breast bounce that fascinated Trey in a variety of ways. Lorilee was too shocked to speak.

Holding Japhy face-to-face, Trey told him, "There's an understanding we need to get started on, Three. Come on." He opened the back door of the apartment, carried the baby out into the frigid air, raised his chin with a finger till his tiny face was more or less aimed at Two Medicine Peak, pointed, and loudly said, "*MOUNTAIN.*"

The baby's tongue protruded, stuck in nipple-cupping position. His mouth corners dribbled milk. His head was wobbling like a bobblehead doll. His blue eyes had been half closed and glazed with comfort. They were now wide-open and blinking fast in the cold.

Trey liked these changes. "That big sucker right there, my boy, is a mountain. Let's hear you say it. *MOUNTAIN!*"

Winter poured in the door. "Bring him in!" Lorilee called.

"*MOUNTAIN,*" Trey repeated.

"He's eight weeks old!" Lorilee shouted.

"Just let me see you *think* it," Trey urged. "Come on. MOUNTAIN."

The baby hung in the cold, gasping.

"You're young," Trey conceded. "But there's two things you need to know. First thing. Huge and scary looking as those beasts are, with one little footstep and handhold at a time, you can climb 'em all the way to the top. Second thing. Believe it or not, baby boy, those icy giants are your *mind*. Your very own ever-lovin' mind."

Trey stepped inside and returned babe to mother, proud as if they'd summited a first peak.

Japhy, meanwhile, hadn't the faintest idea what had happened beyond the broken suction, escaped breast, loss of warmth, comfort, mother, then the father's rough hands and blasts of frigid air. But he was a sensible two-month-old: the next time Lorilee left him alone with Trey, he squalled without ceasing until his mother returned.

Magic Words Hijacked

OVER THE NEXT couple of years Lorilee's women friends expressed incredulity at the number of granite cliffs, domes, and peaks Trey found it necessary to drive, fly, and trek to, then death-defyingly climb. If their alarm was ever expressed in Trey's presence, his blue eyes and heroic grin would blaze up. "We only go around once, ladies!" he'd tell them. "*Chase* your dreams! It's all good!"

Though her friends winced at these assurances, Lorilee had known from the start that a domesticated life was out of Trey's reach—and more power to him. His depth was in his body. He couldn't experience himself, know himself, value himself—or Lorilee and Japhy either, she was realizing—if he weren't free to test his physical limits. If she was to know the light in his eyes and electricity in his touch, something had to give.

She decided this something would be her. She quit performing music in public shortly after she became pregnant. She quit writing songs altogether after Japhy was born. To support Trey's climbing she then quit Grubstake Realty and landed the highest-paying job she could find—just under Japhy's birthplace, it turned out, running the billing department in the basement at Pipestone Community Hospital.

Lore's closest friend, Bess Hern, ran the daycare where Japhy's days were spent, and was outspokenly leery of Lorilee's sacrifices. "Is it fair," she asked, "that while he summits peaks and rock faces all over the continent, you 'keep the light in his eyes,' as you say, by working in a basement and leaving Japhy with me? What about the light in *your* eyes?"

Lorilee pulled a card out of her handbag and passed it to Bess. Her friend looked confused till she found, on the back, a quote by the climber Jeff Lowe, handwritten by Lore herself. Bess read it aloud.

> High levels of uncertainty open doors closed to conservative types. Intelligent, perceptive risk-takers forge opportunities for themselves out of situations that more timid folks would characterize as desperate and threatening.

"Those words," Lorilee said, "are a fair description of Trey's climbing *and* of our marriage. Trey's expeditions keep us poor—if it's accurate to call a deepening canyon of debt 'poor.' But to strip him of the adventures that define him is what I fear most. And I'm a risk-taker too, Bess. I let him climb, and forge opportunities of my own in his absences."

Looking skeptical, Bess asked, "What opportunities are those?"

"A steady zazen practice, for one. The meditations I time to Japhy's nap and bedtime mean a lot to me. Also, Trey is *awkward* with Japh. You know what I mean. *Three, Son of Trey?* But teenagers love Trey. So it's a waiting game, I hope. Trey will gradually slow enough, and Japhy will man up enough, that Trey's adventurousness, outdoor skills, good-heartedness, and courage will become available to his son. Japh just has to be old enough to receive it. Meanwhile Trey's absences, to be honest, allow me to raise Japh as I see fit."

When Bess mumbled, "I don't know, Lore," Lorilee added that when Trey came home from his adventures he was always thriving, his stories were amazing, and his gratitude was profound. When Bess asked how this gratitude was expressed, Lore confessed that when Trey came down off a good climb he was like a gorgeous wild animal and their lovemaking was a wonder of her world.

Bess accepted this with a crooked smile. But other friends—musical compatriots who missed Lorilee's singing and playing, especially—opined that Trey had become a climbing addict, that Lore was his hapless codependent, that their balance of duties was hopelessly unfair, and that their union was going to end badly.

LORILEE COULD NAME the day she began to agree. A weather-jinxed expedition up Denali had taken Trey away for nine weeks, three times as long as planned. The climb left him with frostbite that nipped the tips off two toes and a finger, though they gradually healed, slightly shortened. Charging in the front door undaunted by his near death, Trey had dropped his giant duffel with a thud that quaked the house, enfolded Lorilee and Japhy in his arms, and exclaimed: "Lore! Three! *Denali is now my mind!*"

The words sounded so bizarre that Lore didn't at first connect them to their beloved five Snyder words. Once she did, she was appalled. She held her tongue, but shouting "Denali is my mind" after bagging a summit had nothing to do with climbing seen as a form of poetry written on rock by a mortal body.

Expecting trouble, she felt obliged to restore the original meaning even so. After Japhy was asleep and they'd climbed into the loft, she told Trey, "We need to talk."

He turned his full-bodied attention to her. She said, "The phrase 'The mountains are your mind' is very important to us. We fell in love at the sound of those words. So I need to tell you, Trey, that I see those five words' meaning as being quiet as snow, and feel *we* need to be snow-quiet too, to live their true meaning. I don't mean to hurt your feelings, but I love you too much not to point out that roaring 'Denali is my mind' because you climbed Denali is not at all what Snyder means."

Trey looked not just hurt but shocked by this beginning.

"My love for Snyder's work led me to Eihei Dōgen," she continued. "A thirteenth-century Zen master. An enlightened being, Trey. A *mountain range* in human form, so to speak. Snyder reveres him, so do I, and Dōgen's got a sutra about mountains. Let me read a little to you."

She reached for a thin, well-worn book by the bed and opened to the first page: "'Mountains and waters, right now, are the actualization of the ancient Buddha way. Each, abiding in its phenomenal expression, realizes completeness. Because mountains and waters have been active since before the Empty Eon, they are alive at this moment. Because they have been the self since before form arose, they are liberated and realized. Because mountains are high and broad, the way of riding the clouds is always reached in the mountains, and the inconceivable power of soaring in the wind comes freely from the mountains.'"

Trey looked lost. She tried to coax him. "The reason Snyder says 'The mountains are your mind' is that every mountain's true nature is *alive* and *complete* for all eternity, Trey. And so is *our* true nature. We have always been one with mountains. But it's not *climbing* them that makes this so. It's being free of illusions. It's a disappearing of ego that leaves us at one with the ten thousand—"

"*Whoa, hold it, Lore!*" Trey broke in. "I've got to reel this back down into the world *I* live in, okay? For me, mountains are alive, like Dōgen says, sure they are, but not for the *reasons* he says. For *me* they're alive 'cause *I'm up there on 'em,* giving 'em *my* life. *Giving 'em my life,* Lore. And I think, for me and you, it's the same. We're giving each other our lives. But for me and you, finding our true nature—or finding the *true love between us,* I'd rather call it—is simpler than these Dōgen and Snyder types make it. For me and you, love is about my body and your body, and the warmth and feel of our bodies as we come together, and *that love is not broken, Lore.*" He enfolded her in his arms, then his hands began to move. "Can't you feel it? *Feel me giving you my life, Lore!*"

After his terrible experience on Denali, Lore appreciated his warmth and safety too much to risk hurting his feelings. She let him keep touching her, and her body felt plenty. But her mind was saying, *Wait, though. Our love isn't the topic. The topic is you turning the words "The mountains are your mind" into an ego trip. That twist is a threat to our love!*

"For me and you," he cooed and his hands kept moving and her head began to swim, "love's as simple as this. And for me, climbing's this simple too. *We're not broken, Lore,*" he murmured. "So stop trying to fix us. Let's both of us just love what we've got, which is both of us, *like this.*"

"*But...the self...before form arose,*" she said as her body began to move in his hands. "*The mountains and waters right now,*" she said, "*are the ancient...the ancient...*"

Her thoughts broke up. And what she and Trey experienced was far from broken. But before his frostbite had even healed he drove north to Washington, where he climbed Mounts Baker, Rainier, and Adams in a single late-September week, then dropped down into Oregon where, using headlamps and his astounding fitness, he summited all Three Sisters in a sixteen-hour day. An incredible feat—and a feat soon answered by a sorely needed influx of endorsement money from a few makers of climbing gear. But upon his return home, Trey's new battle cries—"Baker, Rainier, and Adams are now my mind!" "All Three Sisters became my mind in a day!"— sounded so wrong to Lorilee they felt potentially lethal.

Free Remodels

FOUR YEARS PASSED. Trey's spiels about finding the line and writing body poetry on vertical granite grew so polished they began to sound like political stump speeches. But even as the verve fell out of his accounts, he made famous climbing friends, co-starred in climbing films, and won more corporate sponsorship and free gear from outdoor companies, his reputation grew national, then international, and once he added the Southern Hemisphere to his range, he was away on expeditions much of the year. But Lore kept telling herself: *Trey's soul is youngish; he needs the kinds of adventures I free him to enjoy.* And his touch remained electric.

Meanwhile, her little zazen practice flourished. Sometimes when Trey was gone, Japhy was sleeping, and Lorilee was seated on the zafu before her little wooden Buddha, the air of the garage-apartment grew so still and she became so serene that she grew as empty as the air itself. If she happened to stand while in this state, and look out at Two Medicine, the peak was wrapped in the same emptiness into which she'd vanished, and Dōgen's line "In the inner chamber of Buddha ancestors there is no self and others" was an accurate description of the alms of the moment. If Japhy happened to wake from his nap and walk in on her in this state, he too became a small, sweet feature of the unitive and de-selfed emptiness.

Other good things happened in Trey's absence. One day when Japhy was five he opened Lorilee's guitar case, looked delighted by the sight of her old Gibson, and asked, "Can I try?" When she showed him how to strum, he grasped it immediately but the strings hurt his fingers, so she restrung the guitar with gut strings and started teaching him chords. He practiced so diligently his tiny fingertips developed calluses, his enthusiasm coaxed Lorilee back into playing her dulcimer, she began singing again with a joy to match his, and the garage apartment that felt so claustrophobic when Trey was bouncing off its walls had been remodeled, without tools or expense, into a music studio as spacious as the worlds of song.

Then came a second remodel: when Japhy outgrew afternoon naps and started popping in on Lorilee's meditation sessions, he was intrigued. Studying his mother, then her little sitting Buddha, he asked, "Why do you sit just like him?"

"It's called 'zazen,'" she said. "This is an icon of Gautama Buddha. We sit still like the Buddha because, two thousand six hundred years ago, he sat down under a tree, didn't move for days, and found a kind of perfect no one and nothing can undo. And it's findable, *right here and now*. But our minds fool us into chasing endless thoughts instead. Our minds tell us there's no time to sit the way the Buddha did. The mind says, *We've got to keep busy!busy!busy!*"

Japhy laughed and parroted her: "*Busy!busy!busy!*"

"The Buddha showed us how to cut through the *busy-busy* by sitting so still we become empty. His word for this is *śūnyatā*. Emptiness is crucial, he said in better words than mine, because it scoops us out so completely that something astounding happens. Our true nature pours in. Gautama used words like 'no rising and falling,' 'calmness,' and 'extinction' to describe the experience. But I'm getting all wordy nerdy! All you need to know is, sitting like this has worked so well for so long that I've loved and trusted it from the first time I tried it, and love it more and more by the year."

"Can I try?" Japhy asked with the same amiable curiosity he'd shown her guitar.

Lorilee set her zafu down beside him, patted it in invitation, and nodded at the seated Buddha before him. "Make your body, legs, and hands exactly like that and see how it feels."

Japhy plopped down on the zafu, laughed as he fought to pull his feet onto his calves in imitation of the statue, sat up straight, and carefully imitated the Buddha's mudras with his little hands. "What else?" he asked.

The sight of her five-year-old sitting exactly like her spiritual hero moved Lore fiercely. His focus on the posture was total. He even half closed his eyes. She spoke to him of in-breath and out-breath, and of letting thoughts come and go rather than dwelling on them.

"Why is that?" he asked. "I'm just sitting. Why shouldn't I think what I want?"

"Because if you become empty there is no I, and no such thing as want, and what happens in that state is amazing! Listen to my hero, Dōgen: 'To study the way is to study the self. To study the self is to forget the self. To forget the self is to awaken into the ten thousand things.'"

When Japhy repeated, "'The ten thousand things,'" his expression held a satisfaction she'd never before seen. Just like that, he began meditating with her for fifteen minutes a day, giving the tiny garage apartment its second free remodel as a Zendo—

until Trey burst in from an expedition roaring, "*Three J, my man! Lore, my love! Guess what?*" Lore's music-making Zendo mate then vanished, "Three J" became Trey Junior as they bellowed the name of whatever peak or wall had become Trey's mind, and their music studio and Zendo turned back into a claustrophobic pumpkin of a garage.

Contacts

THAT SAME YEAR Lorilee began to get headaches so strong they sometimes made her throw up. Fearing a brain tumor, she paid money she didn't have to see a neurologist, terrified to think he might bankrupt her for life by ordering a CAT scan. After a brief exam, however, the neurologist smiled at her self-diagnosis, asked about her daily life, told her the headaches were from nearsightedness most likely contracted from the basement fluorescent lighting and crappy computer screens at Pipestone Community, and prescribed her first pair of contacts.

As soon as Lorilee adjusted to them her sight improved enormously in ways she hadn't bargained for. She saw for the first time the flinty, hard-worn look of Pipestone, the soul-deadening effect of her job, and the ball-and-chain burden of her and Trey's combined debt. She saw the remarkable gifts and goodness of their son, but also the fragility born of being a smart, sensitive kid in a tough little town. She saw that the musical talent she herself had been neglecting was not just a hobby but a guiding light that would collapse into spiritual blindness if she didn't kindle it back to life soon. With a sinking feeling, she then ignored her love of Trey's touch, turned her vision to the enormous amount of time they spent apart, and began piecing together clues she'd been unwillingly gathering since the addict phase of his climbing had begun. As the clues multiplied she tried to deploy meditation skills to switch her mind off like a light, but the evidence overwhelmed: Trey, she at last saw all too clearly, had been enhancing his expeditions with sexual liaisons. Realizing that the electricity that enlivened her and Trey's love-making emanated in part from other lovers, Lore sank, moaning, to the floor.

The next time Trey returned from a climbing expedition, wrapped her in his arms, announced that Mount Such-and-So was his mind, and began to kiss and stroke her, Lore shocked him by backing forcefully out of his embrace.

"How nice for you," she said. "But I'm glad Japhy's at Bess's, because it's time I checked on whether it's nice for Japh and me. I'm going to ask a few simple, direct questions. Please swear to answer me truthfully. I'm serious."

Trey's "I swear" could not have been more reluctant.

"Did you have a lover on this trek? Or on past treks? And is she, or they, your mind now too?"

Trey's face darkened as his blue eyes began to circle Lorilee's face but never quite meet her gaze. "A climber's mind *trains* his eye," he said. "He trains his eye to find that line the body will be able to follow up through the jumble. And if he's chosen his line well, his mind and body meet the mountain's, skin to stone, stone to skin, and every move and breath are poetry, and the world is exact and perfect. Remember me talking about that?"

"I not only remember those weary metaphors," Lore said, "I bequeathed them to you in the first place. Remember that?"

His gaze fell away from her like a climber falling backward off a wall. Pacing the tiny apartment, a leopard in a sudden cage, he said, "Well, another thing I've worked out is...there's times...when you're up there living that poetry...when another mind-body turns out to be occupying your same line. And a climber's mind stays true, Lore. *He stays true to that line.*"

She looked at him for long seconds. "Since our family depends on this, let's be clear. You're telling me that, to stay true to your climbing lines, you choose to be untrue to me."

Unable to meet her eyes, indignant even so, Trey said, "I stay true to *my truth,* Lore!"

"Which is what?" she asked. "Please remind me."

The life-threatening misdirection she had long sensed slammed home:

"The mountains are my mind!"

How powerful the difference between Trey's adamant "*my* mind!" and Snyder's quiet "The mountains are *your* mind." How easily that single altered pronoun set off an avalanche. How swiftly she, Trey, and Japhy were buried in a rubble that used to be a marriage.

Greatest Meal Ever

THREE MONTHS LATER, on the Saturday Trey promised to help Lore "sort out our material shit," as he put it, she tried to prepare herself with a bout of zazen. The meditation ended in less than a minute when she jumped up off her zafu in a rage and kicked her wooden Buddha so hard she nearly broke her foot and *did* break an earlobe off the Buddha.

When Trey and Japhy arrived an hour later, she had repaired the ear with

Elmer's wood glue, but Trey noticed her limp at once. "What happened to *you*?" he asked.

"Oh, I've been working out," Lore said—then marveled at her words. It was the first time she'd ever flat-out lied to him. How *easy* it was, and what an interesting cheesy aftertaste! Realizing how many times Trey's accounts of expeditions had caused him to taste the same flavor, Lore decided to play some catch-up. "Trying to whip myself into shape for the singles life," she lied. "I'm so excited about all that I guess I overdid it."

Trey gave her a hurt look. Excellent! Even better, her broken-eared Buddha's previously remote smile had taken on a sly, conspiratorial cast.

Then she noticed Japhy, who of course harbored poignant Mom-and-Dad-getting-back-together dreams, gaping at her, utterly crushed.

Determined to shorten the little guy's torment, she limped into the twenty-square-foot space they'd called "the kitchen" and began divvying pots, pans, plates, cups, glasses, knives, forks, placing Trey's share in a box she'd labeled "TREY'S KITCHEN STUFF." Japhy eyed what she was doing, donned the most feral expression she'd ever seen on his kind face, commandeered his dad's pots and pans, sat down amongst them, and started banging the hell out of them with wooden kitchen spoons, shouting, "*Extinction! Extinction! Extinction!*"

Lorilee knelt beside him. "We'll get through this, Japh. Things are going to be different, but all three of us are gonna be okay."

Japhy glared at her, then resumed the banging but at least left out the shouts.

Trey, meanwhile, had stepped at Lore's request into the thirty-square-foot space they'd called "the living room," turned to their modest bookshelf, and begun separating his books from hers by dropping his in a box she'd labeled "TREY'S BOOKS." She'd given him this task because his love of cooking could have made the division of kitchenware contentious. Sorting a library with a nonreader was simple: if the book wasn't about climbing, it was hers.

As Japhy's banging began to give her a headache, Lorilee turned to see if Trey too was in pain—and was surprised to see him smiling happily. At a book. She then noticed, as the book left his hand and dropped into his box, that he'd been smiling at *her* autographed copy of *Axe Handles*. She gasped. She'd been less shocked by his admission of infidelity.

She strolled over and, straining to sound casual, said, "I'd, uh, like to keep that one."

Trey gaped at her in what appeared to be genuine amazement. "You wanna keep *Axe Handles*? Are you kidding, Lore? I drove four hundred miles to fetch this book!"

Her mouth moved, but no words would come out.

Trey chuckled at her "mistake." "Jeez, Lore. Don't you *remember*? Which of us was shut outside Base Camp Books by fire marshal bullshit, then waited in line *forever* for Snyder's George Hancock? Which of us hung out with Maori contour map dude, woman with deer-antler dreads, and the Stoner Jesus bros, then *finally* got in and asked Snyder to write 'The mountains are my mind'? Which of us then risked his life *hundreds* of times to *make* mountains his mind? Your hero's my hero too, Lore. Thanks for picking good heroes. But he signed this for *me*, remember? Take every other book in the house, I don't care. But"—Trey picked *Axe Handles* up, held it to his chest, and patted it for emphasis—"*this* puppy is *mine!*"

Just that fast his blue-eyed gaze became poison. His amazing body and bronzed skin: poison. His energy, strength, presence, and her long trust of all that: poison. The same red rage that cost her Buddha an earlobe boiled up and this time it was volcanic. Lore was about to erupt—when she noticed Japhy had quit drumming and was watching her closely. Japhy, her magic Zendo and music mate. Japhy, whom she had told of "no rising and falling," and "calmness," and *śūnyatā*'s sweet emptiness. Japhy, who knew exactly how often Lore had read *Axe Handles* and how often Trey had. She could enlist Japhy as an ally to reclaim her book—by mangling his call to meditation and music in the year of its birth, shaming his father, and tearing his five-year-old psyche in half.

Into her mind flew a half-remembered aphorism of the Buddha's from . . . a sutra? A calendar at the health food store? She couldn't remember the source, but the gist was this: "The anger you feel toward another, and swallow in silence, is the greatest meal you will ever eat."

The instant this truth rose up, her love for the Buddha demanded her obedience. Yet to suppress so much rage felt potentially cancerous. Turning to her Buddha icon for help, she saw him as an imperturbable dwarf she wanted to limp over and kick some more till she knocked that damned *smile* off his face. *Because please, Buddha, listen!* she wanted to plead. *Trey drove those four hundred miles for* me! *And the love he poured out the next night was for me. And it opened me completely. This sweet boy, peering at us right now, was born of that love, and I've made countless sacrifices to preserve that love. By claiming* Axe Handles *as his, Trey turns the most beautiful thing he ever did for me into* fmog *and* fmush. *How can you say this is the best meal I'll eat? How can you ask me to swallow 'this puppy is mine' and 'Snyder's George Hancock'? Must I really and truly eat my betrayer's pig-ignorant, selfish shit?*

Her rage was so torrid she began to pant. She wanted to shout at her ex-to-be that she'd read every book Snyder wrote at least twice, and *Axe Handles* an easy twenty times, and why? Because its poems were about families *making love, making home, making culture,* and on the thousand and one nights Trey had left her and Japhy alone she'd needed to *feel* that familial beauty even if the family was not hers. She wanted to tell this box-of-rocks-for-brains that his freedoms had come of *her* confinement to a hospital basement where, without mercy, she'd had to bill the futilely oncologized, the surgeon-maimed, the inconsolable survivors of the physically ruined or deceased, while he skittered up Mount This and Mount

That and fucked Miss Tit and Miss Tat, then returned home and called these betrayals *his mind*! She wanted to shout, *Without looking, describe* Axe Handle*'s cover,* watch Trey stand clueless, then fill him with shame by describing, without looking, the orange-nippled goddess sitting cross-leggèd on a green tussock, playing her flute in falling snow, the snowflakes blue against her nakedness but white against the gray sky. *Name* one poem title *from this book that means so much to you!* she wanted to scream. *One* line *even! Recite "Changing Diapers," Trey. That'd be a miracle, since I changed and washed every one of them, so only I saw "How intelligent he looks! / on his back / both feet caught in my one hand / his glance set sideways, / on a giant poster of Geronimo / with a Sharp's repeating rifle by his knee." Recite "Breasts." Tell us how, like philosophers, they "hold back the bitter in mind / to let the more tasty / wisdom slip through / for the little ones / who can't take the poison so young," while you poisoned our young one with betrayal after betrayal. Who served as the* breasts *in this family, and who the* adolescent ass-chaser? *Who gave up her friends, music, life, so you could climb? You* hurt *me, Trey! You* hurt *me, you hurt* me! *And now you ask me to pretend the most loving gift you ever managed to give me was a gift to* yourself?

But even as all of this boiled inside her, Lore looked from her son's wide eyes, to the book in Trey's hand, to her infuriatingly serene Buddha, and somehow managed to say not a word. She had become the poem she loved. She had become "Breasts," filtering poisons to protect Japhy, and Trey too. The effort required was so total that she did finally speak a few lines from the book Trey kept clutching. But not to shame him. She only spoke to summon, from a beloved poem, the strength to remain standing.

"The chill of the air on my nakedness / Starts off the skin. / I am all alive to the night. / Bare foot shaping on gravel / Stick in the hand, forever," she recited, voice trembling as Trey looked from her face to the book in his hand with the expression of a man being cursed by black magic, as Japhy sat, cross-leggèd and calm now, watching them both, his eyes pure pupil.

"Long streak of cloud giving way / To a milky thin light / Back of black pine bough, / The moon still full, / Hillsides of Pine trees all / Whispering; crickets still cricketing / Faint in cold coves in the dark," she recited, her voice cold-cricket faint. "I turn and walk slow / Back the path to the beds / With goose bumps and loose waving hair / In the night of milk-moonlit thin cloud glow / And black rustling pines / I feel like a dandelion head / Gone to seed / About to be blown away."

Trey's expression was that of a scared child caught out in a lie.

Japhy sat tranquil.

Silent as dandelion fluff, a marriage blew away.

The broken-eared Buddha kept smiling.

Pickles

LORILEE SOON MET, and was relieved to like, Trey's of-course-much-younger girlfriend. Liz Holt turned out to be a hardheaded, practical-minded grad student in forestry at University of Colorado, Boulder. After Trey wowed her with the story of the noble old tree-planter at the Snyder reading years before, Liz decided he was a fixer-upper. She was understandably skittish the first time she and Lore crossed paths, because she knew Trey was married when their "climbing lines" had intersected. But she was easy and friendly with Japhy and, at least for now, having some success fixing her fixer-upper. With Liz's help Trey had filed for bankruptcy, trashing his credit but escaping enough debt that, to Lorilee's amazement, he'd made six straight child support payments. He'd also begun calling Japhy "Japh," since Liz punched his shoulder brutally when he called the boy "Three." Liz also helped make sure that, every other weekend, Trey quit climbing and, for two days and a night, became what he himself called "Japh's reliably available unreliable dad."

ONE MORNING A few months after the breakup, Lorilee was prepping for zazen with a little Buddhist history when she came upon a Zen master, Butsugen, telling his monks, "Do not try to be masters of yourselves in any kind of hasty manner." The words struck a deep but dissonant chord. Her restraint toward Trey for the past year, she realized, had been little short of masterful. Butsugen left her doubting whether such great restraint was admirable.

A few days later Lore delivered Japhy to Trey's apartment for his biweekly visit. She smiled ruefully at the way Japhy shot from the car the instant she pulled up to Trey's curb, raced to his father, and flew with perfect trust up into Trey's mighty arms, as Lore herself had done the night Japh was conceived. In a harrowing but apparently familiar routine, Trey spun the boy up over his head like a cheerleader spinning a baton, returned him to Earth, and they tornadoed through the apartment, out the patio door, onto the lawn by the fetid swimming pool, where Trey did a brilliant job of appearing to be helplessly tossed every which way by his scrawny lad.

As Lore carried Japhy's overnight stuff into Trey's apartment she recalled Trey mentioning by phone that Liz was in Boulder for a month of grad work. Finding herself alone in Trey's digs for the first time, Lore tried not to be critical, but was saddened to see what his living room became without the woman in his life. The TV, his other great addiction, was left permanently on. The furniture and end tables were cluttered with partially eaten takeout, ski and mountaineering mags, discarded clothes, climbing videos, and every object and surface in the room was dulled by the pall of grubbiness TV addicts can't see in the cathode glow.

As Lore reached down to snap off the set, she stopped herself. Their son had two parents. The programming and grime in this household were for Japh to see and sort for himself. The objects she could not leave to fate were the two books she'd brought last visit. Lore read Japhy to sleep nightly. Liz Holt did the same, Japhy said. But Trey did not. Lore wanted the books available should the TV fail to scintillate, but *The Hobbit* was now crammed in a teetering stack of hotdog ski videos and *Treasure Island* had joined a swizzle of *Outside, Climb, Alpinist,* and *Playboy* magazines in a galvanized tub meant for firewood. Lore stood Tolkien on end on top of the TV, where even Trey would see it, then stepped over to the wood tub to rescue Long John Silver—when a familiar shade of orange down under the wood chips caught her eye. Brushing the chips aside, she was stunned to see the orange nipples tipping the stylized white breasts of the woman flute player on *Axe Handles'* cover, serene in the falling snow despite all the debris.

Lore felt no such serenity. To find her treasured book buried in a wood bin heated her up fast. Reaching deep for the fortitude to swallow her anger, as Buddha recommends, she remembered Butsugen and realized she was in the act of "mastering herself in a hasty manner." Glancing outside, she saw Japhy whooping it up on a buckin' Trey bronco so real to him that he was kicking his dad's ribs with imaginary spurs and using his hair for reins. Obeying an impulse that had nothing to do with mastering herself, Lore slid *Axe Handles* down the back of her pants and pulled out her shirttail to better conceal it. She then strolled outside, where she hugged Japhy goodbye—and gave Trey a peck on the cheek too, to honor the Oedipal beating he was so cheerfully enduring.

Not till she was walking away did she realize with a swoon of sadness why she'd felt sure she would get away with her theft: her ass had become one of the last things on Earth Trey had any interest in pondering.

WHEN SHE GOT the book home, she set out to relearn a few favorite poems by heart. But *Axe Handles* turned out to be haunted. Its ghosts were a former Trey, her former self, and a love so dead she could understand why Trey had tossed the book in his wood tub. The opening folk song especially, "shape a handle, shape a handle," slammed her with visions of the night they'd left a feast charring to kiss veins that pulse, siphon skin where it peaks, swoon on vertical mind-planes, and conceive a son. The thrill of stealing back her anniversary gift was ephemeral, the melancholy the poems now induced nonstop. So the next time she drove north to Denver she visited the Tattered Cover Book Store, marched up to the Used Books clerk, placed *Axe Handles* before him, and said, "First edition. Signed by the poet. What's it worth?"

The very young clerk had intelligent mascara-lined eyes, skin as white as laser paper, definitionless white arms, pink highlights in his shoe-polish-black hair, and a matching pink T-shirt with a Tattered Cover ID tag that read:

PICKLES
MAY I HELP YOU?

Having watched Trey's muscles ripple for years, Lorilee found the lad adorably refreshing. But when Pickles began flicking through the book to assess its condition, grief welled up so hard she nearly bolted. Mercifully, he was quick. In a surprisingly deep, competent voice, he said, "Hard used. But Snyder's still big, North Point books last, and the inscription's kinda cool. I can give you four bucks cash, or eight in trade."

Lorilee opened the cover and looked for the last time at the inscription:

The mountains are your mind.
! !
—Gary Snyder

She allowed the words to conjure a salmon-egg-colored sun on an evening horizon and herself at age twenty, naked atop Two Medicine beside the astonished and astonishing Trey.

She let the salmon egg set.

She turned to Pickles.

She said, "I'll take the cash."

Third Telling:

The Hard Labor and Unlikely Birth of Dumpster Catholicism

In a murderous time
the heart breaks and breaks
and lives by breaking.
>   —Stanley Kunitz, "The Testing-Tree"

Crush your heart. Be broken.
>   —Shaikh Abu-Said Abil-Kheir

This prayer is surely a mother.
>   —Saint Catherine of Siena

(mostly Portland, 1974 to 1990)

I. How TJ Got Rich

I was digging for gold through the rubble
of a Catholic church
I found a wine bottle and a cardboard box
that I had to search
— Sean Rowe, "The Walker"

IN THE YEAR 1990, one of the world's least-known faiths was born in
the city of Portland, Oregon. Not surprisingly, a Joseph, Mary, and Jesus
were again involved. Quite surprisingly, this Joseph, Mary, and Jesus are
3.2, 2.9, and 0.7 centimeters tall, and the donkey upon which Mary and
Jesus sometimes ride stands 2.4 centimeters at the shoulders. The new faith
collects no tithes or offerings, seeks no converts, and owns no cathedrals,
churches, shrines, abbeys, or real estate of any kind. Its Rome is pedestrian
Portland. Its St. Peter's is the ordinary sidewalks and walking paths of that
city. Its founder is, in his own words, "a permanently munched pissant" by
the name of Jervis McGraff, twin brother of Risa's friend TJ. The name of
the new faith: Dumpster Catholicism.

In 1989, Jervis nearly died due to a terrible event I will come to. In a
strictly metabolic sense he *did* die, then came back. When he commenced
a long, only partial recovery, his favorite form of therapy became walking
those ordinary sidewalks and park paths of Portland. He has continued to
walk them, day and night, for decades and counting. He also enjoys conversing, on his walks, with a huge array of human and other life-forms, some
of them less than visible. As a result, thousands of Portlanders have walked
with Jervis, blithely discussing a panoply of topics. Dumpster Catholicism
is the most famous of these topics. The first time I interviewed Jervis about
his ever-more-popular street faith, in one fell paragraph delivered in the
papery whisper that throat injuries bequeathed him for life, he said,

"*The fuck.* All it is, is I've always loved history, but the only kind of
historian I've ever been is a contrarian. I don't like it that the people who
win all the wars write all the history, encouraging more wars. So when
TJ's and my parents got killed and Holy Mother Church adopted us, I
looked into our adoptive Mother not by reading what her own priests and
historians said but by poking around in the Church dumpster filled with

everything and everyone Mother Church tossed out. With no armies of pious Catholic scholars organizing it, that material is as fragmented and chaotic as a jillion-piece jigsaw puzzle. But I like jigsaw puzzles about the faiths, tribes, men, women, and truths the Church has chopped into puzzle pieces, condemned, and thrown away. The more I poked through the dumpster the more I felt our world itself is a puzzle that can't be solved, in part because Mother Church has caused so many precious parts to go missing. Then I got dumpstered myself, and munched so bad I started walking the Portland streets because that's about all I could do. I walk now for a living, you could say, talking to people, or to dogs and birds, or to angels and other entities, or plants—plants are great listeners. And one day, maybe six months into the walkathon my life has become, Dumpster Catholicism started falling out of me. Nothing revelatory about it, really. I just thought, *The fuck. The things the Church has tossed out would make for the coolest spiritual yard sale the Earth has ever seen!* So I started conducting that sale, chatting to people I walked with about how the world puzzle felt more bearable, if not exactly solvable, when I started plugging in some of the beautiful missing puzzle pieces the Church has persecuted, sexually slimed, smothered in pious deceit, murdered, and dumpstered. It's a thrill and a shock to the people I tell about the great truths, heroically kind humans, huge swaths of the living world, huge numbers of tribes who loved and tended that world, that Mother Church has dumpstered. Some people fly into rages. Others start crying, right there on the street. Others, if they've been persecuted for similar reasons, feel vindicated, even joyful. And more than a few who consider themselves Good Catholics of course tell me to fuck off. Fine by me. I'm not trying to sell anything. Like anybody running a yard sale, I just like offering folks some of the amazing things Good Catholics threw out but I came along and scavenged. So many hundreds of native tribes! Millions of women convicted for the crime of being women! Many of the Catholics' own greatest saints! And the dumpstering is still happening. Wise Father Willigis Jäger silenced by a clique of geezers in red beanies for the 'sin' of being as Buddhist as he is Catholic. American nuns denounced for refusing to bash the gays and poor people they serve. *The fuck.* The word 'catholic' means universal, but given a choice between what Catholicism's bureaucrat caretakers have kept and what they've thrown out, it's no contest. The dumpster is *way* more universal! Which is why so many people have started saying, 'You know what, Jervis? You converted me! Dumpster Catholicism is my faith now too!' I did *not* convert you, I tell 'em. There's nothing to convert *to.* Dumpster Catholicism is just the gigantic old dumpster out behind Mother Church. 'No it isn't!' they say. 'It's the faiths and loves of every Church-violated or scorned or robbed or raped or betrayed or erased person and truth and tribe buried in that dumpster. And what great loves and truths they are! Thanks for showing 'em to us!' Feel what you feel, I tell 'em, but *the fuck!* Don't run around declaring it, okay? You'll just replace bossy Roman Catholic Mom with bossy Dumpster Catholic Stepmom. If we've got anything good or real going it'll only stay real and good if we keep it dirt-poor, cheap as any other good yard sale, and quiet as an alley rat. Okay?"

But as the years passed and people continued to enjoy Jervis's dumpster ramblings, more and more of them declared themselves "Dumpster Catholic converts." And since there is no priesthood or pope in charge of this faith, no canon to study, no vows to swear, and nothing material to be gained or lost by claiming to be a convert, Jervis is helpless to veto their declarations of faith. Thus has a churchless, priestless, popeless, moneyless street religion its founder vehemently claims not to have founded, continued to expand.

For a while Jervis clung to the hope that Dumpster Catholicism would stay confined to the Northwest quadrant of Portland, since that's where he does his walking and talking. But a faith whose time has come is as portable as the hearts it comes to inhabit. Converts soon carried Dumpster Catholicism to cities, towns, and rural outposts all over the Pacific Northwest, south into California and the desert Southwest, onto the internet cloud, and round the globe via ordinary travel till Dumpster Catholics were proclaiming the faith from locales as unlikely as the Hebrides, Bhutan, Kenya, Patagonia, from a surprising number of Catholic monasteries and nunneries, and, via the East-aimed pioneering of Jervis's friend Risa, from the cafes and drift boats and horsebacks and cowboy bars of the Elkmoon Valley of Montana.

"*The fuck!*" Jervis mutters each time he catches wind of these expansions.

JERVIS AND TJ McGRAFF are fraternal twins. They were born in Baltimore in 1958—the same year Jamey was born in Portland. TJ was the elder by nine minutes, and to this day mentions his greater experience to Jervis as often as possible.

The first thing that strikes many who meet the McGraff twins is how unalike twins can be. Both brothers are small in stature but large in presence. Both have balding pates, high intelligence quotients, high energy levels, and shockingly little need for sleep. Both strike people as genderless, as I've described. But that's about as far as their similarities go.

TJ is dark complected, dark-haired where he is haired at all, and his compact face has a constantly solemn look. He is quick to smile but looks like it hurts him when he does. He is introverted but not shy, methodical in his thought processes, extremely organized in his undertakings, and exceedingly responsible. He is also not just well-groomed but a bit of a dandy, with an admittedly unjustifiable fondness for high-end Italian fashion designers and shoemakers.

Jervis, on an extreme other hand, is blond and fair, with a battle-scarred face faintly reminiscent of a pale Mahatma Gandhi, complete with the wire-rims. He is naturally tonsured like TJ, but Jervis's diminished hair is so long it floats out behind his head in a train as he walks. His couture is a cautionary ad against thrift-store bargains. His speech is peppered with commonplace profanities even when he's speaking eloquently about spiritual verities and mystical experiences. He is gregarious by nature, utterly improvisational in word and deed, entirely comfortable among the street people he calls "my fellow pissants," and he doesn't care a whit whether his life strikes anyone but the divine Mystery as responsible. He strikes most of the people he meets as benignly zany, yet many of those same people tell of encounters in which Jervis focused in on them, pierced their every subterfuge, and offered uncannily wise assistance, zany as his methods may have been. He is also, so far as I can tell, the only completely fearless person I have ever known.

The twins' father, Alasdair McGraff, was a successful Baltimore tire merchant, but his inordinate pride in hailing from an auld Scottish clan was evidenced by the names he gave his sons: Tavish Jacobus and Jervis Muireadhach McGraff. (Oy vey!) Alasdair and Marie, the boys' mother, were devout Roman Catholics proud of the fact that Clan McGraff had defied the English ban on Catholicism in Scotland for four and a half centuries and counting. In accord with McGraff Clan tradition, TJ and Jervis attended parochial schools and never missed a Sunday mass.

In the summer of 1974, the elder McGraffs took off on a two-week pilgrimage to their beloved Highlands, exiling Jervis and TJ to a boys' camp where their twin claim to fame was spectacular ineptitude at ball sports. One fine summer's morn in Scotland, meanwhile, despite his impeccable Highland DNA, Alasdair committed the hackneyed American tourist mistake of forgetting himself and briefly driving on the wrong side of the road. Speeding over a blind hillock, he collided head-on with a petrol lorry, which exploded. The McGraff parents were so thoroughly immolated there were no remains to send home. They were thirty-nine years old. They'd left no will and no stated wishes regarding TJ and Jervis. The boys were left without a guardian, trustee, or relative close enough to take them in.

Alasdair had owned Squire's Tires, a chain of fourteen Baltimore/Washington, DC, area stores. Marie had been a successful real estate broker. The franchise, family home, and a vacation home in Maine were put on the market and sold. The fortune went into probate. On the advice of Alisdair and Marie's priest, the boys left Maryland behind. Flying to California, they enrolled at Chaparral Academy of the Sacred Heart, a Jesuit boarding school outside Redding. There, later scandals notwithstanding, the brothers were taken under the wing of some superb Jesuit teachers and were able to grieve and study well enough to finish high school on schedule in 1976. TJ, despite his sorrows, was class valedictorian. Jervis, despite his, was class clown.

The following autumn the estate emerged from probate and Jervis and TJ—now college freshmen at University of Portland and Georgetown U, respectively—found themselves in a bizarre circumstance: even after the estate was ravaged by assessments, attorneys' fees, and inheritance taxes, the brothers had no choice, at the age of not quite nineteen, but to inherit 1.4 million dollars apiece in a one-time lump sum. No limitations. No advisors. To come into that kind of money at that age strikes me as akin to being handed the keys to a high-powered Italian sports car possessed of no brakes. It strains credibility, therefore, to report that the twins' inheritance inspired no notable follies or disasters whatever. Grief dominated TJ's feelings about his sudden wealth. Alasdair and Marie had been penny-pinching workaholics. Their deaths left TJ feeling that, had they lived, his inheritance would have been placed in a trust to which he would have had no access for years. Out of love for his parents, he behaved as if such a trust were in place. Squirreling his small fortune away, he focused on his schooling and gave the money no thought.

Jervis took a more colorful tack. When his ship came in, he attempted a brief playboy phase, but a few weeks of all-night parties with crowds of "party people" sent him flying in the opposite direction. Quitting school for a semester, Jervis took a trip that was anything but a playboy vacation. His mother's favorite saint had been Francis of Assisi. Jervis set out for Italy to honor the same saint. Once in Assisi, however, he was repelled by the swarms of tourists, ostentatious cathedrals celebrating Francis's poverty, and booming Francis-trinket business, so he purchased a World War II vintage canvas Italian Army backpack, set out on foot, and spent three months wandering the hills of Umbria, fasting, and praying in caves and countryside associated with Francis.

At the end of Jervis's trip, when TJ picked his brother up at Dulles Airport outside DC, he found himself embracing an emaciated, sun-baked, joyous ascetic who'd had an experience of which he could not speak, for weeks, without bursting into tears. Through his tears Jervis babbled enough for TJ to deduce that in a cave associated with Francis, an apparently visionary experience involving not Francis but his consort, Clare, had swept down upon him and, to quote Jervis's babbling, "blew the lid off everything I ever thought I knew."

As an aspiring Jesuit scholar with a high regard for Thomist precision, this description didn't cut it for TJ. He pressed for detail. The fuse that lit Jervis's mystical detonation, it turned out, was a famous dream/vision of Clare's, which she described in detail to a spiritual sister. I'll quote and paraphrase part of the sister's transcription:

In her vision, Clare beheld Francis, and when she went to him, the saint "uncovered his breast and said to the virgin Clare, 'Come, take, and suck.'" Clare did so, and "what she was sucking was so sweet and delightful that she had no way to describe it." Afterward, "the nipple or mouth of the breast from which the milk came remained in blessed Clare's lips." Clare then took this nipple into her hands and it took on the properties of "a speculum or mirror" that caused everything in it "to shine with bright perfection." What Jervis experienced in the cave, TJ guessed by his tearful babbling, was this selfsame perfection-creating mirror, but Jervis wouldn't speak of his experience except to quote Clare:

> Place your mind in the mirror of eternity. Place your soul in the splendor of glory. Place your heart in the figure of divine substance, and transform yourself totally through contemplation into the image of his divinity, that you may feel what friends feel in tasting the hidden sweetness that God himself has reserved from the beginning for each of us who love him.

As a non-Christian, I find this lexicon foreign. But in these dramatic gender reversals—the virgin Clare nursing at the breast of Francis; Jervis broken open by a male saint's nipple become a "mirror of eternity"—I'm struck to recall that TJ, on the day he befriended Risa, quoted Augustine ("I made myself a Mother of whom to be born") and said he was her "mother-brother," not just her brother. Many who meet the McGraff twins agree that there is something "both-gendered" about them. Not transgendered, not gay. Their androgyny feels more a spiritual than sexual mystery to those close to them. *Is there a way of being beyond gender?*

Be that as it may, Jervis's Umbrian experience left him burning to emulate Clare and Francis in regard to his wealth—by dispensing of it. Before doing so, he had the courtesy to inform TJ. In one of the many letters that shot back and forth between the universities of Portland and Georgetown during their college years, Jervis wrote,

> By what secret lottery is a lad like the rich, young Francesco di Pietro di Bernardone moved to strip naked in front of his bishop and neighbors and throw everything into Love's fire? There was, let the record show, no democracy in his throwing off of clothes. A majority of those present felt they served Love just fine by tossing a few lire into Church coffers each Sunday. There was no modesty in Francis's act either. The crowd beheld every dangling participle of the lad who felt more inappropriate clothed before his invisible Beloved. By the world's standards, then, Francis's conversion to Love's path was no more modest than a stripper's. So it wasn't Democracy, Modesty, or the World's Standards that caused his stripping to strike joy in the heart of the poor girl Clare or, seven hundred years later, the rich boy, me. I'm writing to warn you, Teej: I aim to keep this joy burning by doing some stripping of my own. You're stronger than me. The money we inherited will turn me into a vapid boob if I don't get poor and naked fast. I'll give it all to you if you want. But if you don't want it, fair warning: my Clare-crazy plans for the future do not include wealth.

When TJ wrote back to tell Jervis he didn't want his money, Jervis, at age twenty, bequeathed $380K to Cesar Chavez's United Farm Workers and $380K to Larry and Girija Brilliant's Seva Foundation, then set aside the modest balance to pay off his college debt when he was through.

An odd way to begin my account of how TJ got rich. But that's how it went.

A FUNNY STORY about TJ: when Jervis returned from Italy in a Clare-induced euphoria, TJ too scheduled a flight to Italy, thinking he'd roam Umbria, fasting and praying in caves vibrating with the sublime energies of saints, and so remain spiritually close to his brother. TJ rescheduled his classes, hopped on a plane, and got a jump on his purification process by fasting on the flight from DC to Rome and on the train ride north to Assisi. But as he was walking from the train station to his Assisi hotel in a hunger-weakened state, he experienced a metanoia quite different from the kind he was seeking. His life-changing experience occurred outside an exquisite little trattoria with sidewalk seating: at the very instant he was trudging past, a dignified old waiter happened to swing a loaded tray of food almost under TJ's nose as he delivered it to a couple. The tray, TJ will tell you to this day, held two little Deruta ware plates in which nested a few large handmade tortellini slaked in butter and fresh sage, beside a pair of perfectly ripe, perfectly sliced tomatoes, a small dish of seasoned olive oil, and two somehow radiant glasses of Chianti. As the waiter delivered this simple meal with an understated precision reminiscent of TJ's own body language, the man and woman smiled blissfully at each other, at the food, then up at TJ—and destiny wrapped TJ in its embrace. He wheeled helplessly into the restaurant, ordered the same simple meal, entered a gastric *Paradiso*, and, to his ongoing shame and bliss, fell head over heels not for Francis and Clare but for Italian cuisine.

MY ACCOUNT WILL begin with its least believable fact: TJ is wealthy today, in large part, because his financial advisor is not a financial advisor: it's his brother, Jervis. That TJ has long solicited and acted upon the investment advice of a voluntarily impoverished street mystic is, of course, madness from a business school perspective. Mention this madness to TJ, however, and he'll calmly tell you how the US based its financial philosophy for half a century upon Federal Reserve chairman Alan Greenspan's and innumerable other US financiers' youthful boners for the fantasy novels of the lurid Russian prophetess of "the virtue of selfishness" Ayn Rand and the Nobel Prize–winning crimes against humanity of the Winner-Blows-Off-Everyone-But-Himself economist Milton Friedman. "I admit that financial advice based not on greed posturing as a virtue but on a Saints Francis and Clare–imitating surrender of self through divine love makes Jervis look pretty eccentric," TJ admits. "But do the math. My brother's financial guidance has proven trillions of dollars more fiscally responsible than the bankruptocracies of Friedman and Rand."

Jervis's economic theories are hard to describe for the same reason it's hard to describe Mahatma Gandhi's golf swing: he has none. His guidance is based on a sense of soul, not a system of thought. The result, for TJ, has been continual self-surrender enacted via the intuitive flashes, moments of guilty conscience, and shocking divestments and reinvestments that have formed the trajectory of his financial success. Simultaneous to TJ's success, the brothers endured extreme challenges in their personal lives. To get both their financial and personal stories told I'll have to double back on the timeline. But all will become clear.

COMPONENT BY UNLIKELY component, here is how TJ McGraff got rich:

TJ was a brilliant student, already destined for a full ride to a first-rate university when his parents were killed. That loss didn't change his college plans but did send him spiraling so deep down into his faith life that, before his senior year of high school even ended, he declared he was going to become a Jesuit priest.

After being orphaned, TJ gravitated toward the monastic view that earthly life, as Saint Teresa of Ávila once put it, "is like a night at a bad hotel," and that the most reliable escape from our wretched accommodations is to undertake an inner journey to an invincible sanctuary the same saint dubbed "the Interior Castle." Throughout his teens and early twenties TJ worked at just this—with the notable exception of his seduction by Italian cuisine and clothes. A daily feature of his hunkered down, celibate, cerebral, and religious life was filched from the yet-unmet Risa's Vedic tradition: TJ spent a portion of each day reviewing the hoaxes, snares, and delusions that had streamed past him, whispering in response to each event, "Not this, not that." (Sanskrit: *Neti, neti.*)

Jervis, during the same years, was an effervescent cross between a street monk and a bon vivant who wondered what could possibly be better than "a night at a bad hotel." In his view, crappy accommodations brought contact with intriguingly messed-up characters, increasing his odds of being able to help fellow guests with messed-up needs. And none of this "*Neti, neti*" stuff for Jervis. Fueled by the Eckhartian adage, "If the only prayer we ever say is *thanks*, it will suffice," he became a hyperactive gratitude altruist who greeted the highs of each day with a spontaneous "How incredible is this?" and the lows with an equally enthused "*YEEEOWCH!* But wow! Thanks for *that* too."

When their parents' estate came out of probate, TJ gave his inheritance the *Neti, neti* treatment. He was a frosh at Georgetown University living on a scholarship so generous he had no need for additional money, so he presented a biblical tithe of his instant fortune—$140,000—to Mother Teresa's Missionaries of Charity, turned the $1,260,000 balance over to a Washington, DC, broker, and approved the broker's proposal to invest the money in what he called "diversified blue chips."

TJ did not approve this proposal because he knew anything about such stocks. He approved it because the broker called blue-chip stocks "safe, time-tried investments that take care of themselves, leaving you free to pursue your education and Jesuit formation without distraction or ethical concerns." That this sounded true to TJ shows how ignorant he was about blue chips and how cagey the DC broker was at roping in abstracted young Catholic idealists. When TJ's stock reports began arriving in his university mailbox, he found them so voluminous and dull that he stacked them unread behind the increasingly extensive selection of Italian clothes in his walk-in closet, hiding his least-favorite source of shame behind his favorite.

Graduating from Georgetown in 1981, TJ chose to pursue his path to priesthood at a Jesuit novitiate in Portland, Oregon. His reason for choosing Portland? His entire family—namely Jervis—was attending the University of Portland. Jervis was still a senior, having fallen a year behind TJ thanks to his Umbrian pilgrimage, and to the volunteer work he'd been doing at halfway houses, soup kitchens, and on the streets of Portland.

As TJ was packing to leave Georgetown, he opened his closet, started removing his clothes from the rod—and was stunned to discover the solid wall of stock reports that had built up behind his clothes. To throw them out would fill several garbage cans too heavy to carry alone. As an aspiring Jesuit headed toward a vow of poverty, TJ was ashamed to dump bald evidence of his wealth in a landfill, so he boxed the reports up, labelled the boxes "BOOKS," and started hand-trucking them to his rented U-Haul to drop off at a recycling center. As he worked at this, several students admiringly told him he must have amassed the biggest private library of any scholar in Georgetown's history. The false impression so shamed TJ that he decided to treat the stock reports as if they *were* part of his library, and lug them all the way to Portland.

Jervis was a history major at U of P, but in four years' worth of letters to TJ he had never described a single class. His letters grew distressingly informative, however, when he spoke of his private scholarly pursuits. His love for Saint Clare and the mystery he'd tapped into in Umbria had blossomed into love for Clare's spiritual heiresses as well. This is how TJ first came to hear the word "Beguine."

The Beguines, according to Jervis's missives, were "a stunningly self-giving movement of feminist mystics" who thrived in the thirteenth and fourteenth centuries in present-day Germany, France, Holland, and Belgium, but Jervis also gave the impression the Beguines were alive and thriving in Portland just down the street from his dorm. As a non-Catholic and non-Christian whose topic in this chapter is money, I'm going to spare the reader the volume and vehemence of Jervis's outpourings in praise of the Beguines, but here is a summary occasionally citing his college letters, which TJ admired enough to save.

When the Beguine movement first started, women were defined by Church doctrine as manqués, which means "malformed men." Properly formed men were even held to be the sole progenitors of children: their manqué wives merely "incubated" their offspring for them. Women were further defined by the Church Fathers as incapable of theological thought and forbidden to study Latin. Thus, since *all* Church doctrine was taught in Latin at all-male schools, women couldn't touch the theology that held them captive. As for economics, all medieval Europe was Christian, all property was owned by the male aristocracy or by the Church, and the bulk of an aristocrat's wealth was passed on to the Church, not the widow, if the deceased patriarch had no male heirs.

How did the Beguines break free of this trap? It started with small gifts from a few aristocratic widows to a first few would-be Beguines. Inspired by a Clare- and Francis-like poverty, the Beguines made maximum use of these gifts, establishing simple, self-sufficient residences they called "beguinages." The women who entered beguinages were not nuns. They represented a whole new take on a life of faith. Beguines were chaste but took no formal vow of chastity, and if they later chose to leave the beguinage to marry they were free to do so. Their communities were self-sufficient from day one, voluntarily poor from day one, free of Church support and Church supervision from day one, and committed to caring for the marginalized, poor, sick, injured, orphaned, and dying from day one.

Beautiful ironies were set in motion. Because the Beguines were self-sufficient they didn't sponge off the populace the way the priesthood did. Because they weren't cloistered, they were widely seen by, known by, and free to share their sense of spiritual wonder with ordinary folk. Because they were forbidden to study theology or assume priestly powers they had nothing to say about the God of threats and punishments and didn't "police" those they served. They just counseled, regaled, educated, fed, healed, and offered safe haven to them, and as a result were loved by the masses almost everywhere beguinages sprang up.

At the time Jervis was assailing his brother with his adoration of the Beguines, TJ was being mainstreamed into the Jesuits by studying the canonical likes of Aristotle, Paul aka Saul of Tarsus, Thomas Aquinas, Ignatius of Loyola—the very lineage Jervis had fled. Precisely here is where TJ's deep love for his brother began to show. He didn't challenge Jervis's outpourings. He just read them, then wrote, "This is all new to me, and it fascinates me. Please tell me more."

Jervis did. The Beguine movement caught fire. Hundreds of beguinages sprang up, thousands of women began falling in love with "Someone, with a countenance, flowing through everything," and since beguinages cost the Church nothing, Rome let them grow unchecked for a time. By 1320 Beguine women represented 15 percent of the adult female population of Cologne. Some beguinages housed thousands of women. In Strasbourg and Basel an estimated one human being in forty was a Beguine. The Beguines rapidly became the largest, most influential women's movement in Europe up until the suffragettes, living radically compassionate, dignified, self-determined lives in spite of a Vatican-enforced caste system as stacked against women as corporate power is stacked against democracy, culture, and the living world today. Dante, upon reading the Beguine Mechthild of Magdeburg, was at last able to give birth to his *Paradiso,* and said he never could have conceived of it without her. Then along came the spiritual genius Meister Eckhart, who saw Beguine mysticism as the pinnacle of Church teachings, nurtured their communities, and set about mainstreaming their Way in his great sermons and other theological works. The Beguines spread like no other contemplative movement in Church history. Why would a woman choose to be a nun in a convent, or the manqué incubator of an over-weening man, when she could, in Christic poverty, move into a beguinage, supporting herself and serving others in a non-cloistered community of master gardeners, musicians, seamstresses, craftswomen, healers, mystical adepts, poets, and true spiritual companions?

Addressing TJ in the somewhat scholarly prose he briefly deployed as a college student but soon jettisoned in favor of street English, Jervis wrote:

So why haven't we heard of this flowering of spiritual audacity that rejuvenated medieval women and Church monastic life? I'm sure you can guess. Our Vatican guardians found the Beguines' freedom intolerable, their ecstasies demonic, their selfless service an embarrassing contrast to the priests' greed for tithes and offerings and spoils of war, their protection of one another from rape and prostitution out of keeping with Everyman's need, and their education of spiritually aware, free-thinking children detrimental to the Vatican preference for uneducated, tithe-paying, indulgence-purchasing flocks.

So in went the Inquisition. And what henchmen they hired! Robert le Bougre was a so-called reformed heretic whose time on the Dark Side gave him a magical ability to detect heretics by simply observing how they moved and spoke. And wouldn't you know it, *droves* of heretics moved and spoke exactly like defenseless female mystics. The Beguines weren't allowed to testify, reason, or plead. They were pre-condemned by being Beguines, then raped or tortured or executed or driven into hiding. The beguinages were ransacked. Their dependent children, poor, and sick were cast out. Their ecstatic art, literature, and music was destroyed. The Church war on these defenseless heroes lasted a hundred years. And have we recovered from Rome's purging of the human experience of divine Love, Teej? Or am I writing to you, seven centuries later, from a Catholic university that doesn't offer a single class on Beguine mystics or house even one of their books?

"O you flowing God in your love! O you burning God in your desire! O you resting God on my breasts!" I swear by my love for Hadewijch, Mechthild, and Eckhart that these beneficent women were kangaroo-tried and annihilated by our Church. And for what crime? Demonstrating that it's humanly and womanly possible to make vital contact, via love, with "Someone, with a countenance, flowing through everything." This is a problem, brother. When Mother Church destroyed the Beguines and condemned the Meister,

She wasn't policing some hippie-dippie band of gyrovagues and one renegade preacher. She was condemning the way Christ Himself is met, loved, and realized by the living soul!

What forbearance it must have taken for TJ, despite his deep immersion in his Jesuit studies, to write back, saying, "This is all new and very troubling to me, Jervis. I want to understand it as fully as possible. If you can find the time, *please*! Tell me more."

In one letter in particular, Jervis did. Another of his spiritual heroes was the thirteenth-century French Beguine Marguerite Porete. Of this woman he spoke with abject adoration, calling her "my dearest M," fully believing, as Beguine legend had it, that she had been "annihilated and deified by Divine Love." If this happened to be true, it was redundant of the Church to annihilate Porete a second time—by burning her at the stake.

The Church's stated reason for Porete's execution was a book of spiritual instruction, *The Mirror of Simple Souls Who Are Annihilated and Remain Only in Will and Desire of Love*. When TJ read Jervis's letter recounting Porete's martyrdom, he was stunned to see the paper warped and ink smeared, in places, because Jervis had wept on it. The climax of that letter:

> *The Mirror*, Teej! An entire book about the vision of Clare born of the breast of Francis! And its survival is a miracle. *The Mirror* was condemned and destroyed by the Church in 1310. Every possible copy burned, and often its owner with it. Though M said, truthfully, that she was not the book's author, she had taken down a divine dictation that still overwhelms with the integrity of its own telling. She paid for her love of the divine with her life. But a succession of unrepentant Beguines and Beguine sympathizers managed to pass the book down, generation after generation, *into the 1950s*. A copy of *The Mirror of Simple Souls* was discovered and Marguerite's inspired work was resurrected like a Christ 640 years after Mother Church believed they'd destroyed it.
>
> What exactly was her heresy? *The Mirror* dared to declare to women everywhere, "We shall be sons of God!" Little surprise that in 1309 the Inquisitors came for the author of this valiant spiritual rebellion against lethal misogyny. Marguerite explained to them that their condemnation of *The Mirror* was the work of "Holy Church the Little," which is governed by Reason and which she faithfully obeyed—with her Reason. But "Holy Church the Great" is governed by a Love, she said, which Reason can no more grasp "than someone can enclose the sea in his eye, or carry the world on the end of a reed, or illumine the sun with a lantern." The Inquisitors' attack on her was rather like a pile of firewood condemning a life-giving fire in winter for not being unburned wood. If they prevailed, who would ever be warmed

by Love's fire again? M had no choice but to defy them. You're out of your depth, she said, and will remain so until you surrender to Holy Church the Great and the Divine Love that rules it.

How vehemently her attackers then stayed locked inside Holy Church the Little! Their head Inquistor, William of Paris, put her on trial by announcing: "*You are vehemently suspected of the stain of heretical depravity.*" Renounce your claims or we'll put you to death, he said. But M had fallen not into sin or error but into what *The Mirror* calls "the total glory of the love of the soul as it is consumed by Divine Love." Unable and unwilling to deny this adored fire, she remained silent.

Her Inquisitors imprisoned her in a cold cell beneath Paris for a year and a half. She remained aflame even so. When they returned to "give her one last chance," the only chance given was to lie that the Love burning in her soul was nonexistent and the book Love had written via her hand constituted the heretical fantasies of a renegade manqué. Unwilling to lie, M remained silent. So Holy Church the Little, *our* church, brother, elected to protect us from the "error" that is Divine Love by burning M in a mundane Inquisition-lit fire.

Come with me to Paris, 1310, and see what this means. See our Church's clerics leading M through the streets as a gaggle of spectacle lovers gabble along after them. See M's stillness as she's bound to the stake. See the bishop tell her she can live if she will lie about "the total glory of the love of the soul" she's experiencing. See M remain silent "in the abyss of absolute poverty," as God's love wrote via her hand. And now, brother, see the rabble react as they hear how easily M could have saved herself by denying Divine Love. See them grow troubled at the sight of what *The Mirror* calls "Love working in her without her." Mind the Inquisitors no more, Teej. M's impossible peace and the ragged onlookers' distress are the story now. Watch them as a torch-bearing minion of our Church lights the oiled brush. See how, as the flames leap up, burning away her gown and hair and M begins to curl and melt the way our parents did in Scotland, she stays inside the divine fire and never falters? See how "a ravishing expansion of the movement of divine Light pours into the Soul"? As her face burns and blackens, not once does she cry out! [Here is where Jervis's ink grew smeared by tears.] It's the ragged onlookers and I who cry the cries M never utters as we realize the Church isn't just destroying an innocent woman, it's outlawing the fusion of Soul to God via Love. As her body burned, M's silence sang what Love itself sang through her hand: "*This Soul has six wings like the Seraphim. This Soul no longer knows how to speak, for she is annihilated from external desires and the will is dead which gave desire to her. This Soul is so enflamed in the furnace of the fire of Love that she has properly become fire, which is why she feels no fire . . . Higher no one can go, deeper no one can go, more naked no human can be.*"

Which makes you and me part of what, brother? When our Church judges M with frigid reason, sees only the black cloud of its own projected depravity, and throws a soul in the throes of the divine fire into the gears and grinders of their mechanized "theology," where does that leave the Church's orphans, TJ and Jervis? I need your answer to this, brother, because the only answer I can find puts the faith of our boyhood out of business, and I don't want to lose you too. Please tell me if you can: how can there ever be another M, another Francis or Clare, another Virgin's Son, if we don't stand "annihilate, without anxiety, no longer knowing how to speak, inside a Church governed utterly by Love"?

When this letter arrived, TJ had entered the penultimate phase of Jesuit formation known as a "regency" and was madly studying Spanish in preparation for two years in Mexico. Jervis's condemnation of the Church attacks on the Beguines shook him to the core. Many an aspiring Jesuit would have reacted with righteous fury. Not TJ. He wrote back,

I stole time I didn't have the other night to read some Eckhart, Jervis. The sermons looked amazing but I was so rushed I went straight to his trial for heresy and read his defense. Stunning! With great humility, equally great precision, and (as far as I can see through a glass darkly) perfect knowledge of Church doctrine, Eckhart demonstrates that if he is condemned on the points his Inquisitors brought forward, they will tacitly be condemning crucial doctrines of Augustine, Origen, Avicenna, Boethius, Aquinas, the Cappadocian Fathers, and Jesus Himself. The Inquisitors then proceed to do just that! Leaving me to ask, as you have asked me, where *does* this leave we who remain Mother Church's charges? Eckhart's triumph at trial is the greatest vindication of mystical union in Church history! He drags his accusers into the Divine Now, and they fail to make any effective arguments against him at all, so they condemn him in a fit of petty frustration over their failure! When I read how, shortly after Eckhart died, Pope John XXII issued a papal bull full of willful misunderstandings and blustering vagaries that pretend to "condemn" the Meister yet again, I fully understood your outraged love for him, and for the Beguines who shaped him. No Inquisitor even tripped, let alone defeated, his shining mind. His defense of mystical union stands to this day. Yet Rome erased his, Clare's, Francis's, and the Beguines' "Someone flowing through everything," replacing Her/Him with a preposterous "God of Reason" that let Inquisitors, imperialists, and sadists spread catastrophe in the now meaningless name of Christ for seven centuries up to today.

Knowing your lack of interest in what the Church is any longer up to, I doubt you even know that the Dominican Order's best scholars and theologians recently completed an exacting study of Pope John XXII's charges against Eckhart that not only exonerates the Meister, it demonstrates him to be the greatest mystical theologian the Church ever produced. But—no surprise to you, I imagine—the Vatican's lead Inquisitor, a Cardinal Ratzinger, didn't even dignify the Dominicans' findings with a response.

I still yearn to be a Jesuit, Jervis. I'm glad my regency will take me out of my troubled mind to Mexico and the outcasts and poor you and I both feel called to serve. But this has hit me hard, and I can't say where my new feelings will carry me. Wherever it may be, Jervis, keep loving your Beguines and Meister, so will I, and our love will keep us close!

—Teej

I realize, dear reader, that the saga of how TJ got rich appears to have strayed far from finance. But in fact I have not strayed at all: shortly after penning his account of Marguerite's execution, Jervis began—via the same gonzo sense of mystical reality that had caused him to soak his description of "dearest M's" immolation with tears—to guide TJ toward a 1980s fortune. *What the fuck!?* the MBA-ed will want to shout. *This Jervis Muireadhach McFreak should be roasting like a marshmallow at some jolly Catholic Tribunal, not guiding his brother or anyone else to riches!* Here's what happened instead:

Though Jervis's possessions were meagre, his dorm room and post-college living space were both so small that he rented a North Portland storage unit. When TJ and his U-Haul arrived from Georgetown, Jervis invited him to share the unit. As a result, TJ's gargantuan collection of unread blue-chip stock reports ended up in a place where Jervis could, if he chose, peruse them. Jervis did just that. The repercussions were profound.

But wait! Reason again shouts. *Why would a Marguerite-Porete-deifying weirdo like Jervis read a single word of a stock report?* Perhaps "dearest M" can best answer this: *for love.* Though Jervis's was not (yet) the self-annihilating Love into which he would soon fall, he spent hours each day striving to live the brotherly love he possessed—and when you see how this works out for TJ, business majors, you might be tempted to write furious letters to your professors for failing to include Porete's *The Mirror of Simple Souls* in your MBA programs.

Fast-forward to March 1986, the year the twenty-eight-year-old TJ entered his regency. TJ's two-year assignment was in Ixhuatán, Chiapas State, Mexico. In last-minute preparation, he visited the storage unit he shared with Jervis to pack a few things for his trip. The moment he stepped inside, he saw that the mountain of stock reports he'd hauled from Georgetown had been pulled from their boxes and placed in towering stacks that rather resembled an architect's model of lower Manhattan. TJ then saw that each "skyscraper" was built of the stock reports of a particular business and that Jervis had paper-clipped several xeroxed magazine and newspaper articles to the summit of each business's stack.

TJ's four-part journey to Ixhuatán began with a PDX to LAX flight on March 16th. He had packing to do, phone calls to make, a mass to attend, farewells to say. But the instant TJ asked himself why Jervis would plow through all those hideously dull stock reports and attach responses, his heart provided the only conceivable answer: *stupendous brotherly love.* Which moved TJ to love Jervis back by ignoring the countless things he had to do, hunkering down on a box of books, and reading the articles Jervis had attached to each stack.

The first thing TJ learned was that his investments, over the course of nine years, had doubled in value. Like the contemplative he'd become, he began muttering, *"Neti, neti, not this, not this,"* delved instead into the paper skyscrapers provided by Jervis, and encountered the elephant that stands stinking in virtually every shareholder's living room: a substantial number of his blue chips—including his General Electric, Monsanto, Exxon, and Halliburton stocks, to name just four—had been busily destroying such features of the planet as the Hudson River, biological diversity, genetic integrity, butterflies, birds, family farms, the world's seeds, aquifers, atmosphere, and native peoples and creatures of many countries and climes, all for the sake of doubling the net worth of one TJ McGraff.

TJ's reaction to this news, though still in the contemplative ballpark, was not so serene: *"Fuck this! Fuck that!"* he chanted as he drove to the nearest phone booth, called his Washington, DC, broker, ignored the man's frantic protests, liquidated his entire blue-chip portfolio, took the capital gains hit with a shrug worthy of a second-century Desert Father, then flabbergasted the broker by ordering him—again over frantic protest—to invest his entire fortune in a single kooky little software company that had just gone public on March 14th. With that he drove home, packed, and said his farewells— including a goodbye to Jervis during which he said nothing of the day's financial activities. Declining Jervis's offer to drive him to the airport (Jervis had never owned a car and was, TJ felt, the worst Catholic driver since the infamously inept Thomas Merton), TJ called a cab and took off for Ixhuatán.

TJ had chosen the kooky software outfit for three frivolous reasons. One: he had literally no time to explore other options. Two: he loved it that the same broker who said that investing in GE, Monsanto, Exxon, and Halliburton "freed him from ethical concerns" was counter-horrified that TJ thought investing in the software company was a fine idea. Three: being something of a nerd himself (long live boyhood ineptitude at ball sports!), TJ had for months been amused by urban myths featuring the software company's nerd genius CEO.

TJ had a golden sense of amusement: the nerd genius was Bill Gates. Microsoft's first decade as a public company created four billionaires and an estimated twelve thousand millionaires. TJ became a double-digit version of the latter ($14 million to start). Upon returning many months early from a troubling stay in Mexico, he chose to leave the Jesuits. (I'll tell exactly why, once this financial account is completed.) In the meantime, TJ had become truly wealthy and needed to respond somehow to that fact. Lacking a vocation, he flashed back on his Umbrian bliss thanks to Italian cuisine, then enrolled in the Seattle Culinary Institute with an eye to becoming a chef and opening a restaurant.

During TJ's time in Mexico, Jervis collected his mail for him at a Portland PO box. The personal stuff he had the Jesuits forward to Ixhuatán. The nonpersonal stuff he stacked in their storage unit. Among the latter was—gulp!—a prodigious tower of Microsoft stock reports, which Jervis had again crowned with critical xeroxed articles. This time TJ wasted no time on Microsoft's gloating accounts of itself: he dove deep into Jervis's dirt. When he discovered thereby that the once-amusing nerd genius had become software's monopolistic answer to John D. Rockefeller during his Standard Oil heyday, he again chanted, "*Fuck this! Fuck that!*" called his DC broker, ignored the man's praise of TJ's uncanny investment prowess, ignored the same man's apoplectic protests, liquidated one hundred percent of his Microsoft shares, and shrugged off the capital gains hit with the detachment of Saint Isaac of Syria. But this time, rather than reinvest, TJ dumbfounded his broker by closing out his portfolio completely, saying, "Thank you, and goodbye."

Next, like a character out of an old Frank Capra movie, TJ stashed his now considerable moneys in a bunch of George Bailey–style savings and loans, then solicited the investment help not of another broker or professional wealth manager but of his six-winged nutjob of a brother. "I'm in a jam," TJ told Jervis. "I've committed to a chef school in Seattle, classes are about to begin, and I need to rush up there to find a place to live. But my restaurant dreams, despite my choice of school, have been whispering, '*Portland, Portland.*' So I was wondering, Jervis, if you'd be willing to scout Portland for me, looking for run-down but solid old buildings with interesting potential restaurant spaces. I also want you to use no real estate brokers, no newspaper listings, and nothing the world deems sensible. Just be your deepest, truest, weirdest self, because if you ask me, Jervis, you and the Beguines and the Meister have had it right all along. I left the Jesuits to try to do work I can truly and deeply *love*. How ironic if I only settled on Holy Restaurant the Little. I want to live, work, and breathe inside *Holy Something the Great*. So turn your intuition on full blast, wander as far, wide, and long as need be, and when you find a restaurant space the Meister and dear M and their self-annihilating Love would be glad to help us operate, let me know!"

With that, TJ left for Seattle, and Jervis set to work as if his brother's mad request had been the most sensible thing he'd ever heard. Consulting no real estate ads or agencies, conducting his search entirely on foot, he felt out neighborhoods in the same nose-in-the-air, feet-on-the-ground, prayer-on-the-breath manner with which a thirteenth-century Beguine might have felt out European towns before siting a beguinage. Hiking Portland for weeks, Jervis trudged several hundred street miles, rain or shine, discussing commercial buildings galore with his spirit guides and neighborhood locals to whom intuition alone guided him. Toting an artist's pad, he also made astoundingly deft graphite sketches of a few intriguing properties, alongside eccentric notes on each property's spiritual ambience. Jervis then mailed his sketches and notes once a week or so—causing poor TJ to turn from his brother's effortlessly excellent drawings to his own awful paintings and smile helplessly.

It turned out that Jervis's six-winged soul army gravitated strongly toward the ambient warmth of old brick, inspiring his once-grounded nine-minute-older brother to ungroundedly exclaim, "Of course, Jervis! I should've known! Stick to brick!"

Sticking to brick, Jervis and his guides were eventually drawn to two structures, both about a century old, both on Portland's West side. One was an enormous rat-infested but basically sound five-story building in Northwest's then-derelict Pearl District. The other was an eccentrically rambling, almost hobbity-looking former sporting goods store standing vacant a block from the Willamette River in the roughest part of the Waterfront District. Powerfully drawn to both buildings but unable to choose between them, Jervis asked the Meister, Dear M, Lady Poverty, the Virgin's innumerable Sons, Clare's eternal mirror born of the breast of Francis, and so on, for a clear sign. When, after five or ten minutes, no such sign manifested, Jervis, with his typical total faith-confidence, took the lack of sign to be the sign, phoned TJ in Seattle, and said, "Your request for a restaurant space didn't work out as planned. As dear M says, 'If we find joy in the knowledge that the Great Love is, we must find joy in the knowledge that we aren't.' The Great Love *is*, Teej. And It located two perfect spaces. So, *the fuck*. You're going to have to open *two* Holy Restaurants the Great."

"Jervis," TJ replied. "Please don't *ever* try to appear sane! My heart was whispering 'two restaurants' all along, but my head wouldn't listen. I'll be right down to buy both buildings!"

And that's what he did. And in 1986, the year Jervis and his thirteenth-century heroes did TJ's real estate shopping for him, the Waterfront and Pearl Districts were enduring street-drug booms, large indigent populations, heightened crime, and the commercial doldrums that result—an added attraction for Jervis since it gave him occasion to serve the raggedy, worse than raggedy, and downright frightening folk who eddied around both hoods. The irony is, Jervis's "deep true weirdness" also proved economically prescient. The brick buildings his spirit guides chose were very spacious, centrally located, and so discounted in price that Teej didn't even need contracts: he bought them both outright. The Waterfront and Pearl Districts then epitomized a mass gentrification of Portland that coincided, throughout the late 1980s and '90s on up to today, with one of the most profitable real estate booms in US history.

Gentrification saddened Jervis when the indigent and ragged folk were shooed away. But the value of TJ's buildings skyrocketed. As he was finishing culinary school, faithfully making more godawful paintings, and falling ever more satisfyingly into deep friendship with Risa, he prepared to pour his remaining cash into remodeling and greening the two buildings. But before doing so, TJ called on Jervis to ask another favor. Unable to decide between the ten talented architects vying to supervise the two big remodels, he asked Jervis to meet all ten in person, turn his intuition on full blast, let the interviews wander as wildly as need be, and choose the architects the Meister and Dear M would choose. Jervis did so. And the stunning green commercial spaces and artists' lofts designed by the two architects he chose were soon some of the most sought after in Portland, generating *really* serious cash flow for TJ.

Tapping that liquidity as needed, TJ set to work creating two Portland restaurants, Rasta Pasta and Étouffée Bruté, both named by Jervis at TJ's insistence. Both were grounded in nouveau Northwest and Italian cuisines. Rasta Pasta emphasized some unlikely Jamaican-Italian fusions, while Étouffée Bruté sported Cajun-Italian entrées that sizzled courageous diners down to their socks. Both restaurants have since changed cuisines and Rasta Pasta changed its name. TJ's practice of the culinary arts is restless. But all his establishments have possessed a certain jouissance that a few patrons who self-identify as "Dumpster Catholics" link to a medieval German mystic genius posthumously condemned but undiminished by a pope, and a French Beguine unscathed—so the Dumpsterites claim—by being burned to death for the crime of daring, as a woman, to become one with an eternally recurring Son.

When Rasta Pasta first opened, the Portland independent paper *Willamette Week* sent their glib food critic, Talia Drucker, down to the Waterfront to test-drive TJ's fare. Drucker's reviews were renowned for giving a long leash to self-adoring chefs or restaurateurs who then more or less hanged themselves with their own megalomaniacal conceits. Drucker took this tack with TJ, but the part of the interview in which he was supposed to hang himself backfired:

> "I'm told you're an ex-Jesuit," I said to McGraff.
> "I wasn't yet a priest. But I came close," he said.
> "What turned you away from it?" I asked.
> "During my trial run at priesthood in Mexico," he said, "a number of terrible events forced me to administer the prescribed Roman Catholic remedies to people suffering extreme grief. As I performed this priestly duty, my ability to see the old remedies as viable spiritual supports sank like a ship in a storm, leaving me lost at sea until a remarkable Mexican, Josef Cabrera by

name, dragged me ashore on a *Tierra Nueva* where the only faith I still experienced was in the invisible structures that enfold ordinary folks whenever a little love or grace flows. As I set out to serve this faith I found that, in my hands, growable, tastable, tangible vegetables, grains, fruit, meat, fish, and wines were far more helpful than the verbiage I'd tried to wield as a priest. This isn't unusual, I don't think. In a poem called 'The Just,' Jorge Luis Borges mentions a man 'who cultivates his garden, as Voltaire wished,' a man who takes pleasure in tracing the etymology of a word though it takes time, two workmen on their lunch hour enjoying a game of chess in a silence so deep the only sound is the sliding of their pieces, a typographer who sets a page perfectly though she dislikes its literary content, and a woman petting a dog, though the dog has fallen to sleep, to be sure its sleep remains sweet. 'These people, unaware, are saving the world,' Borges declares, and I agree. When my church then became such people and their small deeds, I was no longer separate from them, as I had been as a priest. This was a joy. My daily work now centers around holing up in a kitchen each morning to perform self-effacing culinary incantations that, by day's end, hopefully lead to food that enfolds a few people in edible structures through which a little grace might flow."

I nodded throughout McGraff's homily while in my notebook I wrote: "Never heard such high-flown bullshit appliquéd to the low cunning of cookery in my life!"

Then came the ex-Jesuit's wine choice and first course: a pheasant avgolemono alongside a Venezia pinot grigio, neither of which I can accurately review since my palate was hampered by the crow I began eating. Throughout the next four courses, three wines, and dessert I was enfolded in so many incantatory structures that only a Borges could describe the graces pirouetting through the room.

TJ says he's done with the priesthood. I say he's my new priest. Feel like being enfolded in edible structures through which unseen graces flow? Try Rasta Pasta.

II. Risa and Grady's Double-Occupancy Study Carrel

They told me "mind" was neuter, so I sent mine
to my beloved. Now it's making love to her and
won't come back. Never trust a linguist!
        —contemporary Sanskrit proverb

Acting is not very hard. The most important things are to be
able to laugh and cry. If I have to laugh, I think of my sex
life. And if I have to cry, well, I think of my sex life.
        —Glenda Jackson

BARE-CHESTED, DRIPPING SWEAT, cooking under a goosenecked halogen reading lamp, Grady Haynes bellowed, "It's *midnight,* Risa! It's *September first,* Risa! How can a *Seattle apartment* at midnight in September be as hot as the Second Circle of Hell!"

In bed beside him, reading under an identical lamp, but looking so cool and focused she seemed to occupy a different region and climate entirely, Risa murmured, "Read your book, Grady." She did not look up from her own as she spoke.

Grady lifted Heidegger's *Being and Time* and shook it like a giant baby rattle. "This *book* in this Hell Circle is no *book*! It's a *cinder block*!"

"Hrmrr," Risa breathed from the depths of her book.

"*Confusticate and bebother this woman,*" Grady muttered, the diction of Bilbo Baggins being an affectation he had assumed under duress since the age of nine. Who was she jilting him for tonight? He leaned forward to check:

Traditional Art and Symbolism by Ananda K. Coomaraswamy.

Pardon my French, Grady thought, *but frackwaw-fucking-voo! The author's got to be an India Indian with a name like that, and anything olden and Indian turns Risa's already steely concentration into titanium. Vedic runes and mystic titty-twisters will now seize her by the higher chakras till my low chakra needs melt through the floor. Something must be done!*

Grady liked the Circles of Hell concept. He decided to work with it.

"Have you read *The Divine Comedy*?" he asked. "Like, all three volumes?"

"In high school," Risa murmured without bragging, without interest, and without pausing in her reading.

"Well, think back, *sooma-cooma-gooma girl,* and tell me whether you recall, anywhere in Dante's marathon libretto for dyspeptic papists, even an *Italian* capable of reading philosophy in the Circles of Hell."

"Gray*deeee,*" Risa sighed. "We have a deal."

"*Designated Study Nights.* Of course. Keep reading! I'll do a quick *Divina Commedia* scan and answer my question for us both."

Grady closed his eyes, held his breath, plugged his ears, pressurized his face into a bulging red grimace, and spasmed and quaked the bed the way a man might if the entire *Divine Comedy* tore screaming through his brain in six seconds. When he stopped quaking and opened his eyes, he was pleased to see Risa smiling wryly. "Whew!" he huffed. "*Hyperconcentrated Dante.* Serious aneurysm potential! But you know me. *Anything for knowledge!* It turns out that not even the most ultraviolet village in the toe of the Boot ever spawned an Italian capable of reading philosophy in the infernal Inferno! So consider *my* chances of reading Martin effing Heidegger under a Kmart-advertised 'reading lamp' that turns out to be a *halogen head-frying device*! *Fuck me with a blowtorch!* Not even *Heidegger* could read Heidegger in here!"

Pretty good bullhockey, Grady was thinking—till he saw he'd lost her. Though still faintly smiling, Risa had begun filling a notebook with what-ever cosmic verities the preposterously named Coomaraswamy had sent dancing through her head...

A BRIEF HISTORY of what was going on in this bed: on the day Risa had accepted Grady's invitation to move in "on an experimental basis," Grady had believed—*based on direct pre-move ecstatic experience!*—that he'd hit the Erotic Jackpot of a lifetime. True, Risa had immediately insisted on a need for what she called Designated Study Nights. But the second time she referred to such nights she shortened the term to "DSNs," and acronyms sound so innocent! "Living with me won't be like dating me," she'd said. "Ever notice that I only go out on weekends? That's because grades earn the scholarships that put food on my table and a roof over my head. Studying is my *job,* so to speak. And there's more to it than that, Grady. I want to spend my life paying attention to the whole of life. So college, to me, is a window of time in which we get to ponder and interact with the very best things that people of many cultures have ever said, thought, or done. That makes me a nerd, I know. But I intend never to become a Nielsen rating, a consumer lost in a shopping maze, or any variation of my Cathoholic mother or my father's so-called lady friends. I feel called to live as fully and deeply as I can, nerdy or not. So think hard about your invitation. On Designated Study Nights, Monday through Thursday, I'll be visible but unavailable. Will you *really* be okay with that?"

"Oh-my-yes-how-admirable-practical-sensible-and-attractive-plus-I-happen-to-be-an-intellectual-gladiator-capable-of-devouring-philosophic-and-poetic-tomes-till-all-hours-of-the-night-me-ownself!" Grady had blathered. But Risa brushed aside the blather, asked penetrating questions about his living and study habits, then invited Grady himself to establish the ground rules that would govern his Designated Study Night behavior. Which he had done. And which he now, nightly, cursed himself for doing.

A matter of particular concern had been the bed. It turned out they both liked to study on this ambiguous article of furniture, but neither of them had ever before done so, Monday through Thursday, with a Friday, Saturday, and Sunday night sex partner seated inches away. So they hammered out a Two-People-Studying-in-Bed Accord that led to ad-libs (mostly Grady's) and hysterical laughter (mostly Risa's), which agreement was nevertheless binding: on Monday through Thursday, unless otherwise stipulated by both parties, their bed would serve as a double-occupancy study carrel with one scholar positioned on each side.

Risa had moved into Grady's fourth-floor walk-up over spring vacation, Designated Study Nights commenced, and Risa hit the books into the wee hours exactly as promised—which Grady found inspiring, at first. Not only did Risa devour weighty tomes by the bushel basket, she filled notebook after notebook *voluntarily, goaded by no assignment,* with reflections and notes on her reading. When Grady asked about this, she told him that in high school she read a one-page credo by Jack Kerouac, of all people, that advised aspiring dharma bums to create secret scribbled dumbsaint notebooks "for yr own joy." This advice so wowed her at age fifteen that she took up the practice and never gave it up. Grady not only admired her secret notebooks, he realized that, with scores of Western philosophical classics to wade through and intelligently regurgitate to a thesis committee next year, he'd do well to follow her example. But, as Risa's ex-Jesuit pal TJ liked to say, *Schmidt happens.*

The first piece of schmidt to splatter Grady: it turned out that reading Western philosophical classics in close proximity to Risa's living, breathing body converted those classics into the abstracted bleating of a herd of decrepit castrated goats. Second piece of schmidt: once rendered thus illiterate, Grady's mind on Designated Study Nights became a housefly stuck in a jar of honey—a torment so fatiguing that, night after night, he succumbed to Premature Exhaustulation and slept *hours* before Risa abandoned her secret notebooks and reentered the body Grady hoped to ravish. Third piece of schmidt: six months, 130 Designated Study Nights, and 77,000 unsublimated erections later, the only tenet left in Grady's once-promising set of philosophical beliefs was that sex appeal is the cruelest attribute a woman can possess if she also happens to possess excellent study habits.

Grady didn't take his frustration lying down: a few weeks into the DSNs he became an insurgent. Deploying totemic animal magnetism, Tuareg eye juju, incantation, desperation, lotions, potions, love poems, and every other eros-inducing gimmick posited in the *Cosmopolitan* magazines he now found *far* more interesting than philosophical classics, Grady set out to drag DSNs into the realm of eros if it killed him. But, with a single blissful 2 a.m. exception on the weeknight Grady now called Maybe Tuesday, his insurgency not only failed, it caused laws to be enacted against him, inspiring Grady to pen not one but two irate letters to the love-quacks at *Cosmopolitan*, thereby failing to finish a critical essay, delaying his degree work for an entire quarter, costing him several thousand dollars. *Frackwaw-fucking-voo!*

Seven Designated Study Night laws that Grady's behavior in the dual study carrel had so far necessitated: (1) No lascivious ogling of Risa *While Risa Is Studying*. (2) No laying one's scorched jalapeño pepper against the thigh of Risa *While Risa Is Studying*. (3) No lawyerly arguing that the God-given length of the jalapeño caused it to *inadvertently* cross to Risa's side, so the contact was the Creator's fault, not one's own, *While Risa Is Studying*. (4) No crawling under the covers after cruel laws have been enacted against oneself, in order to whimper like a blind puppy in piteous need of mama dog's mammaries *While Risa Is Studying*. (5) No singing "Goodbye, Maybe Tuesday" to the tune of the Rolling Stones' "Ruby Tuesday" at the top of one's lungs at 11:59 p.m. as Maybe Tuesday becomes Never Wednesday *While Risa Is Studying*. (6) No climbing on top of Risa's Montana-Great-Gramma's-Heirloom-Wardrobe to chitter like a batshit pine squirrel whose nuts have been stolen *While Risa Is Studying*. (7) No climbing down from said wardrobe, diving into an imaginary impoundment beneath the bed, and working one's down-turned mouth like a largemouth bass about to explode out of cover and inhale the crankbait that is Risa *While Risa Is Studying*.

None of the laws enacted against Grady troubled him at first, because as soon as a behavior was outlawed he'd invent a behavior that was *not* outlawed. But to combat this, Risa took to getting out of bed, opening her Montana-Great-Gramma's-Heirloom-Wardrobe, and encasing her body, neck to floor, in a size XL puke-gold UW Huskies rooter bathrobe, which meant that their next three nonstudy nights would now be makeup study nights, and Grady wouldn't be *seeing* any, let alone getting any, for many nights to come.

RISA'S SCRIBBLED DUMBSAINT secret notebook entry of September 1, 1989, began:

> *Spelunking A. K. Coomaraswamy again, I find he makes CG Jung sound sorta like Kerouac sounds compared to Jung. What an incomparable scholar-spider, The Coom, weaving polymath webs of precision & depth out of every major wisdom tradition! He's like Gandhi in his distrust of all industrial states, socialist, democratic, or communist, because of the way all three hijack cultures & the living Earth wholesale, then sell them back to their rightful owners defiled & dispirited. But in his trust of primary wisdom sources, Vedic Sufistic Taoist Buddhist Outlier Xian Indigenous, The*

Coom outbelieves even Gandhi! (Note to self: if you meet his like & form crush, remember: five women divorced him!)

Reading his Vedic Temple essay, it's dazzling to think that the human body, the traditional temple, & the cosmos are "analogical equivalents," & that the great temple & cathedral makers knew this, devising cathedral parts to correspond to body parts that correspond to parts of the known & unknown universe. Each "dimensioned form" (Skrit: nirmita, vimita) is explicitly "a house" for the Unseen Unborn Guileless You. (Coom footnote pearl: "In the vault of this my chamber, a large round window above, approachable only by rope, Christ looking through from above, the Beyond visible from below.")

The creation myths of all the world agree, we're not doomed by total separation from the divine! Our being is suspended from above & there is an unseen "Sun-Door" in every body, temple, world, accessible by "ineffable ropes, stairs, or soul threads." Up these ropes, stairs & threads "the sincere ones" learn to climb till they, we!, "emerge from dimensioned structure into the Dimensionless." This sky door, God-aperture, Pali kannika, Greek oculus, "appears of itself & opens unto the eternal." (Another footnote pearl: "This selfsame door is the one at which the Buddhas stand, beckoning.")

I feel beckoned! Thank You! And please, keep beckoning!

As RISA SET down these arcane secrets and Grady tried not to gape at the body movements her happy scribbling aroused, he read the same Heidegger sentence six times in a row, understood it less each time, and began doing a little math: four Friday, Saturday, Sunday nights a month equals twelve, minus up to four nights for menstrual activity equals eight, minus maybe three more puke-gold-Huskies-rooter-bathrobe nights due to misbehavior, equals a total of *six fucks a month*!?!

"Mmm?" went Risa.

"Oops!" Grady cleared his throat. "Sorry. Heidegger's got me thinking out loud."

"Six bucks a month? Why would Heidegger make you think that?"

"No, no," Grady lied. "I said, 'South-facing rocks.' That's what my pal, Born-in-Seattle Dan, said about this apartment when I drove up from Boulder. 'But the windows don't open and there's no AC,' I said. Dan points to the Sound. '*There's* your AC. Get with the Seattle program, Grady. Cool's the norm, gloom's the enemy, and this southwest exposure will bathe you in every ray that pierces the crud cover. Look at that view! Ships on the Puget, snow on the Olys!' Life lesson, Risa. Never trust a guy who calls the Olympics 'the Olys.' '*South-facing rocks!*' Seattle Dan warbles. So I lease the south-facer for a *year* and *BAM!*, it turns into a Circle of Hell straight outta Dante!"

"Try a walk," Risa murmured, scribbling as she spoke. "It's much cooler outside."

"I wouldn't need a walk," Grady ventured, "if the rest of the breast peeking out that sleeveless sleeve would come out to play."

"Time for that walk," Risa said, adjusting her shirt and bending back to her scribbling.

Grady knew from experience that if he took a walk, fresh air would revive him till he got home. Then the stifling air of their Dante-designed Inferno would knock him so deep into sleep that the next thing he'd hear would be his morning alarm. The only way to keep his 2 a.m. chances alive was to ogle Risa precisely *because* ogling was outlawed. Outlawry keeps a fella alert.

Grady commenced the night's outlawry by swinging his eyeballs so far to starboard that the tiny socket muscles holding his gaze in place burned and his vision filled with weird little sparklies that obscured everything he saw. But he was used to this. He was so used to it that he dreamed his eyes got stuck to the far side of their sockets and he had to stagger through a sparklies blizzard to an ophthalmologist who turned out to be an India Indian who informed Grady that he had induced a condition known as "ocular hemorrhoids," after the ancient Greek αἷμα, meaning "blood," and ῥέω, meaning "flow," the only known cure for which was the frequent application of Preparation H to his eyeballs. *Frackwaw-fooping-voo!*

Keeping his eyeballs wrenched and trying to enjoy the sparklies, Grady located his verboten study mate sipping green tea in a leggy half lotus as usual, wearing a ridiculous Huskies-rooter T-shirt rendered glorious due to scissored-away sleeves and no bra as usual. The T-shirt, alas, was deep purple—a color beloved, in Grady's view, by no one but Huskies sports fans, a daft British band, one-eyed one-horned people-eaters, and the author Alice Walker. But when Risa leaned forward to scribble in her notebook, the scissors job she'd done on the sleeves again revealed maybe three square inches of creamy base-of-breast bulge. Defying the puke-gold-U-Dub-bathrobe threat, Grady risked a twenty-degree turn of the head and sighted in those creamy inches with a voracity that enabled him to visualize many more smooth, taut, soft, or sinewy inches of Risa. His reward for his exertions? Aching eyeballs, rapidly approaching Premature Exhaustulation, and Unsublimated Erection #77,001.

He knew he was beating the term to death but still: *Frackwaw-farking-voo!* Though nothing unfair was going on, something unfair was going on. Grady had thought pretty well of himself till he fell boots-over-backpack for this girl who was not only beautiful and intellectually intense but *always* alert and present. In the presence of these qualities Grady's own qualities began to feel trivialized. Her profound concentration turned his distractible concentration into a joke—yet that joke was the only kind of concentration he owned! Better yet, he could concentrate as intensely as anyone on the planet if the thing he got to concentrate on was Risa's body. But his own damned DSN rules had defined that form of focus as "lascivious ogling" and banned it! By being merely smart around Risa's brilliance, his smarts felt suddenly dumb; by being charmingly flawed around her near flawlessness, he felt criticized even though she didn't criticize him; and by feeling amorous seven nights a week, he was coming off as a Lust Monster though every heterosexual lad he knew would be priapic as the god Pan if he had to study next to Risa four straight nights in a *fuckless farking two-person study carrel.* That he'd fallen for a girl of extreme substance was not the problem. The problem was Grady's relationship-founding claim to possess comparable substance. The pretense was killing him! This was TV baseball and Pabst Blue Ribbon weather, damn it. The pennant race was climaxing and he hardly knew who was in it. Why had he stuck his TV in storage and lied that he didn't own one? Why had he said he read poetry and philosophy "till all hours" when both genres turned him cross-eyed by happy hour?

He knew why. He knew *exactly* why. He'd been conjuring the mountain-rugged, incandescently imaginative, celestial-hearted, capacious-brained, almost entirely fictitious poet-philosopher capable of luring Risa into his lair. *And it worked!* Here she sat, her left hip flaring heat into his right— but look at the passion with which she kept scribbling sweet nothings to her Coomaraswamy buzzard. *Frackwaw-swamy-voo!*

IT WAS RISA'S dad, Dave, who'd provided her with the Huskies rooter crap, which she donned for two reasons: one, to look like a doofus when she went running in dodgy neighborhoods; two, to look like a doofus to Grady when she was studying. What annoyed Grady was that Dave seemed well aware of reason two. Very shortly after Risa moved in with him, someone knocked on their door when she was off on a run. When Grady opened up, what appeared to be a nineteenth-century cattle baron stood there, smiling as disarmingly as his daughter, holding a grocery bag full of Huskies rooter garb.

Grady's first impression of Dave: *middle-aged man from Ipanema.* Tall and tan and old and lovely, with silver-streaked brown Wild-Bill-Somebody curls, an archaic but dashing *Maverick* suit, and blue eyes the beauty of which so rivaled Risa's obsidians that it left Grady confused: here stood the DNA he'd gone mad for in a middle-aged man!

With a look of innocence, Dave set his Huskies Grady repellents on the kitchen table, turned to Grady, and said, "There's a cafe I like near here, Grady, and my daughter appears to like you. What say we grab a coffee and get to know each other a little?"

So off they strolled to the nearby Café Kant.

Perched on barstools in a sunny window, they soon discovered they shared a passion for high-mountain meandering. On horseback for Dave. With a backpack for Grady. At the glorious height of summer for both. The minute they starting lobbing favorite mountain ranges back and forth their age difference vanished. Bright-eyed and happy, they kept conjuring high wild places for each other long after their coffees were gone.

"You know what, Grady?" Dave said as he grabbed the tab. "I like you, too. Didn't know if I would, but your love for high country makes me want to share the most alluring such country I know. You ever hear of the Elkmoon Mountains in Montana?"

"Can't say I have," Grady admitted.

"The name honors the late October, early November moon under which bull elk in rut could be taken by a good Indian bowman with a dinky obsidian arrowhead if he could track it as it bled. I grew up in the Elkmoon Valley and love those mountains. Eighty or so peaks in a crescent configuration. Eight- to ten-thousand-footers mostly, plus Steeple Peak at just under twelve thousand. Far from Yellowstone and Glacier, so they're lightly traveled. Granite footing so good you can wander most of 'em freely, trails or no trails. Vast meadows of wildflowers. Creeks with pebbled beds bright as jewels. Delightful air, light, birds, wildlife, plus...an added feeling I can't describe. But I can locate it. It centers around the ten-thousand-seven-hundred-foot Blue Mosque, a dome peak with two freestanding marble spires and three remarkable nearby lakes. I've visited scores of peaks and lake basins, but none like these. You got a pen?"

"For stuff like this," Grady said, "I've got a *memory*."

A pleased nod from Dave. "Lake Pipsissewa could be your base camp. So far up and in that few ever see it. So full of trout, fishermen can't seem to get past it. But after a night's rest and a fish feast, keep going and you'll thank me. As you leave Pipsissewa, Echo Lake is eight miles due west. Sight in the Mosque and head straight for it. Well above timberline you enter a couloir so loaded with blue gentian you're crushing beauty with each step. As you top the couloir you reach Echo, the most perfect cirque lake I've ever seen. Its natural amphitheatre sends your voice bouncing back, but what you holler strikes a triple cliff across the water and morphs into things you didn't say. Sometimes eerie things. That's where my mind would start to bend, and things would begin to...*hey*. You okay there, Grady?"

Grady had closed his eyes and was holding his head as if to safeguard what was being placed in it. "I feel a little weirder than okay, Dave. I'm seeing the Blue Mosque so clearly my head might sprout a minaret in a minute or two."

A surprised smile from the cattle baron. "*Minaret*, you say. The Mosque's two marble pinnacles are actually *called* the East and West Minarets."

Something had come over Grady. Eyes closed, he kept squeezing his head in his fingertips, seeing everything Dave described with a sense of foreknowledge that moved him intensely.

"The Mosque is a *massif*—a huge mountain millions of years ago, broken down by tectonics and weather into something uncanny. Get quiet there and the massif starts to whisper, *I may look gone. But there are ways of climbing what I used to be even now.* That feeling's your call to worship, Grady. That's the muezzin singing you on up to Jade."

Grady's trance deepened. He even heard the distant muezzin!

"I'd advise hiking poles on the arête that leads to Jade. It's on the Mosque's north side, and it's too skinny to pass horses safely. I hobble mine below

Gentian Couloir with a young wrangler to guard 'em on the off chance of a lion. Jade lies at the Mosque's foot, just seven acres in size, and doesn't seem remarkable until you look down into it. The southern third of it is *insanely* deep, cutting back under the Mosque as if it was bored out by a giant drill bit, making it impossible to measure how deep Jade truly is. An old packer woman I once met told me Jade's a meteor crater. Think on *that*. A millions-of-years-old massif wounded by a stone tossed like Lucifer out of heaven. Strangest of all, that stone tapped into a thermal anomaly deep under the Mosque that prevents Jade from icing over. It's tepid even in spring, down-right warm in July, and there's a liveliness to it. When the wind dies there, at night especially, Jade gives off the strangest feelings high country has ever given me. Feelings more of other worlds, or inner worlds, than of this world we think we inhabit. I see you may be tasting that feeling already, Grady. You've got me thinking you'll collect on the gift I'm trying to give. Good on you if you do. *Pipsissewa. Echo. The Blue Mosque. Jade.* Go there."

Grady sat stunned for a few seconds, swore he *would* go, the two men stood and shook hands, and Dave said they'd surely bump into each other again. Grady said he'd like that provided Dave wasn't toting another armload of Huskies rooter crap for Risa. They went their ways smiling, each man feeling he'd just made a friend. But as things turned out, they never saw each other again. As things turned out, Risa and Grady didn't last long together, and Dave didn't last long, period. Yet by describing the Elkmoons, Dave McKeig had changed the course of Grady's entire life.

RISA'S SCRIBBLED SECRET dumbsaint entry of September 1, 1989, continued:

The Sun-Door of the temple is represented in humans by the cranial foramen, which is open at birth, pulsing with each heartbeat. The same aperture is opened at death, in many cultures, when the skull is ritually broken to set free the Unseen Unborn Guileless Perfection. Heads-up, prospective homeowners: the foramen of your skull & sky door of every Gothic cathedral or Vedic temple correspond to the luffer, smoke hole, or skylight of your traditional tipi, wickiup, cliff dwelling, lodge, hacienda, cottage, igloo. (Note to future realtor: Ceiling smoke hole! Must have!)

This "sky door into the Dimensionless" can be opened via grace assaults through which we fall into a Now that opens unto all joy. We humans, same as the cosmos, are <u>hypaethral</u> (Eng. "open to the sky; having no roof")—as demonstrated on the day Jellyfish Man sent me screaming out the door of his Paperback Slaughterhouse & I trip-bashed the books, crawled around cleaning up, found smelly old <u>John Cross</u>, invoked Love Unmanifest, opened the book & accidentally opened a sky door through which Love swooped down in the *form of John's Eagle, corny or not. Footnote pearls:*

*When the <u>angakok</u> (shaman) needs to make a flight, she rises through "the opening that appears of itself" in the roof of her igloo.

*In the temple of which the sky is the roof, the Sun himself is the <u>mokṣa-dvara</u> ("gateway to eternity").

*Mundaka Upaniṣad: "There is no side path leading beyond this realm. But there is a sky path. An ascent can be made from the darkness here below through the Sun-Door above via vertical ascent."

*My own footnote pearl, Emily Dickinson's definition of a poem: When I feel "as if the top of my head were taken off."

Yes! And we imitate this divine lift constantly with our climbing rites, summit-baggings, Half Dome & El Capitan ascents, Jacob's ladders, trapeze art, tightrope walks, elevators, precisely because (take it, AK The Coom!):

"A temple is the universe in a likeness."

"The body is the universe in a likeness."

"And the distance that separates heaven & earth can be annihilated. A bridge lies between. Right here within the body is an Infinite Person, higher than which there is nothing."

Amen. So be it!

"Frackwaw-voo!" Grady finally whispered, turning away from Risa in exhaustion, soon drifting off to the sound of her pen scratching across paper . . .

Who knew how long later he dreamed that something soft landed on his head—and when he opened his eyes, something *had.* All he could see was a wash of Huskies rooter purple that felt about 98.6 degrees and smelled most wonderfully of Risa.

Her reading lamp snapped off. The purple went black.

His head covering was whisked away.

Many smooth yet taut, soft yet sinewy inches of Risa eased up against his backside.

"When an Inuit shaman, the *angakok,* needs to take flight," she whispered in his ear, "she flies up through an opening that appears of itself in the roof of her igloo. Shall we make an opening appear of itself in the roof of this double-occupancy study carrel?"

How gratefully Grady rolled onto his back and nodded.

How slowly a long leg drew itself up his thighs.

Her lips found his mouth. Their hands went a-wandering.

An opening appeared in an impossible fourth-floor roof of their eight-story building.

They took flight.

Their bodies became the universe in a likeness.

(Portland, early 1980s to September 11, 1989)

III. How Jervis Got Poor

Love is as strong as death, and as hard as Hell.
                                        —Meister Eckhart

ONE SPRING DAY during his third year at University of Portland, Jervis McGraff chanced to peer off the same Willamette River bluff over which young Jamey Van Zandt had once flown on a theologically jinxed bicycle. Catching sight of a sailboat on the river far below, he was smitten by the way it cut serenely through the water, peaceably defying the self-important roar of the city, the speedboats, the tugboats and huge barges. A sailboat little different from this one could have sailed the thirteenth-century Rhine at the time of the Beguines' and Meister Eckhart's glory. The thought sent a bliss-shiver up his spine.

I know of no more devout student of his bliss-shivers than Jervis. A flock of ideas flushed and flew like a covey of quail into his mind. *If I gained a real grasp of the disenfranchised people of Portland, might it be possible to start a genuine, latter-day, non-Catholic urban beguinage run by the best of them? I'd base its soul life on Eckhart and the Beguines. And the old Beguine architecture gives guidance on structure. But couldn't a Portland beguinage be housed in a weaponless armada of small sailboats sharing a moorage?*

More bliss-shivers sent Jervis to his bicycle and down to the Willamette River, where he began studying all the moorages. He hadn't gone far when he spied a FOR SALE sign tacked to a hideously weathered twenty-six-foot wooden sloop. The manager of the moorage led him down to the dock to inspect the boat more closely. The fine print on the sign described the scow's condition as "vintage," an assessment so insanely optimistic it reminded Jervis of his favorite mystics' talk of union with God! Examining the sloop with the same optimism, he felt more and more bliss-shivers. The sails weren't too badly mildewed! The hull was so caked with algae you hardly noticed its need to be stripped and repainted! The antique eight-horse Evinrude fired right up on the manager's curses and thirtieth or so pull. Jervis just couldn't get over the fact that the whole vessel was basically a tiny house that *actually floated*! When he squeezed into the cabin and found it as spacious as at least five coffins, it was full-on love at first sight. *What a perfect place to enact what Eckhart calls "the eradication of possessing and having...* " *"The soul must exist in a free nothingness"*! He crept around down there, bumping his head on the four-foot-ten-inch-high ceiling, cracking it even harder on the much lower bulkheads, marveling as he rubbed the rising lumps on his head, at the four circular shafts of light the portholes sent through the gloom.

He bought the sloop that day, and moved a few of his meagre possessions aboard. He named the light rays that streamed through the starboard portholes in the morning *The Meister* and *Marguerite,* and the rays that streamed through the afternoon portholes *Mechthild* and *Hadewijch.* He placed the same foursome's books on little shelves in the path of the appropriate rays and sometimes read a few paragraphs just as the sun lit the pages. Bending himself into Quasimodo configuration, he began stripping, refinishing, and repairing the old tub amid his meditations, and ended up refinishing, repairing, and adoring the same forever-disintegrating vessel for nine years.

Those years did not result in a benign Beguine Armada housed in catamarans, sloops, and ketches on the waters that bisect Portland. But they did deliver Jervis, TJ, and friends some *Wind in the Willows*-type adventures on the Willamette and lower Columbia. The same years gave Jervis a permanently hunched spine and the habit of randomly ducking his head, even under open skies, to avoid braining himself on nonexistent bulkheads. Ever the dutiful nine-minutes-older brother, TJ warned Jervis that his boat was deforming him. Jervis greeted this news with a shrug and a mild, "The fuck. *The soul must exist in a free nothingness.*"

TJ MOVED FROM Washington, DC, to Portland during Jervis's second year on the sloop and eagerly set out to get reacquainted with his brother face-to-face. Thanks to Jervis's torrid letters, TJ was not surprised to hear him speak of the Catholic Church as if he were engaged, as a side hobby, in dismantling and rebuilding it to suit his thirteenth-century Beguine prejudices. What TJ was not prepared for were Jervis's incessant acts of compassion.

Jervis slept on his boat, but spent most of his days on the Portland streets, and his embrace of those he chanced to meet on the streets startled TJ: it was total. In his endless willingness to engage with people he encountered at random, focusing on raw human need, it soon struck TJ that his brother's intuition was uncanny. He could ascertain at a glance the condition of the addicted, afflicted, unhoused, or addlepated, and he never let such a person pass without greeting them and, as the case may be, telling them where to find a halfway house, hot bowl of soup, free winter coat, free dog, or work, if they were capable of it.

An unsought discovery that surprised TJ as much as Jervis's selfless service was his own distaste for such service. When he arrived from Georgetown, he was a Jesuit intellectual who'd been imagining long walks with his brother during which they'd compare reading experiences, follow the threads of their divergent theologies through to satisfying conclusions, and perhaps get to the bottom of Jervis's crazed love for Eckhart and Marguerite Porete. Their walks accomplished no such thing. No conversation ever reached a cogent conclusion, because serving the ragged was Jervis's sole constant. Way too often for TJ's taste, Jervis also enjoyed raucous conversations with such people, swapping outlandish yarns, horrendous jokes, or outright delusions with even the most whacked of them. When the spirit moved, he also bought them cigarettes, cheap wine, and a few times even told people where to score a clean fix. The first time TJ heard his brother connect a junkie to a dealer, he went ballistic. "Are you trying to *kill* that guy, Jervis? What on Earth are you thinking?"

"The fuck, Teej," Jervis calmly replied. "Proverbs 31."

"Remind me," TJ said, dreading whatever he was about to hear.

"'Give strong drink unto him that is ready to perish, and wine unto those that be of heavy hearts. Let him drink, and forget his poverty, and remember his misery no more.'"

"Heroin isn't drink!" TJ retorted.

"But it's that addict's addiction," Jervis said. "And you might have noticed, there wasn't a methadone clinic on a nearby corner. That junkie was scraping bottom. People who don't understand drugs say, 'So let 'em hit bottom, get arrested, go to prison, get clean.' But there isn't a cop on every corner either, and drugs are *dragons,* TJ. They're *way* more powerful than those they flow through. When the drug tells its host, 'Get more of me now!' anyone—you and me too, if we were addicts—suddenly sees the people around them the way a dragon does. As prey."

While his Jesuit twin fidgeted at this information, Jervis shrugged. "The fuck, Teej. Street life ain't pretty. I've run into that guy eight or ten times now. You get a feel for who might go off if they can't get to a hit. You could be wrong. But you can sometimes rehab a junkie if you were wrong. You can't rehab dead prey if you were right."

As the weeks went by, TJ visited Jervis less and less often yet felt increasingly haunted by the stooped, self-sacrificing person his brother had become. On board his wretched sloop, above the yard-long stretch of warped formica Jervis called his "galley," a Catholic Worker calendar hung where other sailors would have hung the Playmate of the Month. On that calendar Jervis's playmates—Gandhi, Cesar Chavez, Mother Teresa, MLK, Dorothy Day, the Berrigan brothers—were photographed serving the halt, lame, pesticided, exploited, diseased, and tyrannized, and under each photo they said things like "There is no such thing as defeat in an act of compassion"; or "Our rule is the daily performance of works of mercy for those in need"; or "The dumping of creation down a military rat hole is worse than it ever was, the wars across the earth are worse than they ever were, taxes are more inexcusable than they ever were"; or "Those who surrender to the service of the poor through love of Christ will live like the grain of wheat that dies."

On their walks, TJ again and again saw Jervis's courage in action rival

that of his heroes, a recognition that filled TJ with a terrible combination
of love and foreboding.

THE MONTHS FOLLOWING TJ's 1986 return to Portland from Mexico were
for a while the happiest of his life. He'd endured a painful but profound
spiritual turnaround. He'd left the Jesuits because of it. He'd then discovered, with a little reminder from Jervis, that his botched early pilgrimage to
Assisi had in fact been a harbinger of his true calling: TJ was as intuitive
with cuisine as Jervis was with street people. When Jervis urged him to stop
trying to understand the streets and do something brilliant with his God-
given culinary genius and the two old brick buildings Jervis had located for
him, TJ took that advice to heart, set to work on housing two restaurants
in old bricks, and his life felt more fulfilling than ever before.

Jervis then surprised TJ in another way: without saying a word about it,
he applied for and landed a job teaching history at rough, tough Westside
Catholic High. The move struck TJ as shockingly mainstream for Jervis—
until he learned that, during his first year as a teacher, Jervis was on the
verge of being fired almost constantly, and that his students adored him.
Jervis then proved himself as spiritually crazed as ever when he admitted to
TJ that he didn't care if he was fired, because his true long-term purpose was
not to teach: his aim was to immerse himself in the lives and difficulties of
Portland's young, tailor an urban beguinage to serve them, and recruit a few
of his more spiritually adventurous ex-students into a neo-Beguine movement housed in an armada of small sailboats on the Willamette River.

Jervis's teaching job so greatly reduced the amount of time he spent on
mean streets that TJ's worries over him were whittled down to a single
concern: his refusal to pay federal income taxes. TJ didn't address Jervis's
civil disobedience openly. If he had, he knew Jervis would slam him with
so many powerful Thoreau, Gandhi, Berrigan bros, Dorothy Day, Simone
Weil, and Chavez quotes he'd end up feeling like a plastic-wrapped slice
of processed American cheese for paying his own taxes. Instead, TJ con-
gratulated Jervis, but asked if it ever bothered him that, by stiffing the feds,
he was emulating some of the most inhumane tax-dodging billionaires and
offshore corporations in the world. He then casually added that it would
be a sad day when Jervis's beloved sloop was confiscated by the IRS and his
hopes of launching a Beguine Armada ended in nothing.

Looking genuinely delighted, Jervis said, "Nice passive aggression, Teej!
I didn't know you had it in you! But as the Meister says, the soul must exist
in a free nothingness." And he went on stiffing the feds. So, as was their
pattern, the nine-minutes-older brother began to lie awake nights picturing
Jervis, once his sloop was confiscated, moving to a freeway underpass to
live among tweakers and street crazies, defending his new accommodations
with the self-abnegating aphorisms of the saints Francis and Clare.

Unable to bear this possibility, TJ took preemptive action. Leasing an
apartment on Northwest 22nd and Hoyt, close to the street life Jervis

loved, and nearly as small, spartan, and gloomy as Jervis's sloop, he kept
the apartment secret until he and Jervis were walking near it one day, then
muttered, "Listen, Jervis. I hate to cop to this, but I leased a dirt-cheap
apartment to house a few of the people I bring to Portland to work on the
Pearl and Waterfront projects. Their hotel bills were killing me. My dump
is just up the block here. Wanna see it and tell me whether I'm abusing my
help?" When Jervis then stepped inside the cheerless box and said, "The
fuck, Teej, I *like* it!" TJ replied, "Damn. *That* can't be good! Guess I was
thinking of my pocketbook more than my guests.

"By the way, though," he oh-so-casually added. "When the place is
vacant, which will be often, there's no reason you couldn't stay here when
it's handy for you. Just promise not to name it 'Proverbs 31 House' and
turn it into a hospice for your beloved rabble."

Thus did the voluntary pauper, Jervis, score the safe but satisfactorily
"bad hotel" he would never have considered if he'd realized TJ had
intended it for him all along.

In September of 1989, TJ temporarily moved to Seattle, where he was
perfecting cuisines as a student at the Culinary Institute and befriending a
young woman named Risa.

Jervis, meanwhile, was going to teach at Westside Catholic again, which
meant taxable income, so he set out to make his sloop IRS-proof. Operating
under the name "Johannes Eckhart," he hired one of his questionable street
pals to procure excellent fake ID for him, and help him falsify the registration
of his boat. "Johannes" then obtained a new moorage on the Willamette
miles upriver from his old one and on the opposite shore, just a twenty-
minute bike ride from Westside Catholic. In mid-August he dry-docked his
sloop and began the arduous process of stripping, repainting, disguising,
and rechristening her. Typical of his humor at the time, he dubbed his boat
the SS *Pygostyle,* a pygostyle being the knob of cartilage on the stern of a
skinned chicken, commonly known as "the Pope's Nose." Lest anyone miss
the intended reference, Jervis painted the outer hull of his vessel Catholic-
cardinal red and added glowering black eyes and flared nostrils to the bow,
causing the white sails, as the sloop approached head-on, to resemble the
towering ceremonial pope's hat known as a mitre, which made the sloop's
prow resemble an apoplectic pontiff's river-gulping face.

On September 7th he completed his long labor but would be unable to
sleep on board for some days due to paint fumes, so he phoned TJ, asked
his permission to stay a week at the Hoyt Street monk's cell, and biked to
the apartment—just as his wily brother had hoped.

What a blow for TJ that his attempt to keep Jervis safe led to the
opposite result.

On the evening of September 11th, Jervis strolled up to Houck's Video on
Northwest 21st, where he rented the two-cassette video of Akira Kurosawa's

Seven Samurai. With films as with sloops as with excommunicated mystics, Jervis was a man of fierce loyalties. He loved it that Toshiro Mifune and the other samurai rescued a village of peasants tyrannized by gun-toting bullies. He loved that the samurai had nothing to gain for themselves by doing so, but chose to uphold their code of honor and live "like the grain of wheat that dies." He did not love that three of his favorite samurai would be gunned down by bandits they could have defeated blindfolded in hand-to-hand combat. But when a friend of Jervis's, Jimbo the Cinema 21 doorman, passed along the great Tom McGuane line "God created an impossible situation," it became Jervis's cherished annual rite to chomp popcorn, wash it down with white wine, whisper McGuane's line each time a low-rent gunman took out a noble samurai, and chomp more popcorn as he wiped away tears.

On his way back to the apartment Jervis ducked into the 22nd Avenue Market, where he purchased a jar of Orville Redenbacher's, a stick of Tillamook butter to melt over it, and a cheap sauvignon blanc to fortify himself during the movie. When he stepped back outside, the sun had dipped behind the West Hills, the late summer heat had abated, and birds had begun vespers. The laurel hedge round the parking lot was alive with chittering sparrows, unseen doves and pigeons were cooing on ledges and roofs, and the starlings in the Johnson Street sycamores seemed to be auditioning as night-club impersonators, imitating bobwhites, congested-sounding meadowlarks, car alarms, and one good imitation of a guy whistling for his dog, Jervis thought, till he spotted a guy on a shaded porch whistling for his dog. "*The fuck!*" he muttered.

As he started across the parking lot, a lone crow came strolling into his line of travel. The bird's slow gait and black garb brought to mind TJ's obsession, during his Jesuit novice days, with something he called "contemplative walking." TJ once made the mistake of including Jervis in this rite. Their one contemplative walk had begun with TJ instructing his brother to be mindful of every muscle as it moved, every ligament as it stretched, every bone as it supported him. Next he was to give thanks for the astonishing gift that is balance, the syncopated rhythms of heartbeat and breath, and the stunningly orchestrated, full-bodied miracle that is a simple forward stride. It all began to strike Jervis as a lot of work. After a half mile or so, when TJ further ordered him to be grateful that he was sharing the same sacred mode of locomotion that had propelled Jesus through the Holy Land and Francis through Umbria, Jervis cut in, saying, "Let us express our joy too, Teej, for the way the disciples occasionally fragranced the Umbrian and Galilean air with a sacred—" And here Jervis exercised his preternatural ability to fart like a rifle shot. TJ jumped halfway out of his skin. Jervis then added insult to injury by saying that the sanctified secrets to his enviable volume were undercooked soybeans and an inviolate sphincter.

As the Jesuitical-looking crow stepped thoughtfully toward him in the 22nd Avenue Market parking lot, Jervis felt so bad about having profaned his only contemplative walk with his brother that he swerved deep into the middle of the lot so as not to disturb the bird.

This swerve proved fatal: behind the blue dumpster in the lot's far corner Jervis heard a thud, followed by an eerie gasp. Thinking a drunk might have tried to dumpster-dive, then fallen in and hurt himself, Jervis strode fast toward the sound. Rounding the dumpster's corner, he was stunned to find a man lying on his back on the asphalt, bleeding from the head and mouth, with two more men standing over him. Both, to Jervis's confusion, wore yellow rubber kitchen gloves. One man wielded a four-foot length of two-by-four, the other a steel Kryptonite bike lock. Both were sweating from the exertion of the beating they were administering. The downed man had shattered-looking hands and was reduced to holding his feet in the air to try to ward off the next blow. Before Jervis could think or shout, one of the men took a tremendous woodchopper's swing, powering the thin side of the two-by-four down onto the fallen man's shin. The cracking of bone was audible. The man's defenses collapsed. The bike-lock swinger took immediate advantage, landing a terrible, spray-spattering blow to the head. The downed man went limp.

On the Catholic Worker calendar beneath which Jervis had breakfasted that morning, Mother Teresa hunched in a Calcutta alley caressing the intact cheek of a leper whose other cheek had collapsed into a festering hole. The eyeball above the missing cheek seemed to gaze incredulously at the camera, an effect due not to amazement but to an enormous fraction of missing face. Below the photo Mother T was quoted saying, "I know God will not give me anything I can't handle. I just wish He didn't trust me so much." For the first time in his life, Jervis experienced the example of his hero not as inspiration but as a weight as horrifically heavy as his childhood Church's lust for other people's gold. He shouldered that weight even so.

He began by loudly clearing his throat.

Two-by-Four and Kryptonite turned—to see a man step from behind the blue dumpster, walk quietly toward them, and stop not six feet away. His proximity of course led them to study him more closely. He stood about five feet three inches and weighed maybe 130 pounds. He had a hunched posture, a premature tonsure, and wispy dark blond side-hair that floated out round his skull like the tail feathers of some bizarre jungle bird. He wore red flip-flops, a pair of torn, dark green Portland State Vikings gym shorts he'd salvaged from a park, and a chartreuse T-shirt with crimson letters that read DYLSEXICS ARE TEOPLE POO. Instead of the revolver or sawed-off shotgun he would have needed to dissuade them from their little murder project, he held a small bag of groceries in one hand and a double video in the other.

Looking hopeful, the little fellow brandished the video at them, revealing an image of a Japanese actor wielding a dangerous-looking sword. The thugs scowled at this image almost politely, as if giving the sword-bearing actor a chance to blow himself up into three dimensions, leap from the box, and join the TEOPLE POO guy in defense of their victim. But Toshiro Mifune was no fool. He remained fixed to the box.

Scores of Portlanders, upon reading newspaper accounts of the tragedy about to unfold, would say that Jervis had been an idiot not to run in safe circles round the parking lot, shouting, *"Help! Police! Help!"* What these second-guessers forget is that, when a person in love with Love sees and hears a two-by-four break leg bone, a bike-lock blast skin, hair, blood, and a bizarre material he fears must be brain from a shattering skull, common sense is shattered by the same blows, leaving nothing in its place but uncommon sense.

Jervis stepped forward, straddling the victim before another blow could fall.

For several pregnant seconds: no movement but the heaving chests of the thugs, the trembling of Toshiro Mifune in Jervis's hand, the blood pooling, impossibly red, on asphalt. But the thugs' eyes had gone reptilian.

Marguerite, Jervis thought. *Bound to the stake. The eyes of her Inquisitors.*

Sensing his body was about to be unmade, knowing his next words could be his last, Jervis invoked his dear M with all his might. *"This soul,"* he told the thugs, *"has six wings like the Seraphim."*

How little metaphysics changes physics. Chitter of sparrows, coo of doves, starlings straining to be meadowlarks, Jervis straining to be M. In a high, trembling voice that sounded doomed even to himself, he said, *"No longer knowing how to speak, obeying no created thing but love, I tell you for your own sakes, leave this man. His soul. Its wings. Go."*

The thugs had heard enough. Two-by-Four jerked his head to one side. Kryptonite nodded and stepped to Jervis's right. Two-by-Four moved left. No way to watch them both as they eased in toward him. *God created an impossible situation.*

The last word Jervis heard in what he now calls "my former incarnation," spoken by Kryptonite: *"Checkmate."*

His last thought: *It's over. My life! It's over!*

His last sensation before the blow that shattered his arm, then the flash that took his consciousness: an impossible eruption from inside the mothering Earth herself, exploding up his legs, buttocks, hardening penis, up his back, neck, head, blasting out the sun-door at the top of his skull in an unstoppable flood of joy.

IV. Grady vs. Two Gorgeous Bald Guys

To displace. To put eyes between the legs, or sex organs
on the face. To contradict... Nature does many things
the way I do.

—Pablo Picasso

BARE-CHESTED AGAIN, COOKING under the goosenecked halogen reading
lamp in the double-occupancy study carrel again, Grady Haynes has, in
defense of his intellect, been making headway in Heidegger's *Being and
Time.* Why? Because Risa is studying at her little writing desk. With her
philosophy-scrambling lower body and legs out of view and the double-
occupancy study carrel to himself, Grady readily grasps the Heideggerian
distinction between "ontological" (the essence of things) and "ontical" (the
thingness of things). He then groks the dictum that our passing moods
doom us to nonreflective immersion in automatism, limiting us to entrapped
reactions rather than creative responses to the world's unfolding.

Where he runs into trouble is when Heidegger and Risa, with the over-
wrought synchronicity of a pair of crystal-groping New Age tofu-jockeys,
join forces: scant seconds after the mighty-minded German chances to
remark that only ecstasy enables the philosopher to fully escape the ontical
entrapment, Risa rises from her desk, causing Grady's entrapment to
feature the perfect pear of her waist and bottom lowering itself onto the
bed beside him. When *Being and Time,* upon the pear's landing, then bobs
up and down in Grady's hands, nonreflective immersion in automatism
floods his imagination with his own favorite form of bobbing up and down.
Gaping at the utterly unstill-life of the pear as Risa proceeds to arrange her
three-pillow backrest, mug of green tea, dictionaries, books, and notebooks
in their usual and accustomed places, Grady is so bowled over he grows
desperate. *If I'm ever going to make it as a philosopher,* he silently vows, *I
must break out of this ontical entrapment NOW!*

With fierce resolve he commences an Olympian attempt to comprehend
this preposterous sentence: "Being does not delimit the highest region of
beings so far as they are conceptually articulated according to genus and
species." Though it takes him ten readings, he *does* by damn wrestle a feeble
meaning from this ostentatious spew. *Good work, Grade-O!* he thinks just

as Risa swings the regions of being she uses for legs onto the bed, her panties flash pink and inner thighs flash cream and tan beneath the dazzlingly
truncated, conceptually articulated bell of her T-shirt, Grady's pulse rate
doubles, his temperature shoots up six or seven degrees, his penis blows
up like a party balloon, and Heidegger's next precision sentence somehow
reads, "*Shlorzalkeich geflugen kunkflarff bleister genugen yowst.*"

Loser! Grady hisses.

Vortkoonkle doofen! the testy German shoots back.

Despite this falling out, Grady vows to continue reading just as soon
as printed words resume even faint legibility: he demonstrates this to
Heidegger by glaring at *Being and Time,* laying it facedown on his lap,
deploying his erection as a bookmark.

Risa, meanwhile, has covered her legs with the snow-white bedsheet and
pulled them into a half lotus that might remind a more ontologically at-
tuned scholar of a yogini, meditating Buddhist, or some such evolved being,
but only causes the ontically entrapped Grady to picture how, beneath the
sheet, the ligaments and tendons of a half-lotussed groin are now stretched
taut as tuned cello strings, causing the hallowed chamber behind the strings
to ever so slightly open and, in some mesmerizing way, to breathe. The
energies released by this visualization assassinate Heidegger for the night,
but do enable Grady to accomplish one last feat with *Being and Time*: by
kegeling the muscled roots of his bookmark, he finds he can make all 498
pages of Heidegger's masterwork bob up and down.

THE CONCLUSION OF Risa's scribbled secret notebook entry of September
12, 1989:

> What a spin The Coom's wisdom sources put on university
> life! The same scriptures & myths the anthro & lit depts
> dissect with condescension he supersaturates with meaning
> & why not? To think the anthro or lit depts can grasp
> love or wisdom like the saints & sages who live it is like
> thinking athletic dept coaches can play basketball like NBA
> stars. Universities are incurably agnostic—yet an agnostic
> approach to the Unseen Unborn Perfection is sheer ego-
> mind silliness. With the heart alone behold It! Don't quibble
> or debate! There IS what Vedic scriptures call "a union to be
> realized within the heart's void" (hrdayakasa). There IS what
> Gir Killeen calls "a blade of flame wedged into the impossibly
> thin season between words."
>
> Flame language! The perfect name for the tongue that
> doesn't contradict empirical thought but transcends our
> need for it. You've felt this, Risa! When masses of barley,
> distilled, become whiskey, when mounds of coal, crushed,
> become diamond, when skeins of human experience become

pregnant stillness, "in a flash, at a trumpet crash," flame words rise up in us without us. When The Coom, in one supersaturated breath, likens an Eckhartian "supreme beatitude" to a Sanskrit "parama bhakti" to a Dantean "piacere eterno" he is not speaking in discursive thoughts: he's speaking in flames, whiskey & diamonds. Dive into Risa-less seeing & read that language! Relish the way the "I" subsides in wonder. Remember how "you" vaporized, at age twelve I think, when you saw the face of Mother Mary hidden in an oil by Odilon Redon? Remember being reduced to nothing but bliss by the hypaethral light that shot in over the Olympics near sundown just last night? Remember the street lady outside St. James's Cathedral on Francis's feast day last year who, when you asked her name, said, "Clare," then cackled, "Gotcha!" then asked for a smoke & when you dug out a Kool & the match flared & she really looked at you, her eyes weren't just looking: they were speaking "the language around which the year revolves, the breathing behind breathing, the sight behind sight, the first, the ancient." And she was a kind of ragged street Clare!

With the heart alone, behold THAT! Don't let CNN's or the anthro & lit depts' agnostic factoids pretend to tell the true story. Subsume "Risa" in the good darkness of the sad/ṣad/ṣadness vault, that each flame word may shine out as bright as it is!

GRADY SNAPS OFF his halogen reading lamp. From a greater height than necessary, he drops *Being and Time* to the floor. *Shlurzle geboogen klaupff!* Heidegger shouts after thunking the hardwood. *Metafizzle-dicked twaddle-drizzler!* Grady silently shoots back.

Turning away from Risa, he ferrets in the magazines beneath his nightstand for a copy of *Ski Colorado!*, then swivels back up onto the bed with a plan. Taking his time, he searches for the coolest-looking photo in the magazine, soon deciding on a full-page shot of a crimson-garbed skier flying down an astoundingly steep mountain face, sending up a plume of sun-shot powder. *Okay, Grady,* Grady adjures Grady. *No more whining. No more Sanskrit cowgirl herding your consciousness like a little dogie into the claustrophobic corral of your own scrotum. Enter the photo. Become the skier. Launch a frigid flying-downhill reverie that negates the heat of the Hell Circle and carries you past Exhaustulation on to whatever does or doesn't happen at 2 a.m.—*

But wait! What's this? *Risa's left leg.* She is drawing it slowly up, causing the snow-colored sheet to avalanche slowly down the leg until *abracadabra,* right in front of Grady's face at an angle so direct he doesn't even have to sprain his eyeballs, an entire naked knee and thigh tower in all their glory!

Okay! Okay then! New plan, new plan, new plan. *Like, uh…like a comparison study.* Yeah! *Like, secretly compare the Ski Colorado! dude shredding down Powder Mountain to the skier-free Mountain of Risa's Thigh.* Yeah! *But, like,* ontologically *compare them, not just* ontically, *getting all heated up by Mount Thigh.* Yeah! *Like, to launch our investigation, why is Mount Thigh—keeping our ontological cool here—about* NINE THOUSAND TIMES *more appealing than little red ski dude's Powder Mountain? Answer me* that, *Philosopher Grady.*

Will do. For starts, Mount Thigh isn't being defaced by some vainglorious skier—which brings me to why I prefer high-mountain backpacking to skiing. In backpacking, the suffering endured as you climb sensitizes you to the gorgeousness when you arrive on high, and your elation lasts and lasts. In skiing, a mechanical lift crammed with party-hardies ratchets you to elevation in minutes, only to turn around and, in seconds, undo all the elevation gain you didn't suffer to achieve, so that way too soon you're DOWN *and the only cure for elation deflation is to get back in the party-hardy line, pay the piper, ratchety-ratchet back up, and bouncy-bounce down again, up, down, up, down,* wanka wanka wanka.

Hmm. Very good, Ontologist Grady. What other philosophy ya got?

Well, Mount Thigh, in contrast to the photo of Ski Colorado! powder, is warm not cold, alive not inert, beautifully groomed without grooming, perfectly sloped without trying, and rooted to the ground zero of a woman who's given me more pleasure in six months than every woman I've known combined. By sighting in an imaginary trail and working my way up Mount Thigh, when I summit at the kneecap I also notice the thigh doing something surprising, namely: exuding charisma! *The way people* do. *What's more, Mount Thigh brings to mind a specific category of person. With its bald kneecapped summit it is exuding the same charisma as the torso and head of a beautifully put-together little bald guy. With Risa's thigh muscles exuding the mannish muscularity of a powerful neck and torso, this fetching little dude is* definitely no woman. *Yet the lack of such features as eyes, eyebrows, a mouth, and a nose give him such* mystique! *I mean, sure, this bald guy is shoulderless, expressionless, has no arms or legs, and doesn't look all that smart either. But how could he? With only a knee for a head* he has no brain! *Speaking purely of his thingness, keeping it* ontomological *or whatever that word was, he's just* a limbless, faceless torso. *Yet if we stop projecting notions such as* an attractive man must have four limbs, broad shoulders, a neck, and a head with a face on it, *I'm moved by the* alternative attractiveness *of this little fellow! In spite of his entire body being a mere thigh and a knee, he's the majority shareholder of one of Risa's legs, propelling her wherever she wishes to go all day, propping her up in bed till all hours of the night, making her look great as he does it, asking nothing in return. And the longer I ponder how helpful and humble*

and alternatively gorgeous this little guy is, the more I feel like praising him.
So by damn I will!

Aiming his thoughts at the shiny kneecap he saw as the bald guy's pate,
Grady thinks: *You know what, little man? You're a strong silent hero to me!*
A role model. So can you and I be friends, do you think? Perhaps even more
than friends? At which point Grady starts to feel a new brand of excitement. He's never asked a fellow male to be *more than friends* before! *What*
exactly did I mean by that? he asks himself. I've never been into guys that I
know of. But doesn't a featureless torso-guy who also happens to be Risa's
naked thigh vex the male-versus-female question? If I was a politician I'd go
ahead and be more than friends with my bald guy, ducking accusations of
homosexuality with a press release explaining how the male for whom I've
fallen is, *in actual scientific fact,* a segment of a *woman.* But *I'm no hair-*
splitting politician! I'm an aspiring philosopher whose sense of The Good
is happiness, pretty much, since, as Saint Augustine famously put it, "Man
has no reason to philosophize except to get happy and stuff," to which the
Declaration of Independence more or less says, "Ditto!" So does my happiness mean I've always had a thing for lithe, strong, armless, legless males?
Will I be drawn to every taut, tanned, featureless torso-type guy to come
sauntering down the sidewalk from now on? Or are my feelings specific to
the denuded man who also happens to be Risa's left knee and thigh?

As he is pursuing these tough queries, some kind of thought tornado
strikes Risa, causing her to rock forward, then back, due to delight it
seems, which causes the remaining portion of bedsheet to avalanche whitely
down—and *Eureka! A second lithe, smooth, taut, tanned bald guy towers*
alongside the first! Just look at them! Grady philosophizes as he ogles the
identical silky-skinned, silent, eyeless, mouthless twins! See how they *mirror*
each other? See how the bald guy to the right reflects the bald guy to the
left so perfectly it's like a perfectly calm mountain lake is parked between
them, reflecting the first bald guy back at the second in perfectly reflected
reflection? *Oh, my little man-twins!* I'm falling so deep into the throes of
whatever the word is for *when-you-worship-something-that-isn't-a-god-as-*
if-it's-a-god-because-screw-it!-close-enough! that I would love to slide over,
throw my arms around you, and experience the godlikeness of your twin
baldnesses. And if I did slide over and do this, I can just *tell*—because women
aren't the only ones who can just tell stuff!—that you'd *love* the feel of my
big torso against your small torsos and bare biceps around your barenesses!
Wouldn't you maybe even start pleading, *Be even* more *intimate, Grady!*
When you've been an armless, legless, eyeless, mouthless bald guy all your
life, you need *the powerful arms you don't have to wrap themselves around*
you, and the mind and imagination you don't have to make up crazy poetic
shit about you, and the lungs, lips, tongue you don't have to breathe-talk-
lick nonsense into you, because what we lack we need! Right, Grady? So go
for it, ooh! do! and we'll thank you in bald-guy thanking ways you never
dreamt of, like squeezing your head between us like we're a humongous

*pair of headphones playing stereophonic bare-body music on your head
that comes in so clear that Lake-Isn't-There hears us, and her waters
start whirling, and you start laughing young-Walt-Whitman-soft while you
squish even wilder nonsense into us, poor lucky Grady squoze between his
giant bald headphones groan-moan-panting sweat-slippery wownesses into
us until, a thigh? a guy? which is which? Who knows or cares when—*

At the ring of the phone Grady lurches, then makes an absurd attempt to
look ontological as he rearranges *Ski Colorado!* atop his bloated schlong.
Without a glance his way, Risa straightens her legs, obliterating both bald
guys, throwing Grady into some weird form of grief until she swings
the legs to the floor, sets out for the phone, the perfect pear reappears,
and Grady is thrown back into his Saint-Augustine-Philosopher-of-Happy
place. Then:

"Hello?"

A sob even Grady can hear, and the words: *"Risa! Something terrible!"*

"My God! *TJ!* What's happened?"

Grady hears: *"horrible injuries...team of surge...might not make
it...not sure I can drive."*

He watches Risa say: "Be there in ten minutes." *Click.* Watches her
throw off her sleeveless Huskies shirt (*Hi, breasts!*), throw on a real shirt
(*Bye, breasts!*), slide into jeans (*Go with God, dearest pear!*), step into
sandals (*I want you too, long slender feet renting the basement under my
bald guys!*).

"Oh, Grady! Jervis, TJ's twin brother, was attacked in Portland. He's
been horribly beaten. Headed into surgery." Car keys. Wallet. A tooth-
brush, hairbrush, and a few clothes fly into her giant ever-ready backpack.
"TJ's beside himself so I'm gonna drive him. I'll call as soon as I know
anything."

She climbs onto the bed and mounts Grady, her no-longer bald guys
at last at least straddling him, her face in his face, eyes in his eyes, wild
hair in his eyes. "You're a scwewy wabbit, Gwady. But, Grampa Brahma
help me, I *do* love you." Lips on his lips. Breath mixed in his breath. But
destraddling him already. Backing away and stepping down already. Backpack obstructing view of fleeing pear. Inferno door opening, *"Bye!"*

Inferno door closed. Sound of running, fading, fading. *Gone.*

"I love you too," Grady says to the wetness she leaves evaporating on
his lips. But when his lips go dry, the room turns instantly oppressive,
Heidegger's thought-snarls lying like wet intestines on the floor, glandular
residues of affair with bald guys skulking through his blood and body,
horrible injuries...team of surge...might not make it...

Abruptly, with feeling, Grady asks the room, *"Who-am-I-what-am-I-
where-am-I-how-am-I?"*

The question feels idiotic, yet apropos to his condition. He likes the
sound of it so much he asks it again: *"Who-am-I-what-am-I-where-am-I-
how-am-I?"*

Looking for clues, he sees Risa's notebook facedown on the bed, picks it up, repeats the question: "*Who-am-I-what-am-I-where-am-I-how-am-I?*" The notebook says:

The distance that separates heaven & Earth can be annihilated.

His brain briefly quiets and an unknown force begins to lift him. Then his brain pipes up: *Hocus pocus. Only ecstasy enables us to escape the ontical entrapment!* Grady splits in two: half faith, half doubt. "*Who-am-I-what-am-I-where-am-I-how-am-I?*" he demands of the notebook.

Right here within the body is an Infinite Person, higher than which there is nothing.

"Within *your* body, maybe," Grady says, wanting Risa's body terribly. But when he looks down at his own body, it seems an insult to The Good to think this walking, talking vat of testosterone could house an Infinite Person.

Setting aside Risa's notebook, Grady gets out of bed, walks to his Hell Circle's big unopenable window, peers out at the city, the night-black Puget, the invisible Olys. "*Infinite Person who annihilates the distance between heaven and Earth,*" he prays to the voidnesses and vastnesses. "*Who-am-I-what-am-I-where-am-I-how-am-I?*"

No answer. His mind feels opaque, body leaden, the room's voidness intolerable. He walks into the kitchen, opens the oven, sticks his head inside, asks the elements, flecked metal walls, and black yam drippings: "*Who-am-I-what-am-I-where-am-I-how-am-I?*"

Weird, cool acoustics and smells, but the same No Answer.

Giving up the search, Grady trudges to the bed and starts to collapse upon it when, on the bed's far side, a shape seizes him by the spinal cord. Crouching like a bowhunter stalking a deer, he creeps round to Risa's side, gazes directly down—*and there lies the perfect pear imprint,* still visible in the sheet.

"*Who-am-I-what-am-I-where-am-I-how-am-I?*" Grady asks the imprint. Risa's notebook lies facedown at the foot of the bed. He picks it up again. The notebook replies:

The body is the universe in a likeness.

And truth bursts so powerfully into the room it drops Grady to his knees. So carefully, so gratefully, he lays his ear and cheek upon the imprint. "*Ohhhhhh!*" he breathes. The shape is still warm.

V. Being Eaten

There is no death that is not somebody's food, no life that
is not somebody's death...The archaic religion is
to kill god and eat him. Or her.
> —Gary Snyder, *The Practice of the Wild*

IT FEELS MANIPULATIVE to tell Jervis's story in a way that leaves the reader
thinking he died. But it feels inaccurate to say, "He lived." Though Jervis's
life does not end in the story here unfolding, it doesn't exactly continue.
Countless human beings, in countless brutal ways, have been so thoroughly
assaulted at some point in their lives that, though they survive, their former
self does not.

The last word Jervis heard in his "former incarnation" was "Checkmate." The first swing of the two-by-four then shattered bones in his left
arm and sent all seven samurai, the sauvignon blanc, and Redenbacher
popcorn clattering and shattering to the pavement. *(Our rule is the daily
performance of works of mercy for those in need.)* Blinded by jagged
bolts of pain, Jervis sagged earthward. A split second before the flash that
annihilated consciousness, an inconceivable blast of Oceanic joy erupted
and filled him. *(There is no such thing as defeat in an act of compassion.)*
The Kryptonite bike lock then crushed the right side of his skull, splintering
the parietal and temporal plates, blasting him into nothingness, obliterating
all awareness of the continued beating that turned his head, throat, and
body into a leaking sack of incalculable damage. *(How can there ever be
another Marguerite, another Francis, another Virgin's Son, if I don't stand
annihilate, without anxiety, no longer knowing how to speak, inside a
Church governed utterly by Love?)*

When the thugs were sure Jervis was dead, they tossed him into the
big blue dumpster with the body of the man he'd failed to save, covered
the gore-strewn asphalt with dead laurel leaves, and vanished, taking their
bloodied yellow kitchen gloves with them.

The dead man was later identified as a full-time Shell gas station
attendant, a single dad with two kids, and, to make ends meet, a meth
dealer. The assailants, though believed to be "higher-level meth dealers,"
were never identified, let alone found.

* * *

JERVIS WAS DISCOVERED at 1 a.m. on September 12th by a college student dumpster-diving for produce tossed by the 22nd Avenue Market. The young man was lithe: he swung up over the high wall of the dumpster and hopped down inside in one athletic motion—then shrieked like a dying rabbit: he'd landed squarely on top of a blood-blackened smear of a man with one eye popped out of its socket.

At the dead man's feet lay a second victim, also horribly disfigured, whose gore-covered T-shirt in the streetlight still managed to read DYLSEX-ICS ARE TEOPLE POO. The words "teople poo" struck the student as such a perfect description of both bodies that he began to laugh, and couldn't stop laughing till he retched. Mind gone, agility gone, he dragged himself from the dumpster, staggered to the market, banged on the glass door, and kept on banging till the frightened shelf-stocking crew realized he was gagging on his words, "Call *yaghh*! the cops. Call *haghh*! the cops."

They called the cops. A Portland police squad car arrived ten minutes later and two unlikely men in blue stepped out: a towering Black officer with a gold tooth and diamond earring and a compact Apache with a graying, extremely tidy, two-foot-long braid. The student tried, between laughter and tears, to say what he'd found. While the Black officer taped off the crime scene, the Indian, an Officer Barrios, climbed up into the dumpster, checked on what, at first sight, he was sure were two dead bodies—and discovered Teople Poo's faint pulse.

Within minutes Jervis was ambulanced the few blocks to Burnside Community Hospital. The ER docs intubated his crushed trachea immediately, then found so many more grave injuries that they did a quick CT scan to help with diagnosis. The entire head and torso seemed to be one massive contusion. Thirty or more bones were visibly chipped or fractured. The worst of three shattered ribs had punctured the right lung. The left eye socket had imploded. The throat appeared to have been stomped by the full weight of an attacker's boot. But the most dire problem was two massive extradural hematomas caused by skull fractures: gushing blood was trapped inside the skull, causing Jervis's brain to compress, slowing his heart rate to that of some trance-pulsed animal: a land tortoise; hibernating bear; basking shark. The neurosurgeon ordered immediate brain surgery, an ENT was called in to work on the smashed and torn throat, a trauma surgeon addressed the rib shards piercing the lung, and a macabre ballet commenced. The order of address was textbook ABC: airway, breathing, circulation. The trauma surgeon inserted a chest tube to drain the pneumothorax. The neurosurgeon drained the intracranial hematomas. The ENT worked wonders up and down the ruined throat. Further procedures were performed as more injuries were discovered or crises arose. Jervis was on the operating table for eleven hours. He flatlined twice. Both times, something beyond desire or will returned him to life.

Flame words rise up in us without us.

TJ AND RISA arrived at Burnside Community early on in the surgery. A nurse, darting through the ER waiting room, glanced at TJ, did a double take, stopped in her tracks. "Are you Jervis McGraff's brother?" she asked.

He nodded. "TJ McGraff."

"Britt Morritz," she said. "Jervis taught my daughter at Westside Catholic last year. She's crazy about him."

"Me too," TJ managed to croak.

"Come with me," said Nurse Britt, and led them to an office adjacent to the ER. A doc in green surgical scrubs, Phillipa something, came in, introduced herself, and told them to take seats. In a voice so gentle it doubled TJ's foreboding, she said that Jervis was in surgery and would continue to be for a long time. When she began running through the list of injuries, Risa took notes for a few moments, but the list grew so long she couldn't keep up. TJ, listening, had to place his head between his knees to keep from fainting. Nurse Britt vanished, reappearing with orange juice for TJ just as Doc Phillipa finished. She and Doc P then invited Risa and TJ to stay in the office as long as they liked, and hurried away.

The juice revived TJ enough to enable him to sit up. "Bathroom," he eventually mumbled. Then he just sat there. Risa offered to help him walk. "I'm fine," he said, then doddered out of the room with the gait of a ninety-year-old man.

Hours crept past. Information crept in. Two small miracles in the sea of horrific hurts: after the hematomas were drained and the pressure on the brain relieved, Jervis's heart rate crept back toward normal; and once the rib splinters were removed from the lung, the lung reinflated and Jervis's breathing resumed without mechanical aid.

But a single simple word had already commandeered TJ's life: "coma."

Hours became days. Days became weeks. Jervis's body remained a breathing, pulsing, but otherwise lifeless planet.

TJ became that planet's faithfully orbiting moon.

(Portland, autumn 1989)

VI. Staying Stupid

The more stupid one is, the closer one is to reality. The more stupid one is, the clearer one is. Stupidity is brief and artless, while intelligence wriggles and hides itself...The more stupidly I have presented this argument, the better I've said it.

—Ivan Karamazov in Dostoevsky's
The Brothers Karamazov

THE ATTACK ON Jervis did not make TJ's business life difficult: it made it impossible. He'd been on the homestretch at Seattle Culinary Institute. He had architects, contractors, and two large crews working for him in Portland. His Pearl and Waterfront renovations were ambitious. Both buildings were old and idiosyncratic. The mortar between every last brick needed to be replaced. Steel infrastructure needed to be added to make the buildings earthquake safe. Problems arose daily. Whenever the trouble-shooting slowed down, the army of workers stood idle. TJ's calendar during these same days was stuffed full of appointments and interviews with potential chefs, sommeliers, and other restaurant staff, and with food suppliers, interior decorators, interior painters, landscapers, sign makers, accountants, lawyers, insurance people. Yet from the moment he set eyes on Jervis's pulverized face and body, TJ had no stomach for anything but sitting at his brother's side.

A week after delivering TJ to Portland, Risa drove down from U Dub after her Friday classes. She found TJ in intensive care, dressed in a green gown, cap, and slippers, hunched in a chair next to Jervis's bed, holding his brother's left hand with his own left while, with his right hand, he fiddled with a tiny drawstring purse hanging from a cord about his neck. The situation struck Risa at once. TJ's lips were moving as if the tiny purse held some kind of sentient creature! What on Earth did it hold, and why did he seem to be talking to it?

After donning her own cap, gown, and slippers, Risa entered the ICU, drew up beside TJ, and saw that, beneath the sterile gown, his dapper clothes had wilted, his face and eyes were exhausted, and, to judge by his odor, he hadn't bathed since she'd last seen him.

Nurse Britt placed a chair beside TJ, caught Risa's eye, and nodded toward the chair's seat. A notepad from an answering service was lying there. Risa picked it up. A quick glance showed her a list of phone messages several pages long. Most of the messages were from architects and contractors. Many of the notes ended in multiple exclamation points.

Risa asked TJ whether he'd returned any of the calls. He shrugged in a vague way, then closed his eyes and kept mouthing words to his tiny purse. Risa squatted in front of him like a baseball catcher, gripped his knees firmly, and said, "*TJ. Come in, please. TJ. Do you read me?*"

When he opened his eyes but kept fretting with the purse, Risa closed her fingers around his hands, stopping their movement. TJ's lips stopped moving too. She said, "I know Jervis means the world to you. I know you're doing everything in your power to send him strength and love. But we need to talk about these." She tapped the list of phone messages.

TJ's expression remained so far away that she went back to gripping his knees.

"I come in peace, TJ. But not the peaceful kind of peace. It won't help Jervis if, when he wakes, *your* life has fallen to pieces. It's time for some practical, real-world decisions. Today, not tomorrow. And if you're incapable of such decisions I'm going to pester you till you hire someone who *is* capable. Got it?"

When he neither nodded nor spoke, she squeezed his knees harder. TJ scowled at her hands as if at some invasive metaphysical force far beyond human control.

"Listen," she said. "Jervis is going to need time. *Lots* of it. And I can see you want to be with him during that time. For that reason, you need a helper you can trust with your *life*. You need to tell this person every last thing you've got going, renovation-wise. They then need to cancel everything that can be canceled. You need them to pay your bills in a timely fashion. The Pearl and Waterfront projects are on schedules that *can't be blown off*. You told me this yourself. So your helper also needs to be a go-between. They can guard your vigil with Jervis but must also be free to bust in and get decisions out of you. Without such a helper you're headed for chaos, and legal trouble too. Are you even *hearing* me?"

TJ roused himself enough to look her in the face. "My problem," he sighed, "which is insurmountable, is that there are only two people on Earth I trust enough to give me that kind of help. And one of them's in a coma. And the other is squeezing the crap out of my knees."

Risa let go, then plunked down in the chair beside him. "I'm honored. But I live in Seattle, I'm a full-time student, I'm art school bound, and I need to win major scholarship dough to swing RISD. I can't slack off. I've also got a boyfriend I really like who's feeling neglected. Who *is* neglected. To work for you here would wreck every last thing *I've* got going."

But TJ was shaking his head throughout her recitation. He'd come to life. "It's *crazy* how much help I need," he said. "But it's also crazy how perfect you are for the job. And we'll keep your life unwrecked. Listen, Risa. Stay in school. Stay with Grady. Just drop a couple classes. Work for me long enough to see Jervis and me through this and I'll pay the rest of your undergrad tuition. Any grad school scholarship money you lose, I'll match. Take my Waterfront and Pearl files to Seattle. You can do a lot of work from there by phone. To save the time you'd waste driving, fly SeaTac to PDX as often as need be, on me. And here in Portland, my house on Skyline is yours—and Grady's when he can make it down to see you. I'll move into Jervis's Hoyt Street monk's cell to be closer to him. What else? Oh. Your salary, starting this minute, is whatever you ask—provided you ask enough."

Risa was stunned by his proposal. She could almost imagine it working. The wild card, most likely, was Grady. Who'd been a wild card from the start. But if he couldn't deal with the first real storm life sent them, did they stand a chance over the long haul?

She said, "I can see already what kind of equation this is. I'll regret it if I help. And I'll regret it if I don't help. Same difference. So...I'll help."

TJ's reaction was strange. His face lit up at her acceptance, but instead of looking at Risa his eyes dropped to the tiny purse, gazed at it as if at a dear friend, lifted it to his lips, kissed it, then slid it inside his shirt. Only then did he stand and throw his arms around Risa.

SHE WENT TO work that day. She had to call Grady and cancel a date to do it. A Silas and Iona Dupree concert no less—Grady's favorite acoustic country duo. He'd already purchased tickets. Excellent seats. She felt so bad she bent over backward to make amends. "As TJ's new Pearl project and Waterfront project go-between," she said, "I have two gigantic messes to sort out. It'll be a week, maybe, before I can get home. But once I catch up I'll be home often. And I owe you big, Grady. So how 'bout this? Let's abolish the double-occupancy study carrel and cancel Designated Study Nights till further notice."

"Now that...Well now. *That's* a deal," Grady said—but after a pause that surprised her. "And when you get here," he added, "we need to talk. 'Cause I've got news. *Good* news, Risa. But too complicated for the phone. It'll keep till I see you. No worries. But now get busy down there so you can get on up here!"

Feeling uneasy, but overwhelmed by the trouble that TJ's renovation projects were in, Risa told Grady she loved him, signed off, and set to work.

THE WATERFRONT ARCHITECT was Gail Brace: a man. The Pearl district architect was Theo Avery, a woman. Both were urbane, charming people, hugely relieved to meet Risa and establish a reliable form of contact with TJ.

The contractors and subcontractors proved less urbane. All men. Their crews all men too. Upon learning that Risa was their boss's lieutenant, incredulous ogling or crooked smiles were the usual first reaction. But after watching these men in action, Risa found herself doing some ogling in return. The amount of know-how and hands-on effort needed to gut old brick buildings without wrecking the bricks, install steel seismic reinforcement, remove every bit of old mortar from the bricks, replace it with new mortar, and construct redesigned walls out of hundred-year-old red clay astounded her. Old heating, power, and plumbing had to be torn out in sync with the brickwork, and state-of-the-art heat, power, and water had to be vented, wired, and piped in. The upgrades all had to work perfectly then vanish, leaving behind seemingly century-old walls, halls, and surfaces that were in fact new but for the bricks. The workmen were well aware that it took money and lots of it to get all this done and they were nobody's fools: as soon as they realized the sight-for-sore-eyes college girl was TJ McGraff's factotum, the more flagrant ogling ended, manners became polite, the levity grew good-natured, and when Risa showed wit and intelligence, she became their respected darling, and working with them the most straightforward part of her job . . .

Whereas working with TJ became the least straightforward. Gail Brace, Theo Avery, and the contractors had inundated Risa the day she met them, with half a hundred things going much less than right. She had a huge capacity for detail (all that Skrit grammar study and metaphysical exegetics). She delivered intricate news of difficulties to TJ as fast as she gathered it. But TJ had become an ever-less-direct route to the solution of his own renovation problems. He pretty much *lived* in a chair beside Jervis, their left hands fused, tracking every beep and blip of his monitors and detail of his care. To reach TJ, Risa had to don a sterile cap, gown, mask, slippers, then capture his attention. But TJ seemed to have fallen into a sympathy coma. She tried coaxing him out into a waiting room to talk but found that, if he couldn't see the rise and fall of Jervis's chest, he got so distracted he couldn't follow her at all.

Bringing the renovation problems to Jervis's bedside increased TJ's attentiveness briefly. But even there, the only topic he was comfortable with for long was his brother. His attempts to send Jervis strength were surprisingly verbal: day in and day out he murmured every praiseworthy detail of Jervis's life, from birth to the present, directly to Jervis's comatose form. At first Risa listened politely till TJ reached the end of a Jervis story, but the stories proved endless. The only way to get a renovation crisis to lodge in his mind, she found, was to establish links between TJ's Jervis stories and the problems she and the builders faced. It was a ridiculous way of connecting, but with no known alternative, she grew skilled at it. A typical conversation a few weeks into the coma:

"Yo, TJ. I talked to Theo Avery this morning. Remember? Your Pearl architect? She told me to tell you the theatre guys from San Fran and New York arrived last night. She said you're turning the gutted old two-story ballroom inside the Pearl into a theatre. You've never mentioned this. Kinda hard to help when you don't say, 'I'm building a huge theatre and you're in charge of that.' Anyhow, you paid for this powwow, bought the theatre guys plane tickets, and I couldn't cancel since I didn't know about it till an hour ago. So they're here. And bursting with design ideas. Theo arranged a meeting with them and hopefully *you*, this afternoon, two o'clock sharp. Can I tell them you'll be there?"

"Jervis once told me angels are real," TJ replied.

"Cool," Risa said. "But about this meeting..."

"We were thirteen. Christmas in Baltimore. Nativity scene on the snowy lawn. Tacky plastic angels with light bulbs inside. But tacky might be Jervis's favorite style. 'Angels are real,' he says, staring out at them. 'And happy to communicate,' he says. 'The thing is, to communicate with angels you have to be willing to listen to the *same boring angel ditties, over* and *over.*'" TJ beamed at Risa, then turned back to his brother's breathing.

"That's funny," she said. "But it's one fifteen. The meeting with San Fran and New York is in forty-five minutes. Does your angel story imply you can't make it?"

"Roger that," TJ said, then chuckled. "The *same boring angel ditties, over* and *over.*"

"Moving on," Risa said. "If you're not coming, Theo needs me to double-check her notes on your specs. Why, you might ask? Because she's about to build the three-hundred-ninety-nine-seat theatre *you* requested, at *huge* expense, with *your* money. We have, let's see, about ten minutes before I have to leave. So let's shoot through her list. If the spec I read is correct, the phrase 'Roger that' is perfect. If the spec is wrong, we'll fix it. Sound like a plan?"

"Roger that," TJ said.

"You asked, first and foremost, that the theatre *not* have a raised stage."

"Roger that," TJ said. "And isn't Jervis's coma starting to remind you of those damned angel ditties sung *over* and *over*?"

"It's, uh...I see what you mean, but prefer a 'Roger that.' Next spec. The seating should come right down to the floor on which the play or concert is performed."

"Roger that."

"And no curtains. You 'hate curtains,' you told Theo, because, quoting her quoting you, 'the players' bodies, minds, and actions and the audience's bodies, minds, and *reactions* should shine back and forth. A great theatrical experience is reflective, like a mirror, but also refractive, like the jewels in Indra's Net.'"

TJ lit up like a plastic lawn angel. "I didn't say that! Jervis said that!"

"Aha. *Jervis* helped with the theatre specs. Good to know," Risa said, seizing the opening. "What else did Jervis tell you and Avery?"

TJ beamed at his inert brother. "'No curtains,' he said. 'Let the set be standing there, sort of gloomy and abandoned-looking in the demi-light while the audience wanders in. That way, when the performers burst up out of the voms and the real light blasts them, it enchants the whole fucking space.' Big on the f-word, my brother. All Baltimore was in our youth. Catholic Baltimore anyway. What else? Oh yeah. 'Three-quarters wrap-around seating,' he says, very insistent. Why, I ask. 'Always reduce artifice,' Jervis says. 'Merge audience and performer. Everybody kind of hovering inside everybody else. The greater the nudity, the greater the union,' Jervis actually said, quoting some mystic or other, Eckhart maybe, Theo faithfully scribbling this down. But I protested. 'We're trying to design a *theatre*, Jervis, not achieve union with God.' 'Exactly wrong, Teej,' says Jervis. 'As we agreed from the start, designing two holy Restaurants the Great and one Holy Theatre the Great *is* our way of seeking divine union. And we'll call her *The Pearl*.' 'After the Pearl District,' I say to Jervis, liking the name. But he shakes his head and says, 'After Dōgen. Who after his own divine union said, "All the universe is One Bright Pearl." '"

TJ continued to smile at his oblivious brother. "Soon as he names it The Pearl, it's like Jervis sees the theatre hovering in the air in front of us. 'She'll need *optional* seating too,' he says. 'Flex-space seating,' they call it. 'Two hundred ninety-nine fixed seats. A hundred more flex.' I try to argue, saying more seats would pay the talent more money. 'The talent,' Jervis says, 'will only thank you when The Pearl turns out to be so intimate the crowd is vacuumed right into the performance. Big showy theatres make for big showy theatrics. Falstaff's bloring. Mick Jagger's prancing. Let the showy types blore at the Coliseum. We're going to make The Pearl—' "

" '—the home of performances,' " Risa cut in, reading from Theo's notes, " 'where every twist and turn of syntax, quaver of voice, scritch of guitar string, intake of breath, twitch of lip or face or finger can be seen and heard so perfectly that everyone is able to hover inside and reflect and refract everyone else.' "

"Exactly!" TJ said, beaming at Jervis's rising and falling chest.

With which Risa thanked him and bolted away. At the 2 p.m. meeting she then confirmed the specs of a ragged street samaritan buried in a coma, Jervis's theatre design won resounding approval and a few nice enhancements from the San Fran and New York consultants, and nearly thirty years later that same Pearl remains a theatrical and musical venue to which great performers flock from all over the world for the pleasure of experiencing a space so intimate everyone hovers inside and refracts everyone else.

THE WATERFRONT AND Pearl renovations threw curves at the builders daily. Walls slated for removal turned out to be weight-bearing, forcing redesign. Potential code violations had to be averted with last-minute alterations. And as Jervis's coma continued, TJ's interest in renovation problems vanished. There came a day, maybe four weeks into the coma, when he stopped tracking anything that Risa told him. The only person now addressing the builders' vital concerns was an unqualified twenty-two-year-old U Dub coed in the habit of calming herself by muttering pidgin Sanskrit under her breath.

The money situation was even more bizarre. Hundreds of thousands of TJ's dollars were being spent and before long only Risa knew why. She warned TJ of this repeatedly. He refused to listen. The one time she truly pressed him, he snapped, "*Please,* Risa! Fill in the needed amounts and I'll sign the checks. That's the best I can do."

"Embezzling from you would be like stealing a Binky from a baby!" she shot back.

TJ thought that over. "More like taking a Gideon Bible from a motel room," he said. "You can't steal what I'm pleading with you to take. For as long as Jervis breathes I'm going to be with him every second. I no longer care about anything else. There's no way I can thank you for taking this on. Eventually I hope to. But for now, Risa, don't tell me a thing. Just act on my behalf. If mistakes are made, seemingly by you, it's *my* fault, not yours. I thank you no matter what. If I go broke on these projects, so be it."

THE LOW POINT of Risa's sojourn as TJ's factotum occurred on the day a small army of workers began installing the ovens, stoves, and ventilation systems in the restaurant space in the Waterfront Building. Due to an earlier coordination failure, a sizable section of finished brick wall had to be torn apart a second time. This alone was very costly. Then the architect, Gail Brace, discovered that six seismic support beams, supposedly hidden behind the brick wall, hadn't been installed at all. A clusterfuck erupted: furious finger-pointing blame games, contractor versus subcontractors versus architect, most of the accusations couched in engineering nomenclature Risa couldn't even grasp. The mistake stood to cost somebody tens of thousands of dollars. She felt adamant that TJ should not have to pay. The renovation couldn't proceed till the crisis was resolved. She studied all the original contracts, listened to the wrangling repeatedly, consulted TJ's lawyer repeatedly. She then compiled a list of questions, took them to Burnside Community, and invaded TJ's vigil.

She found TJ Siamese-twinned to Jervis in the ICU, left hand to left hand as always. "There's a crisis on the Waterfront," she said, then started to describe it. But not two sentences in TJ gave her a pale smile and held up his palm to stop her.

"The fact that these renovations are going on at all is a miracle," he said. "*You're* a miracle, Risa. Thanks a thousand times over. But I can't help. I can't think about this at all."

"Ten minutes!" she pleaded. "I think I need to be the heavy on this one, TJ, and this mess is litigious. *Huge* lawsuit potential! Things could go terribly wrong if I—"

"*Stop!*" TJ pleaded. And tears rose in his eyes. "I...I dreamt last night...he didn't make it."

"Oh, TJ!"

"Does a vivid dream mean a thing is about to happen?" TJ murmured to his brother. "Or, since you dreamed it, has the psyche worked it out, so it no longer needs to happen? I don't know, Jervis. All I know is, I need to thank you, while you're still here, for being brave by the dumpster, though I wish you'd been a coward. I need to thank you for being who you've been all along, especially when I begged you to be different."

Risa felt TJ's attention turn to his brother so completely she doubted he any longer knew she was there. Closing her eyes, she gave herself to his murmuring.

"Thank you for every preposterous thing about you, Jervis. I've complained a *lot,* I know. But the longer you stay in this nothingness, the more sure I am that, if you make it back into somethingness, I'll never complain again. If you decide to stand like a cartoon Odysseus at your crappy sloop's helm again, sailing at night by those blue running lights that don't light up anything, I'll just thank you. If we hit another floating log that stabs a hole in your hull and you say, 'Oops, the bilge pump is busted,' I'll thank you. If you rush down into the hold and nail in a plywood patch that does more damage than the log, and I can't find the life jackets because their cupboard is already underwater, and the *Pope's Nose* leans so far to one side the propeller lifts out of the river so I have to hold a rope and climb off the deck and stand on the algae-slimed hull to keep us upright enough that the propeller stays submerged, I'll only thank you. If you then slide us into a slip I can't even see and your mast falls onto the dock, keeping us afloat just long enough for us to step onto the dock too, and the sloop then sinks in its moorage as you smile and say, 'Voilá!' I promise not to call you a suicidal idiot. From now on, Jervis, thanks is all you get from me."

As Risa listened she was surprised to recall that not once in her life had she seen this man, Jervis, conscious. Yet, through an osmosis born of TJ's prayer-stories, she'd come to know and love Jervis like a brother.

"Thanks," TJ said to his inert form, "for knowing nothing every time I think I know something. Thanks for living the heart's life, not just the mind's, not even in college. Thanks for being afraid of the way I took to using words like 'God' or 'blessed' or 'sacred' as if I knew what they meant. Thanks for being afraid, so far as I can tell, of nothing else on Earth. Thanks for helping me after Mexico, Jervis. 'Stop chasing your thoughts,' you said. Remember? 'Watch people closely, the streams of them, without getting diverted by judging them,' you said, 'and you'll start seeing these little acts of love. They're everywhere, Teej. And if you're dog stupid and fetch those acts the way retrievers fetch sticks, you'll feel better and better.' When you told me that, I *did* try to watch people, the streams of them. But it was hard for me, 'cause I brood on the mass idiocies and twistedness of countless people, then miss the others' acts of love. The acts I did fetch, though, began to impress me not for their greatness but for their smallness. Then one night you asked *me* to do something small. 'How about cooking us a meal that brings back Umbria?' you said. So I did, and so rediscovered my best dog-stupid trick: I *love* to cook for people! Thanks for then taking dear M and the Meister out into Portland to find the Pearl and Waterfront Buildings for us. Thanks for the names Rasta Pasta and Étouffée Bruté too, because both names are stupid. They *are,* Jervis. And that helps *me* stay stupid, fetching love-sticks instead of grandiose restaurant dreams till I came to love both names. I had the Rasta and Étouffée cuisines nailed too, Jervis. They were right in my mouth, and yours. Till the dumpster."

Eyes closed, loving Jervis by osmosis, Risa prayed it would count— prayed that being loved by a stranger somehow counts.

"Thanks for all of that, Jervis. And I'm sorry I can't think about missing seismic support beams with Risa. But I *will* stay stupid enough to hold your hand the way a lab sometimes grabs hold of a stick attached to an entire waterlogged tree, and tugs and tugs on it though it's ten thousand times bigger than the dog. That lab is me, Jervis. And while I stay dog-stupid, Risa has stayed so smart that we've still got a shot at our Holy Restaurants the Great. She's a godsend, same as you. And from now till godsend meets godsend, I'll keep holding and tugging on you. This I promise," TJ whispered, and his head drooped from total exhaustion. But never did he let go of Jervis's hand.

Risa stepped up behind TJ and set her hands on his shoulders. He didn't react.

She kissed the sterile green cap on the crown of his head. He didn't react.

Moved by how perfectly he was keeping his promise, Risa set off to keep her own.

FIVE HOURS LATER she found herself in a conference room with the architect, Gail Brace; the contractor; and the subcontractor who'd been warring over the missing support beams. TJ's lawyer, Brace's two lawyers, and the contractor's lawyer were all present, but Risa forced them, over strident protest, to wait outside the conference room while she conducted what she called "some preliminaries that only concern the builders."

Those preliminaries went as follows: wearing the coldest expression in her repertoire, Risa said, "Please don't interrupt my opening remarks. This is a *building* screwup. Building screwups happen. We will not be discussing who made it because we know you disagree on that. One thing we can agree on, though. It wasn't TJ McGraff's screwup. How kind of him, for that reason, to agree to donate one-quarter of the estimated $45,000 in repair costs. But here's the thing about TJ's kindness. It's a limited time offer. To win his one-quarter payment, each of you, no matter who you think is responsible, must pay one-quarter of the total before leaving this lawyer-free meeting. The only—"

All three men began to speak angrily and at once.

"*I'm* NOT FINISHED!" Risa shouted over them, shocking them to silence. "The only alternative is litigation, and your legal fees will *far* outweigh the repair costs *while nothing gets repaired.* All construction delay costs will then be borne by the loser of the case. *That's* a bill I'd hate to pay. This is why your lawyers are outside. They're *lawyers*. They'll tell each of you you're right, so they *agitate* all of you in order to *charge* all of you. But lucky for you, you're *builders*. You can fix this screwup for $11,250 apiece, get back to making money by doing what you do best, and remain deep in the black on this project. My opinion of going the litigation route is so low that my opening remarks are also my closing remarks. TJ will chip in $11,250 *if* you stiff your lawyers and fill out your checks in the next sixty seconds."

Risa turned her full attention to her watch. "The TJ minute starts now."

Three *extremely* disgruntled men glanced at one another, shook their heads in disgust, produced their checkbooks, wrote a check apiece for $11,250, handed them to a messy-haired college girl with a glare like a lighthouse, and fled the conference room.

Their waiting lawyers were left with nothing to do but be astonished.

Crisis resolved.

(Portland and Seattle, autumn 1989)

VII. Rig Veda vs. Rose

Two passing temporarinesses developed feelings for one another. Two puffs of smoke became mutually fond. I mistook
him for a solidity, and now must pay.
         — George Saunders, *Lincoln in the Bardo*

GRADY, TO RISA'S surprise, showed no resentment over the time she was
spending in Portland. On the contrary, the first chance he got he unleashed
a late-night Seattle-to-Portland phone soliloquy that began like so:

"Risa! I've realized something big. My grad school trajectory has been
wrong all along! What fooled me was that, as an undergrad, I loved
philosophy and poetry so much I figured they were my passion. So I placed
philosophy front and center as a major. Then, as you saw, a graduate-level
reading load of the stuff shot my interest dead. A giant load of poetry
would do the same—I'm sure of that now. The problem isn't the poetry or
the philosophy. It's the whole Grad School Overload Method. It's like being
forced to eat a forty-pound chocolate torte."

"Sooooo...what are you going to do instead?" Risa asked.

With gusto, Grady cried, "Wipe the slate clean and find a whole new
direction in life!"

"Sounds promising! Tell me all about it."

"For starts, I'm ready to be done with school. Even thrilled at the
prospect, if I can find some kind of work I love. So the question becomes,
how does a person in a place as fucked up as America find work they love?
Which immediately puts me in trouble. But it's such *good* trouble! It's good
because the American Industrial answer is, 'See which job pays the most as
it destroys your ideals, self-esteem, body, and brain the slowest, shut your
piehole, man your earth-murdering machine, and get to it, O disposable
termite of industry!' Such a fate is instructively horrible, because it shows
us why vision quests are part of every culture but the corporate anti-
culture. Knowing I need such a quest, I've been rereading the Beats...well,
Snyder, plus a bunch of tribal stuff I only skimmed at CU Boulder, and
I'm *feelin'* it, Risa. Those elders aren't whistlin' Dixie when they say, *Go
ye into wilderness, camp ye out in the Nowhere, take ye a cold hard look
at the nobody you've always been if you'd've shut off the fuckin' TV and*

thought about it a minute. Come to terms with your Mortal Nobodyness, strip yourself down to your Ancient Animal Body and Ancienter Spirit Self, converse ye with the trees, weather, hoot owls, and desolation angels in their language, not yours, and even you, Grady, can catch a whiff of the Old Ways and figure out who the Living World's asking you to be. And I know *exactly* where this stripping down needs to happen, Risa! Can you guess?"

"Grady," Risa said, feeling a burst of affection, "I never know whether you're going to walk, run, swim, yodel, or kiss me, and I love that about you. So please, just tell me."

"Okay!" he cried. "Remember me pissing and moaning when my mind turned to Teflon and philosophy wouldn't stick? I can't believe it took me half a year to ask, *Well then, what* does *stick, doofus?* 'Cause the answer was instant! It's been months since your dad described the Elkmoon Mountains to me and I can *still* hear him. *Echo is the most perfect cirque-lake echo machine, and Jade Lake is the scary-best, deepest, most magic lake in my known universe. It's a continuous hairball oracle up there, boy. Go there, be there, listen to what those lakes give back, and your universe, life trajectory, color of your pee, will all be up for grabs till a new you starts to form.* Duh, Risa! I've loved traipsing through mountains more than anything but you-know-whatting all my life. And I've been worthless to you, me, and the world as a student. *You're* what a genuine, mad-for-knowledge learner looks like. *I'm* what a fey-fuckin'-grad-school-dilettante-stickin'-Heidegger's-brain-up-his-ass-in-hopes-of-a-transfusion-instead-of-using-the-heart-head-an'-body-God-gave-him-for-fear-of-living-an-actual-life looks like!"

"Can you please repeat that sentence?" Risa asked with a laugh.

"Whatever I said, we know it's true! And this is a *happenin' deal.* I got a chunk of my tuition refunded. I'm geared up. I'm *going.* Whatever's next in life for Grady Rhys Haynes, he's gonna hie himself up into the high hoary Elkmoon Lonesome, hike 'em up, down, and sideways from now till snowfall, and see what they help him find out!"

Hearing this, Risa suddenly ached. *The Elkmoons.* Her father's beloved place of pilgrimage, but a place that, for all Dave's glowing descriptions, he'd never once shared with her. Trying not to sound as needy as she felt, Risa said, "If Jervis happens to come out of his coma, I'd *love* to explore the Elkmoons with you."

Grady went silent for several seconds. "I'd love that too," he said. "But it's a big damn *if,* Risa. I leave in two days."

Her insides did a somersault. "*Whoa!* You *are* on a mission. Well then... can I...should I...at least fly up to Seattle after work tomorrow? For goodbyes?"

It took Grady no time at all to work a major transmutation on the term "goodbyes."

"Should you ever!" he roared.

* * *

SHE FLEW UP to find Grady high as a kite. They spent the evening talking about mountains because he could manage no other subject, and when they made love he *still* raved about mountains, indulging some crazed fantasy about one of Risa's thighs being a peak and the other thigh the peak's reflection in a mountain lake, at which point he hugged her thighs in his arms, began rubbing his chest against them, began to yodel (and Grady could do a classic Swiss Alps yodel!), and the yodel gave way to a lascivious parody of John Denver singing, "*O the Colorado Rocky Mountain Thighs! I can feel 'em breathin' fire in muh eyes! When I try to read beside 'em, they just make me wanna cry! Rocky Mountain Thighs!*" by which time Risa was laughing so hard the erotic charge fled until she pulled her legs free, grabbed Grady's head in her hands, shoved a song-silencing breast in his mouth, and the charge came surging back.

They made morning-after love too. But their farewell was wrenching. Grady was off to her father's idea of paradise while Risa was returning to her near-impossible work for TJ. On the flight back to Portland she couldn't shake a feeling that someone close to her was about to shatter. The likeliest candidate was Jervis—and TJ with him. But the farther she flew from Grady and pictured him wandering high mountain wilds alone, it was distressingly easy to picture him so distracted by some lovely vista he stumbled straight off a cliff. Was there some kind of unbreakable thread she could attach to her man to steady him in the Elkmoon wilds and reel him back home when the snows flew?

She found herself recalling a Designated Study Night when Grady, bored to distraction as always, had brought up the subject of guitars. Would Risa mind, he asked, if he bought an old acoustic and tried to learn to play it while she studied? She had thought this an excellent idea, though Grady never followed up. So when her plane landed at PDX, she obeyed an impulse: en route to Burnside Community she detoured past a used instrument store, Artichoke Music. Her impulse paid off. She found a sweet deal on what the salesgirl called "McCartney's *blackbird singin' in the dead of night* guitar." An old Epiphone Texan. The instrument had major cosmetic damage: some rube had left it in a south-facing window for months, causing sunlight to bleach its once-brown mahogany to a garish blond. But it sounded great when the salesgirl strummed it, the price was doable thanks to TJ's generosity, and Risa could just picture Grady compiling an inventory of bleached-blond Texan jokes as he learned to play it.

Then came another impulse: Grady had said he wasn't leaving till the next morning. If she got the guitar there early, she was pretty sure he'd take it with him to the Elkmoons, and curse her fondly each time he had to lug it to his next high-mountain camp.

HER WORKDAY TURNED out to be the kind where problems solved themselves. When she checked in with TJ at day's end, and described the situation with Grady and parting gift she'd bought him, TJ gave her his blessing to deliver the guitar and also gave her the next day off and offered to pay for her flight.

Finding his offer overkind, she decided to drive, caught a short night's sleep, left Portland at 4 a.m., found I-5 nearly empty, and arrived in the U District at 6:45. Carrying the guitar up the four flights to the apartment, she unlocked and eased open the door, smiled to see the inert lump still under the blankets, tiptoed into the breakfast nook, opened the case on the table, slipped the Texan out, then crept toward the bed, thinking to wake him with a guitar chord.

Grady was facing away, curled in the fetal position. He was usually a sprawled sleeper, a bed hog. Seeing him in this posture made her wonder if he'd taken ill. Then she noticed the abrupt rise from his waist to his hip. The rounded softness of shoulder. The rose shoulder tattoo.

A woman. A woman was sleeping in their bed.

Risa turned toward the bathroom. Door open. No one inside. Grady wasn't home. She clung to this. *He left for the Elkmoons early. Loaned our apartment to a friend...*

Then she saw the red backpack leaning against the far wall, fully packed beside Grady's fully packed green one, and knew as clearly as if she'd filmed it: Grady had made love to this woman all night, then stepped out to Café Kant to fetch scones and cappuccinos, same as he'd done for Risa the morning before.

Guitar forgotten in hand, Risa crept closer to the bed. The woman was lovely in sleep. Her shoulder rose was pink-petaled, green-leafed, long-stemmed, magenta-thorned. Her hair, in contrast to her anything-but-boyish body, was cut boyishly short; blond tips, dark brown at the roots; short curls charmingly framing her face. Perfect skin. Adorable button nose. Full lips a little red, a little raw from... whatever she'd been doing with Grady.

Not till Risa began backing away did she rediscover the guitar in her hand. Comparing its two-toned wood to the woman's two-toned curls, its narrow waist and wide hips to the woman's own narrowness and voluptuous rise, the guitar could not begin to compete. No lessons required to play all that! Trying to stop herself, unable to do so, she pictured Grady and Rose, so busy all night, then pictured herself and Grady, so similarly busy the night and morning before. The *very morning* before.

The pain found and stabbed her. She had to collapse into a chair fast.

The Jaipur quilt covering Rose was indigo, one of the few actual gifts Dave had ever given Risa. Cash or checks his norm. She'd made the bed with the Jaipur two nights before to make it "special" for her and Grady. A few lines from the Rig Veda echoed through her:

> *In the beginning, darkness was hidden by darkness. All was*
> *an indistinguishable sea. That which becomes, that which was*
> *enveloped by the void, was born through the power of heat.*
> *Upon that heat, desire arose—the first discharge of thought.*

Upon those hips, Risa thought, gazing at Rose's planetary curves, *desire arose.* Her eyes welled. She had a reason to weep as ancient as the Vedas. But the welling in her eyes suddenly turned reddish-gold. The entire room, she realized, had turned red-gold. Curiosity held her tears in check. Their apartment faced west. The sun rose in the east. Were these the Knowledge Rays she'd hoped to one day find hovering in the air of some last pristine wild?

She turned toward the big Sound-facing window. *Mystery solved by more mystery*: though the sun was unseen in the east, its rays were refracting off two enormous apartment towers to the southwest, causing a rosy brilliance to blink on in hundreds of windows even as it blinked out in hundreds of others. In that rich, refracted light she looked round the room in which two seasons of what she and Grady had called "love" had blinked on, and now out. On her side of the bed on her little treasure shelf the light found a small bronze prayer wheel from Bhutan, a tiny dancing Shiva from India, and a genuine postage-stamp-sized painting of Our Lady of Guadalupe, all from TJ, and the woven nests of hummingbirds, bushtits, and an almost functional purse made of scavenged monofilament by a Bullock's oriole, all from Grady. Across the mound of hip on Grady's shelf: his "phony Shoshone quiver" and the single Chemehuevi-style arrow he'd made (his review: "What a buttload of work!"); the taloned foot of a road-killed great horned owl, now used as a letter opener; a bronze, twelve-inch-tall elk in whose antlers, compliments of Risa, rested the gold fountain pen he used for day poems, the black pen for night poems, and a tiny scroll on which she'd written out the Jim Harrison poem "Homily," from which she'd cribbed the day and night pens idea. In the same rosy light, two bleached blondes, one made of wood in her hand, one sweetly sleeping in her bed.

"'*He the formless assumed myriad forms,*'" she whispered to the glowing objects. "'*He the Infinite became finite. He the Real became the illusory. Were He not here, who would breathe?*'"

Perhaps hearing her, Rose rolled languidly toward Risa and opened her eyes, which were bright blue. Obsidian-eyed Risa had somehow known this. A poignant moment passed during which Rose, with no idea where she was or who Risa was, stretched languidly and smiled.

"When the angakok needs to make a flight," Risa murmured, wishing she possessed this power, "she flies up through the opening that appears of itself in the roof of her igloo."

Rose's eyes grew huge. "Jesus *shit*!" she gasped. In a spasm of terror she sat bolt upright, pulled the bedclothes tight to her body, backed up against the headboard, and secured the quilt with both fists to her chin.

"*Easy,*" Risa cooed as if calming a spooked horse. "*Easy, Rose.* Mind if I call you Rose?"

Rose made a tiny shrug, her fists gripping the quilt so hard her knuckles had turned white. She looked adorably pathetic; a creation of some undersexed Disney cartoonist circa 1950; Chip and Dale's gratuitously voluptuous chipmunk cousin, stuck in a Havahart trap. "Grady *promised* me this couldn't happen!" Rose said. "He swore you two were *done*!"

"It's okay, Rose. Given your location, I agree, we *are* done. He just forgot to tell me is all. Then, judging by your backpacks, I've screwed up your Elkmoon departure by bringing him a going away present." She wiggled the guitar. "This isn't your fault. And I didn't mean to violate your privacy. I just didn't know there'd be privacy to violate. But have you noticed this *light*? Look at your *skin*, Rose!"

The woman looked obediently down at the stunning glow of her flesh, then followed the rosy light out the window to its unlikely source: banks of blazing high-rise windows.

"There's a phrase in the Rig Veda, Rose," Risa said softly. "*Suro ninikta rasmibhih*. 'Wash her with sun-rays.' Lights and hearts blinking on, then blinking out. That's life on Earth. But, since I only just learned Grady's heart for me has blinked out, I need to sit here for a bit. Okay?"

Rose's face showed an array of emotions as Risa spoke: pleasure in the rich light; confusion at the Sansrkit words; red-gold sympathy when Risa described her need to sit.

"There's something wrong with me," Risa said to the light or to Rose or to the Unseen Unborn Guileless Perfection. "Some relationship-dooming crazy dumbsaint obsessiveness. I'm aimed at things so different than most people that even good guys like Grady get lost around me. So please, Rose. Don't think this is all his—"

They froze at a sound: *key entering door.* The door swung open. A grinning Grady strolled in, sure enough toting cappuccinos and scones.

"You *fuck*!" Rose said in greeting.

Turning from her to Risa, Grady's grin did the most spectacular collapse Risa had ever seen a grin do. "I wrote!" he gasped. "*Risa, I wrote!* I mean, I never meant...I mean, the letter's in the mail and explains how I...er. Only then you offered to fly up for goodbyes and...and I didn't have the heart—"

"*Not to lie to and fuck you both!*" Rose cut in.

Grady sank into a chair, looking as if he'd just eaten a quart of mayonnaise.

"Everybody remember to breathe," Risa suggested.

"I don't *want* him to breathe!" snapped Rose.

The red-gold light faded as the sun got on with its workaday business. Taking the hint, Risa stood, leaned the Epiphone against the wall, stepped over to Grady, took the scones and cappuccinos out of his hands, went into the kitchen, and fetched cups and saucers down from a cupboard. "Here's my thought," she said, trying to steady her voice. "Whatever happened here the past two nights is...is not happening now. And two of us didn't know any better. And...and the other one of us has the excuse of...whatever's wrong with me. So we could all use a dose of normal. And scones and cappuccinos are normal. So I'm going to serve us."

"First," Grady said, "please, can I just say that—"

"*NO!*" shouted Rose. "You can't say *anything*!"

Grady wilted down into his chair. Risa removed lids, poured the coffees into three china cups, set a cup and saucer where Grady could reach it, then cut a scone in half, put the halves on two plates, set a plate for herself on the chair by the guitar, delivered the other half to Grady, then set out to deliver the whole scone and a coffee to Rose.

As she undertook this simple task, an incident occurred: when Risa had dressed at 3:30 a.m. in Portland, she'd imagined a very different morning than the one they were having. Accordingly, she'd donned a pair of very tight, frayed, faded, worn-to-white-more-than-blue jeans that signaled the very opposite of what the puke-gold XL Huskies-rooter bathrobe signaled. As she leaned down to deliver cup, saucer, and scone to Rose, what Grady called "the perfect pear" was so graphically ensconced within the jeans' pale frays that he was riveted. His fate then ramped up another notch: as the coffee and plated scone moved from Risa's long slender fingers to Rose's more classically feminine hands, Rose needed both hands to receive them, the Jaipur quilt slipped down when she let it go, and there, like two beneficent wild creatures in their own right, were Rose's breasts.

Of course Risa saw them too: they were right in her face and their beauty explained a lot. But, Risa being Risa, she instantly raised her eyes to the breakfast she was delivering, then to Rose's face, into which she smiled. And because Rose too had modulated into Two-Nice-Young-Women-at-a-Coffee-Klatch mode, she was taking great care not to spill on the Jaipur, and didn't even notice the fallen quilt until cup, saucer, and scone were all safe on the bedside table. As a result, Grady was free to gape—in full-scale brain-melting Female Objectification Mode—at the perfect pear and equally perfect breasts for maybe seven seconds. It seemed a total boon at the time.

BUT THIRTY HOURS and hundreds of road miles later he pulled into an empty Elkmoon Mountains trailhead, donned a very heavy backpack, picked up a guitar case with a bleached-blond Texan inside, and commenced—as he had soliloquized about to Risa but had no intention of actually doing without serious erotic companionship—to trudge up into the High Wild Lonesome and strip himself down to the pissant he'd always been if he'd've shut off the fuckin' TV and thought about it a minute. And on this outing Grady didn't encounter his pissant-hood for an idle day or two. From mid-September into October he wandered the increasingly chill but glorious Elkmoons up, down, and sideways, posing to the peaks such profound existential questions as "*Yo! Infinite Person higher than which there is nothing. Who-am-I-what-am-I-where-am-I-how-am-I?*"

He encountered not one easy answer. Nor, during the October portion of his sojourn, did he encounter any late-season backpackers, rangers, climbers, or even hunters. Immersing himself in stone, wind, weather, and solitude, he was soon wrestling a desolation so merciless he might have welcomed a light mauling by a bear.

Late each night, however, two silent companions did make a wordless appearance in Grady's camp. They always seemed to show up after he'd pitched his tent, gathered wood, started a fire, eaten his awful freeze-dried grub, pulled out the bleached-blond Texan, grown sick of guitar-playing attempts that sounded like a psycho movie soundtrack, stuck the Texan back in her sarcophagus, built up the fire, tried to get sleepy, but instead—amid the chill air, silhouetted pines, merciless mountains, infinite sky—his desolation achieved a purity so intense it burned. This burning, Grady sensed, could have taught him something truly worth knowing if he could have steeped in it. Instead, a lump would rise in his throat, a far more familiar lump would rise in his pants, and Rose's breasts and Risa's fray-ensconced pear would pay such a graphic but disembodied visit that some sort of all-castrati alleluia chorus would bust out in his head, roaring that it would be *a snowy Excelsis Deo* in *HELL* before Grady would be groan-moan-panting any sweat-slippery wownesses into either of those feminine paragons.

AND YET...AND yet...On one of the Elkmoon lakes Grady visited and liked so much he remained beside it for seven days—not one of Dave's big three, Pipsissewa/Echo/Jade; Grady wasn't ready to hike nearly thirty miles in and nine thousand feet up into utter wildness this late in the year, but a damned nice lake nonetheless; High Lake it was called, with voracious brook and cutthroat trout that allowed him to avoid freeze-dried farty food and cram himself full of protein, which improved his dreams, which improved his sleep, which silenced the nightly Hellatious in Excelsis Deo choir—Grady had an unprecedented experience:

What first drew him to High Lake was its sheltering, south-facing cirque. He'd pitched his camp near a shoreline boulder that warmed in the sun each morning, because it fit his back so perfectly it seemed the mountains had spent eons sculpting a recliner just for him. Leaning against his slab each morning, Grady began trying to keep a mountain journal rather like the "scribbled secret notebooks" Risa had kept. Because Risa's journaling, so bodily close beside him, had driven him out of his mind with lust, he was surprised to find that, alone at elevation, he possessed a keen natural attentiveness toward the world enveloping him that had eluded him in Risa's company. Day after day his Elkmoon journal filled with intricate observations of animal and bird behaviors, weather shifts, small day-hike mysteries, geological intricacies, and other modest wonders that grew indelible through repeated acts of careful description. His journaling also tapped into unprecedented introspection. One morning at his lakeside stone recliner, with the bodies of Elkmoon ridges and peaks enfolding him while the morning sun warmed all the world, Grady wrote:

Camped by my lonesome amid the cosmos/temple/body of this mountain range, my obsession with physical bodies is undergoing a transformation. For one thing, lust isn't just lust up here. In a world made up entirely of natural bodies, <u>all of them fucking beautiful</u>, wonder overwhelms lust. And didn't some tony old-timer, Lao Tzu maybe, say, "From wonder into wonder Existence opens"? I feel that! Existence is opening! Why? More and more I feel it's because, idiot though I am, when it comes to bodies mountainous, liquid, celestial, terrestrial, creaturely, and of course womanly, I'm about as wonderstruck as a person can be and still walk! True, I messed up bad by worshipping two female bodies so much that I lied to their owners so I could lie <u>with</u> their owners. Moderation, Grady. <u>But that includes moderation in shame.</u> Amid these gorgeous mountain lake creek tree cloud animal bird weather and night-sky bodies, my heart keeps revealing that a spontaneous love for bodies is the most potent guiding force in me. Why diminish that force because of a rookie erotic wreck I can't undo? Why not work with the forces I feel overflowing and inspiring me miles from any women, and continue to love the wonders right here where I am?

Two nights later, freed of the diminishment shame had cast on wonder, Grady was engulfed by the most powerful cosmos/temple/body experience of his life: he had climbed a seven-hundred-foot ridge just south of High Lake and parked himself on its west-facing summit near sunset, enabling him to see out over a vast expanse of peaks, lakes, forested ridges, talus slopes, gentle meadows, and impassable gorges as he soaked in the last solar warmth and shifting color phases, then lay on his back to watch the sea of stars appear. But once the Milky Way was out in force the shooting stars saddened him for lack of a womanly body with whom to share them. So Grady stood, sighed, and began picking his way down to the hardest hour of his day: facing solitude in his camp in full darkness. His flashlight batteries were dying, he'd brought no lantern or candles, and even books and journaling were nearly impossible by firelight. This left him no entertainment but psycho-movie soundtracks on the bleached-blond Texan. Sinking into misery as he moved toward this fate, he stumbled round a stand of stunted pines, got a first look at High Lake's surface, and gasped: thanks to a perfect night calm, the same billion stars that blanketed the heavens were strewn across a hundred-acre mirror below. Praying no breeze would disturb it, Grady scrambled his way to lakeside and looked directly down upon the water: *stars everywhere!* The sight caused his eyes to fill and dropped him to his knees. Refracted starlight then rose from the water and shone in his wet lashes even as it kept falling from the far reaches of space.

With more reverence than he'd ever felt in his life, Grady whispered, "Flame language!" And the prison of every philosophical distinction between *inner* and *outer* imploded. Water and sky fused in a peace that surpassed understanding. The above fused with the below. Grady had come home to the geophysical edge of a literal, living heaven.

VIII. Eight on I-5

We throw things away as if we think there's a place
called "away."

—Julia Butterfly Hill

"HI, DAVE."

"Risa! Wonderful to hear your voice! To what do I owe the pleasure?"

"Oh, sadness, self-loathing, overwhelming resentment. Stuff like that."

"Sweetheart! Are you all right? You're not! What's happened?"

"Well, I've been working in Portland for starters. But don't ask about that. I—"

"*Portland?* How can you attend U Dub if you're—"

"Dave! Face it. You call so seldom I couldn't catch you up if I talked for a week. So *please*. Just listen. *Promise* me you'll listen."

"But—"

"*DAVE!*"

"Gosh! Okay, okay. I promise to listen."

"Thanks. My first news is happy. It concerns a woman you once knew, Moira O'Reilly. After fifteen years and, my best guess, something like three thousand fifths of Smirnoff, she crawled out of her troll cave. She's in rehab in Woodburn, Dave, and I'm so proud of her I—"

"My *God,* Risa! I had no idea she drank like—"

"*DAVE!* When you interrupt, the thread gets lost or you throw what I'm saying into reverse. *Don't talk. Listen. Hell yes, she drank like that!* She's a devout Catholic whose nuns and priests forced her as a child to memorize the same line they made me memorize. 'A ratified and consummated marriage cannot be dissolved by any human power or for any reason other than death.' A human power named Dave then dissolved her marriage, damning her to hell. To get even, or forget hell, or have fun or something, she chased a few men and, surprise, surprise, rhythm method struck again. Knocked up, unsure of the father, too ashamed to confess, she chose abortion. So her first rhythm method child, me, got to listen to Moira's repeated confessions of having murdered my sibling, doubly damning her to hell. Turned out I wasn't much of a priest at age eight, so Father Smirnoff took over. Then, at Bonneville Power, where she works, came a fall down a stairwell in which she'd snuck off to drink. Pint bottle in her culotte, blood and vodka everywhere. When a coworker tried to help her, Moira roared, '*I'm fine!*' Bonneville Power didn't see it that way. Loss of job and pension if she refused the rehab. But you know Moira. Wait. Correct that. You don't know her at all. She refused. Then came the nightmares. Mine, not hers. *Homeless Bag Lady Mom following me everywhere for the rest of our lives* type thing. But the bad dreams lit a fire in me. I've been working, by the way, on two huge Portland renovation projects. A crash course in Moving and Shaking. Turns out I've got a gift. It felt like child's play to turn to renovating a mere mom."

"Huge renovations in *Portland*? During your final year at U Dub? I'm so confused I—"

"*Citation Two,* Dave. See how the thread just got lost again?"

"Sorry! Very sorry, Risa. Please, go on."

"To renovate Moira I phoned every O'Reilly in or near Portland, three BPA coworker pals, her old priest Father Flaherty, and two young priests I recently heard her say were 'as cute as those early apostles.' *Cute early apostles.* The Smirnoff was really working for her. So it's no wonder that when her clan, priests, pals, and I descended in intervention mode she flew into a rage, calling us 'Hannibal's Ambush.' Nice historical reference, Drunk Lady! When her friends began describing the dangers she poses to herself and Western Civilization—her *driving,* my God—she kept roaring, '*I don't have a problem!*' So I left the room, returning moments later with five full Smirnoff bottles I pulled out of hidey holes. That only made her try to run. And Father Flaherty *did* run! The sight of all that booze made them both thirsty! I figured we'd lost the battle, but then the smallest thing tipped her. '*Mom,*' I said, and her eyes got big. 'I know, I haven't called you Mom since I was little,' I said. 'But if you'll go through rehab, whether it works or not, you'll be no one but Mom to me from this day forward.' Her face clouded then, and I braced for a sob fest, but the ornery Cathoholic jumped back out. 'That's the first nice thing you've said to me since your father left us,' she huffed. 'Which shows how nice you *aren't.* But I'll go into rehab this very day on one condition.' With which she started batting her eyes at the Cute Apostles. 'If you two will drive me,' she said, 'the rest of this bunch can get off its high horse and go home.' So the rest of us did.

"Moira calls her new digs the 'Betty Boop Center.' The Smirnoff translation of Betty Ford Center. She's six weeks in, and had a rough go for a month—DTs, wild mood swings, rage, tears, the works. But she's better by the day, she's made some poignant damaged friends, and she appears to even have some kind of boyfriend."

"That's good, that's excellent, I'm glad to hear it, Risa. But you *have* to understand, I loved Moira very much before we—"

"*YOU* have to understand, Dave, that *this is your third citation for interrupting*!"

"To be treated like a child by my child does not sit very—"

"*WHEN I INTERRUPT YOU, like this, it's hard to remember what you were saying, isn't it?* But you don't just interrupt. All my life you've wiped out my words or fucked up the gist of them by trying to charm me into mute admiration of your pretty, poetic, completely irrelevant interruptions, so my truth never gets told. *That's* why I'm holding you to your damned promise! Don't charm, interpret, confuse, or question. *Just. Bloody. Listen.*"

"............!"

"Tonight's other topic. Working crazy hours in Portland, I only saw Grady every other weekend, and there's still no end in sight to the work I'm doing. So, naturally, Grady started making plans that didn't include me. Quit his master's program. Planned a road trip to clear his head. The trip, especially, made me realize I didn't want to lose him, so I bought him a sweet old guitar and, very early this morning, drove it to Seattle to surprise him. But when I snuck the guitar in our door at sunrise, he'd gone out for coffee and scones, and the woman in our bed had kiss-swollen lips, and a waist and hips *way* sexier than the guitar's. The rose tattoo on her shoulder was cute too. So I named her Rose."

"Oh my *God*, Risa! I'm so sorry you—"

"*OH YOUR GOD!? Is that our topic now!?* Do you even *know* you're breaking your worthless promise for the fourth time?"

"Jesus! You're right. I'm so sorry, Risa!"

"I'll wrap this up so you can get back to confusing and interrupting people who might enjoy it. The main reason I called was to tell you what happened after I met Rose. Grady came in, and Rose was not at all happy to see him, but I played the diplomat and we made nice for a few minutes. Then I left on the long drive I'd just made alone, in reverse, back to Portland. It's my experience en route that I want to share. In the slow lane on I-5, near Centralia, *I turned eight years old again.* I'm not being metaphorical, Dave. I turned so entirely eight I could barely see over the steering wheel. I turned so eight I was sure I'd arrive home in 1975, and you'd be God knows where with God knows who, leaving me to my soused blur of a so-called mother, slumped on the couch slurring insults at the TV, leaving me no choice but to trundle back to my room and turn myself into a weirdo by listening to the scratchy old blues records you gave me to serve as my father. And think, Dave. *Don't speak! Just think.* My poor boyfriend Grady, up until today, was trying to live with and love that wounded, blues-stunted eight-year-old so alive in me still.

"And here's the *déjà doozy,* Dave. Guess where my ex is headed, *but not out loud*! All questions for the remainder of this chat will be rhetorical. *He's headed for the Elkmoons. To find himself.* Or lose *me* anyway. And why there? Because *you* once took him out to coffee and threw an Elkmoon spell over him. Isn't that a mind fuck? *Don't answer!* Rhetorical. It's a *major* mind fuck. Because who else do we know who drove to the same mountains every summer starting the year I became Moira's child priest, then came back to tell me how *amazing* the Elkmoons are, and how I *had* to go there with him, then *didn't invite me year after year,* because he had *lady friends* to take. *'But next year, Risa! The Elkmoons! You've got to see them!'"*

"Risa, you're going through too much, and I've been too selfish and blind, to handle this with a phone call. Let me drive down right now. A phone is just not the way to—"

"Are you interrupting *for the FIFTH TIME to tell me phone calls are fucked!? Do you think I don't know that!?* Do you think that, after fourteen *YEARS* of fucked-up phone fathering, driving down here now would *handle this?* To even *begin* to handle this, Dave, you'd have to time-travel back to when I was seven and leave Moira in an honest, evenhanded way that didn't turn me into *your* worshipper and *her* tormentor. You'd then have to abandon me during the years that followed *without constantly saying, by phone, 'I'm here for you, sweetheart,'* when you were and still are *nowhere* for me. And most of all, Dave, you'd have to *ungive* me the goddamned blues records you used to pick me up and dance to, so that, in your constant absence and Mom's besotted presence, my furious brain wouldn't start chanting to my crushed heart, *Never be soft again! Be steel. Be invincible. Be the Vedic Ātman, Risa. Because look at Moira. Look at yourself. Look at how men rip you to shreds when you're soft!"*

"Risa, please! You've made me sorrier than I can say. And it's all true. But it's only a fraction of the truth. And the rest is a miracle! The rest, dear girl, is that in spite of my failures you've become a brilliant, beautiful, compassionate, entirely appealing—"

"—*mass of hurts and yearnings that left Grady trying to love a woman as fun to be in bed with, most nights, as a garden shovel!* You should have seen him try to court me. Happy as a puppy, he'd say, 'Let's go watch the playoffs at this cool sports bar I know.' Without even pulling my nose from my book, I'd murmur, 'You go,' because the mere *thought* of sports bars, though I've never been to one, conjured Moira's drinking. 'Okay then,' he'd say. 'Why don't you pull on that tight skirt and those beat-up brown boots I love while I round up some of my shitty poems, and we'll go to the open mike at The Small Good Thing to celebrate how great great poetry is by listening to shitty poetry?' A charming invitation if ever there was one. But *miles* beneath the dignity of *Risa the Vedic Ātman Incarnate.* So off I rushed to Portland to work saintly deeds for TJ, *abandoning my beau*—sound familiar?—till finally Grady did what most any appealing young man in an empty bed would do. And when I got a good look at Rose in the rosy dawn light this morning, seeing her whole body singing, *See what it is to be soft?* oh, did I feel my hardness! And I know you and Moira were too fucked up to help yourselves, let alone me. I just wish I'd realized how fucked up that made *me,* and addressed it. I wish I'd *gone* to those open mikes and sports bars with the boyfriend I loved. And if I couldn't handle 'em I wish I'd been brave enough to say, 'Grady! Please, help me! I love you and want to trust you. But how can I when the first man in my life thinks it's love to ask me to dinner *at SeaTac! right before his fucking flight!* where he reads from a book that says I make *happiness fill the space of his sadness,* then runs off down the concourse *happy,* I'm supposed to stand alone and think. That kind of thing would drive a soft girl fucking *insane*! So I'm hard. But I don't want to be. So *please,* Grady. *Help me soften.'* But no such talk ever fell from Vedic Risa's steely lips. So away my man flew to some wonderland that *you,* of all people, planted in his heart!"

"Risa, *please.* This all had to be said. And the parts about me are terrible and true. But hear one thing. I insist. You're *lovely*! Just as you are. I won't hear otherwise. Brilliant *and* sensitive. Steely *and* soft. You're perfection, my girl. And when it comes to the steeliness, don't forget how, when Son House laid that broken bottleneck against those steely strands of American—"

"I can't STAND this! I can't!"

"Oh, Risa! I'm inexcusably sorry! But I can *break* this pattern. No more phone fathering! That's a promise! And thank you so much for this brave..."

As Dave fell silent and realized the phone had been dead for some time, the echo of his own voice nearly made him vomit out of self-disgust.

(Portland, 1989, and Ixhuatán, Mexico, a rewind to 1986)

IX. People of the Purse

God created man to suffer agonies of the heart.
If it had only been a question of obedience
there was no scarcity of angels.
                              —Khwaja Mir Dard

SEPTEMBER VANISHED. PORTLAND, with its brilliant hardwood leaves and angled October sunlight, became a working-class Augustinian City o' God. Blind to the ambient glory, TJ kept vigil at his brother's side, Jervis kept breathing, and his face, despite permanent disfigurement, healed. Much of his body, though emaciated, also healed. Physical therapists began to work his arms and legs. Metabolic disturbances grew rare. No signs of paralysis. Five weeks into the coma Doc Phillipa told TJ, "Keep the faith. He's tenacious. His chances are *much* better than I thought when he was admitted." Then in roared staph infection.

Vancomycin was prescribed and Jervis responded just enough to keep breathing. But he lost even more weight, all talk of his chances ceased, and TJ began to wrestle sheer despair. To lose hope is to lose energy. TJ's long sympathy coma began to exhaust him to a dangerous degree. When he felt too weak to remain at Jervis's side, he'd tell the staff, "If anything changes, you know where to find me," then retreat to the chapel, stretch out on a pew, and try to doze. But the Burnside Community Hospital Chapel presented its own challenges.

It had been designed as a conference room, then converted to a place of worship as an afterthought. It was low-ceilinged, carpeted, and entirely enclosed by windowless walls. But the worst of it was the crucifix. A wooden, Caucasian-looking Jesus hung from a cross that reached from the carpeted floor to the off-white, acoustic-tiled ceiling. He was painted entirely in pastels. His wounds leaked a watery version of red that looked like weak Kool-Aid. His expression evinced no awareness of even his own suffering, let alone anyone else's. Gigantic in the claustrophobic room, the Big Jesus radiated the violent idiocy that only truly bad religious art can. To wait out his brother's coma in such a creature's presence felt like lying in the reeking dumpster in which Jervis had been found.

TJ lay there even so.

* * *

SEVEN WEEKS INTO the coma, Risa walked into the chapel one morning with her usual futile list of Pearl and Waterfront questions. She found TJ in the backmost pew, bent slightly forward in what she took to be prayer. Stepping quietly up behind him to wait until he'd finished, she accidentally got a clear look at what he'd kept hidden in the little purse round his neck all this time: TJ was whispering—and then, it seemed, avidly *listening*—to a tiny, bright-colored Mexican trouble doll. The listening, especially, caused Risa to fear TJ was breaking down completely. Unsure how to react, she slipped soundlessly out of the chapel to ponder her next move. But there *was* no next move without TJ.

A short time later she returned to find him in the same pew, looking utterly spent. Steeling herself, she sat down beside him.

"I came in earlier," she began, "but left without speaking when I saw you were already conversing. With a little trouble doll. Listening to it too, it seemed. Sorry if that sounds accusatory, but that's what I saw."

TJ's surprise overshadowed his exhaustion. Gathering his wits, he said, "You caught me in my sanctuary. It's...an icon for me, the little figure you saw. Very special. And yes, we were...*communing*. That's how prayer works. And Thomas Merton, whom I know you respect, says that the viability of a person's spiritual sanctuary depends on secrecy. A truth we both believe so strongly it feels unnecessary to say it to you. My prayers and icons need to remain secrets, Risa. I'm sure you understand."

"*TJ!*" Risa began, but her voice broke, tears began spilling, and TJ saw a desperation as deep as his own. Angrily swiping at her tears, she let fly:

"I didn't mean to play the boo-hoo card. But listen. At *your request* I upended my school life, crashed and burned my love life, and am still trying my utmost to help you. But in trying my utmost I've been *living* in your damned *sanctuary*, which I don't like doing any more than you or Merton like it! While I've been fighting off crises and lawsuits for you, making countless decisions, and spending countless dollars as if I know what I'm doing when I don't, I've had *no damned choice* but to hear your prayers for *forty-three days*. Meanwhile your *secret sanctuary* blocked every straight answer to my *how-the-hell-do-I-do-this* questions. And yeah, your projects are still afloat. But I was already feeling completely alone when...when Grady fled. So this talking to little dolls thing gets to me. I mean, if all you're doing in your sanctuary is falling to pieces, wow! I'm *really* alone! So if you refuse to explain your little icon dolls, that's your call, TJ. But if it *is* your call, then my call, here and now, is: *I quit.*"

TJ lowered his face, looked lost in concentration for a moment, patted his shirtfront where the little purse lay hidden, and gave a quick nod of resolve. When he then stood and started out of the chapel, Risa took it to mean she should go ahead and quit, and her heart sank. But when he opened the chapel door, he remained standing in it, holding it for her with a pallid hint of a smile. And as she passed through, he said, "*Thank you.*"

Without another word he led them down the four-story stairwell, out a side door of the hospital, into the brilliant sunlight of a working-class City o' God.

They crossed Burnside at Northwest 21st, walked the six blocks north to Hoyt, and took the stairs up onto the porch of Jervis's first-floor monk's-cell apartment. Unlocking the door, TJ again held it for Risa, and again murmured, "*Thank you.*"

HAVING LIVED SEVEN weeks in TJ's elegant townhouse, it was obvious to Risa that he'd left Jervis's apartment just as he'd found it. Her first impression: *indoor homeless camp.* Two wooden fruit crates served as a coffee table and a bedside shelf. The bed was a thin, worn-out futon on the floor in a corner. Venetian blinds made the whole place dark. There was no kitchen table. The "appliances" were a Coleman camp stove, cheap Styrofoam cooler, and toaster oven. One small frying pan, one saucepan, one plate, one bowl, one coffee mug. A half-empty pint of Jim Beam stood by two small Ball jars, the only drinking glasses. A chipped porcelain sink was stained blue where the faucet dripped. No rugs, no curtains, no radio, no art, and an antique TV with no cable. A gooseneck reading lamp stood on the fruit crate by the futon to allow him to read. A few spiral notebooks and a five-inch stack of what looked like letters lay atop the crate, and a row of used books stood inside it, bookended at one end by a pair of bricks Risa recognized from the Waterfront project.

TJ silently offered her a small, canvas-seated, wood-framed folding chair—the only actual piece of furniture in the room. It was so low it left her three inches off the floor beside the books, so she turned to them. The intense focus of Jervis's tiny library appealed to her at once. Three volumes on Tibetan Buddhism, two on Zen, Nikos Kazantzakis's mytho-historic novel *Saint Francis, The Cloud of Unknowing* by Anonymous, and two field guides to American birds filled a third of the row. The other two-thirds were all books by or about the Beguines and their ally Meister Eckhart: Marguerite Porete's *The Mirror of Simple Souls*; Mechthild of Magdeburg's *The Flowing Light of the Godhead*; Hadewijch of Brabant's collected writings; *The Beguine Pearl* by Anonymous; two volumes of Eckhart's sermons; two books of Beguine and Eckhart scholarship by a man named McGinn. That was it, except for the stack of letters atop the crate. Risa's immediate, head-to-toe response: *As soon as can be, I'll read this entire library.*

Continuing to hold his tongue, TJ made green tea in the tiny Yixing pots and teabowls he favored. After serving her, then filling his own bowl, he unthinkingly deployed his weird athleticism: teapot in one hand, teabowl in the other, using legs alone to drop from a standing position into a half lotus on the futon. Jervis's rock-hard monk's bed didn't budge beneath his weight.

Setting aside teapot and bowl, TJ reached over to the fruit crate, grabbed the stack of letters on top, and carefully selected perhaps fifteen pages. Every page was covered with the small, deft handwriting Risa recognized as TJ's own. He introduced the letters by meticulously describing the desolate context in which he wrote them, then began to read to her aloud. His full disclosure took two hours. By the time he'd finished, Risa was so moved she never experienced another moment's doubt about the trouble dolls, or the secret sanctuary TJ had created in which to commune with them.

WHEN AN INCH-LONG steel bolt detaches from an AeroMexico DC-8 cruising at 38,000 feet, drifts seven miles to Earth, and embeds itself in the skull of an eight-year-old girl hoeing weeds in a Mexican cornfield, killing her almost instantly, the term "freak accident" does not appease. The mind continues to grope for explanations. This groping is of course futile. But just as a heart, by nature, can't stop beating, a mind, faced with a fatal catastrophe, can't stop groping. One person who learned this the hard way was a young Jesuit novice sent, in the old Mexican priest's absence, to console the dead eight-year-old's father and friends at her burial. That Jesuit's name: Tavish Jacobus McGraff.

Because TJ would be arriving in this father's life on the day his daughter's body was to be placed in the earth, he felt he should set eyes on the body to prepare himself. Ixhuatán had no proper morgue, but the child had been stored in a walk-in cooler at a market not far from the church cemetery. TJ bicycled there on the morning of the burial, asked to be left alone in the cooler for a while, and stepped inside, hoping for an encounter that might give him a few words to speak at the grave before the child entered it.

What he found in the cooler did the exact opposite. The instant he set eyes on the girl's body he was assailed, first, by the fact that it looked totally unharmed and, second, by its perfect little-girlness. The love visible in the way her hands had been folded was a spear to the heart. Her very small, scuffed but fresh-polished black patent-leather shoes; pretty white dress with a white satin waist ribbon; carefully braided black hair ending in another white ribbon; dimples still visible in the pale cheeks: more spears and arrows. TJ had excelled at science in high school and had a very good memory. In the Ixhuatán cooler that day he could probably have still recited half the Periodic Table of the Elements: *Seven: N, nitrogen. Eight: O, oxygen. Nine: F, flourine.* A beloved child was about to dissolve into that Table. The gulf between the elements and her satin ribbons, mirthful dimples, and perfect black braid shattered thought: the gulf was infinite. At his novitiate TJ had been taught only the canonical solaces. Any such solace spoken at this child's burial would be a platitude tossed like a cigarette butt into a handy hole in the ground.

After long, hard pondering, all that came to TJ was a vision of dropping to his hands and knees at the grave, kissing the dirt at the edge of the hole this child would be entering, then kissing it again once she was buried in it—and not to consecrate the dirt or act of burial. No priest, no church, held any such power. His only aim would be to honor the other-than-human elements receiving the child with the willing touch of his human lips.

This impulse, TJ realized too late, could have been obeyed. To silently kiss the dirt, before and after, might even have led to a few spontaneous, appropriately shattered words for the crushed father and dazed friends. But TJ didn't heed his urge. Overwhelmed by the unanswerable, he clung to the canon, translated a few platitudes into his stiff, foreign Spanish, spoke them to those encircling the child's shockingly unharmed body—and felt his words fall to Earth like junk parts raining down from an AeroCatholic flight to nowhere.

A REPORTER, EDUARDO Nuñez, from the Mexico City newspaper *Reforma*, was scratching notes at the graveside as TJ spoke his platitudes. Nuñez then published a brief article that gave the name of the girl and her father, and wrote of one thing only: the impossible odds against being struck in the skull by a bolt fallen from a jet passing seven miles overhead.

When, within days, newspapers from all over the globe picked up the story, the sheer number of such papers—not to mention the income from serial rights!—astounded Nuñez. Nothing like this had ever happened to him. Most papers even used his *Reforma* headline: **FREAK ACCIDENT VICTIM DIES IN CHIAPAS CORNFIELD.** That his story reduced the girl to a seven-word formula and the father to a nothingness did not impress Nuñez one way or the other. For him there was magic in the fact that **FREAK ACCIDENT VICTIM** clippings kept pouring in from St. Petersburg, Sydney, Prague, Reykjavik, Buenos Aires, Paris, Haiphong. To share this magic Nuñez began mailing photocopies of the clippings, in groups of ten or so, to the young Jesuit he'd briefly met by the girl's grave. "The world now knows of you!" his attached note told TJ. "Share these with the family, good Father. It may appease them! So many people touched by this tragedy! So much concern."

TJ had a slow fuse, but by the time he'd received more than thirty such clippings he telephoned Eduardo Nuñez, took no chances on his rickety Spanish, and said, "Stop sending these, Señor Nuñez. Sensationalism is not *concern.* Her name is *Demetria Annamaria Cabrera,* not *freak accident victim.* And how am I to share *anything* with her family when her mother was murdered by a death squad in Guatemala, her grandmother died soon after, and her father brought Demetria to Chiapas to start a new life. They came to Ixhuatán to be safe, Señor Nuñez, and for a while she was. Write *that.* But then—what a bonanza for sleepwalkers incapable of empathy!—down through the heavens fell the hero of your story: a clever little bolt bent on murder! *Fuck these clippings, Señor Nuñez.* My ridiculous work as Demetria's priest is to help her father discover some inconceivable reason to keep living despite her lost life, lost sweetness, lost playfulness, face, voice, hair, hands. Write *that,* Señor Nuñez!"

Not till he'd slammed down the phone did TJ realize that the man he'd been longing to excoriate was himself. Unable to quell his turmoil, he felt driven to spill his guts to a wise confessor. But TJ's most valued confessor was not an older priest: he was a hunched, sailboat-dwelling, Beguine-loving street samaritan by the name of Jervis Muireadhach McGraff.

Here's the first letter TJ read to Risa in the "monk's cell" that day:

Brother Jervis:

Wasn't it John Lennon who said "Time wounds all heels"? Whoever said it, they were so right. The calendar tells me days are passing, but my life stalled out in self-loathing at Demetria's burial. Have I told you I was so nervous I'd made notes on 3 × 5 preprinted postcards provided by the Oregon Province of Jesuits? Picture it, Jervis! The petrified priestling from El Norte, teetering on the lip of the girl's grave, flip-ping through notecards like Dave Letterman doing a top ten list. Her devastated father watching closely. And what consolations rose from my palmed deck? If only I could forget. *"Estoy más triste que puedo decir."* (I'm more sorry than I can say.) *"A Dios les ama los que se lleva, además de los que deja atrás."* (God loves those He takes, as well as those He leaves behind.) *"Debemos confiar en que, aún ahora, todas las cosas deben llevarnos a la santidad."* (We must trust, even now, that all things are meant to bring us to holiness.) Fuck *me*, Jervis! When our parents died, I fell into a neck-deep hole. My aspirations of priesthood have only deepened that hole, and my words to Demetria's mourners pulled them into it with me. Fuck my tiny-hearted sentiments! I wish Demetria's father had pummeled my face with his fists till I fell on the ground. I wish he'd shouted, *You must trust that my fists have brought you to holiness!*

But what he did, in its way, was worse. What he did was stare at the dirt that held his child captive, then murmur, *"Gracias, Padrecito."* He who'd lost his wife to thugs, his mother-in-law to grief, his daughter to a vicious absurdity. *"Gracias, Padrecito."* Then away we walked, he to his empty hacienda, me to my empty parsonage, where I've thought of him nonstop ever since. The fascination of this childless father, Jervis, is that while no one is strong enough to suffer such a blow and remain whole, countless men, women, and children are strong enough to suffer such blows, be horribly maimed by them, yet survive. The great truth here, then, is our tediously terrifying old friend, the Cross, which we try to wrench into the feeling *Mighty Jesus will save helpless me*. But good souls are hung, same as Jesus, on crosses daily. And Jesus was then taken down by a few fearless women who loved Him. But as far as I can see, this man, Señor Cabrera, and countless others like him, are nailed up and left hanging for the rest of their lives.

I've been to see him twice since the burial. On the first visit I told him how sorry I was for the words I'd spoken over Demetria's grave. I said this at least three times, in three equally wooden ways, then asked if he could forgive me—because *it's always about me!* When Señor Cabrera said there was nothing to forgive, then tossed in another, "*Gracias, Padrecito*," I started to weep. He pointed at his broken porch steps then, which mystified me. In addition to being a rotten priest I own no tools, no carpentry skills, and I'm so stupid I thought he wanted me to fix his steps. Instead he motioned me to sit.

Aha. I sat. Señor C then sat beside me, the broken steps so narrow they forced our hips to touch.

For a long time I expected words to follow. None did. We stayed on his steps, hip to hip, neither of us speaking, for what felt like years. And sitting with Señor C, motionless, silent, was immeasurably more instructive than all the theology I've ever studied then pretended to understand. I needed no epistemology, no Christology, no dogmatics to know I sat hip to hip with a man nailed to an inescapable cross, yet he didn't moan or groan, and he said absolutely nothing. We stared at the toppled stone wall encircling his tiny dirt yard. We looked down at the cruel dirt or up at the cruel sky. We sat together so long I may have forgotten he was there except that, twice, I heard his breath catch as he turned to the gate in the wall. Each time my breath also caught, as I too half expected to see his child come through the gate.

What stepped through instead, after a while, was one of those short-haired yellow curs you see everywhere in Mexico. Obviously seeking Demetria. Obviously our fellow griever, missing the sweet words and handouts he'd always found in this yard. When he saw two silent men instead, one a priestly fool, the other silent in mid-Crucifixion, he slunk away fast.

A flock of pigeons flew over like sad messengers. The sun set like a sad message. The yard grew as dark as my mind. *Gracias, Padrecito.*

But as the first stars came out and I at last stood to leave, Señor C also stood, looked me in the eye, then reached out and embraced me. Picture it, Jervis. Suspended on his cross, he ripped himself free of his nails long enough to hold me in his skinny arms. And so became my teacher. My hero. My ravaged love. He then turned without a word to his empty house, I turned toward my empty parsonage, and we walked in silence into the darknesses we are each called to face.

There's more to tell, Jervis. Much more. But for now I'm too done in by all the crosses.

-TJ

This—the second letter of TJ McGraff to his confessor and twin, again read aloud to Risa as they hunched in the gloom of Jervis's Hoyt Street monk's cell—is the last missive TJ ever wrote as an aspiring Jesuit:

Brother Jervis:

I visited Señor Cabrera again. And this time brought a half-pint of tequila. Which we didn't exactly knock back. But it was good, as we sat on the broken porch steps, our hips again touching, to pass sips of strong religionless communion back and forth as we again considered the dirt yard, stone fence, broken gate, treacherous sky.

Again we remained silent. Again days, weeks, lifetimes passed. Again, in the gate, the yellow cur appeared, saw two forlorn men and no Demetria, and slunk away. But this time, when we at last stood, I thought to part ways, Señor C did something that terrified me. He turned to his little house of heartbreak, house of emptiness, the very wood, nails, and adobe of his cross. And he motioned for me to precede him inside.

The hacienda consisted of a single room. One window in the center of each wall, each so small they cast a light dim as the portholes of your sloop. No bathroom or running water. A Lady of Guadalupe on one window ledge. Two beds a few feet apart, one, as I'd feared, much smaller than the other. The air cool but, as I'd feared, holding a faint fragrance of a child and her things.

I was already trembling when Señor C motioned for me to sit on the smaller bed. It was so neatly made it showed his adoration, which was heartbreaking. But if it had been messy, as if Demetria had been in it that morning, that might have been worse. Made or unmade I felt a shattering reverence for the little bed as I eased down upon it, then an equally shattering gratefulness when Señor C, as is his custom, sat very close beside me.

With his eyes, no words, he directed my attention to the shallow alcove built into the adobe at the head of the bed—and there stood Demetria's greatest treasure: her collection of *muñecas quitapenas*. What we call "trouble dolls." But *quitapenas* also means "take away shame," and shame had been drowning me since the burial. So how medicinal for poor little *Padrecito* that Demetria owned perhaps fifty Take Away Shame dolls.

They were neatly arranged, the men all in tiny vests and sombreros, the women also in sombreros, long colorful skirts, white blouses, miniature shawls. Everyone's hair black. Everyone's skin brown. Everyone's eyes an inscrutable black dot and eyebrows a somehow wistful black dash. Three sheep, two donkeys, a brown-and-white cow, pink pig, and flock of tiny chickens, which Demetria had some-how managed to stand on teensy wire feet.

Still without words, Señor C urged me to touch the dolls, pick them up, play with them if I liked—and how closely he watched for which ones I happened to choose! In scrutinizing those dolls with Señor C watching, Jervis, I discovered there are huge rooms inside small ones, cathedrals inside tiny haciendas. The instant this or that minuscule woman, man, chicken, entered my hands the walls took off for the horizon, the ceiling lifted toward the sky, and jubilation shot through me. *Things before ideas,* brother! Beautiful *muñecas quitapenas* before regurgitated priest-talk about loss.

As if he too felt the room expanding, Señor C was moved, for the first time since Demetria's burial, to speak. His mother-in-law in Guatemala made *muñequitas* for a living till her eyes went, he said. The gringos paid her five US cents per doll and for years she could make fifty a day. But the dolls she made Demetria were special. Far more intricate. Four or five a day at most, and I could see it. The bright colors, simple yet mysterious faces, intricate tailoring of tiny clothes, so enchanted me I forgot my priest suit and exclaimed in garbled Spanish over doll after doll. When I finally thought to turn to Señor Cabrera, he was smiling, but with such agony in his eyes that I knew we were about to go somewhere terribly hard.

He then reached for Demetria's pillow. Lifted it. My breath caught. Underneath lay an exquisite *La Sagrada Familia.* Joseph and Mary in the usual tiny sombreros. *El Santo Niño* with a halo made of a tiny circlet of gold wire. Yet as I stared at them lying there, I could only see them as three beautiful nails, two driven clean through Señor Cabrera's palms, the third into his chest.

He began to describe the precise way in which Demetria had adored them. Every morning before she went out, she stood *La Familia* before her in a dent on top of her pillow, told them of her hopes and plans for the day, and asked for their protection, but never for anything else, he said. Nor did she pretend to speak for the dolls the way almost all children do. Each evening, after washing and drying her hands, she stood them in another pillow dent and spoke to them again, telling how her hopes and plans had or hadn't worked out, thanking them for the day's surprises and pleasures, thanking them for helping her through the hard things. At bedtime she again washed and dried her hands, kissed them good night, taking care to make it a dry kiss, and placed them under her pillow, asking them to love her and keep her safe as she slept, promising to do the same for them.

It was when Señor C spoke of Demetria's request for safety, and promise to give it in return, that the gates opened. He began to breathe in a quick, quiet pant, like a woman in labor. "*La Familia* was sleeping when my child was taken," he whispered. "Though it was daytime, and Demetria and I were out working, they were sleeping. If they had not been sleeping, such an accident could never have occurred."

He labored in silence for a time, unable to speak his next thought. Then:

"El Santo Niño is a baby and cannot be blamed. But I cannot forgive Joseph or Mary for sleeping as the bolt left the jet and started down through the sky. *Her faith in them was so total.*" He was panting terribly now. "To divert the bolt would have been so easy. They had a blessing to bestow, a protection to give. I was so angry at their failure that, several times, I attempted to destroy the holy infant." Gasping for breath, he picked up *El Santo Niño* and told how, on the worst sleepless nights, he several times sat by a candle holding *El Niño* closer and closer, trying to set Him ablaze while Joseph and Mary watched, that they might feel what he felt when Demetria collapsed on the ground. Then his panting stopped, his head fell forward as if his neck had been broken, and he murmured not to me but to the trio in his palm, *"Pero tampoco puedo perdonarme a mi mismo por el hecho de que estaban durmiendo."* (But I can't forgive *myself* for the fact that you were sleeping either.) *"Porque si yo hubiera dicho el nombre de cualquier de ustedes antes de salimos para azadonar el campo por la mañana, yo os lo hubiera despertado a ustedes y nuestra Demetria habría sido protegida."* (For if I'd said the name of any one of you as we went out to hoe the field, I would have awakened you, and Demetria would have been protected.) *"Pero no dije sus nombres. Ni los pensé. Mientras azadonábamos yo me perdi en mis pensamientos. Así que ustedes santos continuaron dormir."* (But I did not say your names, or think them. I was lost in my own thoughts as we hoed. So you Holy Ones slept.)

I was making sounds now, Jervis, stifling sobs. And me losing it caused Señor C to regain his equilibrium. He even smiled. "You'll be a fine priest," he said with impossible kindness. "You learn."

"What have I learned?" I blurted. "I have no idea! Please tell me!"

Speaking extra carefully to be sure I followed his Spanish, he said, "You have learned that, when the padre comes and says of someone's lost loved one, 'It is God's will,' this is blasphemy. But when the *sufferer* says of their lost loved one, 'It is God's will,' this is faith."

When a blast of head-to-toe agreement shook me, Señor C smiled yet again. "See?" he said. "You learn."

I nodded grimly.

He said, "You've learned that, even in public, when all eyes turn to the padre to try to understand a loss, it is sometimes the whole truth to say, 'I don't know why this terrible thing has happened.' To say it happened for a reason, unless you truly know the reason, turns you into a heartless parrot trained to caw 'God loves you' at every suffering person it sees."

More grim agreement from me.

"It also seems you are taught, you priests, to defend your God, but never to blame Him. This is a mistake. When we blame God, two things happen. One, He becomes present. He is now there with the sufferer, taking blame. And two, why *not* blame God? He's *God.* He can take all the blame there is! Go ahead! Blame Him! It keeps Him with you!"

My turn to smile. Who *was* this beautiful broken man?

Taking hold of my hand as if I were a child now, and speaking with a sincerity that widened the walls and raised the ceiling even higher, he said, "You have learned there are no strangers when death occurs. You and I are friends now because death has occurred. This is a small good. But again, the padre is in no position to mention it. Only the one who has suffered the loss can ever mention it. Do you understand?"

I nodded. And he kept hold of my hand. And we sat on Demetria's bed as we had on his broken steps, two friends fallen back into silence. But this silence was anything but peaceful, Jervis. When the strange panting began again, I realized my friend was *literally* in labor. He was in such pain that—I couldn't help myself—I began panting with him. Holding his hand like a midwife, a birth coach, a husband, I labored with him, feeling that if I too panted and coaxed, the burden he carried might be delivered into the world and his agony might ease. Sharing this shattered father's labor was the hardest work I've ever done. By far the hardest. And when his panting at last stopped, it seemed an actual newborn had entered the room. It looked like nothing at all, this infant, but it was palpable, and it had a name.

Its name was *Grief,* Jervis. Grief successfully delivered. And in the presence of this dark newborn I felt completely, clairvoyantly, that something enormous was about to change. Then it did. Señor C released my hand. Turned it over. And into my palm dropped the tiny Joseph. Exquisite Mary. *El Santo Niño.* I just stared at them for a moment, thinking he wanted me to examine their qualities as I had the other dolls. But he wanted *much, much* more than that:

"For you, *Padrecito,*" he said. "These *muñequitas* are for you."

Like a fool, I said, "Oh, I couldn't possibly take these."

Señor C, bless him, became wild. "You *must* take them!" he cried.

I was stunned by his vehemence, but also pleased. That he was being crucified by the loss of his daughter in the presence of her dolls, but still had such fight in him! I felt something had descended from above to meet him, helping him fight back through his demand. "When I remember the pleasure *La Familia* gave my daughter," he said, "I know I could never separate or destroy them. But when I think of my family's deaths, I know I can't keep them. The time has come, *Padrecito,* for you to *truly* help me. *You* must keep them. And you must care for them just as Demetria did. This is a very difficult thing I ask of you."

For the first time in my life, the only time, I fell into a place in which I knew not through thinking but through every cell in my body what it means to be a priest. I stared at the Joseph, Mary, and Jesus in my palm, listening to Señor C not with my mind but with my body and blood.

"I ask that each morning," he said, "you tell the Holy Family your hopes for the day, as my child did. I ask that each night, you tell them how your day went, as she did. I ask that you touch them with clean hands only, kiss them with dry lips only, place them near you before sleep, ask them to guard you, and vow to guard them in return. You must guard, love, and forgive them as I cannot guard, love, or forgive. You must find a way to say their holy names with complete trust, as Demetria did and I cannot possibly do. If you are able to do this, *Padrecito,* I believe *La Familia* will protect my child even now. And may also protect you. And perhaps even me. Yes. If you can do this, they might protect me. For as you must know, I no longer wish to live. Perhaps, in caring for my daughter's *muñequitas,* you and they will change this."

I have not shared a fact up to now, Jervis, because until now it may have seemed silly, and I couldn't bear for anything about this man to seem silly. The name of the father asking me to care for Demetria's Holy Family is *Josef.* And three times, as he was making his request, he reached down and touched each of the dolls in my palm. And the last *muñequita* Josef touched each time was Christ's earthly father. He then raised his hand and touched his heart. And you know how completely I am *not* given to vision, brother. But the third time Josef touched tiny Joseph, then his heart, I beheld the father of Jesus as clearly as I have ever beheld anyone in my life. Sitting so close beside me on Demetria's bed, *La Familia* was being given to me by Christ's earthly father. My body and blood, the hacienda, Joseph's face then opened unto mystery so great that I thought, *Who am I to think I can accomplish this task? Yet who am I to refuse it?* There was no choice in the room. Gazing into the eyes of Christ's father, I said, "I will attempt this, Joseph. I will do my very best. But now I too have a request."

He dropped his eyes and inclined his head to listen.

I said: "You have charged me with caring for *La Familia* as Demetria did. I will give it my all. But it's a long way to El Norte, where we're going. I worry, as Demetria may have worried, about Mary and the infant. And I see two donkeys in her collection. One, I believe, should come with us on our journey, so the holy Mother and Child can ride."

I swear to you, my brother: fool though I be, I am, as I write to you, the blessèd recipient of the completely broken, completely loving smile of the father of Christ. And nothing has ever made me so impossibly happy. As Joseph handed me the donkey he said, "You, *Padrecito,* have become my family's true priest. Family living or dead, our true priest."

Weeping as I smiled at him, I slipped infant, mother, father, donkey into my black Jesuit shirt pocket, and stuffed my kerchief in over them so they couldn't fall out. Joseph nodded his approval. Task given, *Familia* accepted, Joseph melted away and I faced Josef Cabrera again.

I felt certain, as I stood to leave, that Señor C and I will not see each other again in this life. I also felt certain that our connection is endless. In the door of his hacienda, when I turned to him, we neither spoke nor embraced. His eyes simply dropped to my breast pocket, rose to my face, and he nodded just once, so brokenheartedly yet so lovingly that no embrace could add to it.

I stepped out into the night then, and oh, Jervis! The little dirt yard, broken steps, stone fence, unforgivable sky, had all gone beautiful. I remained immersed in this beauty every step of the way to the parsonage. I remain immersed as I write this account. I am immersed each time I tend to and talk with Demetria's *Familia*. And this immersion has finished me as a Jesuit. Why? Because the commission Christ's father placed in my body and blood is ordination enough, and more than enough. Were I to go beyond it and perform the weary wonders priests duplicate like xerox machines, I would again be reciting platitudes on the lip of Demetria's grave. *La Familia* insists I serve her from now on by kissing the good dirt her body has rejoined.

I have not found God, Jervis. But I've discovered an element in the Periodic Table that is, for me, the supreme element, and it has nothing to do with xeroxing old formulas. That element is: *love-at-the-very-moment-it-strikes-us-clean*. Nothing more. Anything more is too complicated, too abstract, too knowing. Thérèse of Lisieux said, "To find a hidden thing, one must hide oneself. One's life must then be a mystery." In seminary, as I was being trained to appear knowing and *never* to hide, Thérèse's words drove me crazy. The same words sing in me now, because nothing I'm saying is being said through my knowing. It's all being said through my loving. When I tried to console those at Demetria's grave with scraps of knowing, I insulted love. Defiled it. *I no longer know!* It's all mystery now and I love, blame, and thank the supreme element for that! A Holy Family standing under my lamp just watched me remove a black shirt and white collar for the last time, and don the one non-Jesuit shirt I brought south. In the window reflection we now see an ignorant, lovestruck man who looks a good bit like you, brother. That man is about to write a note, to be delivered after I leave in the morning, telling his crucified friend to feel, morning and night, for the prayers this new man and *La Familia* will never stop sending him and his daughter. This new man is going to say, "You're right, Josef. I learn. *Amar a alguien o algo, en cualquier lugar, es la única iglesia.*" (Loving anyone or anything, anywhere, is the only church.) We five, counting the donkey, are coming north for as many heartbeats as we're given, dear brother, with no purpose but to love as secretly, faithfully, and long as we can.

Teej

(Portland, October 29, 1989)

X. Tiny Joseph Gives Big Jesus the Speaks

Be a sheet of paper with nothing on it.
                            —Jalal al-Din Rumi

There is a state of reality...in which we actually are no-body and we don't have anything. This sounds very bad. It sounds like total failure, but it is the most beautiful truth that we can ever witness...There is a consciousness in each of us that is nobody...Not American, European, Tibetan, or Chinese.
                            —Anam Thubten, *The Magic of Awareness*

You shall love the nothing. You shall flee the something.
                            —Mechthild of Magdeburg

We ought always to remain in a certain nothingness and annihilation, as one who has nothing, who can do nothing, who knows nothing, and who does not have any power. All salvation consists in this nothing.
                            —anonymous Beguine author of *The Beguine Pearl*

THE NEXT MORNING, on the forty-ninth day of his brother's coma, TJ McGraff stood beside Risa for a moment, staring wordlessly at Jervis as he lay, emaciated but still breathing. He then closed his eyes and began to nod his head. Risa noticed, and turned to hear what he was about to say. But when TJ said nothing, her reborn respect for him ran so deep that she trusted his silence more than any conceivable speech.

What had dawned on TJ was an unprecedented course of action. For seven weeks he had desired one thing in all the world: for Jervis to wake so they could reunite and share the rest of their lives. He'd prayed for this without ceasing till he'd collapse from exhaustion, rest oh-so-briefly, then start praying for it again. But by so doing, he realized, he'd blocked a more radical option. Jervis was lost in a nothingness from which TJ's endless prayers had utterly failed to coax him. What if he stopped trying to coax? What if he tried, instead, to fall into a nothingness in which he gave up all desire for any particular outcome and just sank, sank, sank into what is? Would a surrender that self-annihilating bring Jervis spiritually closer whether he lived or died? TJ had no idea. But after seven weeks spent trying to pray his brother back into the world, the possibility of sinking below consciousness, where Jervis was dwelling, set him to nodding.

TJ gave Risa a quick kiss on the cheek, taking care to make it a dry one. He then left the ICU, walked the Burnside Community hallways till he found an empty waiting room, entered it, and left the lights off. Taking a chair, he placed his elbows on his knees and his face in his hands, turned inward, and with all his concentration began moving toward the nothing-place he'd felt, all these weeks, in the utter inertia of his brother's hand. Time passed on the hospital clock. Earth flew through space. Saving no thought, no yearning, no hope, letting mind and desire fall away, TJ kept journeying till he ceased to be himself at all.

He became an animate nothingness. Time stopped. All objects and all space became abyssal. But the body housing the nothingness had certain habits. Those habits stood nothingness on its feet, enabling it to slowly leave the room.

Nothingness passed people in hallways, passed elevators, and was drawn to open by habit an EXIT door. Climbing an echoing concrete stairwell to the hospital's fourth floor, nothingness strode down the hall to a double door made of thick wood, grabbed the handle of the left door by habit, stepped inside, and found itself in a chapel. Three worshippers seated, alone and far from one another, in the pews. One apparently praying. Two just sitting.

"So be it," nothingness whispered. Taking a seat in the backmost pew, it wiped its hands by habit on a clean kerchief, pulled a little silk bag out of its shirt, opened it, poured a tiny Joseph, Mary, Jesus, and donkey into its palm, dried its lips on the shoulder of its shirt, and carefully kissed each doll, donkey included, as an eight-year-old named Demetria would have wished. Returning Mary, Infant, and donkey to the purse, nothingness dropped them back down the neck of its shirt, picked Tiny Joseph up between thumb and index finger, held him up like a tiny candle, rose to its nothing feet, and started toward the front of the claustrophobic chapel at the regal pace of a priest leading a holy day processional through a mighty cathedral. Time remained stopped. All objects and all space remained abyssal save one very small thing: *Tiny Joseph.*

As nothingness paraded forward it twisted Tiny Joseph between thumb and forefinger, allowing the diminutive periods that served the doll as eyes to peer this way and that. Joseph took in two windows of drab gold glass to each side of the altar, behind which fluorescent lights rather than sunlight shone. He took in a beige carpeted floor reeking of Lysol, a low tiled ceiling, the three people hunched in sterile oak pews. Bearing Tiny Joseph before him like a candle in a cave, nothingness reached the steps leading up to the altar and did not slow. Stepping up to the base of the huge crucifix, nothingness turned its back on the Big Jesus suspended there but spun Joseph 180 degrees so the tiny doll faced Big Jesus. Nothingness then closed its eyes and kept them closed, maintaining immersion in the vortex of itself, till it found these words:

"Tiny Joseph. To know you just as you are—six-colored rainbow vest, blue sombrero, black trousers, yellow wire hands and feet—has been as important to TJ as knowing his brother Jervis. Even during these terrible coma weeks, you've been a solace."

The three worshippers looked up. Two of them—a middle-aged Caucasian man, a young Asian woman—were alarmed to see and hear an exhausted-looking man who was obviously not a cleric trespassing on the altar.

"As you know, Tiny Joseph, TJ loves Jervis beyond reason, the way he loves you," the man said, "and he has prayed for Jervis without ceasing. But after forty-nine days Jervis is skin and bones, overloaded on antibiotics, blood stagnating, every part of him atrophied. And TJ has fallen into despair. You know why. Demetria, her father, and now TJ's brother, either dead or in agony, like your Son. He has tried to pass the best words he can find on to a greater Father, and that his prayers have gone unanswered he accepts. But in this chapel the prayers feel worse than unanswered. They feel *trapped*. Actively smothered. Even *violated* somehow."

The altar trespasser's over-intimate speech aimed in their direction caused the Caucasian man and Asian woman to stand, glare at the fellow in his madness, and march out of the chapel. But the worshipper who'd been praying—a very old, green-eyed woman whose unlikely name turned out to be Rachel Goforth—saw how the young man was holding a tiny, brightly colored object in his raised thumb and finger. A Mexican trouble doll, perhaps? And he was speaking not to his God or to the dreadful crucifix behind him but to the doll! Why did behavior that repelled two worshippers captivate a third? Who can say? I only know that antique, green-eyed Rachel Goforth avidly watched and listened.

"Why does love feel smothered in here?" animate nothingness asked Tiny Joseph. "TJ felt this Big Jesus could be responsible. He tried desperately to get past his feeling that a mere idol can jail prayers, but every time he came here a feeling like a gag reflex rose, as if this awful Jesus was pressing its finger on the back of TJ's tongue. He will not pray in this room again. He will not pray for his brother again. He chooses to say nothing, desire nothing, and sink into nothingness, as Jervis has done. But as he was sinking he had a last feeble thought. Just as he vanished, TJ wondered whether *you*, Tiny Joseph, might know how to break a prayer out of this awful room. TJ is done. Sunk. Gone. Only nothingness holds you, Joseph, and if you choose to speak, or don't, so be it. I only know it's down to you or nothing. Your prayer or nothingness."

Rachel Goforth watched the young man fall silent. Watched his shoulders slump as he stood, eyes still closed, his back to the crucifix, his right hand raised so the doll could study the icon. The man showed no embarrassment over this childlike make-believe. He showed no self-awareness at all.

But Rachel Goforth watched him like an owl, a goshawk, an angel. Who *was* this old woman, I wonder? Is there truth to the old Middle Eastern legends of "spiritual agents" sent down to certain city streets, law-paralyzed mosques, chapels stale with rote-speak, to dissolve an occasional spiritual blockage? Is it possible that, like a relay racer passing a torch to the next runner, Rachel Goforth's bright green eyes were involved in the needle of energy that suddenly pierced the finger and thumb of the nothingness at the altar, right where they touched the tiny doll? To say, "A needle of light passed from an old woman's eyes into a nothingness," feels more truthful than to say, "A prayer was about to be answered," because TJ told the truth: he was done. Gone. And nothingness does not pray. If TJ had been anything more than nothingness, if he'd been a self pleading with its God-concept to "save Jervis," for instance, he may not have noticed the unspeakable needle passing (let's say) from fathomlessness into an old woman, out her electric eyes into a doll's tiny wire hand, thence into a vacated man's fingertip and thumb.

But nothingness noticed. Noticed, then felt the needle pass like a fine thread of fire up the arm into the shoulder, thence downward into the torso. Time passed on the hospital clock. Earth flew through space. Space remained abyssal. Rachel Goforth gazed at TJ, TJ gazed at nothing, and Tiny Joseph gazed at a jumbo prayer-killing crucifix as the fire-thread traveled through nothingness into a chest, infused two lungs, sparked upward past a throat, onto a tongue, which proved flammable, moving in ways that only fire and tongues can—

and a voice emerged. A fusion, it seemed, of a preadolescent Latina and a crotchety old rabbi of the urban East Coast. A fusion invented for comic effect, the average person might think. But there were no average people present. There was no congregation at all save old Rachel Goforth, and all she did, hearing the fused voice, was break into a smile crazed for the green intensity of its delight.

"Nothingness," Tiny Joseph said. "It would be my pleasure to break a prayer out of this room. But to do so I must first give Big Jesus here the speaks."

Tiny Joseph gazed up at the hulking crucifix, curtly nodded his blue sombrero, and in his rabbi-meets-Chicana voice said, "Big Jesus. Allow me to introduce myself. I am Tiny Joseph, a *muñequita* of Christ's earthly father, made in Guatemala by the grandmother of a girl who loved my family and me with all her heart. When that girl died in an insane accident, I was passed by her father, who also loved me, into the keeping of the nothingness through whom I now speak. Whereas *you,* I'm sorry to say, are a beefy wooden Jesus, manufactured in Communist China, perhaps, and at a bargain price by the look of you."

When Rachel Goforth let out a happy snort, the off-white acoustic ceiling tiles turned faintly pink, embarrassed by their failure to maintain a maximum-security prayer-coffin.

"Your appearance isn't your fault," Tiny Joseph told Big Jesus. "But your makers had a duty. Their task was to at least suggest, if not portray, the living mystery of the crucified Son of Love. Instead, they portrayed a dead-faced longhair with yellowish skin suggesting a long diet of junk food, its cheeks and lips absurdly rosy, and its expression, *in mid-Crucifixion!* as blasé as a mannequin's. *Shame on your makers, Big Jesus!* When I first saw you, my thought should not have been *This isn't a chapel. It's an amusement park. This Jesus escaped a carousel. He needs a saddle and a sign:* COME RIDE THE CROSS WITH DEAR JESUS. ONLY 25 CENTS!"

When delighted laughter flew up out of Rachel Goforth, it was too much for the blushing ceiling tiles: they turned diaphanous, then permeable, and Tiny Joseph's words and ancient Rachel's delight shot through the sun-door, Pali *kannikā*, Greek oculus, on to wherever prayers and laughter are most meant to fly.

"I'm no spitting image of Mary's husband either," Tiny Joseph admitted. "I'm very small, I have no heartbeat, and I was born eight thousand miles from the Holy Land. But these are not my credentials. As an image of Christ's father, my credentials are the love with which Demetria's grandmother created me, the love Demetria showered upon me every day and night of her life, the love that moved her father to spare my Infant Son and pass my *Familia* and me on to a loving keeper. We icons run on a simple fuel, Big Jesus. Only when *loved* may we enliven necks and altars, and help those desperate to send love to truly send it to the suffering. This is why the lumpen look of you isn't just disappointing in this chapel. It's a vicious irony assailing hearts with no room in them for irony. If there is to be prayer in this room, then you, poor clunky Carousel Jesus, must vanish. So. *Goodbye!*"

With that, nothingness twisted its thumb and finger and Tiny Joseph spun 180 degrees, so that he too now faced the all-but-empty room. At that very moment, Nurse Britt burst through the door at the back of the chapel, with Risa close behind...

It colors the telling of this story that I, its teller, do not believe in "coincidence" or "luck." My skepticism does. But an impermeable core far deeper than my skepticism has come to believe, like Risa's forest rishis, in a Creator, a Sustainer, and a Destroyer, so my faith struggle is no longer against skepticism. My struggle—like TJ's until he sank into nothingness—is to somehow trust the constant, terrible manifestations of the Destroyer. So it's my faith *weakness,* really, which relishes the fact that, as they strode into the chapel midway through Tiny Joseph's prayer, Nurse Britt was beaming, and Risa was weeping and beaming, forecasting that a terrible act of the Destroyer might, for incomprehensible reasons, have been oh-so-narrowly averted. But the nothingness at the altar saw none of this.

"My Son," Tiny Joseph's rabbi-child voice said. "When I look at Jervis, I see a body being crucified for loving another more than himself. A body like *Your* body. I then wonder why a Jervis or Demetria must be ripped from this world into the beyond *for being like You,* when being like You is precisely what You ask of them? Why can't a few of Your dearest ones stay in this world long enough to wreak a little healing and joy? That's what I must ask. Because look at this poor world without them! Speaking my heart, wrong or right, I say, go ahead, my Son. Ravish Jervis. Bring him into Your embrace, drown him in oceans, give him annihilations and ecstasies, grant his wild wish to be lost in You. But in *this* world! *In this poor world!* Because, O my Son! *Josef Cabrera!* Poor Josef and so many like him! Stripped of their loved ones. Nailed to their grief-crosses. And when You whisk away the Jervis-hearted, Demetria-hearted, Magdalena-hearted, who is left in their crucified lives to take them down?"

Risa listened, stunned. Old Rachel Goforth kept beaming. Looking as if she were about to burst, Nurse Britt started forward again, but Risa took her wrist. "Please!" she whispered. "Let him finish!"

"Isn't it *You* urging me to ask that Jervis and TJ be granted the eyeblink that is the joined lives of two mortal brothers loving away a little of this world's pain? Aren't Demetria, Josef, and Jervis *the very jewels on Your fingers?* Isn't it *You,* my Love, who would be infinitely delighted if Jervis's heart shone again, for a time, amid the darkness of this world?

"I know You will answer these questions as purest Love sees fit. And I will trust Your answer, whether or not I understand. But this is my prayer, my Son. *This is my prayer. Amen.*"

Nothingness had let its arm drop, pulled the purse from its shirt, slipped Tiny Joseph inside, and was about to drop *La Familia* down the neck of its shirt when Nurse Britt hit TJ like a linebacker blindsiding a quarterback. But she also threw her arms around him, keeping him on his feet as she said, "TJ! *Jervis is moving!* He *sees* us! And he nodded when we asked if he can hear us!"

TJ stared at her, uncomprehending. He was the hole in a guitar. The hollowed-out source of a music a no one has been impossibly playing. Risa slid her arm through his, smiled so big her glee gap showed despite her tears, and said, "Just come, TJ. You'll see."

As they passed the old woman in the pew, she stood, green eyes aglow. "I...My name is Rachel Goforth," she said. "And *you,*" she told TJ. "*He,*" she said, dropping her gaze to the tiny purse round his neck. "Oh, I'll just say it! May I please come see Jervis too?"

Nurse Britt extended an arm. Rachel took it. Three luminous women and a hollow-eyed *muñequita* of a man set out for Jervis's room.

THE BED HAD been raised, Doc Phillipa attending, and Jervis looked like an eighty-pound post-human ruin just lowered from an old Roman cross. But his single eye was open, following each of them as TJ, Nurse Britt, Risa, and Rachel Goforth filed into the room. And as they gathered round his bed, the normally implacable Doc Phillipa grinned like a kid who'd mastered a magic trick. "*Listen,*" she said—with which she reached forward and, with her index finger, plugged the trach-tube hole in Jervis's throat.

In a papery little whisper that sounded like nothing his listeners had ever heard, Jervis said, "*The fuck, Teej.* How is he?"

The question meant nothing, the voice everything: TJ flew up through an oculus into joy.

"Who?" asked Nurse Britt. "How is *who,* Jervis?"

"The man I tried to help behind the dumpster."

"He didn't make it, Jervis," said TJ. "I'm sorry. The man you helped is gone. But this is our new friend, Rachel Goforth. And this is Nurse Britt, who for seven weeks has been taking great, great care of you."

"*The fuck,*" Jervis paper-whispered as Rachel and Britt smiled hugely.

"And this," TJ said, "is our lost and found sister, Risa, without whom, I suspect, I'd be gone by now too. So say hi to her, Jervis. Say thanks."

With which TJ took Risa's hand and placed it in his brother's.

Doc Phillipa, meanwhile, removed her finger from Jervis's trach-tube hole, telling them, "You know what he's about to say. And it won't be 'Thanks.' Watch."

"*The fuck,*" Jervis soundlessly said to Risa as, oh so faintly, he squeezed her hand.

Fourth Telling:

Converging Rope Tricks

Any moderately clever cynic can make contemplative effort sound like a cheap rope trick. What the cynics never quite manage to see is the occasional sincere one, sometimes sitting right beside them, quietly weaving invisible rope out of whatever she can get her spiritual hands on. Once in a while, with astonishing focus, she then reaches up, attaches her rope to invisible pitons or climbing cams that faith alone enables her to feel, gives her rope a firm test yank, and, if this ludicrous arrangement holds, begins shinnying her way up out of the pit of disillusionment and despair. The cynics meanwhile, dropping away below, go on wittily yammering.

—Thomas Soames

(Portland, 1989, 1990)

I. Jervis at Sea

I loved her above health and beauty, and chose to have her instead of light: for the light that cometh from her never goeth out...She is the transparent nothing that pervades all things by reason of her pureness...Although she is but one, she does all things. Without leaving herself, she renews all things. And in every generation she passes into holy souls and makes them friends of God.

—*Wisdom of Solomon*

When the Ocean comes to you as a lover,
Marry her, at once, quickly,
for God's sake!

—Jalal al-Din Rumi

WHEN JERVIS AWOKE on October 29th, 1989, he discovered that his left eye was a bandaged empty socket, that his body lay in a hospital bed, and that a woman who looked rather like Dr. Jane Goodall was holding her finger to his larynx as she studied him with a look of great pleasure. "Good morning!" she said.

"*The fuck*," Jervis replied in a papery whisper, causing her to laugh.

When TJ, Nurse Britt, Risa, and Rachel Goforth then burst into the room as previously described, the reunion was brief. Doc Phillipa, despite the Goodall resemblance, was not willing to passively observe primates billowing germs onto a man whose survival was a miracle: she sent everyone but TJ out of the room, then she too left the brothers alone.

For TJ, it was then revelation time.

Jervis's first whispery words: "Can you feel, Teej? Can you feel how everything is now?"

"You're lying in bed," TJ said with a smile, "wide-awake after seven weeks gone. You're talking very softly, but clearly. You're giving me joy, Jervis!"

"You're my Teej, Teej," Jervis said. "But it's not me giving the joy...It's not like before...Nothing's like before...Can you feel how every single thing really is?"

"Just tell me, Jervis. What's changed? What feels different?"

Despite the pauses he needed simply to breathe, Jervis let TJ have it. "*All is an Ocean*. Father Zosima said that...And maybe Dostoevsky made Zosima up...But Zosima didn't make Ocean up...I mean, I see you, see my body, see this room...I hear Portland out the window...But can you feel what it's all immersed in?...Zosima wasn't kidding...There's no inner and no outer. No higher and no lower. No self or not-self. *The fuck, Teej*. All of it really *is* an Ocean."

Jervis's single eye sent TJ a gaze that conveyed how literally and completely he meant it, till at last TJ croaked, "*Jesus Christ, Jervis!*"

Jervis shrugged. "Dunno. Haven't felt him yet. But Ocean for sure."

A FEW MORNINGS into the year 1990, after a four-month hospital stay, Jervis was able, by holding TJ's forearm, to dodder from TJ's car into the Hoyt Street monk's cell.

Once inside, the first thing TJ did was fill Jervis's one small saucepan with water, set it on the Coleman stove to boil, and make tea for them both in his little Yixing teapot.

The first thing Jervis did was toddle over to his fruit-crate bookshelf, ease himself down on the rock-hard futon, slide Marguerite Porete's *The Mirror of Simple Souls* out of the crate, and try, with his single seeing eye, to read. But though his eye saw the words, he couldn't locate the stationary, landlubbing, air-breathing part of himself that could make sense out of printed words. Having discovered a loss that would devastate most literate people, Jervis began calmly sliding his books out of the fruit crate shelf till he'd emptied it. He then flipped the crate onto its back and started piling the books inside, as if packing for a move.

Watching this closely as their tea steeped, TJ was careful to keep his tone light. "Upgrading the Vatican Library, are we?" he asked.

Jervis just kept packing the crate.

Oblivious as ever to his athleticism, TJ held the hot teapot and teabowls as he dropped to the futon, scrunched his legs into a half lotus with no help from his hands, filled both bowls with a high pour to cool the tea, set a bowl on the floor beside Jervis, took a sip from his own, and said, "May I ask what you're doing?"

"Packing my books for Risa," Jervis paper-whispered. "You said she likes 'em, right?"

TJ frowned, but strove to choose his words carefully. "When Risa and I came here near the end of your coma, she expressed interest in the Eckhart and Beguine books. But you've just crated every book you own. The McGinn scholarship, Buddhist books, Kazantzakis's *Saint Francis*. Even your bird books. Why?"

"So you'll mail 'em to her in Seattle," Jervis said. "I'd do it, but I can't lift 'em yet."

TJ controlled himself for a few seconds, then blew: "You've *lived* by these books, Jervis! You nearly *died* for these books. You own a TV that gets no reception to watch one movie once a year, no record player, no CD player, no musical instrument or any other means of entertaining yourself. What do you plan to do here? Conduct a sensory deprivation experiment? Should I mail Risa your shitty chair, stove, futon, clothes, and light bulbs to make the experience total?"

Jervis trained his good eye on TJ. "Just because it's calm," he said, "don't think Ocean isn't here. And just because you see me, don't think I'm the old me. I told you, that me is gone, and this me isn't mine. This me is Ocean's. Drifting as we speak, feeling her every second, breathing her in and out, no inner, no outer, no beginning, no—"

"—up, no down, no look all around, no look at my thumb, no gee you're dumb!" TJ cut in. "I *know,* Jervis! And I don't dispute your...*symptoms.* I'm just asking, symptoms included, why you're giving away every one of your books."

Jervis looked baffled. "*The fuck, Teej,*" came the papery little voice. "I can't swim and read at the same time."

TJ gazed at his brother, saw his seriousness didn't waver, and breathed, "*Jesus Christ!*"

Jervis shrugged. "You keep saying that. Haven't seen him. But Ocean for sure."

LETTER FROM RISA McKEIG, late January 1990:

Dear TJ,

Thanks for Jervis's books! As feared, I love them so much I'm having a hell of a time getting my thesis paintings done. If Catholicism hadn't kicked out the likes of Mechthild, Hadewijch & Marguerite I might not have fled my girlhood faith. How insane of Holy Church the Little to damn their female bodhisattvas! But the good news is, the Beguines are with *us* now, *outside* the effing Church, safe from the pundits & patriarchs who'd do nothing but dissect & codify their blazing hearts if they were still "in the fold."

But the next part of your letter mystified me. I read your description of "Jervis's condition" three times. Each time I had less of an idea what you're talking about. You say: "I'm hoping his sense of being literally 'in Ocean' is a trauma symptom that will ease as he gains strength, so he can lead a pared-down but fairly normal life." For God's sake, TJ! What has Jervis ever had to do with "pared-down" or "normal," & why would you want that for him? Is this the same TJ who, when Jervis was in the coma, lovingly recited tales of his night sailing fuckups, promising Jervis & God you'd never complain of any vessels he might sink if only he'd return to you? Well, here he is, TJ, & according to him *an entire Ocean,* who turns out to be female & infinite, is here with him too, & being in her is bliss! Why in the name of Love would you call this a "trauma symptom," or want it to "ease"? May I humbly suggest you summon your great courage, move the hell out of Holy Church the Little into Holy Church the Great, & never mention Jervis settling for "pared-down" or "normal" again? To quote an Ocean-goer, "*The fuck, Teej!*" When we read Beguine accounts of annihilations, illuminations & awakenings we're not idling the day away in some safe little Marvel comic or *Hitchhiker's Guide* wonderment. We're reading of the soul exploding into our insanely *normal* world in a blessedly abnormal state of awareness! Seconds before his beating, Jervis burst into a state the Bertrand Russells of this world can only slander as "unmitigated rubbish" about rivers entering the sea. Before accepting this, ask yourself what Bertrand might have done if faced with the same two meth thugs in mid-murder & pick your hero! Rather than read books about the Beguines, Jervis has erupted into the Love that erupted in them, shooting far beyond our understanding, but not beyond our love & awe. The same way I adored you the moment you insisted you were not my brother, but my mother-brother, I adored Jervis the moment he woke from his coma & whispered, "Zosima wasn't kidding. All is an Ocean." What could be better than his companionship as we play the game of Love for keeps? I hope I've offended you just enough to help you stop playing nurse & turn the corner on this! I cherish you both.

—Risa

Late night, February 1990. Jervis and TJ alone in the Hoyt Street monk's cell. A single candle, guttering a little, stands on the bookless fruit crate that now serves as a coffee table. Close beside it, Jervis hunches like an injured owl in his crappy little canvas chair.

TJ serves them both tea, sits in a half lotus on Jervis's crummy futon, and speaks words Risa's letter has made available to him: "Your disabilities are still so serious I keep thinking like a nurse, not a brother. A brother wouldn't try to hide from your genuine ongoing experience, or refuse to be your Holy Church the Great companion. What foolishness. I'm sorry to have done that."

Jervis shrugs. Paper-whispers, "You're always my Teej, Teej."

"I *am* your Teej. But *Nurse Teej* isn't. I want the Ocean you love to mean as much to me as she does to you. And when 'the Roman Men's Club,' as Risa calls it, destroyed the Beguines and condemned Eckhart, they rendered themselves, and ratiocinative sorts like me, ignorant of Ocean Language. This Ocean you're feeling, no offense, is a zero to me so far. I do have faith in what you're experiencing, but it's blind faith. I haven't felt a drop of brine, smelled the sea, heard a gull's cry. And maybe that's how it has to be. But if possible, I'd love to be *with you* in this. So if ever you could describe even a little of what—"

It dismays TJ to see Jervis shaking his head before he's even finished. "The way your mind is, Teej, words won't help. Your mind has its hands stuffed in its pockets as you ask to be handed a glass of Ocean. Anything I say to that mind will just fall on the floor and shatter."

"I can get my hands *out* of my pockets!" TJ cries. "I can put my mind *away,* Jervis. I *will* put it away. I've learned how. Just give me a minute."

TJ draws a breath, then pulls the little purse out of his shirt, opens it, fishes out Tiny Joseph. Drying his mouth on the sleeve of his shirt, he kisses Joseph with dry lips only. Taking the *muñequita*'s tiny hand between his index finger and thumb, he aims Joseph at Jervis. "To keep Jervis's words from falling on the floor and breaking," TJ tells the doll, "I need to go away. So will you watch and listen for me, Joseph? And if he hands you a glass of Ocean, will you later tell me how it tasted and sounded and felt?"

Tiny Joseph does the full-body bow that serves as his nod.

TJ nods back, closes his eyes, lowers his head, and dives for nothingness. His neck and shoulders relax. His head inclines toward Jervis. His eyes close and stay closed. His breaths come slow and deep.

The diminutive periods that serve as Joseph's eyes peer at Jervis.

. .

Jervis's glass eye is veered off toward the ceiling, but his good eye peers steadily at the doll. Silent moments pass. When Jervis begins to speak, his paper-whisper is slow and concise, leaving pauses between each statement to help TJ grasp them:

"I can't describe Ocean without help from the Beguines and the Meister...The Meister says, 'A man had a dream, a waking dream, in which he was great with nothingness, as a woman with child. In this nothingness, Ocean was born.' Ocean, the fruit of nothingness, is the endless one, Teej. The shoreless one...She's got no form but contains *all* forms...Never changes but creates all change...We can't find her by seeking because she's already in all the places we search...And I was crazy when I'd plead, 'Be with me, never leave me, stay with me,' because she *was.* She's the Forever Here, and we leave her and leave her even as we claim to love her. She forgives us even so...She's the love that's there the instant we love something or someone, and the love that's still there after we and our someone are dust."

Staying out of it, letting Tiny Joseph do the seeing and listening, TJ allows the words to wash over, soaking him, stirring him, yet remains as passive as the beach sand swirling through incoming and outgoing waves.

The intensity of Jervis's papery voice ramps up: "Here's the hard thing, Teej. Here's the very very hard thing. Whoever life harms, she heals. But almost never in ways we get to see. You need Ocean's own eye to see her work the healing. So to mention her insane mercy sounds like a lie to a human mind. Her mercy *can't* sound true to a mind because it's inaccessible to the mind. We grasp her mercy *when we feel her*. When I'm gone into feeling her, she *is* the mercy, triumphant inside the havoc. When I'm gone into feeling her, creation and destruction are two necessary powers, she's inside both, and she has no preference between them. When I'm gone into feeling her, I too lose all preference. Her insane mercy weaves all of it. Not just parts, like my old me preferred. Not just goodness, like most humans prefer. Not just life, as most prefer. Her mercy weaves the wrecked and the wreckers, the truth-tellers and the liars, the life-takers and life-givers. Because she is, there's this impossible, endlessly destructible yet indestructible whole."

Eyes closed, Tiny Joseph in hand, self long gone, a TJ-shaped nothing-ness listens.

"I'm going to tell my dumpster story now because she feels you wanting to hear it. But it'll only be words. I can't *language* it. So I'll only tell it once—and don't ask questions when I'm done. Okay?"

TJ remains motionless, appearing not to have heard...but Tiny Joseph repeats the curt bow that is his nod.

"Before I flooded I'd tell Ocean all sorts of things. 'I love you.' 'I adore you.' 'Please let me serve you.' I caught glimpses of her in Umbria that dazzled me so blind I'd talk that way. *The fuck*. I did *not* adore her. Too busy jibber-jabbering.

"A thing I've never told. In the Clare cave, what I heard. In the cave Clare said, 'Soul in eternity's mirror, heart at sea. You're ready, Jervis. You're ready.' But her saying my name, saying I'm ready, made me fall to pieces. The soul, when it opens, is vast, vast, vast and empty, empty, empty. That's her splendor, and it was *right there* in that cave. But I couldn't simple me down enough to stay inside it. I'd have stood outside her, sobbing and jabbering, 'I adore you,' till doomsday. I was saved from that doom when I got dumpstered."

Tiny Joseph whispers, "This is what TJ longs to hear described."

"Words *can't* describe it. But Ocean's making Teej long. Listen with that longing. No Teej, Teej. Just the longing."

From TJ, no reaction. From Tiny Joseph, another curt bow.

"I hear a *whump,* then a moan behind the dumpster. I go to it. I find Kryptonite and Two-by-Four killing a man. Knowing it won't stop them, I stand over the man. As soon as they look at me I feel death coming so fast there's only an eyeblink of time to do one thing. *No thinky*. Just one unthought thing. *No longer knowing how to speak, obeying no created thing but love, I give myself up to love completely.* And not my crappy, sobbing, 'I adore you' Clare-cave love. When Kryptonite and Two-by-Four step to opposite sides of me and God creates the impossible situation, finally, *finally!* my old me simples down to something so close to nothing that Clare's, Marguerite's, and the Meister's Love floods everything. And it's so powerful, so blissful, so glorious there's no words for it. As the two-by-four shatters my arm Ocean inundates me. As they obliterate my face and head she immerses me. As they kick, stomp, and beat me to death she surrounds and preserves me. Yet I mean *to death*. The heart Officer Barrios found beating in the dumpster is not mine. It's Ocean's now. And Ocean just loves. So no more talk, okay? Let's feel her nonstop for a while, okay? Will you walk in her with me now, Teej?"

Eyes still shut, thumb and forefinger still holding the doll he has somehow kept aimed at Jervis, TJ comes to himself and his closed eyes begin to stream. "*Okay, Jervis!*" he gasps. "Okay! But Jesus Christ! *Jesus Christ, Jervis!* But okay."

II. Mr. Wrong

It is like one of those traps...in fairy tales. If I accept this gift it is bad and fatal. Its virtue becomes apparent through my refusal of it.
        —Marguerite Porete, *The Mirror of Simple Souls*

AFTER GRADUATING FROM University of Washington with high honors, Risa knew she should have been thrilled to receive a full-tuition scholarship to the MFA program at Rhode Island School of Design. But she also knew why she wasn't thrilled. She'd chosen the most financially advantageous path into the next chapter of her life, knowing that the guidance of her heart, to the contrary, had chosen the path that once caused her to write,

> *The distance that separates heaven & Earth can be annihilated. A bridge lies between. Right here within the body is an Infinite Person, higher than which there is nothing.*

It didn't take Risa long to discover the kinds of places she could be carried by a financially advantageous path lacking heart guidance:

She met Julian Ventano during her first month at Rhode Island School of Design in a graduate seminar called Yeah, Right: Irony as Modus Operandi in Post-Modern Art. The instructor, Julia Gage, was an art historian working on a PhD thesis on art and irony. Two weeks into the semester-long seminar, Julian had dubbed his fellow students "Irony Seminarians" and his class notes, Risa would learn, included these characterizations:

•Not-Quite Dr. Gage: sinewy, whip-smart, lamentably gay, Post-Modern Post-Male associate prof who designed this interesting mess.

•Jonathan Grens: scrawny, wild-eyed, renegade Bible-college-dropout-turned-ceramics-sculptor who adds text to human figures to poke fun at evangelicals. Sample sculpture: a half-life-sized, absolute bombshell "Eve" whose entire body, even her lips, eyelids, nipples, pudendum, is tattooed with 12 pt. type quoting living theologians expounding dead seriously,

hence hilariously, upon "this supremely criminal woman." Grens's title for this work: *6,000 Years Ago: Eve. 38-23-36!*
I love this fucking guy!

•Klaus Hauptmann: misty-eyed German-born Werner Herzog–accented philosophy geek given to interminable discourses upon The Creative Process, Sacred Rites, Art as Empathy, The Exploitation of Indigenous Peoples, and other uppercase prefab totally predictable topics that vacuum the creativity and empathy right out of the room.

•Anna Hallstrom: heroically buxom, pretty-if-you-like-the-cow-eyed-type, boob-negatingly-fatalistic enviro studies devotee who wouldn't know irony if it smashed her in the face. Sample repartee: "What kind of art do you do, Anna?" "I show the ways they are *Killing Our Earth*!" "Who, Anna?" "*They!*" "Could you be less buxom and more specific?" "No! They are *Killing Our Earth*!" "Who, Anna, who?" "*All* of them!" "Which ones?!" "*THEY!*"

•Nita Hymes: Anna's lover, great-grand niece of some famous old linguist-folklorist, owner of the cutest jug ears I've ever seen, and a great pen-and-ink artist. I mean Paul-Klee-Lebbeus-Woods-great. But thanks to Anna's darkly boobulous take on humanity's futureless future Nita's recent work all tests Heinous Apocalypse Positive. The good news is, Nita might really blossom under Not-Quite Dr. Gage's sinewy tutelage. I see subtle sparks flying, and Anna's so busy tracking *THEM!* that she sees nothing. How great if Julia Gage were to become Anna's next evil *THEY!*

•Will Jones: an enormous, enormously skilled woodworker whose latest effort is a line of perverse furniture he dubs "Angst Nouveau." Examples: a set of four alder-wood barstools with seats slanted so steeply to right, left, or forward that they propel occupants onto the floor no matter how sober they are; a Mission-style love seat out the back of which protrude five lethally sharp wooden spikes; a maple analyst's couch with a back so arched it forces the patient's pelvis to thrust toward the ceiling as if on the verge of orgasm. One-liners, really—but so well wrought I'm jealous!

•Moi: an abstract painter secondarily but bon vivant primarily, because there will be no Picassos in my generation. As we Irony Seminarians illustrate, ours is a brood of corporate-cloned, Roundup Ready, obsessively "correct" PMOs (Psychologically Modified Organisms) preprogrammed by the ruling suicide culture to self-destruct if we try to break free of it, and those who deny our doom and strive for "freedom" or "greatness" merely annoy the rest of us by rattling their chains. Case in point:

•Risa O Risa McKeig: a not-unskilled neo-impressionist painter with run-away hair, a voice as deep and dark as her eyes, an *O my!* body, but a chain-rattling addiction to "spiritual imagery" born of ancient Indian wisdoms. The working title of her MFA thesis: "Landscapes of the Inner Eye." Nuff said! But it gets worse: a recent oil she did of a street woman actually moved me till she informed us it had been inspired by a Gandhi quote: "Recall the face of the poorest and weakest man you have seen and ask yourself if the next step you contemplate is going to be of use to him." Gag me with an Ideal! But the joke's on me. Risa's physical presence has turned my mind into a piece of space junk helplessly orbiting her day and night, and my body into Gandhi's "poorest, weakest man"! If the next step I contemplate is to be of use to this man I need to hook up with Risa ASAP, ancient wisdoms and Inner Eyes be damned!

USING RAVE LETTERS of recommendation from the renowned Portland restaurateur TJ McGraff and architect Theo Avery, Risa had landed an assistant manager–bartender job at a high-end Providence restaurant, The Dorrance. One night Julian Ventano strolled gracefully in, chose the barstool directly in front of her, and leveled his high-beams upon her.

Like countless women before her, Risa's first impression was that he might be the most handsome man she'd ever seen. Italian on his father's side, Afghani on his mother's, with an Ethiopian grandparent in the mix, he shone with a paradoxically bright darkness set off by perfect teeth and two-toned green and hazel eyes. His dark curly hair, perfectly proportioned body, and living colors made Da Vinci's Vitruvian Man look like a mannequin by comparison. But Risa also suspected the words "ridiculously handsome" might in some way apply.

Given that, did it fascinate her, or was it weird, that Julian was not a RISD student? During their self-introductions at Julia Gage's seminar, Julian said he lived and painted in Providence, and that was all he said. So. *Pretty painter man with connections sufficient to audit a class he wasn't paying for.* That was all Risa knew. Yet the smile he now leveled upon her set off a jumble of feelings: gratification at being the recipient of his attention; embarrassment at being gratified for such a thin reason; fear that they wouldn't like each other; greater fear that they *would.* This man, she saw at once, was what TJ would call "a lighthouse": his appearance, it haunted her to realize, mirrored her own in that it situated him, whether he liked it or not, upon stony reefs that signaled the opposite of a safe harbor. But what if there was something to learn here? What if he didn't like casting spells any more than she did? *Maybe we could call a truce and form a spell-free alliance,* Risa thought. *Maybe we could even teach each other how* not *to cast spells we don't wish to cast.*

Julian ordered an IPA, then struck up a conversation by asking Risa about her education up until RISD. She needed just thirty seconds to describe her double major at U Dub, her decision to drop Asian religions and focus on art, and the hard-earned scholarship that had brought her to Rhode Island School of Design. "Your turn," she said.

"My education isn't so succinct," he warned just as Jorie, one of the waiters, handed Risa a drink order. "How's your tolerance for detail?" Julian asked.

"How's yours for interruptions?" Risa asked back.

"Watch," Julian said—and he proceeded to feign such deep fascination with his glass of ale that he forgot Risa was even there.

Risa liked this. Jorie's drinks got poured, and Julian's IPA got reduced with total fake concentration. He then made a show of glancing up and acting startled to see her. "Oh!" he said. "Hey! Aren't you, uh...one of the gals from Not-Quite Dr. Gage's Irony Seminary?"

She liked this too—until his smile turned on full blast. *Too much!* The only word for such a smile was "dashing," as in: *capable of sweeping up anyone he chose on a wave of attraction, then DASHING them against the rocks.*

Julian's education monologue: he'd earned an undergraduate degree in the humanities at SUNY Albany, then traveled in Europe, Northern Africa, and the Middle East. "The usual roots-seeking cliché," he said, "and it went on for six years. I've got a big root system." His travels led to an attraction to anthropology, which he also studied at SUNY Albany, earning a master's, and aiming at a PhD. "But the war between biological and cultural anthropologists blindsided me," he confessed. "Have you heard of that rift?"

Risa hadn't.

"The Biologicals, to oversimplify, say anthro is a hard science. The Culturals say it's a form of 'cognitive colonialism' and want to dismantle the entire field. The Biologicals, like most biological organisms, don't wish to be dismantled. So the two factions despise each other. In a world armed to the teeth, I don't like strong antagonistic stances. That's why my PhD thesis was an attempt to bridge the rift. I even admit, though only to you, that said thesis was inspired by Captain Jean-Luc Picard of the USS *Enterprise-D* and *-E*. And I succeeded. Seeing me trying to find common ground between them, the Biologicals and Culturals on my thesis committee *both* shouted, '*Vive la différence!*' and tore my thesis to shreds. I wrote it twice more, trying to please them, wasting another year of my life, then realized the ongoing division between Culturals and Biologicals plays itself out in departmental politics across the land. Since my love for diverse cultures and people *depends* on not taking strong negative stances, anthropology, as a possible profession, had cast me out."

Risa doubted she was hearing the whole story, but didn't mean to show it. Julian, however, saw something cross her face. "I'm nearly done with my tale. But if I'm coming off as the kind of bore who entraps his poor bartender in tedious confessions, please, *shoot me!* I'll only share my education's happy ending if you really want to hear it."

Embarrassed at having been caught out, and mesmerized by his eyes when he flared up, Risa said, "How could your story *not* fascinate? Your academic trajectory was inspired by a French starship captain who won't even be born for three more centuries. Please continue!"

Julian *dashed* her with another smile. "I decided on a different master's degree. I felt there was something incorruptible about drawing and painting. You smile. *Ha.* You're wiser than me. After months of hard prep and multiple applications, I got into Chicago Art Institute. *Incredible,* I thought at the time. I then learned that aspiring painters carry enough chips on their shoulders to stock the casinos of Atlantic City, Vegas, and Monte Carlo combined. Postmodernists versus surrealists versus cubists versus op versus pop. Romanticism and Dada damned to hell, only to rise from the dead as the zombies *neo*-Romanticism and *neo*-Dada. Why can't anthropologists and artists coexist, Risa? No matter what kind of painting I put my hand to, people I considered compatriots looked over my shoulder and *sneered.* Then some started selling their work, while most didn't, and new stacks of shoulder chips formed. I know I sound self-pitying, but take heart! We've reached pay dirt." Julian's tone grew hushed and his smile almost blinding. "Three years ago, in one brilliant stroke, I discovered a way to paint more than ever, avoid artistic dogfights, and sell *all* of my work!"

"Good God! Really? What on Earth is your secret?"

He pulled out his wallet and handed her a business card. Risa grinned crookedly. Julian Ventano painted the houses of Providence and Newport, Rhode Island, for a living.

"Honest labor, I'm good at it, and it supports my true passion," he said.

"Which is?" she asked warily.

"The unassuming life of an arts-and-culture-loving dilettante. An *amateur,* critics could say, with no argument from me. The definition of amateur: 'one who loves, and is fond of, and has a taste for.' No shame in that! Let the cognitive colonialists, neo-deconstructionists, Dada-nihilists and Wawa-pugilists knock themselves out. Maybe it's my divergent roots, I don't know, but I'm incapable of making inviolable choices between *isms,* then savagely defending my choices. I prefer to make houses more weatherproof and elegant inside and out, then spend my leisure enjoying well-made things, art, cuisine, people, places. That way no one presents critical papers at academic conferences savaging my enthusiasm for, say, Julia Gage's incisive intellect. Or Jonathan Grens's anti-evangelical sculpture. Or the way Nita Hymes's adorable little jug ears poke out of her lank hair. Or, it's time to confess, *your* constant half smile, Risa. Which is how I happen to be here. I'm hoping that, compliments of my successful painting career"— another burnished smile sucked her toward the rocks—"you'll join me for a day spent exploring any combination of bistro, gallery, museum, theatre, or live music you might love, be fond of, or have a taste for."

The suaveloquence of Julian's invitation charmed and alarmed Risa equally. Yet she accepted. The instant she did, she felt a sickening *You-have-been-here-before* feeling rooted not in her own life but in her father's. By agreeing to date Julian, Risa was about to experience what Dave would call "chemistry," which would lead to what he called "a relationship," which would very likely devolve into what he called "a romantic conflagration." Yet when she looked not into but simply *at* Julian's green and hazel eyes, glowing skin, softly curling locks, and perfect body, she told herself, *Take the Buddhist approach, Risa. Forget Dave, Moira, and your Abandonment Blues for once. Live in the Now!*

Reflections such as this, she would one day learn from the nice Buddhist couple who run the best distillery in Missoula, Montana, were what inspired them to dub their dangerously seductive rye "Bad Buddhist Whiskey."

JULIAN VENTANO AND Risa McKeig soon discovered themselves to be almost effortlessly compatible in musical, culinary, and travel choices, bleakly compatible in their fears for their increasingly mean-spirited nation-state, and more than merely compatible in what Julian unfussily termed "the sack." After several months of something wildly more involuted than "dating," they decided to shack up together in Julian's airy, arty North Providence loft. Within a matter of days the amped-up intimacy then exposed core psycho-spiritual differences that began to diminish their pleasure in the things they "loved, were fond of, or had a taste for," causing them to resort more frequently to the satisfactions of "the sack," where the erotic harmonies achieved were significant, therefore addictive. Addiction then caused them to experience their core differences as too dangerous to address lest they sabotage the harmonies of the sack. The unresolved core differences and growing sense of danger then led to performance anxieties that brought diminishment to the sack as well.

So this is how Dave used to do it, Risa sighed.

III. Mountains Right Now

I thought I would spend some time wandering like a cloud, calling here and there like a water weed, in the style of the sages of old.

—Eihei Dōgen

IN THE QUIET years after Trey's departure from her life, and for the most part from Japhy's, Lorilee underwent some deep-seated changes in her relationship with the Thus Come One. The transformations began with a seeming triviality: on the day she'd kicked her wooden Buddha in a rage, broken off his earlobe, then glued it back on before Trey arrived to divvy up their possessions, the hasty repair job created an Elmer's Wood Glue ball that dried into a yellowish pearl earring. The effect of this pearl was both piratical and feminine. It erased the slightly smug air of the icon's constant half smile and left Lorilee feeling that an overlooked attribute of the Buddha might be a certain mischievous sisterliness. She liked this feeling so much that she left the pearl on the lobe, dubbed her icon "Elmerina Buddha," and began to meditate with her eyes open so that EB's arch sisterliness remained in view.

One day after nearly two years of these eyes-open zazen efforts, Elmerina seemed to commandeer her little statue and broadcast a message so clearly that Lore was able to write it down. "*I am not so much to be looked at, as to be looked out of. After all, ! ! Who are You?*" From that moment on, Elmerina Buddha became not so much a static icon as an openable door, and Lorilee's sitting became a refuge within, not a straining to become.

This breakthrough bequeathed several boons in the quiet of her new life. Among the first: Lore realized she no longer felt like a second-string Buddhist, sitting on the bench admiring "starters" like Joan Halifax, the Dalai Lama, Ani Tenzin Palmo, Gary Snyder. She felt like a starting player herself now, fully invested and in the game. Another boon: in the comparative peace of a new life as the single mother of an appealingly monk-like boy, she found herself able to fully forgive Trey, to detach from him quickly, and to view post-marriage life not as a duet gone sour but as a chance to perform a vibrant new solo. Her steady practice then fortified her detachment and improved her solo in psychological, spiritual, and physical ways.

An example of the physical: the stouts and IPAs she and Trey used to down as post-work painkillers were suddenly no more necessary than the ten pounds they'd caused her to carry. Going cold turkey, she lived on fruit, raw veggies, and nuts for two weeks, hiked the slopes of Two Medicine Peak daily, grew lean as a teen, felt years' worth of inertia turn into energy, and enjoyed cinching her belts two notches tighter.

A more dramatic physical change: in the first year after her divorce Lorilee's brown hair did an Emmylou Harris number, turning prematurely silver. Most of Lore's women friends advised her to color it back to brown, but one fine Pipestone morning Lorilee's adventurous new self happened past a barbershop advertising a four-dollar special. Remembering the four bucks that *Axe Handles* had put in her pocket, she felt a symmetry, strode inside, sat herself and her Emmylou tresses down in the barber chair, and told Ed the barber, "Exactly an inch long all over, please."

Ed eyed her, and asked if she was sure. "Darn tootin'," Lorilee said. "It's called a Bubbs Creek Haircut. All the rage in my circle."

When the deed was done and Lore climbed out of the chair, Ed gaped at her head to toe, shook his head, and said, "Damned if that ain't the best-lookin' haircut I ever gave a fella."

Ed's gender garbling turned out to be somewhat typical. At age thirty-three Lorilee could have been characterized as a petite, quietly pretty woman. The Bubbs Creek disquieted this quiet in a big way. By exposing her delicate head and thinness of neck, a boyishness appeared that knocked a seeming decade off her age and rendered her breasts and hips bewitch-ingly paradoxical. The silver also caused her black-limned gray eyes to appear even more clear and somehow...*mythic*. One hippety-hop to the barbershop and Lore looked to have stepped out of a wonder tale about the Tuatha Dé Danann or some such beings. The double takes that ensued could be baffling in that they were launched about equally by men and women. Even a few kids couldn't stop staring. Well aware of the attention her unintended "look" was getting, Lore merely sighed, *This too shall pass*. But having spent years in a life that rendered her close to invisible, she did enjoy being seen. So, every two weeks or so, back she'd go to Ed's, where he'd call out, "Another Bubbs Creek?"

"Darn tootin'."

Another fruit of her new life: a newfound intrepidity. When Pipestone Community Hospital underwent a hostile corporate merger, the usual draconian employee shuffle ensued. Because Lore had been a proficient head of billing for many years, her pay had risen to an actual living wage. In the Brave New World in which corporations were acquiring the rights not just of persons but of the particular type of persons known as Flaming Assholes, Lore's proficiency caused her to be summarily fired. Her intrepid new self, however, took this injustice as direction from Green or White

Tara to go forth and live in sunlight instead of fluorescent light, collecting unemployment instead of bilking victims of illness, injury, and loss. In the same intrepid spirit she then surveyed her options. Japhy was in first grade at North Pipestone Elementary and far from wild about it. Trey kept a "base camp" in town and had become a fairly reliable every-other-weekend dad when he wasn't trekking. But the Pipestone job market, as Lore knew too well, would condemn her to work she'd have to struggle perpetually not to hate.

After zazen one night, Lore went to brush her teeth, cast a clear-eyed glance at her reflection in the mirror, saw her face with extraordinary clarity, and felt that face conveying that to live the most mythic possible life in the most mythic possible place was not a whim but a spiritual necessity. So the question became: *What life, and in what place?*

A partial answer was immediate: *Not Pipestone.* She began researching and planning a long meander with Japhy to the north. She'd spent a college summer wandering through a few Rocky Mountain rain-shadow towns and hadn't forgotten how much she'd liked them.

THEN CAME A twist so counterintuitive that Lorilee trusted it at once: despite her determination to leave Pipestone, Two Medicine Peak began to call to her in ways that no wild place had called before.

From the vantage point of downtown Pipestone, CO (elev. 5,445, pop. 4,554), Two Medicine Peak was no peak at all. It looked more as if an Arapaho-cursed Sangre de Cristo ridge had been guillotined in the night, then staggered, headless, bloody-shouldered, and blind into west-central Colorado, where it fell on its faceless face and died. Its disconnection from any range gave it a look so forlorn that, in the twelve years since Lore and Trey had climbed it, she'd seen a grand total of no one anywhere near its summit. Too close to town, too bleak in winter, and a Snyderian anti-lyric told why to stay away in summer. *Axe Handles* p. 20: "The weather record says for August / 0.000 / is the average rainfall here."

On just such a day, half a year after the split with Trey and seconds after her morning zazen, Lorilee simply raised her gaze from Elmerina Buddha on the shrine before her to Two Medicine out the window above—and the pearl-eared icon and scruffy peak struck her as being of one essence: equally battle-scarred; equally implacable; equally feminine and gravid in their silent looming. The Peak also seemed to be conveying that if Lore would literally hike up and gaze not *at* her but *out of* her, she might see, feel, or find something crucial. The feeling was so indelible that she stepped outside with binoculars to scrutinize the Peak's south face, thinking to pick out a climbing line. But the sun blasted her head, back, and legs so fiercely her courage withered.

It was Trey, of all people, who restored her sense that Two Medicine was truly calling to her. On a Sunday evening she'd driven over to fetch Japhy after a dad weekend. Trey's partner, Liz, greeted Lore with her usual curt friendliness and sent her out back, where father and son sat talking by the apartment complex's suspicious-looking swimming pool. "And it's cool, the way you like to look out your skylight at Two Medicine," she overheard Trey saying, "and cool you like knowing your mom and me fell for each other up there. But let me tell you something, amigo. As you grow older you'll learn that there are mountains, and there are MOUNTAINS. And believe you me, Two Medicine Peak is no MOUNTAIN."

To her surprise, Lore felt her heart blaze up in defense of the little working-class peak. Two Medicine's summit was the birthplace of the love that brought Japhy into existence. Trey was defaming that place to suit his "Badass Mountains Are My Mind" conceit. Lorilee hid her feelings, keeping the exchange with Trey friendly. But when she got Japhy home and was tucking him in bed in the loft, she circled back to Trey's belittling of their home peak.

"I've told you that Zen Master Dōgen is a hero to me," she began. "But have I ever tried to tell you why?"

Japhy shook his head.

"Let's start with this. Climbing mountains the way Trey does is a very impressive physical feat. But knowing and loving mountains the way Dōgen does is impressive for far greater reasons. Strange as this might sound, Japhy, I believe Dōgen knows and loves mountains *from the inside out,* which makes Dōgen a kind of mountain himself. Does that make any sense?"

Japhy made his eyes comically big on purpose, making Lore laugh, and again shook his head.

"You're young for Zen teachings. Too young, maybe. But a taste of Dōgen's mountain talk could make a nice bedtime story. Wait here a minute."

Lore climbed down out of the loft, returned with Dōgen's *Mountains and Waters Sutra,* poked around for sentences that spoke some truths she felt needed defending, bent a few page corners, then turned to the boy.

"I know Trey is learning from mountains, and loves them in his own way. But listen to Dōgen's way and you'll feel something very different. Here he is: 'Mountains belong to the people who love them. When mountains love their master, trees and rocks become abundant and birds and animals become inspired. This is because sages and wise people extend their virtue. You should know it as a fact. Mountains are fond of wise people and sages.'"

Whenever Lore was feeling her words deeply, Japhy grew extra still and the pupils of his blue eyes grew big and black. She loved this so much she kept reading. "'A mountain practices at all times, in every place... Mountains, right now, are the embodiment of the ancient Buddha way. Because they have been the self since before all form arose, mountains are liberated and realized.' To put it plainly, Japh, Dōgen is saying that mountains, if we love them deeply enough, are enlightened teachers. Do you think your dad realizes he's scrambling up and down liberated beings who embody the ancient Buddha way?"

Japhy tried to picture it, grinned, and shook his head.

"Here's something that will sound crazy till we think on it carefully. But then it might make surprising sense. Dōgen says that mountains know how to walk. Listen. 'Mountains always abide in ease...And they are always walking...Do not doubt their walking though it does not look like human walking. The Buddha ancestors' words point to mountains walking.' Does that make any sense to you?"

"Nope," the boy said. "But I like it."

Lorilee smiled. "Good answer. Here's a little more. 'Blue mountains master walking, and eastern mountains master traveling on water. These activities are a mountain's practice...Don't slander by saying a blue mountain cannot walk and an eastern mountain cannot travel on water...Without full understanding you drown in small views...There is walking, there is flowing, and there is a moment when a mountain gives birth to a mountain's child.'"

It stirred Lorilee to see her not-quite-seven-year-old solemnly chewing on the old master's words. She tried to help. "I can't claim to understand what Dōgen means by 'mountains walking.' But I know this: the Grand Tetons, in Wyoming, grow about an inch and a half taller each year. And the Elkmoons, up north in Montana, grow nearly two inches. Think of it! In my measly life span, two huge mountain ranges have stepped higher than I am tall!"

Imagining this, Japhy's eyes dilated to pure pupil.

"And the Elkmoons and Tetons aren't just walking," Lorilee added. "Thanks to Earth's molten core, they're *fire-walking*. The part of the earth we see, the 'crust,' it's called, is made of gigantic puzzle pieces called tectonic plates." Japhy's eyes remained pure pupil as she took his hands, stacked them between hers, and moved them in time to her description. "The plates slide over the liquid magma beneath, slowly stacking up on each other, tilting, sending their upper edges higher and higher to form mountain ranges." As she tilted their four hands until all twenty fingers slanted skyward, the boy grinned.

"It was a German, Alfred... *Wegener* maybe, who discovered plate tectonics. But when he went to London and told the Royal Geographical Society, the Brits called him a fool because he was German, Britain's bitter enemy in two wars. 'Mountains' strides do not look like our strides,' Dōgen warns. 'Do not doubt mountains' walking even so.' Piffle, said the Brits, and they ignored plate tectonics for another half century. Only in my lifetime has mountains' tectonic walking been measured and partially understood, proving mountains to be climbers as great as Edmund Hillary—and proving Dōgen, seven hundred years ago, to be a better scientist than the British Royal Geographical Society! How do you s'pose Dōgen knew what he knew?"

Japhy's attention had drifted. Or maybe not. Eyes glued to the moonlit Peak out the skylight, he said, "Maybe mountains don't just walk. Doesn't Two Medicine look like a moon that flew down to visit? Don't you think a mountain could've flew down to Dōgen, so he climbed on board and they flew back up to wherever that mountain lived? Don't you think he could've walked all around up there learning stuff? Look at Two Medicine right now, Mom! Doesn't it look like, if we climbed aboard, it could fly us up and teach *us* stuff too?"

"You sound like Dōgen himself!" Lore said. "Listen. 'There are mountains hidden in swamps. There are mountains hidden in the sky. There are mountains hidden in mountains. There are mountains hidden in hiddenness. This is complete understanding.' And you, my boy, are the child of Trey and me, but of Two Medicine too. Which is something to be proud of. Your dad loves you a lot, and I respect his climbing. But when he puffs himself up and says your birth mountain isn't a *MOUNTAIN*, it could be he's *drowning in small views*."

"Dad and me have tons of fun," Japhy said. "But me and you like cool stuff he doesn't care about. I like having the fun with him and learning the cool stuff with you."

"Mountain's child," Lore whispered, kissing his head.

The boy's lids had begun to droop. "'Mountains hidden in the sky,'" he murmured. "That'd be so cool. Do you really think there are?"

"Are you kidding? With all the galaxies and solar systems and planets flying around the heavens there's *millions* of mountains hidden in the sky. And there's also mountains hidden in *people*. Like here. Check out this one called Mount Mom."

Making herself big and wide-eyed, Lorilee loomed up over the boy, then bent slowly down, a small mothering mountain, hugging him gentler and gentler as his laughter gave way to deep breaths, then sleep.

CLIMBING DOWN THE loft stairs, she intended to read more *Mountains and Waters Sutra*. But when she glanced out the window, Two Medicine, as Japh had noticed, had turned so moonish in the three-quarter moon's light that the best way to study the *Sutra* seemed to be to close it and go sit with the mountain itself.

Filling a blue Ball jar with ice cubes and the space between with white wine, she carried a straight-back chair out under the night sky, sat in it backward, faced the looming peak, and sent up the thought: *What would you have me do?*

How palpably the moonlit peak seemed to convey: *Don't just look at me. Come up and look out of me.*

Lorilee took a sip of wine, smiled, and kept aiming her silent thoughts:

I'm thinking Snyder's phrase "The mountains are your mind" is just part of the story here. What if, as the tribes hereabouts still say, "Wisdom sits in places," and I've been long enough in this place that you, old Peak, have grown a bit fond of me? What if certain specific mountains correspond to specific human minds the way that, say, Cold Mountain corresponded to Han Shan's, or Kailash, in Tibet, corresponds to an entire people's mind? I feel you're safeguarding something, and want me to come up and find it. I feel you might even want me to bring that something back down to other people.

Can a Ball jar of iced pinot gris in moonlight become a hallucinogen that enables a modest peak to infinitesimally nod and whisper, *"Now* you're talkin', girl"?

Lorilee trained her eyes on the Peak and summoned her intrepidity. "If you, Two Medicine, are my mind," she told it, "then my nine-thousand-twelve-foot mental summit is subalpine, which makes me as embarrassing to Trey as a two-digit IQ."

Can a modest Colorado peak shrug ever so faintly in moonlight, conveying that it doesn't care two shits what world-renowned climber Trey Jantz thinks of it? Lore was so inclined to think so that she laughed aloud.

"If you, old neighbor, are my mind," she continued, "then help me not turn Japhy against Trey, or Trey against me. That wouldn't help anyone. But when Trey started saying that only the peaks he has bagged are his mind, he turned peaks into bowling trophies and turned himself against the truth as Dōgen and Buddha live it, which turns him *against himself.* After all, *!   !   Who is Trey?* It saddens me to see Japh's love for a dad on a high-elevation ego trip that looks likely to get dangerous and strange. So could you, Two Medicine, ask your mountain friends to help Trey see that mountains hidden in hiddenness are more important than summits, and that his climbing can't be genuinely heroic until he kills off his *conquered-mountain-as-bowling-trophy* concept?"

Though the Peak offered no reply, she paused to drink everyone's health, Trey's most of all, then turned back to the particular virtues she felt her peak was extending:

"If you, Two Medicine, are my mind," she murmured, "then the Jimmy Carter–era sign marking the way up into me bans motorized vehicles, bikes, horses, and campfires, pissing so many people off it might be the most bullet-riddled piece of prose in Colorado. If you, my tall, scruffy friend, are my mind, then the only trailhead up into my thoughts is a boulder-blocked dead end strewn with broken glass, used condoms, Coors cans, and the rotting roadkills and dumped appliances people lay at your feet like idiot offerings. If you, Two Medicine, are my mind, the only trail to the top of me has flash-flooded out in twenty places, so the only way to summit me is up the crude little switchbacks built by the deer."

Smiling now, sipping more wine, the sense of kinship growing even as her description grew more grim, Lore said, "If you, ugly old beautiful old Two Medicine, are my mind, then a few day hikers, birders, and orgasm-bound teenagers use my lower slopes to advantage. But the heights of me were logged of their ponderosas a century ago, my piñons burned in '88, and no one's replanted me, leaving no shade on my summit, so my wildflowers and grass die so fast that by midsummer the deer no longer browse me, which must be lonely, though you never complain. If you, my scorched, scarred, stalwart old companion, are my mind, then my only north slope body of water, Crane Lake, is a migratory-bird paradise in April, but a shriveled mosquito factory by June, because my only spring-fed stream, Pipestone Creek, is heaven as it meanders through its north slope birth meadow, but doesn't make it two miles before it's dammed and ditched to irrigate a corporate ethanol corn farm miles downstream. So in the canyon where trout, frogs, water bugs, and birds should be thriving on my cold, clear gift to them, I'm a desiccated arroyo choked with hydraulic mining rubble and reptiles."

Her voice faltered then, her meditation went as silent as the silvery Peak, and a mind that enveloped her entire being suddenly yearned— *crazily, ferociously*—for the sensation of trout and frogs swimming and birds flying through her silvery, moonlit, nine-thousand-twelve-foot, Bubbs-Creek-haircutted head.

(Portland, from 1990 to the present)

IV. Ocean-Walking

At last mad, no longer alone.
At last mad, at last redeemed.
At last mad, at last at peace.
At last a fool, at last an inner light.
> —overheard on a city street by the angel Damiel in the
> Wim Wenders film *Wings of Desire*

A man who has...experienced the [God beyond God] no
longer has a place to establish himself. He has settled on
the road, and for those who have learned how to listen,
his existence becomes a call. This errant one dwells in joy.
Through his wanderings the origin beckons.
> —Reiner Schürmann, *Wandering Joy*

IT'S AN ODD quirk of our language that the abbreviations of the words "saint"
and "street" are an identical "St." and "St." (*St. Catherine / Front St. / St.
Francis / Burnside St. / St. Columba / Water St. / St. Julian / Stark St.*) To ask
the same two letters to represent the God-struck one moment and pavement
the next leaves me picturing robes, sandals, and saint-burger mashed into
the pavement by a stream of trucks and cars. So how odd it feels to confess
that in the years 2012 through 2014, while taping interviews for this book,
I took four long Ocean-walks with Jervis McGraff through urban Portland
and found him to be so inarguably streetly, yet covertly saintly, that I
now sometimes dream the Saints Catherine, Francis, Columba, and Teresa
wandering joyous along Front, Burnside, Water, and Stark Streets.

In the decades since Jervis was dumpstered and seven weeks later woke
up in Ocean, he has walked the streets of Portland every single day. Literal
thousands of Portlanders now know him on sight, and he has befriended,
served, regaled, protected, directed, and amused so many of them that
some serious hagiography has arisen in response. Jervis has many times
been compared to the likes of Dorothy Day, Cesar Chavez, Mother Teresa,
Dr. Paul Farmer, and other famed samaritans. But the hagiography stalls
out fast thanks to Jervis's gift for quashing it. His addiction to responding
to countless situations with the exclamation "*The fuck!*" repels those who

confuse the words "sanctity" and "sanitary," and if the praisers aren't repelled by whispered f-bombs his vocabulary grows far more alarming. His
promulgation of the street faith, Dumpster Catholicism, also keeps his halo
nicely tarnished among Roman Catholics thanks to thousands of sidewalk
homilies like this one:

"When the Vatican excommunicated the Meister, exterminated the Beguines, pilloried God by reducing Him to an object of reason, went blind to
the example of Jesus, and turned Roman Catholicism into Europe's go-to
religion for persecution, chauvinism, greed, treachery, and the murderous
conquest of so-called "unconverted" tribes and cultures, they created a
shadow faith that is now the greatest religionless tradition on Earth: Dumpster Catholicism. *The fuck.* What a beautiful irony! To empower and enrich
Holy Mother Church, Rome shitcanned so many wondrous truths, faiths,
and peoples that the contents of the giant dumpster behind the Church
became *far* more holy than the contents of the Church!"

While it's a rare Roman Catholic who smiles happily at such sermons,
more than a few are honest enough to ask for examples of Dumpster
Catholicism's glories, and there is no question on Earth that Jervis's papery
voice answers more formidably and convincingly.

THE METH THUGS who dumpstered Jervis customized him so brutally that
most of his alterations remain visible a quarter century later. His left eye, as
he likes to tell children and pretty women, was "replaced with a glass eye
by a taxidermist. SEE?" He then aims his skewed and blind blue marble at
them and "stares" till they either giggle or run like hell. His voice, thanks
to a thug's attempt to break his neck with a boot stomp, remains the papery
whisper I've described. What I haven't described is how, for a lot of people,
me included, his almost voiceless voice sounds so similar to the thoughts
running through our own heads that it creates an intimacy we find either
endearing or appalling, depending on what we're thinking. As for his looks,
his once-expressive face is now deadpan due to nerve damage, but an eye-
lid slumping partway over his seeing eye gives half his face the look of a
beat-to-hell meditating Buddha. Due to scarring of the thoracic diaphragm
his laugh also vanished, but he remains hilarious even so. He actually does
laugh by shooting air rapidly in and out his nostrils, but the streets are
almost always too loud to hear this. At times Jervis just emanates something
that makes people inordinately happy, as I will soon try to describe.

His most troublesome disability: epilepsy. His massive traumas bequeathed him grand mal seizures that used to cause him to collapse on
Northwest streets, frothing, convulsing, and occasionally chomping his
tongue. Sunlight glancing off water or windows, headlights raking across
him at night, the strobing of a sports bar TV, or any sudden flashes can
set off a seizure. To avoid such stimuli Jervis quit sailing, driving, riding
bikes, riding in cars and mass transit, became a pedestrian pure and simple,
and has not left Portland in a quarter century. A drug called Transorpene

eventually cut the violence of his seizures in half and their frequency by 90 percent. But Transorpene's side effects include weight loss, possible liver and kidney damage, sleeplessness, and acute restlessness, which brings us to the main activity of Jervis's "second incarnation."

Even before he got dumpstered Jervis was a tireless boulevardier. Transorpene turned him into a prodigy. He goes to bed around 1:00 a.m., sleeps three hours, leaves the monk's cell by 5:00, trudges up into the West Hills, and strolls Washington Park, the Rose Test Garden, or Forest Park in the company of retiring owls, slumbering vagrants, and waking birds, rain or shine. As the city comes alive he descends into the bustle and spends the entire day walking with an unending series of companions. These walks have filled his days for so long that I asked how he could stand to spend every hour of his life on the same streets doing the same thing. He said, "Why do you ask how I *stand it*? Why not ask why I love it? What else would I want to be doing? Hacking at a golf ball? *Solvitur ambulando.* 'It is solved by walking.' Augustine said that. I love it because no two days, *ambulandos*, or *solviturs* are ever the same, and the company is sensational. How do *you* stand what gives *you* joy, HG? The same way I do. By feeling joyful."

"I guess you told *me*!" I said, and heard air-laughter shooting in and out Jervis's nose.

Come evening, Jervis stops by Étouffée Bruté for an hour for the easy-to-chew dinners TJ makes him. Then off he goes on a marathon night walk, this one highly secretive. Both the day and night walks are intricate beyond belief, and very different, as we shall glimpse. Between 11:00 and midnight he then meets TJ at the closed Étouffée Bruté bar for a day-ending shot of bourbon. The sole term Jervis uses to describe his ambulations: "Ocean-walking." A description of the Ocean-walker at his task:

Jervis's strides are tireless, and more a quick trudge than a stride. His footwear, rain or shine, is red Converse high-tops, a pair of which he wears out every three to four months. His ever-dirty 501 Levi's manage to appear baggy when animated by his stick-thin legs. His daily T-shirts or sweatshirts are either courtesy of the Goodwill on Burnside or gifts given to him by the Thurman Street Sangha, portraying a serenely seated Buddha on the back and, across the chest in hot pink, I'M A BUDDHIST FOR CHRIST'S SAKE! In rain or snow Jervis adds a hooded green Grundéns® rain slicker that only reaches to his pants pockets, so his jeans and sneakers get soaked and stay soaked, day and night. For a man so damaged and underdressed, these long, cold soakings made TJ fear pneumonia, and he tried desperately to get Jervis to add waterproof boots, rain pants, stocking caps, and the like. Jervis said he would if getting soaked ever made him sick. But year in and year out, in every kind of weather, he has remained the picture of what he calls "perfectly munched health."

He strikes up conversations with people of every description. He also readily converses with animals, birds, plants, trees, and a host of objects and ephemeralities that rationalists hold to be no one at all. His talk is totally open, flagrantly psychic, deep-minded one moment, off-the-wall the next. Risa's description is my favorite: "Jervis reminds me of a Socrates wandering around Athens happily ripped on ganja. He once told me, 'Here's all it is, Risa. My true home is Ocean. My family is streets, weather, and Teej. Breathing and walking are my powers. No-thought is my tactic. And no self is my Ocean-going boat.'"

An odd aspect of walking with Jervis: his nervous system damage makes it impossible for him to walk and talk at the same time. He can *listen* and walk simultaneously but, like a school bus letting out its children, must come to a complete stop before he can let out a sentence. As a result, his urges to speak cause him to slam to sudden halts so often that he is surely the most frequently rear-ended pedestrian in Portland. During rush hour and on weekends it's not uncommon for people to plow into him several times a day.

MY FIRST OCEAN-WALK with Jervis took place on a cool, clear September morn in 2012. After a long drive from Montana the previous day, I looked forward to fresh air, a vigorous stretching of the legs, an enjoyable chat. I had no idea what I was in for.

I started off at his side with my iPhone recording him, thinking I'd interview him as we strolled. But the moment we left the monk's cell he led us down to a Northwest 21st Avenue *jammed* with pedestrians, where I discovered that after twenty-five years of Ocean-walking he's known to many hundreds of Northwest locals. He began slamming to halts to greet so many people that, though I left my iPhone running, my journalistic intent was obliterated. Pedestrians of every description seem to see Jervis as a feature of their own interior landscapes, and I can understand why: he never objects to being stopped, and never needs to be reminded of the intricacies of past exchanges with innumerable people. But when I marveled at this, asking how he's able to track so many lives, he slammed to a halt. "I don't track diddly," he said. "What looks like memory to you is just ping-pong to me. Somebody whacks a thought-ball at me. Ocean strobes a quick image. I make words out of the image and whack it back with a little spin on it. Some people get all happy or moved by that, and say how much I helped 'em. *The fuck.* I don't even know what I'm saying. They're playing ping-pong with Ocean. I'm just the paddle."

Fascinated by this, I wanted to ask follow-up questions, but twenty yards ahead of us a pedestrian in a metallic-blue suit and metallic-green fedora turned to the sensibly dressed matron beside him, pointed at Jervis as if at an escaped orangutan, and gushed, "*There he is!* The man I was telling you about! *Portland's own dear street saint!*"

The matron gave Jervis a thrilled look, turned to the metallic clothes horse, and cried, "*How wonderful!* You *must* find me a home in *his* neighborhood!" When Fedora Man's face turned smug as a cat with a writhing goldfish in its mouth, I realized he was a realtor.

Bestowing several quick namastes as he walked to within a startlingly few inches of them, Jervis slammed to a halt. "The only way to reach Big Truth," he said, "is to stick to little truths every step of the way. Simone Weil said that."

Fedora Man and his prey beamed at this saintly pronouncement. To the matron alone Jervis then said, "That's why I need to say 'The fuck.' Your real estate agent doesn't know me from Attila the Hun, and not only am I not 'Portland's own dear street saint,' I'd a million times rather be called 'Portland's own dear douche nozzle.' Douche nozzles provide a useful service. All phony saints do is headfuck people."

I would later learn that this realtor, upon losing his client, commenced to portray Jervis to all and sundry as a drug-peddling toy-poodle-buggering psychopath who's done more to depress Portland real estate prices than the 2008 financial collapse. I would also learn that, upon learning of this reverence-dispelling slander, Portland's own dear douche nozzle gratefully added Fedora Man to his namaste list for life.

But on that first walk, after watching him appear to make an enemy, I had questions. "Jervis," I said. "You have innumerable street friends, and you're famous for innumerable acts of kindness. Yet you seem to enjoy destroying your repute. The realtor annoyed you by using you to hustle a client. But the woman's admiration seemed sincere. Why are you so allergic to admiration?"

Jervis took a few steps in silence, then slammed to a halt. In the exchange that follows he calls me "HG" due to my nickname, the "Holy Goat."

"Ocean's insane mercy is not 'my innumerable acts of kindness.' Who needs their own dinky kindness when they're sunk in Ocean's mercy? My practice is to *stay sunk*, HG. Allowing people to admire me because of what Ocean's doing is allowing them to dress me in a lie. I'm Ocean's pissant servant, and that's *all* I am."

As Jervis was saying these words a muscular woman runner, holding a Yorkshire terrier under her arm like a football, came upon us from behind. "*Coming through!*" she shouted, causing Jervis to attempt a namaste, but as he raised his arms she stiff-armed them out of her path so hard he nearly fell.

While I muttered a few choice words, Jervis went on talking as if neither the woman's stiff-arm or my muttering had occurred. "This Indian sage, Ramana Maharshi, says that peace is our true nature, and peace is like a big empty attic. To *be* peace, he said, just empty your attic. Before I got munched I loved that idea and started throwing crap out of my attic. But the more I threw out the bigger my attic crap pile grew. Then I got lucky. Two thugs, Kryptonite and Two-by-Four, beat me into a coma and dump-stered me. Seven weeks later I woke up in Ocean, and my attic full of crap was just *gone*. And *I* didn't get rid of it. I just woke up in an Ocean that does everything. An Ocean I feel all day and night and love like crazy. If you love somebody, you don't let people thank *you* for the things *they* did."

We resumed walking, but hadn't taken ten steps when Jervis slammed to another halt. "Helping wrecked people find places to sleep on miserable nights. That's something I'm *known for,* and it's another lie. I'm not living some *Serve the Poor Pissants of Portland* ideal. I just walk, *solvitur ambulando,* until Ocean strobes images of stuff she wants done. To stay in her I do the stuff. If she doesn't strobe I just wait till she does. When people say this is saintly of *me,* they're dragging bogus saint shite into their attic. So I call myself a douche nozzle or worse, make 'em mad, leave 'em disgusted enough to throw their saint shite out."

We walked the better part of a block, then Jervis came to a halt in front of a ground-floor plateglass window. "MOLD ASSESSMENT & SERVICES," read the window. "'It is my life to die, like glass, by light,'" Jervis said. "Thomas Merton said that. And look. Here's what he's saying. Because glass is reflective, the window is showing us to us, standing here on the street. But because glass is transparent, it's also showing us *inside* the Mold office looking like we're underwater. That's plateglass saying what Zosima said. All is an Ocean, inside and outside, all the time. Ordinary extraordinary, all the time. Tides incoming and outgoing, storm waves or no waves, infinite emptiness and fullness, all the time."

When he started walking again, he sent a few namastes sailing up the street to the backsides of two people strolling along more than a block ahead of us. Though I said nothing, I idly wondered if these long-range namastes were an effort to bless as many people as possible. Immediately Jervis slammed to another halt. "*The fuck,*" he said. "After everything we've been talking about, you're *still* thinking saint shite about me?"

I started to lie that I wasn't but realized he'd read my mind, so he'd read my lie. So I just said: "*Uhhhhh.*"

Jervis laughed more air in and out of his nose. "Relax," he paper-whispered. "I hate mind reading. I just can't help it. Since I got munched, certain stuff leaks in, and certain other stuff leaks out. That's Two-Way Post-Munch Leakage. Not sainthood."

Feeling an impulse to make a little trouble, I said, "What if Two-Way Post-Munch Leakage is an attribute of sainthood whether you think it is or not?"

Shaking his head, Jervis said, "*God is not to be thought.* The Meister said that, because as soon as the thought is gone, so is the God. Every time you have a choice between a dirt-simple truth and a God-thought, pick the dirt-simple. Dirt-simples are drops of Ocean. God-thoughts are just *boinka-boinka.* Here's a dirt-simple. The only kind of saint I am is bogus. And know what a bogus saint is to me? Somebody claiming to bless people while he's doggy-doin' 'em from behind. Every time somebody calls me a street saint, I picture me doggy-doin' that poor person from behind. I've never even done anybody from the front, HG, but me doggy-doin' 'em from the back is what the words 'Saint Jervis' make me see. And would a saint picture that? *Fuck no.* And would a saint say fuck no? *Doublefuck no.* Get the picture?"

While I lost my struggle not to laugh, Jervis took off again, but ten steps later came to another halt. "Another dirt-simple," he said. "'All is an Ocean' sounds like a lie to you. You think everything you're seeing today is a city named Portland. You think 'All is Portland' is more honest than 'All is an Ocean.'"

I couldn't help nodding, but Jervis shook his head. "'All is Portland' is *not* honest. This Portland World is more dangerous than Disney World, because people know Disney World is fake. Portland World is just as fake, but its unrealness is so jacked up and under- and over-passed and transient and shot through with brain waves and mind games and dope need and toxic ego juice and dirty deals and combusting cars that, to keep our bodies alive, our mind clutches all that unrealness to itself like it's the only game in town. And once Portland World feels to you like the only game in town, you're just a pinball bouncing *boinka-boinka* through a nonstop unreality machine till your body croaks, your dying mind finally stops all the *boinka*, the soul gives you a parting jolt of joy and glimpse of infinite oceanic swells, and you go, '*Oh my God, it was Ocean all along—fzzzt!*' Lights out. Mind gone. Game over. *That's* why I namaste people near and far. I don't want to forget 'All is an Ocean' for an instant. A person can die in an instant. I did. *Twice,* TJ says. So as I pinball through the Portland *boinka-boinka* I need an Ocean-remembering trick to keep hold of what's real. Mine's this." Jervis shot me with a quick namaste. "Direct hit. Feel anything special?"

"I'm thinking some wild stuff thanks to everything you're saying," I said. "But your namaste didn't make me feel anything."

"That's because a namaste from me *isn't* anything, least of all a saintly blessing. Let's get real, HG. When all is an Ocean, *who needs saintly blessings?* The soul is perfect and the mind's a compulsive liar, so, the Meister says, the soul must exist in a free nothingness. Free nothingness frees you from the *boinka* that tells you you're a *somebody* surrounded by countless *other somebodies.* You're not. You're the soul inside your body, and soul is an emptiness so vast that shoreless Ocean fits inside it perfectly. So fuck the itsy bitsy idea that anybody needs to be blessed by a street saint. The Ocean blessing is so great it includes *all* blessings. The situation ain't broke, so don't run around fixing it. Got it?"

"Got it," I said.

"One more dirt-simple, HG. Why I namaste people going the other way? Ocean never forgets a face or an ass, and the free nothingness that replaced my old Jervis doesn't either, because he's Ocean's. What a gift it is, when people are going the other way, to namaste their asses! Every ass on the street is a two-piece miracle. Three-piece, counting the canyon between halves. Add the amazing extensions of the ass-halves we call legs, plus on nonhumans a tail, and an ass is as distinctive and expressive as a face. Similar too. Two movable cheeks. Important hole between. And so important to know when to keep both holes shut."

While I again struggled not to laugh, Jervis closed his seeing, slump-lidded eye, aimed his skewed glass eye at me, did some kind of glass-eyed read of me, and paper-whispered, "You're a Nature Person."

"Am I, now. Exactly what kind of person is that?" I asked.

"The kind who stares at bluebirds on Montana fence posts 'cause they're beautiful, and at the Auguste Rodin sculptures at Maryhill Museum on the way to Portland 'cause they're beautiful, and at pretty people's ass-halves and leg extensions going all amazing down the street 'cause they're beautiful."

"Guilty as charged!" I said. "It's ornithologically and aesthetically irresponsible not to stare at bluebirds and Rodins, and biologically irre-sponsible not to stare at amazing ass-halves and leg extensions. For civility's sake, though, I try not to get caught at the ass staring."

"You're stupid and good and not a saint, same as me, Nature Person. But I'm an Ocean Person." With which he took off walking.

I caught up. "Any chance you'll explain what an Ocean Person is?"

He slammed to another halt. "'The real Jesus has no name.' The Meister says that. 'No mortal lips are worthy to pronounce Thy Name.' Saint Francis says that. The real Ocean, same deal, has no name, no limit, no end. And she's invisible except when she isn't, and she's thrilling once you give up and realize we're all inside her, and ass-waves and face-waves are washing through her day and night, and here we stand yapping when we could be drifting through the thrill of her. *The fuck*, HG. Can we just walk and feel her now?"

"Just one last question, please. What is it with you and faces and asses? Why not, I dunno, people's pulses? Or their in-breaths and out-breaths?"

"I like pulses. I like in- and out-breaths," Jervis said. "But I *love* how weird it is that something as oceanic as the spirit gets saddled with a face and an ass! Look at the faces rolling toward us right now. *No thinky. Simple down.* See how they're restless as waves, endless as waves, thought-less as waves, obedient as waves? Like here. See the UPS guy's face obeying his miffed mind going, *How do I deliver a damned package to an address that doesn't exist? whoosh*, gone. Or here. Two high school boys, sideways glancing, faces joshing each other all young-man manly. But see the mind of the one with the lip stud going, *I feel such love! Is it okay to really love my friend? Am I gay? Could we—whoosh!* Gone. Or up there! Twenty starling faces shooting over, forty wings, one rhythm, one hunger, one mind, *whishwhishwhishishwhishwhishwhish!*"

Trying to face-read myself, I focused on a tough-looking couple strolling toward us. Though the woman was crying, she was holding the man by the arm and silently laughing as she cried, and the man was grinning ear to ear. "Incoming," I whispered. "This couple, Jervis. What the hell is *their* game?"

"I saw her yesterday, crying to her old boyfriend as she dumped him.

Today she's repeating her performance to make her new boyfriend laugh because she's so good at sounding sincere," Jervis said. "And your thinky part is going, *Aw, poor old boyfriend, getting played like that.* No thinky, HG! Maybe new boyfriend's a grifter, so she's flaunting her skill. Don't judge. *The man who cries out against evil people but does not lovingly pray for them will never know the grace of God.* Saint Silouan said that. To lovingly pray, just look at what is and say, '*Thanks.*' Attic empty. *Heaven of No Thought.* Faces *live* in that heaven. Study them till you see that. Faces *look* like they think, but they *don't.* They're not the mind. Not a single synapse in a face. Yet the no thinky face of that woman crying to her ex to make her new beau smile is as skilled as a Balch Creek kingfisher's face dive-bombing a dinky trout, or a downy woodpecker's face hammering hardwood nine hundred times to tongue out a grub, or a peregrine falcon's face on a Hawthorne Bridge girder dripping rock-dove gore onto the windshield of a horrified commuter. Face grace stops thought and sends us out to sea."

Rattled that Jervis had read my mind so easily, I sought a topic I hoped would keep him out of my mind. "Okay cool, Jervis. Faces I get," I said. "But what is it with you and *asses*?"

"Book of Exodus. 'And the Lord said, Behold, I will put thee in a cleft of the rock, and will cover thee with My hand while I pass by. And I will take away Mine hand, and thou shalt see My back parts.'"

Unsure whether the Bible contained that verse or Jervis had made it up, I asked, "Is *that* your answer to my question?"

"No. That's my answer to a Nature Person who says 'one more question,' then asks three. Unthought love is unbreakable love, and unbreakable love is Ocean, and asses and faces send me so far out to sea I'm brain damaged is prob'ly the dirt-simple on me, plus God knows what the Transorpene is doing to me. I'm a side-effected one-eyed ass- and face-loving ping-pong paddle Ocean uses to thwack a few thought-balls around Stumptown. So have mercy, not *thinky*, and let's walk out to sea. Okay?"

I shut off the iPhone.

"*Behold!*" Jervis paper-whispered, firing namastes at me that made his fallen halo of hair bob like the tail feathers of some bizarre jungle bird.

"*Solvitur ambulando,*" I said, shooting a namaste back.

And out to sea we strode.

Well, *trudged.*

(Pipestone, 1995)

V. Lawn King

If one understands The Way, he should be able to hear
about all Ways and be more and more in accord with his own.
    —Ghost Dog in the Jim Jarmusch film *Ghost Dog*

THE FIRST CHALLENGE of the August day on which Lorilee set out to answer Two Medicine's call: the neighbors. The Peak's shoddy trailhead was a half mile uphill from Lore's garage apartment. The inhabitants of her high-end dead end were accustomed to seeing her power hiking past, empty-handed, dressed for exercise. But as Bob and Shari Hobson's Chrysler LeBaron eased out of the triple-car garage, turned downhill toward the Pipestone Mall, and crept past Lorilee at its usual breakneck six miles per, Shari was so addled by the sight of Lore's more serious gear that she forgot to wave. "Our Martian-haired neighbor," as Bob called Lorilee, was striding along in a heavily loaded backpack with (*what the hell?*) a big metal wastepaper basket strapped to its frame, toting a black mountain dulcimer case they assumed contained a rifle. The chartreuse ball cap with the bright orange DON'T ASK! across the front didn't ease their confusion. As the two women passed within four feet of each other, Shari's pursed red lips and big red hair seemed to broadcast: *Doesn't compute! Not even High Sierra Barbie comes with the wastebasket, rifle case, and* DON'T ASK! *accessories!*

Remembering Dōgen, Lore muttered, "'Drive all blame into oneself,'" and let the Hobsons go.

Heeding her breath, she geared her pace till her breathing and striding were in sync. The rhythms of her body then flew a new Richard Thompson ballad into her mind: "1952 Vincent Black Lightning." Why this tune? Lore wondered—then linked the song's Red Molly to Shari's red lips and hair. The ballad's pace matched her stride so perfectly she felt like singing it, but she only remembered enough of the words to mangle a great rowdy biker song. If she were to sing it, she'd have to roll her own words.

Scanning her route for material, she peered up the road to where it threaded between the Steitzs' and Heidlemanns' meticulously landscaped sidehill yards, turned onto a rutted rock track, and after a quarter mile dead-ended. The Heidlemanns were never home. But old Walt Steitz was almost always outside and alert, tracking everyone and everything. Lorilee liked Walt. He was the hood's last hale World War Two vet, but he never told war stories. Never indulged in Hobson-style gossip. Walt's thing was quick-witted repartee, and several times in passing his place Lore's dry wit had proven so quick she'd trumped him at his own game. He loved her for this. "What that li'l gal might say is anybody's guess," Walt more than once remarked to his wife, Dee Anna. Who'd been dead for three years.

As the rhythm of "1952 Vincent Black Lightning" filled her body, Lore zeroed in on Walt. Though rumored to be a bona fide Pacific Theater war hero, his claims to local fame stemmed from five machines. Walt owned four immaculate classic pickups: a '49 Ford; a '50 GMC; a '54 Chevy; a '57 Dodge. Lore knew this because he drove all four past her garage apartment in sequence, twenty minutes per vehicle, every other day. But Walt's machine of greatest fame was a green and yellow 1982 John Deere Lawn King tractor mower with so many attachments, blades, tines, drags, and extensions that he seemed to use it for everything but mowing his lawn. Case in point: when Lore first spotted him, he was roaring across the grass dodging sprinklers and cactuses and trees, mowing blades idle, with a yard or so of bright pink gravel in the bright yellow scoop in front. Lorilee knew Walt had spotted her, though his gaze remained averted as she approached. This was his style. Pure coincidence, she was to believe, that his tractor mower tasks just happened to intersect her uphill path perfectly.

Not till she was within a few yards did he turn to make a slow, stern study of her backpack, instrument case, purposeful stride, and direction of travel. He clearly wished to interrogate. But since he missed nothing, he'd also taken in her DON'T ASK! ball cap. Like most World War Two vets, Walt obeyed orders, like 'em or not. His curiosity was so intense, though, that he did something he'd never done in her presence: *shut off the Lawn King*! Sure that an interrogation would follow, Lorilee beat the old man to the punch:

"Make you a deal, Walt. You don't ask me what I'm doing, and I won't ask about all that pretty pink gravel you're playing with."

Walt turned in his tractor seat, gravely pondered the desiccated peak above them, turned back, and even more gravely pondered small, delicate, very alone Lorilee. *Incredible,* she thought, *the way some old military guys can read you the riot act without even speaking.* Forced to replay her one card, Lore turned and, just as gravely, stared holes in Walt's pink gravel.

"Campin' trip?" the old man asked.

"Yup," said Lore.

"Anybody ever tell you there's three mountain ranges full of pristine lakes, creeks, and forest within two hours o' town?" Walt asked.

"Seen 'em," said Lore.

"So you've got *special* reasons to camp on a ugly, snaky, dried-up, lonely heap of a peak."

"Somebody *force* you to buy that gravel, Walt? Or are you just kind of a closet pinky?"

Walt cracked a smile so rare it made crackling sounds in his mouth corners. "Sorry to poke my nose, Miss Lore. But if you'd tell me what day you plan to come down, I know one old man'd sleep better the next few nights."

"I'll be two nights out. If you don't see me by sunset the third day, call Search and Rescue."

Walt nodded, then moved, stern gaze first, to the next visual riddle. "You always take a big metal wastepaper basket backpacking with you?"

"This excellent device isn't a wastebasket, Walt."

"What is it?"

"A low-tech amp for my dulcimer."

"A what for your who?"

"I'm a musician, Walt. A rusty one, thanks to single momhood and an old-fashioned need for work that pays. But still." She pointed to Walt's big carport. "If we head into the shade there a minute, I could demonstrate what a wastebasket does for a dulcimer."

Walt nodded militarily, fired up the Lawn King, and Lore followed him down.

Just nine in the morning, but the shade already felt welcome. Walt shut off his engine and sat quiet, watching her closely. His carport, to Lore, had an equestrian feel, the immaculate old trucks like high-end sport horses watching her quietly from their stalls. Strolling toward her favorite—the forest-green '54 Chev—she saw a dark green Lorilee loom like a fish up out of the truck's polished depths.

Shedding her pack, she unstrapped the wastebasket, took her dulcimer from the case, parked on the '54 Chev's running board, set the wastebasket on the polished concrete floor right side up, then gazed up at Walt. "See this?" she asked, running her finger along the wastebasket's rim. "Coated with silicon. Makes it grippy, so my dulcimer won't slide off."

Serious as an officer being briefed for battle, Walt nodded in the affirmative.

She set the instrument across her thighs. "Appalachian-style lap dulcimer. Four strings is the norm. Mine's a five-string built to my specs by a ma-and-pa outfit, Blue Lion. A trouble dulcimers has is, guitars and fiddles drown us out. So mine's oversized, both for volume and heft in the bass clef. Has a few extra frets too, for richer scales and chords. By adding this"—she nodded at the wastebasket—"I'm in the game, volume-wise."

Another nod in the affirmative.

Lorilee tuned up, then plucked a chord so Walt could hear the dulcimer "un-amped." Setting the wastebasket between her legs and the dulcimer on top of it, she then struck the same chord, planning a thirty-second demo of what the hollow metal added. But the concrete floor, cinder-block walls, and trash can created such an enormous sound that Lore herself was stunned. And Richard Thompson's ballad was still dancing in her head.

"Tell you what," she muttered. "I'm gonna try something. Don't listen yet, okay?"

Setting her instrument back on her lap to quiet it, she worked out a simplified, version of Richard Thompson's "1952 Vincent Black Lightning" guitar part, then set the dulcimer back on its "amp," turned to Walt enthroned on the Lawn King, and revved her imagination up as high as it could go: Walt usurped Thompson's outlaw motorcyclist, James. Lore her-self displaced black-leather-clad Red Molly. Shoddy but serviceable verses came on in a flood. Bending forward over the amp, she strummed a single bright chord, then damped the strings to silence and, for shock value, sang her first verse acapella:

Said Lorilee to Walt Steitz,
That's a fine riding mower
With its scoop of pink gravel
Rotary blades and snow-blower.

Jubilant strings erupted from the wastebasket, resounding off the cinder blocks:

Says old Walt to Lorilee,
My ball cap's off to you
It's a John Deere Lawn King 1982
And from my point of view
There is nothing in this world
Beats a trash can amp performance
By a freshly single girl
And no Toro, Snapper, Lawn Boy
Could suit the likes of you
They just ain't got the soul
Of the Lawn King '82
So now listen to my offer
My sweet songbird Lorilee
I have seen better days my lass
I'm nearly eighty-three
So if fate...
Should break my stride...
Let me give you...
My Lawn King...
To rrrrrrrrrrride!

Oh, music hath alarums. Walt's incredulity had doubled the size of his eyes, making him look twenty years younger, and dangerous if not quite handsome. Charmed, Lore riffed a hard-strumming dulcimer solo, then flew by the seat of her pants into her climactic lines:

Come down fast, Lorilee
To Walt Steitz's yard
There's been a sidehill accident
The Lawn King threw him hard!
When she knelt by his side
Walt was staring straight at death
He had run outta lawn
He was runnin' outta breath
But he groaned, "Lorilee my lass
I've no more use for these!"
And he reached for her hand
And he slipped her his keys.
"I see angels on bright riding mowers
Of yellow, green, and chrome
Swooping down with scoops of
Pink gravel to carry me home!"
And he gave her a kiss
And he died . . . . . .
But he gave her
The Lawn King
To rrrrrrride!

As the last notes faded, Walt snatched off his VFW cap, pulled out a hankie, and had to wipe his brow once and blow his nose twice to recover. In a voice gone husky, he said, "Miss Lore! That might be the best thing I ever heard, *period*. This carport and me're gonna feel famous the rest of our days!"

Smiling, she cased up the dulcimer and strapped the magic trash can back on her pack. But when she started to lift the pack, Walt fairly flew off the Lawn King to take it from her. "Will you do me the honor," he said, "of settin' yourself down on this pink gravel so I can run you up to the trailhead?"

"I'll bet you give *all* the girls pink gravel rides to the trailhead," Lore teased.

"Every one who sings and plays like you, I sure do."

It amused Lorilee to assume the zazen posture on a crunchy bed of pink. Walt handed her the dulcimer case, strapped her pack onto the rack behind his seat, mounted, and away they rattled and roared. The engine proved too loud for talk, but halfway to the dead end Walt hollered back, "You still driving that beat-up old silver Civic?"

"Hey!" Lorilee called. "My silver Honda and me are color coordinated. And only a quarter million miles on us. Our best years lie ahead."

"After hearing you play," Walt hollered, "I believe it!"

When they reached the boulders blocking the trailhead, Walt took Lore's dulcimer, gave her a hand out of the scoop, then surprised her by shutting off the Lawn King a second time. "Got a minute for a story about what you were sittin' on?"

Sensing a seriousness about him, Lorilee said, "Sure."

Walt looked off down the hill toward Pipestone, then said, as if to the view, "One morning, three and a half years back, Dee Anna took me by surprise. She asked me to order in ten yards of pink gravel. She collected pink-blooming cacti by the hundreds. Green looks good with pink, she said, and in spring her blooms'd match her choice of rock."

The old man began to struggle. "I loved that woman more'n life, Miss Lore. But that day, damn me, I got all stiff and yard-proud, told her pink rock'd be an embarrassment, and refused to order it. Then, so fast my head still spins, she took sick. Six months later she was gone. And what are cacti famous for? Those spines. Even the names of hers stab me now. *Coryphantha hesteri. Escobaria vivipara.* I've took back what I said ten thousand times. I've tended her cacti like they're *her.* But—" Walt's voice broke. "*Can Dee Anna feel that?*"

Lore was grateful for the sunglasses hiding her welling eyes.

"Here's the truth, Miss Lore," the old man said. "I *am* a closet pinky. This color looks so good to me now, I might bury my whole damn yard in it."

Lorilee had a sudden feeling, and took a chance. Lifting her shades, looking Walt in the eye, she said, "I don't mean to trespass, but I feel this so strong I've gotta say it. *Dee Anna forgives you, Walter Steitz.*" Walt made a sound as if he'd been punched. "She loves you as much as you do her," Lore said. "And for the gravel, and whatever else, she forgives you."

Walt seemed to take two more punches, then turned to stare out over Pipestone. He was quiet for some time. When he turned back to her, she was relieved to see the stern old vet had returned. "*You,* Missy, are awful damn cute in that ball cap. So may I ask, do you carry protection? A handgun? Bear spray? Snake bite kit? Whatever you forgot I'll lend. Out of selfishness. I'd like to keep my favorite music comin'."

Picturing Elmerina Buddha wrapped in the beach towel in the bottom of her pack, Lorilee said, "Got all that covered, Walt."

"Good. Go find what you're looking for then. But can you stop by an' gimme a shout on your way back down?"

When Lore saluted, Walt did the same. He then started the Lawn King, roared off down the rutted track, and Lore turned to tackle the mountain. But after Walt's good company and warnings, the massive, sun-blasted slope made her feel small and alone.

Then came a sound, far below, rising over the Lawn King's roar: old Walt, quavering at the top of his lungs:

And he gave her a kiss
And he died . . . . . .
But he gave her
The Lawn King
To ride!

Taking strength from her own grin, Lorilee started climbing.

VI. On Irony (*Yeah, Right*)

[I]n fear, in hope, in charity, in a rule of life one wishes to keep, in tears, in the desire of devotion, in the bent for sweetness, in terror of God's threats, in distinction between beings, in receiving, in giving, and in many things we judge good, Reason errs.
                    —The Beguine, Hadewijch of Brabant

Make no mistake: irony tyrannizes us.
                    —David Foster Wallace, *Infinite Jest*

BOTH OF JULIAN'S nicknames had caught on. "Not-Quite Dr. Gage" launched her "Irony Seminary" by smiling at each student, then slamming them with this:

"Let me begin our seminar *without* irony by asking whether you share my feeling that we're born to a generation cursed. To define what I mean by cursed, it's hard to beat the prophet Isaiah: 'For the indignation of the Lord is upon all nations... And the streams shall be turned into pitch, and the dust into brimstone, and the land shall become burning pitch. It shall not be quenched night nor day. The smoke thereof shall go up for ever. From generation to generation it shall lie waste. None shall pass through it for ever and ever... The Lord shall stretch out upon it the line of confusion and the stones of emptiness.' Not a bad description of a world with two-thirds of its forests clear-cut, polar ice sheets and glaciers vanishing, mountaintop coal removal, the desertification of Africa, and so on. But I want us to feel free to question the psychological and artistic repercussions of catastrophic data. Has Isaiah just made us better citizens? Better artists? Better friends to our friends? Or is there a tipping point where litanies of horror shove our empathy and creativity where the sun doesn't shine? In a world so terribly out of balance, should we limit the amount of bad news we take in? Or is the honest artistic position to get bashed out of balance by the news, and imbue our art with imbalance and despair? Comments?"

The group's Wheaton College dropout, Jonathan Grens, said, "The preachers of my fundy childhood used *Isaiah* to scare us into filling offering plates, and it worked. But I'd wager good money the Prophet Anna could smoke that old boy in under sixty seconds!"

Julia Gage smiled, glanced at her watch, then at Anna. "Do you accept the challenge?"

Anna drew a busty breath and let fly: "*Hundreds of nuclear facilities storing radioactive wastes with a half-life of ten thousand years, lots of them in earthquake zones! Billions of tons of carcinogens and toxics leaching from landfills and mining sites into groundwater, rivers, oceans, globally! Obliterated mountains, slag-filled valleys, and countless dead streams across American coal country! A marine bird and mammal holocaust caused by mistaking billions of tons of waste plastics for food! Feedlot cattle fattened on grain, offal, and antibiotics, eaten by us, creating medicine-proof super-diseases! Genetically modified dairy cows infected with mastitis pouring pus into our milk! American pus milk, stored in plastic containers, turning men's testosterone into estrogen and women's estrogen into—*"

"MINUTE'S UP!" Julia Gage cut in, and the class broke out cheering. "Take *that*, Isaiah!" "*EVERYBODY NEEDS PUS!*" "You *go*, Prophet Anna!"

Anna just glared, miffed that her litany of horrors had been interrupted.

"So I'm wondering where the age of eco-holocaust and pus milk leaves us as artists," Julia Gage said. "Knowledge is an artistic necessity. But extensive knowledge of an irreparable world maims sensitive psyches, leading to blindnesses that can mess up an entire generation. When the Great Depression and World War Two threatened our grandparents' lives for two decades, a tremendous unified response ended both threats, but cloned their generation as if it were poured out of a factory mold. Yes, they defeated Japan and the Nazis. But when their cloned psyches assumed power on Main Street, Wall Street, and in government, it led to travesties like internment camps for loyal Japanese- and Italian-Americans, the Cold War arms race, McCarthyite blacklists, a near-nuclear holocaust over Cuba, and US-assisted fascist coups all over the world. My parents' generation saw this, but if they mentioned that World War Two idealism got twisted by demagogues into vicious diplomacy, useless military campaigns, and so on, our grandparents' response was blind fury. So our parents' generation blew them off and fought back with massive protest, peace marches, occupied administration buildings, forcing universities to divest from arms dealing, supporting civil rights, and starting a back-to-the-land movement that held promise if it hadn't been so sexist and stoned. But then what?"

"The sixties idealists were co-opted in so many self-indulgent ways that *their* rebellion fizzled too," Klaus Hauptmann said. "There's a pattern here. The idealists of the forties, refusing to bend, became the fascists of the fifties. Then the idealists of the sixties, opposing that fascism, went blind to their own narcissism and hedonism and lapsed into self-parody."

"Which brings us to us," said Julia Gage. "Anyone care to speak to the cloning effects that warp *our* worldview?"

Nita Hymes took the floor. "Anna often talks of rising acidity in the oceans. But I wonder about *our* acidity? It's risen too. And how could it not? The rich own everything, including our token democracy, banks, and corporations, we're led by political half-truths and lobbyists, not leaders, and to try to understand our world we watch news-flavored propaganda delivered in meaningless soundbytes. But doesn't our acidity, like the oceans', cause delicate things to die out *in us*? I feel as if things as fine as coral reefs are vanishing from *people*. Things like a general kindness. Quiet sensitivity. Sincerity. And we Seminarians demonstrate this. I mean, Will's mock furniture is brilliant, but it also stabs its buyers, shoves them into sexually compromised positions, or tosses them on the floor."

This got a big laugh, but Nita remained serious. "Jonathan's work is great too. If that Eve with the full-body theological tattoos had a pulse, I'd beg to be her Adam—sorry, Anna. Meanwhile *my* notion of edgy art is to depict apocalyptic scenarios set on Madison Avenue, Hollywood Boulevard, or Abe's lap at the Lincoln Memorial, earning a grim *ha-ha* from those who get it. So how are we three not cloned? We're not fascists or narcissists. We're *ironists*. A caustic or cynical edge is the only cutting edge we seem able to deploy."

"What I'd hoped to explore," Not-Quite Dr. Gage said, "is squarely on the table. We agree we're cursed in the Prophet Anna's sense. We agree we've mainlined cynicism lifelong. We agree our appetites, entertainments, sense of reality, are controlled by systems we can't defeat or escape. So I can't help wondering why *you,* Julian, are grinning as if we've won a prize."

"I'm grinning because, if we're serious enough about art to recognize it wherever we find it," he said, "we have to admit that corporate cynicism is often a brilliant dark art form and *admire* its devious skill."

"How about an example?" asked Julia Gage.

"The fast-food industry," Julian said with relish. "Think about it. A heavily researched, government-supported, FDA-approved, taxpayer-bilking, corporate *assault diet* targeted us in infancy. Their research quantified the fact that we love sameness, blandness, sweetness, and fat. Disney and the fast-food chains then hired Carl Jung's and Joseph Campbell's evil twins and spawned a food-meets-entertainment industry juggernaut that hooked us like crack cocaine. Let's admit it. Blending feature-length, dumbed-down myths and fairy tales with bland, sweet, fatty food was *genius*! So was popping action heroes into the Happy Meal. Which of the males among us didn't love shoveling that tripe down while we sat in the back seat making mayhem and murder noises as we worked our action figures' weapons?"

As most students laughed, Anna cried out, *"But they're Killing Our Earth!"*

"Of course they are, Anna," Julian said. "But look at the gamesmanship! With nutritious, delicious food to be had all over the planet, they've got billions of us gobbling caffeine, saturated fat, pesticided spuds, Amazon-rain-forest-displacing beef, corn-syrup bombs, feature-length 'toons, and mythic-hero merchandising in the blind hope that mythic qualities are pouring into us—and we're only off by two letters. Mythic *quantities* have made us the most obese, diabetes-infested generation in history!"

While most of the class laughed, Risa noticed Angst Nouveau furniture maker Will Jones blushing for obvious reasons. Will wasn't six feet tall and he weighed at least 250. "Sorry not to join in the fun," he said, "but I grew up in corn-syrup country watching people I love grow as immobile as their couches as they *got* that diabetes. My mom, an RN, blew out her back maneuvering supersized patients. Then *I* supersized. Oops. Sorry, Mom. My heroes in high school weren't action figures. They were people like the farmer prophets Wendell Berry and Wes Jackson, urging us to escape the petro-ag juggernaut by returning to family-run local economies one farm, town, and farmers' market at a time. But we're way younger than those heroes. The timing for us was hopeless. My friends who listen to NPR wonder why I don't. Ever hear of Cargill? Archer Daniels Midland? When I hear Fred Child chirping about Mozart, I don't picture Amadeus. I picture the last decent towns I knew turning ugly when, funny coincidence, Walmarts, meth houses, and Fred's *Performance Today* sponsors all moved in. I was still in grade school when the petro-ag giants bought out the last family farms. The only farms making it now are the corporate dreck purveyors. The best of us, unable to watch, hit the road, and became the irony-addicted urban cynics we still seem to be."

"So aren't these the forces that cloned *our* generation?" Julia Gage asked the class. "Rigged markets, cartels, and corporate gigantism burying farms and hometowns? Urban entrapment if we need culture in our lives? Addiction to acidity and irony in response?"

"Turn toddlers into tricks for Tyson and Monsanto and shit happens," Will said.

"Then is a cynical counterattack desirable?" Not-Quite Dr. Gage asked. "Might ironical protests be the most effective protests we can make?"

As Jonathan nodded vehemently and the other Seminarians grew pensive, Risa sat bolt upright. "Of *course* not!" she cried. And she was off to the races:

"Nonstop irony is a vicious cycle. People think irony expresses some sort of truth. The truth is, most irony is just a verbal trick that swizzles disingenuous words around to convey ridicule, contempt, or caustic humor that makes us *sound* knowing at the very instant we're saying nothing true at all. Irony can't convey truth for a simple reason: *it never means what it says.* But for the same reason, thank heavens, it can't *invalidate* truth. Irony pretends to invalidate things by sounding snarky or snide about them, but if being snide and snarky had that power, *Saturday Night Live* would have invalidated North America by now. I love *SNL,* by the way. Ironic humor relieves tension by treating what hurts as a joke. But when we *equate* irony and truth, some super weird stuff happens. Like, it suddenly feels uncool, or naive, or even *wrong* to sincerely believe in *anything.* Several ironists I've known say, 'There's nothing left to believe in.' But that saying *is* a belief. That's knee-jerk relativism posing as an absolute! And many an ironist holds that pose so fiercely they end up trivializing every moment of their life with *pride,* as if the insincere trivializing of all things is a triumph!"

The Irony Seminarians had fallen into a stunned silence before Not-Quite Dr. Gage managed to flag Risa down. "I want to hear exactly how irony trivializes. But first, Risa, I wonder how in the world, given the cynical state of so many Americans, you managed to reach this understanding in the first place?"

Risa shrugged. "Nothing too profound. I noticed early in high school how my friends' and my senses of irony had grown as addictive as french fries. Name a topic, *any* topic, and it only takes a fry's worth of thought to greet it with a smirk and say, '*Yeah, right.*' By doing that we were dodging serious issues we needed to be grappling with, but if one of us said as much, someone else would smirk and say, '*Serious issues. Yeah, right.*' And we'd snort and change the subject. That kind of irony began to remind me of a football team that, every time it gets the ball, punts on first down because, like, *second down, third down, fourth down?* '*Yeah, right.*' I didn't want to play for that team. So I set out to cure my addiction."

"I can't wait to hear the cure," Julia Gage said. "But first, can you give us a few examples of how irony trivializes lives?"

"Sure," Risa said. "We all know how it works. Most irony is just a reflex, not a considered response. I'll show you." She turned to her right, looked directly at Julian, smirked, and in a caustic tone said: "*Handsome Julian. Yeah, right.*"

There was surprised laughter all over the room, Julian's included.

Risa turned to Not-Quite Dr. Gage, smirked again, and in the same acidic tone said, "*Not-Quite Dr. Gage's Irony as Modus Operandi in Post-Modern Art seminar. Yeah, right!*"

Amid more surprised laughter, Risa turned her smirk upon Anna and Nita. "*Two nice young ladies trying to be in love. Yeah, right.*" The class, including Anna, laughed again. But Nita glanced at Julia Gage, blushed, her gaze fell to the floor, Jonathan hooted, and Anna's smile collapsed.

"Yikes!" Risa said. "Sorry for the awkwardness, Nita and Anna! But that was kind of my point. Just three *Yeah, right*s and I spread unmeaning every which way. And I wasn't even thinking. Just spitting out irony as a reflex. That was an eye-opener in my teens. Hoping to break my addiction, I found my way to some old wisdom traditions as an undergrad. The Vedic tradition of India, especially, held ancient words, ways, and formulas that, if taken seriously, still possess the power to knock the irony reflex out of play."

Seeing her boyfriend's instant scowl, Risa said, "Julian and I scuffle over this. An old Vedic formula in Sanskrit sounds as silly as pig latin if you invest nothing in it but a *Yeah, right.* But invest sincere concentration in certain phrases and they sometimes turn into soul medicine. In Vedic culture it's understood, for instance, that we all possess three bodies—a knowledge body, a truth body, and a begotten body—and to learn to recognize the limits and strengths of each can be life-changing. In contrast, to learn you have three mysterious bodies and respond with a *Yeah, right* leaves you with no body at all!"

Several arms had crossed defensively, and several eyes had opened wide. Among the latter, Julia Gage said, "More please, Risa! Another example?"

"Okay. Say you grew up listening to the awful purple dinosaur, Barney, on kids' TV. When that jackass looks at the kiddies and sings '*I love you, you love me,*' snorting *Yeah, right* is a good way to keep from getting splattered by schlock. But once the *Yeah, right* serves that purpose, people forget to turn off their Barney reflex—and *that's* a spiritual disaster! We in this room, for instance, are trying to deepen our relationship with a fragile pursuit known as art. Imagine that, like me, you're ex-Catholic, female, and cynical as hell about all-male power structures like the Vatican and male priesthood for the way they *still* treat women after umpteen disgraceful centuries. Now imagine that, as an artist, you feel an attraction to the warm organic spin Gaudí's Barcelona Sagrada Família puts on some old cold Catholic imagery. If, due to your distrust of Catholic sexism, your Barney reflex pipes up, *Gaudí's Spanish Fruit and Vegetable Cathedral. Yeah, right!* your attraction goes dead before you've given Gaudí's genius a chance. And why? Because *you elevated the fact that Barney doesn't really love you into a modus operandi.* That's self-defeat posing as hip superiority! That's nuts! I don't know about you all, but my bottom line in art, as in life, is to serve that irony-proof idiot the human heart. I like hearts because their pulsing is steadfast for billions of beats, *never* ironical, and we're *alive* as a result. I like that hearts *ache.* I like that they *yearn.* I want *ache* and *yearning* in my art. So say that, to study the history of heart aches and yearnings, I visit the ancient wisdom wing of the library. If I don't shut off my Barney reflex before opening those texts I'll end up muttering, *Lao Tzu, yeah, right...The Buddha Shakyamuni, yeah, right...Mary Magdelene, yeah, right...* as if those heroes are just three Barneys saying they love me when they don't. See how crazy that is?"

At last taking in the slack jaws she'd evoked, Risa let out an embarrassed laugh. "*Jeez!* Somebody shut off the fire hose! Everybody's talk got me so wound up I blasted your ears off! I'm so sorry!"

While the Seminarians maintained a fraught silence, Not-Quite Dr. Gage said, "Well *I'm* not. In fact I have an awkward confession. When I first set eyes on you, Risa, my irony reflex sized you up in two skin-deep seconds, telling me you were a hip-but-so-what variation on the inescapable old theme *Pretty Ingenue.*"

When some of the class looked startled or offended, Risa smiled her lighthouse smile and said, "It's okay. I get that pretty often."

"But it's *not okay!*" Julia Gage said. "I *believed* my cynical reflex.

Downed it like a french fry. Thank you for filling me with useful guilt over *french-frying you* by bowling me over with a startling wake-up call."

"I second that," said Will Jones with a wistful, lost farm-boy smile.

"Me three," said Nita Hymes.

"I'm more in this camp," Jonathan grinned as he flipped Risa off with both hands.

Risa startled all four of them with another full-on lighthouse smile.

"Seminarians," Not-Quite Dr. Gage said. "I'd planned to tell you about the eighteenth-century thinker Giambattista Vico eight weeks from now. But Risa has fast-forwarded us to conclusions so close to his that I'll introduce you today. Vico was a philosophical enemy of Descartes, and of the so-called Enlightenment. I say 'so-called' because the Enlightenment, in my view, enthroned the kind of reasoning you've been vilifying as 'corporate,' killing off interior coral reefs in the process. Vico offered humanity reflections as unlike Descartes's as Risa's are unlike Jay Leno's. Civilizations have three ages, he contended. The *Divine,* the *Heroic,* and the *Human.* Each is a steep decline from the age previous, the *Human Age* being the last before civilizational collapse. Symptoms of the Human Age as defined by Vico? The acidity Nita described beautifully. The ruthless, reason-driven cleverness Julian admires with his own reasoned cleverness. The ruined farms and towns Will fled. And civil discourse dominated at all times, Vico said, by Jonathan's dangerously close friend *irony.* According to Vico, a civilization laboring under overarching irony loses its way by miring people in what he called *barbarie della riflessione.* Barbarism in our attempts at reflection.

"We'll return to him in eight weeks. For now, though we agree that Disney, McDonald's, and Exxon have us by the brain cells, fat cells, and gas tanks, Risa has floated the thesis that if we're guided by those irony-proof idiots *our hearts,* no corporate power can control our art. Irony treated as an absolute, in reflection as in art, she and Vico agree, is *pathological.* Take care with their thesis, Seminarians. With a disarming smile Risa has fired a hardball at the heads of the committed ironists among us.

"Speaking for myself, I pray irony continues to gleefully debunk pretentiousness, politics, televangelism, and megalomaniacs, and I pray Socrates's charmingly ironic pretensions of ignorance stay with us forever. For comic relief I enjoy low-rent forms of irony too. Between now and our next meeting, however, I hope to switch off every reflex that would cause me to punt a woman as substantial as Risa into a *Person of No Interest* category on first down!

"Until next time, thanks, all of you, for a most intriguing exchange."

(Portland, May 16, 1990)

VII. The Nativity of Dumpster Catholicism

Only in the places of dust and grime and footprint,
only in the failed step and the rusty body, only
in the falling… We meet God on the floor.
                    —Joel McKerrow, "We Dance Wild"

I'VE SAID THAT Dumpster Catholicism collects no tithes or offerings, seeks no converts, owns no cathedrals, churches, shrines, or abbeys. I've said that its "St. Peter's" is the ordinary sidewalks and park paths of Portland. I've said that a Joseph, Mary, and Jesus were again involved: the 3.2, 2.9, and 0.7 centimeters tall Joseph, Mary, and Jesus of Demetria Cabrera, bequeathed by her father Josef to TJ McGraff. I've said that, to honor the promises he made to Josef, TJ has, ever since, kept the Holy Family and their donkey in the little pouch he wears round his neck by day and keeps under his pillow by night. He has also continued to honor eight-year-old Demetria's death each morning by telling her *La Familia* about his hopes for the day, followed each night by accounts of his ups and downs before tucking them in with words of love. What I haven't addressed is the actual moment when Dumpster Catholicism was born on the Portland streets. The blessed event occurred during the first year of Jervis's Ocean-walking, eight months after Jervis himself got dumpstered.

After Jervis discovered his Ocean-walking vocation, TJ decided to make Mondays his Sabbath and closed both his restaurants that day to pursue his favorite form of worship: sharing Jervis's marathon walks. I'm going to leave out the streams of people they greeted on the Monday Jervis's street faith was born, his stop-and-go pace, his innumerable namastes, the chaos of city life and street people that swirls around him, and head straight for the religionless religion's birth. I should also mention that it was TJ, not Jervis, who shared this nativity tale with my shirt-pocket iPhone and me, at the Étouffée Bruté bar one night in 2015, hours after the restaurant had closed. And though TJ was describing an event that happened twenty-five years before, he left me feeling it had happened that very day.

ON THE MONDAY in question, May of 1990, the brothers were deep into the usual blithe stop-and-go conversation, scores of people and hundreds of smiles and namastes interrupting Jervis along the way, when TJ noticed they were passing the 22nd Avenue Market. His gaze flew at once to the far corner of the infamous parking lot: there stood the same blue dumpster into which Jervis had been thrown eight months before. Just as he wondered whether Jervis would react to his transformation point, Jervis veered straight for it, reached the dumpster-side patch of asphalt from which Ocean had erupted as he was beaten to a pulp, came to a halt, and gave the pavement at least a score of rapid-fire namastes. Silly as the gesture looked, TJ felt something electric.

"Every time I come here," Jervis paper-whispered, "I feel so happy to be where Ocean flooded me that she starts flooding me all over again. But lately, Teej, on top of the flooding, she's been showing me an image: a hot, dirty, paved-over place with a dumpster like this one, only bigger. *Way, way* bigger."

TJ asked the obvious question. "What place is that, Jervis?"

"Behind St. Peter's Cathedral in Rome. And yeah, it's invisible. But it's there. You can feel it. I'm talking about the Catholic Church's *own* dumpster. Come to Rome, Teej. Come look in it with me," Jervis said. With which he trudged over to the 22nd Avenue Market dumpster, lifted the lid, and didn't flinch at a stench that made TJ recoil.

"*The fuck*," he said down into the fetid chamber. "Imagine! Roman Catholicism's very own dumpster. So old. So vasty deep. So many so-called *enemies of the Church* thrown in there. Pelagius and the Druids. The Beguines and the Meister and dear Marguerite. So many thousands of European women. So many tribes, languages, ways of knowing, piled helter-skelter, composting like moldy vegetables and meat trimmings and fish guts in there. Heating up and rotting, maybe forever in there.

"*Or maybe not.* That's what Ocean has me feeling. Because, *the fuck*, if a Portland State kid hadn't dumpster-dove in this very steel box, and if Officer Barrios hadn't climbed in to feel for the pulse of a guy who looked deader than dead, I wouldn't be here. So *what about the Church's dumpster,* Ocean's been strobing. If I climb into it and feel around in the rot, might there still be some live pulses in that dumpster too?"

TJ, like most people, loved Jervis's soft, papery, injured voice. But he also suspected this voice allowed Jervis to get away with almost anything he chose to say. So whenever TJ felt especially mesmerized by the voice, as he did now, he got lawyerly. "How could we dive in the Church dumpster even if we wanted to, Jervis? We're a long way from Rome. And even if we went there we'd never gain access to the Vatican archives. But say we *did* gain access. Say we even found a few squelched and buried secrets, a few long-lost spiritual treasures. What difference would that make to a Church with two thousand years of buried secrets and stolen treasures, and a billion faithful despite all the good things their Church has buried?"

"The Vatican archives are where I *wouldn't* go, Teej. Who cares if I can make a difference to the Church or the Vatican or to Roman Catholics? Their history is *their* version of history. The Catholic Church dumpster is *outside* that history, piled deep in the lost stories of those who knew and loved the people, tribeswomen, misunderstood saints, and spiritual treasures the Church killed or threw out. *That's* what I climb in to seek. I want to make the kind of difference to somebody in the Church's dumpster that Officer Barrios made to me in *this* dumpster. I want to dig down through all the persecutions, takeovers, mass smotherings, and stench and feel for possible pulses."

TJ was sufficiently moved by Jervis's papery words to again distrust his feelings, so he stayed in lawyer mode. "That kind of digging would take scholarship, Jervis. Lots of it. And as you told me months ago, you can't swim in Ocean and read at the same time."

"That's changing," Jervis said. "Because of my dance with seizures I can't sit still and read. But all kinds of fishes and jellyfishes can breathe and feed if they keep moving through Ocean's currents nonstop. So I started walking as I read, visiting the downtown library, Powell's, the Portland State stacks, *solvitur ambulando,* feeling for the pulses of Rome-dumpstered hearts. And if I slide a book off a shelf and keep pacing as I read, I can climb down into the stench and feel for pulses for quite a while."

Hearing that Jervis was reading again was so welcome to TJ that he dropped his guard. "Have you found anything of interest?" he asked.

Still gazing into the 22nd Avenue Market dumpster, Jervis said, "If pulses pronounced dead interest you, hell yes, Teej. I find them all the time. Just yesterday I found the pulse of a man dumpstered in 1569. That's why we're here. You must wonder how the pulse of a man four centuries dead could be felt. Come look, Teej. Come smell. Come find out."

TJ joined his brother at the open lid, and did look, and did smell, and the reek was stupendous. But hard as it was to stay at Jervis's side, TJ kept breathing it in.

"The good man the Church dumpstered in 1569 isn't alone in there," Jervis said. "He's in the company of thousands of healers condemned as witches. He's whispering with knowers of the Lady of Fatima's Secret the Vatican keeps smothering though it keeps gasping for breath. He's with Druids, Beguines, the Meister, M's Holy Church the Great, Francis's milky breasts, Clare's mirror, and every other mystery the nonexistent God of Reason condemns or tries to erase because the God of Grace is so un-reasonable. But that same God is so inviolable. And what Ocean whispers is *Rome's victims can pulse back to life.* That's why she had me bring you here, Teej. Get used to the stench. You're gonna acclimatize. We're gonna be together in this. This day, Ocean strobed, you're gonna feel a four-centuries-dead man's living pulse."

TJ was so alarmed by Jervis's prediction he couldn't speak.

"How it went yesterday," Jervis said down into the fetid dark. "Moving from book to book, walk-walk-walking as I read, I found Christians in the Netherlands, two centuries after the Church crushed the Beguines, who began to question infant baptism. Why? Because John the Baptist didn't sprinkle a few drops of the Jordan on Jesus's head then charge Joseph and Mary money for it. You and I were infant baptized, Teej, and what do you remember of it? Same as me, right? *Zero.* Netherlanders old enough to be troubled by that zero started immersing one another John-Jesus-River-Jordan-style. Anabaptists, they were called. The Mennonites, Amish, Brethren, Shakers, Quakers, all came out of that. But the paydays that came of infant head-sprinkles suited the Vatican just fine, so they declared being baptized the John and Jesus way a heresy, and made it punishable by death. *Death, Teej.* For baptizing the way Jesus was baptized. *The fuck!* Our Church began murdering Anabaptists right and left. The men we burned. The women we drowned. How determined was the Church when these lovers of Jesus kept defying them? How many Anabaptists would have survived if it was left to Rome? *None,* Teej. The Amish, Shakers, Mennonites, Quakers. Such cool people. And if Rome got its way, nothing would be left of them but this stench we're smelling. That's why, in the PSU stacks yesterday, I kept walk-walk-reading-reading, feeling for a day when Rome didn't get its way. And, *solvitur ambulando,* in 1569 I found one."

What a relief to TJ when Jervis let the dumpster lid bang shut and turned to face him.

"His name was Dirk Willems. Baptized in secret at fifteen, and so moved by it that he began to let people be baptized in his home. Then he got caught. Sentenced to death."

Seeing where the tale was heading and feeling he might drown, TJ took a page out of Jervis's book and began pacing, hoping movement was life.

"Church prisons were overflowing. They jailed Dirk in a castle. Starved him while he awaited death. Dirk was young. Dirk was tricky. He wove scraps of cloth into a rope, hung it out a window, dropped to the ice-covered moat. Early spring. Thin ice. The good news? Dirk was being starved by our thoughtful Church! The ice held.

"A jailer saw him, gathered a gang, gave chase, but they ran all the way around the thin ice. Dirk got a good head start, crossed another pond, again the ice held, again the pursuers were afraid of it. But Dirk's lead was so serious one man braved the pond. Dirk hears a sound. Turns. The man has fallen through. The gang is afraid. They leave him thrashing in icy water. Dirk has it made! He's a hero to Anabaptists. They'll hide him, help him flee the country. Except, *the fuck, Teej.* Dirk remembers some crazy bird once saying, 'Love thine enemies, bless them that curse you, do good to those who hate you.' Back he runs to the pond. Crawls out on the ice. Rescues the man. Happy ending about to unfold? The way of Christ at least restored at one lonely Dutch pond? Not even close. The rescued man's gang arrest Dirk a second time, the Church tries him again, and Dirk's love of enemy earns him a second sentence of death."

"I can't take this!" TJ burst out. "I feel no pulse at all! All I feel is the same sick-to-the-gut feeling that zealots, Inquisitors, and torturers have given me since we were kids."

But Jervis seemed not to hear: he was gazing at the patch of asphalt upon which he'd been felled eight months before as if seeking something the pavement might still contain. *The eruption point,* TJ felt as he watched his brother. *Ocean's secret blowhole.*

"On May 16th, 1569," Jervis paper-whispered, "Mother Church burned Dirk Willems at the stake for loving his enemy so much he gave his life for him. But here's what I feel, Teej. To call our Church 'Mother,' or 'the Body of Christ,' on such a day is blasphemy. Heresy. Abomination. Our Church, that day and many days, was a gaggle of hypocrites, cowards, and murderers, and the east wind knew it. The wind blew so hard it drove the flames away from Dirk's head and body, keeping him alive and conscious while his legs burned to charred meat. In his agony Dirk began screaming a prayer. *'O my Lord, my God! O my Lord, my God!'* Cries so horrific that one of the spectators counted seventy of them, then fainted. Cries so awful they carried to the next town. How did the Catholics respond? By throwing more wood on Dirk's fire! *O my Lord, my God, Teej! The fuck, Teej! Eli, Eli, lama sabachthani, Teej! The fuck!*"

TJ was shocked to see Jervis's nerve-damaged, expressionless face shed a single tear out of his slump-lidded eye.

"Dirk's love of enemy became famous. It inspired hundreds to keep baptizing the way John the Baptist did Jesus. Our Church kept burning the men, drowning the women, but their victims kept crying out to their God, inspiring hundreds more. Faced with the Christ-likeness of so many, did Mother Church reconsider? Oh, she did, Teej, she did. At Westside Catholic last year I almost got fired three times. The last time was for putting this question on a test. 'In Holland in the 1570s, what famous world religion invented metal tongue clamps to silence the prayers of the Christians they burned at the stake or drowned so that the Christians couldn't cry out to their God?' Most of my students cried, *'Muslims!'* It didn't go over well when their parents learned the tongue-clampers were our very own Roman Catholics."

Sounding as broken as he looked, TJ said, "I'm standing with you on your asphalt Golgotha, Jervis, trying to love and trust what you love and trust. Or *Who.* But if Dumpster Catholicism is just a history of tortures and murders and horrors, how can I? What is there to love or trust in *this*?"

Gazing at the asphalt he'd drenched with blood, Jervis whispered, "*Ocean's mercy,* Teej. No choice. Love the mercy that sounds insane to your mind. Today is the four hundred twenty-first anniversary of Dirk's seventy prayers. His brave roaring needs to escape this dumpster and the stake where he burned. We need to free it. You know how to silence your mind. Now is the hour, Teej."

TJ stared, stunned, as Jervis dropped to his knees. "No dumpster can put a lid on this. No terrible death can stop this. Come down here with me, Teej. *Come feel Dirk's pulse.*"

Feeling no hope at all—feeling nothing but a sick, blind, little-boy wish not to be abandoned by his only family member—TJ sank to his knees beside his brother.

Jervis slid his right arm through TJ's left. "Silence your mind," he said.

With his right hand TJ pulled the tiny purse from his shirt. Held the 3.2, 2.9, and 0.7 centimeters *La Familia* to his heart. Closed his eyes. Became nothing. A free nothingness heard the city internally combusting; heard a laurel hedge alive with chittering sparrows; heard unseen pigeons cooing in trees, starlings imitating sirens, radio static, bobwhites, hard-braking cars. The same nothingness then saw and heard three scenes in succession as clearly as Jervis feels Ocean's strobes.

First: a broad windy field across which drifts the screamed prayer of a man being slowly burned to death—yet his last three moaned "*O my Lord, my God!*" sound eerily exultant.

Second: on this same patch of asphalt, eight months back, something Nameless visits Jervis amid his body's obliteration, sending an insane sliver of spirit so mercifully deep into his wrecked body it couldn't be killed.

Third: at a grave in Ixhuatán, Chiapas, Josef Cabrera stands gazing down at the dirt with an expression so tender that TJ falls out of nothingness and heaves an utterly human sob. And in that intersection—that ever-recurring line of no width between the sobbing and the mortal, the silent and the deathless—TJ feels, then *hears*, a pulse. Then another. Then many, many others.

"You're a good priest," comes the papery whisper. "You learn."

TJ frees his arm from Jervis's and lays *La Familia*, in their tiny purse, upon the oracle point; lays his hands, palms down, on the impossibly unlocked asphalt; places his forehead between his hands on holy asphalt, and begins kissing and kissing the filthy ground.

"That's right," comes the whisper. "That's good, Teej. Hear 'em? *Thank you for remembering us,* they're saying. *O my Lord, my God, Teej. Demetria and Dirk, La Familia, and your donkey too. O my Lord, my God, thank you for feeling and loving us,* the drowned and burned are saying. *Thank you, Teej and Jervis. Thank you! We love and feel you too.*"

"It was a very long time," the Dumpster Catholic TJ McGraff told me many years later, "before the pulses eased enough to allow either of us to return to our feet."

(above Pipestone, 1995)

VIII. Thirteen Tons of Poison Sutra

You must come up here, out beyond the tents, where it is bare and lonely and shaped like loss. Otherwise how will you ever know your unknown self, a bead neither lost nor found, not a bead at all? How will you ever know, for the very first time, what it is you have always wanted?
— Jesse van Eerden, "Work Ethic"

THE BLAZING SOUTH slope of Two Medicine and weight of Lorilee's pack turned her body into a pack mule within seconds. Her thoughts grew mule simple and stubborn. Her twinges of fear fell away with the sweat. For three hours, upward straining usurped thought.

What she found upon summiting was bleak. Not a wildflower or living blade of grass. The pines unscathed by fire dying of drought. Even the cacti stressed. The good news: any nostalgia she might have felt for the time she'd been here with Trey was also dead of drought. All she felt was a new certainty that Earth was truly and terribly heating up. But physical need now trumped even this concern. She had downed two-thirds of her three-day water supply. She'd be heading home tomorrow if she couldn't replenish her supply. The few deer tracks crossing the summit headed in a beeline for the Peak's wilder, cooler north slope. She followed the deer.

The view to the north was vast. Snow-topped mountain ranges rose on both the left and right horizons. Between them, a one-hundred-or-so-square-mile plateau of desiccated ranches, green alfalfa patches, and scrub desert featured microscopic cars and trucks crawling along black seams so distant that no sound reached the summit. Maybe eight hundred feet below and a mile away, Lorilee spotted the patch of color surrounding Pipestone Creek's source spring. She also recalled herself and Trey coming upon a stunning high meadow somewhere downstream of the spring, though a stone shoulder of the Peak blocked it from view. Most of the deer tracks vectored springward. She again followed their advice.

The first few hundred yards were a shattered granite talus slope. No trail. The decline over sharp rock was steep and her legs were wobbly from the ascent. Needing a walking stick to guard against a fall, she found only a few incinerated piñon saplings. She gripped one burned into its roots, tore it from the ground, and in stomping off its spiky branches blackened her hands and jeans. She wiped away sweat, blackening her face. The spring was now needed for two reasons. To alarm possible snakes she banged her walking stick on the granite, spooking a small lizard into a tiny crevice. Lodged in the same crevice was a shape she took to be a bird's skull. Picking it up, she grunted in surprise at its weight. It was a fossilized clamshell, its petrified, perfectly symmetrical halves held open like tiny book covers by solid, gray-black, bird-skull-shaped stone. Speaking for the shell, Lore said: "*Hi. My name is Bivalve. I was born on an ocean floor three hundred million years ago, got bored with it, and hitched a ride on a tectonic plate to this summit. It's lonely up here. Can I come with you?*"

"Yes, you can," Lore said, giving Bivalve a little kiss and slipping it in her jeans pocket.

BY THE TIME she reached the hedge of color surrounding the spring the sound of running water filled her with animal excitement. Plowing through buckbrush, sumac, stunted willow, ignoring scratches to her arms and face, she came upon the creek by stumbling into it.

Turning upstream, she soon found the source pool. She'd forgotten the beauty of it: red sedimentary rock and gray granite bordered by turquoise forget-me-nots, yellow monkey flower, watercress, horsemint, and the coldest, clearest water imaginable surging up through the white sand bottom in a copper-green pool the size of Walt's '54 Chevy bed.

Lore dropped her pack roughly, wondered if she'd broken off a piece of Elmerina Buddha, then shrugged. "I'm beat up too, friend. There's always more Elmer's."

Stripping down to her DON'T ASK! ball cap, she gasped as she seated herself in the chill pool, but threw scores of ball-cap-fuls of water over her head, her face, down her throat. Her body grew mentholated. She used a hiking sock to scrub the ash off her face and hands, then soaplessly washed and wrung out her sweat-soaked clothes. By the time she finished, her teeth were chattering. Opening her pack, she donned fresh hiking socks, long jeans despite the heat to serve as a brush guard, and a Newport Folk Festival T-shirt circa 1990 that splayed Doc Watson's grizzled, one-eyed, now doubly understandable grin across her chest. She stuffed the wet clothes in a side pocket, planning to hang them in camp, donned boots and pack, stood with a groan, found a spindly willow walking stick, and followed the stream.

For half a mile the flow dropped fast down a boulder-strewn gorge. Too heavily loaded to rock-hop, she slid down the dry boulders and ledges, skirting the plunge pools, plowed through streamside brush, and collected more scratches. But several side springs added volume to the creek, pale mayflies soon hovered over the pools, and bright warblers, flashing yellow, flitted out of the willows to hawk them, and little trout leapt at them as if yearning to become birds.

Totally focused on her downstream scrambling, Lorilee was surprised when the brush and boulders abruptly ended and the creek flowed almost silently out into the high meadow she'd remembered. Its wide expanse was nearly level, carpeted in cotton grass, sedge, paintbrush, wild aster, tundra moss. The creek meandered like a child's scribbling, creating cutbanks and oxbows as if seeking a course that would allow it never to have to leave the meadow. The heat lost its intensity. The day's harsh white sunlight softened to shades of citrus. Aiming for a stand of storm-gnarled aspens at the meadow's downstream end, Lore was forced by the meanders to cross and recross. The fords proved a pleasure when raisin-sized frogs leapt from thigh-sized sandbars into sink-sized pools populated with equally tiny trout.

The shade of the aspen grove was instant soma. She dumped her pack, plunked down under the tree closest to the water, shucked her boots where the aspens' roots twined down into the creek, and let her feet do the same. Lying back in dry grass and wildflowers, she stared at treetops and sky, pondering her next moves. While no other place on the mountain compared to this grove in beauty, scores of crushed beer cans, hundreds of empty bullet casings, and a fire ring kicked to pieces evidenced the fact that anybody with four-wheel drive would choose the same campsite.

Digging deep in her pack, Lorilee pulled out Elmerina Buddha, unwrapped her from the beach towel, found her unbroken, set her on the shelf of a boulder aimed at the downstream end of the meadow, and warned denizens of the lower world, *"Enlightened sentry on duty!"* She then wandered the grove on a housekeeping mission, collecting and burying the casings and cans, rebuilding the fire ring, setting up her one-woman tent, sleeping pad, bag. Her wet clothes she hung in an aspen but did not include underwear lest it excite possible male visitors. Her sopped boots she propped on Elmerina's stone shelf, open to the sinking sun. She set her frying pan and saucepans on a rock slab she dubbed "the kitchen," and used a cord to tree her bear-proof food bag. She gathered hundreds of limbs and branches for the next two nights' fires, stomping them into usable lengths. With her camp night-ready, she gave her dulcimer case a glance. *Not yet,* it seemed to say. Lore decided on a stroll.

Pocket binoculars in one hand, water bottle in the other, she found the ground along the creek so soft she set out barefoot through the now-orange light. Strolling without boots or backpack created a floating sensation she found blissful until her memory of where she was headed bit into the bliss: at the meadow's downstream edge the creek eased around a shoulder of Two Medicine and flowed out into what was once a second even larger meadow. Then the Bureau of Reclamation set out to improve it. The flowers, grasses, sedges, oxbows, were converted by bulldozers into a mile-wide alkali playa that resembled a postapocalyptic football stadium parking lot. In the center of the lot lay a tepid reservoir the Bureau had dared to name Crane Lake, though the reservoir had destroyed a sandhill crane nesting ground, warmed the creek's water thirty degrees, turned it saline, killed off its endangered Colorado greenback cutthroat population, driven off the riparian birds, amphibians, and almost all other life-forms, but served America by sending Pipestone Creek down a ten-mile-long pipe terminating at a corporate high-fructose corn syrup farm.

In the August heat the reservoir had become a quarter-mile-wide, manure-colored puddle shimmering with mirages. But defiled water is still water. As Lorilee approached she sent coots, teals, and shorebirds flying across the puddle into a far shore mirage from which a plaintive cry now reached her. Two mystery birds rose by fractions out of the mirage, shone magnified for a few seconds, warped back down into the shimmer, rose and magnified again, and the blue legs, buckskin heads, and upturned bills gave them away:

American avocets. Lore's favorite bird. She trained her binos on them. They were feeding with great energy despite the late hour. A vast expanse of exposed playa lay between them and the nearest scrub cover. They seemed terribly vulnerable. But avocets, Lore reminded herself, have uncanny survival tricks. Within a day of leaving the egg the chicks can run, swim, and dive. They also grow extremely fast, developing plumage identical to their parents' within weeks, so that they don't appear to predators to be the naive fledglings they are. A few years back Lore had been watching a three-chick avocet family in the shallows of Ben Travis Lake, above Gunnison, when a prairie falcon spotted them and went into a kill dive. Lorilee and the avocet mother both let out warning cries. Chicks and mother then vanished underwater, the falcon pulled out of its dive for lack of a target, and an instant later papa avocet struck the raptor, distracting it while mother and chicks vanished in tall shoreline reeds.

Comparing this displaced pair, Lore found their plumage to be that of adult avocets, but noticed that one bird foraged ceaselessly, while the other broke off feeding to follow it around, crying in frustration. The complainer, she realized, was a fledgling just four or so months old despite looking like its parent—and Lore immediately pictured her own fledgling. Japhy sat zazen like an adult, had become a promising guitarist in record time, and for his seventh birthday was given a Swiss Army knife and a whittling lesson by Trey at least two years too soon, Lore felt. Watching the birds, she thought: *Avocet tricks. Japh is still just a seven-year-old boy.*

He'd shown it that morning. When she'd dropped him at Bess's for a two-night sleepover, he was jacked: he'd taken swim classes that had won him permission to play by himself in the irrigation ditch behind Bess's house. When Lore and Bess began chatting, Japh grinned and said, "Ditch?" She nodded, he shot back to the ditch, and when she went back to hug him goodbye he was seated in the shade of a salt cedar, whittling a six-inch-long canoe out of a branch. Spotting her, he pointed to a two-inch-tall rock with a flat bottom that allowed it to stand on end on a larger rock. "This is Search Man," he said, then balanced the rock upright in the canoe. "If you're not back when you said, I'll send Search Man out to find you."

With that, he launched his canoe on the gentle flow—and it capsized in two seconds, sending Search Man to the bottom. They laughed. But now, by a dying reservoir in dying light, watching an avocet child badger its single parent for food it was unable to find, desolation threatened to sweep down like a falcon.

Resisting the feeling, Lore realized the birds could be enacting a line of Dōgen's: "Be disturbed by the truth." *And what's true for them is true for Japh and me too,* she thought. *Sometimes migration is the only choice left.*

Moved to be sharing a necessity with the avocets, she started back to camp.

FULL DARK AND a small fire had shrunk Lorilee's world into a room with aspen trunk walls and a ceiling of interlaced branches, slow-quaking leaves and stars betwixt and between. Her roommates: a tin cup of red wine, her small musical instrument, her serene sentry, Elmerina.

Wanting the fire's warmth, she tried sitting close and strumming the dulcimer as it lay in her lap, but the vast open air reduced its resonance to the dead sound of a plastic ukelele. She left the warmth, moved to the one good sitting log, and set the big wastebasket between her legs and the dulcimer on its rim. Leaning so low her nose nearly touched the heart-shaped sound holes, she sent her strumming and humming down into the echoing chamber. Resonations and oscillations now audible left her ready to whisper up a song. She kept strumming, let her mind drift to await a few good words—and with a speed that dismayed her was attacked by a scrap of sheer musical *crap*.

Like many things she wanted to forget, the scrap was compliments of Trey. One morning at breakfast, late in their marriage, Japhy had asked Lorilee about Appalachian hill music. He'd heard her talk about it but wasn't sure what it sounded like. Charmed by his curiosity, Lore was seeking the best possible musical reply when Trey beat her to the punch. Making his voice satirically high, loud, and twangy, he sang out,

*Way back in the holler
Where Pappy whupped us so hard
We had to eat possum
Once we run outta lard...*

They'd all laughed. Lorilee too. But Japhy was five at the time. Way too young for satires of a tradition about which he knew nothing. Sure, Appalachian music tended toward the woeful. Mountain life was *hard*. But great hill singers had for centuries proven that plaintive responses to hard times can be beautiful; haunting; healing. Lore had been about to prove it when Trey's lampoon shot that possibility dead for the night. She'd felt she owed Japhy and hill music an apology ever since.

Lore had become a musician for nearly opposite reasons. One: at age twelve, her voice began to rivet people, herself included. If the venue was good and she gave herself to one of the old storytelling songs she loved, the effect was startling: kids stopped playing and listened open-mouthed; old men reached for old women's hands; smiles grew far away; eyes shone. But the other reason she'd turned to music was that once she heard a new melody, it snapped shut on her like a leghold trap. *Any* melodies. Puerile pop hits, fatuous ad jingles, self-righteous old hymns—and now, Trey's wretched scrap.

She had long since learned that one way to purge herself of an unwanted melody was to transpose it into something more than it was. She hated to waste precious Peak time on a purging because of Trey. But when out of curiosity she dropped Trey's derisive twang, slowed the scrap's tempo, and hummed it down into the hollow of the wastebasket, the beauty of the little melody surprised her. Trey may even have stolen it from a genuine old Appalachian song.

Picking the tune out on the fretboard and finding the best chords to match, she wed her hum to her strum. To a degree that startled her, the dulcimer and voice rising in a woven strand were wildly more alluring than the ingredients that had gone in. Raising her gaze to Two Medicine, she asked, "*Are you up to something?*"

Don't sing to me, the peak seemed to convey. *Sing* out of *me*.

Gazing out over the meadow the way the Peak itself was doing, she gave herself to the strand. She didn't try for lyrics. (*Do not try to be masters of yourselves in any kind of hasty manner.*) She just used a hum to wed strings to voice till they entranced her. A high shoulder of Two Medicine was aglow. A half-moon nosed into sight. A notion rose with it. Lore placed a capo on the dulcimer's fourth fret, raising the dulcimer into the range of a mandolin, and lifting Lore's voice into its richest range. The capo also let her shift from major to minor and back. A two-mood rhythm entered her strumming hand, inviting desolation and consolation to take turns while her voice created bittersweet tension between the two.

Four lines of a forgotten hill song rose like the half-moon inside her, carrying the same tension, trumping Trey's parodic intent. Chills slid up her spine. Adding lines of her own to the recollected four, she sang them down into the *śūnyatā* of the amp:

> Gonna build me a campfire
> On the mountain so high
> That the blackbirds can't find me
> Nor hear my sad cry
>
> And when the moon lights the valley
> And the deer start to roam
> I'm gonna sing out my sorrows
> Till they leave me alone

Because, lit by this same moon
We two became one
And three seasons later
I bore us a son

Who for five fleeting birthdays
The first verse of a life
Loved a mother and father
Who were husband and wife

And who now, in a ditch
At the foot of this hill
Is launching boats to find Mommy
That sink in the rill

The half-moon broke free of the horizon. She used its light to fetch her notebook and scribbled out the lyrics that had come. Rereading them, her first impulse was to burn them. She was done with Trey. She hadn't climbed and crossed over Two Medicine to relive all that.

But what about the apology I owe to hill music and Japhy? she remembered.

Focusing on the failed love that wounded their avocet boy, words began to pour.

I'm not pointing fingers
I'm not placing blame
We set out for sunlight
But arrived at cold rain

And now a half-moon is rising
In a wide eastern sky
And something inside me
Knows it's come here to die

Like spring flowers in summer
And wild salmon in fall
But I also feel something
That's not dying at all

Something calm as this Peak
That neither sorrows nor longs
But just looms like a guardian
Above the love we have wronged

So I've built me a campfire
On the high slopes alone
Red flames are now flickering
In a circle of stones

And in a circle of sorrow
I feel my heart holding true
To the heart of this high place
I once shared with you

She set down her instrument and stepped out into the meadow to look closer at what she was trying to hold and sing to. The moon's light had turned the looming north face of Two Medicine more sentient than ever. Nine deer out of nowhere now browsed the marshy grasses. The yip of a coyote made them all look up, but went unanswered. They bent as one back to browsing. Lore returned to her log, amp, and intertwined desolation and consolation modes. More verses came to her:

I don't know where love comes from
But I can tell you this
It was we who pulled back
From the flame of its kiss

And having failed love together
We can't rebuild it alone
Though we beg the forgiveness
Of every tree, cloud, and stone

We beheld in our oneness
Because that one is now two
So I've built us a pyre
In the night mountain blue

I have built us a pyre
At the foot of the sky
In these flames let us burn
In these flames let us die
O pretty flames, let us die,
let us die, let us die...

Silence. The way the heavy night air stirred the silence. Way starlight pierced it. Out in the meadow somewhere, creek water fell a hand's span, creating a sound like a distant child's laughter. Two slow crickets kept time.

Lingering on her song's claim to be willing to let failed love die, Lore set her instrument aside, stepped over to the meadow-facing boulder, removed Elmerina from sentry duty, took her over by the campfire, and set her on the ground six feet from the flames. She went to her firewood supply and delved until she found a little pine stick that forked in two. She said, "I hereby christen you the *Broken Love Stick*."

Returning to the fire, she dropped to her knees before it; nodded across the flames to Elmerina; closed her eyes; held the stick to her heart; began conjuring the love that had infused her and Trey the first time they climbed this peak not so many years ago. It was a love, they'd agreed, that rose out of the earth and burst into them the instant Lore spoke the words "The mountains are your mind." On their anniversary four years later, finding the same words inscribed in *Axe Handles,* the same love seemed to fly up out of the bedrock beneath the garage apartment to flood their legs, loins, lungs, bones, blood, till nothing remained of them but the eruption itself. Japhy, she felt more and more since the marriage ended, was not so much her and Trey's child as the son of that bliss-shot mountain-rooted upsurge.

As she knelt before her fire, holding the Broken Love Stick, she felt Two Medicine claiming their boy as what Dōgen calls "a mountain's child." To seal the claim she began to conjure the moment she'd felt the Peak rising up into her and Trey's bodies. For the first time since their son's conception night, she allowed the uncontainable surges to course through her again, but stayed focused, in their throes, on the way the Broken Love Stick forked in two. Raising the fork to her forehead, she held it there for long, intense seconds—then tossed it in the fire. When it burst into flame, the degree to which a severed love did the same left her gasping. She'd believed herself clear of Trey, but as the pronged stick began to vanish, feelings of regret, self-betrayal, heartbreak arose. Fighting the urge to cry, opening her hands repeatedly to fire and icon, releasing each surge of feeling as fast as it came, she let everything she and Trey had ever been to each other turn to vanishing heat, fading flame, glowing coals, cooling ash. She then bowed, touching her forehead to the ground.

To her surprise, at the moment she bowed, a last couplet arose. She whisper-sang it down into the earth:

Trust a seashell discovered
In Two Medicine scree
That awaited your touch
Since this mountain was sea

And it felt like a directive. Reaching in her pocket, she took out Bivalve, circled the fire, placed the fossil in Elmerina's upturned palm. The fit was so perfect it somehow caused a great calm to come rolling down out of every-where. Figuring she was done for the night, Lore decided to settle toward sleep by circling the meadow one time.

Slipping on her sandals, she forded the little stream and wandered out. No trace of the deer now. No coyote cries. Only the tiny fall in the creek making its laughing-child sound. Then, somewhere behind her: *shrill human cries? An actual child, lost in the night?*

No. The sound was airborne, coming fast out of the west, till it passed directly overhead: *the avocets' flight calls*! The fledgling trailing its parent, crying, *Where are we going? What are we doing? It's dark. I'm afraid.* The parent, refusing to slow, tossing back an occasional, *Come! No choice! We go! We go!*

"Good mama," Lore whispered. "'Be disturbed by the truth.'"

Gazing right at the cries, seeing only stars, she tracked the voices as they circled the meadow once, twice, then divided, the fledgling's cries panicky as it flew back toward the desiccated reservoir, the only habitable place it knew. Lore heard the mother chase it down, take the lead again, turn it northward. Again fledgling and mother passed invisibly overhead, side by side, the young bird now making the same call as its mother's: *We go! We're going! We go!*

When they disappeared, Lorilee turned, with an ache in her heart, south to Two Medicine Peak, felt an avocet-like love for its familiar shape, and a fledgling-like fear that the avocets and Dōgen were urging her too to leave. So many years this Peak had defined her place on Earth. So steadfastly it had watched over her and Japhy. "What does Dōgen mean by 'mountains hidden in hiddenness'?" she asked the peak. "Could there be a way to hide you in my *own* hiddenness? If I hide you in me, can I bring you when we go?" The silence answered in the way the night air stirred it; way stars and crickets pierced it; way dark water kept creating a far-off child's laugh.

She had just turned back to her now-distant campfire when an invisible wave washed over, spinning her round to face Two Medicine. The Peak had become a great seated presence. The meadow had become the presence's open palm, Lore herself a small gift placed in the palm. Some kind of *alchemy* sank her to her knees. Thirteen tons of rage once swallowed for the Buddha's and Japhy's sakes became a philosopher's stone. The Peak's north face became a door. The fossil Bivalve, in Elmerina's palm, became the key to the door. Lore's heartache turned the key. Two Medicine opened.

An essence gushed forth. The poison Lore had swallowed was transmuted into a gold converted by Lorilee's nature into folk music: her chosen medium. But, Earth being Earth, there were still challenges to be met.

First challenge: these surges were not humming a few little hill tunes for her to set down on paper. This was an avalanche of songs vying to burst to life through the conduit of one small woman, one dulcimer, one trash-can amp. A friend of J. S. Bach's, after hearing yet another fresh masterpiece Papa Bach had composed with breakneck speed, asked how he managed to think up so many compositions. Bach laughed and said he had no need to *think* at all. His problem each morning was how not to trample all the music that had appeared on his bedroom floor in the night. Two Medicine's upturned palm of meadow had become Bach's floor! As Lore rushed back to camp she felt every small and great object from trailhead to summit to talus to source spring to meadow to avocets to stars scrambling to serve as muses. There was a brief, euphoric moment when easily ten songs were vying to burst into existence at once. She laughed, reached camp, told herself, "*Mono-task!*" built the fire up big, grabbed her composition notebook with musical staffs, her colored pens, sat on her log, took up her instrument, set the amp between her legs, and sent her voice and strings down inside it. Breath-warmed words, resonating steel, and love swizzled together in the amp's *śūnyatā* and flew up into her face as a music unlike any she'd ever made.

Second challenge: the first song she heard was a ballad. But as she began trying to capture it she realized that beginnings and endings are entirely arbitrary where such Buddha ancestors as mountains are concerned, so she settled for beginningless and endless. That's why, on the recording she eventually made of what the Peak was bestowing, Lore is already singing deft lyrics and the dulcimer is already rich as it first becomes audible. And it's why, twenty-three minutes later, with no lessening of intricacy, the voice and instruments refuse to stop expressing themselves as they fade back into silence.

Third challenge: the ballad was coming so fast that setting it down in notation was impossible. But as she began scribbling the first few notes and chord progressions, her right hand suddenly knew music-capturing tricks that Lore herself didn't know. Her hand invented a dots-and-dashes shorthand that let her capture melodies as fast as she could sing them. When lyrics too came on in a flood, the hand jotted just a first few letters of each word and Lore found she could still conjure the entire line. In no time she'd set down ten verses of an outpouring that up till this night would have thrilled her after a full day of struggle. But now, seated in a palm and calm that prevented astonishment from disabling her, she penned *another* ten verses, and then—ever less surprised—ten more. To capture so much so fast was a world wonder, but she ordered herself to wonder later: *more needed to be captured now*! She grabbed a different colored pen and, right on top of a page already glutted with melody and lyrics, scrawled, "Cello comes in here: *," then shot an arrow round to the page-back and set down the first cello part she'd ever imagined. "Mandolin joins cello here: **," she muttered, penning in more untested notes. "Tin whistle avocet flyover comes in here: ***," she wrote, and a full year later the braided cello, mandolin, and whistle parts proceeded to flood listeners' hearts in the very places she'd foreheard them.

Once upon a time in a place called Colorado, a scruffy mountain peak and lone singer-songwriter found a breed of music hidden in hiddenness. Deep into the night, and again the following night, Lorilee sang, strummed, and scratched out songs till she was too wrung out to produce another note. When hidden music kept avalanching down the mountain even so, she just lay back, stared up at the stars and Peak, and sighed helpless thanks. Mountains—her string-worn fingers, muscle memory, and ringing ears informed her body—belong to the people who love them with a reciprocal love greater than even her greatest efforts could capture or contain.

But she did manage to carry four mortal folk songs and one arguably immortal ballad down off the old peak. The mortals she named "Mountain So High," "Bivalve," "Elmerina's Pearl Earring," and "My Old Mountain." The deathless ballad—and the record she released a year and a half later—she named "Thirteen Tons of Poison Sutra."

IX. Heart/Mind vs. Manas

Manas (Sanskrit): the mind; the inner organ which consists of "desire, deliberation, doubt, faith, want of faith, patience, impatience, shame, intelligence, and fear (Bṛhadāraṇyaka Upaniṣad I, v. 3); the inner organ which shapes into ideas the impressions carried by the sense-organs...[and] is the cause of doubt and volition, the other three organs being the *buddhi* (infinite intelligence), *chitta* (mind stuff), and *ahamkara* (I-consciousness).
— Risa's beat-to-crap $1.25 Harper Torchbooks
The Upanishads; notes

ON VACATION ON Cuttyhunk Island, staying in a cottage Julian had painted in exchange for three weeks of free rent, he and Risa were sitting in the breakfast nook, enjoying their coffee as morning sunlight streamed in, when there was a faint knock on the window just above them. They both looked up in time to see a small bird falling groundward. "Very punk, with the tiny red topknot," Julian remarked to Risa. "Looked like a badminton birdie! Any idea what kind of suicidal..."

Realizing he was talking to no one, Julian was stunned to silence. Risa had vanished!

He felt a rush of fresh salt air and realized the back door was open. Unsure what was happening, he picked up his coffee cup and stepped to the window. The bird lay in the flower bed below, immobile, its tiny blood-orange head bowed, eyes closed, beak opening and closing. *Death throes,* Julian thought. Then bright color caught his eye.

At the edge of the lawn thirty feet away an orange cat crouched, tail twitching, then streaked toward the bird. Helpless to stop it, Julian yelled, "*Shit!*" at the window glass, then gasped and lurched backward as some arm-waving lunatic—*No, Risa!*—shot into the frame, screeching, "*HYEEEE! GIT! GIT! GIT!*" scaring Julian so bad he dumped coffee down his Chi Pants as the cat veered off and vanished.

An instant later, kneeling beneath the window four feet from Julian, separated by glass, cupping the bird in her hands, Risa's face took on the medieval madonna look that, paradoxically, always sent a surge through his penis. Placing her lips to her joined palms, she began whispering sweet nothings to the bird inside.

Her speed in reaction to that tiny thud, Julian thought, *was impossible! She dives into* what is *the instant it happens. And now she's holding the bird to her left boo, er...heart, prob'ly thinking that location has magic powers. Getting pretty Out There, girlfriend. Then again, I like being held to that boob myself. But this...*jibber-jabber *of mine.* Shit! *This is my* Barney reflex, *isn't it!*

Thinking he'd never seen Risa so clearly, he went in the kitchen, dabbed at his pants with a sponge, poured more coffee, and joined her as she stepped out of the shrubs onto the lawn.

"Look!" she whispered, opening her hands a little. *"A ruby-crowned kinglet!"*

Just as Julian peeked, the bird's eyes became clear, its body quickened, Risa opened her hands, and the tiny creature nearly slapped Julian's face with its wings in liftoff.

"Oh, *perfect*!" Risa cried as it let out faint calls and winged away. The bloom of happiness on her face was almost blinding. Julian couldn't help smiling back—until she gushed, "Weren't those the sweetest little flight-calls *ever*?"

His smile withered. *Sweetest little flight-calls. Yeah, right.* But he managed to pursue what impressed him. "You saved that bird's life, Risa. You *knew* that cat was coming for it. *How?*"

"When I picked our dinner bouquet last night, I found a pile of feathers under the same window and saw the cat next door. I learned as a kid that when birds thump glass and cats hear it, they check the scene. If the tom was nearby I knew I'd have to move fast."

"*Fast, I guess!* You were greased lightning! But then you calmed completely, holding the bird to your heart, speaking to it. Was that *purposeful,* do you think? Were you *telling it things?*"

"Nothing calculated," she said with a shrug. "I was just cooing. If you'd just smacked an invisible wall and a giant ten thousand times bigger than you picked you up, don't you think terror might kill you though the invisible wall hadn't? But if the giant held you to her heartbeat, and you felt her pulse and breathing slow, wouldn't you sense she wasn't out to devour you? I've saved a lot of window-stunned birds, Julian. If you become nothing but warm hands and empathy, lots revive. And to the ones who don't, you whisper, 'You were beautiful. You're *still* beautiful. Whichever way you go, little one, live forever!'"

Julian split in two. Half of him wanted to sweep Risa up in his arms, carry her into the cottage, throw her on the bed, get naked, hold her to his heart, make love, and listen to her *sweetest little flight-calls.* His other half was thinking: *Fuck me with a fairy feather! Sure, a bird's alive because she computes details with impossible speed. But her awareness of these subtleties feels threatening somehow. Why can't she just sip her coffee and*

*grin when I say a bird looks like a badminton birdie? Why can't we enjoy
our lox and bagels while a cat enjoys a bird like regular people?*

IT WAS HARD for Julian's and Risa's friends to believe a couple so charismatic
could be threatened by a quirk as innocuous as Risa's fondness for pidgin
Skrit. Yet—ever more obviously—they were. A scene from the escalating
struggle:

They had gone out to Yun Deuk's, the fabled Providence Korean restaurant, where they met up with a friend of Risa's, Audrey White, an associate
humanities professor at University of Rhode Island, and with a friend of
Julian's, Kyle Morley, a grad student in anthropology at Brown. As they
drove to Yun Deuk's Julian confided to Risa that Kyle was a great guy and
that, if the chemistry between him and Audrey felt right, Risa shouldn't
hesitate to play matchmaker. She said she looked forward to seeing whether
that possibility opened up.

Risa knew Yun Deuk's so well that she'd decided on her order before
they arrived. So while Julian, Audrey, and Kyle pondered their menus she
leaned back, took a slow look around, noticed the glowing red taillights
of cars streaming past in the rain outside, the crimson-jacketed maître d'
removing the raincoat of a woman whose blouse was red, and the red backs
of the YD menus. She then quietly said, "*Rudra*."

Just that fast, her two syllables of Skrit caused Julian to shoot her a
warning scowl.

It backfired. The anthropology-minded Kyle took the stern look to mean
that Julian and Risa had strongly differing tastes about food. Curious
now, he began paging back and forth through the bilingual menu, saying,
"*Rudra...Rudra...*I don't see it, Risa. Is it a special? Will the waiter tell us
about it?"

"*Rudra*," Risa said with a bright smile, "is the *Destroyer*. Not quite
Shiva, but close enough. I remember a line, maybe from the Puranas: 'When
Rudra, the tawny god, lamented, out of his mouth poured blazing fire.'"

"Whoa!" said Kyle. "A dish so hot it makes you breathe fire!"

There was no such dish and Julian was slicing his index finger across his
throat at Risa. But a chance to wax Sanskritic to an enthused listener was
so rare she said more. "The word stems from the root *rud,* which means
'to cry.' In English we'd never connect a word meaning 'to cry' to the color
red, thence to fire, thence to a theonym for the destructive power of a god.
English words tend to be *centrifugal*. They lose all meaning when their
definitions fly too far out of their original orbit. But a lot of Skrit words,
rudra being a great example, are *centripetal*. They spiral inward, exploding
to more and more intense levels of meaning."

Seeing Julian glaring and sawing at his throat, Kyle laughed. "I can't
believe they'd serve such a thing! Was it some kind of Korean initiation
rite? Does surviving a bowl of *rudra* mean you're a warrior or a shaman or
something? Tell me more!"

"Following the word as it plunges inward," Risa said while Julian groaned and dropped his head into his hands, "*rudra* ceases to mean 'red' and starts meaning 'to howl,' then 'to roar,' then 'to rage.' Further in yet, *rudra* becomes a blazing force of destruction. *Necessary* destruction. Annihilation of the false. But look, Kyle!" She nodded at Julian's face. "There's a *perfect* example of *rudra* billowing inward, gaining greater and greater intensity!"

When Kyle and Audrey turned to Julian and he reddened even more, Risa adopted the manner of an enthused museum docent analyzing a great painting for a tour group: "See how his anger is charging inward now, creating a racing metabolism and actual heat, setting not just his face but his entire body aglow? *That's* the centripetal power of *rudra*. And if we stay detached, not letting his anger cow us, we see that, *my God*, this man is *magnificent* when *rudra* is charging through him!"

Taking Julian's crimson fury to be a hilariously cooperative illustration of Risa's lecture, Kyle and Audrey cracked up.

"Lots of Sanskrit words coax us inward toward an intensified order of things," Risa continued. "*Ooh!* I remember a riff. Sort of!" Turning to Julian, she joined her palms, bowed to him, then recited: "*O Rudra who bestowest happiness and dwellest in Julian's body! Serpents are Thy bracelets, elephant skin is Thy, uh...shirt and pants. And Thy pealing laughter shatters worlds! O Conqueror of death! Please look upon us with Thy most blazing form!*"

Steam now seemed to fly from Julian's nostrils and Audrey realized he was truly angry. But Kyle broke out in applause. "An Academy Award and a *very* cold beer for this blazing man!" he laughed. "But, Risa. Gracious God! How hot *is* this stuff? You've got me so curious I think I'm actually going to try it!"

"Yun Deuk's doesn't serve a dish called *rudra*," she finally admitted. "But if you think you're ready for warriorhood, the kimchi with four stars will fly you straight into an encounter with the Destroyer!"

"Done!" Kyle cried while Audrey laughed and Julian glared at Risa with disgust.

She set out to make peace. "That was my one and only Skrit fit for the night, Julian. It's out of my system. Nothing but English for the duration, I promise."

"Oh no!" he cried. "We're *fascinated*, honey. *Proonda Boonda Goonda. Garuda Neruda Barracuda.* A forty-eight-cards-shy-of-a-full-deck of ancient Sanskrit is just what America needs!"

"Yeah!" Kyle chimed in. "Why stick to English in a Korean restaurant?"

Audrey had been eyeing Kyle with steadily growing pleasure. "Culinary bravery, endless curiosity, and a nature so kind you haven't even noticed that Julian is actually pissed off," she said. "Are you always this quick to make the best of things, Kyle?"

Kyle blushed at the mention of Julian's anger, having taken it for an act. But he was quick to spread graciousness in all directions. "In most situations," he said, "I prefer finding reasons to feel grateful to reasons to feel miffed. But when a situation is truly dangerous, my tendency is a serious fault. Julian tried to warn me, Audrey. When the kimchi arrives, you'll see the kind of disaster to which my optimism can lead!"

When Audrey gazed at Kyle with delight and he smiled back, Risa seized the moment: "You should know, Kyle, that Audrey is much like a cool old Skrit word herself. The closer you get to her, the more you see that she too spirals inward to more and more intense levels!"

When Audrey and Kyle blushed, but kept beaming at each other, Risa turned to Julian with a smile that said: *It's working!*

Julian glared back with unmitigated anger, though the love he'd encouraged her to facilitate was blossoming before his eyes.

IT WAS KYLE who began shining with *rudra* once his kimchi arrived. Laughing as he washed it down with a beer and three waters, fanning his mouth, pouring sweat, he kept at it till his face nearly ignited. But to the eventual applause of waiters, other diners, and the chef himself, he downed every torrid bite.

"Our warrior-shaman!" Audrey cried when he finished. Spiraling inward to a more intense level, she then stood, crossed round to his chair, and kissed him on each blazing cheek, lingering a little to marvel at his skin's extreme heat.

KYLE AND AUDREY left Yun Deuk's arm in arm, headed for a folk club to catch Clannad, an Irish band they'd discovered they both loved. Julian and Risa drove home in silence because Julian was still steaming, which sent Risa into strategic withdrawal.

When they reached their spacious loft, he lit candles in the dining area, dimmed the other lights, and poured them each a glass of red wine, which seemed to suggest a move toward romance. He then offered Risa a chair at their dinner table and circled round to take a seat on the table's opposite side. "Before we relax," he said, "may I get something off my chest?"

Risa took a resigned sip of wine. "Feel free."

"I know Sanskrit was a big deal to you until you discovered that—*hello!*—Hindu culture is impossibly sexist. And I know you think your Skrit scraps are some sort of rebellion against that sexism. But the Brahmins you're counterattacking don't live anywhere near here, Risa, so the person you end up attacking is me. And I've had enough! *Please,* Risa. No more Sanskrit nonsense during our social life, especially!"

"But I wasn't attacking you at all," she said. "I was praising an unusual attribute. When *rudra* boils up in you, honest to God, Julian, you're *stunning.* So I conjured a word that praises the beauty of heatedness: *rudra.* Then Kyle was so cute, thinking it was a blazing-hot Korean dish, that I

308 DAVID JAMES DUNCAN

ran with it. Then you got mad, which got funny so fast I ran with that too. And look what happened! Audrey and Kyle really like each other! Can we be happy about that and try to enjoy each other now too?"

"If you promise to delete Skrit scraps from our life, yes," Julian said.

Risa held her wineglass up before the candle, shut one eye, and stared at the backlit red liquid as she swirled it round and round. "You've never let me explain my attraction to Skrit scraps. It would mean a lot to me if I could. May I?"

Julian heaved a pained sigh, but faintly nodded.

"In my experience, the human yearning for truth really *does* spiral inward. Without truth's inward momentum people get stuck on the surface of things and fall prey to appearances, cheap card tricks, political and religious power plays, banal hocus-pocus. Skrit scraps combat that danger by tapping into truth's inward momentum. *The Vedic mind is concentric,* Julian. It has three layers. *Manas* is the outermost layer. The great trickster of the soul. 'The faith and doubt organ,' the Upaniṣads call it. *Manas* is the machine that churns out opposites: certainty and uncertainty, attraction and repulsion, yes and no, forward and backward. This has its value, of course. But it lacks depth. Lacks heart. The nature of *manas* is to forever declare *I will, I won't, I'm happy, I'm sad, I like this, I hate that,* till a person is so bound up in a self-spun cocoon of mental impressions they go blind to everything but their cocoon. Incarnation after incarnation, the faith/doubt organ binds us this way. But in the Vedas—"

"*Wait!*" Julian cut in. "Hold on, Risa! *Incarnation after incarnation? That's* the kind of pretentious crap that has to go bye-bye! What have you experienced, besides a little teatime chitchat with your friends, that gives you any right to speak of *past incarnations?*"

Swirling her wine before the candle flame again, Risa waited till she was calm enough not to hurl Julian's scathing tone back in his face. "What I experience," she said quietly, "is a feeling of arrogance if I pretend that spiritual giants like the Buddha and Jesus and Krishna don't know more about such matters than I do. Would you contradict Beethoven if he shared secrets about composing symphonies, or diss Martina Navratilova's secrets about crushing top-spin serves, because what they said was beyond *your* experience? It's common sense to believe it when Buddha, Krishna, and Jesus in the Apocrypha all tell us reincarnation is the way of it. That's not *teatime chitchat.* My concepts of *mind* and *soul* are based on truths that realized beings bequeath humanity to free us from illusion. And Skrit scraps connect to this kind of wisdom. May I describe how?"

Julian's face had long since darkened, but he nodded.

As she was framing her thoughts Risa noticed her wine trembling. Julian's left knee, under the table, was bouncing up and down at a high rate of speed. Lifting her glass to stop the wine's shaking, she said, "According to Vedic wisdom sources, inside *manas,* the outer mind, is an incomparably greater mind. American Buddhists call it 'Bodhi Mind.' Tibetans call it *ripka*. The Sanskrit word is *buddhi*. I prefer the term 'heart/mind.' This mind, according to the greats, is infinite, clear, all-loving."

As his knee bounced like crazy, Julian said, "How can the finite *you* speak of the infinite without speaking drivel?"

Swirling her wine again to ease the sting of his words, Risa said, "To paraphrase the greats is not drivel. It's a form of trust known as *faith*. The truth about Bodhi Mind, *ripka,* heart/mind, say the greats, is that if we stop smothering it, it *is* our very own true mind! In sad contrast, the faith/doubt organ wraps us tighter and tighter into the cocoon of opposites that make heart/mind impossible to experience. Why squander my life listening to my doubting organ chant, *I like this, I hate that, I've decided, I can't decide, I'm going, I'm staying, I'm happy, I'm miserable*? That very chant is why we need a sadhana, a spiritual practice, that coaxes us into silence and depth. I've had meditations blissfully erase me *lots* of times, and humble Skrit words and John of the Cross phrases surprise-attack me with joy beyond words. I'm sharing the truth of my experience because I care about us, Julian. If you don't experience such things, fine. But why get worked up over *my* experience? Can't you view my Skrit scraps as an annoying but harmless quirk along the lines of, say, the way your knee keeps bouncing the entire table?"

Julian blushed, stopped bouncing, and snapped, "Your Skrit scraps are a hell of a lot weirder than my nervous tic!"

Risa broke out in an amused smile. "If this is some kind of contest and *weird* equals victory, compare my Skrit scraps to the way you jam your little finger in your ear and, when you think no one's looking, inhale its fragrance like a fine wine. My *manas* finds *that* pretty weird. But a more heartful place in me glimpses the curious little boy in you. Out of affection for that boy I recently did a little ear excavation myself, and there upon the tip of my pinky sat a fleck of lost pumpkin pie filling from *inside my own head*! And when I sniffed it? *Yowza!* An acrid smell like nothing else on Earth!"

Her giggle set Julian's knee to bouncing. He then noticed it and—out of pride, shame, confidence, lack of confidence, faith, want of faith, and a skein of other *manas* dichotomies—forced himself to hold rigidly, miserably still though he was seething.

"Aw, come on," Risa coaxed. "I'm not being derisive. We're funny little creatures, us humans. To wrap this up so we can relax, can you please believe that I love Skrit scraps because they awaken feelings of love? Love's a big deal in spiritual life, right? Sure, the couple thousand Skrit words I remember are pathetic in a scholarly sense, but they're *rife* with a centripetal energy that spirals into depth. I don't just *think* this, Julian. Skrit phrases have led to experiences that are *beacons* in my life and I don't want to lose that. I can be more discreet. But I'm hoping you can learn to ignore my scraps the way I'm ignoring your knee."

Julian blushed deeply, again stopped bouncing his knee, and snapped, "*Finished!?*"

Risa nodded but wished her wineglass was fuller.

"Then I'd like to say a few words as well."

"Of course."

"Back in my anthro days, I actually studied brain science. Unlike you, Risa! And 'brain' is the word I want. Not 'mind.' Not 'mind inside the mind.' Not 'heart/mind.' I mean the mind located in the organ in our heads. Every PhD in the field can tell you that the brain's dynamics give us the perception, the memory, and the consciousness that have led to the greatest achievements of mankind. Yet all I'm hearing from *you* is an eccentric laywoman trotting out prescientific bits of mythology or scripture, calling her bits *holy,* then using her vague concept of *holiness* to lord it over brain science—*even as your brain houses the awareness you're using to critique the brain*! Wake up, Risa! Our brains create art, symphonies, cures for disease, skyscrapers, jet planes, civilizations, and are *by far the most vital* part of us!"

"When it comes to architecture, science, engineering, the tools that build civilizations, *manas* dynamics are vital, I agree. But I hope you're enough of a historian to agree that, without guidance from heart/mind, *manas* dynamics *also* lead to selfishness, blind greed, blind prejudice, corrupt politics and business, diabolical weapons, police states, wrecked ecosystems, wars, and other forces that bring *down* civilizations. And I'm not even damning *that.* But when it comes to what you call 'the greatest achievements of mankind,' we're not on the same page. For me, the greatest achievement conceivable is to merge with ultimate reality. And heart/mind has experiences that show me *Buddha Mind, Christ Mind, Ram Mind* exists. My *manas* thinks heart/ mind isn't worthy of comment because it's not an object it can quantify via laboratory experiments or peer-reviewed studies, but I'm not interested in *manas*'s opinion of what reason can't know. In short, we disagree, Julian. I love the greats who say the Unseen Unborn Guileless Perfection is the essence of our being. *Manas* hears that as nonsense, but seeking spiritual truth with *manas* alone is like trying to play a guitar with my elbows, or hug you with my ears, or—"

"*Get you pregnant with my tongue,*" Julian cut in with a heat that caused Risa's mind to fly off the rails and crash in a dark ravine. *His tongue . . . My cleft . . . His tongue . . .*

Julian stood in the candlelight, glowing with *rudra.* "I just spoke out of something besides the faith/doubt organ. How did I do?"

Risa couldn't reply. Despite everything she'd just said, she felt susceptible to the way they too often detoured around their vital impasses: Julian *shone* in defiance of the spiritual greats, proud of what his tongue was capable of, urging her body to spiral outward and away from heart/mind to join him body to body. Desperate not to succumb, Risa summoned a Skrit scrap she'd taken to heart years ago: *She who knows the bliss of Ātman, bliss that turns away words, bliss the mind never touches, is afraid of nothing. Unassailed by the thought* Why do I do what is evil? *she knows good and evil as Ātman, cherishes both as Ātman.*

Seeing her lips moving, knowing she'd summoned a scrap, Julian showed no impatience. He just blazed, willing to take or leave whatever she chose. And it struck her: while he was effortlessly embodying physical beauty, she was laboriously debating her spirituality when she needed to be embodying it with all her heart. O *Rudra who bestowest happiness and dwellest in Julian's body! Why does his arrogant patience awaken my weakness?*

Their differences were profound, the impasse long. When Risa stood, she meant to simply take her empty wineglass into the kitchen, but as she rounded the table found herself taking a half step toward Julian. Inches at most. She glanced up to see if he'd noticed.

His gaze, still upon her, was dark; exultant; shining.

She set her wineglass on the table. The invisible rope she'd tried to climb to safety snapped. Her dumbsaint memory bank went haywire, seizing on lines from a Beguine book: *You, Marguerite of Hainault, called Porete, are vehemently suspected of the stain of heretical depravity. Because of this we have caused you to be summoned, that you might appear before us in judgment.*

It was Risa who then broke free of the inward spiral and strode round the table; Risa the Sons Only Verse rebel who smothered Julian's lips with her own; Risa the heart/mind defender who let herself be drawn like a moth/hedonist/hypocrite, praying all three were Ātman, to the candle of his face, feel of their glowing skin, flame of his unspeaking tongue.

(Portland, mid-1990s, December)

X. Jervis on World Peace

By means of all created things, without exception, the divine assails us, penetrates us, and molds us. We imagined it as distant and inaccessible, whereas in fact we live steeped in its burning layers.

—Teilhard de Chardin

On a rainy December morning, Jervis and TJ are walking a quiet street at the foot of Forest Park when, apropos of nothing of which TJ is aware, Jervis slams to a halt behind a parked car, eyes its bumper stickers, and in his papery voice rasps, "'Pray for Peace. Visualize World Peace.' What do you think, Teej?"

TJ would prefer not to reply, but figures Jervis might know what he's thinking already. So he speaks, but keeps it short. "Judging by the evidence, I'd say that *world peace* is not even close to the hand this world has been dealt."

"That's it, Teej!" Jervis paper-whispers. "These stickers are ordering us not to inhabit the world we've been given. The way I see it, Earth might be a precious fleck of blazing-hot chili pepper in an infinite vat of mayonnaise. The way I see it, we should wrap our arms around our tiny planet's endless chaos and injustices and suffering while we've got the chance. There are so many shapes and sizes of self-serving pigs, mass delusions, violence, and peacelessness on Earth that the situation should be studied, not wished away. *The fuck.* A VISUALIZE WORLD PEACE sticker shows all the imagination of a DO NOT DISTURB sign. If I drove a car my sticker would say MAKE YOUR PEACE WITH THE RED HOT SMOKIN' PEACE WE'VE GOT!"

TJ can't hide his amusement. "You're pretty worked up about this."

Jervis eyes the offending bumper darkly. "Screw ordering random motorists to remake the universe to suit their prejudices. If the last few centuries had known world peace, a plague of happy fucking would have raised Earth's population by fifty billion and we'd be dead of the effects of *that*."

"Well then," TJ says with a tight little smile, "peace to earthquakes, tsunamis, wildfires, and the Black Death."

Jervis shoots air in and out his nose. "That's the idea. But *let 'er rip, Teej.*"

Standing in the rain in his high-fashion clothes, TJ tries his genteel best. "Peace to warmongers, racist slobs, STDs, unlevel playing fields, undescended testicles, the Bermuda Triangle, and Tornado Alley. *All is an Ocean.*"

"Which accepts all the flowers and coconuts and filth and gore that flows or falls or gets spumed into her forever! That's it, Teej! That's it."

Jervis closes his good eye, peers at God knows what with the glass one, and undergoes some kind of liftoff: "Peace to that royal fuckup 'thy neighbor,' and to Jesus's hilarious command to love him. Peace to my Kearney Street neighbor Dick Strom, and his lucrative investments in weapons for the world's dictators, and corporate theft of the world's poor people's water. Peace to Dick's addict son, Dick Junior, who ripped out and pawned his eighty-year-old grandma's car stereo last month trying to live by his dad's example. Peace to Dick Senior for saying, 'I don't know what's gotten into that boy!' Peace to Jesse Helms for saying, 'I'm not intolerant. I just know what it says in the Scriptures.'"

TJ is surprised by a feeling of expansion as Jervis's paper-whisper begins to sound downright reverent, though his words, at first, sound anything but.

"Peace to my unwanted virginity, Teej. Peace to the decades it's been since a woman touched me with even faint sexual intent. Peace to the insane idea that virgins are pure. *I'm* a virgin. Peace to my useless nighttime virgin erections. Peace to my virgin dream, four nights ago, of standing next to a woman so sensuous that nothing but the circling slide of her wet red tongue over her own wet red lips brought first her, then me, to orgasm. Peace to the fact that every bit of my wrecked body loved that lonely little orgasm. It was a surge of Ocean. A perfect little surge. Peace to the sword Love brought to Earth as Jesus and the Kurukshetra battlefield slaughter Love brought as Krishna and the burned-at-the-stake agony Love gave Herself as Marguerite, Dirk Willems, and Joan of Arc. Peace to the meth thugs who beat my brains and stomped my throat when I imperfectly served the same Love. Peace to the hundred hurts and incapacities that brought Ocean's crushing capacity down upon me. Peace to the storm tides that slam me around like a sloop in a gale with no sails or rudder. Peace to the Transorpene that quells the storms with side effects so strong that giving voice to side effects may be my only purpose in life. Peace to that purposelessness. Peace to the fact that I was just a container of love till Love smashed the container and the Uncontainable came gushing out. Peace to the way Ocean sooner or later pours every fool who thinks they fathom the holy a triple shot of *Old Unfathomable*, tosses it down their throat, throws in a match, and incinerates everything they ever claimed to fathom. Peace to every force, accident, crash, blow, curse, and blessing that murders our complacency. Peace to my wrecked voice for the things a wrecked voice can say that an unwrecked voice can't. Peace to my glass eye and empty eye socket for seeing things that a seeing eye can't. Blackness, for instance.

in Buddhism, when a person's ego is reduced to 'no thing,' that person *becomes mu.* This *no-thing-ness,* this void, this emptiness allows what they call 'the ten thousand things' to flood the empty container, so that all creation is now inside of *you.*"

Walt sat quiet, his expression so neutral that Lore realized Walt was more than a little *mu* himself—which made her want to tell him more.

"Japhy's young but very precocious in some ways," she said. "He plays guitar super well for his age. He has a little Buddhist meditation practice going. And more than that, Walt, he grasps the beauty of Joshu's answer about *mu.* He's an odd bird. Fragile as a bird in some ways, but not in others. I warned him that kids will tease a Mu. He looked me in the eye and said if he becomes Mu he'll be No Thing, and a No Thing *can't* be teased. 'Good answer,' I said, but I still doubt Mu will work as a name. Japh said, 'Teasing a Mu is like teasing Two Medicine, Mom. What does the Peak care?' More solid dharma from my whippersnapper. Then he threw me a curve. The older kids at school have been calling him Jap. I didn't know this. 'No more *Jap,* Mom,' he said. 'I'll come in and eat breakfast soon as you agree I'm Mu!' And out the door he flew. Leaving me stewing. Then you knocked."

"So Mu Jantz, his name'd be," Walt said.

"I guess it would. I'm feeling so resistant I hadn't thought that far."

Walt finished his coffee. "Can I tell you something might surprise you?" She nodded.

"Mu might be just the name for that boy. Names these days are all over the map. I've got grandkids named Snowy and Presley. That's a pet rabbit and Elvis to me, but they're happy kids. Here's what I like about the name Mu. He chose it for himself. He's willing to pay the price of it being odd. And the name will end his dad's JJ and Three J crap."

Lorilee smiled. Hearing a stern but kind old man in a VFW cap say "Mu" a couple times was beginning to normalize it for her.

"One more thing," Walt said. "I reckon it'll cost something to change his name. And I reckon you're strapped. I'd gladly pay to help you let Mu become Mu."

Lore smiled again. "Mu's not the only one whose mind is made up!"

"Can I meet the boy?" Walt asked. "I've got a little something to show you both."

OUT UNDER THE tree, Walt extended his hand and wowed the young Buddhist formerly known as Japhy by saying, "Mu Jantz? Walt Steitz. Very pleased to meet you."

Mu jumped to his feet, shook with Walt, and shot his mom a grin.

Walt then double-dazzled the boy by inviting them to take a ride in his '54 Chev.

As they tooled around Pipestone, Walt grew downright chatty. "The wraparound windows were new in '54. That and the forest green were two reasons my wife let me buy it. Hear how it purrs like a saber-tooth tiger, Mu? Dee Anna purred that way too, so this was to be her truck. But the original 215-inch cube only purred like a mountain lion, and it threw rods. Former owner sold cheap the second time she blew. I scrapped the 215 and dropped in a 235-inch. She's run like a sabertooth ever since. Odometer's synced to the new engine. Not quite 6K on the tiger, see there? Dee Anna and I went for a couple rides, but you're my first two passengers since Dee passed. She would've liked that."

I do like it! a silent voice told a chunk of Walt's head, making him smile. *And why are* you *still driving?*

Walt pulled over and asked if Lorilee would like to take the wheel.

"I've only driven automatics," she said.

Walt shrugged. "Burn out the clutch learnin' and I'll pop in a new one."

Are there forty-year-old versions of this guy? Lore wondered.

For the next half hour Walt instructed, Lore cried, "*Sorry!*" every time she herky-jerked the clutch and killed the engine, and Mu repeatedly laughed.

"Here's an idea," Walt told her. "How 'bout, next time you kill it, you give up on prim little *sorries*, tell Mu to cover his ears, and do some proper Yankee cussin'?"

When Lore began to cuss with skill, an amazed Mu laughed harder—and an amazed Lore immediately began to operate the clutch almost perfectly. "See?" Walt said. "You cuss the tightness away, let the chips fall, the ol' girl starts to like you."

He made the lesson more difficult, coaching Lore on how to stop and go on inclines. He had her drive to the county fairgrounds and practice parallel parking between orange cones in the big grassy lot. Lore did so well Mu was disappointed. He wanted more cusses. After a fourth straight perfect parking job, Walt said, "Could you shut 'er off please, Miss Lore?"

They got out, strolled over to picnic tables under a big stand of poplars, sat down, and admired the forest-green truck from a distance.

You know what to do, said Walt's favorite voice.

"I got a story for you two, and a little surprise to go with it. You ready?"

Mu nodded. Lore didn't know what to think but said, "I guess."

"I'm not a worrier by habit. But the first night you hiked that mountain I tossed and turned and wore myself out pretty good. Second night started the same. Then something crazy as angels on riding mowers happened. Dee Anna showed up. Just her voice, but I could feel her in it. And she sounded good. Happy. *Bossy!* What she told me, Lore and Mu, was this. *Walter Steitz. Give me one good reason why my '54 Chev shouldn't be Miss Lore's?*"

Mu's eyes got huge. Lore cried, "That's *way* too generous, Walt!"

Walt cinched down his cap and scowled like the military man he was. "It wasn't me proposed it. My hands are tied. 'Miss Lore's got a long road ahead and drives a rust-bucket Civic with a quarter million miles on it,' Dee said. '*You've* got four perfect trucks, a newish Buick, and not much road left at all. And one more thing, Walter Steitz,' she added. 'Lore and Mu have music to take to the world and that truck is just a truck. They need a *rig*. Before they leave Pipestone, ask Lore to borrow Mu so you and he can build a sleeping pod for the back. Give 'em a place to snooze on the cheap,' she says. So now I'm lying awake hours on end planning the pod. But Dee Anna *still* wasn't finished! About dawn she orders me to add a cargo trailer to keep your instruments locked up. You can see how this is going, Lore and Mu. Dee's gonna dream-boss me to *death* if I don't get rid of this dang truck. She even bossed me on how to break the news to you."

Lore was smiling now. "How was that?"

The old man busted out a wobbly baritone that stunned Mu and half broke Lorilee's heart:

He reached for her hand, and he slipped her his keys…

With which he did.

And he said, Miss Lorilee my lass,
We've no more use for these.
Before fate can break my stride
Let Dee and me
Give Mu and you
The '54 to rrrrrrrrride!

XII. Dungeon

The souls in Dante's *Purgatorio* suffer the same kind of torments as those in the *Inferno,* but with willing acceptance...We do not suddenly exchange our enslavement to the fogs and sufferings of our condition for a wholly conscious climb to a sunlit summit. What we experience is the total transformation of the nature of darkness itself.

— Father Pat Hawk

How OFTEN HAS a self-deluded, philandering, absentee narcissist father been transformed by a combination of comeuppances into an attentive, loving, spiritually sensitive father? Your narrator, the Holy Goat, would have answered *Never!* had I not met a daughter who swears her father gave just such a transformation a hell of a run.

Dave McKeig's sea change began in 1989, on the abysmally informative morning he answered his phone and heard the voice he loved most in the world forbid him to speak. From a gas station on I-5, Risa had used a pay phone to tell him she'd been usurped by the eight-year-old girl she'd been on the day Dave abandoned her to the mothering of a walking, talking vodka receptacle and the fathering of an unloaded pile of his scratched-up reject blues records. For the next fourteen years, she told him, based on six or seven half-day visits and a score of long-distance phone calls, Dave denied that he'd abandoned her at all. That kind of fathering, she said, would drive a soft girl crazy, so she'd made herself hard. So hard that, early that morning, the young man she loved, tired of her hardness, bedded a softer woman, then fled to the Montana mountain range that Dave of all people had once extolled to him.

When Dave blurted a few words of apology only to realize the phone had gone dead, he finally, fully conjured the eight-year-old hiding in her bedroom night after night, listening to the half-ruined records he and she had once danced to while, out in the living room, her priest-damned and besotted mother gabbled at a TV. Recalling the comfort it had given him to phone this same daughter, usually during his evening wine buzz, just to hear the yearning in her voice as he too gabbled as if to a drinking buddy about his "serial conflagrations" and "lady friends," he fell into a sloeblack, slow, black, crowblack dungeon like nothing he'd ever experienced. His face in the mirror became an object of disgust. His charm struck him as utterly counterfeit. His doting-father pretensions made him nauseous. That Risa was anything more than a neurotic wreck struck him as a miracle. That she'd managed to become the person she was in defiance of who *he* was struck him as an act of heroism worthy of a Homeric epic.

Since the day of that call, Risa had not once phoned him. She also refused to pick up when caller ID identified him. He heard not a word from her as she finished at U Dub. He went to her graduation with a fat check meant to help her with grad school—but she didn't attend the ceremony. He had to mail her the money. Then away she flew to Providence, where her radio silence continued from late May until the following Christmas morning.

When she had finally picked up her phone to field Dave's Xmas call, his heart leapt at the sound of her voice. He then heard her say, "Please don't phone unless it's an emergency. Anything you say, even 'Merry Christmas,' just hurts when it arrives through a piece of plastic held to my ear. It's not that I'm trying to hurt you back. It's just that phones, for us, became hopelessly loaded a long time ago. Since I don't want you to worry about whether I'm alive, let's try postcards. Short ones, please. I'm sorry I can't talk anymore. I'm even sorrier for all the years that made it this way. Bye, Dave." *Click.*

Dave did try postcards, but Risa's responses were so brief and dull they frightened him—till the day he realized each card had consisted of seventeen syllables. She was deliberately penning him the most pedestrian haikus ever written:

I'm fine, thanks for asking. Busy here.
School, work, play, and more. Hope you're well.

He kept sending birthday and Xmas checks, but now cringed to recall that he'd settled on checks in the first place so he wouldn't have to "waste time" researching and shopping for more thoughtful gifts. In a crass attempt to lessen his shame he doubled, then tripled the amounts of the checks, hoping Risa would spend some of the money on a plane ticket and visit him. When her stony haikus mentioned no such plans, Dave experienced the same merciless chest ache he'd so blithely bequeathed Risa from the age of eight to the age of twenty-two.

Abject shame finally drove him to break the postcards-only agreement just long enough to confess to what he was feeling:

Dear Risa,

Last night I sat down to write you a "chatty letter," hoping it might coax you into doing the same, only to realize there's nothing in my life worth chatting about. My work as a loan officer, without the flirtations I've sworn off for fear of another mis-marriage, is the boring practice of usury it always was. Any yarns I might share with you would just reopen wounds I inflicted by being little more than a yarn-spinner to you all these years.

Hoping to find a fresh way to approach you, I've tried therapy. The woman who told me, "Your sincere apology would suffice if your daughter would just see reason," struck me as stupidly blind to my unreason. The man who said, "Let's ease you through this unnecessary low point with a prescription," struck me as a dope dealer. Then came the woman who looked me in the eye and said, "Judging by all you've told me, Dave, I advise you to admit your fathering has been a cruel hoax all along. If you love her, I'm sure you'll admire your daughter as much I do for pushing that hoax away."

This therapist I still see, and here's the truth we agree I must cop to: I abandoned you inexcusably—then said I didn't! The reason I said I didn't is that I've always felt how much I love you. But instead of offering you that love I kept chasing women as self-absorbed as me, telling myself my life apart from you was protecting you from them. Meanwhile I'd left you alone with Moira without the slightest idea of how awful that was. All of this will sicken me to my grave. I deserve your silence. All your life you deserved a father who expressed his love in spontaneous, creative, respectful ways. I talked my love for you to death over a phone.

I've been a liar and a fool, and no words can right this.

I owe you actions that convey love. No more talk.

—Dave

A week later Dave received this postcard reply:

Thank you for finally recognizing your abandonment for what it was.

And I do hope you learn to convey love spontaneously, creatively, and respectfully. I hope that for everyone. But if, anytime soon, you feel you've found a way to show such a love to me in person, don't. I wish you luck with your process. I do not wish to play a part in it.

—Risa

Reading this, Dave felt sick even as he nodded in agreement: he had nothing to share with his lovely daughter but the darkness of his dungeon.

*   *   *

THREE YEARS INTO Risa's sojourn in Rhode Island, Dave stumbled, as it were, upon the stub of a candle lying abandoned on his dungeon floor. It consisted of five one-syllable words that fall at the end of a poem he'd studied a lifetime ago at Princeton. He knew the poem's title, but chose not to turn the candle stub into a graceful taper by looking the poem up. The man who'd penned it, he remembered, was terribly eloquent, and as a lifelong manipulator of his own eloquence the stuff now made him ill. All Dave wanted from the poem was the five-word stub he'd found by feel in darkness.

The stub was from Rilke. Its five blunt words: "You must change your life." As he whispered them aloud they struck a match in his mind. Before its flame could die he held it to the tiny blackened wick of the stub. A light flared, revealing the face he had always loved the most by far—and there was suddenly nothing he wanted in all the world but to *change the life* of the failed father he'd always been.

He had no access to Risa by voice or mail. He could think of no gift on Earth that would lessen his crimes. After long, desperate thought, he realized the only material in his keeping that connected in any meaning-ful way to his child were six boxes of Sanskrit and Vedic literature abandoned in the rafters of his garage. He had never forgotten the love in Risa's voice, early in college, when she spoke of "Skrit Lit." The wonders encountered there had made her glow like campfire embers modulated by night zephyrs. He remembered how, at about the same time she'd delivered the books to his rafters, the glow had gone missing. "Why?" he whispered—and at last found himself aimed, like Rama's bow, at its proper target.

He fetched a stepladder and carried the boxes down out of the rafters. Their heft flooded his mind with questions: *Did she forsake the books she loved most because I forsook the person I love most? If I study the books hard enough, might I come to love and trust them as she once did? If so, might I be able to coax her back toward the wisdom that once helped her glow even in the darkness of my mistreatment of her?*

Dave did not seek answers to his questions. He undertook actions aimed at connecting to his daughter. Carrying the boxes down to his basement den, he fetched an X-Acto knife. In cutting through the many layers of packing and fiber tape, he took note of how hard Risa had worked to *entomb* her once-loved books. He carefully emptied out the books and counted them: 173 volumes. He stacked and measured them, calculating the exact amount of shelf space they'd need. At his garage workbench he built a rough-hewn pine bookshelf custom-sized to Risa's Skrit library. He bought a new reading chair, a standing lamp to set beside it, and a card table to serve as a makeshift desk.

Settling gratefully into his scholar's dungeon, he spent preliminary hours poring over titles, forewords, and scholarly introductions, then shelved the books by category. He pondered his approach carefully, realizing that he must deepen his reading experience by reflecting and journaling about anything and everything that struck him, just as Risa had done. Selecting one of Risa's five Bhagavad Gita translations to start, he sat down in his reading chair and set out to forge, with his grown child's once-loved library, a relationship as intimate and steadfast as his relationship with that child should have been all along.

(Portland, 1990 through 1993)

XIII. The Ocean at Night

a particle is a thing in itself. a wave is a disturbance in something else. waves themselves are probably not disturbed.
　　　　　—Anne Carson, in an email to Sam Anderson

DURING THE FIRST year of Jervis's life as an Ocean-walker TJ vehemently protested the second long walk of the day: the night walk. The purposeless purpose of Jervis's day walks was clearly a blithe, sociably chaotic exchange with countless numbers of Portland's populace. The night walks, in contrast, were furtive and seemingly purposeful, but to hear Jervis describe them was not clarifying. "I wander around obeying a few Ocean strobes. That's all it is, Teej," he'd say—while the dark and more dangerous city and mysterious nature of Jervis's *obedience* made TJ fear nightly for Jervis's life.

As the years passed Jervis's night walks took on a sameness: he invariably wore a little backpack before setting out on small missions, which he reloaded after each mission, sometimes three or four times a night, often with TJ's help. Jervis was mum about details, but as the supplier of much of the contents of Jervis's pack, TJ had long since deduced that the night walks were conducted in the service of certain Ocean-designated people, some of them in dire straits, others seemingly not. TJ himself, at Jervis's request, had loaded the pack with things as varied as money, books, specific articles of clothing, toys, food, poetry, cheap musical instruments, booze, an occasional xeroxed Eckhart sermon or Beguine mystic's rapture, recently written notes from certain people to other people, and whatever else Ocean urged Jervis to pass along. In rainy weather he also carried two wool blankets and two plastic tarps to dispense to people sleeping on streets or in parks—but if Ocean failed to disclose the precise person who was to receive these gifts, Jervis would walk right past people sleeping on cold or rain-soaked sidewalks and return the tarps and blankets to the closet in his monk's cell. I, the Holy Goat, once probed Jervis about this seeming lack of compassion. He told me, "*The fuck,* HG. I'm not a missionary doing mission work. I'm Ocean's. I do the actions in the images she strobes. What the actions do or don't do is up to her, not me. Simple obedience is how I stay inside her. Staying inside her matters more than anything else."

Fair enough for a hardcore mystic speaking of his bride. But as TJ points out, Jervis is incapable of even a mild act of self-protective violence, he takes his night walks unarmed every night of the year, and he conveys Ocean's messages, gifts, payments, inscrutable runes, warnings, thanks, and so on to people in dive apartments, seedy bars, hospitals, back alleys, night-blackened freeway underpasses, homeless camps, and—less dangerously but even more alarmingly—to people dining in Portland's finest restaurants, drinking martinis in jazz clubs, sitting in auditoriums enjoying symphonies, and other startlingly high-end locations he enters at the risk of being arrested and jailed, though that never seems to happen.

Desperately curious about all of this, TJ repeatedly asked Jervis to include him on at least one night walk. Jervis refused. The best TJ could do was convince him to come by Étouffée Bruté after closing, no matter how late, for what their dad Alasdair used to call "a wee dram" so TJ would know he'd survived his night walk. Over their late whiskies Jervis often assured TJ that he wouldn't worry if he knew how completely Ocean dictated where he went, who he saw, what he said and did, and, just as crucially, where he did *not* go, and what people and actions Ocean strobed him to *avoid*. But Jervis's occasional stories of the things he actually did on night walks, despite his assurances, kept TJ's level of concern for him very high.

Years passed and Teej kept trying to put a brave face on it. But in 1993, during a spate of unsolved, possibly serial murders on Portland's night streets, he suffered chronic sleeplessness and grew so haggard that Jervis finally had mercy: on a cold, wet day in March, he told TJ that Ocean had given permission for TJ to join him on a night walk for one hour, from 8 to 9 p.m. TJ found the proposed brevity ridiculous, and said so.

"Take it or leave it, Teej," came the papery reply.

WHEN THE BROTHERS met at the main entrance of TJ's Pearl Building, a Pacific storm had rolled in, a chill rain was blowing sideways, and when Jervis appeared in his unvarying Grundéns rain slicker his jeans were already sopped and his high-top red Converses shot water out the lace holes at every step. Tavish Jacobus McGraff presented a very different picture. Under a London Fog raincoat he had on pressed slacks, perfectly polished lace-up brown oxfords, a light sport coat that left his white dress shirt and silk tie showing at the collar, a natty fedora, and he was using a black umbrella he planned to quickly close and deploy as a sword to ward off street pirates if necessary, like John, the brother of Wendy, in *Peter Pan*.

Jervis's first words: "The fuck, Teej. You look like Bogart in *Casablanca*."

"Is Ocean enforcing a dress code?" TJ fired back. "Since it's only an hour, Jervis, I didn't cancel a kind invitation from friends to have dessert and drinks after."

They set out at 8:00 p.m. precisely. The deluge continued without a break, so TJ figured the streets would be empty, allowing him no real sense of how Jervis and Ocean worked together. But after Jervis had taken them on an incomprehensible zigzag route for about five blocks he zeroed in on a distant lump on the sidewalk. As they drew closer, TJ made out a human shape slumped against a warehouse wall. Closer yet, he was dismayed to see the shape turn into a large, powerfully built man.

As Jervis knelt beside him, shed his pack, and lifted out a blanket and tarp, TJ studied the man more closely, then wished he hadn't. His face, like his fists, was scabbed and scarred, his nose spectacularly misshapen, and his lips had been split so many times they were crosshatched in a way that brought to mind whipping scars. Despite the wind and rain TJ smelled stale alcohol and urine. The man also looked Native American, hence a victim, which caused TJ's fear of him to shame him doubly. But his brutalized face and powerful body looked more than capable of making Jervis a victim too.

"Go on ahead, Teej," Jervis told him. "We're gonna blanket him. We got this."

We. The pronoun resounded. Jervis was in the throes of obedience to his unseen Oceanic beloved. TJ, meanwhile, was standing in a deluge on a dark street, deeply regretting clothing choices that pretty well shouted, *I'm rich! Come rob me!* But he did not *go on ahead.*

Jervis set to work with a thoroughness that struck TJ as suicidal. He lifted each of the man's legs, working the blanket under to protect them from the cold sidewalk. He rocked him from side to side to get the blanket under his butt. He pulled the man's head onto his own shoulder to get the blanket between his back and the cold concrete wall. "*Good enough!*" TJ hissed. "And just *leave* the damned tarp! The rattling plastic will wake him for sure!"

As if TJ didn't exist, Jervis began tucking the tarp under the man's legs, under his ass, wrapped it round his torso, sheltered his head. To TJ the tarp's crumpling sounded like machine-gun fire. Jervis just kept wrapping and tucking.

The speed and inevitability with which the Indian exploded into action caused TJ to shriek like a dying rabbit, then freeze: the man's right hand held Jervis tight by the throat of the Grundéns; his left hand held a knife to Jervis's throat. Sick with fear, TJ closed his umbrella and *became* John in *Peter Pan,* wondering whether to stab the Indian with the umbrella tip *before* he slit Jervis's throat, or after.

But as the man stared wildly into Jervis's eyes, he felt no resistance. He turned to TJ, saw terror. Turned back to Jervis: no fear at all.

"It's pouring rain" came the papery whisper, "so I'm covering you with a blanket and tarp. Then I'll leave and you can go back to sleep."

The Indian looked at the blanket and tarp covering his legs and body, at the rain running off the tarp, at Jervis. He then grunted as if he'd been hit by a brick and passed out, his knife clattering to the sidewalk.

Flooded with relief, TJ said, "Let's go! *Now!*" He then gaped in disbelief as Jervis picked up the knife, closed the four-inch blade, and with great care slid the weapon into the man's pants pocket. Only then did he finish tucking in the tarp to his satisfaction, stand, and without another glance at TJ or the man, trudge away down the sidewalk.

TJ locked step with Jervis, waited till they turned a corner and the Indian was out of sight, then grabbed his brother by the shoulder and went off: "*I* saw it coming, *you* saw it coming, and *still* you prodded and poked him. It's like you *wanted* to get killed! And you came *so close*! *Sooooo* close! And then, *Jesus Christ,* Jervis! Then *you give him his fucking knife back*? Was that *obedience*? Was that your omniscient Ocean strobing, *Give this lethal drunk the switchblade he just held to your throat in case he'd like to finish the job later*?"

Jervis looked mystified. "Ocean didn't have to strobe, Teej. It was *his* knife."

"I can't *believe* this! I feel like *slapping you*. How are you even *alive* if this is what your night walks are?"

"I'm alive because this *isn't* what our night walks are," Jervis paper-whispered.

"How can you say that?" TJ fumed. "What the hell do you mean?"

"*You're* here, Teej."

"Yes I *am*!" TJ cried. "So you're being second-guessed, which goes against your mystical pact with Ocean. But *Christ,* Jervis! Even though *you* survived, you can't know that man won't slit someone else's throat before morning!"

Jervis threw back his hood and let the rain soak him. "Listen to you. We invited you on an Ocean-walk but you didn't come with us. You don't see the night, and you don't feel Ocean. You're just all *thinky talky scared,* forcing me to *thinky talk* with you. And on night walks that could kill us."

"After what you just did you say *I'm* the one putting us in danger?" TJ fumed.

"We blanketed and tarped him, Teej. That's all she asked. You wanted me to rob him because your thinkyness says that'd make Portland safer. I don't listen to *thinky*. If it's *thinkyness* you want, keep getting mad as hell at everything you don't understand, start a radio talk show, and yell worthless thinky crap at your guests."

"Welcome to my show and here's what I think! Your faith in Ocean has you trudging through a crime-filled city for hours every night *wearing a blindfold*!"

Jervis gazed at TJ, closed his seeing eye, read the rain or night with his glass eye, opened the good eye, and said, "You *do* think that. I see that. Okay, Teej. Okay. She's not telling me this, but this one time, if you want, I'll get all *thinky* and *explainy*. Would you like that?"

A fierce nod from TJ.

"Here's what you don't get. Feeling Ocean is *everything* at night. And Ocean can only strobe images to a free nothingness. I stay *gone*. No messing around ping-ponging with people like on day walks. At night she strobes images fast and furious. It takes all my concentration to get to the places in the images, do the actions, speak the words. The free nothingness obeys them because they're *her* places, *her* actions, *her* words. *That's* the safety, Teej. The *only* safety. How would *I* have known, when we left the Pearl, which street had three unfriendlies ready to smash me and roll the guy in the *Casablanca* duds? I didn't. But a free nothingness did when Ocean strobed, *Turn right after a block, go straight for three blocks, turn left for half a block, help the Indian.* That's all it is, Teej. And that's *everything.* You with me so far?"

TJ looked nervously up and down the street, humbled and confused to think Ocean had taken his clothes into account and protected him, and that Jervis *staying gone* had made that possible. "I'm with you," he mumbled.

"Okay. You know how other minds leak into mine because I'm munched. But I haven't told you how murky little movies leak in too. I glimpse times and places that aren't here and now. Things that haven't happened, but might, pour in. The murk movies are like this." He made wild, wavery motions with his hands beneath the streetlights. "Ocean's strobe images are clear and quick as this." He snapped his fingers. "So at night I ignore murk movies. At night her images show what to do and what to leave alone every step, every breath. But to make sense of the knife I'll ignore her for a bit and tell you some murk stuff I saw. Do you want that?"

TJ realized he was way out of his depth. Again he peered up and down the street. No one. "I guess," he said doubtfully.

"Ocean walks me past people like that Indian every night, but has me blanket maybe one in thirty. It's not about blankets, Teej. I told you, I'm not a Salvation Army do-gooder. Ocean uses me to give people things, but the main gift is something *behind* or *inside* the giving. Something I can't see. Her scope is unlimited and I'm limited so I don't ask to see. But I do feel how there's a kind of...*misery of the heart* that gets her attention. Do-gooders do good but can't detect that misery. Ocean's insane mercy sends me right *at* the misery time after time. Your thinkyness is prob'ly thinking, *Why does she ease the misery of some but not others?* It's a useless question, Teej. It's *her* mercy. I'm just the hired help. But in the murk movie just now, here's what I glimpsed.

"In a few days the man we blanketed might pawn the knife I put back. It's worth a few bucks. He might pawn other stuff he's stashed too. *Stolen stuff,* your thinkyness is thinking." TJ winced. Jervis had read his thought as fast as he'd thought it. "But he might use the money to buy a Greyhound ticket to the place he's from. A rez town, maybe. Somewhere piney. Eastern Washington? Idaho? I don't know and it doesn't matter that I don't. But in the murk movie I saw his tremors and terrors on the bus. Saw him in hell by the time he gets to the town. Saw he might climb all sick off the bus, and this old woman might spot him and call out, '*Floyd. Floyd Old Person.*' And the Indian will be afraid, the movie showed, because the old woman loves him and people who love drunks want to cut off their drink. '*The sweats'll get you through this,*' she might say. I heard 'the sweats' and

'Floyd Old Person.' Is Floyd the man we blanketed or the man who leads the sweats? Don't know. Will the man we blanketed *do* the sweats and get human again? Don't know. All I know is, Ocean's up to something with that man's misery of the heart."

A sideways rain gust ripped at Jervis's fallen halo of hair. He didn't react.

"Somehow," TJ admitted, "I believe every word you just said."

"I'm glad," Jervis said. "But we're being *thinky* as hell, so a free nothingness isn't being Ocean guided. Random Portland ping-pong has taken over, and that's the blindfold you *should* be scared of. When I'm not inside a free nothingness, someone bent could come round a corner and hard things could happen fast."

TJ's skin crawled as he looked in every direction. "If telling me this stuff makes us that vulnerable, why are you doing it?"

"So you'll give up talk radio and stop yelling when you don't understand. And so you won't be sad when we obey another image she strobed."

TJ knew what was coming, and felt crushingly sad.

"This night walk is our last. *TJ can't feel me on the streets, so I can't protect him,* was in her strobe. *And when you get thinky to help him understand I can't protect you either.* Ocean-walks at night are beyond understanding, Teej. The little you saw is all I can show you."

Looking miserable, TJ said, "So now I'm supposed to join my friends and not worry as you wander from now till midnight through countless events like the one I just saw?"

"From now till midnight won't be anything like what you saw," Jervis said.

"Why not?" TJ asked.

"Because only Ocean and a free nothingness will be there."

TJ bristled a little. "Without my stupidity distracting you, you're saying, Ocean's strobes guide you nonstop? Can you *promise me that,* Jervis? Is that completely true?"

"It's true, Teej. I promise. And wanna hear what else she strobed?"

TJ looked doubtful, but nodded.

"She strobed that you aren't going to worry about me anymore."

TJ snorted. "How is *that* going to work?"

"The same way Portland pissants and night streets bring out a free nothingness that erases me, feeding people great food and being generous brings out a free nothingness that erases you. *The fuck,* Teej. After all this time don't you see how it works? The free nothingness that erases me gives away what the free nothingness that erases you provides. We're two heads, four hands, and four legs in two places putting our free nothingness at Ocean's service. Then Étouffée closes and we have a dram and say thanks. That's all it is."

TJ peered at the rain blasting past the streetlights, beating on cold asphalt and concrete walls, beating on his very small brother in his squishy Converses, soaked jeans, Grundéns slicker—and there was so little to the man before him that TJ found nothing to disagree with and suddenly trusted his every word. "At least you're dressed for it," he said.

"And you're not," Jervis paper-whispered. "So listen. To meet your friends and get to the dessert, go back to the Pearl the *exact same way we came*. Right in half a block, straight for three blocks, left half a block to the Pearl. No shortcuts. Passing by the Indian included. And take a cab or drive with your friends. Don't test her. Promise her."

What a solace to TJ, there in the rain, cold, and dark, to feel Ocean using Jervis's obedience to protect them both from who knew what. "I promise," he said. "And please thank her for me, Jervis. You'll know just how."

"You're standing in her, Teej. You're breathing her. She's loving you more than you or I know how to love anything. Thank her *your* way, Teej. Mean it."

Mean it. TJ thought this over carefully, then lay his umbrella on the sidewalk. Stepping up to Jervis, he threw his arms around him, lifted him off the ground, and began spinning him in circles with his cheek tight to Jervis's bony little chest. "*Thank you, Ocean,*" he said, "*for my brother, Jervis. And thanks for showing Jervis how free nothingness keeps us in this together. Thanks for targeting misery of the heart, and for Floyd Old Person, and for the Indian Jervis blanketed if he's not Floyd. Thanks for the old woman in the little town, for the sweats, and for strobing how to get me safe to the Pearl. Despite the trillion things I can't feel or understand about you, I feel that you feel me, and I'm very grateful. You know I mean this, Ocean. For all of it, thank you.*"

With that, TJ stopped spinning, set Jervis down with care in case he'd grown dizzy, picked up his Peter Pan sword and reopened it, and stood there on the rain-blasted sidewalk looking serene and dapper as you please.

Jervis shot air in and out his nostrils. "Here's looking at you, kid," he paper-whispered.

With a tight little smile TJ tipped his fedora, they turned in opposite directions, and into the one rain, one night, one free nothingness, away my twin heroes went.

XIV. Carport Coda

My Old Mountain
by Lorilee & Two Medicine Peak
for Walt & Dee Anna

My old mountain you're so faithful
See me bend down on one knee
Hear me say, My gentle mountain
Would you care to marry me
When the city lights your south face
You look like a harvest moon
Who flew a quarter million miles
Just to beam outside my room
Let the circling of the redtail
Be our skyborne wedding ring
And our bower be the deep moss
By your secret northern spring
Let the pika be our preacher
And the sunrise be our vows
Let the words *Death do us part*
Collapse into the Endless Now

**[chorus is improv instrumental: show-off guitar, happy
dulcimer, spooky tin whistle, sisterly fiddle, noble cello]**

My old mountain you're so magic
When you leap to life in May
The world's sadness melts like runoff
From the snowbanks of dismay
Muhammad's people got their Mecca
And the Catholics got their popes
You and me we've got the summer stars
That fleck your dark night slopes
To conquer world-famous summits
To this girl don't mean a thing
I'd rather greet the glacier lilies

On your shoulders in the spring
And wander through your north side meadows'
Dark blue gentian in the fall
You are my own private St. Peter's
You're my secret China Wall

[chorus = show-offy, happy, spooky, sisterly instrumental]

My old mountain you're so steadfast
When the winter storms blast through
I can feel the holy fires
Ancient stars bequeathed to you
And late one night amid a blizzard
I felt you kneel on one stone knee
And say, My child, I live in you
Just as you live inside of me
So let the snowstorms and the heat waves
Do the worst that they can do
The deserts purge and ice preserves
The endless love between us two
Let the breeze that bends my grasses
Be the air that fills your chest
And every deer and hawk and marmot
Be our wild wedding guests
And in the stark gray light of winter
When the guests have gone away
Let our bodies lie together
At the death and dawn of day

O let the eagles and the nighthawks
Forge our skyborne wedding rings
And the deep moss of our bower
Greet us by my northern springs
Let pikas witness from stone pulpits
As we live our marriage vow
There is no death that ever parts
The love inside the endless Now

[instrumental endlessness into fade!]

(Providence, October 1996)

XV. Trojan Horse

Sometimes the nicest thing to do with a guitar
is just look at it.

—Thom Yorke

THIS IS NOT a chapter, just an envoy to a coming chapter. Three days before Risa's twenty-ninth birthday, UPS delivered a twenty-by-eight-by-fifty-inch box to the North Providence loft she shared with Julian Ventano. When she opened it, found a guitar case, and unlatched it, she discovered a vintage Martin D-28 inside. A handwritten note was woven through the strings:

Risa:

You've told me twice through the years that you love folk singer-songwriters and wished you played guitar. If by chance that's still true, Martin D-28s are the flagship American acoustic and this 1960 is in near-perfect shape. Dreadnought body, named for the shape of the early twentieth century Brit battleships. Sitka spruce top. Brazilian rosewood back and sides. Big warm tone growing warmer with age. If it speaks to you I'll be happy. If it doesn't I'll be happy if you do with it as you wish.

Have a wonderful 29th.
—Dave

The Martin was an epic gift, but it threw down a gauntlet. Unbeknownst to Dave, Risa's love for music had nothing to do with any music she'd ever been able to make. In choir back in high school she'd been dismayed to discover that she was more than a little tone-deaf. Unless she leaned in close to a strong-voiced girl singing her part, she invariably drifted off pitch. The D-28 moved her to take on her disability afresh. She began taking guitar and voice lessons from an old hippie folk singer who, back in the day, had toured under the name Goody Stash. She never missed a lesson and was religious about practicing, but took care to hide her efforts from Julian, fearing his caustic wit should he hear her off-pitch singing. Of Dave's gift she simply said, "The guitar's lovely to look at but I don't play, so could you please hang it on a wall peg for me?"

Julian's reply—"Of course. You know what a fan I am of pretty"—came off as cheesy and renewed Risa's determination to play. She kept up the lessons and practiced in secret for six months. Then Goody made a recording of Risa, "so you can self-critique in private." When she then heard her voice objectively, wavering between gratingly sharp and wincingly flat, she called Goody and told him, "Thanks for everything, but it's time I quit torturing music with my attempts to make it." The closest she ever came to making music again was to invent a rite she called "The Can't-Play-the-Blues Blues." Taking the Martin down when no one was around, she'd strike a single chord, then marvel at how long the integrity of spruce and rosewood and tensile strength of steel let the notes go on singing. But that very marvel made her uneasy. This inanimate object was so nearly animate that she felt it had a destiny to fulfill. She began to keep a casual eye out for a musician worthy of it.

A year later, such a musician walked into Risa's orbit, she introduced the guitar, and they worked out a highly unusual trade that made it his. Strangely, by trading away the D-28 it became a kind of Trojan Horse that enabled no fewer than three "Greeks" to slip inside Risa's formidable protective walls. The first was the guitarist himself. The second was our long-lost friend, the actor Jamey Van Zandt. The third was a stranger Risa christened "Dreadnought" in honor of the early British battleship that shared its shape with her departed guitar.

(Portland, summer 1997)

XVI. Barkeep

Two arrows meet in midair.

—Eihei Dōgen

AFTER SEVEN YEARS in Rhode Island, Risa returned to Portland with a master's degree in art, a respectable but not remarkable portfolio of paintings and drawings, and a ridiculously handsome boyfriend. But she did not return with a life's vocation or a true love.

Regarding the vocation: from the time she was a child Risa had dreamed of leading a quiet, retiring life as a studio artist. After completing her MFA in three years, she spent four more years in Providence with Julian, doing exactly that. Funny how often a trial run at a vocation unravels the attraction that launched the education. Though Risa's MFA thesis project strikes your narrator, the Holy Goat, as full of potential, there's no real point in describing it: two years as a studio artist left Risa sure she no longer wanted to be any such thing, and Rhode Island turned out to be a seven-year cul-de-sac in her life's trajectory.

One reason she turned away from art: an ever more troubled sense that her planet was facing utter crisis. The growing woes of nearly every species and country left her feeling that her life, in every way possible, should be given to creative, tangibly expressed forms of love in response. At RISD, Will Jones, Not-Quite Dr. Gage, the apocalyptic pen-and-ink artist Nita Hymes, and the Prophet Anna were the four students who had shared this feeling. Nita and Will stayed in touch with Risa after RISD, and both felt the art market did *not* share their sense of crisis. After several years of artistic and financial struggle, Nita took up computer graphics, expatriated to Reykjavik, and went to work as a graphic designer. Part of her first letter to Risa from Iceland:

Yes I quit making studio art and yes I'll say why. Like you, I want my heart in my work. But after trying to break into a market geared to the decor, pretensions, and amusements of a wealthy class whose riches too often come of ripping seppuku blades through Mother Earth's intestines, my heart rebelled and I chose to make *wake up* art about that ripping. The wealthy were not amused. And gallery owners! I can't count how many times I heard: "Nice technique, Nita, *but lose the message!*" To me, "artist" can't mean a person who pretties up the homes of people "suffering" from glut. I need to express love for the remnants of a planet that isn't yet dead, and grief for the countless places that are. The graphics work I do isn't a tenth as creative as my pen-and-inks, but it does assist those resisting the seppuku blades. And while I can't say I've found peace, I do feel less self-loathing.

Speaking of which: I recently heard from Anna, who has (I kid you not!) gone to work for a nonprofit called the Voluntary Human Extinction Movement, and told me that if I'm "a Serious Person" I must join her. What a fun-loving spirit! I wrote back, "Your movement is redundant, Anna. Industrial humanity already *is* the best possible voluntary human extinction movement. If *you're* a Serious Person you must go to work for ExxonMobil."

Anna didn't reply, and oh how I don't miss her! But I'm surprised by how much I miss *you*, Risa. Yes, this is overt flirting. If you weary of men (and as a Serious Person, *how could you not?*) come see Reykjavik. You'd love Iceland even if you couldn't love me, and whether you fell for me doesn't matter. You break my heart no matter what.

Love,
Nita

After his own multiyear struggle with Angst Nouveau anti-furniture, Will Jones moved to an organic family farm in Wisconsin, where he was given the use of a woodshop in exchange for helping the family with planting and harvesting. With farm work to ground him again, Will lost all interest in woodworking as an avant-garde art form, became a straight-ahead furniture maker and organic gardener, and sounded consistently happy for the first time since he and Risa had met. One of Will's happy Wisconsin letters ended:

Let's face it, Risa. The reclusive artists we worshipped as teens are about as common today as Sumatran rhinos, and make about the same money. You didn't ask for my two cents but here they are: the only way you won't be disappointed with your life is by finding something great to do with it. That's the blessing and curse of being great yourself. Best of luck finding a *What, Where,* and *Who With* to match *you.*

—Will

Risa was touched by Nita's and Will's forthrightness. But the fatal blow to her artistic aspirations had little to do with frustration with the art market or a lack of love for art. It had to do with her greater loves. The first: Sanskrit and Vedic literature. If not for the Sons Only Verse she would never have quit them. The second greater love: the time she had leapt into the breach for TJ, overseeing his Pearl and Waterfront projects during Jervis's coma, she discovered by accident what TJ called "your genius for coordinating and harmonizing people working toward a positive end." No artistic discovery had ever compared. To combine her natural abilities as a shaker and mover with her love for the ravaged Earth felt like her proper direction in life. But shake what? Move who? She didn't yet have a clue.

During her Rhode Island years, Risa and TJ stayed close via phone calls and letters. She tracked every move that turned TJ into a minor Portland mogul, understood his adoration of Jervis better than anyone, and encouraged his mother-brother persona more than anyone. For his part, TJ knew Risa's studio artist dreams had vaporized, and sensed her lack of faith in life with Julian even before she did. He also knew Risa's mother had fallen for a fellow AA member and moved with him to Florida, and that Risa had closed herself off from her father. TJ knew, in short, that the woman Jervis had called TJ's "spiritual littermate" was more or less rootless and without family. So he reached out.

It was a simple matter for TJ to convince Risa to return to Portland to regroup. It was far less simple for Risa to figure out whether Julian should come with her. For half a year he'd been begging her to wander Europe with an eye to them expatriating there. Deeply familiar with the charms, and lack thereof, of life with an arts-and-culture-sampling dilettante, Risa balked. She had no interest in wandering the world's pleasing remnants amid impending apocalypse. She yearned to serve the world in ways that made spiritual and biological sense. But her yearning was so undefined it didn't fare well against Julian's strong lobbying for a permanent move to Europe.

Aware of the growing tension between them, TJ asked Risa if he could have a private talk with Julian about coming to Portland. When Risa said sure, TJ suggested to Julian that he sublet his artist's loft in Providence to keep his options open, join Risa on a trial basis in Portland, and let TJ help them save money for whatever plan they might agree upon. TJ then offered them a rent-free Pearl Building loft, plus all the commercial painting work Julian wanted for better pay than he was getting. When Julian expressed astonishment at his generosity, TJ said, "The things Risa did in my brother's and my time of need go *way* beyond my offer. You'd be doing me a service if you come." And they had a deal.

THEY MADE THE move west and Julian settled into his Portland painting work. TJ then had a heart-to-heart with Risa that culminated in him saying, "It sounds to me as though you, like Julian, need to save as much money as possible before you make some kind of world-serving move. So why don't you come to work for me?"

"Doing what?" Risa asked.

"To fit your talents into my Portland needs," TJ said, "I'd like to hire you to be my boss."

Risa burst out laughing.

"I'm serious," TJ said. "The Pacific Northwest restaurant scene is changing so fast that to stay competitive I need to focus on just two things: new cuisines and local food sources. But to renew my connection to food I need to travel, and to travel I need an Executive VP of Whatever Needs to Happen to take charge of both restaurants. No one could do that better than you. I know you wouldn't want such a job indefinitely, but you'll make great money for whatever you choose to do next while I 'simple me down,' as Jervis puts it, and become a fully informed food-obsessed chef again."

"If I accept your offer," she warned, "the first project I'll recommend is major. To make room for your new cuisine, whatever it may be, we need to remodel, rebrand, and rename Rasta Pasta. That name and matching decor and music are too limiting. The restaurant's next name should suit any cuisine you choose."

"You're the boss," TJ said with a pleased smile.

"Two requests," Risa added. "One: before I have to pull rank on your staff I'd like to bartend for a few months. I'm good at it. I'd like to gain some cred by showing your people I know how to work. I'd also experience the strengths and weaknesses of the space firsthand, and get reacquainted with the restaurant biz by full immersion."

"Fine with me so long as the bartender remembers she's my boss," TJ said.

"She will," Risa assured him. "Second request. Julian has joined a men's group. He'll be out late Tuesdays. You've told me that after you lock up at Étouffée and Jervis comes in from Ocean-walking, you and he share a late-night dram. Any chance I could crash your Tuesday night drams and make that my own little late-night men's group?"

The McGraff boys and McKeig girl had themselves a deal. And Boss Risa, despite doubling as Bartender Risa, tackled the Rasta Pasta remodel straightaway.

IN THE SUMMER of 1997, Jon Van Zandt had noticed his best friend in all the world—his son's dog—was finally, rapidly aging. Jon showed his regard by completely redesigning Romeo's beloved Land Nautilus, making it far more comfortable for a dog now as interested in long naps as in Jamey's adventures. On July 25th, during a torrid Portland heatwave, Jamey filled the refurbished Nautilus's air-conditioning system with a pair of ice blocks, loaded it in the back of his pickup, whistled Romeo up into the cab to ride shotgun, as always, and drove through rush-hour heat to the Willamette River waterfront, where Jamey hoped to dine early at a place that touted itself to be Portland's only Jamaican-Italian restaurant.

Because the events about to unfold feature romance, and because many people, me included, hold romance to be as dangerous as concealed firearms, I'm going to risk the NRA's ire and do a background check on

Jamey's romantic condition as he tooled riverward through the noxious urban air...

JVZ Romantic Background Check, July 25, 1997

For the past decade Jamey had insisted to his sister, Judith, and anyone else who asked, that his life satisfied him completely despite the lack of an all-consuming romance. Jamey lived in a dilapidated but charming penthouse atop a five-story apartment building in an industrialized but surprisingly inexpensive block of Northwest Portland. He was constantly immersed in a modestly remunerative, highly adventurous freelance career as an actor, acting coach, theatrical director, and playwright. He had a wealth of friends and admirers and, as arguable proof of his integrity, a few entertaining enemies. For the fourth straight year he'd written the vignettes for, and would soon be starring in, the Stumptown Shakespeare Ensemble's popular summer comedy series *Urban Arias*. When he'd made his Rasta Pasta reservations by phone and said he'd be dining alone, he took real pleasure in the prospect. Having rehearsed hard with six actors all day, he liked nothing better than no conversation beyond idle banter with a bartender or waiter amid the ambient bustle of a popular restaurant in a three-million-person urb.

To put satisfying perspective on his Rasta Pasta plans, Jamey decided before leaving the poor man's penthouse to phone his sister for their once a week argument over everything under the sun. At the age of twenty-two Judith had married a *nuevo*-Republican electrician with the non-Republican name Carlos Mendez, moved to the sprawling Portland neighborhood of Parkrose, spawned two boys and a girl, and settled into a life of bustling Judeo-Suburban motherhood. Jamey understood how a chaos of parenting tasks might appeal to a mother who'd lost her own mom as a kid, but he didn't try to disguise his love for the bachelor life in the bohemian heart of the city. Rhetorical comparisons of married and single life thus became Jude's and Jamey's favorite phone-war topic.

On the night Jamey and Romeo went to Rasta Pasta, their phone-war volley went like so:

Judith: "Any serious relationships these days?"

Jamey: "Several, thanks for asking."

Judith: "In romance, several is the *opposite* of serious, little brother."

Jamey: "That's what *you* think!"

Judith: "Look in the mirror, Jamey. Your *romantic vignettes* have turned into tedious sequels titled *Fear of Commitment I*, *Fear of Commitment II*, etcetera, as your romantic options shrivel. When I'm playing with my grandkids and you're trapped in a desolate late-middle age, remember I tried to warn you."

Jamey laughed at Jude's diagnosis with real pleasure, and shot back, "Some of the most alluring women in town find my refusal to commit to an all-devouring romance to be the most romantic thing about me. And that refusal *requires* commitment. Unlike you, Jude, I don't consider any romance shorter than the *Oxford English Dictionary* to be a quick cynical fuck."

"There's nothing *romantic* about rooting like a truffle-munching pig through the women of this city," Judith barked, "and nothing funny about a life of licentiousness."

"What's funny," Jamey said, "is that my sister is so self-referentially married and mommified and Disney-channeled that my nonmarried state makes me the star of a porn flick playing day and night in her head. I'm glad Disney's finally doing something X-rated, and it's been great talking, Jude. But now, darn it, it's time to head out into our sick city and start opening shirts and pants till I've munched my truffle quota!"

"Don't you *dare* hang up until I've hung up on you first!" Judith fumed.

"Be my guest, dear sis!" Jamey laughed.

And she was gone.

—End Romantic Background Check—

In a fine twist of fate, Jamey proceeded directly from this smug account of himself to Rasta Pasta and the romantically fateful events of July 25th.

He had two modest objectives for the evening, neither of them romantic. First: find out what the hell Jamaican-Italian cuisine could be. Rasta Pasta had been getting raves for years, but all its name brought to Jamey's mind were absurdities. Ganja-stuffed ravioli. Coconut-hair-covered cannelloni. Piratical blood-laced rum drinks to wash them down. The worst dish on the menu had to be better than his fantasies. But *Willamette Week* had said Rasta Pasta was being remodeled and the cuisine was about to change. Time to solve the Jamaican-Italian riddle before it was too late!

Second objective: Romeo's visible aging moved Jamey to indulge him as often as possible. An after-dinner ritual Roams had long cherished consisted of them driving down to the Willamette as the city cooled and quieted for a riverside saunter, enhanced, for Jamey, by two Dominican Cohiba Miniatures and, for Romeo, by a fresh loaf of bread. The bread wasn't for the dog. In his youth Romeo had fallen in love with the big, gold-plated, tube-lipped, ancient-eyed carp that inhabited the Willamette's depths. A ruckus of mallards and wigeons would make a feast of floating bread bits, so Jamey compressed his bread into balls that he threw in hard, sinking them under the duck ruckus till the epic carp glided in to be revered by Roams's loving gaze. Rasta Pasta was close to Roams's favorite riverside dock, so carp viewing was the postprandial plan—and a fine plan it may have been had Aphrodite, Erotes, Kama, and Xochiquetzal not overheard Jamey dismantling, with cocky eloquence, his sister's concerns for his lack of romantic seriousness.

What fun, the Eros gods agreed, *to plant a vision of feminine near-*

perfection squarely in front of this mortal hotshot and enjoy the psycho-
spiritual carnage she wreaks with a bit of our secret help!

THE FIRST APHRODITIC Mystery to fuck with Jamey's head en route to
Rasta Pasta involved parking. On the streets of Portland on a bustling midsummer's eve, parking is *dependably* an ordeal. So how was it that, just as
Jamey spotted Rasta Pasta down the block, a pink, double-length Cadillac
stretch limo pulled out of not one but two parking spaces directly in front of
the restaurant? "I don't know which I believe less, Roams," Jamey muttered.
"That ridiculous Cupid mobile, or this vacant double parking space."

Pulling his doggy-smelling, no-AC, worthless-for-babe-cruising, 286,000-
miles-on-it, single-guy, green Toyota pickup into the vacated space, Jamey
rolled up all but two inches of the windows, locked the far door, opened the
near one, and let Romeo climb over him and down to the sidewalk, where
he obediently sat to await Jamey as always. Things then took a second swan
dive into the surreal: after stuffing the parking meter full of quarters, standing the Land Nautilus on the sidewalk, and turning to Romeo, he found
Roams staring at the concrete curb so intently that his gaze followed the
dog's—and there, neatly placed on the curb, lay a glinting silver-and-gold
wristwatch. A Seiko quartz chronograph, no less.

"*Fup a dup!*" Jamey breathed. The thing was so garishly unlosable-
looking that Romeo just stared at it without moving a muscle, correctly
believing it to be the cheese in some sort of cosmic snap trap. But the pink
Caddy that was the watch's likeliest source was long gone and the first
pedestrian to come along would not overlook this glimmering prize.

Jamey walked over and picked up the cheese. He'd never worn a
watch. He loathed being reminded constantly of the time. But as an actor
fascinated by the way costumes create character, he slid the thing on and
snapped the chrome latch down tight on his wrist. It felt like a handcuff,
and was an alarmingly perfect fit. "Jude would approve," he muttered.

The Seiko's crystal face, five dials, seven gold hands, and silver and gold
band did give his summer-tanned wrist a certain complicated *something*.
"But you know what's unfair here, Roams?" Jamey mused. "If finding this
watch leads to anything unusual at all, it's going to be the most ham-handed
act of foreshadowing ever! A playwright would *never* get away with planting a chronograph on a curb for some portentous purpose. So *Real Life*
better not get away with planting this ludicrous omen in our path!"

Though Romeo appeared relieved by Jamey's skeptical tone, the ham-
handed Aphrodite, Erotes, Kama, and Xochiquetzal, seeing Jamey about to
eat their cheese, were collapsing all over each other with laughter.

"Here's the plan, Roams. I'm going to give this thing to the restaurant
staff and let *them* try to find the owner, or not, as personal ethics or pawn-
broker decree. But first, just for fun, let's briefly experience the passage
of Time, precision-hacked into one-tenth of a second fragments. What do
you say?"

Romeo's expression said: *I'm panting in this heat, which makes my head nod a little. But that contraption makes me nervous, so don't you dare take my nods as a yes.*

"I knew you'd agree!" Jamey said. "The one rule of this game: guess precisely how long, to the tenth of a second, it will take us to get from this blast furnace to the Rasta Pasta bar for a cool nap in the Nautilus for you and an ice-cold draft for me! And we'll call our game the Hot Street to Cold Brew Race Against Time."

At the repeated word "game" Romeo's ears had flicked into Alert Mode, hoping Jamey was about to hurl the damned Seiko down the street as a fetch toy. Instead he nattered, "What's the world record for this event?" Putting his ear to the Seiko, he said, "*Four minutes fifty-nine seconds.* What a coincidence! My lifetime best in the mile run back in high school." Opening the Nautilus, he cried, "Load up, Roams! We're going for the record!"

With a look of relief, Romeo hopped in the bass case, pulled the lid shut on himself, then pant-smiled through the porthole as Jamey checked the gauges. Temp: 86 but dropping. Oxygen tank: 91 percent full. Jamey turned the valve to ON. "Good to go!" he called through the glass, closing the porthole cover and snapping the case shut.

"Are the contestants ready?" he asked the garish visitor to his wrist.

Have you ever seen a watch more ready? the Seiko glinted.

Jamey activated the stopwatch: *Chiggitychiggitychiggitychiggitychiggitychiggity...*

Thus did his last eleven minutes four and seven-tenths seconds of satisfaction with a love life of mere vignettes and short stories begin hurtling away.

STRIDING DOWN RASTA Pasta's cool, arched brick entryway, Nautilus in tow, Jamey passed a dozen alternating Italian and Jamaican flags hung like banners. When he reached an elegant Italian tile podium, a **PLEASE WAIT TO BE SEATED** sign blocked progress. No host or hostess present. Down the hall to his right he heard the clatter and chatter of early diners. Down the hall to his left, two elegant wooden doors labeled **UOMO** and **DONNA** no doubt boggled the minds of monolingual Yankees desperate to pee. Beyond the restrooms, in the hall's center, stood a large sandwich board upon which someone had neatly written:

BAR ACLOSED AFOR REMODEL ASORRY!
ORDER ADRINKS AFROMMA YOUR SERVER.
AHAPPY HOUR PRICES ALLA NIGHT
ATILLA REMODEL SHE'S ACOMPLETE!

Jamey did not just admire this sign. He wanted to find, praise, and forever befriend whoever made it the way he'd once befriended Lynette and Gary for their sign **DAMSELS IN THIS DRESS**. But there was a problem: *Chiggitychiggitychiggitychiggitychiggitychiggity...*

His pleasure in the sign vanished. Waiting for host or hostess while tiny gold dials chopped the Now into mincemeat felt like waiting for an Idaho congressman to pass a rudimentary sanity test. *He was losing the Hot Street to Cold Brew Race Against Time!*

A lifetime of iconoclasm had taught Jamey a few modest magic tricks. He'd long ago learned, for instance, that when a rote functionary such as a host or hostess fails to manifest, nothing conjures said functionary faster than to indulge in behaviors at which you wouldn't want them to catch you. Standing the Nautilus on its kickstand, Jamey took the stool at the tile podium as if he were the host, hoping for a customer to misdirect. But no customers came.

Chiggitychiggitychiggitychiggitychiggitychiggity . . .

Eyeing the tidy stack of menus on the podium, Jamey looked left, looked right, saw no one, then violently untidied the stack. Still no one. He deranged the flower arrangement. No one. Glancing at the chronograph, seeing his personal best 4:59 mile about to go up in smoke, he opened the little drawer in the tile podium, found a credit card copier and box of green-tinsel-wrapped chocolate mint wafers, unwrapped one, glanced right, glanced left, and ran it through the credit card copier.

Chiggitychiggitychiggitychiggity. But *still* no staff person.

"Fuck it, Roams," Jamey said, and he dropped the Nautilus onto its wheels, turned down the arched brick passageway, and strode fast past the ACLOSED AFOR REMODEL sign into outlawry, as was his nature—just as Aphrodite, Erotes, Kama, and Xochiquetzal had planned. *HA HA HA HA HA HA HA!*

A LONG STROLL down a surprisingly S-shaped hallway brought him to a gated, floor-to-ceiling steel cage that looked like something used to funnel steers into a slaughterhouse. KEEP OUT! said the cage's unequivocal sign. But (*Chiggitychiggity, HA, HA, HA, HA!*) what choice did Jamey have? Drawing a deep breath, he pushed through the gate, cringed at its loud *skreek!* but towed Romeo forthrightly in behind him.

He found himself in a very large, discouragingly dark barroom about which the sandwich board hadn't ABEEN AKIDDING: power tools, power cords, plastic-covered windows, tarp-covered lumber, stacked flooring tiles, bags of grout and sand, and swept piles of detritus were everywhere. At the far end, however, a customerless row of stools lined an exceptionally long and inviting bar. In the dim light behind the bar Jamey then made out movement. A chaotic-haired but servicable female barkeep. Excellent!

He studied the situation carefully. The barkeep's back was turned. A small spotlight illuminated what must be a small sink, too low to see at Jamey's angle, at which she was rinsing remodel dust from a variety of glasses, drying them with a large cotton cloth, and stacking them on blue glass shelves. The darkness accentuated the shaft of light under which she was working. Despite the distance and her turned back, Jamey saw at a glance that she appeared comely. *No distractions,* he ordered himself. *You have a Race Against Time to complete!*

Donning his most affable expression, Jamey towed the Nautilus across the room, stood it on its kickstand, seated himself on the stool nearest the keg taps, unsnapped the insufferable chronograph, set it on the bar, and attempted to make enough of a stir to catch the notice of, but not annoy, the barkeep. She was working fifteen or so feet to his left. Because the bar was closed he expected a possibly officious response and was prepared to turn on the charm, if needed. But she just kept rinsing, drying, shelving. Lost in reverie? Miffed by his breaking of the ACLOSED Commandment? He didn't know and it didn't matter: *Chiggitychiggitychiggitychiggity*...His Hot Street to Cold Brew ordeal needed to end *now*!

To preface the speech about to be launched I must mention that Jamey was the inventor of a longstanding salon called the Book-Movie-Book-Again Club. The way it worked: members read a work of fiction or nonfiction, watched a DVD of the movie made from said work, then gathered of an evening to sip wine, nibble hors d'oeuvres, and rewatch the DVD, pausing the film whenever they liked to read wondrous scenes that the Venal Idiots of Hollywood had butchered or deleted; or, alternately, pause the film to read some of the hopeless twaddle through which the authors would have dragged moviegoers had the wily filmmakers not made deft cuts. At a Book-Movie-Book-Again event a few days prior to his forced entry into the closed bar, Jamey had paused the film to read his club members a lovely passage from Michael Ondaatje's *The English Patient* stripped from Anthony Minghella's nine-Academy-Award-winning film based on that book. For *chiggity*-crazed Hot Street to Cold Brew purposes, Jamey dialed in his most kingly Shakespearean voice and commenced to bowdlerize the crap out of Ondaatje's regal passage:

"I wish, when I die, to have been marked by this generous Earth and by Nature," he intoned as only he can. *"Hence I wish, while I live, to be sculpted by grain-gleaned liquids as Columbia River basalt is sculpted by the high desert rivers it so curvaceously beds. I wish in autumn for amber-hued ales to purl through me in pellucid currents. I wish in winter to be nestled into by night-dark stouts as bears nestle into their breath-warmed caves. And on this heinously hot day of summer that just assailed me with crosstown traffic stress and spew, I wish so desperately for a pint of palest pilsner to pour o'er my teeth, cascade down my throat, bounce off my interior cliffs, and eddy in my slow deeps that my unbounded gratitude and a triple gratuity are as sure to be yours as tomorrow's sunrise."*

Jamey noticed, as he declaimed, that the barkeep was listening keenly, and after a sentence or two began to smile even as she turned decisively *away* from him again. How odd. But the instant he fell silent, she said, *"I. Know. That. Voice. Whoever you are,* I overheard you somewhere within the past few months, saying strange and maybe wonderful things."

"Wonderful enough, perhaps, to reminisce over a cold pale pilsner?" Jamey asked.

Rather than reply in words, the barkeep reached under a shelf and flipped a series of switches. There was an explosion of light. In an instant, Jamey beheld a gleaming maplewood bar, handsome brass lamps with glowing green shades, glistening blue glass shelves covered with all sizes and shapes of glasses, and more than a hundred multicolored bottles of single malts, sour mashes, gins, schnapps, tequilas, vodkas, cognacs, armagnacs, aperitifs, digestifs, sojus, sakes, baijius, and, on their own massive wall rack, wines, wines, wines. He then turned to the barkeep, still turned away but visible in profile in the mirrors behind the bottles, at last beheld her clearly, and at that very moment, with a gleeful nod to one another, Aphrodite, Erotes, Kama, and Xochiquetzal fired up the Drills, Table Saws, Nail Guns, Pneumatic Chisels, and Power Sanders of Love, dialed Jamey's eyes up to Pure Pupil, and commenced a remodel of his interior compared to which the havoc wreaked on the barroom was a light cleaning.

First feature to fly in through his god-widened eyes: a slight transparency of skin at the temples, revealing fragile blue veins that glowed like marine bioluminescence. Second feature: a long, lush, stylistically retrograde chaos of dark hair, piled atop her head against the heat, bound by a crimson ribbon only partially successful at reining in the hairs' anarchistic tendencies. Third feature: far finer, paler little curls, sweet as a two-year-old's, escaping the same red ribbon to curl round her nape. Fourth feature: the neck of which this nape was a part. Up to this moment Jamey would have defined the word "neck" as a noun meaning "the portion of the body that connects the head to the trunk." But there were no heads, trunks, or portions in sight: only a wholeness too beautifully integrated to part out. This barkeep's neck and profile caused Jamey to completely redefine the way sun-tinged contours, fragile blue veins, hidden sinew, ecstatically wild hair, and lovely skin conjoin to form a whole. This barkeep's neck and profile were active verbs the movements of which made Jamey want to pen fan letters to the sperm and egg that had engendered them. This neck and profile poured into him like the pale pilsner he'd forgotten, bounced off his interior cliffs, eddied in his slow deeps, and revised the very chemistry of his body and purpose in life as the Eros gods howled, wiped tears from their eyes, and high-fived each other even as they kept lightning-bolting and Saint Sebastian–skewering the hapless fool below.

But hold up now! Jamey's Body hollered at his Mind. *Enough about* necks *there, Einstein! Time to check out what* I *wanna check out!* With which the Body commandeered Jamey's eyes, slid their gaze quickly downward, and arrived to its bafflement at an oversized, snow-colored, broadcloth banker shirt buttoned to its summit to accommodate a turquoise-topped silver-tipped string tie. The Body was stymied. Though the shirt and tie made the barkeep look like Montana's most winsome cattle baroness, it revealed nothing but vagaries about the bosom inside. *Come look at this,* Jamey's Body called.

Jamey's Mind slid in behind his eyes so he too could see the broadcloth and bolo combo. *A country-and-western type,* the Mind observed.

Know anything about cattle ranchin'? the Body asked.

Jamey's city-bred, city-loving Mind opined, *An incomprehensibly sentimentalized industry controlled for the most part by brutal beef cartels, featuring millions of miles of barbed wire, ecosystem devastation, huge reeking feedlots, criminal slaughterhouses, and munitions galore thanks to NRA propaganda exalted to the level of a mystery religion that sacrifices innocents by the hundreds to its gods. The on-the-ground drudgery, meanwhile, is performed by work-broken cowherds with insanely passionate feelings about the negligible differences between Ford and Chevy pickups. So thank heavens none of this except an occasional medium-rare steak has anything to do with you or me.*

But even as the Mind pontificated, Jamey's god-aimed gaze moved down to the sinuous gray leggings that flowed like twin rivers out from under the wintry high country of the shirt, divinely inspiring his Mind to attempt its first-ever Western drawl: *But ya know what, friend Body? It's dismayin' to me how snide urbanites can be about the proud American few who wander the Great Wide Open caretakin' our long-sufferin' ungulates. I'm even thinkin' you an' me, in the right two-rivered valley flowing down out of snowcapped shirts, I mean peaks, would relish such ranchin' traditions as ropin' an' ridin', four-wheelerin', irrigatin', stall muckin', hay mowin', sashayin', sunfishin', bulldoggin', an' whatever the hell else they got goin' under the Big Sky o' Bolo Tie Land!*

You're not half the jackass I took you for! Jamey's Body told his Mind as the cause of their unanimity shelved a last, long-stemmed aperitif glass, stopped drying, shut her eyes tight, and turned to face Jamey. And *O! Her face when she faced him!*

Cowboy up! Jamey's Mind silently hollered at his Body. *If she's the rancher, we're the boyos for the ropin' an' ridin' life!*

Ratchet up the Fancy Dan talk an' get us there, pardner! Jamey's Body agreed.

Self-blinded by her own eyelids, the beatifically smiling barkeep said, "Pardon me, but there's a game I like to play. During the controlled riots we call a normal Friday or Saturday night I hear hundreds of voices, and I've discovered my ability to match faces to voices is…*phonographic,* you might say. Since I can hardly carry a tune when I sing, it's a consolation when a voice is familiar, like yours, and I sometimes identify its owner via hearing alone, proving I'm voice-smart even if I'm tone-dumb! That's why I shut my eyes. But listen. This bar, as my sign down the hall stated, is—"

"*ACLOSED AFOR REMODEL ATILLA REMODEL SHE'S ACOMPLETE!*" Jamey recited. "I *love* that sign!"

"Thanks!" she said, eyes still closed. "But our assistant manager, Stan, is an ex-cop big on law and order. If he comes in he'll boot you for sure.

So here's my thought. If Stan shows, I'll say we've known each other since forever. Then *you* can finish the pilsner I agree to pour if *I* can finish my little voice ID game. Deal?"

Reeling from his freedom to devour her beauty thanks to her closed eyes, Jamey needed all his acting prowess in order to sound calm as he drawled, "*Deal*."

"What fun!" the barkeep said. "Okay. *Say* something. Anything. Only wait! That *oh so British* rivers of ale speech threw me. How about an accent with, I dunno, one of the outlying British Isles bluster and blore to it?"

Dialing through his theatrical voice bank, Jamey presumed it was himself, not the Eros gods, who sailed him across the Irish Sea and huffed, "*Bluster and blore* is it? Them that amounts to little more than fish-and-chips receptacles might agree with ye. But them as knows world-class oratory when they hear it would *never* call *my* perorations 'blore.' Ye stand warned. Slander me again, unschooled child, and I'll eliminate the middle person and speak my world-class oratory directly to the deep fryer full o' fish and chips!"

Eyes still closed, the barkeep cried, "That's it! The very accent! The rudeness too! It was that *Irish play*—oh, don't tell me—with Cripple Billy and Slippy Helen, by Matthew, no...Matthias...no, *Martin? Yeah! By Martin* McGonnuh...McConnuh...McDonnuh..."

"*We RETRACT the deep fryer accusation!*" Jamey proclaimed. "Ankeny Theatre, nine weeks ago, my Stumptown Shakespeare troupe wrapped up a fine run of Martin McDonagh's—"

"*The Cripple of Inishmaan!*" the barkeep cried, and her smile widened to a grin, and her teeth shone at last, and a quarter-inch gap between her incisors annihilated the near-sanctity of her smile, revealing a rampant gleefulness that was the last straw for poor Jamey. "And *you*," she added, parroting his lilt now, "were that rancid old walking tabloid! That slander pot on legs—*don't tell me your name!*—whose mission in life was to murder his own mum by feedin' her three squares of booze!"

"When ye put it like that," Jamey lilted back, "we should point out we were only playactin', and that outside the parameters of our pretend drama me mum was unharmed by the liquor she so fetchingly drained like a flush toilet."

"And *then*," the barkeep raved, her eyes *still* shut, "when we'd grown to loathe you, we learned that, wretch though you seemed, it was *you* who'd saved Cripple Billy, and *you* who'd given away your meagre savings trying to heal him, and *you* who snuck about quizzin' and gossipin' about him the way you did, because secretly *you loved him*!"

"When ye put it that way," Jamey said, "we don't mind braggin' that his name was—"

"*Johnnypateenmike!*" the barkeep cried, and at last opened her eyes. And their obsidian sheen! Her joy at having placed him! The immense *fun* bursting from betweenst her teeth! Jamey was so undone he feared she'd see his crush and head for cover. Instead, she stunned him by stepping toward him with unguarded delight. "What a chameleon you are! You're not even very hideous or old or demented," she said.

"When ye put it like that, we don't mind saying we selected and directed that fine feck of a play ourself, and that the Stumptown troupe you enjoyed is the brainchild of yours most truly!"

"An honor to meet you." She laughed as she leaned over the glowing maple of the bar, and her smile quieted as her face lit up, and her hand set forth like a quintuple-tipped arrow, met Jamey's hand in midair, and the polite shake each hand gave to each was better than fine. But then, for maybe three full seconds, the barkeep relaxed her grip so that her hand simply rested in Jamey's. And freely given like that, her hand at home in his hand like that, held by his own hand like that, the entire person to whom the hand connected took Jamey's heart by storm. Whichever least way her head or body now moved, a new angle of beauty revealed itself. However far he looked into her eyes he saw there'd always be a farther. Meanwhile the rubble of the bar remodel had been god-blasted into treasure, booze bottles had become exquisite spires of color and light, and Portland had risen from an undiagnosed death to blaze forth as Earth's most vibrantly alive city due to the immortal beauty Jamey had discovered in the guise of a barkeep. Too soul-shocked to realize he was still in accent as he said, "While Johnnypateen's a fine strong name, I go by Jamey Van Zandt in the life I lead in far-off America. And big as was Johnny's news of the fella that pegged his brother's Bible into the sea"—there was a *skreek*ing sound behind them—"it's bigger news yet that you've remembered my voice, watched my Irish directorial debut through to its heartrending climax, and—"

"*Look!*" snapped an angry voice close behind Jamey. "*Look* at this! I go to the kitchen for *two seconds,* come back to the host's station, and some *psycho* has scattered my menus, screwed up the flowers, and squashed a mint in my credit card copier!"

Jamey turned to face a short, muscular, florid-faced, red-headed fella holding the fouled credit card copier in his tough freckled hands. "Would you rinse this please, Risa?" he asked.

Risa!!! Jamey's Mind shouted and Heart shivered and Body sang.

"*What the* . . ." Risa took the copier. "Some people are pure random idiots."

" 'Eejits,' we say in *Inishmaan,*" Jamey remarked in Johnnypateenmikese.

"Hey!" the ex-cop barked. "You can't be here, bub. We're under construction."

Catching Jamey's eye, giving a tiny nod, Risa said, "Jamey the actor, meet Stan the assistant manager. Stan, Jamey's here 'cause I invited him, due to this knockout play he was recently in. We're old friends and wanted to have a drink and catch up after the play, but his fans swarmed him. I've owed him this beer ever since."

"Great, bub," said Stan. "But drink it out in the restaurant. Liability issues."

Kill him! Jamey's Body roared.

At least maim *him a little,* his Mind chipped in.

Next thing Jamey knew, Stan slid up to the bar and stood so close to him the move felt almost sexual—till Jamey saw what had caught his eye:

Chiggitychiggitychiggitychiggitychiggitychiggity...

"*Nice!*" Stan exclaimed.

Jamey hit the button that stopped the chronograph, purely to displease Stan.

Far from displeased, Stan leaned across Jamey in an alarming way as he squinted at the tiny dials. "*Eleven minutes four and seven-tenths seconds,*" he said. "Huh! From *what,* I wonder."

"This," said Risa, sliding Jamey a pint of pilsner and Stan a rinsed and dripping credit card copier and towel to dry it.

"*This,*" Jamey said, lifting his pint to Risa and daring to stare into the twin obsidians.

She didn't blush. Didn't smile. Just stared back, eyes fathomless and unreadable.

Jamey turned to Stan and awarded him a promotion. "Believe it or not, Manager Stan, if you'll allow me a single pilsner at this closed bar, in private, so that Risa and I can catch up a bit, my Seiko chronograph is yours."

"*You're not serious!*" Stan blored.

Jamey bapped the watch like a hockey puck straight into Stan's freckled mitt. "*Goal!*"

Stan gaped at his prize, cackled at its heft, whapped Jamey on the back, said, "Enjoy!" and fairly danced away.

The industrial gate *skreek*ed open and shut. Glancing at each other, Jamey and Risa felt suddenly shy. No voice ID games. No distractions. And from Risa's perspective, Jamey realized, he'd given Stan a damned serious bribe to gain this moment. Everything felt different. Intensified. Serious. *Too* serious, Jamey decided, and veered into small talk.

"Why the remodel?" he asked. "I heard Rasta Pasta's a big success."

"Oh, it was. But TJ, the owner, is a great chef, and the Jamaican-Italian notion limits his cuisine. So he's changing the name to TJ's."

"Mightn't naming his place after himself limit him a different way?" Jamey asked.

"Oh, TJ isn't naming it after himself! He's one of the humblest men I've ever met."

"I'm missing the humble part of a guy named TJ naming his place TJ's."

"He's still not sure *what* to name it, actually. There's a sort of...*iconic person* he wants to honor, Tiny Joseph by name. But tiny TJ is a spiritual secret, which is a big deal to owner TJ. So he's trying out the initialism, which looks like ego, which is just what he *doesn't* want. So now he's unsure."

Risa was straining so hard to establish TJ's sterling character that Jamey began to fear a romantic connection. Trying to sound casual even as his heart headed for the floorboards, he asked, "Might this TJ be your beau?"

She smiled so tenderly that Jamey half died. "I do love him. But the first time he opened up to me, TJ asked me to call him my 'mother-brother.' Which he is. Does a mother-brother beau sound like a good idea to you?"

Jamey's heart rocketed back up into his chest. "Prob'ly not. But if I knew your mother-brother, Risa, I'd assure him that to name his place Tiny Joseph's would give away no secrets, spiritual or otherwise. It'd just be refreshingly odd and unpretentious."

"That's my feeling too, Jamey! I'll tell him what you said. TJ's food is so amazing he could name us Slippy Helen's Fine Feck of a Place and do a booming business. But now, please tell me about this." Her gaze dropped to the Land Nautilus, which lay on its side so Romeo could curl up and sleep. "You're an actor *and* a bass player?"

Debating just how truthful to be, Jamey checked in with the twin obsidians. The forthrightness he glimpsed there left him shaken. *So be it,* he thought. "The instrument in *this* bass case is far more sensitive than a—"

SKREEK! went the industrial gate.

Expecting Stan, Risa and Jamey turned.

In walked Julian Ventano. Risa's face fell. Jamey's face fell.

Seeing he'd broken a spell, Julian's face did not fall: it lit up with battle-strength *rudra*. But in taking stock of his rival he saw a man who surpassed him in height, hence in reach, with a scarred chin and weathered face that had far less to lose than his own. He elected to show Jamey what was what in a decisive but noncombative way.

Strutting up to the bar in front of Risa, he leaned forward and pooched his lips out at her. When Risa, with an unreadable expression, briefly touched those lips with her own, Jamey craved a credit card copier big enough to run this peacock's entire head through it.

"Jamey Van Zandt, this is Julian Ventano," Risa said.

Without a glance at Jamey, Julian cranked up an affected Adoring Look, ran his eyes up and down Risa's body, and said, "I'm an hour early, *love.* My need to be near you just won't quit." But when he pooched his lips out *again,* forcing her to hesitate, look unhappy, but give them a second peck, Jamey realized he *did* possess a kind of copier he could run this fool's head through: his almost Shakespearean gift for incendiary rhetoric.

"Speaking as a longtime actor and acting coach," he began with deceptive calm, "I've got to tell you, *Gilligan* was it? Your greeting just now was smarmy. The smirk as you called Risa 'love'? Pooching your lips at her *twice,* forcing her to either peck back or leave you looking like a hemorrhoid with eyeballs? Kind of her to brave that, but *damn,* Gil. Don't you see the insult, thinking she'd mistake *that* for love?"

Julian reeled as if a small bomb had gone off in his mouth. Risa too felt alarm, but at the same time felt defended from a kind of mistreatment of which she'd been insufficiently aware; even felt, with a rush of shame, that she may have just been kissed by the wrong man. Ducking to a low shelf to hide her face, knowing it held more than the usual quotient of radiance, she busied herself arranging already-arranged glasses and worked to dull her expression. But Jamey was just getting warmed up.

"Out of regard for Risa," he told Julian, "I'm going to share an actor's secret. When someone I'm directing can't feel an emotion the drama demands, I give them a few photos of people in the throes of that emotion, send the actor home to their best mirror, and tell them to rehearse till they can impersonate the photo expressions perfectly. The magic is, nine times out of ten, mastering the expression leads the person to start feeling the missing emotion. The expression you lack, Gilligan, is a genuine face of love. Which is why today's your double-lucky day. Inside this bass case, believe it or not, is a face *filled* with love. Your task is simple. The instant I reveal the face, *inscribe it on your heart*. Then, when you get home, go to your mirror and practice, practice, practice till this expression becomes yours."

While Julian reeled, Jamey turned the Nautilus's starboard porthole toward Risa and the bar lights, unlatched the cover, swung the porthole open, and said, "*Behold the face of love!*"

Romeo's face instantly filled the round glass, smiling blissfully at Jamey, his soft brown eyes shining with *genuine* adoration. "Oh my God!" Risa cried.

Hearing her, Romeo turned, took in her face—and stunned Jamey by beaming just as lovingly at her: Roams *never* shared his look of love with strangers!

Julian then found his voice big time. "Are you OUT OF YOUR MIND, dragging a *DOG* in here? The health department will shut TJ down if they see that ridiculous *mutt*! And my *NAME*, as you very well know, is *JULIAN*!"

"But yelling doesn't change that," Jamey said. "And Romeo's anything *but* a mutt. He's a thoroughbred border collie and, up and down the West Coast, a renowned actor. Nor is he *in here*, as you put it. The Nautilus is anaerobically sealed. Which is a shame, Gillie. To be infected by the love in this land sub would be the best thing that ever happened to you."

"My *name*," Julian fumed, "is *Julian*! And if you don't leave *now* I'm getting Stan!"

"Great idea, Gil! Do fetch friend Stan. He can help me critique your face as you work to master Romeo's expression and, perhaps, experience the joy of seeing Risa the way Romeo does—though, judging by your current expression, that seems highly unlikely."

Livid now, Julian again sized up his combat chances. But since his *manas* did the sizing and Jamey was six foot two, lean, and fit, all Julian arrived at were confidence, lack of confidence, pride, shame, determination, lack of determination, and a skein of other head-on faith/doubt collisions. "That *does it*!" he barked, and off he went, *skreek*ing the industrial gate.

When Jamey and Risa again found themselves alone, this time under threat of an abrupt parting, Risa's feelings grew intense. *There's no time!* she thought. *What could he possibly say with Stan coming?* Then: *Flame language. If he's who I feel he might be, I need to hear flame language!*

"Time is short," Jamey said calmly. "May I cut to what seems to me to be the chase?"

Infinitesimally, Risa nodded.

"First, allow me to say that you seemed loyal to Gilligan despite his awful greeting. This dustup was my fault. I felt he sullied your honor by flaunting and using you like a trophy wife, so I misbehaved. Sorry it got invasive. But the man who could see you clearly and not want to know everything you feel and know and care about is not a man I understand. So I don't understand Gilligan. But yes, I meant to offend him—and if that offended you, I'm *very* sorry. I'm no relationship wrecker. Just a man who, after twenty years in theatre, knows the human face and form. That's why, through no fault of yours, your voice, bearing, keen ear, wit, intelligence, and laughter threw me into a state of awe. So when Gilligan's peacockery snuffed the awe, I called on Romeo to restore it. I wish you the best in every way, Risa. Obviously, so does Roams."

Looking through the porthole, she saw an endless brown-eyed love letter—and Jamey's face was little different as he added, "Although I hope Gil makes you happy in some way I can't see, know that Romeo and I are a lot of fun—and as I see it, so are you, Risa. You brought *fun* to our encounter the first instant! So if you're not finding Gilligan fun, please remember us. Two-headed six-leggèd admirers aren't easy to come by. And the Stumptown Shakespeare Ensemble isn't hard to find."

Though uncomfortable with his audacity, Risa was even more uncomfortable with her hope that some kind of rescue operation had commenced—until the industrial gate made its awful *skreek*. Then she was afraid he'd be forced to leave.

Stunned by how hard her heart was pounding, she watched Jamey lean instantly down over the Nautilus, kiss the porthole glass at the same instant Romeo licked it, whisper, "I love you too!" lock the porthole, lock the sub, and reach for his pilsner. Downing half of it in one throw as Julian barged up, Stan in tow, Jamey laid a twenty on the bar (which was a tenfold tip, not the triple tip he'd promised), pulled the Nautilus onto its wheels, turned to Stan, saw the Seiko on his wrist, and said, "You were made for that chronograph, Stan-O! And thanks for letting Risa and me catch up. As for Gilligan here, I hardly know what to tell you. I'm a bass player, as you see." He tapped the Nautilus. "And my eighteenth-century Klotz is temperamental. But Gilligan here asked to see the old girl, so I risked temp and pressure changes to make him happy. Then, I guess out of insane jealousy that Risa and I had enjoyed chatting, he had some kind of meltdown, started yelling that my bass is a dog, and away he rushed like a second-grade tattletale to fetch you. An astonishing performance! But my bass is too fragile for any more of Gil's shenanigans. So..."

Jamey clapped Stan on the shoulder, shot a crazed smile over Stan's shoulder at an apoplectic Julian, turned and bowed low to Risa, took the Nautilus in tow, began striding away—and as the distance to his long brown ponytail, long body, long strides increased, Risa was both moved and confused to feel herself wanting to cry, *No, wait! Please, come back!*

The industrial gate *skreek*ed open and shut.

"Can you *believe* that asshole!" Julian cried.

"And his little dog too," Risa said. "Romeo's *was* the face of love, Julian. The elusive thing itself. Couldn't *you* see *that*?"

"I thought I was gonna have to *fight* that lunatic fuck! Couldn't *you* see *that*?"

"I liked him," Stan muttered, gazing lovingly at his Seiko.

"I saw a lot of things," Risa said.

"Anyone mind?" Stan asked as he plunked down at the bar, commandeered the rest of Jamey's pilsner, took an absorbed sip, and began fussing with tiny dials.

"*Behold the face of love!*" Julian snarled, eyeing Stan with disgust. "It's bedlam in here, Risa! Can I get a BridgePort ale with a Jack back? And what the *fuck* just happened to *us*?"

"'What the feck,' we say in Inishmaan," she lilted, "where we take it well, when asked for such gifts as a draft and a dram, if him as asks adds a 'please.'"

Julian gawked at her in dismay.

Stan beamed at his Seiko.

Risa poured the drinks.

OUT IN THE heat meanwhile—appetite gone, equilibrium gone, satisfaction with short story or vignette-length romances gone—Jamey drove to the Willamette, parked with the usual extreme difficulty now that the gods were done pulverizing him, and fetched the bread from the Nautilus as Romeo danced in expectant circles. Locking the bass case in his cab, he made his way down to the end of an industrial-strength pier out over the river, plunked down on hot concrete, began squeezing together breadballs, and threw them in hard enough to sink under the wigeons and mallards that flew in for a feed. When, down below them, the Chinese fairy-tale carp sure enough began cutting through the dirty jade water, Roams hummed, danced, and whimpered in adoration. Blind to his delight, Jamey power-smoked both Cohibas without tasting them, watched breadballs sink like hearts in the current, watched the carps' Julian-like smoochy lips inhale every heartball, and unknowingly wore face after face of love for the way a pair of gray leggings flowed down out of a snowy mountain range of shirt, obsidian eyes loomed like portals unto night sky, and a sweet cloudlet of hairs escaped a red ribbon to curl round a nape.

"Risa!" Jamey whispered to each sinking heartball.

The greedy carp just kept sucking them down.

BACK IN THE bar meanwhile, Julian's boilermaker fueled a full-on *rudra* fit:

"I can't *believe* this!" he cried. "Your attraction to that creep is written all over you! And when I showed him you're mine and he insulted me outrageously, you seemed to enjoy it! You know what, Risa? Go ahead.

Make hay with your weird interloper! My faith in us is *gone*. I'm going back to Providence, then on to Europe as I've tried to plan. And if you wonder why, try looking in the mirror, like your actor asshole recommends to unconvincing actors, as I turn and walk away. The woman you'll see there won't do *one damned thing* to stop me!"

As Julian spun and stormed away Risa did look in the mirror. And sure enough, the woman she saw made no move whatsoever.

The industrial gate *skreek*ed open and shut. Silent seconds passed. Then, from far down the S-shaped hallway came a single, faint and furious *"FUCK!"* And back to Providence went Julian, certain that Risa was about to throw herself at Jamey. And back to his poor man's penthouse went Jamey, certain that Risa was taken when in fact she'd been forsaken due to the strength of her attraction to Jamey and Roams.

HA HA HA HA HA HA HA! went Aphrodite, Erotes, Kama, and Xochiquetzal.

Book Two:

Eastern Western

Fifth Telling:

Converging Peregrinatios

The truth about You is in my own heart.
How do You plan to get it out of there?

—Tukaram

When the soul wants to experience something, she
throws an image out in front of her, then steps
into it.

—Meister Eckhart

(Elkmoon Beguine & Cattle Company, Montana, fast-forward to summer 2012)

I. When East Touches West

He mounted the last broken edge of rim to have the sun-fired,
purple sage-slope burst upon him as a glory. Bess panted
up to his side, tugging on the halter of her burro.
—Zane Grey, Riders of the Purple Sage

I have listened to this subtle knowledge.
It falls short of the absolute.

—Gautama Buddha

For WELL OVER a hundred years, Montana has been the home of a genre known as the Western. One would think the favored local genre well suited to the story of the re-inhabitation of a twice-wrecked-and-bankrupted cattle ranch. The ranch in my sights, however, is a four-thousand-acre anomaly known as the Elkmoon Beguine & Cattle Company, five of whose founders are Lorilee Shay, Risa McKeig, Jamey Van Zandt, and Jervis and TJ McGraff, and *that* quintet, as the reader has surely seen by now, would fit in an old-school Western about as readily as a herd of pronghorns fits in an egg carton.

This lack of fit isn't my heroes' fault, or the Western's fault either. But something has to give, and it can't be my heroes if their stories are to be told. So it's got to be the genre. There is precedent for this. The genius of many a Western—Charles Portis's *True Grit,* James Galvin's *The Meadow,* Terry Tempest Williams's *When Women Were Birds,* and Bryce Andrews's *Holding Fire,* to name a quick four—lay in each author's recognition that if they wished to avoid singing a Yippie-ki-yay tale of nothing that exists, they were going to have to bust the genre wide-open. Unbusted Westerns weren't designed to portray anything as nuanced as actual human lives lived in actual Western places. What genre Westerns do, primarily, is entertain, and the entertainment bears considerably more resemblance to classic opera than to the lives of genuine Westerners.

Like the fans of a Verdi or Rossini libretto, the fans of a Zane Grey or John Ford Western expect a prescribed story line performed on an equally prescribed stage. The stories derive, by and large, from the rote, racist, masculinist, triumphalist nineteenth-century "penny dreadfuls" and "Wild

West shows" from which the genre first sprang. The match that ignites the plot is a generic injustice: horses lost to rustlers; ranch lost to a loaded deck of cards; Pa shot in the back over his mining claim; Sis separated from her scalp or cherry while trying to hang the laundry. The inaugural crime then ignites a hero so operatically mannered in his means of vengeance that John Wayne becomes a veritable Luciano Pavarotti and Gary Cooper a Plácido Domingo as tempers combust, horses get rode hell for leather, and hot lead flies. In a Western, we know in advance that Retribution will be enacted via "peacemakers" and "gunplay" upon a sagebrushed, large-bouldered, red-white-and-blue-skied canvas. In a Western, we know the Nutty Sidekick will win our hearts just long enough to prick them when he runs out into a crossfire and gets shot deader'n dirt. In a Western, we know we'll squirm with either desire or embarrassment the instant we sight the heaving bosom of the optionally Sultry or Feisty Female Love Interest. In a Western, we know the Corrupt Patriarch will be protected by a militia of toughs who will fire hundreds of festively inaccurate rounds at Our Hero as he fires back with an accuracy that, over the subterranean groans of the hack Western actor Ronald Reagan, keeps Hollywood stuntmen employed, unionized, and pensioned to this day.

The genesis of the Elkmoon Beguine & Cattle Company can't be a Western because, by that genre's protocol, Lore, Risa, Jamey, TJ, and Jervis would be seen not as needfully eccentric and seminal founders of their vibrant interlocking circles but as alien hallucinations from a galaxy we'd need three or four shots of Rooster Cogburn's whiskey to help us forget. The story of the E.B.&C.Co can't be a Western because a Zane Grey–conditioned visitor motoring onto that ranch property would be flummoxed to find two big greenhouses where the moon-doored outhouses should be; a barn that serves as a combination town hall/concert hall/Zendo/Dumpster Catholic cathedral where the haymows, harrows, and dead tractors should be; a recording studio that makes three times the money of the cattle operation where the bunkhouses should be; and actual Wrangler-jeaned wranglers living in an aspen-and-pine-shaded village of LEED-platinum, Craftsman-style cottages trailing charmingly down a swale in which the scattered bones of General Phil Sheridan's "only good Indians" should be. The Western addict would then cry, "Where in tarnation are the heavin' bosoms, hard-rode horses, hot lead, an' Manifest Destiny till death do us croak?" climb back in their rig, and leave.

The story of the E.B.&C.Co can't be a Western because in a Western there's a "West to be won," whereas the E.B.&C.Co's residents are attempting the labor-intensive recovery of four thousand acres of a West decidedly lost, first by its natives to a human invasion from Europe, then by its settlers to a stacked deck of East Coast robber barons, then by the majority of its populace to a hodgepodge of corporate fantasists and Big Energy or Defense Department Earth rapists whose ravages are seen everywhere across the actual West but nowhere in a genre Western. The E.B.&C.Co's story can't be a Western because the population of the West today is 87 percent urban, the horseback cowboys and family ranches that once hosted the Western genre have all but disappeared, and the enemy wiping out both is a politically hot-wired, anything-but-"free"-market juggernaut that long ago stopped leaving behind quaint Western ghost towns like Shaniko, Oregon, or Bannack, Montana, and started creating ocean-doomed death rows out of entire coastal cities and island nations worldwide. The E.B.&C.Co story can't be a Western because that genre remains too six-gun happy to even reference, let alone portray, a global death economy that extirpates an indigenous language every couple of weeks, an indigenous food crop every four or five days, and reduced Earth's entire population of mammals, birds, fish, amphibians, and reptiles by 68 percent between 1970 and 2015. The E.B.&C.Co story can't be a Western because, within the confines of that nostalgia-blinded genre, "gay" is just a jolly mood, "Buddhists" are Chinese railroad workers laying tracks across the continent for steam locomotives, "God" is the white-skinned left-brained phantasm of a clique of suicidally industrious White Guys, and every acre of Wild West, be it vertical or horizontal, wet or dry, is pleading with those White Guys to be converted into liquid acre-feet, salable board-feet, barbed-wire-fenced sections, divisible lots, combustible fuels, and splittable atoms the White Guys divvy up, privatize, cage, clear-cut, dam, drain, mine, frack, and detonate unfair and square. The E.B.&C.Co story can't be a Western because, since the 1900 heyday of that genre, the world's population has increased nearly eightfold, the use of water twelvefold, CO_2 emissions fiftyfold, and the catch of ocean fish sixtyfold as global food diversity was decimated by more Manifest-Duplicity-spewing White Guys down to fourteen corporate-controlled crops and twelve animal species worldwide. The E.B.&C.Co story can't be a Western because, in the spiritual Death Valley of that genre, every Westerner starved for the numinous and undying has no choice but to rip off the sweat lodges, sacred pipes, and mythologies of tribes from whom the United Straits [sic] of Amerigo Vespucci [sick] already stole everything but a few undesirable nooks and crannies, and if oil, gas, uranium, or gold were later discovered, the nooks and crannies were stolen back, detonated, poisoned, and returned with the capacity to kill. The E.B.&C.Co story can't be a Western because no less an authority than the iconic Western painter Charlie Russell found nothing to say to the booster club of Great Falls but this: "In my book, a pioneer is a man who turned all the grass upside down, strung bob-wire over the dust that was left, poisoned the water and cut down the trees, killed the Indians who owned the land, and called it progress. If I had my way, the land here would be like God made it and none of you sons of bitches would be here at all."

IN MY EFFORTS to portray the psycho-spiritual underpinnings, impending birth, and vulnerable life of the Elkmoon Beguine & Cattle Company, I had written exactly this far, and was strolling their repurposed land taking notes, when I spotted one of the three people who'd envisioned the E.B.&C.Co, Jervis and Lorilee being the unlikely other two. Approaching from fifty yards away, Risa had a clipboard in one hand, fresh-picked balsam root blossoms for a bedridden child in the other, a loaded leather satchel on her left shoulder, and, on her right hip, a little gunslinger-style holster with a cell phone in it, which, as she drew closer, I heard buzzing like a riled nest of wasps. I felt honored when, seeing my yellow legal pad, knowing I was in chronicling mode, she ignored the phone wasps and strolled my way.

"One quick question, Risa," I said. "I'm penning a midpoint essay for our chronicles, explaining why the menagerie you have up and running can't be portrayed within the strictures of the Western genre. But to finish the essay I need to name, or at least describe, a genre that *could* portray it. Any wisdom for me on that?"

"You call that question quick?" she said. "We're a multifarious bunch, HG. To limit us to any genre leaves out tons more than it includes. Depending on which person you ask, the E.B.&C.Co is a tiny but estimable fraction of Vedic cosmic illusion, a toothless Zane Grey yarn undergoing feminist and metaphysical revision, a peephole into Elkmoon Lûmi mythology, a stronghold of Dumpster Catholicism, a barrage of poetics ranging from free verse to cowboy doggerel to the godsongs of Maharashtran poet-saints to Chinese landscape poets to late-medieval mystic chants to bowdlerized dog-added Shakespeare plays to the sometimes heartrending chatter and songs of our own children. What single genre could cover all that?"

"My hope of identifying it," I said, "was to foist that impossible task off on you."

Risa broke out the gat-toothed grin. "You're a devious man. I'm going six ways at once right now, HG, but if you'll email me your anti-Western I'll ponder it tonight and see whether a genre that could contain us comes to me."

I liked this proposal, and soon liked the result. That night Risa wrote:

This lovely, mysterious, hideously assaulted, grotesquely misunderstood world, west to east and north to south, is in thrall to a spiritually bankrupt rape-and-plunder mentality you attribute to White Guys who think they're living out a Western. Charlie Russell nails your despair over this. Thomas Berry nails mine: "The political, religious, intellectual, and economic establishments...are failing in their basic purposes for the same reason. They all presume a radical discontinuity between the nonhuman and the human modes of being, with all the rights and all inherent values given to the human...We perceive the evil of suicide and homicide...yet we have little objection to biocide or geocide. The very magnitude of such activities escapes us."

A key difference between our nation state and the E.B.&C.Co is that the magnitude of such activities does *not* escape us. Biocide and geocide are high on the list of disasters that have us working day and night to close the *radical discontinuity between modes of being*, starting with our own lives in our particular place. I would add that "deicide"—the attempted murder, erasure, or betrayal of deities, angels, spiritual agents, elementals, virtuous sages, holy fools, mystics—comes first on my personal list of laments. Though we Elkmooners are a diverse crew in matters of the spirit, it's fair to say we each yearn, in our own idiosyncratic ways, for an inner and outer wholeness inseparable from Mother Earth's life and wholeness. And though we don't always like it, life on the E.B.&C.Co *forces* us to not just talk but to *walk* the largest possible fraction of that wholeness daily. This walk is so atypical of any nation-state I'm familiar with that to name a genre that portrays us, I feel forced to invent a new one. The "Eastern Western," I think I'll call it, though I'll add that this term designates a spiritual orientation, not a geography, since the dominant industries of every continent but Antarctica are biocidal and deicidal. As a spiritual direction, though, the term "Eastern Western" works for me because, during moments of metanoia, self-giving love, effacement of the ego, or immersion in good work, play, or prayer, an Eastern Western is not just a genre but a habitable location. In the spirit of your fat paragraph on the dangers of the Western, HG, here's my fat paragraph on the virtues of an Eastern Western:

We're all in the midst of having our hearts repeatedly broken by a human assault on the planetary tapestry of life that's fast building toward an inconceivable climax. The magic of an Eastern Western enters through our hearts' very brokenness. When the timeless wisdom of the East touches the brokenness of the West, many hearts don't simply break: they break down into ways of being that tap into ancient, oft-forgotten, expansive ways of being. When East touches West, we're suddenly renters on a glorious planet owned by no conceivable White Guy, and the fiercest possible love for Earth's landforms, living waters, living creatures, and every embodied soul, human and non, becomes entirely justified. When East touches West, no word, deed, or thought is free of spiritual consequence, and those consequences are our stern guiding light. When East touches West, earth, fire, water, ether, and air not only give us life, they continually manifest an Unseen Unborn Guileless Perfection that rules all that is (Upaniṣads). When East touches West, bodhisattvas, Beguine saints, Tibetan lamas, indigenous sages, and holy fools like Jervis know so many things the likes of Zane Grey, Ronald Reagan, and General Phil Sheridan never dreamed of that the latter's bogus knowings don't distract us from our true purposes for more than an occasional few irritated seconds. When East touches West, the central struggle is against cosmic illusion, "all blame is best driven into oneself" (Eihei Dōgen), "all creatures in their preexisting forms have been divine life forever" (Meister Eckhart), "all solace lies hidden in the indestructible soul" (Krishna), the Law of Karma is impartial and inexorable (Bhagavad Gita), and the justice unleashed upon a posthumous human spirit after a skein of subhuman investments in, say, terminator seeds, fracking, tar sands, greed-spawned corporate-run disinformation machines, or bogus derivatives may, of salvific necessity, lead that self-betrayed spirit through the darkest of bardos to a short brute incarnation as a paint huffer trapped in one of the hellholes their financial triumphs helped create. When East touches West, "Nature, the Soul, the Intellect, and enraptured angels all proceed from the One/Many (*al-wahid/al-kathir*), and if the One/Many were to grant you every last thing for which you could think to ask, truly, His kingdom would be no more diminished than is the sea diminished by a needle dipped in the sea" (Ibn al-Arabi). When East touches West, the First Noble Truth is suffering, the Last Frontier is unassailable bliss, our enemies are our teachers, and a "bad guy" is as likely to be shot through with light as with lead. When East touches West, a river-spliced Montana meadow might be visited by a Presence that permeates the heart of a vulnerable female trespasser, enclosing her in a sentient protectiveness that disarms a furious mounted attacker by turning him into a stunned feature of his own interior Vastness. When East touches West, "Depth is height" (Eckhart) and "Elevation is a blessing, not a conquest" (Edward Hoagland) and "There is no democracy in any love relation: only mercy" (Gillian Rose) and "Knowledge is erotic" (Jane Hirshfield) and "The universe, by definition, is a single gorgeous celebratory event" (Thomas Berry) and "Sky is sky, whether it's over Montana or over Tibet" (Jetsunma Tenzin Palmo) and "All the way to heaven is heaven" (Catherine of Siena) and "We are living in a world that is absolutely transparent and the divine is shining through it all the time" (Thomas Merton) and "I was just a container of love till Love smashed the container and the Uncontainable came gushing out" (Jervis McGraff). Early each morning here on the Elkmoon, every man, woman, child, plant, creature, and geographical feature casts a Westward-leaning shadow for the same silent reason: sunrise in the east. So I ask you. Has there ever been a *Western* without an *Eastern Western* beating like a gloriously broken heart inside it?

(Portland and Elkmoon Mountains, Montana, 1992 through 1996)

II. Loom Eye

Between every two pine trees there is a door leading to a new way of life.

—John Muir

THE LAST TIME we saw Risa's ex-boyfriend, Grady Haynes, he was stumbling down an Elkmoon slope in darkness, past a stand of pines a hundred feet above High Lake, when he glanced waterward and gasped: thanks to a perfect night calm, every star in the sky rested upon the black liquid below. Making his way down to lakeside, he peered out over the water: starry depths everywhere. Peered skyward: depths and stars everywhere. The twinned skies dropped him to his knees, an all-enveloping peace more or less pronounced the Elkmoons and Grady man and wife, and a marriage more successful than many began to unfold.

During the winter that followed, Grady sought to finance his mountain marriage by going back to school for a degree in the newfangled field of computer science. In 1992 he then landed a job in Portland, Oregon, at a fledgling software supplier called Dataland. Grady proved a quick study. In his first two years with the company he researched and supervised an expansion of inventory and servicing that soon included computers, printers, phones, the first digital cameras, and hundreds of other world-revising products. He also convinced the owner to change the company's name to Datalyrick. When the revamped company took off like a shot, Grady was appointed general manager. Even so, every summer come August he continued to drop everything, drive through the night to the West Fork trailhead of the Elkmoons, and spend his two-week vacation renewing his mountain love.

Still in the early '90s, Grady made two bold gambles that transformed Datalyrick, and his mountain marriage was responsible for both. The Elkmoon River Valley, with its year-round views of his beloved range, had ignited a desire to move there, which gave him a restless, devil-may-care attitude toward his work. In the winter and spring of '95 he used that restlessness to search out new Datalyrick locations, convinced the owner to leverage the business to the max, and successfully spearheaded the opening of six new stores—two in Portland and one each in Eugene and Bend,

Oregon, and Bellingham and Spokane, Washington. In 1996, finding himself lionized instead of fired, but still pining to move to the feet of his mountain bride, he created more potentially career-ending trouble by organizing an employee buyout of the entire chain. To his amazement, Datalyrick's owner welcomed the takeover, the buyout went smoothly, and the new employee-owners gave Grady a fat raise and made him their executive VP. When his business success then threatened to make him so busy that he'd be steadily diverted away from his mountain marriage, his first move as VP was to double his Elkmoon time by increasing his vacations from two weeks to four. The very first of these extended sojourns proved life-changing.

On all previous two-week Elkmoon junkets Grady had driven like a fiend from Portland to the West Fork, begun hiking at first light, and death-marched the torturously steep twelve miles over Gateway Pass to maximize time in the remote heart of the range unofficially known as the Inner Elkmoons. Because the hiking was brutal, Grady always carried an ultralight tent, an inadequate sleeping bag in which he shivered in thunderstorms, and the lightest possible provisions, water and tea being his only beverages and freeze-dried meals, gorp, and energy bars his usual sorry fare. At the end of two weeks he'd then do another death march down to his car, again drive maniacally home, and return to work at Datalyrick exhausted.

On his eighth consecutive visit to the Elkmoons in '96, with four full weeks to play with, Grady obeyed an impulse to explore a new portion of the range. Taking the East Fork trail for the first time, he set up a base camp at Paintbrush Lake (elev. 7,700). Though Paintbrush was only seven miles into the Elkmoon Wilderness, reaching it required a detour up a steep talus slope that dissuaded hikers headed for the famed Crown of the Continent Lake Basin to the south. Grady had also hired a packer for the first time, an amiable Nez Perce, Sam Rock, whose three-horse string arrived at Paintbrush within hours of Grady bearing an inflatable kayak, a veritable library, by backpacker standards, of seven books, six bottles of red wine, one of whiskey, and a three-person dome tent with a propane stove-heater that enabled him to loll in a Therm-a-Rest chair during thunderstorms that had previously chilled him to the bone. Sam Rock also lent him two bear-proof canisters, which he crammed full of such luxuries as frozen salmon filets, rib eye steaks, corn on the cob unshucked for freshness, bacon, eggs, peanut butter, chocolate bars, and real buttermilk for his famous double-buttermilk pancakes. He refrigerated the canisters deep in a shaded snowdrift.

Grady had chosen Paintbrush because it lay at the foot of Goat Ridge, a towering, three-mile-long dolomite fantasia on the Gothic cathedral motif, featuring mountain goats, golden eagles, pika colonies, profuse wildflowers, and ever-changing displays of light. His plan was to take vigorous day hikes out of his base camp, fly-fish the evening rise, and eat like a king till Sam Rock returned on the tenth day. He'd then send his luxury gear down with Sam, switch to a backpack and his usual ultralight gear, make the purgatorial climb over Goat Ridge, follow a fifty-some-mile network of trails across the Elkmoon Wilderness, spend the rest of his four weeks in the Inner Elkmoons, then hike out down the West Fork, completing a loop of nearly eighty miles, not even counting his day-trip explorations.

This already fine plan got an unexpected upgrade on Grady's second morning at Paintbrush. The Holy Goat will let Grady's Elkmoon Mountain journals take it from here:

I'd had a leisurely breakfast, inflated my kayak, and begun prepping my fishing gear. Most of Paintbrush is deep, but the shallow inlet and outlet create food-rich, weedy shoals, so a lot of its trout winter over and grow to unusual size. I was raring to have at them when a troublingly dark cloud parked atop the Goat and began to rumble. Most morning thunderheads are like politicians: big, noisy campaign promises that by noon come to nothing. But now and then a head will swell into a maelstrom that could turn a fly rod into a lightning rod or throw down a microburst capable of parking an inflatable kayak and kayaker high in a shoreline pine.

As the Goat Ridge rumbling grew downright surly I felt the barometric change and sudden temperature drop that demand full attention. The same change caused every trout in the lake to begin rising, including a specimen, not a hundred feet out, with shoulders like a center line-backer. Feeling half like a predator and half like the thunder god's prey, I hopped in my kayak, paddled to within casting range, and was stripping out fly line when a choir of pikas started _meeping_ in the rock piles and I smelled ozone. An instant later a colossal lightning bolt seemed to fill the entire sky. I sat "bolt upright" and paddled so hard I nearly hydroplaned to shore, flipped the kayak, weighted it with four of the biggest slabs of granite I could lift, rushed into camp, banged in extra tent stakes, gathered and stowed scattered gear, and stashed my books, clothes, and journal in a waterproof river bag. Storm ready, I donned a hooded fleece against the growing chill, brewed my second espresso of the day, set up my Therm-a-Rest chair in the tent's ad-vertised "view vestibule," and was looking forward to all hell breaking scenically loose when, very high on Goat Ridge, I heard what sounded like sheep bells. I grabbed my binoculars to scan...

Holy crap. Some cowboy-hatted numb nut on a little bay horse was leading two pack horses along the ridge summit as the slate-black cloud mass roiled right on top of their heads. The morning sun's rays, underducking the mass, turned the wrangler's denim clothes electric blue against the black. The rumbles deepened. My gut started somer-saulting. The pack animals -- Belgian draft horses I guessed at that distance -- were gigantic beasts. The cowboy and bay looked like a child on a pony beside them. I felt so sure they were all about to fry that I began a mental walk-through of the impending protocol: _climb the ridge, post-storm, to check the dead bodies; hike all the way out,_ leaving my camp and fancy gear vulnerable to theft; drive to the ranger station thirty miles downriver to call in a helicopter for the wrangler's corpse; and God help the dead Belgians and bay. Yet the cowpoke refused to rush. He defied apocalypse for a full ten minutes as the little bay switchbacked down the dangerously steep stony ridge with the hulking Belgians following, their petite bells tinkling comically though my stomach was in my throat. And lo and behold, just as they reached the lake's feeder stream, a quarter mile upslope of me, the rumbling ceased, the pikas stopped <u>meep</u>ing, the thunderhead released its grip on the ridge and slid meekly southward, and I was in awe: this wrangler read sky rumblings <u>way</u> better than I do.

Paintbrush is shaped like a hitchhiker's fist complete with the extended thumb. The inlet stream pours into the thumb. I was camped in the thumb's web. If the wrangler meant to stay I figured he'd pitch his camp on the fist somewhere, giving us both privacy. Instead he rode to within fifty yards of me, then said not a word when one of the Belgians dropped a calling card the size of eight Papa John's jumbo pizzas in a regrettably unboxed pile. Dismounting without comment, he led his beasts to two lodgepoles twelve feet apart, strung a rope from pine to pine, hitched all three animals to it, removed the saddle from his mount and the panniers from the Belgians, then strolled into my camp as if we'd agreed it was half his.

"Howdy," he said in a rusty woman's voice, extending a tough but tiny little hand. "Name's Gladys. Gladys Wax."

Struggling to feminize everything I'd just witnessed, I sputtered, "Grady Haynes," and we shook.

"Might all this fine gear include a folding camp shovel?" she asked.

Mustering the most unwelcoming scowl I own, I said, "Nope."

Gladys met my rudeness with a twitch of a smile, reached in her jacket, produced a sandwich in a ziplock bag, removed it, set the sandwich on a boulder near my fire ring, strolled over to the offending Belgian, wrestled a long-handled frying pan and little blue bucket out of his pannier, strolled back to the pizza pile, slid her hand in the ziplock, and used it as a mitten with which to work the steaming mass into the pan.

"No thanks on brunch!" I called. "Looks good, though."

With another twitch of a smile she headed the other way while I faked absorption in my journal, pretending not to see the hefty raven circling down over her sandwich. Fifty yards up from the lake and well west of my camp, Gladys threw the Papa John's in a brushy declivity, left the frying pan there, took her blue bucket down to the lake, filled it, returned to the pan, soaped, scoured, and rinsed it, and used her jean jacket sleeve to dry it. Every move she made, even hand-shoveling hot crap, was calm, deft, and sensible under the circumstances, and her "Leave a clean camp" etiquette was top drawer.

I was already inclined to like her when the raven made off with the top bread slice of her sandwich, flew low over Gladys's head, and her only reaction was to smile up at the thief and tip her hat.

As she returned pan to pannier and headed my way, I studied her close. Five foot two at most, a good bit of that bootheels and palm leaf cowgirl hat. Faded denim everything. Formerly brown riding boots oiled to a near blackness. Salt-and-pepper braid, same color as the Elkmoon batholith, tucked into her jacket so I didn't see it till she turned to her animals. Spry old body, not an extra ounce on it--nice for the little bay mare. Her face looked seventy to judge by the wrinkles but her stride and movements were so fluid I decided on a weather-riven late fifties. Two camp robbers (_Perisoreus canadensis_) now passed over, carrying the second slice of her sandwich torn in half, and four more parked on the boulder to have at her former lunch's guts. She touched her brim to all of them, took the next good sitting rock over from mine, and remarked: "Always been fond of pirates."

"Good thing," I said. "You've been piratized."

She nodded. "Sorry about the camp-warming present. Both Belgians unloaded when things got rumbly up top. Didn't figure Mormon'd pull the trigger twice."

I tried but failed to fight off a grin. "Your Belgian's name is _Mormon_?"

"And his polite brother is Anonymous," she said. "And my sweetheart, the little bay there, is Ho."

"Like Westward Ho the wagons?" I asked.

"What kinda cracker imitator do you take me for?" she said. "She's Ho like a homey's bitch. I'm her homey."

I found myself grinning again, whereas Gladys still hadn't cracked a smile. I've always liked people unimpressed by their own funniness. I was ready to like Gladys. But her eyes were giving me pause. They were a brilliant blue, narrowed to slits by a nonstop high-elevation squint, and as alert as the bread-swiping raven's. But an unevenness of gaze unsettled me. Her right eye looked wry and ready to shoot the breeze, while her left looked a thousand years old and probed me like an MRI.

Hoping casual chitchat might turn down the probe, I pointed at her scabbarded rifle and asked if Ho was any good with it.

"All three horses like my bolt-action Winchester, since each time I fire it I snack 'em. They may also sense on some level that gunshots let certain wild neighbors know we're not to be screwed with."

"Ho looks to me like a Barb," I said.

I could swear Gladys's left eye dimmed the probe and her right brightened. "You know the breed?"

"I've seen a few up here so I bought a book to find out why. Turns out Barbs were the Berbers of North Africa's favorite mount, and remain the Shoshone's favorite now. Sure-footed, slow to spook, and tireless, my breed book says. The perfect little high-mountain horse."

"You read good books," said Gladys.

She turned to my camp, eyed the overabundance, and scowled. "What's with the high-end safari set up, Grady Haynes? The other four times I saw you, you were backpacking it up over Gateway like you were late for a train."

"I _felt_ late," I said. "Fourteen days a year didn't come close to satisfying my need for these mountains. This year I'm here for a twenty-eight-day stay."

I then reheard what she'd said. "Did you just say you've seen me summit Gateway Pass _four times_?" I asked.

The thousand-year-old eye gave me a quick strip search. "That's about right. Four or five."

"The rock walls on the approach to Gateway are vertical granite," I said. "Except for the trail, there's no place for you and your beasts to even _be_. You weren't _on_ the trail. And what kind of life are you leading that you could have been there to see me four or five different times?"

"An observant one," she replied. "Like yours, judging by what you just said. But answer _my_ question. What's with the Great White Nabob Camp?"

"I got a promotion at work, became my own boss, and awarded myself a month-long Elkmoon vacation every year for as long as I keep the job. I decided to celebrate this first year by eating and sleeping like a king in new terrain. In ten days, though, I'll send the nabob gear down with my packer, overload my backpack, cross Goat Ridge by the usual painful methods, and work my way over to the Inner Elkmoons by a route I've never taken. I felt an urge to come at them from a fresh angle."

Gladys had a way of growing still the instant she grew hyperalert, the way deer and coyotes do. "Interesting urge," she murmured.

"How so?" I asked.

"The Elkmoons have had a hold on certain people for a long time. Those same people like to approach the Inners from a variety of angles, including the one you plan to hike. Ever hear of the Lû mi?"

"You mean the Lemhi?" I asked. "Offshoot of the Shoshone?"

"I do _not_," Gladys said sharply. "The Lemhi are a sad damn story. When Mormon missionaries converted some Agaidika and Tukukika Shoshone, their chief changed his name to Lemhi after some cockamamie Book of Mormon fantasy character. They wanted to try to work with white Manifest Destiny. That Destiny then ran 'em over like a log truck, drove the survivors out of their ancestral home, and turned their defining place names Agaidika and Tukukika into gibberish."

I sighed, "The story of the whole damned industrial world."

"Most of it," Gladys said. "But not the hidden pockets. In the high pocket we're in, the Lûmi are a very different story. They're not a tribe. Just a long-lived breed of secretive mountain pilgrim. The Inner Elkmoons are vital to their way. That's why it touched me to see you barreling over Gateway as if some Lûmi places might be vital to you too. So it gave me a turn, when we topped out on the ridge, to see you camped here like a damned L.L.Bean ad thirty miles from the places I felt you loved. Glad to hear you're crossing over."

When Gladys linked my Elkmoon love to the word "Lûmi" it gave me chills. I wanted to know more but sensed I shouldn't be too eager. "Hungry?" I asked. "I've got bacon, eggs, buttermilk pancakes, Sumatran coffee."

"You know I _am_ hungry. But not for calories. I love to fly-fish but can never make myself pack the gear. I saw your kayak from up top. Now I see your fly rod. A proposition, Grady Haynes. If I can borrow your boat and rod for three hours today and three more tomorrow, Mo, Ho, Anon, and I will return here the same day as your packer and haul a hundred pounds more than you could carry up over the Goat to the Inner Elkmoon camp of your choice."

Her offer was a godsend. To stay on for sixteen days after Sam hauled out my luxury gear I'd need to tote eighty pounds over thirty rough miles. Even so I'd be cutting my food so thin I'd need to catch plenty of trout. If the weather went south I'd end up on a crash diet. Gladys's offer would ready me for anything the mountains might dish out. "In exchange for the help you're offering," I said, "a fairer proposal would be for me to _give_ you my kayak and fly rod."

"I don't see it that way, but how 'bout this?" Gladys said. "When we haul you over the Goat, let my animals bring the kayak too, so I can fish Pipsissewa. Then we'll pack it out and leave it for you at Sam Rock's stables near Elsewhere."

An hour later Ho, Mo, and Anon were hobbled and grazing the inlet meadow, Gladys's tent was pitched a hundred yards from mine, her crazed cackles were drifting across Paintbrush as trout after trout towed my kayak and new acquaintance through sun streaks and shadows, and I couldn't stop wondering. Who _is_ this capable old woman, so at home and happy up here even under threat of lightning? And who are these secretive mountain pilgrims the mere name of which gives me chills?

(Portland and Seattle, summer into autumn 1997)

III. You Have Saved My Life

There's no life
that couldn't be immortal
if only for a moment.

—Wisława Szymborska

IN THE THIRD week of August, while TJ McGraff was exploring sixteen carefully chosen Italian provinces on a long-planned food research trip, his interim boss and restaurant business factotum, Risa, checked his itinerary, then sent him this emergency fax:

Mother-Brother,

I'm writing for a hard reason. A crisis just pulled me off the Rasta Pasta to Tiny Joseph's conversion, which has been going so well we're down to finish work. But it's a question when I'll be able to return. Here's what's happening:

Several hours ago, before I got home from work, Dave broke our no-phone agreement and left a message on my machine. I just listened to it. "Sorry to call," he says, "and sorrier still to shock you, but after two weeks of being sliced and diced by Seattle's finest techno-shamans" (yes, this is how he actually talks) "I'm in the oncology wing at Harborview Medical Center. It's cancer, Risa. Lots of it. My prognosis is poor. But I have much more to tell you and the rest verges on the miraculous. Thanks to you I have gone through sea changes. Thanks to you I feel almost ready for this. Thanks to you I even feel a kind of elation."

This totally mystifies me, TJ, because not only have I *not* helped him, I've banned him from my life for years and feel sick with shame as I type this.

Another reason he called: his "great friend Bart Simonsen," a lawyer, is "helping us with estate planning." Typical of our relationship, I've never heard of Bart, or of Dave owning anything resembling an estate. As far as I know he owns a house in Seattle, period. But he says my help is "urgently needed to complete my bequest to you," left

Bart's number, asked if I'd catch the soonest possible flight to Seattle, and said this Bart person volunteered to pick me up at SeaTac. I tried to call Dave back to say how sorry I am and learn more about his condition, but the hospital told me he was unavailable. That scared me into booking the next flight.

At Tiny Joseph's, as I said, we're down to installation and finish work. Of course the need to monitor that is huge, so I've hired Othello to be my eyes when I'm in Seattle. He and I will go over everything by phone daily, and I hope to slip down to inspect from time to time. But oops. I said *Othello*. I mean Daniel Bern. He and I got into a Shakespearean "merry war" at work when he decided I was *Much Ado*'s Beatrice, who I'm nothing like, so I called him Othello, who he's nothing like... but *why am I telling you this?* I guess a little shock has set in.

Before I started this letter I called Dave's friend Bart, called a cab, threw stuff in a suitcase, and the cab's outside. But I repeat, TJ: yes, this is a crisis for me, but not for you. Othello's a sharp cookie. Don't abort your trip. Just call me and we'll work out the best plan. Love love love!

Risa

Two hours later Bart Simonsen met Risa at the SeaTac baggage claim.

She liked him on sight. Kind hazel eyes; good-humored face; a slight Western drawl similar to Dave's. He also insisted, Dave-like, on carrying her suitcase.

As they headed for short-term parking she asked how he and Dave met. "Freshman year, Princeton, he was the lone Montanan, me the lone Idahoan amongst five thousand funny-talkin' Eastern bluebloods. We became each other's Western home ground."

Risa wanted to hear more, but Bart was on a mission: "Listen, Risa. I really look forward to getting to know you, but we've got a lot of ground to cover before we get to the hospital, so right now we need to cut to the chase. Dave's always been too much the cowboy. He toughed out what he called 'tummy trouble' for two months. It was pancreatic cancer. Metastasizing. Now it's everywhere. His prognosis could hardly be worse. The doctors can give you details but I'm going to skip to the bottom line. Dave believes Harborview will be the last roof he sleeps under, and I do too. I can't tell you how sorry I am."

Bart gave Risa a moment to take this in. She needed years. Dave was dying *now*. Her mind went into a tailspin. What made his doom hurt even worse was the fact that she'd shunned him for the last *eight years* of his life.

Bart stepped up to an immaculate crimson Ford Explorer with dealer's plates still on it and set her suitcase in the back. As she climbed in Risa was surprised to see white leather seats, a sunroof, a custom Bose six-speaker stereo, a CB radio, and more. Bart and the decked-out vehicle didn't match.

After starting the engine, Bart left it in park. "Something you should know, Risa. Dave's been my closest friend for thirty years and change. I know his foibles and his virtues. But when I mention the foibles, bear in mind..." Emotion stole Bart's voice for a moment. "Bear in mind *I really love your dad*. You and I are losing someone who's played an epic part in our lives. So I wonder. Can we skip the getting-to-know-each-other part and start a friendship? I know he was a lousy father. I know he's hurt you. I also know good things about him you don't know. If we jump into friendship I can mention both good and bad stuff without tiptoeing around. What do you think?"

Risa studied Bart's kind eyes for a moment, then extended her hand. Bart took it. They shook. As they started toward the city they wore matching sorrowful smiles. The smiles lasted five minutes, then I-5 northbound came to a standstill. "Must be a wreck," Bart muttered.

"It's a *nightmare* being stuck with Dave dying up ahead!" Risa burst out. "Can I get out and run?"

Bart said, "We've got so much ground to cover, you're about to feel you *are* running. Everything related to Dave is going to come flying at you faster and harder than I'd like. I'm sorry for that, Risa. But we should get started even so."

"That's why I'm here," she said.

"The first thing is this factory-fresh, tricked-out SUV with the Thule canoe rack, CB radio, and custom everything. It's not mine. But, starting today, Dave would like it to be yours."

Risa's feelings did a somersault. "I knew he hated my old Volvo. But are you telling me he hates it so much he replaced it with a *crimson Exploiter* without asking what kind of car I might actually like?"

Bart smiled as he winced. "'The Crimson Exploiter.' Let's call it that. But that's not what happened. This rig was to be Dave's. It won't be. We're sitting in your dad's last indulgence in his Highland love of finery. Before he got sick his aim was to return to his Montana roots for the rest of his life. Launch date: April. The Crimson Exploiter was his escape vehicle."

As soon as Bart shared the car's purpose, the crimson paint, sunroof, deluxe stereo, and impractical white leather all turned so stupidly poignant a lump rose in Risa's throat. "If he weren't dying," she croaked, "this decked-out harlot of a car would strike me as the best purchase he ever made."

"I feel the same," Bart said. "Four years back Dave finally got a clear read on himself for reasons he'll tell you. *Great* reasons, Risa. Involving you. He became a changed man, and I mean *completely*. Amid a hundred new insights, he'd seen that Montana was the one place that might restore a late wholeness to him, and he was so desperate to end his addiction to lady friends that he asked me to help him plan his Montana escape in secret. I only agreed when he promised: *no last-minute new woman joining his Montana plans.* Dave not only heard me, Risa, he pulled it off. Ready or not, this makes you an heiress. This vehicle is part of your inheritance. So is his home, which was recently appraised at 850K. Dave didn't want to tie you down with it so it's currently occupied by a woman, the one former lady friend I could mostly stand, who's staging it for sale as a favor to Dave, all proceeds of which sale will go to you. She's moving out September 30th and it'll go on the market October 1st. A nice twist is, she's a stickler for spare interior decor, even in the full basement and two-car garage, so Dave had to move fast to put what she calls Dave's 'endless piles of old ranch junk' in storage. And *I* would call this junk treasure, including all kinds of heirlooms from your namesake, Grandma Stella the Elkmoon Valley homesteader. Dave was approaching the move like a homesteader himself. Two huge moving vans transferred enormous loads of things perfect for life in Montana. Two E City storage units await you, and I urge you to take your time with their contents. I'll give you the keys to the units tomorrow."

"It *kills* me that Dave won't get to live his great escape," Risa said.

"Keep your eye on the best part of this, daughter of Dave. Starting four years ago his Montana dream, and your part in a very different kind of effort, made him happier than I've ever seen him, even despite his doom. You will see and feel this, Risa."

Risa tried to imagine, but couldn't. The I-5 traffic began to creep forward. They drove in silence for a while. "How are you feeling?" Bart asked.

"Spun in directions there's no way to understand. I've never even seen Montana. I'm losing my dad. But we're moving toward him. What's left of him."

"He's still there," Bart said, "and I'd like to talk frankly, as a close friend who loves him, about some of his biggest blunders. You okay with that?"

"We don't have time to wonder if I'm okay, Bart. Just go ahead."

"Thanks for grasping that, Risa. First blunder. Despite being a great talker and storyteller, Dave has always been close-lipped about his deepest hurts. The cowboy way, I guess. He's had a broken heart all his life. Losing the Elkmoon ranch and his Grandma Stella, *bam, bam,* is what broke it. You know that. From my perspective, heartbreak turned a kind and capable man into one of the biggest fools I ever met in three ways. One, his dead-end career at the bank. A shocking underachievement for a man so gifted. Two, his taste in *lady friends.* More gross underachievement. Three: his treatment of you. And the three were intertwined. I can't imagine what it was like for you as a kid, but it drove my wife, Cindy, and me crazy that Dave couldn't see why a string of romances begun over loan contracts wouldn't work out just fine for him and his child."

The skyscrapers of Seattle came into view. Risa hardly noticed. "I can tell you what it was like, Bart. All of Dave's women except Moira struck me as the same type. Superficially attractive via synthetics. High-maintenance as hell. Self-centered. And cold as ice *especially* when they tried to feign warmth. Pardon a barroom expression, but to me as a kid, watching Dave choose that kind of woman again and again was a total mind fuck."

Bart nodded. "The last time my wife, Cindy, and I had Dave and one of his women to dinner Cindy told me, 'Never again, Bart. Socializing with Dave's women is like sitting in a closed garage with the car engine running.'"

Risa smiled. "I have *got* to meet Cindy."

"You will. And when you do, ask her about Dave's biggest blunder. When he left you with Moira after the divorce, he didn't just break *your* heart. He broke his own. And Cindy nailed his motivation. 'Dave loves that girl more than anyone or anything on Earth,' she told me. 'That's *why* he left her with Moira. He thinks the life he's leading would contaminate Risa. Thinks he's keeping her *pure*. As if a heartbroken and abandoned *purity* is preferable to a little rough-and-tumble contamination. And as if alcoholic *Moira* is capable of keeping anything pure!'"

This analysis didn't just ring a bell for Risa, it smashed an enormous gong. "Good *God*! Another mind fuck! If Cindy was here I'd spill my guts."

"You'll meet her tomorrow," Bart said. "But we agreed we're friends. If it helps, please, Risa, spill away."

"That word 'purity.' Oh, that's big! It makes me realize Dave opened a vein in me that's still bleeding. Subconsciously, but still, the part of me wounded by being abandoned as a kid always wondered just what I was abandoned *for*. So, at RISD, I got involved with a man I found *aesthetically pleasing,* and that was *it*. Physical *aesthetics,* the entire attraction. Yet I stayed with him for *five years*. And why? Cindy named it. I wanted to annihilate any *purity* that would ever cause a man to *put me away for my protection*. But you know what happened instead, Bart? Thanks to the edifying shame of a five-year romantic ride to nowhere, I not only grew to understand Dave's similar rides, I was ready to forgive and love him in spite of them!"

With brimming eyes she turned and gave Bart a smile so big it revealed the gap between her teeth for the first time. It nearly knocked him over. "A pure child's heart could *never* have felt that forgiveness!" she cried. "But my contaminated heart loved him just as he is! I was *so* ready! I couldn't wait to sit down with my reprobate dad, talk story over too much wine, laugh all night at our scuzzy-hearted antics! But instead...four hours ago...his brave voice on my phone machine. 'Cancer, Risa. Lots of it.' How useless, the waves of forgiveness I'm feeling!"

Risa and Bart got busy with Kleenex and a handkerchief for a while. "*God,* Cindy's going to like you!" Bart said. "And listen to your attorney on this one, Risa. Your love and forgiveness have never been so needed as now. And if you ask me, my friend Dave is one very lucky dad."

* * *

WHEN BART PARKED in the garage beneath Harborview Medical Center, he said, "There's one more estate item I want to mention before we go in. I *should* leave the description of it to Dave, since this was his achievement. But he's so self-deprecating he wouldn't be fair to himself. So may I please spill his best beans?"

Mystified, Risa nodded.

"When you were nine, you may remember, Dave divorced Mitzy just a year after he'd divorced Moira. I was in law school, Cindy and I were expecting, the pregnancy got complicated, and life was hard, so when Dave came over one night, drank too much, and confessed to us that he had created nothing solid in his life, or in *your* life either, I blew a fuse. 'True,' I said. 'The way you're going, that child you claim to love so much will end up as fucked up as you are. But what can you do to change that? Nothing! Manly men are manly, hot loan clients are irresistible, fate is cruel, and that beguiling young daughter of yours is just shit outta luck.' You should've seen Dave's face, Risa. If Cindy hadn't been unwell he would have clocked me.

"He stormed off without a word and Cindy and I didn't see him till our son's third birthday. But when friendship resumed, Dave and I grew close as ever. So close I thought we knew each other's secrets. Not till his recent cancer diagnosis, when we cracked into estate matters, did I learn that, within days of me telling him his daughter was SOL, he took out a half-million-dollar life insurance policy with one beneficiary: *you*. A remote way of loving somebody, maybe. But think on this. While keeping Moira's child support steady, paying alimony to both his exes, and going nowhere career-wise, Dave kept that policy paid up in hope of helping some dream of yours eventually come true. I'm damned proud of him for that. I hope you are too."

"Bart!" Risa piped. "All of this is...*really* a lot! So before I...go in to see him...I need to just sit here and cry awhile. Okay?"

Bart gave her the kindest nod ever, and waited outside the car.

THEY ENTERED THE building, took the elevator up to oncology, and turned down the long hall toward Dave's room. As they neared his door, Bart said, "I feel this will go best if you two meet solo. Don't you?"

Risa nodded. Bart opened Dave's door, gently closed it behind her—and there lay her father, opening his eyes at the sound of the door's closing.

She saw in an instant how much the cancer had taken. He was being eaten alive. It took all her strength to register this and still give him a full-on smile.

But oh, Dave's reaction! His bony, jaundiced face turned so joyful at the sight of her that his love hit her in a wave, her heart flew all the way back to age seven, she adored him as unconditionally now as then, and there was no way not to throw herself into his arms. "*I'm so glad to see you!*" she sobbed. "*And so sorry it's been so long. I'm so sorry, Dave! I'm so sorry!*"

Holding her as tight as he could, which was not tight at all, he murmured words that made no sense to her: "There'll be no more sorries between you and me, Risa. Never again, ever. Because, listen to me. *You have saved my life. Believe it, my girl. You have saved my life.*"

(late July 1997)

IV. Genesis

> Our concern is with the person, the Who, going up the mountain.
>
> Also we ask, Who is already up there, calling? Who is the person in the person, prompting the whole endeavor?
> —James Hillman, "Peaks and Vales"

From the Elkmoon Mountain Journals of Grady Haynes:

"Keep an early morning eye out," Gladys Wax told me as she, Mo, Anon, and Ho left Lake Pipsissewa yesterday. "The weather patterns we're having, you might wake up on the first page of Genesis." She then rode off with a blithe wave, leaving me no idea what she was talking about--till it happened:

At first light this morning I woke in a perfect stillness, poked my head out of the tent, turned to the lovely lake I remembered camping beside, and it was gone: uncreated in the night. A gray fog lay so heavy upon me I couldn't see the edge of Pipsissewa twenty feet away. I crawled out, pissed, washed, built a bigger than usual fire against the cold, made espresso. I'm now sitting on a log ten feet from water I still can't see, hear, or sense except as an odor so faint it's more an intuition than a smell. A fifty-acre lake and the intricate ridges and peaks encircling it vanished. Egypt Peak, rising from the east end of the lake a short walk away, is only a memory. No wind. No sound. No world. I'm hunched in a void of the sort my poet hero Jim Harrison calls "the gray egg." Even time seems to have stopped. The world is so stripped it feels like a Before Time. If this were my permanent reality I'd be terrified, but I don't rise to the fear. I sit motionless, as with every kind of mountain weather, trying to open to the gray nada itself; appreciate it; fuse with it.

After a duration I can only call "two slowly sipped drams of espresso," the nothingness begins to exude a hint of somethingness and Gladys's <u>first page of Genesis</u> sure enough begins to unfold:

•The grayness directly overhead takes on a faint turquoise tint as a contradictory darkness looms out of the gray to the east: Egypt Peak! The fog right in front of me, fog closing me in, begins losing its obdurate thickness. When I run my hand through it, I sense it grows restless, coming to life. The Gray Egg inches toward silver and at the same time begins to feel gigantic. The fog moves and thins, brightening in all directions. A golden ghost of Egypt Peak now looms like a glorious yolk inside Harrison's Gray Egg.

•As the fog thins it begins to spiral. Objects and living creatures remain visibly nonexistent but the grayness, whiteness, gold, and turquoise are not static. They gyre. Everything that is, is in foment and ferment.

•Thirty or so feet of lake water returns to view. Two minutes later it's eighty feet. The fog doesn't leave the lake, but rather than smother the waters it now haunts them. White robes with no Trappists in them, white dervish skirts sans dervishes, begin tearing themselves free of the rug of fog to spiral across the lake in search of something more substantial to become. An on-earth-as-it-is-in-heaven feeling sweeps over me as Egypt Peak's gold intensifies and Pipsissewa's obscured surface grows faintly visible to the opposite shore. As my mist-cooled eyes take it all in I feel like a re-peatedly firing synapse inside the mind of the "no one" the old poets say we meet in the mountains. Today, this no one turns out to be a painter possessing brushes, but no visible hands and only a few obscured colors. Nevertheless I feel her gazing at the empty canvas that up till now was the Gray Egg.

•Change, the painter whispers, and the mist-monks and dervishes turn from off-white to diaphanous silver, rise up in disintegrating spirals, and begin departing the water like an army of spirits. Change, she repeats, and beneath the spirit army a trout rises, first life-form of the day, stun-ning Pipsissewa's night thoughts with expanding rings of silver. Change, she whispers again, and just past the rise-rings a black silhouette emerges, a genuine water bird, I realize, swimming fast, perturbed, it seems, by the racing vapors and spirits on all sides. Looking this way and that, swimming faster and faster amid foment/disintegration/creation, it lets out a cry I recognize as a loon's and sets off running, each spattering footstep creating an explosion of silver, till she's airborne and fleeing, then gone.

•Change, says the no one we meet in the mountains, and a hatch of pale morning duns begins, countless trout rise to greet it, and their crisscrossing silver rise-rings create a unitive new form of beauty. Though the air seems dead calm, hundreds more mist-forms, driven by windless convection, stream west to east across the water, moving almost as fast now as the loon that fled them, till I can no longer keep up with the unseen painter's gifts. Mist-bodies detach from mothering lake, rise toward enveloping mountains and sky, and it's Spirit World Rush Hour: pure energy and essence flying forth to animate the Elkmoons' awakening forms, bequeathing each its daily quota of life. Yearning to take part, I set aside my cup, stand, close my eyes, extend arms to the sky, and invite my own quota to enter me.

•When I reopen my eyes, the painting has become wildly more exact-ing. Colors and forms have gained full specificity. Whitebark pines and talus slopes appear on the far shore, violet-green swallows pierce the fading mist-dervishes, the silver rise-rings now dazzle the eye, and more plants, geographical features, and creatures than I can name have joined me. Six red and four gold crossbills approach from across the lake and vanish in the pines behind me. A golden-mantled ground squirrel scuffles up to my fire ring, a raven calls, and everywhere sunlight touches water I see thousands of the tiny, backlit, mote-sized insects that, if you focus your eyes one way, fly left to right over the lake surface, but if you focus another way fly right to left.

•<u>Change</u>, says the no one and, stage left, the transference of life force brings massive ridges into view and, in the V between ridges, the first snowcapped peaks of the Elkmoons. <u>Change</u>, says the no one and, stage right, mist parts to reveal the low indigo lumps of the distant Tamarack Range. <u>Change</u>, says the no one, and a total dispersal of every last shred of mist enables Elkmoons and Tamaracks to cast their reflections upon opposite ends of a now fully revealed, afternoon-languid lake.

•<u>Rest</u>, says the no one as a pair of gray jays land five feet from me and the first day of Genesis ends.

I had just finished the above account and tossed my journal in the tent when I happened to glance west at the ridge summit two-thirds of a mile distant and 900 feet above. The previous night, as sunset played across the sky, I was struck by the summit's smoothness. Not a deer, elk, or goat silhouette; not a tree. But as the mist dispersed to reveal the summit once again, three silhouettes stood in plain sight against the bright sky.

I ducked in my tent, grabbed binoculars, darted out, trained them on the shapes. Already there were just two, halved in size, seeming to sink into the ridge, leaving the summit smooth again--but not before I recognized two human-sized heads atop our species' distinctive shoulders.

<u>There was someone</u>. Three someones. And due to the blindingly thick predawn fog I knew they hadn't scaled this difficult ridge this morning. Whoever was up there had spent the night. So the question became: <u>To what end?</u>

I recalled Gladys saying, <u>The other four times I saw you</u>. Recalled how undaunted she was by a Goat Ridge thunderhead that had her Belgians shitting pizzas and me prepping for apocalypse. And where, by the way, is Gladys now? What's going on atop these highest Elkmoon ridges? Why would three voyeurs expend the time and effort to peer down upon the lowly likes of me? I feel I'm being studied. Perhaps even courted!

Who were--or more precisely, <u>who are</u>--the Lûmi?

(Harborview Medical Center, Seattle, summer into autumn 1997)

V. The Face of Love

Anything we pay for with our lives
does not cost too much.
                                          —Antonio Porchia, *Voices*

Fax from TJ, in the Fiumicino Airport, Italy, to Risa in Seattle:

Dear Risa,

I caught up to your fax in Anzio. It floored me. I'd have written sooner but had many things to do quickly and many things to cancel. I'm on my way home, and don't fret that. This hard passage has me reliving with fresh gratitude the salvific help you gave Jervis and me eight years ago. The work I've been doing here is mostly done, and what I didn't quite finish doesn't compare to a chance to meet your father. I'm so sorry about this, Risa! But how can I not also sense a great healing in the reversals you describe? I need to *see* this! I'll sleep on the plane, meet with Othello for a Tiny Joseph's walk-through tomorrow, then up to Seattle I come.

                                          Arms around you,
                                          TJ

Fax from Risa in Seattle, to Othello at Tiny Joseph's to give to TJ when he arrives in Portland:

I knew you'd do this and I thank you, TJ. You're my true mother-brother and I need both of you right now. Come meet my beloved, heartbreaking father at last!

                                          Love,
                                          Risa

The face of love.

During her Harborview vigil Risa remained haunted by the phrase—and by the actor who'd so forthrightly informed Julian he lacked such a face. When the actor then opened a porthole of his bass case and there was Romeo, the ingredients of love's face were so obvious! Gentle but keen eyes gazing at her, so unconditionally delighted that she existed that they wanted nothing but to go on gazing, and voilà, a mirror was created: she trusted love's gaze so completely she gazed back, love was delighted by love in two faces at once, and Julian's face turned into a pretty plastic chess piece that Romeo's face unintentionally wiped off the board. And hadn't Jamey, before leaving the bar, sent her the same gaze? *Two-headed six-leggèd admirers aren't easy to come by*, he'd said, every word sounding heartfelt and undefended. But he was an *actor*! How could she know if the actor's face was as sincere as his dog's?

The faces she didn't doubt were those she witnessed throughout her long days at Harborview, her father's face first and foremost. As cancer ate away at Dave he spent increasing spans of time asleep or drifting. But every time he came out of a nap or Vicodin haze to find Risa at his side, his face lit up just the way Romeo's had.

Sensitized to the expression by repeated exposure to it, Risa noticed, as she wandered the hospital, that faces of love are often at odds with prognoses. Visited by a loved one, tended by a kind nurse, many a terminal patient's face shone with adoration or gratitude that patients in full recovery didn't show at all. She also noticed that faces of love are not just direct two-way mirrors but mirrors capable of casting love over long distances, and into the unknown. When TJ, the day after his return from Italy, arrived at Harborview as promised, Dave's first words to him had been, "Splendid to meet you at last, Tavish Jacobus McGraff! And how's that Ocean-going brother of yours?"

Hearing the modifier "Ocean-going," TJ's love for Jervis broke out on his face, then shifted target, becoming love aimed at Dave for having honored Jervis despite his dire condition. When TJ then shared a few antic tales of Jervis's recent acts of holy foolishness, Dave's face of love took long-distance aim at Jervis even as it maintained contact with TJ, and Risa felt all three men loving one another, though two of them would never meet.

As her hospital days turned into weeks, such faces became islands near which she'd drop anchor, resupplying her courage and capacity to love.

CAMPED IN DAVE's room as he slept away the last day of August, Risa grabbed her laptop and managed to find a website for the Stumptown Shakespeare Ensemble of Portland. There were photographs of Jamey in several roles, mostly Shakespearean, and of Romeo too. But when she studied them, man and dog were so subsumed by their roles that she found no trace of the loving expressions that had so moved her at Tiny Joseph's in July.

There was an announcement for what the Stumptown troupe called "our world famous dog day divertimentos, *Urban Arias*." They'd been playing at Portland's Ankeny Theatre for three weeks, the reviews were raves, and she found herself remembering the rich timbre of Jamey's voice, his fascinating face, his forthright, funny yet substantial manner. But *dog day divertimentos*? A skein of farces in the midst of her father's miraculously sweet-natured suffering was the last sort of entertainment she would choose.

Dave woke just then, his face of love instantaneous soon as he saw her in her usual chair. Taking in her open laptop, he asked what she was looking at. She handed him the computer open to the Stumptown troupe's site. While Dave donned his reading glasses and perused it, she told of her first meeting with Jamey, of Julian's interruption, of Jamey's rude but revelatory diagnosis of Julian's lack of love, and of how Romeo's face, peering at her through a porthole in a bass case, did not so much knock Julian out of her heart as make her realize he'd never occupied that vital chamber at all.

Dave drew himself up painfully and broke out his skeletal smile. "A little rough-looking, this Van Zandt fellow. But in a good way, don't you think? And he sneaks this angelic dog into bars and restaurants in a bass case and gets away with it, yet gave away his secret to show *you* the dog's face? May I ask how you felt about this tall, dark pirate, Risa?"

"I admit to a hint of a crush," she said. But Dave's pallor, wasted smile, and hopeless prognosis made her add, "I lied. Within minutes I formed a *massive* crush. When the tension between Julian and Jamey got intense, I even half wanted to be the cause of a fight so I could throw myself into the arms of the victor, who I knew would not be Julian! When, in words, they *did* fight, Jamey won with ease. But Julian's impotent fury made the situation so awkward that, like a gentleman, Jamey left. Yet as he strode away I nearly called him back with Julian standing right in front of me! I wanted that so badly, Julian felt me wanting it, and moments later he was gone from my life too."

Weak as he was, Dave lit up. "But Jamey isn't gone! Risa! You're not helpless here. These reviews of *Urban Arias* are great, and tonight's the last night of their run! *What time is it?* Not yet two! You can make it! Go see Jamey and Romeo in action! Go *laugh* for an evening, my girl. You haven't left my side since you arrived. Take a night off in Portland, stay somewhere posh on me, and maybe, after the play, you can coax Jamey and Romeo out for a drink and a dog biscuit!"

Though she loved his enthusiasm Risa saw he'd utterly spent himself. He nodded weakly. "I know. I'm three-fourths gone. All the more reason for you to do this. You *so* deserve faces of love in your life."

"I've got one right in front of me, and my love for that face isn't going anywhere. Rest, Dave. I'll be here when you wake. Believe me. There's nowhere on Earth I'd rather be."

(Bend, Oregon, 1997)

VI. Dearest Walt,

Mu and I fell in love with Rocky Mountain rain-shadow towns, and settled on Elkmoon City, Montana, when I became the morning short-order cook at a cafe in the 120-year-old Black Queen Hotel, which got us a great deal on a cool corner apartment three floors up.

Mu is ten now, if you can believe that, and starts fifth grade in two weeks. But at the moment we're still on our first honest-to-gosh concert tour, sad to be down to our last four gigs. If you studied your "Hand Wash Cold Water" liner notes you know it's Mu singing those good harmonies and playing solid backup guitar, so I've been telling him we need a _band_ name, not just _my_ name. But months ago I made him our manager because he's ten times better at it than me. And Mu says: "_Thirteen Tons_ is still selling with no name on it but yours, so our band name is _your_ name. Don't argue with your manager, Mom."

We're in Bend, Oregon, tonight at a pub called McMe-namins. As we rolled into town Mu spotted a garage that restores classic cars, made an appointment, and got us a light tune-up. The '54's purring like a sabertooth again and I swear, Walt: Dee Anna's ride sells more records than our concerts. People love it so much that when Mu says, "The Chev's not for sale but the CDs are classics too," they buy our CDs out of love for the truck!

I know you said no more thank-yous but here are the cold hard facts: this rig keeps hauling us everywhere, the lock-on trailer keeps our instruments safe, the sleeping pod and KOAs save us hundreds in hotels, and to start each day by climbing into this old girl is to start each day happy. That's your kindness, Walt. That's a fact. Mu and I send you nothing but the military salute you like. But you better duck, because mine comes with a sneak hug and a kiss!

Love,
Lorilee

VII. Grady at Elevation 8,400 Feet

Lately I've been catching myself saying, "Holy shit, I'm not here alone." I've never had that experience before the past few months. I've felt this strange, eerie feeling that I wasn't alone, and I'd better know it.

—Bob Dylan

From the Elkmoon Mountain Journals of Grady Haynes:

No clouds, no wind, brilliant sun, blindingly blue sky. Lake Pipsissewa is an off-white granite aspersorium, light-flooded as holy water should be. Just east of camp a lone golden eagle rides a thermal flowing up Egypt Peak's eastern flank. Lodgepoles and rare white pines cast long shadows across the water as trout trouble the stillness, creating expanding bull's-eyes as Gladys Wax lounges in my inflatable kayak at the lake's center, casting flies into the bull's-eyes. From my perspective at water's edge, the lake is sky blue and broad, the eagle is jet-black and tiny despite its seven-foot wingspan, and the trout engaging Gladys are invisible but for the silver rings of their rises. The nature of things is so straightforward and clear up here. Sun lights Earth, warms waters, awakens life, becomes countless life-forms, and a fool named Grady sits in the clutches of all this until a peace as literal as the nature of things befalls him.

Last night by our campfire, however, orange flames flickered nonstop in the Informant's eyes as a conversation that began innocently enough soon left me far from peaceful...

"People spook at the word 'supernatural,'" she began, "and Stephen King and the horror movie industry get rich off that silliness. But all supernatural means up here is: a little more natural than regular old natural. 'Extra-natural' is what I call it. A good term to understand."

"Are you willing to help me understand it?" I asked.

"Only if you're willing to let go of what you think you understand."

"Can you help with an example of an understanding I need to let go of?"

"Sure. Let go of the fact that the advertising on a box of cornflakes says they're <u>natural</u>. I once poured a little box of them out on the ground up here, and the wild critters and birds wouldn't touch the stuff. Why?

They've got <u>extra-natural</u> things to eat that only this part of the world can provide. You and me are on to that, Grady Haynes. We're alike in one small but specific way."

The way she went quiet, as if she'd finished her thought, forced me to either leave a topic I couldn't bear to leave or sound like a fool. As usual, I chose the fool. "In what specific way are we alike, Gladys?"

"The natural world is run by natural laws, but we sense that those laws change at elevation. In the high places of the world there's a legitimate <u>above world</u>. An extra-naturalness enters in. Cornflakes no longer cut it. I've felt that in every high range I've ever visited. But you and I feel it here in the Elkmoons like nowhere else."

I was so touched to hear her unite us in this way that I went confessional. "My Elkmoon love has turned into the closest thing I have to a marriage, and I'm grateful for it. But my mountain marriage seems to be ruining my chances at the other kind. I've brought two girlfriends up here. Both seemed outdoorsy. But neither felt a trace of the <u>extra-naturalness</u> or the <u>above world</u>, so the depth of my love for this place eventually struck them as some kind of psychological malady."

"Then your girlfriends weren't friends after all," Gladys said. "Your malady is not loving these mountains <u>enough</u>. This is the one place on Earth you've never felt like a tourist for one second. What better proof that you belong? You are of this place. But every summer, after being at home here, you tell yourself, I've got Datalyrick to run. My work is important. And the pay's so good I can stay in the Elkmoons for a month every year. So you abandon them for an eleven-month Datalyrick diet of cornflakes that exiles you from the extra-natural love of your life."

To be told I <u>belong</u> to the Elkmoons one second and abandon them the next made me feel elated and insulted in such quick succession that the two feelings crashed head-on, canceling each other out. Gladys saw this, let out an odd little bleat of satisfaction, and went back to fussing with the fire.

This old woman has gotten under my skin like no female I've met since my botched grad school love, Risa. I assume Gladys is a packer by trade -- she's very skilled with Mormon and Anonymous and their tack and panniers. But I've never seen her pack anyone but herself, and she's not listed online or in phone directories. All I really know is that, during the warmest third of the year, she wanders the Elkmoons nonstop -- whereas I, she told me last night, "live like a damned sea anemone. Every summer the Elkmoons pry your closed heart open, and you drive elated down to Portland thinking it'll stay open. Then the cynicism, empty wit, and blinders that come of dealing with a world defined almost entirely in commercial terms cause your anemone heart to close and you're back on a soul diet of cornflakes, hoping the Elkmoons can open you next year. <u>Know this, Grady Haynes. A day's coming when they won't.</u> Your annual abdication of the mountains that heighten your consciousness doesn't cut it. Your Elkmoon life should be dictating the terms of your Portland life, not the other way around."

392 DAVID JAMES DUNCAN

Her diagnosis both scared and angered me. I told her I have to earn a living, I'm great at my job, I can't live all winter under an ice sheet like the trout in Pipsissewa, and her attacks on my Portland life were getting old. In reply she let out a sort of goat snort and fussed with her perfect little fire...

But whoa! That's a nice trout she just hooked. Came two feet out of the water in a cartwheel spraying silver like a firework. When she borrowed my rod, I told her I'm low on protein. That too earned a goat snort. If she lands that fish she'll release it for sure -- and last night by the fire she sort of explained why:

"Most of these trout are like us. Not from around here. The goldens are from the Sierras, the rainbows from Kamloops country in BC, the brookies from Maine. Yet they've made themselves so at home they can overwinter here. That should encourage you. Any living thing that overwinters in places this high and cold has my respect. Marmots, trout, goats, pika, people."

When I idly remarked that a winter up here would kill all the people I know, Gladys said, "Get off it, Cornflakes Haynes. People of the Andes and Himalayas live twice this high and thrive."

I asked if she'd spent time in the Himalayas. She said, "To sit in the heart of the Elkmoons talking about meeting the Oompa Loompa Lama in Bhutan is like sitting beside the living Buddha chattering about your weekend at Disney World."

God, she was cranky! "I'm easy," I said. "What do you want to talk about?"

"How 'bout some high-elevation physical facts, to start?" she said.

"Great," I said.

"What does the word 'atmosphere' mean to you, Grady Haynes?"

"One definition," I said, "would be the gigantic ring of air encircling our planet. Another would be the ring of grumpiness surrounding this campfire."

"More an ocean than a ring," she said, ignoring my jab. "An all-enveloping ocean of air, sixty miles deep, which everything alive -- including your corn-flakiness and my grumpiness -- has to thank for its existence. Atmosphere is a big damn deal."

I haven't described Gladys's fire keeping. She preps by breaking or sawing limbs into two-foot lengths. Whether she's talking or listening she then places each length with great particularity. She likes a circular fire, roughly three feet in diameter, that burns almost smoke-free and quiet. Never a blaze. To stay warm by a Gladys fire you've got to sit close. With a beaver-stripped willow wand she then pokes at her blaze as if the fire would forget how to burn without her help.

"Something to remember about that ocean of air," she said. "It has great depth, same as the oceans. And that depth weighs on us, just as the ocean weighs on divers. The atmosphere puts fifteen pounds of pressure per square inch on us at sea level. You wanna grasp that, set a fifteen-pound weight on a one-square-inch base, then set it on your head. Youch! That's a lot of pressure, you'll realize. But at eighteen thousand feet there's only eight pounds per square inch holding you together. Half the pressure. That's worth studying. Atmospheric pressure gets oxygen into our blood, body, and brain by squeezing it through tiny air sacs and membranes. 'Passive diffusion' it's called. And think on _this_. What's held firmly inside us at sea level starts trying to bust out at high elevation, giving us shortness of breath, hypoxia, splitting altitude headaches, inability to think, pulmonary edema. And what does it do to us to reduce, by half, the pressure not just on our bodies and brains but on our spirits? Our imaginations? Our consciousness? Our libidos? Look closely at your own experience and I'm sure you'll see that, at high elevation, things you never feel or imagine in Portland start reverse-pressuring their way out."

As Gladys kept fussing with the fire I felt her fussing with my mind to get it burning a certain way. It felt intrusive as hell, but fascinating as hell. Why, as a mountain lover, hadn't I pondered these metabolic mysteries before?

"Something else about the atmosphere at elevation," she said. "The higher you go, the more the light changes. At eleven thousand feet there's twenty percent more light than at sea level, with more topography to capture it. When the Inner Elkmoon marble turns the terrain white, you're getting extra-naturally _saturated_ with light. The atmosphere changes color too. If you kept climbing higher than mountains go, the sky would move through the blue and violet spectrum to ever darker indigo until you'd enter the blackness of space."

I stared up into that darkness so intently that when something clanked on the ground beside me I startled. It was a flask.

"I'm not done with you, Grady Haynes, and a fella stuck listening to a lecture deserves a snort."

I unscrewed the lid, took a pull, tasted good bourbon, and told her that if my grad school profs had thought of this I'd still be in school.

"You still _are_ in school," she said. "Only a fool would think we ever graduate from mountains. Tonight's assignment: grasp that landscapes encourage some things, and suppress others, and you can use that to your life's advantage. Specific weeds, trees, wildflowers, birds, critters, prefer certain elevations and terrains, and not others, for all kinds of reasons. It takes a long cover of snow to produce glacier lilies. Takes ninety-degree heat to incubate giant mullein and the furry leaves that are nature's best toilet paper. Takes thousands of years for pine forests to coax the finches we call 'cross-bills' into evolving the skewed beak that lets 'em tear open pine cones for the nuts. And the same specifics sculpt _people_. Those who live lifelong on sixteen-thousand-foot Andean terraces and Tibetan plateaus aren't put together like us. They have twenty percent more blood. Sixty percent more hemoglobin. Red blood cells bigger than ours. Blood much thicker than ours. And to pump that blood, hearts a fifth or more bigger than ours. Bigger lungs too, and barrel chests to house 'em. Shorter, stronger legs with better oxygen flow to handle the daily ascents and descents. Extremities loaded with arteries and veins so much more dilated than ours that they just about _never_ get frostbite. And all this is only the physical."

Egypt Peak and the pale ridges below had been aglow with moonlight all evening though the moon had remained hidden. A two-thirds moon now rose over the ridge and shone across Pipsissewa's entire surface, lighting up Gladys's face. Seeing her ancient eye trained upon me, I got the feeling she was just getting warmed up.

"A mystery worth studying," she said, "is what elevation does to con-sciousness. One thing it changes is receptivity. Tell me if I'm right, Grady Haynes. For you, strong reception kicks in as you traverse those last four miles of West Fork switchbacks up to Gateway Pass, and holds steady from Boundary Lake up to Pipsissewa. But as you ascend Gentian Couloir toward the base of the Blue Mosque the reception cranks up so hard you sometimes feel the long-gone massif still hovering in the sky over your head."

"It's true!" I cried. "But how on Earth can you know that so specifically?"

"Very few people can tote seventy pounds from the West Fork trailhead to Boundary in a day. Something's gotta lift 'em. I've seen that lift in you. Are you aware of how important that is? Have you paid attention to how your sense of lift is inviting you, specifically, on up to Jade Lake at the foot of the Mosque?"

"I have felt something pulling me, but what makes you so sure it's Jade Lake?"

"Jade," she said, giving the fire a hard poke that sent up sparks, "is some-thing special. A causeway into little-known heights and depths. A few rare places in this world help a person blossom into who their part of the world needs 'em to be. Jade is such a place. The reception there, day or night, can turn extra-extra-natural. The Lûmi have known this for centuries."

That word again. Loom eye, she pronounces it. The thought of a high hidden people native, five months of the year, to these very peaks, lakes, cathedral ridges, unseen massifs, sent tremors through me.

"To more fully imagine the Lûmi, remember what those high Andean and Tibetan plateaus do to humans physically. At elevation our imagination, consciousness, spirit, bodies, are literally elevated. And elevation does things. Creates things. And uncreates other things. Again to our potential advantage. Elevation can unmake the mental ruts and overcrowding that trap our think-ing. On a high peak in the Alps, a climber named Emile Javelle once looked out over the world and was swallowed alive by a vastness that overwhelmed him. Years passed before he could even speak of it. When he did, he said that any philosophy, religion, or science that tells us what the universe is, or what our place and purpose here are, is a blindfold, not a seeing. 'The further the vision of our eye extends,' Javelle said, 'the greater the mystery becomes.'"

Gladys kept glancing at me, then tending the fire, glancing, then tending. "How to shed our blindfolds and live the mountain mystery? You're chasing that. I see it in you every time we meet. You're here for the reception, in both senses of that good word. This is why Jade is invaluable. Do you know the word 'apophatic'? An apophatic truth doesn't give you anything. It takes things away. Erases falsehoods and delusions the way an Alps vast-ness erased Javelle's philosophy and science. Make no mistake, Grady Haynes.

<u>Jade holds that power</u>. The Lûmi revere that lake's ability to remove the blindfolds created by the crushing loads of crap we think we know."

Remembering the silhouettes on the ridge above Pipsissewa, my heart pounded. "You're saying the Lûmi <u>still</u> come up here to remove their blindfolds?"

Poking the fire chaotically now, messing up the even burn she'd so carefully maintained, she said, "There's no real point in talking about what your life as a low-elevation cornflake bars you from experiencing."

Hurt, then euphoria, then hurt again. This time it made me mad. "You love to denigrate my Portland life. But I come up here to wage war against that life! And it works. When I arrive at the trailhead, hoist my pack, start hiking, start hurting, everything gets dead simple. One foot in front of the other. Sweat out the city habits, blindnesses, poisons. Gulp mountain water. Relish the elevation gain, vertical rock faces, increased intensity of light, purgative pain. Hike and hurt, hike and hurt, higher and higher. And when I make it over Gateway and set eyes on Boundary and the Mosque, I'm floodlit by their mystery. The skill I lack is an ability to find mystery and wonder at low elevation, which should be possible too. Instead of denigrating Cornflakes Grady, how about helping me <u>leave him behind</u>?"

The Informant said and did nothing for three minutes of silence that felt like an hour. Then, lo and behold, she faintly smiled as she said, "How to carry elevation's gifts down has been a Lûmi practice for centuries. One method they advise. <u>Carry the mountains down out of the mountains</u>. Never leave them behind. That sounds like crazy to a head full of cornflakes, but mountains are hell on cornflakiness. Keeping them with you is no crazier than Buddhists and Christians carrying their Buddha and Jesus icons and rosaries wherever they go. If you learn to carry mountains skillfully enough, high-elevation truths can reverse-pressure their way out of you in lowly Portland. Get that going and you'll really be on to something."

The way she looked at me left me eager to feel for high-elevation sensations on low-elevation streets. "I won't forget that," I said. And I haven't.

"So here's another tool to help carry mountains down," she said. "Your chosen locations up here are too conservative. You're a lakeshore guy. With the exception of Jade's shores, I urge you to be a high ridges guy, and not just in fair weather."

"I love the ridges, Gladys, and hike them every chance I get. But thunderheads form fast up there, and my fear of <u>those</u> monsters is primal!"

"That fear is what makes the ridges such a key mountain feature to befriend and carry down to low elevation," she said. "Sure, lightning kills some folks. But on Cornflakes's turf so do coronaries, cancer, car wrecks, diabetes, pneumonia, mass murderers, and the wear and tear of bad work on a high-paying hamster wheel. Find places of safety at elevation so you don't fear thunderheads and that familiarity begins to protect you down low."

Her words had doubled my heart rate. "I've searched some ridgelines, and found a few intriguing things. But can you tell me more about what to look for?"

"On the longest, most connective high ridges, have you noticed some faint old footpaths?" she asked.

"I have! Since I couldn't find boot tracks, I thought ungulates made them. But then I found a few unobtrusive cairns alongside them. Quite small, but each stone stacked so that gravity presses it inward, like a drystone wall. Something moved me to take one cairn apart. In its center I found a small green rock. Nephrite, I think. I'd been meaning to ask you about that."

"Two things," the Informant said. "One. When you follow cairn-marked trails, look for offshoots. They're so rarely used, and so well erased by winter snow, that they're very hard to spot. But if you find even a suspicion of one, follow it. Some lead to storm and lightning-proof rock shelters and small caves."

Again my heart pounded. A series of such shelters could make the high ridges traversable, or even inhabitable!

"As for the cairns," she continued, "ignore any that look clumsily made. That's the work of random hikers. The small, inward-leaning cairns are the ones to look for. But don't disturb 'em. And for God's sake don't steal the jade piece."

Even by firelight she could tell I was blushing. "Didn't mean to embarrass you," she said. "But if you kept a nephrite piece, put it back. Bad juju to keep it. Don't fret. Just restore it, rebuild the cairn with the same skill that created it, and mark the spot on your map. If you find another cairn, try to see on your map how it connects to the first one without losing or gaining much elevation. That could lead to more. The cairns are way markers on a gigantic circle that, in English, we might call the 'Lûmi High-Elevation Purification Loop.'"

"Good God!" I cried. "A North American high-mountain loop that _purifies_? It sounds like the Tibetan pilgrimage round Mount Kailash!"

"More like Kailash than Dante's Mount Purgatory anyway. The Lûmi purification takes place in _this_ world, not the next, and participation is voluntary, not mandatory. But to tell you what the Loop does in words is wrong-headed. For a Loop pilgrim the payoff is in stupendous efforts of the body that shut down the grinding gears and cheap tricks of a pilgrim's mind. No ego stinks worse than a _spiritual ego_, and the Lûmi Loop was designed to murder that prince of darkness. It traverses several hundred long ridges, threading through one thousand and five peaks and nineteen deep river valleys. But it's best begun from Boundary, which you bolt to every year as if you knew that. And it ends -- after so many years of effort that most pilgrims write the Loop off as a lunatic fantasy -- on Jade's eerie shores, where a rare Loop-completing pilgrim rises up into a _Seeing_ compared to which eyesight is a blindness. There's a book that tells of all this, _Lûmi Singings_."

I'm embarrassed to admit that I went crazy. "A _book_? _Lûmi Singings_? Good Lord! As soon as I get home I'll buy it and devour it! I can't wait!"

Cringing at my every word, Gladys said, "Three things, Grady Haynes. One, you're sitting here _on_ the Lûmi Loop, blind to everything _Lûmi Singings_ would tell you because you want a book, not the mountains. Two: you won't find the book. Three, the atmosphere up here is highly charged, as you sense. But you don't yet sense that this charge is not your special little friend. The powers that reign here are dead neutral in terms of how they strike people, same as the lightning and just as dangerous. Foremost among these powers are fun-house mirrors that can get you lost and keep you lost for life -- and a strong will, overheated imagination, and spiritual ego stand you right in front of 'em. You can't reach the mountains that can be carried within by mentally raiding them and thinking that claims them. Force yourself upon the Elkmoons and they turn into a maze you'll never escape even as your compass and map lie that you know where you are. The work up here, the way up here, is to erase self. And if that sounds more like getting lost than finding a clearly defined Way, you're beginning to hear me."

"But, Gladys!" I argued. "When it's my love for the Elkmoons that makes me want to read Lûmi Singings, why shouldn't I find it and relish every word?"

"Go ahead and try," she said. "And when you fail and give up, remember an old lady who once told you to approach this place differently than you have up to now. While resting at Boundary before heading farther up and in, shut off your willpower like a circuit breaker. Imagine nothing. Let the Elkmoons be the Elkmoons in their subtlest details and in their majesty. No helping 'em out. No deciding what it all means. For time out of mind, mountains have known exactly what they're doing. It's their knowing you seek, not your own. Stop trying to give yourself little mountainy presents. Diminish you till there is no you. Vanish into what is, Grady Haynes. It changes everything."

I said, "I know!" And saw the Informant flinch. And didn't take the hint. "Two years ago I was hiking that smooth, half-mile-wide escarpment at the base of Egypt Peak when two mountain goats bloomed out of the rock forty feet above me. They had nowhere to hide. I shucked my pack and whipped out my Nikon. Took six or seven seconds max. But when I lifted the camera the goats had vanished. It was extra-natural, Gladys! A cheetah couldn't have crossed that escarpment that fast! And if mountain goats can vanish, I figure I can too."

"I saw! I shucked! I lifted! I figure! I can!" she scoffed. "You cast yourself as the hero of these moments like a dog rolling in something he thinks makes him smell fascinating, but those goats you spooked are residents who never leave the mountains for an instant, even in the dead of winter. Do you want to gawk at photos of true kings of these mountains or be the mountains, Grady Haynes? If you'd captured those goats and sold the shot to National Geographic their readers would see what you saw. Goat Cornflakes. Next time something blooms out of the rock, don't pick the blossom! Freeze thought. Dead calm, body and mind. No need to capture a thing. Let granite be granite, eyes be eyes, and goats be goats on a rock face being rock."

The fire she'd so avidly tended was dying. Instead of feeding it she poked it to pieces, as she'd done to me. And she wasn't finished. "If it wasn't so peaceful tonight I might not be annoyed by the peace-shattering sound of you rummaging through your head for more <u>Deeds of a Mountainy Man</u>. But it <u>is</u> calm, so I hear what you're coming up with. <u>Cornflakes</u>. Have fun crunchin' 'em if that's your idea of fun. Me, I'm gonna get these old bones to bed, see if I can't sneak inside a big mean granite spire, and spend an eon or two flippin' off those show-offs, the stars."

She'd done it again: left me so elated, then so humiliated, that the two feelings crashed head-on, knocking each other out.

But there was something new about this crash: I saw I had it coming, let my feelings hurt until they didn't, lay back against a log, froze thought, and let nine shooting stars be nine shooting stars I let shoot but didn't lay claim to.

She left early the next morning and I missed her, as always. But for the following two weeks I abandoned the lake basins, hewed to the high ridge-lines, restored the nephrite I'd taken to its drystone cairn, let mountains be mountains, and entered a prolonged state of self-effacement like nothing I'd ever experienced. One day I crested a high white marble ridge, beheld a sun-warmed pond in a grassy declivity four hundred yards down its far side, went dead calm in body and mind, and descended, emptied of self, till there was a small, limpid, grass-bottomed pool in a declivity's center and nothing more. Not till the sun dipped below the ridge and my teeth began to chatter did I find myself sitting naked, waist deep in a pool and a peace that continued for two more perfect days.

But after my trip-ending twenty-eight-mile hike out, eighteen-hour drive, and nine-thousand-foot descent to my Sacajawea Village Luxury Townhouse at elevation forty, I felt so distanced from my peace place that I got out my mountain journal, found the entry on the sun-warmed pool, read it to reassure myself--and all it did was make me shout, "<u>Limpid grass-bottomed Cornflakes!</u>," Frisbee my journal across the room, and pour myself a fat whiskey.

<u>Reception</u>. At low elevation, God help me, I have next to none--and reception, I realize more by the year, is a matter of life or death. <u>With</u> reception, I once learned that water, night stars, light-years, and light speed can come to rest on a lake's surface tension and in a human heart at the same instant, unveiling a universe shot through with bliss and beauty. <u>With-out</u> reception a swarm of Datalyrick customers are destroying the planet, and for eleven months out of twelve I sell them <u>mental telepathy equipment for mentals</u> to speed the destruction. After nine mountain summers my failure to carry the Elkmoons' gifts down to Portland has filled eleven-twelfths of my life with hypocrisy, and when I try to imagine what sort of messiah-therapist-shaman could rescue me, I picture the same figures every time: <u>silent, watchful silhouettes atop an occasional towering Elkmoon ridge</u>.

Preposterous as it may sound to those with fifteen pounds of pressure per square inch preventing what's inside them from busting out, I feel my sole chance at becoming the person my part of the world needs me to be is to locate, and hopefully befriend, an actual living Lûmi.

VIII. Hail Debbie, Full of Grace

Give me some kind of rain for to make me see.
—Lightnin' Hopkins

JAMEY VAN ZANDT was towing the Land Nautilus, recently remodeled by Jon with added comforts for a very old Romeo, down a crowded Northwest 23rd sidewalk at his usual long-strided four miles per hour, when a stooped little man doddering along at perhaps a mile per hour blocked his way. Jamey began to pass on the left. As if he had eyes in the back of his head and a death wish, the man veered left just as Jamey was about to fly by him, then slammed to an abrupt halt. Jamey plowed into him so hard the fellow would have landed on his face if Jamey hadn't lunged forward, caught him by the hood of his sweatshirt, and yanked him back up onto his feet. "We're *so sorry!*" Jamey cried. "Are you all right?"

The little fellow gave Jamey a namaste. "My fault," he said in a papery whisper.

I'M A BUDDHIST FOR CHRIST'S SAKE! added his sweatshirt.

"No, no," Jamey said. "We ran into *you.* Are you sure you're okay?"

"Sometimes English confuses me. You call you *we.* But I only see *you.* Is this the same kind of trickery that allows a woman to put on a *pair* of panties, but only *one* bra?"

"Nothing of the sort!" Jamey laughed. "Look." He tapped the porthole of the Nautilus and Romeo's face loomed, smiling his serene Andalusian smile. "Romeo makes us a we."

The man squatted by the Nautilus and peered through the porthole as a stream of pedestrians veered awkwardly around them. "*Finally!*" he paper-whispered to Roams. "A fellow Portlander who understands our true Oceanic situation!"

Though he'd no idea what the little fellow meant, Jamey squatted down and opened the Nautilus. "I'm Jamey, and this is Romeo," he said as Roams stepped out onto the sidewalk.

"Jervis McGraff," said Jervis as he extended the back of his hand so Romeo could sniff it. When Roams instead offered his right paw for a shake, two passing pedestrians burst out laughing, but laughter was old hat to the actor in Roams. He kept his paw extended. "*The fuck!*" Jervis breathed as he and Romeo shook. "*This dog obeys no created thing but love.*"

Moved by this odd locution, Jamey said, "Jervis and Roams. What say we head for a place where obeying no created thing but love won't get us trampled?"

Jervis nodded, causing his Saturn-ring of long gray-blond hair to bob like the tailfeathers of some bizarre jungle bird. With the empty Nautilus in tow, Jamey turned west on Northrup and left the traffic and crowds behind. Yet Jervis slammed to another halt so abrupt that Romeo plowed into the backs of his legs.

"Full disclosure, Jamey," he said as he squatted down to pet Roams. "I've seen every Shakespeare play you and Romeo ever fucked with, and loved 'em all. My fave? You as Lear and Roams as the faithful dog able to see through your enemies' lies when the mad king couldn't, faithful to you even as you went completely nuts. What an actor, this soul-dog! When Goneril had him killed, Roams had the whole place sobbing, though I'm so munched my sobs just whistle in and out my nose."

Jervis's skewed gaze took aim at Jamey now. "More full disclosure," he said, scratching Roams behind the ears. "Because I'm munched, I leak, which makes me see stuff I'm not trying to see, and know stuff I'm not trying to know. Sorry to know this, Jamey, but somehow I see you're in love, and your love is unrequited."

Jamey reeled. "How could you *possibly* know that!"

"Don't ask unless you're strange-tolerant," Jervis warned.

"I'm in theatre. Of course I'm strange-tolerant." Jamey eased closer to Jervis to hear.

"All is an Ocean," he paper-whispered as he gave Romeo's arthritic lower back a fingertip massage that had him marching in place, groaning with pleasure. "Father Zosima said that. People think Dostoevsky made Zosima and his Ocean up. But in 1989 I got beat into a coma, and when I woke seven weeks later I was in Zosima's Ocean. I still am, believe it or not. Ocean communicates in strobe images, not language. Lots of her images are faces I can read because I live on the streets and see thousands of 'em a day. Your face said you're in unrequited love. But Ocean didn't strobe who smote you."

Jamey heaved a riven sigh. "Her name's Risa! Risa McKeig!" (Hearing his brother's closest friend named, Jervis's poker face didn't so much as twitch.) "July 25th. Place called Rasta Pasta. They were remodeling. The bar was closed. I snuck in anyway. Risa was cleaning bar glasses, so for a while it was just her and me, and she was...*ye gods, where to begin*! Super smart, kind, funny. And so beautiful! Gorgeously out-of-control hair. A low voice I can't stop hearing. Her whole heart in her dark-eyed gaze. And this unlikely glee-gap in her front teeth that gives her an imperfect beauty a thousand times better than perfect beauty! But this beau of hers showed up. Gilligan. A talking table scrap who pretended to own her and pass it off as love. That riled me enough to defend Risa by opening Romeo's porthole and showing her what it is to be seen with love. And she did see. I then gave Gilligan pro bono advice he took so poorly I had to leave. But I swear Risa felt something for Roams and me, and I can't get her out of my mind, so I went back to her bar recently, Tiny Joseph's it's called now, and it was mobbed, and the bartender shouted, '*She's in Seattle!*' But her number's not listed there or here. So unless something changes I'm not just unrequited, Jervis. I'm *fucked*."

"Before you decide you're fucked, a little more about Ocean," Jervis paper-whispered. "Back on 23rd, it was she who strobed, *Veer left, then stop*. I didn't know why. I obey without a why. I veered. I stopped. And you crashed into me. Ocean wanted us to meet, Jamey. And when Ocean wants people to meet, *ways lead unto ways*." Jamey was beginning to question Jervis's sanity when, calm as could be, he added, "In this case, for instance, my brother TJ *owns* Tiny Joseph's"—Jamey gaped—"and we both know Risa"—Jamey gasped—"and her imperfect beauty *is* more beautiful than regular old beauty." Jamey's whimpering caused Romeo to wag his tail as he marched in place to Jervis's massage. "But you need to stay calm, Jamey, because two currents are running through here. The tiny current of the little I know, which can't help you, and the giant Ocean gyres that can help if you give yourself up and let her gyres carry you."

"For me to attempt this, please say what you mean by *give yourself up*," Jamey said.

"If TJ or I put you in touch with Risa now, your contact would be crap. She's doing heartwork with her dad, who's dying of cancer. Work that'll nurture the rest of her life. No room for you in that. But *you* have heartwork to do too. Ocean just strobed this. Very rare."

Unable to contain himself, Jamey stood up and roared, "Let me at it!"

Jervis also stood. "*Calm,* Jamey. It takes calm to settle into heartwork. Your task, Ocean strobed, is to stop driving away the first woman you ever loved."

Confused, but eager to obey, Jamey said, "Aha! Well, okay then. That would be a woman named Lia, way back in Ashland days. Except...hold up, Jervis. I didn't drive Lia away. She dumped me! So I guess Ocean missed the target on that one."

"All is an Ocean, Jamey. *All*. She is the Great One. Her *All* includes every conceivable target, so how could she possibly miss one? Her strobe flashed that there's a sorrow in you like a sorrow in me. I don't know what it is. But for some reason I feel I should say this. When I was fourteen, my parents were killed in a head-on crash in Scotland."

A feeling so Oceanic washed over Jamey that his hair stood on end. "Of all the beslubbering, fen-sucked, beef-witted predicaments! If I ask myself what kind of crackpot you are, Jervis, my honest feeling is, *you're Ocean's dead honest oracle*! Your fathomless friend just told the orphaned *you* to tell the half-orphaned *me* to get his head out of his ass and remember the facts of his own scurvy life. The first woman I ever loved was my *mother*! Whom I drive so far away I didn't even think of her when you asked your 'first woman' question. She died on my fifth birthday. Her name was Debbie."

"Now we can begin," said Jervis. "Come on, Roams and Jamey. *Solvitur ambulando.*"

The trio set out on what Jamey later learned was called an Ocean-walk. Unexplained by Jervis, their rambling soon struck Jamey as absurdly purposeless until Jervis read his mind clearly enough to remark, "Destination isn't what matters. *All is an Ocean.* What might matter is, you've done some weird shit in your life. Ocean is working through it. Her turning us one way and not another helps her help you. I can't explain how. But Ocean's strobes have helped so many people it would be an insult for me to ask after the hows and whys."

Hearing this, the walk's purposelessness began to fascinate Jamey. At one point Jervis led them back and forth on the same forty-foot length of sidewalk perhaps thirty times, doing abrupt about-faces so Marine-like in execution that even Romeo smiled at the absurdity of it. But Jervis was teasing out the history of Jamey and Debbie's shared birthday-deathday, and Jamey the Princeling was dodging his queries with evasive, lighthearted accounts of his debacles. By slamming to halts and doing about-faces, Jervis gradually silenced the Princeling, drew out the Darkling, and the sudden about-faces weren't funny anymore.

Surrendering to Jervis's tactics, Jamey began pouring out his futile attempts to make contact with his dead mom; his rage and theological warfare with God; his annual birthday disgraces, agonized doubts, injuries to self and others. When he finally wound down, the least military-looking person Jamey had ever seen slammed to another military halt. "A question for you. Since you despise the abbreviation *Debbie,* why do you answer to the name *Jamey* instead of James?"

The question picked Jamey's heart like a lock. When he first tried to reply, his voice failed him. When words did come, Jervis became the first person ever to hear Jamey say, "With the last shred of vivacity she ever mustered in my sight, my bald-headed, swollen-faced, horrid-breathed mother took me by the shoulders, flashed the wreckage of her beautiful smile, and said, 'Promise me you'll *always* be my Jamey. *James* is too drab. *Jamey* suits your lively little face to a T.' Then she died. Leaving me to be her Jamey forever, I figure, since she won't be asking me to do much else to please her."

Speed-shifting into Princeling mode, Jamey added, "But damn, Jervis! You call this heartwork? Everybody has sorrows. What's the purpose of dragging my long-departed little woes out into the glorious light of an Indian summer day?"

Jervis spun on Jamey and drew so close that his upturned chin nearly touched Jamey's chest: "You're a *Shakespearean* and a *tragedian* and you don't know the answer to *that*? Unexamined woes turn to *shite* in a human heart. You drag your heart shite out into the light of consciousness so your writhing shite demons shrivel up and die. You drag heart shite out so it doesn't become a fetid poison you eventually spew on the woman who wins your heart. *The fuck*. If you want good contact with *any* woman, *ever,* your contact place with Debbie can't be a festering black hole you keep pretending isn't there!"

At the words "black hole" the Darkling flew into Jamey like a bird on fire. Breathing hard, fighting to contain him, Jamey sputtered, "Okay! Okay! You win, but back off, Jervis! Don't *poke* at me like this. Just tell me how to drag out and shrivel up my heart shite."

Jervis stood stock-still and closed his eyes. "Most mothers are just mortal pissants, same as you and me," he paper-whispered. "But *Motherhood* is a goddess you have seriously dishonored. You need to make prayers to the goddess, Jamey. Prayers of atonement. You're not Catholic, so a *Hail Mary* would just be *boinka-boinka*. But a good tragedian's prayer to the Motherhood goddess could be as simple as this: *Hail Debbie, full of grace.*"

The Darkling roared back to life. "If attaching my mother's puling name to that old bromide is prayer, fuck praying! And just for the record, Jervis, I made great contact with Risa at first. Her pissy pet peacock, Gilligan, was our only problem."

With a speed completely out of character, Jervis stepped forward and rapped Jamey hard on the breastbone. "*Feel it?*" came the papery whisper. "*Feel the black hole in there?* Wanna punch me because I banged on it? Wanna run off and screw some poor whore, or raise hell with motorists, or shit in the Ocean, or tell me to fuck off because your mom died three and a half decades ago and left you *a poor little fella*? Wanna refuse to hail Debbie and fall in love with Risa, only to discover Risa loves an Unseen Unborn Guileless Perfection that enrages you because your mom suffered a lot, so you tell Risa to fuck off too?"

The thought of doing such a thing to Risa caused the Darkling rage to fizzle out in an instant. "Okay. Shit! Sorry, Jervis. I see it now. I do. I need to climb down into my black hole and clean house somehow. But what kind of lame deity would want to hear my forced and faithless little prayer down there?"

"The *Motherhood goddess,* fool! And she's been anything *but* lame! Don't you ever ponder your bent nose bone, your giant chin scar, and the tongue you drove so many teeth through you almost bit it off? You live in a motherhood blackness you've never explored with *any* love or skill. You maimed a bakery truck driver in that blackness. You shoplifted steaks, handed them to cops, nearly lost Roams to animal control, got the clap, nearly killed people, nearly killed yourself in that blackness."

"You can't shame me with what I just confessed," Jamey said weakly.

"Then let's shame you with this. *You've left your mother lying in that blackness!* All these years you've *never* tried to free her from it. Her death, for you, is all about *you.*"

Jervis's furious whisper shook Jamey to the core.

"Here's a strobe," he said. "A direct gift from Ocean to you. This is rare, Jamey. She strobes that *Hail Debbie, full of grace,* is your lamp. She's telling you to stop feeling how you felt, go down into blackness, and use your lamp to find out how *Debbie* felt. Say your Hail Debbies till her face and grace *actually show up.* Say them some more, until *leukemia* shows up. Say them as Debbie, full of grace, fights with all her might to get well, only to *fail* to get well. Say them as Jon brings you to visit her and she lies there helpless, wasting away in front of you, studying your slumped little shoulders and scared little face, seeing you're *afraid* of her now because of the sickness she can't help. Say your Hail Debbies *as she dies on your birthday,* unable to avoid that terrible timing. *The fuck* is all *I'm* saying, Jamey. I'm a pissant and fool, same as you. It's *Ocean* strobing you to take a five-word lamp down into your mother darkness, and see and honor what you've *never* seen or honored. *Who Debbie was.* How *good* she was. What she had to give up and go through despite that goodness. It's time to honor her love not just for you but for her *own* life, her friends, your dad, her full deep breaths, her once-beautiful body, long legs, and gorgeous ass halves going all coordinated down the sidewalk. Confession alone doesn't touch this. It's time for contrition and penance, and don't even *pretend* to want absolution. That's Ocean's job, not ours. Your assigned work is to light a five-word lamp, climb down inside your black hole, hunt Debbie's grace till you find it, and *give it back to her. The fuck!* How old *are* you, anyway? *Hail Debbie, full of grace,* no matter where or what she is now. *Hail Debbie, full of grace,* till your whole heart means it and she *feels* you meaning it. *Hail Debbie, full of grace,* Jamey. That's all Ocean's got for you today."

Jamey was so undone he couldn't even nod to show he understood. But there was no need. Romeo, as he listened to Jervis and felt Jamey's emotions in response, never once quit panting and nodding.

"I walk dogs for a few friends," Jervis said. "Closest thing I've got to a job. How about, while you seek Debbie's grace, I walk Roams? I'll wind us down to Étouffée Bruté by dark. When you and Debbie and Debbie's grace have met, that's where we'll be. Okay?"

Jamey stood frozen, recognizing the five-year-old inside himself, traumatized at the prospect of being abandoned. When he managed a nod, Jervis took the Nautilus in tow and trudged away. Romeo turned back and gave Jamey a questioning look. "Go," Jamey said, and Roams happily followed Jervis and the land sub.

Feeling a stricken urge to run after them, Jamey whispered, "*The fuck.*

How old *are* you, anyway?" and managed to stand motionless until they rounded a corner two blocks away.

JAMEY'S FIRST RECITATION was a raging failure. The instant he said, "*Hail Debbie, full of grace,*" he stopped cold. "Fucking *ridiculous!*" he snapped. "This I *will not do!*"

But in a perfect Jervis impersonation, he added, "*Said the Princeling to the Darkling. The fuck, Jamey. Light the lamp and do the damned heartwork.*"

He sighed. The first cold rain of autumn began to fall. Not dressed for it, he sighed again. "Okay. Okay, Jervis. Here goes.

"*Hail Debbie, full of grace,*" he declaimed in his resonant actor's baritone.

You just turned prayer into performance, he imagined Jervis saying. *Don't* act. Invoke! *For once in your beslubbering fen-sucked life,* find Debbie, *and* be *with her!*

"Bossy, bossy. But dammit, you're right. Okay. Maybe it's as simple as..."

"*Hail,*" he said in time to a stride up the sidewalk; "*Debbie,*" he added on the next stride; "*Full,*" he said on the third, "*Of grace,*" he added with a fourth.

Crapola! Why did it feel so *awkward?* One stride per word made each word feel like a bowling ball dropped on the sidewalk.

How about a word timed to the first step, then two steps with no words, the Jervis voice suggested. *Turn your prayer into a waltz and you could dance for her as you pray.*

"*What an idea,*" Jamey murmured. And with no further ado, away he whirled. "*Hail*" (two, three) "*Debbie*" (two, three) "*full*" (two, three) "*of grace*" (two, three), "*Hail*" (two, three) "*Debbie*" (two, three) "*full*" (two, three) "*of grace*" (two, three)...

Yeah! Better! Coordinating steps and words and upping his heart rate and breathing removed his anxiety about not believing in prayer. He didn't expect a thing. He just waltzed along until rhythm, words, and steps merged. "*Hail*" (two, three) "*Debbie*" (two, three) "*full*" (two, three) "*of grace*" (two, three)...

Maybe five minutes in, though the rain was falling much harder, Jamey realized he was smiling. Yet as he waltzed his way down Thurman past commuters walking home from work, several of them greeted his chant with fierce scowls. Wondering why, he tried to see himself objectively—and burst out laughing. Hail *Debbie?* The scowlers, he realized, must be Catholics who thought he was so stupid he couldn't get Mary's name right!

Ever the contrarian, and an excellent dancer as well, Jamey began to greet the scowlers by placing his arms round an invisible Debbie and *flying* past them, spinning her in time to his chant: "*Hail*" (two, three) "*Debbie*" (two, three) "*full*" (two, three) "*of grace*" (two, three), "*Hail*" (two, three) "*Debbie*" (two, three) "*full*" (two, three) "*of grace*" (two, three)...

He waltzed across Vaughan Street and down into the industrial district, the pedestrians thinning, the rain a near downpour now, and as he spun his way along he found himself going blind to the city for a reason beyond hope: he began to see his mother more clearly than he had since he was five. "*Hail*" (two, three) "*Debbie*" (two, three) he kept breathing, till there she towered "*full*" (two, three) "*of grace*" (two, three) on tiptoe "*Hail*" (two, three) high above him "*Debbie*" (two, three), her body lithe in a pale blue dress dotted "*full*" (two, three) with hundreds of tiny red flowers "*of grace*" (two, three) as she peered "*Hail*" (two, three) into an enormous rose bush "*Debbie*" (two, three), then sent her long arms "*full*" (two, three) and slender hands "*of grace*" (two, three) into the bush, separating blossoms and leaves "*Hail*" (two, three) till her face "*Debbie*" (two, three) disappeared in the green cave, then emerged "*full*" (two, three) beaming like the very lamp "*of grace*" (two, three) he thought his prayer could never light "*Hail*" (two, three), her arms, hands, face, body "*Debbie*" (two, three), blue dress, tiny flowers "*full*" (two, three), then bent down to him "*of grace*" (two, three) with a smile "*Hail*" (two, three), clutched him under the arms "*Debbie*" (two, three), and swept him "*full*" (two, three) up into her face "*of grace*" (two, three), kissing him "*Hail*" (two, three) even as she pinned his arms "*Debbie*" (two, three) tight to his sides "*full*" (two, three), whispering, *Thorns!* "*of grace*" (two, three) as she clutched, lifted, and eased him "*Hail*" (two, three) into the green cave, *Look!* she whispered "*Debbie*" (two, three), and tucked among the thorns "*full*" (two, three) from which her grip "*of grace*" (two, three) protected him, Jamey saw the bird-thrown bowl "*Hail*" (two, three) in which five eggs glowed "*Debbie*" (two, three), the same pale blue "*full*" (two, three) as her dress "*of grace*" (two, three). Keeping his "*Hail*" (two, three) strides light and waltzing steady though his clothes had soaked through "*Debbie*" (two, three), but fighting emotion "*full*" (two, three), Jamey's memory did a jump cut "*of grace*" (two, three). She was climbing "*Hail*" (two, three) from a car's front seat now "*Debbie*" (two, three) as he watched "*full*" (two, three) from the back seat "*of grace*" (two, three) as her door closed "*Hail*" (two, three) and his opened. And as she "*Debbie*" (two, three) stood tall on the sidewalk "*full*" (two, three) a fierce wind "*of grace*" (two, three) blasted shoulder-length hair the color of backlit autumn grass "*Hail*" (two, three) and whipped it wildly against her face "*Debbie*" (two, three) till her trout-quick hand captured it "*full*" (two, three) and held it tight to her cheek "*of grace*" (two, three). Then— somewhere north of Vaughan Street, Northwest Portland, October of '97— thirty-four years vanished as a thirty-nine-year-old five-year-old waltzed brokenly past unseen buildings "*Hail*" (two, three), blinded by the beauty of the smile she "*Debbie*" (two, three) gave him as she bent down to offer him her left hand "*full*" (two, three) as her right still held her hair "*of grace*" (two, three) in check. But as he steadied "*Hail*" (two, three) on the sidewalk, her right hand "*Debbie*" (two, three) willingly left her cheek "*full*" (two, three) so her autumn-yellow hair "*of grace*" (two, three) again whipped her face fiercely "*Hail*" (two, three), and she smiled even

so "*Debbie*" (two, three) because she'd freed the backs of the two fingers "*full*" (two, three) that now glided softly along her thirty-nine-year-old's cheek "*of grace*" (two, three), causing Jamey to stop waltzing,
    stop chanting,
    close his eyes,
    touch his cheek,
    and stand crushed,
    by purest gratitude,
    steeping in the presence of the very love with which she loved him.

(Portland, September 1997)

IX. Grady at Elevation 40 Feet

High El Grady's thesis:
Corruption never has been compulsory. When the cities lie
at the monster's feet there are left the mountains.
                    —Robinson Jeffers, "Shine, Perishing Republic"

Lead me to the rock that is higher than I.
                                        —Psalms 61:2

Low El Grady's antithesis:
Sudden loss of altitude is the main clue to my veering moods.
A change is taking place, some painful growth, as in a snake
during the shedding of its skin—dull, irritable, without
appetite, dragging about the stale shreds of a former life.
                    —Peter Matthiessen, *Nine-Hearted Dragon River*

At twenty our bodies start to go to pieces.
We were built to go downhill and not to climb.
                                        —James Ensor

From the City Journals of Low-Elevation Grady Haynes:

It is 1997, and the American people are loaded, and the American people
are lost. It is 1997 and the iconic New York author Norman Mailer is so
lost he's just published a book purporting to be the memoirs of Jesus Christ.
It is 1997 and America's 101st senator, Tony Blair, is so lost he's living
in the prime minister's house in London. It is 1997 and Vice President Al
Gore is so lost he's wandered off to China, and Speaker of the House Newt
Gingrich is so lost he's jetted off to China to prove he's more *importantly
lost* than the damn fool liberal Gore.
    It is 1997 and America's Oz the Great and Powerful is Federal Reserve
Chairman Alan Greenspan, American Beat poet Allen Ginsberg has just
died, and the RMS *Titanic* has sunk for the second time, this time taking
out Leonardo DiCaprio, breaking Kate Winslet's heart. It is 1997 and a
syndicated astrologer, seeing exciting connections here, publishes a column

in over a hundred Rupert Murdoch–lobotomized US newspapers dubbed
GINSBERG, GREENSPAN & DICAPRIO ALL BORN UNDER SAME SUN
SIGN! It is 1997 and the Gallup Corporation has stepped in, probed the
sun-sign claim, and determined that Alan, Allen, and Leo were born in
March, June, and November, respectively. But it is 1997, so Murdoch and
all his papers stand by their astrologer, refusing to retract the sun-sign
claim, causing Gallup to take aim at Murdoch's Disinformation Empire
with a hard-hitting public opinion poll. Among the findings: 69 percent of
US women under the age of forty find the *Titanic*'s second sinking "*way
more tragic*" than the first, 78 percent of Americans have never heard of
Ginsberg or Greenspan, and 23 percent of Americans identify Alan and
Allen on the Gallup questionnaire by checking the box that reads: "balding,
sexually ambiguous, aging, or possibly dead Jewish poet/financier with
oversized black glasses." It is 1997 and America's gender-ambiguous, arguably defunct Federal Reserve Chairman Alanis Grinspleen is so troubled by
the poll's potentially deleterious effect upon the US dollar that he/she calls
a meeting of the Reserve Board, wheels and deals behind closed doors, calls
an international press conference, and the entire free market world listens
with bated breath as Gurnsprain announces:

> I have seen the best financial minds of my generation destroyed
>   by dot-com derivative junk-hedged hostile-mergered madness,
>   dragging themselves shrivel-cocked down Wall Street at dawn—
>   ambition-stoked MBAs who goose-stepped through grad school
>   thrilling to the tactics of free market warfare, masturbating
>   ecstatic at the jimmied back entrances to the Lotteries of Liquidity,
>   hollow-eyed high on cathode glow, burning for Cuban 'gars and
>   single-malted secretaries splay-leggèd in their boardroom backrooms,
>   slathering rabid for the inside offshore Senate-vetted fix,
>   weirdwired sleepless on speculation-pubed bank-balled
>   yackety yack, *I'm retiring at thirty to the Ronald Reagan Golf, Yacht, and
>   Jellybean Ranch! Hasta la vista, baby, to the SEC-suckered cowards of
>   finance!—INCINERATED INSTEAD IN A MOLOCH AVENUE
>   NIGHTMARE!* manacled to slave-rat cubicles for eighty-hour
>   workweeks screaming, *Buy!No!Sell!No!Buy!*, shit-spraying their
>   outsourced toilets, tension-puking in the security-cammed stair-
>   wells, bleeding down the pant legs of their data-breached, melted-
>   mortgaged Goldman Sachs suits,
>   *meat*
>   for the Corporate Machine,
>   cast down on pavement,

"So I have decided," Goonspawn concludes, "to lower the Fed another
point."

*   *   *

IT IS 1997 AND Datalyrick VP Grady Haynes is so lost he has split in two. He now comes in alienated high and low elevation versions of himself, and the drivel he's writing here is as close as he's come to *carrying the mountains down out of the mountains* as the Informant advised. It is 1997 and High El Grady is so enamored of the human-shaped phantasms he glimpses on high Elkmoon ridges during his prolonged near-death experiences on the High-Elevation Purification Loop that he's decided low elevation is the root of all evil. It is 1997 and Low El Grady, meanwhile, is sitting in the upstairs drawing room of his Sacajawea Village Luxury Townhouse on the banks of Portland's Willamette River (elev. 40) thinking, *For nine straight summers the high-altitude fascist who shares my body has squandered every fucking vacation of our life.* Hoping to nix the coming summer's death march, Low El affably remarks to High El that he's decided to get back into Buddhism, *So what say we go on a not-too-rigorous Buddhist retreat this summer instead of the usual mountainy masochist thing?*

It is 1997 as High El growls, *When were you ever* into Buddhism *in the first place?*

It is 1997 as Low El drags his legs into a painful half lotus and groans, *I've studied plenty of Buddhist sages.*

Name one, hisses High El. *No wait! Quote one.*

Chögyam Trungpa, Low El replies. Quote: *Everybody loves something, even if it's only tortillas.*

Elkmoons! High El groans to his distant mountains. *Help me* lose *this buffoon!*

It is 1997 and Grady's salt-of-the-earth kid brother, Rafer, and Rafer's troublingly luscious wife, Lynn, have driven down to Portland from culture-starved Pendleton, Oregon, to enjoy their biannual "romantic city weekend" while kindly Low El overnight-babysits their four-and-a-half-year-old son and three-year-old daughter, Hugo and Hallie. Or is it Corky and Kiley? Bugler and Riley? What's more, babysitting Bugler and Riley has been surprisingly tolerable this evening thanks to a gift from Rafer: a Missoula, Montana, rye hooch that spent two years toiling, troubling, and bubbling in a pot still and aging in charred oak casks before it was bottled and most excellently christened Bad Buddhist Whiskey, awakening in me both the aforementioned desire to get back into Buddhism and the means by which to do it! It is 1997 and the view out my picture windows, the Bad Buddhist elixir, and the sight of the kids falling to sleep on my drawing-room hide-a-bed have inspired both a sincere prayer (*Buddha! Please don't let them pee the bed!*) and my first Buddhist poem. Look, High El!

> The goddamned moon shimmers on the
> goddamned river. A goddamned breeze stirs
> the goddamned trees. What is there to
> yearn for this boundless goddamned
> evening? Rejecting the usual carefully

cultivated illusions since I can't get my
hands on any, my babysitting duties and
reborn love for the dharma cutting off
the Portland house of cards completely,
I turn from the goddamned thief skulking
across the moonlit condo lawn to my
sweetly sleeping niece and nephew and
ask, What's the goddamned difference?

It is 1997 and High El is roaring, *Do you know how a Lûmi destroys his illusory self, funny man!?* On the High-Elevation Purification Loop he ascends and descends and reascends so many peaks and valleys in succession that he hikes that dirtball not to death, which would allow the lower self to reincarnate, but to *extinction*! And when we reach the Elkmoons next summer that's exactly what I'll do to YOU!

Oy vey, dear reader. It is 1997 and I, Low El Grady, am harmlessly funning with a little free verse and Buddhistic booze while altruistically babysitting my kid brother and luscious Lynn's kids, whose names, by the by, I know perfectly well to be Hugo and Hallie, but who fall over laughing when I call them Corky and Kiley, so *they themselves made up the names Bugler and Riley*. But easygoing humor so horrifies thin-lipped grim-browed High El that, when summer arrives and I'm dying for the Scandinavian or Caribbean vacation my fun-loving nature and material successes deserve, my same-body doppelgänger will drag me off on another month-long assault on his mountains in an attempt to annihilate his fun-loving better half for all eternity!

Can we blame gentle Low El for wishing a certain high-elevation masochist would choke to death on an Elkmoon spruce grouse bone that doesn't quite kill me?

(Portland, late September 1997)

X. Murk Movie Beguinage

The solution to our plight, I think, is likely to be something
no other culture has ever thought of, something over which
!Kung, Inuit, Navajo, Walbiri, and the other traditions we
have turned to for wisdom...will marvel at as well.
            —Barry Lopez, *Crossing Open Ground*

AT ÉTOUFFÉE BRUTÉ, ten minutes till midnight, TJ pours the bourbons. Jim
Beam for the downwardly mobile Ocean dweller. Bulleit for himself.

TJ sets the shot glasses on the glowing bird's-eye maple of the bar, circles
round, takes the stool next to Jervis, levels his usual intense gaze upon his
glass, and starts spinning it in his fingers. Incredibly intent stare. Endless
precision spin. But for record amounts of time he neglects to drink his drink,
and both brothers decline to speak. For TJ, the day-ending dram is all about
staring at whiskey until something ineffable at last moves him to inquire into
his brother's eighteen-hour day of Ocean-walking, and they've performed
the rite so many times that TJ's inquiry consists of a single syllable:

"*So?*"

"So," Jervis paper-whispers. "Never mind the night walk. There's something from my day walk. Have you ever seen the Stumptown Shakespeare
Ensemble perform, Teej?"

"Just once," TJ says, still staring at and spinning his Bulleit. "*Lear*. When
I heard of an added dog, I feared tomfoolery, but you hounded me to see it,
insisting that Lear's dog obeyed no created thing but love. And sure enough,
I couldn't believe how moving the dog made the play. His love for his liege
was utterly visible, as was the king's love for his dog, though his madness
doomed them. And when Goneril finally poisoned the dog, my *God*, that
dog could die! Half the crowd broke out sobbing. It was a performance I
want to remember forever, so I've not been back since."

Jervis takes a sip of Beam, then paper-whispers. "The Lear you saw is
named Jamey Van Zandt, the dog is named Romeo, and Roams is a king
too. And I got to walk him today."

TJ turns away to hide a smile. He doesn't want Jervis to know he's more
at ease with his love of animals than his love of Ocean. Animal love is so
much more manageable! But TJ's relief doesn't last long.

"Something else, Teej," Jervis says. "Jamey has met Risa, and he told me he really felt something for her."

TJ's bourbon stops spinning. During late-night McGraff Brothers' dram stories, TJ's bourbon *never* stops spinning.

"He says he loves her, and I felt that too, but I also felt the time's not ripe. He's got heartwork to do first. But get this. The instant Jamey said he was willing, Ocean *gave* him some heartwork. I walked Roams while he went to work on it, we met here at six, and soon as he saw us coming Jamey yelled, '*Ocean is helping me like crazy, Jervis!*'"

With a stillness so total it's clearly dread, not calm, TJ asks, "Does Risa have feelings for this actor fellow, do you think?"

"No strobes on that. Ocean's not a dating service. But after tonight's Ocean-walk, heading back here to the Pearl, there was a murk movie that included them both."

TJ's bourbon goes unspun as he says, "But murk movies are very inaccurate, right?"

"They're not a fraction as clear as strobes are. But this murk movie connected to a later strobe, and murk movies that connect to strobes have truth to them."

"Better tell me about it then," TJ sighed.

"Jamey and Risa were part of a group of broken-open lowly people who started what, through the murk, looked very like one of the Beguine communities the Roman Catholics wiped out. But coed, with kids included, in America this time, and *Dumpster* Catholic this time. Risa seemed central to this beguinage being born. Soon too it seemed in the murk."

TJ starts spinning his drink so fast that whiskey spills—another unprecedented event in the annals of McGraff midnight drams. And Jervis notices. He has always been aware that the love between TJ and Risa is platonic only on Risa's part.

"Yep," he paper-whispers. "A full-on beguinage, it seemed in the movie. And wow was it piney! Is South Dakota piney? Idaho? It's sad to think of Stumptown Shakespeare losing Jamey and Roams. But for a new Dumpster Catholic Beguine movement over Idaho Dakota way? Worth it, maybe."

TJ seizes his Bulleit, empties the entire shot, pounds his chest as he wheezes, circles the bar, and pours himself a second shot. Three straight unheard-of midnight dram events!

"Let me be sure I've got this right, Jervis. According to an unreliable murk movie, Risa, this actor, his dog, and other people 'over Idaho Dakota way' are going to resurrect a religious order of women mystics destroyed eight centuries ago by the Church, and fairly soon."

"The Beguines weren't an order," Jervis says. "Just Jesus lovers. And the movie didn't show Romeo. Roams is old. It's time his body became human maybe, since his heart already is. The murk-movie people just seemed like grounded women, men, and kids somewhere piney. But when the movie ended there was a quick strobe showing we shouldn't speak of this to Risa or Jamey. They'll get thinky if we do, and the dumpster beguinage might not come to be."

"*Christ!*" TJ snaps. "Is this supposed to make me want to pack my bags and head over Idaho Dakota way?"

"There's more at the murk-movie level. Not a strobe. But do you wanna hear it?"

"Do I have to?"

"You'll like it, Teej."

"We'll see about *that!*"

"The piney beguinage seemed to connect strongly to Portland. The Pearl Building was vital to it in a murky but good way. And *you* were the mother-brother of whom that connection was born. So don't get thinky. Just know that you, me, Risa, Jamey, and no created thing but love might have some cool stuff to do before long."

Confused, disgruntled, and fascinated all at the same time, TJ gives Jervis a pained glance and asks, "Anything else?"

"Nothing that's not thinky," Jervis says, and he closes up like a tomb.

"*Thank God,*" TJ sighs. He then raises his glass, hoists a tight smile onto his face, and adds, "Here's to whatever comes of no created thing but love here in the Pearl and over Idaho Dakota way. And for Christ's sake, people! *Don't get thinky, and don't forget the piney!*"

Shooting air in and out his nostrils, Jervis clinks TJ's glass.

The brothers set to work on their drams.

XI. Dear TJ

Fax from Risa in Seattle to TJ in Portland:

Mother-Brother:

He died at 4:30 this a.m. after a month of miracles. My child heart, broken by his abandonment, doubly broken by him denying it, feels healed by an outpouring of more love and truthfulness in four weeks than in all of his life up to now—and what a delivery system he used! For the past three years he conducted a secret love affair with Skrit Lit. His sources were every book, journal entry, and class note from *my* college affair with the heart and mind of India, which I abandoned in the rafters of his garage.

All month his sense of wonder, sense of gratitude, physical courage, never wavered. He hurt tons but swore off morphine and lorazepam to keep his mind clear, making it through on Vicodin so we could chatter like a couple of Skrit nerds, and did we ever! Between naps and pain waves we swapped bhakti poems, *Mahabharata* and *Ramayana* yarns, hours of Vedic crazy dumbsaint talk. Not long before he launched he then astounded me with a story about Gandhi's incredible moment of death, which he festooned with Kabir, Tulsidas, and Valmiki verses lifted from *my* old notebooks! Before taking flight he also bequeathed me an instant aunt and uncle, Cindy and Bart, whom I'll be staying with tonight.

I can't say when I'll make it back to work, TJ. My heart's so full I can't confine it yet, and I've got a road trip to take. Destination: a subalpine Montana meadow where I'm to scatter Dave's ashes, and two Elkmoon City storage units Bart says Dave has stuffed full of gifts. They cremate tomorrow, which feels impossibly wrong after so much intimacy. I'm staying right here with his body till they take it away, hoping he'll feel me kissing him goodbye.

If the cremation stays on schedule I'll scatter his ashes on Oct 8th, my 30th b-day. It feels right to be in the place he loved more than any other on that day. I'll call sometime after the scattering, but don't worry if my silence runs at least a week past the 8th. He loved his Montana home valley like I loved Skrit Lit. I want to give myself to his place as completely as he gave himself to the very heart of me.

All love to you and Jervis,
Risa

(Oregon, Washington, Idaho, Montana, October 6 and 7, 1997)

XII. Both an Angel and a Storm

Three chords and the truth.
That's all a country song is.

—Willie Nelson

If only.

—Ona Kutar

ON OCTOBER 6TH, a little before 3 p.m., Risa got a call in Portland from the crematorium in Seattle. They said they were working late. Her father's ashes could be picked up that day if she could make it there by 7:30 p.m.

This was the timing she'd hoped for. Dave had drawn her a map of how to get to his high Montana meadow from Elkmoon City. If she drove long and slept short, she could reach Dave's mapped meadow on her thirtieth birthday. Why did this feel crucial to her? Dave had showered her with the Crimson Exploiter, the worth of his Seattle house, a life insurance payoff, and two storage units apparently stuffed with Montana-appropriate gifts. To use her birthday to release him in his meadow was the last gift she could ever bestow in return.

She packed for probable cold night camping in under an hour, choosing the Crimson Exploiter, not her old Volvo, because Dave's Montana escape vehicle felt right for her first experiences of his birthplace. She filled a thermos with hot Lapsang souchong, cream and honey, and a cooler with sandwiches and snacks, and hit the road.

I-5 from Tacoma, north, was bumper-to-bumper, but creeping along at five to twenty miles an hour. Risa made it to the crematorium with just minutes to spare. Their rigamarole wasn't too time-consuming. The marbled plastic urn containing Dave's ashes was mauve. Jarringly wrong! But there was no time to change that.

She set out for Montana at 8 p.m. Breaking free of rush-hour traffic on I-90 east, her escape velocity was strong. But miles and miles of the freeway were being resurfaced by night crews, often allowing just one lane to move at a time. It slowed her by more than two hours as she wound over the Cascades. Construction ended in the night-blackened pines of Cle Elum. She made good time in the rain-shadow country, past chaparral and the last increasingly small pine forests, past the huge green circles of center-pivot irrigation lands, the oceanic swells of the Palouse with its vast dryland wheat farms, past Ritzville, Sprague, Spokane, Coeur d'Alene.

In the Idaho panhandle fatigue hit Risa suddenly and hard. She checked the clock: 2:50 a.m. Too late for motels, too early for cafes and coffee. She passed a string of sad-looking little mining towns—Smelterville, Kellogg, Wallace, Mullan, *Compressor District*? (that's what the sign said)—but had to stop by the Compressor off-ramp to down a sandwich and drain her Lapsang for the caffeine.

As the interstate corkscrewed up into a high mountain nowhere, no place to stop and rest except a shoulder with trucks blasting by, Risa grew so sleepy she turned off the heater, downed her windows, and let the car grow so frigid her chattering teeth rattled her back to wakefulness. As she summited Lookout Pass, Risa slowed down and looked out. Pitch-black for a moment. Then came a sign she'd waited lifelong to see:

WELCOME TO MONTANA!

Her spirits had already risen when the next sign invited her, as Dave had promised, to drive any damn speed she liked so long as it was "reasonable and prudent." Risa pulled over, opened her door, set her sandaled foot down in Dave's birth state, turned to the urn, and said, "We're homing in! But you know what, Dave? *Fuck mauve.* First store I see we're getting what's left of you a new container."

As the Exploiter snaked its way down into Montana the headlights lit upon names Dave used to mention: THOMPSON FALLS. PLAINS. GLACIER PARK. KALISPELL. ST. REGIS. MISSOULA. To see the names was to yearn to hear Dave say them. Dark asphalt became pale concrete the same instant a green and white sign said, ST. REGIS RIVER. Realizing she was on a bridge, Risa saw a young, handsome Dave swivel at the steering wheel, craning his neck to glimpse the water far below. The image moved her to do the same, but she'd seen nothing but blackness when her right tires hit a rumble strip and, very nearly, the concrete wall of the bridge. Veering back into her lane, she told the urn, "*Jeez!* I had no idea your swivel and crane move took such skill!"

More miles of near black. Drowsy again after her adrenaline rush, Risa turned on the radio. On the only station she could find, a twangy-voiced DJ was so broken up by static that she started to snap him off, then heard, "*Next up, Willie Nelson's fresh take on the Silas Dupree classic 'Both an Angel and a Storm.'*" She'd never heard of the song, but her college boyfriend, Grady, had loved the Duprees and Risa had a soft spot for Willie. Over the radio's crackling an acoustic guitar set out in slow waltz time. When Willie chimed in, crackling be damned, she cranked it:

My long-gone bride and cowboy pride
Left me so lost and confused

Hopped on my Harley, turned up Bob Marley
And rode to church for Good News
But when the news was her body
Squeezin' past me through the pews
I cried, Mercy, please don't curse me
Sweet King of the Jews

"Holy crap!" Risa laughed. "Are you hearing this, Dave?"

The ashes jounced along in their mauve container, saying what ashes say. But when a Dobro slid in under the guitar, Risa felt a fraction of the man who could talk story like a Dobro slide into the Exploiter to listen—and oh, Willie Hugh! That old hippie cowboy could make honey out of another songwriter's fresh morning stool...

My will is strong, but church was long
Soon she was all I could see
Whether she'd kneel, or just set still
It was a love dance to me
We stood for song, her legs were long
Her voice was bright and sincere
And when she eyed me as if to try me
The Lord destroyed all my fear

"*Damn*, Dave!" Risa said. "If Willie sang an ode to John Wilkes Booth, Lincoln's death day'd be as big as the Fourth! That hymny organ's got me drawlin' an' almost bawlin', an' I heard that Dobro make your throat catch even though it's ashes."

Hear me, Creator, it's You made her
And You who lured me in here
My tree of knowledge says she's my college
An' I'm enrollin' in there
Reception line, chills down my spine
My gaze gets lost in her hair
Her blazin' eyes, her rump and thighs
O Lord, I'm walkin' on air
When she prays it's all Jesus
But when she loves me I'm torn
That's why I call her
Both an angel and a storm

Now a woman joined Willie in high haunted harmony, creating eros of a high order. The woman's voice was clear, noble, eerily familiar. Risa felt as if a lady of great beauty and virtue had strode into a ragged biker bar, seen Willie crooning on the smoky stage, stepped fearlessly up beside him to bust out a harmony—and suddenly Risa had it: "*Emmylou!* You *wouldn't!*"

But, oh, Emmylou would...

> *We blast Bob Marley on my Harley*
> *And find her home on the hill*
> *And when we kiss, a sea of bliss*
> *Is all my stoned soul can feel*
> *She reads my body like a Bible*
> *Takes my lost soul by force*
> *An' when she holds me, holy rolls me*
> *I thank the Lord for my divorce*
> *Yeah, when she prays I see Jesus*
> *But when she loves me I'm torn*
> *That's why I call her*
> *Both my angel and a storm*

Driving with her knee so she could hold her head in both hands, Risa asked the radio, "When did the night hallucination music of truckers get so *gorgeous?*"

> *I thank You, Lord, that I've been floored*
> *I praise Your works to the skies*
> *Crazed by her hips, mad for her lips*
> *I crash an' burn in her eyes*

The guitar, band, and choir vanished, a ritardando made the voices feel like slow cirrus clouds sliding across a crimson sky at sunset, and when a lone French horn joined Emmylou and Willie in aching three-part a cappella Risa nearly expired from happiness:

> *Yeah, when she prays it's sweet Jesus...*
> *And when she loves I'm torn...*
> *That's why I call her both my angel...*
> *And a storm.*

"Pope John Paul!" Risa shouted into the night. "Saint Willie *today!* What's it take, *two* miracles? That face, those braids, that voice. His conversion of cowpies into hymns! There's five miracles countin' both braids! *Saint Willie Hugh.* What a ring it's got! You'd convert a million in a day!"

On the far side of the freeway, under the lights up ahead, she saw gas pumps and a twenty-four-hour gambling and guzzling establishment that could have been the scene of the musical crime she'd just relished:

The Ten Thousand Silver Dollar Saloon

"*Saint Willie, guide me,*" Risa prayed, and took the exit.

Giving the saloon-casino a miss, she pulled up to the pumps, took in the rough old pickups parked everywhere, and made a mental note to stop by a rental car agency to filch stickers that claimed the Crimson Exploiter belonged to Alamo or Hertz. She filled up, washed the windshield, strolled into the convenience store, used the restroom, washed her face. When she came back out, the clerk at the counter, a smoked-and-honey-cured-looking bouffant blonde, said, "You're up with the coyotes, hon."

Copying the blonde's patois in accord with Saint Willie's guidance, Risa said, "You too, hon. Hey, I got an odd request for ya. I need three bags; two brown paper, one plastic. Nothin' but the bags, please."

"Listen, hon," the gal said as she handed them over. "In Montana that don't qualify as one bit odd." She eyed the dollar Risa offered. "But *that* does. You keep that, hon."

Feeling a little wash of affection, Risa bought Dentyne with the buck, thanked the woman, and headed out the door.

Back in the Exploiter, she placed one paper bag inside the other, then both inside the plastic. Grabbing the urn, she removed the lid and tried to be invincibly matter-of-fact as she began pouring Dave's ashes into the bags. The remains were pouring in smoothly and Risa was doing okay—when a parade of unexpected bone fragments clattered down like smashed chess pieces, raising a cloud of Dave-dust that spun in the still air of the Exploiter, refusing to settle. Inside that galaxy of dead fatherness, Risa felt paralyzed.

"Fight it!" she ordered herself. Shaking the remaining bones and ashes abruptly into the bags, she waved aside the Dave galaxy, rolled the bags shut, throttled the urn like a neck, slammed on the lid, kicked open her door, stomped over to the convenience store trash can, shoved the urn in through the swing top, and relished the bang of it hitting bottom.

Inside, the bouffant blonde looked up, startled. Risa waved and mouthed, "Sorry!"

The blonde's return wave and worn smile were right out of a Saint Willie tune.

As Risa stepped up to the Exploiter she noticed its crimson growing more scarlet. Turning in a semicircle, she found the source: on ridges high above the Clark Fork Valley, the tips of a thousand night-darkened larches had turned gold thanks to an unseen but rising sun.

Just that fast the day took on the bruised beauty of a Dobro solo.

"One last time," Risa whispered as she belted the bagged ashes back into the passenger seat. "*Fuck mauve.* Before this adventure's over you'll merge with the colors that created you. No others needed. Colors you loved all your life. No others."

Firing up the Exploiter, she turned, reasonably and prudently, back onto the freeway, and east into the sere palette of Montana.

XIII. Becoming Pope

Consider the obvious! I did!
    —C. G. Jung (to Alice O. Howell, in a dream)

ON A SWELTERING July day the same year Risa later arrived in Montana, on the 22,000-acre holding known as Valley Land & Beef Incorporated, three Black Angus cows—healthy calf producers, all—mired themselves in the quick-mud of a spring-fed pond at dusk. This brought the number of cattle trapped in the same pond to fourteen in five years. Ranch foreman Kale Broussard had long since left a water trough a safe fifty yards from the quick-mud, but in hot weather cattle prefer to stand belly deep in mire, cooling as they sip. The habit reminded Kale of his lifelong dance with whiskey, giving him sympathy for the beasts. When he learned it was the daughter of his new hand, Eddie Dominguez, who'd discovered the mired cattle, though, it spooked him. The pond was a quarter mile from the nearest ranch buildings and twice that far from Eddie's Airstream. Kale had seen cow moose with calves at that pond, bear and cougar tracks circling the mud shoreline, stripped deer carcasses in the surrounding willows. Dusk, for predators, is suppertime. A solitary eight-year-old had no business being there at all, let alone at dusk. He and Eddie would be having a talk pronto.

With too much office work to break free, Kale rounded up three weary hands and sent them to the pond, reminding them to take waders or hip boots and a come-along.

Kale's phone rang three hours later. His 320-pound second in command, Hub Punker, said they'd managed to save one cow by using three ropes, two pulled by horses, a third by the winch on Hub's pickup. The cow, once freed, Hub said, "plowed off through the willows like a rhino in a shit coat." The winch strangled the second cow and dragged her out of the pond dead. Hub had Doty Nolan haul that one to town and dump her behind the butcher Don Steadles's place. Don had agreed to clean and carve the croakers if Land & Beef Inc. would give him half of each. By the time Hub and Eddie reached the third cow she'd writhed herself in up to the neck, and no Doty Nolan meant no winch. Shovel work, and lots of it, was what was needed. Dusk was upon them, the men were spent, but Hub had his thinking cap on: he and Eddie nailed together an arrangement of two-by-fours and worn pickup tires, propping the cow's head above water. Hub then tranquilized her and they called it a day. Come dawn they figured she'd be miserable but breathing.

Kale thanked Hub, said he'd meet the crew pondside at 6 a.m. sharp, hung up, and went to bed. Sometime around 3 a.m., however, he woke from a weirdly sexual dream to the far-off sound of bawling, realized what he was hearing, threw on his clothes, grabbed his thirty-thirty and jacklight, and drove an ATV fast, to the pond. A pack of coyotes had light-stepped it over the quick-mud, found they couldn't reach the cow's submerged throat, and so began chewing her neatly propped face off, nose, muzzle, brows, ears, and eyes first. They vanished at Kale's engine noise. The blind and faceless cow had quit bawling, but was nightmarishly gurgling. Leaden with guilt for having failed to think of coyotes, Kale shot her in the temple.

He drove the ATV home and napped in his clothes. No dreams this time. But it felt like a dream when he and the crew returned to the pond at six to find a cloud of magpies, ravens, and one golden eagle swarming in frustration over the cow's entirely submerged body, her skull and the top of her spinal column stripped clean, her bloody, emptied eye sockets staring at the sky. The coyotes had returned, eaten everything the two-by-fours and tires propped above water, and vamoosed.

"Cool opening shot for a Western," remarked the unflappable Eddie.

By laying out plywood sheets, Doty Nolan and Eddie managed to get a rope around enough carcass that Hub could winch the faceless cow, then the two cowboys, out of the goop. They looked like Mud Men of New Guinea when they emerged, but no one laughed, knowing next time it was their turn. The carcass looked so violated that rather than haul it to Don Steadles's, Kale fetched the backhoe, buried the cow deep, and had the men cover her with staked-down hog wire and a gob of big rocks so bears couldn't dig her back up. He then gave the boys the morning off, donned clean clothes, climbed in his white Ford F-250, and headed for his least favorite building in Elkmoon City and all the valley, whacked fundie churches, H&R Block office, and morgue included: the Grand Lodge on the Elkmoon.

GRAND LODGE. THE name pretty well said it. Seven hundred of the biggest, most beautiful ponderosa pines left in Montana converted, to the tune of fifteen million bucks, into a three-story log palace for men of commerce with outdoorsy pretensions, then named as if the KKK skulked inside—and perhaps it did.

Valley Land & Beef Inc. was a small subsidiary of, and tax shelter for, the international banking Goliath, NorBanCo, for whom and by whom the lodge had been built. The man who'd christened the Grand Lodge, Charles Keynes Schiller III, also owned a name that pretty well said it. Schiller was a Dallas born, country-club raised, Exeter Academy and Yale educated blueblood who'd spent a decade corporate climbing in Chicago and Atlanta while answering to the name C. K. Schiller. But when his overlords sent him to Montana to mastermind the development of their 22,000-acre holding, C. K. exhumed a nickname he'd been given by Exeter classmates who hadn't understood that Dallas country clubs aren't exactly the cowboying portion of the Lone Star State: "Tex."

The moniker worked no wonders: Tex Schiller turned out to know exactly as much about cattle ranching as Kale Broussard knew about corporate climbing. Kale's first impression of Schiller had felt a little random: *Parisian concierge lost in cattle country.* The intuition turned out to be prescient. Tex's strong suit was hiring as many "service people" as needed to keep the Grand Lodge grounds looking like a PGA country club, the massive draped window treatments spotless, and the Charlie Russell knockoffs, Ahab Gilhooley glass gewgaws, two-hundred-thousand-dollar ninety-seven-key Bösendorfer grand piano, elk-horn chandeliers, indoor and outdoor bars, and twenty suites in immaculate condition. He also kept the restaurant's cuisine at the four-star level no matter how many psychotic chefs he had to import from Europe. The "Concierge" had corporate sportsmen to impress, his efforts *did* impress, and none of this would have bothered Kale at all were it not for one small detail: the Concierge was also in charge of the 22,000 acres surrounding the lodge, including Foreman Kale Broussard, his cattle, and his cowboys. When disagreements arose, Tex was *very* fond of saying, "I'm NorBanCo's man on the ground in Montana. You're *my* foreman, Broussard, not your cows'. End of story."

But Kale was living a very different story. When he was a boy, eight families, his own included, owned adjoining family ranches on those same 22,000 acres. An Elkmoon Valley Bank president, Becker Brandt by name, then began snapping those ranches up. Beck had a vulture's nose for families in distress and his banking work provided great intel. He purchased three spreads from widows of World War Two victims, two from aging couples with no offspring, one from a family ready to try city life, and one from a family whose only child drowned in Elkmoon River runoff. Kale's meagre 2,000 acres were located in the very center of Becker's otherwise contiguous 20,000 acres. Naturally Becker came calling. Kale told him he'd best get used to being neighbors, because Kale would never sell. Then the medical bills from Kale's mother's cancer death and his father's dementia cleaned him out, Beck descended upon Kale again, and after brutal negotiation Kale was left with the 20 acres surrounding his family home and barn, and 100 acres atop Schoolhouse Bluff, named for the century-old one-room Testament Creek School Kale mothballed but continued to maintain. Becker had been Kale's classmate at that school. His refusal as a banker to assist ranchers who'd formerly been neighbors, the better to predate their land, made him the first person Kale had ever fantasized about killing—so Kale felt a little guilty when Becker *was* killed, in a drunken water-skiing accident.

The twist Kale didn't see coming as a result of that death: Elkmoon

Valley Bank and its holdings were then swallowed like an after-dinner mint by NorBanCo. Overnight the ranches and wilds that had been the scene of Kale's entire life became a high-end development scheme under Tex Schiller's governance. Tex then hired Kale as ranch foreman, not in admiration of his ranching skills but because of steely orders from Corporate to not let Broussard out of sight until NorBanCo acquired his two inholdings. Schiller's determination to acquire Kale's land was total, so he was not pleased the day Kale's lifelong friend, Lou Roy Skinner, told him, "Tell you what, Tex. You wanna buy something from Kale he might actually sell, you gotta better chance makin' an offer on his arms and legs."

The Concierge's stewardship of the lands Kale loved then left him feeling as though he *had* sold off his arms and legs. The number of cattle Tex forced him to run was based on grazing data gathered before the invasion of noxious weeds and droughts caused by climate breakdown. The budget Tex granted for road and fence maintenance, weed control, irrigation gear, vehicles, and other necessities was a consistent one-fourth of what was needed. The budget for working horses, which the steeper gulches and Testament Creek Canyon demanded, was nonexistent. "Use the ATVs I pay for!" Tex would bark, though he paid for nothing and was speaking of terrain so precipitous his ATV advice was a cowboy death warrant. Money for maintaining the sound but aging buildings left by departed ranch families was nonexistent, but created a look of desolation that a visiting NorBanCo CEO had found "charmingly forlorn," so decay was allowed to continue until the buildings collapsed. Cashing in on even this crumbling, Tex committed a literary crime against one of Kale's favorite writers, Annie Proulx, by renaming NorBanCo's impending recreational citadel the Brokeback Ranch & Country Club, leaving the tumbledown family ranch ruins standing to make sense of the name. Typical of NorBanCo's fortunes, and Kale's too, Tex's rip-off name was then met with rumors that Proulx's *New Yorker* yarn "Brokeback Mountain" would soon be a full-fledged Hollywood motion picture, enhancing his development's cachet.

It did nothing for Kale's mood that Tex earned ten times what Kale did, or that every half-cracked Euro-chef Tex "yarded across the pond," as he put it, made more than all five of Kale's cowboys combined. But the protocol by which Kale could express his grievances was classic mega-corporate: he could talk his troubles over with Jesus, or he could go fuck himself. Last time Kale checked, NorBanCo was the third largest investment firm in the world: $88 billion in assets in two dozen countries, office towers in nineteen cities including Tokyo, Copenhagen, Paris, London, Dallas, Singapore, and soon, Tex promised, at the Grand Lodge on the Elkmoon. But it wasn't as if the Elkmoon was being picked on: NorBanCo owned half a million acres of failed ranches in Montana alone; the acres that were the scene of Kale's entire life represented just 4.4 percent of their in-state holdings, and Valley Land & Beef Inc. was basically just corporate sleight of hand: NorBanCo's interest in the Elkmoon holding was the recreational potential and viewsheds that represented the development's chief value. Until such time as NorBanCo sliced and diced the entirety into ranchettes, mountain bike trails, ski runs, hunting grounds, fishing beats, golf links, and so on, Kale and his "boutique cows and cowboys" (an actual Concierge quote) were there to serve Grand Lodge guests as "colorful but silent features of our bucolic Western Landscape" (another Texism). The fact that boutique cows and cowboys had non-colorful and very audible needs about which Kale was not silent infuriated the Concierge.

KALE ARRIVED AT the Grand Lodge at 8 a.m. sharp, ordered himself to remain impervious to whatever was about to happen, strode with purpose through the Great Room but, as always, came to a halt before the ten-foot-tall, four-inch-thick door of Tex Schiller's ground-floor office. It was the half-life-sized bronze head of Chief Sitting Bull door-knock beneath Tex's name that stopped him. Kale was far too serious a student of Western history to grab that hero by his cheekbones and bash his eagle feathers against a metal plate. He used his fist on the door instead. But he and the Concierge had been over this many times: a hell of a lot of pounding had to go on before Tex deigned to answer, and when he did answer his words were "Oh. Broussard. I thought that feeble thumping was the maid emptying wastebaskets. Next time, use the Chief. That's what he's there for."

Kale swallowed his desire to give Tex an example of what a "feeble thumping" felt like, but did not accept the proffered chair. Holding his Stetson over his unbreakfasted and grumbling belly, he deployed his most understated tone as he told of the mired cattle. Having once been asked by the Concierge, "What were you *thinking*, hiring a Mex up in these parts?" Kale left the Dominguez girl out of his account, but did not leave out the fourteen animals mired in five years, or nose, eyeball, and spinal surgery the coyotes had performed on last night's still-living cow. Without hope, but with firm clarity, he concluded: "For half a decade I've asked you every year for funds to fence off that pond. It's time, Tex."

In the eternally offended tone that had won him his nickname, the Concierge huffed. "Cowboy bull hockey rides again. I pay you to *contain* those animals, not drown them. Why can't you and your cows be low-maintenance like the elk and deer?"

Having expected this, Kale managed to flex neither fists nor jaw.

"Guess what, though," Tex added. "There's government funds for this kind of crap now. With wetlands involved, maybe even a stewardship prize. Which would up land value. Which would keep the board off *my* ass when I'm forced to defend *your* ass. Research it, Broussard. Target a prize, apply for grants, and fence your swamp. Receipts for every man-hour and expense. All the proper permits. I'll paint your negligence as a chance for Brokeback's visionary investors to capitalize on our 'harmony with nature.'"

"Thanks," Kale murmured, with which he turned, strode past Sitting

Bull with an expression to match, crossed the parking lot, climbed in his F-250, calmly closed the door—then slammed his left fist down so hard on the armrest he sent a crack shivering down through the entire synthetic door panel. Summoning the default curse he'd been deploying in his lifelong battle against compulsive swearing, he barked, "*Lordy!*"

When he got home, Kale called the nearest Ford dealer—a hundred forty gas-guzzling miles distant—asked for the repair costs, and got an eight-hundred-dollar estimate.

"*Lordy!*"

TWO MONTHS LATER, proper permits in hand, Kale popped the Ford into low-range and eased down through the aspens toward Cowkiller Pond. His windows were down and the September air was pellucid, but his cab was claustrophobic in ways that no breeze could clear. Kale was his own unpaid secretary and his traveling office was the back seat of his cab. At the moment, that "office" contained six phone books, a large leather briefcase that could no longer close due to all the paperwork generated by trying to raise cattle under the second-guessing of Tex Schiller, a file bulging with riparian fencing designs and receipts for materials, and a file jammed with regs from federal, state, and county agencies. As the big Ford heaved and jounced down through the aspens to the pond, Kale glanced back to see that both files had opened and swirled their contents together on the floor. "*Lordy!*"

He parked two hundred yards from the work site, directly across the pond. His cowboys took it badly when he micromanaged, so he faced every direction but toward his crew, but he was in fact spying, and for a reason. Kale had located four potential funding sources and a stewardship prize, as Tex had requested. But before those sources produced any cash, van-load after van-load of county and state bureaucrats would inspect their handiwork, and Kale's crew had never heard of a gated watering station or game fence like these. A screwup would force Kale, hat in hand, back to the Concierge. The choice between that and a little surreptitious spying was no contest.

The purpose of the watering station was to give cattle hot-weather access to a solid-bottomed, belly-cooling bay from which to drink. The suspension-fence around the rest of the pond was designed to prevent cows from miring in quick-mud, but still allow wildlife to reach the pond to drink. The design's ingenuity pleased Kale no end. He'd watched a herd of elk charge such a fence in the Madison River Valley, assumed it would be destroyed when the elk thundered into and flattened it, then gaped when the entire fence sprang back up, undamaged by the entire herd passing over. The secret: one post in five was an oversize gatepost, but the next four smaller and lighter posts weren't sunk at all; they were suspended in the air by extra stout but barbless wire, so when moose or elk charged the fence it collapsed, only to stand back up once the animals passed. Smaller animals—pronghorns, deer, black bears—could pass under the wire without harm, and cattle and horses respected the fences—*if* they were built perfectly. For that reason Kale had managed to hire a temporary cowboy despite Tex's grumbling, Max Bowler by name, who had worked on the Madison River fencing project.

Holding a few papers high while he peeked through them at his crew, Kale reminded himself of the bumper sticker: JESUS IS COMING. LOOK BUSY! But his parking spot was perfect. The boys had no idea how well their voices carried over the pond. Eddie Dominguez, with his usual understated humor, was off-loading fencing material while whistling "Don't Fence Me In." Hub was showing Doty Nolan and the new man, Max Bowler, the design Kale had gone over with Hub three times the night before.

"These plywood boxes, here," Kale heard Hub saying, "are molds for two concrete footings for our watering station. Overdoing it, maybe, but the bogginess forces us. These super-stout gate-like sections, here, are the watering station's cow-proof iron sides."

Hub's voice was drifty over the water. Kale's mind drifted with it. *Iron sides*. Wasn't there an old TV show of that name? Same guy that played Perry Mason maybe, portraying an Indian detective in a wheelchair? Chief Ironsides? Picturing Tex's Sitting Bull door knocker, Kale hoped he had the Indian part wrong.

Young Max Bowler, inspecting the diagram, began expressing such enthusiasm that Kale lowered his Stetson to hide his grin. *I was so right to hire that young man,* he thought.

Then came a string of words that threw a kink into his grin:

"Yep," Hub told Max. "The Pope's fulla all kinda slick ideas. But be ready. 'Cause every time Pope gets an idea, it's us not him'll be bustin' our ass out in the elements."

What was Hub saying? The design and diagram were Kale's own. Who was this *Pope* character? And why, despite the cool fall air, was Kale suddenly roasting?

As if in reply to his questions, Hub said, "Case in point. It's time for us to slide on farty ol' duck waders an' do battle with quick-mud. Meanwhile, in F-250 Cathedral acrosst the waters there, *His Holiness* just basks in the zephyrs."

When the cowboys chortled and glanced his way, it hit Kale like a brick: the *Pope character* was none other than himself! Worse yet, Hub's nomenclature was so practiced that the nickname had clearly been around a good while. But did they mean "Pope," as in *John Paul Two*? And if so, how *could* they? Kale was a once-in-a-blue-moon mass-attending Catholic and liked JP2 well enough. But *damn*! Last time he'd seen Christ's vicar on TV he was bobbling along in the back of a pickup in Africa or Cuba or some such place, looking like an albino hunchback as he tried to bless crowds without getting coldcocked by his see-through bulletproof cage. Kale was still two years shy of fifty. JP was what, *ninety*? More to the point,

Kale was a straight-backed, square-shouldered, six-foot-two, two-hundred-twenty-well-fed-but-still-formidable pounds. Plenty formidable enough to drive Hub Punker like a fence post neck-deep into the pond muck. *F-250 Cathedral? His Holiness just basks in the zephyrs?* Kale literally began to growl. Next time he heard a certain nickname aimed his way, he'd give fair warning. The time after that, Hub or whoever would be spitting a few teeth.

A FEW MORNINGS later, though, Kale was shaving by blind feel in the shower, as was his custom, when he nicked the base of his left ear almost as badly as the boys had nicked his name. Applying pressure to the cut, he turned off the shower, fetched a Band-Aid from the medicine cabinet, closed it, and was peering in the mirror to place the Band-Aid just so—when he noticed the man peering back at him. He and that man then did a double take that escalated into a close, grim study of each other's physiognomy:

Once a rather handsome hombre if he did say so himself, Kale expected the mirror to reflect a weathered version of the same hombre. In fact, his reflection argued, Kale's fifth decade was sneaking up on him like coyotes in the night, chewing on features he'd long taken for granted, and spitting them back onto his face in a scary good likeness of Karol Wojtyla a few years before he became pontiff. The longer Kale stared the more inescapable the resemblance grew. It didn't seem out of the question that if he white-washed his skin, donned his big white terry-cloth bathrobe, drove down to St. Luke's in Elkmoon City, and stood stock-still during the next church rummage sale, he'd fetch a decent price as a piece of JP2 statuary.

Kale's mood plummeted toward depression. The instant it did so, the face in the mirror grew even *more* John Paul Twoish. "*It's a goddamned trap!*" Kale yelled.

But then he felt guilty. And why? He'd just yelled "goddamned" at the living pope's look-alike. "You'd never use that word, would you?" Kale asked his reflection.

The pope in the mirror shook his head. Nope. He sure wouldn't.

This exchange amused Kale...which made his eyes twinkle...which improved his looks...which lessened the resemblance. Kale *grew reflective,* as the saying goes. Recognizing upon his face the onslaught of forces that drive good men to drink, lesser men to evangelical post-life-insurance policies, still lesser men to plastic surgeons, and all men, eventually, to the wrong side of the grass, he realized his fists were a ridiculous response to his nickname. A *problem,* by definition, is a potentially soluble difficulty. His face's problem was *insoluble,* which meant it wasn't a problem at all: it was one of those ever-unfolding events known as "an inexorable change." And the only way to deal with inexorable changes in himself, Kale had learned from countless futile attempts to defy them, was to surrender and accept them.

Well then, he thought. What *about* that terry-cloth bathrobe? *What if, instead of wishing Karol's mug hadn't snuck onto mine, I try to* welcome *the dang thing?*

Intrigued by the possibility, he scampered to his bedroom with a grin so impish he looked more like himself at age ten than JP2 at any age. He donned the big white terry-cloth bathrobe. He yanked the red and black Pendleton off his bed, stripped off the white top sheet, folded it into lengthwise quarters, and wrapped it round his robed white shoulders to serve as a vesture. He then rushed, with chuckles of anticipation, to the kitchen, where he rummaged through his least-used drawers till he found the off-white tea cozy with the red needlepoint bucking horse on it. A strict coffee drinker, Kale had never before deployed this device, but he'd saved it because it had been handmade for him years ago by his then fourteen-year-old daughter, Marla.

Feeling the need for fresh sight of his transmogrified face, Kale strode back down the hall to the bathroom, turned on every light including the heat lamp, placed the tea cozy sideways on his head so the red bucking horse showed front and center, summoned his full ranch foreman authority, then gazed straight into the mirror, determined to see once and for all just how strong their resemblance was.

"Ho...Lee...*Shit!*" Kale whispered as a bigger, outdoorsier John Paul Two ringer whispered, "Ho...Lee...*Shit!*" right back.

Kale let out a horsey nicker, then felt rude to have done so. But again, why? *Because he was nickering into the face of a visage millions hold to be Christ's vicar on Earth!* Realizing this, Kale nickered louder. Which of course caused Karol to nicker back. "Behave now!" Kale said, and the two men summoned their respective ranch foreman and papal dignities and stared at each other for several solemn seconds. Then, the way friends do, they exploded, losing it so bad they bucked the red stallion right off their head.

"No offense, Karol," Kale wheezed as he restored the papal head horse, "but I reckon my only chance at handsomeness from now on would be an ex cathedra declaration by you that you yourself are handsome."

"And I can do it, my son," intoned JP2, "with one casual wave of my unerring hand."

This drew more chortles out of both of himself.

Kale let his face sag: *Pope.*

Hoisted it up into a smile: *Kale.*

Sag: *Karol.* Hoist: *Kale.*

"*Lordy!*" the two men averred.

"The bad news," Kale told Karol, "is that gravity eventually wins. On that day, it's goodbye Kale and howdy Pope till death do us part!"

"But the good news," Karol reminded Kale, "is that, for as long as you remain foreman of this or any other ranch, the head of the holy Roman Church will be visually reinforcing every order you give your crew."

Kale laughed. Karol laughed back. "I'm late for work, Your Holiness.

But *dang*, it's been a weird pleasure. I'm gonna miss you a little out there today."

"My son," said JP2. "There is no need to miss me, for truly"—Karol patted Kale's big cheeks with their shared hands—"I shall never again be far from you!"

Rumbling with affection, Kale returned to the bedroom, put the bedsheet back where it belonged, remade the bed drum-tight, hung up his bathrobe, donned a blue Roper shirt, Wrangler jeans, and lace-up Tony Lamas, then went to the kitchen to collect his lunch.

Ready for work. But was he ready for the boys? Flashing on the Hub Punker phrase *His Holiness just basks in the zephyrs,* Kale began to rumble again. "JP pardner?" he asked the empty room. "Any ideas?"

"Yes, my son," Kale's new pal said. "Here you are." And into the lunch box, between the sandwiches and thermos, went the off-white cozy with the embroidered red bucking horse.

When Kale reached the ranch buildings, Max Bowler, Doty Nolan, Lou Roy, Eddie, and Hub were all smoking and chewing and loitering and gabbing as they awaited the daily doling out of tasks, as usual. But as Kale stepped down from his cab and the men encircled him, he nodded at them with far greater solemnity than usual, set his lunch box on the hood of his big white pickup, felt a grin try to rise up, bulldogged it down into a grimace, and launched this speech:

"Boys. As a man grows older he grows resistant to change, but the changes refuse to quit coming. His body, for instance, changes. Things he once did with ease start to do him damage. Things he did for pure pleasure all of a sudden just hurt."

Max Bowler was nodding thoughtfully. Such an amenable giant, this lad.

"Or his face, maybe, changes," Kale continued, "till he might look so damn different even his name could seem to be up for grabs."

Five cowboys grew very quiet and stood very still.

"What got me thinkin' this way," Kale said easily, "was a certain nickname's been making the rounds. First time I heard it, I admit, I wanted to beat the living puke outta the man said it. And I could do it. I could pound that particular cowboy into the dirt—*this* year. But next year might be different. Or the next fella that slung the nickname might be a brick shithouse of a man like Max here, pardon my metaphor. And there's another angle on this too. An unexpected angle. A thing called *fairness*. I need to show you boys a little something."

With a grave expression Kale turned to the hood of his truck, carefully opened his lunch box, and produced the bucking-horse tea cozy. The cowboys stared, uncomprehending. Foreman Broussard then removed his white Stetson, pinning its brim to the hood with his lunch box so a breeze wouldn't toss it in the dirt. Next, very slowly and solemnly, he fit the off-white cozy upon his head, red bucking horse front and center. He then turned to face his men.

Four cowboy mouths fell wide-open, but the fifth, Eddie, began to emit straining sounds that doubled him over and threatened to leave him on the ground. Summoning the majestically slow movements he'd discovered in his bathroom mirror, Kale raised his big right hand in regal greeting.

"Fellas," he said. "*Hark. Verily.* Some nicknames are fair. You wanna call me what you been calling me, feel free. All I ask is, do it to my *face*, not behind my back. Gimme that much and I beat the puke outta no one. Deal?"

While Eddie went on spasming, the rest of the crew scratched their whiskers, moved dirt around with their boot toes, gazed off at the ridges across the river, picked at a scab on their knuckle, and mumbled things like "I, er, I, uh, gee, boss."

"*Come on, you pants-piddlers!*" Kale roared, causing his red bucking horse to buck. "I'm trying to ratify your wit and lay this thing to rest. I want at least one of you to look me in the face an' call me what you've *been* callin' me when you think I can't hear."

Not only were the boys unable to look or call, Eddie, for survival purposes, was forced to stagger away from the circle entirely.

"Aw *hell*," Lou Roy finally muttered. "Nuffa this shit. Let's get to 'er ... *Pope.*"

"Thank you, Lou," Kale said. With which he removed Marla's cozy, set his white Stetson back on his head, checked on Eddie—who recovered with the cozy out of sight—and put his cautiously grinning crew to work.

(Elkmoon Valley, rewind to May 1997)

XIV. Airstreamers

Reasoning is important. But any form of reasoning that refuses to give way to intuition is akin to choosing not to scrape the ice off your windshield before driving to work in the morning.

—Thomas Soames

KALE BROUSSARD AND Lou Roy Skinner would prove as important to what unfolded in the Elkmoon Valley as Risa McKeig when she arrived in the autumn of 1997. But whereas the encounters between Kale and valley newcomers were almost always smooth, first encounters between Lou Roy and a few newcomers were a very different kettle of fish.

Two newbies who would prove crucial in the Elkmoon, twenty-nine-year-old Eddie Dominguez and his eight-year-old daughter, Rosalia, arrived in Elkmoon City in May of '97 with no home, no school, and no job prospects. Eddie was driving a smoke-spewing early '70s Silverado with Arizona plates, burning a quart of oil per tank of gas, pulling an old Sundowner trailer loaded with his quarter horse, Madre, Rosalia's pony, Bub (accurately short for Beelzebub), and every tool, toy, utensil, and article of clothing they owned. They'd been living in campgrounds and rest areas for more than a month, sleeping amongst their belongings in the unheated, unplumbed bunkroom of the trailer.

After camping in a rest area on the lower Elkmoon River, they arrived in E City hungry, cruised Main, and decided on an eatery in a hundred-twenty-year-old, four-story orange-brick building, the Black Queen Hotel. The ground floor restaurant, the Ambivalent Cafe, sported two double-sided signs in the window that lived up to its name. One sign: SORRY. WE'RE OPEN. Flip side: HURRAY! WE'RE CLOSED! The other sign: NO SHIRT, NO SHOES, GREAT SERVICE! Flip side: ALL PUBLIC HEALTH INSPECTORS FOUND ON THESE PREMISES WILL BE PUBLICLY INSPECTED! But the vintage hippie owners, Poke and Lisa Kettle, looked friendly in a photo and the diners in the cafe were amiable.

Eddie bought an *E City Weekly* in the lobby. Rosalia picked their table. When Eddie, as usual, stuck his nose in the want ads, she wandered back out to a corkboard she'd seen in the lobby. The top of the board featured a long row of three-dollar bills with Bill Clinton's face on them. The corkboard itself was covered with handbills advertising well-digging services, farriers, free roosters, used farm equipment, frozen whole, half, or quartered sheep and cows, a square dance center, a four-square gospel church promising to beam members up out of the Apocalypse, and a three-by-five-inch card with a hand-printed message to which Rosalia, by pure luck, was drawn like a magnet:

> WANTED: Full-time all-around ranch hand. Experience a must. Call Foreman Kale Broussard, Valley Land & Beef.

And a phone number followed.

Rosa plucked out the pushpin and shot to her table with the card: "*Dad!*"

The lobby had a pay phone. Before their breakfasts arrived, Eddie and Rosalia had a late-morning appointment with Foreman Broussard.

Lou Roy Skinner had been a working Elkmoon Valley cowboy from the age of fourteen. He became a saddle bronc champ in his early twenties, a cutting horse champ in his early thirties, a cutting horse trainer at forty, and worked under Kale as a hand for Valley Land & Beef when horse training opportunities ran thin. Lou Roy was widely respected. But he was also a man with an odd secret: the portion of himself he had so successfully attached to horses had a pigmentation issue. Nothing serious. Just potentially embarrassing for a man who took cowboy dignity seriously. So it was fortunate that Lou's two-year marriage to a rodeo queen had ended when they turned twenty-two and his queen left the valley. At age fifty-two Lou Roy was not amorous, his seater-bottomus was of no interest to anyone but the horses to which he skillfully glued it, and he seemed likely to carry his secret to his grave.

But as TJ McGraff once said to Risa: *Schmidt happens.*

In 1997, schmidt came looking for Lou Roy in the form of a little girl.

In driving up the valley Eddie saw an asphalt bicycle path paralleling the highway the entire nine miles from E City to the Land & Beef entrance. The path was well engineered, and Eddie realized it suggested financial clout and local political clout too. When he followed the signs into Valley Land & Beef Inc., the cattle operation buildings disappointed him: all made of metal, with a cold industrial look. But when Kale drove up in a white Ford F-250 Eddie liked the look of him immediately.

After shaking hands, Kale told Eddie his interview would take place on horseback, and that they'd mount up at Kale's barn. He led them two miles to an inholding, Kale's old family home. Eddie took no chances on Rosalia and Bub. He unloaded and tacked up Madre, squeezed Rosa onto the saddle in front of him, and out they rode with Kale on his huge roan gelding, Eisenhower. As Kale led Eddie and Rosalia over rolling hills their glimpses of the wild river bottom and towering pine-covered hills put a light in Eddie's eyes.

"The look of this place causes hearts to soar," Kale told him. "But here's a reality check. Three generations of family ranchers did okay here till two world wars knocked 'em into early graves or the beef cartels knocked 'em out of business. Those days are a lost world now, Eddie. The Land & Beef boss I answer to is one Charles Keynes Schiller, who changes his name to Tex when he flies out from Dallas and slips into his four-hundred-dollar pre-faded jeans and thousand-dollar Luccheses. Tex is my problem, not yours. But his boss is a multinational called NorBanCo, and that's everybody's problem. NorBanCo board members love rare steak, as do we, but have no idea it's healthy grass and cattle that steaks come from. Our jobs will continue into the foreseeable future, but it's only fair to warn you. Staying employed by Land & Beef Inc. is a battle we will one day lose.

"Now, how about Rosalia hops down and you and Madre show me what you can do."

Eddie settled Rosalia on a sunlit log.

Kale put him on trial, first, by asking him to rope, upend, and release a calf. Liking what he saw, Kale upped the degree of difficulty, asking Eddie to work two feral steers from a brush-choked willow bottom out into the clear. Madre moved the steers with ease while Eddie sat her, looking like he had nothing to do with it. Kale had him move five Black Angus cattle in a wide circle. The circle looked choreographed. Finally Kale had him separate three calves from their mothers. When Eddie and Madre pulled this off in a way that left the mothers more or less calm, Kale let his approval show with two curt nods.

He led Eddie to a reinforced corner post, they talked fencing, and Kale liked what he heard. At a slumping gate they talked gates. More to like. Satisfied, Kale said, "There's a couple things for us to discuss, and a specific place I'd like to do it. Let's gather up Rosalia."

They rode back to the child. As Eddie was lifting her into the saddle Kale heard her say, "Can we tell him?"

Through clenched teeth Eddie murmured, "*I told you no, Rosa. Don't ask again.*"

They rode out across the ranch in the direction of the river. Kale pointed out a spring creek tributary, two golden eagles, a small herd of pronghorns, a badger den, but he had to pretend not to notice Rosalia throwing her elbow back into Eddie, whining, "We need to tell." Finally Eddie caught her arm and gripped it so firmly she let out a yelp.

Kale reined Ike in. "All right, Eddie. What's up?"

"Father-daughter disagreement, sir. We worked it out." But Rosa shook her head.

Kale eyed them. "How about Rosalia gets down again, Eddie, and you and I ride far enough away to make this private?"

Eddie looked miffed as he lifted Rosalia and set her on the ground, but was extra gentle with her because he was angry. "Don't you move or say a word," he said. "I'm really mad at you, Rosa." But Kale could hear his affection even as he scolded.

The two men rode a hundred yards off, reined in, and faced each other. Rosalia stood glaring at them, looking fierce but very small. "First off," Eddie told Kale, "I'm sorry I caught her arm like that. But she was outta line. On the drive up I told her not to bring up what brought us to Montana. I was real clear. She tried to force me to do it anyway. If a single dad's kid gets away with stuff like that, things head downhill fast."

"I was a single dad myself," Kale said. "Anything more you care to tell me, Eddie?"

"I think you see I'm a decent cowboy. I'm also a jack of several trades. Carpentry's my strong suit. I can build or repair just about anything made of wood. I don't like bragging, but I'm a hard worker. If I'm not, you'll know in a week and that'll be that. I only say it because I hope I get that week to show you what I can do."

"Listen," Kale said. "I raised a daughter solo, same as you're doing, and want to give you that week. But something's haywire. You need to trust me enough to tell me what brought you here, Eddie. Once that's in the open, I hope we can work it through."

Eddie heaved a stricken sigh. "All right. The first thing to know is, I'm a fifth generation Arizonan. Not an illegal. People are so quick to think that. Second thing, our connection to Arizona is done. I want Rosalia and me in Montana for good. And I brought us here knowing that hardly any Chicanos live in these parts, because I wanted that. The reason I want it is what I didn't want to get into. I'll go there, Mr. Broussard. But only if you promise to keep what I tell you between you and me. You'll understand why once I say it."

"I can promise that," Kale said.

Eddie drew a breath. "Three years back I had to divorce Rosa's mother. I loved her a lot, but her trouble was hard drugs. I gave her many chances. But she couldn't stay clean. I had divorce papers drawn up. She wouldn't sign. Kept coming back for money, which was hell on Rosalia, who of course loved her. When I told her to stop coming, she went off like a bomb and wanted to kill me, but had nothing but her hands to attempt it with. I got a restraining order. She came back anyway. I made the call. The police hauled her off screaming death threats and worse. Terrible for Rosalia. And she wasn't done. The next time she came back was late at night, and she brought the kind of men who think nothing of doing horrible things to people. People talk about a drug war. A war is two sides fighting.

This was murderers on one side, me and Rosa on the other. I don't even own a gun.

"To save us I lied to those men, and lied skillfully. I hoped to trap them and almost did. But they'll kill me on sight if they ever see me again. We had to disappear so completely I had to change our names. I know how bad that sounds, but I researched it and paid top dollar. Valid driver's license, social security number, birth certificate, the works. None of that will come back to bite you, sir. But if what I just told you costs me a chance at this job, I still ask, for our safety, that our secret goes no further than you."

Kale gave Eddie a long look. Eddie did nothing but meet his gaze. "Thanks for squaring with me. I'm gonna give you a try, Eddie. But that means giving Rosalia a try too. And that concerns me. For your safety and hers, I'd like a few private words with her."

Eddie nodded. "I'd be glad of that, sir."

They rode back to Rosalia. Eddie dismounted and, without a word, set her, alone, on Madre, then strolled away.

While she sat the horse, looking a bit stunned, Kale rode in close. "You like this place, don't you?" he said.

She nodded, but not eagerly. She knew something was up.

"Your dad's a good man. I like him a lot. You do too, don't you?"

Another nervous nod.

"There was just one thing about his interview I didn't like, Rosalia. Your elbow work. I'm foreman here, young lady, and if I hire Eddie there are rules. *Strict* ones. For *your* safety. Those rules will often mean not getting your way. But if you can't abide by my rules your dad can't work for me. It's that simple. Do you understand?"

Big-eyed and very attentive now, Rosalia nodded.

"Will you shake with me on this?"

Looking very small and solemn, she extended her little hand and they shook.

Kale waved to Eddie. He strolled back and mounted up behind Rosa. "Time to talk turkey, and there's a place I'd like to do it," Kale said. "Schoolhouse Bluff. Let's head."

TEN MINUTES OF easy cantering brought them to a half-mile-long, 80- to 150-foot bluff overlooking the Elkmoon River's broad cottonwood bottom. Two Airstream trailers were perched a quarter mile apart, both twenty yards back from the decline. Across the river a sizable tributary flowed into the Elkmoon out of a deep ponderosa-forested canyon. In an equidistant triangle with the Airstreams was a no-longer-used one-room schoolhouse with a fresh-painted sign: TESTAMENT CREEK SCHOOL.

"That old school looks well cared for," Eddie remarked.

"I keep it up because I owe it," Kale said. "Student body averaged fifteen kids, age six to fourteen. Not the way they do things nowadays, but I'll tell you what. That little building and one great teacher put me on a path to Harvard."

Rosalia had no idea what *a path to Harvard* meant, but she loved the look of the many-paned windows, the unused but carefully tended little ball field, and a single towering swing hanging from a high limb of the schoolyard's lone ponderosa.

Kale and Eisenhower led them at a walk toward the Airstream to the east. "My parents owned two thousand acres here till they took sick," he told Eddie. "Their care drained me dry. A banker named Becker Brandt had bought out eighteen thousand acres of neighboring ranches by then. Mine and another, the McKeigs, made it twenty-two thousand. I was real unhappy about that. It didn't help that Beck and I went to Testament Creek School together and were sports teammates and friends. So to make Beck unhappy I kept hold of my family home, barn, corrals, orchard, and garden on twenty acres, and the hundred acres surrounding this bluff. Best view property for miles and it protects the schoolhouse. Beck's long gone so now my inholdings make NorBanCo unhappy, which I like just fine."

Kale dismounted near the Airstream and tied Ike to a thick-boled willow in front. Eddie lowered Rosalia to the ground, then tied Madre to the same tree.

"Front door's around back," Kale said. "Come on, Rosalia. I'll show you why."

They circled the trailer to a wooden deck built out from the back "front door"—and Rosa and Eddie were struck speechless: the view of the Elkmoon River, a hundred yards south and eighty feet below, was stunning enough, but to the west lay thirty winding miles of valley and the first white crowns of the Elkmoon range. The Airstream's biggest window was squarely aimed at all of that beauty.

"Here's the deal," Kale said to Eddie. "Land & Beef offers my cowboys free rent in a bunkhouse. But if I hire you, Rosalia will be the only child on the ranch and life in the bunkhouse gets...*colorful*. Whereas this Airstream is vacant. Tight quarters but snug. Good well water. School's nine miles off in E City, but a bus comes to road's end at seven and drops kids off at four. My daughter rode it for twelve years and didn't grumble too bad."

Eddie nodded, but looked almost frightened as he gazed at the view.

Kale unlocked the door and switched on lights. "Step on in, both of you, and get a feel for it. More like a sailboat's cabin than a hacienda, really. I'll wait out here."

As if the Airstream were a church, Eddie removed his hat, stepped inside, and gazed in reverent disbelief out the back window at the river valley and mountains. Rosalia, meanwhile, threw herself on the little bed, peeked in the closet, tried the faucet in the tiny bathroom, the shower in the tiny stall, the kitchen sink. "Everything's so little and cute!" she said. But when she joined Eddie at the window her voice dropped to a whisper. "We're *sailing*. This place is sailing, Dad. The waves are made of mountains!"

The more thrilled Rosalia looked, the more Eddie looked troubled.

"If it's Madre and Bub you're worried about," Kale said through the open door, "they can board at my barn. Lou Roy trains horses there. He'll show you the ropes."

Looking completely miserable now, Eddie said, "It's perfect, sir. It's perfect. And I hate to ask, but...well. What's it rent for?"

Kale waved as if shooing a fly. "Keep out the mice and mildew and you're doin' me a favor, Eddie. Help me maintain the old schoolhouse, making it two favors, and let's forget rent the first year and just see how it all goes."

When Eddie looked astonished, Kale said, "Let me warn you. Life on this bluff's no picnic. Blizzards hit full force. Lotta snow to plow. We'll have to put snow tires and a blade on your pickup. I've got an extra. The pickings entertainment-wise are damned slim. The little black and white gets the History Channel and PBS, but PBS has its own blizzard blowin' through it. Besides wildlife your only neighbor, in the other Airstream over there, is Lou Roy, a good man and great friend to me, but we're hardly the village it takes to raise a child. If you like it here though, and if I like your work, it could matter that these acres are mine. NorBanCo will be calling off their cattle operation before long and the day they do we're unemployed. If you and I get along, you'll still have a home."

"I'll hope for that, Mr. Broussard. And two TV stations is perfect. We love the outdoors, we love to read, and Rosalia's been wanting me to teach her guitar."

"And how to fly-fish!" she hollered.

"And look at that river," Eddie said, shaking his head. "Truth is, I can't think of a place on this Earth we'd rather be."

"Well hell then, Rosalia and Eddie," Kale said. "Let's ride back to our rigs and get you moved in."

Rosalia shrieked in the manner of an excited horse, pawed the floor with one foot, tore out the door, and began galloping circles round the Airstream.

"If you're the kind of horse can read," Kale called on her first pass, "my daughter, Marla, left her favorite books at my place. Want me to bring 'em by?"

Rosalia tossed her black mane in a *yes* and galloped away.

"If you'll pardon my asking," Kale said once she'd rounded the corner, "how're you fixed for cash, Eddie?"

Eddie grimaced. "That's why the rent scared me. Thirty bucks to my name, sir."

When Kale pulled a money clip from his pocket and peeled off a three-hundred-dollar advance against Eddie's new nine-hundred-dollar-a-month job, Eddie couldn't speak.

The very next day he enrolled the only Chicana within a hundred-mile radius at E City Elementary, went to work for Valley Land & Beef, and Lou Roy Skinner had himself a pair of new neighbors.

What a schmidt-load of difference, Lou would learn, one small new neighbor can make.

XV. Tarkio. Ouzel. Father. Ṣad.

Sometimes human beings have to
just sit in one place and, like, *hurt*.
——David Foster Wallace, *Infinite Jest*

DAYLIGHT CREPT UP. Black and white forest turned green, gray meadows went blond, the eastern sky did some gorgeous bleeding, then a colorless high ceiling turned slowly blue. As I-90 crossed the Clark Fork, Risa swiveled and craned the way Dave would have to glimpse the river. Far below, mesmerizing green current sent up spirals of mist pierced by slant rays of sun, creating such beauty it hurt. "You should *be* here," she blurted. Then listened, with care, to the way no one replied.

An ache filled her. For lack of a more palpable father, she spoke to the ache:

"Remember how, from the time I was tiny, you told me Elkmoon stories? About the ranch, the river, the owls in the cottonwoods. Your Aussie cow dogs, Dylan and Thomas. Your sorrel quarter horse mare, Shirts. The last few mostly tragic town Indians. Your animal and bird stories, mostly tragic too."

Her ache, like a radio, tuned in a random Dave story in reply:

To hypnotize a chicken, Risa, you just lay it in the dust and draw a line straight away from its beak. That's all it takes. It'll lie there staring cross-eyed at that line till nightfall erases it . . .

Turning her attention to the passing land, she began trying to locate particulars that had made her father love Montana so. The first detail to catch her eye: on the freeway median, a whitetail doe so violently disassembled she resembled a Picasso. "*Not that,*" Risa whispered.

Three or so miles later, this time on the shoulder, "*Aw, a dead lab.*" Only wait. Just as she passed it, the dog turned into a disintegrated truck tire. *Whew! Good trick. But not that.*

Not ten minutes later, hundreds of small round stones appeared in her lane too late to dodge them, but when her tires hit them there was scarcely a sound. *Elk crap*, she realized. *And still three-dimensional means the herd just crossed. Definitely that!*

A few minutes later, standing stock-still in a vast hayfield, the bull elk she spotted was larger than seemed possible, till it too started to shape-shift and she realized she was staring at her first bull moose. Its rack seemed the size of the Exploiter's entire hood. Its towering butt was aimed at the freeway, but its eyes were so riveted by a line of pines Risa felt sure they were concealing a sexually ripe cow. "Sing her 'Both an Angel and a Storm,'" she suggested.

Knowing Dave would have laughed, she was unsure of just how his laugh sounded, and the heartache of that tuned in Ache Radio as it broadcast an even longer random tale:

One time Dad offers me and Charlie two cents bounty per bird for every grain-robbin' English sparrow we can kill in the barn. We're maybe six and eight. Good military training, Dad said, plus we'd be servin' the Lord. Has it ever taken more than that to turn a country boy into a patriot assassin? Mother gave us oats for bait. Supporting her troops. Charlie used his BB gun. I hid between four hay bales, two on each side, a fifth bale to sit on, waiting till a bird bent over the oats, then swatted it with Mother's kitchen broom. In two days we killed a hundred and six. Sixty-two kills mine. I was so proud to have outmurdered Charlie I about popped, not to mention the buck-and-a-quarter Dad put in my pocket. One penny of that a gratuity. So generous, my dad. But as any God-servin' killer will tell you once it's too late, get ready for your post-traumatic stress. For half a century I've had broom-busted wing-broke burst-eyeball thrashing-to-death sparrow nightmares. I toss 'em bread in the parks, fries in the drive-thru parking lots. I burn candles to Saint Francis and make prayers to Raven. The sparrows just keep thrashing.

Risa nodded. Why wouldn't they?

The freeway again crossed the Clark Fork. Before she could think, she was craning to see it. This time the higher sun poured peach and pink shafts through the mist onto an enormous blade of swirling mercury. "*Jeez!*" she whispered. "No *wonder* you craned."

Ignoring her discovery, Ache Radio continued to broadcast:

I was eighteen and Charlie twenty when Dad and Mother divorced. Old enough not to care, we told each other. But having no Elkmoon to go home to, Charlie went to 'Nam and I went Ivy League. Silver star for Charlie, honor roll for me. Lookin' good on the outside. But you've seen who Charlie's become. And here's a story 'bout me. It's sophomore year at Princeton. I'm earnin' straight A's and my girl's a knockout. But like every woman I've been with, she can't get enough of me, because I can't locate enough of me to give. She tells me she wants to move in, thinking then she'll find more of me. I tell her no. Listen to why. If my knockout moved in, I couldn't stop under the big horse chestnut on my way home each day to collect forty or so nuts till my pockets are stuffed. Then when I get to my room I pour 'em out over the big rag rug, sweep the horde of others out from under the couch, lie down in the lamplight, turn the rug into my Elkmoon Valley rangeland, turn the chestnuts into my Herefords, an' start herdin' 'em with my hands, calling, "Hyaw! Git up there! Hyaw!" their rusty sides and rolling shadows so real I hear 'em lowing. Think of it, Risa. A twenty-year-old man choosing not to live and lie with a beautiful girl so he's free to lie there like he's five, cowboyin' chestnut-cattle with his hands. Downside was, it was nuts all right. Upside was, I was pretty soon runnin' over a thousand head and owned my whole spread free and clear.

The poignance was too much. "No more *pitiful sweetness*," Risa said. "Some other flavor, please, Ache. How 'bout a *Horrors of Nature* tale? Uncle Charlie's faves."

Ache Radio liked this request:

Last fall hunt I did with Charlie, early the first morning, I'm out cold in my frost-covered sleepin' bag when I hear a locomotive about to hit us. I open my eyes. A huge-racked mule deer buck's standing seven feet away, snortin' like a steam engine, wondering what on Earth we are. Charlie's awake. Sleeps by his rifle since 'Nam. Without even sitting up he one-arm-raises the rifle slow. Shoots that animal almost point-blank in the chest. Buck takes off prongin', on what fuel I'll never know. Makes it a hundred yards before he drops. Charlie cuts open his chest, me watching. That buck's heart is in three separate pieces, and I swear, Risa, all three are still beating. Tell me how that's possible.

"It's not, Ache. I don't think it is. But it's a story. More please."

Ache Radio obliged:

Aspen camp in the Glory Meadow. Foggy morning. In the pond down past Ten Cedars I'm scoping a great blue heron with my rifle to see if it's catchin' brookies. No better breakfast than a panful of small brookies. Over my right shoulder a golden eagle streaks in a kill-dive straight as a Phantom jet. Heron just keeps fishin'. Eagle's talons hit it so hard it nearly beheads it, then swoops up and around to finish the kill. Great blue takes off flyin' all crazy, head floppin' against its chest. Makes it fifty, sixty feet then piles in a heap into the pond and it's a haiku. "Great Blue falls in. The sound of the water!" The golden circles the haiku, screaming and screaming. Got nothin' outta the deal but hungrier.

"And round we come to the chorus," Risa said in Dave's Miller Low Life drawl: "*Most incredible place on Earth, my girl. Elkmoon Country. I'll take you soon, I promise.* And the years pass, the stepmoms an' lovers dictate, we go a grand total of nowhere, but still I believe you. And now look, Dave." She patted his ash bags. "Regular family vacation we got goin'."

The freeway again crossed the Clark Fork. The most crossed and recrossed river in the federal highway system, she remembers Dave saying. Bridge after bridge, so chance after chance to see him *not* swivel and crane and *not* see the water. Chance after chance, then, to ache, until she starts to tremble. *You have saved my life,* he'd kept telling her during their short, sweet chance to finally, truly, know each other. A wonder beyond hope. But it swept by so fast that all five stages of grief were now balled up inside her at once.

Every human's capacity for sorrow has limits. Feeling her limit about to be surpassed, Risa saw an exit sign that said: TARKIO. She'd never heard of it, never heard Dave speak its name, so there were no Ache associations.

She left the freeway and came to a stop sign and graded gravel road.

NO SERVICES, NO EXIT, said a sign. DEAD END, said another.

"Tell me something I didn't already know," Risa murmured.

She followed the dead end down into the Clark Fork canyon. Heavy pine forest and granite walls closed in. No bridge when she reached the river, so no visions of Dave craning. Just an industrial-strength steel-doored outhouse, a concrete boat ramp, and a lot of talkative green water.

She parked, shut off the engine, and stared out at the current, hoping it might carry her sorrow away. But the Dave Ache possessed the inward telescoping power of some great Skrit word. "No way to escape this kind of centripetal power," she whispered to her ache. "The only direction the great spirals let you go is *in*."

Knowing she was about to relive Dave's transition from a breathing *he* to an unbreathing *it*, knowing this would take all her strength, Risa zipped all four windows down, inhaled the pine-rife air as if preparing for a deep ocean dive, sent her thoughts flying to the last few hours of Dave's life, whispered, "Sad. Ṣad. Ṣadness," and spiraled in.

HOSPITALIZED ROUND THE clock, scarcely able to move, pain constant and tremendous at times, Dave yet again refuses morphine and Ativan to summon what clarity he can for a last talk. In the high, breathy voice that's replaced the light Western drawl she loved, he says, "I'm sorry the Exploiter's all crimson and white leather, Risa. I'm glad my Highland love of finery wasn't passed down to you. But last time I looked there were 387 miles on it. A disgraceful odometer reading in a world beautiful as this one. So please. Exploit the Exploiter. Find the beauty."

"I will," she promises.

Summoning the most Jolly Roger–like grin she's ever seen, he adds, "There's a string attached. A string I hope leads to something you'd love to find. Pen and paper?"

Risa has a politically incorrect fondness for Pilot throwaway fountain pens. Delving in her bag, she finds a black and a blue. Hands the dying blues lover the blue.

"Paper?" he asks.

She delves again, finds a computer-printed page from Bart: directions to Dave's storage units in Elkmoon City. She hands it over.

Dave sees what page it is, flips to the blank back without comment, sets to work. Within seconds Risa sees he's drawing a map, and by the lovestruck look in his death-yellowed eyes and answering needle in her heart she already knows what it will depict if he lives to finish it: *most beautiful place on Earth, my girl. And I'll take you there. I promise.*

The empty air over the Clark Fork sends a feeling that somehow causes her to mutter, "Wouldn't it be dumb, Dave Ache, if a big old eagle flew by about now?"

Not ten seconds later, flying upriver from the west and Idaho, here it comes: massive black wings and body; regal white head and tail; pale eyes peering down on the world with such cold authority that the world too takes on a cold, authoritarian pall. Even so, Risa tells the Ache: "*Dumb.* Just like it was dumb watching you kill yourself mapping a place that only ever hurt me. *Have your dying fun,* I thought. *But your special place isn't special to me. Your endless lady friend pilgrimages there made sure of that.*

"Only, just as this timeworn disappointment hit, you stopped drawing, looked up, and leveled the most crucified but uncomplaining look on me. And your eyes had ceased to be a father's eyes and were just, I dunno, this innocent, nameless, journeying soul's eyes, about to take off out of a body the way souls have done forever. A lot of father-to-child promises being broken by that departure. The kind the psych books say wound us for life. But the look in your eyes revealed the very essence of you acknowledging, *Yes, my girl. Promises broken.* And then—I don't know how you pulled this off—then that innocent, ageless soul smiled at me, out of you, as if *no* promises were being broken, causing your nearly dead face to say what Krishna says. *The soul is unborn, enduring, constant. It can never not be. Weapons don't cut it, fire doesn't burn it, waters don't wet it. And bad as people hurt each other, Risa, no soul has ever hurt another soul. Not mine. Not yours. Not even once.* And everything in me cried out: Yes, Dave! Yes, it's true!

"As if you knew your map was safe now, you bent back to the making of it. And as you worked I think maybe you sensed, as I did, Yama, Lord of Death, in the very act of lowering his little silver noose down into your body to capture your thumb-sized life. But you started enthusing over your damned map even so! Calling me *perfect girl* and *mouse-mouse* and *bear-bear* like I'm still six or seven, sounding like some incorrigible scoundrel out of Robert Louis Stevenson, you raved, as you mapped, about everything I'd touch and feel and adore when I reached your perfect place, forcing Yama to enthuse right along with you. Dying Dave strong-arming the all-powerful Dharma Raja into letting you chatter like a happy kid about some stupid meadow in Montana even as His wire noose cinched tight, ready to yank the very life out of you. *God,* I love you for that, Ache!

"But then...then that very love became the struggle...because your Elkmoon treasure map was really an *anti*-treasure map. *Proceed to the X and bury treasure forever,* the map orders, you being the treasure. Knowing I was hearing your storytelling for the last time, my heart cracked in two. *But listen, Ache.* I let your Stevenson scoundrel charm pour into me even so. That's how it's *always* been for us. From day one we loved the sight and sound of each other even though we broke each other's hearts. The heartbreaker this time was the energy you kept pouring into your map, because it was for me. So pure, so playful, so *all-giving,* the effort you poured into *Risa's* map. Nothing like the divided energies I'd shared with your *lady friends.* As you drew the way the Elkmoon cuts through its upper-most meadow I watched the longtime bank employee emptying his account. Steadying your tremors, forcing Yama to let you be a happy papa one last time, you started printing fishing advisories beside the bits of mapwater to which they applied. *Early Sept: throw hoppers against these undercuts. Use 2X. BIG browns!* Then: *Early Oct: blue-winged olives & 6X for the rainbows rising in every glide!* Absurdly late for such advice, the gasps of effort more and more pained. But nothing more important, in our world or Yama's afterworld, than for *perfect girl* to know where and when to cast which fly. And you know what, Ache? That kind of enthusiasm sells! I *will* try to fish those undercuts and glides."

On the Clark Fork's far shore, at Tarkio, a whitetail doe and fawn catch Risa's eye, but her focus is so intent they seem to be passing through the meadow on Dave's map.

"You force Yama to follow you on to other meadow features. The boggy pond you call *Moose Hotel,* where I'm to watch out for *some pretty rough customers.* The tiny hot spring no one knows, *just your size, Risa, right here, in the bull pines upslope of the bog.* You draw *the Indian camp in the quaking aspens, where we found so many arrowheads after big rains.* Then *the black bear den at the foot of the thousand-foot talus field. And here on the ridge, the eagle nest in the ancient ponderosa. Six feet deep, that nest. Been there a thousand years.* Lots of *thousands* in your death talk as thousand-armed Yama's noose started lifting you from your body. But, departing life be damned, what care your wrecked body took to draw me the glacial erratic boulder behind which Charlie hooked a nine-pound brown, draw every bend in the quarter mile of river down which he chased it, then draw the tail-out where he beached it and—being *never-love-nobody, nuke-them-gooks, damn-if-that-daughter-of-yours-didn't-up-an'-grow-an-ass-on-her* Charlie—killed it.

"Bank account empty, your face then went so gray I think Yama Himself might have lent you the juice to draw the grove of ten cedars around which, you whispered, *You might scatter me in kind of a faery ring, the way cottonwoods and mushrooms grow. Maybe save a handful for the river there too.* Who was I loving then, Ache? Whose hands quaked like aspens as you started to pass me the map, but groaned, *Wait!* set your jaw, set pen back to paper, and wrote the idiotic title 'Glory Meadow' across the top, wrecking the whole thing if either of us were sane? Who then underlined those crazy words *twice,* insisting *Ātman* to *Ātman* that yes, Risa, *Glory and nothing less awaits you here.* This meadow is *exactly* where it lives!

"Whoever you were now, Ache, your little-boy treasure map and destroyed face and body made the love rise up so hard I fell on your wrecked breastbone and chest, and you not only took the blow, you kind of held me, stroked my hair a little, a pretty much dead dad tending his sobbing child while cancer—what a great Hollywood heavy!—cancer sneered at our love, tears, map, mortal bodies, embrace, and kept pulling the trigger, unnecessarily blasting you again and again and again!"

Tears stop her. She pulls out her shirttail, wipes the mess from her face, looks up, and sees the same world-darkening eagle, coming from upriver this time, gliding east to west. "*Make up your mind!*" Risa sniffles through her tears.

At river's edge a water ouzel flits into sight, then alights on a log jammed by current into an elephant-shaped boulder. Water bulges over the front of the elephant, running swift and smooth, three inches deep, over its massive gray back. Spying something edible in the bulge, the ouzel shoots forward and submerges itself, the river flowing so evenly that an animate gray ouzel becomes a nub of inanimate gray elephant back. The sight somehow fortifies Risa, showing her how a nub of life might, with courage, dip smooth as this ouzel into the current of death and make its way along under there. She turns back to her beloved Ache:

"Final trajectory. A brand new holiday: *No-More-Dave Eve.* An instant came when I knew I was no longer your *mouse-mouse,* your *perfect girl,* your anything. And how the rest went from your side, only you and Yama know. But from mine? *Listen, Ache.* I held your hand for *hours* after it stopped squeezing back. TJ my inspiration, you my Jervis. I held it through the nurses' lawsuit-inspired protocols: changes of position, groin-and-ass washings, the insane machines spewing numbers as if death's demolition work might lead to some number besides zero. And through *all* of that, Dave, *you fathered me.*"

For a few gasping breaths she's close to a state of overwhelm. But the river never stops flowing, the ouzel never stops burying its little body in the bulge flowing over the stone elephant, and again the bird's blithe courage steadies her.

"Sounds impossible, I know, *fathering* a child with all volition gone. But you *did,* Ache. You did. First, you fathered me by living *far* longer than humanly possible. You stayed with me the way mist stays on mountains after rain, the way September stays part of the best Octobers. You lived on five or six rattling breaths and fifteen or twenty erratic heartbeats a minute as I watched you, amazed, carefully counting them. For an hour, two hours, you kept doing this, a wonder worthy of that heart-blown-to-three-pieces buck of Charlie's. And then—*know this, wherever and whoever you are now*—you fathered me by becoming my own personal Northwest native myth. Back to nature you went, your jaw working the way a dying salmon's does, eyes blind but open like the salmon's, aimed at places only you and they know how to find. The totem pole at the center of the sea. The old McKeig ranch on the best day of your boyhood. And then, *oh, Ache,* then you fathered me by going *beyond* nature, your last sounds genderless, nearly bodiless, and *far* from language. *More* than language. Inhumanly purposeful, your last two out-breaths. *Majestic,* I want to say. Showing me our final departure can be uncanny. Miraculous. In some harrowing way even *beautiful.* I know this now. You gave me this gift so much later than possible that, again too late—*how could I have forgotten*—I cried, *Father! My Father!* The word I'd refused you since I was thirteen!"

She splinters now, sob-racked, eyes awash. But even amid grief's surges the tear-blurred ouzel remains merged with Elephant Rock, holding her splinters together, enabling her to fuse one last time with Dave's departure.

"Finally," she whispers, "soul-quiet, soul-free, small as a thumb and willing now, you fathered me by sliding away as if into water. And I felt it: *gone!* And tried to follow. Tried to sense: *Where? Can I touch your spirit with mine? Help you on your way? Shove you off into the strongest, safest current somehow?* But my body stayed on shore, and the body you'd abandoned became all that was left.

"*But listen, Ache.* Then even *it* fathered me...by becoming...so quickly meaningless. *He wasn't this. And you're not that,* your emptied body told my body. Everything in me then rose up to say, *Thank you, David McKeig. Thanks for your life and late love, my father.* And *God,* how I hope some last mist of you feels that!"

A final shuddering sob, heard by who knows what or whom.

The severe calm of absence.

> *When the sun has set, moon has set,*
> *fire gone out, speech stopped,*
> *what serves as light*
> *for woman or man?*

Long October shadows. Tireless current.

The words current never stops saying to stones.

One current-defying ouzel, refusing to wash away just as a father so long refused.

Her halting breaths reliving Dave's last halting breaths.

Her life loving his no matter how lifeless the brown paper bags' contents.

Lone woman in an empty canyon, incarnating a few lonely magic words: *Tarkio. Ouzel. Father. Ṣad.*

(Elkmoon Valley, summer and autumn 1997)

XVI. Appaloosa in Hell

The Heaven of No Thought should not be regarded as upward, nor the Lowest Hell as downward. The Lowest Hell is the entire phenomenal world; the Heaven of No Thought is the entire phenomenal world.

—Eihei Dōgen

HAVING HIS LIFE ruined and sanity seriously compromised turned out to be a Five Step Program for Lou Roy Skinner. What made his plight even harder to defend against was the fact that it was designed almost entirely by the eight-year-old girl now living in the Airstream next door. In chronological order, the five steps:

1. Unseen Lion

One evening a couple of weeks after Eddie and Rosalia had moved into their Airstream, Rosa was enjoying an out-of-body reverie on the Testament Creek School's towering ponderosa swing when—not a hundred feet away, but unseen round the corner of the schoolhouse—a gunman opened fire, rapidly emptying five rounds from a Mossberg tactical shotgun into a stand of pines seventy yards past Rosa's swing. The blasts paralyzed Rosalia and brought Eddie tearing out of his Airstream carrying a kitchen knife, expecting men from his past had arrived to kill them. When Lou Roy then stepped round the corner of the schoolhouse, shotgun in hand, and started toward Rosa, she screamed, certain that she was about to die. Lou Roy froze instantly, lay the Mossberg gently on the ground, showed her his empty palms, and didn't move a muscle till Eddie reached the swing and, glaring fiercely at Lou Roy, took Rosa in his arms.

"Awful sorry for the scare, Eddie, but we might of just got lucky," Lou Roy said. "I was headed over to show you my new shotgun when I seen a she-lion crouched in the closest lodgepoles there. She was all eyes for Rosalia, twitching her tail the way that says *prey*. With no time to warn the poor girl, I gave the cat a buckshot shower I do believe helped. She was still goin' full-bore when she crossed that rise a quarter mile north of us there."

Eddie thanked Lou Roy profusely and asked Rosalia to do the same, but she remained paralyzed with terror. And she hadn't seen any lion. All she knew for sure was that Lou Roy had inflicted the worst fear she'd felt since drug-runners separated her from her mother forever. Did she conflate Lou Roy with those men? Sure. Did she believe a lion had been eyeing her with dark intent? Maybe. But just as dark to her mind was the fact that Eddie believed in Lou Roy's lion so completely that he forbade Rosalia to visit the swing or schoolyard alone, separating her from her favorite place to play.

2. JB Jones

Eddie Dominguez was born on June 30th. A week before his birthday, Rosalia told the staff at Wiggles & Giggles Daycare in Elkmoon City that Eddie had given her permission to walk the two blocks to JB Jones's Hardware at lunchtime to buy something Eddie needed at work. What the daycare staff didn't know was that, for altruistic purposes, Rosalia was lying. Eddie was great with tools, but carried the few he owned in a waxed cardboard fruit box with a baling twine handle that made him resemble the illegal alien he wasn't. So when, back in March, Eddie was buying a few nails and screws at JB Jones's Hardware, Rosalia checked out the spiffy tool belts. She then ate food her classmates didn't want for the rest of the school year, saving most of her lunch money to buy Eddie a belt.

When her lie was believed, Rosalia walked down to JB Jones's Hardware, stepped inside, and nodded to JB, who was manning the cash register. When three men came in just then and started gabbling with JB, Rosalia headed back to the belts, and was elated to discover she'd saved enough to buy Eddie the thirty-dollar Carhartt that was her favorite.

Starting back to the cash register, belt in hand, she overheard JB asking his chunky white compatriots, "What d'ya call a busload o' Mexicans going over a cliff?"

"Tell us," one of the men said.

"A good start," JB rejoined, and a few raucous cackles fell out of the men.

Rosalia showed what she was made of by walking up and setting the tool belt on the counter. JB's face downshifted to an embarrassed smile. The three strangers blushed and wandered off on errands. But a fifth man had appeared who remained at the counter, staring holes in JB's face. Unfortunately for this man, Rosalia failed to notice that he was seething. All she saw was that it was Lou Roy, whose shotgun blasts had filled her with terror. She made her purchase in silence, left JB Jones's Hardware, and prayed all the way back to Wiggles & Giggles that every man she'd just seen would be driven over a cliff. More bad luck for Lou Roy: she kept the encounter secret from Eddie to keep his birthday gift secret. Had she shared what she'd seen she would have learned that Eddie and Lou had become trusted friends. More holes in her understanding: Lou Roy had seen her studying the belts through the hardware store window, guessed who she was shopping for, and stepped inside thinking to add a few tools to Eddie's belt, only to be sidetracked by JB's joke. Nor did Rosalia know that the instant she left the store, Lou got in JB's face. "You goddamned fool," he had fumed. "What did that little girl ever do to you?"

"Oh, come on," JB said. "You know I was only jokin'."

Moving in closer, Lou Roy said, "Next time I hear you tell a joke that funny in Rosalia's hearing, your goddamned dentures'll be your lunch."

He then, unbeknownst to Rosalia, strolled JB's aisles and purchased several tools he knew Eddie needed for his birthday belt.

3. Hoot

A few days later Rosalia was out by the front gate at Wiggles & Giggles, waiting for Eddie to pick her up, when a man coming down the sidewalk spotted her, swept off a mangled straw cowboy hat, gave her a bow, and started chatting at her unasked. His name, he said, was Hoot Clark, he was E City born and raised, and he'd been the sole editor and writer of a long gone weekly, the *E City Standard,* but was now, in his own words, "your distinguished town drunk, with unpublishable opinions about every person and place in town."

Though his sloppy friendliness was a little scary, Rosalia's agenda overcame her fear. She asked Hoot if he knew JB Jones and Lou Roy Skinner. Hoot did. She asked if he thought they were racists.

"What a question from a child so young. Let me ponder," Hoot replied. "JB's got dumb-shit jokes for all occasions, but the meanest ones are about crackers like himself. He's more numbskull than racist. And Lou Roy is no such thing. Decades ago he captained the Elkmoon Eagles, shortest team ever to win the Class A state hoop crown. There were three Indian starters on the team, and two more who'd come blazing off the bench. They ran big white ranch boys into the ground, and Lou Roy was their floor general. Before horses bowed his legs and smoking fried his lungs, Lou could fly. Funny twist, though. He was the one suffered for his skin color. The Eagles' great Nez Perce shooting guard, Sherman Arm Horses, dubbed him *Appaloosa.* High praise, I figured, since that's the Nez Perce breed of choice. But the nickname made Lou furious. I couldn't think why till the locker room celebration after the championship. When Lou Roy come out of the shower, Arm Horses moved his head in his direction, and I damn near fell over. Turns out Lou Roy's got big purplish-brown birthmarks all over his rump just *like* a damned Appaloosa!"

How sweetly Rosalia smiled as she filed this fact away.

4. Lying to the Max

The next morning, a Tuesday, Rosalia accompanied Eddie to the Broussard barn early, telling him, "I need to ride Bub. He's gotten all fat and lazy."

She hadn't been on the pony in months, so Eddie helped set her up in a little round pen outside the barn. She and Bub then circled the pen at a listless pace till she spotted what she was waiting for: Max Bowler in his hopped-up Jeep Wrangler.

Ending her ride abruptly, she left Bub in the pen, threw in some hay, stepped into the parking area, accidentally-on-purpose crossed paths with Max, and struck up a conversation. Thanks to the scores of books Kale had bequeathed her, her high intelligence, and the daily urbane chats between Eddie and the Pope, Rosalia's diction and vocabulary were highly precocious. Well aware of the charm precocious kids hold for some adults, she set out to charm Max, and began by asking him what he thought of the other cowboys. Max said the Land & Beef crew seemed like an exceptional bunch. Rosalia agreed, and began sketching them to Max like so: "Kale says Hub Punker isn't the sharpest knife in the drawer. But if you call him 'our lead cowboy,' he'll lend you his truck, tractor, bulldozer, and backhoe if you ask. So you better not ask."

Max smiled big, revealing teeth of a wondrous whiteness. His musculature was even more extraordinary. And if his dimples were any deeper he'd have to plug his cheeks with corks or something to keep his food from falling out. "You're a trip, Rosalia!" he laughed. "How about Doty Nolan?"

"My dad says, 'Doty Nolan is Doty Nolan and that's all there is to say about Doty Nolan.'"

Max laughed. "That's been my impression too! So tell me about Eddie."

"Eddie's the best dad in the world, but he won't let me brag about him so that's all I got."

"How about Kale then?"

"Best boss ever. Best neighbor ever. He likes his real name better than 'the Pope,' but we call him the Pope anyway because we respect him, like Catholics respect John Paul Two."

"And how about Lou Roy?" Max asked—and Rosalia made her move:

"Lou Roy is Kale's oldest friend. He was a great rodeo cowboy, and he's still a great horse trainer. That's why the boys call him what they do."

"Which is what?" asked her goon-to-be.

"'Appaloosa.' Out of respect for the breed and the cowboy. Same as Kale's 'the Pope' out of respect," Rosalia said—and immediately felt queasy. But she didn't retract it. "I gotta put Bub back in his stall before he bites somebody. Thanks for talking with me."

"You have a great day, Rosalia!" Max said, and away he strolled, cocked and loaded, thinking Rosalia the most perspicacious eight-year-old he'd ever met. Which she probably was. And she was also, during the moment just passed, the worst informed and meanest.

Max didn't see Lou Roy for two days, but Rosalia's sketches of the crew rang so true that his trust of her words remained total. So when, first thing Thursday morning, Lou came ratcheting toward him across the barnyard, Max showed his respect by touching a finger to his Stetson and saying, "Mornin', Appaloosa, sir."

Lou Roy froze on the spot, so Max stopped too, thinking a pearl of wisdom was about to fall from the sagacious old horseman's lips. Cocking his head and peering up at Max out of his glacier-silt-green eyes, Lou Roy hoisted the grimace he used for a smile up onto his face, drew a big breath as if about to speak—and uncoiled the hardest sucker punch he had straight into Max Bowler's nose.

Next thing Max knew he was sitting in horse hotchnik with blood gushing from both nostrils. But it was surprise and placement, not force of blow, that had felled the mighty young cowboy—and what better push button than a nose to activate blind rage? With an impossible handspring and a roar that brought the rest of the crew at a run, Bowler exploded off the ground, let his blood fly, and moved in on Lou Roy like the skilled boxer he was. Lucky for Lou, even in his rage Max withheld his right-handed haymaker, knowing it could end in manslaughter, and started throwing left jabs at a rate of about one per second. Lou Roy's skinny arms flew up in defense. Max's fist blasted through them like a bull moose through a pair of cattails. Driving the old cowboy backward, popping him in the mouth, cheeks, eyes, chest, at will, Max let him keep his feet solely for the pleasure of landing more blows. When Lou Roy went punchy and fell on his back, Max pounced, pinning him down.

"*Listen, shitball!*" he roared as his blood cascaded into Lou's face. "They told me your name was *Appaloosa* the way the Pope's is the Pope, out of respect. And maybe that wasn't true, *before*. But it's true now, and I want to hear you say it! '*My name is Appaloosa Skinner.*'"

"*Fuck you,*" Lou wheezed.

Max freed Lou Roy's arms to give him half a chance, but his jab blasted an arm so hard that Lou's fist smashed his own face. "Speak up! '*My name is Pappy Appy.*'"

"*Fuck you, Bowler.*" Wham!

The crew circled closer as an old schoolyard-style litany commenced:

"'*My name is Lou Roy Lou Boy Appaloosa Skinner.*'"

"*Go to hell, Bowler.*" Wham!

This went on a long time. Lou Roy never repeated the nickname. When his face began to resemble steak tartare and his fuck-yous grew nearly inaudible, Max couldn't keep it up.

Helping the old cowboy stand, Max felt like a stupid bully as Lou gimped away.

5. Exile

The damage Rosalia desired was done, and more than she wished for followed. The nickname spread through the valley like wind-driven fire, and Lou Roy's reaction to it didn't change. He'd known lifelong that equine misbehavior can often be corrected with a quick, hard smack on the snout. The same smacks delivered to men in their twenties and thirties got very different results. Most were just curious to see whether, as rumor had it, the name of a fine breed of horse caused the renowned old cowboy to go berserk. Lou never disappointed. If he was headed to the Stockman's and three or four passersby murmured the nickname, he'd try to take them all on. The first man he hit would then put him on the ground.

Weeks passed. Lou Roy lost a front tooth. His contusions never healed. He got so punchy he once swung at a cowboy he'd merely imagined said the nickname. Lou was fifty-two the day he became Appaloosa. He'd smoked hand-rolled Bugler cigarettes thirty-six of those years. He weighed 140 pounds in boots, clothes, Stetson, and a thick belt with a heavy rodeo buckle. His severely bowed legs had been horse-sculpted to glue him to a mount, not keep him on his feet when a name-nicker counterpunched. He never came close to winning a fight. Nor was he the sort of tumbleweed who could escape his problem by riding off into the sunset. Except for the West's rodeo grounds and riding arenas, the Elkmoon Valley had been his entire world from birth. Beyond the edge of that world, so far as he knew, you fell off. The fact that every person in his world now knew of his gluteal anomaly made him just about perfectly unhappy. Being *named* after it made him downright insane. Pappy Appy Skinner had himself a serious problem—

for which reason so did Foreman Kale. Four of Lou's lost fights had taken place on Valley Land & Beef property during work hours. Their contracts included a no-fighting rule. Kale had convinced Tex Schiller to stretch that rule to "three strikes" after the American legal system did the same. But Lou Roy was not a three strikes friend to Kale. He was family. When the Pope was a boy, Lou had taught him more about horses, cattle, riding, and wrangling than Kale's father and grandfather combined. During the years the Broussard ranch was sinking, Lou Roy had volunteered to work for Kale for room, board, and no pay, and shared his bronc-riding winnings to keep the ranch afloat. When the bank finally foreclosed, Lou and Kale had split a bottle of whiskey, confessed their abject need to live nowhere on Earth but the Elkmoon Valley, bit the bullet, and went to work for the same financial entity that had cannibalized the valley's family ranches, theirs included. Riding the melting iceberg that was the life of a cowboy, they'd been each other's solace for thirty years. They were now likely to lose that solace due to a dozen or so modest blemishes on Lou's ass.

"You're right about one thing," Kale growled on the day he called his friend onto the carpet. "Your nickname *is* an insult—to Appaloosas! How can a man your age be vain about his goddamned ass? You won't have to own it much longer!"

"This ain't about my ass an' you know it," Lou Roy fired back. "It's about my *name*. My father was the all-round rodeo champ, Big Roy Skinner. My brothers are Delroy, Elroy, an' Kilroy Skinner. I been Lou Roy since birth. I'm gonna die Lou Roy. An' I'm tired o' gettin' beat to shit. You wanna help end this thing, Kale, spread the word. I got better weapons than fists, an' if this Appy crap don't stop I'll be packin' 'em. A man my age has a right to his own goddamned name."

"If you want to work here *you're giving up that right*!" Kale roared. "You're getting beat to shit because you belt people! For God's sake, Lou! Cowboys *tease,* and when the teasing gets results they double down on it. If you hope to stay in this valley it will *be* by the name *Appy* till they get bored with it, and you need to hear me. *Throw one more punch and you're gone. Carry weapons of any kind and you're gone.* And not just from Land & Beef. From my barn and Airstream too. You've used up every chance you had. This negotiation is *over*."

But even as he delivered his ultimatum Kale saw no light of reason dawning in his old friend's eyes. On the contrary, the threat of being cast out of his world filled Lou Roy with reason-proof rage. So, like the gentleman he was, Kale tossed in a quid pro quo:

"Here's what we're gonna do. You need practice saying 'Appaloosa' in private, where the only man in need of punching will be you, and there's work that needs doing up at Three Forks Meadow. Five miles of shoddy fencing. Screwed up troughs and water lines. Salt to pack in. A busted fence and tangle of lodgepoles from a microburst to saw up. You can stay in the line shack. I cleaned it last elk season, but take mouse and packrat traps. You have *got* to get this under control. When you're ready to go, let me or Eddie know. We'll tend the horses you don't take along."

Still too furious to speak, Lou Roy gimped out of the office. But a couple of hours later Kale and Eddie saw him pile his pickup full of gear, lead his favorite horse, Grey, into the trailer, and call his little cow dog up onto the front seat.

Eddie and Kale nodded as he drove past. Lou didn't give them a glance.

"I feel for him," Eddie said.

"Me too," Kale said. "But if things don't change he could go criminal over this. He's *got* to cool down. I'll gather him some good eats and whiskey, drive up, and try to talk sense to him in a few days."

XVII. Skrit Lit at E City Storage

It will be the task of our generation not to seek great things, but to save and preserve our souls out of the chaos, and to realize that it is the only thing we can carry as a prize from the burning building.

—Dietrich Bonhoffer

IT'S 3 A.M. ON Risa's thirtieth birthday. Completely spent, she glides into Elkmoon City, finds E City Storage, and parks the Exploiter behind the storage units where nobody can see it. She creeps into shrubs in the drought-stricken landscaping. Pees. Returns to the SUV. Reclines the seat as far back as it will go:

Gone.

FAINT FIRST LIGHT and a gurgling stomach. All quiet. Doze.

Open one eye to fall colors. So few. The land so sere. Open a second eye to squint at a crimson sliver of sun the width of a paper cut: that slice of beauty and a grumbling stomach wake her. She revisits the stricken landscaping, sees no one. Pees. Gets back in the Exploiter, shakes and face-pats herself awake, drives.

She finds a truck stop on Main, cleans up in the restroom. Loads up on eggs, hash browns, ice water, coffee.

She returns to E City Storage. Locates units A and B. The garage-sized metal doors face east. She unlocks and lifts each door in turn. In unit A, early morning sun floods a space stockpiled floor to ceiling with every useful-looking furnishing, tool, and piece of indoor and outdoor equipment and furniture sufficient for a dozen people to start a life in Montana. Despite Bart's hints, the abundance blindsides her. Had Dave been planning to open a store? Adopt three or four extra families? Lead a chosen people to a promised land? She strolls the aisles, marveling. Exhaustive kitchenware, rugs, lamps, appliances. Enough outdoor gear to start a sporting goods store. A selection of six tents ranging from a one-person ultralight to a four-person elk-hunter's tent complete with stove and stovepipe chimney. Four state-of-the-art backpacks and six sleeping bags. Three chainsaws? Why? Two Skilsaws, a high-end table saw, a lathe, and every woodworking power tool and hand tool imaginable.

She leaves unit A less than halfway through it and scans unit B. Same story. A spanking new ATV. A snowblower. A rototiller, several wheelbarrows and manure carts, gardening tools sufficient to start a farm. Beekeeping supplies to add a honey business. Enough saddles, tack, and panniers to lead an eight-horse pack string into the Elkmoons tomorrow if she knew how to ride and where she'd be going. Two butterfly nets; two long-handled minnow nets; two wet suits with snorkels, fins, goggles. A locked metal gun cabinet Risa unlocks, and shakes her head at a firearms collection sufficient to start a war. On a handsome wall rack, five split-cane and six graphite fly rods, each of them with its own reel and line, plus three wicker creels and two large satchels full of see-through boxes bristling with trout flies.

Overwhelmed, she locks B up, returns to A, and tries to simply squeeze down a skinny aisle through the merchandise to the back wall and what appears to be a bookshelf. When she finally reaches the wall, an enormous portion of her inner self suddenly opens its long-closed eyes: the rough-cut pine bookcase contains every last volume of her long-abandoned Skrit Lit library. The books fit so precisely it's obvious Dave designed the case for them. "And for *me*," she whispers. Atop the case, wedged between bronze bison bookends, stands a row of unfamiliar volumes against which leans a large, gaudy-colored, India Indian dancing Krishna card. She opens it:

Risa:

When you shunned me (as deserved), I can hardly believe the good that came of it: I grew so desperate for some form of contact with you that a means of achieving it smacked me in the head, and down from my garage rafters came your 173 Skrit Lit volumes! I haven't braved the 33 in Sanskrit. I'd need a younger brain and a Dr. Kool for that. But the other 140 I have pored over for three years, and Skrit Lit has opened up what your man The Coom might call a *God-aperture*. I've been stunned by joys, mysteries, and insights galore. I've cherished your Dr. K class notes, endless curiosity, mind-bending marginalia, dumbsaint reflections. As tokens of my inexpressible thanks, please find, between the bison, 29 additions to your Skrit Lit collection: 26 are from publishers American, European & Asian (Happy B-day & Xmas '95, '96 & '97!); the other 3 are in the tradition of your self-invented genre, "crazy dumbsaint notebooks," dumbed down since they were penned by yrs truly. But they truly are my sincere, sustained attempt to interact with the Vedic cosmos as lovingly as you have. I needn't go deeper here; my notebooks go as deep as I could dive, and now a health crisis has come calling. However this crisis goes, dear one, never forget: you are treasure, your library is treasure, and the two combined have guided me to desperately needed late treasure in myself.

> So much love to you!
> Dave

Between the bronze bison, sure enough, stand three volumes titled *Dave McKeig's Dumbsaint Sanskrit Lit Notes*. Sliding them out, Risa spots an old rocker atop a wall of jam-packed storage containers, lifts it down, carries Dave's notebooks and the rocker out into chill morning sun, sits, and finds the chair fits her perfectly. Noticing a white tag wired to its arm, she untwists the wire. "Grandma Stella's fave," the tag says in Dave's tidy hand.

"Of course it is," Risa whispers. "And not one but *three* dumbsaint notebooks. On *Skrit Lit*. Handwritten. For *me*," she breathes. Her eyes pool. A door swings open inside her. Stepping through it, she arrives in a profoundly familial, pine-scented, Montana-meets-Sanskrit inner landscape in which she feels entirely at home for the first time in her life. Opening *Volume III* near the end, she begins reading at random, and is not surprised that the blindly chosen passage sets off fireworks. Dave has written:

> The aims of Skrit Lit are complex. The basic medium is brilliant stories. The *Ramayana* and *Mahabharata* alone tell hundreds of them. But hidden in the stories' aim, I feel over and over as I reread favorites, is an energy that tirelessly aligns us with that which never dies. *Ātman. Paramatma.* The *ākāśa* in the heart. *The Divine Beloved.* These books shouldn't be opened by anyone unwilling to die into the Undying. And my astounding daughter was ready for that at nineteen! Maya's great trick, she learned, is to lure the "I" into facing outward at all times so it can't catch a glimpse of the Self. Oh, Risa! If ever you find this page, my life itself thanks you for giving me a means to turn around and face the Undying! Skrit Lit is the best thing to happen to me since February 25th, 1963, when I sat on the floor of the Quarry Street Coffee House in Princeton at the feet of Mississippi John Hurt. But Hurt was gone in three hours. Skrit Lit is more like the long river he's named for. What conversations we've had, these books and I, rafting downriver for three magic years!
>
> Another twist original to you: the greatest marginalia I've ever seen! What an inspired defacer of books you are, peppering page edges with exchanges that double the text's power! Precision Skrit definitions, miraculously apt lines from world wisdom classics, mystical poems, Coomaraswamy footnotes, Dr. K class notes, handwritten pages of dumbsaint reflections, intimacies, and insights so right, so resonant, right there on the printed pages that inspired them! Best of all to me

are your...what to call them? *Spiritual detonation symbols?* Cork-screwing spirals alongside passages that so move you, you snatch up a pen and people the spiral with tiny human figures climbing like souls up Mount Purgatory. Circular doors located at the very tops of pages, as if the beloved passage below cut a hole in the top of your skull and you escaped into sky. What a gift, the guidance the younger woman but older soul has given her purblind old dad! How many fathers and daughters, *ever,* have shared anything as personal and universal and profound?

Next night: Risa! I woke at 3 a.m. to an insight I'll set down hoping you one day find it. When I abandoned you to Moira at age eight, I left you locked in a terrible cage. But as soon as you left home and fell in love with Sanskrit and Vedic truth, you smashed that cage open and flew into a series of awakenings that continued for two solid years! Your notebooks *revel* in them, as have I!

But how is it that, despite the years of discovery and joy, early in your third Skrit year a single fey sentence from the Upaniṣads wounded you to the quick? The "Sons Only Verse" you call it. For months now I keep failing to see how this mediocre caste system relic could stab you so deep, *especially* when your first response was so perfect! Don't read that worthless verse again, my girl! *Read your response to it aloud,* as I have several times, furious with happiness each time!

Dear Pseudo Rishi,

I won't lie. The grenade you somehow slipped into the Upaniṣads broke my heart. But some of us lapsed Catholic girls know how to deal with this kind of shit. When Aristotle, Aquinas & the Church fathers teach that a woman is a malformed man known as a manqué, or when some big-shot early Xian like Tertullian teaches that the wombs of women are "filth" & the children in our wombs "loathsome curdled lumps feeding on muck," we turn as tough as this cruel foolishness forces us to be. When it comes to defining our minds, hearts & bodies, YOU, Sons Only Fool, are a manqué rishi, Aristotle, Tertullian & Aquinas are manqué theologians & I thank the Unseen Guileless Perfection for the womb She gave me to distinguish me from the penis-fetishizing likes of you! My Skrit-fired heart burns for Truth in the body the Unseen bequeathed it & if you think I'll let that fire die to passively await an incarnation as some niggle-scriptured Brahmin's pampered baby boy you've got another hundred thinks coming. There is a path, extremely fine and extending far! It has touched me, I have discovered it! That beneath which the year revolves, the breathing behind breathing, sight behind sight, hearing behind hearing, thinking behind thinking, the first, the ancient. With the heart alone I have beheld it & that heart is beating inside a knowledge-body (*sambodhakāya*) & truth-body (*dharmakāya*) like yours, but a begotten-body (*nirmanakāya*) that, thanks to a Cathoholic Irish American, a philandering Montana Scot & my beloved Unseen Mother/Father, is double-breasted, girl-hipped & gratefully vaginaed & the time for you vaginaphobes to start freaking is NOW. This girl aims to show the Highest Mysteries a love so true it will break even your mother-hating heart, causing the spurned word WOMAN to fall inside you, saving you, at long last, from YOU!

You just handed the Sons Only Verse author his ass on a platter, Risa! But you don't accept your own victory. You keep feeling the Verse emanating hurts that caused you to abandon Skrit Lit! *Why?* How does it help to take refuge in a "one-woman Sanskrit Oral Tradition" made of memories alone, so that your most cherished language and source of faith is now written in disappearing ink?

Having read the entirety of your Skrit class notes and dumbsaint notebooks I kept asking myself how one antiquated sexist relic could wound you so deeply, and here's the insight that woke me this night: on the day I first carried your six cardboard boxes down out of my garage rafters, I was stunned by the way you'd run whole rolls of filament tape round and round every box as if to mummify the wisdom and love the books bestowed! As I cut through that tape I realized I was cutting through impotent rage. And tonight it hit me: this was *never* the fury of the woman you are. *This is the fury of the eight-year-old girl I abandoned.* I just spent three years riveted by your love for Vedic Truth and "the highest mysteries." Those years leave me certain that the person who can bring peace to the wounded child isn't me: *it's the woman you are now.* Listen to you, Risa! In the margins of your Gita you call Krishna "the eternally recurring Beyond Male who enflames hearts with no regard for gender, space, or time." Yes! You say in a hundred places that Ram and Krishna *are* the Highest Mystery and you adore them with all your bhakti heart. You *are* the woman the hurt child needs! So may I ask why you've abandoned that child, as I once did? Why are you behaving as if the undying Beyond Male, upon hearing some puffed up Brahmin regurgitate the Sons Only Verse, would just nod His weary head and say, "Ah yes, My fine priest. Your Verse is wonderfully correct. All these female poet-saints, Qawwali singers, gopis, Beguines, bhikkhunīs, and dumbsaint scholars with their enflamed hearts, passion for Truth, and joy in My Presence can just forget about Me. What a burden, the oceans of adoration from their strangely made bodies, voracious minds, and annoyingly loving hearts. Thank you for your reminder, faithful Brahmin. As the scriptures say, only pompous, privileged males like you and your fatuous first son will ever know Me!"

For God's sake, soul's sake, and your wounded child's sake, Risa! Be who you *are*! While I pissed away three decades as a blues cliché and Moira sulked on Planet Smirnoff, you sewed your heart to the Beyond Male, set forth without fear, and discovered the Unseen Unborn Guileless Perfection, Kabir's and Tulsidas's *Ram,* Mirabai's and Lal Dêd's *Narayana,* Tukaram's *Vithoba,* your amazing friend Jervis's *Ocean,* and more. The door to a life in that stupendous company is wide-open! *Enter,* my intrepid daughter! Love's Lord awaits you *certain* of the day you and the eight-year-old fly into each other's arms, then turn to the task of rescuing Him from every manqué rishi, blowhard Brahmin, and misogynist priest who dares pretend that caste, tyranny, sexism, and manqué maleness lay claim to the divine!

Sitting, truth-frozen, in her great-grandmother's rocker in warming light, Risa closes her eyes and whispers the trouble verse aloud. *"The highest mysteries must never be revealed to one whose passions have not been subdued, nor to one who is not a master's pupil, nor to one who is not a Brahmin's son."* And the words mean nothing! Both weapon and wound have vanished. In a sleep-deprived state of wonder she whispers, "It's just as you say! My eight-year-old and I *are* in each other's arms! And it's *crazy* the way you keep fathering me! When I had a Dave for a dad, I had *no* father. With your ashes, three notebooks, and two storage units for a dad, you've become the best father ever!"

Risa bows her head, whispers a few sweet nothings to the Beyond Male, and takes her feet. She returns Stella's rocker to unit A, marches to the Exploiter's front passenger seat, lays the books upon it, seat-belts Dave's bagged ashes in place, unfolds his deathbed map, and props it on the dash to serve as the state-of-the-art GPS she feels it's about to become.

She circles round, climbs in, and takes the wheel. "Come on, best father ever!" she says to the map, bags of ashes, and books bursting with afterlife. "Let's bust the Lord of Love out of storage and take your molecules on home!"

XVIII. Pope vs. Preambles

Go to your bosom, knock there, and
ask your heart what it doth know.
                —Shakespeare, *Measure for Measure*

THE SAME SUMMER and fall that converted Kale into a Pope converted the one house in Elkmoon City on the national historic register. A severe gray and white three-story Victorian, built in 1899 and occupied by a string of town mayors, was purchased by one Ida Craig, formerly of Jackson Hole, Wyoming. Ms. Craig then raised an E City's worth of eyebrows when she painted her Victorian cornflower blue, added pink trim and a controlled riot of faux-rococo detailing, and turned her first floor into E City's go-to emporium for New Age cosmetics, healing magnets, crystals, herbs, meditation supplies, yoga mats, Hindu god and goddess statuettes, posters of Tibetan Buddhist tankas, and the like. Ida then converted the enclosed wraparound porch into a charming espresso bar and reading room, the second floor into a surprisingly decent mainstream bookshop, and put up a big red neon second-story sign dubbing her tripartite establishment IDA'S IDEAS.

The local response to this broadening of Elkmoon City's cultural horizons was not warm. The general consensus was that she was positioning herself to cash in on the proposed Brokeback Ranch & Country Club nine miles out of town, and the developer's plan to lure well-heeled urban aliens to an Elkmoon "planned recreational community" that would convert E City's populace, as Brokeback brochures actually put it, into "the colorful yokels and locals of *your* very own sleepy Western shopping town" sent steam out their ears.

But when Lou Roy's name got nicked and his rage grew lethal, the terrain changed for Kale. If anyone could talk Lou down, it was he. But his talking points, he felt, would require detailed knowledge of how admirable Appaloosas are, and there was but one bookstore on Earth that Kale could reach on his lunch hour...

What a comeuppance for the Pope to hide his white F-250 in an alley off a side street three blocks from Ida's Ideas, pull his signature white Stetson low over his eyes, approach via the alley in hopes of not being seen, turn straight toward the Victorian's cloying colors, charge down a walkway of tangerine-colored pavers enveloped in sex-organ-colored peonies billowing out of Greco-Roman-goddess planters, take the six pink-trimmed blue steps in two strides, grab the crystal door handle, wince at the jingling Nepalese goat bells as the door swung wide, step inside, reel at a scent tsunami of aromatherapeutic gels, ointments, eye-bag annihilators, and hand youthifiers, then raise his eyes and espy, not two horse lengths in front of him, Ms. Ida Craig herself.

"Well, *hello,* cowboy!" she piped in a voice that stunned Kale both for its childlike pitch and how thrilled it sounded. "I just now opened and you've already made my day!"

Wondering how he'd done that, Kale felt his face turn florid, touched his Stetson, and murmured, "How do, Miss Ida. I'm Kale Broussard."

"Your reputation precedes you, sir!" she piped.

Trying to grasp how that could be, Kale gave Ida a head-to-toe glance and flew fathoms deep into anti-understanding. Ida stood six feet tall in teal and tan cowgirl boots, enabling her to look the six-foot-one Kale straight in the eye. An ankle-length sheer teal skirt left her legs as bewitchingly obscured as two trophy rainbows on the spawn in an April Elkmoon River tail-out. The same legs were as long as Kale's, incomparably more shapely, yet so powerful in appearance they brought to mind a female NFL running back, yet the boots at the legs' base were so teensy it seemed Ida's feet had ceased to mature on the same day as her voice. Her eyes were brightest blue. Her charmingly cut hair was a red so neon she matched her outdoor IDA'S IDEAS sign. Her face was delicate, with a sweet bow of a smile, a porcelain complexion that testified to the efficacy of her skin youthifiers, and a chin invitingly soft in its lines yet not at all doubled, unlike most of the chins that flirted with Kale.

All of this bewitched him. But it was the bosom hovering a shockingly short distance beneath her chin that unbuckled the belt upholding his sense of reality. Ida's breasts were so immodest in size and jutted so far out in front of her that the cowboy in Kale, thinking of his unruly roan, Eisenhower, was tempted to ask if the makers of her bra perhaps also manufactured a line of tack. What an irony, her saying *his* reputation preceded him when, to his keen carpenter's eye, Ida preceded herself by an easy seven inches. Though she was standing still as she smiled at him, her femininity kept charging so hard that he stepped backward, nearly collapsing a rack of body lotions and soaps. "Miss Ida," he finally managed to say. "I . . . this is damned awkward . . . but I'm in a hell of a crisis with one of my hands." Kale glanced at his hands, scowled, shook his head. "A cowboy I mean. And you're . . . I, uh . . . there's more going on than I can . . . *damn!* My basic deal is this. I need a few of the best books there are about Appaloosa horses and I need 'em fast."

Ida set her child-sized feet, running-back legs, and preambles to her constitution in motion, seating herself at her computer in seconds. "There's nothing on my shelves—I'm sure of that," she piped. "But let's see what my distributors have to offer!"

Kale's bamboozlement was so total he heard *nothing on my shelves* as stupendous false modesty, and *my distributors* as a synonym for the two imperialists overrunning the territory between Ida and her screen. When the desired titles appeared, she cried, "Oh, Kale! There's...let me count...*eight choices*! You'd better come look over my shoulder."

Certain of what a blunder *that* vantage point would be, Kale took it up anyway, and as he leaned down close to read the screen his finest fears came true. A riot of fragrances, power sources, and cantilevered delicacies rose up to greet him, his frontal lobes began doing loop-de-loops, and he backed off a good eighteen inches to get doubly in the clear. Hoovering out his wallet, he blurted, "I'll take all eight!" since that was as close as his Ida-addled brain could get to the dozen red roses he wished he was ordering for her.

When Ida ignored the idiocy of his order and began arranging for the books to be delivered to Kale's lifelong Downriver Road address, he fell so out of character that he lied, saying his reliable mailbox was unreliable so could she please ship them to her store. "But, Kale!" Ida piped. "Three distributors could mean three separate trips to town!"

"I'm in town all the time," he lied. "Funny I don't bump into you more." Rashly visualizing the possibilities of such a bump, Kale panicked, threw it into reverse, and blurped, "*Say!* You're new in town, Ida, and I'm a Born Here who knows most everybody. If it'd help your business any I'd be glad to take you to Loco Creek Steakhouse one of these nights to help you sort the nuts from the bolts among the locals."

Swiveling to face him, Ida's prow sent him another step back. "Oh, *Kale*! I'd be *thrilled*!"

Smiling so big he hurt his face, Kale tucked the book receipt in his Roper shirt pocket, touched his Stetson, said, "Till then then, Ida," bolted out the door, took the alley to his truck, and fell so deep into a Loco Creek Steak & Date reverie that he was three miles out of town before he realized he'd named neither a day nor a time. "*Lordy!*"

He pulled a U-turn, drove back to the first payphone near E City, fished out the receipt, punched in the number, and heard his all-time-favorite high-pitched voice pipe, "Ida's Ideas."

"Kale here, Ida."

"Oh, how *wonderful*!"

"Yeah. Well. *Say*. I'm so rattled over this Appaloosa deal I forgot the date part of dating. Would it work to pick you up six o'clock Friday right there at your shop?"

"Oh, Kale. I'm so excited *I* forgot that part too! Six Friday would be ideal!"

"Till then then, Ida."

"'Till then then.' What a cute way to say it! Oh, Kale, this is already so fun!"

"*It kinda is, idn't it. How do. Toodle oodle. Till then then.* I got a pile of 'em for ya, Ida."

"Oh, you're so funny! And I'm so happy!"

"Well. Say. Six Friday then, Ida."

"Well! *Say,* Kale!"

"Are you *teasing* me, Ida Craig?"

"I kinda is, idn't I!" she giggled. "Six p.m. Friday, cowboy! *Toodle oodle. Till then then!*"

"Bye, then, Ida."

"Bye-bye!"

Click.

"*Lordy!*"

(Upper Elkmoon Valley, October 8, 1997, and October 2012)

XIX. Infinite Guest

This beauty is not a doorway into something better. This beauty is my other half. This sky, this majesty, is my other self.
> —Sharman Apt Russell, *Standing in the Light*

> The whole of the great earth is my own True Body.
> The whole of the great earth is the real Human Being.
> > —Eihei Dōgen

IN THE LAST three miles before Montana's Elkmoon River reaches the crescent-shaped range of peaks that give it its name and pristine waters— last three miles before valley and pavement end, the gravel road forks and steepens, and the river forks into three separate tribs plunging down brutal ravines; last three miles before the Elkmoon's legendary rainbows, cut- throats, and browns give way to little plunge-pool brookies you can only drop a fly directly on top of, then flip, hysterically flopping, over your head into willows in which a bull moose could be standing, ready to give the same sort of flip to you—the valley first opens wide, allowing the river to meander, intact and unhurried in its headwater wholeness, through a last vast golden-grassed meadow.

The instant Risa sighted the meadow she knew she'd entered Dave's map. And given the closeness of peaks, thinness of air, brilliant gold of cotton- woods, father ashes beside her, she was slammed by a sense of how all living things, including even the Elkmoon, must come to an end. But those very endings left no stretch of river so vulnerably beautiful. With Indian summer on the wane, the sky had turned a blue so deep and dark it wouldn't have surprised her to see star fields in broad daylight. Clouds of insects hovered starlike over the bends and oxbows as trout ignited concentric silver fires upon the river's same dark blue. "*Early October,*" she whispered, quoting the map she could now see, eyes shut: "*Blue-winged olives & 6X for the rainbows rising in every glide!*"

She drove the meadow's three-mile length, marveling at how abruptly the mountains rose from its wide plain, then turned around and drove back to the meadow's sole pullout, where she parked. Zipping down her windows, she heard the Elkmoon's soft current, smelled cottonwoods and pines, smelled the mineral fragrance of mountains. "*Great-Gramma Stella. Father Dave. Lord of Love*," she said. "*I smell home.*"

Her eyes then fell to a cattle gate made of pine poles and barbed wire, and a kind of Sons Only Verse smacked her: three plywood signs, fresh-painted in blood-red Montana semi-English, hung from the wire, the top sign proclaiming,

No HuNTiN No fiSh iN nO NUTHiN!
   the next one hollering,
ABSoLuTly nO NeveR! Don'T eveN ThiNK aBouT iT!
   and the bottom sign promising,
PErpETaitoRS will be VIOLatED!

"Must even your wild grave feature a *manqué male overlord?*" she sighed to Dave's ashes.

For a defiant moment she considered carrying the remains directly out into the meadow and proceeding with her task. But she'd waited her entire life to enter this family-hallowed ground. To feel rushed or under threat would diminish her ability to receive it.

She zipped her windows and set out to seek permission. Downstream of the meadow she'd seen no dwellings for miles, so she turned and drove upriver, looking for a ranch, home, ranger station, or uniformed person in a vehicle she could flag down. She'd gone just a mile past meadow's end when the paved road gave way to washboard gravel, then forked in two on the East Fork and West Fork roads. She squandered half an hour following each spur up into ridges so steep they blocked the view of the mountains, encountering no beings or structures but mountain ravens and wherever they hid their nests.

Driving back down to what she now called "our friendly neighborhood perpetaitors' parking lot," she reopened all her windows, shut off the engine, gazed at the glowing waters and grasses beyond the blood-red signs, and sighed, "*What now?*"

Whisper of water clarity of air fragrance of pines enflamed cottonwoods grief love gratitude, answered the vast meadow.

Plucking Dave's map from the dash, she splayed it open. To see the quavering of the map's every line was to see the dying tremble of Dave's long fingers. Noticing the near-identical shape of her own fingers, they too began to tremble. To have come so far, hold such a strong claim on a place, and be denied entry caused her to remember Lafayette Mboya, with his contemptuously regal smile, defining what he called "Indian position": *The constant sense of violation felt by a people who once entered everywhere, now able to enter almost nowhere.*

An eerie yearning began to rise from the ground up into Risa. She found the map's "Aspen Camp," raised her binoculars, and located the stand of white-barked, quaking, brilliant-leafed trees a half mile distant. She noted the "Moose Hotel," zoomed in on a shimmering beyond the aspens, and had no doubt the pond was frequented by the "rough customers" she was to watch out for. She found the thousand-year-old eagle nest, scoped the giant living larch's lightning-split crown (not a ponderosa, as Dave remembered), and there was the six-foot-wide, six-foot-deep nest to which generations of eagles kept adding layers. That multigenerational artifact then reminded her that Uncle Charlie was childless; that she was Dave's one and only; that Montana's Clan McKeig would continue or come to an end in her very body. Her mind flew from the month-long vigil at Dave's bedside through her eight-hundred-mile drive, nights of near sleeplessness, birthday-morning discovery of a lifetime's worth of lovingly stored gifts, and drive to precisely *here*, where the ground-born yearning was so strong that Dave's deathbed map became living meadow and his promised trout kept igniting silver fires on the water. The blood-red signs lost every shred of power. There was no choice here at all. "*Lord of Love, Unmanifest,*" she whispered. "*Become Manifest. Stay with me as I take his molecules on home.*"

She pulled a fresh-inherited Rand McNally Atlas from the storage space under her armrest, thumbed through it till she reached Nebraska, tore out the full page depicting the western half of the state, and on the nearly featureless map-scape stretching from Chadron to Valentine to O'Neill wrote to the painter of the blood-red warnings:

To Whom It May Concern:

I like your signs! Scary! But I need permission to trespass & looked for it upstream & down & couldn't find a soul. Here's my story: my dad, Dave McKeig, grew up on a downriver ranch my Great-Gramma Stella McKeig homesteaded. This meadow was their favorite place on Earth. Five days ago, the night he died, Dave drew a map of this meadow from memory & asked me to scatter his ashes here. I just drove 800 miles to do that & found your signs. I can only hope you agree I have to do this. I'll be very careful to secure your gates & I'd be glad to do some work in exchange for my trespassing. I hope to meet you later on. Thank you.

—Risa (Marisa Stella) McKeig

As she stepped out of the car and placed her note under the driver's side windshield wiper, a watcher in the woods a half mile distant, peering at her through a rifle scope, set the rifle aside and loaded a tactical shotgun with eight shells. To her ash-bags-and-dumbsaint-journals-dwelling father Risa muttered, "Wouldn't you know the cedars where I'm to scatter you are on the far shore. Why didn't I look for hip boots in the units? There's prob'ly nine pairs."

She donned wading sandals, folded the map, slid it in her shirt pocket, took the triple-bagged ashes in hand, locked the car. As she stepped down to the barbed-wire gate, the distant watcher filled his revolver with six bullets, then slid it in his holster.

The five-strand gate ended in a vertical pine stave fastened to a gatepost by a strong wire loop. She tried to lift the loop with her free hand. Couldn't. Set down the bagged ashes. Strained at the loop with both hands. Couldn't budge it. An old Dave adage made her smile: *It takes two fly-fishers but only one Montana rancher to work those damned wire gate loops.*

As she squeezed between the barbed strands without disturbing the gate, then picked her way down through locust and chokecherry to the river, the watcher muttered to his saddled and ready horse, "Typical big-city missy. Thinks her fancy fuckin' SUV's a free pass to any damn place she drives it. But this is one place comes with a little greetin' committee."

He mounted, and nudged his horse forward through the pines.

RISA ROLLED UP her pant legs and crossed the river in a shallow ford. The submerged stones were gorgeously varied—greens, gray-blues, oranges, pinks, and browns—the water clear and so cold her feet ached.

On the far shore she rolled her jeans down, then gazed out over the great meadow's last vast exception to vertical granite. The mountains enclosed her so decisively she felt like a passing thought inside their deathless mind. A few ravens strolled the yellowed grass like golfers, bending over frost-paralyzed grasshoppers as if over putts, only to swallow them whole. In the blue overhead the night's billion stars hid inside light. On the smooth glides of the Elkmoon the rise rings were so bright they went on dazzling after she closed her eyes. The dazzle conjured a Dave-awakened Skrit scrap:

> *Here in this body is a dwelling place.*
> *Within the dwelling place is a small space.*
> *What is there in this space that we should seek to perceive?*

Her resurrected Skrit love sent more lines:

> *As vast as the space around us is this space within.*
> *In this small space are contained earth and sky,*
> *fire and wind, sun and moon, lightning and stars.*

Light poured down in diaphanous shafts. Without warning an Unseen Presence poured down inside the shafts, burst into all things, and kept pouring, as it pierced meadow, mountains, and Risa through and through. She tried to greet what she felt with her meagre Skrit scraps. The October sky (*Antariksa?*) became breath and entered her nostrils (*nāsārandhra?*). Meadow soil and grass (*mṛd* and *ghāsa?*) became skin (*tvacā?*). Joy avalanched down from talus slopes, glaciers, a green infinity of pine-tips. The power (*prabhu*) that lifts mountains (*śaila?*) lifted her bones (*asthi?*) as well. Scents of stone, ice, solar-heated pine duff; scents of grasses, river-skin, foreverness. Snowmelt streamed down granite visages as tears began streaming down her face. The forested ridges and dark hair of her head merged, and where her hair parted at the opening known as *vidṛiti*, "the cleft," the Presence powered down and into and through.

What does a young woman do when vast Presence pours in at the cleft?

Shakes with joy, apparently, and greets her Guest with a whispered shard of the Upaniṣads:

Know the embodied soul. Though it hides in the hundredth part of the point of a hair divided a hundred times, it is infinite. Not female. Not male. Not neuter. What body it takes, with that it is united.

The rings of fire on water transpierced her. Presence poured in through her light-wounds. Her ears (*shrotra?*) heard a distant gun blast as her eyes (*sundare netre?*) took in, across the wide meadow, an orange horse and black-hatted rider approaching at a gallop. But it was not Risa who faced the charging horse or furious man. The Presence stood her in a towering wild nave so assailed by love that every iota of mountains, meadow, river, fast-closing horse, and cowboy unfurled within that love. Shouts punctuated by gunshots rose over the pounding hooves: "*This ain't a fuckin' nature preserve!*" BLAM! "*And your fancy fuckin' red car*" BLAM! "*gives you no fuckin' right to strut past my signs!*" BLAM!

Stay in Me, the Presence conveyed not in words but via the love that was its very being.

IN THAT SAME meadow, while researching these chronicles fifteen eventful years later, I, the Holy Goat, had grown so uncomfortable with what I was hearing from Risa that I asked just whose love she felt she was experiencing as she was being attacked.

Gazing up at the mountains and sky, she said, "The love *is* the Whom. *The I/You fusion* is the Whom. Via nothing but love the Whom conveyed, *I am here. I am in you. Don't find it too much. Remain in Me.* So I did. '*God damn it, woman! No trespassing means YOU!*' the cowboy was roaring as an Unseen Perfection kept flooding me with the feeling that all was perfect just as it was. Mortal body backed against a river; father ashes in arms; horse charging fast. *Perfect.* The fine festive holes the rider kept shooting in the sky. *Perfect.* Another woman judged guilty without a trial, expected by a raging male to receive or dodge bullets, stones, curses, or possible defilement. *What body it takes, with that it is united. Perfect.*"

Those were Risa's words, just as I recorded them. And all I could picture was a lone woman standing helpless against violence at least, and sexual violence at worst—horrors that play out all over this world every godforsaken day. So when Risa kept insisting the Presence kept her free of fear, imagination failed me and her account and I parted ways.

The trinity that made some sense of her apotheosis for me (sorry, Risa!) was Lou Roy Skinner, his infamously spotted ass, and his excellent quarter horse, Grey. And Lou's account of that fusion is no scene from a mystic's autobiography. It's straight out of a Western—though a Western colored, I have to admit, with elements of what Risa might call "an Eastern, beating like a broken-open heart inside it."

"The trespasser's calm as I charged her," Lou Roy told me years later. "That an' her smile. You can't fake a smile that calm. It troubled me. But it didn't slow me any. I had an anger beat into me so deep it had to bust out. I aimed to herd this woman straight into the river, soak her good, drive her through the brush like a fool stray heifer to her fancy-ass car, an' send her back to whatever hot-shit place she came from. Spacin' my shots to make 'em last, I put seven shotgun an' six revolver holes in the sky. She stayed so calm it was *me* started to spook.

"But when I was maybe sixty yards out, I seen she wasn't even lookin' at me. Her eyes were aimed up into mountains and sky. By her lights, I figured, I was some rural lowlife not worth a glance no matter what I said or did. All I seen then was red. I slowed Grey to a fast trot an' veered him toward her, aimin' the Mossberg right at her smilin' face, one shell left. Her eyes were wide-open. She saw me comin', plain. When her calm stayed put, I went so crazy it makes me sick to say what I done. Meanin' to terrify, I shot the last shell into the air above her close enough she'd hear the hiss o' buckshot, then aimed Grey straight at her, aimin' to knock her aside or run her over, I didn't care which.

"But Grey had his own ideas 'bout what was happenin'. *Grey,* mind you. Born knowin' his business an' trained *me,* is how that went. But one habit I couldn't cure him of. Once he'd cut a calf from a group an' confuse it to a halt, he'd want to walk up an' smell it. Even nuzzle it if I'd of let him, which of course I would not. But for this woman he overrides me. With me spurrin' him hard, hurtin' him bad, he comes to a full halt an' breaks free of the anger I'm pumpin' into him. I can't believe it. The woman's still gazin' off into some happy place all her own, an' I feel twinky even *sayin'* this, but seein' her gazin', Grey wants her attention so bad he lowers his front end till he's *bowing* almost, askin', *May I have this dance?* He then migrates on into her happy place with her, hops sideways left, sideways right, paws an' happy-snorts, all without my permission. I jerk him up hard. Eyes glued to the woman, he defies me, goin' prongy as a damn mule deer, puttin' on a show. I'm still outta my head wantin' to hurt somebody. But guess what saved me, HG?"

What a glow in Lou's glacial-silt-colored eyes as he said, "*My ass!* When I'm on a good horse, my seat is part o' that animal. My head's still wantin' Grey to charge her, but my ass hates this idea so bad it sides with my horse, an' it's a *mutiny* out there. An ass an' horse takeover! My reinin' hand goes slack, my ass forces my hands to give Grey his head, an' he *really* turns it up now, gambolin' like a two-month-old goat. You can picture how *that* went. To stay on board *I* have to goat-gambol too. My legs, torso, hips start gyratin' every which way. Weirder yet, I'm *enjoyin'* it, an' the weight of the Mossberg is interfering, so I toss six hundred bucks worth o' shotgun off into the grass like a ninety-nine-cent squirt gun run outta water.

"I see the woman watchin' us now, her smile lit up beyond any smile I ever recall seein'. My horse an' ass like this so much they give me an impulse. With just my thumb an' forefinger I lift my revolver all dainty from the holster, toss it in the same grass as the Mossberg, an' raise my hands like *she's* got *me* at gunpoint. Figured this'd be funny. Turned out it was, but not how I planned. To stay on Grey, hands up, I have to loosen my waist an' pelvis an' start makin' high-speed hula moves like nothin' I done since my saddle-bronc days. I try to make amends anyways. Belly dancin' like an idiot, arms whippin' outta their sockets, talkin' at a shout 'cause I'm workin' hard, I holler, '*Whoever you are, Miss, my horse an' me never seen your like! I'd say I'm sorry I scared the tar outta you, but you're so unscared I'm not sure I even did what I done!* I'm not sure where I even *am!* I've lived in this valley my whole damn—*EASY, Grey!*—whole damn life, an' I'd of swore till today that Valley Land & Beef holds grazin' rights to this meadow. But my horse here—*GOD DAMN IT, GREY!*—has decided, an' I'm inclined to agree, that as of now this whole corner of the world belongs to *you!*'

"Knowing he'd won our argument because my ass told him so, Grey comes to a standstill an' just stares at the woman, an' *damn.* Our standstill sure improves the view. 'Whoever you are,' I says, 'Grey an' me feel you're somethin' special. I was hopin' maybe if you could use a bit of that specialness to erase every fool thing I done up to now, I'd sure like to start our deal over. Whatever brung you to this meadow, I'm for it. Whatever you need, just ask. I'm at your service, is what I'm sayin'. Somethin' tells Grey an' me that's how it's gotta be. I'm Lou Roy, by the way. Lou Roy Skinner.'

"'Marisa Stella McKeig,' the woman says back. An' though Grey's standin' stock-still, then's when I about come off him. 'No damn way,' I says. 'Yes damn way,' she says, crankin' her smile up into a grin, an' out comes the same front tooth gap her Great-Gramma's grin had. 'You're them!' I says. 'I see it plain! I knew Stella as a boy, Marisa Stella! The grand ol' lady o' this whole valley is who *she* was! I named two mares Stella and Marisa after her, an' still live an' work land she homesteaded—land you McKeigs an' my friend Pope Broussard owned side by side. An' I can't imagine that son of a bitch Charlie's *your* dad, so his kid brother Dave must be.'

"When she nods an' grins even more, I says, '*Damn,* Marisa Stella. Wait'll the Pope meets you! He's gonna poop party hats! Wait'll we show you the land he an' she run. If I don't roll me a smoke fast I'll *never* get over what a jackass I been. You mind?'"

"'Feel free,' she says, an' while I pull out my makin's she steps over to stroke Grey till I light up, then reaches to shake my hand. *Lord, what a face, an' what a hand.* 'I go by Risa,' she says. 'An' Dave an' Stella loved this meadow more'n any place on Earth. That's what brung me,' she says. Then her smile gets...not bigger, but *glowier* as she says, 'Dave died a few days ago,' and she hefts these paper bags I finally see she's carryin', which pretty well busts me open. 'These are what's left, an' I'm sorry to trespass,' she says, 'but I come to plant him where he asked, an' tried for permission but found no one. I explained this in a note under the wipers at my car. If you know how to arrange it, Lou Roy, I'd love to camp a couple nights here so's my dad an' me don't have to rush our goodbye.'

"I feel so low-down by now I can't even look at her, and she sees my shame clear. So what does she do? *Forgives me fast as poor ol' Jesus!* 'You couldn't see my note from down here,' she says. 'You were doin' your job is all, Lou Roy. It's okay.'

"'It ain't one bit okay,' I says. 'This is public land an' grazin' rights don't change that. It's *you* belongs here, Miss Risa. Anybody says different, I'm your reinforcements from now on.'

"I roll a second smoke then, which settles me enough to follow her 'cross the river to fetch her rig. Then back we come an', down toward the cedars over the river there, set her up a real nice camp. *Provin'* she forgave me real as Jesus, she then invites me to share her camp."

WHEN RISA AND I, the Holy Goat, visited what she still calls the Glory Meadow fifteen years later, she pointed out the pines out of which Lou Roy had charged. Imagining his rage, her aloneness, his gun blasts, I wanted *way* more detail on how she'd managed to stay calm. Waving a hand at the looming mountains, she said, "It wasn't *my* calm. A limitless Presence flooded me, but don't you hate lame words like 'limitless Presence'? I do. If I could borrow your pen and pad a minute I could draw a sort of...*pictograph,* I guess, that gives a better idea of how it felt."

Baffled, I handed her my utensils. Risa dropped into a squat, steadied the pad on a knee, and took her time with her artwork. "One moment I was the me I am now," she said. "The next, all sorts of veils lifted and the entire world—Lou Roy, Grey, and me included—became something more like this..." She handed me the pad, upon which she'd drawn this:

$$(((((( ))))))$$

I asked what I was seeing.

Risa said, "A mystery so far beyond words that punctuation marks feel more truthful. Imagine the first pair of parentheses depicts the mountains enclosing this meadow like a gigantic manger. Imagine the rest of the parentheses are a glimpse I got of concentric spiritual planes of ever greater intensity, which was so overwhelming that the tiny blissclamation point in the center is all that was left of me. Imagine the whole experience was *hypaethral,* meaning 'open to the sky,' 'having no roof.' But you ask how I stayed calm as if words could make this understandable, HG, and words are just words. If I say, 'the Soul of the World seized mine,' does anything seize you? If I say, 'I felt overtaken by the infinitely loving Son and Mother the Beguines and Meister revere, and the Oceanic tide of bliss-shot adoration flowing back and forth between Son and Mother suspended the universe like clothes on a clothesline made of pure Mother to Son to Mother love,' are my words bursting with bliss the way the experience was?"

When I crossed my eyes, Risa nodded and shot me the glee grin. "Told ya. That's why the punctuation marks. Inside the concentric planes the blissclamation point is realizing: *it is forever this moment.* Reach inside yourself for that point and maybe *you'll* feel the foreverness too. But *words* aimed at such an experience are trying to catch a thunderhead in the gopher trap of American English. The Great Love *de-selfs* us, making of us Itself, so the storytelling problem here is wonderful: *there are realities infinitely greater than words or stories can contain.* That's why, same as you, I like Lou Roy's explanation better than mine. If you want more words for your chronicles, maybe just say it started *joying* out, the way it blizzards in a blizzard, and the mountains, meadow, rise rings on the river, Dave's ashes, Lou's gun blasts, Grey's dance, were joying too. It was that joy, by the way, that Lou fell in love with, *not me,* and bless him, he figured that out pretty fast, stopped worshipping me, and just became my great friend. So can we move on to that?"

"I guess," I grumbled.

"Not fifteen minutes after they'd charged me, Lou and Grey led me up to the Exploiter. As Lou opened the gate with the blood-red signs he gave me a scowl and growled, 'Go on ahead, Missy. Drive that fancy-ass trespasser mobile down into my meadow.' I did, grinning as I eased past him, waited while he closed the gate, and began to wonder why he was so slow when he stepped up to my open window holding something behind his back. 'Li'l present,' he said, and around swung his PErpETaïtoRS wïll be VIOLaTED! sign. I thanked him, leaned out the window, pulled my map of Nebraska request-to-trespass out from under the wiper, and gave it to Lou. When he honored me by framing it on the wall of his Airstream, I epoxied his PErpETaïtoRS sign to my refrigerator door to scare off looters. I've loved that sign and its painter ever since."

I saw that Risa felt she'd wrapped things up. She saw this didn't satisfy me. "You want more apotheosis verbiage, don't you?"

"I don't know what I want," I said. "I only know that what happened in this meadow that day led to a whole lot of good things for a whole lot of people."

"But not via language," she insisted. "The veils that lifted, revealing the Guest, descended when Lou said the Pope was gonna poop party hats and I cracked up, and that's as it should be. Only the spirit has the spiritual experience. If our egos lay claim to it they counterfeit it. And words just *graffiti* it. The one person I know who may be living a nonstop spiritual experience is Jervis, but as he would tell you, that's because he belongs to *Ocean,* not to himself, so his experience is Ocean's, not his own. Accuse Jervis himself of being holy or saintly and he'll cut you off with disclaimers like—"

"I got this!" I cut in, and made my voice all papery: "'Every time somebody calls me a street saint, I picture me doggy-doin' that person from behind. And would a saint picture that? *Fuck no.* And would a saint say "Fuck no"? *Doublefuck no.* Get the picture?'"

Oh, that glee-gap grin of Risa's!

"One last question?" I pleaded.

"If it's truly the last," said she.

"Say what you like about egos, it was *your* spirit that had the experience, *you* who fell in love with the life and mystery humming through the entire Elkmoon, *you* whose enthusiasm started drawing down-to-earth, kindhearted, but somehow thwarted people together, and *you* who started helping them get unthwarted with your kindness, generosity, and key friends. To connect and help so many people in such a short amount of time didn't seem humanly possible to some of those you helped. Rumors still circulate that, a bit like Jervis, *you* possess some kind of transcendent guidance system. Is there anything to that, Risa? I'm serious."

"You know," she said, and her brow knit as she appeared to mull this hard. "There *is* something along those lines. I call it the Spectroscopic Flashlight. Let's see if I can conjure it." Fastening her fists to her right and left temples, she pointed her index fingers at me and wiggled them wildly while glaring a hole in my face. Then out popped the glee grin and, when she saw my exasperation, a giggle fit too. "Like lots of people," she said, "some sort of intuition flashlight sometimes turns on in me and lights the way. But that's a *grace,* not an *appliance.* I don't even know how to turn it on. And when it *does* turn on it lights only the next few steps to be taken, which often scare the hell out of me. When I take them anyway, things sometimes work out in such unforeseen ways that I've come to trust the flashlight enough to take even scary steps most of the time."

"Is it lighting any steps right now?" I asked.

"Give it up, HG," she said. "Who needs an intuition flashlight when my rumbling animal stomach is telling me you're as hungry as I am, and could use a drink too. And we both love a certain hole-in-the-wall eight miles down the road. I'm vegetarian these days, but a mac and cheese and whiskey sound mighty good. And who violates an Angus perpetaitor better than the Elsewhere Bar & Grill? Shall we?"

Our grins crashed head-on. "*Doublefuck yeah!*" I paper-whispered.

(Glory Meadow, aka Three Forks Meadow, upper Elkmoon
River, October 8, 1997)

XX. Release

In the alms of this moment, the humble scornless million
hands of water...No obstacles in my heart,
everything a frailboned kindness.
           —Teddy Macker, "The Kingdom of God"

GOLDEN COTTONWOODS AND quaking aspens silhouette to black. Snow-flocked mountains silhouette to blue, then black. Sky briefly ablaze, then indigo. A planet. A first few stars. The vast wash of stars.

Small campfire in darkest blue air. Quiet river louder as the air chills and thickens.

"I've got something I need to do," Risa says.

Lou Roy and his Australian kelpie, iPooch, turn to her, dark eyed and quiet as a pair of deer. She nods at the grocery bags she's tended all day.

Lou's answering nod is curt. "Need company?" he asks. "Or help?"

"Dave asked that I"—her voice catches—"asked that I release him where the river passes a stand of cedars. The only cedars I saw today were just downstream of us. But there were only seven. Dave wrote 'Ten Cedars' on my map."

Lou Roy nods. "Microburst took three of 'em just last winter. Your dad got it right. Eddie Dominguez and two high schoolers harvested the shakes come spring. You'll see the upended rootwads and sawdust. The missing three are roofin' my friend Kale's barn."

Risa stands, ashes in hand. The cowboy and kelpie watch. "I'll be back," she says.

"Sure you want to go it alone?"

She smiles. "It's a hundred yards away."

Lou Roy shakes his head. "It's a whole lot farther 'n that an' you know it."

Eyes brimming, but still smiling, she says, "When you put it that way, I'd like to bring iPooch if she'd like to come."

Hearing her name, the dog is at her side in an instant, looking up, awaiting orders.

Weird how my dog fell for this woman same as Grey.

Risa turns on her headlamp. "Come on, friend."

Lou watches them move, in a wobbly beam of light, off toward the black silhouettes of seven big trees.

POURING FROM THE bags as she walks a faery ring circle amidst the seven cedars, Risa likes the way gray ash looks atop golden brown pine duff, and the faint clatter of bone chess pieces troubles her no more. "I love you, molecules of Dave, Dad, Father," she murmurs.

At the sound of her voice, iPooch's tail *whumps* the duff.

"I wouldn't say a seeming frivolous thing if I wasn't sure you'll like it. So, one last time my dear father, *fuck mauve*. You're amidst *your* colors now. Your home colors. You need no others."

More tail *whumps*. "I love you too, iPooch."

Still a lot of ash in the bags though the requested ring is complete. Surprising how much matter an incinerated body leaves behind.

She leaves the cedars for the river. Drawn to a place where the flow is quiescent, she lies belly-down atop an undercut bank. iPooch sits alertly behind her, staring out at the night. Risa gazes at the slow eddy two feet below her face. Lets its movement take her.

Night's hair catches in the river's slow circling. Blurred stars reflect and refract. She pours and pours borrowed loan officer back into his boyhood flow, but saves a last couple of small handfuls. Not sure why. Just not ready to be done.

BACK AT THE fire, Lou Roy hands her a small but brimming tin cup. "Whiskey."

Her grateful smile, tears brimming but not spilling, slays him. When she stood up to his weapons and charge, he sees now, he fell into some kind of love. Sure, he's old and she's young. Sure it's hopeless. But he can gaze when she's not looking, and just the sight of her is healing. When he remembers his Mossberg aimed at her face, remembers spurring Grey to run her down, his stomach slides into places so horribly wrong he realizes, *This war is over. They can call my ass Appaloosa, Polkadot, Spotty, whatever they want. Honors the best damn part o' me.*

Pretending to be fire-gazing, he raises his eyes. She's in her sleeping bag, sitting up, watching the night sky same as iPooch. Not saying a word, or looking as if she wants to. Just draining the cup sip by sip, making no face at the burn.

Damn! Lou thinks. *Even handles her whiskey. I forgot this craziness where every tiny thing about a person makes you wanna bow to what they are.*

She sets aside the cup, removes and folds her jacket to serve as pillow.

Almost the instant her head touches the jacket, she's asleep.

Lou Roy pours another cup. Rolls a smoke. Settles in.

That face. That wild hair.

* * *

RISA WAKES IN the night to the feel of iPooch fitting herself against the back of her sleeping bag. Fourteen billion stars. Lou Roy's quiet snoring. She remembers his intro of the kelpie: "Kale tells me he's saving up big to buy some new-fangled computer comin' out next year. Wave of the future, he says. Called a iMac. *What the hell kind of future is that?* I ask him, then have me an idea. I drive to the pound, find this little cow dog cost me nothin', drive up to Kale's, an' tell him, 'Meet iPooch, boss. She's got my back on all o' this iShit.'"

Feeling Risa's stifled giggle, iPooch's tail whumps the ground four times. The whumps feel like a request. Risa replies by thumping the ground in front of her four times. iPooch hops over her, walks three tight circles round the spot Risa thumped, then lies on it. Risa invites her to settle, but iPooch keeps sniffing the night air and scanning the sky. At sunset she tracked the flights of ducks, magpies flocking to roost, a pterodactyl-sized heron. Now she tracks a shooting star. Sky-aware, this canine. Rare. Risa strokes her body. Black hair of a fine sleekness. No real fur at all. "You got any siblings at the pound?"

Whump, whump, whump.

Risa checks Lou Roy. Kind of a soothing snore, and she loves what the fire does to his face, tanned and gullied from a long life outside. She's well aware of his crush. By the positioning of the firewood she knows he kept building up the fire to create light by which to see her till fatigue coldcocked him. Poor old guy. *Perpetaitors will be violated.* But he kept his feelings to himself. Rode them like a well-trained horse. Kept his dignity. Protected hers.

The night has turned cold. She eyes the grocery bags flickering in the light, the last handfuls inside. Sees no reason for her earlier hesitation.

Quietly unzipping her sleeping bag, she takes her feet. iPooch stands too. Risa is touched, as she slips on her boots, to think the dog is coming to the river with her. iPooch then curls up on the warmed place her body left on the opened bag. Risa grins. "Smart girl."

Whump, whump, whump.

She steps down to a white sandbar glowing faintly under a sliver of moon, sits down next to the flow, reaches into the innermost of the triple bags, takes the last of the ashes into her hands, clenches her hands closed. She lies by the flow, on her back this time. Mountains looming so close. October sky so clear each star's conflagration feels intimate despite the impossible reach. Light-years and light speed come to rest on the river's shimmering skin, creating pinpoints so countless they truly do make a wavery milk.

She trembles with... *cold? intensity? immensity?*

In her shirt pocket: this very meadow, so lovingly mapped by her father's dying hand.

In her hands: the last remnants of his body.

In her head: some kind of heat-lightning from the day's run-in with the Unseen.

Gratitude approaches the zenith that erases. She stifles a sob as *vidṛiti,* the cleft, begins to open once again. The vault of night rains down, but gently. The bliss brims over, spills onto sand, shimmers in the mica flecks. Stars of heaven, stars on water, stars seen eyes shut. The same and the same and the same.

"*Father,*" she whispers. "*True Father. Thank You for touching me the way the stars touch this dark water. Thank You for allowing the Elkmoon to birth her own kind of quavery stars.*"

HALF WAKING TO tend the long night's fire, Lou Roy sees iPooch asleep on Lore's empty bedroll. He sits bolt upright. Listens. Hears a sound by the river. Words? A sob? Sounds so private he knows not to interfere. But he peeks—and startles:

The young woman, Stella McKeig's great-granddaughter, lies flat on her back at water's edge staring straight up into night sky, digging her fingers into the sand beneath her as if to hold herself to Earth . . .

EYES ON THE vault, she furrows the molecules into the Earth with blind fingers as her eyes sew her handiwork to shimmering sky. Silence singing mountains true. Prayer no longer possible. Only prayer's answer possible. Every small and great thing, herself included, so present, so broken open, there's only a great openness with which to behold it all.

"*No goodbyes, now or ever.*
"*Just these born and burning stars, held.*
"*This born and burning Earth, held.*
"*My born and burned Elkmoon father, home again. Held.*"

XXI. First Beguine Audience with a Pope

"In the mountains" means the blossoming of the entire
  world.
—Eihei Dōgen

HAVING FORDED ITS first river, the Crimson Exploiter looked proud of itself, parked on crushed grass between two incomparably more indigenous-looking Elkmoon vehicles: Kale the Pope's '94 Ford F-250 and Lou Roy's rust-splotched yellow '75 Chevy Cheyenne.

The three vehicles' respective owners are sitting round a campfire in plastic chairs Kale has brought, stuffed on elk steak, foil-wrapped fire-roasted potatoes, a tomato and mozzarella salad Lou Roy merely eyed askance, and a store-bought apple pie he inhaled. Among the other supplies Kale has delivered, the notable item at present is a bottle of George Dickel, a Tennessee whiskey that Risa, as a Kentucky bourbon purist, secretly finds unpalatable, but on this night gamely endures.

The cowboys, several small tin cups into it now, turn to a tried-and-true drinking topic. "Erosion," Lou Roy calls it.

"Herdin' cattle on an ATV may seem a small thing," he tells Risa. "So does punchin' plastic ID tags into calf ears. What you don't see is what's gone missing. The love between man an' horse. *Gone.* A spring brandin' an' castratin' party where the families an' friends raised the calves get dirty gettin' it done, then eat, drink an' laugh till they can't move. *Gone.* Efficient stuff, erosion. Pretty soon we won't need to rope, herd, ride, work, or eat at all 'cause ranchin' will of eroded away and plastic ID tags'll be danglin' from *our* ears."

"How about we change the subject, Lou?" the Pope suggests.

"Not till you promise the West we were born in won't of washed away before I next bring erosion up. And not even you, my Harvard friend, can make that promise."

Kale gives his big white Stetson a shake. "I know what he means, Risa. I was born an optimist, so a lot of changes strike me as improvements at first. Subarus instead of F-150s? I think: *Safer family vehicles.* More espresso shops than bars? *Maybe a better kind of drinking problem.* More boutiques than hock shops? *Well, one serves the shopping addicts, the other the gambling addicts.* But more developers than ranchers? More realtors than ticks? And now, NorBanCo's plan to triple the valley's population by luring a bunch of Brokeback country-clubbers onto the land your dad, Lou Roy, and I grew up on, turning us, say the ads, into the colorful yokels of *their* shopping town? That's not even erosion. That's us being sent into exile though we've stayed right here at home.

"And another thing that troubles me, Risa. Before NorBanCo even arrived, when the Elkmoon Valley Bank was buying out family ranches, Lou and I fought as hard and long as we could. But quite a few locals who could have held on, didn't. The educated, mostly. In college they'd learned a few of the horrors of westward expansion. Since the land had belonged to the tribes, they decided, as non-Indians, they had no lasting claim to it. So off to the cities they moved, letting their land, neighbors, and legacy go for funny money to bankers who then handed it all over to NorBanCo. What kind of favor is it to the tribes to cash out your land and home to entities with no human name at all? Entities with no respect for the way the tribes lived? I can't enter my corporate boss's office without grabbing the face of a Sitting Bull door knocker. You know why his tribe loved Sitting Bull? He was so fearless, so resourceful, so sure the Earth would provide that over and over he gave everything he had to his people. Make a door knocker out of a leader like that and install greed-driven ignorance in his place and what chance does your valley have? It seems to me, to wrap this sorry sermon up, that every place with anything right about it goes to hell soon as it falls into the hands of these multinationals. The one way to preserve and defend a place's rightness is to *inhabit it,* intimate, knowledgable, and vigilant as can be. An absentee board of cash-kissers has never done that and never will. It makes me sick, what we've come to. I feel I failed the land, failed the tribes who lived here forever, failed most of the best things I've ever known."

Lou Roy's dirty black Stetson shakes in disagreement. "I seen how hard you fought, Kale, an' how hard you *still* fight. It ain't you. It's *erosion.* The West is washin' off to some point on the compass that idn't West at all, an' the people pourin' in never even arrive. They appear to, but look closer. They're standin' on E City corners peckin' at gizmos that bounce their brain off a satellite, shoppin' for shit in every city but E City, a neighbor an' friend to no one. Brokeback *Ranch* my famous ass. There's not a rancher on all their acres. What the Elkmoon's got goin' is an invasion of *gizmo peckers,* an' that's *all* it's got."

"If Lou Roy and I could cork it a minute," Kale puts in, "I'd be interested to know what *you* think of where this country's headed, Risa."

She smiles. "So you want *my* sorry sermon?"

"I do, actually. I really do."

"Well, I know what you both mean. But it's hard to feel frustrated when I just spent two of the best days of my life in this meadow with these incredible mountains hovering overhead, feeling my father and some kind of God the Mother hovering overhead too. Asking myself why these days and nights feel so perfect, what Lou says rings true. Without devices and broadcasts, *what is* is the broadcast. And *what is* is a wonder! I spent a long time today just watching caddis fly larva crawl off the river bottom onto dry rocks, leave the sand and pine needle sleeping bags they'd built with their own special glue, and transform themselves into big orange insects that open their wings, fly up into the air to find mates, then air-drop their eggs on the water to become next year's October caddis flies if a trout doesn't eat them. For the suspense, the mystery, the transformations, caddis flies rival human drama. I watched a northern harrier, gliding low over the grass, do the craziest midair flip, reverse direction as it dropped to the ground, then up it flew again, calm as could be, with a vole in its talons. I watched a giant flock of cedar waxwings circling this enormous meadow all afternoon, turning this way and that as if the hundreds of them shared the same one mind—and that's the mind I pray to stay inside of. Everything intricate and real and connected to everything else. Everything alive needing to eat, so sure, there's a lot of death. Each trout rise all day ended the life of a cool little mayfly my dad called a blue-winged olive. But the birthing is endless. And the carcasses and kills make the beauty bitter-sweet. Which is the flavor of what's real. Flavor of paradox, dark chocolate, good coffee, mortal life. Flavor of John of the Cross saying, 'Moaning is connected with hope.' I'm well aware that, while the harrier was doing its gold-medal-worthy backflip and killing its vole my car radio could've told me an earthquake just killed four hundred people in a fresh-shattered country, and a shooting rampage left eighteen dead in a devastated city, and a madman abducted three kids playing on a trampoline and abused and killed them and horrified millions. But there's no doubt in my mind that we weren't created to connect ourselves nonstop, via gizmo-pecking, to every horror suffered by the six billion of us instead of attending to what *is*, right here where we *are*. Like, today a flock of white-crowned sparrows landed in a weed patch near me, and while the rest began to feed, one intrepid fledgling left them to hop right up to me. As we were studying each other— this white-crowned three-inch-tall flying person and me—we were standing inside a blue, green, gold, and at sunset crimson orb of life. And if you ask me, the endless unnatural-death-list we call 'the news' did not shoot that gorgeous orb full of holes or abduct, rape, and kill it. If you ask me, being in tune with trout rises, harrier grace, caddis transfigurations, white-crown friendliness, hawk kills, deer carcasses, and the ashes of those we love gives human and animal suffering the bittersweet dignity of a great old blues tune. Which was my dad's favorite music. So it's little wonder he and Stella worshipped this place. I doubt I answered your question, Kale, but setting my dad's molecules free last night, then seeing what I'd released him into all day, has my heart full to brimming, and that's the only sermon in me right now."

Lou Roy eyes Risa shyly, then stands to feed the fire.

"I love hearing what the day gave you," Kale says. "And I hate it when I can't stand by the same appreciation. The feeling that bucks me off is how, if my parents' dying hadn't been so costly, I wouldn't have lost their ranch. So if you don't mind me asking—though *only* if you don't mind—I wonder how losing his ranch, then his Grandma Stella, set with Dave."

Risa takes a sip of whiskey and gazes into the brightening flames. "In the end I loved my father to pieces. But Dave himself would tell you, losing the ranch, then Stella, broke his compass. He became a man lost in deep woods. He had all kinds of talent and smarts but stayed in a no-brainer bank job for life, amusing himself with stupid affairs galore and two even stupider marriages. Three years ago, though, something happened. A lot of people in midlife realize they've wasted their life and wish they could change it, but very few actually dump the habits and social circles that prevent huge change. Dave pulled that miracle off. He went back in secret to a kind of school. He stuck to a plan to swear off skin-deep relationships and start life over in this valley, moved a whole bunch of goods perfect for Montana into storage here to serve that life, and kept himself aimed in the best direction he knew. And it sounds tragic that, just before he would have freed himself, he took sick and was gone fast. But I spent his last month with him and, suffering included, it was the best month we ever had. He stayed aimed in his best direction to the last breath, and left me feeling the Big Mercy helped him hold to that direction in the unseen. So when I think how happy he'd be that I'm sharing a fire and whiskey with two men who knew Stella, knew the land he neighbored, knew all his favorite Elkmoon places, a sweetness saturates his departure, turning it bittersweet. Like the best blues. Like real life."

Kale shakes his head. "As a father who raised a daughter, I've got to tell you, Risa. Every word you just said does your dad so proud I can feel his pleasure."

Lou Roy knows it's coming, fears its coming, looks across the fire, and there it is: the grateful glowing smile, tears brimming but never quite spilling. Lou can't take that look. It makes him want to drop to one knee, hand her his sword as if he had one, and swear *fealty* to her, or some such stupid stunt. Turning away from her, he rolls another smoke and hunts his mind for a story that might move the light around on her face in a less devastating way. When he feels he's found one, he passes Risa the Dickel.

"Enough o' my plain bitter bitchin', Miss Risa. Here's a differ'nt flavor story. *Bittersweet.* You haven't heard this either, Kale. You okay with me tellin' this?"

"Let 'er buck," says the Pope.

"Last week I tackled that thick-forested fence line runs from Mink Creek down to the river. Tall skinny lodgepoles growin' dense as they get. The elk an' moose damage wudn't bad. Thought I might get off easy. But as Kale warned, I come on a snarl of forty-some trees downed by a microburst. Trunks tangled ever which way. Fence buried beneath. Wire snapped. Posts splintered. The tangle too thick to get my truck close. Grey an' me fetched the chainsaw an' got to it. I limbed an' Grey dragged out the logs one by one. Bucked an' stacked eleven cords of stovewood in a place my truck could fetch it. Built a huge slash pile. Planted new posts an' strung an' stretched wire. The fence come out good by dusk on day six.

"So I'm cut up an' corpse tired, it's more'n half dark, an' I'm ridin' the woods side of Mink Creek to the ford, when I spot a glow down where creek meets river. Meadow's posted. We're ten river miles upstream of any water I ever seen boated. I tell Grey, 'Shush,' an' ease toward the glow, worried some nut's out to burn down the world. Grey snorts an' backs up a few steps. I've walked him right into some fella out to take him a night crap, I figure."

"Keep it civilized," the Pope puts in.

"Keep your hat on, Kale. I'm sayin' I *figured,* not what happened. I wouldn't waste Risa's time on some bunkhouse potty joke."

"Sorry, Lou," the Pope says solemnly—then shoots Risa a sidelong grin.

"Fella says he didn't mean to startle us. Has a good way with Grey. Name's Taylor. Little red-headed fella. Turns out he's not only not takin' a crap, he's lookin' for *me.* Says he an' his friends heard me workin' while they fished all day. The fishin' was good, Taylor says, which made 'em feel guilty, which earned me a drink and a bite if I want 'em. Bison burgers, he says, but drinks first of course. Day I had, I says why not.

"Turns out there's four of 'em camped on a little sandbar. Andy, Al, and Aaron, fly-fishers all. Sounds like a band, I says. *Taylor an' the A Words.* They like this. They're floatin' the Elkmoon despite it's so small up here, in these itty-bitty pontoon craft, an' every damn thing they own matches the boats. Itty-bitty tents. Itty-bitty coolers an' camp stoves. An' they're all settin' in itty-bitty no-leggèd ass-on-the-ground chairs. Taylor offers me his no-leggèd. If I was to set in *that,* I says, I'd never make it to my feet again an' the day you buried me stuck to it you'd lose a slick little chair. They like this too.

"I set on a log. Taylor raids his itty-bitty cooler for my drink. A beer I figure, since it's coolered. But he pulls out this white box, 'bout yea big. I turn to the A Words an' see they're *all* holdin' white boxes, yea big. Not a bottle in sight. 'Here ya go,' Taylor says. Box is cold an' slimy as a fresh-clobbered trout. 'Vanilla Enriched Rice Milk,' it says. Just my luck, I'm thinkin'. After six days workin' off the ass he's named for, *Appaloosa Skinner* gets invited for a drink to the only camp in the West where four teetotalers are guzzlin' yea-big boxes o' rice slime."

Kale lowers his Stetson brim to hide his astonishment. How *serenely* Lou Roy joked about his infamous blemish! *This young woman has healing powers,* Kale thinks. Meanwhile Risa can't stop laughing, which makes iPooch's tail keep whumping the ground, which makes her laugh more, plus the first godawful Dickel she downed rearranged her priorities so severely that the second Dickel tastes pretty okay. "What did you do, Lou?" she asks.

"Played the noble horseman," he says. "'Scuse me, fellas, but I was so eager for this fine drink I done the unforgivable. Forgot to tend the horse worked harder 'n me all day. Anybody got a fry pan I can borrow? I got grain in my saddlebag, but Grey'll scatter it in the sand an' give himself sand colic. I'll wash your pan up good, after.

"I figure I'm SOL with everything bein' itty-bitty, but Taylor an' the A Words go into a mad scramble an' offer me *four* little fry pans, which double as lids on their itty-bitty mess kits. Packin' my box o' rice goop like I love it to pieces, I thank Tay for his pan, leave the firelight, limp over to Grey in the shadows, pour my goop in the pan an' whisper, 'Grey, ol' friend ol' pal! I don't know if these poor fellas are Mormon or what, but look what they're drinkin'! You have *got* to help me out here!'"

The less Lou Roy laughs at his own humor the more Risa's laugh and iPooch's tail make up for it. "What did Grey think of enriched vanilla rice milk?" she asks.

"Traitor wished Taylor an' the A Words would adopt him!" Lou says. "An' here's the punch line. When I get back to the fire after washin' Tay's pan, there's three bottles o' them fancy malt scotches an' a bottle o' Beam on my settin' log, an' when Tay an' the A Words see what this does to my face, they laugh so hard one o' the A Words falls like a beetle flat onto his back, which idn't easy in a ass-on-the-ground chair."

Risa's laugh and iPooch's tail whumps are so contagious Lou slips up and briefly smiles.

"'The Beam's yours if it suits you,' Tay says. 'Oh, it does, I says,' an' pass 'em their scotches. Once we set to, they want to know *everything* 'bout our valley an' mountain ranges, what all lives here, which tribes, homesteader history, crimes against the tribes, till I wished Kale was there to fend 'em off. But what brought my story to mind, Miss Risa, was how it come out so good that when I forded the river home, relyin' heavy on Grey, shape I was in, the world an' all I'd been through felt just like you say. *Bittersweet*."

Risa nods quietly, and out comes the smile that causes Kale to peer at her face harder and Lou to turn away, fast, toward the mountains and stars.

Sixth Telling:

Converging Mothers

Just as God is our Father,
so God is also our Mother.

—Julian of Norwich

Before heaven and earth came to be, there was
something nebulous, silent, isolated, unchanging
and alone, eternal, the Mother of All Things. I do
not know her name.

—Lao Tzu, *Tao Te Ching*

I preferred her before sceptres and thrones, and
esteemed riches as nothing in comparison to her.
Neither compared I unto her any precious stone,
because all gold in compare to her is as a little
sand...I do not hide her riches, for she is a treasure
unto man that never faileth...For in her is a spirit
holy, one only, manifold, subtle, lively, clear, un-
defiled, plain, not subject to hurt, loving the thing
that is good quick, which cannot be letted, ready
to do good, kind to man, steadfast, sure, free from
care, having all power, overseeing all things.

—Wisdom of Solomon

(Elsewhere, Montana, fast-forward to 2012)

I. The One True Seven-Hearted Holy Goat

Try this for openers: the art of a region begins to come mature
when it is no longer what we think it should be.
—William Kittredge, *Owning It All*

IN 2012, THE year I began work on these chronicles, Kale Broussard
bequeathed me a nickname that has stuck to me like a full-body tattoo. It
happened like this:

One pleasant if apocalyptically warm late-winter morning I drove from
the cabin I lease in Elsewhere down to the Elkmoon Beguine & Cattle
Company, parked near the office, stepped onto the porch, and perched on
the porch rail so I could finish the little cigar I'd been puffing on the drive.
Hearing the office door swing open behind me, I turned to see Kale step out
and continue holding the door with an expression of surprising tenderness.
Then out stepped the bardic folk singer Lorilee Shay. The instant she saw
me Lorilee beamed, and I was smitten, as always when I see her. But there
was more. Amongst the intricate little populace at the E.B.&C.Co there's
always more.

The more this time was that I hadn't seen Lore for a month since she'd
fallen out of remission. Chemo and radiation had, for the seventh time, reduced her to an alarming thinness, intensified her clear, black-rimmed gray
eyes, and replaced her hair with a silver down that left her delicate head
so vulnerable-looking I wanted to shelter it in my hands. Her devastated
beauty reminded me of Earth herself, yet her smile, in impossible contrast,
was completely uninjured. That smile flew into me like a wind from another
world. Every door and window in me fell open to receive it, clearing a
path all the way in to my riven heart. So when Kale took in the goaty
beard-but-no-mustache I'd sprouted in solitude and said, "Well, if it ain't
the Holy Goat," his timing was perfect: I was standing somewhere so far
from words or wit that I didn't realize till later how memorably my name
had been nicked.

I've got a mouth that seldom hesitates to defend me if need be. When the
nickname began to spread, I could have fended it off with ease. But I soon
found I didn't want to, because there's more: on these four thousand acres
there's always more. On the morning Kale nicked my name I'd been delving

into the E.B.&C.Co for three months. I'd picked through hundreds of letters and photos both personal and historical, thousands of emails, hundreds
of pages of journal entries, a skein of Jamey-VZ-altered Shakespeare plays.
I'd studied plat maps, deeds, business records, blueprints. I'd recorded and
transcribed over a hundred ten hours of face-to-face interviews with nineteen
E.B.&C.Co residents and twelve current and former friends and neighbors,
learning of adventures, wrecks, and revelations ranging from nefarious to
hilarious to erroneous to erotic to harrowing to outright heroic.

Why did I want all this at my fingertips? Because the E.B.&C.Co, as the
psalm has it, *restoreth my soul*. All my adult life I've felt the global industrial
juggernaut masquerading as "civilization" has trapped us in a greed-driven
apocalypse that scarcely a species, humanity included, will escape in the
end. In the summer of 2003 the jaws of this trap opened enough to let
me glimpse possibilities beyond demise. The freeing sensation began during
my first strolls and tour-guided drives around the newly formed Elkmoon
Beguine & Cattle Company, a couple of times with Risa, once with Kale,
twice with Lou Roy, and several times with Lorilee Shay.

Though I was more impressed after each such tour, I wasn't sufficiently
impressed to shake off a strong aversion to communal living. But over
the next few years the E.B.&C.Co folks eased me through a slow-motion
conversion. For starters, despite its populace of thirty, the place didn't *feel*
communal. Every one of the residents had more freedom to determine the
contents of their days than anyone I knew working typical nation-state
jobs. Even better, in an epoch of worldwide industrial devastation, the
E.B.&C.Co residents were living lives of practical integrity and economic
self-sufficiency, treating land, water, plants, animals, and one another with
sensitivity, tolerance, humor, and something new and invaluable to me, but
hard to define. I've seen countless op-eds calling for a "change of consciousness" if humanity is to survive. I've seen *zero* op-ed descriptions of what
this new consciousness looks, feels, tastes, sounds, and lives like from day
to day. But how slow I am to make crucial connections! Almost every time
I visited the E.B.&C.Co I was at some point blindsided by a wandering
joy that spontaneously permeates the place, its life-forms, its people, their
interactions, yet *years* had to pass before I realized the wandering joy *is* the
needed change of consciousness!

My yearning to write of the E.B.&C.Co was born of that revelation, and
I began my research that very day—March 19, 2012—as my shirt-pocket
recorder took down this Kale Broussard description of their collective
genesis:

All through the '90s up to 2003 we were in the same trap as
most everybody, bumblefuckin' around in a post-money economy and
post-democratic democracy, working shit jobs for shit pay to profit a
"corporate person" bent, far as I can tell, on drowning a quarter of
Earth's populace under rising seas while the rest of us live out some

hideous sequel to *Mad Max*. In a civilized world, nations become nations in order to offer their citizens collective strength. In our world, the way I see it, Big Banking, Big Energy, Big Government, and all the other Biggies calved off of the civilized world long ago, becoming big mean free-floating icebergs that smash into every country, ripping holes in their hulls that drowned millions and leave the rest of us in constant danger of goin' down. We're facing biological and ecosystem holocaust while the men doing the damage cry, "My heck, you people, mugging the planet in industrial back alleys creates job, jobs, jobs!," the profiteers stand up and cheer, and who can hear Earth's mortal moaning amid that ruckus?

Once in a while, though, God knows how, a seemingly small event will sneak up and give birth to thousands more. That event, for us, was a day on the upper Elkmoon, October of '97, when Lou Roy Skinner rode down the legally trespassing Risa McKeig in what started out to be a hate crime. But when Lou ran out of bullets and Grey refused to be weaponized, he and Risa saw deep into each other, and a mutual trust was total. Lou Roy began showing Risa Elkmoon places that flew into her like wild birds. She began seeing ways humans could enhance those places, giving Lou a deeper grasp of his world than his lifelong own. Lou was old and Risa was young, so romance had no shot at wrecking their deal. They just enjoyed the hell out of the way Elkmoon country, seen by the two of them, became potentially better country than either of them had ever seen alone.

Lou and I are close. Risa hadn't been in the valley four days before her effect on him began to affect me. I'd felt for years that the possibilities for improving the life of our populace and place had been ripped away by NorBanCo's development plans. Risa didn't care two hoots about those plans. All she cared about was her direct relationship with the life of the land, river, and mountains, what the land suffered to grow, what kind of creatures and plants inhabited it, right down to its weeds, bugs, moss, and lichen, ruled by her burning desire to throw nothing out of balance. Anything more grandiose than that—which was everything NorBanCo had in mind—was to Risa just a bunch of cheap tricks performed by moneyed fools oblivious to an all-important sphere known as Mother Earth. Watching her treat NorBanCo's antics like white noise, when the same noise had tormented me for a decade, initially made me wonder whether she was running on brilliant intuition or optimistic oblivion. But she was soaking up the intricacies of our place and connecting to our best people so fast that I underwent a sea change. The Elkmoon started showing Lou Roy and me the same fresh possibilities it was showing Risa.

That's when a little group of us began to talk of sharing an Elkmoon spread as free as possible of Biggie control—a dream millions of dollars beyond our means. But Risa is no mere dreamer. She connects to people in a spirited way that connects to *more* spirited people. She lured her well-heeled friend TJ here from Portland, and in two days he'd become one of my most trusted friends. She fused hearts with Lorilee Shay, and the two of them drew another powerhouse woman into our group, Ona Kutar. These newcomers then put us at ease by having no interest in a private fiefdom that shut out locals. On the contrary, they asked us locals what had gone wrong, then teamed up with us to set some things right.

City mice and country mice began eating their stereotypes of each other for breakfast, lunch, and dinner. Quicker than quick we began scheming and dreaming of a shared spread as easy on the Earth and free of Biggie Everything as could be. Risa and TJ returned to Portland, Ona to her career, the three of them began setting aside money toward our dream, we cowboys kept working NorBanCo's rich-brat fiefdom, watching for cracks in its armor. And though I'll never understand it, a magic flared up. A kind of *holiness,* I want to say. Our dreaming held so steady that, six years in, fifteen of us defied our fears, laid our money on the table and our lives on the line, and purchased the four thousand acres you're looking at.

God help us, we then got into such a knock-down drag-out over what to call our place that some of us began hunting lawyers to split off from the rest. But our best peacekeeper, Lorilee, spoke for the holiness when she said, "The solution to this is simple. We choose a name none of us like. Then no one wins, loses, gloats, or pouts." That's how the lob-eared crock-kneed name Elkmoon Beguine & Cattle Company came to be, and I tell you what. We all disliked and liked that name so lukewarmly that peace was instantly restored.

The real work began. Thousands of sweat-drenched acts of atonement toward our land, water, soil, forests, livestock, wildlife; endless acts of forgiveness and makeshift diplomacy toward neighbors and one another. Sooner than expected we saw we *were* cobbling together ways of life better than any we could have led in the Biggies' flailing nation-state. In a place where six cowboys had been doomed to extinction by a multinational, thirty folks of all ages and kinds, cowboys included, are doing better than just okay working for no one but our collective selves. Income has crept up on outlay to where we're turning small profits on several cottage industries and a small cattle biz. We now share eleven well-chosen vehicles instead of the forty or so wrecks and gas hogs we owned before. We're off the grid and green energied. We hunt, fish, bee-keep, ranch, farm, and forage 60 percent of our food. We've scraped some broken lives up off some cold city pavement and helped 'em rehab to where they're part of us now. We support so many locals and their businesses and good causes that the slanderers who tried to talk us to death have been forced to cork it, at least for now.

Here's my feeling, HG. The only planet we're ever going to live on is undergoing a global demolition the Biggies call an upgrade because they're still squeezing cash and wage slaves out of it. But look close at history and you'll see that empires don't just implode. Some of them crumble into humbler, friendlier little countries or regions in spite of the surrounding failed empires. Here on the E.B.&C.Co we've managed to become a solvent, spiritually awake, thirty-person dryland lifeboat that's helping hundreds. What might this world be if Earth-gentle lifeboats became the common social unit? I don't claim to know. All I know is, a little bird keeps telling me that the more lifeboats people launch as the Biggies grow greedier and the climate goes berserk, the more people might reach some humble little home-lands safely.

But can I ask a favor before you start spinning our tale? Though some of the folks living here are mighty charismatic, please don't make them all saintly shiny. The West's already got a Book of Mormon. One's more than plenty, don'tcha think? Show how we rose out of dirt and desperation. Show we remain so fragile a run of hard luck could sink us. Show how broken open and strange tolerant we had to be to even *consider* this grand misadventure. But don't leave out how deeply moving life on our big dryland lifeboat can frequently be.

BURNING TO TRY, I retired to my cabin upriver, set to work roughing out a list of seminal events in the lives of the E.B.&C.Co settlers, and sat down to write of them—when something knocked me out of my authorial comfort zone. That something, I realized after a week of failure, was *affection*. Getting to know the E.B.&C.Co residents in depth, my role as their mere chronicler had turned into a cherished circle of friendships. I needed the authorial detachment Chekhov calls "coldness," or the trifecta James Joyce calls "silence, exile, and cunning," but couldn't achieve either given my entanglement with people whose secrets, flaws, and fragilities made me care about them all the more.

This impasse drove me to something at which most writers excel: whining about our writing to other writers. Targeting the E.B.&C.Co's semi-resident playwright, Jamey Van Zandt, I lured him upriver to the tiny Elsewhere Bar & Grill, dinner and drinks on me, ordered him a double shot of Islay single malt scotch that cost as much as his dinner, and the instant his drink arrived commenced to whine:

"As you know, Jamey, I've begun to portray the back stories, birth stories, and pretty dang triumphant survival stories of your repurposed ranch. And I knew it would be challenging. But something's making it impossible. The trouble, I feel, is that I got fast-tracked into everybody's good graces during our interviews and am now seen as everybody's friend. But the *real* story of the E.B.&C.Co's genesis isn't always friendly. I need to trespass in awkward, private, and humiliating places, and everyone's friendliness is smothering this need to death."

As he listened Jamey didn't take a sip of his drink. Just inhaled its fumes. He'll spend ten or more minutes nosing a fine single malt as if that's its sole purpose, suddenly throw a fat swig in his mouth, chew it a while, down it, shake himself like a river-sopped dog, and sigh some such profundity as "*Dang!*"

I said, "I've pondered this hard, Jamey. The only way to pull this weave of tales off is if the most painful, troubling, and revealing disclosures become *self*-disclosures. In short, I need to enlist a handful of Elkmooners to serve as embedded co-authors. And if they *do* enlist, the confessions I'll seek will be so raw, contentious, and revealing that I'm not sure I have the guts to ask."

Snout still in his scotch fumes, ignoring my angst completely, Jamey said, "Here's a mystery, HG. All over the globe the word 'whiskey' is spelled w-h-i-s-k-e-y. How is it that the Scots, of all people, delete the *e*?" His voice became a brogue so thick I felt as if my ears had filled with haggis. "Goegh faeguerre *thaey'd* beae the fey dribblin' brattlers to raemoove a lettre frome thay aft ende of oure goddish giftie," quoth he.

His pseudo Gaelic already had me grinning when the mystery moment arrived: lifting his glass, he threw some scotch in his maw, chewed it like food, downed it, did the wet-dog shake, and wheezed, "No worries, HG. In theatre, *raw, contentious,* and *revealing* is our daily bread. I'll make sure the embedded co-author asks for you."

Desperate to hold him to that, I shot to the bar, ordered him a second Islay, and set it before him. Smiling at it, Jamey said, "So who *are* these co-authors?"

"For starters, *you*," I said.

"Given the liquid bribes, I figured," he said, and his intriguingly broken nose went back to imbibing the smoke, malt, and peat scents of the Scottish archipelagoes. "Who else?"

"Kale and Risa, of course. TJ for his business genius, Pearl Building, intimacy with Risa and Jervis, and some kind of Beguine nothingness state I want to understand better. Rosalia for her contrary ranch brat angle on the whole Elkmoon scene. And Grady for his crush on high country and the Lûmi whether the latter exist or not."

"*Done*," Jamey said. "And they'll all say yes. I know they will. So. Whine-fest over?"

"Not quite," I said. "There's one more ask."

He took an uncharacteristically normal sip of his drink. "Name it."

A stone rose in my throat. "You can guess."

He read my face. "We all need her for a host of reasons, and we're not likely to have her much longer. But if I were you, HG, I'd drive down to the E.B.&C.Co tomorrow, find her, and just look at her. Without asking a thing. She's turned transparent. Her face will tell you, without a word, what can or can't be asked of her at this time."

SO THAT'S HOW I happened, next morning, to be finishing my little cigar on the E.B.&C.Co office porch when Kale opened the door, Lorilee stepped out, Kale eyed me and said, "Well, if it ain't the Holy Goat," and Lore's sure-enough transparent smile knocked me so far out of my ordinary self that I was left hovering in a void between...well...between my *holiness* and my *goatness*. And that void was *vast*. I seemed to float in it, weightless, an astronaut fallen off his space station, boundlessness in every direction.

I asked Lore the nothing her smile invited, we gently embraced, I pretended I'd come to interview Kale, and made the best of my fib by recording the description of the E.B.&C.Co's genesis you've just read. I then drove back to my cabin in Elsewhere—where I sat frozen in the pine-needle-paved driveway, unable to move until I confessed my true condition: I was in *Lore-shock*. Somehow she makes me realize I need to kill all desire for ordinary romance and strive to love in the way she loves, embracing every person and chapter in her life, including even her impending death. My chances of pulling this off? About the same, I figure, as humanity's chances that Anthropocene Tyranny won't delete us all.

But when I dragged myself into the cabin, made tea, sat down at my desk, and turned to the mountain range of research on my eight-foot plywood side table, a wonder befell me: the instant the nickname "Holy Goat" entered the room, the mountains of research became the possession of a Hovering Bard *seething* with Chekhovian coldness and Joycian silence, exile, and cunning. I, the Pope-christened Holy Goat, began writing of the E.B.&C.Co residents' idiocies without pulling punches, of their spiritual heroics without New Age maunder, and of things as hard as shattered loves, shattered lives, and Lorilee's impending death without trepidation or sense of trespass. As the HG, I worked deep into the night, woke wired, wrote long again, and the next day again, and so it continued. I cloistered my newfound self in solitude, stayed away from the E.B.&C.Co, missed the place and people terribly, and portrayed them all the more vividly for that very reason.

Jamey, meanwhile, issued invitations to the hoped-for embedded co-authors, all of them began writing with candor and skill to the topics I assigned—and we've come to my happy secret: in the very spirit of the E.B.&C.Co, the collaborative efforts of we who Jamey dubbed "the One True Seven-Hearted Holy Goat" have authored these chronicles from inception. Risa's dumbsaint notebooks, correspondence, favorite lines of wisdom literature, and my interviews of her have contributed more than anyone else. Kale's contributions, also substantial, have been oral, recorded mostly in the cab of his F-250 as he goes about his ranch tasks. Jamey,

Rosalia, and TJ have contributed emails, letters, written sketches, and many more interviews, Jervis a few choice pieces of guidance from Ocean. Grady gave me full access to his Elkmoon Mountain journals. This material was then reworked by me for concision, consistency, and narrative flow.

Now to get back to whining: with so many contributions pouring in on top of my own efforts, I soon identified more than a hundred possible chapters at the same time I developed *no* strategies on how to bring order to so much material. Overwhelmed by the options, I spent two hyper-caffeinated days developing what I called "comprehensive and fail-safe organizing principles," leading to a comprehensive and fail-safe splitting headache. But the splitter gave me one good idea: I wrote to Jamey again, said I'd been buried in a story avalanche, enclosed one of my fail-safe organizing principles, and asked what he thought of it, fully expecting him to blow it to smithereens and rescue me from the rubble. And it worked! Three days later this JVZ missive arrived in my Elsewhere PO box:

Your Goatliness:

Allow me to begin by clearing the air up there in Elsewhere: "Fuck forever the ghastly term 'comprehensive and fail-safe organizing prin-ciples' and repeat after me. The millionfold story of the E.B.&C.Co is untellable, and what a relief! Now I, the Holy Goat, can turn to whatever I'd most enjoy telling and abandon my assault on the impossible."

To rejuvenate your sense of enjoyment I recommend this: the next time Ona Kutar comes to the Elkmoon, ask the kids to take you to see her bead collection. It's mostly Venetian, Middle Eastern, African, and India Indian in origin; glass and ceramic beads of all kinds; inlays of precious metals, mother-of-pearl, ivory, semiprecious stones. She's collected a huge number and the kids are so in love with them they make a bead pilgrimage to Ona's every time she comes home.

When you join them, watch Ona as she opens the multilevel mahogany trunk containing the beads. The Diva, the Guitar Legend, the Activist, the Farming Generalissimo, all vanish. A girl-like Ona of pure focused wonder takes their place. She's so contagious when she gets this way! Try to catch what she's got. As the kids set about build-ing their own little rosaries they're dumbstruck by the beads' beauty and their freedom to handle them. And though each rosary is worth many hundred dollars, Ona lets each child wear their creation home. At Risa's urging they string the beads on wire pike-fishing leader, the ace fly-fisher Rosalia ties all the knots, and they're "catch-and-release rosaries" they return to Ona after exactly one week. But, with Ona's blessing, they wear the rosaries on what they call "Quests," wandering the river bottom, forests, and fields in search of mysteries the beads help detect, and it's awfully easy for a questing child to get distracted. Last year Willa set a rosary down, forgot where, and we've been searching for it ever since. But get this: when Willa broke into tears and confessed, Ona just told her, "What a beautiful surprise for somebody someday!" With which she pulled out her collection, helped Willa build another rosary, and let her wear it home that same evening.

Late last night it hit me, HG: assembling your Elkmoon chapters should feel little different than making bead rosaries feels to Ona and the kids. Guided by pure focused wonder, keeping it playful, do a flyover of your countless tales, select one, tell it with a full heart, pick a second tale that connects to the first via color schemes and wonder themes that mesmerize the kid in you, and keep going until your story beads have created a rosary that leads your readers on a little Quest.

What can't be taken lightly is the thread connecting your story beads, so let's talk about that. It can't be wire pike leader, for starters. In all but certain rare kinds of light—blue June dusk; golden day in October; midwinter moonlight amid fresh snowfall—the connecting thread won't even be visible. But not because it's weak. It's invisible because it's made of spirit. Vague as that may sound, "spirit" or "soul thread" is exactly what sews the people, mountains, and sky together here, and not by organizing or systematizing us, but by *piercing us.*

Talk to Risa about this. She'll tell you that the difference between *systematizing* lives and *piercing* them is the difference between living in cold obedience to a Chairman Mao, Ayn Rand, or Vatican manifesto versus living by intuition, Ocean strobe, myth tellings, and *bárdachd.* I've heard you marvel at how, all day every day, the E.B.&C.Co throws the Industrial Suicide Machine into reverse and drives the opposite direction. It's true. But it's not accomplished by cult leaders and laws. We are *not* an intentional community. We're an *unintentional menagerie* as unalike as Ona's beads, joined not by didactic intent but by hearts pierced by unseen threads. It's an old, old magic. When even two such hearts align, things happen. Not easy things but, more often than not, *moving* ones. And when thirty pierced hearts came together here, we more and more often found ourselves feeling the wandering joy you realized was the needed change of consciousness everybody keeps yakking about but refuses to shut up and feel.

So where to begin? The hell if I know. *Don't overthink it* is all I tell myself when starting a play. I often just stare at my hands till my fingers start wanting to twiddle the keys. Then out might come a few lines as unpretentious as, maybe:

Look at this nowhere place with the dopey name, Elkmoon Beguine & Cattle Company. What the fuh? Yet two dozen adults, six kids, the

*inhabitants of two pregnant bellies, and a constellation of friends con-
join here with animals, birds, and a river moving through. Sky flowing
over full of weathers, jets, and birds from ten-foot-winged trumpeter
swans to bushtits. Serious mountains to the southwest birthing our
river. A strong link to a city two days west, wedding itself to us via
love, commerce, and those who like TJ and me choose to live both
places. And how rich our pierced and interwoven lives turn out to be!
How had we forgotten this?*

A sample string of story beads? *Everything* beautifully broken,
which is everything pertaining to Lorilee these days, opening ever
deeper as she fades, a sunset in the act of becoming night sky, us
half-asses struggling to keep up, at a loss for words or even facial
expressions to wear in her almost unbearably poignant presence.
Sometimes her illness feels to me as if a maniac is smashing Ona
beads with a hammer and shards are flying into our eyes, mouths,
hearts. But have you watched Willa, Fionn, and Rosalia tend our
ailing one lately?[2] Three spirit guides/angels/best friends at the unlikely ages of seven, thirteen, and twenty-two carrying nibbles of
food, love letters, drawings, feathers, flowers, or fresh catch-and-
release rosaries to Lore daily, provisioning and beautifying her for
whatever comes next. The strolls those four take of an evening *fell*
me with their poignancy, Lorilee the wobbly toddler now, Willa's
small hand giving her courage, Rosalia the ever-tender nurse, Prince
Fionn steadying Lore with his slender shoulder as they toddle past
the garden, horses, barns, ponds, baptized every step in a mystery
Lorilee keeps proclaiming, though the rest of us can't let go enough
to hear, "How alive death feels once your life is completely given."
When I compare my own fucked-up first grief to the beauty of Fionn's
and Willa's adoration of our dying songbird, vegan Regina's love for
tobacco-chewing steak-loving Buford, Kale's great friendship with
the urbane urbanite TJ, everybody's quiet respect for Jervis's Ocean
strobes, or Ona and Lou Roy's redneck love for whitefishing together
in midwinter with Pabst for social lubrication and maggots for bait,
I ask myself how *any* of this came to be. How have so many unalike
strangers become so intimate as they remain so unalike? Why does
spirit thread keep piercing these particular acres? Are there hidden
niches all over the earth being similarly pierced, and brutalized and
abandoned corners of our planet moving toward rebirth the way our
corner has been doing? In answer to such questions you then take
your spirit thread in hand, ponder your pile of story beads, thread

---

2   The Holy Goat begs the reader's pardon for giving away the existence of
young Willa Shay Van Zandt and her older brother, Fionn Kabir McKeig.
These are Jamey and Risa's children, whom I'll introduce later but allow
Jamey to mention here because their adoration of Lore is so beautiful.

one that charms you, choose the next for its relationship to the first, and keep going till you've made us laugh, cry, and love our lives, our living world, and the Unseen a wee bit more.

I'll be home awhile now, and can strategize, write, or address a dram with you as needed, my turn to buy. Clearer than clear nights these days. "An' all them nosey damn stars," quoth the ()-leggèd bard Lou Roy.

Love,
Jamey

()-leggèd...
Everything beautifully broken...
How alive death feels once your life is completely given...

If I couldn't work with the likes of that I was hopeless. I tacked Jamey's letter to my wall for counsel and comfort, sat down to my desk, shipped on a chestful of air, and on the out-breath whispered, "*Story beads in color schemes and wonder themes, pierced by the unseen thread...*"

Two years later, having been companioned, regaled, rescued, and inspired innumerable times by the wildly generous hearts of Risa, TJ, Kale, Jamey, Rosalia, Jervis, and Grady, our united effort has made it to here. It's on my gratitude-sopped heart to bring us on home.

II. Nine Cool Unlikelihoods

The sound of water says what I think.

—Chuang Tzu

IN SEPTEMBER OF 1997 the multinational conglomerate NorBanCo announced an exclusive Elkmoon Valley development plan they dubbed the Brokeback Ranch & Country Club. With the help of state legislators whose allegiance to the plan was purchased for a pittance, strapped Montana taxpayers were footing the bill for infrastructure changes with no idea they were being bilked by an absentee cabal of the richest people in the country. NorBanCo's Montana man on the ground, Charles Keynes "Tex" Schiller, forecast at their annual shareholders meeting in Dallas that the development would be "fully built, paid for, and populated in three to five years." To Kale Broussard's delight, the development was then threatened with a lawsuit by Annie Proulx's publisher for pilfering the word "Brokeback" from Proulx's famed *New Yorker* short story "Brokeback Mountain" and ordered to drop the name. When NorBanCo refused and solicitors on both sides of the tiff began to make excellent money, the negotiations of course went horribly. Determined to move the development forward regardless, NorBanCo set out to show Proulx's publisher that their kleptomania was an honor by running a foldout ad for the Brokeback Ranch & Country Club in the October issue of *Better Homes and Gardens*. During the same week Risa McKeig arrived in Montana, seven million *Better Homes* subscribers were presented with digitally produced images of what 22,000 Elkmoon acres would look like "graced," as the ad put it, "by Brokeback's 50 luxury ranchettes, 150 high-end townhouses, 700 spacious condos, championship eighteen-hole golf course, nearby ski runs, mountain bike and running trails, six miles of private spring creek fly-fishing beats, 13,000 acres of exclusive hunting grounds, extensive network of paved solar cart paths, an indoor tennis, squash, and racquetball club, an Old West–style mall of boutiques, haberdasheries, galleries, restaurants, delicatessen, yoga studio, and fitness center, and—our crowning achievement—*the Grand Lodge on the Elkmoon*." At the bottom of the page a row of staged action photos depicted "Brokeback's pioneering co-owners enjoying their world-class sportscape via snowmobile, drift boat, kayak, bicycle, trail horse, dressage horse, polo pony, and Western saddle horse in a year-round indoor-outdoor paradise where"—sing it "Brokeback Mountain" if the lawyers can work it out!—"*it got to be all that time a yours a-horseback makes it so goddam good*. Won't you join us?"

THE MORNING AFTER the ad appeared, the best cowboy on Kale's crew, Max Bowler, knocked on his door before work. The instant Kale opened up, Max said, "Sorry I couldn't give you proper notice, sir, but I quit. Effective today."

Kale ran a hand over his face as if to wipe away his dismay. The attempt failed. "Can you step inside long enough to tell me why?"

Max entered, took a chair at the kitchen table, declined the coffee Kale offered, and slapped *Better Homes and Gardens* down on the table open to the ad. "I found this at E City Market yesterday and spent the night feeling sick. NorBanCo claims this is a three- to five-year plan, but potential investors are driving all over the ranch right now while we push around a few cows to provide local color. We call ourselves cowboys, but throwaway props in a bogus Western is all we really are, and I've met the girl I'm gonna marry, Kale. Kira won't be part of that. We found a fixer-upper house and barn on thirty acres, we're gonna make an offer, and I've got strong notions about a better kind of beef if I can figure out how to market it. And before you tell me the cattle biz is rigged, we *know* it is. But I'd rather try to slip through a crack in the scam beside the woman I love than serve NorBanCo one more day. Sorry for the short notice, Kale, but if you were me I believe you'd do the same."

Kale sighed, stood, and said, "Do me one favor, Max. I'm a lifer in this valley and get along with most everybody. When things get rough, as they're sure to do, don't be the strong silent type whose notion of strength withers his family. Reach out, and if there's any way my posse or I can help, we will. Can we shake on that?"

The two men shook work-rough hands, went their separate ways, and if the world's disenfranchised would only agree to live by the dictates of weazened corporate logic, NorBanCo was about to win big. But from the week of Risa's 1997 arrival, steady on into the summer of 2003, a skein of cool unlikelihoods began to befall some like-minded people, their paths and dreams began to intertwine, and as Jervis McGraff likes to put it, "Ways began to lead unto ways."

Unlikelihood #1: New Reasons to Say Lordy

Ida Craig strolled into a packed Loco Creek Steakhouse, took aim at Kale when he stood at their table, and snap-crackle-popped a half dozen cowboy cervicals as her Junoesque figure swept by on impossibly small turquoise-and-tan-booted feet.

Kale blushed as she closed all distance between their prows to give him a quick hug and peck on the cheek. Shooting a dark look at the oglers, Kale worked Ida's chair. The instant she was seated a server named Callie— a whip-smart patron of Ida's bookstore and espresso bar—appeared with Kale's double Knob Creek on ice and Ida's Oregon pinot gris, and no sooner did the drinks touch the table than Callie asked if they'd like Kale's usual rare T-bone and Ida's medium-rare grilled halibut. They nodded, thanked her, clinked glasses, took a first sip of their drinks, and Ida casually asked Kale how his day had gone. A pent-up Pope then burst out with this:

"I've whitewashed the topic of work since the day we met, Ida. It's time you knew the score. I hired my cowboys to raise cattle. But once this Brokeback deal gets going they'll be wanting lawn boys and busboys, not cowboys. That day's a little ways off according to Tex, but it's coming sure as death and taxes, and caused my best man, Max Bowler, to quit today. If I followed his example I could sell my inholdings to NorBanCo for a killing, move up valley, and not have to watch my home get turned into an all-hats-and-no-cowboys Disney diorama. But when I try to put a cash value on the view from Schoolhouse Bluff, or the home my barn gives Lou Roy's cutting horse operation, or what forty years of every kind of bird feeder has done for the wild birds in my garden and yard, or what'd happen to Eddie, Rosalia, and Lou if NorBanCo lorded the land beneath their Airstreams, I can't find it in me to sell. So let me put this plainly, Ida. I'm no ranch foreman. Not anymore. I'm more like a chess king on a board with one pawn left, name of Lou Roy, and all sixteen of my opponent's pieces are coming at me like a storm."

Ida set down her wineglass, laid a hand on Kale's, turned her full femininity upon him, and her girl-voice was fiercer than he thought possible as she said, "You listen to every word I'm about to tell you. You're your crew's and cattle's loyal foreman, the land's true steward, and NorBanCo's exact opposite. And there are *good* changes coming to this valley. I don't just hope for that, Kale. I'm certain of it."

"I wish I thought so," he sighed. "But every change I see coming, I dread."

Leaning so slow and deep into Kale's air space she sucked the dark thoughts right out of him, Ida breathed, "Then it's time to look right beside you, cowboy, 'cause there's all *kinds* of change I'm capable of bringing to your valley all by myself. Changes that you in particular, alongside me in particular, are *very* likely to enjoy."

When Kale recovered enough to burble, "*Well! Say!*" Ida giggled, moved his hand to her strong shapely thigh, and began toying with his digits in ways that caused Kale to wave down Callie and beg her to box their meals pronto no matter the degree of doneness. "We'll heat it up at home," he told her, then blushed at the double entendre. When Callie delivered the boxes with a puckish grin, Kale and Ida stood, he offered his arm, and they strode past the neck-popping cowpokes and out the door, forgetting their boxed dinners as completely as Kale had forgotten his double Knob Creek.

Following Ida's white Audi home in the white F-250, he squeezed truck next to car in the driveway, gossip be damned, walked Ida into the cornflower Victorian, wove uneasily through the boutique and bookstore, and endured stupendous loop-de-loops as he followed six voluptuous feet of Ida up two flights of skinny stairs to her third-floor boudoir. In that eyrie, exactly as promised, Ida then brought earthshaking changes home to the Elkmoon's last best foreman. Swept into intertwinings and swoons he had never dreamed possible, the Pope showed his quality. His strongest oath all night was an occasional, "*Lordy, Ida! Oh, Ida! Lordy!*"

Unlikelihood #2: The City Lights of Elsewhere

At dawn the day after Kale, Lou Roy, and Risa shared a campfire in the Glory Meadow, Kale freed Lou Roy from exile and Lou moved back to his Airstream on Schoolhouse Bluff for a day of unpacking, resettling, and tending his horses.

The next morning, early, Lou Roy picked Risa up at her motel for a tour of the Elkmoon Valley. When she climbed onto the bench seat of Lou's faded yellow and rusted Cheyenne, iPooch broke the Montana State Tail Whumping Speed Record in greeting her. "Come sit in my lap before you turn me into a soufflé!" Risa told her, and up she hopped.

"Best way to learn a valley," Lou opined as they left E City, "is start at the top, turn back around, an' follow the river down checkin' out side valleys, tribs, tiny towns, historic sites, an' cool little secrets as we go."

"Mind if I take notes?" Risa asked. "I want to learn this valley inside and out."

"Scribble away," said Lou Roy. "An' here's a tip will help. Pine forest has a way of all lookin' the same, an' lots o' these places you'll want to find again. So each time we turn off Downriver Road, write the nearest milepost marker. I'll help you spot 'em."

Lou Roy's style as tour guide was to pull up to a feature of interest, park the old Cheyenne, down his window, roll a smoke, light up, and say next to nothing. "Too much talk scribbles over what's callin' to the eye," he said.

Risa liked his spare commentary just fine. Treating the valley like a Skrit Lit classic, she took copious notes, adding sketches, maps, bird and animal sightings, personal observations, and a few crazy dumbsaint notes too. A few of the morning's highlights:

Downstream of the Glory Meadow the valley spread out over a surprisingly level floor, most of it forested with four species of conifers. Downriver Road cut straight lines through the trees but the river meandered, sometimes near the highway, sometimes as much as a mile away from it. Near milepost 66 Lou turned onto an unmarked track, jounced through pines to river's edge, downed his window, rolled his smoke, and waited to see what Risa would see.

Across the river was a cliff with strata that fanned out like the tail of a turkey gobbler. "Betcha five bucks I can name that cliff in five tries," Risa said.

"No bet," Lou Roy said. "Gobbler Rock. A name so obvious it's dumb, an' that's what I like about it. Folks drive in, gawk at the tail, maybe shoot it a couple times, an' leave without noticing the creek tricklin' outta the willows just downstream. See it?" Lou looked over and saw that Risa was already sketching the shiny-rocked hint of creek leaking out of the willows. "Cross that tail-out, stand in the outflow, an' you'll feel Gobbler Creek is warm. Steams like a locomotive in winter, but the track we just drove is under eight, ten feet of snow then. Come summer, bring a friend, follow Gobbler two miles up, an' the sweetest hot spring in the Elkmoon's likely to be nobody but yours."

A quarter mile past milepost 65, Lou Roy's secret was a hanging valley into which he would climb in November. "With luck I'll down an elk, lower it in quarters down the cliff there, an' Grey an' Goober, hobbled at the bottom, will tote my elk an' me out in one go."

Between posts 60 and 59 Lou Roy eased into a pullout and pointed crossriver to the mouth of a trib. In the crown of a larch towering over the creek perched two bald eagles. "Ospreys leave in September, so brown trout on the spawn timed *that* right," he said. "But eagles winter over. You're lookin' at Two Pound Creek. Can you guess why?"

An inch into Lou Roy's cigarette an eagle went into a dive, sank its talons in the riffle at the mouth, lifted off with a good brown, landed on a gravel bar, the eagles made sushi of it, and Risa said, "Two pounds is the average size of the creek's spawning browns."

"Bingo." Lou and his glacier-silt-green eyes gave her a glance of approval.

At milepost 44, with nothing but forest in sight from the highway, a road sign read:

ELSEWHERE, MT
POP 40
ELEV 4385

Lou turned right, followed a gravel road riverward, and before they reached water they entered a pine-forested hamlet of thirty-some cottages and modest board-and-batten buildings. Lou parked by one of the buildings, downed his window, and again said nothing. But Risa was quick. Spotting a weathered board that faintly read, ELSEWHERE BAR & GRILL, she cried, "My dad loved this place!"

"Makes two of us," Lou said. "Four tables an' five barstools, same as forever. Trout risin' off the back deck. Opens at five, closes at nine, so we're six hours early, dang it. Big pours on drinks. Great steaks. Folks tell Mitt Gruneau, the owner, he'd triple his business if he'd put a billboard on the highway an' improve his sign. 'Why would I do that,' Mitt says, 'when a crappy sign an' no billboard pulls in just the number I like to serve?'"

Risa was making a note to return, look Mitt up, and ask if he remembered Dave when Lou Roy's face brightened and iPooch began to cry with excitement. Lou opened his door, the dog flew over him, and Risa climbed out and joined them peering skyward. "There we go!" Lou said, pointing directly overhead.

Risa gasped. A half mile up, against a pure blue so dark their bodies and white wings shone like the lights of a celestial city, their black wingtips causing the lights to spark on and off, *six thousand? eight thousand?*—she couldn't even guess how many snow geese trumpeted as they flew.

"Hard to beat that," Lou Roy said. "Let's save the rest of the valley for next time an' go check out NorBanCo's big doings, Kale's inholdings, an' the lands your family once owned."

Unlikelihood #3: Risa Gives the Concierge Nothing

Nine miles shy of E City Lou Roy turned onto a heavily oiled gravel thoroughfare as wide as two lanes of an interstate freeway. "What's with the oil?" Risa asked. "Isn't it toxic?"

"NorBanCo's man Tex likes toxic," Lou muttered. "What he hates is dust in his lodge."

A six-by-sixteen-foot sheet of steel hung under the enormous log arch they drove under, with two-foot-tall letters plasma-arced clean through the steel proclaiming, **VALLEY LAND & BEEF INC**. They drove slow past a cavernous metal warehouse in which Risa glimpsed a huge snowplow and two even bigger road graders. Next came an enormous gravel pit with a loader and four dump trucks in its depths, the source of the oiled high road.

Suddenly iPooch let out a string of high-pitched dog words. They'd reached the stockyard loading docks where Land & Beef cattle shipped out. No cattle present, but the odor kept iPooch singing till Lou Roy barked, "*Squirrel!*" which made her fall silent and peer madly in all directions. Eyeing her antics, Lou turned talkative. "Kelpies are great herders, but it's sheep they're geared to, so I keep iPooch distracted around cattle. The breed's famous trick is called 'backing.' When a gob of spooked sheep jam into a fenced corner, a kelpie'll charge like a maniac, jump right up over their faces onto their backs, run atop 'em to the fence, drop to the ground, an' raise enough hell to force 'em out to where a horseman can slide in an' move 'em forward from behind. Trouble is, iPooch sees cattle same as sheep. First time she tries backin' a herd of Angus, *she'll* be the one ends up hamburger."

Beyond the cluster of industrial buildings they came upon an anomaly: an old-fashioned white-washed clapboard Grange Hall. "Your McKeig forebears used this building for three generations," Lou Roy said. "Weddings, wakes, place to vote, square dances, every kind o' meeting. Now Doty Nolan an' our new man, Buford Raines, bunk here. A calf roper, Buford just turned twenty-four. Replaced Max Bowler, best man we had, but it could be we come out good. Kale says Buford's the best all-round cowboy he's ever hired, an' Max, who I like despite losin' teeth to him for bein' a dumb shit, found a woman, their own place, an' a foreign breed o' health food cattle he hopes to market."

They drove out onto rolling grasslands pretty as a picture, but as fast as iPooch relaxed Risa grew tense. The beauty of the open country made it all the more troubling to see hundreds of survey stakes laying out the impending ranchettes, condos, golf course, and mall. "With the ad campaign going I'm surprised building hasn't started," Risa said.

"They'll wait till a percentage buys in, Kale says, then poop out the whole deal in one spring, summer, an' fall. If you hope the hordes aren't comin', take a look over this next rise."

They crested a swell. A half mile ahead, atop tableland fifty or sixty feet above the river, stood the most ostentatious log structure Risa had ever seen. "What do they call *that*?"

"*The Grand Lodge on the Elkmoon*," Lou muttered. "Four stories and thirty-thousand square feet o' what Tex calls 'Old West luxury.' Every dead log old-growth Montana ponderosa, yet every tree Tex plants is as nonnative as he is. Even the lawn's trucked in from Oregon, same as the golf course'll be. Montana-grown grass idn't phony enough to suit 'em."

Everywhere Risa looked the aura was mega-corporate, and the bustle suggested NorBanCo was taking the valley by storm. A heliport with three parked choppers included a behemoth with front and rear blades. An asphalt parking lot sported thirty or more high-end SUVs and pickups, with parking space for a hundred more.

Four hundred yards shy of the lodge the road dipped into a stand of cottonwoods, and Risa had a notion. "Could you hold up, Lou? Seeing we've reached the enemy fortress, I'd like to do some recon solo, so I don't incriminate you or Kale. I won't be twenty minutes."

Lou Roy parked under the trees and checked his pocket watch. "Make it fifteen an' we're on time for the good lunch the Pope's making us."

"Deal," Risa said, and took off at a fast trot toward the Grand Lodge bustle. She wove through service people in electric carts and delivery vehicles driving to and fro among a multitude of outbuildings. Men were using a compressor to blow the water out of the lawn's sprinkler system to winterize it. The lawn itself must have covered twenty acres. Six men in formation were swinging around leaf blowers so loud it seemed they were trying to scare the leaves back up onto the trees. Risa slowed to a walk, tied back her hair, strode up the eight massive stone steps onto the lodge's wraparound roofed veranda, reminded herself to look self-important, and entered the gigantic main doors.

The first four people she encountered were maids. When Risa smiled, all four dropped their gaze as if lack of eye contact was mandatory. Executive types passed by, many of whom did the opposite of drop their gaze, some of them dressed like golfers despite the lack of golf course, others like fly-fishers or hunters so unconvincing they seemed to be playing dress-up.

At the entrance to the lodge's Great Room, Risa snatched a brochure from a display table and strolled in. To her surprise the room was empty, but the look of it made her mutter, "*Whoa! Our Lady of the Hostile Merger Cathedral!*" Massive log roof beams and trusses loomed so high overhead it seemed the owner might be a fairy-tale giant. Above the beams the subdued light from recessed skylights might have generated a feeling of reverence had the ninety-seven-key Bösendorfer Imperial grand piano, gaudy Ahab Gilhooley glasswork, Charlie Russell rip-off paintings, and Nouveau Manifest Destiny decor not been designed to induce abject envy over the room's cost. "Our second and third stories," the brochure crooned, "offer luxury suites with twelve-foot ceilings, private Jacuzzis, fully stocked kitchenettes and bars, bear and bison skin rugs, and—" Risa tossed the brochure onto the strings of the Bösendorfer in disgust.

At the room's far end she spied a ten-by-six-foot wood and ironwork door, noticed a small sculpture affixed to it, and realized she was seeing Tex Schiller's Sitting Bull door knocker. Feeling instantly furious, she had a furious idea. Why not "knock" on Tex's door by kicking the crap out of it with her boots, impersonate a Brokeback client in love with one of the luxury ranchettes, then tell Schiller that his outrageous door knocker changed her mind, convincing her that the whole Brokeback development was a scam?

En route to Schiller's door, however, she lost momentum. An ambient sense of suffering hung heavy in the air. When she stopped walking and tried to determine the source, her attention fell on ten enormous ponderosa-pine boles, thirty feet tall, deployed as pillars to support the enormous crossbeams and trusses. Stripped of their bark, lacquered, and spotlit to create dramatic shine, the boles bore a disturbing resemblance to sweat-slicked human torsos. Their sunwise straining was so muscular it felt *alive*. Torn from their forests, bound by massive black bolts and ironwork, the pillars fairly wept that they'd been ten of the most magnificent trees left in Montana, and what was left of them was in torment. Risa's eyes filled. "*Organ of speech departed,*" she whispered. "*Eyes gone. Ears extinguished. Mind snuffed out.*"

She reached Schiller's door. Sitting Bull's astounding face, though miniaturized, was disturbingly well rendered. But so many oily white hands had grabbed his cheekbones to bang his warbonnet against a bronze plate that the nose and cheeks had turned a green to match her queasiness. "Enough!" she snapped, and she spun on her heel, crossed the Great Room and entry hall at full stride, stepped out into blinding sunlight on the veranda—

and collided *hard,* shoulder to shoulder, with a man glancing at a newspaper as he turned to enter the lodge. They each spun to apologize. The sight of Risa then caused the man to eye her up and down with a smile that made her feel as if she'd been seated in a warm puddle of questionable origin. "*Well* now," he drawled. "How do *you* do?"

Realizing she'd collided with the Concierge himself, Risa's intuition flashlight turned on full blast: *Give this man nothing! Get away NOW! No eye contact, no words, no voice. Run!*

Her obedience was total.

Midway through his second scotch at happy hour, Tex would ask his bartender, an Elkmoon local, "Is it a thing in Montana for a beautiful woman to run smack into a man, say not a word about it, respond to his friendly greeting by runnin' like a greyhound for a distant grove of trees, meet up with a small dog that flies up into her arms, catch him like a football, hop in a piss-yellow pickup driven by a shady lookin' old cowpoke, and tear out of the grove as if ten squad cars are after 'em?"

The bartender considered it, then said, "Nope. Not even in Montana could such a thing happen. My advice, Tex. Lay off the *Dukes o' Hazzard* reruns an' let's freshen that drink."

Unlikelihood #4: Two Fists Against the Dark

As Lou Roy and Risa left the cottonwoods he started quietly cursing at the way NorBanCo's oiled high road forced all motorists to pay obeisance to the Grand Lodge by driving a semicircle around it from a reverent three-hundred-yard distance. Lou couldn't stop cursing until they approached another massive metal warehouse, where he took a left as if to access its loading dock, but veered into a stand of pines—and Risa was stunned to find them traversing a dusty ranch road like those of a Montana a century gone.

Risa sighed with relief and downed her window. iPooch climbed onto her lap and stuck her head out into the breeze. All human structures vanished. The dust of the road was so deep in places that Lou's tires splashed it aside with a sound similar to water. "Funny how the driest thing goin' makes a noise so wet," he mused. The road ran south to the Elkmoon River's edge. A side channel came so close the pickup felt more like a boat as it flushed ducks and herons from beaver ponds. A northern harrier, cruising low over cattails, veered so close Lou had to brake. "Careful there, handsome," he muttered, then pointed ahead. "You're gonna like this, Miss Risa."

A quarter mile in front of them a massive granite hoodoo, two hundred feet in diameter and three hundred feet tall, loomed up by the river. Risa did an astonished double take: the Elkmoon flowed close by the hoodoo on its west side, disappeared behind it, and on the east side came flowing straight back at them! The two flows ran so close together in such opposed directions that Risa first thought they were two separate rivers. "The Elkmoon River pulled a U-turn behind a single big rock!"

"Pope says it's a 200-degree turn. The big curved cliff across the water's what changes the river's mind. Didn't look possible, does it?"

"Does this place have a name?" she asked.

"The hoodoo's called Block an' Tackle Rock. The river turnaround is Elbow Bend. Soon as we round the bend and leave the river you're gonna meet your family history on former Broussard and McKeig land."

Instantly in love with the way the very psyche of the land changed, Risa feasted her eyes upon the sloeblack, slow, black, crowblack landscape of her father's boyhood nights and days. She had expected beauty. She had not expected the five big glacial furrows they began to traverse. As the pickup dropped into each quarter-mile-wide trough the world grew intimate and sheltered; atop the next crest it turned as expansive as an inland sea. The contrasts mesmerized. So did the inhabitants. Atop one swell, six prong-horns eyed them from a distance. In the trough beyond, a mother coyote was teaching two gangly pups to hunt rodents. On the next swell's summit the eagle perched on a fence post was not a bald but a golden—the first Risa had ever seen.

As they topped the fifth swell a broad bench of nearly level land came into view, and the McKeig and Broussard forebears had taken full advan-tage. Two enormous fields stretched out before them, one planted in hay, one in alfalfa, both long since harvested. "Over nine hundred arable acres," Lou Roy said. "Your fore folks' bread an' butter. It's Land & Beef cattle feed now. We harvested July 5th. There'll be no second cutting with this drought. But look sharp. We're comin' up on somethin' extra special."

Beyond the harvested fields a gleaming spring creek meandered through junipers, sage, pines, and cottonwoods. When the road drew close, Lou pulled over and parked. They climbed out and stepped up to the pellucid flow. Water weeds waved like slow green flames between banks burgeoning with horsemint and pale blue forget-me-nots. "Used to be they called it Spring Creek," Lou Roy said. "But when your great-gramma passed, as I'm sure Dave told you, they changed the name to Stella Creek."

Risa eyes welled instantly. "He *never* told me! I had no idea, Lou Roy!"

Lou rolled a Bugler, and smoke rode his words as he said, "Easy, Risa. Hearin' a story 'bout a thing we can't see, we don't feel much. Seein' the thing the same time its name connects to your people, the feelin' goes deep. I'm sure Dave was waitin' to give you that big feelin' in person."

Hearing Stella's name as she studied the way the flow wound north for a sinuous half mile, then entered the Elkmoon in a lagoon covered with silvery rise rings, Marisa Stella the Younger felt herself being planted like a tree. Though her feelings were sad, the beauty of the place imbued her sorrow with a richness she'd never known. She longed to return to *precisely* this place, letting Stella Creek's pensive flow have its way with her from now till the day she was no more.

Then she remembered something perfectly awful: "*This* is the place NorBanCo's going to turn into private fishing beats with gazebo bars and asphalt cart paths!"

"That's why you needed to see it now," Lou said. "Times like these, Miss Risa, it can hurt to hell just to love a good thing. Take your time memorizin' Stella the way nature made it." And he strolled away, leaving Risa to the hurt of the pure flow, green flames, rise rings, and beloved name of the good doomed thing.

WHEN THEY CONTINUED their exploration by truck, two ponds came into view. The first, ten acres in size, was encircled by a half-moon of cottonwoods and sported two rafts of ducks. "That pond's spring fed and food rich. There's six or eight browns the size o' salmon in there, so Tex give it the name Big Salmon Pond to invite fools to come catch an' kill 'em. An' see the four new duck blinds on each of the pond's four sides? The day Brokeback's up an' runnin' there'll be ten or twelve shotguns per duck."

Picturing the greenish pall on Tex's Sitting Bull door knocker, Risa began to seethe.

"The small pond ahead's called Cowkiller. Hot days they'd wade in to cool an' get stuck on the quick-mud bottom. The lucky ones drowned. The unlucky, come night, fed the predators. Took Kale years to convince Tex that cattle with eaten-off faces weren't good for his business or ours. We solved that last month with the damnedest fence you ever saw. No barbs in the extra-stout wire, and if moose or elk charge it the whole fence collapses, then stands right back up. Deer jump it. Pronghorns crawl under. Cattle leave it be."

Lou Roy's pleasure in the fence helped Risa cool down a little. The road on both sides grew lined with Lombardy poplars so massive they formed a long leafy tunnel. "Dave mentioned this tunnel!" Risa said. "Stella's homestead is coming up!"

Lou Roy said nothing but seemed to slump a little. As they emerged from the poplars they came upon hand-built stone fences created by the laborious clearing of big, rectangular fields, obvious evidence of a ranch. But not a structure in sight.

Risa's heart sank as Lou pulled over. "Hated to tell ya, Miss Risa. Stella's place is gone. Her home had a beauty they don't try for no more. Burned to the ground two years after Dave's folks sold it. Chimney fire. Folks bought it didn't know what creosote was. But it was Tex ordered the barn, outbuildings, fences, potato cellar, pump house, cattle sheds, an' orchard all tore down an' burned. An' our crew's the ones had to burn it. Talk about salt in a wound. All of it in good shape—an' what kinda fool burns a fruit orchard? Kale fought Tex hard. He wanted that barn for me. 'Not part of the Brokeback Vision,' Tex kept sayin'. 'We're returnin' it all to Mother Nature.' Hope I live to see that ass-bite do the same."

The sense of rootedness that had poured into Risa by Stella Creek vanished. Some kind of Vedic-Western rage rose up in its place. "This *Nor-BanCo-owned NorBanCo-asphalted NorBanCo-razed-and-burned bullshit* is bullshit!" she fumed. "*There is a path, extremely fine and extending far! That beneath which the year revolves, the breathing behind breathing, the first, the ancient! With the heart alone I have beheld it!* This land is the beating heart of the entire valley and it's not gonna roll over and play dead for some fucked-up fake-Western golf ranch. This place is gonna push back! I can feel it, Lou Roy!"

Lou donned the near-grimace that was his smile and eased the truck forward. "I didn't follow the half o' that, but I caught this much. NorBanCo owns a lot, but they sure as shit don't own you or Kale. You're gonna love his inholdings, Miss Risa. They're what the Butte Irish would call 'two fists against the dark.'"

As they were topping the next long incline a lightning rod seemed to rise out of the earth, followed by a cupola, then the cedar shake roof of the barn upon which the cupola perched. "I'm thinking that shake roof was three Glory Meadow cedars last year," Risa said.

Lou shook his head in admiration. "You don't miss much, do you?"

When the twenty-acre Broussard inholding was fully in view, Lou Roy stopped so Risa could study it. "See how it worked? This trough gave the Broussards winter shelter an' privacy year-round. Previous trough did the same for the McKeigs. The two families shared ditches, water sources, helped each other with brandin' an' roundups, did what neighbors do. Then Vietnam left your Uncle Charlie feelin' he gained a right to shoot any bird or animal year-round. Ducks with nestlings. Does with fawns. Kale warned him twice. But when Charlie shot two trumpeter swan cygnets Kale collected them and turned Charlie in. He went to jail rather than pay the fine. Never spoke to us again. Seemed a real bad deal at the time. Then Dave's folks sold the place, Stella died, along come NorBanCo, an' when we met Tex an' his bosses we wished the Lord would give us back good ol' mean ol' Charlie."

As they approached Kale's acreage it took on the intricately tended, homespun, historic look Tex purged wherever he found it. Sixteen big ponderosas—"yellow pine," Lou called them—shaded the big yard and fifty-year-old log home that had replaced the homesteader cabin. A lawn rife with dandelions and clover was unsprayed so horses could graze. Seven-foot-tall post-and-pole fencing with hog wire kept out elk and deer, enclosing the lawn and large garden. At the front gate a red, white, and blue mailbox perched atop a twelve-foot pole, sporting the words: AIR MAIL. Every outbuilding was handsomely weathered, hand rather than factory built, and sported the river rock and mortar foundations that had preceded concrete. Late-blooming pink, purple, and white hollyhocks flourished in every foundation's crack.

On Lou's face rare emotion showed as, parking by the barn, he said, "My second home thanks to Kale." To restore his stoic facade he turned to iPooch, feigned excitement, and huffed, "Mouse!" The kelpie flew over his lap and out the window, hit the ground running, tore into the barn, and began jamming her face into the cracks between stacked hay bales. Lou Roy and Risa followed her in.

The barn was sound despite its seventy-plus years. Having grown up in the Northwest, Risa was constantly surprised by wood's longevity in Montana. The big riding arena was entirely utilitarian. Fresh-groomed footing. No grandstand. A half dozen old wooden stools for spectators to park on. "My kinda barn," Lou said. "Just a big quiet space to get serious with horses in."

He ducked into a tack room, brought out a bucket of battered apples, handed it to Risa, led her to the stalls. Up ahead she heard a nicker. "*Grey!*"

Lou Roy let her snack and fuss over him, then introduced her to his six current cutting horses, Kale's big roan Eisenhower, Eddie's mare Madre, and three fit-looking quarter horses belonging to Buford Raines. Of a sullen little pony Lou said, "Rosalia's mount. *Beelzebub.* Don't offer him an apple an' find out why."

As they turned to leave, iPooch trotted up holding a mouse by the tail— but then dropped it on purpose and streaked out of the barn. Pope's F-250 had rolled up outside.

As Risa and Lou left the barn he roared, "*Sons a bitches!*" Ten wild turkeys were creeping into the orchard of thirty or so trees. "How 'bout you tell the Pope howdy while I race them gobblers to the year's last pears?" Lou said. Risa nodded and they were off.

Kale awaited her beneath the AIR MAIL box. "Welcome to my home, such as it is," he said, waving her ahead up the sidewalk to the front door, unlocked as always, onto a sleeping porch with several shelves of books, farther into a book-laden living room, then even a book-laden dining room, and on into his kitchen. As he began making what he called "roast beast sandwiches," iPooch parked beneath the platter of beef he'd pulled from the icebox and peered up at him with her charm turned on full blast. "Dream on," Kale growled as he sliced the beef thin with startling speed and precision.

"So tell me, Risa. What was the best thing you saw today, and what was the worst?"

"Three-way tie for best," Risa answered. "One: an enormous flock of snow geese *way* high over the Elsewhere Bar & Grill. My dad loved that place. The geese brought his love to life. Two: the former Broussard and McKeig spreads with their glacial swells and troughs, ponds and huge fields, animals and birds. Three: Stella Creek. Seeing what Stella and Dave lost, I now have a feel for why Stella took sick, and why Dave lost his bearings once she and his home were gone."

"Wish I didn't know the feeling," Kale said. "How 'bout the worst thing?"

"Two of those," Risa said. "One. Having driven the entire valley, I believe the McKeig and Broussard spreads are the living heart of it, and Tex's plans for that heart make me heartsick. The other worst. Those ten giant ponderosa pillars holding up the beams in the Grand Lodge Great Room. They made it feel like a torture chamber in there. I fled the room before I broke down crying."

Kale peered at Risa. "When I was a boy my mother once called Dave's Grandma Stella 'a sensitive,' like the word was a noun. I'd never heard it used that way. You just made me want to use it again. Those pillars were as majestic as ponderosas get. Two were tribal medicine trees. NorBanCo greased political palms to get at them, but their taking was a crime. Three tribal elders, an Indian lawyer, and a half dozen University of Montana students drove up to defend the first medicine tree from NorBanCo's logging crew. I went too, and stood close by, but couldn't join the circle round the tree 'cause I'd be fired. 'No protest' is in my contract—and the day I'm fired a *lot* of vulnerable things will go unprotected."

Kale stopped building sandwiches, reached in a cupboard, and poured two shots of whiskey. "Given our topic, whaddya say, Risa?"

"No thanks," she said, then wished she'd said yes when Kale downed them both.

"The elders called the ancient ponderosa a Grandmother Tree. A Nez Perce girl studying forestry told me they're communication hubs. With hands that moved like a hula dancer's, she showed how their root systems and the mycelial network team up to send nutrients and water through huge swaths of forest. I had a head full of questions for her when three squad cars rolled in and six cops got out, gripping nightsticks. When the elders and kids locked arms round the Grandmother and I didn't join 'em, something in me died. When I saw a trooper shoving the Nez Perce girl's face into his hood though she lay docile as a fawn, I nearly went to prison for a long damn time, and still half wish I had. *The last look that girl gave me. My impotent fury. Ten forest Grandmothers dead to serve corporate vanity.* I'll carry all that to my grave."

"Close one!" Lou Roy called out as he ratcheted in the back door with six pears, two of them turkey pecked. While Lou cut away the pecks, washed, and sliced them, Risa took the iced tea Kale made into the dining room and set the table. Lou served the pears, Kale the sandwiches. The nutty bread and late butter lettuce were pleasant surprises to Risa, the mountain of rare beef slathered with hot horseradish no surprise at all.

As they ate, Kale pointed out the dining room's log walls. "Yellow pine. Standing dead, every one. First beetle kill I ever saw. The wiggly incisions are the tunnels they leave as they eat their way through the cambium. My dad liked standing dead, wigglies be damned, because they're sun-dried and cured and hold their straightness. Ancient ponderosa's a different story. When Grand Lodge doors an' lintels kept going cattywampus, Tex would call the builders, blaming *them* nothing stays plumb. The trouble was Tex himself using huge logs he didn't let cure. The builders fought back. An inspector NorBanCo couldn't buy made Tex watch as he measured crossbeams, lintels, and walls, then came back after three months and measured again. There's logs all over that Lodge twisting upward, downward, and both kinds of sideways. I'm no *sensitive*, Risa. But a Nez Perce girl I can't get out of my dreams might say that what you felt in that Great Room are ten forest Grandmothers, blinded like Samson by the Philistines, in some tormented kind of communication with an incompletely killed forest they feel around them on all sides."

Seeing Risa's harrowed expression, Lou was pure gentleness as he passed her the pears.

Unlikelihood #5: Greater Good Headquarters

As the old Cheyenne left Kale's home the road curved away from the river and wound up Schoolhouse Bluff—Kale's second fist against the dark. Three hundred yards short of the summit Lou Roy pulled into a stand of pines, parking in front of a padlocked length of cable strung between trees to keep cars from taking the grass track leading up to the school. As they climbed out and leaned into the incline iPooch streaked ahead to scare off the hopper-hunting magpies. "I like retired traces like this," Lou said as he ratcheted along. "Keep cows an' vehicles off a track a few years, give it a mow now an' again, an' it takes on a gentleness. We'll reach that school feelin' better'n if we drove up. On foot a fella actually *arrives*."

As they topped out at the schoolyard, a fella named Risa sure enough arrived. "Compared to what your families lost," Lou Roy said, "the hundred acres Kale saved here ain't much. But it's a shit ton better'n nuthin'. The bluff edge has long views prettier'n any Brokeback can offer, the river bottom's all floodplain an' can't be developed, but thanks to Montana law it *can* be fished, hunted, camped, boated, an' rode."

The place was everything Risa had hoped it might be. The views up and downriver, and across to the Testament Creek Canyon, were spectacular. The schoolyard featured a quaint old kid-sized baseball field, a towering rope swing hanging off a lone ponderosa, a rooftop cupola with a big bronze school bell and lightning rod. Lou pointed out Eddie and Rosalia's Airstream two hundred yards east and his identical Airstream four hundred yards west, their views so grand behind them the trailers looked like silver ladybugs.

The Testament Creek School was a hip-roofed square, twenty-six feet tall at the peak, painted white. Three of four walls had a centered eight-by-eight-foot window consisting of sixty-four one-foot panes. The fourth wall, opposite the front door, had a slant-roof addition that housed a simple kitchen and small bathrooms still labeled GIRLS and BOYS.

Instead of going inside, Lou Roy circled to the front entrance, sat down on the steps, and said, "Mind joinin' me a minute, Miss Risa? I got a little somethin' to say."

When Risa sat, Lou Roy's glacial-silt eyes locked in on the Elkmoon peaks forty miles west. Having long since noticed how he gazed into distances to make room for the larger things on his mind, Risa summoned her full attention.

"So I drop by Kale's last night an' he pours us a Dickel. I take a sip an' says, 'I got a request.' Kale says, 'A bigger Dickel?' I keep it serious. 'Sometimes we know a thing without knowin' how we know it,' I says. 'Here's one such thing. Risa McKeig belongs to this valley the way ol' Stella did. Sees it clearer'n anybody, same as Stella. You know this, Kale. I seen it in your eyes that first night with her by the fire.' Kale says, 'I do feel that. What's your request?'

"I says, 'When Risa comes to the Elkmoon, not just this trip but *every* trip, you need to let her turn your schoolhouse into a headquarters.' 'Headquarters for what?' he says. I says, 'Hell if I know. Risa's the one'll know. She knows all kinds o' shit we don't. An' whatever she decides, people'll be better off because of it. All we need to do is set back an' watch it happen.' Kale says, 'You know what, Lou? I saw Stella in Risa so clear at lunch yesterday that what you're sayin' makes some kind of lunatic sense.' An' he pours us more Dickel, we drink to your headquarters, an' that's where it stands. If you feel called, Miss Risa, the Pope'd like this school to house what you feel it's *meant* to house. An' me, Kale, an' Eddie'll help you fix it up how you want. An' Rosalia'll drive us all batshit while we do." Facing Risa at last, he asked, "Whaddya say?"

Now it was Risa who gazed west to the Elkmoon Mountains. "I say that's a super kind offer. And I love this bluff. The quiet here has a liveliness to it and I feel the Elkmoon Valley's own lively mind might be its cause. So, for starters, how would it be if I slip inside the school alone, get real quiet, and try to sense how the valley itself might feel about your offer?"

"That right there," Lou said, "is what I mean about you knowin' shit I don't. Take all the time you need. I'll be close by." With which he stood, whistled iPooch, and walked off to the bluff edge to scan the Testament Creek Canyon across the river for elk.

Risa stepped up to the schoolhouse door, lifted the open padlock from the hasp, swung the door open. At the sight of a century-old schoolroom flooded with warmth and light she froze. Closed her eyes. Whispered, "*Hoping You don't mind repetition: Lord of Love unmanifest. Become manifest. Draw Yourself out of Yourself. Touch me. Were You not here, who would breathe?*"

She stepped inside.

THIRTY OR SO minutes later Risa emerged with a face freshly washed in the schoolhouse sink and a shirttail soaked from drying it. Lou Roy was waiting on the steps.

"You cleaned up," he said.

"I did," Risa said.

"An' took your time in there," he added.

"I did," she said.

"I'm thinkin' this ol' valley had a thing or two to say."

Oh, it did. Which was why Risa stood silent, pondering how much to reveal. She knew Lou would like hearing how she stood gazing for long minutes out each of the sixty-four-paned windows, east, south, and west. She knew he'd like it that when she reached the west window and found ten miles of shoreline cottonwoods streaming twin rivers of golden leaf light while the Elkmoon streamed blue betwixt the gold, she couldn't tear herself away. But she also knew she'd be pushing it if she told how the sun then achieved a lower angle that backlit the cottonwoods the same instant it turned the blue Elkmoon to blazing mercury. And there was no question that if she attempted to tell how the three rivers were joined by what felt like the Unseen Unborn Guileless Mind of the Valley, how the top of her head again opened at *vidriti,* the cleft, and how a fourth river of Love unmanifest became manifest and she wept so hard for gratitude it left her a royal mess, hence the face wash and shirttail cleanup, Lou was almost certain to say, *That right there's what I mean 'bout you knowin' shit we don't.*

So she kept it simple: "As far as I can feel, Lou Roy, this old schoolhouse invites us to use her to try and coax the greater good of the entire valley to come out and play. And by 'greater good' I mean every life-form that dwells here, not just the humans—and by 'life-form' I also mean air, wind, weather, water, rocks, light, and subtler presences for as long as we're lucky enough to be here."

Lou Roy smiled his wince of a smile, shook his head and dirty black Stetson just once, and said, "That's good to hear, Miss Risa. That's real good to hear."

Unlikelihood #6: The Boy by the River

Deep into the night in the Testament Creek School, Risa was awakened by the exact same dream she'd had the night before. This had never before happened to her. Both dreams began with her walking in sunlight by the Elkmoon River, then glancing down to find, trundling along at her side, a clear-eyed, messy-haired, adorably rough-and-tumble-looking boy of four or five. Each time they stepped over uneven river cobble or drew close to fast water the boy would reach for her hand—and how she loved the feel of that trusting little hand. When the river gentled and the shore grew grassy or sandy, he'd release her hand and wander free, and she loved his independence as much as the feel of his hand. In both dreams the boy never spoke, so Risa didn't either. In both dreams the air was so clear, the light so vivid, every stone, tree, water plant, bird, pool, riffle so articulate in shape and color that the river radiated joy. When the boy would then look up into Risa's eyes, the same joy, distilled, flew into her with such intensity that her pounding heart woke her, alone in the dark, wanting nothing more than to be back by the river with the little wild boy.

The second time she dreamed him, the possibility that such a child might be making his way toward her caused Risa to whisper to him: "Where are you, little boy? *Who* are you? Is there any way I can help you make your way toward me? And in our next dream, will you talk to me? I want to hear your little voice! I want to sit on a log by the river, set you in my lap, and cut the pitch knots out of your messy hair. I want to piggyback you up the bluff, sit with you on the schoolhouse steps, and feed you raspberries, brown sugar, and cream. I want to bring you inside, kiss your little forehead when it frowns, kiss your cheeks when you smile, and tell you stories and stories to sweeten your sleep. Oh, unseen unborn little river boy! Where did you come from, where are you now, and what is making me love you so?"

Unlikelihood #7: Ode to a Booby-Trapped Name

On Saturday morning, October 12th, Risa unlocked the cable blocking the track up to Testament Creek School, drove the Crimson Exploiter on up to the school's front door, and began carrying a multitude of items inside. On her fourth trip to the car, a petite young Chicana stood by her open back hatch, gaping at her as if at a heavenly host.

"Well, hello!" Risa said. "You must be Rosalia Dominguez."

Rosalia was so transfixed she could barely take the hand Risa offered. In her eight months on the Schoolhouse Bluff, no woman of any description had visited, *ever*. Now this impossibly fascinating woman was carrying furnishings, kitchenware, and clothing inside! Rosa trembled as she piped, "Are *you* the one moving in?"

"For a couple weeks, yes. It's exciting, Rosalia. With Kale and Lou Roy's help I'm going to fix the school up so others can stay here too. And I plan to keep coming back. I really love the Elkmoon Valley. Three generations of my people are from here, and I dearly hope to become the fourth. But now, my friend, may I please have my hand back?"

Rosalia blushed, released Risa's hand, and they smiled huge smiles.

Eddie Dominguez came strolling over. Rosalia introduced him. Eddie asked if he could be of use. "Eventually, yes, thank you, Eddie," Risa said. "But I'm too disorganized for now. If Rosalia would like to hang out, though, I'd love her company."

Eddie smiled at his daughter's ecstatic face. "Fine by me. But if she gets to be a handful, Risa, or more likely six or seven handfuls, feel free to send her home."

When Rosalia shot eye-lightning at Eddie, Risa lifted a box out of the Exploiter for her to carry. "Today's all about handfuls, Eddie. Rosa's just the helper I need."

Eddie strolled back to their Airstream—and as soon as he was out of earshot Rosalia sure enough turned into six or seven handfuls. At not quite nine, she was a nonstop juggler of experimental personas: Hyper-Imaginative Kid, Crackpot Psychologist, Vulnerable Child, Shameless Local Gossip, Passionate Amateur Naturalist, and more. But underlying each was a motherless girl in an all-male world, starved for the example and friendship of a grown woman. In a single chatter-filled hour, Risa became the grown woman of her dreams.

Her first act as Rosa's friend: Risa noticed a jittery silence fell over her every time Lou Roy was mentioned. The reaction was so severe, and its probable cause so obvious to Risa, that after Rosalia went home she did a little detective work.

A brief chat with Eddie informed her of the mountain lion and shotgun scare. A quick exchange with Kale led to a longer call to Max Bowler. A trip into E City and JB Jones's Hardware then told Risa everything she needed to know.

FIRST THING THE next morning—Sunday, October 13th—Lou Roy volunteered his services to Risa as promised, borrowed the Crimson Exploiter, and drove to E City Storage to pick up a list of items Risa had requested for the school's conversion to an Elkmoon Greater Good Headquarters. During his absence Risa invited Rosalia over for tea, casually lured her into a heart-to-heart, and was soon met with an emotional explosion. She soothed Rosalia as best she could, but soothing words from a kind woman turned out to be something Rosa craved so desperately that even the soothing left her distraught, knowing Risa would be leaving in a couple of weeks. No matter how many times Risa promised she'd be back, Rosalia was still raw with emotion when the Exploiter came tooling up the grass track.

When Lou stepped round to the rear hatch, draped an enormous load of lace curtains over his arms, ratcheted up the schoolhouse steps, shoved open the door, and called out a friendly "*How do!*" Rosalia took one look at him and burst into tears again.

Dumbfounded, Lou Roy turned to Risa. "If I done somethin' I don't know I done, tell me quick so I can fix it!"

Before Risa could speak, Rosalia cried, "It's not you, Lou Roy. It's me! I got everything about you *wrong*! When you saved me from the mountain lion, I thought you were just scaring me to be mean. When you told JB never to tell another Mexican joke around me, I thought you'd laughed at the joke. And you only went into JB's to buy tools for the birthday belt you saw me buy Eddie. *And then I got mean!* I learned your high school nickname from Hoot Clark. I found out what Appaloosas look like. And it was *awful* of me to trick poor Max into calling you that. Then everything went *crazy*! I don't know how many times you got beat up trying to get your name back, and I can't ever fix that! All I can do, Risa says, is tell you I'm sorry, and I really, really *am*! But if I were you, Lou Roy, *I'd hate me*!" And out poured more tears.

With the pile of lace curtains still draped over his arms, Lou plunked down on a chair, took the calm, firm tone he used to settle riled horses, stroked the curtains as if they were the horse, and said, "Hey now. You tellin' me all this was brave, okay? An' trickin' Max into callin' me Appaloosa shoulda been funnier'n shit, okay? The craziness was mine, Rosa. But look what come of it! Here sits Miss Risa, about to be our neighbor, and we wouldn't even know her if some jackass name of Appaloosa didn't get sent to Three Forks

Meadow to cool off. And in that meadow it was me—not you, Rosalia—
who tried to scare Risa off with gunfire when she only wanted to lay her
dad's remains to rest. But even for that she forgave me so fast my head's
still spinnin'. So what kinda fool would I be not to forgive you? 'Forgive'
ain't even the word. I *thank you* for the booby-trapped nickname brought
Risa to us. So how about, startin' now, you, me, an' Risa just enjoy bein'
friends? How would that be?"

Rosalia's smile had six wings like the Seraphim as she cried, "I'd *love*
that, Lou Roy!"

Unlikelihood #8: Folk Night at the Ambivalent Cafe

Lorilee Shay had been the morning short-order cook at the Ambivalent
Cafe for three years, but the job was nothing like as grim as one might
imagine. True, cooking breakfasts in E City's favorite cafe paid just $5.15
an hour. True, it ate thirty hours a week Lore could have devoted to music.
But the positives were many. Poke and Lisa Kettle, the old hippies who ran
the cafe, loved Lore and Mu so much they gave them the third-floor corner
apartment with the best view in the Black Queen Hotel for free. Meanwhile
Lore's ongoing meditation and music practices had so transformed her that
her job as breakfast cook had become a spiritual practice: with the cafe's
big grill facing the ten-stool counter, she had endeared herself to so many
E City residents that if she'd run for mayor she'd have won in a landslide.
Likewise, Mu's illegal fifteen-hour-a-week job bussing tables, precocious
music-making, Buddhist practice, calm disposition, and wild imagination
had endeared him to so many that he'd become that rarity in America's
societal ruins, a happy ten-year-old affectionately known and held by his
community. The three years Lore and Mu had spent revering Dōgen's
Mountains and Waters Sutra within striking distance of the Elkmoons had
spawned a love for mountain wanderings they could bring down to the
valley floor as music. And for two and a half years, May through October,
Poke and Lisa had let Lore and Mu turn the Ambivalent into a Sunday
night folk venue that attracted surprisingly good musicians from all over
the country to show a modest but warm crowd what they could do.

In short, Lore and Mu were *not* seeking life changes as they strolled
down from their apartment to Sunday Folk Night at the cafe. They loved
the lives they had going. But not seeking change is no guarantee our lives
aren't about to drastically change.

A GOOD CROWD by E City standards filled the cafe. Maybe seventy people in
attendance, a dozen or so of whom Lore had never even served a breakfast.
Joined by their cello and mandolin playing friends, Chris and Glenn from
Butte's Trout Grass Studio, Lore's foursome took the stage last.

They opened their five-song set with "My Old Mountain" and Lorilee
poured herself into it, as always. But she was also one of those rare

musicians who enjoys studying faces in the crowd as she performs, and three faces at a table front and center captured her interest immediately. Young Rosalia Dominguez and the grizzled old cowboy Lou Roy Skinner were sitting with a stunning dark-haired woman, and the three of them gave off an air of being in some kind of love. This was especially striking to Lore since, as town gossip had it, Lou had recently lost a *lot* of fights due to a nickname Rosa was said to have given him. The reverence with which the regal woman was watching and listening to Lore was matched by the reverence with which Lou Roy and Rosalia watched her listen. The trio began to give Lore heart pangs. Something unknown but vital seemed to hang in the balance. For no reason she could name she felt she *must* establish deep contact with this woman. So, after their first song, she huddled the band.

"I'm of a mind to bag the four tunes we agreed on and go epic just the once," she said. "Chris, Glenn. You up for the 'Sutra'?" Two happy nods.

"Mu, got the F whistle?" He smiled and lifted it out of his guitar case.

"Great! Okay. Deep breaths, everybody. I'll start solo, super pianissimo. You'll feel when to join me." Three more focused nods.

Lore turned to the crowd, scanned them with a smile, paused for a moment at Lou Roy, Rosalia, and the regal woman's table, and sent them a smile. She then lowered her face and let her long, motionless silence gain everyone's attention. Face still lowered, she began singing a cappella in a scarcely audible whisper, added dulcimer of matching softness, and incrementally raised the volume with a foot pedal as she straightened up to sing. The trio she'd hoped to reach was already riveted. So were Kale Broussard and his belle, Ida, and Max Bowler and his bride, Kira.

"Thirteen Tons of Poison Sutra" unfurled. Four verses in, Lore scanned the room again and noticed another strong response from a woman standing against the back wall. Wearing shades, an orange and black San Fran Giants ball cap, and a sweatshirt sporting the words ADD TO CART below an image of a virtual Amazon shopping cart more or less containing her breasts, she seemed a character for sure. But as the song gathered power the woman's mouth moved as she silently sang along, apparently knowing every word of Lore's twenty-three-minute epic.

As catharsis overtook the lyrics and joy overtook Lore and the band, she wondered why this ballad always raised the room to the joy level at the moment it passed into its deepest sorrow. When she voiced the marriage betrayal and the breasts filtering the betrayal's poisons, the regal woman's welling eyes added urgency to Lore's voice. As Rosalia lay her head against the woman's shoulder and Lou Roy looked so shaken he rolled a smoke and had it in his lips before he remembered he couldn't smoke it, Mu kindled the tiny F tin whistle, he and Lore created the mother and child avocets' departure, Lore's voice broke precisely where mythos, Mu's soaring, and the crowd of transported faces invariably broke it, and Lore was stunned, despite her own emotion, to see tears absolutely *cascading* from under Add to Cart's shades while the regal woman's face shone as though a harvest moon had risen inside her very skin.

Their last notes were still faintly sounding when the inwardly lit woman, Lou Roy, Rosalia, Kale, Ida, Max, and Kira took to their feet as one, and the entire crowd followed suit. Yet—amid E City's Sunday Folk Night's first-ever standing ovation—Lore and Risa gazed at each other as if they were the only two people in the room, somehow knowing they'd just found a spiritual sister of the highest order.

Unlikelihood #9: How Come We Can Even Walk?

Skipping her four a.m. meditation the next morning, Lorilee went to work at five and enjoyed the irony of cooking breakfasts for almost exactly as many Elkmooners as had cheered her the night before. Knocking off at eleven, she trudged up to her apartment, lay down on the couch for a rest, and was just dozing off when someone knocked on her door.

Lore rose, opened up—and there, smiling broadly, stood the woman who'd gushed tears, this time without a Giants cap, sunglasses, or ADD TO CART shirt to disguise her.

"Good *God!*" Lore cried. "You're Ona Kutar! I *love* your stuff!"

"And you're Lorilee Shay and I *worship* yours!" Ona told her.

Lore invited her in, offering her a chair at the kitchen table. Before sitting, Ona pulled a folded Ambivalent Cafe placemat from the back pocket of her jeans and unfolded it. "Your son's guitar, tin whistle, and solid harmonies knocked me over last night," she said. "Then at breakfast this morning, bussing tables, he knocked me over again. How old is Mu anyway?"

"Ten until January."

"Just ten? That's crazy!"

"Why? What did he do?" Lore asked.

"He took a short break from bussing, sat in a corner with his day pack, pulled out scribbled notes I rightly guessed was research of some kind, and started writing neatly in a spiral notebook. Total concentration. Me so curious I couldn't stand it. When his break ended and he came by to bus my table, I introduced myself. I liked that he'd heard of me but didn't blink an eye. Just said, 'Glad to meet you, Ona. I'm Mu.' I told him your music is out of this world. He said, 'Thanks.' Nothing more. I asked what he was writing. He said, 'Science paper.' I asked, 'What about?' And his reply was so wild I flipped over my placemat, begged him to start over, and took notes. Check this out, Lore."

Ona unfolded the placemat: "'Here is our astronomical reality this quiet morning,' said your son. If we were standing on the equator, Earth's rotation would have us traveling at fourteen hundred miles per hour. At the same time we're revolving around the sun at sixty-seven *thousand* miles an hour. Meanwhile the sun is orbiting the Milky Way at about *four hundred sixty-five thousand miles an hour.* 'So I hate to tell you,' Mu says—looking like he *loved* telling me—'that the Cosmic Background Explorer satellite just discovered that the Milky Way's two hundred billion stars including all their planets and solar systems, *plus* a whole cluster of *other* galaxies called the Local Group, just *one* of which is the Andromeda galaxy with its *three hundred billion* stars, are *all* speeding toward the Hydra constellation at about *1.34 million miles an hour.*' With a devilish grin he added, 'And I left out that Earth is wobbling on its axis. You're really coordinated to keep all that coffee in your cup, Ona!'"

Lorilee was laughing now.

"'Since you're older and wiser than me,' Mu continued, 'can I ask *you* a couple questions?' How foolish I was to nod yes! 'How come we can even *walk*?' he said. 'How come, traveling at insane speeds in four different directions at once, there are such things as calm evenings, still waters, silence, feelings of peace? What kind of impossible gyroscopes are keeping our chairs and tables and us from being blown out the cafe windows or into its brick walls? What's stopping all seven continents and oceans from being hurricaned off the planet till all that's left of what used to be Earth is a smudge of intergalactic space crud?'

"As his ride to school, thank God, showed up, I said, 'Great to meet you, Mu. And now if you don't mind, I need to wash down three ibuprofen with four whiskies, take a twenty-four-hour nap, and sign up for six months of trauma therapy.' '*Great to meet you too, Ona!*' Mu says with a cherubic grin, and off he scoots to school."

"That's my boy," Lore said, evincing the same steady calm Ona had admired in Mu. "His mind's so active I helped him skip a grade last year. Boredom was luring him into interests more worrisome than intergalactic space crud."

"If boredom's still an issue for him, or you, Lore," Ona said, "it's time I told you why I'm here. My band and I just cut a retrospective double album called *Life Works ('Cept When It Don't)*. Starting in late February we're gonna tour twenty-five American cities, take a rest till summer, then tour twenty more in Europe. I loved your first two albums so much I had my brilliant assistant, Regina Cloud, seek out your next performance so we could see how you struck us live. Through some kind of internet voodoo Regina found your Ambivalent Cafe gig, we flew up to watch, and *oh my hell!* In a venue that did nothing for you, you blew us away. I've got an afternoon flight out, so I'll cut to the chase. How would you and Mu feel about opening for the Ona Kutar Band on our US tour and, if that goes as well as I know it will, our European tour too? Uh-oh! *What's wrong*, Lore?"

Not till Ona reacted did Lore realize she'd been shaking her head. "Sorry! That was my *I can't believe this is happening* headshake. I'm so stunned I can't think!"

"Then let me unstun you a little," Ona said. "Touring will feel a bit crazy at first. But as Mu might say, invisible gyroscopes hold a good touring band together. My manager, Richie, and four-man band are excellent company and they'd look out for you both. My assistant, Regina, is the world's youngest great vegan chef, a total sweetheart, and I'll eat one of my boots if you two aren't instant friends. Our crowds get a little rowdy but are almost always warm. The tour bus is cozy. The pay would be excellent, the music-making a thrill, and to help my fans become your fans I can also imagine you, me, and Mu doing a...*Lore*! Which kind of headshake are you doing now?"

"I'm so overwhelmed I'm down to just one idea, Ona. Mu is our manager. He has a calming effect on me. What say we hop in my truck, kid-snatch him out of school, and talk this thing over like three intelligent ten-year-olds?"

"What a solid idea! Let's do it."

And down the stairs and out the Black Queen's back door they went. But when Lorilee stepped up to the hotel's rickety carport and unlocked a classic green '54 Chevy pickup in perfect condition, Ona slammed to a halt. "This is the last straw!" she barked. "This can't be your truck, you and Mu can't be you and Mu, and I'm not in some backwater called *Elkmoon City* trying to talk two of the most evolved beings on the planet into touring with the no-account likes of me. Tell me when this dream's *over,* will ya?"

Lore laughed. They hopped in. They kid-snatched Mu. They strategized like intelligent ten-year-olds. And Ona's weird dream ended up lasting for eight great musical months.

III. Blue Empty

Many of us have been running all our lives.
Practice stopping.

—Thich Nhat Hanh

LORILEE WAS BY nature an unusually serene person. But as the reality of touring with the Ona Kutar Band sank in, she realized that, much as she'd liked Ona, the impact on her and Mu's lives was sure to be substantial. Though Mu was nothing but exuberant about the prospect, Lore advised him to keep the tour secret. "I'm *serious*," she said. "If word of this gets out in E City our breakfast customers will drive us so crazy we'll want to quit. And we can't *afford* to quit. The Kutar Band tour is top secret."

Though Mu was fine with secrecy, Lore remained so on edge that after Ona left town she skipped another morning's meditation, made tea, and sat at the kitchen window pondering what course of action might calm her. Her first move was obvious: she needed to hike, *today* if possible, to her favorite centering place: a ridge a couple of miles upriver of E City Park. "Blue Empty," she called it. Her second idea was to get together with the wisest friend she knew and raise her touring-with-Ona concerns. But in pondering who that person might be, she realized there was no one she wanted to confide in half as much as the radiant woman at the Ambivalent Cafe concert night before last—and she didn't even know the woman's name.

Putting the idea on hold, Lore went down to work and, as happens in small towns, one of her first customers was Lou Roy, who took a stool close to Lore's grill, broached the subject of a newcomer he'd been showing around, Risa by name, and Lore realized he was describing the Folk Night mystery woman. Ten minutes later she had Lou's account of Risa's fearlessness, charm, noble Elkmoon lineage, altruistic plans for the Testament Creek School, healing of the rift between Lou and Rosalia, and cell phone number.

Lore called Risa on her break.

THREE HOURS LATER Lore eased the '54 Chevy down Parish Lane, passed St. Luke's Church and graveyard, turned into E City Park, and parked in the shade of the rare western cedars towering over the pond. Moments later Risa's Crimson Exploiter rolled up beside her. They climbed out smiling, and embraced as if they'd been doing so for years. "It's so good of you to come," Lore said. "I don't know many people who'd call an invitation to hike to a place called Blue Empty 'irresistible.'"

"Fair warning, Lore. My love of mysticism is extreme to the point of nerdy. If you don't stop me I'll be rattling on about Vedic sages, bhakti poets, and medieval Beguines, all of whom revere a *nothingness* that sounds like Blue Empty to me. As for my nerdiness, after you called I memorized a nerdy verse to consecrate today's adventure. Mind if I recite it?"

"I'd love that," Lore said.

"The speaker is Nāgārjuna, an India Indian Buddhist from the time of Jesus." Closing her eyes without a hint of self-consciousness, Risa let fly with an intensity that stunned Lore:

Sarvaṃ ca yujyate tasya śūnyatā yasya yujyate.
All is possible when emptiness is possible.
Sarvam na yujyate tasya śūnyaṃ yasya na yujyate.
Nothing is possible when emptiness is impossible.

Lore stood frozen a moment, then cried, "That took my breath away! I'm *so* glad we're doing this together!"

"Me too," Risa said, stunning Lore again with a first glimpse of her glee gap.

They walked to the backs of their vehicles, where Lore slid out a hard-used old external frame backpack. Risa looked at it, laughed, and slid out an almost identically outmoded pack. "External frame twins!" she said. "I fell so in love with this old beauty that I wore it to U Dub every day till graduation, lugging around a small library, a huge magnifying glass, binoculars, and a rotation of bird, plant, tree, bug, and other guidebooks. The pack has protective powers too. The people who found it dorky and shunned me were *exactly* the people I wanted to avoid!"

"I understand that magic," Lore said. "My external frame helped me befriend a scruffy Colorado peak named Two Medicine, which bequeathed me eight years of marriage, my son Mu, a spiritually exhilarating divorce, and co-wrote every song on my album *Thirteen Tons*. The songs then inspired a great old friend of mine, Walt Steitz, to give his classic pickup to Mu and me!"

"Heck yeah!" Risa laughed, and they slid into their matching antiques.

As they set out, Lore said, "We're headed two miles west and eight hundred feet up deer trails. Much steeper than hiking trails. Let's take it slow so we can talk. You lead, I'll follow."

"Sounds good," Risa said, and set off at an easy pace.

"The place we're headed won't look like much," Lore told her. "A microburst snapped a ponderosa in half a decade ago. The bottom half's alive and offers shade. The fallen top half is dry pulp now, a nice seat for zazen on the sloped ground. But it's the view that, for me, is an emptiness-inducing wonder."

"While you do zazen, are you okay with me doing my own little practice?" Risa asked.

"Sure. May I ask what that is?"

Risa stopped walking and turned to face Lore. "For your ears only, it's in the bhakti tradition. Path of love. My focus is a name I keep secret. Working with a divine name is a fairly universal practice. The Hesychasts, Hindu *japa yogins,* Tibetan Buddhists, the Mount Athos monks, and many more invoke a divine name. My faves are the Indian poet saints, and a rare few Americans who take a name. For Mirabai and Lal Dêd it's *Narayana,* one of Krishna's names. For a ragamuffin Portland street mystic I know, it's *Ocean.* For Kabir, maybe the best known name poet, it's *Ram,* short for Lord Rama. 'What is a man without Ram?' Kabir says. 'A dung beetle on a busy road.' Another great Ram poet, Tulsidas, is gentler. 'If you would have light within and without, place the Name of Ram on your tongue like a lamp on the threshold.'"

Pleasure shone in Lore's eyes. "Do you *always* talk like this?"

Risa thought it over. "Pretty much, yeah, I'm afraid so!" And they laughed.

"I'm not asking you to give away secrets, but is it possible to say a little about how you work with your secret name?"

"I take guidance from *The Cloud of Unknowing,* the author of which is our old friend Anonymous. *The Cloud* advises that the word we choose be simple, and that it *not* be a theological idea we have to ponder. Better a simple word or name to which we feel drawn, sans thought. We then, quoting Anonymous, 'fasten this word to our heart so that it never goes away.' The word serves as a shield at times, a spear at other times. We use it to 'block' or to 'strike down' thoughts and let them 'dissolve in a pool of forgetting.' If our thoughts offer to 'analyze' our Word and its meanings, we let the Word spear that thought so mercilessly it staggers away bleeding and, hopefully, dies. But of course thoughts, mine anyway, have more lives than cats and zombies put together! So the *Cloud* quote that helps me the most goes like this." Again Risa closed her eyes before reciting: "'It is not a matter of analyzing or elucidating. No one can truly think of God. It is therefore my wish to leave everything that I can think and choose for my love the thing that I cannot think.'"

When Risa's eyes opened, Lore was shaking her head in wonder. "You really *are* like this!"

"Only with those I trust. And trust hit last night the instant I first saw you."

"Same with me," Lore said. "And we'll speak of it no more, choosing for our love the thing we cannot think."

"And keep silence until we get to Blue Empty?" Risa asked.

"*Yes.*"

WHEN THEY REACHED the broken ponderosa, shed their packs, sat in the duff, and took in the view, Risa immediately saw what drew Lorilee to the place: the South Whitetail ridges on which they were seated formed a huge C curve. Seven miles across the valley, the North Whitetails formed a matching C bending the opposite way. The two curves formed an enormous circular bowl cleanly broken in half by the Elkmoon River.

"May I speak?"

Risa smiled. "Of course. But you're so kind for asking, Lore!"

She smiled back. "My ex is a conqueror of mighty peaks and walls, but my love for mountains has two sources: Zen Master Dōgen's *Mountains & Waters Sutra,* and Appalachian mountain music. The latter gave me a soft spot for working-class hills like this one. Modest mountains lead to lyrics I can carry down to the people in the valleys below—whereas, name me one good folk song with Everest or K-2 in it."

Risa smiled. "Good point! So have you carried any songs about your Blue Empty experiences down?"

"You know, I haven't," Lore said. "They're too uncanny. To speak of them could sound like spiritual bragging, which I would hate, since they're not *my* experiences at all. This place experiences *itself* without ceasing, and somehow I disappear into that experience here."

"Wow!" Risa said. "Can you say more about these disappearances?"

Lore lifted an enormous beach towel out of her pack, unwrapped what was inside, and the instant Risa caught sight of Lore's Buddha icon she felt strong affection. "That pearl earring is priceless! How it *feminizes* him. I've never seen a Buddha I felt more drawn to. It reminds me of the femininity of many Krishna images."

"I call her Elmerina Buddha, since her first pearl was an accident, made of Elmer's wood glue when I broke and repaired her ear. I recently asked Eddie Dominguez to refinish her head to toe, repair her cracked lobe, and replace the glue with a real pearl."

When Lore handed the icon to Risa, she marveled at the way the pearl feminized the slender waist, rounded countenance, plucked-looking eyebrows. "I'm smitten, Lore. Elmerina invokes everything I love about the divine feminine! Don't answer if the question is impertinent, but how do you and Elmerina experience Blue Empty?"

Lore drew a deep breath, and visibly calmed as she released it. "It was so simple. The first time I came here I sat exactly where you're sitting and situated Elmerina beside me. We faced north toward the valley bowl. An experience of emptiness rose up, and in one breath my only awareness was of the bowl. Name, sex, genus, species, vanished. Thoughts, narratives, angst, self-consciousness, gone."

"What remained?" Risa asked.

"The blue tint we see in the air today. It does something mysterious. In Zen circles they talk of 'beginner's mind.' But in Blue Empty there's no beginner, no mind, no ideas. *Everything present* is what's present. Self vanishes. Earth pours form after form into the bowl—like the three hummingbirds we heard a moment ago; the clouds of insects down over the Elkmoon; the waxwings leaving their snags to snatch them; the two redtails showing us invisible thermals by spiraling upward without a wingbeat. Dōgen said, 'To study the way is to study the self, to study the self is to forget the self, and to forget the self is to awaken into the ten thousand things.' There are the things, but none of them are thought. Dōgen's forgotten self, like your *Cloud of Unknowing* friend Anonymous, chooses for its love the endless things it cannot think."

A long silence followed during which two forgotten selves did nothing but love the things arrayed before them. When a raven then passed over, loudly calling down, Risa turned, and found Lore gazing at her with such unabashed tenderness it made Risa blush.

Lore said, "You just caught the forgotten self choosing for its love the tributaries of blue veins that pattern your temples, throat, backs of your hands. See how beautiful they are? That's the cosmos at work in your body, as beautiful and purposeful as the river below!"

Risa looked at her hands, forearms, the undersides of her wrists. The tributaries *were* beautiful. So were Lore's. "Dōgen's saying about forgetting self reminds me of Hadewijch of Brabant, a Beguine, saying the soul is small, a mere creature, until touched by the One who is great. Allowing that touch, the soul grows so vast she can never be filled. How mind-stopping that a mere creature inside us is capable of that unimaginable expansion!"

Lore's continued smile and direct gaze caused Risa to blush again. She couldn't recall ever receiving such a gaze that wasn't followed by an attempted embrace or kiss, but Lore's eyes held something beyond embraces and kisses. Perhaps the touch of "One who is great." When her gaze then turned back to the river-sundered bowl and remained just as tender, Risa found herself a little breathless—and maybe a little bereft.

"I don't know why Blue Empty opens precisely here," Lore said. "I only know that, once it does, the peace is so all-pervading it seems there's nothing it can't contain. The forgotten self enables this. Perhaps the forgotten self *is* this sundered bowl. But here's a little mystery, Risa. Sometimes, despite the self's forgotten state, memories of painful old events enter the bowl here, real birds fly through events that had no birds in them, and the old pains are imbued with the solace of the living birds."

"I'd love to hear an example of *that*!" Risa said.

"One cold, bright day, late October, I was lost in the ten thousand things when one of the things became a memory of my ex, Trey, defending his infidelities with the words 'I'm true to my truth, Lore!' At the very moment that hurtful memory arrived, a line of sandhill cranes—nineteen of them— flew into the bowl at just my elevation, calling as they sailed right *through* Trey's words. And how harmless, even childlike, his words became! The cranes moved with such Pleistocene authority the words *were drawn into them,* and the pain they'd once caused rode away on long legs, massive wings, crimson foreheads, and two-million-year-old cries."

"*Beautiful!*" Risa breathed.

Lore caught sight of movement far below them. Someone was plodding their way up the deer trail. "Mu!" Lore cried, and stood up to wave.

When he reached them, Lore introduced him to Risa. As they shook hands, Risa saw that Mu's eyes had the same dark rim round the irises as Lore's, but his were bright blue, not gray, and their dark rim was indigo, not black. This variation on a theme smote Risa with her dream of the little river boy, leaving her wondering what kind of eyes he might have.

Dropping his day pack, Mu said, "I saw Mom's truck pass the school, so I rode up and locked my bike to it. Okay if I join you?"

"That's impossible," Lore said. "There's no one here but the forgotten self to join."

"Uh-oh!" Mu said, shooting Risa a grin. "Mom Roshi's been dishing out the *śūnyatā* talk."

"It's true," Risa said.

Mu nodded. "Most kids go to Sunday school, but Mom sent me to the Śūnyatā School. She opened one in E City. Did she tell you? She taught it so well that all her students and the school building disappeared!"

Risa laughed, but Lore said, "Fair warning. He can do this indefinitely."

Risa gave Lore a look. "*Really?*"

"'Fraid so," Lore said.

"I'm not convinced," Risa told Mu. "I think you're out of ideas already."

"Oh dear," Lore said. "You're in for it now."

"Just tell me when to quit," Mu calmly told Risa. "A few things I love about emptiness? One, it's my name. *Mu* is the Chinese word for 'no thing.' That's me. Two, emptiness doesn't know if it's here or not here, or what it's doing or not doing. How could it? It's empty. But without knowing what it's doing it does its work perfectly, all over infinity, for all time! Isn't that amazing? Need an infinite emptiness to keep your universe from getting all balled up in a humongous glob? Need a gazillion tiny emptinesses between musical notes so orchestras can hit each note at the right instant? Need two feet of emptiness between your pants and the stupid urinals at our school to keep from splashing your pants? Need a giant desert emptiness to keep the Grand Canyon grand? Or a ninety-three-million-mile emptiness between Earth and sun to keep us from becoming a two-second fireball? 'Can do,' says Emptiness without saying a thing."

Mu smiled a cocky little smile that he showed no signs of slowing. But in response, Risa's gat-toothed grin appeared for the first time. Mu's cockiness vanished. Visibly startled, he stared at Risa so intently her glee grin intensified, which made him blush and look away.

Seeing her boy thunderstruck, Lore was delighted. She'd grown concerned about what a ten-year-old's cockiness might turn into at fifteen. Gluing his eyes to a pine cone on the ground, Mu asked, "So what do *you* love about emptiness, Risa?"

"Oh. Well. Let me see. I'll start with what a friend calls a 'dirt simple.' I love what emptiness does for buttermilk biscuits. Leave out the baking powder and biscuits are wheaten stones fit to break your teeth. Yet what does the powder actually do? Injects countless tiny emptinesses into flour, salt, and buttermilk. Nothing more. Yet those tiny *śūnyatā*s, fresh out of the oven, are the *no things* into which the butter and honey so delectably melt."

Mu dared a glance at Risa. "You wouldn't happen to have some biscuits, butter, and honey in your giant pack would you?"

"Of course! And an oven too," Risa said as she delved into her pack, handing Mu an apple and two big chocolate chip cookies she'd been saving to fuel herself and Lore on the return hike.

Mu thanked her, then impressed her by breaking the cookies into thirds. "What else do you love about emptiness?" he asked as he passed her the biggest piece.

When Risa's half smile turned glowingly pensive, Mu was in trouble in a whole new way. "I love that emptiness has a purity that can't be violated," she said. "People can despise her, attack her, pollute or slander her, pretend she doesn't exist, rip through her in cars and jets, pretend she isn't here, there, or anywhere. But every attack or denial leaves her as pristine and pure and omnipresent as she always will be."

If blushing and staring at pine cones were any indication, Mu's crush had just doubled. "You turned emptiness into a *she*!" he said. "How come?"

"I could be wrong, but I connect *śūnyatā*'s purity to the divine feminine once known as Sophia. It irks me that a sexist Roman men's club stripped Sophia of her femaleness and gave her the silly name "the Holy Ghost." Misnaming her doesn't change her. Let's wrap our emptiness talk up with a few words about her very essence." With that, Risa closed her eyes and recited, " '*Sarvaṃ ca yujyate tasya śūnyatā yasya yujyate. Sarvaṃ na yujyate tasya śūnyaṃ yasya na yujyate.*' "

Gazing, slack-jawed, at the emptiness through which the sentences had floated, Mu asked, "What language is that? What did it mean?"

"The language is Femalese," Risa said with a straight face. "A lingo women have invented to restore mysteries stolen or sullied by men's clubs. As for its meaning, ask your mom. She's fluent in Femalese."

Trying to regain his lost cockiness, Mu said, "Mom! Risa is lying that you can speak some kind of *śūnyatā* piñata lingo called Femalese."

Matching Risa's straight face, Lore said, "Translating Femalese to

English, the sentences mean, 'All is possible when emptiness is possible. Nothing is possible when emptiness is impossible.' "

With delight in his eyes, Mu turned from his mother to Risa, back to his mom, and said, "All I know is, you two are *cool* together!"

"And all I know is, *you* two are cool together," Lore told Mu and Risa. And she turned to her seven-mile-wide begging bowl, and Mu opened his knife to divide the apple into thirds, and Risa drank in the company of this remarkable mother and son, moved by how deeply they understood, loved, and inhabited one another, but unaware of how deeply they'd penetrated her own heart.

(Inner Elkmoons, summers and falls, 1994 through 2000)

IV. An Elkmoon Geographical Précis

Mountains occupy phases and scopes of place and time that make a mockery of language.
> —Robert Macfarlane

To the eyes of the man of imagination,
nature is imagination itself.
> —William Blake

From the Elkmoon Mountain Journals of Grady Haynes:

A series of events has been transforming my life in ways I'm unable to describe without detailing the geography in which the events take place, because physical immersion in the geography is the transformative event.

Sixteen designated trails with hundreds of spurs crisscross Montana's Elkmoon Wilderness. The immersion has been occurring in the landscape known in Lûmi lore as the Inner Elkmoons. The Inners are reached most directly via the West Fork trail to Gateway Pass, a twelve-mile hike said to be the most brutal in the entire Elkmoon trail system. By contrast, the East Fork trailhead, which begins not ten miles up the road from the West Fork, attracts fifteen times the hikers and horse packers for understandable reasons: that trail begins in stately ponderosas, climbs at a not-too-challenging pace, reaches the lakes of the beautiful Crown of the Continent Lake Basin just six miles in, and accesses the famed climber's destination Steeple Peak (elev. 11,900) just two miles past the basin. But these landscapes are more than thirty miles from the Inner Elkmoons, and in ways I don't understand, the Inner Elkmoons carry a charge these other mountains don't. I took the East Fork trail just once, reached the picture-postcard lakes of the Crown Basin, and felt so purposeless trapped in mere picture postcard beauty that I didn't remove my pack: I just turned around, hiked out, drove to the West Fork trailhead, slept on the ground by my truck, and the next day set out for Gateway via the usual brutal ascent. As of this writing I have now made that ascent bearing a seventy- or eighty-pound pack seven summers in a row.

The West Fork trailhead is located just past a gas station that looks like it was bombed out in a post-Soviet internecine war, in a no place called

Forks (elev. 4,600) consisting of a dusty parking lot poorly shaded by scraggly lodgepoles, with a USFS outhouse, a ramp for offloading horses, and not much more.

The trail to Gateway Pass (elev. 8,100) has two distinct sections. The first seven miles parallel the West Fork of the Elkmoon River's obnoxiously loud cataracts in a narrow ravine. A welcome flat, known as Halfway, silences the river as it oxbows across a boggy half-mile-long plain, but I only pause there to refill water bottles.

The real ordeal begins past Halfway, where the trail switchbacks up a towering, shadeless, south-facing ridge. Much of the footing is shattered scree very hard on feet and legs. Three miles of switchbacks then get you over a summit that should feel like a victory--where the trail, and your heart with it, drop a mile down into a boulder-strewn ravine, losing 900 vertical feet to reach the footbridge over the upper West Fork.

On the ravine's opposite side, four miles of even steeper trail stand between hikers and Gateway's summit, and make me hurt in spectacular ways. Yet the Inner Elkmoons begin to lift me. With eerie reliability this sense of lift causes my personality to split: at the same moment High El Grady thrills to see the rock beneath him become a single, gargantuan, 160-million-year-old batholith, Low El starts whining about "mystical masochism." But we're entering High El's terrain now. I pay the Sacajawea Village Luxury Townhouse whiner no heed.

By the time I summit Gateway and sight in the glistening blue of Boundary Lake (elev. 7,900), even my aches and pains feel elated. The lake is gorgeous upon approach. From a high cliff at its eastern end, Six Falls Creek zigzags down the rock face in six distinct falls. From the lake's west end, where I overnight, the falls sound like a jazz drummer working a snare with wire brushes, giving the place a feeling that's both soothing and anticipatory. In my pine-sheltered, granite-floored, star-roofed camp the simple acts of removing my pack and boots, pouring a whiskey, and sticking my feet in Boundary's waters then steep me in all the euphoria I can contain.

The one time the Informant found me in Boundary camp, she too seemed to love it. By the fire that night she grew downright expansive, and let me take notes in my journal even though she was telling secrets--an unprecedented liberty. I will set down her words, but words leave out the effect of her company. Deploying a beaver-stripped willow wand as her baton, Gladys conducts more than tends her small symmetrical fire as if it were an orchestra, making a music of embers and flames. She speaks in a light Western drawl, pausing constantly to gaze at the lake, the mountain silhouettes, the stars, so at ease with silence that her pauses are as moving as her words. From the beginning I've loved everything about our shared fires: her useful insults; unvarying faded denim; two different eyes, one so warm, one so ageless. Have I admitted I love her company more than that of any woman I've known since I proved too callow for Risa McKeig back in grad school? Every summer, when I first hear the tiny bells on her hulking Belgians, then enter Gladys's mountain-tough presence, her world so envelops me that there is no other. From my notes that night, here's what our Boundary camp moved her to say:

"A lot of Lūmi myths and legends have become fragmented, and a lot have been lost altogether. But if people keep exposing themselves to the land where the legends take place and the creatures who live there, lost parts sometimes appear out of nowhere and can be grafted to remembered parts. The best myths and legends grow toward wholeness the way a starfish can regrow its central ring-disk and five whole tentacles out of a single surviving limb. And coming here year in and year out, making hard hikes like you did today, you're doing your starfish work. Listen close for rhythmic sounds, Grady Haynes. Sounds soft as the softest whisper. Japanese mountain poets spoke endlessly of the wind in the pines and wavelets lapping lakeshores because sounds send meaning that doesn't weigh us down in words. Heeding such sounds is starfish work, and you don't need permission to do it. The permission is given by the sounds."

The Informant's suggestion that rhythmic sounds can regrow Lūmi legend-parts lit my heart up so bright the lake and mountains took on a glow. The rippling campfire flames and Boundary Lake wavelets were suddenly a joy. Inside our shared dome of firelight, even the lint balls on the sleeves of my old hooded sweatshirt attained some kind of perfection!

"Lūmi legends," she said, "rise out of a wild so intricate that the big vague place we call 'Montana' only obscures it. This wild is rhythmic, and the rhythms, where they're not drowned out by earth-eating machinery, are still playing nonstop. Don't doubt that. Lūmi knowing isn't a collection of worn-out old stories. It rides in rhythms we can feel and hear in every least thing around us. Seasons are rhythmic. Migrations too. I like the word 'chant' in this context. Sunrises and sunsets, snowfalls and snowmelts, birth and death taking turns, are a fugue of rhythmic chants waiting to be felt. And the chants remind me to mention, Grady Haynes, you find your returns to Portland tragic because of elevation loss. What's with that nonsense? Elevation change isn't loss. Do your starfish work! Losing and regaining elevation is as rhythmic as the seasons. The chants of snowfields become trickles become streams become rivers become ocean become water vapor become rain and snow-laden clouds traveling inland re-create water's forms including the walking talking body of water that is you. In the beginning the spirit of God moved across the face of the body's waters too, so why not leave here eager for the mountain-to-river-to-sea-to-vapor-back-to-mountain journey? Celebrate your bloodstream as you drive it down to Portland. Feel your heart forcing the blood to travel as far as it can get from the heart to sustain all of you, only to turn back toward it as surely as you keep returning here to the Inners."

As she snatched up her baton to poke at the fire I felt her poking at a fire in me, and words rose with the sparks. I said, "I read an anthology of

Indian lore in college that felt strangled by bad translations and academic anthropologists. But one old chant, even in English, stuck in me like an arrow in a tree. What you've been saying makes me wonder if it stuck because it's the kind of thing starfish work can regrow. Do you mind if I say it so we can see?"

"Hell yes, I mind if you <u>say</u> it," the Informant groused. "It's a <u>chant</u>, Grady Haynes. You've got to chant it."

God, I love this old woman's persnicketiness! I sat quiet a moment, drew a breath, and gave it my best:

"How shall I begin my song
in this blue light that's settling?
In the great night my heart will go out.
Toward me the darkness comes rattling.
In the darkening blue my heart will go out."

"<u>Ermm</u>," went Gladys, but there's no spelling the sound. It's like a mother llama's soft bleat the first time its baby tastes her milk.

"<u>Ermm</u>," I bleated back.

She took up her baton and resumed conducting. Sparks flew up and vanished among stars. "Another thing about starfish work," she said. "Lots of folks think that when the US cavalry and missionaries rolled in, their bugles and pump organs blared the wild instruments and orchestra into oblivion. More nonsense! For the same reasons that high places are very hard to live in, they're <u>protected</u>. Soldiers and missionaries scarcely touched them, and even when they were <u>in</u> them they remained deaf, dumb, and lost. The wild instruments survive, their notes still open doors, and those who think spirit contact requires some big ol' thunderbird- type god have confused wisdom with mountaintop coal removal. A hoverfly can open us. A patch of lichen on a rock. The amazingly deep trenches dug in a single summer by the trillion footfalls of a little freeway of red and black ants. The silent seconds it takes the sound of falling stones to travel a mile across a valley, becoming the audible clatter that draws our eye to the ant- sized bull elk who caused it, trotting away."

"<u>Ermm</u>," I bleated as the lint balls of perfection reappeared on the sleeves of my sweatshirt.

From the west end of Boundary the main trail turns north into the Scatter Lakes Basin, a maze of Lilliputian lakes linked by charmingly tiny clear creeks. To hikers who've endured the West Fork ascent, this fairy- tale landscape sings like a siren. Few leave it to pursue the mysteries of the Inner Elkmoons. But where the trail turns sharply left down to the Scatter Lakes, a faint trace turns northwest, created not by trail crews but by moose, elk, mountain goats, deer, threading through a land so open that if you lose the trace it doesn't matter: just aim at Egypt Peak (elev. 9,500) and eight semi- level miles carry you to Lake Pipsissewa (elev. 8,400).

With its shoreline stands of rare white pine, unusually prolific insect hatches, and great fishing, I call Pipsissewa "The Commissary" and depend on its trout protein when planning these treks. Down in the valley the river's mayfly, stone fly, and caddis fly hatches last from March all the way into October. At Pipsissewa the same three kinds of insects spring to life in a furious summer a quarter the length of the summer below. So do the wildflowers: on the eight-mile hike from Boundary to Pipsissewa, I once catalogued seventy species in a day.

After a restful day or two and fish feast or three I follow Pipsissewa's inlet creek three miles west up an easy incline as the Blue Mosque, now eight miles distant, seems to rise out of the ground. All trees but those of the weather-torn and stunted Krummholz vanish, as do the game trails. But the terrain gains visual logic as it funnels up a couloir dense with blue gentian toward a massive cirque cradling Echo Lake (elev. 8,700).

Echo more than lives up to its name. Devoid of trees but for the willows obscuring its outlet stream, it's enclosed on three sides by curved and towering cirque cliffs white as the cliffs of Dover, and, acoustically speaking, it's a sort of Hollywood Bowl. Stand near the outlet and shout at the cliffs and they bounce your voice back nearly two seconds later, and faintly double-echo it two seconds after that. Being at different distances and angles, the cliffs also alter the echo. On a still night a shouter's original words can be so radically different from what bounces back that the Informant warned me never to overnight at Echo. Over the centuries, she claims, provocative words have flown back and forth across the water, leading to insults or allurements that throw occasional visitors into rages or mad attractions, causing more than a few narcissists to drown in an effort to kill or make love to the voices on the far side.

On the three-mile climb to the base of the Blue Mosque the salt-and-pepper batholith granite gives way to beige dolomites and off-white marble, and my sense of having entered what Gladys calls "a legitimate 'above world'" increases with every step. The summer aridity and clarity of air intoxicate. Much of the marble is sculptural in an unsettling human way. The high-elevation sky and brightness of the rock flood all things with more light than any other kind of landscape.

Then comes a high, thin, quarter-mile-long arête that must be braved. Any other route to the Mosque involves a long detour and rock-hopping across boulder fields, a terrible idea for anyone unbalanced by a heavy pack. The arête's name is Daniel's Bridge, in honor of a nineteenth-century naturalist, Matthew Daniel, who Axel Volkmann cites in LÛmi Singings. Daniel rhapsodized about the process whereby rock, carried by tectonics to great depth, encounters heat and pressures that metamorphose lesser rock into marble. He linked this to the LÛmi, describing them as "humans whose extreme efforts on the Purification Loop transform them in ways as beautiful as the high Elkmoon marble." One such extreme effort is crossing Daniel's Bridge: the arête falls away on both sides at an angle so precipitous that a simple misstep could be fatal, and a fifty-yard stretch narrows to a mere blade of rock with patches of sedimentary sandstone so rotten it can break off under a hiker like water-logged particle board. I use two collapsible trekking poles to cross the arête, probing the rock before me at every step, and in bad light, rain, or winds I don't cross at all. At the beginning of the bridge is a hidden, man-length bed of white sand where I've twice overnighted to await safer conditions.

The arête ends a third of a mile shy of the northern base of the Blue Mosque (elev. 10,700), a very impressive marble dome with two remarkable pinnacles forming east and west "minarets." The Mosque is a massif, once several times its current mass and several thousand feet taller. Broken down through the ages by harsh weather and the sinking caused by tectonic subduction, the Mosque remains majestic even so. From its summit the views of vast wilderness and night skies are out of this world, but, strange to say, I've haven't overnighted up there even once. The reason I haven't is a small lake at the foot of the Mosque, which Volkmann and the Informant hold to be the pulsing heart of the entire Elkmoon Range: Jade Lake (elev. 9,007).

Daniel's Bridge is so rarely crossed that there's not even a faint path to Jade, but an easy stroll brings you to twenty or so acres of lake-encircling tundra the Informant calls the Flying Carpet. Jade itself is but seven acres in size, and the four acres adjacent to the Carpet are only knee-to-neck deep. At the foot of the Mosque, however, Jade's other three acres drop off to astonishing depth. The cause of this anomaly, geologists, Volkmann, and the Informant for once agree, was a meteorite roughly 240 feet in diameter traveling at unusually high speed.

High mountain lakes are natural phenomena that should conform to nature's laws. Jade rebels against such laws in two flagrant ways.

Rebellion One: bullets travel up to 1,800 miles per hour. An impressively deadly speed. But meteorites travel an unimaginable 30,000 to 160,000 miles per hour. When the 240-foot-diameter molten super-bullet struck the base of the Blue Mosque at an angle, it bore so deep under the Mosque's north flank that it connected with tectonic seams and layers of limestone that, over long periods of time, enabled Jade's snowmelt-created waters to tunnel deeper into the earth than scientists can accurately measure. Jade, in other words, is fathomless. Trying to experience some sense of this on my first visit, I swam to the center of the deep end holding a fly reel loaded with 80 feet of fly line and 220 feet of backing, where I treaded water as I lowered a grapefruit-sized stone. The stone took all 300 feet of line straight down and never touched bottom. The deeps beneath me then gave me unmanageably awestruck feelings that sent me swimming fast as I could to shore.

Rebellion Two: Jade also possesses warmth. When the snows melt enough to render it accessible in June, Boundary, Pipsissewa, and Echo remain iced over, but Jade, the highest lake in the chain, is ice-free and tepid to the touch. For perspective on this, Conundrum Hot Springs in the Elk Range of Colorado are the highest such springs in North America at 11,200 feet, but they're cradled in a volcanic basin where rain and snowmelt are heated by fumaroles. The entire Elkmoon Range, in sharp contrast, is volcanically inactive, and Jade's heat source remains undetermined to this day. This anomaly has driven some geologists almost literally crazy. Most agree that, immeasurably deep under the Mosque, Jade's waters intersect with a heat thread that, even in winter, warms the water all the way back up to Jade's surface, keeping it ice-free year-round except during the most frigid Arctic fronts. Planes doing winter flyovers have verified this with photos. But a faction of geologists has never stopped hammering on the fact that the Elkmoon Range possesses no measurable geothermal activity, moving them to lambaste the heat thread theorists so furiously you'd think the divisive cliffs of Echo Lake goaded them to impotent rage.

Contending that mountains are better approached as living mysteries than as knowable geologic quantities, Volkmann veers off in a different direction entirely. In Lûmi Singings he comes at Jade's warmth via a Lûmi creation myth depicting a male–female polarity between heaven and Earth, and between the star-shard at Earth's core and the sun in particular. The Informant takes this literality even further: she once serenely informed me that the meteorite that created Jade "was less an insensate ball of flame than an extra-natural gamete that shot down from the heavens, sought and entered a kind of fallopian tube under the massif that preceded the Mosque, struck an unthinkable ovum, and fertilized it." In amplification of her theory she likes to quote the scholarly old Reynold A. Nicholson translation of Rumi's Mathnawi:

> From the other stars
> this embryo received only an impression,
> until the Sun shone upon it.
> By which way did it become connected in
> the womb with the
> beauteous Sun?
> By the hidden way that is remote from sense-perception.

While the Informant's gamete-and-ovum talk strikes my reason as preposterous, it has felt dauntingly apropos to my body and being every time I've camped at Jade. Overnighting on what I want to call "her" shores, I have invariably experienced her waters as alive, and sentient. Sleeping by her in a dead calm, especially, sends me on night sea journeys that so assail my sense of reality and self that the words "reality" and "self" vaporize, and a brooding consciousness that seems to inhabit Jade's depths opens celestial, terrestrial, and subterranean seams in me. The stars above and star fragment at Earth's core energize each other from opposed directions, creating shocks of wonder and yearning that "inter-be," as Thich Nhat Hanh might put it. Impossible sounds rise from what should be silent waters: the creaking of oarlocks; an invisible someone drawing breaths an instant after each of mine; the sounds of every kind of water but the stilled lake before me, including, twice now, a frightening <u>swoosh</u> sound that brought to mind poet Michael Donaghy's description of an angel's voice as "the noise of a pond thrown into a stone." At first light I wake on Jade's shores feeling slept <u>with</u>--and honesty compels one painful example of how literal this feeling can be.

The last time I shared a fire with the Informant at Pipsissewa, the first thing she asked was when I'd last been up to Jade. When I admitted I hadn't been there for two years, she grabbed her willow wand and took on gravitas as she stoked the flames. "It's time you knew," she then told me point-blank, "that Jade is the starting point and end point of the entire Lû mi High-Elevation Purification Loop."

Oh, did <u>that</u> rattle my cage!

"Why haven't you been back?" she asked.

"That would make for a gnarly story," I muttered.

"I'm a gnarly old lady," she growled. "Tell me the damn story."

I've never met a person whose crankiness I so respect. I rolled out my tale:

On the long hike back down from the Inner Elkmoons three summers before, I was in my usual camp on Boundary Lake's west shore, hating to leave, when, shortly before sunset, a solitary woman hiker arrived across the lake. Because I was in trees and shadow and she stood in blinding sunlight three hundred yards away, she couldn't see me. From the distance she looked appealing. As she removed her pack and boots I grabbed my Leicas and was shaken to see, from what now seemed a thirty-foot distance, that she was stunning. The very next moment she crossed her arms low over her belly, took hold of the bottom of her sweat-soaked, sleeveless brown T shirt, and in one graceful sweep removed it, revealing a taut, tanned torso and stunningly pale, swaying breasts. She then stepped out of her shorts and undies, dove into Boundary, and swam a small circle, making what sounded like love cries against the cold. When she returned to shore, gleaming in the evening light, my eyes devoured her. Donning fresh black bikini underwear, socks, and her hiking boots, she pillaged my sanity by adding no jeans, no shorts, no T shirt. As she strained her way into her pack, the juxtaposition of tanned muscle and sinew to loose sway of pale breasts overthrew my government. When she hiked off into the Inner Elkmoons all but naked, I kept seeing sinew and sway long after dark. It shames me to say that I was only able to sleep by vowing to break camp in the morning and seek her out.

The Informant listened to all this with an attentiveness that never hinted at judgment or surprise. Her deadpan listening kept my account dead honest:

I broke camp at dawn. When I reached Pipsissewa in late morning, I immediately spotted a blue dome tent on the far shore. A moment later I spotted the woman sunbathing, belly down, on a log at water's edge. The log wore no bark. The woman wore no clothes. But my intentions went way beyond voyeurism. Pretending not to have seen her, I eased out of my pack, set up my fly rod, and did some serious fishing. Killing and cleaning six foot- long golden trout. I did not pitch a camp.

An hour before sunset I donned my pack, circled the lake, walked close by the woman's camp, feigned surprise to see her tent, then her, and strolled over to say hello. We struck up a chat that grew so amiable it led to me offering a shared meal of trout amandine, whiskey, and dark chocolate. She accepted. The hoped- for sparks began to fly. As we were finishing our second whiskies I had her nearly weeping with laughter when she pulled herself up short, gave me a troubled look, and confessed that she had a fiancé who wasn't half as funny or handsome as me. I confessed that I'd been living for three years with a woman named Nance who was not a small fraction as beautiful as she.

As if revealing the deceitful truth absolved us, she slipped inside her tent, hung up a charming candle lantern, and invited me in. As soon as I entered she slid out of her jeans, rose to her knees before me, crossed her arms, took hold of the base of a now white sleeveless T shirt, lifted, and again smote me with the paradox between her tanned and sinewy body and pale, swaying breasts. The obvious guilt- inducing pleasures then happened and happened.

When we woke in the morning and looked at each other, the first thing we saw was matching shame. We dressed in haste. I told her that, since my pack hadn't been unpacked and I had a very long hike out, I'd eat energy bars on the trail rather than take time to breakfast. She nodded, looked very sad, and asked where I called home. When I said "Portland," she fell silent and I sensed a battle going on inside her. We both lost that battle when she murmured, "Me too." We couldn't meet each other's eyes as we exchanged the kind of contact info our partners wouldn't discover. Her conflicted, lost- looking smile as I turned and hiked away no doubt matched my own.

The Informant was watching me so keenly yet acceptingly that I felt she'd known from the start where my story was headed. The story line, I now sensed, was not her quarry. She awaited a turn quite different from my predictable lust and shame.

And I'd reached it. When I returned to Portland, I told her, I tried my wretched best to forget the woman, and six weeks passed without betrayal. But my Sacajawea Village Luxury Townhouse is Low El Grady's turf. Resisting temptation was a day and night torment. So was Nance's trust in me. The night Low El decided to phone the beautiful hiker I tried to stop him by quoting the Dalai Lama: "Beware the difference between happiness and pleasure."

Low El snorted, _Fuck happiness!_ and made the call.

The hiker and I met at noon the next day in a cheesy generic motel near the Portland Airport. During our first liaison the pleasure was almost un- bearable, the happiness nonexistent. That was the day the Dalai Lama began to impress even Low El. At our second encounter I learned it was possible for a woman to have wild multiple orgasms with a man and despise him for it. The third time we met we quickly stripped, coupled like dogs to keep from having to see each other's faces, and every emotion but self- disgust fled. Her mountain tan, like mine, had long since faded, her breasts had become inert balls of fat in my hands, and I can't imagine what sort of lascivious orc I'd become in her eyes. When I recognized the sex as being in service to that orc, I pulled out and collapsed beside her. "What's wrong?" she asked. I said, "It was the Elkmoons that made us beautiful to each other, the Elkmoons we're still trying to find in each other, and it's never going to happen." The woman nodded, her eyes filled and overflowed, and with her cheeks streaked by tears she was beautiful to me again.

Hoping to escape before the tears evaporated, I rolled away to gather my clothes -- and hurt myself! The hotel mattress had filled with stones.

The Informant was nodding as I told of waking in shock on the stone shore of Jade with the tears I'd seen on the woman's face evaporating on my own. A dream that seemed to last weeks had taken a fraction of a night. Its cast of characters featured no one but me and, I very strongly suspected, the eerily sentient lake at my side.

When Gladys asked if my condition included "any peculiarities," I considered lying. But she sees into me far too easily not to confess: I'd come in my underwear not once but twice for sure, and quite likely three times. Her nod was so matter-of-fact I let out a strangled laugh. I told her I was relieved not to have betrayed Nance but couldn't stop wondering what kind of voodoo had invaded me, because I'd never experienced anything like the exhaustion I felt not just on the hike down and drive home but for weeks afterward. Fearing my epic wet dreams had given me chronic fatigue syndrome, my mountain fortitude was so depleted and self-respect so tainted I hadn't been back to Jade since.

"The Lúmi way is built on secrecy," Gladys said, "so I'm not going to mudpuddle around in this. Just know you're far from alone in having had such a dream at Jade. And what happened was not as simple as a horny young fool profaning Jade's power. Remember me saying high elevation can cause things buried in us to reverse-pressure their way out? What's happening to you is apophatic, not psychotic. Apophatic experience doesn't give us things. It takes things away. Jade holds a power to draw falsehoods, delusions, obsessions, lusts, out of us the way a poultice draws pus from a wound. That's one reason why it's the culmination point of the Loop. What happened to you was a victory, not a defeat. You were exhausted because, at a Jade-deep level, your energy sources are being switched out. The long loneliness is beginning to leave you. Who do you suppose you'll become once ol' Cornflakes Grady is gone?"

"I'll tell you who's gone," I said. "Nance. A few weeks after the dream I took a two-night business trip. When I got home to the townhouse, Nance had left me for a Vancouver, BC, art dealer who, her note said, 'loves me, not some distant damned range of mountains!' And what you call the long loneliness is not leaving me. I felt so weak and desolate after that dream that here's what I've feared ever since. If one or two of the silhouettes I keep glimpsing on high ridges don't invite me up to the party one of these years, the mere memory of a dream woman could lure my Low El doppelgänger off on a Vegas or Cancún or Riviera debauch that fucks me up so bad I'll never make it back to the Elkmoons again."

Expecting anger, I was instead met with a gaze so piercing it hurt. "What makes you think you haven't been at the party all along?" the Informant asked.

I stared at her, speechless.

"Don't complain to _me_ about mountains being mountains," she said. "Your Low Elevation sidekick is in a world o' hurt and _he_ at least knows it. That's why he's pleading for a debauch. But it's not gonna happen. Do you need me to tell you why?"

I thought hard, and came up empty. "I'm afraid I do."

Her power eye gave me the thousand-year-old stare. "Your inner Hamlet knows he's got a dark king to kill. Low El Grady is that king. When you get down to Portland, you'll find all your relationships in greater flux than ever, and Low El's desolation will be overwhelming. Admit why this is so. A minute ago you said, 'when I got home to the townhouse.' Feel the lie? You inhabit no such home, and Nance knew it, named her true rival, and wisely left you. Low El's home is _gone_, making it easy for you to finish Low El himself off now. Why?

"_Ah, Grady Haynes! Into the great night your heart has gone out. The Elk-moon mysteries have come rattling._ Your heart's home, the only true home you've got, has walls made of mountains under constellation chandeliers."

Her diagnosis opened me wide to the peaks and stars above us, my strength began returning in a flood, and who but the Informant can make me feel so dismantled one moment and so moved and purposeful the next?

I said, "I'll haul myself up to Jade next summer, and _every_ summer for as long as I'm able. And that's a promise I make not to you, or to myself, but to the powers that sent the meteor that awakened Jade and the star shard and sun heat that warm her."

The Informant stood, handed me her beaver-sculpted baton so I could conduct the fire, then peered up and said to the night sky, "It turns out my camp mate isn't the complete waste of stars I once feared he might be." With which she traipsed off to check her horses, washed her face in the lake, and retired to her tent.

But I stayed on long by the embers, my eyes on the stars I was no longer a waste of, my heart going out and out as, down through the diaphanous blue, the mysteries continued to come rattling --

making it child's play, when I reached Portland three days later, to sell every one of my controlling shares in Datalyrick and, as the lower world so foolishly puts it, "retire," at the age of thirty-four, into the never-retiring service of my Elkmoon home.

V. The Squire and the Pope

Some things you just raise hell about and hope
somebody smarter than you can fix it.

—Wendell Berry

ON THE EVENING of October 16th, Risa called TJ in Portland, and he was
so thrilled to hear from her that he fell out of character, blurting, "What a
relief to hear your voice! Tell me *everything,* Risa! *Please! Now!*"

"It's been an epic two weeks, TJ. 'Everything' could run long."

"But so much was about to happen. *Please.* Run long!"

"Well, a good place to start is this room. I'm sitting in a hundred-and-
four-year-old one-room schoolhouse I've been offered rent-free, which is a
story in itself. And I'm staring out the west window at one of the most
beautiful views in the world, another intricate story. The school is owned
by a ranch foreman, Kale Broussard, who grew up next door to my dad,
who lost his family ranch not long after Dave lost his, and who feels like
an instant life friend. And on the life friend front, let's add another cowboy, Lou Roy by name; a not-quite-nine-year-old named Rosalia, her dad,
Eddie; and a mother-and-son folk-singing duo, Lorilee and Mu. That's six
life friends in less than a week if you're counting. Which brings me to
a big feeling I've been having nonstop: Great-Gramma Stella's and Dave's
favorite place on Earth has been hiding inside me all my life. It is fast
becoming my favorite place too."

Sounding excited, TJ broke in, "Your big feeling might correspond to
something Jervis has been feeling too, Risa. When and where did the
feeling start?"

"The day I arrived in the Elkmoon, my thirtieth birthday. When I drove
up to release Dave's ashes in a meadow he and Stella loved, I got swallowed
by a Presence that took the form of every tree, stone, body of water, vista,
creature, plant, smell, and sound, which, come to think of it, might be the
way Ocean takes form for Jervis on Portland streets. It was total joy amid
a total homecoming. And it left me wanting to help coax a, uh, *what to
call it?* 'Community' is too *communal* a word, and 'tribe' and 'village' are
too tribal and villagey. Let's just say 'a circle of people' who are of and for
the living world and one another in ways the modern world subjugates and

makes impossible. I feel my coaxing needs to be so gentle it's no coaxing at all. It would just be *an alertness,* an *allowing,* so the circle could form *itself.* Is there a word for this, TJ?"

"As you and Jervis know better than I do," TJ said, "for *many* self-forming circles of women and the places and people they once served, 'Beguine' was the name for each woman, and 'beguinage' the name of each circle."

"That's *exactly* what I feel could self-form here!" Risa said. "I just didn't want to sound *grandiose,* since the Beguines were so spectacular. The people I'm meeting here aren't grandiose at all, but there's a readiness in them. They're close to broke, most of them, because the high-paying Earth-wrecking jobs went bust here a few decades ago. And none of them want the double-mortgaged house, soul-crushing jobs, or lifelong debt the American Dream scam has become. What they want, some of them quite openly, is to move out of the failed nation-state and serve the living continent they love. They want compassionate change *now,* and all I see preventing them is their near-complete lack of money. And now for some crazy talk, TJ! I know you and Jervis belong to Portland the way elk belong to the Elkmoon, but I feel you connect to *here* too. I know Jervis can't travel and belongs where he is. But what *can* travel here, as a model, is the way he moves through Northwest like a shuttle providing the weft that weaves a spiritual tapestry. Day and night he lives the *unknowing knowing* that self-forms circles of compassion and cooperation—and the way you *enable* his generosity models the other key ingredient, TJ. If you simply met the people here I'm sure you'd feel a broken-openness in them that allows them to feel possibilities most people can't. Kale and Lou Roy, for instance, are old-school cowboys whose lost way of life left them ready, just three days after meeting me, to offer me the use of this schoolhouse. And not for a few nights. They asked me to turn it into the headquarters of whatever I feel it most needs to headquarter. And when I said it should headquarter the greater good of the entire valley and every living thing in it, they began giving me every kind of help they can. What kind of middle-aged men trust a near stranger that fast?"

"What kind of near stranger," TJ said, "responds to an offer to use their schoolhouse by saying it should headquarter the greater good of their entire home valley?"

Too revved to even notice the compliment, Risa said, "That reminds me, I have a headquarters question. The schoolroom will need to sleep six or eight people at times. To keep it from looking like an Army barracks, and to create privacy between beds at night, we need pleasing dividers that can be easily removed by day so the big schoolroom reappears. Any idea how to achieve that?"

Risa waited so long for a reply that she thought they'd been cut off. "TJ? Are you there? Did my crazy talk snap the phone lines? *Hello?*"

"I'm here," he said. "But I'm also feeling most of the way *there.* Ready for *my* crazy talk?"

"Please!"

"When you were in Seattle with Dave, Jervis and I sat down to a midnight dram, and out of the blue he said that Ocean strobed that there's going to be a beguinage in this country. Dumpster Catholic, not Roman, this time, he said. And co-ed, so that amor and eros and the innocence and chaos kids bring will be part of it. Ocean also strobed—and Jervis harped on this—that the beguinage will be 'somewhere piney.' So before we get carried away, tell me. Does that spectacular view from your schoolhouse have any pine trees in it?"

"Time to get carried away!" Risa cried. "From the sixty-four-pane west-facing window, two low mountain ranges, the North and South Whitetails, parallel the Elkmoon River forty miles to its headwaters. And both ranges, much of the valley floor, and all but the snowcapped peaks of the wilderness area beyond are covered with so many pines that by the time some mortal counted them, millions more pines would have been born!"

"Well then, fasten your seat belt," TJ said, "because Ocean strobed that *you*, Risa, are one of the mothers of whom this *piney beguinage* of Jervis's is to be born! And *I'm* the mother-brother whose Pearl Building and businesses will connect to your beguinage for the greater good. But we're under strict orders not to get *thinky* or it won't happen. And I'm so excited by your Big Feeling that the only way I can *not* get thinky is by hopping on the next possible plane so you can show me the pines, life friends, and Greater Good Headquarters in person!"

"Oh TJ! As soon as I was offered use of the schoolhouse I began checking flights between here and Portland. A 6 a.m. flight will get you to Salt Lake by 7, a 9 a.m. gets to Bozeman by 10:30, and a puddle jumper will land you in E City by noon. To prepare you, E City International is a two-hundred-foot-long Quonset hut with no control tower, no baggage claim, no security, and no amenities. But through a cyclone fence to the south you'll see a crimson Ford Exploiter with a cute black and tan cow dog standing beside it. That will be iPooch. And the lunatic waving both arms at you will be me."

"Inshallah, I'll be there. And oh! Those dividers? What are the dimensions of your schoolhouse?"

"Thirty-six by thirty-six. Thirteen hundred square feet plus two water closets and a tiny kitchen."

"That could sleep ten! Okay. To avoid the barracks look we'll order Japanese latticework paper walls, sliding shoji doors, and tatami flooring, so *everybody* has privacy. All easily removed when you want the big room back. You'll need to store it all outside the school, so if you meet a good carpenter, line him or her up and I'll spring for a heated storage shed."

"What is Ocean up to?" Risa cried. "Your idea's perfect and you haven't even seen the place. And the carpenter, Eddie Dominguez, lives two hundred yards away."

* * *

BY EARLY AFTERNOON the next day, TJ was seated in Great-Gramma Stella's rocker at the Testament Creek School's west window, stunned by the ocean of pines establishing a Dumpster Catholic beguinage's *piney* criteria so many times over that, when he heard someone coming up the steps, he wouldn't have been much surprised if Hadewijch of Brabant walked in. When Risa then entered, followed by the first two working cowboys TJ had ever seen, her gat-tooth delight was out in full force: "TJ McGraff. Meet Lou Roy Skinner and Kale the Pope Broussard."

As the cowboys took in the Portlander it was their turn to be stunned. Though TJ had set aside his mouse-gray fedora and matching scarf, he was still decked out in a sage-colored Italian linen suit, an apricot shirt with mother-of-pearl cuff links, and two-tone beige and brown slip-on leather shoes, also Italian—with tassels, no less. When the sartorial gulf between restaurateur and cowpokes did nothing to prevent the cowboys from removing their white and black Stetsons and shaking TJ's hand, TJ opened his carry-on, produced a bottle of Bulleit bourbon and four highball glasses, and the conversation grew friendly so fast that, not ten minutes in, Kale posed one of the most unexpected questions TJ had ever fielded:

"Lou and I esteem Risa so highly," he said, "and she esteems you so highly, that we'd like to offer an Elkmoon experience we offer to very few, TJ. Have you by chance ever pushed cows around with a horse?"

TJ bottled up his incredulity with his tight little smile. "Answer me this, Kale. Do I *look* as though I ever pushed cows around with a horse?"

With a masterfully straight face, the Pope replied, "No, sir, you do not. To my eye, you look more as if you just stepped out of a villa on the seaside cliffs of Portofino, Italy, in the year 1928, and are headed into town to join Cole Porter for dinner. But that dinner wouldn't prevent you from discovering, tomorrow morning, that pushing cows around with horses might pleasantly surprise you."

Kale's uncanny grasp of TJ's sartorial intent inspired him to ask, "If you had three words to describe this pleasant surprise, what would they be?"

Summoning his full papal authority, Kale intoned, "*Bloody. Good. Fun.*"

TJ laughed his tight little laugh. "Tempting," he admitted.

"Then might I interest you in a quick run into E City and treat you to some rougher, readier duds?"

"In pondering what Montana might toss at me," TJ said, "I mail-ordered a pair of Carharrt overalls and jacket in a color the label called 'rust,' which I find troublingly close to 'orange.' But before I commit to cow-pushing, a question. Might one of you own a mount equipped with a five-mile-an-hour governor on its engine and a roll bar to protect the rider?"

Lou Roy didn't miss a beat: "I got just the animal, TJ. Stocky coal-black quarter horse name o' Physics. The governor an' roll bar aren't visible, but you'll feel 'em. Physics moves like a road-grader, an' is just as impossible to speed up or knock down."

Of all the natural and unnatural wonders that led to the nativity of the

Elkmoon Beguine & Cattle Company, the one I most wish I could have witnessed was TJ, Kale, and Lou Roy tacking up Physics, Eisenhower, and Grey the next morning, mounting up, and riding out onto the range for three hours that left the cowboys debilitated by laughter as an orange-overalled, more or less ecstatic business genius pushed around cows on a mount that moved exactly like a road-grader with hooves and a tail.

LITTLE SURPRISE, THEN, that a few days later a seminal friendship blossomed between TJ and Kale. They'd agreed to spend half of the day driving around NorBanCo's holdings in Kale's F-250, combining his usual ranch foreman work morning with a tour of the former Broussard and McKeig family ranches.

Tackling chores first, Kale made four brief calls and three quick stops to set the day's tasks for his Land & Beef Inc. crew. This deep into October they were down to dismantling sprinkler systems in harvested fields, closing irrigation ditch headgates, repairing damaged fences, and, in Hub Punker's case, doing maintenance on roads with the heavy equipment he more or less lived on. As Kale introduced TJ to Buford, Doty Nolan, Eddie, and Hub, they were all so friendly that TJ later asked Kale if they were always this way.

"Buford and Eddie, yes," Kale said. "But Doty and Hub would have had no use for a city slicker if they hadn't heard from Lou Roy that, on his first day in Montana, this city slicker risked buckbrush scratches and locust thorn punctures to push around cattle on Lou's horse Physics. That lowered suspicions. Then, when you and Risa stopped by the Grange Hall bunkhouse this morning to pick up the partitions you bought us so the schoolhouse can sleep a crowd, Hub overheard you and Risa strategizing about how to be generous to locals without offending them. From that moment Hub claimed full credit for recognizing your heart of gold and nicknamed you 'the Squire.' And take it from the man he *poped*, TJ. Hub's nicknames outweigh peoples' real names by as much as Hub outweighs other people. In these parts, you'll be 'the Squire' for life."

Their tour of the former homesteads with which Risa had fallen in love left TJ in high spirits. It was stunningly beautiful land despite a decade of corporate misrule. When they reached NorBanCo's overbuilt roads and the Land & Beef Inc. buildings and stock pens, Kale's mood darkened in a hurry. As a restaurateur with beef on his menus, however, TJ was interested in this darkness, and began to probe it.

"So, Kale. In Oregon there's a renaissance of small family farms, organic gardens, community-supported ag, weekend farmers' markets, co-ops, and so on that now serve a lot of restaurants, my two included. Is anything similar stirring in cattle country?"

"I wish," Kale said. "But the profit margins for small growers were destroyed years ago. Free-market corporate globalism did 'em in. The only family ranches left are passed down by multigenerational landowners, some of them good people. Other so-called family ranchers are just rich hobbyists, Ted Turner the big name, with the big bucks and ego to match."

"I want to understand the mechanisms that make family ranches fail. Can you give me a case study?"

"I can, but it hurts," Kale said. "My former crewman, Max Bowler, best cowboy I had, is driving his family into poverty trying to raise cattle the right way. What hurts is knowing he'll be broke in under a year. Where it all goes to hell is when a family takes their cows to market. Have you ever seen a video auction, TJ? Or a giant industrial feedlot?"

"I haven't."

"What the industry calls 'finishing' cattle turns mild-mannered star-gazing grass-grazers into terrified commodities in the cartel feedlots. Steak lovers don't ask why the lots fatten animals to butcher at twelve hundred pounds. They assume beef is beef and added weight maximizes profit. But feedlot cattle are prisoners of an economic war. What does that look like? Living on moldy hay-coils with rotting snakes and rodents in them, getting hauled long-distance in aluminum trailers that scare them literally shitless, and on the lots they're bloated on petro-grains from the oil industry, antibiotics from the drug industry, and offal from the animal euthanasia industry till they're slaughtered in terror by ex-cons, undocumented migrants, addicts, and other unfortunates who hate what they're doing, so they can't help but do it badly. We then eat the results of that."

"*Jesus!*" TJ burst out. "But please go on."

"Stop me when you've had your fill," Kale said.

"I want to grasp this," TJ insisted.

"Corporate markets undercut the humane competition, driving it out of business. It's that simple. Beef cattle consist of how they're bred, where they live, and how they're treated by the humans they live under. When I was a kid, my dad and I moved our cattle over the land you just saw, caring for them from birth to death, and for the land too. When we'd bow our heads over our beef, the word 'sacrifice' humbled us as we tasted our healthy land's spring and summer bounty. That approach didn't suddenly vanish because ranchers became incompetent assholes. Big Chain Big Bargain Big Everything strangled their profits to death. And that's enough outta me, TJ. I need to cool down."

But TJ had become less a kindly Squire than a bird dog on a hot scent. "Tell me *exactly* what Max is up against by trying to do it right, Kale. I like details."

"Max and Kira break my heart. There's a detail. You never saw a more fit couple ready to give ranching their all. So last winter Max sold a little E City tract home he'd made payments on, Kira left an apartment she shared with former college girlfriends, and they made a down payment on a noxious-weed-infested thirty-acre farm and moved into a borrowed camper. The farmhouse was an ad for why not to remodel older houses. Dry rot, mold, mice, spiders. New drywall needed. Warped linoleum to rip out. New joists needed to support the new flooring. Kira teaches school so she couldn't help till June. But Max was in love, and that man can *work*. With help from Kira's kid brother and, now and then, me, he put in fifteen-hour days without a break. By Fourth of July he'd converted a potential hovel into a handsome, solid home. Then school let out, Kira tackled the land, and she's a workhorse too. She purged it of knapweed, hound's-tongue, and Russian thistle singlehanded while Max rebuilt every fence and gate, reroofed the barn, replumbed the well, and set to work on his dream. Raising Scottish Highlands. Do you know the breed, TJ?"

"Long, shaggy hair they can hardly see out of, and horns that could work as Harley-Davidson handlebars."

Kale smiled. "Well said. That shaggy hair insulates so they don't need gobs of fat for warmth, making them lower in cholesterol than other breeds. When Max speaks of 'em, he'll say stuff like, 'These beasts have thrived in the Highlands and Western Isles far longer than Christendom,' and I'm hearing bagpipes and starting to hope. But by doing everything right, it's all going wrong for them one small thing at a time. In August Kira went back to teaching, then learned she was pregnant, unplanned. Meanwhile Max had handpicked ten heifers, twenty-five cows, and a good bull he penned on an acre close to the house to track breeding efforts. But he bought his herd with a mortgage from bank vultures who saw what he'd done with the house and told him, 'Highlands! Great idea, Max. Sounds like the next big thing!' He got grazing rights high in the Whitetails dirt cheap, because Highlands thrive higher than other breeds. He planned to graze them into October. But his old Ford could only trailer four animals at a time. Took him nine trips to get his herd up there, fuel bills killing him, and on the ninth trip his engine went gunnysack. I rescued the animals stuck in his trailer and offered to bring down the rest, but Max refused. Sold a Jeep Wrangler he loved like a pet to rebuild his rattletrap Ford. Without him knowing, I kept an eye out for hay deals and stocked him up for winter. When he came home and saw it, he went off on me, saying he can't stand to feel beholden. 'Then don't, dammit!' I told him. 'Pride and strength aren't the same thing, Max. Confusing the two cost me a good marriage.'

"Max said sorry and accepted the hay. But the setbacks snowballed. He'd planned to camp out with his herd, but while seeing to his Ford he lost three heifers and a cow to a lion. Now it's mid-October, Kira starting to show, Max with thirty-two animals plus late-winter calves to feed until late spring. And once his animals are ready *he has no market*. He'd planned to create a niche market by touring West Coast cities, educating a clientele with tastings and talk of stewardship and heart health. But leaving pregnant Kira to feed his herd all winter while her teaching brings in their only income was a nonstarter.

"Next setback: Highlands need two years, not one, to reach a market-able weight. The payoff is the flavor, which is as good as beef gets. But they don't dress out like feedlot breeds. The cuts look different, and steak lovers are about as fond of change as South Carolina senators, plus the existing market is steakhouse and supermarket chains. What chain CEO will listen to a small-time wrangler trying to sell funny-looking cuts by lecturing him on cholesterol? I hate my own fortune-telling, TJ, but I see Max selling his herd at a loss by midwinter, forfeiting all his acres but the two around the house, trading his old pickup for a sedan safe for Kira and the baby, and begging me to give him back the Land & Beef job he hated."

It confused Kale that TJ looked nothing but stimulated by Max's woes.

"These complexities are new to me, and formidable," he said. "But finding new ways to do business is a passion of mine, and Max's plight gives me ideas. I'd like to fine-tune them with you, and talk with Max and Kira before I head back to Oregon. There's a chance I can set up the kind of small market they need."

Kale pulled the truck over and killed the engine. "This I gotta hear."

"My two restaurants, and those of a score of restaurateurs I know from Ashland, Oregon, north to Bellingham, Washington, do things with beef that interest no steakhouse or supermarket chain in America. The Highlands' lower cholesterol and great flavor are big pluses to chefs, and the less like feedlot cuts, the greener the source, and more substantial the land stewardship and heart health info, the better. What I'd do first is buy Highland cuts I'll run down myself, since Max's animals aren't ready. My chef friends and I will then get busy in my Portland kitchens, and if this beef tastes like we hope, we'll set up a consortium that does an end run around the cartel and create the market the Bowlers need. There's a thriving Oregon outfit selling organic ground beef to burger joints. We could do the same with Max's product. But our first move is to talk to him and Kira."

"*You,* sir, are a force of nature," Kale said.

"Not really. But I'm trying to keep up with one."

Kale asked, "Might that force go by the name of Risa?"

TJ shook his head. "Yep. Case in point. While we were pushing around cows yesterday, Risa invited Rosalia, Eddie, Lore, and Mu to E City Storage and told Eddie to bring his horse trailer. Risa's dad left her two units crammed full of hardware, furniture, sporting goods, and heirlooms galore. Lore told me that when they arrived, Risa said, 'Last week Americans celebrated Europeans stealing the Americas from the millions who already lived here. Today is *Un-Columbus Day.* I want to celebrate discovering those who already live here by giving them things, not taking them.' Having seen that her friends were poor, proud, and independent, Risa set upon them, saying stuff like, 'Look at all this *junk* my dad left me, Eddie! You've got woodworking skills. Can you get this Skilsaw outta here?' When polite Eddie tried to refuse, Risa looked so miffed he accepted. But before he even began to load it she added, "That heavy damned table saw and wood lathe are blocking access to everything I need. Do I look like a woodworker, Eddie? Do me a solid and get those behemoths outta here.' With all five of them pushing, up a ramp into Eddie's trailer rolled thousands of dollars worth of superb power tools. Eddie then hid in his trailer for fear she'd give him more, so Rosalia, Mu, and Lore were next. Risa had seen Lore's apartment. Calling classic kitchenware, lamps, and furniture 'crap I just don't need,' she showered Lore with what Lore needed. Having seen Mu's shitty kid's bike, she gave him a new mountain bike, helmet, saddlebags, and bike lock. Having seen Rosalia loving her fly-casting lessons with Eddie, she said, 'Let's see if Dave left some fishing crap lying around.' Minutes later Rosalia's hauling off a video of *A River Runs Through It,* a split-cane fly rod, and two vintage fly boxes loaded with flies Dave had hand-picked for the Elkmoon River and its tribs and arranged by season. Risa then phoned me to ask after another task. 'Yep. Done,' I said, and I met her, Eddie, and his trailer at the shop space he didn't yet know I'm fronting him in town. When we rolled his lathe and table saw inside, Risa powered them up so fast that Eddie was reduced to pleading, 'Thanks, but *please*. No more!'"

"Can she *afford* such generosity, TJ?" Kale asked. "Will *Risa* be okay?"

"What makes Risa okay is different than most people. Someday I'll tell how, when my brother was in a coma and I couldn't even breathe if I wasn't holding his inert hand, she dropped out of college, took over *all* my enterprises, and saved my sanity, restaurants, businesses, and possibly my life. That's why I'm here, Kale. As long as I'm breathing, what's mine is Risa's, and whatever she's doing for others, I'll help. And here's another thing. Happy as it makes her to give stuff away, it makes her even happier when others share the same spirit. If you and I just keep doing what we're doing, she won't just be okay. She'll be more fun than just about anybody you ever met. So let's talk to the Bowlers. And I haven't had time to tell you that my Portland builder and architect friends want to help Eddie with this idea he has to update the old Sears Craftsman Cottage kits. Think what *that* could do for us Elkmoon schemers and dreamers if we acquire land! So if somebody, say *you*, Pope, were to invite Eddie over to Ida's Ideas, hand him classic books on the Craftsman movement, plus blueprints of what some great Portland architects are doing to update those cottages..."

"Amigo," Kale said. "I like the way you think. Let's see if we can't make Lou's pal Miss Risa more fun than anybody the bunch of us ever met!"

VI. What Threads, Dreams, and Fragments Grow the Whole?

I awoke at three, feeling terribly sad, and feeling rebelliously that I didn't want to study sadness, madness, melancholy, and despair. I wanted to study triumphs, the rediscoveries of love, all that I know in the world to be decent, radiant, and clear.

—John Cheever, *The Stories of John Cheever*

The Fastening of Heaven

Dumbsaint Notebook Entry, Testament Creek School, October 17, 1997:

The Elkmooners' instant regard for TJ, & his for them, has me pondering spirit threads again. I first learned of them in my Desert Fathers class at U Dub back in 1988. The Coptic monks of Egypt called them "indestructible connecting lines," but this term would have fallen out of my memory if Dr. Kool didn't stroll into Skrit Lit the next day, step up to his blackboard, & with his trusty robin's-egg blue chalk write:

sutratman
sutr = suture; atman = soul
sutratman = soul-suture

I was still reeling at the beauty of this word when I realized that Lore's favorite Buddhist texts, the Diamond Sutra, Heart Sutra, Mountains and Waters Sutra, are called what they are because sutr is the literal thread that binds these holy texts together.

Feeling a mystical reality seeking entry to our world, I made green tea when I got home that night, opened The Coom's Metaphysics, combed through his treasure trove footnotes, & hit the jackpot:

Plato's term for soul-suture: "the fastening of heaven."
Rumi's term: "the cord of causation."

Plotinus's: "our tutelary spirit, not bound up with our nature, not the agent in our action, belonging to us as belonging to our soul, as the power which consummates the chosen life."

And American poets have discovered this magic, too! Denise Levertov speaks of a thread, finer than spider's silk, that pulls at her, keeps her company, guides her. William Stafford speaks of a thread we can follow as it pierces things that change, yet itself never changes. That these spirit threads, as Plotinus says, aren't ours, that they're the soul's own unbreakable extensions, is why they have the ability to fly over any distance in space, or backward & forward in time, connecting us to whoever or whatever the soul chooses to assist in their birth or blossoming. And not often, but sometimes, the soul's blossoming allows us to see with its clear eye, not our own. Holding my thread as I pictured my years with Julian, for instance, I finally saw us as a bouquet of flowers wilted from the very start. Holding my thread as I conjure my friendships with Jervis & TJ, & everything that happened during my last month with Dave, & everything that's happened since his deathbed map led me to the Glory Meadow & Lou Roy & then to all these good people, I sense ALL our threads trembling on an Unseen Weaver's Loom as she fashions us into a tapestry inconceivably more wonderful than anything we could create for ourselves! When it comes to breaking out of cages, driving money-lenders out of temples, or giving tyrannical leaders & institutions the slip, soul-suture is the most irascible of Mysteries—& I use the word irascible advisedly:

"Irascibilis," declares the Meister, "is the soul's upward striving power. She can't tolerate anything that would be above her & has such perfect confidence in God & in herself that she feels God has nothing in his whole being that is off-limits to her. She can't tolerate even God being above her unless he is in her & she in him, & she has & is all that God has & is."

ZOWIE!

So what does the irascible soul have to do with what's coming together here in the Elkmoon? My feeling tonight is: Everything! There is a palpable thread in every person convened here, living or deceased, that goes among things that change, but doesn't change:

* I sense Dave's thread operating in the lifelong Elkmoon heartbreak that led to his late conversion transformation into

an Elkmoon-worshipping mystic who, even after dying!, guided me with his deathbed map and dumbsaint-notebooks into the Presence of the Unseen Unborn Guileless ((((((!)))))).

* And I sense Kale's thread in his irascible love for an Elkmoon ranch he adores despite losing all but his twenty-acre & hundred-acre pieces of it—yet as soon as Kale's & TJ's threads crisscrossed in the Unseen Weaver's tapestry I could see & feel Kale moving toward a home place even _better_ than his childhood promised land.

* And I sense Lou Roy's thread in his lifelong loyalty to Kale. His service to that soulful foreman & his inholdings is a daily allegiance that's turned Lou into a Human Inholding himself!

* And who but a dead soul could fail to sense Jervis's thread guiding him through the unseen Ocean he never leaves as he wanders the lucky pavement of Portland whispering his gospel of "Simple down!" "No thinky." "No created thing but love." "I'm not my own, I'm Hers!"

* And TJ's thread is his total love for his Ocean-going brother & for a La Sagrada Familia given to him by a flown child & a father on a cross who help TJ disappear into a nothingness out of which compassion, empathy & generosity flow & flow.

* And Lorilee's thread glows in the marriage of her voice to her dulcimer, & in her unstinting reverence for a pearl-earringed Buddha, & for a scruffy Colorado peak, & for a seven-mile-wide Elkmoon Valley begging bowl, all of which tell Lore: "I am not so much to be looked _at_ as to be _looked out of_. After all,   !   !   Who are You?"

How simple, the reason the company of these people feels so very right: they don't ever let go of their threads.

A Letter and Song from Lorilee in Elkmoon City, MT, to Ona Kutar in Sausalito, CA:

Same Day You Left E City, 1997

Dear Ona,

Before you look at this song, know that I hold no expectations. If you feel nothing for it, just toss it. I only send it because you reacted so strongly to "Thirteen Tons." Five years back, on the same solo campout during which Two Medicine Peak became my songwriting partner and we wrote the *Thirteen Tons* album in one night, I felt so drained I thought I'd compose nothing for a month.

But as I was summiting Two Medicine on my hike home the next day, close to heat prostration, another song began to come to me. The odd thing was, the incoming music was nothing I could perform. A raw rock and roll voice and untamed virtuosity on electric guitar were required. But this music was circling overhead, requesting clearance for landing. Who was I not to help it down?

I pulled into the shade of a boulder and tacked down the melody, but the lyrics were defying me. They only came to me in fragments, and when I tried to lengthen them into complete thoughts it felt wrong. Then it hit me: *the fragments* are *the song.* Where the words break off they could be *way* more powerfully completed by a raging guitar than by words. *But wait,* I thought. *Somebody's done this.* And I recalled *your* voice and guitar duet at the end of "Zappalachia." I repeat, I expect nothing, Ona. I just hope this encounter between us five years before we met might fascinate you as much as it did me.

Love,
Lore

Frag Song

General musical idea: Legato 4/4 w/churchy chords resolving every eight beats, creating rock liturgy. Not pop, not folk, not a diva vehicle. Slow <u>rock</u>, as regal in feeling as, say, the opening of "Hey Jude," but every lyric breaks off midsentence to be emotionally completed by an electric guitar that sometimes enhances but other times <u>crushes</u> the fragment's intentions. In what key? Whatever's best for the vocalist. Likewise my chord suggestions are just crude notions of how it might go. The gist? Let "Frag Song" do from start to finish what Ona does on that last byte of "Zappalachia": words conveying no more than small broken sayables so an unbroken Fender can sing or insinuate or roar the Unsayable.

Verse One:

The day you said you'd crossed a...	*D, D, G, D...*
I only felt you'd lost the...	*D, D, G, D...*
The shattered glass inside my...	*G, G, C, G...*
Bled out the things I swore I'd...	*D, D, G, D...*
I know we promised we would...	*A, A, G, A...*
But when you laughed and spurned my...	*G, G, D, G...*
I had to torch and burn my...	*A, A, G, A...*
And disappear to hide my...	*A, A, G, A...*

[Voice cuts off, electric guitar grabs its note and emotion, and entire band closes the turnaround's D, D, G, D, then sets sail for eight bars, or sixteen, or however many the musicians feel will fly...]

Verse Two:

So when you said you'd found true...	D, D, G, D...
I couldn't turn to even...	D, D, G, D...
Or move my lips to say I...	G, G, C, G...
Or touch you in the way I...	D, D, G, D...

[next four guitar phrase finishers are <u>FEROCIOUS</u>]

The lies you...	A, A, G, A...
And when you...	G, G, D, G...
The sins you...	A, A, G, A...
And then you...	A, A, G, A...

[Voice cuts off, band completes turnaround's D, D, G, D, and guitar and band again sail for as long as feels right. Then key change brings Ona up three steps, into that wrecked thing she does with her voice as her lyric-finishing Fender solo soaring over acoustic guitars, organ, band, and choir...]

Chorus:

But even now the mountains...	G, G, C, G...
And all the summer stars are...	D, D, G, D...
Out of the cleft the waters...	G, G, C, G...
Let the lost sons and daughters...	D, D, G, D...
When Her touch sails across the...	E, E, D, E...
Your wild tears will wash the...	D, D, G, D...
Yeah even now the mountains...	E, E, D, E...
And all the summer stars are...	E, E, D, E...

[All voices and instruments complete the G, G, C, G, then lift and loop through the huge Fender solo...]

Verse Three:

You say you can't believe the...	G, G, C, G...
And nothing can relieve the...	D, D, G, D...
And all the love we never...	G, G, C, G...
And all the wounds we ever...	D, D, G, D...
But there's a hidden way that...	E, E, D, E...
Bringing a day you'll see the...	D, D, G, D...
And broken dreams become the...	E, E, D, E...
That opens out upon a...	E, E, D, E...

Chorus:

And even now the mountains...	G, G, C, G...
And all the summer stars are...	D, D, G, D...
Out of the cleft the waters...	G, G, C, G...
Let the lost sons and daughters...	D, D, G, D...

When Her touch sails across the...	*E, E, D, E...*
Your wild tears will wash the...	*D, D, G, D...*
Yeah, even now the mountains...	*E, E, D, E...*
And all the summer stars are...	*E, E, D, E...*
Out of the cleft the waters...	*G, G, C, G...*
Let the lost sons and daughters...	*D, D, G, D...*

[All voices, instruments, and untamed guitar complete the turnaround and continue as long as the spirit moves, and Blinky fades it out while it's all still soaring...]

The Boy by the River Sees a Man on the Other Side

In this dream, Risa and her river boy are walking Schoolhouse Bluff when the boy begins to tug on her hand, leading her quickly to the bluff's brink. Coming to a standstill, he ignores the majestic vistas upriver and down and peers into the cottonwood bottom directly across from them. Suddenly he tenses, seeming to track movement, though he doesn't speak or make a sound. So odd, the boy's silence. What child, on seeing something unusual, wouldn't say, *A bear! A moose! A fox!* From this boy, though he's electric with excitement, not a sound.

But look! Right where he's gazing. A *man*. A lone man is making his way through the cottonwoods, appearing, disappearing, reappearing under the canopy. He's easily three hundred yards away, walking with speed, much of the time erased by the leaves, yet the boy seems not only to recognize him but to be thrilled by him.

And *now* look! When the man reaches a small clearing, he stops, and turns toward the bluff. The boy pulls his hand free of Risa's and waves frantically. The man spots him at once, raises his right arm, and in big sweeping movements waves back. The boy bursts out laughing: the first vocalization he's ever made! Then the man sees Risa, raises his other arm, and waves so vigorously the boy turns to her, beside himself now with laughter! Though they hear nothing but the river, the man looks to be laughing too. Who *is* this person who elicits such emotion in the boy? Why does his waving to Risa fill *her* with longing too? She wants to run down the bluff, swim the river, find him, study his face closely, and, if she trusts what she sees, find out what connects him to her little river boy.

But what's *this*? Words on the air! Though the man's voice is inaudible, he's placing his hands on his chest, repeatedly unfolding his arms and hands toward Risa and the boy, and these gestural broadcasts are launching faint but sometimes audible words upon the air. *Let the fields come close,* Risa hears—and the boy lights up, feeling them too! *Let the fields be joyful, and all that is...* something something. *For the Lord? Before the Lord?* something. *And he cometh to greet the world with...* something something.

As his broadcast ends the man sets out as if he's coming to find them, Risa feels. But when he vanishes under the leafy ceiling the boy turns frantic. Running back and forth along the bluff edge, trying to spot movement, he's so upset to have lost sight of his man that Risa too rushes along the bluff trying to spot the man, but sees not a trace of him.

Suddenly the boy is in front of her, gripping her hand tight, his little face fierce with determination. And in an adorably froggy little-boy voice, out come his first words! "*I know where he is, and how to find him*! For *both* of us. I *can*! And don't worry about the river! *I know how to cross*! But it has to be *now*! Right now!"

The instant Risa releases him the boy turns and tears down the bluff, grabbing brush and small trees to keep his feet, his speed impossible for one so young—and Risa wakes on her camp cot, breathing so hard it's as if she too just tore down to the river.

Hoping the dream means that the man and boy are connecting, she sits up and peers out at the night. The boy's so small to be alone in that darkness! "*Be careful!*" she says aloud, then remembers TJ asleep across the room. Why are these dreams so insistent, and coming in chapters now? Who *is* the boy, or the man he's in search of? How could they recognize each other at such a distance if they didn't already know each other? Why does the man inspire such joy, such distress, and such courage in the boy? Is the Elkmoon's far shore a world accessible from our side? Is there something I could be doing to reunite the boy and man?

Too agitated to sleep, she slips into her robe and out the schoolhouse's back door.

Her bare feet, expecting dew, find the grass frozen. First hard frost of the year. Her feet begin to ache painfully. She ignores the hurt, rushing across the schoolyard to the drop-off, but the river bottom is a black void in the night, the bright cottonwoods a blur of sallow gray. Craning and straining to see the way the boy did, for what other connecting place is there, the small clearing in which the man stood seems never to have been. Feeling a desperation she doesn't understand, she steps to the very brink of the bluff, lays her own hands upon her breastbone, and starts unfolding her arms and hands the way the man did. "He *knows* you!" she cries, trying to hurl her words and feelings across the river. "Whoever you are, the boy knows and *needs* you! And he needs *me* too. And when you threw your words toward us we felt them so strongly! And what I felt…*what I felt*…"

Emotion sweeps her away: "I felt the entire valley answering! And its fields *do* wish to be joyful, and all that is therein! And the Lord *does* something something! This boy, these fields, these forests all *need* you! And I don't know who you are, or whether it's you or I who must cross the river. But I felt you too knowing that *we three must find one another!* Oh, tell me, Elkmoon! Tell me Unseen Guileless! *How do I find the man who threw such joy into the river boy and me!?*"

The Mythic Birds Keep Coming

The following letter, a CD, and a xeroxed story manuscript were mailed by Ona Kutar from the Salt Lake City Airport to Lorilee at the Black Queen in E City, and crisscrossed in transit with Lorilee's "Frag Song," which she had mailed to Ona the same day:

October 15, 1997

Dear Lore,

This should be three letters since it raises three topics. But our lives are about to intertwine, and I've got a window between flights here at SLC that I won't have once I'm home so I'm shooting you all three letters.

Letter #1: Allow me to speak sincerely about our upcoming tour. You and Mu are leading beautiful, quiet lives, and the last thing I want our tour to do is warp your lives with stress, so here are some thoughts on how I aim to reduce stress, and please share your own ideas about this with me whenever you like.

To my mind, an opening act should never feel like a sideshow to kill time before the main act. The opener should be treated as respectfully as the headliner. And you *will* be. Your storytelling songs are miracles of an old bardic power the world has nearly forgotten. To be sure our crowds can feel that, Richie and I are picking venues suitable for acoustic musicians, not for monsters of rock. No sports arenas and crowds of umpteen thousands. Great acoustics and appropriate scale will support you all the way.

The other help I want to offer: to sensitize my fans to you and Mu I'd like to dust off my acoustic Gibson, join you to open your sets, and do two or three covers in *your* style. We three will give crowds the heart-shivers, Lore. I *know* we will! Then I'll get lost and you two can shiver 'em on your own.

Letter #2: That little audience at your cafe concert last night felt like a roomful of long-lost friends. Crowds in a rare few places used to give me that feeling, but not for years, and it's led to some strong feelings.

The Ona Kutar Band is Mu's age, Lore, and it's been an epic decade. But the life of a year-round rocker disconnects me from everything I love about life on a living planet. I've dreamt for years of spending November to April touring, but May to October settled in one place. I want to fly-fish when the bugs are hatching, not when my tour frees me for a day when the fishing sucks. I want a farm big enough to share with everybody I love. And I sense a basic goodness in E City that has left much of America. Walking incognito through town this morning, folks met my eyes, smiled, and even *spoke* to the unmet stranger. I've missed that for two decades! So, fair warning: I'm gonna scheme with manager Richie and my brilliant assistant, Regina Cloud, about how such a move might work. And if my dreams should pan out, I'm gonna build a sound studio and hand you a key so that, year-round, you can record every musical idea you choose to set down.

Letter #3: Anyone who's heard "Thirteen Tons" knows that fabulous music can rise like a phoenix out of the ashes of a marriage. The enclosed CD is one such mythic bird that exploded up out of my own marital ashes. I won't try to dignify it by claiming this is a thoughtful gift from me to you. It's just an act of extreme mischief my band and I wreaked upon my ex's all-time greatest hit at our *Life Works* sessions in LA last month. Silas's "Feminine Side" was definitely written to provoke a response from me. But neither he nor I had any idea that my band's response to his hit would leave poor Silas looking like Wile E. Coyote smoldering in the crater of a rock and roll bomb he detonated himself! Since my topic is reducing stress, I was going to feign a virtue I don't possess and promise not to perform this looney tune on our shared musical adventure, Lore. But the boys in my band claim our take on "Feminine Side" has reduced female stress on a national level and saved a few thousand marriages, so I'm leaving the Yes or No up to you.

I can't wait to hit the road with you come late Feb!

Love,
Ona

A Postcard from Lorilee in E City to Ona in Sausalito:

O Ona! Your Feminine Side query makes me happy! There is no bird I'd rather watch repeatedly than the rock phoenix that came screaming up out of your marital ashes to uncork that mash-up of Silas's take on the feminine! Just FYI: I've got a humbucker & an FX box I once in a blue moon attach to my extra-large extra-loud 4-string dulcimer that might surprise you. Think it over. It would be a died & gone to heaven joy to help you dismantle that idiotic song!

Love,
Lore

VII. Ona's Severe Twang Phase

> That song is kind of a rhino in hot pants on a burnt
> rocking horse with a lariat shouting, "Repent, repent!"
> —Tom Waits, "Gravel Pit," *The New Yorker*

ONA WAS IN the voice booth singing a scratch vocal for her engineer to reference while, out in the live room, the four handpicked musicians of her band were feeling the friction, playing out-of-their-gourds great. In the control room, meanwhile, the engineer, Blinky Fitzpatrick, was riding the soundboard, blinking in the frenetic way he did only when a band was doing what he called "sky-larking" (definition: *pouring forth their full hearts in profuse strains of unpremeditated art*) when suddenly, for no apparent cause, Ona quit playing and hollered, "*God damn it! CUT!*"

The boys clattered to a halt, and gaped at her. "We were killin' and grillin' that thang, Ona!" "Jeez, *I* was sure feelin' it." "What's the matter, babe?"

"Somethin' just feels *way* off," she growled.

"But what?" "You were cookin' with jet fuel, Ona." "We were too."

Richie Horgan, Ona's longtime manager and crisis counselor, was peering out at her through the control-room glass. "Wussup, Ona?" he called in through the talk-back.

"Wussup," she said, "is that life is complex, paradoxical, and contrary as hell and *I want that in my art.* I want the yes that means no, the no that means maybe, the love that might also mean hate, the hate that always means fear. So what am I doing pumpin' out Top Forty platitudes about 'moons' and 'swoons' that rhyme way less interestingly than Dr. Seuss? Have you heard that new album *Hand Wash Cold Water* by the folkie Lorilee Shay? *There's* a woman pouring pain, mythos, complexity, and daring into music meant to transform us. It *can* be done. But nobody buys her CDs, and guess why? They shot their wads on mine! Wussup is, I'm overly famous, this band is the best, my voice is sounding great if I do say so, the groove is unholy good, it's a big-seller-to-be. Sure. Fine and dandy. But even as we're nailin' it I'm thinkin', *Jesus Gawd, listen to what I'm sayin'!*"

In a tone that stripped away the joy she'd been creating, Ona recited,

"You just don't know *ah, ah, ah, ah,*
"You just don't know *ooh, ooh, ooh, ooh,*
"We cannot know ooh-wah, ooh-wah,
"So let's just go *hoo, hoo, hoo, hoo.*

"Wussup, Richie, is, *who needs this ass-scratching chimpanzee drivel?*"
Seeing his skills were needed, Richie stepped into the live room.

"I remember the day you dreamed 'Hoo Hoo' up, Ona. In the drum-machine-and-synth-oppressed world of 1986, you said you wanted to send a love and joy song direct from your guitar's body into human bodies, and that the way to do it was to write lyrics so dumbed down they left you nothin' to talk out of but your guitar, giving listeners nowhere to go but into their bodies. That concept was so great it took over the album, *Iona Gittar* went triple platinum, 'Hoo Hoo' is now a national monument, and when you, me, and Sony were planning *Life Works* and they objected to 'Hoo Hoo' you told 'em, '*Bullroar! Look at the band I put together. 'Hoo Hoo' stays so the boys and me can boogie.*' Your dream came true, Ona, and to the tune of something like 3K an hour out of *your* pocket, you and the boys were just nailin' 'Hoo Hoo' to the wall. Then you quit on us. This confuses me. It's *your* smash hit, *your* handpicked band, *your* victory over Sony, and 'Hoo Hoo's never going to sound any more like Jane Austen than 'Louie Louie' sounds like Dostoevsky. So how about setting classic literature aside, doing what classic *rock* can do, and *shakin' this joint?*"

The musicians parked on their amps or stools and got comfortable. Waiting out Ona's roadburn, self-doubt, and angst fests went with the gig, but she was way too fun—and lucrative—to tour with for them to feel mutinous.

"What's wrong," she argued, "is that every guitar-driven hit I play takes ten seconds to achieve power, two minutes to reach the git-fiddle solo, and at three minutes it's over. What's wrong is, I spend my life serving the world a bunch of *audio quickie fucks.* What's wrong is, we lay down the rhythms of *sexual congress* in a span of time too short for a woman to get anything but *groped,* I sing of '*love that lasts forever,*' and when we fade at a hundred eighty seconds to make way for the Chevy Tahoe ad we wonder why the polar caps are melting, ADHD rules the *infotainment* industry, and poo-brained politicos win every election. Why do you think? *Because stars like me have eradicated the American Memory by stuffing it full of hoo-hoo shit on a drumstick!* Sorry to call a spade a spade, boys, but that's our gig. Thanks for the codependency."

Catching a barely perceptible nod from Richie, the boys began trying to calm her: "Call it what you like, Ona, it beats guttin' chickens all day at the factory farm." "Beats climbing into septic tanks to replace broken pumps like I used to do." "Beats stuffin' unHappy Meals down obese kids and diabetics all day."

Seeing it wasn't working, Richie gave an ever so slight headshake. The band fell instantly silent. God, Richie loved veteran studio musicians! *So* good at being conducted. He turned to Ona. "Would you mind hearing the unvarnished What Richie Thinks?"

"Gimme both barrels," she said.

"We're old friends, you and me. But in times of friendship. This isn't such a time. Your love for the world and desire to address its problems are wonderful out in the world. *But this isn't that world. This is a recording studio.* You've mastered a straight-ahead feel-good art form at a level reachable by about ten people on Earth, not two of 'em women. And you're only at the *funding* stage of your next problem-solving expedition. First things first, Ona. To fund your ideals, you and your band first need to blow the roof off this pricey music-making facility."

"You're making sense, Richie, you always do. But some day, God help me, I'm gonna find an art form that doesn't trap me in the shallows." (Scarcely moving his lips, drummer Jack Kite murmured, "*Here comes.*" The band, in unison, donned their most "interested" expressions.) "Like in *Marchy Dark's fiction*!" Ona enthused. (None of the boys even rolled their eyes, though they'd long since secretly dubbed these outbursts "Marchy Darklies.") "That woman gives birth to *worlds*. Spawns lives of every kind. An' we get to live the ups an' downs of 'em. Her women are my best friends! Even the bitches. Ha! No surprise. An' her men? *Shit howdy!* How come Marchy's made-up men feel ten times more real than the man I squandered my youth on?"

"Reality was never Silas's strong suit," Richie said.

"Still isn't," Robby Bray, the rhythm guitar man, said. "Y'all hear that new hit o' his?"

"'*Feminine Side*'?" Jack Kite asked with a wince.

"That's the one."

Richie had begun madly slicing a finger across his throat, but this time the boys missed it. Ona's ex-husband had written a flagrantly sexist, facetiously feminist anthem called "Feminine Side," and created a nationwide gender feud and furor that turned his tune into a megahit. In a televised country channel interview Silas then denied any culpability for the furor, saying, "I don't see the beef. That li'l tune idn't aimed at *country* women. I *love* country women—and they *know* it!" (Wink, wink.) "'Feminine Side' is just a harmless li'l SCUD missile aimed at ol' Iona Dupree—or whatever she orders folks to call her now."

Ona had to hand it to Silas. In four cheerfully poisonous sentences he'd made her sound like country music's answer to Muammar Gaddafi. She hadn't dignified his dig with a response. But when "Feminine Side" rose to the top of the country charts the real fun began. Silas's fans, infiltrating Ona's concerts during the Kutar Band's recent *Dervish of the Purple Sage* Tour, began shouting for *her* to play Silas's sexist megahit. Hoping to avoid a George-and-Tammy-style tabloid shitstorm, Ona took pains to ignore the chanters and keep giving her loyal fans what they'd come for. But at a concert just a month ago a knot of rabble-rousers started a chant that got maybe a third of the audience roaring: *"Fem-uh-nin Side! Fem-uh-nin Side!"* The takeover of *her* fans by Silas's fans felt sanity-threatening. To quell them Ona changed the playlist, busted out "Jackalope," one of her greatest hits, and all was well as she opened with the scorching guitar solo. But when she launched into the lyrics, something inside her went *sproing!* and a *severe* country twang leapt out of her for the first time in her life. Ona had been shocked to silence. "I was raised in *San Francisco* for chrissake," she'd told the crowd, trying to laugh it off. But when she lit into "Jackalope" a second time, she *again* twanged the lyrics involuntarily!

Gossip over the incident chased her to the next concert, this time fully half the audience took up the *"Fem-uh-nin Side!"* chant, and when Ona tried to quell them with a slow ballad her voice *again* went twangy. The country music rags and TV twaddlers jumped all over it. Those in Silas's court claimed her twang was deliberate mockery, proving her intolerance toward everybody who wasn't an overeducated urban liberal like herself. Stupendously unflattering photos of Ona accompanied magazine rants about her refusal to accept her ex's healthy sexuality when, in truth, Silas himself had lost count of the number of bimbos he'd bedded. Then Ona was targeted for her magnanimity. She'd donated herself and her bands, often at great personal expense, to concerts to curb world hunger, educate oppressed Muslim women, combat HIV in Africa, create havens for Tibetan refugees. The country gossips who'd worshipped Iona Dupree threw this back in Ona Kutar's face, claiming her concerts "for non-Christians and foreigners" demonstrated her detestation of America, whereas patriots like Silas supported what was needful in the Age of Terror. The absurdity of the slander left Ona speechless. Her sole reply to her detractors, she vowed, would be to rock the bullcrap clean out of them with her two-CD retrospective, *Life Works ('Cept When It Don't)*. But there in the Axman Studio live room, her band knew Silas's hit had put Ona through hell. In response to another discreet nod from Richie, they tried to show solidarity:

"Dupree seems to think he's some kinda funny man." "Funny as an impacted wisdom tooth." "Funny as an IRS audit." "Funny as a rubber turd on your mom's coffin."

"Funny as the flag-wavin' self-parody he's decided to be," Ona said with a shrug. "Anybody names his Stratocaster after Ronald Reagan obviously has no idea what a *muse* is. But I gotta admit, Silas makes me laugh almost as often as he makes me mad."

"That's *way* too generous," Richie said. "His guitar work is dumbed-down grunge, his lyrics are antique Andrew Dice Clay, and 'Feminine Side' is an all-time low."

Jack Kite chimed in. "That song's so misogynistic that when it came on the radio in Albuquerque two nights ago, my wife phoned as it was playing, steaming mad at *me*! 'Jeez, Ava,' I said, 'it's *Dupree's* tune and *your* radio station. I'm in LA, I hate the song, I've never worked with Dupree and never will. Why don't you call the station to complain, hon?' '*Don't you tell me what to do!*' Ava fires back. 'You men're a buncha sex-obsessed trolls, an' this *theme song of yours* should be convicted of *ear rape!*' 'Theme song of *mine*? How does *that* work?' I said—and Ava hung up on me!"

"But that's hilarious!" Ona insisted. "Without even leaving Nashville Silas voodooed your marriage, my concert tour, and half of America with his song. Marchy Dark could make hay outta that. Speaking of makin' hay, you fellas ever read her novel *Dwight Yoakam's Legs?*"

The boys all shook their heads *regretfully*.

Ona took on a wild look. "Good God in heaven, *here's* an idea! Let's *us* do it. 'Feminine Side'! An' play it in a way that squeezes every drop o' sass out of that stupid song's face!"

The boys broke out in nervous chuckles.

"I'm not kidding!" she said, strapping her guitar back on. "I get to be Silas! To play that thing'll *purge* me. Come on, gents! One time through, giving it all we got, an' I'll behave for the rest of this session."

The boys still looked dubious, but Ona was bobbling like the lid of a saucepan on high boil. "She's *definitely* not kidding," said Richie.

"It's in D," Ona said, and struck the chord. "Four-four time, like a military march. Think: *all male firing squad leading a woman out to shoot her for no reason.* World's oldest three-chord turnaround. Bridge, the same three in different order. And when we get to Silas's solo, *my guitar gets to play God.* You with me? Sure, it's therapy. Jack's marriage and me *need* therapy!"

"For the record," Jack said, straightening up in preparation, "it was *me* Ava shot for no reason. But gimme the pace o' this firing squad."

Shutting her eyes, Ona felt for it in her body: "*Hup. Two. Three. Four.*"

Jack set down a military beat with drum rolls that conjured all the good cheer of a kangaroo court martial. The band laughed. Ona started toward the vocal booth, then stopped herself. "I better hang with you fellas in the live room. My guitar and me are about to have a hell of an argument. You'll need to see it to stay with us."

No objections from the band.

When Ona bent down and began dialing in her sound, rhythm man Robby and bassist Sleeves Davis were riveted. When "the Ophelia of the Grand Ole Opry" had left Silas and gone into seclusion, there'd been an explosion of rumors as to the identity of the four electric guitar masters who'd helped turn demure acoustic Iona into electrified Ona. Every album since had included a thank-you such as, "More kisses to my Four Horsemen of the Decibel Apocalypse." But she'd never named them. As she settled on the sounds she'd be bringing, Robby and Sleeves whispered back and forth about whose influence they were hearing: "Her touch is so light. That's Billy Gibbons's deal!" "Maybe. But holy shit! That was a *Prince* lick right there!" "But her gear is old-school. One mechanical pedal to crank her amp so she can drive the tone with no effects. That's Neil Young's MO." "Right on. No Klon either. Only *real* distortion. But hey. What's this thuggery she's doin' now? Joe Walsh shit-faced?" "When was Joe ever not shit-faced?" "Joe's stone-cold sober now, Robby!" "No way!" "Yes way." "Shit yeah! Go, Joe!" "Time to gird our loins, hombre."

Happy with her prep work, Ona popped in her earbuds. The boys did the same. She gave them a conspiratorial grin, then began playing the basic three-chord riff in time to the beat Jack had set. On her second pass Sleeves kicked in on bass, Robby on rhythm, and both men blushed when, by the way they nailed it, it was obvious they knew the song perfectly well.

"*BUSTED!*" Ona laughed. "*Louder!*" she added. "And *WAY* more shameless!" She ripped off a few chords to show them what she meant.

Still crimson, but grinning, the boys did as told and then some. The groove started to gel.

Jiggy Croft, on keyboards, was listening hard but looking baffled. When he wasn't doing studio work he was a jazz player. Never heard of Silas Dupree. Avoided Republican Country like an all-hats-and-no-cowboys pandemic. But when he got a feel for what the guitars and drums were doing he unfurled a Liberace glissando to make the mood strange, started banging away, and the groove took a turn toward vintage Who with a great piano man sitting in. Ona's and Robby's guitars turned as edgy as predators smelling blood. To sharpen that edge Jiggy ditched his piano long enough to dial in a Who-ish synth part, which he programmed, then shut off, on standby if needed.

"*Hell* yeah, Jiggy!" Ona called. "We'll burn them Icarus wings off 'fore we're done. Here's how I'll ask for 'em." She popped her cowgirl hat on, then did a right-armed Pete Townshend windmill move that knocked it off. Jiggy nodded and went back to banging.

Ona returned to the basic riff and let the boys work it. Her windmill and Jiggy's synth had set something off. Robby reached over and cranked Sleeves's bass higher. Sleeves donned a haughty expression and started Entwistling rapid-fire finger-tipped bass arpeggios. In answer, Ona attempted something Townshendesque for the first time in her life, Sleeves ramped up his Entwistling, and everyone was grinning as their efforts began to feel like the foreshocks of a killer earthquake. Sure, the chords were high school. What they hadn't remembered was the idiot joy that came of *blasting* them this way.

When the groove was way more dialed in than mere therapy required, Ona went to full volume and ran through the turnaround four times, but the imbecilic bridge just once, "'cause I hope to surprise you guys, and me too, when we get there. Jack, we're loving the Who references, but *please*. Even if we conflagrate, *no Keith Moon*. Those cymbal crashes would set off my tinnitus, I'll be done sleeping, and our session'll go entirely to hell."

Though Jack nodded, Richie Horgan waved both arms, caught his attention, and made praying hands. "Got it. No Moon!" Jack told him.

"To start, Jack," Ona said, "gimme two bars of court-martial drum solo.

Then you and I will kick it up to full-bore. Fellas, give Jack four bars with just me. Then, from your first stroke, *BLAST IT!*" Four happy nods. A couple nudged gain and volume knobs.

Ona wiggled her cowgirl hat at Jiggy. He made a windmill with one finger. Ona nodded, then went dead still, her head bowed for several seconds the way she'd made famous. She gave Jack the coolest of nods. He played the two-bar firing-squad solo. To everyone's incredulity, given how relentlessly Silas's smash hit had hounded her, Ona lit out on a perfect replica of Silas's dead-simple, dead-raucous opening lick on his oversized Stratocaster, Big Ron. Four bars later the band exploded in behind them. Cranking her voice up so rough Richie feared she'd wreck it for life, Ona let fly:

BABE-BABE-BABE-BABE-BABE HEY NOW!
I'm so in touch
With my feminine side
I'm on my back
Climb aboard
Take a ride!
You kept on accusin' me
Of too much cowboy pride
But if you'd been
My LOCO MOJO
I'd be your bride!

Richie marveled. Ona's voice and body, without even trying, turned the snickering sexism of Silas's lyrics into something counterinsurgently sexy, her guitar work was epic, and the band already sounded far better than the band backing Silas's megahit.

I'm so dang comfy
With the she part o' me
That I pour me my Jack Daniel's
With an upraised pinkie
An' that ain't all I coulda raised up
If you'd thought how it could be
If you had just stopped yer preachin'
An' climbed up there on me!

When she reached Silas's idiot bridge, Ona stunned the boys by dialing in a Devo delivery so convincing Jack later said he hallucinated her Stetson turned into a toilet plunger:

I hoped to lie on my back
An' suffer your brute attack
I hoped your halter and reins

Would jerk the thoughts from my brain
If the tight squeeze of your thighs
Had put some stars in my eyes
I could have cooked an' crocheted
Because you ROCKED ME THAT WAY, HEY, HEY!

At the "HEY, HEY!" on the megahit video, Silas did indeed fall flat on his back. A stunt. Padded landing. But well performed, detractors hated to admit. The camera angle shot to the ceiling, aimed straight down, and viewers saw the floor beneath Silas was a big round American flag spinning in slow circles. With a miniature dolly hidden under his back and gummy rubber added to the down sides of his boots, Silas, in time to the music, walked in counter-circles to the flag as he played a hard-driving Big Ron solo while a crowd of "cowgirls" in little star-spangled vests offered their bosoms to the spinning stage, "thrilled" by Silas's thick-fingered gittarin'.

As Ona reached the same Guitar Moment she kept her feet, sported no red, white, and blue and added no theatrics. But the instant she launched a chord-rich chord-shredding solo Richie felt it in his marrow: *she'd caught fire.* Loving the feel of jazzman Jiggy's rock-hijacked piano, Sleeves's Entwistling, Robby's driving rhythm, Jack's even-keeled drum heroics, Ona performed the windmill, knocked off her hat, summoned Jiggy's Icarus synth down from on high, and proceeded to transform Silas's galumphing Big Ron solo into a crazed kissing cousin to Pete Townshend she hadn't known she owned. Sounding like two guitars celebrating an apocalypse, leaving gaps in which the synth and band blazed, extending and varying her chord-shredding, she unearthed a bag of tricks so astonishing even to herself that when it was time for the last verse she shook her head, her guitar stayed on the bridge, and the boys followed her inspired madness into a '70s Valhalla a second time, ecstatic third time, levitating fourth time, no end in sight.

Richie meanwhile had entered rock samadhi. Yes, this diversion was costing Ona a fortune, but her hands had turned into wings, the whole room had taken flight, she was healing herself, igniting the band, setting the tone for the rest of the session—and if Silas could hear what she was doing to his Running-in-Patriotic-Circles chug-a-lug he'd grab Big Ron by the neck, smash him to splinters Townshend-style, throw himself down on his spinning Old Glory, and bawl his little boy brains out.

Damn! Richie muttered to himself. *If only Blinky had been ready to capture this!*

But wait. Richie spun round and peered in the sound booth.

Ohhhhh yeah! Manning the board, blinking like mad, grinning like the fool he wasn't, Blinky Fitz was turned on, tuned in, taking it all prisoner. What a Christmas gift for poor Silas! Looking higher than Richie had seen her in years, Ona burned her solo's Icarus wings off in a sonic sun as promised, did the little hip crank that meant *last verse*, the boys read her like a book, and all instruments, amps, and efforts fused as Ona set Silas's closing thoughts on gender in their crosshairs:

BABE-BABE-BABE-BABE-BABE HEY NOW!
I'm so in touch
With my feminine wiles
I'd have lain me down in cacti
If you'd rode me in style,
You just can't keep accusin' me
Of too much cowboy snide
When if you'd been
My HOOHAW BRUJO
I'd be your bride!
Yeah, you keep on accusin' me
Of too much macho pride
When if you'd been
My LOCO MOJO
I'd be your bride!

Silas's smash hit ended with a big unison one-note bang—but as the Kutar Band watched Ona approach that dead end they read her jubilant *NO WAY!* Jiggy unleashed the Icarus synth again, and back they flew into the bridge, flying still higher into the rapture that had jumped them out of the least likely source imaginable. In the sound booth Blinky was *gone*, skinny arms in the air waving in some kind of Tree-Frog-Comes-to-Jesus ecstasy. Meanwhile Richie, feeling something weird going on below him, glanced down and found his feet doing a deft Scottish jig he'd never before seen, let alone learned, and the next instant had a vision of the faux bootleg DVD that would make this record look outlawed. *Oh,* Richie could see it! Plain black words on a pure white CD cover to make the thing look outlawed:

ONA KUTAR
BOOT LEGGÈD

And below the words, beginning with a foot hidden in a ragged ol' cowgirl boot, nothing but a woman's long, tan, naked leg all the way up to an unseen but breathtakingly implied rest of her. A leg so provocative it left you feeling life with the woman up top might be like living full-time in a Mandan sweat lodge, but *bring it on*! A leg that, coupled with Ona's bliss-shot transfiguration of her ex's ham-handed he-man solo, helped turn Silas's greatest hit into Ona's nineteenth Grammy.

(Elkmoon Valley, October 1997)

VIII. Cottonwoods vs. the Corporation

That civilisations fall, sooner or later, is as much a law of
history as gravity is a law of physics. What remains after
the fall is a wild mixture of cultural debris, confused and
angry people whose certainties have betrayed them, and those
forces which were always there, deeper than the foundations of
the city walls: the desire to survive and the desire for meaning.
— Paul Kingsnorth and Dougald Hine,
The Dark Mountain Manifesto

Through the coulee a river of cottonwoods runs.
In winter the river runs dry, all but a trickle.
But autumn the water's golden and its running
drowns out even the real river's running.
You can breathe inside this water, too, and let
its conflagration raze the brain's old homestead...
A long time ago when God was reading the earth
the angels interrupted, pleading for another galaxy.
He made this stand his bookmark. Some frigid nights
you can almost hear the dusty spine unfolding.
— Chris Dombrowski, "Cottonwoods," *Ragged Anthem*

THE OCTOBER 20TH gathering in the Testament Creek School convened at
2 p.m. on a Sunday. The day was clear and calm. A week of rain and snow
and a forty-degree drop in temperature was forecast in two days, making
the year's final sixty-degree day poignant. TJ had been scheduled to return
to Portland that morning, but when Lorilee told him how the approaching
storm would blast forty riparian miles of cottonwood leaves into and
down the Elkmoon in huge undulating shoals, creating yet another form of
October beauty he'd never seen, TJ canceled his flight, lent his chef talents
to the celebratory meal, and drove Risa to Portland later that week in the
Crimson Exploiter.

The meal in the schoolhouse was planned for 4:15, a time Risa chose
because, at 4:25 precisely, the sun dropped into the low western cleft of
the Elkmoon Valley, backlighting the cottonwood gold and the river-blade

of silver for moments so glorious she felt it would consecrate the school's conversion into Elkmoon Greater Good Headquarters without need of a single spoken word. The guests were Lou Roy, Kale, Lorilee, Mu, Eddie and Rosalia Dominguez, Max and Kira Bowler, Regina Cloud, Buford Raines, Ona Kutar, TJ, and Risa, with Ida Craig scheduled to arrive late. Hub Punker put in an appearance, but only to see if the Squire was living up to his nickname. The instant Hub spotted TJ's sage-colored Italian suit, new Ariat cowboy boots, immaculate pink dress shirt, and buffalo skull bolo borrowed from Risa, he gave the Squire a grease-stained thumbs-up, and left.

The schoolhouse interior had been converted into a restaurant by Buford, Regina, and Lore. Lounging in the low sun outside, Kale, TJ, Lou Roy, Eddie, Risa, and Ona were scheming about their ever more openly expressed hope to reinhabit a portion of the valley as a group committed to lives as frugal and easy on the planet as the Brokeback Ranch plans were the opposite. This conversation occasioned the first time Risa and TJ shared their admiration, as a community role model, for the spiritual and material independence of a fourteenth-century movement of European laywomen who called themselves Beguines.

Intriguing ideas about sharing appliances, vehicles, group health insurance, group property insurance, daycare, and material goods to reduce expenses and Earth wounds so absorbed them that only Kale noticed Ida Craig's white Audi pull in among the parked cars down at the locked cable blocking the track up the bluff. When Ida emerged holding a sheaf of papers and three bouquets and began powering up the hill with a Junoesque blend of strength and grace, Kale was astonished afresh to be her chosen man. But her speed was extreme. Something was up.

Rather than draw attention to her, Kale suggested the group wander back into the school, took the lead, and set a pace that caused their stroll and Ida's uphill charge to reach the schoolhouse door at the same moment.

"Oh, Kale!" she cried in the voice so out of keeping with her figure that those who'd not yet met her gaped. "I was closing up shop when a *New York Times* story appeared online. Can we gather? I think everybody will want to hear this!"

"Circle round!" Kale called as Ida, looking like Mount Olympus's own schoolmarm, handed out xeroxed copies of the *Times* story to the twelve adults and two kids.

The gist: confident of an eventual legal victory, NorBanCo had bulled ahead with the development name Brokeback Ranch & Country Club, sinking a fortune into lawyers and more lawyers, promotional brochures, signage, national ads, and, most recently, a Brokeback logo they attached to sweaters, T-shirts, hoodies, ball caps, golf shirts, golf balls, and other merchandise. In the meantime, Annie Proulx and her publisher had signed a movie contract for her story "Brokeback Mountain," giving exclusive control of its title to the producer to protect subsidiary rights, concessions, spin-offs, and their own very different merchandising. The *Times* story then quoted movie industry and intellectual property insiders who agreed the producer's claim on the word "Brokeback" was bulletproof and that further NorBanCo use of the word was now actionable to the tune of millions.

Some whooping and hollering greeted the news, but to Risa's and TJ's surprise, Kale only looked pensive. He then quietly asked Ida, Risa, TJ, and Lou Roy to slip out one at a time, bring no one else, and meet him on the brink of the bluff.

They did as asked and Lou Roy arrived last. "What's up, Pope?"

"That's some good news Ida brought," he told them. "But it hit me as I heard it that it's high time I share with you four, but *only* you four, two secrets I've been keeping for over a year. Both concern what we might call 'infestations,' but of two very different kinds.

"First infestation. In September of *last year,* not this, I went bowhunting in the South Whitetails, as I've done every year since boyhood with good results. But I'd barely got started when I was derailed by the condition of the forest. In stand after stand of pines, pitch tubes—these sappy globs that run down the trunks out of boring holes—were oozing from every tree. Woodpeckers then slammed the holes till they're gaping. The cause: *pine beetles.* I gave up my hunt, explored hundreds of acres, and for the past thirteen months I've explored almost all of their forestlands. Things are *far* worse now. Tens of thousands of trees riddled. The infestation is unstoppable— and we're talking *South Whitetails* here, folks. Think about that."

"Their entire development's viewshed!" Risa said.

Kale nodded. "The vaunted views from the Grand Lodge, proposed ranchettes, condos, townhouses, clubhouse, mall, are aimed at *billions* of pine-murdering critters the size of a grain of uncooked rice. In a few months, every potential picture window in their touted outdoor paradise will have a perfect view of a lifeless rust-orange forest. Yet NorBanCo hasn't begun to respond. Their entire board is made up of Texas clones swearing by their Fox News Oracle that climate breakdown is a hoax perpetrated by Al Gore."

"But doesn't this endanger *all* forests?" TJ asked. "Isn't this a disaster for us too?"

"Yes to the danger," Kale said. "But let's look at the disaster—and stay with me, TJ, because I'm no longer speaking as the owner of two little inholdings I've kept just to be a burr in NorBanCo's britches. I'm speaking out of the Elkmoon dreaming that you, Risa, and your brother, Jervis, have encouraged us all to be doing.

"Beetle-killed forests are a tragic loss, but only for a time. And when it came to our ability to control our destiny here, we were never in the game so long as the viewshed stayed green. That's why I've kept quiet. This infestation changes *everything.* What outdoorsy fat cat would invest in a recreational paradise of tree carcasses? A mass exodus of investors is about to reduce their land to fire-sale prices, whereas those of us with faith in natural regeneration and no desire to turn a quick profit might *enjoy* watching a blighted landscape return to intricate green life."

"But aren't dead trees extra susceptible to fire?" TJ asked. "Am I wrong to find this terrifying?"

"Wildfires *are* terrifying and climate breakdown makes them more so. But there's a hell of a lot we can do to prep, and I've been prepping all year. The land we dream of recovering—the four thousand acres of the former McKeig and Broussard holdings—is the most defensible land NorBanCo owns. Both spreads have excellent water sources even in drought. The huge open fields turn the scattered stands of trees into small, defensible targets. There are no buildings to protect since Tex knocked them all down. With help from Buford, who knows how to keep quiet, I've irrigated the dickens out of that land, creating big, fireproof green belts. We still need an ability to douse spot fires without being dependent on NorBanCo's equipment and we're on it, buying water tanks to go in the backs of our pickups, and our own used ATVs to reach terrain our trucks can't. Ida and I are also pricing used fire trucks."

Ida's smile showed a mischievous streak Risa had never noticed. It made her glee grin appear, which Ida spotted, and a little more mischief flew back and forth between them.

"NorBanCo has no interest in ranching, or in the health of their forests," Kale continued. "Their Fort Worth accountants advise them to buy huge holdings and do almost nothing to steward them, so they generate 'net operating losses'—NOLs—to negate taxes and other costs. Except for their development lands and horse and bike trails, NorBanCo sees their twenty-two thousand acres as one giant NOL. That's why Tex ignores their wild lands and irrigates nothing but the Grand Lodge grounds and his development sites. But this infestation is *way* more than an operating loss. Huge change is upon this valley, and yes, a lot of it's negative. But only half their forest land is infested. And on the land we covet the positive is this: Tex's Brokeback Ranch dream is about to become an unsellable development graveyard that NorBanCo will unload for sure. A hell of a lot of damaged but *very* inexpensive property will then be changing hands."

While TJ looked reassured by Kale's words, Risa did not. "You said *two* infestations," she said. "I hate to even ask, but what's the other one?"

Kale gave her a look that surprised her for its tenderness, then leveled the same look on Ida, TJ, Lou Roy. "I'm looking at it," he said. "You four and the folks in that school are an 'imagination infestation' that began the day Risa arrived. Risa *has* turned the school into our true Elkmoon headquarters. Ida *has* shored me up when I needed it most. TJ *is* a collaborative business genius offering folks help beyond their wildest dreams. And Lou's cowboy basics, every time my hope gives out, have steadied me lifelong. Our dream of inhabiting this land in creative ways is coming closer by the day. And those beetle hordes are a fist that's *already* hit NorBanCo smack on its glass jaw."

Wearing his tight little smile, TJ said, "You're a dangerous man, Pope. The fire threat scares me, but I trust your judgment that the acres we want are defensible. And the beauty of that land, the goodness of these people, and my brother Jervis's nonstop hints that remarkable things could happen here excite me *way* too much to back out now."

"I can't tell you how glad I am to hear that!" Kale said.

"Risa," Ida said, her mischievousness still visible. "Reading your face, I have no doubt that you're thinking thoughts we'd like to hear."

Risa smiled. "I was thinking about NorBanCo, actually. Yes, they're an enormous multinational, and in some ways very powerful. But lately I'm more struck by all the ways they're powerless. By legal definition they're an anti-visionary, non-tax-paying, money-grubbing machine whose moral imperative in the Elkmoon—an urge to turn ninety billion dollars into ninety-one—is bonehead math, not an imperative. Their methods are greed-skewed reason, cultural, historical, and biological ignorance, and hubris. Their guidance comes from abstracted minds in distant office towers, their bylaws make expressing their humanity illegal, and the pile of money they serve has no pulse and no soul, which not only makes our imagination infestation inconceivable, it makes us *invisible to them*. Which is *perfect*."

Though her friends' eyes were shining, TJ checked his watch, panicked, and said, "If I don't get to the kitchen our dinner's an NOL!" And away he streaked before they could thank him for his ongoing good deeds, which was just the way he liked it.

WHILE THE IMPENDING disappearance of the Elkmooners' archenemy from this chronicle could strike some readers as a loss of suspense, I don't like bogus suspense any more than I like bogus climate facts, NOLs, or Corporate Persons. The truth is, Risa Evenstar, TJ Gamgee, and Kale Baggins did not outwit the Dark Lord of Power, nor did Max Solo, Buford Skywalker, and Lou Roy the Jedi elder take out a single NorBanCo stormtrooper. *NorBanCo took itself out.* Their acceptance of the lie that climate chaos is a conspiracy designed to cripple capitalist profits left them helpless against the most vicious threat to every sylvan development in the Canadian and American West: the raging wildfires and insect infestations annihilating millions of acres of forest every year. Kale's prediction of NorBanCo's slow, self-crippling response to the crisis was on the money. It turned out to be a six-step program that went like this:

One, at the January of '98 meeting in Dallas, the NorBanCo board unanimously agreed they had solved the last glitch slowing their wonderful development by voting to change the name Brokeback Ranch & Country Club to Grand Lodge Ranch & Country Club.

Two, when six thousand more acres of viewshed pines responded by turning the same color as TJ's orange Carhartts, the board launched their June of '98 meeting in London by unanimously blaming Tex Schiller for being as ignorant of pine beetles as they were, and ordered Tex to solve their dead-forest glitch with a helicopter logging operation. When Tex obeyed, a parade of flying tree corpses and nonstop smoke from a gargantuan forest funeral pyre filled the Grand Lodge skies, and even cautious queries into investing ended.

Three, at their January of '99 meeting in Honolulu the board agreed to hire consultants from the forest products industry to convince the development's panic-stricken early investors that flying tree corpses and pyre smoke were to their benefit. The consultants responded with a four-color brochure worthy of the Koch Brothers, claiming that NorBanCo's heli-logging operation "demonstrates our ongoing dedication to maximum forest health and fire control to safeguard *your* visionary Grand Lodge investment."

Four, at the June of '99 meeting in Copenhagen the NorBanCo board was stunned to learn that early investors responded to their brochure by realizing they were getting hosed, hiring a team of lawyers, and demanding full refunds of their down payments on homesites. When NorBanCo denied the request, the investors responded with a multimillion-dollar lawsuit citing multiple instances of fraud in the development's prospectus and legal descriptions. At the January 2000 meeting in Singapore the board then learned they'd been forced to settle the lawsuit for a dollar amount even more onerous than what they'd paid their army of lawyers to lose the case.

Five, at the June 2000 meeting, again in Dallas, NorBanCo's CEO, one Cecil Danforth, surprised no one when he informed the board that their visionary Old West mall, luxury ranchettes, townhouses, golf course, fishing beats, and hunting grounds had spiraled down the toilet. The board then unanimously voted to repurpose the Grand Lodge as a conference center open in June, July, and August to make the exorbitant cost of upkeep tax deductible, and awarded Tex Schiller an 80 percent pay cut to handle lodge upkeep and security for the nine months the place was mothballed.

Six, when Tex's Montana years culminated in a 24/7 job as a janitor/security guard in wintry solitude, he defied the contractual clause that forbade him to overnight anywhere but the lodge and began paying scotch-soaked visits to the Loco Creek Steakhouse and motel next door. When word of his absences spread, a tactical team of pranksters paid a visit to the renamed Grand Lodge & Conference Center, threw black plastic over its impressive sign, erected a somehow familiar-looking handmade replacement, photographed it with the lodge looming behind, and the photo went viral, leaving NorBanCo famous across ten western states for owning a ponderosa palace named "The BroKeBAnK RaUNcH & CLimaTE cLUb."

NorBanCo's hold on their ailing lands forced the Elkmoon Dreamers to wait from 1997 to 2003 to learn their fate—a length of time that would cause most such collectives to dissolve. The Elkmooners did the opposite. They knew NorBanCo's presence had been reduced to an abandoned lodge and blueprints less substantial than a ghost town. They knew Tex was so obsessed with trying to preserve his lodge that he let

Kale run Land & Beef Inc. free of his misguidance, leaving the Elkmooners free to soak the fire danger out of the arable land they coveted. Meanwhile, on Kale's inholdings, the Elkmooners kept improving their plans to become organic farmers, organic beef providers, kit cottage builders and suppliers, wilderness outfitters, Earth-loving educators of many kinds, and much more.

BACK TO THE October 20th Greater Good Headquarters banquet:

As the 4:25 cottonwood witching hour approached, TJ's servers rolled out a variety of hors d'oeuvres, put finishing touches on salads and side vegetables, and took orders for the main course of vegetarian or carnivorous lasagnas. The vegetarian entrée featured spinach, four cheeses, shallot slivers, and TJ seasonings unlike anything most of them had ever tasted, and the result was sublime. The carnivorous option added a zingy elk sausage so locally sourced they could look out the west schoolhouse window and see it: a rusty white box freezer on the plywood porch of the elk hunter Lou Roy Skinner's silver Airstream.

TJ's culinary charisma had kept Rosalia hovering close, peppering him with questions the replies to which made her laugh so infectiously that Lou Roy ratcheted over to eavesdrop. En route, however, he glanced out the east schoolhouse window at the ball field—and there in the golden light, on the long-disused grass-covered pitcher's mound, Regina Cloud straddled Buford Raines, who lay on his back gripping her hips in his strong tanned hands, laughing while she leaned down to tickle him with her almost Rapunzel-length brown hair, keeping up a rocking movement that so closely resembled clothed coitus that Lou sighed, "*Ho! Lee! Jeez!*" But when Rosalia started over to see what caught his eye, the wily old Jedi faked a cough and said, "'Scuse me. What I'm tryin' to say is, *Ho Lee Jeez, Rosaleez!* Let's pick us a place to set at one o' them pretty tables."

Them pretty tables were a pair of weather-grayed four-by-twelve sheets of plywood resting on sawhorses, transmuted by elegant off-white embroidered tablecloths, eight candles in silver holders, and fourteen place settings compliments of the Valley matriarch Stella McKeig's heir and great-granddaughter, Risa. While Lorilee poured and Mu delivered long-stemmed glasses of wine and apple cider, a long-since relaxed Ona Kutar strolled out to ask Buford and Regina if they perchance remembered how to stand up and walk.

Five minutes later, fourteen good humans age nine to fifty-four convened at the tables before the sixty-four-pane west-facing window, spun their chairs toward the long view at Risa's urging, and Kale invited Lou Roy, of all people, to say the blessing.

Risa thought Kale was teasing and Lou would demur. Instead, without missing a beat, the one-trick Dickel drinker raised perhaps the first long-stemmed glass of red wine he'd ever held, took an uncertain sip of an epic bordeaux provided by TJ, winced, recovered, touched each guest's face with his glacial-silt-green eyes, and said, "Lord. I figure, You bein' all-knowin', You know the only prayer my dad Big Roy Skinner ever said at dinner was 'If you see bad do good. Amen.' An efficient prayer, Big Roy's. I also figure You read hearts easier'n I read Ernest Haycox Westerns since You're the manufacturer. So You already know I bring Big Roy up 'cause o' what we got goin' right here. Never in my life have I seen so many folks, the second they see the need of another, try to meet it so fast it's like each person is out to be each other's prayer answered."

As smiles of surprise greeted Lou Roy's blessing, the old wall clock reached 6:40, Rosalia cried, "*Look!*"—and the diners were struck silent as the setting sun eased into the valley's cleft, turning mile upon mile of leaves and water a backlit gold and frontlit silver that transformed an infinity of forms into astonishments. Continuing down onto the snow-flocked tips of the distant Elkmoons, the now crimson sun painted the peaks with alpenglow as it burrowed down inside them, leaving embers in fourteen hearts as fourteen soul-threads were ever more intricately woven through a single tapestry.

"To wrap it up, Lord," Lou Roy resumed, "the gifts out our window whittle my prayer down to this. Whatever kinda heaven trickery You got goin', we thank You, from way down here, for this whole God dang schoolhouse deal."

Amens and laughter brought a memorable God dang moment to a close.

IX. Out of the Cleft the Waters

I believe in the beauty of all things broken.
> —Terry Tempest Williams

WHEN ONA HAD flown to E City to see Lore perform at the Ambivalent Cafe, she brought along her twenty-four-year-old Girl Friday and chef, Regina Cloud. After Lore, Mu, and friends took the stage, Ona was so blown away by their performance that she didn't notice, leaning against a wall twenty feet to her right, a lanky, kind-faced, incessantly smiling cowboy with eyes for no one but Regina.

Regina remained professional in her attention to her boss until tears began to cascade out from under Ona's sunglasses. She then figured it was safe to turn to the young wrangler and smile, lighting him up so bright that before "Thirteen Tons" wound down they'd pantomimed their eagerness to exchange names and phone numbers. When the crowd rose for the standing ovation, the buckaroo—Buford Raines by name—slipped behind Regina and a piece of paper entered her hand. She whispered, "I'll call tonight!" When Buford beamed and blurted, "Goll *dang*!" Ona, three feet away, turned to give him her sweetest smile, believing he was exclaiming over Lore's music. Regina, meanwhile, experienced the same "Goll *dang*!" as the most disarming declaration of love she'd ever heard.

Goll *dang* courtship is easy when the faucet turns on that hard!

AS REGINA WAS driving Ona to E City Airport the next morning for their return flight to SFO, Ona asked how she'd felt about their visit to the Elkmoon. To Ona's surprise, Regina cried, "I'm totally smitten!"

Unaware that their conversation was now traveling down two very different roads, Ona cried, "Me too! I need to get back to San Fran for umpteen reasons, but I can hardly stand to leave!"

"Me too!" Regina agreed.

"Then whoa hold it," Ona said. "*Here's* an idea. How 'bout we reschedule your flight and you stay on? You can pick Lorilee's brain, explore the Elkmoon Valley and town, check out local color, amenities, saloons, real estate, and report back to me in the evenings. If it goes well I'll clear it with

Richie, and in a week I'll fly back and you can drive me around showing me what you've found."

With a sweetheart smile that completely disguised her true motives, Regina said, "I'd love to do that for you, Ona!"

So Ona boarded her plane and flew to San Francisco solo. But when she taxied home to Sausalito, the normally level-headed Regina had left a message on Ona's answering machine saying that she was "unexpectedly occupied in a very good way, but too busy for phone calls for the next three days."

No phone calls! Three days! And nothing for me to do but wait? What the hell are you thinking, Regina?

But there was no way to read her, and nothing to do but wait.

On Regina's second day and night of radio silence Ona went to bed furious with her. But when she woke in the night, her anger had turned to intense concern verging on panic. She sat up in the dark considering a call to the police, snapped on a lamp, and saw it was 3:30 a.m. Pacific, which was 4:30 a.m. Mountain. Realizing she knew someone awake at that hour whose deep natural calm might soothe her, she dialed at once.

Lorilee picked up. "Hello?"

"Lore!" Ona cried. "Sorry to interrupt your meditation but I'm frantic! Has Regina Cloud called you recently? Have you seen her? She's gone dark on me!"

"Regina's *way* better than okay, Ona," Lore replied. "What's happening is wonderful!"

"What on Earth is going on, Lore? Tell me!"

"Breathe deep and calm yourself," Lore said. "The only reason Regina didn't call is, she wants to surprise you. She and a young cowboy, just her age, are head over heels and it bodes nothing but well. His name's Buford Raines, we all love him, and he's so well connected here that Regina is gathering kinds of local knowledge most folks *never* learn. They can't wait to share it with you. And I can't wait for you to see them. They're *adorable* together."

"*Head over heels? Adorable together?*" Ona blurted. "Thanks, Lore, but I gotta scram!" With which she hung up, redialed, booked that morning's tedious triple flight, SFO to SLC to Bozeman to Elkmoon City, threw clothes in a bag, and was out the door.

WHEN ONA TOUCHED down in E City, she disembarked with the only other two passengers, watched the plane and passengers fly and drive off as if fleeing a plague, walked into the dimly lit Quonset hut that served as the airport terminal, encountered not a soul—and began to enjoy herself because, as she remarked to the empty Quonset, "This whole scene is right out of a Marchy Dark novel!"

She tried Regina's cell again. When it replied, *The party you wish to reach is unavailable,* Ona chuckled. "Of course she is!"

She asked directory assistance for an Elkmoon City taxi service. There were none. She asked for rental car agencies. The nearest one with a name she'd heard of was a Rent-a-Wreck ninety miles away. When the sole rental car listing in E City turned out to be called Big Ron's Rides, Ona said, "Of *course* that's its name! Good one, Marchy!" And she made the call.

In a cocky twang a man said, "*Hey there hi there ho there!* Rowdy Lord speakin'."

Rowdy Lord! Ona thought. *Too good, Marchy!* And the twang pretty well confirms what I feared Big Ron's Rides was named after.

Realizing her famous identity might now be a liability, she hijacked the identity of her favorite character in the Marchy Dark classic *Dwight Yoakam's Legs*. "Howdy, Rowdy," she said with a little twang of her own. "My name's Louise Parcheesi, I just landed at E City Airport, and I'd like to rent me a car."

"Oughta be a breeze, Louise," quoth Rowdy. "Course I'll have to drive it out from town, pick you up, and you'll need to drop me off back here."

Hoo boy! Ona thought. *Little over the top there, Marchy!* But the ever-unflappable Louise Parcheesi replied, "Of course you'll have to drive it out. The joys of country living. What kind of vehicle will we be sharing, Rowdy?"

"Choice o' two," he twanged. "My main ride's the '88 Silverado."

"Like a rock, those Chevys," said Louise. "And only a decade old. Great! How many miles on your rock, Rowdy?"

"Three hunnert an' ten thow, but hold up for the full menu. I just scored me a Jeep Wrangler broke the heart o' Max Bowler to lose. I was you I'd go with the Wrangler."

"Well then, let's say you *are* me. I'll take it. How long till you get here, Rowdy?"

"Eight minutes if the light in town's green. Eight an' a half if it's red. Long damn light."

"Good precision on the time, though," Ms. Parcheesi observed. "May I trouble you with a last question, Rowdy?"

"Ready, aim, fire," he twanged.

"Any chance Big Ron's Rides is named after Silas Dupree's guitar?"

"*Jeez Louise!* Are you *psychic*?" Rowdy cried.

"Nope," Ona said. "Just happily divorced. I'll be out front and you can't miss me. I'm the one human between this Quonset hut and Mars. See you in eight or eight and a half."

"On muh way, hun," Rowdy twanged.

Hun? Hoo boy!

SIPPING TEA AT her third-floor apartment window after working the break-fast shift at the Ambivalent, Lorilee was gazing absent-mindedly down Main Street when Max Bowler rolled in and parked in front of the cafe. She was surprised. Max hadn't come to town for lunch since he married, he never ate lunch later than noon, and it was pushing 2 p.m. She was even more surprised when Ona Kutar, not Max, climbed out of Max's Wrangler, entered the hotel at high speed, and thirty seconds later was banging on Lore's door. When Lore opened up, Ona burst in and gasped, "Thank *God* you're here!"

Greeting Ona's frantic air with her usual serenity, Lore said, "Always a pleasure, Ona. But a bit of a surprise. What brings you north again so soon?"

"Regina and that *cowpoke*!" she cried. "How did this *happen*? Regina's the best personal assistant I ever had by *light-years*! I'm *lost* without her! And her cuisine is third-generation vegan genius by way of France! How bad *is* this romance?"

"No offense, Ona, but you look and sound famished. Let me feed you. Scrambled eggs and toast okay?"

Ona's face fell. "Without Regina, that's pretty much what I'm down to."

"A little garlic and cheddar in the eggs?"

"Oh, Regina!" Ona keened. "*Are you hearing this?*"

"If you haven't made motel reservations," Lore said, "Mu enjoys the couch. I'm sure he'd offer you his room if you'd prefer to stay here with us."

"Oh, I'd *love* that!" Ona cried. "Thank you both!"

"You're welcome. But there's a house rule my guests must abide by."

"What's that?"

"I'm Lorilee, not Regina, this is E City, not Sausalito, and I'm a nonvegan breakfast cook because a vegan cook would bankrupt the Ambivalent Cafe. But my straight-ahead breakfasts send a mob of Elkmoonians to work happy five days a week, and you need such a breakfast *fast*. So please. No more insulting the cook or menu."

"I'm so sorry, Lore! I'm a wreck *and* a boor!"

"Way too hungry is all you are. Garlic and cheddar in the eggs then?"

"Sounds perfect, Lore of E City. Double sorry, and thanks."

"Take the chair by the window and enjoy the sun," Lore said as she set to work. "And here's some news you need as bad as breakfast. When Mu gets home in half an hour, we three will take my truck to the Testament Creek School to meet up with our new friend, Risa, and others. Among the others will be Regina and Buford, neither of whom have abandoned you. Regina took your brain-picking advice and called me soon as you left, we hit it off in every way, and we're meeting to prep the school for a party tomorrow. But before we get there you need to regroup. Buford is a one in a million, Ona. All heart and innocence, yet whip-smart. Regina kept quiet about him only because they're gathering Elkmoon intel for you, Ona, and it's time to grasp that very cool things are happening to Regina, Buford, and, unless you flare up and blow it, you. And while you're working on that, a question. How come you're driving Max Bowler's Jeep Wrangler?"

"Max, whoever that is, apparently sold it to one Rowdy Lord at a two-rig rental-car start-up called Big Ron's Rides."

"Damn. Could I borrow the key to move the Wrangler around back? It'd break Max's heart to see it right where he used to park it. I'll grab your suitcase for you too."

A PILE OF cheese eggs, two toasts with homemade pear butter, and a travel cup of strong coffee later, a revived Ona was riding in the '54 Chevy with Mu and Lore, drinking in the sights, sounds, and fragrances of the big river valley en route to Schoolhouse Bluff, when she suddenly smacked her forehead, spun on Lore, and cried, "*Holy hallelujah!*"

"Say what?" Lore asked.

"'*Frag Song!*'" Ona blurted. "I worked on it yesterday. I don't know how you did it, but the me you channeled on that Colorado peak was *born* to perform this tune! And when I shed this mortal tube amp, *please* chisel the words 'The fragments *are* the song' on my tombstone!"

"Wow!" Lore laughed. "Thanks, Mortal Tube Amp. What sold you on it?"

"The brilliant obvious: inviting my guitar to steal the story stick from those broken-off lyrics. You may have noticed, Lore, that the more worked up I feel the better I play. Yesterday, while freaking nonstop over Regina, I moved 'Frag Song' down into my B-flat sweet spot, changed a few words to tap into my own heartbreaks, and my freaked-out Fender fragment-finishers turned it into somethin' like this."

Without warm-up or warning Ona began stomping her boot, hard, on the floorboard, set up a strong rhythm, then belted the fragment "*Out of the cleft the waters!*" at a decibel level that *proved* she was a mortal tube amp. Still stomping hard, she added "*Let the lost sons and daughters!,*" shifted into a vocal imitation of her Fender, and crushed the lyric's mood into riotous resolution, continued into a fade-out accompanied by moody decrescendo boot stomps, then fell silent, turned to Lore, and asked, "Can even *you* believe the incredible gift you gave me?"

Mu was gaping, and Lore was laughing. "I know what I gave you, Ona, and it wasn't *that*! Your talent is insane! You could make an album using your voice as the Fender and an album using your Fender as the voice and they'd be equally great!"

"But it was you who kicked the cap offa that well. I've *never* made sounds like I just made in my life, and your 'Frag Song' is why. So who's the insane talent here?"

"*Both* of you!" Mu burst out.

"Speaking of talent, Mu," Ona said. "When we record 'Frag' in LA, I need to be freaking out again, and from what your mom says of Regina and Buford my freak-out source has flown. So Mu. Can I *please* phone you from the Axman Studios live room? And will you please tell me again how we're screaming through space at four lethal speeds including nine million miles an hour into the Klingon Galaxy where, the instant Earth's gyroscope breaks, all that'll be left of our planet and us is a smudge of intergalactic crud spew? Paying gig, Mu. I'm serious. That speech could make my Fender lose its shit in ways that'd go down in rock history."

With the same serene smile Ona admired in his mother, Mu said, "Sure, Ona. I can terrorize you with Earth's reckless driving any time you need it."

"*God*, I love this little family!" Ona sighed.

X. A Seeing That Didn't Stop Where It Once Used To

I am learning to see. I don't know why it is, but everything enters me more deeply and doesn't stop where it once used to. I have an interior that I never knew of. Everything passes into it now. I don't know what happens there.

—Rainer Maria Rilke,
The Notebooks of Malte Laurids Brigge

ON OCTOBER 22, THE day before Risa would drive back to Portland with TJ, she joined Lorilee for a farewell meditation at Blue Empty that turned unforgettable in several ways.

A few minutes into their effort, when Lore turned toward the seven-mile-wide begging bowl, Risa felt her enter a peace so pervasive it swallowed Risa too. All things were suddenly *floating...No thought...No time...The outwardness of things not outward...Inwardness of things not inward...Gate of heaven everywhere...*

When Lore finally stirred, Risa touched her knee and told her, "*Thank you!*"

Lore smiled. "You're welcome. But for what?"

"I doubt this is even sayable," Risa said. "But I felt you vanish into an emptiness so boundless that it somehow pulled me in after you. It was beautiful, vanishing into that, knowing you were in there too. So thanks."

At a moment when almost anyone would have voiced a reply, Lore, as was her wont, gazed at Risa so tenderly that Risa realized no words would be forthcoming. Two friends just sat beneath a broken pine above a river-broken begging bowl, gazing at each other. No compulsion to look away, break it off, blush at the intimacy of such a protracted study of a loved face.

"We remind me of a cedar and a Bohemian waxwing," Lore finally said in the serene voice Risa had come to love. "Different species. Yet we hardly differ at all."

Lore reached for her backpack, delved in a side pocket, and pulled out a little notepad covered in handwriting. "I've been loving the Eckhart sermons you gave me, and comparing the German Meister's and Master Dōgen's differences, and I've seen that the terms 'sermon' and 'dharma talk' serve our need for meaning in the same way. This morning I turned their words into a little conversation that sort of shows this. Wanna hear it?"

"Yes!" Risa said.

"The Meister: *The eye in which I see God is the same eye in which God sees me. My eye and God's eye are one eye, one seeing, one knowing, one loving.* The Master: *This grass or that tree are not grass and tree, nor are the mountains and rivers mountains and rivers: they are one bright pearl.* The Meister: *Run into peace!* The Master: *Mountains flow!* The Meister: *Jesus is empty and free and maidenly in himself.* The Master: *At the moment of giving birth to a child, is the mother separate from the child? You should study not only that you become a mother when your child is born but also that you become a child.* The Meister: *If I spent enough time with the tiniest creature, even a caterpillar, I would never have to prepare a sermon. So full of God is every creature.* The Master: *Unlike humans, fish are not ignorant of each other's intentions. It might be natural for us to have minds like fish in a dwindling stream.* What a pleasure it is, Risa, to fly down out of Blue Empty and land amid our own waxwing not-differences."

As Lore spoke, her clear eyes, serene smile, and wisdom words filled Risa with such affection that she closed her eyes to bask in it—when *immediately,* behind her eyes, she saw one of them standing by a bed, the other one lying in it, and the one in bed was dying. The clarity of the image stormed her. She then saw it was she who was standing, Lore who was dying, and her dread of this loss tore so deep that, to preserve the smile Lore was still sending, Risa pulled it together enough to say, "I'm gonna take a little stroll. Back in a bit."

Out of love she then walked far enough away that she could break down sobbing without being seen or heard. Out of love she vowed to the Unseen Guileless Perfection never to mention what she'd seen. Out of love she prayed that what she'd seen was false, or could be prayed false. Out of love she then pulled out her shirttail, cleaned up her face, tucked her shirt back in, put on her sunglasses to hide her reddened eyes, and stood, stunned to realize the simple act of walking back to her friend might now require more strength than she possessed.

Out of love, she knew not how, Risa then returned to Lore wearing the same *Run into peace, Mountains flow* smile she found waiting on the face of her beloved friend.

(Portland, late October 1997)

XI. Risa's No Night Stand

The soul is tough, sometimes deceived,
but will kill rather than marry falsehood.
—Martin Shaw, *Scatterlings*

The clock struck eleven. The renowned folk singer, Patterson Davy, was in town, ten days into a thirty-concert tour, three thousand miles from home, famished and spent after an unusually good performance thanks to the outstanding acoustics of a Portland theatre called The Pearl. The good restaurants were closed. The night was rainy. Davy faced two choices. He could hole up in his room at the Barrington, raid the basket of junk food, down the four 1.7-ounce bottles of mediocre whiskies in the mini-bar, and wake in the morning feeling desolate before flying to Seattle for his third concert in three nights. Or he could defy his deflation, walk the few blocks to the ground-floor bar and grill directly below The Pearl, and hopefully arrive in Seattle fortified. Étouffée Bruté, the bar was called. Silly name, but of good repute, and open till midnight.

Borrowing an umbrella at the front desk, Davy hiked the few blocks, scoped Étouffée's warm glow from the sidewalk, stepped inside, and encountered the anonymous human warmth he liked best after a concert. He hung his umbrella on the back of the barstool farthest from other diners and drinkers, and sat. Five stools to his left a bizarre little street person was also taking a seat, wearing a sopped rain slicker, jeans, and red Converse high tops that were creating puddles on the floor thanks to the rain he'd obviously spent hours in.

A barkeep en route to the puddle-maker, bearing a single shot of whiskey, slid a menu in front of Davy and said, "Back in three minutes." As she tended the dripping street guy Davy couldn't help but notice she was a stunner, wearing an oversized white dress shirt but black leggings sized ever so right. He began to study the menu she'd handed him, but grew distracted when he realized he could hear every word the barkeep was saying, yet not a syllable of her street friend's replies. And what on earth was she telling him?

"Mechthild of Magdeburg says, *Whoever is seriously wounded by true love will never become healthy again unless she kisses the same mouth by which her soul was wounded.*"

Did the barkeep really say that? Davy wondered. *Or am I so hungry I'm hallucinating?*

"In the Glory Meadow a great love wounded me," she said, "and I long to kiss its mouth. I do *not* long to get kissy with another *man's* mouth. Given my history, my romantic atheism makes perfect sense and TJ knows it. But my dreams of a little river boy have left me longing for a love that doesn't erase me the way the great love does. A love I can hold in my physical arms and walk by the river with. TJ, knowing I researched artificial insemination, keeps listing the risks. But they're not life-threatening, and he knows he'll be part of the life of any child of mine. He's just *fussing* over me, Jervis. That's what mother/brothers do."

Davy watched the man reply, yet from ten feet away heard not a sound.

"Exactly," the barkeep said. "If it works, I'll have a one-member family in Montana just like my dear friend Lore and her son. If it doesn't work, I've got you, Mr. Fussy, and the Elkmoon spirit-thread holders. So what's to lose? I need to help this gentleman then check on my flock, which will probably take till closing. If I don't make it back, have an oceanic night."

Patterson Davy watched as the little street fellow bowed his head shockingly low in farewell, and kept it bowed. In what was apparently a rite between them, the barkeep stood on tiptoe, leaned all the way across the bar till her lips reached the man's natural tonsure, and kissed that naked target dead center as Davy gaped. *Who were these people?*

TAKING IN HER new customer, Risa recognized, from posters all over The Pearl, Patterson Davy, the hero of tonight's concert, about which her customers had raved. She was idly wishing she'd seen the concert when the intuition flashlight turned on full blast, shining bright upon her river boy, upon Davy, and upon the 1960 Martin D-28 that Risa had hanging on a wall-peg just four floors overhead. The Holy Goat asks you, dear readers, *Do you remember that guitar, Risa's 29th birthday gift from Dave?* It appeared a lot of pages ago, though only a year ago in time. And the intuition flashlight message could not have been more clear. Resting upon the barstool Risa was about to approach were a pair of testicles brimming with musical DNA. If she was serious about pursuing her river boy, and if the boy was to have any chance of being musical, she must show Mr. Davy the D-28 and, if he loved it, propose a straight-across trade: his sperm for her Martin. *Who are these people* is right, Patterson Davy!

Are you insane? Risa told the flashlight. *He'll call the cops and who could blame him!*

As always, when she questioned the flashlight it simply disappeared. *Calm down, take his order, and no crazy talk,* she told herself. *Just see what develops. And if nothing develops, fine.*

It calmed her a little to remind herself that Davy was only about her tenth-favorite male folk singer. Very good guitarist, great lyricist, and he and his lady vocalist made sweet harmonies. But he'd leaned career-long on a breathy, overly gentle tenor to deliver his poetics. He busted loose a grand total of *never*, and ethereal men just weren't her thing.

But a donor who isn't your thing is perfect! the flashlight piped up. *He'll deliver the goods, vanish, and you needn't think of him again. How many musicians this gifted do you expect to meet alone at a quiet hour? This is your chance to reel in your sweet river boy!"*

Oh, little boy, she thought. *What am I about to try in hope of finding you?*

She drew a deep breath, whispered, *Lord of Love Unmanifest, help!,* stepped up to Patterson Davy, served a glass of water, and gave him her most professional smile. "Welcome to Étouffée. I'm Risa. How are you tonight?"

"*Famished!*" Davy gasped—and whoa! That *breathiness.*

"Well, you're in luck. Our bar menu's the best in town," she said, preparing to launch her polished spiel. But as Davy leaned in to listen she began transplanting his features onto a four-year-old ragamuffin walking hand in hand with her along the Elkmoon, and liked what she saw so much that a white lie leapt out. "I won't blow your cover," she said. "But our owner, TJ, loved your concert so much that he popped in afterward to say that, if you came in, I should offer you the three best appetizers on the menu, the bottle of wine of your choice, and not one but *two* desserts, all on the house, with TJ's sincere *Bravo!*"

"*Good Lord!*" Davy exclaimed over TJ's nonexistent admiration. "If the owner's serious, I'm partial to Bordeaux and Cabernet."

After a little thought, Risa opened a 1993 Owens Sullivan cab from the new Walla Walla wine country and poured Davy a taste. He swirled it in his glass, sipped, and exhaled, "*Sensaaaational!*" Yikes.

Risa poured, set the glass before him and, when his eyes dropped to the menu, went back to studying him. Thick brown hair with blond highlights. Big manly beard. High hairline. Noble forehead. Intelligent brown eyes consistent with his intelligent lyrics. Stature on the shorter side, but not a deal breaker.

"I don't know why, Risa, but curtain calls reduce me to idiocy," he said. "Given your perfect wine choice, would you mind helping me with food choices?"

"My pleasure. Given the way you said *famished,* I recommend our most substantial salad. Tomatoes Five Ways consists of heirloom tomato, tomato gelee, tomato leather, tomato sorbet, tomato powder, buttermilk, mustard greens, fennel fronds, and compressed melon."

"*Yessssss!*" Davy exhaled in a way that just didn't do it for her—but the flashlight had a point: her lack of attraction began to strike her as ideal. And to broach this certifiably insane topic, his meal needed to be out of this world.

Risa focused, and for once didn't curb her natural charm despite the dangers: "If it were me, Mr. Davy, I'd follow up the Five Ways with the Albacore Crudo. Wild-caught off Oregon eight hundred miles out of region thanks to our handy global climate crisis. Served in a jasmine-tea-cured tonnato sauce with touches of jalapeño, citrus, onion ash, and sour gherkins, topped with a potpourri of borage, capers, garlic chips, herbs, yogurt, and lime. If those dishes speak to you, I'll get them started while you ponder your third choice."

Expelling five times the breath needed, Davy said "*My heavenssss yesssss!*" and Risa grew genuinely solicitous: his performance *had* reduced him to idiocy.

"I heard there were *three* encores," she said. "You must be running on fumes! May I bring some bread so the wine doesn't completely cream you?"

"*Ohhh yesssss! Thank you sooooo much, Rissssa!*" Davy huffle-puffed.

She served Mr. Davy the sourdough baguette with olive oil and balsamic, strolled casually to the kitchen to place his salad and albacore orders—then raced away, unseen, out Étouffée's side entrance up the four flights to her studio apartment, where she lifted the D-28 off its peg, dusted it, placed it in its case, took the elevator back down, locked the guitar in TJ's office, dropped back into casual mode, and returned to her target.

Davy had annihilated the Tomatoes Five Ways, put healthy dents in the bread and Owens Sullivan, and the Albacore Crudo had arrived. When his first bite caused his eyes to roll back in their sockets, river walks with her dream child began to feel like a distinct possibility.

One more entrée and two desserts needed. Entrée? "How would you feel, Mr. Davy," Risa asked, "about an appetizer instead of another main dish to save room for more sustained pleasure? TJ's crab cakes are the best in the West, but leave room for your desserts."

"*Lord yesssss!*" Davy exsufflated. "This meal is *supernatural!*"

After delivering the order to the kitchen and asking a sous-chef to deliver the cakes to Davy, Risa chose Davy's desserts, returned to TJ's office, fetched the guitar, left it just out of sight at the end of the bar, and peeked at her target. The crab cakes had arrived. Davy ate, Davy drank, Davy licked his plate, Davy turned into silly putty, and on came merciless Risa. "No consultation needed on your desserts," she said. "I have a strong sense of you now, Mr. Davy," she said. "Correct me if I'm wrong. The Apple Cake features crème fraîche, pine nut brittle, petite basil, pine nut milk, a lace cookie, and the best vanilla ice cream you'll ever taste, made right here by TJ himself."

Davy used his spoon to assemble a bite that included all the ingredients, including the cookie. His redundant review: "*Lord yesssss!*"

"And our Chocolate Crèmeux," Risa set it before him with an under-stated flourish, "features huckleberries, huckleberry sorbet, caramel, and a salted cocoa cookie."

Davy's first bite of Crèmeux blinded him so completely that he didn't notice Risa turning off the house music and dousing all the bar lights but a few nine volts to set the maplewood bar aglow. Placing the guitar case on the bar just out of Davy's reach, she asked no one in particular, "How does that Joni Mitchell song with the mind-bending guitar part go?" Knowing the effect it would have, she then dared to sing, a capella:

> The sight of ghost jets leaving contrails
> Seven miles up off the ground
> Fires up a cargo cult in me
> Behold the nothing I've then found

Davy was jerked by the ears out of his trance. The beautiful barkeep couldn't sing to save her life! Her low alto either wobbled beneath or warbled wincingly above the pitch, but never quite held it. "Sorry for that," she said. "But my hope was that if I violated Étouffée's airspace with my tone deafness, it might move you to purge the air with *this*."

With which she opened the case, lifted out the Martin, placed it on the spotlit maple, and prayed, *O unseen unborn river boy. May he love the D-28 as much as I love you!*

"*Ooof!*" went Patterson Davy, sounding truly gut punched, and Risa knew she had a mad guitar lover on the line. "What vintage is *this*, Risa miracle?"

"1960," she said. "Dreadnought body, named for the shape of the early-twentieth-century British battleships. Sitka spruce top. Ebony fretboard. No longer obtainable Brazilian rosewood back and sides. Big warm tone growing warmer with age. May we do the same! Please give it a spin."

Taking the D-28 in hand, Davy deftly spun it 360 degrees, fine-tuned it, gathered himself, struck a single chord, and the tone and length of its sounding visibly shook him. "If this is one of the nothings that fall from those ghost jets, I'll join Joni's cargo cult today!"

"Is that a promise?" Risa asked. *Oh, little river boy. He's nibbling the bait!*

Giving himself to the instrument, Davy played the very riff Risa loved from "Ghost Jets," began to transpose and transform and toy with it, and for long minutes grew so lost in what the Martin awakened that only when he stopped playing and the last few diners and drinkers broke into applause did he realize he'd played perhaps the best improvisation of his life.

"*Beautiful!*" Risa said, a bit breathy herself as she imagined his virtuosity in her river boy.

Though Davy nodded thanks, his expression suddenly changed. "Something to know," he said with an entirely present smile. "Miraculous food, wine, and instruments don't dull perception. They heighten it. I've just re-called that when I staggered in, post-concert, you spoke some odd phrases to your quiet street friend. For instance: *my romantic atheism.* Also: *artificial insemination.* I too am being played, Risa. With genius. And I believe I understand why. You need to ask a question so awkward it frightens you.

But what if I enjoyed your performance so much I'd be honored by the question regardless of what I decide? Would that make it easier to ask?"

Risa nodded, and found her courage. "The Martin was a gift from my dad, who died recently. I still love him dearly."

"I'm very sorry," Davy said with palpable kindness.

"Thanks. The D-28 was such a generous gift that it must seem ungrateful that I'd part with it. That's why I sang the Joni lines. I needed to show you that my musical disability imprisons his gift's greatness. If this guitar were to become yours, Mr. Davy, would you play it often and treat it with great care?"

"I'd treat it like a Stradivari Long Pattern fiddle and play it in Seattle tomorrow night. But the time has come, Risa. What would I need to offer in return?"

The intensity of her blush burned her, but Risa managed to speak it: "A one-in-five shot at a musical child. And this is not a proposition. This is Biology 101. I've got the ovum. An impersonal test-tube needs the other ingredient. I also want to be dead honest, so I confess: *I fibbed.* The owner, TJ, is on the Oregon Coast. Your dinner was on me. "

Davy smiled. "I sensed that. Thanks for coming clean. But now tell me. How might this proposed exchange work?"

Risa flipped over the single-page bar menu, wrote on the back, and handed Davy the name, phone number, and address of a fertility clinic and sperm bank. "I've thought it out carefully. The favor would take a small fraction of your morning. No money involved. The guitar would arrive at the clinic at your convenience. I wouldn't. My friend Daniel Bern, a tall handsome African American you can't miss, would arrive, carrying this guitar case. A nurse would admit you and ask a few questions. You would donate. The nurse would label the donation so I can identify it, but a pseudonym is fine. Daniel will then hand you the Martin, no strings attached except for your promise and mine to keep our trade secret forever."

"I'm at the Barrington," Davy said. "How close is the clinic?"

"About eight blocks due west," Risa said.

"I leave for the airport at noon," Davy said. "Would it work if I get to the clinic at 9:30?"

"Perfectly," Risa said.

"We have a deal," Davy said, and they gave each other a fresh look, feeling strangely moved. "And I wish you, and I hope *yours*, the very best, Risa." He extended his hand.

"Same to you and yours," Risa said as they shyly shook.

And Patterson Davy proved a perfect gentleman. He even gave Daniel a receipt the next morning. It read, "*Tens of millions of swimmers exchanged for one 1960 Martin D-28. May the kindest of them all join you soon.*"

SIX DAYS LATER Risa ovulated, dashed to the clinic, and deployed Davy's donation.

Fourteen days later she learned it took. One would imagine she'd have been delighted. But unexpected feelings had complicated the success. From the moment she'd cut the guitar-for-sperm deal, her dreams of the river boy had ceased. Her strong sense of his gender vanished with the dreams. Despite vowing to think of him never, she thought of Patterson Davy hundreds of times a day and at night listened to his albums. Meanwhile her pregnant and hormone-rife body proved to have its own strong feelings, and no vow, prayer, or spiritual practice she knew prevailed against them. She began wrestling indecision and worry at pregnancy's every twist and turn. She lost her certainty that the swap was inspired by intuition flashlight. She became so secretive about her condition that it took her a week to work up the courage to tell Lorilee (who was nothing but delighted), and two weeks and a huge glass of wine, despite the risks, to work up the courage to call TJ.

"Mother/brother!" she heard herself blurt with leaden fake-cheer. "I'm pregnant, and *so* happy about it! Can you please be happy with us?"

TJ burst out, "*Happy?* Not good enough, Risa! I'm *thrilled*! Tell your bambino that he or she has a doting uncle in waiting!"

They chittered back and forth for a while, and TJ signed off by saying, "I'm going out to shop for baby clothes *this minute*!"

"Gender nonspecific at this point!" Risa reminded him.

"That's me," TJ said.

"I meant the *clothes*, you nimnam!" she said, and they laughed as they signed off.

Risa then walked straight into the bathroom, looked in the mirror, watched her eyes fill, and told her reflection, "*This is, by light years, the stupidest thing you've ever done in your life!*"

"No it's not!" she argued even as tears began to spill. "This is my sweet river boy—or girl—come calling! And either one will be wonderful!"

"This creature could be anything from a genius to an imbecile to a serial killer," the face in the mirror told her. "You have *no idea* what's growing in your body."

Anger killed her tears. "*That*," she snapped, "is pure *manas drivel* and I refuse to listen! *Grind away, faith/doubt organ! You're nothing but a hormonal brain's exhaust fumes!*"

Planting herself defiantly before the mirror, she pulled up her shirt, placed her hands on her very unpregnant-looking belly, stroked it to soothe the passenger inside, and told it, "Welcome, sweetness. And pardon the *manas* fumes. Human minds carry doubts and fears galore in their outermost layer, but my heart/mind loves every atom of you! And I believe I can spare us future *manas* fumes. I traded a guitar with a body shaped like an old British battleship for the ingredient to create *your* body. The shape's called a *Dreadnought*. Two nights ago my dad visited in a dream, beamed at my belly, cried, *Welcome, tiny Dreadnought!*, and laughed so happily that I laughed too, waking myself up. And as I lay in the dark knowing the inch-long *you* were inside me, a battleship-sized love rose up, my fears vanished, and from now till the day you're in my arms, my *tiny Dreadnought* is who you'll be!"

LAST WEEK OF November, 1997. Midnight. Étouffée Bruté.

TJ sets two shot glasses on the maplewood bar, fills his own with Bulleit and Jervis's with Beam, circles the bar, takes the stool next to his brother, levels his gaze on his drink, and starts it spinning. Super intent stare. Interminable precision spin. But instead of the usual curiosity about Jervis's Ocean-walk, TJ keeps clenching and releasing his jaw muscles, spinning the drink, clenching, releasing, spinning.

"What is it, Teej?" Jervis asks.

"Risa was artificially inseminated three weeks ago. She told me a week ago that it took. Pretends to know nothing about the donor but she's a terrible liar. Did you know she was pregnant, Jervis? Does Ocean tell you such things?"

Since his injuries and coma, Jervis has seemed incapable of being surprised. At this news, he shrugs. "No, Ocean doesn't tell me such things. She sustains the universe, Teej. If she strobed a nano-fraction of her doings my head would explode. But I know Risa wanted this. She must be very happy."

"It's hard to tell," TJ says, still clenching and unclenching his jaw as he spins his shot. "She's keeping the baby secret till it shows, but I don't think she's afraid of people knowing. What she fears, I feel, is being in Montana with an infant and no partner. She's also grown compulsive in new ways. Her Rembrandt glow has always caused trouble at the bar. She insists on bartending even so, and with a *madonna glow* added to the Rembrandt at the same time her body has grown...well...more *voluptuous,* I've never seen a woman exert such a pull on men. Othello and I run interference when we can, but it's a *barrage.* Grotesque come-ons. Point blank marriage proposals. And have you seen the way she sometimes bolts into the walk-in cooler? It's morning sickness, Jervis. At *night.* I think the noxious flirtations trigger it. She tries to sound chipper, telling me morning sickness means less chance of a miscarriage. But imagine being hit on by creeps while trying not to throw up! She's built this pitiful hidey hole behind the kegs and beer crates. She darts back into it, vomits into a plastic container, screws on the lid to trap the smell, cleans up with little wipes and mouthwash, and steps back into the bar as if nothing happened. Her magnetic pull then brings on the next fool. She's strong, we know that. But is anybody strong enough to—"

Jervis lays hold of his brother's drink-spinning hand. Surprised, TJ falls silent.

"Why are you telling me all this?" Jervis asks.

TJ sits motionless, debating, then draws a breath. "I'm sure you know, but I've never come right out and said this. Risa is the only woman who's ever made me sorry I can't be the one and only in her life. *Bitterly* sorry.

Our drive to Portland from Montana was especially hard. We came the slow way, down the Clearwater, overnighted in Walla Walla, had a great dinner, and it was an almost unbearable joy to be mistaken for a couple all evening. But somehow I've always known that, if I try to make what we have romantic, I'll destroy it."

"It's good you know that, Teej. But know this too. *You're* one of the men she's exerting that tremendous pull on. And being so close to her, you're by far the most vulnerable."

TJ takes a very large swig of Bulleit and wheezes, "*Tell me about it!* But I'm worried. I want to help her, but don't see what more I can do. I guess I tell you this in the hope that, if you ever pray to Ocean, you'll ask her to protect and help Risa through this."

Shaking his head, Jervis paper-whispers, "To ask the source of the insane mercy moving through everything to change what's unfolding is asking her to fix what's never broken."

TJ resumes clenching and spinning. "Given the state of the world, Jervis, you must know how hard it is for me to believe that. Risa wanted a child and no man to go with it for small, vulnerable reasons. Being pregnant makes her even *more* vulnerable, and your Ocean often strikes me as too vast and invulnerable to care about the small and vulnerable. Meanwhile Jamey, the actor I guess Ocean murkily suggested could be the man for Risa, is a confirmed Portlander who can play no part in her Montana plans. So how can *he* be her man?"

In the most caustic whisper TJ has ever heard Jervis use, he says, "Listen to *Mr. Thinky* get everything wrong! Calling Ocean *my* Ocean. Saying she's too vast to care about the small or vulnerable even as she creates, sustains, dissolves, and re-creates every small vulnerable thing there is. Listen to him forget the steeliness that's kept Risa available, the coming move to Montana that's kept her available, the unwed pregnancy that's kept her available. *The fuck*, Teej. *What Seymour loved best in the Bible was the word 'Watch'!*" Salinger wrote that. So do us a Salinger and tell Mr. Thinky to simple down and *watch*. The zillions of things constantly happening in Ocean don't need *our* tiny ideas about how they're supposed to go. *Just watch!* And if, watching Risa, you see her about to misadventure, help her turn it into an adventure. It's that simple."

TJ stops spinning his whiskey, sits silent a moment, then says, "*Damn it, Jervis.* Guilty as charged. Sometimes Ocean's omnipotence freaks me out so badly I blind myself to her on purpose, my mind starts racing, and I get *totally* thinky! I *do* need to simple down. And I *can.* I've been working on this. *Watch!*"

Through the cloth of his shirt, TJ takes hold of the little purse dangling inside, draws a slow deep breath, releases it, keeps hold, closes his eyes, grows perfectly still—and though he can't see it, Jervis's expression has grown as close to tender as his scars and nerve damage allow. "You've got a great love inside you," he paper-whispers. "A love you'll never make love to. A love pregnant with a baby you didn't choose. A love that, year after year, breaks you more and more open. To stay so open knowing you'll never be your love's one and only has got to hurt like hell. And I'm sorry for your hurt. But I'm *amazed* by your faith, Teej. You're not munched like me. You don't feel Ocean all day the way I do. Your faith is *greater* than mine. So let's do a double Salinger and *Watch!*, knowing we've got cool stuff to do, and soon. Stay with Ocean, brother. It's gonna get good. I don't know just how or when, but it is. She promises."

Still clenching *La Familia*, eyes still closed, TJ murmurs, "When you're my Jervis, Risa's my Risa, and Ocean's my Ocean, what choice do I have, brother? What choice have I *ever* had?" He then opens his eyes meaning to challenge Jervis, but is stunned to silence by the tenderness of the look the twin's damaged face and single eye are giving him.

For the first time maybe ever, Jervis then raises his glass to propose their toast. "You keep making the choice Jamey's dog Roams makes. The best choice there is, Teej. *Here's to your obedience to no created thing but love.*"

"And to the woman, brother, and Ocean who give me no choice," TJ says darkly—but then gives on darkness and sends Jervis his tight little smile.

XII. Mahatma Gandhi's Magic Word

Let not they who have not heard this story be astonished.
Rama is infinite, his perfections infinite, and
boundless the extent of his stories.

—Tulsidas

TEN WEEKS INTO her pregnancy Risa's morning sickness ended and she began to thrive. Eleven and a half weeks in, she entered what she promised TJ would be her last week of bartending and, with no queasiness to contend with and an end in sight, took fresh pleasure in the work, regaining the deft multitasking skills and simultaneous calm that only the best of barkeeps can maintain amid a crush of customers.

On the evening of January 30th, moments before her very last shift, TJ asked Risa if she had any parting requests. "I do," she said. "There's a story I need to tell to you, Jervis, Othello, and anybody still hanging around at last call. It's a Holy Church the Great story, TJ. When the intuition flashlight shone on it, I resisted, because it's so rooted in India it probably won't translate to Americans. But to lay my bartending career to rest with this story will keep the most meaningful promise I ever made to my father. Which is reason enough to tell it."

"I love the sound of this," TJ said. "Anything the staff or I can do to assist?"

"The story has to be told before midnight. It'll take maybe ten minutes, so at a quarter to twelve I need quiet. Any idea how to achieve that if it gets loud and crazy?"

"Empty wineglasses and spoons to Othello and a few others I trust. We'll *tink* like mad till you've got your quiet."

"Perfect!"

BUT FIVE HOURS later, at 11:05, the bar crowd had swelled beyond all expectation. Word of Risa's last night had spread till it seemed every off-duty restaurant employee within miles had rolled in for a last chance to witness her ability to serve a raucous throng with speed, wit, and calm. The mood grew as boisterous as Étouffée Bruté ever got. Three of the bar's reigning sports hounds, Will Battle, Doc Doyle, and Noam Davis, were holding forth on excruciating basketball minutiae amid a posse of far-gone hoop nuts. Two of the bar's more notorious philanderers and several potential prey were sharing three tables, maneuvering toward or away from later liaisons via rhetorical flights of fancy Risa took care to tune out. Her friend Othello, normally a master of regal detachment, had gotten sucked into a debate with Theo Bollingsworth, the one-time British Shakespearean a young Jamey Van Zandt once aced out of a role as Mercutio, inspiring Bollingsworth to quit acting, expatriate to the US, and establish himself as Portland's Christopher Hitchens impersonator in his *Willamette Week* column "A Dyspeptic's Guide to Everything," which it certainly was.

At 11:20 Jervis stepped in from his Ocean-walk, took the stool TJ reserved for him, and when Risa set down his shot of Beam he gestured her close. "Teej just told me you've got Holy Church the Great words to say, and this crowd has gone cuckoo. A few words from the Meister for you: 'One must learn an inner solitude, wherever one may be.'"

Risa was so grateful for the calming sentence that she reached across the bar and stroked Jervis's grizzled cheek. His eyes dropped to his bourbon. He later told TJ, "Risa's touch has Ocean in it." TJ sighed and sang a common refrain: "Tell me about it."

Risa sustained inner solitude for a few minutes, but by 11:30, still serving a cacophonous crowd, Dave's deathbed Gandhi story was the only drink she any longer wanted to pour. Shortly after his September cancer vigil had begun, a kind old Jesuit priest Dave had known since college came to see him at Harborview. The priest had spent half his life in India, where he'd earned the nickname Father Coolie due to endless acts of humble service to others. In parting with Dave, Father Coolie told him the story of the last instant of Gandhi's life. Dave's telling of the same tale to Risa on the second to last night of his life had slain her with its poignancy and power. By 11:40 she felt so seized that the bar crowd, rather than trouble her, seemed to envelop her the way a Delhi crowd had enveloped Gandhi as he walked to his death. Bullets were coming and only the assassin knew it. It moved Risa deeply that, at the moment she needed him, TJ again appeared at her side. "Ready?" he asked. When she kissed him on the cheek, his gaze dropped to the floor: *Risa's kiss has Ocean in it.*

"My tale's magic lives so far from American bar banter that it'll just confuse most people," she told TJ. "But a rare heart or two, who knows? All I know is, I owe it to my dad to tell it, and hope you, Jervis, and Othello will be able to feel why."

TJ nodded, then strolled down the long row of barstools, distributing spoons and wineglasses to four people he trusted, saying, "Follow my lead." He kept a glass and spoon himself, gave the last to Othello, scowled Theo Bollingsworth to silence, and murmured in Othello's ear, causing him to turn to Risa at her pouring station and send her his most kingly smile.

When TJ returned to Risa, he said, "I just realized what might be a problem. The tinking will make people think you'll be offering a toast."

She lit up. "That'll work! It will help to frame my story as a toast!"

TJ nodded, caught the attention of his cohorts, waved his spoon like a symphony conductor his baton, and his orchestra began tinking their half dozen wineglasses. The crowd of perhaps sixty grew surprisingly quiet.

Othello stood, tall and imposing. "This night," he declaimed in his operatic bass, "is the last of Risa McKeig's bartending career, and TJ has invited her to share some parting words. Let us show our gratitude for her graciousness and God knows how many perfectly poured drinks by giving her ten minutes of our attention."

The applause and cheering surprised her. The crowd, for the moment, was truly hers. She wasted no time: "I'm going to propose a toast that needs an introduction. Fifty years ago today, January 30th, 1948, Mahatma Gandhi was assassinated in Delhi, India."

Raising his glass high, Will Battle called out, "How fun! Cheers, everybody!"

Othello waited out the laughter, then said, "Will, my friend. If that's your idea of giving Risa your attention I'll call you a cab. A better option: Keep still till she's finished and your next two drinks are on me."

Will pinched his lips shut with the fingers of both hands, creating a sort of duck bill that got more laughs.

Inner solitude, Risa thought, then forged on: "Today is also the four-month anniversary of my father's death. He was a great teller of tales. Two days before he died he told me a true and uncanny story I'd like to share as my parting gift to this wonderful bar and all of you. The story of Gandhi's last moment alive."

"*Go Risa!*" shouted a man in the back, but his encouragement sounded terribly forced.

Inner solitude. "As the nonviolent hero of India achieving independence," Risa said, "Gandhi was the most beloved man in India, if not the world, at the time. But as the British government packed up to leave, India's out-numbered Muslim populace grew so afraid of an all-Hindu government that their leaders chose to split India in two. Hundreds of thousands of Muslims set out for what is now Pakistan. Hundreds of thousands of Pakistani Hindus set out for India. The double migration became a blood-bath. Riots broke out all over the country. When Calcutta was set ablaze, Gandhi moved to a house in the Muslim quarter and protested the violence by fasting to the verge of death. The riots raged on even so."

"Oh, excellent barkeep!" Theo Bollingsworth called out. "I celebrate every drink you've so charmingly poured us. But why must you pour us *this*?"

"Gandhi kept a lifelong spiritual secret, Theo," she said. " 'If that secret is not on my lips at the moment of my death, you should consider me a fraud,' he told his close ones. Today is the fiftieth anniversary of a death that proved an emaciated, outrageously courageous mortal to be the extreme opposite of a fraud. If the act I describe disappoints you, Theo, feel free to rip into me in your next Dyspeptic's Guide."

Though Theo made a show of pulling a pen and notebook out of his old tweed jacket, Risa had invited her father's wasted "face of love" into her inner solitude. Her voice grew charged: "Gandhi kept preaching Hindu-Muslim unity, risking his life on both sides. He urged Hindus to bring Muslims to their temples to read from the Qur'an. He vowed to live with Muslims in Pakistan till the violence stopped. He went to the capital to make his case known to the world, and did—which should bring me to the heart of this story. But here in the West, *that heart has been cut out.* We know that a fundamentalist, Nathuram Godse, intercepted Gandhi on his way to public prayer and murdered him. And that is *all* we know. We've stripped his death of its incredible power. And I'm standing here because my dying father told me, 'Americans need this story,' and I promised him I would tell it."

"*These are the voyages of the Starship Risa,*" one of the philanderers intoned, "*going where no barkeep has gone before!*"

Bollingsworth gazed skyward and groaned, "Beam me up, Scotty!" People cackled.

Feeling the crowd slipping away, Risa surprised them by returning fire at Theo. "In Richard Attenborough's movie *Gandhi,* Ben Kingsley's portrayal of the Mahatma won an Oscar. A few armchair critics, our own Theo Bollingsworth among them, called it a travesty to cast the British-born Kingsley as India's hero. This is unfair to the point of slander. Kingsley was born *Krishna Pandit Bhanji,* he's half Gujarati, and it's hard to imagine a more qualified actor giving a better performance. Who would damn a great performance of *Hamlet* because the Danes who played Claudius, Gertrude, and Hamlet weren't from Denmark?"

"Theo Bollingsworth!" one of his non-fans bellowed, and the laughter was raucous.

But Risa's reaction to the laughter was inspired: grabbing a highball glass, she poured an extremely generous Johnnie Walker Black on ice and said, "Will someone please deliver this to my friend Theo as my apology for singling him out?"

Othello, amid uproarious glee, delivered the scotch with aplomb. Bollingsworth then had the grace to raise his glass to Risa and, with an expression some in his vicinity believe was an actual, cynicism-crippled attempt at a smile, gave her a little bow.

Risa had the crowd back. "We've reached the deleted heart of the story," she said. "In the evening light of Delhi, Gandhi set out walking to a public prayer, so weak from fasting that he was supported by two young women. Godse stepped into his path, smiled a smile of hatred, raised a pistol, and shot him three times. The first two bullets ripped into Gandhi's chest. One bullet tore an exit wound out his back. His heart would get eight or ten more beats, his gushing lungs two or three failing breaths. Given the reverence so many Westerners feel for him, one would think Gandhi's choice of words would interest us. He spoke only two, and what he said is well known in

India. We also know he spoke eloquent English, and his dying words were not *in* English—a choice made with all the force of his life and faith behind it. Yet the West still insists on translating his two words into English!"

Risa's attention to detail lost some of her audience. When people began conversing amongst themselves, the quietest, most damaged-looking man in the room drained his shot glass, took his feet, and began loudly banging the glass on the bar. Reading Jervis's intent, Othello bellowed, *"SILENCE!"* A startled silence fell. In his gentlest voice, Othello said, "Please give Risa three minutes to tell us what gave Gandhi's two words their power. She offers this as a gift. Accepting it is so little to ask."

Attention returned.

Risa said, "In India, Lord Rama and Lord Krishna are divine incarnations equal to what Jesus is to many in the West. The loving repetition of Ram's name is a cherished act of devotion. Here's the father of Indian poets, Valmiki: 'Dear Rama, Lord of the Worlds! Nothing You do ever fails! Nothing is forever except Yourself! One glance from You and people again sing the ancient songs!' Here's the famed poet Kabir: 'One Ram speaks through each individual mind. One Ram spreads throughout the whole Creation...Without Ram's name, the worlds into dying worlds disappear.' Having long since given himself to this secret practice, Gandhi, with his very last breath, spoke these two words and no others." With more emotion than the crowd had ever seen from her, Risa gasped: *"Hai Ram!"*

Most looked confused or uncomfortable. A few looked stunned.

"Hearing him speak," she continued, "Godse shot him a third time. *Too late!* Gandhi's one Ram spread throughout Creation. He died into the arms of He who sets people singing the ancient songs. And hell *yes* my father's dying made this story powerful to me in ways I can't give you. But how *dare* we cram this miracle of courage into our silly little Western comfort zones! With no Ram tradition to aid them, English-speaking journalists, filmmakers, newscasters, biographers, have *erased* Gandhi's taking of his beloved's name by claiming he said, '*Oh God!*' As Jervis likes to say, 'The fuck! *Oh God!* is the title of a terminally cute Carl Reiner movie starring George Burns as God!'" (Othello later told TJ that Theo Bollingsworth literally *writhed* with dyspeptic delight at this line.) In a voice blending heartbreak and fury, Risa said, "The Attenborough crime my father couldn't forgive? Trapping Kingsley's Gandhi in a script that made him take the bullets, then groan in a voice falling off in despair,

Ohhh-
　　Gaa-
　　　　aaa-
　　　　　　aawd!

"The difference between that sound and Gandhi's '*Hai Ram!*' is the difference between abject shock and diamond focus! Between a reflexive death-groan and an invincible love! Between a man shocked by his murder and a man hurling himself into his Lord's arms! 'How much more difference can there be?' my father asked as his life too was giving out. 'If you ever get even an awkward chance to tell this to a few of our countrymen,' he gasped, 'please, tell it true!'"

At the moment many in the crowd felt Risa was about to break down, she astonished them by upending a Maker's Mark bottle over a shot glass, righting it in an instant, and raising the quarter-shot she'd poured: "My parting toast to Valmiki, Kabir, Gandhi, and my father? May we never again imagine a despairing '*Oh Gawd!*' Gandhi never spoke! Let's raise a fiftieth anniversary glass to a last-breath '*Hai Ram!*' that left three bullets nothing to enter but the imperishable name of a hero's secret love and Lord!"

Glasses were raised and drained, Othello let out a "*HEAR, HEAR!*" Jervis appeared to be attempting a dance step, TJ looked downright soul-shocked, and a few listeners were clearly moved. But most of the crowd looked nothing but relieved that Risa was done. Within seconds the philanderers were back to philandering, the sports nuts were parsing sports, and the gossips, casting glances at Risa, were whispering, "Pregnant, is what I hear. And no man in the picture. Big white shirt to hide the evidence. And did you see her down that whiskey? Her poor baby!"

Then, from an alcove at the far end of the bar, there came a sound like a clipper ship's sail being ripped in half by a mid-Atlantic gale. The entire crowd spun toward it. *What the hell!?*

A man sitting alone, his back to everyone, gave himself away as his shoulders quaked, lungs heaved, and the storm within him shredded a second sail. Turning from the man, to Risa, back to the man, Will Battle declared, "They're *both* bonkers!" But Jervis and TJ knew whose heart had been stormed, and smiled to see Risa abandon her pouring station and head straight for the wild sounds.

Their source wasn't hard to locate. Everyone near a tall man with a dark brown ponytail gawked briefly, then turned away from his awful failures to contain himself. "It's that *play actor*!" a woman said. "I saw him in... oh, what was it? *The Secret of Roan Inish?*"

"Well, Darby O'Gill's losin' his shit over *somethin'*!" Will Battle blored.

"Risa's Hindu blarney?" an incredulous hoop nut asked. "*How? Why?*"

The man put his face in his hands and ripped a third sail.

"Talk sports!" Will told his huddle. "It always bucks a fella up to hear the guys talkin' sports." Will cranked his volume: "*How 'bout that Rasheed Wallace!? Looks like the Blazers finally got it goin' on!*"

"Will!" Othello cut in, handing him a fresh whiskey. "We have a deal. Let them be."

THOUGH HE WAS facing away from her, Risa had recognized Jamey immediately. How could she forget a man who, not half a year ago, showed her a border collie hidden in a bass case he promised would be wearing "the face of love," and Romeo *had* been? Could this same man be as moved by Gandhi's kept promise to a secret love as she? Feeling so uncertain she trembled, she reached out and touched his shoulder.

Jamey spun, stricken and tear-streaked, but smiled at once at the sight of her. Direct as an avalanche, as Lou Roy once described her, Risa said, "If all this emotion has anything to do with Gandhi taking Ram's Name, *you and I need to talk!*"

With a wild-eyed look of joy, Jamey said, "Oh, we do, Risa! We do."

When she took the chair across from him, she couldn't help but see a crowd lining up at her pouring station, many of them looking her way. "*Damn.* Sorry, Jamey. I need ten minutes to pour the last calls. But don't you dare leave! Promise?"

He nodded, but just as Risa stood, TJ slid into her work station and caught her eye. *I've got this!* he mouthed, waving the back of his hand as if to shoo her and Jamey away.

Risa blew him a kiss, sat back down, and said, "This should be good! TJ wants to cover for me. Sweet of him. But he's famous for ridiculously heavy pours, so a crowd will swarm him. And he's just as famous for getting drink recipes all screwed up."

Ten or more customers mobbed the station when TJ went into action, two of the first three he served were trying to return their drinks, and a laughing man holding a full martini glass was saying, "TJ! Fifty percent *vermouth* is a potion Godse would've served to Gandhi!"

Jamey turned back to Risa. "Sorry to seem...*obsessed,* maybe. But your story slammed me so hard I'd like to touch on why."

"That's why I'm here!" Risa said.

"When you moaned that '*Hai Ram!*'" Jamey began, but paused as a tremor passed through him, "something impossible happened. Your two words brushed my unbelief away like a few crumbs off a table. Then, beautiful as you are, Risa, and much as I've hoped to see you again, you vanished into mere instrumentality as some kind of Presence flew me back to the day I first heard Gandhi's name. My tenth birthday. And in an instant, that day and all thirty birthdays since were transformed! It overwhelmed me! I'd need quiet and time to tell the story and we've got neither. But may I show you one little relic to give you a faint idea of what you and the Presence just transformed?"

When Risa nodded, Jamey fished out his wallet, unfolded it, slid a small card out of a leather slot, laid it in her palm—and she found herself staring at a rectangle of beige paper worn to the softness of cloth. Holding the table candle near, she recognized an ancient Multnomah County Library card. "Flip it over," he said.

She did, and read these words, block-printed in pencil by a ten-year-old's hand:

Jan 30, 1948, Gandhi shot dead
Jan 30, 1958, Jamey VZ born

Jan 30, 1963, Debbie VZ dies of leukemia
Jan 30, 1968, Dead Debbie Dead Gandhi and
Live Jamey meet in Woodstock Library

"Good God!" Risa breathed. "These coincidences are *brutal*!"

"So it has long seemed," Jamey said. "Debbie was my mother, and her death on my fifth birthday took years to sink in. The deeper it sank, the more I hated any power or being that would unleash such hideous synchronicities. But *now*, Risa. *Now*..." He began trembling so hard he turned away for fear of ripping another sail. "I can't speak of it yet. But my birthday-deathday story owes your Gandhi/Ram story a full telling. So *please*. Will you keep this little card as a promissory note until my debt is paid?"

"But this is holy writ, Jamey! A Book of Job in haiku, written by a little boy!"

Jamey shook his head in wonder. "That very description tells me, who better than you to safeguard the holy? Please, Risa. Keep it for me!"

Slipping the card into her big white banker shirt pocket, she stroked the pocket as if soothing a living creature.

A long pause followed in which they just sat smiling at each other, unsure where to go after such momentous contact. "I've never seen you here," Risa ventured. "What brought you to Étouffée on this night of all nights?"

Jamey brightened. "A new friend suggested I come. A man I met on a sidewalk when he suddenly veered in front of me, then stopped so fast I nearly flattened him. He'd veered on purpose, he said, because an invisible Ocean 'strobed' him to cause our collision."

"Jervis!" Risa cried.

Jamey smiled. "What a wonderfully improbable man. When it came out that he knew you, I didn't hide my admiration. And though he'd only just met me, he had instant advice for me. But not his own. This was *Ocean's* advice, he whispered. Lunacy, I might have thought if the lunatic and Romeo hadn't fallen instantly in love!"

"Those two had nowhere to fall," Risa said. "Pure love already fills both of them. But may I ask what advice Ocean and Jervis had for you?"

"The strobe conveyed that my interest in you was fine, but my timing wasn't. I had work to do first, related to my mother. 'Heartwork,' Jervis called it. Ocean then assigned me a walking prayer to recite on the streets in my mother's honor. As the child victim of a berserker God, as you know from my Job haiku, I told Jervis no thanks on the prayer. His papery little voice then launched a soliloquy that *obliterated* me over the awful way I've treated my departed mother. But theatre prepares us for some things. Jervis's words were so inarguably damning they were *beautiful* to me! I began reciting the Ocean-assigned prayer, and four months later hardly recognize myself. This morning, for instance, when my old birthday-deathday rage would have devoured me, I simply thought, *What would I most enjoy doing on my fortieth?* And since Jervis had told me tonight was your last at Étouffée, I thought I'd—"

"I'm so dense!" Risa interrupted. "Your library card just told me but it didn't register. *Happy fortieth, Jamey!*"

He glanced at the 12:15 on his watch. "Thanks to you and Gandhi it *was* happy. But what an unhappiness looms now. Jervis tells me you're moving to Montana, and that it's a great move for you. I have no right to feel crushed by this, Risa, but I am. My connections, work, friends, old dad, old dog, all tie me to Portland, so the best I can offer is a *very* fond farewell. You're truly remarkable, Risa. You possess a...what to call it?...*forthrightness of soul* like no one I ever met. From the bottom of a heart you've overwhelmed *twice* in two meetings, thank you for both overwhelms! I wish you every joy in Montana!"

With that, Jamey stood, picked up his coat, and shocked Risa by extending his hand to shake hers and leave! Ignoring the hand, completely refusing to facilitate departure, she said, "Listen, Jamey! Before you exile me to Montana before I'm ready to leave, I need to tell you some things that are *spectacularly* awkward."

"Well!" he said with an amazed and relieved smile. "*Awkward* is one of my middle names."

"I have to warn you. My awkwards don't pussyfoot around."

"Let them thunder like a herd of elephants," he said.

"Very well. My first thundering awkward is this. I'm eleven weeks pregnant."

As his eyes widened Risa braced herself against some lame version of *Who's the lucky guy?* So when, with what looked and sounded like absolute sincerity, Jamey cried, "*Congratulations*, Risa! How *wonderful!*" it nearly undid her.

"Thanks!" she sputtered. "Jeez, Jamey. Since my most thundering awkward went okay, how would you feel about sitting back down and hearing another?"

"I'll journey as high up into the awkwards with you as you care to go," he said as he sat.

"Well then. News of my condition is being spread by the kind of gossips who feel that pregnant women who don't yet show should have a neon sign bolted to their foreheads flashing the words, 'FORGET IT! SHE'S TAKEN!' I mention this because I want you to know I'm not. *Taken,* that is. Because—here's the awkward—*I like you,* Jamey. By which I mean, I like you a *lot!*"

With no seeming self-awareness Jamey's hand flew to his heart. "My God, Risa! And I don't even *have* a God! I'm thrilled to hear this!"

Oh, *that hand thrown onto his heart!* Risa felt her *liking* getting out of control. "Can you bear another awkward?" she asked.

"The more the better!"

"When I finished my Gandhi story and everyone went back to what they'd been doing, that was what I had expected. What I hadn't expected were sounds exploding out of someone as if Gandhi's death had just happened before their eyes. When I then saw it was you who kept exploding, there's no other way to put this: *it pierced me*. You pierced me, Jamey. And now that I know what it is to be pierced, I know that no man ever pierced me before, and only one came close. And that man, in the 'ACLOSED AFOR REMODEL' bar last summer, was *you*."

The madness was contagious. Though Risa had turned crimson again, fearing she'd said way too much, Jamey looked thunderstruck as he leaned toward her. "I felt the same last summer, I feel the same now, and there's more, Risa! Right *now* there's more! When you just said, 'no man ever pierced me before,' I felt yet *another* piercing. And it was so awkwardly intimate, but so beautiful, that *permission*, I feel, is what's needed before I describe it."

Risa went quiet. Beginning with Dave when she was seven, *awkwardly intimate* male revelations had been nightmares in real life. Why would this man's be different?

Well, she thought, because he is different. Like, the day we met, when he saw that Julian didn't truly love me, he turned outrageous, started calling him Gilligan, used Romeo's face to prove Julian's face loveless, and didn't care that Julian flew into a rage—because it was true. Within minutes of meeting me he showed me I'd spent years not being loved, and not loving. He dared that to protect me from settling for such a life. And now he's felt something piercing, intimate, beautiful. How can I not ask to hear it? "Permission granted," she murmured.

At the same moment Jamey's face lit up, he dropped like a baseball catcher down into a squat before her, leaving Risa close to horrified. *Is he about to propose to me like some barroom creep?* But wait: he was squatting, not kneeling, and he wasn't even looking at her. He was staring straight ahead at her banker shirt, smiling so brightly that when he said, "May I?" she had no idea what he was asking and in her confusion nodded yes.

When he reached out, placed his long hands gently on each side of her waist, and held her there, she was flooded by feelings so conflicted she couldn't move. Leaning forward till his lips weren't twelve inches from her navel, he murmured, "*Hey, tiny traveler.* Wasn't that *you* I felt slip in just now?" And what a light in his eyes when he turned to her. "The instant you said I pierced you, Risa, something flitted around you like a moth round a lantern. I wouldn't have believed it possible if your *Hai Ram* hadn't left me feeling *anything's* possible. The moth then flew inside your shirt, flitted around a bit more, and dove—*joyously*, I felt—inside you!"

When Risa, at that moment, felt a mothlike flittering inside her, a dream world subsumed her, a ragamuffin river boy took her hand and gazed into her eyes, and she burst into sobs.

"*Aw!* What is it, Risa?" Jamey cried. "What's the matter?"

"*Let the fields come close!*" she gasped. "*Let the fields be joyful, and all that is something something!*"

Feeling her intensity, though her words made no sense, Jamey slid his chair close and held her. "*For the Lord something something!*" she cried. "And *he cometh. The man across the river, he cometh!* Which made our little boy *so* happy! *I know where he is!* he told me, *and how to find him! For both of us. I can! Don't worry about the river! I know how to cross!* he said, and ran for the water. Oh, Jamey! Was Gandhi's *Hai Ram* the crossing? Did our river boy find and bring you as promised? Is the man I've so long and stupidly searched for really here?"

Jamey reached to the neighboring table and handed Risa two napkins. Streaming tears, but radiant, she wiped her eyes with one, violently blew her nose in the other—and a throat cleared close beside them.

Manifesting out of nowhere, TJ stood holding a large drink in a small snifter. "Risa and Jamey," he said. "What I just accidentally witnessed was absolutely incredible. I'm so sorry to have interrupted. But take a look at Jervis."

They turned to the bar's distant end and saw Jervis on his feet, the better to shoot them namastes by the seeming hundreds. As Jamey stood and sent a few back, Risa noticed her backup had manned her pouring station and was serving the last-call drinks.

TJ set the snifter down before Jamey. "Lagavulin," he said. "Jervis tells me you relish this potion of our people and we're honored to stand you a dram. My brother is very fond of you, Jamey, and even *more* fond, it seems, of your wonderful dog."

When Jamey took TJ's proffered hand, he merely held it in both of his. No manly shaking. TJ was stunned, then moved, by this odd break with rote tradition. "Risa speaks of you the way Jervis speaks of Romeo," Jamey said. "It's truly a pleasure, TJ."

Smiling his tight, intelligent smile, TJ studied Jamey's face with keen curiosity. When he then turned to Risa, his smile softened in a way that showed Jamey he adored her, wanted Jamey to *know* he adored her, and no matter what hold Jamey or anyone else had on her, TJ would go on adoring her for as long as he breathed. When he noticed Jamey simply smiling and nodding, TJ's smile then softened for Jamey as it had for Risa.

She stood and embraced TJ.

"I'm never sure what to make of it when Jervis says things that strike me as sensible," he said when she released him. "So please, tell me what you two think of his notion that, after her bartending finale, Risa might like a post-work shower and change of clothes in the office as Jamey enjoys his dram, and then..." TJ shifted into a Jervis impersonation as hopeless as his bartending, though they did like the content: "*The fuck.* Get outta here, both of you, and get busy doing nine hundred thousand wonderful things together!"

(Portland, January 31, 1998)

XIII. Barzakh

The greater the nudity, the greater the union.
                              —Meister Eckhart

THE FUCK. RISA showered, changed, and they donned their coats and set out to do nine hundred thousand wonderful things together. But a nattering, chattering, unrecognizable-to-herself Risa's first words were: "So, Your Fortyness! Wanna stroll up to the twenty-four-hour caffeine joint, Coffee Zombies, eat too much of their stupidly good coffee cake, and get wired on dark French 'cause so what if we can't sleep? Then, since everything'll be closed, we'll circle back to my place in the Pearl, regroup, and maybe hop in my car and head east up the Gorge for the sunrise, or west to the coast for the rain rise, or stay put and stay up swapping life stories, Jervis stories, or Ram stories. It's up to you, dear man, because *damn*! Fortyness is biblical!"

When Jamey just gazed at her, smiling the smile she'd adored in his dog, Risa smiled back, fell silent, they fell in stride, and there was something so guileless and perfect about the way their coats brushed together that she took his arm, drew him closer, their strides fused and hips gently collided, and when their strides and collides reached the lights and bustle of Coffee Zombies they turned to each other, shook their heads at the same instant, and Jamey planted himself on the sidewalk at a dramatic dancer's angle. Reading his intent perfectly, Risa took three swift steps right *at* him, made a wildly trusting leap into his arms, and Jamey caught and spun her into an about-face worthy of Fred Astaire and Ginger Rogers.

Beaming to know they'd accomplished the first of the nine hundred thousand wonderful things, they hiked the nine blocks back to the Pearl Building and into the lobby. Steering Jamey past the elevator to preserve their arm-in-arm- and hip-to-hip-ness, Risa led him up the four flights of stairs, down the hall to her door, and unlocked it.

They stepped inside. A single soft lamp had been left burning, allowing Jamey to see that her studio apartment was a single high-ceilinged room, maybe six hundred square feet, with a kitchen space, walk-in closet, small bathroom, low futon bed. But the moment they removed their winter coats and set them aside, the apartment vanished, so delighted were they just to stand there seeing so much more of each other.

"Can I describe three things I love that you've done so far tonight?" Risa asked.

Dazzled by her request, Jamey said, "Please!"

"The first. When I was telling the Gandhi story, you said that I 'vanished into mere instrumentality.' I love that as a barkeep especially. I can't tell you how sick I am of men telling me all these things my appearance was supposedly doing to them when I was doing nothing. When you saw me vanish into instrumentality, subservient to the Presence, you left me feeling, *She who loseth her life shall save it.* Thank you for granting me the freedom to disappear!"

"You're welcome," Jamey said. "Your clarity about inner things is incredible, Risa."

Her expression grew more intimate, mildly shocking, deeply moving. "The second thing that struck me appalled me at first. When you squatted down before me, not caring how weird it looked, I didn't know you'd felt a flitter. I was ready to run for the hills! But then I felt the moth flittering myself, and *my God! Overwhelm!* I have more to tell you about dreams of an adorable boy and an impossible river crossing. But now, can we give ourselves completely to our freedom to be no one but you and me, alone together?"

"Nothing would make me happier!" Jamey said.

"So the third thing that struck me *still* strikes me—but stay where you are, because where we are is what's creating the third thing, okay?"

Jamey planted himself afresh where he stood, seven feet in front of her.

"There's an Arabic word I've fallen in love with," Risa said. "The word *barzakh.* Found it in a book by a twelfth-century Sufi sheikh, Ibn al-Arabi. A *barzakh,* he said, is the border that separates any two things, but can also be said to *join* the two things. In Ibn Arabi's words, 'A *barzakh* separates a known from an unknown, a negated from an affirmed, an existent from a nonexistent.' But since the *barzakh* is neither the one thing nor the other, yet joins them, it partakes of the powers of *both* things."

"Whew!" Jamey said. "That's so deep I'm not touching bottom, Risa. Can you, maybe, describe something I've seen or felt that fuses the powers of two things?"

Risa closed her eyes, pondered a moment, nodded, reopened her eyes. "Picture a big, wide, moon-drunk Oregon beach. See the ocean's huge swells rolling in, turning into breakers? See the breakers crashing toward us, crushing solid rock into fine sand with their power? But see the played-out waves and riptides, loaded with the same sand, sneaking back out to sea underneath the showy breakers? High tide or low, wet or dry, that wide strip of sand is neither ocean nor land. It's a barzakh *rife* with the power of both! What defiance the tiny sand-grains exert, in that violent meeting place, to maintain the barzakh's beachness as ocean's power keeps crushing the rock to sand!"

"I see it, I feel it!" Jamey said.

"Which brings me to the barzakh you and I create," Risa said as she ran her hand through the air before them. "I have no idea why this is so, but much as I loved it when we were walking arm in arm, I feel our closeness even *more* in this empty space between us. Tell me, Jamey. Am I a metaphysicated fool who needs to drink more beer and watch more sports? Or is this space uniting us even though we're not yet united in literal ways? Can you too feel the barzakh making the not-yet-physical physical and our untouched bodies feel touched?"

Jamey closed his eyes and ran his hand through the air. "If I greet this space with reason alone, I'd recommend the beer and sports. But if I tie my reason like a dog to a tree and open up to what the space between has me feeling, it's all about moon-drunk waves crashing in and sliding back out over sand that defies ocean's power over the very land it keeps crushing. Your description of barzakhs also makes me aware I have more than one kind of mind. An outer and an inner one, maybe. And I *love* the one that's experiencing our barzakh!"

Risa glowed as she whispered, "I *adore* this feeling!"

Jamey shared a moment's delight. Then his face saddened. "But Risa. Aren't you also implying that if I cross the barzakh, and touch you, I'll destroy something you adore?"

How incomprehensibly delighted she looked as she said, "*Yes!*"

"Then how," Jamey asked, "am I ever to cross, or touch you?"

As her tooth gap emanated sheer glee, she said, "I have no idea! But as the only man in a barroom crowd who saw me vanish into instrumentality, got slammed by Ram's Presence, and sensed a mothlike quickening in me even before I did, I'm *sure* you'll come up with something!"

Though he suspected her of teasing, Jamey took her challenge seriously. His expression grew concentrated, his gaze turned off to the side, and he stood silent for a length of time that surprised and moved her. He then lit up as an idea struck, but gave it time to settle rather than blurt it half formed. "I *do* have a notion, based on the *ridiculous* joy I felt when we simply came in, took off our coats, and were able to see so much more of each other. That moment makes me wonder how it might affect our barzakh if, while preserving the space between us, we slowly, calmly, *seriously* begin removing *everything* that's concealing us from each other? What better way to feel how untouched bodies affect the space *between* bodies than to become naked for the first time, at the *same* time, seven feet apart?"

Risa's smile banked down to a glowing ember. "I *knew* you'd come up with something. And a strong yes to seriousness. No *vava-voom* silliness. No words even, I don't think. Just silence, patience, and courage as we stalk the barzakh and each other like three rare wild birds. *Oh, Jamey! What an idea!* Are we really going to do this?"

Rather than speak, Jamey sent his fingertips to the top button of his night-blue shirt, undid it, and the next three, then paused to wait for Risa.

Removing her string tie and laying it on the closest chair, she undid four buttons of the fresh banker shirt she'd donned after her shower, and Jamey saw that she was wearing a camisole the color of old ivory and, beneath it, no bra. And so it began. Wearing faint smiles of concentration, keeping the same slow pace, taking time to fold and set aside each piece of clothing, they studied each other, and the space between each other, till there was nothing more to remove. Free to speak, they then said nothing. Free to approach and touch, they chose not to. Why? Because some Sufi Sheikh of Yore once extolled an imperceptible something/nothing thingy called a barzakh! What a spell Risa had cast to cause Jamey to invent such a game! And what a spell Jamey had cast that she willingly played it!

Yet to the surprise of neither of them, their faces grew limned with wonder as, via proximity, eyesight, unseen extensions of being, an exquisite tension *did* permeate the space between. Seven feet from Risa, Jamey forthrightly fed upon her wild hair, blue-veined temples, obsidian eyes, unceasing hint of smile, sent his gaze down her neck, shoulders, arms, took in the small breasts, alert and shy as week-old fawns, relished the barely perceptible swell of belly, long legs, elliptic hips, dark gateway between. Just as forthrightly, Risa studied Jamey's face, enamored of the contrast between its weathering and its kindness; its scars and its tenderness of gaze. Dropping her eyes to his body, she took pleasure in its length, litheness, maturity; smiled at his incongruously hairless chest and little-boy nipples; admired his unconcern over the levitation trick the sight of her had inspired in his lingam. When her gaze then focused on the barzakh, she detected shimmers of color and floating pockets of emotion, and felt closer exploration was needed.

"How would it be," she asked, "if each of us, in turn, took a single stride into the barzakh and, still without touching, felt the feels as we arrive there?"

Jamey gave her a courtly bow, then took a stride toward her. Risa's pulse and breath quickened. The greatly reduced space ramped up the *known, unknown, negated,* and *affirmed* instantly. She took her own stride. Twenty inches apart now, they perceived beauties and blemishes previously imperceptible: the near bioluminescence of her blue-veined temples; the now-perceptible scars that showed it was catastrophe, not DNA, that had sculpted Jamey's aquiline nose; the astronomical blossoming of nebulae and color variations in what were formerly simply his warm brown and her obsidian-dark irises; the night sky faintly visible inside the tiny skylights we call pupils. As Risa ran her hand back and forth through the now-negligible border space, a previously unseen beauty radiated from her depths, outward, causing the words *Risa, full of grace* to flood Jamey with feelings so potent he couldn't speak.

"Your respect for the barzakh has been heroic," she murmured. "But what the diminished space has me feeling now is a need to do this." She took seven backward steps to the low futon, lay down on her side, and gazed up at him. "What does it have *you* feeling?"

Saying nothing, Jamey reached back, unbound his hair, shook it free, stepped over to the bed, and surprised her by dropping to his knees beside it. She rolled onto her back, wanting to bury her hands in his hair and pull him to her, but suppressed her want, the better to witness how he might approach and touch her for the first time.

He leaned slowly forward and down, his body so long and the bed so low that, though his knees remained on the floor, his torso loomed just inches over hers. With great care he planted his palms to either side of her, supported himself with his arms, and his face approached hers. First contact: *lips, touching her forehead oh so lightly*. Still silent, forgoing all bodily contact and use of hands, the lips began exploring her face. When the small sensations made her smile, his lips moved to the smile, brushed over its lift and creases, imbibed as best they could the feelings beneath or behind. The intimate sound of his breathing, light insistence of his lips, enveloping canopy of his hair, began to intoxicate. "Come up," she whispered, backing away to make room. "Please. *Come up.*"

He did, but knelt beside her without yet embracing her, his body, hands, erection so close their heat was palpable, yet only the lips continued to touch.

Her smile turned wry. "I'm sure Ibn Arabi himself commends your reverence for the barzakh. But I love your voice, and sense Dreadnought does too, and you haven't said a word since this exploration began. Please, voice of Jamey. Trespass in the barzakh."

"Who, pray tell, is Dreadnought?" the voice murmured as his lips continued to explore.

"Our little moth," she whispered. "But don't make me explain. Just give us the voice I've loved from the moment I first heard it."

A nonexistent commandeered an existent. A negated was suddenly affirmed. A lips-voice-skin barzakh sprang to life, the lips-voice his, skin hers. "From the moment I first saw you, I knew that if ever I were allowed to be free with you, like this..."—the lips-voice moved to her neck and nape—"you'd be my one and only in an instant. And yes, I said, 'my one and only,' knowing it would set off a *too much* feeling in your doubting place. But nothing in me knows how to resist you, Risa, your doubting place included."

She closed her eyes, lay deathly still, and in spite of knowing he was Dreadnought's beloved man from across the river, struggled terribly with the *too much* feeling. *My romantic atheism!* she thought. *My steeliness! I'm impossible!*

But even as she thought this his lips kissed each closed eye to soothe it, kissed each bluish temple to soothe it, kissed the thoughts behind her eyes to soothe them, his good voice murmuring as it worked: "You *need* the doubting place I see and feel. The admiration of unadmirable men has plagued you." The lips-voice made their way down her neck to the clavicle, crossed half that proud bone as if crossing a bridge, but jumped off into the cleft between breasts knowing this was another *too much* move. "But the barzakh is *genius,*" it said of itself as it grazed upon her left breast. "Such a beautiful necessity!" it said as it grazed the right. "And don't you feel how, even lips and voice to skin, like *this,* both a negated and an affirmed remain in place? I will *never* lay claim to the space that joins but also separates. Where's the love in wanting to *possess* you? Even if we become a kind of Juliet and her Romeo; a Beatrice and her Benedick; a Eurydice and her Orpheus," the lips-voice murmured as it moved, name to name, from breast to breast, "the space that partakes of the power of both belongs to neither of us."

Soothed by his understanding but feeling what her body now longed to get her into, Risa's steeliness flared up. "Listen, Mister Sufi Shakespeare Barzakh Beach Poet or whoever you think you are," she began. But when his mouth broke into a smile at her feistiness she thought, *He truly* does *get me!* And no matter how many times the lips switched breasts, they found the other breast such a momentous discovery that, over and over, she felt discovered afresh. As her shoulders began to roll and nipples to vie to be the next to meet the lips she murmured, "*Please* don't compare...a flawed, easily confused mortal...to the Bard's or Greeks' *immortals*...Because I like you...a *lot,* it seems...and all I could ever, *ohhh!*...be to a worshipper, *unh!*...is a false idol."

He lay beside her at last, framed her hips with his hands, and the lips-voice barzakh started down her body toward the hands. But as waves of pleasure swept through her, Risa's doubting place spiked. "Where are you *going?*" she asked, genuinely anxious.

"To court a doubter," the lips-voice kissed and whispered as they worked their way, oddly, out to the point of her hip. "Here's an erogenous nothing place," they said as they began feeding on the skin and bone of the hip point as if it were soma. "But feel how, when love suffuses touch, touch turns unconditional, and there *are* no nothing places?" Of its own accord her body began to move, her doubting place to drift out to sea. "Isn't Cape Hip suggesting," came the murmur, "that we've been overtaken by powers to be welcomed, not feared?"

The barzakh made its way across her belly to the opposite hip point, again found soma, added tongue, and it took all her willpower to keep from thrusting. "Cape Hip," she breathed, "and Cape Other Hip, have been overtaken, I admit it. But *still,* Jamey. I, *still*...maybe *don't!?*"

The lips-voice stopped cold. The surges in her head and body subsided. She felt grief at the loss. Jamey's eyes were nothing but kind as they met hers. "I will *always* stop when you ask," he said. "But can you tell us why you've stopped us?"

She leaned up, took his head in her hands, pulled him to her, smothered his mouth with her mouth, then let him go. "I'm sorry! I'm so sorry!" she cried, stunning him with an obvious wave of grief. "But I can't stop seeing how...just four months ago...my father's vacated body showed my body how soon *every* bodily thing, *this* included"—she gave a mournful little thrust—"is just *gone!*"

Gazing at her with a face of love laughably like Romeo's, Jamey said, "May I remind you of something you know far better than I do?"

Her nod was that of a confused child.

He dropped back down to a hip point, for a third time found soma, but the instant he felt her experiencing it he abandoned the hip, slid up till they were face-to-face, and cupped her face in his hands. "The Presence Gandhi's magic words called down into our barzakh is a *deathless* answer to my agony at age ten," his good voice said. "The barzakh came to me through you to me, Risa, *and* to me through you, and *we're still inside it.* We're not just you, me, and a fleeting Presence. We're inside a mortal-meets-immortal barzakh partaking of the powers of all three. What do you, or I, or Dreadnought have to fear by trusting a mystery so beautiful?"

Encircling and enclosing him with her limbs and body in every way she could, Risa breathed, "*When you put it like that...*"

And a moon-drunk *negated* melted into an *affirmed.* Waves incoming and outgoing washed over and through. The sea and sands of the barzakh remained no one's as they partook of the power of both. And love fed love to love as they fed each other to each other with their hands.

Last Telling:

On Earth as It Isn't in Heaven

Remember the earth whose skin you are.
——Joy Harjo

There is a world of sentient beings in a blade
of grass said Dōgen, a decade before Eckhart,
continents away, said a piece of wood contains
the rational image of God, for which the clergy
burned him at the figurative stake. Christ the
carpenter also chose a skin-to-skin departure.
——Chris Dombrowski

If the soul had known God as perfectly as do the
angels, it would never have entered the body. And
if the soul could have known God without the
world, the world would never have been created.
The world was made for the soul's sake that the
soul's eye might be practiced and strengthened to
bear the divine light...The soul's eye could not
bear this light unless it were steadied by matter,
supported by likenesses, and so led up to the divine
and accustomed to it.
——Meister Eckhart

(Elkmoon Mountains and Elsewhere, Montana, 1996 through 2002)

I. Notes on the Lûmi

An intake of breath is not just oxygen, a pulse is not just the rush of blood but also the taking in of divinity through an orifice, and as it moves through, it becomes a spark. To be inspired is to have accepted spirit in the lung and heart, to watch it circulate through miles of blood vessels and capillaries whose tiny fenestrations allow oxygen, nutrients and grace to leak into the tissues of muscle and consciousness, then be taken up again, reoxygenated, and returned.
—Gretel Ehrlich, *A Match to the Heart*

From the Elkmoon Mountain Journals of Grady Haynes:

It's time I summarized what I've learned of the Lûmi, and my first admission will strike anthropologists, ethnologists, and academics as ludicrous: I will never share the knowledge I've gained of these elusive mountain pilgrims in book, lecture, or video form with people schooled by mere college degrees. The kind of knowledge I've gathered can only be grasped by people deeply in love with, and bodily familiar with, a particular range of mountains.

More unacceptable admissions: as long and hard as I've studied the Lûmi, I have no desire to prove they exist by producing one of them to be dissected by the dominant "culture." (Yes, those are scorn quotes around "culture.") They would never agree to be "produced" and I agree with that disagreement. Likewise, since the Lûmi don't believe in chronological time, why should they verifiably exist in it? Their claim to an unwanted fame is their complete lack of fame, and they're so skilled at seeming not to exist that academic scholarship and journalism can't engage them at all. In the seven years I wasted combing libraries I located just three articles that reference supposed "Lûmi people." All three appeared in the kind of Western tourist magazines that exist primarily for the real estate ads, and all three were so pompously portentous and silly that they brought to mind an observation attributed to Mark Twain: "Researchers have already cast much darkness on the subject, and if they continue their investigations we shall soon know nothing at all about it."

Nothing at all is exactly what the Lûmi want the public to know about them. Their lore makes clear that anyone who accepts the term "First World

Nations" has accepted political and commercial takes on "reality" that destroy their ability to grasp even basic geophysical facts, let alone grapple with Lû mi subtleties and mythological realities. This is why, when communicating with so-called First World nation-states, the Lû mi keep themselves out of the equation. Twelve years of exploration have taught me that what these high-elevation secret-keepers have to offer can only be experienced via long, keen attention to mountain ranges capable of drawing an occasional dirt-humble seeker up into the immense imaginations of the mountains themselves.

My notes on the Lû mi derive from five sources:

First source: all the mountains I've explored, but the Inner Elkmoon Mountains supremely.

Second source: eight campfire conversations with Gladys Wax, the age-less old packer I call "the Informant" when the Lû mi are our topic. Her backcountry horse-packing business, I've suspected for years, is no business at all but a subterfuge. Our first two meetings took place miles and weeks apart in 1996, and we've met once every year since up to this year, 2002. All but our '96 encounter took place in the Inner Elkmoons during August or September. The marriage between the Informant and her landscape was obvious from the start. What has snuck up on me is my ever deeper regard for her. Who else in my life has forgiven my faults so blithely? Whose intimate mountain knowledge has made me ache with longing for over a decade? Whose occasional lambastings have left me feeling that greater aware-ness is not only possible but owed to our beloved mountains? Every year, when she rides away with Mormon and Anonymous in tow, I ache knowing twelve months will pass before I see her again -- if I see her again. Even if I don't, she's been the most influential person in my life precisely because she doesn't care about anything I do, think, or feel beyond its effect on my reverence for the Elkmoons. Receiving her acceptance, rather than her judgment, has moved me to change behaviors that would have grown worse had she sat in judgment. Of Low El Grady's hedonism, for instance, she once said, "It's nothing but a seamy little truth about you. There's no way to approach Big Truth but to address the seamy little truths that divert us along the way. We don't transcend the rocks and roots in the trail, Grady Haynes. We stub our toes, turn our ankles, and fall on our faces till we learn to see the damn things and stop wrecking ourselves."

Third source: the dreams I've had on the shores of Jade Lake, some of which have affected me as powerfully as peak events in my waking life, an example being my dream affair with a woman who at dream's end turned out to be myself, yet my partner considered the dream itself an act of infidelity, and dumped me!

Fourth source: a growing body of evidence that I, and perhaps all visitors to the Inner Elkmoons, are being observed by some very aware, very quick-to-vanish people. Spotting human silhouettes against the skyline soon caused me to start carrying a pair of Leica Trinovid 10x42 binoculars, enabling me to spot a few humans possessed of uncanny knowledge of Elkmoon high ridges, and great skill at vanishing if I seek them out. By traversing the ridges after those sightings I've discovered four substantial rock overhangs, one habitable cave, and a rock shelter of partial human construction, all of them capable of sheltering a hiker from lightning, rainstorms, or unseason- able snow. The same ridgelines feature small, well-made cairns of two kinds, some of them way-markers, some perhaps messages to fellow travelers.

Fifth source: a book owned by the Informant, authored by one Axel Volkmann, titled Lûmi Singings. Five straight summers, beginning in '98, the Informant has allowed me to read from it for exactly nineteen minutes -- a minute, I presume, for each of what Volkmann calls "the Nineteen Valleys of the Lûmi cosmos." As I read, Gladys keeps me in sight, making sure I take no notes and pull no fast ones with cameras or recording devices. The first time I read in the book I found her time limit amusing, but the second time Lûmi Singings set fire to my imagination, leaving me desperate for more. After returning the book to Gladys I retire to my tent and write down as much as I can recall as the words are vanishing from memory, capturing a few paragraphs verbatim, and paraphrasing a few more. But to call my brief dips in the Singings frustrating is an understatement.

A summary of what I've gleaned even so:

The Lûmi art, work, path, practice, is to allow identity, face, ego, and name to disappear into high mountains roughly five months of the year, then melt down into the valleys for roughly seven months, calling no attention to their summer sojourns. When they come down, the Lûmi "vanish" by becoming ordinary members of the populace. No Amish beards, brimmed hats, long dresses, small bonnets; no Buddhist shaved heads and red or orange robes. In the lowlands the Lûmi guard their secrets by becoming bus drivers, baristas, mechanics, high school basketball coaches, and maybe mountain-defending activists too. And they might prove to be the kindest barista, coach, or activist you ever met, but good luck catching them out as Lûmi when, at low elevation, they're superstitions even unto themselves. When May then rolls around, they tell their neighbors, "I travel in summer. See you next fall." And away into their chosen high country they go.

The Informant feels bad for the Canadian First Nations and American Indian tribes when she compares them to the Lûmi. "Being born of specific river valleys, estuaries, desert cliffs, defines them," she says. "But specific geog- raphies leave them vulnerable to enviro degradation, attrition, and treaties that too often provide little more safety than outright lies. The Lûmi, in contrast, are nomadic pilgrims who move seasonally through their high places engaged in practices so subtle that if strangers happen upon them, they drop what they're doing before it's seen that a practice exists. Good luck stealing that."

I once asked the Informant if the way the Lûmi disguise themselves struck her as cowardly, compared to the tribes' steady presence in their places.

She said, "Disguise is a necessity for many of the most fragile and beautiful creatures on earth to exist. When a chrysalis is a chrysalis, it isn't a butterfly. It's a tough, camouflaged pupa protecting the coming butterfly by being unrecognizable as such. I'm moved by the tribes' loyalty to place, but it's heartbreaking how often it saddles them with abandoned uranium mines, nuclear test sites, species holocaust, extreme poverty, and so on. To say tribal lifeways are 'misunderstood' by modern industrial culture is too kind. 'Industrial culture' is an unending assault on living things. The Lûmi elude assault. The high country they pass through offers little that exploiters value, and much high country is protected by wilderness designation. There's no comparing their tradition to the challenges facing the world's tribal peoples."

"A related question," I said. "Didn't you once tell me that most Lûmi are DNA mongrels, and that you consider this a good thing?"

"If I said 'good' I didn't mean 'superior.' Only different. To attach neither pride nor shame to racial purity or impurity appeals to me since we're increasingly a planet of mutts. But tribal assimilation tends toward tribal extinction. As an outsider I have no right to speak of blood quantum issues. In precolonial times the Lûmi were all tribal, and ninety percent of them died of the smallpox and German measles Europe brought. Centuries passed during which there were almost no Lûmi. But the Loop and the lore were preserved, starfish work filled in some gaps, and their lifeways survive though their numbers are small."

"Do the Lûmi even know their numbers?" I asked. "Or want to know them? It seems to me that a census is antithetical to what defines them."

Looking amused by my question, Gladys said, "Here's a story about a census taker. The second time I ran into a fella name of Grady Haynes, he told me he hadn't seen a single Lûmi he could be sure of, and no wilderness ranger, backpacker, or horse packer he'd met had even heard of them. But when I met the same fella a year later, he'd realized a few of those same rangers and packers may have been Lûmi, telling him they'd never heard of themselves. How can you take a census of tricksters like that? And here's another thought. Wouldn't it be an even slicker trick if some likable fella -- say, that same Grady Haynes -- wandered these mountains for years with no idea that the Lûmi, from the beginning, had recognized him as one of their own?"

Seeing she'd gobsmacked me, Gladys lifted a finger to her lips, inviting a silence in which the door to my soul fell ajar, and from that moment until she doused the fire I felt perfectly whole and at peace in Gladys's company for the first time.

During the five years I've known of Lûmi Singings I've searched for it online, in countless bookstores, and in every university library in Idaho, Montana, Oregon, and Washington with no success. When I complained of the book's scarcity, the Informant told me, " 'Scarce' isn't the word. Your search is in vain. Every copy but mine was either destroyed or hidden the year Lûmi Singings was published."

I asked who would disappear such an innocuous book.

She said, "I would guess the Lûmi themselves were involved, for the obvious reason: the book threatens their anonymity. My Belgians are named Mormon because I suspect the Utah Mormons helped disappear the <u>Singings</u> and Anonymous because anonymity preserves the Lûmi way. The Lûmi are formed by mountains, not by books."

Who <u>is</u> this intrepid old woman who holds Lûmi knowledge so lightly that she shrugs at the destruction of the only known book detailing their myths and practices? I was about to pursue this pointedly when she turned the tables on me:

"You know, Grady Haynes. The kind of knowledge you're trying to dig up is no small thing. In Tibetan Buddhist tradition, hidden teachings of this kind are called <u>terma</u>, and a person who brings such teachings to light is a <u>terton</u>, a time-honored title for a considerable achievement. Are you worthy of such an honor?"

"When the only people capable of bestowing that honor remain hidden," I said, "how would I know? All I know is to keep searching."

Gladys said nothing, but her weathered old face did not disguise her approval.

<u>Lûmi Singings</u> was published in an edition of one thousand copies in 1979. I first saw Gladys's copy in 1998. After much futile searching it occurred to me to contact the Library of Congress -- and the book was catalogued! But when I took steps to travel to DC to read it, the congressional librarian I had contacted wrote to tell me their three copies, though still on record, could no longer be found. That really took the wind out of my sails. To make matters worse, Southern Idaho University, including SIU Press, was dismantled and absorbed by other schools in the Idaho state system. Searching that system for SIU faculty or employees of SIU Press, the one person I reached by phone -- once an accountant for the Press -- said, "I worked with numbers, not titles or author names. I have no memory of Axel Volkmann or <u>Lûmi Singings</u>."

And that was that. As of this writing -- Christmas Day, 2002 -- I've found nothing but the banal magazine articles I mentioned. I've also inquired at seven tribal headquarters, speaking with Shoshone, Kootenai, Blackfoot, Salish, Spokane, Wishram, and Nez Perce leaders, elders, and scholars. The one Shoshone elder who'd heard of my heroes turned stone-faced and said, "The Lûmi are a scurrilous myth. Trickster shaman-type crap. You're wasting your life." No other Indian I've talked to (if they're telling the truth!) has even heard of the Lûmi.

When I mentioned the Shoshone's response to the Informant, she said, "Stop barking up the tribal tree. The Lûmi allegiances are to high elevation, the Loop, the lore, and secrecy. They might be from any tribe, or none. Any religion, or none. There are no safe generalizations. Some don't have families because the Loop and secrecy are so demanding. Others have big families who can cover for a mom or dad who vanishes for five months every year. The one meaningful Lûmi characteristic is the depth and weathering of character their high hidden landscapes create."

"High hiddenness. Secrecy. Disappeared books. Dead ends," I muttered. "I feel as if my two days a year with you are as close to the Lûmi as I'll ever get."

Gladys unleashed her crazed cackle. "You're not even that close, Grady Haynes. I'm just a scurrilous myth! Trickster shaman-type crap!"

When I did not share her levity, she said, "I repeat. The terton knowledge you seek is no small thing. I'm impressed by your diligence. It honors what you seek."

I said, "Here's all I know about diligence. If there is no wind, row. If there are no oars, laugh."

She let out another cackle. "Good one, Grady Haynes!"

And on with my futile terton seeking I went.

In 1999 I offered a $500 reward to six book-finding agencies for a well-preserved copy of Lûmi Singings. Nothing. In 2000 I upped the offer to $5,000 for a used copy in any readable condition at all. More nothing. The world's sole book on the Lûmi has become a kind of Lûmi itself.

Do I lament this? To be honest, the part of me that regrets the lack of Lûmi material is at war with the part of me delighted by the same lack. If these people exist, they're some of the most admirably nonexistent people in existence! The little I've learned in seeking them has also borne its own fruit by forcing me, seven vivid summers in a row, to experience the same purgatorial climbs and mesmerizing high country the Lûmi — or some remarkably skilled imposters — still know. That alone has been changing me body and soul. Herewith, my discoveries to date.

— Grady Rhys Haynes, Christmas 2002

Lûmi Findings

• The One-Thousand-and-Five Summits and Nineteen Valleys can be known, and are known, by those who have become Lûmi. (Volkmann, Lûmi Singings, preface, p. xvi)

• During "the Myth Times" (neither Volkmann nor the Informant define this vague term, but it seems to imply cyclic narratives that predate concepts of chronological time), the Nineteen Valleys could be "known" by a long-lived man or woman via "rigorous walking." (Volkmann) The Nineteen Valleys can no longer be known in this way because property rights, no-trespassing laws, thousands of miles of barbed-wire fences, irrigation ditches, and highways have set people apart from and against one another, making the Nineteen Valleys impossible to traverse on foot. The Lûmi World in its completeness has thereby "become impossible to know via what the Lûmi call 'land-knowings.' But the Nineteen Valleys are still known by what they call 'river-knowings' and 'above-knowings.'" (Volkmann)

•According to the Informant, the Lûmi's loss of the ability to Know the Valleys by land was foretold in the <u>Singings</u> "millennia ago." I didn't comment, but "millennia," plural, strikes me as a hell of a long time for any lineage of mere mortals to claim to be tracking any Kind of Knowing at all.

•During my 2001 nineteen-minute session with <u>Lûmi Singings</u> I memorized, then snuck into my tent and wrote down, the following passages. All sentences and words in quotation marks are very close to verbatim Volkmann. The parenthetical remarks are paraphrased Volkmann:

"There will never be a time when the Lûmi will not live among the people. But there will be a time when a majority of people will dishonor the gifts the Lûmi bring. The gulf between such people and the gifts will bring about the perishing of" (a massive number of the people and the gifts.) But a "reduced world" will survive, the Lûmi and "terrestrial humanity" will survive, and (after centuries of struggle) "great new gifts will be sung back into being." [Song XI]

"In the dark time to come, there will be one great hunt. Then, the Great Hunger. As the dark time approaches, the Nineteen Valleys will become impassable and life-giving Knowledge will fail nearly all but the Lûmi." Small families, small elites of the wealthy, and single hog-rich individuals "will behave as if they possess the authority of an entire people. Their tendentious behavior and crude thought-forms" (will be laughable to the Lûmi). "Tremendous harm will be done to the world's creatures, lands, seas, skies, and cultures even so." [Song XI]

"The Lûmi of the dark time will be <u>takh-nekh-wakhul</u>" [takh = no; <u>nekh</u> = exterior; <u>wakhul</u> = sign; "no outward sign"; incognito]. "The One-Thousand-and-Five Summits and Nineteen Valleys, though reduced, will comprise a Complete World even so," and "a renewed terrestrial humanity" will survive in reduced numbers and "live as a strand in harmony with other living strands." [Song XI]

•When I read that a reduced but "Complete World" and terrestrial humanity will survive and seek harmony, I nearly wept with relief. I then glanced up to find the Informant gazing at me, perfectly aware of my feelings. With effort I made my face deadpan, but I continued to feel elated to learn that, after a world catastrophe,

the time of <u>takh-nekh-wakhul</u> will end, broken people, places, and creatures will slowly heal, new life-forms and deep Knowings will again shine forth, and the Lûmi Way will be one of (many old ways rejuvenated, not just restored). [Song XIV]

•Though the Informant won't verify this surmise, the term "Complete World" seems to imply the existence of a viable wisdom culture <u>and</u>

that culture's specific geography. The oneness of land and culture is so central to the Lûmi worldview that the terms applied to each are often interchangeable. Four related axioms I've gathered from Lûmi Singings. One: when "land-knowings" of the Nineteen Valleys are unobtainable, "above-knowings" and "river-knowings" suffice. Two: the Lûmi's favored high-elevation places and the "above-knowings" they inspire are far more ancient, and once sustained far more people, than anyone would guess today, and the archaeological evidence of this is abundant to those who know where to look. The Informant herself has shown me treasures I'm forbidden to describe, some of which anchor my love of their high places. Three: though the Lûmi's takh-nekh-wakhul state appears to give free rein to the orcs, dictatorial dolts, and dark wizards now in political and industrial power, "true knowers always do their work." Four: the ruling anti-culture is so pervasively delusional that there would be "no true knowing in this dark time" if the Lûmi and unspecified others like them were not takh-nekh-wakhul (incognito) as they continue their vital work.

•Trying to grasp what is meant by the term "Complete World" with just two of my nineteen minutes left, I read that while there are many thousands of summits to the south, west, and north of the particular One-Thousand-and-Five referenced in Lûmi Singings, "to seek the knowledge of too many peaks causes true knowing to wither." I'm reminded of Soto Zen founder Dōgen saying, "What you receive with trust is your one verse or one phrase. Do not try to understand the eighty thousand verses and phrases." In support of this perspective, the Singings maintain that each individual creature, human or otherwise, constitutes "a Song," and that every Song but "the Origin Song" fills a "necessarily limited" span of time and portion of space. A limited geographical space and time is appropriate to human beings, the Lûmi maintain, "for wisdom's sake." Too great a geographical territory or span of time "spreads thin" the kind of knowing that "strikes like a lightning shaft, revealing the Great Knowing."

•According to Volkmann, the One-Thousand-and-Five Summits and Nineteen Valleys become known to those Lûmi who, "at the waxing of their song-span," leave people and place behind, attempt the High-Elevation Purification Loop, and, if the traverse is successful, "reenter the Origin Song and rise into the Seeing." Once "rising" occurs, every summit among the One-Thousand-and-Five, every valley of the Nineteen, and every "life-form, power, and principality above and below is felt, heard, tasted, smelled, seen, and known" regardless of season or weather, including winter blizzards, summer thunderstorms, impenetrable fog, extreme heat, extreme cold, and so on. As I interpret Volkmann's summation of Lûmi terminology and belief, "The Seeing" results in unassailable power, love, knowledge, and bliss. But while Vedic nirvikalpa samadhi, Sufi fana-fillah, and Christian "mystical union" would seem to convey the same meaning, the Lûmi lexicon is composed not of metaphysical or theological terms but of geographical, meteorological, geological, botanical, biological, and other physical and phenomenal terms and images -- an insistence that, for what it leaves out, reminds me of the Buddhist insistence on refusing to speculate about or debate over God. Thich Nhat Hanh says it beautifully: "To me the best theologian is the one who never speaks about God...If you are not able to touch the phenomenal world deeply enough, it will be very difficult, or impossible, to touch the noumenal world."

•Because my own pilgrimages through the Elkmoons continue at times to induce a personality split caused by loss or gain of elevation, I was relieved to see this split described by Volkmann as "part and parcel of the Lûmi Way." He went into some detail, describing would-be traversers of the High-Elevation Purification Loop that left me more tolerant of the way I divide into a valiant but arguably cold "High El" persona, who wanders the luminous numinous Elkmoons in a state of energetic wonder, and a twaddling "Low El" fond of decadent comforts, self-regarding sophistry, and a dilettante's life in Portland, horrified by marathon hikes driven by what he calls "High El's belief in a Wonderment Song said to lift fanatics like himself into a 'higher seeing' that could be achieved in minutes for $39.99 in a hot-air balloon."

•"For a Seeing Lûmi," Volkmann writes, "nothing can be misperceived or misknown. Perception and experience are infallible and limitless in that state, and the One-Thousand-and-Five Summits, Nineteen Valleys, and Self-Being are a unity, though a unity that doesn't disturb humanity's inherent diversity." I assume Enlightenment to again be Volkmann's topic, but the Singings never use such terms and the Informant gets extremely cranky if I compare Lûmi lore to other wisdom traditions. She calls this "going to Vatican City to study Chenrezig." The Lûmi lexicon reminds me of no other tradition in its emphasis on the bodily and psycho-spiritual experiences the Elkmoons' and other Loop ranges' extreme weather and topography put high-elevation pilgrims through. The Informant's fiercely held position is that the Lûmi path is in no way theological or philosophical: it is the sum total (summit) of natural and extra-natural experiences, be they arduous or blissful, encountered while moving our small, destructible bodies through this challenging landscape until a rare pilgrim's integrity results in a never-to-be-expected encounter with the Origin Song and the Seeing.

•Returning to the phrase going to Vatican City to study Chenrezig: every time I've tried to compare "Self-Being" or "the Seeing" to the climax terms of other wisdom traditions, the Informant has literally begun to make growling noises, and on the shores of Pipsissewa this past summer (2002) her displeasure ramped up to a shocking degree.

The brevity of my session with the Singings had frustrated me so deeply that, by the campfire, I began badgering her to define "Self-Being." But no matter how I phrased my speculations she ignored me so completely I finally snapped, "How can I aspire to something I've never once heard described? How could the Seeing of the Self-Being _not_ boil down to what Buddhists call Nirvana, Vedantists call mukti, and Christians call mystical union with a capital G God?"

The Informant donned a thoughtful expression as she picked a baseball-sized rock out of our fire ring. _Aha!_ I thought. _She's finally going to illustrate the Seeing somehow._ How right I was : without warning she hurled the stone at me, drilling me so hard in the ribs that I collapsed in a gasping heap. Pain kept me up half the night, and as we parted ways the next morning the Informant asked how I was feeling. "Shocked!" I gasped. "I think you cracked a rib! Filling my lungs on the elevation gain to Jade is gonna hurt like a _motherfucker_!"

Donning a mock-sweet smile, the Informant said, "The Lû mi have a term for hurting like a motherfucker. It's called 'Mystical Union with a Capital-R Rock.'"

Of course Low El Grady was appalled by the rock, the wisecrack, and the smile and urged me to hightail it down to Portland and never return. Meanwhile High El greeted the severe pain of donning his pack by thinking, _Now we're really getting somewhere!_

•Having made the Informant sound unhinged and myself sound like the acolyte of a sadist, here's another perspective: I have, as said, wandered the Elkmoons fourteen summers in a row. Though I first met the Informant at Paintbrush Lake in August of '92, then for three years didn't see her at all, it's the seven straight summers from '96 to 2002 that give me pause. The Inner Elkmoons comprise roughly 34,000 acres of a 1450-square-mile wilderness only slightly smaller than Glacier National Park. I wander the Inners spontaneously according to weather, whim, and occasional intuition. I never tell Gladys the dates or where I'll be camping because I never know, and have no way to contact her. So how have she, Ho, and her Belgians worked a Wise Men Finding the Manger miracle to find my tiny camp seven years in a row? The year after the rock to the ribs she found me napping in a small dome tent buried under four inches of August snow in the Scatter Lakes Basin -- a place I'd never camped until the snow forced a detour. A few years previous I got caught in a bad thunderstorm, left the trail, scrambled two hundred feet up through talus to a rock overhang I'd discovered on a previous trip. Sheltered from the rain and lightning but hidden from view in every direction, I woke in the morning to the smell of smoke, assumed a bolt had ignited a nearby tree, then began to smell a cafe breakfast. I stepped out of the overhang. Two hundred feet below, Ho, Mo, and Anon stood munching their morning grain bags near a fire in the middle of the trail upon which Gladys had made us hash browns, scrambled eggs, and coffee. "Okay!" I said as I joined her. "With no obfuscation, please, how did you find me this time?"

"Mountains are talkative if you shut off the mind chitter and listen," she said. "You just have to know which mountains to believe."

While High El thrilled to think the mountains track his whereabouts and share the intel, Low El opined that only an imbecile would fail to realize the Informant long ago hid some kind of tracking device in his backpacking gear.

•A final fruit of my "Union with a Capital R Rock": I had made my way up to Jade, the injured rib knifing me every breath of the way, set camp on the soft tundra close to the lake, and again slept fitfully due to rib pain. But at some timeless hour of the night I dreamt that no less a being than God visited me there at Jade, and the form God chose to take was female. Though no more visible than a heat shimmer over a sunbaked road, God the Mother swung low as the proverbial sweet chariot, a shimmery arm reached toward me out of nothingness, She reached into my body without shedding blood or inflicting pain, gripped my cracked rib in Her right hand, and Her touch was bliss as she slid, smooth as a knife from a sheath, three inches of rib bone out of me. In the loving heat of Her hand the bone then melted into a liquid the color of mercury, which began to set, becoming claylike though it retained its stunning mercury color. She fashioned this substance into a tiny woman whose body and close-shorn hair were the same shining silver, and the woman's three-inch height and metallic fluidity caused her nakedness to appear exquisite, but sexually neutral. Then the mercury began to cool, turning to flesh as the woman began to stir, and the comeliness and grace of her form and movements aroused me despite her size. Given the other female present, this shamed me, but God the Mother came to my rescue, dressing the woman in adorably tiny brown hiking boots, beat-up little blue jeans, and a sleeveless T shirt of forest green. Mother God then set the woman in <u>my</u> hand, vanished without a trace, and there I stood gazing at an exquisite, newly minted woman kneeling, face lowered, on one knee in my palm. As she then raised her face and looked up into my eyes, three things slammed me.

One: as her astounding eyes met mine, I suffered a thunderbolt dunderbolt loveblast like nothing I'd ever experienced.

Two: the painful way she took to her feet left me certain she was mortally wounded in some way, and not long for this world.

Three: I woke alone on the shores of Jade, looked at my palm, found it empty, pulled open the flap of the tent, saw that the impossibly deep waters in the predawn light were the same green as the wounded woman's T shirt, and somehow knew that God's gift woman is as real as Jade, that I'm going to meet her one day, that she's going to be as completely lovable and mortally wounded as I'd dreamt, and that my love will turn to heart-break. When I then broke down sobbing, Low El Grady paid a visit.

"<u>Pathetic!</u>" he snarled. "<u>Bad-ass Glad-ass</u> the Lûmi Info Bitch <u>viciously</u> cracks your rib for no reason, scoffs at your pain, and you're so goo-goo about this touchy-feely Lûmi shite that your subconscious plays right into her abuse, causing a female <u>Gawd</u> to highjack your dreams, give the old Adam's rib yarn a jujitsu flip, and make you the butt of a women's lib joke starring the AARP magazine version of Tinker Bell! When you look deep into Granny Tink's eyes, you then burst out sobbing at the tragic grandeur of it all. <u>Frackwaw-voo!</u> What kind of idiot <u>are</u> you?"

"The Kind who invented the wonder phrase 'Frackwaw-voo,'" I calmly replied. "Thanks for liking my favorite gratitude-expletive enough to use it."

"Frackwaw you!" quoth Low El.

•It is said in the Singings that there have been Lûmi in these mountains and valleys "since humanity was born," and that "the One-Thousand-and-Five Summits, Nineteen Valleys, and Lûmi People created one another in the endless Now of the First Night and Day." Though these phrases stop my reason cold, they connect, sans reason, to my enormous regard for the Informant, grouchy and in one instance violent though she can be, to say nothing of my love for the tiny broken woman Mother God bequeathed me in a dream, possibly triggered by Gladys's well aimed stone. Which returns me to the seemingly crucial question: Is the Informant a living Lûmi? She's never come out and said so. But how can she if the Lûmi are takh-nekh-wakhul (no outward sign) in this lust-, greed-, and anger-crazed age of the world?

Sharing her campfire on the shores of Pipsissewa again last summer, fussing with the fire's symmetry as always, the Informant, apropos of nothing we'd been doing or saying, all of a sudden said, "There's something you're ready to Know. The purpose of Lûmi life is to reinhabit the Now of the First Night and Day."

Cutting off any question with which I might have peppered her, she added, "To speak more of this is without purpose."

With no goading from me she then added: "It is without purpose because, though any story is a saying, every story but the First Saying has a limited life span. The First Saying has no life span."

In what was amounting to a soliloquy by her niggling standards, she said, "The First Saying becomes audible, in our little cosmos, when a pilgrim has traversed the One-Thousand-and-Five Summits and mastered the One-Thousand-and-Five Sayings. At which point the pilgrim too has no life span."

Cool as a cup of water freshly lifted from a mountain spring, she said, "I seem to describe an impossible task. But Know this, friend Grady. The One-Thousand-and-Five Sayings are learned in a split second."

Becoming friend Grady at the same instant I was told of an experience that defies the limits of space, time, and memory filled me with an energy I'd never Known.

"When a Loop traverser sets eyes on the Gahan-Ka'isht," she said, "they see an ordinary person, but that person is singing, or effortlessly ringing, with a continual note. The One-Thousand-and-Five Sayings are all contained in that incomparable note."

A storm of gratitude struck as I realized that not only was the Informant sharing huge secrets, she'd come a hell of a long way via trails dangerous on horseback and worked an eleventh straight Wise-Woman-Finds-Grady's-Manger miracle to do it. The charged look in her ancient eye then struck a match, an Other-than-me flared to life in my place, my self-doubt, self-consciousness, self-disgust fell away, and whoever now breathed in me did not just look <u>at</u> the old woman seated across the fire; his gaze entered the gaze she was sending, fused with it, and at the same time I was me gazing at her, I was her gazing across at me. We didn't just <u>mirror</u> one another. We <u>were</u> one another, separate but fused as if "in the Now of the First Night and Day." And what are those old Greco-Roman or Sanskrit words for the Source Flame that is our very life? <u>Agni?</u> <u>Helios?</u> <u>That</u> Flame, pouring out of my eyes in a stream smooth and dense, met the same Flame pouring from her eyes, the flames fused, what I want to call an "Immensity of Mercy" welled up out of the batholith beneath us, my limits were exceeded, the container named Grady burst, exploding out to fill the next available container: the One-Thousand-and-Five Summits and Nineteen Valley fast-nesses of the Lûmi Cosmos! The Immense Mercy poured from night shadows into all creatures, all vegetation, all objects, infusing the eagles on their aeries, the hummingbirds awaiting the nectar of gentian fields, the ladybugs enduring eight or nine frigid months under mountaintop scree. In the fiery exaltation of the inpouring and outflowing Helios gaze, the Mercy just as improbably permeated pika pellets, moose flops, biting flies, predator kills, and a self-involved hundred-seventy-pound agglomeration of flesh, blood, neuroses, dirty Smartwool socks, pitch-stained jeans, way-making boots, and immortal spirit the Informant had always taken the trouble to call "Grady Haynes" until the Mercy upgraded him to "Friend Grady," causing everything Low El and High El once hated about each other to be mercy-attacked, mercy-infused, mercy-erased, and their long-running effort to destroy each other was not only over, it was no more worthy of note than the winter-sterilized bird dropping lying atop the largest rock in our fire ring.

I somehow felt directed to reach out and pick up this bird dropping. The instant I did so the Immensity of Mercy seemed to complete its work, and I began spiraling outward till I found myself back in my workaday body and mind. And if I might lapse into my workaday parlance, the Informant's response to all of this was <u>so fucking perfect</u>: with the most understated, birdlike expression of wonder I've ever seen, she did a little chin cock, the way an old-school cowboy does on the day he first fully accepts you as part of his world and crew.

I didn't just revel in the cool of her gesture: I appropriated it. Gazing up at the mountains, I said, "Fourteen straight summers I've hied on up here, seven of 'em to cross paths with you because the mountains told you where I'd be." I did the chin cock. "I figure this, plus the two-way seeing that just befell us, makes me local enough in these parts to have earned some kind of local name. What do you think?"

"Not only was I thinking the same," she said, "a name just came to me."

"What name might that be?" I coolly asked.

"Bird-Dropping-Me," said she.

I looked at the little present between my right thumb and index finger. "<u>Bird-Dropping-Me</u>. It <u>does</u> have the right ring to it, doesn't it?"

The Informant smiled the closest thing to a loving smile I was ever to see on her face, considered me in silence, then took on gravitas the way she can.

"I'm going to say two simple things, and you need to hear them perfectly. Just _you_, Bird-Dropping-Me. Not those other two ding-dongs you used to drag up here."

Bird-Dropping-Me was amenable to this request.

"One," she said. "What just happened was a birth. A child of the mountains has been delivered into the world to which he belongs. To see that finish line is not to cross it. The mountain child is just our partner, Bird-Dropping-Me. But his birth is as real as these mountains."

Bird-Dropping-Me gave her the chin cock.

"Two. In case you think you just saw your destiny revealed, I repeat. To traverse the Loop is too much for a human life span. It would break you a hundred times. That's why, to see with the Lûmi Seeing, we don't wait lifetimes. We _leave time_ via a coming and going as extra-natural as the arrival and departure of the Elkmoon snows."

Leaving those words suspended in the firelight, my friend did her ablutions by the lake, and retired to her tent. But I stayed on by the embers under slow-circling stars, praying to the peaks a little, crying a little when they'd whisper back as never before, my heart going out and out as, down through the diaphanous night blue, the mysteries continued to come rattling.

In the morning the Informant groused and grumbled as she broke camp, refusing my help as always as she heaved her panniers up onto Mo and Anon. Noticing that her ability to work with the Belgians was giving out half broke my heart, but turned every moment we'd ever shared invaluable. Mounting up, she lined her horses out, nudged Ho close, gave me a look that did nothing to disguise her affection, then reached in a saddlebag, dug out a leather sheath, and handed it to me. "Don't let the two ding-dongs even _touch_ this," she growled. "This parting gift is for no one but Bird-Dropping-Me."

The words _parting gift_ broke my heart the rest of the way, making my hands a little shaky as I took hold of the sheath and drew out an old arborist's saw. Unfolding the curved twelve-inch blade from the hardwood handle, I found it razor-sharp, with excellent bite, like the gift's purposefully cranky giver. From that day forward every fire I've built has been as tidy and close to smokeless as Gladys's own.

When I thanked her with a final cool chin cock, she let out her llama bleat, nudged Ho forward, raised her left hand high and kept it high, without once looking back as she rode out of sight, and my heart hurt in ways it had never hurt before. But so did it keep pumping the blood as far from the heart as it can go until, at the end of every least capillary, back it turned toward the heart's life-giving chambers, enabling my very pulse, when I set out the next morn for low elevation, to assure me I needn't strive to be more than, and have nothing more to lose than, every earthly drop of water on its prayer-wheel journey, mountains to rivulets to rivers to ocean to rising vapor to cloud banks -- and ever again inland to the mountains it blankets in the Beginning we call snow.

(Portland and the Oregon coast, January 2000)

II. Romeo Shows Jamey the Door

All beings are. They never are not. They are either alive or between. There is, hypothetically, a split second between life and the between that is properly called death. A boundary. A line with no width. Something ultimately not there except as an arbitrary border.
—Robert Thurman, *Circling the Sacred Mountain*

ON FEBRUARY 19TH, 2000, Jamey Van Zandt held his best friend in his arms, nodded to the doctor standing over them, then watched that doctor, in obedience to his nod, end his friend's life via lethal injection.

This world being a cauldron of war, violent separation, murder, injustice, suffering, it sounds anticlimactic to admit that this friend was just a black and tan border collie. But it's true. Jamey loved a lot of people a little and a few people a lot, but in duration of intimacy he'd been closer to Romeo than to any human he'd ever loved, and even in degree of intimacy, he had, in many ways, been closer to Roams than to Risa and their toddler, Fionn—of whose birth I will speak later. Jamey and Risa had become very close fast, but Risa had not spent eighteen years imbibing his every gesture of hand, meaningful or meaningless word, facial expression, odor; eighteen years jumping up out of sleep just to track Jamey's unconscious pacing as he talked on the phone, guard his wee-hour insomnia attacks, join him on every trip to the garbage can, corner convenience store, mailbox. Nor had Risa insisted, as Romeo had every morning of his life, on following Jamey down the hall to lie outside the bathroom door as Jamey moved his bowels, greeting him when the door opened, *seven thousand times in a row,* with grins, dancing, and tail wags of such contagious delight that Jamey too sometimes felt he'd accomplished something remarkable in there. For eighteen years he and Roams were a six-leggèd, two-headed, one-tailed unit so constantly fused that most people found them ridiculous at first. But as years would pass and they'd bump into the Jamey-Roams Unit again, something would flip like an egg over easy inside them, and the ridiculous would become the exemplary. Yes, Romeo was "just a dog." But he embodied a love that came within a single condition of attaining the transcendent level known as "the unconditional," and the only condition

628 DAVID JAMES DUNCAN

Romeo placed on his love was a burning wish that Jamey never, even briefly, leave his sight.

So that's who, on February 19th, Jamey held in his arms. That's whose adoring brown eyes he gazed into, then turned from, to nod to the animal doctor. That was the beloved sixty-pound piece of himself he then watched die via the requested injection.

WHAT DID THIS sundering do to the now two-leggèd and tailless survivor? When I later asked, Jamey quoted Emerson: "There is a crack in everything God has made." He then told me that Romeo, as his parting gift, cleaved the very crack in Existence that serves the spirit as door, offering a deathless exit out of the doom to which birth fatally binds us. "This isn't hocus-pocus," he insisted. "The door was palpable. Invisible, yes, but as real as a sudden zephyr. I felt it all through my body."

To preface this door, all that need be said is that eighteen years caused the canine portion of their oneness to grow ancient while the human portion did not. Romeo's sight and hearing faded. His teeth became nubs. Arthritis turned his paws into something more like flippers. The hard month of January then delivered the coup de grâce. Behind the Poor Man's Penthouse was a sidehill yard with a concrete goldfish pond. In exchange for maintaining the pond and picking up the dog berries, Jamey won Romeo lavatory rights among the azaleas above the pond. One cold morning he let Roams out to use his lavatory, whistled for him twenty minutes later, and walked out wondering why he failed to come. Romeo's hips had collapsed, sending him rolling down the embankment and through the thin ice of the pond, where he stood submerged to the neck. And because Jamey, years before, had forbidden him to bark in the yard early lest he wake the neighbors, Roams had kept silent. Dying of hypothermia, he would have stood in the icy water obeying Jamey's order till his spirit left him. "Tell me of a higher love if ever you hear of one," Jamey told Risa when he carried Romeo up into the penthouse.

Within two days a sinus infection developed, and grew chronic. The recommended drugs didn't cure the infection but they did make Romeo incontinent. Mortification at every indoor mistake was now as palpable in his eyes as his love. Too sick to remain at Jamey's side even in the Nautilus, he stayed home alone for the first time in his life. When Jamey, Risa, and Fionn were out, the infection caused him to sneeze convulsively to clear his sinuses, but the arthritis destroyed his ability to control the sneezes, so he'd smash his muzzle on the floor, causing profuse nosebleeds. These too mortified him. When Jamey and family got home, bloody paw prints showed how Romeo had hobbled round and round the apartment, trying between sneezing fits to lick up the blood he kept spilling. Trips to the vet accomplished nothing.

One morning Jamey called Romeo so he could take him outside. Romeo stepped out of the Nautilus, took two steps, went splay-leggèd, and collapsed on the floor. Watching from the kitchen, Risa began to cry as Jamey stood him back up, but Romeo lay back down, gazing up at Jamey with an expression Risa and Jamey clearly saw as a plea for the only help remaining. As Roam's namesake had put it,

Let me have a dram of poison, such soon-speeding gear
As will disperse itself through all the veins
That the life-weary taker may fall dead,
And that the trunk may be discharged of breath
As violently as hasty powder fired
Doth hurry from the fatal cannon's womb.

In the tiny Oregon Coast town of Hebo a college friend of Risa's—a laconic Chinese American, Gai Lee—was the practicing large animal vet. With a lump in his throat, Jamey said, "On this one I'm weak, Risa. Will you please make the call?"

She did. Gai said to bring the dog before they opened at eight the next morning. Jamey thanked Risa, hesitated, then said, "One more request, please. I need to do this alone."

"Are you sure?" she asked.

"What I'm sure of," he said, "is that I don't want anyone, especially Fionn, to see what Romeo's and my parting might do to me."

Risa threw her arms around him. "I understand. I'm so sorry."

AT 4:30 A.M. THE next morning Risa bundled up Fionn, carried him outside in the dark, and they watched Jamey close a fold-up camp shovel inside the Nautilus and set it in the bed of his old green Toyota pickup. When Roams limped up to Jamey and Jamey lifted him into the shotgun seat from which Risa had displaced him, the dog's best Third World elder smile in months caused Risa to finally lose it. Her sobs as she hugged Roams left him confused and guilty-looking. Which made her sob harder. Which made Fionn start to cry. Which made Romeo look as if even he were crying. Which made Fionn start to laugh. Which cheered Risa just enough to circle to Jamey's open window, kiss him, and say, "While it still seems faintly possible, *go!*"

THEY REACHED HEBO in three hours. Jamey found the Large Animal Clinic, drove as prearranged around back, and parked in a spruce-lined, mist-shrouded meadow. Romeo took one look at the meadow and began blissfully panting, anticipating a hike. Gai Lee then stepped out the back door of the clinic, his drams and soon-speeding gear at the ready.

Romeo's pant changed to one of fear. He knew Gai at once for what he was: *a damned animal doctor.* When Romeo was young, a vet had saved him from a bad case of salmon fever, but in so doing she'd committed the unforgivable sin: separated him for two whole days from Jamey. Roams never forgot. As Gai approached, Jamey felt heartsick to realize Romeo's distrust of vets foresaw this event all along.

While Jamey greeted Gai and paid him in advance, Roams trotted across the meadow to a huge Sitka spruce, did his spryest leg-lift in years, then beamed his inimitable smile back at Jamey as if to say, *See? Limber as can be! Strong stream! No need for that quack.* How Jamey wished Romeo could trot off into the mist, leaving him with that smile. When, instead, he cantered back, gimpy but wagging his tail, Jamey grew so nauseated by the sense of betrayal that he half collapsed in the wet grass. While Gai watched in silence, Jamey ordered Romeo to lie down beside him. Roams hadn't disobeyed him yet. Turned out he never would.

Jamey slid Romeo—old, pained, and knotted up again—onto his lap. Roams panted hard, kept a suspicious eye on Gai, but tried to smile up at Jamey, grateful for their awkward intimacy. Gai said, "Ready?"

Even as he thought, *Never,* Jamey clamped his hand round Romeo's muzzle to protect the vet, and nodded. Gai slipped a tourniquet around Roam's foreleg, produced the sedative syringe from his white lab-coat pocket, said, "This is the relaxer," and drove the fluid into Romeo before Jamey could fully take it in.

An instant later the fatal syringe was poised in Gai's hand. Loathing Gai's efficiency but recognizing the desperate lateness of his and Roam's united life, Jamey put his theatrical training to work, drove Gai from his mind, and locked his gaze to Romeo's. He couldn't bear to say, *It's gonna be all right.* He couldn't bear to say anything. But as he drank in Romeo's last moments of life, the words *unforgivable mercy* floated into his head, and stayed there. An odd concept. Yet here its recipient lay, still adoring, still beautiful despite age and fear. Jamey leaned down over Romeo, placed his lips to his ear, and softly whispered, *"No created thing but love."* Romeo panted, smiling his inimitable smile.

Gai's glance asked the final question. Jamey nodded. In went the syringe. Actor that he was, Jamey's calm appeared real as he asked, "Will it be fast?" But when Gai murmured, *"Very,"* something amorphous and black rose in Jamey's chest, then flopped over in a spilled heap. And whatever that black thing is, Jamey says it's never left. It's flopped over and spilled inside him, still.

Yet Romeo kept on panting. *He kept on panting!* Jamey tried not to run with this; tried not to pray Gai had grabbed the wrong syringe; tried not to picture himself saying, *We gave it a shot, but fuck this, Roams! Let's go home!* Gai even made Jamey's heart pound when he began to look a little panicked.

Then came the snap. Jamey felt it throughout Romeo's body, and his own. And that's what the snap made of a dog: a body. A smiling Romeo no more. But a split second after the snap, or simultaneous to but *inside* it, Jamey felt an opening in the atoms that compose the very wall of this world. *Who can open the doors of His face?* asks the Book of Job poet. But the question is rhetorical, a faith statement in disguise. The poet is sure the only possible answer is an awestruck: *No one*. Yet at the instant of the snap a six-leggèd oneness created by eighteen years of intimacy experienced something unforeseen: simultaneous to the nervous system recoil that ended their union, a perfectly crafted, airtight door opened,

Jamey felt his beloved friend shoot silently through it,

felt the door close,

tk!

felt a slight suction at its closing,

and a thing that wasn't there was there. An unseen door.

Jamey was transported. What struck him most was the door's perfect minimalist beauty. As the life of his canine better half flew through it, Jamey experienced an opening in the world-wall so exquisitely crafted that *there was nothing to it*. Death's door, as Romeo's life passed through, revealed the handiwork of an aesthetic so sublimely minimal that the artifact created—*death itself*—wasn't there. Roams's body had been vacated in a split second. The body remained. But the being was gone with an ease so exquisite it left beingness intact:

tk!

Gone where? Jamey wondered. *Into what?* Who knew? But myths and legends abounded, and he vowed to ponder them with a *tk!*-opened heart. In defiance of every expectation he'd had, the shooting away of Romeo's life struck him as a work of what Risa called the Unseen Guileless Perfection's own art. To feel the door open and close was to experience the Unseen's very carpentry. Not a glimpse of a miracle. There was nothing to hold on to, after, but an emptied dog. Yet Jamey was left, after the *tk!* and tiny suction, with an overpowering sense that his closest friend had departed entirely intact, and that this world was just one of a now-palpable two. The darker, sadder one, with singing winter wrens and thrushes, cold mist, and shaggy old spruce trees in it. Gazing at those trees—gazing at the very spruce Romeo's last piss must still faintly warm—Jamey's jaw went slack and he was a child again, hunched on a rug with sister Jude, gazing at their dead mother's elaborate old wooden advent calendar. Twenty-five camouflaged countdown doors. A gift hidden behind each. Staring at tree, meadow, moving swatches of mist, Jamey felt the gift he'd named Romeo hovering just behind the spruce bark, mosses, water vapor, intact in every way that counted, sending the *feel* of his adoring smile back through the world-wall to his beloved man. The solace came in waves, defeating grief. He was holding Roams's body in his hands, awash in the same sheer wonder he'd felt when Fionn slid into the midwife's hands, then Jamey's own, from a realm whose advent door had, impossibly, consisted of Risa! He hadn't understood then. He didn't understand now. He simply experienced Romeo's life passing out of this world not as the *opposite* of Fionn's life passing into it but as its equal. Everything that made Romeo himself, his body excepted, felt no more dead as he departed than Fionn's antic character had felt dead moments before his little body arrived.

"I'll leave you now," a somber voice announced.

Gai. Poor Gai Lee! His face as sad as Jamey's was awestruck. "I'm very sorry," he murmured, then turned and trudged toward the clinic. Still awestruck, Jamey watched the heavy metal door open, watched Gai step through it, watched it close, *tk!* and it suddenly felt wrong not to share his joyous glimpse of life's seamless continuity with Gai. Jamey started to lay Roams's now-meaningless body aside, intending to stand, pound on the clinic door, and attest to the fear-shattering news: *No call for grief, Gai! No sorrow! Romeo just showed me the door our lives pass through intact!*

But as he lifted Roams's body Jamey took in data his hands had been gathering that knocked his grieflessness for a loop: Romeo's passing had cured his abandoned body of its arthritis. The limbs, paws, torso, so twisted and pain-knotted for years, were suddenly loose and lithe as they'd been in his prime. *The door did this!* Jamey marveled. *Even our abandoned bodies are put at ease by the Unseen's carpentry!* He felt this. Knew it. Adored it for a moment. But the same litheness, draped languidly across his thighs, created a conflicting desire for the physical prime that went with it—and with that desire every detail of Romeo's wondrous departure went to hell.

Exploring the corpse with his hands, smitten by its "youthfulness," Jamey underwent total eclipse. His awareness of a sublimely minimalist art vanished. The sense of two worlds vanished. Craving not the deathless realm the *tk!* let him sense but a Pharaoh-like immortality of body for his dog, he ran his hands over Roams's litheness and was moved to offer not a prayer of acceptance but a scrap of soliloquy from his own histrionic pope: "*O true apothecary! Thy drugs are quick. Thou detestable maw, thou womb of death, I enforce thy rotten jaws to open!*" And once the Shakespearean shinola started to fly, "*Never was a story of more woe than this of Jamey and Romeo.*" Burying rather than cherishing the *tk!* Jamey took his feet, gathered Romeo's body imagining it to be the entire dog, lifted that false entirety in his arms, and staggered to his truck, woe-struck by the *detestable* speed of a corpse's falling temperature.

Laying Roams's head in his lap, he drove as planned to the headland where his mother's ashes had once been thrown off the cliff by his father, only to be blown back into her bereft children's faces and lungs. Stepping out of the cab, deaf to winter wrens, thrushes, fragrances of fields, forest, and sea, Jamey lay Romeo and the folding shovel in the Land Nautilus and began dragging the load up the headland, vowing to find a grave site Romeo would choose for himself. But just a quarter mile in, espying an ancient, storm-torn spruce, the tragedian felt drawn to this mawkishly majestic stage prop. Big mistake. Old spruces have astoundingly tough root systems. To get the hole deep enough to safely bury Roams's body Jamey exhausted himself hacking spruce roots with his little shovel, raising quarter-sized blisters in both palms.

When the grave was just a yard deep, the blisters burst. Tossing the shovel aside, Jamey dropped to his knees, lifted Romeo's body, lay it in the hole, and curled it up the way Roams used to curl himself for sleep. Then came crisis: *Romeo's eyes opened*. He reached down and closed them. They reopened. He closed the lids again, held them shut awhile. When they opened yet again, Jamey imagined volition, sobbed, *"Unbearable!"* leaned down into the grave, kissed Romeo's skull repeatedly, straightened up, gripped the shovel in his wrecked palms, dumped in a bladeful of dirt, watched it sully his beloved friend, felt an absolute wrongness of perspective, and gave way to a frenzy bent on nothing but escape. Sweating the kind of theatrical flop sweat he'd never once sweated on a stage, he shoveled till he ran out of dirt, burying the soft brown eyes, tan eyebrows, weathered paws, regal tail, smiling black lips, wrecked teeth, and coat so inattentively that he noticed none of these features. His greatest wish now was to dig Roams back up and rebury him with loving attention, but the palms of his hands had begun to resemble Christ's. Feeling he'd exhausted his options despite betraying his love, Jamey splayed himself across the grave and sobbed until he couldn't.

By the time he dragged the empty Land Nautilus back to the truck and hit the highway for Portland, he felt so full of self-loathing he stopped at four taverns en route, downing a pint in each. Four hours later he arrived home drunk, picked up Fionn when he toddled up, kissed him, gave Risa a brief hug but spared her the kiss after Fionn went, *"Eeuuu!"* then walked down the hall and got in the shower.

After reading Fionn to sleep, Risa heard the shower still running, knocked on the bathroom door, got no response, and called, *"Incoming!"* Opening the shower stall, she found Jamey sitting naked in the stall corner, hugging his knees, teeth chattering violently, the hot water long gone, drunkenness gone, gazing at the shower stall door with clear-eyed awe. Risa stepped out for a towel, stepped back in, shut off the water. "Got a little wake going, do we?"

"Something *imp-puh*-possible happened today!" he said through his shivers. "*Ruh-right* as he died, *ruh-ruh-Roams* showed me a door. The most *buh*-beautiful door!"

Risa reached down, seized his wrists, helped heave him to his feet, steadied him in the corner. Alarmed by how frigid his skin felt, she began roughly toweling him to warm him.

"I can show you!" he cried, and reached behind her, closing them in the stall.

Considering his nakedness, Risa entertained sexual thoughts. What better way to bring him back from the far galaxy into which he'd been abducted? But with the wide-eyed look of a toddler, Jamey simply pushed the stall door back open. *Tk!* went the plastic latch, causing him to gaze at empty air as if beholding an archangel. "The most *buh-beautiful* sound ever!" he cried. "And I *betrayed* it! And *ruh-*Roams's *guh*-gift to me with it!"

Risa's eyes welled. Her strong man had become the broken child whose fifth birthday gift had been a dead mother. "I should've hired a sitter!

Should've come with! This was too much to take on alone. But Roams was in misery, Jamey. It had to be done."

"*Nuh-not the betrayal!* Eighteen years we spent *buh*-building the *buh*-bond that led to the *tk!* And I betrayed it! With his *buh*-body dead, Roams turned back to me as he was leaving! Obeying *nuh-no* created thing but love, he turned back. *We go on, Jamey!* his face conveyed. He made sure I knew! So why didn't I cry, *I love you so much! Travel in joy, my Roamy Roams!* Why did I *deny* what he was giving me, turn to the body I'd ordered Gai to kill, and cry out to *that, Come back to me!*"

Risa marveled. Here stood the actor who claimed stage-crying had destroyed his ability to cry for real, blue-lipped and Tinkertoy-dicked, dredging up tears so fat they made loud *splat*s on the shower stall floor. "This day has *chuh-changed me!*" he gasped. "Romeo's door *chuh-changed me!* I vow to *suh-stop betraying the Unseen!*"

She took him in her arms then, and let him quake till he grew still. And the reason Risa has never forgotten Jamey's sworn fealty to the Unseen is that he *did* change. The word "death," he has insisted ever since, can never again mean "final end of story" without betraying the love Romeo somehow sent back from beyond death's door.

Moved to explore Risa's wisdom books for the first time, he found a Sufi term in a Coomaraswamy footnote that captured his feeling. "The word *al-hayrah*," The Coom averred, "designates a state wherein the pilgrim begins to circle in astonishment round a place, person, or point they find rationally incomprehensible yet endlessly desirable."

Risa continues to revere a subalpine meadow that opens unto an Infinite

((((((())))))

!

Jamey can't stop revering a death-defying

tk!

But their astonished circling is identical.

III. Perfect, Not Cruel

Our wounds are the fathers and mothers of our destinies.
  —James Hillman, *Senex and Puer*

THROUGHOUT THEIR YEARS in E City, Lorilee and Mu's love for backpacking the Elkmoons had steadily grown, but had also been steadily frustrated. In their early Montana years Lore had longed to hike farther up into the range than the young Mu could go. By the time he hit his teens he'd gained so much size and strength that they could hike wherever they chose, but their tours with the Ona Kutar Band had brought them enough fame to make a living performing their own music if they pursued every good gig that came along, limiting them to frustratingly brief Elkmoon excursions.

As they were working out their summer of 2001 tour schedule they blocked out an eight-day Elkmoon outing in July that would allow them to reach a destination that fascinated them: the mountains at the head of the West Fork called the Inner Elkmoons. During their years as a breakfast cook and busboy, Lore and Mu each heard customers speak of how the aches, pains, and sometimes intense weather endured to reach "the Inners" bestowed mysterious benefits. Lore also once heard two backcountry wanderers agreeing that the route over Gateway Pass was under some kind of surveillance by secretive high-elevation observers who sounded like something out of native myth, and to show fortitude when climbing up into their country was said to lead to profound insights, and perhaps even to contact with the mysterious observers.

One morning Lore was having tea and scones at Ida's Ideas when an American Indian man of perhaps forty, sporting a long braid, sat at the next table with a similarly braided five-year-old girl who announced to Lore, "*I'm Tallulah!*"

Lore gave her a smile as the man said, "It's a fact," and set Tallulah up with the colored pencils Ida left on tables so customers could draw on the paper tablecloths. After a brief but intense burst of coloring Tallulah left her table, walked up to Lore, and announced, "I have a horse! And my dad has lots!"

"Can you draw one for me?" Lore asked.

"No!" Tallulah proclaimed. "Horses are too hard!" And off she wandered to visit Ida Craig in her emporium, where she could always depend on receiving some small gift.

Turning to the man Tallulah-style, Lore proclaimed, "*I'm Lorilee!*"

Sam chuckled. "Hi, Lorilee. I'm Sam Rock."

"So what do you do with lots of horses?" Lore asked, and when Sam said he was an Elkmoon packer, she asked if he knew the high country beyond Gateway Pass.

"Very well," he said.

"Then maybe you can advise me. In late July, with eight days to work with before a sixteen-city business trip, my son and I want to explore that country. Any advice on how or where to spend that amount of time?"

"A week's a short trip, but you can at least get the lay of the land," Sam said. "If it's hot, though, you'll want to spend the first night at Halfway, a meadow just seven miles up the West Fork. You won't be tired, but after Halfway come seven more miles of very steep uphill trail, and the first three are cut into south-facing rock walls, all unshaded, no resting points. On a ninety-degree day those walls reach a hundred thirty degrees by noon. Heat prostration's a real thing. My horses and I tackle those cliff walls in morning cool."

"What if we wore headlamps and left the trailhead at 4 a.m.?" Lore asked.

Sam looked surprised, then impressed. "I don't see why that wouldn't work very well."

Neither did Mu and Lore.

But on the July day they set out from E City at 3 a.m. their long-faithful '54 Chev burst a radiator hose, overheated near the Glory Meadow, and they were out so early that flagging down help burned six hours. Once they were towed back to E City, running down the right hose then ate an entire second day.

With just five days to work with they reached the West Fork trailhead at 4 a.m., hiked with a vengeance, passed Halfway at 6, traversed the three miles of rock wall in morning cool, and reached the disheartening midpoint elevation loss down into the West Fork canyon at a quarter to eight.

Crossing the footbridge, they eyed the final four miles of switchbacks up to 8,100-foot Gateway Pass, and were heartened to see the most brutal ascent of their journey was the most beautiful. The entire path ribboned up a solid granite batholith, the footing was excellent, and though the near whiteness of the rock grew blinding and the 30 percent grade was unrelenting, Lore began to experience a sense of lift that added power to every stride. Under the influence of junior high cynicism, Mu had taken to scoffing Lore's perceptions if he found them too subtle, so she said nothing about the lift. It was Mu himself who stopped in his tracks, turned back to Lore, incredulous, and said, "*Do you feel an invisible escalator carrying us up this incline?!*"

In full agreement that a gravitational anomaly was aiding them, mother and son summited Gateway smiling despite having covered fourteen miles and 5,500 feet of elevation gain, loss, and regain in a third of a day. Their first sight of Boundary Lake then struck them stupid with happiness. Floating the easy mile to the pine-shaded campsite Sam Rock had recommended, they set up their tent in a euphoria, then spent a perfect afternoon exploring the Lilliputian rills and lakelets of the Scatter Lakes Basin.

RETURNING TO CAMP as the air cooled, they were finishing an early dinner when they heard clip-clops on the far shore. A rider in denim clothes and cowboy hat appeared aboard a bay mare, leading two enormous pack horses. When the rider doffed the hat and waved it, she revealed herself to be a smallish old woman. When Mu waved back, the woman traversed the third-mile of shoreline separating them, tethered her horses, and set up camp not fifty yards from Lore and Mu. With no one else on the entire lake, Lore found this presumptuous, but Mu, watching the woman closely, was struck by her easy competence in tending her horses and setting up her camp. When she finished her labors and headed straight for them, Lore began stacking wood by the fire ring to hide her annoyance, but Mu gave the woman his most disarming grin, extended his hand, and said, "Hi. My name's Mu, spelled M-u. And this is my mom, Lorilee."

"Glad to meet you, Mu and Lorilee," the woman said. "My name's Gladys Wax, spelled W-a-x, and my mom was named Rowena."

Mu invited Gladys to share the backrest Sam Rock had hewed into a pine log near the fire ring on previous visits.

Settling in the duff beside him, Gladys set aside her hat, revealing a silver French braid so skillfully woven that Lore began to like what Mu liked: everything this small, sturdy elder did evinced skill. Finding her example contagious, Lore took pleasure in sculpting a ball of dry lichen, placing a precision tipi of twigs over it, igniting the lichen, enjoying the twigs' flare, and adding incrementally larger branches till a bright fire drove off the night chill.

Gladys sent her a twitch of a smile. "Visitors aren't common here, Lorilee. That West Fork trail's a bear. What brings you two to Boundary?"

"We're musicians with a liking for songs about mountains. At an E City cafe where we work, we heard talk about the high country past Gateway that made us want to see it."

"Mind if I ask what kind of talk?"

"Rumors of spiritual benefits created by the hardship of getting here. Guardians of high-elevation secrets in the passes. An impossibly alive lake at the foot of the Blue Mosque. It sounded like woo-woo till I met a packer, Sam Rock, who seems grounded as can be, and encouraged us to come. But Mu and I experienced a little woo-woo ourselves. Those last miles of switchbacks up to Gateway gave us a sense of lift so strong that Mu says there's an invisible escalator inside the rock, and I felt the same thing."

Gladys let out a cackle. "Confession time, Lore and Mu. If you ask me, your *music* has an invisible escalator inside it! And you two are just who I hoped you'd be. Would you care to hear a few secrets about what Boundary Lake borders?"

Lore said, "Please!" And though Mu said nothing, his pupils had turned as big, black, and receptive as a barred owl's.

"Well then. What would you say if I told you of a seventeenth-century scientist, Johannes Kepler, who defied the Catholic Church's claim to own all sacred knowledge and risked his life declaring that Mother Earth has a living body, same as us, and is endowed with an amazing soul, same as us, and *breathes*, same as us only different?"

"I'd say that Kepler sounds a little like Zen Master Dōgen," Lore replied, "who eight centuries ago told his Japanese monks that *mountains* are alive, same as us, and *enlightened*, same as a rare few among us, and *walk* same as us only different, though until the 1960s no one but a German named Wegener believed that tectonic plates enable mountains to walk up off the ocean floor and bring their seashell collections with them."

"So let's take Wegener, Dōgen, and Kepler a bit further," Gladys said. "What if I told you there are places on Earth's body where we can feel her breathing, and sense her soul, and one such place isn't far from here, though part of the hike is dangerous? What if I told you that, at the base of the Blue Mosque, there's a little lake, Jade by name, with waters that never freeze though she lies at nine thousand feet? Yet the Mosque isn't volcanic, and Jade's heat isn't 'geothermal' as that term is defined. What if I told you that Jade's deep end was dug in one blow by a huge, high-speed meteorite, followed by centuries of snowmelt that bore so deep into limestone down under the Mosque that geologists doubt they'll ever find the lake's bottom? What if I told you that, if you camped on the soft tundra close to Jade, and in the quiet of the night asked Jade herself, using personal pronouns, why she's so warm in a place so high, a voice might rise up and ask where *you* think the warmth is coming from? What if, seeming to hear a lake speak, you think *woo-woo*, only to hear whatever is speaking ask, 'Have you considered body heat? Not geothermal or volcanic heat, as scientists keep seeking but can't find, but the warmth of an ensouled and breathing body intimate with every kind of body—solar, celestial, terrestrial, subterranean, human, animal, avian, angelic—because all these heats are of a piece with My vast living body?' "

Oh, did Gladys seize hold of them with that! Fastening her gaze on Mu's barred-owl eyes, she said, "What if I told you that strange and wonderful friendships can form between Jade's waters and humans? What if I told you of a secretive people, intimate with these mountains, who hold that Jade's warmth rises out of Earth, and a more mysterious being who Earth houses? What if I told you of an old lady who lives in friendship with Jade and the great ones who enliven her, and friendship gives the old lady a guardian's duty to protect mountain secrets, but also a greeter's duty to tell a rare few souls that, from this camp, they're a day's hike from a place that could seat them in the presence of two females the Lûmi believe are running the whole heaven and Earth show?"

Shifting her gaze so abruptly to Lore that her heart lurched, Gladys said, "What if I told you, who sings so beautifully of the human-mountain marriage, that if you were to risk the hike to Jade and touch these mysteries, they might touch you back and whisper, to paraphrase a couple lines from the great Anna Akhmatova, that the miraculous still comes close to our ruined houses, enabling a rare brave one to meet *a being not known to anyone at all, but wild in her breast for centuries*? A being unimaginably healing? A being for whom, faced with the mortality of all that we love, we sooner or later burn?"

Having set Mu's and Lore's imaginations afire, Gladys's lively old face, with an abruptness that stunned them, changed from that of a queen's secret messenger to a weary old horse packer who, message delivered, had no more authority to speak. With a dull "Past my bedtime. Good night," Gladys retired to her tent. And in the morning she rose early, broke camp, and after another terse farewell, rode away without a smile, wave, or glance.

Watching her disappear, Mu turned to Lore and blurted, "Mom! What the hell!?"

Feeling bad for herself and worse for Mu, Lore said, "Her departure was rude, I agree, and hurtful after romancing us the way she did. But I suspect she had her reasons."

"Such as *what*?" Mu fumed.

"Making sure we don't mistake the messenger for the message, is my guess."

Looking, for once, as young and vulnerable as he was, Mu said, "So how are we supposed to find the message without her?"

They put their heads together, based on Gladys's clues. Knowing they'd need two full days to get down to the trailhead and home, where they'd have just two more days to prep for their tour, they agreed they had but a single day to work with. They spent it well, hiked the eight miles to Pipsissewa at top speed, ate a quick lunch, and climbed Gentian Couloir as the looming Blue Mosque grew ever more majestic. As they passed Echo Lake and Mu bounced a few shouts off the cirque cliffs, their spirits rose. But as they came over a crest and beheld Daniel's Bridge, the sun dipped shockingly early behind the Mosque, and in the peak's gloomy shadow the blade-thin arête was what the mountain poet Thomas Merry called a "neck of stone, one / soul wide, chasm / gaping silent on either side."

That neck of stone was, *flagrantly*, the danger of which Gladys had spoken. They set out to cross it anyway, but hadn't gone far when Mu stepped on a patch of slick mudstone, his feet flew out from under him, he landed on his face, and though he wasn't much hurt, if he had slid off the stone neck to either side it could have been fatal.

Their momentum vanished. With a lake said to hold the warmth of an ensouled and breathing being not two miles away, Mu was the first to say it: "Mom. We're twenty-eight miles from the truck. We'll be whipped when we get down with two days to prep for our tour. We need to leave now."

Two brutal days later they reached the Black Queen, slept long, and discovered over a late breakfast that they both had dreamed of the unmet Jade. In Mu's dream the lake's waters, or a sentient being inside them, had called him, "*My son.*" In Lore's dream, she had stood in Jade immersed to the neck as the waters sent such immense surges of life's indestructible energy that she woke shedding tears of joy. Filled with a yearning they had no time for, Lore proposed they at least take an hour to clean up their backcountry gear and packs, store them in Mu's closet, and add maps and provision lists for a serious Jade pilgrimage the following summer. They did so, and the prep left Mu happy. "Nothing will stop us next year!" he declared, and Lore felt the same.

But two unforeseen events *did* stop them. The first: in late October, Mu was one of just twenty Montana high school students, and the only freshman, chosen by their art or music teachers to audition for full scholarships to a summer-long art and music school in the Sierra foothills of Southern California. The school was renowned, the odds of being selected almost nil. Unbeknownst to Lore, Mu had written an essay, composed, performed, and recorded a song for voice and guitar, and won one of the four scholarships—a remarkable honor for a freshman, but an honor that wiped their 2002 Jade pilgrimage off the calendar and map.

The second event: the twelve-week camp was three times longer than Lore and Mu had ever been apart, and Trey had arranged to take Mu down the Grand Canyon afterward, lengthening their separation. On the long drive back to the Elkmoon after dropping Mu off at the Bozeman airport, Lore was struck by an empty-nest heartache she couldn't shake. As she neared E City and the Elkmoon peaks appeared on the far horizon, she realized that nothing prevented her from making a Jade pilgrimage on her own. The prospect eased her heartache at once. Her only hesitation was that Jade was important to Mu too.

She went to bed of two minds, and was of two minds when she woke, so she headed for the place that reliably left her of one mind: the broken ponderosa at Blue Empty.

When she took her seat in the pine duff and turned to the seven-mile begging bowl, a radiant July morning had turned Earth's generosity profligate. Among the alms in the bowl were thirty or more browsing whitetail deer, a family of four otters after crawfish in the river, and huge hatches of mayflies and stone flies that sent hundreds of birds of many species veering through the blue.

The Dōgen moment arrived. Self forgotten, a nameless awareness awoke amidst the ten thousand things, among them an unmet mystery that, for all its wildness, felt as though it had lain hidden in Lore's breast for centuries.

So moved was she by its arrival that she undid two buttons of her faded blue work shirt, reached inside, and felt for her pulse beneath her heart-side breast so as to touch *solar, celestial, terrestrial, subterranean, human, animal, avian, angelic* mysteries with her very hand. For a numinous moment a de-selfed self was then able to find the timing perfect, not cruel, when her hand discovered not only that wildness but also two small, very real lumps in that same heart-side breast, then three more in the right.

How swiftly the forgotten self returns when impermanence arrives. "*A being unimaginably healing,*" Lore gasped as the wildness vanished, the lumps remained, and tears began to stream. "*A being for whom, faced with the mortality of all that we love, we sooner or later burn.*"

(Inner Elkmoons, August 2003)

IV. Moondial

Bred as we, among the mountains,
Can the sailor understand
The divine intoxication
Of the first league out from land?

—Emily Dickinson

From the Elkmoon Mountain Journals of Grady Haynes:

July 31: Forty days into the ninety-day Inner Elkmoon immersion I craved for years, I've encountered something unexpected: in one of the most intact high havens left in North America I've spent a large part of each day either on edge or in grief. The Elkmoon snowpack is one of the smallest on record. July drought and heat have been merciless. Forests all over the West are tinder, including coastal rain forests. The Inner Elkmoons' surviving glaciers, once impervious to summer, look like dust-coated burial mounds. As I hiked past Boundary Lake on my way in, the only surviving waterfall of Six Falls Creek was so reduced its drops made a slow ticking sound, like a sad old grandfather clock. The Pacific clouds' path to the Rockies is broken, the planet itself broken, by humankind. Human unkind.

Even so, the Blue Mosque is a wonder, Jade Lake a wonder of wonders, and extended time with them has caused their hold on me to deepen. On fair nights -- and all the July nights have been fair -- I forgo my tent and sleep on the Flying Carpet tundra close by Jade's impossibly warm waters, star-watching myself to sleep. Dreams and half-waking trances then take me on journeys so strange I bewilder myself.

In summers past my packer, Sam Rock, has resupplied me just once, with a bear-proof canister he cables to a boulder near Lake Pipsissewa and hides under scree. On this three-month sojourn I've hired Sam to ride as close as he can get and resupply me every ten days. He and his Appaloosa, Looking Glass, lead a two-horse string up the West Fork to Gateway, past Boundary, Pipsissewa, and Echo, dropping my supplies at the foot of Daniel's Bridge. Sam trusts Looking Glass's sure feet more than his own, but no horse can safely manage that crumbling arête. I use my backpack and trekking poles to hump the supplies up to my Jade camp. Each of his deliveries entails a sixty-mile round trip for Sam, but we relish our arrangement. I get fresh supplies and news of the world delivered as close to on time as mountain weather allows. Sam gets good wages, big tips, long rides through high country he loves, and freedom from his tedious summer cash cow: taking string after string of tourists on hot two-hour trail rides out of Elsewhere.

I also value Sam's ability to protect high-country secrets. When he crests a rise opening out on new territory, he reins in, scans the land with binos, and if he spots hikers on his route or climbers on the mountains, he and his string disappear like veritable Lûmi until the coast is clear. He was due to arrive today actually, and it's getting dark. I would guess he overheard campers whooping it up at Echo and veered east to bivouac until they're gone.

August 1: Sam made it to Daniel's Bridge first thing this morning, unloaded, and left with my fresh supply list after I made him lunch. In three backpack loads I got the supplies over the arête to my camp, stowed everything, and had dinner.

At 8 p.m. I moved my bedroll and pillow down onto the Flying Carpet. Far from sleepy, I lay back to watch the Perseids meteor shower, but as usual ended up muttering, "Six in an hour? What a miser you are, Perseus."

Seeing the long, thin shadow cast by the Mosque's 140-foot east minaret easing toward me across Jade's waters, I had the odd feeling that the shadow possesses intelligence. We've all seen sundials. The minaret shadow was a natural moondial, and I felt it was probing Jade's depths with the same fascination I feel for this improbable body of water. As the moon crossed the sky east to west, the moondial's shadow crossed Jade's waters west to east, and its tip passed conspiratorially over my very feet. "Are you trying to tell me something?" I asked it.

August 2: In response to my feeling about the moondial last night, I hiked up to the east minaret after breakfast, thinking to position myself at its base, steady the Trinovids on a rock, and scan all the terrain that the moonshadow darkened last night, seeing if anything struck me as evidence of the Lûmi. On reaching the minaret, however, I chose to circumambulate it before I began scanning—and stumbled into near-certain evidence of a place the Lûmi know: a large natural rock shelter.

Hidden on the minaret's east side, invisible from Jade below and the Mosque above, the shelter is a wide-open overhang. Lit by morning sun to its back wall, it formed inside the same off-white marble as the spire towering overhead. Twenty-two feet long and ten to fifteen feet wide, the shelter is high-ceilinged enough that at six foot one I can stroll its length without ducking. I was also struck to see the stone floor includes a declivity the size of a bathtub, filled two feet deep with pure white sand. The sand on the trails from Boundary up to Jade is a gray-brown blend of granitic grit and thin soil. The only pure white sand I've seen is in the man-sized declivity at the foot of Daniel's Bridge, where I've twice spent nights awaiting safer weather before crossing the arête. I believe the white sand was carried to both places by humans who wanted a bed softer than solid rock. The thought that those humans were most likely Lû mi made me jumpy until I examined the rock shelter thoroughly. The only sign of recent visitors are the tracks of mice who look to have been playing on the white sand of the tub.

Wondering how an overhang formed in the minaret, I stepped outside to reconnoiter, and my eyes were soon drawn to a nearly vertical Mosque cliff face a hundred yards below me and three hundred yards above Jade. Though the face appeared to be solid marble, five circular holes in it looked rather like empty eye sockets. Scrambling down to the nearest socket, I was able to crawl eight feet inside it, recognized the rock to be a limestone deposit amid the marble, and realized the open space of the rock shelter must have been limestone too. I imagine the deep snows of centuries lying against the water-soluble calcite at the base of the minaret, dissolving the limestone during the melts of millions of springs.

Doubly fascinated by the rock shelter now, I returned to it, paused before entering, gazed up the 140-foot spire, stepped inside, lay my hand against the ceiling, and the thought of so much weight directly overhead gave me a swooning sensation. Keeping my hand flat against the ceiling, I closed my eyes, grew still--and the stone felt <u>impassioned</u> in my palm. How else could it sustain such a steeple for centuries?

The stone's passion somehow entered me, creating such a strong desire to make the minaret my summer's home that I rushed down through four hundred yards of talus to Jade's shore, broke down my camp, and packed my worldly goods up to the minaret in four increasingly exhausting trips. But within three hours of having discovered the shelter I was seated in my Therm a-Rest chair, pondering white sand mouse tracks with a mouse-sized bourbon in hand, offering a libation to the sand as I asked the minaret's permission to take shelter. I felt no opposition.

In honor of what led me to it, I've named my shelter "Moondial."

August 3 through 12: I've spent the past ten days repeatedly exploring the network of Inner Elkmoon ridgelines that fascinate me most. I'm now able to traverse them, and to disappear from sight, with a speed that few hikers could match. It wouldn't be difficult for me at this point to emulate the elusive silhouettes keeping watch on visitors. But though I long to encounter a Lû mi, I feel the likeliest way for this to happen is to simply man my post at Moondial. It's my strong sense that, if we're meant to meet, it must be they who choose to come to me.

August 13: The year's first powerful thunderstorm formed yesterday out of impossibly clear blue skies, soon engulfing the Mosque in microbursts little gentler than tornadoes, followed by lightning and torrential rain. Though the rains didn't much surprise me, the wind drove the rain so hard into

Moondial that it poured down the shelter's back wall continually for four hours. I stayed in my tent and managed to stay dry, but the shelter's stone floor forbids the use of tent stakes. I had to bodily reinforce my tent poles and walls to prevent the poles from being pretzeled and the tent from being torn -- a serious matter since I don't have an extra. T storms come in clusters in August and I've fallen in love with Moondial's mystery, vistas, and proximity to Jade, so I'm going to try to build a rock wall at one end of the shelter, creating a crude room inside which my tent and I will be protected.

After breakfast, as a welcome sunbath made my sopped gear steam, I set out in search of appropriate wall-building rock. The Inner Elkmoons are almost entirely granite and marble, and the Moondial is miles above marshy terrain that creates clay. But I vaguely recalled seeing sedimentary rock along Daniel's Bridge. Hiking down, I sure enough found a shale deposit not two hundred yards from the arête's summit.

I know from experience that shale can be split into rectilinear bricks with a hammer and chisels, but I have no such tools. To lay such bricks in a wall I'd also need some kind of mortar, so I tried what seemed a feeble idea: picking up a smooth slab of shale, I scraped it with my hunting knife, creating a pile of dry powder as fine and slippery-feeling as talc, wet it with my water bottle, and lay the fine gray mud between two smooth pieces of shale. It created a surprisingly strong bond. Once Sam runs down some tools I hope to get into the bricklaying business.

August 14: I hiked down to Jade to resupply my water and take a brief swim this morning. But, as always, I left the water in a near panic when immersion made me feel I was literally disappearing. Never have I been so fascinated, or so intimidated, by a seemingly inviting little body of water. I'd say I want to get to the bottom of this mystery, but I've come to believe the Jade mystery is literally fathomless.

I dried, dressed, and kept an eye on the crest of the trail up from Echo Lake, anticipating Sam's afternoon arrival with fresh supplies. At 4 p.m. I was about to give up when he and Looking Glass crested the rise, leading his two hardest working pack horses, pointedly named Armstrong and Custer.

When we met at the foot of Daniel's Bridge, Sam greeted me by describing the storm on the Mosque from his viewpoint at Lake Pipsissewa. "A weird sight," he said. "The skies were clear in all directions. The thunderheads amassed on the Mosque and nowhere else, looking like gigantic gray bison stampeding in circles, snorting lightning nonstop. I got so worried I sang you a little protection song."

Having never heard my Nez Perce friend say anything so traditional, I said, "How good of you, Sam. Is it kosher to ask what sort of song?"

Donning a Grim Warrior Face worthy of a commemorative postage stamp, Sam said, "Puff the Magic Dragon." Without a hint of humor, though he'd smote me with glee, he then lifted a big ziplock out of an insulated saddle-bag that doubles as his cooler whenever he finds ice or snow: inside were enough chilled Pipsissewa trout for two good meals. "At dusk," he said darkly, "eat these for strength, for tonight you must dance long to thank Puff for saving you from the Sky Bison."

With that, Sam began unloading his horses while morosely chanting:

Puff's head was bent in sorrow / green scales fell like rain,
Puff no longer went to play / along the cherry lane...

Then came the treacly melody:

Oh, Puff the Magic Dragon lived by the sea...
"Join me, Grady!"

I would have if laughter hadn't crumpled me. Amazing what lyrics a good dad with young kids will commit to memory.

August 15: I crossed Daniel's Bridge this morning to make Sam breakfast before he rides out. As we sipped espresso I asked him if creating a stormproof room in Moondial would be a profanation of a place the Lû mi might hold sacred.

Sam donned his Grim Warrior Face and said, "You will have to ask Puff."

Taking that as a no, I handed him my supply list: chisel-tip rock hammer; two mason's chisels; work gloves; traction cleats to steady me on the arête; a large waterproof oilcloth; two five-gallon buckets for hauling more water up from Jade than my bottles can carry; a dozen climbing pitons; and the cargo pack I'd left in my cabin in Elsewhere. The cargo pack has lots of straps and a strong aluminum shelf at the base that allows it to carry such items as the seventy-pound hindquarters of a bull elk -- or stacks of the shale bricks I hope to fashion. Sam proposed that in late September I ferry everything I can't pack out to the base of Daniel's Bridge, and he'll make a late run with his horses to fetch it all home.

Pondering my list, Sam said, "I'd add one small item. Us backpackers are idiots, wrecking our bodies the way we do. Last summer I read a study of Nepalese porters conducted by Belgian scientists. They gave tumplines to a big group of Sherpa and Tamang men, women, and children, age eleven to seventy. Tumplines wrap around the forehead, distributing load-weight to the head, neck, and entire back, not just the shoulders. The porters trekked a hundred kilometers from Kathmandu to Namche, an elevation gain of ten thousand feet, with many more thousands of feet of ascent and descent en route. They covered it in seven to nine days. Tumps allowed the women to carry an average seventy percent of their body weight, and the men averaged ninety percent. I ordered a tump the same day and the difference is unbelievable. What do you weigh, Grady?"

"At the end of winter, one-eighty. By midsummer, one-seventy."

"And you're strong. How much do your packs usually weigh?"

"Sixty pounds _feels_ ideal, but forces me to leave out stuff I wish I had.

Seventy to eighty gets miserable, but until I hired you that's what I'd end up carrying."

"With a tumpline, and by slowing your pace," Sam said, "you could tote hundred-fifty-pound loads easy."

"Over the thirty miles from the West Fork trailhead to here? I don't think so!"

"I'm an out-of-shape horseman who weighs one ninety, much of it fat. With my tumpline last fall I toted a hundred forty pounds, including the inflatable kayak you lent me, up to fish High Lake without having to mess with horses. I was barely even sore from it."

"Well then damn, Sam! Bring me a tumpline!"

"Any particular brand?" he asked.

"I trust you to choose."

"This is wise," Warrior Sam intoned, "for I shall first seek Puff's counsel."

August 26: Sam returned as scheduled late this morning, off-loaded my tools and supplies at the foot of Daniel's Bridge, and turned right back around so he could make it down to Boundary by dark. One of his daughters has a birthday in two days and wants a horseback camping party. "On the way up," he said in parting, "I stopped by the canister near Pipsissewa and resupplied it for your hike out. The forests lower down are so scary-dry you might have to hightail it sooner than you'd like. I left calorie-heavy foods, mostly canned so they'll keep, some first aid stuff for the trail, a pint of bourbon for whatever the hike might do to you, and more."

I tipped Sam heavily for his kindness, and away he went.

Attaching the new tumpline to my Kelty backpack, I got everything but my slate-making tools and old cargo pack across Daniel's Bridge, hid those by the slate near the top of the bridge, and hauled everything else up to Moondial in two loads that topped out at a hundred or so pounds apiece, blessing Sam and all those porters.

The next morning I set out early, collected my tools and cargo pack, and set to work at the shale deposit. I was surprised by how easily a rock hammer and chisels split soft, layered shale into slabs. I let the slabs vary wildly in thickness, since bricks of any thickness can be puzzle-pieced into a wall, but I was careful to make each slab as flat as I could cut them and roughly twelve-by-twenty-four inches in size.

As the making and hauling of oversized rectilinear bricks became my sole purpose in life I fell into the simple mind that's my favorite thing about manual labor. My anxiety over drought, fire danger, and climate apocalypse fell away. The tumpline let me tote loads of 120 or so pounds, the traction cleats stabilized me so well I didn't even need my trekking poles, and the trip to Moondial was short enough that I hauled fourteen loads in two days, giving me way more slate bricks than I'd need.

On day three I returned to the arête and hid my excavations under talus and scree, leaving Daniel's Bridge looking pristine, then hiked up and set to work on my wall. My first task--scraping shale bricks into powder with a hunting knife for four hours--was as tedious as it sounds. But the adhesive goop that resulted turned walk building into a pleasure. At the end of three days, Moondial featured a slate-solid nine-by-nine-foot chamber with a two-by-two-foot window through which I can watch sunrises without leaving my bedroll. I set four extra-long slabs in the wall sideways so they jut into the room to provide shelves. I built two shale tables out of thirty-inch slabs, one inside the room for meals when it's cold, one by the white sand tub for meals with a spectacular view. I fashioned three two-foot-tall benches, half hoping for guests. I folded the big oilcloth over four times and duct-taped the layers together to create a thick door. I then lay my palm against my 140-foot-tall ceiling, asked permission to hammer in pitons, felt nothing ominous, and nailed the door up. The morning and evening chill hasn't entered the room since.

As the sun was setting I nailed in three more pitons, two for an indoor clothesline, one to hang an overhead lantern. I then collapsed in my Therm a-Rest chair on the white sand tub, feeling quite civilized to set a tin cup of bourbon on the little table I'd made.

As orange light and ravens played over the mountainscape, I felt so pleased with Moondial's new addition that I hoped a thunderstorm would put it to the test.

How many times do we have to hear it?

Be careful what you wish for.

(Inner Elkmoons and Elkmoon Valley floor, August into September 2003)

V. In the Heat of the Mother's Palm

[Christ] said not, "Thou shalt not be tempested, thou shalt not be travailed, thou shalt not be dis-eased"; but he said, "Thou shalt not be overcome. And all manner of wounded and vanished things shall be well."
> —Julian of Norwich, *Revelations of Divine Love*

From the Elkmoon Mountain Journals of Grady Haynes:

August 30: Amid the much colder nights of late August I began yearning for evening campfires, but my choice of home had come at a price. Moondial is well above timberline. The closest firewood I knew of was a stand of weather-stunted larch in a ravine north of Pipsissewa, seven miles away. I knew this wouldn't have stopped the Lû mi from bringing up loads of it, and reminded myself I'd been called a "child of the mountains," and christened "Bird-Dropping-Me," so it wouldn't stop me either.

At 12:30 p.m., August 30th, I loaded the cargo pack's side pockets with tumpline, headlamp, water bottles, arborist saw, traction cleats, two sandwiches, the Trinovids, and off I went. I have a ground-eating stride and elevation loss was on my side. A mile shy of Pipsissewa I turned south to the ravine and found two larch blowdowns with limbs perfect for my needs. The cargo pack's capacity made me ambitious. I set to work at 2:45 and in an hour built a towering, tightly bound load of four- to five-foot staves to haul to Moondial, where I'd saw them into lengths so uniform I could imagine Gladys's llama bleats as I enjoyed their heat. Attaching the tumpline, I hoisted my ungainly load with full-bodied ease and set out for the Mosque.

On my return trip the weather took a sharp turn. As I toiled up Gentian Couloir the day's overhead flow of clouds gained speed and bulk. Though the Mosque blocked my view to the west I twice heard distant thunder. When Echo Lake lay perfectly still despite the swift and heavy clouds, I sensed it was a deception, set down my load, donned traction cleats, and shortened my trekking poles so I could bend low if the wind kicked up. My precautions were very nearly not enough. When I reached the rotten rock blade half-way across the bridge, a brutal gust struck my load broadside, knocking me so badly off-balance I had to throw my poles backward to force myself to fall forward, grab the arête's top edge in my hands, then grab it a terrifying second time when my first handfuls crumbled into pebbles and sand. I clung there listening to my trekking poles clatter hundreds of feet down the arête, wondering how long my body would have lasted in their stead.

Weakened by the close call, I bent so low I could scramble like a chimpanzee, using hands as much as feet, and made it across despite more equally strong gusts. As I started up the slope to Jade I was relieved to feel the Mosque break the gusts down into less dangerous whirlwinds. As I then crested the rise that brings the lake into view, I was stopped in my tracks by what seemed a hallucination: not two hundred yards ahead of me, a woman was serenely swimming a slow circle around Jade's fathomless deep end.

Thinking she might be part of a group, I ducked low and veered off into the boulder field east of Jade to protect Moondial's secrecy. Dumping my load of larch, I grabbed the Trinovids, crept back up the rise, hid in the shadow of a huge glacial erratic, and surveyed the scene.

The lake was wind-whipped at my end but comparatively calm where the woman swam, thanks to the shelter of the peak. Her backpack lay on a big white marble slab on Jade's far shore, fully loaded except for a sleeveless blue T shirt, worn jeans, hiking boots, and a towel. I'd launched my swims from the same slab all summer, and been immersed in states so inexplicable that I was tempted to give up on secrecy and compare notes with the woman when her swim was done. But everything I love about Jade and Moondial could be lost if they were targeted on the internet or even in wilderness guidebooks, and who knew what kind of person the swimmer was.

Glassing the terrain in all directions and the Mosque to the summit, I saw no one, and my guardedness turned toward admiration. Knowing the tens of thousands of carefully chosen steps, achingly short breaths, and feelings of desolation required to reach this place alone, I felt the swimmer's bravery would show in her face, and refocused the Trinovids as her slow circle turned her toward me. Nothing in my life compared to the concentric shocks I then experienced.

First shock: the instant her face came close in the binos, I turned inside out. Her calm clear eyes, close-cropped silver hair, and every other detail but the blue of her discarded shirt matched the woman God the Mother had sculpted out of liquid mercury and placed in the palm of my dreaming hand. But just as this registered, _second shock:_ a deafening tsunami of rolling thunder came pouring over the Mosque for a solid thirty seconds -- the most sustained and threatening thunder I've ever heard. It relieved me to see the woman at last turn toward the marble slab and speed up to a crawl stroke. When she stepped up out of the water and I saw that she was naked, it hardly registered that she was, as the King James might sayeth, _wondrously wrought._ I was sure she'd rush to her pack, throw on clothes, seek shelter instantly. Instead she walked slowly up to her pack, picked up the towel, and began to dry off so slowly that I wondered if she was literally deaf. When she then turned round to gaze at the lake, _third shock:_ her chest bore two waxy-looking half-moon scars. _Her breasts were completely gone._ Yet as I took in her condition, knowing what it takes to get here even without the challenges the scars implied, the depth of her yearning flew across the water, and _fourth shock_: I was hit by a _thunderbolt dunderbolt loveblast_ as extreme as the one in the God the Mother dream. The delicacy of her lake-lit features, industrial assault on her chest, and nakedness of her surrender to Jade were what the long-lost Risa would have called "flame language." The Trinovids were an assault on that language. I lay them down. When the honest distance then left me seeing, to scale, a three-inch figure indistinguishable from the woman Mother God once set in the palm of my dreaming hand, I had to tear my eyes away and lay back on the rocks to try to remember how to breathe. But, _fifth shock_: the sky overhead had become a gigantic roiling threat! When a second wave of rolling thunder shook the very batholith and even then the woman didn't appear to respond, I was slammed by the intuition that Jade Lake had bequeathed her some kind of overwhelming euphoria or sense of eternity that now threatened her very life.

I didn't think the word "Lōmi" even once. The vigilance the word implies simply seized me. At Moondial I keep a duffel loaded with wilderness first-responder gear: two Mylar survival bags; SAM splints for broken bones or sprains; a serious first aid kit; climbing rope; duct tape; extra towels. As the swimmer turned to dress I took off up the mountain, leaping and scrambling my way to the shelter in record time, circled the minaret for the view to the southwest, and went weak. A sky-wide armada of gigantic thunderheads was bearing down on the entire Elkmoon Range. The head in the lead, not a mile off, towered so high it topped out in the flat anvil shape caused by the boundary between troposphere and stratosphere. Lightning flashed nonstop inside the anvil. The heads farther off were unleashing rains so dense they turned the air beneath them black. A green smudge on the horizon told me the sun had set. Inconceivable violence was moments away -- and in Jade's not yet assaulted corner a double mastectomy survivor was completely without shelter.

I shot into Moondial, grabbed the responder duffel, and had just donned it when the first true storm gust smashed the shelter, hurling sand from the stone tub up into my face. Spitting the stuff, trying to wipe it from my eyes, I stepped out into winds so brutal I feared they'd start an avalanche. The anvil-topped thunderhead engulfed me -- and no doubt the Jade swimmer too. The temperature plummeted. When I put on my headlamp, its beam left me lost in a dizzying swirl of dense vapor. Lightning flashed in all directions, showing no route to the woman safer than any other. Sorely missing my trekking poles, I began staggering down through four hundred yards of shattered rock, blinding flashes, and convulsing, high-speed cloud matter in search of God the Mother's hapless gift to me.

Elkmoon Valley Floor

By sundown, August 30th, fire lookouts and planes had tallied some three hundred lightning-caused fires in Western Montana, including nine in the

South Whitetails. Early the morning of August 31st, fire crews and slurry bombers had at them, and were having some success. Though the blazes were many, most were born of a single bolt striking a tree. But in late morning a breeze out of the southwest flickered to life, built to a steady twenty-five miles an hour, and the ninety-eight-degree afternoon heat added fifty- to sixty-mile-an-hour gusts.

O *happy fires!* They rolled east over the Whitetails, roaring through forests climate-cooked to a 100 percent ignition rate. They made spectacular runs up timbered ridges, sending walls of flame four and five hundred feet in the air as they summited. Tens of thousands of acres were devoured faster than wildlife and many birds could flee. Ground crews and smoke jumpers couldn't get within miles of the fires' fast-charging front edges. Stately ponderosas, despite their fire-resistant bark, torched bole to crown in as little as thirty seconds. Huge stands of densely packed lodgepoles did not so much ignite as explode, making the *whoooomph!* familiar to knuckle-heads like me who've started bonfires with gasoline, but at a decibel level more like the sonic booms of fighter jets. The lodgepoles burned so hot and fast they ignited the duff and kept burning downward, leaving behind moonscapes that looked as if no such thing as forests had ever existed.

Kale and the Elkmooners had been preparing for such a crisis. Ona Kutar was in California when the fires blew up, but she, TJ, and Risa had sprung for four ATVs that Kale's crew had equipped with 125-gallon water tanks, pumps, and hoses, making them independent of NorBanCo's equipment. Kale's F-250 was rigged with a 325-gallon and Doty Nolan's old Dodge pickup was rigged with a 200-gallon. With help from Ona's super-gifted assistant, Regina Cloud, everybody had BlackBerrys or two-way radios with a four- or five-mile range except Lou Roy, who refused them. Verizon's new wireless network also enabled the laptop owners, Risa and Regina, to communicate with the world, which importantly included TJ in Portland and Ona Kutar wherever she roamed. And Ona had purchased a laptop for Mu and Lore.

Risa called Jamey late on the 30th. He was in Portland for a Stumptown Shakespeare Ensemble performance of *As You Like It,* playing the famously melancholy Jacques, but he had long since become a welcome member of our "imagination infestation." Seeing wind in the E City forecast for the 31st, Jamey told Risa, "I've called in my understudy to play Jacques, schemed with TJ, and we're aimed at Montana in his new Land Cruiser rather than a jet in case the fires shut down E City Airport."

The twenty acres round Kale's home, barn, and hundred acres at School-house Bluff lay three to four miles downriver of the Grand Lodge. The fires likeliest to endanger the inholdings kept their distance on the 30th, but when the winds blew up on the 31st all hands were called on deck, knowing they were in for a marathon fight. Stationed at Testament Creek School, Regina Cloud served as command central to Kale's field commander, the pair of them working with BlackBerrys and identical contour maps to coordinate and direct the crew's efforts. Teenagers Mu and Rosalia were stationed in the school's cupola with binoculars and a two-way radio, directing three volunteer firefighters guarding the hundred-acre surround.

The first volunteer, Risa, manned the tank-added ATV Dave had left her, dousing every flare-up the teenagers called in. The second volunteer, Ida Craig, had achieved hero status a month previous when she sprung for a used wildland fire engine, named it *The Commonweal*, and with no help from the overbusy Kale became expert in its use. The truck had four-wheel drive, a 500-gallon water tank, and the ability to "pump and roll," meaning it could be driven with the pump engaged and a firefighter manning its powerful hose, unlike urban fire trucks that can only pump when parked and connected to a hydrant. The third volunteer, Max Bowler, had appeared out of nowhere to man that very hose. Ida then proved so intrepid at the wheel, and Max so quick to create routes to flare-ups with his chainsaw, courage, and brute strength, that they worked wonders to guard the bluff, the entire length of Aspen Swale, and Kale's home and twenty acres while Lou Roy safeguarded Kale's barn and all their horses.

The great weakness in their defense was that, as Land & Beef Inc. foreman, Kale had to answer to Tex before he and his crew could tend to the inholdings' defense. Then, to Kale's distress, Tex stopped answering his phone when the fires blew up at midday. This made it impossible to get into locked buildings that housed NorBanCo's firefighting equipment, forcing Kale to send Doty Nolan, Eddie, and Buford on the Elkmooners' own ATVs to douse spot fires on NorBanCo's land.

As sunset approached and containment remained inconceivable, the public utilities grid that powered the Grand Lodge, Kale's inholdings, and Schoolhouse Bluff went down. Lou Roy started the diesel generators that ran Kale's sprinklers so he could keep soaking the shake roofs of the house and barn, and the schoolhouse was rich in heirloom kerosene lanterns for light. But when Buford called in to say that his, Eddie's, and Doty's efforts were like fighting a hundred dragons with three squirt guns, Kale could no longer bear Tex not answering his phone. He called that trio back to Schoolhouse Bluff to regroup, then got on a two-way to Hub Punker, telling him to drive his D9 bulldozer to the lodge, find Tex, and offer to blade fireproof swaths of dirt around any NorBanCo structures under threat.

Ten minutes later Hub called back. "You're not gonna like this, Pope," he said. "Tex seen me comin', roared down in his Escalade, screamed that my Cat and me should bleep the bleep back the way I come, and get this. There's not a light burning in the lodge or outbuildings, no diesel generators running, no sprinklers, and no crew. I never seen a soul 'cept Tex."

"*Christ!* Stay within plain sight of the lodge where Tex can see you, and if he yells at you, refuse to move. We'll join you shortly." Kale then called Regina and asked her to have Eddie, Buford, and Doty meet him at his barn as fast as they could get there.

From the Elkmoon Mountain Journals of Grady Haynes:

I'd made the Moondial to Jade hike a hundred times. I knew the lake to be 400 steep yards distant. The first 350 yards were talus, the last 50 yards even more jagged rock from the meteorite strike, and never had I descended amid nonstop thunder and lightning as winds slammed me like invisible fists, forcing me to drop down and grab talus in both hands to keep from being blown over. If the swimmer was trying to pitch her tent it would be ripped from her hands. I prayed she was heading for the boulder field where I'd left my cargo pack. She could roll under a boulder's curved base, wrap herself in her bedroll and unpitched tent, and wait out the lightning and winds. That was my plan for us if I found her. But the kaleidoscopic cloud shreds, lit by my headlamp, set off a vertigo that erased all sense of how much ground I'd covered. When a brief lull arrived, I turned the lamp off, stood still with eyes closed until the vertigo eased, peered down through the cloud mass, and was amazed to glimpse a wobbling headlamp maybe 300 yards below me. Though it vanished in an instant, I at least knew the woman was seeking safety.

I'd covered perhaps half the distance toward her when another lull arrived. I again doused my headlamp. An unlikely ally -- lightning -- then seared my retinas with four images like freeze-frames in a movie. In the first, the woman was hunched low, traveling directly away from me, steadying herself by holding on to stone, as I was doing. In the second flash I saw she was indeed angling toward the boulder field, and felt sure I'd find and be able to help her. But the third flash put my heart in my throat. One of her hiking boots had gotten stuck in a crevice and she was leaning hard right to free it. Then the fourth flash brought horror: before she could free her foot, lightning struck so close to her that either the bolt, or her response to it, showed her falling backward and downhill in the opposite direction from the way she'd been straining, with nothing to land on but jagged rocks. Certain that she was very badly hurt, if not lightning-struck and dead, I scrambled toward her thinking things couldn't be worse -- when the clouds burst, releasing something more like a falling lake than rain. I was half crushed by it. Trying to hold the angle and distance to the woman in memory, I scrambled across the shard-scape till it seemed I'd gone too far, then doubled back at a lower angle, intending to comb the area one swath at a time when, not thirty yards away, I glimpsed a faint, torrent-obscured light.

I was elated until I reached her. Then I doubted she was alive. She lay flat on her back on shattered rock, looking as if she'd been <u>thrown</u> there. Her head was far lower than her feet. Her right boot was still trapped in the stone crevice, her ankle surely torn at an angle so terrible I believed she'd have been screaming if she were alive.

The deluge was frigid. The woman was drenched. I knelt beside her, removed my duffel, took out and folded a towel, lifted her head from the cruel rocks, pillowed it on the towel, and saw my hands were covered with blood. Removing her headlamp, I used it like a flashlight to examine her -- and saw little puffs of vapor leaving her nose and mouth! When I cried, "<u>You're</u> <u>breathing!</u>" her eyes opened. Her pupils were enormous, a sure sign of shock, and her gaze was so unfocused I doubt she even saw me. But she saw some-thing. "<u>Whatever you are</u>," she whispered, "<u>I'm finished. Please take me.</u>" Her eyes then began jittering in a way I've never seen, and she passed out -- but the puffs of vapor, thank heavens, kept coming!

I went to work. Grabbing her trapped boot in both hands, I had to strain cruelly to free it. Her feet now lay side by side, the right ankle sickeningly floppy. Lifting her in my arms, I set her down against a smooth slanted boulder, then stabilized her ankle by wrapping it thickly, boot and all, in duct tape. Opening her pack, I plundered a towel and as much dry clothing as I could stuff in my duffel, found a hand-knit wool hat, slid it onto her head. Though there was no way she'd hear me, I said, "Sorry, but I need to free my shoulders," and strapped my duffel tight to her small shoulders and back. I then slid her feet in close to her butt, gripped her left wrist in my right hand, pulled her up into standing position, shoved my left arm through her legs, and heaved her onto my shoulder in a firefighter's carry. I found her so much lighter than expected I feared she must be lifting out of her body. <u>You will meet her</u> <u>one day</u>, the Jade dream had foretold, <u>and find her completely lovable but</u> mortally wounded. <u>Your love will then turn to total heartbreak.</u>

"But not yet!" I growled at any deities or powers who might be eavesdrop-ping. "And we're <u>mortals</u>, you deathless hotshots! When <u>isn't</u> heartbreak coming for us? Just let us reach Moondial with no more lightning strikes or breakage, okay?"

Do divine powers respond to crank prayers? I don't know. I only know I started up-mountain through a veritable waterfall bearing a terribly injured woman I'd first met in a beautiful dream. And even unconscious, don't ask me how, she steadied me every step of the way.

Elkmoon Valley Floor

Kale and crew met at his barn and set out for the Grand Lodge in two pick-ups and two ATVs. Vigilant en route, they encountered a multitude of small brands and one spot fire, all of which they quickly doused. As they rounded the radical curve at Block an' Tackle Rock, they stopped their vehicles to gape: the South Whitetails across the river were an inferno, and the viewshed of the entire development was *already* annihilated. The modest threats to the land Kale and crew had just protected seemed miraculous by comparison. The reason: *Elbow Bend.* Driven northeast by very high winds, the wildfire roared right past the two-hundred-degree turn it would have to make to attack Kale's home and Schoolhouse Bluff.

Four hundred yards on they found Hub Punker hulking on his D9, keeping watch on the lodge as ordered. "No change, Pope," he said. "Not a light. Not a sound. Not a soul. Tex's Escalade still parked on the steps up to the main lodge entrance."

"Let's find him, Hub," Kale said, and the big man maneuvered his bulk up into the Pope's Ford. The crew fell in behind, following in reverse the promenade that half circled the lodge. As they neared the huge parking lot they were surprised to see headlights approaching via NorBanCo's over-built road in to the lodge from Downriver Road. Regina had told Kale the police reported NorBanCo's high road to be on fire in places, and probably crossed now by several fallen and burning trees.

Kale and crew turned onto the slate pathway to the lodge's main entrance and parked behind Tex's Escalade as the mystery vehicle that had dared the fiery road pulled in behind them—and out of a char-stained and branch-scraped white Land Cruiser stepped Jamey and TJ, the latter garbed in the famous orange Carhartts. "If you two aren't a sight for sore eyes!" Kale laughed.

"Same goes for you, Pope," said Jamey. "You wouldn't *believe* what TJ drove us through!"

"I'm so glad you two made it, and we'll talk story later," Kale said. "Here's how things stand now. The power's out at the inholdings, but our people are fine. The boys and me are here to defend the lodge but nothing we see adds up. No crew. No backup generators or sprinklers. And Tex is inside in the dark some damn where, refusing to answer his BlackBerry when Regina or I call."

Even as Kale spoke, Tex stepped round the far end of the south side veranda, gaping across the river at the South Whitetail conflagration. "I don't like this lights-out no-generator no-sprinklers situation one bit," Kale said. "With their development up in smoke, I'm thinking Tex is getting crazed orders from corporate. I need to read him the riot act before he does something rash. He's not gonna enjoy my warning, so you all better wait here."

"Let me join you," TJ said, "but just a second, please." TJ pulled a small rectangular device Kale didn't recognize out of his Carhartts, punched at it, then slid it in the bib pocket of his overalls.

As they started down the veranda Tex at first looked frightened to see them. Then his fear blew up into anger. "You're not needed, Broussard!" he shouted. "Your crew neither! We've got this under control!"

"Who's *we*, and in what world is hellfire *control*?" Kale shouted back. "All I see is you doing nothing with brands burning all over your lodge roof and grounds. We're here to fire up the generators, get the lights and sprinklers going, and douse the brands."

Stomping toward them now, Tex hollered, "I'm just off the phone with *our* firefighters. Our truck is en route. Men I *trust* will deal with this the instant they get here."

"*The road in is on fire!*" Kale roared. "They *can't get here*! TJ just drove it. Tell him."

"It was a nightmare!" TJ said, playing his part. "When a big fallen ponderosa blocked the road, my Land Cruiser got us through a gulch, dodging fallen trees and fire all the way. We barely made it back onto the road. No fire truck could make that detour."

"My men put out the ponderosa and are *removing* it!" Tex shouted. "We've *got* this, I tell you! What you all can do is get down to the country club and ranchette sites and keep the big fields there from burning!"

In a sidelong whisper, TJ told Kale, "There is *no* fallen ponderosa."

"This situation is a no-brainer, Tex," Kale told him, "which gives me the feeling you're trying to frame me. How could I justify leaving a multimillion-dollar lodge undefended to protect summer-dead grass and structures that only exist as blueprints? We'll fire up your system, soak things till your men arrive, and *then* we'll leave."

Fury lifted Tex's voice into his bizarre *Concierge* falsetto. "This is not a discussion group! Do the job I *ordered* you to do!"

With a calm born of knowing where his next words would lead, Kale said, "No way in hell can I obey an order that suicidal to this place."

"Then here's your very last order!" Tex yelled. "You're *fired*, so's your crew, and that changes things! As of now you own a right-of-way in to the crappy old house, barn, and schoolhouse you can fuck off and try to save if you want. But that's *all* you own. If I see *any* of you wandering NorBanCo lands you'll be arrested for trespass!"

"Good luck with *that*," Kale told him. "You're a weak and pitiful man, Tex."

Back at the vehicles the crew encircled Kale and TJ.

"What did he say?" Hub asked.

"You heard," Kale said. "We're fired. All of us."

"We heard that," Buford said. "But did he say why?"

"No. But a decade under Tex leaves me sure of one thing. The Grand Lodge is his precious darling. I'm sure the son of a bitch is being forced by much meaner sons o' bitches to let fire take the lodge so they can collect the insurance. They may also hope to frame *me* for abandoning the lodge, so thank God TJ heard our argument."

"Sorry Kale," TJ said, "but in a court of law anything I claim to have heard would just be my word against Schiller's, with Tex backed by NorBanCo's team of hotshot lawyers."

As Kale's face fell, TJ added, "But *this* should hold up in court." And out of his Carhartt bib came the minicassette recorder he used for business affairs, which he turned on—and out came every word of Kale and Tex's exchange. As the crew listened, sometimes roaring with laughter at how damning the evidence was, TJ glanced back at the lodge—and just inside the darkened main entrance stood Tex, motionless, his expression thoughtful, listening. Within weeks this odd moment would strike TJ as the most fortunate event of the night.

"Sorry we're fired," Kale told his men. "But these fires have taken out NorBanCo so our jobs were gone anyway. And I'd like to offer temp work at time-and-a-half wages to anyone willing to help me protect the old McKeig and Broussard acreage. It's obvious that NorBanCo wants as much of their land to burn as possible so they can claim it as a giant operating loss. My aim is to fuck with that plan as much as possible, and no way will Tex try to arrest us for saving *his* land. That'd make NorBanCo's villainy too obvious."

"I'll make that pay double," TJ added, causing Buford to don a rare scowl.

"No can do, Squire," he said, looking stern. Then he beamed and added, "But how 'bout this? Let's all of us go save the whole shitaree an' you two pay us nothin'!"

Another round of laughter and the Greater Good crew was all in.

"Before we take off for Schoolhouse Bluff," Kale said, "let me call Regina for the latest intel. And while she and I chat let's get Hub down to his Caterpillar."

A few minutes later Hub was back on the D9 and Kale was fully informed: "It's one a.m. and we're tired," he said. "But if we're gonna get this done, the night is young. Schoolhouse Bluff is fire free thanks to Risa, Mu, and Rosalia, and Ida, Max Bowler, and *The Commonweal* have been dousing anything that glows from my barn all the way up to the schoolhouse. But somebody agile enough to walk my barn roof needs to spell Lou Roy. A sprinkler slid off the roof and I don't want Lou trying to put it back up. Whoever goes, wet cedar shakes are damn slippery. Behind the tack room door is a pair of spiked rubber golf galoshes I wear up there. Use 'em."

"I'm on it, Pope," Buford said. "Anything else while I'm there?"

"Regina asked if Ida and Max can refuel my generators going forward. They can. Take my BlackBerry, and once you right that sprinkler, ask Regina where you should join us on the four thousand acres. It's gonna be a David and Goliath show out there tonight. We need you."

"I'll bring my slingshot," Buford said, and away his four-wheeler tore.

"Three E City volunteer fire trucks got the Downriver Road and NorBanCo high road fires out," Kale said. "But we all know Tex was lying. There's no NorBanCo fire engine or crew at all. Regina's going to follow the volunteer trucks back to E City, evacuating a few kids en route so their parents can focus on defending their homes and barns. The kids will stay at Ida's. How Regina also found time to leave us a pile of sandwiches in the schoolhouse I don't know, but we need 'em. Risa's our phone maven now. She says she hopes somebody, maybe you, TJ, can spell Rosalia and Mu in the schoolhouse cupola. They've been doing a bang-up job as lookouts for twenty hours straight."

"Good God!" TJ said. "I'd be honored."

"I asked Risa for advice given what she sees from the bluff. She read my mind. The hundred-percent ignition rate means we choose our battles, she said. It's gonna hurt to watch places we love burn without a fight, but the former Broussard and McKeig lands are where we'll make our stand. Those big alfalfa and hay fields are downright soggy from our good work all summer. Our job is dousing the brands and small brush fires before they torch the scattered stands of pines. And when stands torch, listen to me, boys, *back the hell off*! No heroics. We'll protect Stella Creek, the two ponds and their trees, and as many beautiful places as we can. But we will *not* overreach and die. Anything I'm forgetting?"

"My Cat's no help where you're headed," Hub said. "Let me scrape that swath of brush east of your barn down to bare dirt. Even wet, that shit could torch."

"Good man, Hub," Kale said. "Are we all on the same page then?"

A round of nods and they were off.

From the Elkmoon Mountain Journals of Grady Haynes:

September 1: At 9:30 a.m., twelve hours after I lay the drenched and unconscious woman down in Moondial, she opened her eyes. She remained motionless, simply gazing at the marble ceiling. Unspeakably relieved, but not wanting to startle her, I whispered, "Careful not to move your right leg. Your ankle's very badly injured."

She turned to me and stared, no doubt wondering who I was, but gave a small, careful nod. <u>Comprehension!</u> More relief.

I told her my name. She told me hers. <u>Lorilee.</u>

I said, "You've been out for twelve hours. I found you after you got hurt last night, and carried you here. <u>Here</u> is a rock shelter a quarter mile above Jade, in which you swam before the storm. Do you remember any of that?"

She whispered, "Swimming, trying to find shelter, yes. Then, nothing."

I said, "Each time you speak I feel relief, Lorilee. You came so close to being lightning-struck, and stayed unconscious so long, I feared the bolt had hit you. But no way could you be this clearheaded if you'd been struck. May I tell you about your injuries so you can be careful of them?"

She gave a careful nod.

"Your ankle will need surgery. It's in a SAM splint I shaped to fit you, then wrapped in an ACE bandage. You've got three deep bone bruises on your back that'll hurt for days, but almost no bleeding, and no breakage that I could feel. But there's a much deeper gouge and lump on the back of your head. I put Polysporin in the gouge but no bandage. Better to pillow it with towels. It was probably a concussion in addition to the wound, so <u>please</u>, take it very easy."

"I've no choice, believe me," she whispered.

"Our only plan for today and tomorrow is rest. Any needs at all, ask me. I'm going to get you back to civilization, Lorilee. And <u>you're</u> going to heal, ankle included. It's going to be a process, but it will happen. We start now with total rest."

"First, a question," she said. "I'm wearing your long johns and lying in your sleeping bag. What happened to my pack?"

"To carry you here I had to abandon it. My zero-degree bag is the only bag we've got till I can fetch yours. When we arrived, you were seriously hypothermic, which is deadly. Your clothes are drying on the line above you. I dried you with towels, warmed you with friction, dressed you in my long johns since they're big enough to slide over the SAM splint. Even then you stayed so cold I had to share the bag to warm you. Sorry if that seems overly familiar, but letting you die was not an option."

She gazed at me so long I feared she was finding what I'd done creepy. Instead, she melted me with a smile. "The situation <u>demanded</u> intimacy. I'd be dead without you. Once in the night, in a cold painful fog, I felt warmth begin to envelop me, and dreamed a friendly animal was sharing its body heat. I realize now I was right. If I could move, I'd give that animal a thank-you hug."

Undone by her grace under duress, I said, "I'm completely at your service."

"That's good," she murmured, "because I require service right now."

"Name it," I said.

"My bladder is bursting."

"I've thought on that."

I hopped up, sat on one of my little slate benches, set a five-gallon bucket on the floor between my legs, patted my thighs, and said, "I'll work out a way to give you privacy tomorrow, but for now, welcome to Moondial's handicap-accessible flush toilet. My thighs are the toilet seat. I'll carry you here, help you stand on one leg, ease you down, look the other way as you use the bucket, then put you back to bed. The flush is a pleasant stroll to a ravine sixty yards from Moondial. May I?"

When she nodded permission, I picked her up in my arms with extreme caution, and had no difficulty positioning her and holding her steady. But nothing in my life prepared me for the joy I felt at the sound of a woman whose life I'd feared lost throughout the night simply piddling and sighing with relief.

Elkmoon Valley Floor

Lou Roy Skinner was bone-weary, but uneasy. When Buford had met him at Kale's barn and said the Grand Lodge power was off and no one was protecting it from fire, all Lou could think about was the irrigation canal NorBanCo shared with Kale's inholdings. Known as Six Mile Ditch, its headgate was three miles upriver of the Grand Lodge, its outflow three miles downriver from Kale's barn, and its entire length was lined with sun-seared grass. For close to a mile that grass lay directly across river from the South Whitetail holocaust. While winds from the west were still blowing burning debris east, the wind was weakening. If it died down completely the burning debris would change direction, making Six Mile Ditch's dried-grass banks a fuse leading to every building, horse, and person Lou cared about most.

Unwilling to pull anyone off the threats Kale and crew were facing, but knowing he wouldn't sleep till he rode the ditch watching for flare-ups, Lou Roy ratcheted over to Kale's sleeping porch and opened a cupboard entirely filled with U-Haul moving blankets. Built thick to pad furniture, the blankets could hold a lot of water. Kale and his dad had quelled small flare-ups with similar blankets years ago. Lou Roy took three out of the cupboards, went to the barn, saddled Grey, strapped two blankets behind his cantle and lay a third across his lap. Nosing Grey around the barn and up onto the backhoe-built banks of the ditch, Lou Roy set out upstream in the direction of the Grand Lodge.

His uneasiness proved out in no time: as the wind dropped to a breeze it grew swirly, making the direction of airborne brands unpredictable. In the first five hundred yards he came upon six small spot fires. He doused them all with a sopped blanket, preventing his fears from coming true. But half a mile farther he reached a burning brush clump too big for even two soaked blankets. He had to ride from ditch to fire and back five or six more times to put the clump out. The soaked blankets weighed twenty-five pounds apiece, making fifty-pound loads, but Grey gave excellent help. He'd step down into the ditch and wait as Lou saturated the blankets without having to dismount, then stand steady though the blankets drenched Grey as they drained to a weight Lou Roy could manage. Lou would then dismount, walk alone to the flames, and hurl the blankets where they'd do the most good.

At 2:30 a.m. he made the turn at Elbow Bend and saw that the South Whitetail fires across the river had devoured the forest so completely they were dying down for lack of fuel. He covered the mile of ditch that had worried him most, dousing a scatter of small spot fires without much difficulty. But not far from the lodge, he came upon a burning stump so full of pitch it destroyed his first blanket and burned large holes in the second. Lou then stood too long on ash-concealed embers near the stump, burning a hole in his right boot sole and singeing his foot.

Down to one blanket, knowing his judgment was going, Lou checked his pocket watch: 3:10. Past time to leave Grey at Kale's then check in at the schoolhouse. But he was just two hundred yards from the Grand Lodge and had never seen it dark and silent. Falling into a trance, he sat Grey motionless, staring at the ponderosa palace—when the lights came on in Tex Schiller's big corner office. Curious, Lou nudged Grey into the dense cottonwood saplings covering the back side of the ditch and rode as close as he dared. Two hours later, back on Schoolhouse Bluff, he told Kale and Risa what he then saw:

"As you know, Tex's office has south- and east-facin' windows that give him views of his entire development that's never to be. I almost felt for him, seein' him alone like that, with the world's finest view of his an' NorBanCo's total failure."

"How come he still had lights?" Risa asked.

"The lodge is high-end," Kale said. "In a power outage banks of batteries keep lights and phones on, freezers full of food frozen, and generators can keep it up for days if repairs are slow to come. Sorry to interrupt, Lou. Go ahead."

"For a good while Tex paces his office like a caged animal. Then he picks up his phone, makes a call, an' is soon red-faced, wavin' his arms, yellin' so

I have no kids and she has a teenaged son with the remarkable name Mu; learned she and Mu are musicians who perform together. But we pursued none of these topics. I could see her drawing strength from Moondial's cloistered quiet. Her color improved. Her eyes stopped glazing over. Her face relaxed -- and my, she was pretty as her remarkable eyes became clear and present.

We said nothing until there was need. I stayed close enough to be of instant service. I caught up in my journal. I loved watching her sleep.

September 3: Lore woke late, looking wonderfully alert. After I helped with her morning ablutions she said, "I'm done with horizontal. I'd like to sit up today."

I fetched my trekker chair and helped her into it. Having never seen the ten-ounce kits that turn Therm-a-Rest sleeping pads into comfortable chairs, she said, "I feel like royalty in this thing!"

"Then it's yours," I told her. "I have two more at home."

I made us pancakes for breakfast and fried Lore our last egg, then fetched two buckets and many bottles of water from Jade Lake to Moondial, heated water, did the dishes, and was about to hike down to fetch Lore's pack when I noticed her wincing at me. "Are you in pain?" I asked.

"Of a kind," she said. "I'm feeling a call of nature. I'd love to have privacy for that. Is there any chance I can achieve that?"

"I've pondered this," I said. "Give me five minutes, max."

I hammered two more pitons into the ceiling at the foot of our bed, hung climbing rope down to the ground, built a V-shaped bench of slate beneath, set a bucket in the V, helped Lore over to the bench, handed her the two ropes, waited till she'd steadied herself and said, "I'm good," and I went outside. When she pulled the task off and called me back, she looked so happy it was hard to remember her constant pain.

I asked if she was okay being alone for half an hour. She said yes, but asked to sit out in the sun. This made me happy for a reason that was rapidly intensifying: I got to carry her in my arms again. Such carrying was vital to my ability to help her, so we'd developed an etiquette to keep it from feeling loaded. We donned poker faces. Very important. I then helped her stand on one leg, placed an arm round her back as she placed her arms round my neck, and she turned her face away while my other arm lifted her by the legs to horizontal. I then walked her to the desired location, set her down in the trekker chair, and facial expressions were again allowed.

I handed Lore her sun-bleached old ball cap with the command DON'T ASK!, left her sunscreen, water, a cup of almonds and raisins, and the Trinovids, then set off down the steep quarter mile to her pack.

When I reached it -- and saw by day the jagged rocks upon which Lore had fallen -- my stomach nearly turned. Add gravity's force to a dead fall and those shards were lethal weapons. It was eerie to realize that the terrible injury to her ankle may well have prevented the sharp rock to the back of her head from being fatal.

Her pack was light, thirty-five pounds at most, so I carried it to the boulder field where my cargo pack of larch staves was stashed, strapped her pack to mine, attached the tumpline, and hauled the double load up to Moondial in one trip.

When I found Lore asleep in her chair, I quietly stacked the larch, spread the contents of her pack and sopped sleeping bag on clean sunbaked marble, and set her first aid and toiletry kits beside her. When Lore woke and saw them, she dug out a vial of tiny arnica pills, dropped two on her tongue, and said, "_Thank you!_ What's next?"

"Now we have a big decision to make. I'd like you to help me think it through. And to make our situation clear I need to be blunt. Is that okay?"

"Of course."

"We're thirty miles deep into serious backcountry, and very high up. You have a terrible ankle injury, and a deep gouge on your head. You've figured out a way to go to the bathroom solo, but do you think you could prepare food, dress yourself, and stay safe if I left you here?"

The sad face she made at this prospect was what I'd hoped for. "It would be very hard. Maybe even impossible. But why do you ask, Grady? Are we splitting up?"

"You tell me," I said. "If I set you up here and took off like a shot, I believe I could get to cell coverage in two very long days and, I hope, get a Life Flight helicopter up here on day three. If I carry you down to the trailhead, caring for you all the way, I think we'd need three very long days, and luck, to get you into a chopper on day four. I'm sure the world below is on fire, so the Elkmoon Wilderness area is probably closed, which means we wouldn't encounter a pack string with a mount. To turn _me_ into your mount, I'll need the rest of today to prep. So we must make the call now. And I'm not going to lie. I would much prefer that we stick together."

Lore cried, "Me too!" and embraced me.

My head spun and I nearly kissed her. To cover my faux pas I said, "Let's head inside and start making stuff for the trail!"

"Okay," she said. "But don't say what you're making! I want to guess."

I knelt to lift her in my arms again. But when we tried to don our poker faces, we couldn't keep from smiling and the unkissed kiss still hovered close.

I set to work with a vengeance to keep us focused. Delving in my clothes stack for my third-string pair of Levi's, I grabbed my sewing kit, pulled out the scissors, and said, "Ready to start guessing?"

When Lore nodded, I cut both pant legs off just below the pockets.

"What on Earth!" she cried.

Explaining nothing, I set the legs aside, picked up the cutoffs I'd made, and was using carabiners and Levi's belt loops to attach them to the ropes that gave her bathroom privacy when Lore said, "A Levi's sling to ice and elevate my ankle!"

"_Correctamundo!_ Jeez, you're a good guesser!"

"But where's the ice? Is there a glacier up the Mosque?"

Still explaining nothing, I grabbed needle and thread and in minutes turned the amputated legs into sacks by sewing them shut at the cuffs. Slipping on work gloves, I said, "Be right back," ducked outside, and circled to the always-shaded north side of the minaret, where an inch-deep layer of slush from the thunderstorm hadn't melted. Scraping it into the pant legs till they bulged, I lugged them back inside.

"Your ingenuity is endless!" Lore exclaimed.

"Easy there," I said. "Ingenuity is just part of wilderness living--and ingenuity's dark side is total fuckups. I'm good at those too."

"Ingenuity and humility!" she teased.

I proposed removing her SAM splint so the ice could better chill her ankle. She agreed, lay back, and when I got the bandage and splint off I went queasy: her ankle had become a sickly stew of grays, greens, and mustards and her foot was cold to the touch. Can a blown-out ankle cut off so much circulation that the foot dies? I didn't know. I only knew she needed surgeons, and for days to come all I could offer was pain relief. I got the ankle elevated and iced, and another dose of Advil kicked in. But when Lore called me a miracle worker and said she hardly hurt at all, I couldn't even fake a smile. The state of her ankle increased my sense of urgency tenfold.

"What's next?" she asked.

"A task I'm unsure of. I'm going to convert my Kelty backpack into a saddle-pack to carry you. To do that I need to cut leg holes in the nylon main compartment. If the cuts rip on the trail we're in something worse than trouble. So. While I cut and smooth two larch walking sticks to serve as my forelegs as your beast of burden, could you read my notes on backpack to saddle-pack conversion, and think hard on how we might strengthen the main compartment after the leg holes have been cut?"

"Sometimes my hands get the best ideas when my brain stays out of the loop," Lore said. "Can I have a pencil and paper so I can doodle?"

I set to work, Lore set to reading my notes and doodling, and a half hour later, as I was smoothing my finished forelegs, she cried, "Come look!"

She'd made two cartoon drawings, one a front view of me wearing the saddle-pack and her smiling over my shoulder as she rode in it, the other a back view with two new additions. Across the top of the Kelty pack frame she'd added a larch stave, and from the stave she'd hung a sling that ran under her bottom then back up to the sling. "A weight-bearing sling's a great idea," I said, "but what's it made of?"

"The rain-fly from my tent! My hands thought of it!"

"That," I cried, "is the genius idea I couldn't come up with! Will you please be my advisor as I try to execute your design?"

"My pleasure."

Before cutting leg holes in the nylon I handed her my soft tailor's tape measure and asked her to measure the circumference of one of her thighs at the very top of her leg. She gave me an arch look, but obeyed, then announced, "Twenty-two inches. Who knew?"

I moved us outside for ventilation and Lore sat close as requested. I drew twenty-four-inch leg holes with a Magic Marker, cut them out with an X-Acto, cauterized the edges with a butane lighter for added strength, and lined the melted nylon with three layers of duct tape for even greater strength. Selecting a straight, strong stave from the pile outside, I peeled off the bark then sawed it to fit the top of my pack frame, leaving it a foot longer on the right so my strides wouldn't bump Lore's bad ankle. I then wired and taped the stave to the top of the pack frame. "How's that look?" I asked.

"Like my ride home," she said with a smile.

"On to the next feature." I ducked inside, brought out my sewing kit and amputated Levi legs, and ripped out the stitches that had turned the legs into snow bags. But I'd done nothing but thread a needle when she cried, "Thanks for the Levi's stirrups you're making to support my good and bad ankle in the saddle!"

"You're so quick it's scary," I told her.

Twenty minutes later, the sling and stirrups hung from the stave, adjusted for comfort, and my confidence in our saddle-pack had flown from marginal to almost total.

September 4: We both woke early, excited to be just three tasks from departure. One: we'd sort out and pack everything we'd need on the trail. Two: I'd pack up and haul everything we didn't need to the base of Daniel's Bridge, where Sam and his horses could find it and haul it home. Three: I'd leave a clean camp.

When we finished selecting needed supplies and food, I fit it all into our day packs, which I would attach to the saddle-pack once Lore was in it. Her 115 pounds, my 170, and about 65 pounds of food and gear would turn me into a 350-pound beast of burden. Doable? Not sure. But we could cache stuff if my load overwhelmed.

Lore asked me to carry her in to the cookware so she could make us beans and rice for supper. As I gathered her in my arms her poker face failed her, becoming a look of undisguised affection as she said, "_I'm so excited!_" I was too.

As she began to make dinner I turned to leaving a clean camp, a formidable task. I'd been seduced by Sam's pack horse deliveries into ordering many nonessentials. I packed up the slate brickmaking tools, an extra two-burner stove, a large Coleman camp lantern, a stupid amount of unneeded clothing, an eight-book library, and my fishing gear, and could barely hoist the load onto my back. But the tumpline, traction cleats, and larch forelegs did get me across Daniel's Bridge.

Wrapping the gear, cargo pack included, inside our retired oilcloth door, I roped it shut and buried it under scree, hoping Sam could fetch it before the autumn snows.

When I got back up to Moondial, I gorged on Lore's rice and beans, then moved us outside as the mountain cooled. While Lore sipped chamomile tea and I a dram of bourbon, greatly increased low-elevation smoke and a sky full of high cirrus put on a red-spectrum light show that ran from pink to flaming orange to a somehow soothing sea of blood crisscrossed by ravens and a scatter of bats.

Lore's sleeping bag was bone-dry after a day in the sun, so I brought it in and started making her a bed of her own. "Hold on," she said. "Am I allowed a vote? You're _very_ careful of me, you don't snore, and if we share your bag we could take just one bedroll on the trail."

Seeing that her proposal knocked me sideways, she smiled and said, "_Good._"

Our bedtime had taken on a routine. I'd seat her on the bench under the support ropes to pee, take the bucket outside to empty in the morning, lend her my down coat to use as a bathrobe, carry her to her trekker chair at the top of our shared bag, fetch her a saucepan of hot water for a cloth bath and cup of cold to brush her teeth, then step outside and do my own ablutions under the stars.

I'd taken advantage of the day's sun to wash and dry the long johns Lore had worn every night since her rescue. When I brought them into the slate room, she'd removed my coat and was down to a thin T shirt. I knelt to help her slide the long johns over her SAM splint. But Lore said, "No thanks. It's warmer this evening." And oh, her skimpy little T shirt and lovely legs freed from my dumpy long johns...

Keeping to routine, I set a dim solar light on the floor by the down vest I use for a pillow, slid into the bag, lay on my back, and held still as Lore began working her way in, keeping her left leg against my right and her splinted ankle away from me. When her head drew even with mine, she lay on her back beside me, as usual. Then, very much not as usual, she eased her left side up against me, sighed as her head came to rest on my shoulder, and cautiously, but also incautiously, slid the back of her left leg over the front of my right, relaxed it, and left it lying between my legs. "Knowing I can't do more," she said, "is being entwined, just this much, okay for you?"

"_Oh man!_" I breathed.

"_Good._ It feels nice to me too. Now a request. When my ankle gets painful in the night, I make sounds. Every time I do you pop up to help me. My request: don't pop up. If I need you I'll say so. Your load tomorrow will be insane. You need all the rest you can get."

I said, "I like putting out for you. I like it a lot."

She said, "I feel that so deeply it's time I shared some difficult things."

I tried to brace myself, but had no idea what to brace against. Sensing my uneasiness, she took my hand and held it. "Here's the hardest thing. Though I don't have the breasts in which it started, I still have the cancer I hoped their removal would remove. It's in remission, but probably not gone."

Her taking my hand. Head on my shoulder. Naked leg at rest between mine. Knowing her prognosis might crush me, she was trying to console me as she spoke of what was crushing her. It left me reeling.

"Another thing. In case you've wondered, I chose to look the way I do because my cut-rate insurance didn't cover reconstructive surgery. Radiation and chemo almost cleaned me out, and my son is likely to lose me sooner than we wish. So I want what money I've managed to save to be his."

Meeting her needs had become so automatic that I blurted, "I have money."

She turned, brow furrowed, and studied my face. Hearing myself in light of her expression, I said, "That came out stupidly. Sorry, Lore. I didn't mean to imply, <u>I have money so you can have breasts.</u> I only meant that if the woman I'm looking at, just as she is, has needs I can help with, Mu's needs included, I sold a software company I half owned not long ago and have more money than I need."

Her furrow vanished. Her head returned to my shoulder. "Explanation accepted. About my prognosis, I'm sure you have questions, but I thank you for not asking them. I prefer to deal with medical stuff when I have to and not think about it when I don't. I said as much as I've said because I sense strong feeling between us. To let those feelings grow without you knowing my prognosis isn't fair."

"So now I know. And my strong feelings are free to grow as they will."

"As are mine," Lore said. "And having shared the hard part, I feel it's time I shared the most uncanny part of my prognosis. Last year at Boundary Lake, then again at Boundary just last week, I met an old horse packer you happen to know."

"<u>Gladys?</u>" I cried.

Lore's smile went into full bloom. "She loves you, Grady. Even though she calls you 'my dear Bird-Dropping-Me'! She said I might run into you around the Blue Mosque. Who would have dreamt that would go as it did. But how right she was. And that old woman, crankiness and all, is a harbinger of hope."

Now I was reeling for several reasons, some of them beautiful to me.

"The first time we met I hadn't a clue I had cancer. Later, I realized Gladys had sensed it. Why else would she have told Mu and me that Jade's waters are imbued with a power that heals whether we live or die? A healing for the <u>long</u> journey, she called it. Last year those words only made me curious to see Jade when it fit Mu's and my schedule. That was two breasts ago. This year I felt <u>commanded</u> to come. And how glad I was when, on my way up, Gladys again showed up at Boundary."

"<u>God,</u> I miss that old woman! How is she, Lore?"

"Still spry. Wise as an owl. Still riding Ho. She gave Mormon and Anonymous to a family in Dixon to turn into plow horses. Two Sicilian donkeys carry her gear now. She loves how much easier they are on the trails and ground around her camps."

"But what went on between you?" I asked. "Tell me, if you can, about the hope."

"Our two encounters were very different. When Mu and I met her last year, she got us <u>very</u> excited about Jade, but then, in an instant, turned the magic off completely. It hurt Mu. Last week she asked me to tell Mu he's wonderful and said she was sorry for his hurt, but had no choice. I asked why not. I'm embarrassed that I remember her reply perfectly. She said: "Your remarkable nonjudgmental receptivity has prepared you for something no one I've met has been ready for. Mother Earth and her Unseen Companion want to meet with you, alone, in Jade. Not camped beside it, Lore. In it.'"

Lore's words encircled me in a whirlwind.

"From then on Gladys spoke of nothing but Jade's importance and powers, held nothing back, then handed me a book, _Lúmi Singings_, open to a rite she said to write down, learn by heart, and perform in Jade's waters -- 'to open them,' she said. On the day you saw me swimming I'd done that, and Jade _did_ open. I stayed immersed for two life-changing hours before I set out swimming, when you saw me."

My mind flew into a high-speed revision of my first glimpse of Lore. _Two hours_ immersed! This was impossible for me. As I said, every time I'd enter Jade I was overwhelmed by a dissolving sensation. The feeling was blissful, but it was a bliss born of _being unmade._ The water also seemed to convey that I might be needed in some way that meant I _shouldn't_ give way to dissolving. Recalling how serene Lore had looked as she swam, it dawned on me that her spiritual capacities are far beyond mine, and that serving _her_ might be what the mysteries ask of me. As if to confirm what I was feeling, Lore reached across me with her left hand, gently pulled at my hip, and whispered, "Please lie close."

How gladly I did so.

"Tomorrow demands too much for us to speak of Jade's gift tonight," she said. "For now I'll just say that, in the throes of it, fear of death, and of the coming storm, was impossible. Not till the second huge thunder rolled over did it strike me that the gift Jade has given is important to _many_, that the storm could destroy me, and that, if it did, the gift would be lost to all. You know better than I do what happened then."

Her voice dropped to a whisper as she lay her hand on my cheek. "How can it be that the storm _did_ destroy me, yet here I am? How can it be that your rescue of the gift's bearer also rescued the gift, though you don't even know what the gift is? I feel once again that, live or die, Jade has given me wondrous things to share with a few others. You're as responsible for this as I am. And one more thing. If we make it down, I'm going to see my oncologists again. I'm going to fight this, Grady. You and Jade have reversed my intended direction of travel. How do you feel about that?"

I lost it. "_I can't tell you!_" I gasped. "_Live long, long, long, Lorilee!_"

She began stroking my cheek to calm me, but I couldn't hold it in. "I'm sorry! Sorry, Lore! I just _really, really like you,_ is all!"

"Well, I really, really like you too. So let's put our liking to bed with us, and wake it up again at dawn."

VI. Seeking the Below

When the inner and the outer are one, and the above is
like the below, then you will enter the kingdom.
                                   —Jesus, Gospel of Thomas

And I saw the river over which every soul
must pass to reach the kingdom of heaven
and the name of that river was suffering,
and I saw the boat which carries souls across
the river, and the name of that boat was love.
                                   —Saint John of the Cross

BEGINNING THE DAY they left Moondial, Grady and Lore's descent demanded efforts so extreme that Grady's journal-keeping came to a halt. It wasn't until I, the Holy Goat, began work on these chronicles in 2012 that I was able to cobble together this partial account of their descent thanks to interviews we did eight years after the fact:

On the morning of their departure Grady seated Lore on one of the benches in the slate room, helped her pull on the saddle-pack like a bizarre pair of shorts, and guided her floppy right ankle and foot into its Levi's stirrup for safekeeping. Sliding into the pack straps, he carefully stood. As Lore's full weight left the ground he felt the joy she took in being the height of a standing human, figuring out where to place arms and hands, position legs and body, lean right or left to see round him, meld her contours to his. Taking up his forelegs, Grady walked them out into sunlight and asked Lore to lean as far as she wanted to either side, then to lean back and look skyward. As she did so he tested the effect of her shifting weight on his balance. The saddle-pack's low center of gravity and Grady's four-leggèdness so steadied him that she was able to move at will. "Are you ready to do this?" Grady asked.

Lore said, "That question's only answer is whatever happens as we try."

AS THEY LEFT Moondial a great calm had descended. The entire sky turned an even off-white that made the world feel, Lore said, "like a single huge room." The smoke was dense in the valleys but faint at elevation, a boon given the desperate work Grady's lungs began doing.

When they reached water's edge at Jade, it was mirror calm and pallid as the sky. Lore whispered, "Please stop," and pointed at a flat-topped boulder. Grady seated her on it, slipped out of the pack straps, turned—and saw that Jade had usurped her. The way she gazed at the waters reflected their warmth and depth, turning her *regal* in a way that caused strange words to form in Grady's mind: *I'm carrying a Lûmi. A takh-nekh-wakhul (no outward sign) Lûmi of the Dark Time.* They sat silent for what Grady remembered as an hour and Lore remembered as "an unveiling outside of time." When she was ready for him to help her mount up, she turned first to the lake, Mosque, minarets, and whispered, "*Thanks for every molecule of this, Your place. Thanks for housing every creature that ever was, that now is, and that ever shall be.*"

Her words made Grady feel shy of her despite their extreme physical closeness.

CROSSING DANIEL'S BRIDGE was very different from Grady's two solo crossings the day before. Because Lore wasn't bent by a massive load or half blinded by extreme effort, she guided his every step with whispered directives: *Bear right. Not that much. Perfect. A little left now. See that reddish sand? Mudstone beneath, maybe. Poke every bit of it before you step. Watch the striated rock after the sand too. It looks rotten.* Grady's task was to make countless stabs with his larch forelegs into every bit of the bridge that Lore found doubtful—and not once did they falter. By the time they crossed the arête Grady's animal trust in his rider was total.

Before long, however, the rider's trust in her animal was not. Grady planned to make Pipsissewa by nightfall, and his progress had been determined for a long time. But as they reached Gentian Couloir his strides had weakened, while his determination had not: a dangerous combination. At the brink of the couloir Lore stroked his cheek and whispered, "*Whoa, Grady horse.* Your legs have turned to rubber. Time to rest and refuel."

They dismounted in the ink-blue blossoms and filled up on water. When Lore handed Grady two energy bars, he said he wasn't hungry. "Trust the one of us whose mind hasn't flatlined from exertion," she said. "You need these. I insist."

While Grady chewed his unwanted cuds, Lore got out the Trinovids and studied the smoke-blanketed foothills, soon spotting three air tankers, tiny as gnats in the distance, passing in and out of the smoke as they dumped slurry on unseen flames. Lore had hoped a packer, ideally Sam Rock, might happen along and give them a ride out, but the tankers left her sure the Elkmoon Wilderness was closed. Seeing the mountains to the east buried in dense smoke, she prayed the wind didn't change direction. Realizing they faced dangers they hadn't anticipated, she said, "We're on our own, Grady. One stumble and fall would finish us. So please forget about reaching Pipsissewa. Just focus on your next step. I'll be feeling for when you need to stop. I'm also noticing how steep this couloir is. What's your strategy here?"

"First, thanking you," Grady said. "The energy bars restored my ability to think." He showed her the tips of his larch forelegs, which were smashed to a pulp by his stabbings on Daniel's Bridge. He sharpened the pulp to points with his hunting knife, attached traction cleats to his boots, helped Lore into the saddle-pack, and descended the couloir in a sideways four-leggèd crab walk, on two legs of larch, and two legs of his own. On the steepest pitches he even walked backward, as if descending a ladder, stabbing the staves into the ground *behind* them to serve as brakes. When the couloir ended on the good footing of the Elkmoon batholith, Lore again stroked his cheek.

Their progress remained slow and steady, hours passed, and Lore simply tracked the angle of the sun and energy in Grady's body until she said, "We're done. You're rubbery again. But look where you managed to bring us!"

Due to total focus on his next step, Grady hadn't noticed they were trailing along a little spring creek. The spring rose from the base of a small cirque, flowed a short distance through sand and rock, then disappeared under a brilliant green moss carpet forty yards long and five to ten yards wide. When the rill reappeared at the moss's downstream end, it broke up into a multitude of tiny channels that poured over a five-foot granite slide, whispering down into a quiet pool. Lore marveled at the sight. "Don't those strands of water look as if we're in a jet at thirty-five thousand feet, peering down on some great river delta?"

Feeling more like a jet out of fuel and about to crash, Grady could only grunt as he freed her from the saddle-pack, picked her up in his arms, seated her in the trekker chair at pool's edge, and removed her bandage and splint. Just as Lore eased her ankle into the chill water she whispered, *"Straight behind you! Fifty yards out!"*

Just as Grady turned, some forty elk cows and calves and a magnificent bull strolled unawares over a swell in the batholith, spotted the two of them, stuck their noses high in the air to verify them by scent, turned, trotted a brisk quarter mile, and appeared to sink into the earth among treetops that struck Grady as somehow familiar. For one thing, they were a baffling gold color. "Are those the larches that donated your forelegs?" Lore asked.

"Gosh! I'm so brain dead I didn't recognize 'em," Grady sputtered. "We're closer to Pipsissewa than I thought. In the morning I'll resupply from the canister Sam hid near the lake. For tonight's dinner I'll heat the leftover rice and beans we packed."

"I'm so sorry you're having to do absolutely everything," Lore said.

"And I'm sorry I'm shitty company. But at least I can still help you out."

AN HOUR LATER, sated bellies and a tiny fire left them lying in their shared sleeping bag under smoke-dimmed stars. Turning to Grady, Lore said,

"Given our ultimate destination and the people you'll encounter there, it's time I told you a little story I once heard about your former self. Ready?"

Grady blinked in surprise. "Ready for stories of my former self? *Not likely!*"

But Lore began speaking in the manner of an old myth-teller in love with the strangeness of her tale. "Once upon a time, for one summer and fall, you had a girlfriend whose dark hair was as uncontainable as her mind."

Solving the riddle instantly, Grady grew short of breath.

"She was tall, stunning, and even more beautiful inside than out. Her great loves were mystical traditions—the Beguines, Eckhart, the Vedic and bhakti traditions of India. She was also funny, and you could see her humor approaching before it arrived. When her grin expanded, a gap in her front teeth appeared through which all kinds of mischief poured."

"*This is stupendous!*" Grady blurted. "How long have you known her, Lore?"

"Six years. We swapped stories about our exes early on, and she named you, but at Moondial I was too pain-addled to make the connection until day four. Knowing an almost impossible hike lay ahead of us, I then chose not to distract you with such an epic coincidence. But with the scariest stretch of our hike over it's a joy to tell you, Risa is the closest friend I've ever had. There are no words for how dear she is to me! You should also know that, when she spoke of your time together, her glee grin always appeared first, most of her tales were hilarious, and even when she described finding Rose in your bed she placed no blame. She said your life needed purpose. She felt the Elkmoons would provide it. When she learns that sense of purpose saved my life, she's going to levitate! What are you feeling, Grady?"

"*Crippled* with happiness! That our descent will connect the two best women I've ever met is unreal! And that Risa forgives our sloppy breakup rids me of a shame I've carried for years. But, Lore. If I don't sleep now I'll be walking into tree trunks tomorrow."

They eased into the entwinement they loved, Lore up against Grady with her head on his shoulder, the back of her left leg lying between his two. But before he could summon a single "*Oh man!*" Grady was *gone*.

IN THE MIDDLE of the night he woke to Lore coughing so violently it forced ankle movements that left her fetal with pain. Grady began to hack too. The smoke had climbed the Elkmoons, burying them alive. Their eyes burned and lungs ached in ways they'd never known. Lore's coughs and cries of pain were a nightmare. Grady had but one feeble idea for a next move. They'd brought Lore's ultralight one-person tent in case of rain. Grady set it up, removed the rainfly butt-sling from the saddle-pack, spread the fly over the mesh sections of the tent to seal out smoke, and secured the fly with duct tape. He then lay Lore at the tent's entrance, lay on his belly beside her, and she dragged herself onto his back and held on as he crawled them inside. "Our cotton T-shirts are the only air filters we've got," he said. "Let's use them and hope for the best."

After a gruesome couple of hours their coughing eased enough that they were able to doze. A few bad dreams later, Grady woke to the sound of Lore moaning. He switched on a lantern. She was hot to the touch. He dipped a washcloth in water and began wiping her forehead, neck, arms. She grew hotter. He added Tylenol to her Advil and kept wetting her skin, which heated the cloth so fast it felt useless.

Lore began to whisper in what sounded like a delirium, yet made an awful kind of sense: "We're trapped in the Industrial Fallout Bardo, Grady. Everything in which we place faith turns into falsehoods here. Listen. *The solace of nature. The majestic Elkmoons. The ten thousand things that appear when self disappears.* What solace? What majesty? What ten thousand things? There's nothing in this bardo but smoke and lies."

"You're burning up and I want to cool you. That's no lie," Grady said. "And smoke this bad does something good. It's smothering the fires, Lore. The air will improve. Don't give up. Tell me what I can *do* for you. There's got to be something."

"There is," she said, her voice an eerie rasp. "Stop placing faith in me being all right. We're not here to be all right. What we feared has arrived. This fever means my foot is dying—and don't pray for it not to. The Fallout Bardo will turn your prayer into a lie."

Heartsick with helplessness, Grady kept wiping her with the cloth.

SEPTEMBER 7TH BROUGHT a sallow light and a hundred or so yards of visibility. Between coughing fits they told each other the smoke had lessened. They knew it was a lie, but their food supply was down to its last day. In the windless calm of a Rocky Mountain Indian summer, wildfire smoke can remain dense for weeks. They needed Sam's canister. To reach it, the Fallout Bardo had to be traversed.

Grady reckoned them to be less than two miles from Pipsissewa. All landmarks were erased, but he told Lore he'd find the lake by compass. They set out, and he kept up a slow trudge despite his hacking cough. Lore's faith in his trudge lasted for four hours before she said, "We've walked far too long not to have arrived. Tell me we're lost so the bardo turns our lostness into a lie."

"It's already a lie," Grady wheezed, and he pointed. Fifty yards ahead was water's edge. "I've slid many a trout onto that triangular rock. Unless the Fallout Bardo has the power to rearrange the world's furniture, a hundred yards to the left we'll find three gnarled old white pines and a perfect campsite beneath them."

They traversed the yards. There were the pines, with massive boles and bark like dragon scales, near a fire ring and plenty of wood that Grady had stashed in June. But the smoke turned the charismatic camp into a lie. Their sole, sorely insufficient shelter was the tiny tent. Setting it up and helping Lore inside, Grady handed her a can of bear spray. "Sorry to leave you, but we need the contents of Sam's canister desperately. I'll be back as soon as I can."

"I won't say 'Stay safe' so the bardo can't make my words a lie."

"Thanks," Grady said, and vanished.

Who knew how long later, Lore woke to the tent door unzipping.

Grady shoved his heavily loaded day pack through and followed it, smiling. Sam Rock had been prescient. He'd left cough drops, eye drops, four of the filtration masks used by firefighters, antibiotic ointment, arnica cream, more Tylenol, two ACE bandages, adhesive moleskin for Grady's ravaged feet, and enough high-calorie food to last an easy five days.

Grady refueled. Meds and masks eased their coughing. They slept like the dead.

INHABITANTS OF THE twenty-first-century West know this brand of story too well, so I'll speed it up: on the 8th they woke to a mere fifty yards of visibility. Depression rendered them speechless. Their planning session was Grady wheezing, "I can get us to Boundary in this shit," and Lore rasping, "Let's go." The lake was eight miles due east. Grady's straining under his load forced him to breathe so hard that his cough turned into paroxysms that stopped him cold. Three miles took four hours. Well short of Boundary, Lore pleaded with him to put up the tent. Once inside they collapsed in their clothes, and for seventeen hours stirred just enough to inadequately address thirst, pain, hunger, and bladders in need of emptying.

They woke on the 9th as half-paralyzed pieces of human wreckage, but Grady found a desperation gear of small but unceasing steps that got them to Boundary. He pitched camp on an unfamiliar stretch of lakeshore. After settling Lore in the tent, he donned his headlamp and was stepping down to the lake to refill water bottles when he tripped on a root nub, fell forward on the steep slant of the shore, and slammed the batholith hard, bone-bruising both knees, the heels of his hands, and his forehead. Pain kept him awake half the night.

On the 10th, still smoke-smothered, Lore bandaged Grady's hands and knees enough to let him grip his larch forelegs and dodder the level mile to Gateway Pass. Reaching the brink of the 30 percent grade down to the West Fork footbridge, one of the most beautiful views in the world resembled a back alley leading into hell. "What do you think?" Lore asked.

"No resting places between here and the footbridge, or on the long climb up the canyon's far side. My grip is weak. My knees barely bend. I need food, meds, and rest. Sorry."

She stroked his cheek. "No apologies. Your efforts have amazed me."

As Grady tottered along the canyon rim seeking level ground for a camp, a small good thing happened: they came upon a single ancient five-needle white pine with a massive, sun-spiraled bole. Its enormous roots gripped boulders they'd broken to pieces centuries ago. Walled in by these roots was a bed of white sand identical to the sand near the foot of Daniel's Bridge and in the marble tub at Moondial. "*A Lûmi bed!*" Lore whispered.

In the misery of the Fallout Bardo, this kindness to unmet wayfarers made Grady cry. Stunned by his tears, Lore defied her smoke-wrecked voice and, for the first time ever, sang to him, ad-libbing lyrics to a classic the way she'd once done for Walt Steitz:

If from the Fallout Bardo you and I make our escape
I'll carry in my heart this tree that gives our bed its shape
Though Earth can't help but share with us the awful wounds she's
*   borne*
Come in, the white pine sings, I'll give you shelter from the storm.

Early morning, September 11th, Grady woke to shaking tent walls and Lore's face smiling at him from inches away. "It's been blowing for hours," she said. "The air smells fresh. Peek outside and see if it's a lie."

Unzipping his salamander exit, Grady peeked. "*The Fallout Bardo is gone!*" he cried.

Pulling on his boots, he defied knee and hand pain, maneuvered Lore outside, scooped her up in his arms, carried her to the rim of the canyon, and not till he set her on a sun-warmed rock did he see that they were still dressed in dirty underwear. Eye bags, haggard faces, filthy hair, and all, they laughed and cried.

As Lore basked in clean air, early sunlight, and vistas to the horizon, a rush of energy exploded the helplessness that had weakened Grady for days. He delivered her trekker chair and clothes, then hot water and washcloths to bathe, then coffee and breakfast. After eating, he washed their dishes with sand, broke camp, loaded Lore, manned his larch forelegs despite his wounds, and made heavy use of the crab walk to saddle-pack her the four miles down to the West Fork footbridge.

He had just seated her on a low streamside rock to soak her ankle in a plunge pool when Lore gasped, "*Good God! Look up the trail!*"

Grady turned. Not three hundred yards up the steep slope leading to Halfway, two shirtless men in running shorts were approaching at break-neck speed. To avoid a fatal fall into the canyon their concentration was total. They weren't forty yards off when they finally glanced up, gaped, slammed to a halt, grinned, and approached at a walk.

Their names were Garrett and Coy. They offered handshakes till they saw Grady's bandages, then smiled down at Lore but saw her ankle, bandaged and splinted. When she asked if the wilderness wasn't closed due to fire after all, Garrett said, "We're poaching it."

Confused by her fever, Lore said, "In a wilderness area? What are you poaching?"

"Just access," Coy said with a grin. "The Wilderness *is* closed.

We're long-distance trail runners. When the smoke cleared, we drove up and lit out for Boundary for our first run in an awful week. But what the hell's happened to you two? You've been through a war! Congrats on the ingenious pack alteration, but how serious is that ankle injury?"

"Can you answer?" Lore asked Grady. "I feel queasy."

"It's bad," he told them. "Happened in the storm that started the fires. We were thirty miles into backcountry and nine thousand feet up, and yes, getting here has been a war. We'll head to a hospital soon as we make it down."

Coy's expression took on authority. "I'm an ex-paramedic and still treat athletic injuries at the college where Garrett and I teach. May I have a look?"

When Lore nodded, Grady and Garrett lifted her in the trekker chair, carried her up to a level stone slab by the trail, and Grady removed her bandage and splint. When Coy saw the ankle, he blurted, "*Christ!*" As he examined the injury closely he grilled Grady about its cause, Lore's levels of pain, fever symptoms, queasiness, then didn't mince words. "I hate to reward your courage with this, Lore, but your ankle isn't sprained. It's totally dislocated, and cutting off so much circulation that the foot is dying. I advise a Life Flight to Missoula and we're here to serve. We'll break records getting to the nearest cell coverage to call the flight in. Any advice on where to find that coverage, Grady?"

"There's none in the mountains or on the upper Elkmoon. But if Elsewhere didn't burn there's a landline in the tiny store and post office. It's ten miles downriver from the trailhead."

"Elsewhere survived," Coy said. "I'm guessing a Life Flight could be here in four to five hours. Can you make it to the big meadow at Halfway inside of that, Grady?"

"I'll get us there in three hours," Grady said.

"If for some reason a chopper can't come," Garrett said, "Coy and I will be at Halfway in five to six hours with a stretcher to carry Lore to a bed in the back of my van, and drive you to Missoula ourselves. That's a promise."

"The two most underdressed saints I ever met," Lore managed to say.

"Need energy bars? Chocolate? Gas money? A couple of dirty shirts?" Grady asked.

They patted their fanny packs. "We're set," Garrett said. "A pleasure to help."

"Have faith, Lore," Coy added. "Surgeons work miracles on injuries like yours."

And they were off up the slope at an improbable rate of speed.

ENERGIZED BY HOPE, Grady covered the four miles to Halfway in under three hours. En route, Lore told him their time was short and she needed to speak of things that required complete calm and quiet. "There's a place," Grady said, and struck out for a stand of lodgepoles in the meadow's very center. "My hidden camp for years," he said.

The pines enclosed a quiet oxbow, and the instant Grady seated Lore in the mottled shade, her face shone with pure solace. The streambank was grassy, its edges dense with forget-me-nots. Brook trout lazed in the slow, deep flow. Grady fetched Lore the raisins and almonds she always managed to nibble despite lack of appetite. "To say what needs saying," she said, "I need to lie down."

Grady spread their bedroll, helped her settle, and lay down beside her.

"When I saw Gladys ten days ago," she began, "she told me that if I was able to reach Jade, immerse, and speak the rite said to open the waters, I must use a voice as close as possible to silent. 'Half the breath of the softest whisper,' Volkmann says in the *Singings*. For that softest of voices to be heard"—she sent Grady an unexpected smile—"I need intimate access to your ear."

Grady sighed happily, rolled onto his back, and lay still.

Lore moved every part of her body but her right leg and ankle against him, placed her lips at the entrance to his ear, and began putting so little breath into her words that the main sounds were just her lips, tongue, and inner walls of her mouth breaking tiny bonds of saliva. Yet her barely audible words held Grady spellbound. This was not the helpless woman with whom he'd staggered through the Fallout Bardo. This was, once again, the Lore who struck him as a *tahk-nehk-wakhul* (no outward sign) Lûmi of the Dark Time.

That resemblance makes what I, the Holy Goat, *don't* say more important than what I say: Lore's half-whispers swam them through deep secrets of the Lûmi. Those secrets must be kept. I realize that, in our strife-torn world, secrecy is distrusted due to association with wars, espionage, criminality, betrayals, hacking, identity theft, and so on. But knee-jerk broadcasts of what *should* remain secret have turned countless world wonders into lost mobs of clueless tourists. The truth is, we've never left an ancient world in which, to be fully human, we must enter a sanctuary in which it's possible to surpass the merely human. When Lore's lips moved to Grady's ear, they both entered such a sanctuary. Until the Life Flight arrived her lucidity never faltered as she brought Jade's gift to life in him. If what she shared were to reach a website and Lûmi locations went viral it would destroy what makes these people and places who and what they are—and don't think I haven't protected all that in these chronicles: the Inner Elkmoons and Boundary Lake aren't so easy to find.

After Lore departed in the Life Flight, Grady stayed on by the oxbow that night and half the next day, writing out every fragment of her outpouring that he could recall. True to the Lûmi need for secrecy, he shared those fragments with Lorilee alone, and she created a handmade booklet of them that she carried with her everywhere for the rest of her life. The forthcoming chapter, "The Queendom-Come Shards," are the words in that small booklet.

As for my own account of Lore and Grady's descent from Jade, I'll end with a letter Lore sent shortly after we concluded our 2012 interviews:

Dear HG,

After reading your account of our descent, I was moved to add this personal aside. Please consider including it in your chronicles:

I know a few people who speak of the spiritual path as if it's an app on a handheld device that enables them to take recreational Spiritual Path Hikes whenever the urge strikes. While I try not to judge such talk, I don't hurt my head trying to believe it either. It's simply the truth that, for me, no such path has ever existed. What I've experienced, so far as I can describe it, are effacements of self that allow something vast and merciful to envelop me in a Now outside of time. Some of these disappearances arrive via practices: meditating at Blue Empty; performing music in bluish venues; being seized by the cries of avocets; holding the antiquity of a fossil named Bivalve in my hand; surrendering to a once-in-a-lifetime ability to translate Two Medicine Peak's emanations into five songs in one night.

These visitations are so unlike a walk down any kind of path that I had written that metaphor off completely, when fate arranged that I spend eight days with my arms and legs wrapped around the straining body of a man creating a path in exactly the way Antonio Machado and Gautama Buddha describe. Machado: "Wayfarer, the only way / is your footsteps, there is no other. / Wayfarer, there is no way, / you make the way by walking." The Buddha: "No one saves us but ourselves. No one can and no one may. We ourselves must walk the path."

You already know that Grady saved my life at terrible cost to his own. You know he was my sole means of being doctored, warmed or cooled, nourished, encouraged, dressed, able to answer the call of nature, helped outside or in, be put to bed. But what no one but me will ever know is how it felt to ride on his back over the seven days he served as our sole means of locomotion, our only functioning pair of stone-bruised feet, our much more ingenious second pair of hands, our far stronger arms, legs, lungs, pulse, giving my body agency when it had none of its own. This man who rued his exhaustion-dulled wit was carrying a hundred-eighty insane pounds over twenty-eight brutal mountain miles through smoke so crippling it's given him chronic asthma for life. This man and I absorbed so much smoke that our skin kept releasing the reek of it for three days and nights after the skies cleared. This man who'd never heard the Gospel of Thomas promise that "When the inner and the outer are one, and the above is like the below...then you will enter the kingdom," carried a gift from the Above of a lake the Lûmi consider the beating heart of their cosmos to the Below of our impending Elkmoon Valley home. This man, upon reaching that home, set about doing such excellent starfish work alongside my dearest friends and son in a place "the Corporate Person" wanted cremated that our descendants may one day grow back an entire living star.

On our white sand bed among the white pine's roots, that last night at Gateway, this same man, knowing nothing of the good to come, had used himself up so completely that, as I was kissing him my thanks, he passed out into a sleep so deathlike that, until I lay my ear upon his heart, I feared he'd fallen into something worse than a coma.

To quell the tears that rose to feel him so gone, I kept on kissing him.

VII. The Queendom-Come Shards

Anyone who has swum through Love's depths
Now with deep hunger, now with full satiety
Neither withering nor blossoming can harm
And no season can help:
In the deepest waters, on the highest gradients,
Love's being remains unalterable.

—Hadewijch of Brabant

THE CREATION OF the Queendom-Come Shards came about primarily be-cause Lore's departure from Halfway turned out to be horrific. Lying by the oxbow with Grady, lowering her voice to the half-whisper the Lûmi recom-mend when speaking the unspeakable, she poured out her Jade experience for nearly an hour. Her account left them moved beyond words—with no way of knowing an eight-thousand-foot ridge and sharp bend in the West Fork canyon formed a total acoustic blockade just downstream of them.

With little more warning than a lightning strike, the silence at Halfway exploded in a roar of engine and whammering of blades as the Life Flight approached like a Cobra gunship. The blast of sound hurled Lore into PTSD. Reliving the lightning bolt and fall that nearly killed her, she began hyperventilating, her skin went clammy, her lips turned blue. Trying to protect her, Grady lifted her into the trekker chair and wrapped her in his arms, but the chopper dropped onto the meadow so close to them that rotor downwash blasted their faces with flying debris. When a male nurse and female paramedic immediately descended from a bi-fold side door, pulled down a bright red stretcher, and turned Lore's way, her long courage at last collapsed. *"DON'T LET THEM TAKE ME!"* she cried. *"I WANT TO STAY WITH YOU!"* *"SORRY I'M YELLING!"* Grady hollered, *"BUT I'LL SEE YOU SOON! YOU NEED THIS SURGERY! THIS IS SO YOU CAN WALK!"* *"WHAT!?"* she shouted. *"WHAT!?"* And the medics were upon her. *"I'M JAKE! THIS IS ARDITH! WE'LL LEAVE THE SAM SPLINT ON TILL WE GET YOU IN THE FLYING HOSPITAL!"* Lifting her out of Grady's arms, they lay her on the stretcher. *"I DON'T WANT THIS, GRADY! AT LEAST COME WITH ME! PLEASE!"* she cried as Ardith rubbed her shoulder—to soothe her, Grady thought. *"HE*

CAN'T! CABIN'S FULL!" Jake bellowed. "BUT HE'S HURT! HE'S JUST HIDING IT!" Lore cried. "I'LL BE FINE, LORE. YOUR ABILITY TO WALK IS AT STAKE! WE'LL MEET UP SOON!" Grady hollered. "THAT'LL TAKE THE EDGE OFF!" Ardith yelled and Lore turned to see she'd given her an injection she hadn't felt. The "friendly" shoulder rub had numbed her with lidocaine. "I DIDN'T WANT THAT! WHAT WAS THAT?" she cried. "FENTANYL!" Ardith hollered.

Lore let out a weak "NO!" as they strapped her to the stretcher. Grady handed Jake her wallet: "LORE'S I.D.!" "THANKS GRADY!" Jake bellowed. "GREAT JOB BRINGING HER SO FAR! TAKE CARE ON YOUR HIKE OUT!" "No!" Lore whimpered as they hoisted her and set out under the blades. Grady closed his eyes as the downwash blasted him, hoping she saw the blind kisses he kept blowing her. But as the chopper lifted off Lore wasn't even on board: she was free-falling off the breast of her beloved Mother into a dark, doped oblivion.

WHEN THE LIFE Flight rounded the high ridge downstream, its slamming and roar vanished as fast as it had arrived. Alone in the silence after twelve days of extreme intimacy, Lore's parting distress left Grady gutted. He lay down on the indentations left in the bedroll by their bodies, let himself sob to release his dismay, and like a stone tossed into the deep end of Jade, plummeted into fathomless sleep.

HE WOKE BY the Oxbow to early sunlight and a murmuring of slow water so like Lore's half-whisper that he remained motionless, surrendering to the sound. Time ceased to pass, replaced by a conjuring. Long portions of the sentences Lore had as much kissed as whispered into his ear flowed past in a current so slow and easy to capture that he was unwilling to let them flow away.

He left the bedroll, dressed, dug out his mountain journal, made espresso, seated himself in Lore's stream-side chair, and set down every word the waters made available. With Grady's apologies for gopher-trapping Jade's gift in American English, but in support of Lore's belief that his rendering of her half-whispers do anchor a few profound Lûmi truths, here are:

The Queendom-Come Shards
Lore's first two sentences are inscribed on my heart:
The Lûmi name for Earth is Sun House. To tell you of Jade's gift is to tell you why this name comes as close as words can to truth.

PARAPHRASING, OR SOMETIMES QUOTING, Lore's half-whisper:
Deep inside the Earth, but directly connected to Jade, is a gift inherent and overwhelming which an occasional rare human can glimpse, or even access. This gift, if received in full, makes the ensouled and embodied Earth *the Enlightenment Planet.*

* * *

LORE'S IMMERSION IN Jade revealed what she called "a male/female polarity inherent in the universe." Lûmi mythology gets at this polarity by describing the relationship between Earth and Sun. In *Lûmi Singings*, Volkmann marvels that the Sun is burning *four million tons of himself per second*. Without Sun's total self-immolation the endless life-forms Earth creates and sustains could not exist.

THE LÛMI SEE a tragic side to Sun's sacrifice. Earth is the intimate mother of the countless life-forms she and Sun create out of his energy and her body, but the Sun must remain distanced from their co-creations, lest he incinerate them.

Rather than pity the Sun, Lûmi mythology sees Sun's isolation as a limitation that can be overcome. They call Earth's core her star-heart. In *Lûmi Singings* Volkmann says this heart is not molten liquid, as many imagine. It's an unimaginably pressurized 9,800-degree Fahrenheit solid. Yet even so, say the Lûmi, this solid is a *house*. The ensouled and embodied Earth is the house's famous resident, but it also houses a more mysterious resident whose Presence Lore experienced in Jade.

SHE INTRODUCED HER immersion experience to me with the Informant's favorite Rumi lines: *By which way did Earth become connected in the womb with the beauteous Sun? By the hidden way that is remote from sense-perception.* For the Lûmi, this *hidden way* is the downward path the meteorite opened up beneath the Mosque, allowing Jade's waters to travel so deep they made contact with what they describe as "the divine female present everywhere and in everything." But inside Earth's star-heart this deity existed in what the Lûmi call a *Beyond State*—"an uncreated state transcending all forms of consciousness and unconsciousness," Volkmann writes, "untouched by Time and Space, impervious to the heat and pressure of Earth's core."

The meteorite's arrival, say the Lûmi, coincided with the divine female leaving the *Beyond State* to enliven Jade's waters. Their myth about this says that the divine female summoned the meteorite "to make a Way," establishing a point of intense contact with Earth, ongoing to this day.

IN *LÛMI SINGINGS* Volkmann introduces the divine female by saying that, just as every man, woman, and child is composed of a mortal body and an undying soul, and just as the Sun is composed of the mortal body blazing in the sky and an undying spiritual Sun—the *Suraj*, it's called in India—so is Earth composed of a mortal planet body and an undying resident who is every earthly body's spiritual Mother.

The Lûmi cosmos, Lore breathed into me in the half-whisper, was born of the arrival of this Mother from the Beyond. She is an Omnipresence named in languages the world over. She is the *Gahan-ka'isht,* the Lûmi holy of holies. She is the Greek's *Sophia*, the embodiment of infinite creative power. She is Solomon's *divine wisdom, who because of her purity pervades and penetrates all things*. She is Lao Tzu's *eternal Mother of All; the Mysterious Female; She who was before heaven and earth came to be*. "And how I love Lao Tzu," Lore said, "for humbly adding, *I do not know her name*."

IN THE JADE rite Lore had memorized, the pilgrim is to enter Jade up to her clavicle, remaining receptive and free of thought as she immerses. She is then to open her hands to a Sun ray and bend it down into her heart, without a thought as to whether this is possible. What the Lûmi call "hidden properties of the heart" then shunt the ray down into Jade's immeasurable depths. "But before the waters even reached my waist," Lore told me in the half-whisper, "I had an overpowering sense that I'd entered the *wound* the meteorite left in the Earth, and that this wound is the *activator*, the *awakener*, of the Mother's full creativity. And no wonder the feeling frightened you, Grady. Awake and active, the Mother makes our individual existence unnecessary the way a drop is unnecessary to the Ocean. But what becomes of the fragile individuality that allows a drop to be a drop? *Joy!* Fearlessly surrendering to all that She is, I felt Jade urging me to leave the marble slab and swim circles over the deeps created by her wound. I obeyed instantly."

As soon as Lore set out swimming slow circles, "love and touch became inseparable, and it was the same loving touch, in the myth-language about Jade, that is the Mysterious Female's great gift to the Sun. Without her touch Sun only experiences himself. Because of her touch, every least form that Earth and Sun co create is now experienced by both of them as the fruit of Earth's boundless creativity and Sun's blazing self-sacrifice, blissfully fused."

And the Mother of All is the infinite opposite of a being capable of performing just one act at a time. As Lore navigated the wound-water, her experience became intensely personal. "The lake's temperature so perfectly matched my own that I felt no boundary between my body and Jade's Mother-infused body, which gave me access to some of what's hidden in her at the same time it gave Jade *total* access to what's hidden in me. I sensed her experiencing me *completely*; felt her at-oneness with my cancer, my sacrificed breasts, my chemo and radiation; my every thought, feeling, fear, passions; my music, son Mu, Risa, all my friends, and the solace of being known in such compassionate completeness left me sobbing with gratitude."

From that moment on, immersion in Earth/Sophia's presence suffused Lore with shock after shock of wonder even when the Mother's revelations were forbidding. Lore felt, graphically, how even as Earth is being decimated by humanity, she is giving birth. And these births are not like animal or human births. Earth's child is not so much Earth's infant as she is Earth herself, re-creating herself via innumerable nativities. Lore saw newborn creatures and objects unknown to her—things that perhaps didn't exist till the moment Lore perceived them. The births were occurring in out-of-the-way places all over Earth's body: extreme ocean deeps; extreme mountain heights; all the way down in Earth's core; inside a far subtler world within our world. "Though Earth is the one giving birth to regenerative multitudes and Sun the one energizing them," came the half-whisper, "the *instigator* of the births is the Earth/Sophia unity. The feeling was crystal clear: *Earth/ Sophia, being Creativity herself, can no more* not *create than can the Sun/ Suraj unity not shine.*"

SOPHIA OFFERED LORE a spirit-thread of Earth's, Sun's, and Sophia's united love. The instant Lore took hold of it she experienced a gigantic circling movement shared by all life-forms, by the elements earth, fire, water, air, ether, and by forms that science considers lifeless such as gases and stone. Inside the great circling, what we call *death* is not a form's end but its passage into a remaking. Innumerable living things born of Earth's body, Sun's energy, and Sophia's creativity pass the departing form's essence on to its next mortal vessel. In full surrender to this, Lore experienced the breakdowns and deaths of all created things and beings, herself included, as inseparable from the love in which she still stood immersed. "But as Volkmann insists, *there is no understanding this.* The great joy is beyond understanding."

SOPHIA AIMED HER toward all the violence, unmaking, and strife of the Now and showed her hard things. She revealed that four humans are born per second in our time and only two die, an impossible imbalance Earth/Sophia must address for vibrant life to be restored. She revealed that the industries savaging Earth will not willingly cease, "so they will cease *unwillingly*, in disastrous ways they've brought down upon themselves." She revealed that the exploiters of fossil fuels, especially, have weaponized Earth's climate to a degree so extreme that the exploiters themselves have no more chance of escape than the species, ecosystems, and cultures they've sent into oblivion. "Yet, imperceptible to horror-struck reason, the love remains."

SOPHIA REVEALED THAT the sixth Great Extinction will be terrible, yet no more permanent than the previous known five. She revealed that when gaping voids appear in the human-savaged Chain of Being, Earth/Sophia unleashes an evolutionary opportunism that fills these voids with creative speed, power, and variations beyond imagining. She revealed that it's never too late to align with this creativity, for it lives wild in our breast through the centuries. She revealed that hope lies not just in the dwindling life-forms eking out an existence under the monstrous impacts of industry, but in new life-forms that will rise out of the industrial monster's carcass. She revealed that what feels like apocalypse to those who savage the Earth is not a punishment meted out by a vengeful God, but a strict karmic equation balancing countless acts of violent human folly to restore fecundity and beauty to our ensouled planet's body. She revealed that this restoration can only be done at nature's regal, non-human pace, "yet no matter what sufferings befall humans because of that slow pace, *the love remains*."

SHE REVEALED, IN the strangely piercing near-silence of Lore's half-whisper, "that all created things and beings move unstoppably through death and rebirth because, just as Dogen has it, *All the universe is one bright pearl that reaches to the eternal present, and in the eternal past never ceased to be.* And just as Julian of Norwich has it, *we shall be tempested, we shall be travailed, we shall be dis-eased, we shall pass through death, but we shall not be overcome, and all manner of wounded and vanished things shall be well.*"

WITH THAT LORE'S lips left my ear, she rolled onto her back, we gazed up into blue morning sky, and when she spoke again she used her ordinary soft voice:

"To get to the heart of what Jade left me feeling, I'll share an intuition of Risa's. The night before I set out for Jade I called her to say I was going into the Inner Elkmoons alone to seek what Gladys called *a being for whom, faced with the mortality of all that we love, we sooner or later burn.* I feel my burning, I told her. I must do this while my body still can.

"*Then take this with you*," she said, and in seconds she emailed a poem she felt might speak to what I'd experience. It's by a thirteenth-century Marathi poet, Jnaneshwar, who Risa called *great the way Sita/Ram are great.* (Typical Risa!) I haven't memorized it, it's in my pack somewhere. But I remember the first and last couplets, and the gist.

"First couplet: *Without the God, no Goddess. Without the Goddess, no God. How sweet is their love!* Then come all these mind-stopping paradoxes: *The universe is too small to contain them, yet they live joyously inside the most infinitesimal particle… The life of one is the life of the other and not a blade of grass can grow without them both…Two sarods making one music, two roses one fragrance, two lanterns one light.* And the last couplet: *Appearing separate, forever joined, mirrors each revealing the other, she is his pure partner and can't live without her Lord, and He, the One who can do all things, without her cannot even appear!*

She rolled into and against me, and again found the cave of my ear:

"The heart of a mountain is never its summit," came the warm breath; the inner walls of mouth, lips, tongue breaking tiny bonds of saliva. "Like Jnaneshwar's God and Goddess, the Elkmoon heart pulsing in Jade reveals a *Sun/Suraj Earth/Sophia* Twoness-in-One in which endless self-giving is creation's purpose and its bliss. That's why, in honor of Earth's union with her mirrored beloved, the Lûmi gave our planet the self-giving name Earth/Sophia herself would choose: *Sun House.*

(the impending Elkmoon Beguine & Cattle Company, autumn 2003 through 2016)

VIII. Holy Purchase the Great

I am increasingly attracted by the idea that there can be
at least small pockets where life and character and beauty
and meaning continue. If I could help protect one of those
from destruction, maybe that would be enough.
                                                    —Paul Kingsnorth

You have to have this sense of faith that what you're
moving toward is already done. That it's already
happened. And you live as if you're already there.
                                                    —Congressman John Lewis

THE EVENT THAT banished NorBanCo from the Elkmoon Valley for good
occurred six weeks after the Grand Lodge burned, when Tex Schiller and
NorBanCo CEO Cecil Danforth were deposed by the insurance company
investigating the fire. Danforth had phoned Tex beforehand to be sure their
stories aligned, then wrote this deposition statement:

> From my home in Dallas at 3:58 a.m. Central on the night of the
> fire, I spoke by phone with our excellent man in Montana, Charles
> Keynes Schiller, and was anguished to learn that our magnificent lodge
> and grounds had lost power, that countless burning brands driven by
> raging winds had overwhelmed Schiller's efforts to protect the lodge,
> and that even as we spoke it was burning to the ground. Knowing all
> was lost, I prioritized Mr. Schiller's safety and ordered him to evacuate
> while he still could.

Tex, meanwhile, had been scapegoated for a pine beetle plague that
NorBanCo's entire board had completely ignored, insulted by Danforth
with a massive pay cut and demotion that reduced him to a security guard/
janitor, and rewarded for a decade of service with an order to burn down
the lodge he considered his greatest achievement. Tex's rage over those
betrayals are why, when he peeked out of the lodge on the night of the fire
and saw that TJ had recorded him firing Kale's crew at Danforth's order,
it occurred to Tex to emulate TJ, deploy the mini-cassette recorder in his

office, capture his and Danforth's last phone conversation and present his boss with a deposition surprise:

> From the Grand Lodge veranda on the night of the fire I spoke by phone to CEO Cecil Danforth twice. During the first call Danforth had threatened me with career-ending slander if I refused to douse the lodge with diesel and burn it down. The diesel was meant to run generators to power the lodge's and grounds' sprinkler systems in case of a public utilities power outage. When that outage occurred, my crew arrived promptly to start the generators and protect the lodge, but Danforth ordered me to fire the crew, arrest them for trespass if they tried to save the lodge, lie that burning brands driven by high winds overwhelmed me, leave all my personal possessions in the lodge to make his lie more convincing, and burn it to the ground. His previous threats overwhelmed my better judgment and I poured the diesel as ordered. But before lighting it I called Danforth a second time, said I couldn't obey his orders, and recorded the attached tape of his screams and threats as proof that I was acting upon his brutal demands. I have also attached two August 31 Western Montana weather reports proving the wind Danforth describes as "raging" had died down to 2 to 3 mph and reversed direction, as I tried to tell him, causing the fires to turn back on themselves and burn out. I have filed suit against NorBanCo collectively and Danforth personally for the trauma it has caused me to be forced to this reprehensible act.

When the nickname "NorBanCo CEO arsonist Diesel Danforth" proceeded to make business news headlines and talk-show punch lines, NorBanCo hastily put their Elkmoon Valley holdings up for sale, and opportunity tilted so entirely in the Elkmoon dreamers' direction that schedules were cleared and travel plans made.

On November 4th, 2003, at 10 a.m., the firmly committed gathered at Testament Creek School to rough out a purchase offer for the land they'd given their all to protect. The group consisted of TJ, Risa, Jamey, Kale, Lou Roy, Ida Craig, Regina Cloud, Buford Raines, Ona Kutar, Max and Kira Bowler, Doty Nolan, Hub Punker, Eddie and Rosalia Dominguez, and two newcomers, Gret Greeley, who'd become indispensable to Eddie getting the cottage business going, and Gret's partner, Luann Coats, an ace accountant helping us negotiate the financial mysteries of being an unintentional menagerie. Having stayed in close contact for the past six years, the group had established a thriving Highland beef consortium, the Craftsman cottage kit business, and put Kale in charge of a purchasing team consisting of Risa, TJ, Ona, Risa's Seattle lawyer friend Bart Simonsen, and Regina Cloud, and Regina's emailed summaries of the team's meetings had kept everyone else so well informed that, at the schoolhouse gathering, Kale had only to take the floor and launch the proceedings.

"As most of you know," he began, "Lorilee, Mu, and Grady Haynes, the hero who saved Lore, are in Missoula for a follow-up procedure on her ankle surgery. Grady called early today to say it went guardedly well. I'll also mention that, during our call, Grady made a huge donation dedicated to the long-term maintenance of our menagerie provided the purchase goes through." There were surprised murmurs. Grady's folk hero status kept growing. "As I turn to our chances," Kale continued, "rather than keep repeating 'if our purchase goes through,' I'll speak as if it will, and tell you why I believe this when I get there.

"But first, an inventory. Twelve thousand of NorBanCo's twenty-two thousand acres burned to the ground, leaving them ten thousand scattered acres of unburnt land, sixteen miles of overbuilt roads, three gravel pits, a burned airstrip and heliport slowly returning to nature, two big undamaged warehouses, one large metal hay roof, and a few toolsheds now miles from any structures requiring tools. We hope to buy the warehouse near Elbow Bend and use it to expand our cottage kit business. It's just five minutes from Aspen Swale, where we've agreed to site our village.

"Speaking of that village, we invite your opinions as our covenants come together. You can track all of this in Regina's bulletins. To avoid ostentation in the Brokeback Climate Club tradition, we've agreed on the five sizes of cottage Eddie offers, and are firm on size of footprint, height, and the wood's natural color. Two acres will attach to each cottage, connecting to an abundance of commons. An architect friend of Risa's and TJ's will be sending blueprints of how the Swale will operate in terms of water, power, plumbing, and so on. Her drawings of the village's appearance are so stunning that my biggest concern is how little Eddie is charging for his cottages."

"I'll be okay, Pope," Eddie said with a smile.

"Then on to our best news. Three thousand acres of the former McKeig and Broussard spreads are intact, all arable acres included, thanks to every hero in this room." (The firefighters, male and female, ages fourteen to sixty, grinned at one another.)

"In the debit column," Kale continued, "nine hundred of our hoped-for thousand acres of South Whitetail pine forest burned. But we still want it. The burn abuts our land, giving us a nice buffer from future development, and the loss of timber drops the price to near nothing. We'll replant with larch and ponderosa, planted sparsely so our descendants can defend our forest in the future. You'll be surprised by how fast a burn can return to life if we protect the saplings from ungulates. But what am I forgetting? Oh yeah. Regina, can you briefly explain the purpose of your email bulletins to the few of us who haven't yet seen 'em?"

"They summarize our purchase strategies," Regina said, "plus every aspect of the menagerie we're putting together, and your opinions on all of that are welcome up to the deadline dates. We're moving fast because NorBanCo, like any outlaw, wants the quickest getaway possible, and that's good news for us. I've got every bulletin on file. Just ask if you need them."

"Thanks," Kale said. "Moving on, the Testament Creek Canyon and its big ponderosas are unscathed, a huge relief. The Elkmoon river bottom is also intact. And Stella Creek is flowing at fifty-five trout-friendly degrees past zero asphalt-cart paths and gazebo bars for conquistadors with fly-fishy pretensions. Big Salmon Pond is also in fine shape, and its name is now Ten Acre Pond, which is its size, not lame hyperbole of Tex's. Speaking of size, on tiny flies she ties herself, Rosalia has caught two browns in Ten Acre that Eddie estimated at seven pounds each. She also refused to clobber and taxidermy them, kissing them on the nose and releasing them instead. NorBanCo responded with a press release sharply critical of Rosa's un-American mercy upon potential wall trophies."

Kale got a good laugh, especially from Rosalia. With emotion in his voice, he added, "Getting down to it, it's a pleasure say that the one hundred acres of Schoolhouse Bluff and twenty round my home, barn, and buildings are intact solely because of all of you, so from here on they *belong* to all of you. I'll live in an Eddie cottage. Those who've been in my house know my eccentric dad built long skinny hallways between each of the five bedrooms. The educators among us say that will make for excellent class or conference rooms, each out of earshot of the others. We're abuzz with plans to teach visitors how to learn their land, switch to green energy, grow crops and livestock, safeguard forests and waters, learn the flora, fauna, and watershed, and all kinds of other good stuff.

"We'll take a short break now. Ida wants coffee, tea, and scones in our bellies before we get down to brass tacks."

When the circle re-formed, fortified by Ida, Kale got right to it:

"The main reason why I feel our purchase offer will be accepted is the arson trial. Cecil Danforth's head rolled. Tex Schiller walked. NorBanCo was disgraced. Though Tex drove me nuts for a decade, his eleventh-hour truth-telling continues to serve us. An example: NorBanCo wanted Sotheby's, the purveyor of luxury properties worldwide, to sell their Elkmoon holdings. Sotheby's told NorBanCo to take a hike. That forced their Elkmoon rep to hire an E City realtor, Ludeman Ricks, a good friend of mine ever since he let my daughter, Marla, crash his all-boys Little League team. Ludie called me four days ago to warn that NorBanCo's land would go on the market yesterday. That's how we knew to gather. They're asking eleven million dollars for the twenty-two thousand acres, eight million dollars less than they paid eleven years ago. But they're dreaming. No offers have come in. Better yet, their rep told Ludie that NorBanCo's wealth is about to work in *our* favor. All they want is to get out of the valley of their disgrace and erase the memory, and they think in billions. The four thousand acres we covet is chump change.

"In short, now is the hour to make our move. But before we do, listen. Our resources vary hugely. If you can't afford to contribute, please don't.

For six years everybody in this room has contributed to our togetherness in ways we'll always be grateful for."

Gracious as Kale sounded, when he took a seat next to Ida the silence grew awkward. Planning an untested collective is one thing. *Investing* in it is something else again.

Leave it to Risa to change the mood. "I'll start," she said. "We've waited six years for this, and I've loved our cooperative ventures and look forward to many more. But I've run up against something I didn't expect: the short dark days of Montana winters. Ona? Care to share what you told me when I whined to you during the January cold and dark?"

"Sure. I told Risa about a midwinter gig my band and I played at a combination barn and bioshelter near Shelburne Falls, Massachusetts. No money in it, but the owners are friends, and *damn* did their space lift our music. Rough-hewn interior, thirty-foot ceilings with skylights, ceiling fans wafting warmth to the floor. And the plants, flowers, and summer fragrances with a blizzard blowing outside did something magical to our performance."

"Thanks," Risa said. "Ona's experience seeded a notion many of you have already given a thumbs-up. When my dad died, I inherited a life insurance payout, and TJ is so generous when I work for him in Portland that I haven't touched that nest egg. It's 750K now. I hereby commit all of it to building us what I wanted to call the Beguine, Buddhist, and Delta Blues Barn and Bioshelter, but Kale did an intervention. We'll just call it the B Barn, to match Kale's A Barn, short for Animals. But to give the letter *B* a little more punch I'm going to paint the barn's exterior Lorilee's favorite indigo blue."

Risa's extreme generosity raised a chorus of astonished whispers and a few glances that were almost fearful. She took it all in stride. "To our daydreams of what's coming," she said, "switch out midwinter cabin fever for the fragrance of greens and blossoms under a ceiling so high our thoughts can soar. Imagine social nooks, meditative crannies, and a small indoor pond stocked with koi who'll tickle Rosalia with their barbels if she kisses them. Picture a breakfast cafe menued by TJ and Regina, an indoor theatre for movies, and a huge main room for whatever we dream up: candlelit storytelling, sewing bees, lariat-tossing, fly-tying, ping-pong tournaments, yoga, and, *hell yeah*, Ona's band making magic while a blizzard blows outside. The Shelburne Falls barn crew is committed to the project and drawing up plans. If our purchase comes together, construction could start this summer."

I, the Holy Goat, am going to jump in to say that Risa didn't just break the ice. Our infant menagerie was crowning in the form of a glorious blue barn that pushed a generosity button in everyone. The first person to respond was Ona. She'd been conspiring by email with her Wyoming novelist friend, Marchy Dark, who wanted to write a book portraying a few great musicians as their music was being conceived and track them through the ups and downs of composition, recording, early performances, and a first few tour dates. Marchy had invited the Ona Kutar Band, and Lore and Mu, to be the musicians in the book so they could market and tour their CDs and her book together.

"At that point," Ona said, "Marchy and I had some kind of mind meld. I confessed that I was fried on recording in LA and Nashville. If our land purchase goes through, I told her, I want my next studio to be here. Beguine Records, I'll call it, after these cool women mystics Risa has a few of us reading about.

"Marchy wrote back proposing that since the recording studio would be a big part of her book, we should *both* build it. 'But I know me well enough to limit my share to forty-nine percent,' she said, leaving me the controlling partner at fifty-one percent, so when we get in fights I'll always win. '*You're* the musical genius, not me,' Marchy said.

"And here's another idea appropriate to this community once it gets rolling. Risa's Beguine books tell how, whenever an individual Beguine chose to leave the community, the room in which she'd lived, even if she'd paid for and built it herself, stayed with the beguinage. Risa has said this will apply to the B Barn, Kale has said the same of his former home, and I feel the same about Marchy's and my studio. If Marchy and I move on to other projects, Beguine Records will remain where it is and belong to our ongoing circle, not us. Maybe Lore's manager, Mu, could carry the torch for it next."

When Mu smiled and said, "Sounds good to me," our stalwart Pope, from his seat beside Ida, began to quake.

Ida took his arm. "Are you all right?"

"Not yet!" Kale said. "But I'm about to be. The generosity and foresight in this room has turned spectacular so fast I see I dropped the ball! I hereby add to the purchase pot the 200K I've been saving for, I dunno, my burial plot I guess."

To the surprise of everyone, Ida turned on Kale with the scowl of a miffed four-star general and in her utterly un-general-like voice ordered, "Nothing doing, cowboy! *You're* the one who held on here forever, giving the rest of us a chance to join you. Swear to keep your savings for *your needs,* and I'll double your purchase offer to 400K here and now."

Kale gaped at her a moment, then laughed. "*I swear, Ida! I swear!*"

"I want to do more too," Ona said. "But first I have a question for Jamey."

"I'm all ears," he said.

"I believe you're the reason why people keep calling us 'an unintentional menagerie,' not 'an intentional community.' I'd like to understand why this odd term is important to you."

"It's important, no offense anyone, because nearly all communes fail," Jamey said. "And strong human intentions are the main reason they do. *Intentionality* misses the mark as soon as it leads to *mental straining toward a fixed end.* Monsanto, the NRA, Ayn Rand's absurdly unimaginable fiction, Vatican edicts and so on, herd human lives into cold obedience to a manifesto with great *intentionality,* and look at the results. Sordid intention is so contagiously bad it's caused good intentions to become famous for paving the road to hell."

"*Good Lord, Jamey!*" Ona burst out. "What's the antidote?"

"Paying heed to what *pierces* a life, not what systematizes or tyrannizes it. Being pierced leads to living by intuition, Ocean strobes, myth tellings, openness to grace, the bardic wonders in Lore's music, brown trout kissing, susceptibility to wild creatures, conversing with birds, incredibly unlikely friendships, and other wonders. Think on our genesis, Ona. Kale says our alliance was born the day Lou Roy and Risa met up in the Glory Meadow, where Lou's *intention* was a hate crime. But with Grey's help that run-in unintentionally pierced Lou Roy, launching a friendship that soon led Lou to convince Kale to turn his schoolhouse over to Risa, enabling *her* to turn it into the Greater Good Headquarters in which we're headquartering our hearts out as I speak. Lou being pierced was *a holiness,* Kale says to this day. And I would add that it was entirely unintentional. Wouldn't you agree, Ona?"

"I agree enough to make a serious pledge to this menagerie," Ona said with a mischievous twinkle in her eye. "But I'm attaching three *intentions* to my pledge *because that's the kind of selfish old cow I am, Jamey*. Intention One: if Rosalia promises to master a drift boat, teach me to fly-fish, float me down the Elkmoon twice a month or so each summer, and let me pay for every float, I'm one-third committed. Intention Two: if Lou will train my young gelding, teach me how to ride him, and let me pay his going price, I'm at two-thirds. Intention Three: if Regina will continue to keep my life in order and let me pay her for it so I have time to grow you all a giant garden every year and share the bounty, I'm at three-thirds. This place is a life dream come true. If my intentions are met, I'll match Risa's three-quarter mil, and my loot goes entirely toward the land purchase. What do you say, threesome?"

Rosalia and Regina were stunned speechless by Ona's offer, so Lou Roy spoke up first. "My feeling, Ona, is that our winter whitefishin' trips are so damn fun, an' Regina's smoked whitefish pâté is so damn good, that the pleasure o' teachin' you to ride has got to be a wash. But for breakin' in an' trainin' your horse I *do* need what I'm worth. So. Next time you an' me go whitefishin', the Pabst an' maggots are on you!"

When the laughter died down, Rosalia spoke up. "I already guide Eddie in a raft I can handle fine, Ona. Ask my dad for his guide review." Eddie gave Rosalia a double thumbs-up. "So even *this* summer I can guide you," Rosa said. "But I have some selfish intentions too. *You* have to tow the raft and do the driving. I'm only fourteen!"

"You're the guide for me, girl!" Ona laughed.

"My feeling," Regina told her boss, "is that your life is in good order with or without me, and you pay me plenty for the little I do for you. So what I'd like to do come spring, if you're willing, Ona, is help upgrade your garden to a farm big enough to feed us, and serve E City and valley residents too. If we offer CSAs and a farmers' market we'll get to know all kinds of neighbors we wouldn't meet otherwise. We need fruit and vegetable PR to silence the miscreants who claim we're a cult."

Ona grew quiet as her eyes moved from face to face, taking us all in. Her voice then broke a little as she said, "Good humans, we have ourselves a second 750K deal and I couldn't be happier!"

That huge act of divestment was the moment we knew the E.B.&C.Co was in the birth canal and its head was crowning. It was TJ who then delivered the baby.

"Before I contribute," he said, "let me say a few words about my brother. Most of you have heard how, when he woke from his awful injuries and coma back in 1989, Jervis began to experience a mystery he calls Ocean. You've also heard how Ocean communicates through blasts of images Jervis calls 'strobes.' I can't define what I haven't experienced, but I *can* swear to this. In the fourteen years I've helped Jervis respond to strobes, they've led to countless deeds of so much benefit to others that my feeling has become, 'By their fruits shall ye know them.' So you should all know that Jervis has been strobed not once but *many* times that this very place and this group of people are going to help coax a way of life into being that will set an example of value to thousands. And I'd like to put my money where my trust is. Please do me the honor of covering the rest of our land purchase, whatever it turns out to be."

After six years of waiting, our land acquisition didn't feel real until our purchase group and Ludeman Ricks met with the NorBanCo rep the next day, found her frantic to get out of Montana, agreed on a figure in two minutes, hammered out a contract in half an hour, and ten days later the deal closed. What has our purchase of four thousand acres led to during our first thirteen years?

I keep liking the way Kale Broussard puts things. "As I've said for years," he told me recently, "the demolition the Biggies call an upgrade has Mother Earth in convulsions. But here on the E.B.&C.Co, swimming against that grim tide, we've become a solvent, spiritually awake, dryland lifeboat housing close to fifty counting the kids, helping hundreds of neighbors, visitors, customers, and clients besides. If Earth-gentle lifeboats were to become the common social unit, could we turn enough things around to survive? I don't know anything on a huge scale, HG. But I know this. If the Biggies' demolition work brings it all down tomorrow, we'll go down knowing we were the dryland mariners who never once thought Mother Earth owed us whatever we could rip out of her and we owed her nothing in return. We were the navigators who proved city and country folk, carnivores and vegans, and people of all kind of faiths can live and work together in a harmony that gets slapped now and then, but learned to minimize the sting of the slaps with forgiveness. We were a small circle of citizens who, as

America's politics went totally to hell at the end of your chronicles' time-frame, thanked Lou Roy for warning us, *'Don't butt heads with buttheads. And don't drag the head-buttin' they call the news into our good home.'* We were the unintentional menagerie who knew grace when it pierced us, and so heeded a holy fool governed by an Ocean we could only infer by the fruits of his words and actions, revered the women among us governed by the example of mystics and all things selfless, and found more to worship in what the Roman Church and its Kings and Queens cast out or killed than in what it kept in. And we're the ones still listening as an unseen bird, no bigger than a tiny calliope we'll never forget, keeps telling us that the more lifeboats we can help others launch, the more folks have a shot at crossing this world storm to reach some humble little homelands safely."

IX. Cure for Staph

If the flesh came into being because of spirit, it is a wonder.
But if spirit came into being because of the body, it is a
wonder of wonders. Indeed, I am amazed at how this
great wealth has made its home in this poverty.

> —Jesus, Gospel of Thomas

The real mother of a child is not just she who
gave it birth but she who gives it milk.

> —Ibn al-Arabi

The required food is milk.

> —James Hillman

RISA WAS IN bed alone, wearing a well-worn *Stumptown Shakespeare Ensemble* t-shirt of Jamey's that had her thinking about him. Their six-year-old, Fionn Kabir McKeig, and infant, Willa Shay Van Zandt, were both asleep, hopefully for the night. Jamey had stayed late at his desk, trying to finish a play. When Risa peeked in on him earlier his smile looked spent. "I won't be long," he said. Ten minutes later she heard him get in the shower.

The play had been commissioned for the inaugural season of a new Portland theatre in the heart of downtown. Out of the eight plays to be featured, all the other playwrights were nationally renowned. Jamey was the sole local hero invited to take part. But opening night was six months away, his play was seven weeks tardy, and though he blamed only himself, Risa knew that, from the night they united six years ago up to tonight, Jamey's devotion to her, to the two babies she'd carried, and to their children once born had been unceasing.

She also hadn't forgotten that he somehow found her irresistible throughout both pregnancies. "How could I not?" he'd said. "You were pregnant the night we fell in love!" Though he only turned amorous when her invitations were flagrant, she surprised herself, when she was carrying Fionn, with how often they *were*. She loved the way that, as she and the baby expanded in size, Jamey's foreplay expanded in playfulness and always included the passenger he dubbed *Froggy*. Every time she wished to engage, Jamey would slide under the covers, place his lips on the drum of her eventually racing-striped belly, and say, *Froggy? You awake in there?* Warm hands on her hips, lips to her womb, he'd courteously ask, *Mind if I borrow Mum for a while?*, then listen for the longest time for a reply. And sure, the game was childish. But Froggy had been sired by a stranger and conceived in a test tube, and Jamey refused to abandon mother and child to that stark laboratorial script. *Froggy's deliberating!* the lump under the blankets would stage-whisper—and Risa would actually grow excited to find out what her inhabitant would decide. *Ah! Sounds promising!* the lump would say. Then: *Oh, thank you, Froggy!* And out Jamey would pop: *Great news, Risa! Froggy says that me borrowing you is simply a matter of whether a particular fetus in its particular mum is up for a little ride. And Froggy loves little rides!* How movingly he then transformed the body Risa had taken to calling the minivan into an object of adoration as they became the universe in a likeness.

But when birth night had begun with an epic breaking of water, all clowning vanished and the term "birth coach" didn't begin to describe Jamey's attentions. He made her feel like the star of the Miracle Play he took Froggy's birth to be. Charming the nurse-midwives with his focus and kindness, politely declining offers of drugs or techno intervention, volunteering, during the mood swings of transition, as Risa's human backrest, punching bag, shoulder to moan into, he served her tirelessly. When Earth's seven billionth human then slid onto a planet in utter crisis, Jamey's joy filled the room as he cried, *It's the River Boy, Risa! Froggy turns out to be our little River Boy!*, and Risa doubted whether even the father of Jesus loved the baby he had so famously *not* sired more than Jamey loved theirs.

Six years later Jamey reprised his superb service as Risa gave birth to his DNA's own Willa. Then—immediately, *crucially*—he began weaving Fionn into a family-of-four script full of comedic affection that enabled the boy to see his sister as welcome and wildly amusing, *especially* when she was blowing out a diaper, suffering meltdowns from colic, or screaming as she cut new teeth.

THIS, MORE TRULY, was the man whose play was now running late. And as Risa lay alone, pondering him, she was stricken with alarm to realize that they hadn't made love even once since before Willa's birth! Two demanding homes, Portland and Montana, two kids, two absorbing worlds, two careers, and so many friends, but still: how had she lost track of this vital gift? And not a word of complaint from her man.

The one meaningful apology she could offer, she felt, was to begin making it up to him this very night. But oh, family life! There was a complication. For the third night running, Willa had refused to nurse, shrieked when Risa tried to insist, settled down only when Risa completely gave up, and went to sleep leaving Risa's breasts full to bursting.

The rejections had begun three nights before, when Jamey's Wild Bird Dinner Theatre had turned Fionn into an osprey. While Willa watched from her high chair, Jamey raised Fionn up toward the ceiling in his big strong hands, emitted piercingly accurate osprey cries, and narrated in a perfect David Attenborough accent as he flew Fionn round the kitchen, held him in a high osprey hover, and eyed the six inches of cold water in the kitchen sink that served as their river. When Osprey Fionn then dove into the river and managed to grip a Colorado Greenback Cutthroat trout (baby dill pickle) in his toe/talons, the boy's laughter grew so infectious that Willa began to call out, "*Gaw! Gaw!*" Jamey then flew Fionn to his perch atop the kitchen cabinets, where the impossibly agile boy lifted his foot to his mouth and ate a trout as Willa kept *gawing* and David Attenborough declared, "Being endangered is the unfortunate cutthroat's problem, for Osprey Fionn, Lord of the Waters, devours whomsoever he pleases." As feared, an hour later Risa's attempt to nurse Willa met with so many spat nipples that there was no denying that *Gaw* translated to: *I wanna be Osprey Willa in Dad's next Wild Bird Theatre! I do NOT want my mouth stopped up by a boringly predictable BOOB!*

So there Risa lay, alone and in pain, scribbling in her dumbsaint notebook:

> *Lao Tzu nursed till he was eight, Fionn till he was two & a half. Willa has quit cold turkey at seven months & the pain in my breasts is epic! I can't stop picturing a totem carving in the museum in Victoria B.C.—Haida, I think— of a woman with two bulging, apoplectic faces on her chest where her breasts should have been. At twenty I considered those faces mean & wrong. Breasts anthropomorphized, I felt, should be benign, slow-witted, nurturing creatures. That was then. Now I not only know those faces spoke truth, I'm wearing them!!*

Hoping to divert herself by reading, she knew her nightstand books to be too obsessed with metaphysics and mysticism to address her mammalian hurt. Circling the bed, she sat on the floor by Jamey's stack, began working her way down through novelists, playwrights, poets, then gaped to see, on the very bottom of the heap, the black leather cover of what appeared to be a Bible. *Jamey? A secret Bible owner?*

Extracting it, she found the cover so thickly coated with dust that she doubted he'd ever opened it, and was relieved: Jamey's spirited life and complete lack of exposure to religion struck her as entwined. But the Bible was a King James translation, the first she'd ever seen. Curious, she took it to her side of the bed, removed a sock, dusted the cover, and began examining her find.

Dubbing it *The King Jamey Version*, her first discovery was that the book didn't simply open. A layer of polyester-reinforced black cloth hid the pages behind a closed zipper. Stranger yet, the zipper's pull tab was a brass cross. As Risa grabbed it and started unzipping, her mind leapt to a graphic image of unzipping Jamey. Whoa! Shoving the image out of her mind, she murmured, "*Whew! Sorry, Boss! I crave my man even more than I thought.*"

In keeping with a childhood habit that left her imagining an Arabic-speaking incarnation, she began exploring *The King Jamey* from back to front. *Huh.* Interesting. In the very back was a complete biblical concordance: every significant word in both testaments referenced by chapter and verse. In her pain, it gave her an idea. "Ahoy, Jeremiah and Zachariah!" she said. "You still in there? If so, I could use your help. My name is Risa, I'm a nursing mother, my infant has broken off relations with my breasts, and after three days they feel like the world's two worst ice cream headaches. Any chance you could guide me to a line or two of scripture with the power to ease aches?"

Searching the concordance for *Ache,* she was astonished to find *Achan, Achar, Achim, Achish, Achmetha, Achor* and *Achsah,* none of which she'd heard of, but nary an *Ache.* "Is mine too feminine a pain for you rough tough patriarchs to even consider?" she asked.

When the prophets maintained a stony silence she gave up on them, called on their wives and paramours, opened the concordance to *breasts*— and hit the jackpot! Twenty-seven references to Breasts plural, fifteen to Breast singular, and eleven to Breastplates, "*which are just what mine feel like!*" she muttered just as Jamey walked into the room.

"What was that?" he asked, sending her a cheerful though weary smile.

"Oh, nothing," she sighed. Glancing up, she saw that he was bare-chested, his shoulder-length hair hanging loose to dry. But uh-oh! He was wearing his only pair of pajama bottoms—dark blue flannel with gold stripes down the outer seam of each leg. He called them his U.S. Cavalry pants, and they were marital code. Though he and Risa preferred to sleep naked on nights the kids might sleep through, when he bought the pants he told her, "My love for making love with you goes without saying. But you once told me you found Ronald Reagan *even more sexually repugnant than Nixon* when he called the U.S. Cavalry's long slaughter of Indians *the most romantic time in America's history.* I bought these figuring that, on nights when we're exhausted, Reaganite Cavalry pants will help us catch up on our sleep."

Hypothetically, she thought as she studied him. But his smooth hairless chest, long clean hair, and compassion in donning a lampoon of Reagan's genocidal sense of *romance* sent a little current through her groin. As he lay back beside her his torso flexed, then relaxed in a way that made her want to say, *Do that again, will you? Several times, please!* Smelling the inexpensive conditioner he used so that she could hoard the expensive kind, she also smelled kindness, which sent another hint of current through her. *Here I sit*, she thought, *holding a book with a bunch of Sex-As-Sin tales zippered inside, when, Lo!, a long, strong, potential co-sinner arrives in my* bed. *Reagan be hanged! What could be more alluring than shirtless Jamey in his mock Cavalry pants?*

Crossing his hands behind his head, Jamey stared up at the ceiling as he said, "You're holding my sixth birthday gift from Gramma Nan, presented on my mother's negative first deathday. Check out the card in the front."

Risa flipped to the front, found the card, and read:

Dear Jamey Boy,

Our Debbie resides in a much better place now, and this book tells of that place and how to get there. Wishing you a very special birthday as you begin your journey Up Yonder.

—Your Nanna

In disbelief, Risa said, "How thoughtful! Blind to the fact that *Jamey Boy's* first motherless birthday might be a little rough, Nanna tells him his Mom's better off without him and hands him the most contentious book on the planet!"

Still gazing at the ceiling, his breathing slow and calm, Jamey said, "The instant I read those words I zipped her gift shut and vowed not to unzip it until God Him or Her self tells me, *Your mom is happy now despite her brutal early death. And this book, despite the self-righteous legions who swing it around like a riot baton, is worth reading.* Since neither thing has happened, this is an occasion. My Bible's first unzipping since I jailed Nan's card inside it."

"I'm so sorry! Want me to zip it back up?"

"Naw. The King James language from Shakespeare's time is said to be beautiful. Give it a go. Just not out loud, please. Hearing it would break my vow."

Turning to *The King Jamey* concordance, she looked up one of the references to breasts and was stunned to read this:

To whom shall God teach his knowledge? And to whom shall he explain his message? Them that are weaned from the milk, and drawn from the breasts.

Risa's mind lit up. Jamey had *never* been weaned, because he'd never nursed—and he had recently told her that despite an increasing love for some kind of *tk!* and Romeo-inspired spirituality, he remained a "Don't-know-God-from-nuthin'" type guy.

To whom shall God teach his knowledge if they have not been weaned and drawn from the breasts?

Risa rolled onto her side and peered at her man. Feeling her move, Jamey rolled onto his side and peered back. What a compliment, the way his gaze zoomed from far away to up close and grateful. "How's *your* life going, beautiful woman in my bed?" he asked.

"I'll live," she sighed. "But I'd sure like to complain a little. Would you mind?"

"When non-complainers complain, there are reasons. Tell me every reason."

"There are two," she said, hoisting one of her breasts in her hand. "I can't *believe* how fast Willa gave them up, or how much they hurt tonight."

Jamey sat up at once. "Hot water bottle? Ice packs? Meds? Double shot of bourbon? Bourbon can't hurt with Willa off the milk. You ask. I fetch."

"I was picturing something...*different*," Risa murmured.

"Paint me this picture," he said.

Risa sat up, crossed her arms over her belly, grabbed her *Stumptown Shakespeare* shirt at her hips, uncrossed her arms as she lifted it, tossed it aside, and lay back down, naked.

"*Look*," she ordered.

Achan, Achar, Achim! Jamey looked.

"At how *hard* they are, I mean. See it?"

Oh, he saw. He saw and saw. "Isn't *fullness* a kinder word?"

She shook her head, adamant. "A hardness this hard deserves no kind words. *Feel.*"

Achish, Achmetha, Achor! He reached out, tentatively felt, and his face filled with empathy. These weren't baby-feeding devices. These weren't sex objects. These were *malady*. "Jesus, Risa! What can I do to help? Anything. Just say."

Closing in on what she hoped for, Risa said, "I've been wondering whether, if I roll over..." with which she rolled over, "and we made spoons..." with which she backed her nakedness into him, inviting him to lie behind her like a spoon behind a spoon, "you could reach around..." with which she led one of his arms over her ribs and around, then snaked his other arm under her waist and up and around, "*and if you held them...*" with which she placed each of his hands on each of her breasts, "and maybe *kneaded* them...*real* slowly and gently...we could see...whether kneading...helps."

First hearing the word *kneading* as *needing*, Jamey realized his mistake but let it stand in his mind as he began, at the pace she urged, to gently knead and need.

Risa closed her eyes. Felt how it felt. "The slowness is good," she murmured. "But not so light. Try to *find* the hurt. To *capture it in your hands.* I don't know how. Just try."

As she made small sounds of disapproval or approval he experimented, adding strength, gently lifting, keeping the movement slow, seeking the hurt.

"*Yeah... Good...*" she finally breathed. "*That's good.* But they're starting to drip." She reached for the drawer of her nightstand, handed Jamey two cloth diapers, and backed into him again. He kept kneading, wiping away the drops as they appeared.

"Yeah," Risa sighed. "*Just right.* And another thing they'd like, I think, is if we talk to them. They feel so...*rejected.* So *jilted* by the baby they transformed themselves for. Would you mind if I sing their blues a little?"

"I'd *love* to hear what kind of blues your breasts compose," he murmured.

Laying her hand on one of his kneading hands, sighing with pained pleasure, she said, "They feel that, small as they were before the milk, they were kinda sweet looking. Then they grew. *Impressively.* But, rejected, they've shot past impressive to *bloated,* and when the bloat is over they'll be all stretch-marked and saggy. They'll be *dugs,* is what they'll be. So the breasts they used to be...for *you,* I felt...are sad. They sacrificed what appeal they held for you to serve Willa. And their services were so quickly—"

"I *understand,*" he cooed as he kneaded. "*Poor spurned Mama. Poor abandoned breasts. Such wondrous fruit, ripe on the wondrous tree. And Willa refuses to climb up and harvest.*"

"They *knew* your voice would help," Risa sighed. "And so, since you're being poetic, might a poem. Do you know any that soften hardness? And please keep lifting as you knead. The anti gravity is...*mm-mmmm.*"

"There's a Jack Gilbert poem I wish I knew," Jamey said as his hands sent *mmmmmm* into ache. "In giving each other to each other, men and women *get into bed with the Lord,* I think is his phrase. But love alone is not enough. Because our bodies are going to die and be put in the ground, he says, we must eat through the wildness of the beloved body in our bed to free the body *inside* the earthbound body. Something like that."

With an abruptness that surprised him, Risa removed his hands from her breasts, rolled over to face him, and he felt as if three people were staring at him: lovely, hurting Risa and, to be honest, two rather stupid-looking cyclopes gawking out of her chest. But her voice was rapt as she breathed, "That's it! The breasts *inside* my breasts were *also* abandoned. Their wildness not found, not *eaten through,* not freed. Their fruit was just abandoned to fall off the tree and rot in there. Food for ants, flies, and yellowjackets in there."

Her dark eyes found Jamey's and began boring in, till he saw she wasn't looking *at* him: she was gazing past the pigmented epithelium, aqueous humor, retina, into the impressions and memories behind them, searching so hard for something that he wanted to help her find it. But she didn't want him to know she was seeking the ache she often sensed in *him.* The ache that made him a "*Don't know God from nuthin'*" type guy. Despite his claim that her love for him had worked a great healing, how easily she located what had *not* healed:

Once upon a time a newborn contracted staph boils from a hospital, was treated with sulfa drugs, had an allergic reaction, and was taken, new to the world, away from his mother so that, despite her love, she couldn't even touch him. Taken away so long that she went dry, couldn't breastfeed him ever, so the wild body within his little body was never reached. Then, the day he turned five, his mother was also taken! Put inside the earth forever on his birthday! So now he felt not just unreached, but cursed. Birthday after birthday, deathday after deathday, he then went mad trying to find and fight what cursed him. For thirty-five years he fought and failed, fought and failed, until, one birthday/deathday, he comes upon me *of all people, telling my father's Gandhi story in a bar of all places. And amid all the distractions of that impossible venue, this man alone ate through the wildness of my tale to take and eat the two words that turned murder into apotheosis. Inside that consecration, how could I not* love *and* trust *him as I've trusted no other? But the veils that lifted descended again, leaving him only me as medicine, and what power do I have to mend such a wound? Might the real power lie in the way his hurts, and mine, are calling to each other tonight?*

Though Jamey couldn't read her face, he sensed her intensity. "What on earth are you seeing, Risa?" he asked. "What are you feeling?"

"Appalled at myself, and apologetic. I didn't realize till you were in the shower that we've gone without sex for seven months. That's *terrible!* We must insist while there's still time. We need to eat our way through the unhealed wildness I sometimes feel in both our bodies and glimpse in your eyes." Rolling onto her back, then gazing at him with a gravity that riveted him, she spoke two syllables as unforeseen as Gandhi's last two:

"*Hungry?*"

Achmetha, Achor, Achsah! The child stares. Stares. The child is staring at her as she shows, pure, voluptuous, her breasts of shining metal. And not only does she invite it, she lays her hands to each side of his face, aims him at what he has never in his life tasted, and guides him toward a wildness within them that, unreached, can only hurt and hurt.

Stunned, Jamey opens his mouth. The instant he places lips and tongue upon the overburdened shape his consciousness flies into a different mode entirely. Psychic material, genetic material, spirit and matter become indistinguishable. He breathes as if running for his life though he's done nothing at all. Just touching, just *feeling* this loaded mortal breast with his mortal mouth nails him, body and soul, to the cross upon which all mortal love is suspended. "*Eat*," she whispers, positioning his head. "Please. *I need you to eat.*"

Enclosing the nipple, he dares a tentative suck. But picturing Willa at the same breast, he feels so gigantic and awkward he starts to laugh, losing the connection. "I feel like the big dumb Giant in some kinky fairy tale!" he gasps.

"Be *still!*" Risa orders. "Be *here.* I *need* that big dumb Giant, so do you,

and this once-in-a-lifetime offer is no time for polite, Mr. Polite Pajamas."
She tugs the Cavalry pants by the waist band down as far as she can reach,
catches the band with her toe, extends her leg, sliding them off, and returns
his head, *sternly*, to her breast of shining metal.

Hardly believing what he's doing, Jamey makes moves he's watched
Fionn and Willa make, latching on in earnest, giving earnest suck. "*Good,*"
Risa coos. "*That's good. Be hungry for me, Good Giant. Find the hurt. For
both our sakes, find it and draw it out.*"

The Giant, wonderstruck, goes to work. The nipple's leathery dryness
turns slick. The milk flows faster. As the breast's metal vanishes Jamey
grows metal of his own, but savors nuances even so. This beverage, this
flavor, is the fruit of the tree of his love's entire length. *Joy.* Her in-breaths
and out-breaths grow heavy as the breast releases and flow increases. *Joy.*
The milk is sweet yet thin; not filling; *better* than filling; a food so absorb-
able it flows straight into his bloodstream, heart/mind, marrow, extremities,
without burdening his stomach at all. Head to toe to fingertips their bodies
grow hungry, the breast no longer the one thing he wants, relief from ache
no longer the one thing she wants. Eros storms their efforts, their every
move dual-purposed now. *Joy.*

But... but, but... troubles arise!

First trouble: the breast turns *torrential*. The milk is coming so fast it
takes athletic effort and all his concentration not to spill the miraculous
stuff everywhere. *But, but,* ...

Second trouble: sexual excitement, coupled with effort, is causing him
to breathe harder and harder, but the breast fills his mouth so completely
that he can only suck air through his nose, and his nostrils can't flare
wide enough to supply the oxygen needed. He remembers seeing Fionn like
this, mouth latched tight to breast, face red, consternated, wind whistling
in and out his tiny nostrils at a furious pace. Hearing his big bike-crashed
nose making the same sounds in a lower register, Jamey resists the comedic
aspect of his nose gale, reminds himself, *Be hungry! Find the hurt!*, keeps
drinking. *But, but,*

Third trouble: the more prolonged his efforts the more truly in-
fantile his consciousness grows until it toddles off a cliff, landing
in some atavistic trauma-scape where, even as he's gulping and his
sexual self remains wildly alive, *he begins to weep!* Ancient sorrows
assail physical joys. Even as the gushing breast mothers he's attacked
by staph boils, sulfa drugs, no mother milk, no mother; by birthdays
spent leukemia-mothered, black-hole-mothered; by shame to be alive. *Eat
through it, Good Giant! Find the bodies within our bodies! Yes! Yes!
But, but,*

Fourth trouble: as natal consciousness keeps nursing, his faith-doubt
organ pops like a bubble, the Unseen Guileless lets down a bliss-drop, natal
consciousness drinks it, words/thoughts/names vanish, ecstasy surges—and
Debbie full of grace smiles down upon him through a wall of glass, blonde

and blue-eyed, face so kind so sad so gentle, so close she's all but here! *Yet she can't touch him he can't touch her they can't touch!* He lets out a moan that connects with hope. Risa full of grace lets out an answering moan. The Unseen Guileless serves her too a bliss-drop. The bliss finds, suffuses, floods the body within her body, she lets out a cry, her wild body takes over, her Kuan Yin Sophia breast vaporizes glass, milk pours and pours into exiled infant-man, instantly absorbed, everywhere inside him now, numberless hurts compassion-mothered as he moans, drinks, streams tears down her ribs. Clutching him hard, she begins to move, and the wild body within him tries to move with her, *but, but*

Fifth trouble: so awkwardly! Drunk on the food of infants, he can no more manage what union asks than could an infant. It is her hand that guides him till his hurts/lust/hunger enter so deep she no longer merely mothers, she *houses* him now, a planet sustaining her long-injured inhabitant, his pain/ardent life/plays/losses/gains/gratitude her whole purpose now, woman's wildest fruits flowing into man's wildest depths, his gasping breaths so like sobs that the head she keeps kissing is one moment a newborn's, the next her lover's, the next a darkling king risen from the tomb in which mother-death long entrapped him, the tomb dissolving now, a freed and entire man adoring his mother planet now, *except, except...*

Sixth trouble: "Switch sides!" she gasps, causing Jamey to freeze in confusion. But Planet Risa thrusts her *other* breast in his face, and *oh ho!* He catches on, latches on, thrusting as he sucks, suckling as he thrusts, the second breast divesting so fast he's gasping drowning downing so much milk, so much giving receiving giving, so much come-take-eat-bliss-opened-oculus-moon-breast-lowered-from-above-love that, for an infinite instant, their name-stripped grief-struck joy-shot fusion makes of them the oceanic Mother/Father out of whom all humanity crawls, feels a call, sets out seeking, escapes some cages, loves and chooses, loves and ages, loses all, dies and flies,

an evanescence so briefly, hurtingly, cheatingly loved,

an evanescent essence so gloriously, guilelessly, unboundedly loved.

AND WHAT AN act by the actor to remember the purpose of feet, rise from the bliss bed, and vanish—to reappear seconds later with a frayed cotton towel held to himself, a second such towel in hand, his eyes rapt but touch matter of fact as a mother's as he tends, cleans, dries his love, then lies down beside her to find ocean swells still surging in over their bodies, breaking upon the sands of the barzakh, sliding back out to sea, reprising, reprising, subsuming, subsiding, leaving two humans on Earth as it isn't in Heaven, awestruck to have felt, even once, such great wealth make its home in their mortal poverty.

X. Governance by Wandering Griefs and Joys

...Then a woman
told a story. Of a donkey
beaten near to death with a length
of rebar. And then, somehow,
his sudden erection. The sudden erection
of the collapsed donkey despite eyes
mangled to mush. Despite
one bleeding ear, two useless legs.
And then the woman said,
I am ready for the beaten body.
She said, I am the grass of this meadow.
She said, I am the mother
of all the waters holy.

—Teddy Macker, "May"

The Inward-Turning Spiral (2016)

SOMETHING HAPPENED TO me, the Holy Goat, when Grady Haynes wrote in his Elkmoon Mountain journals, "As long and hard as I've studied the Lûmi, I have no desire to prove they exist by producing one of them to be dissected by the dominant 'culture'... They would never agree to be 'produced' and I agree with that disagreement. Likewise, since the Lûmi don't believe in chronological time, why should they verifiably exist in it? Their claim to an unwanted fame is their complete lack of fame, and they're so skilled at seeming not to exist that academic scholarship and journalism can't engage them at all."

Pondering these words, I was struck by a realization that, during the years the people I've been chronicling have inhabited the E.B.&C.Co, chronological time has come to mean less and less to them—and I owe it to them to be true to that. The chronological presumption that we're "progressing into a better future" has not just blinded humans to the fullness of the moment, it's put the very survival of life on Earth in doubt. Risa, Kale, Lore, Jamey, and others here would gladly tell you that our efforts to honor the Now involve us less in time than in timelessly recurring cycles and seasons and, in terms of consciousness, inward-turning spirals that allow hearts and minds to rise like a redtail hawk up a thermal, arriving not at the Thanksgivings, Black Fridays, and mirthless Santas of calendars, but amid the wandering griefs and joys that truly guide and sustain us. That's why our populace, as they've grown increasingly sensitive to the unseen, encourage me to tell the stories in which they sometimes catch a thermal and rise, no matter when the story unfolded in time. A few memorable examples:

Wandering I: Schizm (October 2008)

In the mid-nineteenth century the stentorian Brooklynite Walt Whitman proclaimed, "Behind the tally of genius and morals stands the stomach, and gives a sort of casting vote."

In the late twentieth century the incorrigible Manhattanite Fran Lebowitz voted her stomach's preference when she declared, "My favorite animal is steak."

In the early twenty-first century, six years into the existence of the E.B.&C.Co, our menagerie's own Rosalia Dominguez, at the age of nineteen, cast a very different vote when she decided that the raising and slaughtering of Scottish Highlands for income was a crime against every compassionate belief we hypocrites claimed to hold. To complicate matters, Rosa mentioned her feelings to no one so she could conduct a covert war against the beef consortium that TJ, Kale, Hub Punker, Doty Nolan, Max and Kira Bowler, Buford Raines, and Regina Cloud had turned into our most profitable early business. (Yes, Regina helps the consortium despite her veganism. She's become a skilled wrangler too. Her Romeo, Buford, manages the cattle operation, and "Love trumps diet," she gently insists. Buford says nothing to this, but grins as he crosses the same divide by devouring plate-loads of his Juliet's delicious vegan cuisine.)

So how was Rosalia, operating alone, able to wage war against so many? *The Homeric Hymn to Hermes* lists some of the qualities needed:

> *Then there was brought to light this wily, cunning, night-watching, dream-bringing, cattle-driving bandit child.*

Imagine Buford riding out at dawn on his horse, Vegan (sincerely named in Regina's honor), arriving at the E.B.&C.Co's grazing land to move forty young Highlands onto their next electric-fenced twenty-acre quadrant—to find the entire herd has vanished. Imagine tracking hoofprints and cow pies through three strategically opened gates, down a mile and a half of dirt roads and old bulldozer tracks, at last spotting the cattle scattered across the steep, talus-strewn slopes of a towering North Whitetail ridge dense with browse from the 2003 fires. Imagine Buford calling Kale, and Kale ordering half his crew to saddle up horses to handle the treacherous terrain, while the other half rush to the ATVs to meet the cattle and drive them home once they arrive on safer ground—only to find the ATVs' spark plugs have all been removed.

Imagine Lou Roy having a fine morning supervising three high school girls as they whitewash the schoolhouse in exchange for cutting-horse lessons, when Ida Craig drives up with the news of the scattered herd. Imagine Lou hops in his Chevy Cheyenne to drive down to the A Barn, saddle up Grey, and help rescue cattle—only to hear the faithful old truck cough, sputter, and die for the first time in its life. Imagine fussing with the engine for half an hour to no avail, towing the truck ten miles to his E City mechanic, and learning after many expensive misdiagnoses that Karo corn syrup has been poured in his gas tank. Imagine replacing spark plugs, fuel filter, fuel lines, and gas tank and *still* the engine sounds like it's contracted whooping cough as it tries to make it up even a minor incline.

Imagine Buford, Regina, Doty, Max, and Kale combing the dangerous Whitetail talus slope for two days on horseback, then ATVs, to get the Highlands down into a fenced ten-acre enclosure adjacent to Aspen Swale, where our first twelve Eddie Dominguez kit cottages are under construction by six different Sapphire County contractors and crews. Imagine, the very night the Highlands are returned to the enclosure, hearing them loose again in the Swale, shitting on building materials, trampling wildflowers, browsing on young fruit trees, planter boxes of basil and tomatoes, and late-blooming perennials planted by our eager cottage owners. Imagine Kale remarking to Buford that these deeds could only have been done by someone with inside knowledge of the Highland operation and all the E.B.&C.Co roads and landscapes, possessed of very impressive cattle-driving skills as well. Imagine Lou Roy, with a sinking heart, gimping across Schoolhouse Bluff to Eddie and Rosalia's Airstream, to find Rosalia's Morgan mare penned up behind a storage shed for easy night access because, she told Eddie, she's doing a study of Buford's holistic grazing practices for school. Imagine Lou Roy finding, on the table under the already enormous willow he planted to shade Rosalia and Eddie's Airstream nine years ago, a weather-beaten paperback titled *The Monkey Wrench Gang*. Imagine Lou taking the book home to find Edward Abbey advising readers that Karo corn syrup dumped in the gas tanks of developers will slow them down considerably.

Imagine the hurt inflicted when this child we love equates us with the developers we resisted, outsmarted, and outlasted. Imagine our entire populace having to drop everything to attend an emergency town hall meeting on Schoolhouse Bluff the night Rosalia's guilt is discovered. Imagine the several attendees who can't find last-minute babysitters so squalling infants and toddlers add teeth-grinding tension to the room. Imagine watching the famously gifted but infamously willful Rosalia take the floor and declare to all present, "I know what I've done the last few nights has caused a lot of trouble. That was my intention. I wanted us to gather so I could ask us all a serious question. Is there anything worse than raising animals who trust us from birth, shooting the males dead after two years, chopping them to pieces, and selling them to rich people in distant restaurants when there are countless less evolved forms of life to eat, and countless better ways for us to make a living?"

Imagine Kale the Pope replying with icy calm, "Yes, Rosalia, there are things much worse. One is watching a young woman we love and trust, driven by blind certainty, sabotage our livelihoods and endanger our lives, though we're raising and harvesting our cattle in the most Earth-beneficial way it's ever been done."

Imagine Rosalia retorting, "The best I can do for people who think a horrible wrong is Earth-beneficial is make it as hard as possible for them to keep doing it."

Imagine Eddie, who's worked his tail off for years to house us more elegantly and economically than we ever dreamed possible, saying with a tremor we've never heard in his calm voice, "Rosalia. I've never been so ashamed. To speak like this to Kale, who housed us when we were homeless and became a grandfather to you; to drive cattle into the Swale and trash our neighbors' yards and plantings before their cottages are even standing; to speak this way in front of Risa and Lorilee, who've mothered you, spitting on their kind and compassionate mothering; to ruin Lou Roy's truck, scatter our cattle, and create days so dangerous it could have killed one of our friends, are *crimes*. You're a criminal of a low order, and if anyone presses charges you'll do time in a detention facility that will expose you to dangers we can't protect you from. You owe a lot of people a lot of your college money once we tally the amounts. And, here and now, you owe every person in this room the most sincere apology you ever made."

"In other words," Rosalia said, trembling now far more than Eddie, "blame the one who calls you out, act like we have no say in how we make our livings, and go on doing something horribly wrong!" With which she stormed out of the schoolhouse, causing her "enemy," Buford, to ask Regina to please go find her and try to soothe her.

High-stress high-volume ugliness then filled the serene old schoolhouse as Hub, Doty, Max, and Kira agreed we should call the police and have Rosalia arrested, while Kale, Risa, Ida, and Buford urged we give her a second chance.

It was a surprise to all but Risa, who somehow sensed before he spoke that he'd detected an unseen thermal in the room, when Jamey rose to his feet wearing a gentle smile and said, "I propose a recess, during which everybody with kids or animals to tend can go home. I'll then propose, to a smaller, calmer group, what I feel is a graceful way out of this crisis, we'll discuss it, and we'll fill the rest of you in on how our discussion went in the morning."

When no one objected and many looked relieved, Jamey asked Hub, Doty, Max, Kira, Kale, Ida, Risa, Lou Roy, Buford, and Eddie to please join him in a seated circle, the room emptied by two-thirds, and the named parties moved their chairs accordingly.

"I've got no skin in this feud," he began, "except my friendship with all of you. Rosalia's hell-raising has shocked and angered us. But that girl's a loved friend to me too, and I strongly believe we can bring this thing to a close without calling the cops or giving her a criminal record. I was scheduled to go to Portland in four days, but if Eddie will let me take Rosalia with me, I'll leave tomorrow. Think of me as a parole officer who vows she will *not* be a repeat offender. But know too that I hope to help heal her of a wound I feel has caused this crisis, a wound she and I share. I lost my mother in a very cruel way when I was five. Rosa lost hers just as cruelly when she was seven. Just sit quiet with that a minute."

You could have heard a pin drop. No one saw this coming. But when Eddie Dominguez, looking stunned and moved, slowly nodded his head, Kale and Risa nodded too.

"If you'll let her come with me tomorrow, Eddie, we'll compare our losses together. A glimpse of mine, to help the rest of you understand: when my mother died on my fifth birthday in the same hospital where I was born, I buried that cruel coincidence so deep you'd think I never had a mother. But every year, when our shared birthday-deathday rolled around, impotent rage burst out of me in ways as dangerous as what's been bursting out of Rosalia. This is where Portland comes in. I called TJ before our meeting tonight because his brother, Jervis, sees things most of us can't. On a long Ocean-walk in 1997, Jervis diagnosed my idiot refusal to grieve my mother, and assigned me a simple prayer. When I snarled that I didn't believe in prayer, Jervis, in his damaged, papery whisper, read me a riot act that reduced me to rubble. Long story short, he forced me to repeatedly say the prayer I didn't believe in, and I made stronger contact with my mother than I had since I lost her. My plan for Rosalia is simple: we'll talk mother loss en route to Portland, and the next day Jervis has agreed to take Rosalia Ocean-walking. After dozens of such walks with him, I fully believe he might help Rosalia in ways the rest of us can't. What do you say, folks?"

Max Bowler spoke up first. "Sounds nutty on the face of it, Jamey. But we can't leave Rosalia on the loose here. What's to lose if you think this is worth a try?"

Hub Punker turned red as a beet and blored, "*What's to lose!?* Cattle and cowboys, that's what! That girl needs to be *punished*!"

"I just changed my mind for two reasons," Kira Bowler said firmly. "One, we all owe TJ a ton, and Rosa holds a special place in his heart. Two, if we turn her over to the cops and they put her in Sapphire County Juvenile Detention, I know from former students there are dangers there we wouldn't wish on anyone. I couldn't live with myself if we jailed her and something awful happened. I'm all for the Jamey and Jervis plan."

When Hub sputtered, "*Turncoat!*" and Doty Nolan nodded, Ida Craig stared holes in them and said, "Name-calling? *Seriously?* I'm a hundred percent behind Jamey's plan."

"Makes two of us," Kale rumbled—and Hub and Doty went silent for the night.

Lou Roy then reached deep into the kindness he tries to hide and turned to Eddie. "I know you're upset about my truck. Don't be, Eddie. I was overdue for a new rig. It's my pal Rosalia I hope we repair fast, an' Jamey's tossed us an idea *miles* ahead o' anything else I heard this sorry night. Can we bag this nonsense an' let Jamey an' Jervis get to it?"

The instant Eddie nodded, Kale said, "Then we're good to go. Thanks, everybody, and extra thanks to you, Jamey and Eddie. Meeting adjourned."

Wandering II: Including Joaquina (October 2008)

The next morning, as Jamey and Rosalia crossed Western Montana, he kept the talk light for the first couple of hours. But after a pit stop near the Idaho border, when he and Rosalia climbed back in, he said, "Before we get back on the road, are you willing to step, as gently as possible, into troubled waters we have in common, Rosalia? Would that be okay?"

Though her posture stiffened and she stared straight ahead at nothing, she nodded.

"A big reason I wanted to make this trip with you is that I lost my mom when I was five. Her name is Debbie, and I say *is*, not *was*, because I still feel her strongly sometimes. I'm wondering what your mom's name is, and whether you sometimes feel her."

Just that fast Rosalia burst open. "Her name was *Joaquina*, and not even Risa or Lore have ever asked me that! And I *try* to feel her all the time. But nobody speaks of her! Nobody *looks* for her! Do they think because awful men used drugs to take her captive, Joaquina was awful too? She was my *mother*! She could still be alive! *How could Eddie make us abandon her? Why did he make us run?*"

Her intensity redoubled Jamey's effort to remain calm. "Thank you for opening up, Rosa. You fill my heart with good trouble and my mind with questions. But let's go slowly and carefully. To start, I wonder what you make of this. Last night Risa and Kale briefed me on why you and Eddie came to Montana a decade ago. They said Eddie risked his life for Joaquina several times before you left Arizona, but when she brought the drug men to your home he had to lie to save you both. If they saw Eddie again, he believes they'd kill him. Kale and Risa believe it too. I know you trust Kale and Risa. So I feel there's something even bigger than trust going on. My first question: What's happening *inside of you* that's turned you so fiercely against the cattle operation and your finest friends?"

"I lost Joaquina, and you lost Debbie. I trust that," she said. "So I'll try to answer. But it's very hard to talk about. I'll prob'ly cry at the worst parts. But I'll try!"

"Cry when you need to, with my thanks," Jamey said.

"On our last night in Arizona, two of the men who took Joaquina captive found our house. And yes, Joaquina led them to us. But who can blame her? They would have hurt her, maybe killed her, if she didn't. They were terrifying, both of them—and they'd come to terrify us. The hardest thing…" Rosalia's voice broke up, and she began to tremble. But she raised her hands in the air and shook them as if shaking off water, took a huge breath, and surprised Jamey with how quickly she was able to continue. "I'd found two feral kittens. Really small ones, their eyes just opening. Calicos. I kept them in a shoebox by my bed and fed 'em milk out of a dropper. When one of the men saw them, he walked over to them, turned and smiled at Eddie and me, and at Joaquina, then shot both kittens dead." Now the tears came. "I couldn't understand anything Eddie said to the men! I was too young to know what they wanted! But I can't *not* hear those shots even now! I can't *not* hear Joaquina's screams! I can't not see the bullet holes in the floor after they took my mother away."

"Oh, my *God*, Rosa! I'm so sorry!"

"So that's why," she said brokenly, "loving the Highland calves from the day they're born, seeing how gentle they get during two and a half years of trusting me, I can't stand the shots that kill them. I just *can't*! And I'm sorry I put people I love in danger. But I'll *never* be able to stand those shots!"

Jamey was gentleness itself as he said, "You shouldn't *have* to, Rosa. From now on we'll protect you from them. I volunteer and others will too. We'll go climb a mountain, canoe a lake, take you wherever you feel most at peace. And another thing, Rosalia. There's a beautiful side to what you've been attempting. May I describe it?"

Looking mystified, she nodded.

"You knew it would be impossible to *truly* free the cattle, but you freed them as best you could anyway, twice in two days. Why? Because it was your way of trying to free your mother. *That's* the beauty. In impossible circumstances, you're still trying to love Joaquina."

Something in Rosalia released, and she cried hard. "Kleenex in the glove box," Jamey said, and she used lots of them. But again, after shaking her hands in the air as if to dry them, she was able to steady.

"'Bless you' is not a phrase I use," Jamey told her. "Who am I to think I can bless anybody? But something bigger than me is urging me to say, 'Bless your attempts to love your mother. Bless them, Rosalia.'"

A few more tears. A few more Kleenex. No words. But such grateful dark eyes.

"This exchange has been huge, and we should give it a rest," Jamey said. "But we're on our way to Portland for a reason, so there's one more thing to say. Jervis is a very unusual man. Two men as bad as those who took Joaquina once injured him terribly. You'll see his damages. But you'll also soon see that he is all about *love*, Rosalia. And when he senses yours for Joaquina, he's going to help you do *way* more than scatter cattle and endanger friends with it. He's going to help you increase your love, and give it new and better places to go."

"Oh, I hope so!" Rosa cried. "And bless *you*, Jamey, for helping me this way!"

Wandering III: The Listenings (2008 and 2009)

Word never slipped out. By late December, all that clued Risa in to a major change was Rosalia's palpable happiness, and the glowing smiles that appeared on her face and Lore's every time they set eyes on each other. They clearly had a secret they relished keeping.

With her usual acuity, Risa noticed the glow was brightest on mornings when she found Lore- and Rosalia-sized tracks leading into, then out of, the windowless, doorless shell of the unfinished B Barn first thing in the morning. On the last Monday in 2008, Risa woke in the dark, took a 6 a.m. walk, and through binoculars saw what she'd hoped for: the shine of two flashlights stepping out of the barn shell together. Not wanting to damage something dear to her friends, Risa didn't speak of it, but did keep investigating.

At 5:15 a.m. the following Monday, January 5th, 2009, she donned her warmest clothes, grabbed a flashlight, strolled down through Aspen Swale to the shell of the B Barn, stepped through the doorless door into the 17-degree-Fahrenheit great room, and beheld Lore's icon, Elmerina Buddha, facing three votive candles burning on a chair in the room's center, while Rosalia and Lore sat in two more straight-backed chairs, lit by the same candles. They remained so motionless and still for such a long time that Risa sensed their ardor, and hated to disturb them. But she also didn't want to seem a spy. So she cleared her throat.

Lore and Rosalia turned, smiled, and silently gestured for her to approach. Risa did, but whispered, "I sensed you might be praying. If I should leave, just say so."

Before she could say another word Grady Haynes stepped out of the darkness into the candlelight. "I invited Grady to join us," Lore whispered to Risa. "And next week I planned to invite you. Please join us if you like."

Grady carried two chairs over, gave one to Risa, and they settled on four sides of Elmerina and her candles. "Lore calls what we're doing 'a Listening,'" Rosalia said. "Every Monday since I found her here in early November we've done this. And Lore came out by herself a few times before that. Can you tell us why, Lore?"

"In a book Risa gave me," Lore whispered. "Mother Teresa said two things that struck me. One: 'May God break my heart so completely that the whole world falls in.' Two: 'When I finally see Jesus, I'll tell Him I loved Him in the dark.'"

"*Wow!*" Grady whispered.

"Then I happened to see an exchange," Lore continued, "between the CBS newsman Dan Rather and Mother Teresa that went like this:

"Dan Rather: 'What do you say to God when you pray?'

"Mother Teresa: 'I don't say anything. I just listen.'

"Dan Rather: 'Well, what does Jesus say to you?'

"Mother Teresa: 'Oh, he doesn't say anything either. He just listens.'

"Moved by her faith in listening, I looked up the times of sunrise, got up early enough to love Elmerina and Jesus in pure dark for forty-five minutes, and chose the shell of the barn so I'd be sheltered from wind and snow. Every Listening has been so beautiful I've continued every Monday since."

Grady smiled. Risa smiled. Rosalia smiled. Elmerina always faintly smiles.

Lore then raised her index finger to her lips, blew out the candles, and there they sat in Mother Teresa's Jesus-loving dark.

THE FOLLOWING MONDAY the same foursome, same three candles, and Elmerina convened at the usual time—then turned toward the sound of boots entering the barn. Into the candlelight stepped Kale, Lou Roy, Buford Raines, and Regina Cloud. All four newcomers had been invited by Lore. All four were dressed in winter coats, Stetsons, cowboy boots, and work gloves for the early morning cattle feeding after. All four added chairs to the circle.

Feeling a little tense given Rosalia's militant veganism, Risa and Kale both glanced at her to check her reaction to the newcomers' arrival—and Rosa looked so overjoyed that tears glistened in her eyes. When Buford noticed this, his eyes welled too, and he and Rosalia smiled long and steady at each other.

"It looks to me like you all must be hearing what you're listening for," Kale said. "But can you please tell me what that is exactly?"

Grady said, "*She who was before heaven and Earth came to be.*"

Risa said, "*The Unseen Unborn Guileless Perfection.*"

Rosalia said, "*The silence that comes of loving a spiritual hero in predawn dark.*"

Lore said, "*A love in the room that doesn't need sound waves to be heard.*"

Buford said, "Dang! Where do you all come up with this stuff?"

"A fandangled forgotten thing they call 'book learnin',' " Grady twanged.

"Before a Listening," Lore said, "one of us sometimes whispers a few words in praise of silence, so long as the words take less than a minute. I brought words today. May I?"

There was something unaccountably thrilling to Risa that one of the heads that nodded yes was Lou Roy Skinner's.

Lore's voice dropped to a whisper. "In a book called *First Church of the Higher Elevations*, the author, Peter Anderson, tells of a Western tourist arriving at a Buddhist monastery high in the Himalayas. After walking up and greeting a monk, the tourist asked, 'What do you do up here?' The monk said, 'We pray and seek wisdom.' The tourist said, 'But that's not really doing anything.' The monk smiled and said, 'In that case, we don't really do anything.' "

Lore's smile inspired seven more. And after forty-five minutes that felt like no time at all, all eight of them smiled again, and left the barn without a word.

THE FOLLOWING WEEK, once the same group was seated, Kale said, "I liked Lore's short homily last week, so I brought an even shorter one. Two sentences by Pico Iyer that put me in a listening mood. Ready?"

Everyone nodded.

" 'Silence is the tribute we pay to holiness,' " Kale whispered, " 'We slip off words when we enter a sacred place just as we slip off shoes.' " When Kale then leaned over, slid off his cowboy boots, and set them by his chair, Buford, Lou Roy, and Regina did the same, Risa, Lore, Grady, and Rosalia all slipped off their shoes, and Rosalia's affection for them swelled into something so great that it felt as though her feud against the beef consortium had never been.

BY SATURDAY, FEBRUARY 9th, the days had lengthened enough that the listeners came at 5 a.m. to guarantee their customary darkness. To the surprise of all, when Lore blew out the candles they heard two uninvited listeners join them. Thirty-two feet up the east wall, through a large circular hole that would eventually be a stained-glass image of Jade Lake and the Blue Mosque, a silhouetted pair of barn owls perched for an instant, disappeared by entering the barn's blackness, and the Listeners heard them begin building a nest atop the coming window's spherical framing.

The nest was soon completed, the female laid a clutch of eggs, by mid-March the eggs hatched, and the offspring had a major effect on the Listenings. Hungry baby barn owls have a screech little less distressing than the wail of an Irish banshee. When the parent owls flew in to feed them, the owlets got so competitive the Listeners were driven to laughter by the sounds. But when the Listenings began and the screeching didn't stop, the laughter died.

The Listeners toughed it out for a month. But at the Listening that fell on April Fools' Day, when the nearly adult-sized, much louder owlets started up, Kale said, "Anybody besides me care to move to the dining room of my former house until our pet banshees fledge?"

Expecting they would consider this in silence, the group was surprised when Rosalia launched a homily that shamelessly violated the one-minute limit.

"The last time I was in Portland I was recording a conversation with Jervis," she said, "when I mentioned that our Listenings had been invaded by five shrieking owlets. I'm so glad I was recording! When I asked Jervis what he would do if he were us, he gave a long answer I've listened to maybe ten times, so I can pretty much share it. 'If I were there, ' Jervis said, 'I'd do what the Meister recommended when he said, "Run into peace!" To me, this means that when the owlets start shrieking, you remember they're your neighbors, then love thy neighbor as thyself by running into bigger, tougher kinds of peace than you're used to. Why hold to a prejudice that peace shouldn't alarm our eardrums? Why shouldn't the peace of a Listening consist of parent owls cruising in through a no-glass window to rip warm mice, voles, and baby cottontails to shreds for their screaming owlets? Isn't one of the best homilies in the Bible, "Take. Eat. This is my body, which is broken for you"? Isn't another great homily, "Jesus wept"? Your Listenings bring you the lowing of cattle neighbors your cowboys raise to sacrifice, and isn't that a good thing? How could peace exclude sacrifice?' Jervis asked. 'How could peace exclude the consortium that puts a roof over Max, Kira, Lou Roy, Doty, Kale, Buford, and Regina's heads? How could peace exclude the restaurant work that is Teej's spiritual practice? How could peace exclude droves of people from E City to Portland to Ashland to Bellingham to whom your sacrificed cattle give jobs, the hundreds of diners they give pleasure, and the challenge you're now meeting, Rosalia, when you watch your carnivorous neighbors dig into a steak and love them no less for it?'

" 'How did you know I've come to love them no less?' I asked Jervis.

" 'Because I've seen you grasp on our Ocean-walks,' he said, 'that peace is nothing more than the most perfect attention a complicated circle of people can pay to every moment, which is a peace hard to reach amid wailing and anger and violence and lamentations and countless other deafening things going on in the world at all times. But if peace were easy to reach, would it be worth finding? If your peace excluded hungry owlets, was it ever peace to begin with? Wouldn't Eckhart advise you to run into the great screeching blue barn peace you've got for the chance it gives you to truly love thy owlets as thyself? And when they fledge and fly, don't you s'pose peace might surprise you with the heartache of missing them, screeches and all, leaving you delighted if more shrieking neighbors are born in your barn next year?' "

So touched was the circle of Listeners by Jervis's words that they *did* run into the blue barn's screeching peace, and soon noticed that their challenging owlet neighbors had left them more resiliently at peace with their challenging human neighbors in every other walk of life.

Wandering IV: Beginning the Beguine (Portland, 2008)

When Jamey drove Rosalia to Portland, he was confident that Jervis would somehow give her love for her missing mother new and better places to go. But he had no inkling of how ready Rosalia was for Jervis, and TJ too, or of how far and fast the three of them would travel down what was, for Rosa, a completely unprecedented path.

Their very first Ocean-walk was revelatory to her. Recognizing this immediately, TJ and Jamey let Eddie, Lore, and Risa know that something transformational was happening, and that Jervis and Rosalia needed more time. Eddie, Lore, and Risa all told them to take all the time they needed to reach the best possible result. So it was that Rosa stayed on in the Pearl Building for two solid weeks and took twelve marathon Ocean-walks with Jervis. And while a hundred-page description would scarcely scratch the surface of what their walks contained, it's not hard to describe the cumulative effect:

Rosalia was transformed. Jervis's intricate, unflagging love for Ocean as she guided him through the wildly multifarious people, creatures, and contents of his city, rather than blow Rosa's circuits as it sometimes did mine, blew her previous worldview away. Mysteries comparable to what Skrit Lit and the Beguines brought to the young Risa, what Gladys Wax brought to Grady, what Blue Empty brought to Lore, befell Rosalia, and she was as surprised as anyone when her appetite for Dumpster Catholicism and Ocean and street people and self-giving proved prodigious.

Seeing this, Jervis and TJ not only took her under their wing, they welcomed her, after just a week, into the intimacy of their late-night drams, where Rosalia's dram of choice was kombucha, and where the secretive talk touched on TJ's adoration of Demetria Cabrera's trouble dolls, everybody's love for Dumpster Catholicism, the mind-bending complexity of Ocean's strobes, the rock steadiness of Risa's love for Eckhart, the Beguines, and the Unseen Unborn Guileless Perfection, and Lore's steady love for Blue Empty, Dōgen, and Jade. "How you all operate, and what you live by," Rosalia wrote to Risa and Lore, "keeps pouring into me, and I want it to take me over completely. I want to be immersed the way Lore was as Jade! I want to actively serve the mysteries, as you all do!"

The way she'd been serving in Montana then came under the influence of all she'd been experiencing in Portland. She had, for instance, been farming lentils as a protein substitute for the cattle, because the slaughter of Highlands enraged her. As Rosalia emulated Jervis and TJ, her motivation completely softened. Another influence Portland had on her Montana life: back in high school Rosa had been a champion of misfits and outcasts— male, female, and Other. She had shown a gift for saving some of them from bullies, fanatical preachers, abusive parents, or advising them on pregnancies, broken homes, how and when to come out of closets, and other tricky life passages. Going away to college had put this invaluable service on hold. Jervis and TJ encouraged Rosalia to revive it, and to dream big about who some of her rescued misfits might become if Rosa herself took the lead. In her last letter to her spiritual mothers before Jamey brought her home, she revealed her dream:

Dearest Risa and Lore,

Jervis keeps saying we three remind him of the Beguines, and the more I read about them, the more I see their resemblance to you two. They made their own rules without institutional guidance, studied and emulated their spiritual heroes, earned their keep by working hard and serving others, and were most serious of all about their spiritual practices, so like you two. And their way of life spread all over the Low Countries and was serving tens of thousands when what Jervis calls the Catholic Gestapo decided to destroy them. When I asked him why priests hated them so, Jervis said it was because the best of the Beguines married *all* their loves, including all creatures, all creation, all marginalized people, and, so unlike the priests, zero institutions, political powers, or riches stolen from conquered other peoples and poured into Church coffers. And that's where I began to see a resemblance to me. Jervis and TJ think as a team, as you must know. They're crazy about my hope to keep helping persecuted Elkmoon locals, so TJ helped Eddie back me, as you know, by building the two kit cottages by my lentil farm. He and Kale also turned the old Airstream over to me. On the farming front, TJ has ordered a couple truckloads of cheap bamboo fencing to protect our lentils from deer. And that reminded Jervis of the enclosing walls that protected the Beguines' privacy and safety, so next thing you know Jervis and I schemed and TJ invested in a better grade of bamboo fencing that will give privacy and safety to the cottages and Airstream that house us, so we'll really and truly resemble the Beguines. Then on our Ocean-walk just today, Jervis went on a roll, listing so many cool things that Montana neo-Beguines could be doing that it's 11:30 at night and my head is still spinning! I need to join them for their drams and my kombucha now, but here's just one of a dozen ideas Jervis had: I should explore turning my fishing guide, boating, and outfitting skills in all new directions, like running multiple-day float trips you two could conduct as river-riding spiritual retreats, giving the locals we'll be helping—and the refugees of wars and climate catastrophes Jervis says are coming—peace and healing on the waters.

But I'm gonna pop if I don't share the greatest thing of all from the Ocean-walk: I've been devouring the same Beguine books Risa studied, I'm completely in love with them, and when you two and I feel I'm ready, Jervis said, "TJ—through powers vested in him on the authority of no institution or created thing but love—will be honored to ordain you North America's first Dumpster Catholic Beguine." He then closed his good eye, saw who knows what with the glass one, and stood so still I felt it was Hadewijch herself who whispered, "I never felt love, unless as an ever-new death, until the time of my consolation came, when God granted me to know how we shall love the Humanity in order to come to the Divinity, and rightly know both in one single Nature. This is the noblest life that can be lived," leaving me sobbing on God knows what Portland street corner as I realized a Risa-and-Lore-guided, TJ-ordained, Jervis-blessed, Buddhist-for-Christ's-Sake Dumpster Catholic Beguine is everything I've ever dreamed of being!

But please don't tell Eddie. I wanna smash him with a huge hug and tell him myself!

> All the love in the world,
> ~Rosalia

Wandering V: In His Vast Wasteland (Summer 2012)

"My heart," Lorilee told Risa as they were driving home from Missoula after yet another bout of chemo, "has ceased to struggle against my cancer. Of course body and mind are in a panic. So soon doomed. But since receiving Jade's gift my heart doesn't engage. I choose to remain quiet as I can amid the pummeling, and to embrace Blue Empty when it ends. I can't hike up to the broken ponderosa to peer into the begging bowl except on the two days a week Grady carries me up in the saddle-pack. But I can still totter along the lower river trails inside the bowl's contents. I think you'd like it that the last time I did that, a week or so ago, the hot wind in the cottonwoods flew me to the winds on the plains of Mamre in which, you once told me, 'the Lord appeared to Abraham in the heat of the day.'"

"I can't believe you remembered that!" Risa said.

"I didn't," Lore said. "The wind and cottonwoods did."

"You're reminding me of our old Dōgen and Eckhart game. Of the hot wind and cottonwoods out of which the Lord appeared, I hear the Meister saying, 'Whether you like it or not, whether you know it or not, secretly all nature seeks God and works toward Him.' (Or as blessed Julian adds, Her.)"

Lore smiled. "After chemo, I feel more like the fish in that Dōgen line we loved. 'It might be natural for us to have minds like fish in a dwindling stream.'"

Risa grinned and kept the game going: "'God never tied salvation to any pattern,' the Meister said, so dwindling streams and flooding streams are *both* a Way."

With a smile impossibly happy for a face so drawn and pale, Lore said, "You're so right. 'When there is much mud,' Dōgen said, 'the Buddha is large.'"

"The Meister would love that! How would he reply? Let me think…Got it! 'God's ground is my ground, and my ground is God's ground.'"

"'Buddha's mud is my mud and my mud is Buddha's mud,'" Lore said, and a small laugh caused a cough, then she choked slightly, then a fierce coughing fit left Risa fearing her heart would crack in two. "But now," she whispered, "as cough medicine, may I please hear Nāgārjuna, in his own tongue, say that everything is still possible when emptiness is possible?"

Risa needed several slow breaths to calm before she managed to recite, "'Sarvaṃ ca yujyate tasya śūnyatā yasya yujyate.'"

"The perfect terminal cancer strategy," Lore sighed, giving Risa a look so tender that the Meister quote Risa was about to add fell to pieces in her mouth.

"'In his solitary wildness,'" she said brokenly. "'In his vast wasteland,'" she whispered.

Then her voice left her completely, and emptiness made possible two women heading south through Montana on Interstate 15, holding hands as they smiled through their tears.

Wandering VI: Clouds and Curtains in Their Bodies (October 2015)

"Sure I'll talk about the truck Ida and TJ purchased for us," Kale told me, the Holy Goat, as we met for drinks and dinner at the Loco Creek Steakhouse.

"*The traveling abattoir*, some call it, as if a French word can disguise its purpose. A slaughterhouse and meat locker on wheels is what this one is. But grim as that sounds, I'm not ashamed of it. Our ability to ready our own animals for market ended our need for the international beef cartel, freed us of the feedlots, and allows our cattle to die where they were born, same as I hope to do. So when Don Steadles and his sons drive the abattoir up, I feel duty bound to help move the steers to the killing place. I can't pull the trigger. I just watch, and they wound me, those killings. But ever since Risa told me that her man, Meister Eckhart, said, *Every creature is a word of God*, I feel an *obligation* to be wounded by each steer's death."

"Has there ever been a slaughter day," I asked Kale, "where each thing that happened felt like it couldn't have gone better in spite of, or maybe because of, this wound you choose to feel at each death?"

Kale took a pull on his Knob Creek, thought a moment, and said, "Since we worked out how to conduct their life's end, it's much the same every time. Things happened just last fall that hit me where I live. But it was after the killings and butcher work and the abattoir drove away, so it doesn't really speak to your question."

"Then I change my question," I said. "Tell me *anything* about a slaughter day that hit you where you live."

Kale settled the way he does before he unspools a story. "I was smoking a little Dominican cigar I believe you once gave me, HG, not to rip off something sacred from the tribes, but just to smell something besides the departed creatures I'd loved. I was sitting on a boulder amid the gore-covered ground where eight steers had just died, so I was surprised to see Regina Cloud headed in my direction. Feeling sure she'd veer off, I turned away toward the sunset and steeped in my feelings. Next thing I knew, Regina was beside me, wearing an expression so kind it shook me a little. I then saw that, to reach me, this sweet woman, vegan from birth, really, had gotten blood all over her pretty fake-leather boots. That shook me a little more. When she then sat on the boulder beside me, reached an arm around me, and gave me the longest, gentlest half hug I've ever received, I was in trouble.

"'I've been spying on you all day,' she said, 'and you know what I keep seeing? How much you love the young cattle that die here. It's in your body language, and in your eyes this instant. You're all alone up here being heartbroken, Kale. That's why the hug.'

"'Well, thanks,' I said, 'but can we not speak of it just now? Because as anyone will tell you, Kale the Pope does not cry. But if we talk more of this, he might.'

"So she didn't say a word. She did something worse. She lay her head on my shoulder and just left it there. And *good God, HG*. That moment, eyeing the blood on her boots amid the sad scent of Highlands, I felt so much love for this secret daughter and this way of life and death we've all got going here, I could hardly bear it. 'The reason I feel broken up,' I managed to mumble to Regina, '*is a choice*.'

"'Explain it to me,' she said, leaving her head where it was.

"'More sensible cattlemen choose not to love creatures they know they're going to kill,' I said. 'They keep it cold. Which I understand. But I prefer to appreciate each steer from birth to death, its early doom at our hands included. Highland calves aren't smart, but they're incredibly charming, and so in love with the world their love sneaks up on some of us. Me and Buford get slammed by it, as you know. Short as their lives are, the land on which we tend them becomes storied by the goofy things they do, their mad random gambols and games, the dangerous fixes they get themselves into. Our rescues of the goofiest of them put us at serious risk at times. Then they reach two-and-a-half, and our brave rescues are undone by Don Steadle's unerring rifle shot. I choose to ache over that because the refusal to ache over the ending life of an Eckhart *word of God* is why giant industrial feedlots and slaughterhouses are the way it's done now. Far better to ache, is my feeling, than to pile horror upon horror on every animal and human involved in their departures.'

"Did Regina have anything to say to that?" I asked Kale.

"Her head on my shoulder said everything. Until I blew it. *Do you know Wendell Berry's hog-killing poem?* I asked, and her head left my shoulder. *What am I saying? I told her. Of course you don't! Sorry, Regina! But it's a prayer, really, asking for the quickest, calmest kill possible, which is the best thing we can offer. Let them stand still for the bullet,* Wendell writes, *and stare the shooter in the eye. Let them die while the sound of the shot is in the air, let them die as they fall.* And if it was up to me I'd recite those words to diners wherever our beef is served. I'd tell how our little Golgotha, thanks to Don's dead-steady aim, *does let them die as they fall. I loved that animal on your plate,* I'd say, *and I delivered him to where we killed him, and I kept loving him as he fell. What you're tasting was for once done right.* But what diner on a date wants to hear that?

"'*This* diner,' Regina told me. 'I came up to bloody my boots in what happened here, and to hear you describe it, for which I thank you. But I also ask a favor, Kale. It would help Buford and me a lot if you'd talk to us both the way you're talking to me now, because we're not just in love with each other. We're in love with this whole place and don't wish to know it in some fractured carnivore-versus-vegan way. We want to know what's *real* here, and to love whatever's lovable. And *you're* the Elkmoon longtimer wise enough to help us with that.'

"'Well,' I said. 'If Buford's not too busy, there's no time like the present.'

"So down the hill she went to where, at the end of the hard day he works daily, Buford was still tending horses. And I saw nothing but what's real as Regina reached him and right away kissed him, work dirty though he was. I saw what's real in the way she threaded her arm through his; in how he inclined his head to listen to her; in the easy rhythm of their walk as they set out toward me; the deep wear and dirt in their clothes as they drew closer; the October light in their eyes as they arrived."

"Regina's right," I told Kale, "that you're the one to convey what's real here. You're an eloquent man, Pope."

"Ah, but Regina outdid me, HG. Listen," he said. "When the two of them arrived at my rock, her first words were, 'The next animal you ask Don Steadles to drop, Kale, I want to be there with Buford, watching. I want to see for myself that it dies as it falls. And then I want to see it butchered, and help if I can. I want to know what this place we love turns a calf's body into, and how best to take that body apart to feed people. Can I bear that? I don't know. But it's time I tried.'

"She sought strength then, HG, by drawing a deeper breath. 'And after it's been hung, and aged,' she said, 'and a maestro like you, TJ, or Buford grills it, I want one bite of Eckhart's *word of God*.'

"Hearing this, Buford's jaw dropped so low I could see his whole chaw. 'Just one bite,' Regina said in that calm, even voice of hers. And though Buford got his mouth closed, his eyes had filled. 'I want to taste the body and the blood,' she said, which *really* got to poor Buford. 'That *grassiness* you talk about. That *Elkmoon June and July bounty*. That September field you save all summer—*their going-away present*, you call it. That's a sweet way of talking, but unless I taste of it, it's just pretty words. For the steer's sake, and mine, I need to know, just the once, the flavors of these animals you and Buford so love, and sacrifice even so. Because there's another pretty word some visitors like to bring to the Elkmoon: *holistic*. But if that word doesn't mean what's actually being done here, it doesn't mean a thing. So who am I to refuse one bite of what sunlight, grass, the life's work of my husband, and miracle combined to create a soft-eyed, red-banged, thirty-month-old Highland steer? I want that to enter me,' Regina said while Buford leaned over his tomato sauce can hoping his Skoal spurt would blind me to his spurting tears.

"To save myself from a similar fate, I looked past Regina to a bunch of our kids laughing as they scared ravens and magpies off the gore in the kill zone while Eddie, Doty, and Risa kept mopping up, and Buford set up sprinklers to wash the blood back into the earth and the tears off his face. It then felt so right, HG, to leave Regina's man in peace, offer her my arm, cross the bloodied ground, and say to her the things I've wanted to say to diners as she and I studied the place we gave the steers their last supper; place the bullet struck; place they fell; place where they were slaughtered; tracks of the departing abattoir in the dry Indian Summer grass.

"So we continued up through fields our steers grazed all the way to the horizon, where I described to Regina the towering clouds and huge gray to black curtains of rain that grow the grass from March on into summer heat. And if you're still fishing for what caused me to raise the Elkmoon water table, HG, the time has come: it was Regina, saying to me in a voice only sheer wonder can create, 'So clouds and curtains were in their bodies as they fell.'"

"Beautiful!" I whispered.

"Yes it was," Kale said. "But the total number of tears summoned by that beauty was *two*, dammit. So don't go turning it into a *deluge* in your chronicles."

"Only the two, Kale. Swear to God. And in honor of each, my two favorite new bourbons are headed for the cabinet you've shared with me all these years."

"That a trace of spirits might remain in our bodies as we fall," quoth Kale.

God, I love the things that man says and feels.

Wandering VII: New Eyes

Letter from Trey Jantz in Pipestone, Colorado, to Mu Jantz on the E.B.&C.Co, February 2012:

Dear Mu,

Last week I returned from four summits in the Andes to your news of Lore's crisis. Thanks for filling me in. I can't tell you how sorry I am that it seems to have become a losing battle. And thanks even more for reminding me that no one we know glimpses the life beyond ours more clearly than Lore.

Living with this hard news for a week, Mu, has more or less plucked out my eyeballs and replaced them with new ones. I don't expect you to believe this without proof, so let me tell you some of what I'm seeing and you can decide for yourself. I see that my four recent Andes climbs brought me no joy at all. I see, after all my years of raving about climbing lines, that it's not those lines we follow most of the way up the Andes now but hundreds of abandoned high-elevation village sites and drought-killed farm and grazing lands.

I see my pals and me shouldering our way through former herders and farmers camped in Lima and Cuzco ghettos because an industrial world they wanted no part of destroyed their glaciers, sucking their waters and way of life dry. I see my climbs captured in films in which every item I carry or wear is chosen for endorsement money. I see my pals and me plowing along blind to the world, while you've become a multitalented young man living to serve and inspire others, same as Lore has always done. And I'm so in awe of you both, Mu, and so sick of being self-serving, that I beg you to accept the enclosed check. You'll know what to do with it.

Because I wish it was so much more I also want to float an idea by you and Lore. If it wouldn't disturb you, I'd love to offer my labor to your community from April Fools' Day to September's end for the next three or four years. I can afford it, I promise to be as unobtrusive as possible, and I say three or four years because I'll get better at it if I do it longer. With your okay I'd rent a little apartment in E City, slip out to your ranch each morning, do any work you ask of me, and slip back into town each night. No pestering. No pay. No task too humble. Carpentry, grunt work, pest control, weed control, painting, any handyman chores that come up.

Just say no if it doesn't feel right, but know I only want to do this to slightly lighten the heavy burden you and your mother are carrying.

Love,
Trey

Letter from Mu Back to Trey, February 2012:

Dear Dad,

Thanks for writing, thanks for the generous box of money, thanks for your offer, and yes, there are things you could do for us on the E.B.&C.Co. Mom suggested a one-month trial to see how it goes. I agree because she's Mom, but just between us, I'm all for your plan. You and E City will be a great fit. The climbers in town will be dazzled to meet you, there's fun stuff to do here even though it's mostly quiet, and you'll love the Loco Creek Steakhouse and Ambivalent Cafe.

As for the work, our head farmers are named Regina and Ona, but Ona's busy these days in ten ways at once, and Regina's hampered by her toddler, Lily Cloud Raines, plus she and Buford are hoping to have another kid. So in the months you named, April thru Sept, we need emergency farm help in a big way. Normally I'd step up, but I'm maxed out helping Mom. Despite her health she's full of great ideas, both musically and on behalf of our menagerie. She needs me to help capture and implement the ideas. This is a hard but very special time for us.

So fair warning, Dad: our farm labor shortage is serious, and not just this year, so your multiple-year offer sounds perfect. Harvest starts with radishes and greens in April, simultaneous to planting, and runs all the way into October tomatoes, pumpkins, winter squash. Translation: how strong is your back? The soil needs improving non-stop. Translation: are you willing to haul and spread chicken and cow manure ad infinitum? Weeds are also ad infinitum. And you mentioned pest control. Translation: holy crap, Dad! This could make you a hero to us. We have a gopher and ground squirrel crisis. If you choose to address it, here's some detail on what you'd face.

You've heard me mention our ranch fireball, Rosalia Dominguez. She's like an annoying but lovable sister to me. Lovable in her ad-oration of animals. A terror thanks to the same love. In the past she was a militant vegan, but contact with Lore and our other great heart, Risa, has convinced her to quit trying to talk multigeneration cattle growers, hunters, and anglers into swapping their love for hunting and fishing for growing lentils. True, lentils do well here, our best chefs work wonders with them, but Rosalia is nuts about fishing her-self. I'm not trying to make her sound hypocritical or dumb. She's as tenderhearted as she is ornery, and downright saintly when it comes to helping every kind of misfit being scapegoated, human or non. But the same quality has made Rosa believe that if we would all study interspecies communication and ask our gophers and ground squirrels "with great love" to go away, they will! The rodent welfare state this has created is killing our farm operation, we needed to declare war years ago, and if you'll go to work on this crisis I promise to protect you from Rosalia when we're deciding what methods to use.

If this doesn't appeal to you, I'd still be glad of a visit. If Mom ever recovers enough to free me for eight days I'd love to show you our favorite mountains. I'm not a climber, just a high-country wanderer like Mom's beau, Grady, but the Inner Elkmoons are something special. Standing neck-deep in this crazy warm lake at 9,000 feet was life-changing for Mom, and now for Grady and me, and might be for you too. That lake's hidden powers are why, hard as things are, we're not as broken up as most people would be over Mom's prognosis. Another thing about the Inners: if you see the place where Mom tore up her ankle, then try to imagine how Grady got her from there down to here as we make the hike out, you'll know why we all love him.

Come what may, thanks for writing, Dad. Your offer is huge, and I'm very glad for your new eyes. Just that is a lot.

Love,
Mu

Wandering VIII: Nephrite

From the Elkmoon Mountain Journals of Grady Haynes:

There came a morning in the spring of 2013 when Lorilee felt good enough to attempt a last solo hike up to Blue Empty, and settled Elmerina beside her so they both faced the valley-wide begging bowl. The air was tinged with the faint blue she loved and the gifts of the bowl were profligate. But when the moment arrived when she forgot the self and awakened to the ten thousand things, one adamantine thing among the ten thousand remained the joy-devouring cancer that could no longer be slowed, and it took all her strength not to break down sobbing. Feeling like Blue Empty's betrayer, but also like the one betrayed, she limped on her bad ankle back down toward E City Park, haunted to realize that the only escape from her plight now was to journey beyond the end of her life.

When her '54 Chevy pickup came into view, she was startled to see a white Volkswagen camper van parked close beside it. There were no other vehicles or people around. She didn't want company. Slowing her approach, she saw a man sitting at the wheel, and was about to hide in the trees until he drove away, when he jumped out of his van, turned to her, and his body language and every feature exuded such kindness that her curiosity to learn who he was made her forget her plight.

Joining him by her truck, he told her, "Greetings. I'm Jimmy Fong, and I believe you're Lorilee Shay. If so, I have a message for you."

"I'm Lore," she admitted, feeling shy. This man seemed so accomplished in his humanness, she told me later, that he reminded her of the first time Lore met Risa.

"The message is unusual," Jimmy said. "Please interrupt and ask questions if you feel a need."

"I will," Lore said.

"Someone who loves you, but must do so from a distance, told me you often come down out of the South Whitetails to a classic green Chevy pickup parked by the E City Park pond. This person said that, should I encounter you, I should tell you that she loves me too, to build a little trust between us. She then shared your diagnosis. I'm very sorry to know of it, Lorilee, and don't mean to pry, but the one who loves you insisted that I deliver her message. She told me to state with the certainty she herself feels that, at Jade Lake ten years ago, you were able to immerse, and to experience beings entering and exiting our world, and to fully grasp that, for the Atman, there _is_ no termination. I'm a little embarrassed to speak to you this way but do so out of esteem for the one who esteems you. Does this make any kind of sense, Lorilee?"

"That was the most implausible greeting anyone's ever given me," Lore said. "And it makes perfect sense. As I believe you know, Jimmy, the greatest mysteries are wonderful _because_ they're so implausible. But where are you going with this?"

"The one who loves you invites you to be at the West Fork trailhead in three days, on May 19th, around nine in the morning, and asks that you bring Bird-Dropping-Me with you. The forecast is for heavy rain. A little group, dear to the one I speak for, is fond of traveling under cover of rain. Before we set out we also wanted to connect with you and Grady, and present you with a few small thank-you gifts."

"Still implausible, Jimmy," Lore said. "Just the way Bird-Dropping-Me and I like it. We'll see you there."

"It feels nuts," I groused as Lore and I set out in my little pickup early on the 19th, "to be driving to the West Fork with no backpack, no supplies but a lunch and thermos of tea, and no plans to continue past the trailhead. It's like being invited onto the doormat of our heart's home, and not allowed inside."

"Since I haven't been able to make the hike for a decade," Lore said, "it feels pretty normal to me. Look on the bright side, Grady. Since it's pouring, you at least got to pack our lunches and rain gear. And don't pretend you're not excited. Jimmy's group is 'fond of traveling under cover of rain.' Why do you suppose that would be?"

Although neither of us would say it outright, we hoped Jimmy's "someone who loves you" might be Gladys, of whom we'd heard nothing for several years. And we also dared hope that Jimmy and the rain-travelers might be her high-elevation intimates.

The drive through steady rain was soothing, as are all rainy drives since devastating conflagrations became the Mountain West's summer norm. Past Elsewhere we left campgrounds and cell service behind. Lore asked me to slow to a crawl as she gazed out over what Risa and Lou Roy still call the Glory Meadow in honor of the encounter that prefigured the E.B.&C.Co's genesis. "It doesn't seem the same place with the mountains obscured," Lore said. "Doesn't it move you to know the people we're going to meet will be journeying into that obscurity? Later this very day, it will erase them!"

Seeing Lore smile, in part because she herself is being erased and has great faith in that, I couldn't speak or even look at her, knowing I'd lose it completely.

At the bombed-out-looking gas station where the road forks in three, we chose the steepest: West Fork Road. A half mile along, Lore got her wish: we were erased by the dense gray of the clouds, and Lore appeared moved beyond words by it. A mile or so farther, I was rounding a tight curve when Lore cried out and I slammed on the brakes: we'd come face-to-face with a twenty-foot Winnebago--the last thing we expected weeks before tourist season. I had to back up a hundred yards to find a place where it could squeeze by us. As it did so, the old man at the wheel gave us a huge grin and exuberant wave. "Talk about _lost!_" Lore said.

"Or maybe not," I said. "But if that ol' boy's face implied what I suspect it did, Lûmi secrecy is not his strong suit."

We reached the lodgepoles, USFS outhouse, and horse ramp three hundred yards below the trailhead. "Many big road- and trail blocking snowbanks, and zero vehicles," Lore said. "Perfect conditions for those we hope to meet."

"And it's raining even harder up here," I added.

Feeling Gladys so strongly that we never once said so, we donned our rain gear, and I slipped on the day pack with our lunches and tea. Lore needed both hands to work the trekking poles she's long needed to support her bum ankle. As we started up toward the concrete obelisks and signboard that mark the trailhead proper, we came upon fresh tire tracks. "The old man's Winnebago," Lore said.

Yep. Then came a patch of mud, close by the tire tracks, down onto which many boots had very recently stepped. The Winnebago had been full. I could distinguish nine separate patterns of boot soles. "What are you thinking, Lore?" I asked.

Utterly delighted, she turned to me full on and said, "Wayfarer, the only way is your footsteps, there is no other. Wayfarer, there is no way, you make the way by walking." I joined my palms and bowed.

The wayfarers' boot prints, after milling around a bit, set out for the trailhead. We did the same. Just as we reached the obelisks and signboard Lore gripped my arm as she gazed ahead, riveted. In the shelter of a stand of bull pines seventy yards up the trail, eleven strangers sat upon rain-cleansed kinnikinnick beside heavy packs, watching us with an intensity perceptible even at that distance. "We're still in bed, dreaming," I murmured. "When we wake they'll have disappeared."

"Not this time," Lore said, raising a hand to them and smiling. "The Chinese American waving back is our inviter, Jimmy Fong. And look at them closely, Grady, because I'm sure you've seen several of them before. A few silhouetted on the high ridgelines. Two or three running little pack strings that, like Gladys's, never pack anybody but the packers. One maybe working a drive-through coffee stand in a mountain town in winter, delivering a smile with your coffee that nearly knocks you over. Some, on days of heavy Inner Elkmoon trail use, disguised by costumes and silly behaviors. Uncomfortably dressed hikers toting field guides to wildflowers they misidentify with per-fectly straight faces. Out-to-lunch-looking wanderers in wrinkled Orlando Disney getup photographing themselves endlessly, the mountains meaningless except as a backdrop."

"All things I've seen, as you know," I said. "But if you're telling me these particular people are those Inner Elkmoon Lûmi wayfarers, I'm not taking another step until you say why you think so."

"I don't think so," Lore said. "I'm not thinking at all. Just saying what I feel due to what I see. The pleasure they're taking in weather so raw that any normal hiker would call off the hike. The calm of faces as apparent as their curiosity about us as we gather at the trail leading up into the most powerful and mysterious place we know. No matter who these men and women are, Grady, how can we not feel honored to meet them?"

I joined my palms and gave Lore another little bow. At seventy yards, all eleven of the watchers smiled to see this, and several joined their palms. _Alert!_

We started toward them, and as we drew closer we sensed a circle of men and women as keenly aware as our E.B.&C.Co intimates. They ranged in age from maybe thirty to seventy, with calm expressions and weather-autographed faces revealing each to be the intimate of storms as terrible as the one that nearly took Lore, and of experiences as transcendent as the night, on my very first Elkmoon pilgrimage, when the Milky Way lay upon the glass-smooth waters of High Lake, placing me on the edge of a literal and living heaven. These people had known wildlife encounters, weather, extreme terrains and mountain experiences as vivid as any Lore or I have had. But there was one run of experiences they had not had: _Lore's long immersion in Jade, subsequent ankle and head injuries, and my rescue of her._ This mattered so much to these eleven that they had summoned us and brought gifts. As I came fully awake to this, their intensity shook me.

They'd set up an overhead tarp to shelter two trekker chairs at the base of a pine. The group faced the pine in a semicircle. Jimmy Fong gestured us to the chairs.

Once seated close by, I recognized several faces, as Lore had predicted. I even recalled chatting with a few on Inner Elkmoon trails, though I'd no idea of their purposes and practices at the time. "We've brought gifts if you're willing," Jimmy said.

Lore and I nodded, and the pilgrims began to rise one at a time, walk over, kneel in the kinnikinnick before us, and each of them presented us with two gifts. The first, times eleven, was a beautiful piece of the green nephrite the Lûmi hide inside their way-marking ridgeline cairns -- an act of shared secrecy that left us feeling deeply accepted. Their second gifts were a small item each pilgrim had personally selected.

The first, given to Lore by a woman who looked Tibetan, Nepali, or Bhutanese, was a photograph of six Buddhist pilgrims: five monks in maroon or ochre, four young and muscular, one an elder, and an unlikely young woman, also Tibetan looking, prostrate in utter reverence in a deep blue dress. All were in motion as they bowed or lay facedown, in slant sunbeams, to the original Bo Tree in Bihar, India, where the Buddha's enlightenment had taken place. The photo washed my eyes so clean that I easily perceived the same disciplined reverence in the eleven before me, and in Lore as she sat among them, smiling like Elmerina Buddha herself.

My first gifts were presented by a tall, rail-thin man whose almost emaciated skinniness was contradicted by a deep, strong, West Texas drawl that took me by total surprise. Then so did his gift: a telephoto lens photo of a magnificent mountain lion seated on a boulder, alert as the teacher's pet in a classroom, gazing at a tiny dome tent pitched by a lake perhaps two hundred feet away. As I slowly recognized the tent as my own, and the lake as Pipsissewa, the Texan grinned and gave me a little nod that said, _Look closer!_ I then spotted myself in the photo, hunched at lakeside, filling the bottom half of my espresso pot, with no idea that I was being considered by the teacher's pet lion as a possible breakfast. When I turned to the West Texan, we burst out laughing, and so did everyone else.

A blue-eyed, auburn-haired, Irish-looking woman handed Lore a small lidded jar and told her, "You make me so glad I live in Montana that I'm returning a little of what I'm glad for." When Lore removed the lid, a homemade cottonwood salve filled our dark rainy pine grove with the musky-sweet scent of a sunny late June cottonwood bottom. Following Lore's lead, we all closed our eyes a while and just breathed it in.

The oldest-looking man, calling himself "an Oregon Coast lifer," presented me with an agate that had formed inside a hermit crab shell and retained the shell shape perfectly, though the creatures and forces that had sculpted it were tens of centuries gone. "A sister for my similar seashell, Bivalve!" Lore said with a smile.

A lovely woman, Middle Eastern or maybe southern Italian in appearance I would guess, handed Lore a wooden box, inside of which lay a foot-tall ceramic sculpture of a woman seated cross-legged and buddha-like, her dark eyes possessed of a thousand-mile gaze that brought to mind a white-tail doe. But her hands could form no mudras, for she was in fact a beautifully sculpted Deer Woman, her arms narrowing to inhumanly thin forelegs and, in place of hands, the delicate hooves of a whitetail doe.

"So _true_!" Lore told the woman, eyes welling. "I _know_ this doe!"

And so it went, eleven times over, every gift a small astonishment.

Then Jimmy Fong rose to his feet. "One more," he said, handing Lore a sealed letter inside a ziplock, and me a small wooden box. The letter was addressed:

Lorilee Shay & Bird-Dropping-Me
% First Pine Grove up West Fk. Trailhead
at 9 a.m. the day Jimmy says

Lore asked me to open the box. Inside were the two most exquisite pieces of nephrite we'd ever seen. Lore then opened the envelope, began reading the letter to us all, and spirits rose to hear the unmistakable style of the one we'd been hoping for:

Dear Lower West Fork Gathering,

Let me first confess that I track you via Jimmy by eating my words, since our communications are all thanks to tech devices I've maligned from the day they were invented. I'm also embarrassed to admit that I'm in Spain, sending my love from more age-appropriate mountains, and a cottage far closer to the beach below than the summit above! It turns out that, as Meister Eckhart attests, the soul does indeed grow younger, but these flesh-and-blood vehicles our souls drive around in do not. I've outlived my Inner Elkmoon access. A close call on a precipice with Mormon and Anonymous warned me this was coming. The pack goats with which I tried to replace the Belgians then caused an even closer call with a large predator that sealed the deal.

So Spain it is, my loves. But remember: Spain it also *isn't*. There will be no separation between us ever. I refuse it. Refuse with me and all will be well.

Lore paused in her reading, the whole group of us glanced at one another -- and again we burst out laughing, this time at the ferocity of our expressions of refusal to be separated from the Informant. Lore continued:

Though I sent a couple of jadeite trinkets for you, Lore and Grady, no gift comes within light-years of what I feel for you two, and for *all* of you.

Lore, you will always be my Jade Lake Lore the Baptist. Bird-Dropping-Me, you are my ever-true Child of the Mountains. Yet who but the Elkmoons and the motley fourteen of us know this? *Perfectly done, all of you!*

Hoping my affection, by the time it arrives, will have dried enough to not feel gooey, I send Gateway, Pipsissewa, and Boundary Love, pitching Grady shit about being a Cornflake Love, crying in the night to Lore's mountain songs when no one can hear me Love, crying over Mu's gorgeous tin-whistled avocet Love, Blue Mosque massif and fathomless Jade Love, and heart overflowing Love at the way each of you risk and consecrate your lives to enter and adore our beloved mountain friends and teachers, each abiding in its phenomenal expression, realizing completeness, active since before the Empty Eon, alive at this moment, the self since before form arose, liberated and realized.

How can I end but with boundless gratitude, and the truth Lore grasped for all of us in Jade: *Earth/Sophia, being Creativity herself, can no more not create than can the Suraj-Sun unity not shine. The great joy is beyond understanding.*

—Gladys

(Portland, November 2013)

XI. Lorilee at The Pearl

And a woman in a wheelchair
is singing a fado
that puts every life in the room
on one pan of a scale,
itself on the other,
and the copper bowls balance.

—Jane Hirshfield, "Fado"

AT THE PEARL theatre benefit concert for Lorilee, three bands and eight solo singer-songwriters performed a single song each, during which a whole lot happened. Most of the E.B.&C.Co populace had come down from Montana and were having a host of responses. And Trey Jantz had driven from Colorado "to support Mu," he told me, but instead broke the record for the number of times I've seen a man cry in two hours. Yet as Jervis McGraff had foreseen decades ago, the lack of a raised proscenium stage enabled "every twist and turn of syntax, quaver of voice, scritch of guitar string, intake of breath, twitch of lip or face or finger to be seen and heard so perfectly that everyone is able to hover inside and reflect and refract everyone else."

When Ona Kutar walked out onstage with her famed Fender electric but no band, no drummer, no form of support at all, I was afraid she might break down and go the way of Trey. What a magnificent relief when, instead, she said, "Lorilee once parked on a mountaintop in hundred-degree heat to write this for me. What a friend, and what a gift," then flew straight into "Frag Song," standing strong and dry-eyed as the two voices— Ona's own and her raging Fender's—poured forth "in profuse strains of unpremeditated art" her heartbroken love and fury over Lore's fate. By the time she reached the final chorus—

> *Yeah, even now the mountains...E, E, D, E...*
> *And all the summer stars are...E, E, D, E...*
> *Out of the cleft the waters...G, G, C, G...*
> *Let the lost sons and daughters...D, D, G, D...*

—the audience was so close to shipwreck that no one but the object of everyone's affection could possibly have followed the gorgeous havoc Ona left in her wake.

AND SO IT came to pass. The lights dimmed as low as they go. The stage was rearranged in darkness, under cover of which a few things were heard being placed onstage. When the lights came up, frail, silvery Lore was suddenly just *there,* in the wheelchair to which she'd taken, by a small table that had also appeared center stage.

Upon the table: a glass of water; a five-string dulcimer; a little F tin whistle.

Lore retracted the arms of her chair, picked up her five-string, set it on her lap, leaned the mike a little closer, and we prepared to be undone. She then ignored her instrument and began to speak as serenely as if we were all sitting in morning sun under the broken ponderosa at Blue Empty:

" 'Every song is a comeback,' Jeff Tweedy once said. And I agree," she began. "But, given my own situation, I'll add four words to Jeff's five: 'Every song is a comeback—even if it's fatal.' "

Lore's calm as she spoke her doom. It undid us, but also united us. I've never heard a crowd fall so silent or feel so emotive so fast.

"When I first learned I had breast cancer, I talked it over with my spiritual sister, Risa, who's in the front row tonight. I told her how, up to then, whenever my hero, Zen Master Dōgen, used the phrase, 'You must fully penetrate these words,' I always found the words well worth penetrating. But when the words I was given to penetrate became 'breast' and 'cancer,' I wasn't able to penetrate them at all.

" 'Maybe, to help you now,' Risa told me, 'Dōgen and love need to be swizzled together in some new way. You know how we swooned over his saying, "The whole of the great earth is your own True Body. The whole of the great earth is the real Human Being." I wonder, if you swizzle those words and love together and try to penetrate them now, what you honestly feel?'

"I swizzled my best, and immediately felt what had changed. I told Risa, 'I used to hear that Earth is our True Body and think, *What a beautiful truth.* But hearing that now, I feel, *What is my one little case of terminal cancer compared to what's been done to the whole of the great Earth?* How can I see the real Human Being's conflagrating forests, obliterated glaciers, plastic-choked and rising seas, dead coral reefs, vanishing species, as anything but our True Body's innumerable breasts, *cancered?* Yet where is there to turn but back to my ravaged Mother? Even if establishing life on other planets were possible, I would never have left Earth's riddled old breasts even to have saved my own. So what I've realized,' I told Risa, 'is that Earth is no longer just my Mother. She's my stricken sister too.'

"Gazing at me the way she does, our tears welling the way they do,

Risa said, 'Your love for Buddhists and mine for the Beguines have danced together a long time, Lore. I wonder if Mechthild of Magdeburg could help you penetrate the words "breast" and "cancer" when she compares Mary's joy as she suckled the infant Jesus to her agony at His suffering as she stood near the cross. Thirteen centuries later, in the endless Now of vision, Mechthild saw that same Mother-Son joy-agony pouring compassion over unending sorrow and wrote what she saw: '*His wounds and her breasts opened, and the wounds poured forth, and the breasts flowed, and Mary's desolate soul was completely restored as he poured the sparkling red wine into her red mouth. And Mary's breasts became so full that seven streams poured out of each breast over Mechthild's body and over her soul.*'

"Oh, that *did* penetrate. 'That helped,' I told Risa.

"To which she said, 'It helped me too, at first. But here's my struggle now, Lore. What Mechthild saw is a glory. An exalted glory. But most days you and I are just two unexalted little friends in Montana trying to help everything and everyone we love make it through somehow. And the unexalted need compassion too. So in trying to help you penetrate the words "breast" and "cancer," what might help me most would be to forget all about exalted glories, and look at you—just *you*, Lore, just as you are— and be free to call you "dearest one."'

"You know how these things go," Lore said. "I started to cry, and said she can call me 'dearest one' whenever she likes if I can call her 'Darlin'.' 'Oh, you *can*,' Risa said. 'You can.'"

As many in her audience crumbled, Lore's Jade-deep empathy kicked in. Sending out a grateful smile, she said, "I share this taste of our friendship, first, to thank you *all* for being friend enough to be here. At this late hour, as the sound of rain and smell of fallen leaves slip into The Pearl to befriend us too, everyone in this room feels like a *darlin'* and a *dearest one* to me. And the other reason I shared Mechthild's vision is, it helped inspire a last song, which is to say, *a comeback, even if it's fatal*. And what a joy it is to have this chance to sing it to you. To the surprise of no one, I named it 'Breast Song.'"

I can describe to you how Lore bowed her head over her dulcimer, placed her left hand on the fretboard, her right upon five silver strings, and set up a droning rhythm that alternated between the major and the minor, creating a sonic pregnancy. But no words can touch the way her one-of-a-kind voice rose out of her ravaged body, sending her calm, consenting melody into the faintly blue air. In my writerly poverty I could only give you her verses stripped of the music that was their purpose and triumph, mangling the wonder and mystery of it in the gopher trap that American English becomes when it overreaches.

"Breast Song" has five verses. I can only bear to trap the very last. I'll introduce it by saying that, due to the spiritual cross-pollination that had long gone on between Lore and Risa, "Breast Song" gives thanks to heroes from Lore's Buddhist, Blue Empty, and Jade-loving inner life, *and* from Risa's more polyamorous inner life.

The moment that shook the crowd hardest came four verses in when, for the first time, handsome young Mu walked out into the light. Picking his tin whistle up off the table, he took a stand close by his mother, and it was hard enough to lay eyes on the grown boy who Lore's breasts, in her earlier verses, had died trying to protect from the poisons of this world. When Mu then trembled, just a little, in that perfect venue it was visible to all, and The Pearl audience was so devastated I couldn't imagine how he'd be able to go on.

But oh, what magic in music's ability to lend some people impossible strength: the instant Mu sent breath into his tiny whistle he steadied, his soaring notes lifted the crowd from ruin, Lore flew up into her highest octave, Mu's part turned out to be a counterpoint hovering like a hummingbird inside the blossom of Lore's voice, and they became the very reality of a mother and son bleeding life into each other inside that blossom. Her final verse:

> *O Mirabai and Magdelene,*
> *Sita-Ram and Marguerite,*
> *When sorrow tries to crush my heart*
> *I reach through time to touch your feet*
>
> *My boy is grown, first love long flown*
> *My ghosted breasts still bless them both*
> *Proving two voids upon my chest*
> *More faithful than my wedding oath*
>
> *Great gifts assail us then fly*
> *But love can't bid itself adieu*
> *And is it not this very wound*
> *That haunts my holy heroes too*
>
> *Mothers, my opened and closed flesh*
> *Now sisters us in love and strife*
> *And breasts are wounds through whence a woman*
> *Bleeds her life into the Christ's*
>
> *O breasts are wounds through whence a woman*
> *Bleeds her life into the Christ's*

When dulcimer and whistle reprised a verse sans words, it resurrected the feeling behind Lore's every word, behind her courage and Mu's, behind their completely given lives, and the song-ending silence was so fraught it left the audience incapable of even marring it with applause.

Inside that eerie *śūnyatā,* knowing their charmed musical alliance had come to its end, Mu turned to Lore, bowed slow and deep, lifted her dulcimer from her lap, set it on the side table, and helped her to her feet. When next they embraced, gently but not briefly, then turned to us, each with an arm round the other, and bowed, the melting of everyone into everyone else was so replete that, amid an attempted standing ovation, many were unable to stand.

It was the last time Lorilee Shay ever took a stage.

(Elkmoon Beguine & Cattle Company, summer solstice 2016)

XII. Running Hand

When the light is just right
if you squint, you can make out
the wiring to the one bird they all are,
thousands
of swarming black starlings
going suddenly vertical, stalling,
doubling back on themselves.
In China it's called "running hand,"
this brush stroke that flows
over the paper, nobody in charge.
    —Tom Crawford, "The Eucharist"

EARLY AFTERNOON, SUMMER solstice, thirteen years into the existence of the E.B.&C.Co and two years after Lorilee took flight (and don't think I won't get back to *that* story), I set down the last sentence of these chronicles, titled them *Sun House,* placed them in the stunning walnut box Eddie Dominguez, Earth, and Sun made to house them, locked my Elsewhere writing cabin, hopped in the dinky but indomitable green Toyota pickup I'd bought from JVZ when his family outgrew it, and drove thirty-eight miles of sun-shot river valley to present the book to a gathering of those about whom and with whom it had been written.

But when I turned right at 1144 Downriver Road and drove under the towering log arch, Valley Land & Beef Inc.'s huge steel letters had been replaced by a weathered plank into which Eddie Dominguez had wood-burned the humble words ELKMOON BEGUINE & CATTLE CO, inspiring me to take a detour. Before making my presentation I wanted to ponder our entire property and the good ways we've altered it, and I knew the place to do it.

Traversing the entire E.B.&C.Co, I crossed the Elkmoon River at the Rifle Creek bridge, headed up a Forest Service road into the South Whitetail burn, took a spur to the base of a disused bulldozer track, put chains on my pickup, and switchbacked to the summit of a 5,200-foot ridge. Locking the chronicles in the truck's toolbox, I grabbed binoculars, strolled through blackened spars and June grass thick with daisies, lupine, and bear grass onto a high granite promontory, and began a scan of the twice-bankrupted acres we've resettled even as so much of the West and world have been brutally unsettled.

Twelve hundred feet below me lay the Elkmoon's braided channels and bottomlands. On higher ground upstream are our nine hundred acres of arable benchland, the meandering miles of Stella Creek, the tranquil lagoon at Stella's mouth, and our three ponds, one of them new. Atop Schoolhouse Bluff, the one-room school remains our Greater Good Headquarters. Not far below, the twenty-three Craftsman cottages that house most of us nestle among the car-free acres of Aspen Swale, reached on foot when we're carrying armloads, or by a solar-powered golf cart with a little trailer when we've larger items to carry. Our reward? The wildflowers of the Swale untrammeled and in full bloom, thanks to the absence of trucks and cars.

A hundred yards on are the chicken pens and coops, then a newish post-and-pole paddock that will hold our working horses by nightfall. A quarter mile below, Kale's vintage garden and orchard now belong to everyone, and his rambling family home is now a library and four classrooms for a multipurpose school so interestingly visionary that only a treatise could describe it, and a treatise writer I am not. Next comes the A barn, still providing riders and horses an excellent utilitarian arena. Then the B Barn and bioshelter, which for years has been the great, unifying gift that Risa had hoped it would be.

Our cottage industries employ most of us, but because we're trying to keep our adult populace under forty we also employ fifteen to twenty neighbors from E City and the valley. This is good for relations with our surrounding community, and great for the wild creatures who, as Rosalia puts it, "got here first and can't talk or vote, so our land use errs in wildlife's favor for a change." As a result, scattered amongst our varied landscapes are critters uncountable, employed and decorative, tame and wild, furred and feathered, scaled and finned, two-leggèd, four-leggèd, and in a trapped-but-Rosalia-rescued ermine's case, three-leggèd, building their nests, burrows, barns, dens, aeries; casting their shy glances, keen gazes, trout flies, magic spells; leaving their tracks, redds, nests, carcasses; producing growls, howls, colloquy, yawp, bird calls, and love songs until it comes time to produce a death.

It all looks so idyllic from my elevation that I have to remind myself: the commitment to live down there is serious. I've watched it cost all but four residents what financial advisors would call "everything," by which they mean a near-total lack of retirement accounts, contingency plans, slush funds, bomb shelters, escape routes. I've also learned firsthand the way that life down there is a blessing or a curse depending, each morning, on whether a person grasps the day by the handle or the blade. Having grasped many a day by the blade myself, I tried for years to spare the Elkmooners my bloody-handed company. But as I peer down on our home from my high perch this evening I'm nothing but glad my independence is many years gone—for who in their right mind would choose to be independent of a Montana river valley at 6 p.m. on a perfect midsummer's eve?

Our four thousand acres are sky-dominated, and look harsh and sere from up here. But the harsh appearance can soften in scant seconds. As the sun eased horizon-ward, the willows lining Stella Creek flared briefly orange in defiance of their obvious green. A subtle thing, this color shift, but in the Rockies in late June it coincides with the afternoon's heat-caused convection wind dying down into zephyrs, till on the best days the very nature of Nature changes. A blue, breathable peace permeated the visual desolation till you saw it wasn't desolate at all. Though it was hours until sunset, nighthawks joined hosts of swallows and waxwings, shooting through clouds of river-born insects with a grace that made the bugs' sacrifice feel like a chosen merging with longer-lived life-forms. Every shadow darkened and lengthened, every contour of tree, boulder, grasses grew richer in color, and a calm befell the valley that was no mere cessation of wind. It was the Elkmoons' own translation of the phrase "the peace that passeth understanding." It was what Gladys Wax calls "the Church with no walls." It was what Lore, in her swan-song CD, had called "the thickening," since birds that all day were soaring now swam with greater effort through the weightier air.

It was also what Kale calls "the Lord's Cocktail Hour," which brought to mind a gift he bequeathed me when I first began chronicling this place back in 2012. In accord with our arrangement, I returned to my truck, jounced back down the ridge, crossed the river and drove to the main nexus of buildings, and strolled through the B Barn to the freezer room. That there was no one around made me feel thievish, but Kale himself presented me with the key I now used on his private whiskey cupboard. Opening its double doors, I pondered five pricey single-malt scotches, then eight solid bourbons, but selected a Missoula rye dubbed Bad Buddhist Whiskey because I was charmed by its honest name.

Kale favors china cups and saucers for whiskey, his rule being "Break one while drinking and you're on the wagon for two weeks"—so of course neither of us have ever broken one. I grabbed his largest cup and saucer, poured in three fingers, scribbled an IOU though Kale says my money's no good here, grabbed his ice pick, opened one of our four big chest freezers, and shoved around butcher-papered and labeled antelope, venison, elk, and Highland beef portions till I found a thirty-pound chunk of glacier ice from Steeple Peak, the Elkmoons' highest. The "USE REVERENTLY!" sticky note made me mutter, "Yeah, yeah." But I did picture Steeple's stately shape as I stabbed off glacier shards, slipping them into my rye till it turned glacier cold and my cup ranneth over. I then revisited my IOU, wrote, 'It was really four fingers plus a deliberate half saucer of overspill,' and locked my note in the Pope's cupboard.

It was Lorilee's ex, Trey, who cut and toted the big shard of glacier down off the Steeple each September. He had learned the rite from high-altitude *paqos* in Peru in his free-climbing glory days. Ritual fasting was part of it, so he was weak going up, even weaker lugging the ice down, yet he insisted on going it alone, saying, "I've got blunders to make up for." The purpose of the rite, he told me, is "to love the Elkmoons' glaciers back to health." That's a Trey quote, mind you. The rhetoric of Vertical Rock Mystics dwells high above my preferred elevations. "According to my *paqo* pals," Trey said, "sharing a reverently obtained shard of glacier with your village enables these cool human-faced, bird-bodied mountain gods to pour reverence for peaks into human hearts, usually between about three and five a.m. The reverence then leads to activism, intelligent policy making, and eventually the end of the Dark Age of fossil fuel." In Trey's defense, I'll add that he also loves NFL football and calls his favorite team the Green Bay Paqos.

Swiping a folding chair from the B Barn's meeting circle, I stepped back outside, trudged down the barn's still blazing south wall, eased into the shade of an ancient juniper at the southwest corner, and leveled my chair amid the roots. A remarkable old tree, this juniper, loaded with tiny green berries that by high summer turn a gin lover's powder blue. Before the B Barn was built and the juniper fenced off, a century's worth of cattle rubbed its lower bark smooth as polished furniture. For reasons unknown, a sense of well-being floods me as I run my hands over this smoothness, inspiring me to remove my boots and socks, sink my feet in three-inch-deep dust as soothing as talcum powder, dribble my Bad Buddhist spillage into the dust of Pachamama the way Trey showed me, raise my cup to the Elkmoon Mountains, and call out, "Cheers, Tipus!"

Only wait. Isn't a tipu some kind of tree? Cup still raised, I tried, "*Sláinte, Pupus!*" But damn it. Isn't *pupu* Hawaiian for the cheese and crackers I wished I had to go with my rye? What sane person doesn't want health restored to glaciers, and there I sat toasting the wrong brand of pu!

"*Salud* anyhow, little god-dudes!" I said, then sampled the cup's contents, and *Whoa!* Even if I couldn't name them, I was positive that every human-faced bird-bodied god I know digs Bad Buddhist!

LORD'S COCKTAIL HOUR update: the air was so still that Earth seemed to have stopped spinning, and Time to have stopped creating old age, sickness, and death. Meanwhile Space had quit creating isolation via vast distance and begun creating a vast intimacy instead. The air was now officially pale orange, the shadows dark blue, and Rumi's beauteous Sun was a swelling, wavery-edged *Primo Uomo* you could almost hear conflagrating four million tons of himself per second to enliven Earth's house of insects-become-birds, melting-snow-become-rivers, bare-hills-become-grass-become-cattle/deer/antelope/elk/rabbits/voles/mice. On the edge of Aspen Swale I saw our new spring-fed pond—Six Acre Pond, we call it—had been found so amenable to our blessed nonhumans that it was being scribed by crisscrossing V's of baby teals, mallards, coots, grebes, and widgeons. On the benchland beyond the pond, in the center of our farm, stood Ona Kutar, the farm's genius locus. Ona remains a music giant, global-minded activist, and huge-hearted Renaissance woman, so it pleased me to see her doing nothing but stand there at her ease, drinking in the orange-hued beneficence that in this place, for a time, had overthrown the forces of chaos.

In the giant fields beyond and below, Buford had just moved thirty Highlands into their next electric-fenced quadrant. A wheel-line sprinkler metronomed water over the patch the cattle had left, a lone pronghorn buck munched greens under a misting sprinkler head, and though there were no deer in sight when I had arrived under the juniper half a whiskey ago, seven mule deer had appeared. Since I hadn't seen them approach, my Bad Buddhist–enhanced intellect concluded that they'd climbed up out of the network of deer tunnels they had excavated, clever as America's fabricated enemy the Vietcong. *Eat my dominoes, hungry ghost of Robert Strange McNamara!*

Beyond the fields, down in the river bottom, the cottonwoods were enjoying serene sex, inseminating the air with a snow of seed-bearing fluff that turned Van Goghish in hue in this light. On an unseen porch in the Swale behind me, Eddie Dominguez started up on his guitar. Two great and three very good guitarists live and play here—and then there's Eddie: self-taught in all he does, he applies the math skills vital to carpentry to his music by sawing two or more famous songs into fractions he nails back together in time signatures like 5/4, 7/16, and 9/8. If my ear had it right he was forcing "Begin the Beguine" and "Let It Be" into a togetherness to a beat so weird no one but Ona could even tap a foot to it. The Pope suspects Ona and Eddie are an item since she calls his playing "perverse genius" and listens to it avidly, confirming Kale's suspicion that Eddie's playing gives traditional cows and cowboys irritable bowel syndrome. Even so, Kale respects Eddie so much that, rather than even hint that he stop playing, Kale heads for the nearest bathroom and God help the cows.

Our glacier-ice fetcher, Trey Jantz, working overtime as always, stepped blue-jeaned and bare-chested round the barn corner wheeling a heaped barrow of aged chicken manure up toward Ona. At fifty-four Trey's still such a hunk that, in this spellbinding light especially, I could think of several E City women and droves of big city men who'd pay him a living wage just to walk by them dressed like he's dressed once a day and smile.

"Trey!" I called. "Just the pundit my meditations require. What's the name of those Andean mountain pu's? I'm drinking the health of Elkmoon glaciers with Pope hooch and Steeple ice and wanna get it right."

"*Apus!*" he called back with that blazing alpine grin that almost made *me* want to pay to see it. "And did you remember to make your offering to Pachamama?"

"Darn betcha!" I said. "One good taste of Bad Buddhist rye and she sighed with such pleasure she derailed nine coal trains down in Wyoming. Pacha and me are all over this climate chaos deal."

"Great work!" he shouted with a sincerity that delighted me since, well, *look at us*. I was barefoot in the shade, sipping whiskey and talking twaddle, Trey was shoving a huge load of chicken shit up an incline, and *he was* thanking *me*!

Next Lou Roy eased round the B Barn corner on his aging orange quarter horse Grey, leading the yearling Andalusian Ona was going to name T Jeff, but in these changing times decided to name Sally, after Jefferson's enslaved concubine and true love, Sally Hemings. This will, I guess, make her our menagerie's first transgender resident once he's gelded. However Sally identifies, she sends me her cute nicker and her *Will you be my friend?* look. That colt, says Lou, is the most social horse he's ever met. She sends the same nicker ahead to the working horses in the paddock, but can't join them yet because she's still got her balls. A cranky gelding might castrate a colt if given a chance. Ona will eventually get Sally de-nutted, but the longer she keeps her cojones the shorter and more muscular she'll be, and that's the physique Ona wants for her. In an appealing way, as her zillion fans will tell you, Ona is sturdy and muscular herself. Many dressage riders seek mounts whose appearance flatters their own. I can't say I've seen that dream come true too often, but my opinion shouldn't count. To me, dressage ladies circling arenas in blazers and top hats look like seriously lost vaudeville actors bobbing round and round an aquarium on well-trained orcas.

Lou Roy's and Grey's faces were as impassive as old baseball mitts as they passed by, but the sun was low enough I could see past the Stetson brim to Lou's eerie glacier-silt-green eyes taking in my indolence. Keeping it terse, the way he likes, I muttered, "How do." Lou didn't give me a glance, just touched a finger to his brim, but I felt a wash of friendliness even so. Same deal when our trucks pass on a road. He never looks, honks, changes expression. Just raises his index finger two inches off the wheel. Something crosses into you, even so.

He'll fetch his Nigerian dwarf goats in next, he'll do it on foot, and it won't be pretty. At seventy-one Lou remains as smooth on horseback as a swan on a pond, but once he dismounts he's so ( )-leggèd he ratchets along as if Grey's entirety is always betwixt him. Dealing with goats was once miles beneath his pride, "but pride swallowed," quoth Kale the Pope, "is the daily vitamin upon which this place runs." Though Lou's notion of vitamins is his evening double Dickel, when Ona complained that the noxious weeds proliferating along our fenced farm's outer edge were too close to the vegetables to be sprayed, Buford said, "Goats'd take care of it." To which Trey said, "If they broke loose, hundreds of hours of hard labor would be their lunch. We'd need a world-class goat-staker."

That was all it took. Though head lettuce and sweet corn are the only vegetables I've ever seen pass Lou's lips, he said, "Get me some o' them Nigerian dwarf goats an' I'll tether the sumbitches so solid you'll think I unscrewed the legs." Two days later Ona bought seven of them, and Lou liked them so much he bought seven more out of his own paltry savings.

Every day since he's unscrewed the legs, and the weeds are about done for. I do admire the way folks vitamin up and get things done around here.

IT WAS OUR original ranch brat and first Dumpster Catholic Beguine, Rosalia, who made me aware of an attribute a lot of us Elkmooners hold in common. She calls it "the second skin that protects by far the greater of our two living bodies." When I asked her to explain herself, she described something I'd been experiencing for years, but didn't have a name for. She said, "If I wake in the wee hours and lie perfectly still, I never feel alone in the dark. I feel surrounded by the people, animals, plants, birds, fishes, rivers, grasses, trees, land, and skies inside and outside of me. If I don't move or speak, but just lie still, I can then feel my way around the land, barns, cottages, forests, and fields as my second skin ranges over what's dying back into the Earth and can't be helped, and what's in need of immediate help when I begin my day."

Rosalia helped me realize that almost all of us do some version of this. Lou Roy, for instance, will rove the skin, teeth, ears, eyes, withers, quarters, fetlocks, hooves of each of his horses, grateful for the thriving ones, mind-doctoring the ailing ones, who'll be the first things he'll tend at sunrise. He then mind-doctors his dwarf goats, mind-checks the health and recent honey harvest of his thirty beehives, then plans a hunting or fishing trip till it puts him to sleep.

When Buford wakes, his second skin sees where irrigation needs to happen in the hay and alfalfa fields, moves on to how the grazed land looked yesterday so he'll know when the Highlands' hoof work has given maximum benefit to the soil without damaging the dozen or so kinds of grasses. Buford plants nowadays with a no-till drill that's eliminated our need to plow our grazing land, thereby conserving so much water that even in dry years our water table's on the rise. If Regina stirs beside him, her second skin begins picturing the salsa she'll make from the last of the year's tomatoes, the chutney from the last pears, the pesto from the last basil and black walnuts from the old Broussard family trees. Then she might start tweaking her smoked whitefish pâté recipe, adding cloves! anise! peppercorns!— wonderful ideas when you've fallen back to sleep and don't know it.

Meanwhile Ona's second skin hears the night sighs and cries in the greenhouse and farm beds, senses when to transplant what, which plots she'll let lie fallow for a year, what's ready for harvest, what's bolting, and which marauding rodent, bug, animal, weed, or weather pattern threatens her produce. Come morning she then notifies her right-hand man, Trey, whose second skin, ten miles away in his E City apartment, remains so obsessed with ground rodents that he likes it that Hub Punker has nicked his name to Caddyshack Jantz.

THE LAST THING I want to share about the Elkmoon Beguine & Cattle Company is this: when your home place and its multitude of life-forms become your second skin, the death of a loved one feels very different than it did before you acquired that skin. I mean, sure, death disappears us in a way that inarguably ends our life story. But as we repeatedly wander these many acres of life-forms, landforms, and water bodies year after year, we sometimes experience messages from *beyond* the ends of life stories. There are places in these parts that send such messages year in and year out, Jade Lake being the big one, but Lore's seat under the broken ponderosa at Blue Empty also continues to speak. More than a few of us have hiked up there, seated ourselves in the duff, inhaled the fragrance of the bole's puzzle-piece bark on a hot summer day, and felt gray-eyed Lore hovering inside us saying things like, *If you're going to cry for me again, Dear Holy Goat who's fooling no one with his disguise, make sure this time it's for joy!*

For Risa the two great message places remain the Glory Meadow cedar grove near Dave's freed molecules and the spring-fed forget-me-not-lined pools that form when our Elkmoon side-channels diminish in July. No child who wades and wanders those microworlds with Risa forgets the frogs, muskrats, baby ducks, motionless newborn fawns, or roils of baby skunks that begin creating their second skins. For Regina Cloud the place beyond the ends of stories are the dips in the hills across the river in November, which catch and hold the mist she calls *qi*, turning the landscape so Chinese that when she points out *qi* pockets to Jamey-the-Quote, he recites Li Po, Ryokan, Cold Mountain, and other poets he didn't know he knew, then completely forgets them as soon as the *qi* disperses.

Another link to our creatures: those who can impersonate them. Buford talks to pine squirrels by squeezing air pockets between his molars and his cheeks, making a sound that, to humans, sounds just like the squirrels. But Buford delights in the fact that there are unintended insults in his chickaree dialect that cause squirrels to come running from hundreds of feet away, park on branches just out of his reach, and curse him furiously.

Not so for Jamey: his osprey calls remain so authentic that the genuine birds abandon their hover over fat trout in the Elkmoon glides, fly to the nearest cottonwood snag, and call down to him as many times as he's got the patience to reply. He can also coax crowds of ravens into overhead circlings for call-and-response exchanges that can last till his voice gives out. In the spring he's fond of locating treetop raven nests by simply listening for young ravens shattering the forest peace with their awful attempts at adult raven calls. Pitying the parent birds assaulted by this caterwaul, Jamey stands beneath nest trees demonstrating his nearly perfect raven call to the fledglings, who soon grow curious, stop screaming, listen, and learn. By late July their calls have so improved and Jamey's efforts are so appreciated that as many as eight parent ravens sometimes circle fifty or sixty feet over his head, calling down thanks—a courtesy that caused the E.B.&C.Co populace to follow Jamey's lead and change the old British term "an unkindness of ravens" to "a kindness."

How can we not see such exchanges as kindnesses after all we've done to terrorize these creatures and their world? I recently read that an average 1.4 million whitetail deer were killed on the Lower 48's highways each of the past ten years. Yet in the midst of this holocaust an occasional deer—with me it's almost always a lone doe—will stop browsing when she sees me, step toward me instead of shying away, and regard me for the longest time. Can you too feel the doe transmitting when she gazes at you like this? Her message doesn't translate into words, but who needs words when there she stands, exchanging pure attention with a member of a species that, in a single American decade, murdered fourteen million of her kind simply to hurl themselves through space at more lethal speeds. Compare that to the Holocaust and cry. Another mystery: more than a few times I swear I've felt people I loved and lost briefly *borrow* that doe's gaze. My second skin loves these exchanges so much that, when I get behind the wheel at night, a storm in me refuses to even turn on a radio lest I sink into an oblivion that would blind me to the next glowing pair of eyes at highway's edge.

All I'm trying to say, really, is that only our keenest attention can sustain a life-giving connection between our kind, Earth and Sun's other offspring, and the Sun House itself. Lives swirl up into being and come to an end here in the Elkmoon, as everywhere. But so do occasional nonhuman lives connect to a human life's end so powerfully that the human takes up residence in a place inside us, *freed* of time. The Irish champion of mystical love John O'Donohue held that time is not a calendar product, but "the parent or mother of presence." The Vietnamese master of mindful love, Thich Nhat Hanh, said of his own death as he was serenely dying it,

> *Since before time, I have been free.*
> *Birth and death are only doors through which we pass...*
> *So laugh with me,*
> *hold my hand,*
> *let us say good-bye,*
> *to meet again soon.*
> *We meet today.*
> *We will meet again tomorrow...*
> *We meet each other in all forms of life.*

In that spirit, let me lead us up an inward spiral into the presence of a last few wandering griefs and joys. Let me tell you of a bird who united seventy human hearts in a Now we can all still summon, though our union took place twenty-five turnings of a calendar month ago. Let me end with the wonderfully inconclusive departure of everybody's love, Lorilee Shay.

(Elkmoon Beguine & Cattle Company, April 2014)

XIII. Sky Door

Let very old things come into your hands.
Let what you do not know come into your eyes...
May the spring of a foreign river be your navel.
May your soul be at home where there are no houses.
Walk carefully, well loved one,
walk mindfully, well loved one,
walk fearlessly, well loved one,
Return with us, return to us,
be always coming home.
                    —Ursula K. Le Guin, in her prophetic novel
                                    Always Coming Home

FOR TWO DAYS, for just twenty minutes each day so we don't overwhelm her, everyone thanks or gently kisses or weeps or smiles with Lorilee. Next to last in the line but first in the quality of their smiles are Lore's end-of-life guardian angels, Fionn and Willa, Rosalia, and Lily Cloud Raines, Buford and Regina's five-year-old. And last in line come the bullet-through-a-windshield smiles of Lore's true love, Grady, and son, Mu, though their parting kisses are surely the most needed. Before leaving, the ever mindful Mu also sets Elmerina Buddha, Bivalve, and Lore's five-string dulcimer on a side table not for Lore, who is past need of such things, but to steady his dear friend Risa with three beloved icons.

At Lore's request, only Risa, and a hospice nurse on call, then remain with her in the cottage Eddie and crew built us, specifically, for departing this life. Though Lore's thoughts have become slow as the sun's slide across the sky, as the cottage's first guest she is invited to name it. Risa waits a good five minutes for Lore to respond, all the while looking so gone Risa isn't sure she's conscious. Then, in a slow-motion whisper, she says: *"Sky Door."*

Risa's eyes fill. "Sky Door it ever shall be."

DESPITE HOW CLOSE Lore seems to taking flight, Risa's vigil is running long. A third day and night pass; a fourth. Every four hours Jamey and a rotating companion give a gentle knock on the cottage door. If Risa doesn't answer

Jamey does a code knock that means he's leaving tea and nourishment on a covered tray, compliments of TJ or Regina, for Risa to nibble or to ignore. Sometimes she steps out on the porch for a private word with Jamey, and how it haunts me to see them in the distance, Jamey's head bent low to hear her whispered updates, praise her strength and courage, embrace her before she slips back in. Then, as soon as she's gone, he stands there frozen, looking utterly riven and lost.

Not long past dawn on the vigil's fifth day, Jamey heads for Sky Door with Grady in tow. Seeing them coming, Risa steps onto the porch. In the early sunlight Grady sees that her still untamable hair is rapidly turning silver and her famously glowing face is wan. He aches to see how completely she's pouring herself out for Lore—but her expression also holds a pallid excitement. Leading them away from the door, Risa says, "For a day now I've been telling Lore she's got our blessing, and can set sail as soon as she feels the call. Not an hour ago, something released: I feel her slowly departing now. I pray it won't be much longer."

Hearing this, Grady nods to Risa...but before I continue, dear reader—especially those readers who have not yet guessed which of our characters is your chief chronicler—I, Grady, have been hiding in plain sight by allowing the Holy Goat to sometimes interview me as if we are two people. Yet I beg to continue, even now, to occupy that anonymous scribe, for I can't begin to speak to what follows as the person I am. My sole hope of getting through this chapter is to peer down out of Joycean "exile" and Chekhovian "coldness" to speak of things, as the HG once put it, "as hard as shattered loves, shattered lives, and Lorilee's impending death without trepidation or sense of trespass." For Grady this is no such occasion. For Grady it's time to lie helpless in the shards of his own shattering while the Holy Goat alone takes a second run at Vigil Day Five:

"For a day now," Risa tells Jamey and Grady, "I've been telling Lore she's got our blessing and can set sail as soon as she feels the call. Not an hour ago, something released: I feel her slowly departing. I pray it won't be much longer."

Hearing this, Grady nods to Risa and mumbles, "Thanks. Thanks for every single thing you're doing for her, Risa. I know it's hard. Thank you."

With which he turns on his heel, blows past the B Barn, strides fast up through the cottages of Aspen Swale, breaks into a gasping run as he mounts Schoolhouse Bluff, charges across the school grounds, over the bluff edge, down into the Elkmoon river bottom, collapses on the trunk of a wind-felled cottonwood, waits for his breathing to calm—and instead bursts out in the uncontrollable sobs he's held in all the years since he carried his love, broken, down out of the Elkmoons from Jade. "*Lore!*" he gasps. "*Lorilee!*" he sobs. "It was *you* bearing *me* up as I carried you down, and you who carried me eleven years as you fought to stay with us. I *know* it's time to fly, I know you're not afraid, I *want* this for you. But what am I to do, now or ever, with this chasm that's opened between us?

Am I to hike back to the barn, sit amongst our friends, and pretend I'll ever know or love anyone remotely like you?"

As prearranged, Jamey shares Risa's sense of Lore's impending departure with Rosalia, who makes a call to Regina and Buford, another to Poke and Lisa Kettle at the Ambivalent Cafe, and a phone tree is activated. Within half an hour a crowd of Lore's friends begins to arrive, parking as instructed near the E.B.&C.Co office, proceeding on foot to the B Barn. More than a few veer off en route, tiptoe onto the porch of Sky Door, and don't dare to even whisper as they set flowers, wild bird feathers, unusual stones, children's drawings, poems, love notes, on the seats of two big Adirondack chairs till both are overflowing. They then tiptoe off the porch and stride the sixty yards to the blue barn that serves as our concert hall, town hall, Zendo, Dumpster Catholic cathedral: our "enchanted place," Neruda would call it, "where we dance our clumsy dance and sing our sorrowful song."

In the B Barn's high-ceilinged main room, seventy-two folding chairs borrowed from St. Luke's Parish await guests in a crescent of six rows. As Lore's admirers file in they shake hands, embrace, nod, or speak, only to cover their mouths in alarm, remembering the request for silence. Once seated they then look uncertainly around, wondering who among them might know what they're supposed to be doing.

When only two chairs remain empty, an equally uncertain-looking Kale takes his feet, walks to the front of the crescent, turns to us, and says, "Welcome, one and all. Thank you for coming. The reason we've gathered is something new to us. Risa has let us know that Lore appears to be leaving this world as I speak. We're hoping it's possible to help her with that journey, and since Lore is a lover of silence, we've chosen to forgo words. Rosalia Dominguez will explain what we have in mind."

Over in Sky Door, at the sound of passersby, Risa sometimes leaves Lore, peeks out at them through her great-grandmother's lace curtains, returns to Lore, and whispers who she saw—though Lore no longer responds. Lore's last words were spoken two days ago when she whispered an equation that has transfixed her for years: "*Every time I disappear, something perfect happens. I'm ready, Risa. Time to disappear.*"

Those three short sentences seemed to take so much out of her that her breathing ever since sounds like she's climbing a mountain—yet the effortful breathing seems to coincide with a lack of physical pain. A solace. What Risa can't help but lament is that Lore seems to have relinquished her beautiful soft voice. "I'll never hear it again, will I?" Risa whispers.

Saying nothing, Lore continues climbing the mountain that leads out of this world.

In the B Barn Kale sits, and Rosalia walks up front, trembling a little.

"As you know from our calls," she says, struggling to find her voice, "we believe Lore is dying right *now*. So we want to encircle her with a rite she invented. The rite started when we got into a feud that I caused. For a while in my teens I believed I knew what creatures shouldn't be dying to feed us, since we could eat other things instead, and my ideals decided to hell with everyone else's. I did bad things to those I disagreed with. Kale even feared our little lifeboat—that's what he calls our home here, *a lifeboat*—might split in two. But one frigid winter night, a Monday, I couldn't sleep due to the trouble I'd been causing, so at five fifteen I bundled up, grabbed a flashlight, and came out to this very room.

"The B Barn was a hollow shell then, with barn owls nesting on the studs just under the stained-glass window up there. I hoped to see newborn owlets. About here where I'm standing there were five rickety wood chairs where the barn builders ate lunch. Soon as I came in, I startled. Someone was sitting in one of the chairs. No heat or light. Nine or ten degrees Fahrenheit. When my flashlight shone on Lore, who was on chemo and radiation at the time, all I could think was that she'd catch pneumonia and die. I set my flashlight on a wicker seat so its beam shone soft, and said, 'It's too cold, Lore! What are you doing out here?'

"Smiling so sweetly, she made a zipping gesture across her lips, then pointed at her ears, hidden in a thick wool hat. Extending her mittened hands out away from her ears, her big circular gesture conveyed that she was listening to the entire world. Next she reached out with her hands as if to pull everything she was hearing toward her. When her hands then came to rest on her heart, as if placing every sound on Earth there, I started to cry."

Reliving it, Rosalia starts to cry. So do many in the crescent, including an unashamed Buford Raines, whom Rosa hated as an enemy at the time of the story she's telling.

"Lore patted the chair beside her, inviting me to join her, put a finger to her lips to show we wouldn't be talking, then closed her eyes. The best thing I've ever done in my life was take that chair. What we shared, she simply called 'A Listening.'"

Wiping away tears, Rosalia looks from person to person. "Lore's face, as she listened to the world, grew so peaceful it was *intense*. An intense peace caused by the *force* of one's listening. I'd never felt such a thing. It reminds me now of Rilke lines that Risa later shared: 'Listen, my heart, as only saints have listened. When the gigantic call lifted them off the ground, they kept on, impossibly, kneeling and didn't notice. So complete was their listening.'

"I never saw Lore lift off. But how many of us have carried around stories so hard to tell we couldn't speak them? How many times has Lorilee sensed this in us, lifted us with her listening, and out our hardest stories poured? The reason we've gathered is simple. Our friend is lifting off in answer to a gigantic call. We want to thank her, and hopefully help her, with our own intense listening. To get started, try remembering a time when she gave her listening to you. So many of you came today! Thank you! We're so grateful! And now..." Rosalia makes Lore's big, circular, listening-to-the-world gesture, brings her hands to her breast, and whispers, "*Listen, my heart, as Lorilee has listened.*"

When Rosalia sits, looking half broken, ten-year-old Willa Van Zandt puts her skinny arm around her, leans over, and kisses Rosa's shoulder. The rest of us steady our breathing—or fail to steady it at the sight of Willa's kiss—and we begin.

It feels way awkward at first. For one thing, we look wrong. Lore's black-rimmed gray eyes and deep serenity gave her such a visible and loving presence. The thought of those eyes departing makes many feel more like weeping than listening. It also feels as though we're too many. Seventy humans can't help but carry a lot of capriciousness into a silence. But as some begin, as Rosalia suggested, to conjure a time when Lore's listening coaxed a hard story out of them, we gain focus, until we *feel* one another's focus. The silence takes on a unison quality, as when a choir creates harmonies in a first few shared notes. Seven minutes in, our shared love for Lore is filling the room, and who knew our listening would take on such a *choral* quality? Keen listening is receptive by definition, but as we focus on Lore our listening begins to feel like an outpouring that, moments later, is transformed by an unexpected attendee:

The B Barn's biggest door is open wide, allowing eight by twelve feet of sunlight and fresh air to stream in on us from behind, but it's the three-foot-wide door in the barn's north wall through which the entry takes place. As Grady Haynes tries to slip in after an emotional fracas and face-wash down by the Elkmoon, past his ear shoots the first hummingbird of the year. A calliope. Finding itself in a vast room with seventy people beneath it, it begins to explore the room in a slow hover, and the care with which it moves causes Rosalia to feel it's a messenger. It's hard to remember, during the seven or eight months we live without them, that calliopes are the size of a small tube of lip balm and the weight of a Lincoln penny. Yet the presence of this one holds such authority that person after person begins gazing up at it, proving to Rosalia that yes, *this* is a messenger.

Fifteen-year-old Fionn, watching the bird keenly, has been working for years on a so-far-unsuccessful imitation of the easy knowledge of his hero, Kale the Pope. The flaw is, Fionn has no idea how resonant his changed voice has become, whereas the Pope's knowledge carries no further than the person upon whom he's bestowing it. Lou Roy is sitting by Fionn. Audible to at least half the gathering, Fionn whispers to him, "*Calliope! Male!* The purple beard's how we know. Smallest bird in the Americas, Pope says. So small they can die in an orb weaver's web! But tough for their size. And grouchy too—like Lou Roy, the Pope says."

"*Hey now,*" Lou whispers.

"They're so grouchy they won't fly in flocks, same as Lou, Pope says."

"*Easy there,*" Lou Roy whispers, spearing Fionn with his glacial-melt-green eyes.

"But brave like Lou too, Kale says."

"That's better," Lou whispers.

"Lindbergh soloed three and a half thousand miles across the Atlantic, Pope says, but every single calliope solos *five thousand* miles to reach Montana from Mexico! And the *Spirit of St. Louis* flew low. Calliopes migrate at twelve thousand feet. Think how strong and cold the wind gets up there, Pope says. That bird above us flew all those miles *alone*, through *that*!"

Tracking the hummer, failing to realize many of us hear him too, Lou whispers, "*Fuckin' miracle bird, idn't he...*"

WHILE IN SKY DOOR, sixty yards away, Lorilee, eyes closed, sighs out her first word in two days and third to last word in this life: "*Risa.*"

Risa clouds up at the same instant she smiles, keeps smiling as tears fall, and is so hopelessly moved she climbs onto Lore's bed and lies against her, placing her hand on Lore's far shoulder, lying her cheek on the near one. Lore just continues her motionless climb.

THE CALLIOPE EXPLORES the B Barn for a while, but begins to feel trapped despite the room's great size, and a calliope's instinct, if trapped in a building, is to escape skyward. The bird doesn't even register that the big barn door is open. Seeking escape in only the top twenty feet of the barn space, he begins to cheep and fly faster, then sights in, thirty feet up the east wall, a circular multicolored blaze of light. Taking the yard-tall orb of stained glass to be a sky door, the calliope zips straight for it, bangs it with his tiny body, regroups, bangs it again, glues himself to the hopeful colors, and his cheeps grow frantic.

Realizing the bird's in real trouble, Rosalia leaves her seat, leans down to Trey Jantz, whispers a request, then dashes out of the barn to the pump shed by the pond to fetch a long-handled minnow net as Trey runs to the A Barn to fetch the twenty-four-foot stepladder. And as all seventy of us register the tiny bird's distress, something very rare begins to occur:

A metaphor is normally an intimate thing; a nut we crack open in private to eat the hidden kernel by ourselves. A metaphor futilely beating itself against brilliant glass while someone we adore is dying a stone's throw away feels very different. Many of us fall into the same recognition at once: the B Barn is no longer just a barn, the hummer no longer just a bird, we seventy no longer an idle audience. Despite the great variety of our spiritual perspectives, most of us are now feeling the same thing. If Risa were with us she might express it like this: *Isn't the B Barn the very image of Lore's failing body? Isn't the calliope her exquisite spirit trapped in that body, seeking release? And isn't the stained-glass orb the Latin oculus, the Pali kannikā, the very sky door through which she needs to escape?*

Oh, it is! we feel. *It is!* And having seen her endure so much for so long to remain with us, we *want* the escape her calliope spirit seeks. Yet just as much—*exactly* as much!—we *never* want her to escape. Because *the sight of her! The sight of her! Tell me, O inconceivable God of mercy. By what mercy must we give up forever the sight of our loved one's clear eyes, serene presence, and peace-bestowing ability to unburden our hearts with her listening?*

At which point we are undone en masse by Rosalia's messenger: a lone hummingbird. Eyes welling, hearts aching, we watch the tiny creature embody Lore's effort to take flight. And to hear a man the size of Hub begin to quake, then helplessly begin to blubber; to see Lou's glacier-melts grow rapt as a Byzantine icon's as he gazes out from under his dirty Stetson, "watchin'," as he'll later put it, "April's first effin' miracle bird duel an orb of light"; to see Lore's orphan-to-be, Mu, gazing up at the bird with the same clear-eyed intensity we've adored in his mom; to feel seventy humans, each in their unique way, experiencing the barn as our friend's body and the hummer as the Upaniṣadic person the size of a thumb, trapped in the body's ravages, fills the B Barn with purpose and power as great as any cathedral that ever stood.

Only TJ McGraff seems oblivious to the metaphor that Lore's departure, the bright window, and the calliope are creating—but in truth Teej has sunk, as is his practice, into a nothingness that hears, in the gaps in Hub's woe, faint cheeps and a tiny body battering itself against glass. Nothingness then sights in the flying gemstone fighting the multicolored brilliance, feels an answering commotion inside its shirt, undoes the top two buttons, reaches in, and pulls out a tiny silk purse suspended on a cord. I must mention that all 320 distressed pounds of Hub are seated right beside the nothingness whose high-end Italian duds, tasseled two-tone shoes, and intelligent voice cause Hub to call him nothing but "the Squire." And Hub knows there would be no E.B.&C.Co without the Squire; knows he might not have a home without the Squire; deeply respects the Squire. But Hub has also felt, from the day they met, *way* out of his depth in the presence of the Squire's indeterminate gender. So when the Squire reaches in his shirt, draws out a tiny purse, loosens its drawstring, and pours four tiny dollies into his hand, Hub begins gasping for breath. He feared something like this! Yet he can't wrest his eyes away from the Squire's dollies! Judging by the tiny sombreros of two of them, Hub thinks: *Mexicans. Wouldn't you know!* From the baby doll's halo he then guesses, *A Mex Mary, Joseph, an' Jesus baby and, what the hell, a Great Dane? No, wait. Mary's donkey!*

But what's this now? The Squire is drying his lips on the sleeve of his cream-colored linen sport coat, which is weird, but not *that* weird. But by the time the Squire takes up each doll and tenderly kisses its tiny face, donkey included, Hub is gasping like a beached puffer fish. What a relief when the Squire finally drops mother, infant, and donkey back into his doll purse and the purse back inside his shirt!

But what in the name of Holy Annie Oakley is he doing with his Mex Joe doll? Holding it up to his face, he is not only whispering to it, his fingers are causing eensy Joseph to nod and whisper eensy replies! Mesmerized,

Hub goes blind to the Squire's fingers and sees nothing more nor less than the Mexican father of Jesus raise his tiny face to gaze up at the glowing stained glass and tiny bird. The Squire then starts emitting a sustained high hum that Hub properly hears as Christ's earthly father trying to console the wee creature!

Mmmmmmmmmmmmmmmmmmmmmmmmmmmmmmmmmmmmmmmmmmmmmmmmmmmm...

Then comes the departure of anything Hub recognizes as reality: *in Buford's lap, three chairs to Hub's left, right on pitch, five-year-old Lily Cloud Raines takes up the Mex Joe doll's same eensy note!*

Mmmmmmmmmmmmmmmmmmmmmmmmmmmmmmmmmmmmmmmmmmmmmmmmmmmmm

Mmmmmmmmmmmmmmmmmmmmmmmmmmmmmmmmmmmmmmmmmmmmmmmmmmmm...

DAYS WILL PASS before Hub learns from Buford that Lily Cloud's impulse was not random. Two nights previous she had rioted when Buford and Regina refused to let her, Willa, and Fionn monopolize the home-theatre in the B Barn loft by watching *Lord of the Rings* for the forty-seventh time. Instead, Lily was forced to join Grady, Jamey, Fionn, Willa, and her parents for a film called *As It Is in Heaven*.

Lily's riot had been fueled by being banned from the Sky Door cottage. Knowing full well that Lore was dying, Lily saw no reason why only Risa got to be with her. Having lived a portion of each day at Lore's side for the past three months, Lily had cheered Lore up so many times that she felt sure she could keep cheering her up to the moment her life ended. So if she couldn't be with Lore for some dumb grown-up reason, she at *least* deserved the consolation of watching Sam and Frodo defy death. But Regina said, "No dice, Lils," and Jamey laid a Dad Voice on Willa and Fionn, telling them the movie was "the perfect story to accompany what we're going through with Lore." But the film turned out to be in a foreign language with subtitles Fionn read so loud that Lily curled up in a quilt in an Adirondack chair, squeezed her ears between two pillows, and her eyelids grew heavy.

Just as she began to drift off, Fionn and Willa let out a unison "*WHOA!*" Lily peeked—and there stood the conductor of a fancy symphony in front of a big audience, having a terrible nosebleed all over the fancy tuxedo he was wearing. When Willa tittered at his plight, Fionn snapped, "*Don't be a stupid little kid, Willa!*" Jamey shushed them, and Lily hoped the film would follow the conductor on to his death since she couldn't follow Lore on to hers. "He has a very weak heart," Jamey whispered, "and his love for music is so strong it will kill him if he keeps conducting."

"No fair!" Lily cried, and everybody laughed for some reason. But sure enough, the conductor stops conducting and journeys up to some crummy village in the north, where he moves, all alone, into an abandoned school-house not a tenth as nice as Testament Creek School. In the village nearby he then meets a scruffy church choir of screwed-up country people, disobeys his doctor, starts conducting the scruffies, and they sound so awful that Lily dozes off in seconds and sleeps hard...

So who knew what all has happened when she finds herself wrapped in a quilt in Buford's lap, wakened by the tall blond boy in the scruffy choir making weird humming noises because, it seems, their weak-hearted conductor has gone missing. *But look!* The screwed-up country choir is now on stage in a cathedral even bigger than the B Barn, packed with hundreds of other choir members—and when the tall boy keeps making weird *hrrmmm* noises, a few of the village choir members start *hrrmmming* along with him, turning the sound into rudimentary music—and in the giant church *hundreds* of singers follow their lead! No one sings, exactly. But as they make their oceanic unison *mmmmmm* sound, other choir members begin to add harmonies to it, and such a huge, swelling, joy-struck music fills the church that Jamey turns the volume way up, causing it to pour through the B Barn and out into the Elkmoon night where Risa and Lore can surely hear it in Sky Door, which makes Buford and Regina, then Grady, then even Jamey weep as they smile and hum along. Lily too smiles as she sends a high *mmmmmm* of her own to Lore though she can't be with her. But as the choir keeps choiring and Lily's favorite grown-ups keep cry-humming, a man staggers like a drunk into a basement lavatory of the cathedral, collapses on the floor, and cracks his head against a toilet as he falls. "*The conductor with the music-wrecked heart!*" yells Fionn, and not only is he right, the conductor is dying for real this time, and *does* remind Lily of Lorilee, because even though he's done for, he's *smiling*, same as Lore did the last time Lily saw her. And why is he smiling? Because, through a tinny loudspeaker on the lavatory wall, he hears his scruffy choir merge with the huge cathedral choir upstairs, creating the gigantic swelling sounds.

"*Look at his ear!*" Willa gasps, and Lily sees it shooting little splurts of blood in time to the conductor's wrecked heartbeats. But he goes on smiling even so, letting what he loves kill him same as Lore must now be doing. And after eight or ten beats, sure enough, the splurts stop, Willa yells, "*Dead!*" Jamey says, "*Just watch, please*," as he wipes away tears—and then comes the part of the movie Lily will love forever!

As the huge choir keeps soaring and Buford / Regina / Grady / Jamey keep smile-crying, the gigantic sound brings the dead conductor back to life all cleaned up and beaming. And he's walking through a huge grassy field in summer, feeling seed tips with his fingertips just like Lily does in summer. And he hasn't wandered far when a boy just Lily's size jumps up out of the tall grass, holding a violin. "*The conductor as a kid!*" Willa yells. "*Very good,*" Jamey says though she's supposed to cork it. And Buford / Regina / Grady / Jamey *sob* through their smiles as the conductor picks his little boy-violinist-self up in his arms, starts dancing with him, and Lily's happiness is so huge she no longer misses *Lord of the Rings,* though she *still* feels she should be in Sky Door with Risa to help Lore depart...

* * *

...ALL OF WHICH is why, in the B Barn, when Lily hears Tiny Joseph's *mmmmmmm* coming out of TJ, she knows *exactly* what she can do for Lore: she takes up the *mmmmmmm* to help Tiny Joseph same as the giant choir helped the crummy country choir! And if, as she hopes, everybody in the B Barn joins her and Tiny Joseph, she just *knows* they'll fly a cleaned-up beautiful Lore up into a golden field where her little girl-self will jump out of the tall grass holding a dulcimer, and Grown-Up Lore will sweep Child Lore up in her arms and dance with her like the conductor danced with his little boy-self, and Lily can hardly *stand* how much she hopes to meet Child Lore in the dream-field after Grown-Up Lore hopefully dies soon! So her job right *now*, Lily just *knows*, is to get these boring B Barn grown-ups to sing like all the choirs in the movie so the singing really *does* fly Lore home to her girl-self in the summer field. And how she *loves* Fionn and Willa for grasping what she and Tiny Joseph are trying to do, joining them to create a four-part,

Mmmmmmmmmmmmmmmmmmmmmmmmmmmmmmmmmmmmmmmmmmmmm
Mmmmmmmmmmmmmmmmmmmmmmmmmmmmmmmmmmmmmmmmmmmmm
Mmmmmmmmmmmmmmmmmmmmmmmmmmmmmmmmmmmmmmmmmmmmm
Mmmmmmmmmmmmmmmmmmmmmmmmmmmmmmmmmmmmmmmmmmm...

BUT FIONN'S NOTE, loud as always, is off-key by a fraction so grating it hurts Lou Roy's left ear, so Lou leans down and hits the same *mmmmmmm* so loud it floods Fionn into holding the pitch. Then Eddie Dominguez, on the far side of Lou, smiles at Willa and Lils and takes up their note, and Rosalia, next door to Willa, does too, and a dozen or so people in the crescent, including Grady, Buford, and Regina, start humming harmonies like in the movie, the humming takes on beauty, and shy Emile Smith, the menagerie's tech whiz so Hub named him Email, chimes in with some mind-bending notes that let the cat out of the bag: Email can really sing! And the Pope and Max Bowler, on opposite sides of the crescent, look across at each other, knowing from St. Luke's masses what each of them can do, nod their white and brown Stetsons just once, and lay down Tiny Joseph's original note a Grand Canyon octave lower and **BIG**, creating a fundament that grounds everyone's hums.

Mmmmmmmmmmmmmmmmmmmmmmmmmmmmmmmmmmmmmmmmmmm
Mmmmmmmmmmmmmmmmmmmmmmmmmmmmmmmmmmmmmmmmmmmm...

AT GROUND ZERO next to TJ, meanwhile, Hub is gaping at the Mex Joe doll upraised in the Squire's hand, so flabbergasted by what it hath wrought that he's thinking, *Goodbye God Bless America, hello Dumpster Catholic cowboys an' weird-ass Beguine hum-fests!* But since he can't beat 'em and most days even likes 'em, Hub joins 'em, and the Irish tenor that pours out of his hugeness turns out to be surprisingly sweet and right on pitch.

For Ona Kutar, meanwhile, sitting next to Mu, the calliope's growing exhaustion makes Lore's dying so present that she puts an arm round Mu's shoulder and keeps a tight hold. But Mu is so taken with Email's eerie harmony that he takes it up too, sounding so bright and strong despite what he's losing that Ona removes her arm, dips her head, heaves a single wracked sob to get it out of her system, then sits up, sucks it up, and starts sliding her voice over and around and through every hum and harmony in the entire room.

Hearing *that* musical wonder, Jamey, quite a singer himself, tries to join in. But having seen a Tiny Joseph doll, his own Fionn and Willa, and Lily Cloud ignite this eruption, and knowing Risa can hear it, and Lore too if she lives, he's so overcome that he can only lean forward, place his head in his hands, stare at the floor, and listen as Ida, close by the Pope, adds a quavery high soprano, Poke Kettle starts *boing*ing the main note like a Jew's harp, Lisa Kettle and a bunch of Lore's old Ambivalent Cafe customers add volume, her Butte folk music friends Chris and Glenn add diatonics in Dorian mode, Eddie's gay man and gay woman cottage builders join in, and what Kale dubs the Pretty Cool Under the Circumstances Choir fills the barn with a great,

Mmmmmmmmmmmmmmmmmmmmmmmmmmmmmmmmmmmmmmmm
Mmmmmmmmmmmmmmmmmmmmmmmmmmmmmmmmmmmmmmmm
Mmmmmmmmmmmmmmmmmmmmmmmmmmmmmmmmmmmmmmmm
Mmmmmmmmmmmmmmmmmmmmmmmmmmmmmmmmmmmmmmmm
Mmmmmmmmmmmmmmmmmmmmmmmmmmmmmmmmmmmmmmmm
Mmmmmmmmmmmmmmmmmmmmmmmmmmmmmmmmmmmmmmmm
Mmmmmmmmmmmmmmmmmmmmmmmmmmmmmmmmmmmmmmmm
Mmmmmmmmmmmmmmmmmmmmmmmmmmmmmmmmmmmmmmmm
Mmmmmmmmmmmmmmmmmmmmmmmmmmmmmmmmmmmmmmmm
Mmmmmmmmmmmmmmmmmmmmmmmmmmmmmmmmmmmmmmmm
Mmmmmmmmmmmmmmmmmmmmmmmmmmmmmmmmmmmmmmmm
Mmmmmmmmmmmmmmmmmmmmmmmmmmmmmmmmmmmmmm!!

To support Ona's riffs, Regina summons a Bedouin-sounding trill that causes poor Grady to double over, hide his face in his hands, and hike up in memory to Blue Empty the way he and Lore did many times late in her illness thanks to their trusty old saddle-pack. But with no Lore to carry after having carried her so far, Regina's trill shatters Grady the way the meteorite did the stone beneath Jade, and he needs neither eyes nor Trinovids to see Lore leave the lake naked, step up onto the marble slab, take up her towel, and turn to regard the waters that reveal the infinite births Earth and God the Mother make of infinite deaths. But, blinded by the tears he's streaming, Grady can't see whether Lore still bears this world's scars, or the coming world's healed and whole breasts.

Lou Roy, meanwhile, bent low to keep Fionn on pitch, is peering out from under his brim at seventy human and one avian hummers, wondering how in heaven's, hell's, or any other principality's name this can be happening. This choir has convened via a multitude of migrations as unlikely as the calliope's, their sound is sending what Lou guesses Risa's fancy books would call "bliss" shootin' through him, *an' what in the name of Roy Rogers an' Dale Evans is a stove-up ol' wrangler like me doin' even* thinkin' *a word like* bliss, *let alone havin' it flood his whole sorry carcass?*

THE SOUND POURS out of the barn, through the spring day, into the open window by the bed where Risa lies holding Lore's hand, and by the hand's cooling and Lore's increasing slowness of breath Risa believes she is beyond hearing the love arriving and arriving from so many. Lore then stuns her by faintly whispering a second to last word: *"Mu."*

Elated to have this pearl to share with him later, Risa whispers, "Yes! Mu! He's with us, we adore him, he's right in the heart of all the love you're hearing. So, dearest darlin'. When you feel ready, we release you. I mean it. Feel free to take flight."

But when Lore, showing no sign of having heard her, continues to draw breaths, Risa grips her harder, unable to let go at all as...

...A STONE'S THROW away, Trey and Rosalia burst in through the big door of the B Barn, Trey carrying the twenty-four-foot stepladder, Rosalia the long-handled minnow net. As the Pretty Cool Choir keeps the hum coming, Trey gets the ladder planted in seconds. Eddie, Gret, the Pope, and Max all grab hold of it, still bringing their song as all eyes begin to move to Trey—but before anyone can even *imagine* his first move Trey has shot up the ladder to its second-highest step. All eyes are now captured by him as he gestures down to Rosa. She climbs just high enough to pass him the long-handled net. As the calliope, eight or nine feet above Trey's head, bats against the glassy brilliance, Trey strains his body and arm upward, creeps the net to within inches of the exhausted bird, but before he can make a sweep it spooks up over the stained glass to the circular wood trim above, perches out of Trey's reach, and the choir loses focus as groans rise from below. *What can Trey do?* they wonder.

The only thing possible: true to the trajectory of his entire life, he steps fearlessly onto the one-from-the-top step labeled THIS IS NOT A STEP! strains and stretches upward again, touches the tiny bird with the mesh of the net, spooks it back into flight. When it again lands on the wood trim just out of reach, more groans arise.

Ona Kutar, focused on the music, does not like this break in what the choir was sending Lore. Drawing a huge breath, she starts bringin' it, pulling from a place so deep and pure that everyone hears it, and responds, till the B Barn is vibrating like a giant resonator guitar:

Mmmmmmmmmmmmmmmmmmmmmmmmmmmm
Mmmmmmmmmmmmmmmmmmmmmmmmmmmm

The calliope remains on the window frame at an angle impossible for Trey to reach. But on the ladder's very summit is a bright red-and-black warning, DANGER. USTED PODRÍA PERDER SU EQUILIBRIO. Catching the eyes of Kale, Max, Gret, and Eddie, Trey nods his intent. They grip the ladder like roots upholding a massive tree. Calm and steady, Trey steps onto the ladder's very summit as...

...INSIDE SKY DOOR, Risa discovers that the grief and love pouring in from so many good people frees something that's been locked in her bones for days. Adding her own feeble *mmmmmmm*, she feels her chest, body, two-handed grip on her friend relax, then release, marveling that a home-spun choir has enabled her to lie shoulder to shoulder with Lore, no longer holding her at all, as...

...TWENTY-FOUR FEET IN the air, his depth in his body where it's always been, Trey balances atop a ridiculously small aluminum rectangle that can't fully support even the soles of his shoes, extends his long arm and net, strains his utmost, and as the calliope again takes flight he makes a sweep, at last capturing the creature! Twisting his wrist to flip the mesh over the net's rim, he traps the bird in its soft center—a brilliant move! But as the choir cries out gratefully Trey begins to sway. *Badly!* A mass gasp rises and horror seems a certainty when Trey begins beating the minnow net against the air like a long thin wing. It's just enough! He catches his balance, steadies, stills the net, backs three steps down so his knees can brace against the ladder. We all glimpse the bird now, a shard of green sea glass trapped in the net's white mesh. Overflowing with relief, the choir takes up the hum with heightened intensity:

Mmmmmmmmmmmmmmmmmmmmmmmmmmmmmm
Mmmmmmmmmmmmmmmmmmmmmmmmmmmmmm
Mmmmmmmmmmmmmmmmmmmmmmmmmmmmmm

Mmmmmmmmmmmmmmmmmmmmmmmmm
Mmmmmmmmmmmmmmmmmmmmmmmmm
Mmmmmmmmmmmmmmmmmmmmmmmmm
Mmmmmmmmmmmmmmmmmmmmmmmmm
Mmmmmmmmmmmmmmmmmmmmmmmmm
Mmmmmmmmmmmmmmmmmmmmmmmmm
Mmmmmmmmmmmmmmmmmmmmmmmmm
Mmmmmmmmmmmmmmmmmmmmmmmmm
Mmmmmmmmmmmmmmmmmmmmmmmmm
Mmmmmmmmmmmmmmmmmmmmmmmmm
Mmmmmmmmmmmmmmmmmmmmmmmmm
Mmmmmmmmmmmmmmmmmmmmmmmmm
Mmmmmmmmmmmmmmmmmmmmmmmmm
Mmmmmmmmmmmmmmmmmmmmmmmmm!!

Trey passes the net down to Rosalia.

Taking it in hand, tears in her eyes, she rushes out the open B Barn door.

Trey climbs down, sees seventy faces beaming at him as they hum, and smiles a completely confused smile. *What is going on here anyway?*

Buford raises a hand to catch his attention, sets Lily Cloud in his lap, points a finger at the chair she emptied between himself and Regina, slides the tomato juice can out of his shirt pocket, spurts in tobacco juice, slips the can back in. As Trey steps over and takes a seat, Buford claps him on the back and whispers, "Great work!" Lily cries, "*YAY, TREY!*" and Regina, in a bewildering show of thanks, touches her forehead to Trey's shoulder.

He smiles at each of them, then turns his attention to the ongoing sound. Focused on bird and balance, he hadn't allowed himself to wonder why this choir exists or what it hopes to achieve. Now it slams him: *every note and breath of this strange music is for Lore.* He tries to imagine how the sound might affect what she's going through. Can't. Tries to imagine what it's doing to Mu. Can't. And just that fast, seated in a perfectly steady chair, Trey again loses his balance. Were he up on the ladder or on a vertical wall he'd be in free fall.

But Buford feels it, reaches round Trey's back, grips him hard by the shoulder, and Regina stops humming, lets fly with an ululation, lays a calm hand on the back of Trey's neck as Lily beams up at Trey nonstop. And this strange combination—beaming child/calm touch/eerie trill/soothing hum/ Buford's strength—enables a magic word to grip Trey as hard as Buford is gripping his shoulder: *Crux. Lore is at the last crux! Help her!*

The music-rife air envelops Trey. He sucks it into his lungs and body like food. Each person in this great drum of a room, he feels, is releasing breath, voice, and greatheartedness the way mountains release their ice and snow in spring. *How has Lore lived, what gifts has she given, to inspire this response in so many?* He doesn't know. He betrayed her repeatedly before he truly knew her, and now she's leaving. The ferocity of this failure awakens Trey's ferocity of body, stops his trembling, and his voice is strong as he joins the choir and Lore at the crux.

But what strengthens one man can weaken another: now it's the Pope who's struggling. *Oh, the Pope is struggling.* Seated on his right is Mu, on Mu's right is Ona, and Mu is bringing his notes nonstop as he is losing his mother, which is courage, which is Mu's nobility, and no surprise. Kale's struggle is with Ona's left arm, which is wrapped round Mu's shoulder not twelve inches from Kale's eyes. Several times he saw a tremor he thought was Ona's big feeling as she sang to steady the lad, but now he sees the tremors aren't hers: they're coming so hard out of Mu that they shake Ona's arm. How can a young man quake that hard and still bring his music? Leaning back to peek, Kale sees Mu's kind, intelligent face has gone so wide-eyed he resembles little Lily Cloud—and that look, Kale realizes, is born of certain knowledge that the astounding closeness Mu and his mother cherished all his life, *at this moment, to these beautiful sounds,* has become an unbridgeable gulf. When Mu shudders again, Kale's empathy shudder is so violent he shakes Ona's and Ida's chairs, leans forward, covers his face the way Grady and Jamey have done, and though Ida begins rubbing Kale's back, he fears Mu's next tremor could unglue him completely.

Seeing three men as strong as any she knows in such a state, Ona grows desperate to change things, heighten things, alter the mood and mode radically—and who better than she to know how? As she sends her voice soaring, she turns the choir's "*mmmmmmmm*" into the most powerful possible "*Ahhhhhhhhhhhhhh.*"

The instant he hears this, Jamey is able to sit up and join her, and who can resist those two voices? When Mu too takes up the *Ahhh,* Kale and Grady straighten and join them, person after person follows their lead, and the B Barn human crescent burgeons into a seventy-fold refusal to let desolation so much as touch Lore's parting flight:

Ahhhhhhhhhhhhhhhhhhhhhhhhhhhhhhhhh
Ahhhhhhhhhhhhhhhhhhhhhhhhhhhhhhhhh
Ahhhhhhhhhhhhhhhhhhhhhhhhhhhhhhhhh
Ahhhhhhhhhhhhhhhhhhhhhhhhhhhhhhhhh
Ahhhhhhhhhhhhhhhhhhhhhhhhhhhhhhhhh
Ahhhhhhhhhhhhhhhhhhhhhhhhhhhhhhhh!!!

ROSALIA ARRIVES BENEATH the open back window of Sky Door, gripping a net enclosing the tenth-of-an-ounce veteran of a five-thousand-mile solo migration that ended this day. The fresh power pouring from the B Barn fuses with her love for her more-than-surrogate mothers in the cottage, but her proximity to one dear mother in the act of leaving, the other in the act of losing her, drops Rosa to her knees.

Dew soaks through her jeans. Sun warms her back. The year's first green grass rises thin as infant hair from the muddy ground. At a fence not forty feet away a pair of two-month-old Highlands watch her, their trusting eyes obscured by auburn bangs, and Rosalia's love for two women, two calves, soaring choir, tender grass, tiny bird, becomes a great brimming. With all the attentiveness in her, she unfolds the net and encloses the calliope in the soft hut of her hands. As gently as possible she moves the hut first to her heart, then to her mouth, where she pours gratitude for the brimming over the hut's occupant in the form of a long exhaled "*Loooooooooooooooooorrrrre…*"

INSIDE THE COTTAGE, hearing the choir's brave liftoff, Risa feels certain that Lore will now lift out of her body. At that very moment Lore instead moves her lips ever so slightly, and an utterly unexpected puff of air faintly forms her beloved word, "*Blue.*"

So stunned is Risa to hear a word this close to the departure gate that tears stream a good while before she realizes something else: Lore's breathing and pulse have stopped.

OUTSIDE THE COTTAGE, as the sacrificial calves stop gazing and begin to graze, Rosalia hears Risa let out a moan fit to uproot a sequoia. *Moaning is connected with hope.*

Knowing exactly what has happened, Rosa stifles a sob and bows her head not to pray but to peer with all her might at a messenger more potent than any prayer she knows how to summon. She opens her hands to sunlight: the calliope lies on its side, motionless in her palms; unhurt; not even frightened, it seems. Just unaware that it's free. Soon, through the window, Rosalia knows she'll hear Risa reading words Lore chose, from *Mountains and Waters Sutra*, about her longing to disappear.

Risa's voice then arrives, though it breaks up every few words: "*Because mountains and waters have been active since…since before the Empty Eon…they're alive this moment…*" (a violent sob)…"*And because*

they've been the self since...since before form arose, dearest darlin'"
(a softer sob)... *"they're liberated and realized...And because mountains
are high and broad...the way of riding the clouds is always reached
in the mountains...Always Lore!...and the inconceivable power of...of
soaring in the wind...comes freely from the mountains now.* So, my
love, *soar!"*

Risa falls silent.

The calliope begins to thrum in Rosalia's hands.

INSIDE SKY DOOR, gazing at Lore's perfect stillness, Risa ponders her
closed eyes. At first she was touched by them. It's rare for eyes to close
at death. But she has so loved regarding and being regarded by those
black-rimmed gray eyes that being cut off from them brings the first wave
of grief. Lore's expression is, as undertakers say, *peaceful*—but who wants
to settle for what undertakers say? This peace is too sudden, too final, too
closed off!

Unable to interact via sight, Risa obeys a dumbsaint impulse; bends
slowly down; places her lips gently upon Lore's; lets this touching become
a kiss; lets the kiss linger. *How still you are. How strange and...somehow
helpful...a kiss that brings no hint of a response.*

A little surprised by what she's doing, Risa wonders if she's taking some
kind of advantage. But a papery voice within whispers, *No thinky, just
feel!*—and it feels nothing but right to let her breath mingle with Lore's
no-breath; feel her warmth fend off Lore's growing coolness; feel life and
death get entangled, admiring each other as they pass like the day's hawk
and the night's owl at dusk.

But *what is this?* Rain splashing onto Lore's face! Wondering where on
Earth it's coming from, Risa is not quick to realize that her eyes are crying
though she herself is not. The unfelt tears make her wonder what else she's
not feeling, inspiring another dumbsaint impulse: Wanting contact with
every material and immaterial trace of Lore as it departs the form Risa has
so loved, she lies down next to Lore's body, throws her left arm over Lore's
bony chest, lays her left leg across Lore's rail-thin thighs, and whispers, "I
haven't felt you leave. I won't move until I do. I'm here, Lore. Nowhere but
here until you choose to take flight."

THE CALLIOPE, THOUGH free, remains on its side, thrumming in Rosalia's
open hands. Obeying her own dumbsaint impulse, Rosa leans toward the
bird, thinking to pour another warm *"Loooooooorrre"* over it—but as
she draws close the calliope rolls upright, comes wildly alive, vaults into
the air, and whirs upward, an iridescent arrow with no shaft, seeking a
vanishing point higher than cottonwoods, higher than pine-covered ridges,
higher than mortal sight, piercing Rosalia through as it vanishes into
empty blue.

* * *

SIMULTANEOUSLY, WRAPPED AROUND Lorilee fifteen feet away, Risa closes her eyes, giving herself blind to whatever comes. Hearing a whir out the window, she wonders what caused it. At the instant of wondering she feels life erupt up through Lore's body and streak out the sky door at the top of her skull.

Risa gasps, and falls in:

$$((((((\ (\ )\ )))))))$$
$$!$$

The sky is vast, straight into the heavens.
A bird flies just like a bird.
O Unseen Guileless! Deathless Love!
Even in Montana,
how I long
for Montana!

Acknowledgements in Four Stories

Seventeen years ago, in a world in which the problems facing humanity and every living thing had overwhelmed our politics and many a politician's sanity, I came to feel the world situation is so darkly mythic; epic; overwhelming, that only a collectively mythic and epic response stood a chance of righting the countless wrongs. But though I'd seen countless op-eds calling for a change of consciousness if humanity is to survive, I'd seen zero op-ed descriptions of what this consciousness looks, feels, tastes, sounds, and lives like as it addresses inescapable biological and spiritually realities with the love, truthfulness, and justice they demand.

This impasse set me dreaming of an outpouring of stories in what the praise poet Anne Porter called "an altogether different language." I was suddenly attracted to tales that felt like walking El Camino in Spain, where it's simply ordinary to befriend total strangers taking the same walk; or like a hundred day spiritual retreat in a place far from our species' raging and asphalt and fumes, which at age nineteen I did in a mountain fastness I can still summon by simply closing my eyes. I kept quiet about my new literary efforts, figuring many would consider me mad to attempt something so potentially optimistic in a time so dark. But as May Sarton once said (and I only know Sarton said this thanks to Maria Popova's splendid blog, *The Marginalian*) "There is no place more intimate than the spirit alone." Soothed again and again by that very intimacy, I began to marvel at how many of my friends still believed spiritual forces can be summoned with mythic, mystical or poetic language sincerely said, because we've seen it done, or have once or twice done it ourselves. And the stories began to come. Then they began to intertwine in ways that increased their potency. And they didn't stop coming for sixteen years, when *Sun House* was at last complete.

Upon learning the manuscript was 360,000 words long, some of my friends laughed and asked who had time for what even my esteemed editor called "this beautiful behemoth" in an age of governance by tweets and "news" shelled out by logarithms while even the logarithms are rendered nonsensical by the invasion of clickbait and ads? My reply, "Everybody puking sick of tweet governance and ad-prostituted logarithms," didn't appease the skeptics. But as it turns out, everyone in these acknowledgements not only gave *Sun House* time, they thanked me for what it gave them in return, leading me to want to thank them not with a rote list of their names, but with the brand of words I love best: stories.

First story: **The Virtues of Kick-ass Criticism**

My fellow Oregon ex-pat, William Kittredge, near the end of his life but still sharp as a tack, requested and read an early draft of 600 *Sun House* pages when I was mired neck deep in what I called "the middle muddle from hell." Bill then had the toughness and concern to send me some criticism so brutally honest and desperately needed that I replied:

> Many thanks, Bill, for your disgruntled reading! There is so much good, grounded, physical, racy and rough material to come that I'm in disbelief at how slowly things were unfolding, and how many times I sent people into quiet places to have itsy bitsy insights. Since your welcome ass-kicking I've been charging through the manuscript making notes like: "*Feck!* This scene is not fun enough, funny enough, sexy enough, or grounded enough! *DELETE!*" And into the void it goes. For Christ's sake, Bill (and that's a prayer, not a curse), thanks for being mean and real enough to shake me out of my torpor!

Bill then read a chapter I'd intensified in the manner he'd asked for and sent back a note I'll cherish till I move, as Bill liked to say, "to the other side of the grass."

> David,
> What a pleasure to see you kicking in!
> This ought to be a beauty!
>   Bill K

Second story: **The Primacy of Women**
Naming every person who helped inspire this book over sixteen years would make for an absurdly long list. But it would also include so many kindnesses that I'm going to split the difference and name perhaps a quarter of those who've helped me, begging the pardon of impossibly many others: you know who you are and I thank you.

The New Mexico writer, William de Buys, penned a soliloquy in praise of *Sun House* and me that included these lines: "I know of no one who better captures the beauty of the natural world or who better communicates the ineffable experience of transcendence whether through music making, meditation, or love-making. The primacy of women in this man's writing also calls out to me. He does those of us bearing XY-chromosomes proud." I'd like to thank some of the women who created this primacy, beginning with Celia and Ellie Duncan, my daughters, the raising of whom left me capable of writing either gender with love and understanding, thanks to my liking for being jerked up short by women when my love and understanding fail me. In a frigid outdoor Seattle interview for a profile the writer Jimmy Watts did of me in last fall's issue of *The Flyfish Journal*, Jimmy wrote what he saw:

> Duncan wears two long sleeve collared shirts with a craft knitted blue scarf horseshoed around his neck. "My daughter Celia made it," he says, wearing it like a hug.

Scattered on the acre behind you hidden under the salmon-berry and sword fern," I tell David, "are five Sequoia-starts your daughter Ellie gave me a couple years ago. A few hundred years from now they may be the only conifers still here.

Holding his blue scarf from Celia and eyeing Ellie's Sequoias, David remarks that he loves sitting in the backseat while his daughters choose the destination and drive. He says he wrote *Sun House* as a gift to his daughters, and to all the generations facing the epic and the overwhelming.

More women who inspired and improved this novel: my longtime literary and spiritual sister, Melissa Madenski, and the remarkable family she raised solo after her 34-year-old husband's early death of no diagnosable cause—yet out of that smashing, so much love and poetry! The whisky distiller, artist, and poet Jenny Montgomery, who alongside husband Ryan and son Heath pour inspiration as well as lubrication into Missoula's rich culture. The poet Jane Hirshfield, whose work I've esteemed since we met at a Montana writer's retreat in 1997 just after our beloved border collies had died, such a sweet thing to bond over; the writer Becca Hall, whose advice on my novel's Second Telling helped me refine a key female character and fend off the Men Can't Write Women crowd; and, last and far from least, the Saturday afternoon living room contemplative group formed by Marianne Spitform, Jenny Montgomery, Miriam Morgan, Lawrence Duncan, Ann Stevenson, Anita Doyle and me was a seven year immersion in an atmosphere that transcended gender scuffling. Our opening silences and the remarkably One-minded conversations that rose out those silences caused me to write my friend Wendell Berry and say, "I've finally found my church."

Counterparts to the living room women is "an unintentional menagerie" of men who first met on rivers to fly fish, but enjoyed each other so much that when 11-year-old Luca Dombrowski dubbed us "a bunch of spiritual rednecks" we rolled with it. We consist of the tender-hearted lawyer, Bret Simmons, the brilliant singer songwriter, Jeffrey Foucault; the poet, memoirist, and fishing guide, Chris Dombrowski; the Death Cab for Cutie drummer and scholar of all things rhythmic, Jason McGerr, the veteran fireman, writer, and builder of split cane fly rods, Jimmy Watts, and last and least, me.

Third story: **Murmurations of Humans**

My estimable friend, Barry Lopez, came to believe late in life that if human beings are to survive, we must learn to operate like starlings once they've gathered in flocks of tens of thousands to migrate in the fall. Winging through the skies in dense formations called murmurations, their reflexive attention to the four or five birds adjacent to them is so superb that they never collide despite their sharply veering flight patterns. There are gigantic murmurations in the farm valleys of California that peregrine falcons attack, screaming through flocks of thousands at 180 miles an hour, but the starlings veer away so preternaturally fast that the bewildered falcons often give up and find a vole or field mouse for supper. Barry's description of how this skill could address what threatens humanity:

> The flock is carving open space up into the most complex geometrical volumes, and you have to ask yourself, *How do they do that?* The answer is, *No one's giving anyone else instructions.* You look to the four or five birds immediately around you. You coordinate with them ... One of the birds you're using as a guide for your maneuverings is itself watching the birds around it to coordinate its movements ... It's an aggregate of birds, and to behold them is to take in something ... in which there's no leader, no hero, no driver. That to me is the way around the dilemma of scale [we humans face]: a much greater level of coordination and reference toward others. You must rid yourself of the idea that only one person knows, and understand that genius might be manifested in one man or woman in a particular moment, but that the quality of genius that characterizes humanity is actually possessed by the community."

Being of the same murmuration as Barry, I'd had the same insight a decade earlier, citing another visionary, the poet Tom Crawford, in a poem titled "The Eucharist":

> *When the light is just right*
> *if you squint, you can make out*
> *the wiring to the one bird they all are,*
> > *thousands*
> *of swarming black starlings*
> *going suddenly vertical, stalling,*
> *doubling back on themselves.*
> *In China it's called 'running hand,'*
> *this brush stroke that flows*
> *over the paper, nobody in charge.*

Other humans with whom I've been honored to murmurate: Michael Snell, my steadfast agent since 1983; Sherman Alexie and Diane Tomhave, dear friends since they first fell in love in 1994; Linwood Laughy and Borg Hendrickson, with whom Montanans and Idahoans fought a mega-Goliath off our living rivers; Steve and Diane Pettit, though the weight of the *Sun House* xerox I gave Steve to read nearly killed him!; my Alaska brother Hank Lentfer and his better half, Anya. My Oregon coast brother and sister, Frank and Jane Boyden, and their son Ian, my dear friend, an authentically Indigenous tribe of three. My early editors Kevin Odermann, Thomas Schmidt, Brian Doyle, Tom Crawford, Steven Hawley, and Chip

Blake, emeritus editor of *Orion,* whose hands-on help with the manuscript surpassed all but one person: Michael Pietsch.

Michael's work on *Sun House* far surpassed any edit I've received. He bestowed more loving attention on *Sun House* than all the editors of every book and magazine piece I've published, combined. There would simply be no *Sun House* without him. Just one reason for that: the ten contract extensions he granted me. Any other publisher would have said *Off with his head!* when I asked for a third. Michael didn't just grant time: he had nothing but praise for the steady improvements he found in eight partial versions of *Sun House*, and his hands-on stewardship of the finished manuscript through copy-editing and multiple design issues brought splendor to a hardcover so beautiful I'm left speechless with gratitude.

Fourth story: **Inner Sanctum**

Though I strongly agree with Thomas Merton that spiritual secrecy is the guardian of spiritual integrity, there is a select group of people with whom I have murmurated so long and intimately that at times they've stepped briefly into my heart's inner sanctum. First and foremost is Casey Bailey, my Jesuit then Trappist spiritual brother from the first day of college, on to India, Nepal, and back to Oregon, where it's been a joy to walk the woods at Our Lady of Guadalupe with him decade after decade. More intimates I think of as "the Stanford five," met at the southern end my solo hitch-hikes to Stanford from Portland as a restless high school teen: the brilliant Sufi scholar Carl W. Ernst and his artist partner, Judith Ernst; the Classics scholar, Sanskritist, and my dear friend since 1968, John Bussanich; and the nonpareil Erico Nadel, who, due to a stunning coincidence I must protect with secrecy, became the half patron saint, half beloved holy fool of this novel.

More inner sanctum companions: the renowned Nashville music publicist Erin Morris Huttlinger (think Vince Gill) who jumped ship into literature after reading *Sun House*, whose acumen, clarity, quick witted camaraderie, and tireless devotion to this novel made a wrap-up that could have felt like punishment a pleasure; the poet, teacher and orchardist Teddy Macker, who seems to live on a teeter-totter with me at the other end; for years we've taken turns being the confused acolyte, then the clear-sighted friend who cuts to the physical and spiritual quick and brings us back into balance; the professional astrologer and amateur scholar of travesties neither of us can forgive the Roman Catholic Church, and an absolute anchor to me during the worst storm of my life, Anita Doyle; the great unpaid scholar of world spiritual luminaries and master, Markar of South Carolina, who does what he does, as Eckhart advises, out of no created thing but love; and finally, from beyond hope, the stunning friend of 20 years and recent arrival at the center of my life, Chantal Strobel, a walking talking font of culture, compassion, and service to her enormous central Oregon community, and a font of joy for me.

May we give it all away before it's taken. May the Beguines begin again. *O my Lord, my God, Teej.* May we feel and love what you and Jervis and the Meister feel and love.

A *Sun House* Bibliography

I've seen countless op-eds calling for a change of consciousness if humanity is to survive, but precious few op-ed descriptions of what a changed consciousness looks, feels, tastes, smells, sounds, or lives like. This is the void *Sun House* set out to address. That the times are dark is life-threateningly obvious. But that light shines brightest out of darkness explains why so many seekers are finding new ways into solace. Many of the seekers in *Sun House* who become finders are based on personal friends over the past half century who've done the same. Their spiritual practices include traditional Buddhist meditation; Eastern Orthodox forms of prayer; remarkable intimacy with the natural world; particular art forms visual, musical, or readable, in which they lose themselves daily; a highly active call to compassion and service; and prayer or love practices whose practitioners keep their lips sealed in keeping with Thomas Merton's insistence that spiritual secrecy is the guardian of spiritual integrity.

Something I've come to love about such practices: *They're contagious.* Time spent with fellow practitioners tends to beget enthusiasm for one's own practice. As Jervis McGraff often says, "*Ways lead unto ways.*" This bibliography is an honest, though not exhaustive, list of books that have helped me, many of my friends, and the dramatis personae of *Sun House* find and maintain our ways.

A gentle word of warning: While the books of stories in this list are safe to read to your heart's content, the books of pure metaphysics and mysticism should be handled with care. These topics can hit a reader like a triple espresso or a triple shot of whiskey, and it's not easy to know in advance which of the two you will imbibe.

I usually read mystical or metaphysical material first thing in the morning, when my mind is most clear, and often a single deep insight fills my cup. Wisdom sages warn readers of proper dosages the way druggists do. Of his tradition's great spiritual genius, St. Isaac of Syria, Ieronymos the Clairvoyant warns,

> Every day one page of Abba Isaac. Not more.... In Abba Isaac you will behold your thoughts, what they are thinking. Your feet, where they are going. Your eyes, if they have light and see. There you will find many sure and unerring ways in order to be helped.... In the morning or at night, suffice it that you read one page.

Half a world and centuries away, Sōtō Zen Master Dōgen issues a similar warning to his monks: "What you receive with trust is your one verse or one phrase. Do not try to understand the eighty thousand verses and phrases." And today in the United States, at St. John's Abbey in Minnesota, Kilian McDonnell, OSB (101 years old as of this writing, so he must be doing something right!), warns of delving too deep in the writings of saints in his book *Swift, Lord, You Are Not,* when he says, "Shepherding the saints is like herding cats."

That said, I offer a list of works that helped create several of my own contemplative circles, and the similar circle in *Sun House:*

Myths of the Hindus and Buddhists, by Sister Nivedita and Ananda K. Coomaraswamy, Dover Publications, 1967.

note: 400+ pages of the greatest myths of India, drawn mostly from the Mahabharata and Ramayana. Safe to read in large doses!

The Kalevala: Or Poems of the Kalevala District, compiled by Elias Lönnrot and translated into prose with foreword and appendices by Francis Magoun, Jr., copyright 1963 by the President and Fellows of Harvard College.
note: A "conflation and concatenation" of hundreds of songs "narrative, lyric, and magic," sung in preliterate Finland by peasants, collected in the mid-nineteenth century by one David E. D. Europaeus, made into a book by Elias Lönnrot, translated into English by Francis Magoun. The songs were told by a pair of bards in "parallelisms," a narrative device that involves expressing same idea in different words twice per verse, like so:

It is my desire, it is my wish
to set out to sing, to begin to recite,
to let a song of our clan glide on, to sing a family lay.
The words are melting in my mouth, utterances dropping out,
coming to my tongue, being scattered about on my teeth...
Let us clasp hand in hand, fingers in fingers,
so that we may sing fine things, give voice to the best things
for those dear ones to hear, for those desiring to know them
among the rising generation, among the people which is growing up

This narrative style, sung to the plucked strings of a kantele, enabled peasants to keep the oral culture of preliterate Finland healthy for centuries.

The Voice of the Bard: Living Poets and Ancient Tradition in the Highlands & Islands of Scotland, compiled and introduced by Timothy Neat with help from John MacInnes. First published in 1999 by Canongate Books.
note: The attempted "regularization" (i.e., obliteration) of Scots Gaelic by the British conquerors of Scotland did not succeed, and I didn't know this until I visited Scotland in 2006 and learned from *The Voice of the Bard* and other sources that dozens of living bards are creating *bàrdachd* and songs within a tradition, writes Timothy Neat, "that goes back unbroken to the pre-Christian Gàidhealtachd." A fine Wikipedia entry on Gàidhealtachd speech and culture extends to many regions and a multitude of smaller pockets almost everywhere that Scots have settled, globally.

Courting the Wild Twin, by Martin Shaw, published in 2020 by Chelsea Green, and Martin's other books, can be safely read in large doses without fear of herding cats.
note: In *Sun House* a high-elevation female elder tells a neophyte mountaineer: "The best myths and legends grow toward wholeness the way a starfish can regrow its central ring-disk and five whole tentacles out of a single surviving limb." I consider Martin Shaw one of the finest and most audacious starfish growers of our time—and my admiration extends to his recently confessed love (considered scandalous by some of his fans) for an uncompromised and uncompromisable Jesus imperceptible to fundamentalist or Judeo-Suburban Xianity.
My response to Martin's new love? *Pour that good man a Lagavulin!*

Axe Handles: Poems by Gary Snyder, published by North Point Press, San Francisco, 1983.
note: One of the great starfish growers of the generation before Martin's and mine.

My favorite edition of the Upanishads continues to be a 1964 $1.75 Harper Torchbook paperback abridged, translated, and edited by Swami Nikhilananda, because in fifty years that battered old book has not disappointed me once. "Life is like Sanskrit told to a pony," sang the legendary Lou Reed. "Lucky pony!" sing Risa McKeig and I.

A Concise Dictionary of Indian Philosophy: Sanskrit Terms Defined in English, by John Grimes, published in 1996 by State University of New York Press, Albany.
note: The subtlety and profundity of Indian philosophical terms in this dictionary are truly consciousness-expanding. Grimes's book is also a wonderful companion volume to both the Upanishads and to Roberto Calasso's masterpiece, *Ka.*

Ka: Stories of the Mind and Gods of India, by Roberto Calasso, translated by Tim Parks, published in 1998 by Alfred A. Knopf.
notes: *San Francisco Chronicle:* "One closes the book with the sense of having tasted a way of thinking about the world that, despite being magical, probes the most fundamental questions about mortality, desire, time, selfhood and cosmos." *New York Times:* "A giddy invasion of stories—brilliant, enigmatic, troubling, outrageous, erotic, beautiful."

I unabashedly revere the following three Beguine female writers and their defender, Meister Eckhart, and say of them what Bernard of Clairvaux said: "Today we read the book of experience. If one wishes to understand what is read here, one has to love."
Hadewijch: Writer, Beguine, Love Mystic, by Paul Mommaers with Elisabeth Dutton, published in 2004 by Peeters Publishers.
note: Hadewijch of Brabant is a mind-blowing writer. Her letters of instruction to her acolytes are loving with a love that transcends the human, and as with Mechthild and Marguerite, I advise that she be read in small doses. Her words reach heights at which spiritual altitude sickness is hard to avoid. I took six months to read this slender book, filling its margins with jubilant comments, resonations with other wisdom sources, and exclamations of abject reverence until it became the most heavily annotated book I own.

Here, Hadewijch speaks the essence of Beguine mysticism:
All that a human comes to in his thought of God, and all that he or she can understand of him or imagine under any image, is not God. For if humans could grasp him and conceive of him with their sense images and with their thoughts, God would be less than humankind, and a person's love for him would soon run out.

Mommaers and Dutton continue:
The *other,* and all the more *the entirely Other* [God], never enters our thoughts and words....Hadewijch describes the desiring way of approaching God as follows: "Love rejoices that it falls short in the face of what God is." This "failing" should not be interpreted as a lack of activity....The desiring movement towards God compels humans to...try to enter so fully into what the Other *is* that, overwhelmed by Reality, they outdo themselves and are thus enabled incomprehensibly to touch God. *Ghebreken,* "to fall short," is, then, a positive term which refers to the moment when the human person is freed from selfness.... what Hadewijch describes as "being conquered in order to conquer."

Mechthild of Magdeburg: The Flowing Light of the Godhead, translated and introduced by Frank Tobin, published by Paulist Press, 1998.
note: Dante credits Mechthild's portrayals of her human heart interacting with the heart of God as enabling him to pen the *Paradiso* portion of the *Divine Comedy*. Her stunning work also anticipated the Spanish mysticism of Teresa of Ávila and John of the Cross.

Marguerite Porete: The Mirror of Simple Souls, translated and introduced by Ellen L. Babinsky, published in 1993 by Paulist Press.
note:

> And why would the Holy Church understand these queens, these daughters of the King, sisters of the King and spouses of the King? Holy Church could understand them perfectly if Holy Church were within their souls. But no created thing enters within their souls except God alone who created the Souls, so that none would understand such Souls except God who is within them.
>
> —Marguerite Porete

The Complete Mystical Works of Meister Eckhart, translated by Maurice O'C Walshe with a foreword by Bernard McGinn, published in 2010 by the Crossroad Publishing Company.
note: "The more ourselves we are, the less self is in us." —the Meister

The Collected Works of St. John of the Cross, translated by Kieran Kavanaugh and Otilio Rodriguez, published in 1979 by the Institute of Carmelite Studies, Washington, D.C.
note:

> And I saw the river over which every soul
> must pass to reach the kingdom of heaven
> and the name of that river was suffering,
> and I saw the boat which carries souls across
> the river, and the name of that boat was love
>
> —John of the Cross

Two meaty volumes, *Metaphysics* and *Traditional Art & Symbolism,* by Ananda K. Coomaraswamy, both edited by Roger Lipsey and published in 1977 by Princeton University Press. The Coom's *Christian and Oriental Philosophy of Art, The Transformation of Nature in Art* and *The Dance of Shiva* are also available as used books and reprints.
note: When I chose to quit college to become a storytelling writer due to a *still small voice* heard on a holy hill in India, these five volumes (also beloved by Risa) became the core curriculum of an unofficial "graduate writing program" grounded by blue-collar jobs and the help of two brilliant scholar friends, John Bussanich and Carl W. Ernst.

Waiting for God, by Simone Weil, published in 1951 by G. P. Putnam's Sons.
note: It makes me inordinately happy to share a birthday with this woman who

chose, as have I, to live a life of faith outside any church but the one with galaxies for chandeliers.

My sole copy of *The King James Bible & Concordance* was inherited from my brother John, who died at 17 when I was 13. While this volume is a vital aid to eavesdropping on the roilings and boilings of the Christian schizmas, the Christ doesn't need Christianity to be Christ any more than Earth's oceans need sailors to be oceans. The Christ state transcends religions, Jesus remains my favorite non-Christian, and Jervis's Dumpster Catholicism and Rosalia's Dumpster Catholic resurrection of the Beguines feel more holy to me than the myriad factions laying claim to religiose faith scraps I recognize nowhere in the words and actions of the transcendent Christians in this bibliography.

The Bijak of Kabir, translated by Linda Hess and Shukdev Singh, with essays and notes by Linda Hess, published by North Point Press in 1983. Out of print in the original but still available from many used-book sites.
note: One of the most thought-provoking books of poems and commentary I've read. There are times when Kabir remind me of Dr. Samuel Johnson's line, "I like a good hater." But with Kabir what can sound like hate is an incendiary love for ultimate truth. A sample:

Hermit, nature has unnatural ways.
She smiles on a pauper and makes him a king,
she turns a king to a beggar.
She keeps the clove tree from bearing fruit,
the sandalwood from blooming.
Fish hunt in the forest,
lions swivel in the ocean [...]
Kabir says: Ram is king.
Whatever he does
is natural

Reflections on a Mountain Lake: Teachings on Practical Buddhism, by Ani Tenzin Palmo, published in 2002 by Snow Lion Publications.
note: This serene yet bracing book helped me realize that a work of fiction, perhaps especially during the world's current Dark Night, can aspire to sing little songs about a Pure Land "quivering," "transparent," "full of wisdom light," and keep us sane by doing so. Tenzin Palmo's work to house and nourish Tibetan women aspiring to monastic life, and to defend gender equality in an extremely masculinist tradition, is also in the very spirit of the Beguine mystics, Meister Eckhart, and the secrecy in which love dwells.

Sun House's Elkmoon Mountains would not exist were it not for the many mountain ranges I've wandered in Oregon, Washington, Idaho, Montana, and California, and there are no finer guides to their treasures than the mountain guidebooks of Daniel Mathews, the most "Elkmoon specific" of which is *Rocky Mountain Natural History: Grand Teton to Jasper,* published in 2003 by Raven Editions. Of which Dan wrote

This book is for
the fourlegged people
the standing people
the crawling people
the swimming people
the sitting people
and the flying peopl

that people walking
with them may know
and honor them

Amen.

The Ascetical Homilies of Saint Isaac the Syrian, translated from
ancient Greek and Syriac, published by the Holy Transfiguration
Monastery in 1984.
note: For those of an ascetic bent with a passion for prayer, these 84
homilies strike me as everything they're cracked up to be. But once
I read my one daily page of Abba Isaac, I can't help hungering,
too, for the hope-rife pages of *The Revelations of Divine Love* by
Julian of Norwich; for the life's work of the great Trappist Thomas
Merton; for Brother David Steindl-Rast's ongoing gratitude practices even in the darkest of times; for the anthology of fine Zen
Buddhist writing *The Roaring Stream,* edited by Nelson Foster and
Jack Shoemaker; for *The Practice of the Presence of God* by the
gentle Brother Lawrence; for Desert Mothers as well as Fathers;
for the likes of Mirabai, Lal Ded, and the 43 centuries of female
poets in Jane Hirshfield's *Women in Praise of the Sacred;* for the
Maharashtran poet saints, Chinese and Japanese landscape poets,
myriad tribal mythologies of oral cultures older than writing, and
for more wonderful wisdom sources than could ever be listed for
the same reason the number of pines in Montana's forests can
never be known: Mother Earth is constantly creating wise humans
and trees.